The Kingkiller Chronicle:

Day One: THE NAME OF THE WIND
Day Two: THE WISE MAN'S FEAR

For more about The Kingkiller Chronicle
visit www.patrickrothfuss.com

THE WISE MAN'S FEAR

THE KINGKILLER CHRONICLE: DAY TWO

PATRICK ROTHFUSS

DAW BOOKS, INC.

DONALD A. WOLLHEIM, FOUNDER

375 Hudson Street, New York, NY 10014

ELIZABETH R. WOLLHEIM
SHEILA E. GILBERT
PUBLISHERS

www.dawbooks.com

To my patient fans, for reading the blog and telling me what they really want is an excellent book, even if it takes a little longer.

To my clever beta readers, for their invaluable help and toleration of my paranoid secrecy.

To my fabulous agent, for keeping the wolves from the door in more ways than one.

To my wise editor, for giving me the time and space to write a book that fills me with pride.

To my loving family, for supporting me and reminding me that leaving the house every once in a while is a good thing.

To my understanding girlfriend, for not leaving me when the stress of endless revision made me frothy and monstrous.

To my sweet baby, for loving his daddy even though I have to go away and write all the time. Even when we're having a really great time. Even when we're talking about ducks.

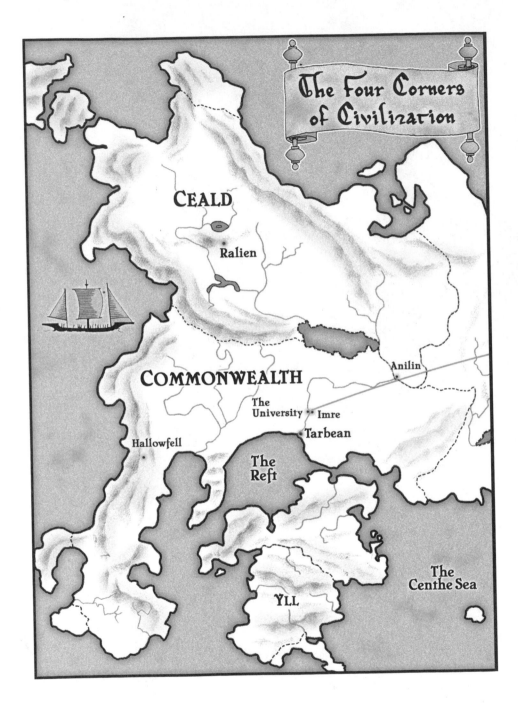

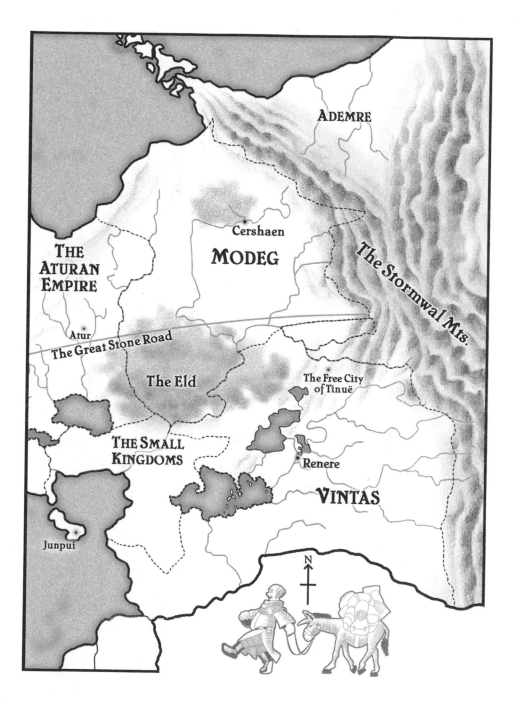

ADEMRE

MODEG

Cershaen

The Stormwal Mts.

THE
ATURAN
EMPIRE

Atur
The Great Stone Road

The Eld

The Free City
of Tinuë

THE SMALL
KINGDOMS

Renere

VINTAS

Junpui

N

A Silence of Three Parts

DAWN WAS COMING. The Waystone Inn lay in silence, and it was a silence of three parts.

The most obvious part was a vast, echoing quiet made by things that were
lacking. If there had been a storm, raindrops would have tapped and pattered
against the selas vines behind the inn. Thunder would have muttered and
rumbled and chased the silence down the road like fallen autumn leaves. If
there had been travelers stirring in their rooms they would have stretched and
grumbled the silence away like fraying, half-forgotten dreams. If there had
been music . . . but no, of course there was no music. In fact there were none
of these things, and so the silence remained.

Inside the Waystone a dark-haired man eased the back door closed behind
himself. Moving through the perfect dark, he crept through the kitchen,
across the taproom, and down the basement stairs. With the ease of long
experience, he avoided loose boards that might groan or sigh beneath his
weight. Each slow step made only the barest *tep* against the floor. In doing
this he added his small, furtive silence to the larger echoing one. They made
an amalgam of sorts, a counterpoint.

The third silence was not an easy thing to notice. If you listened long
enough you might begin to feel it in the chill of the window glass and the
smooth plaster walls of the innkeeper's room. It was in the dark chest that lay
at the foot of a hard and narrow bed. And it was in the hands of the man who
lay there, motionless, watching for the first pale hint of dawn's coming light.

The man had true-red hair, red as flame. His eyes were dark and distant,
and he lay with the resigned air of one who has long ago abandoned any
hope of sleep.

The Waystone was his, just as the third silence was his. This was appropriate, as it was the greatest silence of the three, holding the others inside
itself. It was deep and wide as autumn's ending. It was heavy as a great river-
smooth stone. It was the patient, cut-flower sound of a man who is waiting
to die.

CHAPTER ONE

Apple and Elderberry

BAST SLOUCHED AGAINST THE long stretch of mahogany bar, bored. Looking around the empty room, he sighed and rummaged around until he found a clean linen cloth. Then, with a resigned look, he began to polish a section of the bar.

After a moment Bast leaned forward and squinted at some half-seen speck. He scratched at it and frowned at the oily smudge his finger made. He leaned closer, fogged the bar with his breath, and buffed it briskly. Then he paused, exhaled hard against the wood, and wrote an obscene word in the fog.

Tossing aside the cloth, Bast made his way through the empty tables and chairs to the wide windows of the inn. He stood there for a long moment, looking at the dirt road running through the center of the town.

Bast gave another sigh and began to pace the room. He moved with the casual grace of a dancer and the perfect nonchalance of a cat. But when he ran his hands through his dark hair the gesture was restless. His blue eyes prowled the room endlessly, as if searching for a way out. As if searching for something he hadn't seen a hundred times before.

But there was nothing new. Empty tables and chairs. Empty stools at the bar. Two huge barrels loomed on the counter behind the bar, one for whiskey, one for beer. Between the barrels stood a vast panoply of bottles: all colors and shapes. Above the bottles hung a sword.

Bast's eyes fell back onto the bottles. He focused on them for a long, speculative moment, then moved back behind the bar and brought out a heavy clay mug.

Drawing a deep breath, he pointed a finger at the first bottle in the bottom row and began to chant as he counted down the line.

Maple. Maypole.
Catch and carry.
Ash and Ember.
Elderberry.

He finished the chant while pointing at a squat green bottle. He twisted out the cork, took a speculative sip, then made a sour face and shuddered. He quickly set the bottle down and picked up a curving red one instead. He sipped this one as well, rubbed his wet lips together thoughtfully, then nodded and splashed a generous portion into his mug.

He pointed at the next bottle and started counting again:

Woolen. Woman.
Moon at night.
Willow. Window.
Candlelight.

This time it was a clear bottle with a pale yellow liquor inside. Bast yanked the cork and added a long pour to the mug without bothering to taste it first. Setting the bottle aside, he picked up the mug and swirled it dramatically before taking a mouthful. He smiled a brilliant smile and flicked the new bottle with his finger, making it chime lightly before he began his singsong chant again:

Barrel. Barley.
Stone and stave.
Wind and water—

A floorboard creaked, and Bast looked up, smiling brightly. "Good morning, Reshi."

The red-haired innkeeper stood at the bottom of the stairs. He brushed his long-fingered hands over the clean apron and full-length sleeves he wore. "Is our guest awake yet?"

Bast shook his head. "Not a rustle or a peep."

"He's had a hard couple of days," Kote said. "It's probably catching up with him." He hesitated, then lifted his head and sniffed. "Have you been drinking?" The question was more curious than accusatory.

"No," Bast said.

The innkeeper raised an eyebrow.

"I've been *tasting*," Bast said, emphasizing the word. "Tasting comes before drinking."

"Ah," the innkeeper said. "So you were getting ready to drink then?"

"Tiny Gods, yes," Bast said. "To great excess. What the hell else is there to do?" Bast brought his mug up from underneath the bar and looked into it. "I was hoping for elderberry, but I got some sort of melon." He swirled the mug speculatively. "Plus something spicy." He took another sip and narrowed his eyes thoughtfully. "Cinnamon?" he asked, looking at the ranks of bottles. "Do we even have any more elderberry?"

"It's in there somewhere," the innkeeper said, not bothering to look at the bottles. "Stop a moment and listen, Bast. We need to talk about what you did last night."

Bast went very still. "What did I do, Reshi?"

"You stopped that creature from the Mael," Kote said.

"Oh." Bast relaxed, making a dismissive gesture. "I just slowed it down, Reshi. That's all."

Kote shook his head. "You realized it wasn't just some madman. You tried to warn us. If you hadn't been so quick on your feet . . ."

Bast frowned. "I wasn't so quick, Reshi. It got Shep." He looked down at the well scrubbed floorboards near the bar. "I liked Shep."

"Everyone else will think the smith's prentice saved us," Kote said. "And that's probably for the best. But I know the truth. If not for you, it would have slaughtered everyone here."

"Oh Reshi, that's just not true," Bast said. "You would have killed it like a chicken. I just got it first."

The innkeeper shrugged the comment away. "Last night has me thinking," he said. "Wondering what we could do to make things a bit safer around here. Have you ever heard the 'White Riders' Hunt'?"

Bast smiled. "It was our song before it was yours, Reshi." He drew a breath and sang in a sweet tenor:

Rode they horses white as snow.
Silver blade and white horn bow.
Wore they fresh and supple boughs,
Red and green upon their brows.

The innkeeper nodded. "Exactly the verse I was thinking of. Do you think you could take care of it while I get things ready here?"

Bast nodded enthusiastically and practically bolted, pausing by the kitchen door. "You won't start without me?" he asked anxiously.

"We'll start as soon as our guest is fed and ready," Kote said. Then, seeing the expression on his student's face, he relented a little. "For all that, I imagine you have an hour or two."

Bast glanced through the doorway, then back.

Amusement flickered over the innkeeper's face. "And I'll call before we start." He made a shooing motion with one hand. "Go on now."

The man who called himself Kote went through his usual routine at the Waystone Inn. He moved like clockwork, like a wagon rolling down the road in well-worn ruts.

First came the bread. He mixed flour and sugar and salt with his hands, not bothering to measure. He added a piece of starter from the clay jar in the pantry, kneaded the dough, then rounded the loaves and set them to rise. He shoveled ash from the stove in the kitchen and kindled a fire.

Next he moved into the common room and laid a fire in the black stone fireplace, brushing the ash from the massive hearth along the northern wall. He pumped water, washed his hands, and brought up a piece of mutton from the basement. He cut fresh kindling, carried in firewood, punched down the rising bread and moved it close to the now-warm stove.

And then, abruptly, there was nothing left to do. Everything was ready. Everything was clean and orderly. The red-haired man stood behind the bar, his eyes slowly returning from their faraway place, focusing on the here and now, on the inn itself.

They came to rest on the sword that hung on the wall above the bottles. It wasn't a particularly beautiful sword, not ornate or eye-catching. It was menacing, in a way. The same way a tall cliff is menacing. It was grey and un-blemished and cold to the touch. It was sharp as shattered glass. Carved into the black wood of the mounting board was a single word: *Folly*.

The innkeeper heard heavy footsteps on the wooden landing outside. The door's latch rattled noisily, followed by a loud *hellooo* and a thumping on the door.

"Just a moment!" Kote called. Hurrying to the front door he turned, the heavy key in the door's bright brass lock.

Graham stood with his thick hand poised to knock on the door. His weathered face split into a grin when he saw the innkeeper. "Bast open things up for you again this morning?" he asked.

Kote gave a tolerant smile.

"He's a good boy," Graham said. "Just a little ditherheaded. I thought you might have closed up shop today." He cleared his throat and glanced at his feet for a moment. "I wouldn't be surprised, considering."

Kote put the key in his pocket. "Open as always. What can I do for you?"

Graham stepped out of the doorway and nodded toward the street where three barrels stood in a nearby cart. They were new, with pale, polished wood and bright metal bands. "I knew I wasn't getting any sleep last night, so I knocked the last one together for you. Besides, I heard the Bentons would be coming round with the first of the late apples today."

"I appreciate that."

"Nice and tight so they'll keep through the winter." Graham walked over and rapped a knuckle proudly against the side of the barrel. "Nothing like a winter apple to stave off hunger." He looked up with a glimmer in his eye and knocked at the side of the barrel again. "Get it? Stave?"

Kote groaned a bit, rubbing at his face.

Graham chuckled to himself and ran a hand over one of the barrel's bright metal bands. "I ain't ever made a barrel with brass before, but these turned out nice as I could hope for. You let me know if they don't stay tight. I'll see to 'em."

"I'm glad it wasn't too much trouble," the innkeeper said. "The cellar gets damp. I worry iron would just rust out in a couple years."

Graham nodded. "That's right sensible," he said. "Not many folk take the long view of things." He rubbed his hands together. "Would you like to give me a hand? I'd hate to drop one and scuff your floors."

They set to it. Two of the brass-bound barrels went to the basement while the third was maneuvered behind the bar, through the kitchen, and into the pantry.

After that, the men made their way back to the common room, each on their own side of the bar. There was a moment of silence as Graham looked around the empty taproom. There were two fewer stools than there should be at the bar, and an empty space left by an absent table. In the orderly taproom these things were conspicuous as missing teeth.

Graham pulled his eyes from a well-scrubbed piece of floor near the bar. He reached into his pocket and brought out a pair of dull iron shims, his hand hardly shaking at all. "Bring me up a short beer, would you, Kote?" he asked, his voice rough. "I know it's early, but I've got a long day ahead of me. I'm helping the Murrions bring their wheat in."

The innkeeper drew the beer and handed it over silently. Graham drank half of it off in a long swallow. His eyes were red around the edges. "Bad business last night," he said without making eye contact, then took another drink.

Kote nodded. *Bad business last night.* Chances are, that would be all Graham had to say about the death of a man he had known his whole life. These folk knew all about death. They killed their own livestock. They died from fevers, falls, or broken bones gone sour. Death was like an unpleasant neighbor. You didn't talk about him for fear he might hear you and decide to pay a visit.

Except for stories, of course. Tales of poisoned kings and duels and old wars were fine. They dressed death in foreign clothes and sent him far from your door. A chimney fire or the croup-cough were terrifying. But Gibea's trial or the siege of Enfast, those were different. They were like prayers, like charms muttered late at night when you were walking alone in the dark. Stories were like ha'penny amulets you bought from a peddler, just in case.

"How long is that scribe fellow going to be around?" Graham asked after a moment, voice echoing in his mug. "Maybe I should get a bit of something writ up, just in case." He frowned a bit. "My daddy always called them laying-down papers. Can't remember what they're really called."

"If it's just your goods that need looking after, it's a disposition of property," the innkeeper said matter-of-factly. "If it relates to other things it's called a mandamus of declared will."

Graham lifted an eyebrow at the innkeeper.

"What I heard at any rate," the innkeeper said, looking down and rubbing the bar with a clean white cloth. "Scribe mentioned something along those lines."

"Mandamus . . ." Graham murmured into his mug. "I reckon I'll just ask him for some laying-down papers and let him official it up however he likes." He looked up at the innkeeper. "Other folk will probably be wanting something similar, times being what they are."

For a moment it looked like the innkeeper frowned with irritation. But no, he did nothing of the sort. Standing behind the bar he looked the same as he always did, his expression placid and agreeable. He gave an easy nod. "He mentioned he'd be setting up shop around midday," Kote said. "He was a bit unsettled by everything last night. If anyone shows up earlier than noon I expect they'll be disappointed."

Graham shrugged. "Shouldn't make any difference. There won't be but ten people in the whole town until lunchtime anyway." He took another swallow of beer and looked out the window. "Today's a field day and that's for sure."

The innkeeper seemed to relax a bit. "He'll be here tomorrow too. So there's no need for everyone to rush in today. Folk stole his horse off by Abbot's Ford, and he's trying to find a new one."

Graham sucked his teeth sympathetically. "Poor bastard. He won't find a horse for love nor money with harvest in mid-swing. Even Carter couldn't replace Nelly after that spider thing attacked him off by the Oldstone bridge."

He shook his head. "It doesn't seem right, something like that happening not two miles from your own door. Back when—"

Graham stopped. "Lord and lady, I sound like my old da." He tucked in his chin and added some gruff to his voice. *"Back when I was a boy we had proper weather. The miller kept his thumb off the scale and folk knew to look after their own business."*

The innkeeper's face grew a wistful smile. "My father said the beer was better, and the roads had fewer ruts."

Graham smiled, but it faded quickly. He looked down, as if uncomfortable with what he was about to say. "I know you aren't from around here, Kote. That's a hard thing. Some folk think a stranger can't hardly know the time of day."

He drew a deep breath, still not meeting the inkeeper's eyes. "But I figure you know things other folk don't. You've got sort of a *wider* view." He looked up, his eyes serious and weary, dark around the edges from lack of sleep. "Are things as grim as they seem lately? The roads so bad. Folk getting robbed and . . ."

With an obvious effort, Graham kept himself from looking at the empty piece of floor again. "All the new taxes making things so tight. The Grayden boys about to lose their farm. That spider thing." He took another swallow of beer. "Are things as bad as they seem? Or have I just gotten old like my da, and now everything tastes a little bitter compared to when I was a boy?"

Kote wiped at the bar for a long moment, as if reluctant to speak. "I think things are usually bad one way or another," he said. "It might be that only us older folk can see it."

Graham began to nod, then frowned. "Except you're not old, are you? I forget that most times." He looked the red-haired man up and down. "I mean, you move around old, and you talk old, but you're not, are you? I'll bet you're half my age." He squinted at the innkeeper. "How old are you, anyway?"

The innkeeper gave a tired smile. "Old enough to feel old."

Graham snorted. "Too young to make old man noises. You should be out chasing women and getting into trouble. Leave us old folk to complain about how the world is getting all loose in the joints."

The old carpenter pushed himself away from the bar and turned to walk toward the door. "I'll be back to talk to your scribe when we break for lunch today. I en't the only one, either. There's a lot of folks that'll want to get some things set down official when they've got the chance."

The innkeeper drew a deep breath and let it out slowly. "Graham?"

The man turned with one hand on the door.

"It's not just you," Kote said. "Things are bad, and my gut tells me they'll get worse yet. It wouldn't hurt a man to get ready for a hard winter. And maybe see that he can defend himself if need be." The innkeeper shrugged. "That's what my gut tells me, anyway."

Graham's mouth set into a grim line. He bobbed his head once in a serious nod. "I'm glad it's not just my gut, I suppose."

Then he forced a grin and began to cuff up his shirt sleeves as he turned to the door. "Still," he said, "you've got to make hay while the sun shines."

———————

Not long after that the Bentons stopped by with a cartload of late apples. The innkeeper bought half of what they had and spent the next hour sorting and storing them.

The greenest and firmest went into the barrels in the basement, his gentle hands laying them carefully in place and packing them in sawdust before hammering down the lids. Those closer to full ripe went to the pantry, and any with a bruise or spot of brown were doomed to be cider apples, quartered and tossed into a large tin washtub.

As he sorted and packed, the red-haired man seemed content. But if you looked more closely you might have noticed that while his hands were busy, his eyes were far away. And while his expression was composed, pleasant even, there was no joy in it. He did not hum or whistle while he worked. He did not sing.

When the last of the apples were sorted, he carried the metal tub through the kitchen and out the back door. It was a cool autumn morning, and behind the inn was a small, private garden sheltered by trees. Kote tumbled a load of quartered apples into the wooden cider press and spun the top down until it no longer moved easily.

Kote cuffed up the long sleeves of his shirt past his elbows, then gripped the handles of the press with his long, graceful hands and pulled. The press screwed down, first packing the apples tight, then crushing them. Twist and regrip. Twist and regrip.

If there had been anyone to see, they would have noticed his arms weren't the doughy arms of an innkeeper. When he pulled against the wooden handles, the muscles of his forearms stood out, tight as twisted ropes. Old scars crossed and recrossed his skin. Most were pale and thin as cracks in winter ice. Others were red and angry, standing out against his fair complexion.

The innkeeper's hands gripped and pulled, gripped and pulled. The only sounds were the rhythmic creak of the wood and the slow patter of the cider as it ran into the bucket below. There was a rhythm to it, but no music, and the innkeeper's eyes were distant and joyless, so pale a green they almost could have passed for grey.

CHAPTER TWO

Holly

CHRONICLER REACHED THE BOTTOM of the stairs and stepped into the
Waystone's common room with his flat leather satchel over one shoulder.
Stopping in the doorway, he eyed the red-haired innkeeper hunched intently
over something on the bar.

Chronicler cleared his throat as he stepped into the room. "I'm sorry to
have slept so late," he said. "It's not really . . ." He stalled out when he saw
what was on the bar. "Are you making a pie?"

Kote looked up from crimping the edge of the crust with his fingers.
"Pie*s*," he said, stressing the plural. "Yes. Why?"

Chronicler opened his mouth, then closed it. His eyes flickered to the
sword that hung, grey and silent behind the bar, then back to the red-
haired man carefully pinching crust around the edge of a pan. "What kind
of pie?"

"Apple." Kote straightened and cut three careful slits into the crust covering the pie. "Do you know how difficult it is to make a good pie?"

"Not really," Chronicler admitted, then looked around nervously. "Where's
your assistant?"

"God himself can only guess at such things," the innkeeper said. "It's quite
hard. Making pies, I mean. You wouldn't think it, but there's quite a lot to the
process. Bread is easy. Soup is easy. Pudding is easy. But pie is complicated. It's
something you never realize until you try it for yourself."

Chronicler nodded in vague agreement, looking uncertain as to what else
might be expected of him. He shrugged the satchel off his shoulder and set
it on a nearby table.

Kote wiped his hands on his apron. "When you press apples for cider, you
know the pulp that's left over?"

"The pomace?"

"*Pomace*," Kote said with profound relief. "*That's* what it's called. What do people do with it, after they get the juice out?"

"Grape pomace can make a weak wine," Chronicler said. "Or oil, if you've got a lot. But apple pomace is pretty useless. You can use it as fertilizer or mulch, but it's not much good as either. Folk feed it to their livestock mostly."

Kote nodded, looking thoughtful. "It didn't seem like they'd just throw it out. They put everything to use one way or another around here. Pomace." He spoke as if he were tasting the word. "That's been bothering me for two years now."

Chronicler looked puzzled. "Anyone in town could have told you that."

The innkeeper frowned. "If it's something everyone knows, I can't afford to ask," he said.

There was the sound of a door banging closed, followed by a bright, wandering whistle. Bast emerged from the kitchen carrying a bristling armload of holly boughs wrapped in a white sheet.

Kote nodded grimly and rubbed his hands together. "Lovely. Now how do we—" His eyes narrowed. "Are those my good sheets?"

Bast looked down at the bundle. "Well Reshi," he said slowly, "that depends. Do you have any bad sheets?"

The innkeeper's eyes flashed angrily for a second, then he sighed. "It doesn't matter, I suppose." He reached over and pulled a single long branch from the bundle. "What do we do with this, anyway?"

Bast shrugged. "I'm running dark on this myself, Reshi. I know the Sithe used to ride out wearing holly crowns when they hunted the skin dancers. . . ."

"We can't walk around wearing holly crowns," Kote said dismissively. "Folk would talk."

"I don't care what the local plods think," Bast murmured as he began to weave several long, flexible branches together. "When a dancer gets inside your body, you're like a puppet. They can make you bite out your own tongue." He lifted a half-formed circle up to his own head, checking the fit. He wrinkled his nose. "Prickly."

"In the stories I've heard," Kote said, "holly traps them in a body, too."

"Couldn't we just wear iron?" Chronicler asked. The two men behind the bar looked at him curiously, as if they'd almost forgotten he was there. "I mean, if it's a faeling creature—"

"Don't say faeling," Bast said disparagingly. "It makes you sound like a child. It's a Fae creature. Faen, if you must."

Chronicler hesitated for a moment before continuing. "If this thing slid into the body of someone wearing iron, wouldn't that hurt it? Wouldn't it just jump out again?"

"They can make you bite. Out. Your own. Tongue," Bast repeated, as if speaking to a particularly stupid child. "Once they're in you, they'll use your hand to pull out your own eye as easy as you'd pick a daisy. What makes you think they couldn't take the time to remove a bracelet or a ring?" He shook his head, looking down as he worked another bright green branch of holly into the circle he held. "Besides, I'll be damned if I'm wearing iron."

"If they can jump out of bodies," Chronicler said. "Why didn't it just leave that man's body last night? Why didn't it hop into one of us?"

There was a long, quiet moment before Bast realized the other two men were looking at him. "You're asking me?" He laughed incredulously. "I have no idea. *Anpauen.* The last of the dancers were hunted down hundreds of years ago. Long before my time. I've just heard stories."

"Then how do we know it *didn't* jump out?" Chronicler said slowly, as if reluctant even to ask. "How do we know it isn't still here?" He sat very stiffly in his seat. "How do we know it's not in one of us right now?"

"It seemed like it died when the mercenary's body died," Kote said. "We would have seen it leave." He glanced over at Bast. "They're supposed to look like a dark shadow or smoke when they leave the body, aren't they?"

Bast nodded. "Plus, if it had hopped out, it would have just started killing folk with the new body. That's what they usually do. They switch and switch until everyone is dead."

The innkeeper gave Chronicler a reassuring smile. "See? It might not even have been a dancer. Perhaps it was just something similar."

Chronicler looked a little wild around the eyes. "But how can we be sure? It might be inside anyone in town right now. . . ."

"It might be inside me," Bast said nonchalantly. "Maybe I'm just waiting for you to let your guard down and then I'll bite you on the chest, right over your heart, and drink all the blood out of you. Like sucking the juice out of a plum."

Chronicler's mouth made a thin line. "That's not funny."

Bast looked up and gave Chronicler a rakish, toothy grin. But there was something slightly off about the expression. It lasted a little too long. The grin was slightly too wide. His eyes were focused slightly to one side of the scribe, rather than directly on him.

Bast went still for a moment, his fingers no longer weaving nimbly among the green leaves. He looked down at his hands curiously, then dropped the half-finished circle of holly onto the bar. His grin slowly faded to a blank expression, and he looked around the taproom dully. *"Te veyan?"* he said in a strange voice, his eyes glassy and confused. *"Te-tanten ventelanet?"*

Then, moving with startling speed, Bast lunged from behind the bar toward Chronicler. The scribe exploded out of his seat, bolting madly away. He upset two tables and a half-dozen chairs before his feet got tangled and he tumbled messily to the floor, arms and legs flailing as he clawed his way frantically toward the door.

As he scrambled wildly, Chronicler darted a quick look over his shoulder, his face horrified and pale, only to see that Bast hadn't taken more than three steps. The dark-haired young man stood next to the bar, bent nearly double and shaking with helpless laughter. One hand half-covered his face, while the other pointed at Chronicler. He was laughing so hard he could barely draw a breath. After a moment he had to reach out and steady himself against the bar.

Chronicler was livid. "You ass!" he shouted as he climbed painfully to his feet. "You . . . you ass!"

Still laughing too hard to breathe, Bast raised his hands and made weak, halfhearted clawing gestures, like a child pretending to be a bear.

"Bast," the innkeeper chided. "Come now. Really." But while Kote's voice was stern, his eyes were bright with laughter. His lips twitched, struggling not to curl.

Moving with affronted dignity, Chronicler busied himself setting the tables and chairs to rights, thumping them down rather harder than he needed to. When at last he returned to his original table, he sat down stiffly. By then Bast had returned to stand behind the bar, breathing hard and pointedly focusing on the holly in his hands.

Chronicler glared at him and rubbed his shin. Bast stifled something that could, conceivably, have been a cough.

Kote chuckled low in his throat and pulled another length of holly from the bundle, adding it to the long cord he was making. He looked up to catch Chronicler's eye. "Before I forget to mention it, folk will be stopping by today to take advantage of your services as a scribe."

Chronicler seemed surprised. "Will they now?"

Kote nodded and gave an irritated sigh. "Yes. The news is already out, so it can't be helped. We'll have to deal with them as they come. Luckily, everyone with two good hands will be busy in the fields until midday, so we won't have to worry about it until—"

The innkeeper's fingers fumbled clumsily, snapping the holly branch and jabbing a thorn deep into the fleshy part of his thumb. The red-haired man didn't flinch or curse, just scowled angrily down at his hand as a bead of blood welled up, bright as a berry.

Frowning, the innkeeper brought his thumb to his mouth. All the laughter faded from his expression, and his eyes were hard and dark. He tossed the half-finished holly cord aside in a gesture so pointedly casual it was almost frightening.

He looked back to Chronicler, his voice perfectly calm. "My point is that we should make good use of our time before we're interrupted," he said. "But first, I imagine you'll want some breakfast."

"If it wouldn't be too much trouble," Chronicler said.

"None at all," Kote said as he turned and headed into the kitchen.

Bast watched him leave, a concerned expression on his face. "You'll want to pull the cider off the stove and set it to cool out back." Bast called out to him loudly. "The last batch was closer to jam than juice. And I found some herbs while I was out, too. They're on the rain barrel. You should look them over to see if they'll be of any use for supper."

Left alone in the taproom, Bast and Chronicler watched each other across the bar for a long moment. The only sound was the distant thump of the back door closing.

Bast made a final adjustment to the crown in his hands, looking it over from all angles. He brought it up to his face as if to smell it. But instead he drew a deep lungful of air, closed his eyes, and breathed out against the holly leaves so gently they barely moved.

Opening his eyes, Bast gave a charming, apologetic smile and walked over to Chronicler. "Here." He held out the circle of holly to the seated man.

Chronicler made no move to take it.

Bast's smile didn't fade. "You didn't notice because you were busy falling down," he said, his voice pitched low and quiet. "But he actually laughed when you bolted. Three good laughs from down in his belly. He has such a wonderful laugh. It's like fruit. Like music. I haven't heard it in months."

Bast held the circle of holly out again, smiling shyly. "So this is for you. I've brought what grammarie I have to bear on it. So it will stay green and living longer than you'd think. I gathered the holly in the proper way and shaped it with my own hands. Sought, wrought, and moved to purpose." He held it out a bit farther, like a nervous boy with a bouquet. "Here. It is a freely given gift. I offer it without obligation, let, or lien."

Hesitantly, Chronicler reached out and took the crown. He looked it over, turning it in his hands. Red berries nestled in the dark green leaves like gems, and it was cunningly braided so the thorns angled outward. He set it gingerly on his head, and it fit snugly across his brow.

Bast grinned. "All hail the Lord of Misrule!" he shouted, throwing up his hands. He laughed a delighted laugh.

A smile tugged Chronicler's lips as he removed the crown. "So," he said softly as he lowered his hands into his lap. "Does this mean things are settled between us?"

Bast tilted his head, puzzled. "Beg pardon?"

Chronicler looked uncomfortable. "What you spoke of . . . last night . . ."

Bast looked surprised. "Oh no," he said seriously, shaking his head. "No. Not at all. You belong to me, down to the marrow of your bones. You are an instrument of my desire." Bast darted a glance toward the kitchen, his expression turning bitter. "And you know what I desire. Make him remember he's more than some innkeeper baking pies." He practically spat the last word.

Chronicler shifted uneasily in his seat, looking away. "I still don't know what I can do."

"You'll do whatever you can," Bast said, his voice low. "You will draw him out of himself. You will wake him up." He said the last words fiercely.

Bast lay one hand on Chronicler's shoulder, his blue eyes narrowing ever so slightly. "You will make him remember. You *will.*"

Chronicler hesitated for a moment, then looked down at the circle of holly in his lap and gave a small nod. "I'll do what I can."

"That's all any of us can do," Bast said, giving him a friendly pat on the back. "How's the shoulder, by the way?"

The scribe rolled it around, the motion seeming out of place as the rest of his body remained stiff and still. "Numb. Chilly. But it doesn't hurt."

"That's to be expected. I wouldn't worry about it if I were you." Bast smiled at him encouragingly. "Life's too short for you folk to fret over little things."

Breakfast came and went. Potatoes, toast, tomatoes, and eggs. Chronicler tucked away a respectable portion and Bast ate enough for three people. Kote puttered about, bringing in more firewood, stoking the oven in preparation for the pies, and jugging up the cooling cider.

He was carrying a pair of jugs to the bar when boots sounded on the wooden landing outside the inn, loud as any knocking. A moment later the smith's prentice burst through the door. Barely sixteen, he was one of the tallest men in town, with broad shoulders and thick arms.

"Hello Aaron," the innkeeper said calmly. "Close the door, would you? It's dusty out."

As the smith's prentice turned back to the door, the innkeeper and Bast tucked most of the holly below the bar, moving in quick, unspoken concert. By the time the smith's prentice turned back to face them, Bast was toying with something that could easily have been a small, half-finished wreath. Something made to keep idle fingers busy against boredom.

Aaron didn't seem to notice anything different as he hurried up to the bar. "Mr. Kote," he said excitedly, "could I get some traveling food?" He waved an empty burlap sack. "Carter said you'd know what that meant."

The innkeeper nodded. "I've got some bread and cheese, sausage and apples." He gestured to Bast, who grabbed the sack and scampered off into the kitchen. "Carter's going somewhere today?"

"Him and me both," the boy said. "The Orrisons are selling some mutton off in Treya today. They hired me and Carter to come along, on account of the roads being so bad and all."

"Treya," the innkeeper mused. "You won't be back 'til tomorrow then."

The smith's prentice carefully set a slim silver bit on the polished mahogany of the bar. "Carter's hoping to find a replacement for Nelly, too. But if he can't come by a horse he said he'll probably take the king's coin."

Kote's eyebrows went up. "Carter's going to enlist?"

The boy gave a smile that was a strange mix of grin and grim. "He says there ain't much else for him if he can't come by a horse for his cart. He says they take care of you in the army, you get fed and get to travel around and such." The young man's eyes were excited as he spoke, his expression trapped somewhere between a boy's enthusiasm and the serious worry of a man. "And they ain't just giving folks a silver noble for listing up anymore. These days they hand you over a royal when you sign up. A whole *gold* royal."

The innkeeper's expression grew somber. "Carter's the only one thinking about taking the coin, right?" He looked the boy in the eye.

"Royal's a lot of money," the smith's prentice admitted, flashing a sly grin. "And times are tight since my da passed on and my mum moved over from Rannish."

"And what does your mother think of you taking the king's coin?"

The boy's face fell. "Now don't go takin' her side," he complained. "I thought you'd understand. You're a man, you know how a fellow has to do right by his mum."

"I know your mum would rather have you home safe than swim in a tub of gold, boy."

"I'm tired of folk calling me 'boy,'" the smith's prentice snapped, his face flushing. "I can do some good in the army. Once we get the rebels to swear fealty to the Penitent King, things will start getting better again. The levy taxes will stop. The Bentleys won't lose their land. The roads will be safe again."

Then his expression went grim, and for a second his face didn't seem very young at all. "And then my mum won't have to sit all anxious when I'm not at home," he said, his voice dark. "She'll stop waking up three times a night, checking the window shutters and the bar on the door."

Aaron met the innkeeper's eye, and his back straightened. When he stopped slouching, he was almost a full head taller than the innkeeper. "Sometimes a man has to stand up for his king and his country."

"And Rose?" the innkeeper asked quietly.

The prentice blushed and looked down in embarrassment. His shoulders slouched again and he deflated, like a sail when the wind goes out of it. "Lord, does everyone know about us?"

The innkeeper nodded with a gentle smile. "No secrets in a town like this."

"Well," Aaron said resolutely, "I'm doing this for her too. For us. With my coin and the pay I've saved, I can buy us a house, or set up my own shop without having to go to some shim moneylender."

Kote opened his mouth, then closed it again. He looked thoughtful for the space of a long, deep breath, then spoke as if choosing his words very carefully. "Aaron, do you know who Kvothe is?"

The smith's prentice rolled his eyes. "I'm not an idiot. We were telling stories about him just last night, remember?" He looked over the innkeeper's shoulder toward the kitchen. "Look, I've got to get on my way. Carter'll be mad as a wet hen if I don't—"

Kote made a calming gesture. "I'll make you a deal, Aaron. Listen to what I have to say, and I'll let you have your food for free." He pushed the silver bit back across the bar. "Then you can use that to buy something nice for Rose in Treya."

Aaron nodded cautiously. "Fair enough."

"What do you know about Kvothe from the stories you've heard? What's he supposed to be like?"

Aaron laughed. "Aside from dead?"

Kote smiled faintly. "Aside from dead."

"He knew all sorts of secret magics," Aaron said. "He knew six words he could whisper in a horse's ear that would make it run a hundred miles. He could turn iron into gold and catch lightning in a quart jar to save it for later. He knew a song that would open any lock, and he could stave in a strong oak door with just one hand. . . ."

Aaron trailed off. "It all depends on the story, really. Sometimes he's the good guy, like Prince Gallant. He rescued some girls from a troupe of ogres once. . . ."

Another faint smile. "I know."

"...but in other stories he's a right bastard," Aaron continued. "He stole secret magics from the University. That's why they threw him out, you know. And they didn't call him Kvothe Kingkiller because he was good with a lute."

The smile was gone, but the innkeeper nodded. "True enough. But what was he *like?*"

Aaron's brow furrowed a bit. "He had red hair, if that's what you mean. All the stories say that. A right devil with a sword. He was terrible clever. Had a real silver tongue, too, could talk his way out of anything."

The innkeeper nodded. "Right. So if you were Kvothe, and terrible clever, as you say. And suddenly your head was worth a thousand royals and a duchy to whoever cut it off, what would you do?"

The smith's prentice shook his head and shrugged, plainly at a loss.

"Well if *I* were Kvothe," the innkeeper said, "I'd fake my death, change my name, and find some little town out in the middle of nowhere. Then I'd open an inn and do my best to disappear." He looked at the young man. "That's what I'd do."

Aaron's eye flickered to the innkeeper's red hair, to the sword that hung over the bar, then back to the innkeeper's eyes.

Kote nodded slowly, then pointed to Chronicler. "That fellow isn't just some ordinary scribe. He's a sort of historian, here to write down the true story of my life. You've missed the beginning, but if you'd like, you can stay for the rest." He smiled an easy smile. "I can tell you stories no one has ever heard before. Stories no one will ever hear again. Stories about Felurian, how I learned to fight from the Adem. The truth about Princess Ariel."

The innkeeper reached across the bar and touched the boy's arm. "Truth is, Aaron, I'm fond of you. I think you're uncommon smart, and I'd hate to see you throw your life away." He took a deep breath and looked the smith's prentice full in the face. His eyes were a startling green. "I know how this war started. I know the truth of it. Once you hear that, you won't be nearly so eager to run off and die fighting in the middle of it."

The innkeeper gestured to one of the empty chairs at the table beside Chronicler and smiled a smile so charming and easy that it belonged on a storybook prince. "What do you say?"

Aaron stared seriously at the innkeeper for a long moment, his eyes darting up to the sword, then back down again. "If you really are . . ." His voice trailed off, but his expression turned it into a question.

"I really am," Kote reassured him gently.

". . . then can I see your cloak of no particular color?" the prentice asked with a grin.

The innkeeper's charming smile went stiff and brittle as a sheet of shattered glass.

"You're getting Kvothe confused with Taborlin the Great," Chronicler said matter-of-factly from across the room. "Taborlin had the cloak of no particular color."

Aaron's expression was puzzled as he turned to look at the scribe. "What did Kvothe have, then?"

"A shadow cloak," Chronicler said. "If I remember correctly."

The boy turned back toward the bar. "Can you show me your shadow cloak then?" he asked. "Or a bit of magic? I've always wanted to see some. Just a little fire or lightning would be enough. I wouldn't want to tire you out."

Before the innkeeper could to respond, Aaron burst into a sudden laugh. "I'm just havin' some fun with you, Mr. Kote." He grinned again, wider than before. "Lord and lady, but I ain't never heard a liar like you before in my whole life. Even my Uncle Alvan couldn't tell one like that with a straight face."

The innkeeper looked down and muttered something incomprehensible.

Aaron reached over the bar and lay a broad hand on Kote's shoulder. "I know you're just trying to help, Mr. Kote," he said warmly. "You're a good man, and I'll think about what you said. I'm not rushing out to join. I just want to give my options a look-over."

The smith's prentice shook his head ruefully. "I swear. Everyone's taken a run at me this morning. My mum said she was sick with the consumption. Rose told me she was pregnant." He ran one hand through his hair, chuckling. "But yours was the ribbon-winner of the lot, I've gotta say."

"Well, you know . . ." Kote managed a sickly smile. "I couldn't have looked your mum square in the eye if I hadn't given it a shot."

"You might have had a chance if you'd picked something easier to swallow," he said. "But everybody knows Kvothe's sword was made of silver." He flicked his eyes up to the sword that hung on the wall. "It wasn't called Folly, either. It was Kaysera, the poet-killer."

The innkeeper rocked back a bit at that. "The poet-killer?"

Aaron nodded doggedly. "Yes sir. And your scribe there is right. He had his cloak made all out of cobwebs and shadows, and he wore rings on all his fingers. How does it go?

On his first hand he wore rings of stone,
Iron, amber, wood, and bone.
There were—

The smith's prentice frowned. "I can't remember the rest. There was something about fire. . . ."

The innkeeper's expression was unreadable. He looked down at where his own hands lay spread on the top of the bar, and after a moment he recited:

There were rings unseen on his second hand.
One was blood in a flowing band.
One of air all whisper thin,
And the ring of ice had a flaw within.
Full faintly shone the ring of flame,
And the final ring was without name.

"That's it," Aaron said, smiling. "You don't have any of those behind the bar, do you?" He stood on his toes as if trying to get a better look.

Kote gave a shaky, shamefaced smile. "No. No, I can't say as I do."

They both startled as Bast thumped a burlap sack onto the bar. "That should take care of both Carter and you for two days with plenty to spare," Bast said brusquely.

Aaron shouldered the sack and started to leave, then hesitated and looked back at the two of them behind the bar. "I hate to ask for favors. Old Cob said he'd look in on my mum for me, but . . ."

Bast made his way around the bar and began herding Aaron toward the door. "She'll be fine, I expect. I'll stop and see Rose too, if you like." He gave the smith's prentice a wide, lascivious smile. "Just to make sure she's not lonely or anything."

"I'd appreciate it," Aaron said, relief plain in his voice. "She was in a bit of a state when I left. She could do with some comforting."

Bast stopped midway through opening the inn's door and gave the broad-shouldered boy a look of utter disbelief. Then he shook his head and finished opening the door. "Right, off you go. Have fun in the big city. Don't drink the water."

Bast closed the door and pressed his forehead against the wood as if suddenly weary. *"She could use some comforting?"* he repeated incredulously. "I take back everything I ever said about that boy being clever." He turned around to face the bar while leveling an accusatory finger at the closed door. "That," he said firmly to the room in general, "is what comes of working with iron every day."

The innkeeper gave a humorless chuckle as he leaned against the bar. "So much for my legendary silver tongue."

Bast gave a derogatory snort. "The boy is an idiot, Reshi."

"Am I supposed to feel better because I wasn't able to persuade an idiot, Bast?"

Chronicler cleared his throat softly. "It seems more of a testament to the performance you've given here," he said. "You've played the innkeeper so well they can't think of you any other way." He gestured around at the empty taproom. "Frankly, I'm surprised you'd be willing to risk your life here just to keep the boy out of the army."

"Not much of a risk," the innkeeper said. "It's not much of a life." He hauled himself upright and walked around to the front of the bar, making his way to the table where Chronicler sat. "I'm responsible for everyone who dies in this stupid war. I was just hoping to save one. Apparently even that is beyond me."

He sank into the chair opposite Chronicler. "Where did we leave off yesterday? No sense repeating myself if I can help it."

"You'd just called the wind and given Ambrose a piece of what he had coming to him," Bast said from where he stood at the door. "And you were mooning over your ladylove something fierce."

Kote looked up. "I do not *moon*, Bast."

Chronicler picked up his flat leather satchel and produced a sheet of paper three-quarters full of small, precise writing. "I can read the last bit back to you, if you'd like."

Kote held out his hand. "I can remember your cipher well enough to read it for myself," he said wearily. "Give it over. Maybe it will prime the pump." He glanced over at Bast. "Come and sit if you're going to listen. I won't have you hovering."

Bast scampered for a seat while Kote drew a deep breath and looked over the last page of yesterday's story. The innkeeper was quiet for a long moment. His mouth made something that might have been the beginning of a frown, then something like a faint shadow of a smile.

He nodded thoughtfully, his eyes still on the page. "So much of my young life was spent trying to get to the University," he said. "I wanted to go there even before my troupe was killed. Before I knew the Chandrian were more than a campfire story. Before I began searching for the Amyr."

The innkeeper leaned back in his chair, his weary expression fading, becoming thoughtful instead. "I thought once I was there, things would be easy. I would learn magic and find the answers to all my questions. I thought it would all be storybook simple."

Kvothe gave a slightly embarrassed smile, the expression making his face look surprisingly young. "And it might have been, if I didn't have a talent for making enemies and borrowing trouble. All I wanted was to play my music, attend my classes, and find my answers. Everything I wanted was at the University. All I wanted was to stay." He nodded to himself. "That's where we should begin."

The innkeeper handed the sheet of paper back to Chronicler, who absentmindedly smoothed it down with one hand. Chronicler uncapped his ink and dipped his pen. Bast leaned forward eagerly, grinning like an excited child.

Kvothe's bright eyes flickered around the room, taking everything in. He drew a deep breath, and flashed a sudden smile, and for a brief moment looked nothing like an innkeeper at all. His eyes were sharp and bright, green as a blade of grass. "Ready?"

CHAPTER THREE

Luck

EVERY TERM AT THE University began the same way: the admissions lottery followed by a full span of interviews. They were a necessary evil of sorts.

I don't doubt the process started sensibly. Back when the University was smaller, I could picture them as actual interviews. An opportunity for a student to have a conversation with the masters about what he had learned. A dialogue. A discussion.

But these days the University was host to over a thousand students. There was no time for discussion. Instead, each student was subjected to a hail of questions in a handful of minutes. Brief as the interviews were, a single wrong answer or overlong hesitation could have a dramatic impact on your tuition.

Before interviews, students studied obsessively. Afterward, they drank in celebration or to console themselves. Because of this, for the eleven days of admissions, most students looked anxious and exhausted at best. At worst they wandered the University like shamble-men, hollow-eyed and grey-faced from too little sleep, too much drink, or both.

Personally, I found it odd how seriously everyone else took the whole process. The vast majority of students were nobility or members of wealthy merchant families. For them, a high tuition was an inconvenience, leaving them less pocket money to spend on horses and whores.

The stakes were higher for me. Once the masters set a tuition, it couldn't be changed. So if my tuition was set too high, I'd be barred from the University until I could pay.

The first day of admissions always had a festival air about it. The admissions lottery took up the first half of the day, which meant the unlucky students who drew the earliest slots were forced to go through their interviews mere hours afterward.

By the time I arrived long lines snaked through the courtyard, while the students who had already drawn their tiles milled about, complaining and attempting to buy, sell, or trade their slots.

I didn't see Wilem or Simmon anywhere, so I settled into the nearest line and tried not to think of how little I had in my purse: one talent and three jots. At one point in my life, it would have seemed like all the money in the world. But for tuition it was nowhere near enough.

There were carts scattered about selling sausages and chestnuts, hot cider and beer. I smelled warm bread and grease from a nearby cart. It was stacked with pork pies for the sort of people who could afford such things.

The lottery was always held in the largest courtyard of the University. Most everyone called it the pennant square, though a few folk with longer memories referred to it as the Questioning Hall. I knew it by an even older name, the House of the Wind.

I watched a few leaves tumble around the cobblestones, and when I looked up I saw Fela staring back at me from where she stood thirty or forty people closer to the front of the line. She gave me a warm smile and a wave. I waved back and she left her place, strolling back to where I stood.

Fela was beautiful. The sort of woman you would expect to see in a painting. Not the elaborate, artificial beauty you often see among the nobility, Fela was natural and unselfconscious, with wide eyes and a full mouth that was constantly smiling. Here in the University, where men outnumbered women ten to one, she stood out like a horse in a sheepfold.

"Do you mind if I wait with you?" she asked as she came to stand beside me. "I hate not having anyone to talk to." She smiled winsomely at the pair of men queued up behind me. "I'm not cutting in," she explained. "I'm just moving back."

They had no objections, though their eyes flickered back and forth between Fela and myself. I could almost hear them wondering why one of the most lovely women in the University would give up her place in line to stand next to me.

It was a fair question. I was curious myself.

I moved aside to make space for her. We stood shoulder to shoulder for a moment, neither of us speaking.

"What are you studying this term?" I asked.

Fela brushed her hair back from her shoulder. "I'll keep up with my work in the Archives, I suppose. Some chemistry. And Brandeur has invited me into Manifold Maths."

I shivered a bit. "Too many numbers. I can't swim those waters."

Fela gave a shrug and the long, dark curls of hair she'd brushed away took the opportunity to tumble back, framing her face. "It's not so hard once you get your head around it. It's more like a game than anything." She cocked her head at me. "What about you?"

"Observation in the Medica," I said. "Study and work in the Fishery. Sympathy too, if Dal will have me. I should probably brush up my Siaru too."

"You speak Siaru?" she asked, sounding surprised.

"I can get by," I said. "But Wil says my grammar is embarrassingly bad."

Fela nodded, then looked sideways at me, biting her lip. "Elodin's asked me to join his class, too," she said, her voice thick with apprehension.

"Elodin's got a class?" I asked. "I didn't think they let him teach."

"He's starting it this term," she said, giving me a curious look. "I thought you'd be in it. Didn't he sponsor you to Re'lar?"

"He did," I said.

"Oh." She looked uncomfortable, then quickly added, "He probably just hasn't asked you yet. Or he's planning on mentoring you separately."

I waved her comment aside, though I was stung at the thought of being left out. "Who can say with Elodin?" I said. "If he isn't crazy, he's the best actor I've ever met."

Fela started to say something, then looked around nervously and moved closer to me. Her shoulder brushed mine and her curling hair tickled my ear as she quietly asked, "Did he really throw you off the roof of the Crockery?"

I gave an embarrassed chuckle. "That's a complicated story," I said, then changed the subject rather clumsily. "What's the name of his class?"

She rubbed her forehead and gave a frustrated laugh. "I haven't the slightest idea. He said the name of the class was the name of the class." She looked at me. "What does that mean? When I go to Ledgers and Lists will it be there under 'The Name of the Class?'"

I admitted I didn't know, and from there it was a short step to sharing Elodin stories. Fela said a scriv had caught him naked in the Archives. I'd heard that he'd once spent an entire span walking around the University blindfolded. Fela heard he'd invented an entire language from the ground up. I'd heard he had started a fistfight in one of the seedier local taverns because someone had insisted on saying the word "utilize" instead of "use."

"I heard that too," Fela said, laughing. "Except it was at the Horse and Four, and it was a baronet who wouldn't stop using the word 'moreover.'"

Before I knew it we were at the front of the line. "Kvothe, Arliden's son," I said. The bored-looking woman marked my name and I drew a smooth ivory tile out of the black velvet bag. It read: FELLING—NOON. Eighth day of admissions, plenty of time to prepare.

Fela drew her own tile and we moved away from the table.

"What did you get?" I asked.

She showed me her own small ivory tile. Cendling at fourth bell.

It was an incredibly lucky draw, one of the latest slots available. "Wow. Congratulations."

Fela shrugged and slipped the tile into her pocket. "It's all the same to me. I don't make a special point of studying. The more I prepare, the worse I do. It just makes me nervous."

"You should trade it away then." I said, gesturing to the milling throng of students. "Someone would pay a full talent to get that slot. Maybe more."

"I'm not much for bargaining, either," she said. "I just assume whatever tile I draw is lucky and stick to it."

Free from the line, we didn't have any excuse to stay together. But I was enjoying her company and she didn't seem terribly eager to run off, so the two of us wandered the courtyard aimlessly, the crowd milling around us.

"I'm starving," Fela said suddenly. "Do you want to go have an early lunch somewhere?"

I was painfully aware of how light my purse was. If I were any poorer, I'd have to put a rock in it to keep it from flapping in the breeze. My meals were free at Anker's because I played music there. So spending money on food somewhere else, especially so close to admissions, would be absolute foolishness.

"I'd love to," I said honestly. Then I lied. "But I should browse around here a bit and see if anyone is willing to trade slots with me. I'm a bargainer from way back."

Fela fished around in her pocket. "If you're looking for more time, you can have mine."

I looked at the tile between her finger and thumb, sorely tempted. Two extra more days of preparation would be a godsend. Or I could make a talent by trading it away. Maybe two.

"I wouldn't want to take your luck," I said, smiling. "And you certainly don't want any part of mine. Besides, you've already been too generous with me." I drew my cloak around my shoulders pointedly.

Fela smiled at that, reaching out to run her knuckles across the front of the cloak. "I'm glad you like it. But as far as I'm concerned, I still owe you." She bit at her lips nervously, then let her hand drop. "Promise me you'll let me know if you change your mind."

"I promise."

She smiled again, then gave a half-wave and walked off across the courtyard. Watching her stroll through the crowd was like watching the wind move across the surface of a pond. Except instead of casting ripples on the water, the heads of young men turned to watch her as she passed.

I was still watching when Wilem walked up beside me. "Are you finished with your flirting then?" he asked.

"I wasn't flirting," I said.

"You should have been," he said. "What is the point of me waiting politely, not interrupting, if you waste such opportunities?"

"It isn't like that," I said. "She's just friendly."

"Obviously," he said, his rough Cealdish accent making the sarcasm in his voice seem twice as thick. "What did you draw?"

I showed him my tile.

"You're a day later than me." He held out his tile. "I'll trade you for a jot."

I hesitated.

"Come now," he said. "It's not as if you can study in the Archives like the rest of us."

I glared at him. "Your empathy is overwhelming."

"I save my empathy for those clever enough to avoid driving the Master Archivist into a frothing rage," he said. "For folk such as you, I only have a jot in trade. Would you like it, or not?"

"I would like two jots," I said, scanning the crowd, looking for students with a desperate wildness around their eyes. "If I can get them."

Wilem narrowed his dark eyes. "A jot and three drabs," he said.

I looked back at him, eyeing him carefully. "A jot and three," I said. "And you take Simmon as your partner the next time we play corners."

He gave a huff of laughter and nodded. We traded tiles and I tucked the money into my purse: *one talent and four.* A small step closer. After a moment's thought, I tucked my tile into my pocket.

"Aren't you going to keep trading down?" Wil asked.

I shook my head. "I think I'll keep this slot."

He frowned. "Why? What can you do with four days except fret and thumb-twiddle?"

"Same as anyone," I said. "Prepare for my admissions interview."

"How?" he asked. "You are still banned from the Archives, aren't you?"

"There are other types of preparation," I said mysteriously.

Wilem snorted. "That doesn't sound suspicious at *all*," he said. "And you wonder why people talk about you."

"I don't wonder why they talk," I said. "I wonder what they say."

CHAPTER FOUR

Tar and Tin

THE CITY THAT HAD grown up around the University over the centuries was not large. It was barely more than a town, really.

Despite this, trade thrived at our end of the Great Stone Road. Merchants brought in carts of raw materials: tar and clay, gibbstone, potash, and sea salt. They brought luxuries like Lanetti coffee and Vintish wine. They brought fine dark ink from Arueh, pure white sand for our glassworks, and delicately crafted Cealdish springs and screws.

When those same merchants left, their wagons were laden with things you could only find at the University. The Medica made medicines. Real medicines, not colored stumpwater or penny nostrums. The alchemy complex produced its own marvels that I was only dimly aware of, as well as raw materials like naphtha, sulfurjack, and twicelime.

I might be biased, but I think it's fair to say that most of the University's tangible wonders came from the Artificery. Ground glass lenses. Ingots of wolfram and Glantz steel. Sheets of gold so thin they tore like tissue paper.

But we made much more than that. Sympathy lamps and telescopes. Heateaters and gearwins. Salt pumps. Trifoil compasses. A dozen versions of Teccam's winch and Delevari's axle.

Artificers like myself made these things, and when merchants bought them we earned a commission: sixty percent of the sale. This was the only reason I had any money at all. And, since there were no classes during admissions, I had a full span of days to work in the Fishery.

I made my way to the Stocks, the storeroom where artificers signed out tools and materials. I was surprised to see a tall, pale student standing at the window, looking profoundly bored.

"Jaxim?" I asked. "What are you doing here? This is a scrub job."

Jaxim nodded morosely. "Kilvin is still a little . . . vexed with me," he said. "You know. The fire and everything."

"Sorry to hear it," I said. Jaxim was a full Re'lar like myself. He could be pursuing any number of projects on his own right now. To be forced into a menial task like this wasn't just boring, it humiliated Jaxim publicly while costing him money and stalling his studies. As punishments went, it was remarkably thorough.

"What are we short on?" I asked.

There was an art to choosing your projects in the Fishery. It didn't matter if you made the brightest sympathy lamp, or the most efficient heat-funnel in the history of Artificing. Until someone bought it, you wouldn't make a bent penny of commission.

For a lot of the other workers, this wasn't an issue. They could afford to wait. I, on the other hand, needed something that would sell quickly.

Jaxim leaned on the counter between us. "Caravan just bought all our deck lamps," he said. "We only have that ugly one of Veston's left."

I nodded. Sympathy lamps were perfect for ships. Difficult to break, cheaper than oil in the long run, and you didn't have to worry about them setting fire to your ship.

I juggled the numbers in my head. I could make two lamps at once, saving some time through duplication of effort, and be reasonably sure they would sell before I had to pay tuition.

Unfortunately, deck lamps were pure drudgery. Forty hours of painstaking labor, and if I botched any of it, the lamps simply wouldn't work. Then I would have nothing to show for my time except a debt to the Stocks for the materials I'd wasted.

Still, I didn't have a lot of options. "I guess I'll do lamps then," I said.

Jaxim nodded and opened the ledger. I began to recite what I needed from memory. "I'll need twenty medium raw emitters. Two sets of the tall moldings. A diamond stylus. A tenten glass. Two medium crucibles. Four ounces of tin. Six ounces of fine-steel. Two ounces of nickel . . ."

Nodding to himself, Jaxim wrote it down in the ledger.

———————————

Eight hours later I walked through the front door of Anker's smelling of hot bronze, tar, and coal smoke. It was almost midnight, and the room was empty except for a handful of dedicated drinkers.

"You look rough," Anker said as I made my way to the bar.

"I feel rough," I said. "I don't suppose there's anything left in the pot?"

He shook his head. "Folk were hungry tonight. I've got some cold potatoes I was going to throw in the soup tomorrow. And half a baked squash, I think."

"Sold," I said. "Though I'd be grateful for some salt butter as well."

He nodded and pushed away from the bar.

"Don't bother heating anything up," I said. "I'll just take it up to my room."

He brought out a bowl with three good-sized potatoes and half a golden squash shaped like a bell. There was a generous daub of butter in the middle of the squash where the seeds had been scooped out.

"I'll take a bottle of Bredon beer too," I said as I took the bowl. "With the cap on. I don't want to spill on the stairs."

It was three flights up to my tiny room. After I closed the door, I carefully turned the squash upside down in the bowl, set the bottle on top of it, and wrapped the whole thing in a piece of sackcloth, turning it into a bundle I could carry under one arm.

Then I opened my window and climbed out onto the roof of the inn. From there it was a short hop over to the bakery across the alley.

A piece of moon hung low in the sky, giving me enough light to see without making me feel exposed. Not that I was too worried. It was approaching midnight, and the streets were quiet. Besides, you would be amazed how rarely people ever look up.

Auri sat on a wide brick chimney, waiting for me. She wore the dress I had bought her and swung her bare feet idly as she looked up at the stars. Her hair was so fine and light that it made a halo around her head, drifting on the faintest whisper of a breeze.

I carefully stepped onto the middle of a flat piece of tin roofing. It made a low *tump* under my foot, like a distant, mellow drum. Auri's feet stopped swinging, and she went motionless as a startled rabbit. Then she saw me and grinned. I waved to her.

Auri hopped down from the chimney and skipped over to where I stood, her hair streaming behind her. "Hello Kvothe." She took a half-step back. "You reek."

I smiled my best smile of the day. "Hello Auri," I said. "You smell like a pretty young girl."

"I do," she agreed happily.

She stepped sideways a little, then forward again, moving lightly on the balls of her bare feet. "What did you bring me?" she asked.

"What did you bring *me?*" I countered.

She grinned. "I have an apple that thinks it is a pear," she said, holding it up. "And a bun that thinks it is a cat. And a lettuce that thinks it is a lettuce."

"It's a clever lettuce then."

"Hardly," she said with a delicate snort. "Why would anything clever think it was a lettuce?"

"Even if it *is* a lettuce?" I asked.

"Especially then," she said. "Bad enough to be a lettuce. How awful to think you are a lettuce too." She shook her head sadly, her hair following the motion as if she were underwater.

I unwrapped my bundle. "I brought you some potatoes, half a squash, and a bottle of beer that thinks it is a loaf of bread."

"What does the squash think it is?" she asked curiously, looking down at it. She held her hands clasped behind her back.

"It knows it's a squash," I said. "But it's pretending to be the setting sun."

"And the potatoes?" she asked.

"They're sleeping," I said. "And cold, I'm afraid."

She looked up at me, her eyes gentle. "Don't be afraid," she said, and reached out and rested her fingers on my cheek for the space of a heartbeat, her touch lighter than the stroke of a feather. "I'm here. You're safe."

The night was chill, and so rather than eat on the rooftops as we often did, Auri led me down through the iron drainage grate and into the sprawl of tunnels beneath the University.

She carried the bottle and held aloft something the size of a coin that gave off a gentle greenish light. I carried the bowl and the sympathy lamp I'd made myself, the one Kilvin had called a thieves' lamp. Its reddish light was an odd complement to Auri's brighter blue-green one.

Auri brought us to a tunnel with pipes in all shapes and sizes running along the walls. Some of the larger iron pipes carried steam, and even wrapped in insulating cloth they provided a steady heat. Auri carefully arranged the potatoes at a bend in the pipe where the cloth had been peeled away. It made a tiny oven of sorts.

Using my sackcloth as a table, we sat on the ground and shared our dinner. The bun was a little stale, but it had nuts and cinnamon in it. The head of lettuce was surprisingly fresh, and I wondered where she had found it. She had a porcelain teacup for me, and a tiny silver beggar's cup for herself.

She poured the beer so solemnly you'd think she was having tea with the king.

There was no talking during dinner. That was one of the rules I had learned through trial and error. No touching. No sudden movement. No questions even remotely personal. I could not ask about the lettuce or the green coin. Such a thing would send her scampering off into the tunnels, and I wouldn't see her for days afterward.

Truth be told, I didn't even know her real name. Auri was just what I had come to call her, but in my heart I thought of her as my little moon Fae.

As always, Auri ate delicately. She sat with her back straight, taking small bites. She had a spoon we used to eat the squash, sharing it back and forth.

"You didn't bring your lute," she said after we had finished eating.

"I have to go read tonight," I said. "But I'll bring it soon."

"How soon?"

"Six nights from now," I said. I'd be finished with admissions then, and more studying would be pointless.

Her tiny face pulled a frown. "Six days isn't soon," she said. "Tomorrow is soon."

"Six days is soon for a stone," I said.

"Then play for a stone in six days," she said. "And play for me tomorrow."

"I think you can be a stone for six days," I said. "It is better than being a lettuce."

She grinned at that. "It is."

After we finished the last of the apple, Auri led me through the Underthing. We went quietly along the Nodway, jumped our way through Vaults, then entered Billows, a maze of tunnels filled with a slow, steady wind. I probably could have found my own way, but I preferred to have Auri as a guide. She knew the Underthing like a tinker knows his packs.

Wilem was right, I was banned from the Archives. But I've always had a knack for getting into places where I shouldn't be. More's the pity.

Archives was a huge windowless stone block of a building. But the students inside needed fresh air to breathe, and the books needed more than that. If the air was too moist, the books would rot and mildew. If the air was too dry, the parchment would become brittle and fall to pieces.

It had taken me a long time to discover how fresh air made its way into the Archives. But even after I found the proper tunnel, getting in wasn't easy. It involved a long crawl through a terrifyingly narrow tunnel, a quarter hour worming along on my belly across the dirty stone. I kept a set of clothes in the Underthing, and after barely a dozen trips, were thoroughly ruined, the knees and elbows almost entirely torn out.

Still, it was a small price to pay for gaining access to the Archives.

There would be hell to pay if I were ever caught. I'd face expulsion at the very least. But if I performed poorly in my admissions exam and received a tuition of twenty talents, I'd be just as good as expelled. So it was a horse apiece, really.

Even so, I wasn't worried about being caught. The only lights in the Stacks were carried by students and scrivs. This meant it was always nighttime in the Archives, and I have always been most comfortable at night.

CHAPTER FIVE

The Eolian

THE DAYS TRUDGED PAST. I worked in the Fishery until my fingers were numb, then read in the Archives until my eyes were blurry.

On the fifth day of admissions I finally finished my deck lamps and took them to Stocks, hoping they sold quickly. I considered starting another pair, but I knew I wouldn't have time to finish them before tuition was due.

So I set about making money in other ways. I played an extra night at Anker's, earning free drinks and a handful of small change from appreciative audience members. I did some piecework in the Fishery, making simple, useful items like brass gears and panes of twice-tough glass. Such things could be sold back to the workshop immediately for a tiny profit.

Then, since tiny profits weren't going to be enough, I made two batches of yellow emitters. When used to make a sympathy lamp, their light was a pleasant yellow very close to sunlight. They were worth quite a bit of money because doping them required dangerous materials.

Heavy metals and vaporous acids were the least of them. The bizarre alchemical compounds were the truly frightening things. There were transporting agents that would move through your skin without a leaving a mark, then quietly eat the calcuim out of your bones. Others would simply lurk in your body, doing nothing for months until you started to bleed from your gums and lose your hair. The things they produced in Alchemy Complex made arsenic look like sugar in your tea.

I was painstakingly careful, but while working on the second batch of emitters my tenten glass cracked and tiny drops of transporting agent spattered the glass of the fume hood where I was working. None of it actually touched my skin, but a single drop landed on my shirt, high above the long cuffs of the leather gloves I was wearing.

Moving slowly, I used a nearby caliper to pinch the fabric of my shirt and pull it away from my body. Then, moving awkwardly, I cut the piece of fabric away so it had no chance at all of touching my skin. The incident left me shaken and sweating, and I decided there were better ways to earn money.

I covered a fellow student's observation shift in the Medica in exchange for a jot and helped a merchant unload three wagonloads of lime for half-penny each. Then, later that night, I found a handful of cutthroat gamblers willing to let me sit in on their game of breath. Over the course of two hours I managed to lose eighteen pennies and some loose iron. Though it galled me, I forced myself to walk away from the table before things got any worse.

At the end of all my scrambling, I had less in my purse than when I had begun.

Luckily, I had one last trick up my sleeve.

———————

I stretched my legs on the wide stone road, heading to Imre.

Accompanying me were Simmon and Wilem. Wil had ended up selling his late slot to a desperate scriv for a tidy profit, so both of them were finished with admissions and carefree as kittens. Wil's tuition was set at six talents and eight, while Sim was still gloating over his impressively low five talents and two.

My purse held one talent and three. An inauspicious number.

Completing our quartet was Manet. His wild grey hair and habitually rumpled clothes made him look vaguely bewildered, as if he'd just woken up and couldn't quite remember where he was. We had brought him along partly because we needed a fourth for corners, but also because we felt it was our duty to get the poor fellow out of the University every once in a while.

The four of us made our way over the high arch of Stonebridge, across the Omethi River, and into Imre. Autumn was in its last gasp, and I wore my cloak against the chance of a chill. My lute was slung comfortably across my back.

At the heart of Imre we crossed a great cobblestone courtyard and walked past the central fountain filled with statues of satyrs chasing nymphs. Water splashed and fanned in the breeze as we joined the line leading to the Eolian.

When we got to the door I was surprised to see Deoch wasn't there. In his place was a short, grim man with a thick neck. He held out a hand. "That'll be a jot, young sir."

"Sorry," I moved the strap of my lute case out of the way and showed him the small set of silver pipes pinned to my cloak. I gestured to Wil, Sim, and Manet. "They're with me."

He squinted at the pipes suspiciously. "You look awfully young," he said, his eyes darting back to my face.

"I *am* awfully young," I said easily. "It's part of my charm."

"Awfully young to have your pipes," he clarified, making it a reasonably polite accusation.

I hesitated. While I looked old for my age, that meant I looked a few years better than my actual fifteen. To the best of my knowledge, I was the youngest musician at the Eolian. Normally this worked in my favor, as it made me a bit of a novelty. But now . . .

Before I could think of anything to say, a voice came from the line behind us. "It's not a fake, Kett." A tall woman carrying a fiddle case nodded at me. "He earned his pipes while you were away. He's the real thing."

"Thanks Marie," I said as the doorman gestured us inside.

The four of us found a table near the back wall with a good view of the stage. I scanned the nearby faces and staved off a familiar flicker of disappointment when Denna was nowhere to be seen.

"What was that business at the door?" Manet asked as he looked around, taking in the stage, the high, vaulted ceiling. "Were people paying to get in here?"

I looked at him. "You've been a student for thirty years, but never been to the Eolian?"

"Well, you know." He made a vague gesture. "I've been busy. I don't get over to this side of the river very often."

Sim laughed, sitting down. "Let me put this in terms you'll understand, Manet. If music had a University, this would be it, and Kvothe would be a full-fledged arcanist."

"Bad analogy," Wil said. "This is a musical court, and Kvothe is one of the gentry. We ride his coattails in. It is the reason we have tolerated his troublesome company for so long."

"A whole jot just to get in?" Manet asked.

I nodded.

Manet gave a noncommittal grunt as he looked around, eyeing the well-dressed nobles milling on the balcony above. "Well then," he said. "I guess I learned something today."

━━━━━━━━

The Eolian was just beginning to fill up, so we passed the time playing corners. It was just a friendly game, a drab a hand, double for a counterfeit, but coin-poor as I was, any stakes were high. Luckily, Manet played with the precision of a gear-clock: no mislaid tricks, no wild bids, no hunches.

Simmon bought the first round of drinks, and Manet bought the second. By the time the Eolian's lights dimmed, Manet and I were ten hands ahead, largely due to Simmon's tendency to enthusiastically overbid. I pocketed the single copper jot with grim satisfaction. *One talent and four.*

An older man made his way up onto the stage. After a brief introduction by Stanchion he played a heart-achingly lovely version of "Taetn's Late Day" on mandolin. His fingers were light and quick and sure on his strings. But his voice ...

Most things fail with age. Our hands and backs stiffen. Our eyes dim. Skin roughens and our beauty fades. The only exception is the voice. Properly cared for, a voice does nothing but grow sweeter with age and constant use. His was like a sweet honey wine. He finished his song to hearty applause, and after a moment the lights came back up and the room swelled with conversation.

"There's breaks between the performers," I explained to Manet. "So folk can talk and walk around and get their drinks. Tehlu and all his angels won't be able to keep you safe if you talk during someone's performance."

Manet huffed. "Don't worry about me embarrassing you. I'm not a complete barbarian."

"Just giving fair warning," I said. "You let me know what's dangerous in the Artificery. I let you know what's dangerous here."

"His lute was different," Wilem said. "It sounded different than yours. Smaller too."

I fought off the urge to smile and decided not to make an issue of it. "That sort of lute is called a mandolin," I said.

"You're going to play, aren't you?" Simmon asked, squirming in his seat like an eager puppy. "You should play that song you wrote about Ambrose." He hummed a bit, then sang:

A mule can learn magic, a mule has some class,
Cause unlike young Rosey, he's just half an ass.

Manet chuckled into his mug. Wilem cracked a rare smile.

"No," I said firmly. "I'm done with Ambrose. We're quits as far as I'm concerned."

"Of course," Wil said, deadpan.

"I'm serious," I said. "There's no profit in it. This back and forth does nothing but irritate the masters."

"*Irritate* is rather a mild word," Manet said dryly. "Not exactly the one I would have chosen, myself."

"You owe him," Sim said, his eyes glittering with anger. "Besides, they aren't going to charge you with Conduct Unbecoming a Member of the Arcanum just for singing a song."

"No," Manet said. "They'll just raise his tuition."

"What?" Simmon said. "They can't do that. Tuition is based on your admissions interview."

Manet's snort echoed hollowly into his mug as he took another drink. "The interview is just a piece of the game. If you can afford it, they squeeze you a little. Same thing if you cause them trouble." He eyed me seriously. "You're going to be getting it from both ends this time. How many times were you brought up on the horns last term?"

"Twice." I admitted. "But the second time wasn't really my fault."

"Of course," Manet gave me a frank look. "And that's why they tied you up and whipped you bloody, is it? Because it wasn't your fault?"

I shifted uncomfortably in my chair, feeling the pull of the half-healed scars along my back. "Most of it wasn't my fault," I amended.

Manet shrugged it aside. "Fault isn't the issue. A tree doesn't make a thunderstorm, but any fool knows where lightning's going to strike."

Wilem nodded seriously. "Back home we say: the tallest nail gets hammered down first." He frowned. "It sounds better in Siaru."

Sim looked troubled. "But the admission interview still determines the lion's share of your tuition, doesn't it?" From his tone, I guessed Sim hadn't even considered the possibility of personal grudges or politics entering into the equation.

"For the most part," Manet admitted. "But the masters pick their own questions, and they each get their say." He began to tick things off on his fingers. "Hemme doesn't care for you, and he can carry twice his weight in grudges. You got on Lorren's bad side early and managed to stay there. You're a troublemaker. You missed nearly a span of classes toward the end of last term. No warning beforehand or any explanation afterward." He gave me a significant look.

I looked down at the table, pointedly aware that several of the classes I'd missed had been part of my apprenticeship under Manet in the Artificery.

After a moment, Manet shrugged and continued. "On top of it all, they'll be testing you as a Re'lar this time around. Tuitions get higher in the upper ranks. There's a reason I've stayed an E'lir this long." He gave me a hard stare. "My best guess? You'll be lucky to get out for less than ten talents."

"Ten talents." Sim sucked a breath through his teeth and shook his head sympathetically. "Good thing you're so flush."

"Not as flush as that," I said.

"How can you not be?" Sim asked. "The masters fined Ambrose almost twenty talents after he broke your lute. What did you do with all the money?"

I looked down and nudged my lute case gently with my foot.

"You spent it on a new lute?" Simmon asked, horrified. "Twenty talents? Do you know what you could buy for that amount of money?"

"A lute?" Wilem asked.

"I didn't even know you *could* spend that much on an instrument," Simmon said.

"You can spend a lot more than that," Manet said. "They're like horses."

This made the conversation stumble a bit. Wil and Sim turned to look at him, confused.

I laughed. "That's a good comparison, actually."

Manet nodded sagely. "There's a wide spread with horses, you see. You can buy a broken old plow horse for less than a talent. Or you can buy a high-stepping Vaulder for forty."

"Not likely," Wil grunted. "Not for a true Vaulder."

Manet smiled. "That's it exactly. However much you've ever known someone to spend on a horse, you could easily spend that buying yourself a fine harp or fiddle."

Simmon looked stunned by this. "But my father once spent two hundred fifty hard on a Kaepcaen tall," he said.

I leaned to one side and pointed. "The blond man there, his mandolin is worth twice that."

"But," Simmon said. "But horses have bloodlines. You can breed a horse and sell it."

"That mandolin has a bloodline," I said. "It was made by Antressor himself. It's been around for a hundred and fifty years."

I watched as Sim absorbed the information, looking around at all the instruments in the room. "Still," Sim said. "Twenty talents." He shook his head. "Why didn't you wait until after admissions? You could have spent whatever you had left over on the lute."

"I needed it to play at Anker's," I explained. "I get free room and board as their house musician. If I don't play, I can't stay."

It was the truth, but it wasn't the whole truth. Anker would have cut me some slack if I'd explained my situation. But if I'd waited, I would have had to spend almost two span without a lute. It would be like missing a tooth or a limb. It would be like spending two span with my mouth sewn shut. It was unthinkable.

"And I didn't spend *all* of it on the lute," I said. "I had a few other expenses crop up too." Specifically, I'd paid off the gaelet I'd borrowed money from.

That had taken six talents, but being free of my debt to Devi was like having a great weight lifted off my chest.

But now I could feel that same weight settling back onto me. If Manet's guess was even half-accurate, I was worse off than I'd thought.

Fortunately, the lights dimmed and the room grew quiet, saving me from having to explain myself any further. We looked up as Stanchion brought Marie up onto the stage. He chatted with the nearby audience while she tuned her fiddle and the room began to settle down.

I liked Marie. She was taller than most men, proud as a cat, and spoke at least four languages. Many of Imre's musicians did their best to mimic the latest fashion, hoping to blend in with the nobility, but Marie wore road clothes. Pants you could do a day's work in, boots you could use to walk twenty miles.

I don't mean to imply she wore homespun, mind you. She just had no love for fashion or frippery. Her clothes were obviously tailored for her, close fitting and flattering. Tonight she wore burgundy and brown, the colors of her patron, the Lady Jhale.

The four of us eyed the stage. "I will admit," Wilem said quietly, "that I have given Marie a fair amount of consideration."

Manet gave a low chuckle. "That is a woman and a half," he said. "Which means she's five times more woman than any of you know what to do with." At a different time, such a statement might have goaded the three of us into swaggering protest. But Manet stated it without a hint of taunt in his voice, so we let it pass. Especially as it was probably true.

"Not for me," Simmon said. "She always looks like she's getting ready to wrestle someone. Or go off and break a wild horse."

"She does." Manet chuckled again. "If we were living in a better age they'd build a temple around a woman like that."

We fell silent as Marie finished tuning her fiddle and eased into a sweet roundel, slow and gentle as a soft spring breeze.

Though I didn't have time to tell him, Simmon was more than half right. Once, in the Flint and Thistle, I had seen Marie punch a man in the throat for referring to her as "that mouthy fiddler bitch." She kicked him when he was on the ground, too. But only once, and nowhere that hurt him in a permanent way.

Marie continued her roundel, the slow, sweet pace of it gradually building until it was trotting along briskly. The sort of tune you would only think of dancing to if you were exceptionally light on your feet, or exceptionally drunk.

She let it build until it was beyond anything a man could dream of dancing to. It was nothing like a trot now. It sprinted, fast as a pair of children racing. I marveled at how clean and clear her fingering was despite the frantic pace.

Faster. Quick as a deer with a wild dog behind it. I started to get nervous, knowing it was just a matter of time before she slid or slipped or dropped a note. But somehow she kept going, each note perfect, sharp and strong and sweet. Her flickering fingers arched high against the strings. The wrist of her bow hand hung loose and lazy despite the terrible speed.

Faster still. Her face was intent. Her bow arm a blur. Faster still. She braced herself, her long legs planted firmly on the stage, her fiddle tucked hard against her jaw. Each note sharp as early morning birdsong. Faster still.

She finished in a rush and gave a sudden, flourishing bow without a single mistake. I was sweating like a hard-run horse, my heart racing.

I wasn't the only one. Wil and Sim each had a sheen of sweat across their foreheads.

Manet's knuckles were white where he gripped the edge of the table. "Merciful Tehlu," he said breathlessly. "They have music like this every night?"

I smiled at him. "It's still early," I said. "You haven't heard me play."

———

Wilem bought the next round of drinks and our talk turned to the idle gossip of the University. Manet had been around for longer than half of the masters, so he knew more scandalous stories than the three of us put together.

A lutist with a thick grey beard played a stirring version of "En Faeant Morie." Then two lovely women, one in her forties and the other young enough to be her daughter, sang a duet about Laniel Young-Again I'd never heard before.

Marie was called back onto the stage and played a simple jig with such enthusiasm that it set folk dancing in the spaces between the tables. Manet actually stood for the final chorus and surprised us by demonstrating a pair of remarkably light feet. We cheered him, and when he took his seat again he was flushed and breathing hard.

Wil bought him a drink, and Simmon turned to me with excitement in his eyes.

"No," I said. "I'm not going to play it. I already told you."

Sim deflated into such profound disappointment that I couldn't help but laugh. "I'll tell you what. I'll take a turn around the place. If I see Threpe, I'll put him up to it."

I made my slow way through the crowded room, and while I did keep an eye out for Threpe, the truth is I was hunting for Denna. I hadn't seen her come in by the front door, but with the music, cards, and general commotion there was a chance I'd simply missed her.

It took a quarter hour to methodically make my way through the crowded main floor, getting a look at all the faces and stopping to chat with a few of the musicians along the way.

I made my way up to the second tier just as the lights dimmed again. I settled in at the railing to watch a Yllish piper play a sad, lilting tune.

When the lights came back up, I searched the second tier of the Eolian: a wide, crescent-shaped balcony. My search was more a ritual than anything. Looking for Denna was an exercise in futility, like praying for fair weather.

But tonight was the exception to the rule. As I strolled through the second tier I spotted her walking with a tall, dark-haired gentleman. I changed my path through the tables so I would intercept them casually.

Denna spotted me half a minute later. She gave a bright, excited smile and took her hand off the gentleman's arm, motioning me closer.

The man at her side was proud as a hawk and handsome, with a jawline like a cinder brick. He wore a shirt of blindingly white silk and a richly dyed suede jacket the color of blood. Silver stitching. Silver on the buckle and the cuff. He looked every bit the Modegan gentleman. The cost of his clothes, not even counting his rings, would have paid my tuition for a solid year.

Denna was playing the part of his charming and attractive companion. In the past I had seen her dressed much the same as myself: plain clothes meant for hard wear and travel. But tonight she wore a long dress of green silk. Her dark hair curled artfully around her face and tumbled down her shoulders. At her throat was an emerald pendant shaped like a smooth teardrop. It matched the color of the dress so perfectly that it couldn't be coincidence.

I felt a little shabby by comparison. More than a little. Every piece of clothing I owned in the world amounted to four shirts, two sets of pants, and a few sundries. All of it secondhand and threadbare to some degree. I was wearing my best tonight, but I'm sure you understand when I say my best was not particularly fine.

The one exception was my cloak, Fela's gift. It was warm and wonderful, tailored for me in green and black with numerous pockets in the lining. It wasn't elegant by any measure, but it was the finest thing I owned.

As I approached, Denna stepped forward and held out her hand for me to kiss, the gesture poised, almost haughty. Her expression was composed, her smile polite. To the casual observer she looked every bit the genteel lady being gracious to a poor young musician.

All except her eyes. They were dark and deep, the color of coffee and chocolate. Her eyes were dancing with amusement, full of laughter. Standing behind her, the gentleman gave a bare hint of a frown when she offered me her hand. I didn't know what game Denna was playing, but I could guess my part.

So I bent over her hand, kissing it lightly in a low bow. I had been trained in courtly manners at an early age, so I knew what I was doing. Anyone can bend at the waist, but a good bow takes skill.

This one was gracious and flattering, and as I pressed my lips to the back of her hand I flared my cloak to one side with a delicate flick of my wrist. The last was the difficult bit, and it had taken me several hours of careful practice in the bathhouse mirror to get the motion to look sufficiently casual.

Denna made a curtsey graceful as a falling leaf and stepped back to stand beside the gentleman. "Kvothe, this is Lord Kellin Vantenier. Kellin, Kvothe."

Kellin eyed me up and down, forming his full opinion of me more quickly than you can draw a short, sharp breath. His expression became dismissive, and he gave me a nod. I'm no stranger to disdain, but I was surprised how much this particular bit stung me.

"At your service, my lord." I made a polite bow and shifted my weight so my cloak fell away from my shoulder, displaying my talent pipes.

He was about to look away with practiced disinterest when his eye snagged on the bright piece of silver. It was nothing special in terms of jewelry, but here it was significant. Wilem was right: at the Eolian, I was one of the gentry.

And Kellin knew it. After a heartbeat of consideration, he returned my bow. It was barely more than a nod, really. Just low enough to be polite. "Yours and your family's," he said in perfect Aturan. His voice was deeper than mine, a warm bass with enough of a Modegan accent to lend it a slight musical cant.

Denna inclined her head in his direction. "Kellin has been showing me my way around a harp."

"I am here to win my pipes," he said, his deep voice filled with certainty.

When he spoke, women at the surrounding tables turned to look in his direction with hungry, half-lidded eyes. His voice had the opposite effect on me. To be both rich and handsome was bad enough. But to have a voice like honey over warm bread on top of that was simply inexcusable. The sound of it made me feel like a cat grabbed by the tail and rubbed backward with a wet hand.

I glanced at his hands. "So you're a harper?"

"Harpist," he corrected stiffly. "I play the Pendenhale. King of instruments."

I pulled in half a breath, then closed my mouth. The Modegan great harp had been the king of instruments five hundred years ago. These days it was an antique curiosity. I let it pass, avoiding the argument for Denna's sake. "Will you be trying your luck tonight?" I asked.

Kellin's eyes narrowed slightly. "There will be nothing of luck involved when I play. But no. Tonight I am enjoying my lady Dinael's company." He lifted Denna's hand to his lips and gave it an absentminded kiss. He looked around at the murmuring crowd in a proprietary way, as if he owned them. "I will be in worthy company here, I think."

I glanced at Denna, but she was avoiding my eyes. Her head tilted to the side as she toyed with an earring previously hidden in her hair, a tiny teardrop emerald that matched the pendant at her throat.

Kellin's eyes flickered over me again. My ill-fitting clothes. My hair, too short to be fashionable, too long to be anything other than wild. "And you are. . . a piper?"

The least expensive instrument. "Pipist," I said lightly. "But no. I favor the lute."

His eyebrows went up. "You play court lute?"

My smile stiffened a bit despite my best efforts. "Trouper's lute."

"Ah!" he said, laughing as if things suddenly made sense. "Folk music!"

I let that pass as well, though less easily than before. "Do you have seats yet?" I asked brightly. "Several of us have taken a table below with a good view of the stage. You're welcome to join us."

"The lady and I already have a table in the third circle." Kellin nodded in Denna's direction. "I much prefer the company above."

Outside his field of vision, Denna rolled her eyes at me.

I kept a straight face and made another polite bow to him, barely more than a nod. "I won't delay you then."

I turned to Denna. "My lady. Might I call on you some time?"

She sighed, looking every bit the put-upon socialite, except for her eyes, which were still laughing at all the ridiculous formality of the exchange. "I'm sure you understand, Kvothe. My schedule is quite full for the next several days. But you could pay a visit near the end of the span if you wish. I've taken rooms at the Grey Man."

"You're too kind," I said, and gave her a much more earnest bow than the one I had given Kellin. She rolled her eyes at me this time.

Kellin held out his arm, turning his shoulder to me in the process, and the two of them walked off into the crowd. Watching them together, moving gracefully through the throng, it would be easy to believe they owned the place, or were perhaps thinking of buying it to use as a summer home. Only old nobility move with that easy arrogance, knowing deep in their guts that everything in the world exists only to make them happy. Denna was faking it marvelously, but for Lord Kellin Brickjaw it was as natural as drawing breath.

I watched until they were halfway up the stairs to the third circle. That's where Denna stopped and put a hand to her head. Then she looked around at the floor, her expression anxious. The two of them spoke briefly and she pointed up the stairs. Kellin nodded and climbed out of sight.

On a hunch, I looked down at the floor and spotted a gleam of silver where Denna had been standing near the railing. I moved and stood over it, forcing a pair of Cealdish merchants to detour around me.

I pretended to watch the crowd below until Denna came close and tapped me on the shoulder. "Kvothe," she said anxiously. "I'm sorry to bother you, but I seem to have lost an earring. Would you be a dear and help me look for it? I'm sure I had it on me just a moment ago."

I agreed, and soon we were enjoying a moment of privacy, decorously searching the floorboards with our heads close together. Luckily, Denna's dress was in the Modegan style, flowing and loose around the legs. If it had been slit up the side according to the current fashion of the Commonwealth, the sight of her crouching on the floor would have been scandalous.

"God's body," I muttered. "Where did you find him?"

Denna chuckled low in her throat. "Hush. You're the one who suggested I learn my way around a harp. Kellin is quite a good teacher."

"The Modegan pedal harp weighs five times as much as you do," I said. "It's a parlor instrument. You'd never be able to take one on the road."

She stopped pretending to look for her earring and gave me a pointed look. "And who's to say I won't ever have a parlor to harp in?"

I looked back to the floor and gave as much of a shrug as I could manage. "It's good enough for learning, I suppose. How are you liking it so far?"

"It's better than the lyre," she said. "I can already see that. I can barely play 'Squirrel in the Thatch,' though."

"Is he any good?" I gave her a sly smile. "With his hands, I mean."

Denna flushed a bit and looked for a second as if she would swat at me. But she remembered her decorum in time and settled for narrowing her eyes instead. "You're awful," she said, "Kellin has been a perfect gentleman."

"Tehlu save us all from perfect gentlemen," I said.

She shook her head. "I meant it in the literal sense," she said. "He's never been out of Modeg before. He's like a kitten in a coop."

"So you're Dinael now?" I asked.

"For now. And for him," she said, looking at me sideways with a small quirk of a smile. "From you I still like Denna best."

"That's good to know," I said, then lifted my hand off the floor, revealing the smooth emerald teardrop of an earring. Denna made a show of discovering it, holding it up to catch the light. "Ah! Here we are!"

I stood and helped her to her feet. She brushed her hair back from her shoulder and leaned toward me. "I'm all thumbs with these things," she said. "Would you mind?"

I stepped toward her and stood close as she handed me the earring. She smelled faintly of wildflowers. But beneath that she smelled like autumn leaves. Like the dark smell of her own hair, like road dust and the air before a summer storm.

"So what is he?" I said softly. "Someone's second son?"

She gave a barely perceptible shake of her head, and a strand of her hair fell down to brush the back of my hand. "He's a lord in his own right."

"*Skethe te retaa van,*" I swore. "Lock up your sons and daughters."

Denna laughed again, quietly. Her body shook as she fought to hold it in. "Hold still," I said as I gently took hold of her ear.

Denna drew a deep breath and let it out again, composing herself. I threaded the earring through the lobe of her ear and stepped away. She lifted one hand to check it, then stepped back and gave a curtsey. "Thank you kindly for all your help."

I bowed to her again. It wasn't as polished as the bow I'd given her before, but it was more honest. "I am at your service, my lady."

Denna smiled warmly as she turned to go, her eyes laughing again.

I finished exploring the second tier for the sake of form, but Threpe didn't seem to be around. Not wanting to risk the awkwardness of a second encounter with Denna and her lordling, I decided to skip the third tier entirely.

Sim had the lively look he gets around his fifth drink. Manet was slouched low in his chair, eyes half-lidded, his mug resting comfortably on the swell of his belly. Wil looked the same as ever, his dark eyes unreadable.

"Threpe's nowhere to be found," I said as I took my seat. "Sorry."

"That's too bad," Sim said. "Has he had any luck finding you a patron yet?"

I shook my head bitterly. "Ambrose has threatened or bribed every noble within a hundred miles of here. They'll have nothing to do with me."

"Why doesn't Threpe take you on himself?" Wilem asked. "He likes you well enough."

I shook my head. "Threpe's already supporting three other musicians. Four really, but two of them are a married couple."

"Four?" Sim said, horrified. "It's a wonder he can still afford to eat."

Wil cocked his head curiously, and Sim leaned forward to explain. "Threpe's a count. But his holdings aren't really that extensive. Supporting four players on his income is a little ... extravagant."

Wil frowned. "Drinks and strings can't amount to much."

"A patron's responsible for more than that." Sim began to count items off on his fingers. "There's the writ of patronage itself. Then he provides room and board for his players, a yearly wage, a suit of clothes in his family's colors—"

"Two suits of clothing, traditionally," I interjected. "Every year." Growing up in the troupe, I never appreciated the livery Lord Greyfallow had given us. But these days I couldn't help but imagine how much my wardrobe would be improved by two new sets of clothing.

Simmon grinned as a serving boy arrived, leaving no doubt as to who was responsible for the glasses of blackberry brand set in front of each of us. Sim raised his glass in a silent toast and drank a solid swallow. I raised my glass in return, as did Wilem, though it obviously pained him. Manet remained motionless, and I began to suspect he had dozed off.

"It still doesn't add square," Wilem said, setting down his brand. "All the patron gets is lighter pockets."

"The patron gets a reputation," I explained. "That's why the players wear the livery. Plus he has entertainers at his beck and call: parties, dances, pageants. Sometimes they'll write songs or plays at his request."

Wil still seemed skeptical. "Still seems like the patron is getting the short side of it."

"That's because you only have half the picture," Manet said, pulling himself upright in his chair. "You're a city boy. You don't know what it's like growing up in a little town built on one man's land.

"Here's Lord Poncington's lands," Manet said, using a bit of spilled beer to draw a circle in the center of the table. "Where you live like the good little commoner you are." Manet picked up Simmon's empty glass and put it inside the circle.

"One day, a fellow strolls through town wearing Lord Poncington's colors." Manet picked up his full glass of brand and jigged it across the table until it stood next to Sim's empty one inside the circle. "And this fellow plays songs for everyone at the local inn." Manet splashed some of the brand into Sim's glass.

Not needing any prompting, Sim grinned and drank it.

Manet trotted his glass around the table and entered the circle again. "Next month a couple more folk come through wearing his colors and put on a puppet show." He poured more brand and Simmon tossed it back. "The next month there's a play." Again.

Now Manet picked up his wooden mug and clomped it across the table into the circle. "Then the tax man shows up, wearing the same colors." Manet knocked his empty mug impatiently on the table.

Sim sat confused for a second, then he picked up his own mug and sloshed some beer into it.

Manet eyed him and tapped the mug again, sternly.

Sim poured the rest of his beer into Manet's mug, laughing. "I like black-berry brand better anyway."

"Lord Poncington likes his taxes better," Manet said. "And people like to be entertained. And the tax man likes not being poisoned and buried in a shallow grave behind the old mill." He took a drink of beer. "So it works out nicely for everyone."

Wil watched the exchange with his serious, dark eyes. "That makes better sense."

"It's not always as mercenary as that," I said. "Threpe genuinely wants to help musicians improve their craft. Some nobles treat their performers like horses in a stable," I sighed. "Even that would be better than what I have now, which is nothing."

"Don't sell yourself cheap," Sim said cheerfully. "Wait and get a good pa-tron. You deserve it. You're as good as any musician here."

I kept silent, too proud to tell them the truth. I was poor in a way the rest of them could hardly understand. Sim was Aturan nobility, and Wil's family were wool merchants from Ralien. They thought being poor meant not hav-ing enough money to go drinking as often as they liked.

With tuition looming, I didn't dare spend a bent penny. I couldn't buy candles, or ink, or paper. I had no jewelry to pawn, no allowance, no parents to write home to. No respectable moneylender would give me a thin shim. Hardly surprising, as I was a rootless, orphan Edema Ruh whose possessions would fit into a burlap sack. It wouldn't have to be a large sack either.

I got to my feet before the conversation had a chance to wander into un-comfortable territory. "It's time I made some music."

I picked up my lute case and made my way to where Stanchion sat at the corner of the bar. "What have you got for us tonight?" he asked, running his hand over his beard.

"A surprise."

Stanchion paused in the act of getting off his stool. "Is this the sort of sur-prise that's going to cause a riot or make folk set my place on fire?" he asked.

I shook my head, smiling.

"Good." He smiled and headed off in the direction of the stage. "In that case I like surprises."

CHAPTER SIX

Love

STANCHION LED ME ONTO the stage and brought out an armless chair. Then he walked to the front of the stage to chat with the audience. I spread my cloak over the back of the chair as the lights began to dim.

I laid my battered lute case on the floor. It was even shabbier than I was. It had been quite nice once, but that was years ago and miles away. Now the leather hinges were cracked and stiff, and the body was worn thin as parchment in places. Only one of the original clasps remained, a delicate thing of worked silver. I'd replaced the others with whatever I could scavenge, so now the case sported mismatched clasps of bright brass and dull iron.

But inside the case was something else entirely. Inside was the reason I was scrambling for tuition tomorrow. I had driven a hard bargain for it, and even then it had cost me more money than I had ever spent on anything in my life. So much money I couldn't afford a case that fit it properly, and made do by padding my old one with rags.

The wood was the color of dark coffee, of freshly turned earth. The curve of the bowl was perfect as a woman's hip. It was hushed echo and bright string and thrum. My lute. My tangible soul.

I have heard what poets write about women. They rhyme and rhapsodize and lie. I have watched sailors on the shore stare mutely at the slow-rolling swell of the sea. I have watched old soldiers with hearts like leather grow teary-eyed at their king's colors stretched against the wind.

Listen to me: these men know nothing of love.

You will not find it in the words of poets or the longing eyes of sailors. If you want to know of love, look to a trouper's hands as he makes his music. A trouper knows.

I looked out at my audience as they grew slowly still. Simmon waved enthusiastically, and I smiled in return. I saw Count Threpe's white hair near the rail on the second tier now. He was speaking earnestly to the well-dressed couple, gesturing in my direction. Still campaigning on my behalf though we both knew it was a hopeless cause.

I brought the lute out of its shabby case and began to tune it. It was not the finest lute in the Eolian. Not by half. Its neck was slightly bent, but not bowed. One of the pegs was loose and was prone to changing its tune.

I brushed a soft chord and tipped my ear to the strings. As I looked up, I could see Denna's face, clear as the moon. She smiled excitedly at me and wiggled her fingers below the level of the table where her gentleman couldn't see.

I touched the loose peg gently, running my hands over the warm wood of the lute. The varnish was scraped and scuffed in places. It had been treated unkindly in the past, but that didn't make it less lovely underneath.

So yes. It had flaws, but what does that matter when it comes to matters of the heart? We love what we love. Reason does not enter into it. In many ways, unwise love is the truest love. Anyone can love a thing *because*. That's as easy as putting a penny in your pocket. But to love something *despite*. To know the flaws and love them too. That is rare and pure and perfect.

Stanchion made a sweeping gesture in my direction. There was brief applause followed by an attentive hush.

I plucked two notes and felt the audience lean toward me. I touched a string, tuned it slightly, and began to play. Before a handful of notes rang out, everyone had caught the tune.

It was "Bell-Wether." A tune shepherds have been whistling for ten thousand years. The simplest of simple melodies. A tune anyone with a bucket could carry. A bucket was overkill, actually. A pair of cupped hands would manage nicely. A single hand. Two fingers, even.

It was, plainly said, folk music.

There have been a hundred songs written to the tune of "Bell-Wether." Songs of love and war. Songs of humor, tragedy, and lust. I did not bother with any of these. No words. Just the music. Just the tune.

I looked up and saw Lord Brickjaw leaning close to Denna, making a dismissive gesture. I smiled as I teased the song carefully from the strings of my lute.

But before much longer, my smile grew strained. Sweat began to bead on my forehead. I hunched over the lute, concentrating on what my hands were doing. My fingers darted, then danced, then flew.

I played hard as a hailstorm, like a hammer beating brass. I played soft as sun on autumn wheat, gentle as a single stirring leaf. Before long, my breath began to catch from the strain of it. My lips made a thin, bloodless line across my face.

As I pushed through the middle refrain I shook my head to clear my hair away from my eyes. Sweat flew in an arc to patter out along the wood of the stage. I breathed hard, my chest working like a bellows, straining like a horse run to lather.

The song rang out, each note bright and clear. I almost stumbled once. The rhythm faltered for the space of a split hair. . . . Then somehow I recovered, pushed through, and managed to finish the final line, plucking the notes sweet and light despite the fact that my fingers were a weary blur.

Then, just when it was obvious I couldn't carry on a moment longer, the last chord rang through the room and I slumped in my chair, exhausted.

The audience burst into thunderous applause.

But not the whole audience. Scattered through the room dozens of people burst into laughter instead, a few of them pounding the tables and stomping the floor, shouting their amusement.

The applause sputtered and died almost immediately. Men and women stopped with their hands frozen midclap as they stared at the laughing members of the audience. Some looked angry, others confused. Many were plainly offended on my behalf, and angry mutterings began to ripple through the room.

Before any serious discussion could take root, I struck a single high note and held up a hand, pulling their attention back to me. I wasn't done yet. Not by half.

I shifted in my seat and rolled my shoulders. I strummed once, touched the loose peg, and rolled effortlessly into my second song.

It was one of Illien's: "Tintatatornin." I doubt you've ever heard of it. It's something of an oddity compared to Illien's other works. First, it has no lyrics. Second, while it's a lovely song, it isn't nearly as catchy or moving as many of his better-known melodies.

Most importantly, it is perversely difficult to play. My father referred to it as "the finest song ever written for fifteen fingers." He made me play it when I was getting too full of myself and felt I needed humbling. Suffice to say I practiced it with fair regularity, sometimes more than once a day.

So I played "Tintatatornin." I leaned back into my chair and crossed my ankles, relaxing a bit. My hands strolled idly over the strings. After the first chorus, I drew a breath and gave a short sigh, like a young boy trapped inside on a sunny day. My eyes began to wander aimlessly around the room, bored.

Still playing, I fidgeted in my seat, trying to find a comfortable position and failing. I frowned, stood up, and looked at the chair as if it was somehow to blame. Then I reclaimed my seat and wriggled, an uncomfortable expression on my face.

All the while the ten thousand notes of "Tintatatornin" danced and capered. I took a moment between one chord and the next to scratch myself idly behind the ear.

I was so deeply into my little act that I actually felt a yawn swelling up. I let it out in full earnest, so wide and long that the people the front row could count my teeth. I shook my head as if to clear it, and daubed at my watery eyes with my sleeve.

Through all of this, "Tintatatornin" tripped into the air. Maddening harmony and counterpoint weaving together, skipping apart. All of it flawless and sweet and easy as breathing. When the end came, drawing together a dozen tangled threads of song, I made no flourish. I simply stopped and rubbed my eyes a bit. No crescendo. No bow. Nothing. I cracked my knuckles distractedly and leaned forward to set my lute back in the case.

This time the laughter came first. The same people as before, hooting and hammering at their tables twice as loudly as before. My people. The musicians. I let my bored expression fall away and grinned knowingly out at them.

The applause followed a few heartbeats later, but it was scattered and confused. Even before the house lights rose, it had dissolved into a hundred murmuring discussions throughout the room.

Marie rushed up to greet me as I came down the stairs, her face full of laughter. She shook my hand and clapped me on the back. She was the first of many, all musicians. Before I could get bogged down, Marie linked her arm in mine and led me back to my table.

"Good lord, boy," Manet said. "You're like a tiny king here."

"This isn't half the attention he usually gets," Wilem said. "Normally they're still cheering when he makes it back to the table. Young women bat their eyes and strew his path with flowers."

Sim looked around the room curiously. "The reaction did seem . . ." he groped for a word. "Mixed. Why is that?"

"Because young six-string here is so sharp he can hardly help but cut himself," Stanchion said as he made his way over to our table.

"You've noticed that too?" Manet asked dryly.

"Hush," Marie said. "It was brilliant."

Stanchion sighed and shook his head.

"I for one," Wilem said pointedly, "would like to know what is being discussed."

"Kvothe here played the simplest song in the world and made it look like he was spinning gold out of flax," Marie said. "Then he took a real piece of music, something only a handful of folk in the whole place could play, and made it look so easy you'd think a child could blow it on a tin whistle."

"I'm not denying that it was cleverly done," Stanchion said. "The problem is the way he did it. Everyone who jumped in clapping on the first song feels like an idiot. They feel they've been toyed with."

"Which they were," Marie pointed out. "A performer manipulates the audience. That's the point of the joke."

"People don't like being toyed with," Stanchion replied. "They resent it, in fact. Nobody likes having a joke played on them."

"Technically," Simmon interjected, grinning, "he played the joke on the lute."

Everyone turned to look at him, and his grin faded a bit. "You see? He actually *played* a joke. On a lute." He looked down at the table, his grin fading as his face flushed a sudden embarrassed red. "Sorry."

Marie laughed an easy laugh.

Manet spoke up. "So it's really an issue of two audiences," he said slowly. "There's those that know enough about music to get the joke, and those who need the joke explained to them."

Marie made a triumphant gesture toward Manet. "That's it exactly," she said to Stanchion. "If you come here and don't know enough to get the joke on your own, then you deserve to have your nose tweaked a bit."

"Except most of those people are the gentry," Stanchion said. "And our clever-jack doesn't have a patron yet."

"What?" Marie said. "Threpe put word out months ago. Why hasn't someone snatched you up?"

"Ambrose Jakis," I explained.

Her face didn't show any recognition. "Is he a musician?"

"Baron's son," Wilem said.

She gave a puzzled frown. "How can he possibly keep you away from a patron?"

"Ample free time and twice as much money as God," I said dryly.

"His father's one of the most powerful men in Vintas," Manet added, then turned to Simmon. "What is he, sixteenth in line to the throne?"

"Thirteenth," Simmon said sullenly. "The entire Surthen family was lost at sea two months ago. Ambrose won't shut up about the fact that his father's barely a dozen steps from being king."

Manet turned back to Marie. "The point is, this particular baron's son has got all manner of weight, and he's not afraid to throw it around."

"To be completely fair," Stanchion said, "it should be mentioned that young Kvothe is not the savviest socialite in the Commonwealth." He cleared his throat. "As evidenced by tonight's performance."

"I hate it when people call me *young Kvothe*," I said in an aside to Sim. He gave me a sympathetic look.

"I still say it was brilliant," Marie said, turning to face Stanchion, planting her feet solidly on the floor. "It's the cleverest thing anyone's done here in a month, and you know it."

I lay my hand on Marie's arm. "He's right," I said. "It was stupid." I made a vacillating shrug. "Or at least it would be if I still had the slightest hope of getting a patron." I looked Stanchion in the eye. "But I don't. We both know Ambrose has poisoned that well for me."

"Wells don't stay poisoned forever," Stanchion said.

I shrugged. "How about this then? I'd prefer to play songs that amuse my friends, rather than cater to folk who dislike me based on hearsay."

Stanchion drew a breath, then let it out in a rush. "Fair enough," he said, smiling a bit.

In the brief lull that followed, Manet cleared his throat meaningfully and darted his eyes around the table.

I took his hint and made a round of introductions. "Stanchion, you've already met my fellow students Wil and Sim. This is Manet, student and my sometimes mentor at the University. Everyone, this is Stanchion: host, owner, and master of the Eolian's stage."

"Pleasure to meet you," Stanchion said, giving a polite nod before looking anxiously around the room. "Speaking of hosting, I should be about my business." He patted me on the back as he turned to leave. "I'll see if I can put out a few fires while I'm at it."

I smiled my thanks to him, then made a flourishing gesture. "Everyone, this is Marie. As you've already heard with your own ears, the Eolian's finest fiddler. As you can see with your own eyes, the most beautiful woman in a thousand miles. As your wit discerns, the wisest of . . ."

Grinning, she swatted at me. "If I were half as wise as I am tall, I wouldn't be stepping in to defend you," she said. "Has poor Threpe really been out stumping for you all this while?"

I nodded. "I told him it was a lost cause."

"It is if you keep thumbing your nose at folk," she said. "I swear I've never met a man who has your knack for lack of social grace. If you weren't naturally charming, someone would have stabbed you by now."

"You're assuming," I muttered.

Marie turned to my friends at the table. "It's a pleasure to meet all of you."

Wil nodded, and Sim smiled. Manet, however, came to his feet in a smooth motion and held out his hand. Marie took it, and Manet clasped it warmly between his own.

"Marie," he said. "You intrigue me. Is there any chance I could buy you a drink and enjoy the pleasure of your conversation at some point tonight?"

I was too startled to do anything but stare. Standing there, the two of them looked like badly matched bookends. Marie stood six inches taller than Manet, her boots making her long legs look even longer.

Manet, on the other hand, looked as he always did, grizzled and disheveled, plus older than Marie by at least a decade.

Marie blinked and cocked her head a bit, as if considering. "I'm here with some friends right now," she said. "It might be late by the time I finish up with them."

"When makes no difference to me," Manet said easily. "I'm willing to lose some sleep if it comes to that. I can't think of the last time I shared the company of a woman who speaks her mind firmly and without hesitation. Your kind are in short supply these days."

Marie looked him over again.

Manet met her eye and flashed a smile so confident and charming that it belonged on stage. "I've no desire to pull you away from your friends," he said, "but you're the first fiddler in ten years that's set my feet dancing. It seems a drink is the least I can do."

Marie smiled back at him, half amused, half wry. "I'm on the second tier right now," she said, gesturing toward the stairway. "But I should be free in, say, two hours. . . ."

"You're terribly kind," he said. "Should I come and find you?"

"You should," she said. Then gave him a thoughtful look as she turned to walk away.

Manet reclaimed his seat and took a drink.

Simmon looked as flabbergasted as we all felt. "What the hell was that?" he demanded.

Manet chuckled into his beard and leaned back in his chair, cradling his mug to his chest. "That," he said smugly, "is just one more thing I understand that you pups don't. Take note. Take heed."

When members of the nobility want to show a musician their appreciation, they give money. When I first began playing in the Eolian, I'd received a few such gifts, and for a time it had been enough to help pay my tuition and keep my head above water, if only barely. But Ambrose had been persistent in his campaign against me, and it had been months since I had received anything of the sort.

Musicians are poorer than the gentry, but they still enjoy a show. So when they appreciate your playing, they buy you drinks. That was the real reason I was at the Eolian tonight.

Manet wandered off to fetch a wet rag from the bar so we could clean the table and play another round of corners. Before he could make it back, a young Cealdish piper came over to ask if there was any chance he could stand us a round.

There was a chance, as it turned out. He caught the eye of a nearby serving girl and we each ordered what we liked best, and a beer for Manet besides.

We drank, played cards, and listened to music. Manet and I had a run of bad cards and went down three hands in a row. It soured my mood a bit, but not nearly as much as the sneaking suspicion that Stanchion might be right about what he'd said.

A rich patron would solve many of my problems. Even a poor patron would be able to give me a little room to breathe, financially speaking. If nothing else, it would give me someone I could borrow money from in a tight spot, rather than being forced into dealing with dangerous folk.

While my mind was occupied, I misplayed and we lost another hand, putting us down four in a row with a forfeit besides.

Manet glared at me while he gathered in the cards. "Here's a primer for admissions." He held up his hand, three fingers spearing angrily into the air. "Let's say you have three spades in your hand, and there have been five spades laid down." He held up his other hand, fingers splayed wide. "How many spades is that, total?" He leaned back in his chair, crossing his arms. "Take your time."

"He's still reeling from the knowledge that Marie is willing to have a drink with you," Wilem said dryly. "We all are."

"Not me," Simmon chirped. "I knew you had it in you."

We were interrupted by the arrival of Lily, one of the regular serving girls at the Eolian. "What's going on here?" she said playfully. "Is someone throwing a handsome party?"

"Lily," Simmon asked, "If I asked you to have a drink with me, would you consider it?"

"I would," she said easily. "But not for very long." She laid her hand on his shoulder. "You gents are in luck. An anonymous admirer of fine music has offered to stand your table a round of drinks."

"Scutten for me," Wilem said.

"Mead," Simmon said, grinning.

"I'll have a sounten," I said.

Manet raised an eyebrow. "A sounten, eh?" he asked, glancing at me. "I'll have one too." He gave the serving girl a knowing look and nodded toward me. "On his, of course."

"Really?" Lily said, then shrugged. "Back in a shake."

"Now that you've impressed the hell out of everyone you can have some fun, right?" Simmon asked. "Something about a donkey. . .?"

"For the last time no," I said. "I'm done with Ambrose. There's no percentage in antagonizing him any further."

"You broke his arm," Wil said. "I think he's as antagonized as he's going to get."

"He broke my lute," I said. "We're even. I'm ready to let bygones be bygones."

"Like hell," Sim said. "You dropped that pound of rancid butter down his chimney. You loosened the cinch on his saddle. . . ."

"Black hands, shut up!" I said, looking around. "That was nearly a month ago, and no one knows it was me except for you two. And now Manet. And everyone within earshot."

Sim flushed an embarrassed red and the conversation lulled until Lily returned with our drinks. Wil's scutten was in its traditional stone cup. Sim's mead shone golden in a tall glass. Manet and I got wooden mugs.

Manet smiled. "I can't remember the last time I ordered a sounten," he mused. "I don't think I've ever ordered one for myself before."

"You're the only other person I've ever known to drink it," Sim said. "Kvothe here throws them back like nobody's business. Three or four a night."

Manet raised a bushy eyebrow at me. "They don't know?" he asked.

I shook my head as I drank out of my own mug, not sure if I should be amused or embarrassed.

Manet slid his mug toward Simmon, who picked it up and took a sip. He frowned and took another. "Water?"

Manet nodded. "It's an old whore's trick. You're chatting them up in the taproom of the brothel, and you want to show you're not like all the rest. You're a man of refinement. So you offer to buy a drink."

He reached across the table and took his mug back from Sim. "But they're working. They don't want a drink. They'd rather have the money. So they order a sounten or a peveret or something else. You pay your money, the barman gives her water, and at the end of the night she splits the money with the house. If she's a good listener a girl can make as much at the bar as she does in bed."

I chimed in. "Actually, we split it three ways. A third to the house, a third to the barman, and a third to me."

"You're getting screwed, then," Manet said frankly. "The barman should get his piece from the house."

"I've never seen you order a sounten at Anker's," Sim said.

"It must be the Greysdale mead," Wil said. "You order that all the time."

"But *I've* ordered Greysdale," Sim protested. "It tasted like sweet pickles and piss. Besides . . ." Sim trailed off.

"It was more expensive than you thought it would be?" Manet asked, grinning. "Wouldn't make much sense to go through all of this for the price of a short beer, would it?"

"They know what I mean when I order Greysdale at Anker's," I told him. "If I ordered something that didn't actually exist, it would be a pretty easy game to figure out."

"How do you know about this?" Sim asked Manet.

Manet chuckled. "No new tricks to an old dog like me," he said.

The lights began to dim and we turned toward the stage.

The night rambled on from there. Manet left for greener pastures, while Wil, Sim, and I and did our best to keep our table clear of glasses while amused musicians bought us round after round of drinks. An obscene amount of drinks, really. Far more than I'd dared to hope for.

I drank sounten for the most part, since raising money to cover tuition was the main reason I'd come to the Eolian tonight. Wil and Sim ordered a few rounds too, now that they knew the trick of it. I was doubly grateful, otherwise I would have been forced to bring them home in a wheelbarrow.

Eventually the three of us had our fill of music, gossip, and in Sim's case, the fruitless pursuit of serving girls.

Before we left, I stopped to have a discreet word with the barman where I brought up the difference between a half and a third. At the end of our negotiation, I cashed out for a full talent and six jots. The vast majority of that was from the drinks my fellow musicians had bought me tonight.

I gathered the coins into my purse: *Three talents even.*

My negotiations had also profited me two dark brown bottles. "What's that?" Sim asked as I began to tuck the bottles into my lute case.

"Bredon beer." I shifted the rags I used to pad my lute so they wouldn't rub against it.

"Bredon," Wil said, his voice thick with disdain, "is closer to bread than beer."

Sim nodded in agreement, making a face. "I don't like having to chew my liquor."

"It's not that bad," I said defensively. "In the small kingdoms women drink it when they're pregnant. Arwyl mentioned it in one of his lectures. They brew it with flower pollen and fish oil and cherry stones. It has all sorts of trace nutrients."

"Kvothe, we don't judge you." Wilem lay his hand on my shoulder, his face concerned. "Sim and I don't mind that you're a pregnant Yllish woman."

Simmon snorted, then laughed at the fact that he had snorted.

The three of us made our slow way back to the University, crossing the high arch of Stonebridge. And, since there was nobody around to hear, I sang "Jackass, Jackass" for Sim.

Wil and Sim stumbled gently off to their rooms in Mews. But I wasn't ready for bed and continued wandering the University's empty streets, breathing the cool night air.

I strolled past the dark fronts of apothecaries, glassblowers, and bookbinders. I cut through a manicured lawn, smelling the clean, dusty smell of autumn leaves and green grass beneath. Nearly all the inns and drinking houses were dark, but lights were burning in the brothels.

The grey stone of the Masters' Hall was silvery in the moonlight. A single dim light burned inside, illuminating the stained glass window that showed Teccam in his classic pose: barefoot at the mouth of his cave, speaking to a crowd of young students.

I went past the Crucible, its countless bristling chimneys dark and largely smokeless against the moonlit sky. Even at night it smelled of ammonia and charred flowers, acid and alcohol: a thousand mingled scents that had seeped into the stone of the building over the centuries.

Last was the Archives. Five stories tall and windowless, it reminded me of an enormous waystone. Its massive doors were closed, but I could see the reddish light of sympathy lamps welling up around the edges of the door. During admissions Master Lorren kept the Archives open at night so all the members of the Arcanum could study to their hearts' content. All members except one, of course.

I made my way back to Anker's and found the inn dark and silent. I had a key to the back door, but rather than stumble through the dark, I headed into the nearby alley. Right foot rainbarrel, left foot window ledge, left hand iron drainpipe. I quietly made my way up to my third-story window, tripped the latch with a piece of wire, and let myself in.

It was pitch black, and I was too tired to go looking for a light from the fireplace downstairs. So I touched the wick of the lamp beside my bed, getting a little oil on my fingers. Then I murmured a binding and felt my arm go chilly as the heat bled out of it. Nothing happened at first, and I scowled, concentrating to overcome the vague haze of alcohol. The chill sunk deeper into my arm, making me shiver, but finally the wick bloomed into light.

Cold now, I closed the window and looked around the tiny room with its sloped ceiling and narrow bed. Surprisingly, I realized there was nowhere else in the four corners I'd rather be. I almost felt as if I were home.

This may not seem odd to you, but it was strange to me. Growing up among the Edema Ruh, home was never a place for me. Home was a group of wagons and songs around a campfire. When my troupe was killed, it was more than the loss of my family and childhood friends. It was like my entire world had been burned down to the waterline.

Now, after almost a year at the University, I was beginning to feel like I belonged here. It was an odd feeling, this fondness for a place. In some ways it was comforting, but the Ruh in me was restless, rebelling at the thought of putting down roots like a plant.

As I drifted off to sleep, I wondered what my father would think of me.

CHAPTER SEVEN

Admissions

THE NEXT MORNING I splashed some water on my face and trudged downstairs. The taproom of Anker's was just starting to fill with people looking for an early lunch, and a few particularly disconsolate students were getting an early start on the day's drinking.

Still bleary from lack of sleep, I settled into my usual corner table and began to fret about my upcoming interview.

Kilvin and Elxa Dal didn't worry me. I was ready for their questions. The same was largely true of Arwyl. But the other masters were all varying degrees of mystery to me.

Every term each master put a selection of books on display in Tomes, the reading room in the Archives. There were basic texts for the low-ranking E'lir to study from, with progressively more advanced works for Re'lar and El'the. Those books revealed what the masters considered valuable knowledge. Those were the books a clever student studied before admissions.

But I couldn't wander into Tomes like everyone else. I was the only student who had been banned from the Archives in a dozen years, and everyone knew about it. Tomes was the only well-lit room in the whole building, and during admissions there were always people there, reading.

So I was forced to find copies of the masters' texts buried in the Stacks. You'd be amazed how many versions of the same book there can be. If I was lucky, the volume I found was identical to the one the master had set aside in Tomes. More often, the versions I found were outdated, expurgated, or badly translated.

I'd done as much reading as possible over the last few nights, but hunting down the books took precious time, and I was still woefully underprepared.

I was lost in these anxious thoughts when Anker's voice caught my attention. "Actually, that's Kvothe right over there," he said.

I looked up to see a woman sitting at the bar. She wasn't dressed like a student. She wore an elaborate burgundy dress with long skirts, a tight waist, and matching burgundy gloves that rose all the way to her elbows.

Moving deliberately, she managed to get down off the stool without tangling her feet and made her way over to stand next to my table. Her blonde hair was artfully curled, and her lips were a deeply painted red. I couldn't help wondering what she was doing in a place like Anker's.

"Are you the one who broke the arm of that brat Ambrose Jakis?" she asked. She spoke Aturan with a thick, musical Modegan accent. While it made her a little difficult to understand, I'd be lying if I said I didn't find it attractive. The Modegan accent practically sweats sex.

"I did," I said. "It wasn't entirely on purpose. But I did."

"Then you must let me buy you a drink," she said in the tone of a woman who usually gets her way.

I smiled at her, wishing I'd been awake more than ten minutes so my wits weren't quite so fuddled. "You wouldn't be the first to buy me one on that account," I said honestly. "If you insist, I'll have a Greysdale mead."

I watched her turn and walk back to the bar. If she was a student, she was new. If she'd been here more than a handful of days I would have heard about it from Sim, who kept tabs on all the prettiest girls in town, courting them with artless enthusiasm.

The Modegan woman returned a moment later and sat across from me, sliding a wooden mug across the table. Anker must have just finished washing it, as the fingers of her burgundy glove were wet where they had gripped the handle.

She raised her own glass, filled with a deep red wine. "To Ambrose Jakis," she said with sudden fierceness. "May he fall into a well and die."

I picked up the mug and took a drink, wondering if there was a woman within fifty miles of the University Ambrose hadn't treated badly. I wiped my hand discreetly on my pants.

The woman took a deep drink of her wine and set her glass down hard. Her pupils were huge. Early as it was, she must have already been doing a fair piece of drinking.

I could suddenly smell nutmeg and plum. I sniffed at my mug, then looked at the tabletop, thinking someone might have spilled a drink. But there was nothing.

The woman across from me suddenly burst into tears. This was no gentle weeping, either. It was like someone had turned a spigot.

She looked down at her gloved hands and shook her head. She peeled off the wet one, looked at me, and sobbed out a dozen words of Modegan.

"I'm sorry," I said helplessly. "I don't speak—"

But she was already pushing herself up and away from the table. Wiping at her face, she ran for the door.

Anker stared at me from behind the bar, as did everyone else in the room. "That was not my fault," I said, pointing at the door. "She went crazy on her own."

I would have followed her and tried to unravel it all, but she was already outside, and my admissions interview was less than an hour away. Besides, if I tried to help every woman Ambrose had ever traumatized, I wouldn't have time left for eating or sleeping.

On the upside, the bizarre encounter seemed to have cleared my head, and I no longer felt gritty and thick with lack of sleep. I decided I might as well take advantage of it and get admissions out of the way. Sooner begun is sooner done, as my father used to say.

On my way to Hollows, I stopped to buy a golden brown meat pie from a vender's cart. I knew I'd need every penny for this term's tuition, but the price of a decent meal wasn't going to make much difference one way or the other. It was hot and solid, full of chicken and carrot and sage. I ate it while I walked, reveling in the small freedom of buying something according to my taste rather than making do with whatever Anker happened to have at hand.

As I finished the last bit of crust, I smelled honeyed almonds. I bought a large scoop in a clever pouch made from a dried corn husk. It cost me four drabs, but I hadn't had honeyed almonds in years, and some sugar in my blood wouldn't hurt when I was answering questions.

The line for admissions wound through the courtyard. Not abnormally long, but irritating nonetheless. I saw a familiar face from the Fishery and went to stand next to a young, green-eyed woman who was waiting to queue up as well.

"Hello there," I said. "You're Amlia, aren't you?"

She gave me a nervous smile and a nod.

"I'm Kvothe," I said, making a tiny bow.

"I know who you are," she said. "I've seen you in the Artificery."

"You should call it the Fishery," I said. I held out the pouch. "Would you like a honey almond?"

Amlia shook her head.

"They're really good," I said, joggling them enticingly in the corn-husk pouch.

She reached out hesitantly and took one.

"Is this the line for noon?" I asked, gesturing.

She shook her head. "We've got another couple minutes before we can even line up."

"It's ridiculous that they make us stand around like this," I said. "Like sheep in a paddock. This entire process is a waste of everyone's time and insulting to boot." I saw a flicker of anxiety cross Amlia's face. "What?" I asked her.

"It's just that you're talking a little loudly," she said, looking around.

"I'm just not afraid to say what everybody else is thinking," I said. "The whole admissions process is flawed to the point of blinding idiocy. Master Kilvin knows what I'm capable of. So does Elxa Dal. Brandeur doesn't know me from a hole in the ground. Why should he get an equal say in my tuition?"

Amlia shrugged, not meeting my eye.

I bit into another almond and quickly spit it onto the cobblestones. "Feah!" I held them out to her. "Do these taste like plums to you?"

She gave me a vaguely disgusted look, then her eyes focused on something behind me.

I turned to see Ambrose moving through the courtyard towards us. He cut a fine figure, as he always did, dressed in clean white linen, velvet, and brocade. He wore a hat with a tall white plume, and the sight of it made me unreasonably angry. Uncharacteristically, he was alone, devoid of his usual contingent of toadies and bootlickers.

"Wonderful," I said as soon as he came within earshot. "Ambrose, your presence is the horseshit frosting on the horseshit cake that is the admissions interview process."

Surprisingly, Ambrose smiled at this. "Ah, Kvothe. I'm pleased to see you too."

"I met one of your previous ladyloves today," I said. "She was dealing with the sort of profound emotional trauma I assume comes from seeing you naked."

His expression soured a little at that, and I leaned over and spoke to Amlia in a stage whisper. "I have it on good report that not only does Ambrose have a tiny, tiny penis, but he can only become aroused when in the presence of a dead dog, a painting of the Duke of Gibea, and a shirtless galley drummer."

Amlia's expression was frozen.

Ambrose looked at her. "You should leave," he said gently. "There's no reason you should have to listen to this sort of thing."

Amlia practically fled.

"I'll give you that," I said, watching her go. "Nobody can make a woman run like you." I tipped an imaginary hat. "You could give lessons. You could teach a class."

Ambrose just stood, nodding contentedly and watching me in an oddly proprietary way.

"That hat makes you look like you fancy young boys," I added. "And I've a mind to slap it right off your head if you don't piss off." I looked at him. "Speaking of which, how's the arm?"

"It's feeling a great deal better at the moment," he said pleasantly. He rubbed at it absentmindedly as he stood there, smiling.

I popped another almond into my mouth, then grimaced and spit it out again.

"What's the matter?" Ambrose asked. "Don't fancy plum?" Then, without waiting for an answer, he turned and walked away. He was smiling.

It says a great deal for my state of mind that I simply watched him go, confused. I lifted the pouch to my nose and took a deep breath. I smelled the dusty smell of the corn husk, honey, and cinnamon. Nothing at all of plum or nutmeg. How could Ambrose possibly know. . .?

Then everything came crashing together in my head. At the same time, noon bell rang out and everyone with a tile similar to mine moved to join the long line winding through the courtyard. It was time for my admissions exam.

I left the courtyard at a dead run.

———

I pounded frantically on the door, out of breath from running up to the third floor of Mews. "Simmon!" I shouted. "Open this door and talk to me!"

Along the hallway doors opened and students peered out at the commotion. One of the heads peering out was Simmon's, his sandy hair in disarray. "Kvothe?" he said. "What are you doing? That's not even my door."

I walked over, pushed him inside his room, and closed the door behind us. "Simmon. Ambrose drugged me. I think there's something not right in my head, but I can't tell what it is."

Simmon grinned. "I've thought that for a . . ." He trailed off, his expression turning incredulous. "What are you doing? Don't spit on my floor!"

"I have a strange taste in my mouth," I explained.

"I don't care," he said, angry and confused. "What's wrong with you? Were you born in a barn?"

I struck him hard across the face with the flat of my hand, sending him staggering up against the wall. "I was born in a barn, actually," I said grimly. "Is there something wrong with that?"

Sim stood with one hand braced against the wall, the other against the reddening skin of his cheek. His expression pure astonishment. "What in God's name is wrong with you?"

"Nothing's wrong with me," I said, "but you'd do well to watch your tone. I like you well enough, but just because I don't have a set of rich parents doesn't mean you're one whit better than me." I frowned and spit again. "God that's foul, I hate nutmeg. I have ever since I was a child."

A sudden realization washed over Sim's face. "The taste in your mouth," he said. "Is it like plums and spice?"

I nodded. "It's disgusting."

"God's grey ashes," Sim said, his voice hushed in grim earnest. "Okay. You're right. You've been drugged. I know what it is." He trailed off as I turned around and started to open the door. "What are you doing?"

"I'm going to go kill Ambrose," I said. "For poisoning me."

"It's not a poison. It's—" He stopped speaking abruptly, then continued in a calm, level voice. "Where did you get that knife?"

"I keep it strapped to my leg, under my pants," I said. "For emergencies."

Sim drew a deep breath, then let it out. "Could you give me a minute to explain before you go kill Ambrose?"

I shrugged. "Okay."

"Would you mind sitting down while we talk?" He gestured to a chair.

I sighed and sat down. "Fine. But hurry. I've got admissions soon."

Sim nodded calmly and sat on the edge of his bed, facing me. "Okay, you know when someone's been drinking, and they get it into their head to do something stupid? And you can't talk them out of it even though it's obviously a bad idea?"

I laughed. "Like when you wanted to go talk to that harper girl outside the Eolian and threw up on her horse?"

He nodded. "Exactly like that. There's something an alchemist can make that does the same thing, but it's much more extreme."

I shook my head. "I don't feel drunk in the least. My head is clear as a bell."

Sim nodded again. "It's not like being drunk," he said. "It's just that one piece of it. It won't make you dizzy or tired. It just makes it easier for a person to do something stupid."

I thought about it for a moment. "I don't think that's it," I said. "I don't feel like I want to do anything stupid."

"There's one way to tell," Sim said. "Can you think of anything right now that seems like a bad idea?"

I thought for a moment, tapping the flat of the knife's blade idly against the edge of my boot.

"It would be a bad idea to . . ." I trailed off.

I thought for a longer moment. Sim looked at me expectantly.

". . . to jump off the roof?" My voice curled up at the end, making it a sort of question.

Sim was quiet. He kept looking at me.

"I see the problem," I said slowly. "I don't seem to have any behavioral filters."

Simmon gave a relieved smile and nodded encouragingly. "That's it exactly. All your inhibitions have been sliced off so cleanly you can't even tell they're gone. But everything else is the same. You're steady, articulate, and rational."

"You're patronizing me," I said, pointing at him with the knife. "Don't."

He blinked. "Fair enough. Can you think of a solution to the problem?"

"Of course. I need some sort of behavioral touchstone. You're going to need to be my compass because you still have your filters in place."

"I was thinking the same thing," he said. "So you'll trust me?"

I nodded. "Except when it comes to women. You're an idiot with women." I picked up a glass of water from a nearby table and rinsed my mouth out with it, spitting it onto the floor.

Sim gave a shaky smile. "Fair enough. First, you can't go kill Ambrose."

I hesitated. "You're sure?"

"I'm sure. In fact, pretty much anything you think to do with that knife is going to be a bad idea. You should give it to me."

I shrugged and flipped it over in my palm, handing him the makeshift leather grip.

Sim seemed surprised by this, but he took hold of the knife. "Merciful Tehlu," he said with a profound sigh, setting the knife down on the bed. "Thank you."

"Was that an extreme case?" I asked, rinsing my mouth out again. "We should probably have some sort of ranking system. Like a ten point scale."

"Spitting water onto my floor is a one," he said.

"Oh," I said. "Sorry." I put the cup back onto his desk.

"It's okay," he said easily.

"Is one low or high?" I asked.

"Low," he said. "Killing Ambrose is a ten." He hesitated. "Maybe an eight." He shifted in his seat. "Or a seven."

"Really?" I said. "That much? Okay then." I leaned forward in my seat. "You need to give me some tips for admissions. I've got to get back into line before too long."

Simmon shook his head firmly. "No. That's a really bad idea. Eight."

"Really?"

"Really," he said. "It is a delicate social situation. A lot of things could go wrong."

"But if—"

Sim let out a sigh, brushing his sandy hair out of his eyes. "Am I your touchstone or not? This is going to get tedious if I have to tell you everything three times before you listen."

I thought about it for a moment. "You're right, especially if I'm about to do something potentially dangerous." I looked around. "How long is this going to last?"

"No more than eight hours." He opened his mouth to continue, then closed it.

"What?" I asked.

Sim sighed. "There might be some side effects. It's lipid soluble, so it will hang around in your body a bit. You might experience occasional minor relapses brought about by stress, intense emotion, exercise. . . ." He gave me an apologetic look. "They'd be like little echoes of this."

"I'll worry about that later," I said. I held out my hand. "Give me your admissions tile. You can go through now. I'll take your slot."

He spread his hands helplessly. "I've already gone," he explained.

"Tehlu's tits and teeth," I cursed. "Fine. Go get Fela."

He waved his hands violently in front of himself. "No. No no no. Ten."

I laughed. "Not for that. She has a slot late on Cendling."

"You think she'll trade with you?"

"She's already offered."

Sim got to his feet. "I'll go find her."

"I'll stay here," I said.

Sim gave an enthusiastic nod and looked nervously around the room. "It's probably safest if you don't do anything while I'm gone," he said as he opened the door. "Just sit on your hands until I get back."

———

Sim was only gone for five minutes, which was probably for the best.

There was a knock on the door. "It's me," Sim's voice came through the wood. "Is everything all right in there?"

"You know what's strange?" I said to him through the door. "I tried to think of something funny I could do while you were gone, but I couldn't." I looked around at the room. "I think that means humor is rooted in social transgression. I can't transgress because I can't figure out what would be socially unacceptable. Everything seems the same to me."

"You might have a point," he said, then asked, "did you do something anyway?"

"No," I said. "I decided to be good. Did you find Fela?"

"I did. She's here. But before we come in, you have to promise not to do anything without asking me first. Fair?"

I laughed. "Fair enough. Just don't make me do stupid things in front of her."

"I promise," Sim said. "Why don't you sit down? Just to be safe."

"I'm already sitting," I said.

Sim opened the door. I could see Fela peering over his shoulder.

"Hello Fela," I said. "I need to trade slots with you."

"First," Sim said. "You should put your shirt back on. That's about a two."

"Oh," I said. "Sorry. I was hot."

"You could have opened the window."

"I thought it would be safer if I limited my interactions with external objects," I said.

Sim raised an eyebrow. "That's actually a really good idea. It just steered you a little wrong in this case."

"Wow." I heard Fela's voice from the hallway. "Is he serious?"

"Absolutely serious," Sim said. "Honestly? I don't think it's safe for you to come in."

I tugged my shirt on. "Dressed," I said. "I'll even sit on my hands if it will make you feel better." I did just that, tucking them under my legs.

Sim let Fela inside, then closed the door behind her.

"Fela, you are just gorgeous," I said. "I would give you all the money in my purse if I could just look at you naked for two minutes. I'd give everything I own. Except my lute."

It's hard to say which of them blushed a deeper red. I think it was Sim.

"I wasn't supposed to say that, was I?" I said.

"No," Sim said. "That's about a five."

"But that doesn't make any sense," I said. "Women are naked in paintings. People buy paintings, don't they? Women pose for them."

Sim nodded. "That's true. But still. Just sit for a moment and don't say or do anything? Okay?"

I nodded.

"I can't quite believe this," Fela said, the blush fading from her cheeks. "I can't help but think the two of you are playing some sort of elaborate joke on me."

"I wish we were," Simmon said. "This stuff is terribly dangerous."

"How can he remember naked paintings and not remember you're supposed to keep your shirt on in public?" she asked Sim, her eyes never leaving me.

"It just didn't seem very important," I said. "I took my shirt off when I was whipped. That was public. It seems a strange thing to get in trouble for."

"Do you know what would happen if you tried to knife Ambrose?" Simmon asked.

I thought for a second. It was like trying to remember what you'd eaten for breakfast a month ago. "There'd be a trial, I suppose," I said slowly, "and people would buy me drinks."

Fela muffled a laugh behind her hand.

"How about this?" Simmon asked me. "Which is worse, stealing a pie or killing Ambrose?"

I gave it a moment's hard thought. "A meat pie, or a fruit pie?"

"Wow," Fela said breathlessly. "That's . . ." She shook her head. "It almost makes my skin crawl."

Simmon nodded. "It's a terrifying piece of alchemy. It's a variation of a sedative called a plum bob. You don't even have to ingest it. It's absorbed straight through the skin."

Fela looked at him. "How do you know so much about it?"

Sim gave a weak smile. "Mandrag lectures about it in every alchemy class he teaches. I've heard the story a dozen times by now. It's his favorite example of how alchemy can be abused. An alchemist used it to ruin the lives of several government officials in Atur about fifty years ago. He only got caught because a countess ran amok in the middle of a wedding, killed a dozen folk and—"

Sim stopped, shaking his head. "Anyway. It was bad. Bad enough that the alchemist's mistress turned him over to the guards."

"I hope he got what he deserved."

"And with some to spare," Sim said grimly. "The point is, it hits everyone a little differently. It's not a simple lowering of inhibition. There's an amplification of emotion. A freeing up of hidden desire combined with a strange type of selective memory, almost like a moral amnesia."

"I don't feel bad," I said. "I feel pretty good, actually. But I'm worried about admissions."

Sim gestured. "See? He remembers admissions. It's important to him. But other things are just . . . gone."

"Is there a cure?" Fela asked nervously. "Shouldn't we take him to the Medica?"

Simmon looked nervous. "I don't think so. They might try a purgative, but it's not as if there's a drug working through him. Alchemy doesn't work like

that. He's under the influence of unbound principles. You can't flush those
out the way you'd try to get rid of mercury or ophalum."

"A purgative doesn't sound like much fun," I added. "If my vote counts
for anything."

"And there's a chance they might think he's cracked under admission
stress," Sim said to Fela. "That happens to a few students every term. They'd
stick him in Haven until they were sure—"

I was on my feet, my hands clenched into fists. "I'll be cut into pieces in
hell before I let them stick me in Haven," I said, furious. "Even for an hour.
Even for a minute."

Sim blanched and took a step back, raising his hands defensively, palms out.
But his voice was firm and calm. "Kvothe, I am telling you three times. Stop."

I stopped. Fela was watching me with wide, frightened eyes.

Simmon continued firmly. "Kvothe, I am telling you three times: sit down."

I sat.

Standing behind him, Fela looked at Simmon, surprised.

"Thank you," Simmon said graciously, lowering his hands. "I agree. The
Medica isn't the best place for you. We can just ride this out here."

"That sounds better to me too," I said.

"Even if things did go smoothly at the Medica," Simmon added. "I expect
you will be more inclined to speak your mind than usual." He gave a small,
wry smile. "Secrets are the cornerstone of civilization, and I know you have
a few more than most folk."

"I don't think I have any secrets," I said.

Sim and Fela both burst out laughing at the same time. "I'm afraid you just
proved his point," Fela said. "I know you have at least a few."

"So do I," Sim said.

"You're my touchstone," I shrugged. Then I smiled at Fela and pulled out
my purse.

Sim shook his head at me. "No no no. I've already told you. Seeing her
naked would be the worst thing in the world right now."

Fela's eyes narrowed a little at that.

"What's the matter?" I asked. "Are you worried I'll tackle her to the
ground and ravage her?" I laughed.

Sim looked at me. "Wouldn't you?"

"Of course not," I said.

He looked at Fela, then back. "Can you say why?" he asked curiously.

I thought about it. "It's because . . ." I trailed off, then shook my head.
"It . . . I just can't. I know I can't eat a stone or walk through a wall. It's like
that."

I concentrated on it for a second and began to get dizzy. I put one hand over my eyes and tried to ignore the sudden vertigo. "Please tell me I'm right about that," I asked, suddenly scared. "I can't cat a stone, can I?"

"You're right," Fela said quickly. "You can't."

I stopped trying to rummage around the inside of my mind for answers and the odd vertigo faded.

Sim was watching me intently. "I wish I knew what *that* signified," he said.

"I have a fair idea," Fela murmured softly.

I drew the ivory admissions tile out of my purse. "I was just looking to trade," I said. "Unless you are willing to let me see you naked." I hefted the purse with my other hand and met Fela's eye. "Sim says it's wrong, but he's an idiot with women. My head might not be screwed on quite as tightly as I'd like, but I remember that clearly."

———————

It was four hours before my inhibitions began to filter back, and two more before they were firmly in place. Simmon spent the entire day with me, patient as a priest, explaining that no, I shouldn't go buy us a bottle of brand. No, I shouldn't go kick the dog that was barking across the street. No, I shouldn't go to Imre and look for Denna. No. Three times no.

By the time the sun went down I was back to my regular, semi-moral self. Simmon quizzed me extensively before walking me back to my room at Anker's, where he made me swear on my mother's milk that I wouldn't leave my room until morning. I swore.

But all was not right with me. My emotions were still running hot, flaring up at every little thing. Worse, my memory hadn't simply returned to normal, it was back with a vivid and uncontrollable enthusiasm.

It hadn't been that bad when I was with Simmon. His presence was a pleasant distraction. But alone in my small garret room in Anker's, I was at the mercy of my memory. It was as if my mind was determined to unpack and examine every sharp and painful thing I had ever seen.

You might think the worst memories were those of when my troupe was killed. Of how I came back to our camp and found everything aflame. The unnatural shapes my parents' bodies made in the dim twilight. The smell of scorched canvas and blood and burning hair. Memories of the ones who killed them. Of the Chandrian. Of the man who spoke to me, grinning all the while. Of Cinder.

These were bad memories, but over the years I had brought them out and handled them so often there was hardly a sharp edge left to them. I remembered the pitch and timbre of Haliax's voice as clearly as my father's.

I could easily bring to mind the face of Cinder. His perfect, smiling teeth. His white, curling hair. His eyes, black as beads of ink. His voice, full of winter's chill, saying: *Someone's parents have been singing entirely the wrong sorts of songs.*

You would think these would be the worst memories. But you would be wrong.

No. The worst memories were those of my young life. The slow roll and bump of riding in the wagon, my father holding the reins loosely. His strong hands on my shoulders, showing me how to stand on the stage so my body said *proud*, or *sad*, or *shy*. His fingers adjusting mine on the strings of his lute.

My mother brushing my hair. The feel of her arms around me. The perfect way my head fit into the curve of her neck. How I would sit, curled in her lap next to the fire at night, drowsy and happy and safe.

These were the worst memories. Precious and perfect. Sharp as a mouthful of broken glass. I lay in bed, clenched into a trembling knot, unable to sleep, unable to turn my mind to other things, unable to stop myself from remembering. Again. And again. And again.

Then there came a small tapping at my window. A sound so tiny I didn't notice it until it stopped. Then I heard the window ease open behind me.

"Kvothe?" Auri said softly.

I clenched my teeth against the sobbing and lay still as I could, hoping she would think I was asleep and leave.

"Kvothe?" she called again. "I brought you—" There was a moment of silence, then she said, "Oh."

I heard a soft sound behind me. The moonlight showed her tiny shadow on the wall as she climbed through the window. I felt the bed move as she settled onto it.

A small, cool hand brushed the side of my face.

"It's okay," she said quietly. "Come here."

I began to cry quietly, and she gently uncurled the tight knot of me until my head lay in her lap. She murmured, brushing my hair away from my forehead, her hands cool against my hot face.

"I know," she said sadly. "It's bad sometimes, isn't it?"

She stroked my hair gently, and it only made me cry harder. I could not remember the last time someone had touched me in a loving way.

"I know," she said. "You have a stone in your heart, and some days it's so heavy there is nothing to be done. But you don't have to be alone for it. You should have come to me. I understand."

My body clenched and suddenly the taste of plum filled my mouth again. "I miss her," I said before I realized I was speaking. Then I bit it off before I could say anything else. I clenched my teeth and shook my head furiously, like a horse fighting its reins.

"You can say it," Auri said gently.

I shook again, tasted plum, and suddenly the words were pouring out of me. "She said I sang before I spoke. She said when I was just a baby she had the habit of humming when she held me. Nothing like a song. Just a descending third. Just a soothing sound. Then one day she was walking me around the camp, and she heard me echo it back to her. Two octaves higher. A tiny piping third. She said it was my first song. We sang it back and forth to each other. For years." I choked and clenched my teeth.

"You can say it," Auri said softly. "It's okay if you say it."

"I'm never going to see her again," I choked out. Then I began to cry in earnest.

"It's okay," Auri said softly. "I'm here. You're safe."

CHAPTER EIGHT

Questions

THE NEXT FEW DAYS were neither pleasant nor productive. Fela's admissions slot was at the very end of the span, so I attempted to put the extra time to good use. I tried to do some piecework in the Fishery, but quickly returned to my room when I broke down crying halfway through inscribing a heat funnel. Not only couldn't I maintain the proper Alar, but the last thing I needed was for people to think I'd cracked under the stress of admissions.

Later that night, when I tried to crawl through the narrow tunnel into the Archives, the taste of plum flooded my mouth, and I was filled with a mindless fear of the dark, confining space. Luckily, I'd only gone a dozen feet, but even so I almost gave myself a concussion struggling backwards out of the tunnel, and my palms were scraped raw from my panicked scrabbling against the stone.

So I spent the next two days pretending I was sick and keeping to my tiny room. I played my lute, slept fitfully, and thought dark thoughts of Ambrose.

Anker was cleaning up when I came downstairs. "Feeling better?" he asked.

"A bit," I said. Yesterday I'd only had two plum echoes, and they were very brief. Better yet, I'd managed to sleep the whole night through. It seemed I was through the worst of it.

"You hungry?"

I shook my head. "Admissions today."

Anker frowned. "You should have something, then. An apple." He bustled around behind the bar, then brought out a pottery mug and a heavy jug. "Have some milk too. I've got to make use of it before it turns. Damn iceless started giving up the ghost a couple days ago. Three talents solid that thing cost me. I knew I shouldn't have wasted money on it with ice so cheap around here."

I leaned over the bar and peered at the long wooden box tucked away among the mugs and bottles. "I could take a look at it for you," I offered.

Anker raised an eyebrow. "Can you do something with it?"

"I can look," I said. "Could be something simple I could fix."

Anker shrugged. "You can't break it more than it's already broken." He wiped his hands on his apron and motioned me behind the bar. "I'll do you a couple eggs while you're having your look. I should use those up too." He opened the long box, took out a handful of eggs, then walked back into the kitchen.

I made my way around the corner of the bar and knelt to look at the iceless. It was a stone-lined box the size of a small traveling trunk. Anywhere other than the University it would have been a miracle of artificing, a luxury. Here, where such things were easy to come by, it was just another piece of needless God-bothering that wasn't working properly.

It was about as simple a piece of artificing as could be made. No moving parts at all, just two flat bands of tin covered in sygaldry that moved heat from one end of the metal band to the other. It was really nothing more than a slow, inefficient heat siphon.

I crouched down and rested my fingers on the tin bands. The right-hand one was warm, meaning the half on the inside would be correspondingly cool. But the one on the left was room temperature. I craned my neck to get a look at the sygaldry and spotted a deep scratch in the tin, scoring through two of the runes.

That explained it. A piece of sygaldry is like a sentence in a lot of ways. If you remove a couple words, it simply doesn't make any sense. I should say it *usually* doesn't make sense. Sometimes a damaged piece of sygaldry can do something truly unpleasant. I frowned down at the band of tin. This was sloppy artificing. The runes should have been on the inside of the band where they couldn't be damaged.

I rummaged around until I found a disused ice hammer in the back of a drawer, then carefully tapped the two damaged runes flat into the soft surface of the tin. Then I concentrated and used the tip of a paring knife to etch them back into the thick metal band.

Anker emerged from the kitchen with a plateful of eggs and tomatoes. "It should work now," I said. I started eating out of politeness, then realized I was actually hungry.

Anker looked over the box, lifting the lid. "That easy?"

"Same as anything else," I said, my mouth half full. "Easy if you know what you're doing. It *should* work. Give it a day and see if it actually chills down."

I finished off the plateful of eggs and drank the milk as quickly as I could without being rude. "I'll need to cash out my bar credit today," I said. "Tuition's going to be hard this term."

Anker nodded and checked a small ledger he kept underneath the bar, tallying all the Greysdale mead I'd pretended to drink over the last two months. Then he pulled out his purse and counted out ten copper jots onto the table. A full talent: twice what I'd expected. I looked up at him, puzzled.

"One of Kilvin's boys would have charged me at least half a talent to come round and fix this thing," Anker explained, kicking at the iceless.

"I can't be sure. . . ."

He waved me into silence. "If it isn't fixed, I'll take it out of your wages over the next month," he said. "Or I'll use it as leverage to get you to start playing Reaving night too." He grinned. "I consider it an investment."

I gathered the money into my purse: *Four talents.*

———

I was heading toward the Fishery to see if my lamps had finally sold when I caught a glimpse of a familiar face crossing the courtyard wearing dark master's robes.

"Master Elodin!" I called as I saw him approaching a side door to the Masters' Hall. It was one of the few buildings I hadn't spent much time in, as it contained little more than living quarters for the masters, the resident gillers, and guest rooms for visiting arcanists.

He turned at the sound of his name. Then, seeing me jogging toward him, he rolled his eyes and turned back to the door.

"Master Elodin," I said, breathing a little hard. "Might I ask you a quick question?"

"Statistically speaking, it's pretty likely," he said, unlocking the door with a bright brass key.

"May I ask you a question, then?"

"I doubt any power known to man could stop you." He swung open the door and headed inside.

I hadn't been invited, but I slipped inside after him. Elodin was difficult to track down, and I worried if I didn't take this chance, I might not see him again for another span of days.

I followed him through a narrow stone hallway. "I'd heard a rumor you were gathering a group of students to study naming," I said cautiously.

"That's not a question," Elodin said as he headed up a long, narrow flight of stairs.

I fought back the urge to snap at him and took a deep breath instead. "Is it true you're teaching such a class?"

"Yes."

"Were you planning on including me?"

Elodin stopped and turned to face me on the stairway. He looked out of place in his dark master's robe. His hair was tousled and his face was too young, almost boyish.

He stared at me for a long minute. He looked me up and down as if I were a horse he were thinking of betting on, or a side of beef he was considering selling by the pound.

But that was nothing compared to when he met my eyes. For a heartbeat it was simply unsettling. Then it almost felt like the light on the stairway grew dim. Or that I was suddenly being thrust deep underwater and the pressure was keeping me from drawing a full breath.

"Damn you, half-wit." I heard a familiar voice that seemed to be coming from a long way off. "If you're going catatonic again, have the decency to do it in Haven and save us the trouble of carting your foam-flecked carcass back there. Barring that, get to one side."

Elodin looked away from me and suddenly everything was bright and clear again. I fought to keep from gasping in a lungful of air.

Master Hemme stomped down the stairs, shouldering Elodin roughly to one side. When he saw me he snorted. "Of course. The quarter-wit is here too. Might I recommend a book for your perusal? It is a lovely piece of reading titled, *Hallways, Their Form and Function: A Primer for the Mentally Deficient.*"

He glowered at me, and when I didn't immediately jump aside he gave me an unpleasant smile. "Ah, but you're still banned from the Archives, aren't you? Should I arrange to present the salient information in a form more suited to your kind? Perhaps a mummer's play or some manner of puppet show?"

I stepped to one side and Hemme stormed by, muttering to himself. Elodin stared daggers into the other master's broad back. Only after Hemme turned the corner did Elodin's attention settle back on me.

He sighed. "Perhaps it would be better if you pursued your other studies, Re'lar Kvothe. Dal has a fondness for you, as does Kilvin. You seem to be progressing well with them."

"But sir," I said, trying to keep the dismay out of my voice. "You're the one who sponsored my promotion to Re'lar."

He turned and began climbing the stairs again. "Then you should value my sage advice, shouldn't you?"

"But, if you're teaching other students, why not me?"

"Because you are too eager to be properly patient," he said flippantly. "You're too proud to listen properly. And you're too clever by half. That's the worst of it."

"Some masters prefer clever students," I muttered as we emerged into a wide hallway.

"Yes," Elodin said. "Dal and Kilvin and Arwyl like clever students. Go study with one of them. Both our lives will be considerably easier because of it."

"But . . ."

Elodin came to an abrupt halt in the middle of the hallway. "Fine," he said. "Prove you're worth teaching. Shake my assumptions down to their foundation stones." He patted at his robes dramatically, as if looking for something lost in a pocket. "Much to my dismay, I find myself without a way to get past this door." He rapped it with a knuckle. "What do you do in this situation, Re'lar Kvothe?"

I smiled despite my general irritation. He couldn't have picked a challenge more perfectly suited to my talents. I pulled a long, slender piece of spring steel out of a pocket in my cloak, then knelt in front of the door and eyed the keyhole. The lock was substantial, made to last. But while large, heavy locks look impressive, they're actually easier to circumvent if they're well-maintained.

This one was. It took me the space of three slow breaths to trip it with a satisfying *k-tick*. I stood up, brushed off my knees, and swung the door inward with a flourish.

For his part, Elodin did seem somewhat impressed. His eyebrows went up as the door swung open. "Clever," he said as he walked inside.

I followed on his heels. I'd never really wondered what Elodin's rooms were like. But if I'd guessed, it wouldn't have been anything resembling this.

They were huge and lavish, with high ceilings and thick rugs. Old wood paneled the walls, and tall windows let in the early morning light. There were oil paintings and massive pieces of ancient wooden furniture. It was bizarrely ordinary.

Elodin moved quickly through the entryway, through a tasteful sitting room, then into the bedroom. Call it a bed*chamber*, rather. It was huge, with a four-post bed big as a boat. Elodin threw open a wardrobe and started removing several long, dark robes similar to the one he was wearing.

"Here." Elodin shoved robes into my arms until I couldn't hold any more. Some were everyday cotton, but others were fine linen or rich, soft velvet. He lay another half-dozen robes over his own arm and carried them back into the sitting room.

We passed old bookshelves lined with hundreds of books and a huge polished desk. One wall was taken up with a large stone fireplace big enough to roast a pig, though there was currently only a small fire smoldering there, keeping away the early autumn chill.

Elodin lifted a crystal decanter off a table and went to stand in front of the fireplace. He dumped the robes he was carrying into my arms so I could barely see over the top of them. Delicately lifting the top off the decanter, he sipped at the contents and raised an eyebrow appreciatively, holding it up to the light.

I decided to try again. "Master Elodin, why don't you want to teach me naming?"

"That's the wrong question," he said, and upended the decanter onto smoldering coals in the fireplace. As the flames licked up hungrily, he took his armload of robes back and fed a velvet one slowly into the fire. It caught quickly, and when it was blazing away, he fed the others onto the fire in quick succession. The result was a great smoldering pile of cloth that sent thick smoke billowing up the chimney. "Try again."

I couldn't help but ask the obvious. "Why are you burning your clothes?"

"Nope. Not even close to the right question," he said as he took more robes out of my arms and piled them into the fireplace. Then Elodin grabbed the handle for the flue and pulled it closed with a metallic clank. Great clouds of smoke began to pour into the room. Elodin coughed a bit, then stepped back and looked around in a vaguely satisfied way.

I suddenly realized what was going on. "Oh God," I said. "Whose rooms are these?"

Elodin gave a satisfied nod. "Very good. I would also have accepted, *Why don't you have a key for this room?* or *What are we doing in here?*" He looked down at me, his eyes serious. "Doors are locked for a reason. People who don't have keys are supposed to stay out for a reason."

He nudged the heap of smouldering cloth with one foot, as if reassuring himself it would stay in the fireplace. "You know you're clever. That's your weakness. You assume you know what you're getting into, but you don't."

Elodin turned to look at me, his dark eyes serious. "You think you can trust me to teach you," he said. "You think I will keep you safe. But that is the worst sort of foolishness."

"Whose rooms are these?" I repeated numbly.

He showed me all his teeth in a sudden grin. "Master Hemme's."

"Why are you burning all of Hemme's clothes?" I asked, trying to ignore the fact that the room was rapidly filling with bitter smoke.

Elodin looked at me as if I were an idiot. "Because I hate him." He picked up the crystal decanter from the mantle and threw it violently against the back of the fireplace where it shattered. The fire began to burn more vigorously from whatever had been left inside. "The man is an absolute tit. Nobody talks to me like that."

Smoke continued to boil into the room. If it weren't for the high ceilings we'd already be choking on it. Even so, it was becoming hard to breathe as we made our way to the door. Elodin opened it, and smoke rolled out into the hallway.

We stood outside the door, staring at each other while the smoke billowed past. I decided to take a different tack on the problem. "I understand your hesitation, Master Elodin," I said. "Sometimes I don't think things all the way through."

"Obviously."

"And I'll admit there have been times when my actions have been . . ." I paused, trying to think of something more humble than *ill-considered*.

"Stupid beyond all mortal ken?" Elodin said helpfully.

My temper flared, burning away my brief attempt at humility. "Well thank God I'm the only one here that's ever made a bad decision in my life!" I said, barely keeping my voice this side of a shout. I looked him hard in the eye. "I've heard stories about you too, you know. They say you toffed things up pretty well yourself back when you were a student here."

Elodin's amused expression faded a bit, leaving him looking like he'd swallowed something and it had gotten stuck halfway down.

I continued. "If you think I'm reckless, do something about it. Show me the straighter path! Mold my supple young mind—" I sucked in a lungful of smoke and began to cough, forcing me to cut my tirade short. "Do something, damn you!" I choked out. "Teach me!"

I hadn't really been shouting, but I ended up breathless all the same. My temper faded as quickly as it had flared up, and I worried I'd gone too far.

But Elodin just looked at me. "What makes you think I'm not teaching you?" he asked, puzzled. "Aside from the fact that you refuse to learn."

Then he turned and walked down the hallway. "I'd get out of here if I were you," he said over his shoulder. "People are going to want to know who's responsible for this, and everyone knows you and Hemme don't get on very well."

I felt myself break into a panicked sweat. "What?"

"I'd wash up before admissions too," he said. "It won't look good if you show up reeking of smoke. I live here," Elodin said, pulling a key from his pocket and unlocking a door at the far end of the hallway. "What's your excuse?"

CHAPTER NINE

A Civil Tongue

MY HAIR WAS STILL wet when I made my way through a short hallway, then up the stairs onto the stage of an empty theater. As always, the room was dark except for the huge crescent-shaped table. I moved to the edge of the light and waited politely.

The Chancellor motioned me forward and I walked to the center of the table, reaching up to hand him my tile. Then I stepped back to stand in the circle of slightly brighter light between the two outthrust horns of the table.

The nine masters looked down at me. I'd like to say they looked dramatic, like ravens on a fence or something like that. But while they were all wearing their formal robes, they were too mismatched to look like a collection of anything.

What's more, I could see the marks of weariness on them. Only then did it occur to me that as much as the students hated admissions, it was probably no walk in the garden for the masters either.

"Kvothe, Arliden's son," the Chancellor said formally. "Re'lar." He made a gesture to the far right-hand horn of the table. "Master Physicker?"

Arwyl peered down at me, his face grandfatherly behind his round spectacles. "What are the medicinal properties of mhenka?" he asked.

"Powerful anesthetic," I said. "Powerful catatoniate. Potential purgative." I hesitated. "It has a whole sackful of complicating secondaries too. Should I list them all?"

Arwyl shook his head. "A patient comes into the Medica complaining of pains in their joints and difficulty breathing. Their mouth is dry, and they claim to have a sweet taste in their mouth. They complain of chills, but they are actually sweaty and feverish. What is your diagnosis?"

I drew a breath, then hesitated. "I don't make diagnoses in the Medica, Master Arwyl. I'd fetch one of your El'the to do it."

He smiled at me, eyes crinkling around the edges. "Correct," he said. "But for the sake of argument, what do you think might be wrong?"

"Is the patient a student?"

Arwyl raised an eyebrow. "What does that have to do with the price of butter?"

"If they work in the Fishery, it might be smelter's flu," I said. Arwyl cocked an eyebrow at me and I added, "There's all sorts of heavy metal poisoning you can get in the Fishery. It's rare around here because the students are well-trained, but anyone working with hot bronze can inhale enough fumes to kill themselves if they aren't properly careful." I saw Kilvin nodding along, and was glad I didn't have to admit the only reason I knew this was that I'd given myself a mild case of it a month ago.

Arwyl gave a thoughtful *humph,* then gestured to the other side of the table. "Master Arithmetician?"

Brandeur sat on the left-hand point of the table. "Assuming the changer takes four percent, how many pennies can you break from a talent?" He asked the question without looking up from the papers in front of him.

"What type of penny, Master Brandeur?"

He looked up, frowning. "We are still in the Commonwealth, if I remember correctly."

I juggled numbers in my head, working from the figures in the books he'd set aside in the Archives. They weren't the true exchange rates you would get from a moneylender, they were the official exchange rates governments and financiers used so they had common ground for lying to each other. "In iron pennies. Three hundred and fifty," I said, then added. "One. And a half."

Brandeur looked down at the papers before I'd even finished speaking. "Your compass reads gold at two hundred twenty points, platinum at one hundred twelve points, and cobalt at thirty-two points. Where are you?"

I was boggled by the question. Orienting by trifoil required detailed maps and painstaking triangulation. It was usually only practiced by sea captains and cartographers, and they used detailed charts to make their calculations. I'd only ever laid eyes on a trifoil compass twice in my life.

Either this was a question listed in one of the books Brandeur had set aside for study or it was deliberately designed to spike my wheel. Given that Brandeur and Hemme were friends, I guessed it was the latter.

I closed my eyes, brought up a map of the civilized world in my head, and took my best guess. "Tarbean?" I said. "Maybe somewhere in Yll?" I opened my eyes. "Honestly, I have no idea."

Brandeur made a mark on a piece of paper. "Master Namer," he said without looking up.

Elodin gave me a wicked, knowing grin, and I was suddenly struck with the fear that he might reveal my part of what we had done in Hemme's rooms earlier that morning.

Instead he held up three fingers dramatically. "You have three spades in your hand," he said. "And there have been five spades played." He steepled his fingers and looked at me seriously. "How many spades is that?"

"Eight spades," I said.

The other masters stirred slightly in their seats. Arwyl sighed. Kilvin slouched. Hemme and Brandeur went to far as to roll their eyes at each other. All together they gave the impression of long-suffering exasperation.

Elodin scowled at them. "What?" he demanded, his voice going hard around the edges. "You *want* me to take this song and dance more seriously? You want me to ask him questions only a namer can answer?"

The other masters stilled at this, looking uncomfortable and refusing to meet his eye. Hemme was the exception and glared openly.

"Fine," Elodin said, turning back to me. His eyes were dark, and his voice had a strange resonance to it. It wasn't loud, but when he spoke, it seemed to fill the entire hall. It left no space left over for any other sound. "Where does the moon go," Elodin asked grimly, "when it is no longer in our sky?"

The room seemed unnaturally quiet when he stopped speaking. As if his voice had left a hole in the world.

I waited to see if there was more to the question. "I haven't the slightest," I admitted. After Elodin's voice, my own seemed rather thin and insubstantial.

Elodin shrugged, then gestured graciously across the table. "Master Sympathist."

Elxa Dal was the only one who really looked comfortable in his formal robes. As always, his dark beard and lean face made me think of the evil magician in so many bad Aturan plays. He gave me a bit of a sympathetic look. "How about the binding for linear galvanic attraction?" he said in an offhand way.

I rattled it off easily.

He nodded. "What's the distance of insurmountable decay for iron?"

"Five and a half miles," I said, giving the textbook answer despite the fact that I had some quibbles with the term insurmountable. While it was true that moving any significant amount of energy more than six miles was statistically impossible, you could still use sympathy to dowse over much greater distances.

"Once an ounce of water is boiling, how much heat will it take to boil it completely away?"

I dragged up what I could remember from the vaporization tables I'd worked with in the Fishery. "A hundred and eighty thaums." I said with more assurance than I actually felt.

"Good enough for me," Dal said. "Master Alchemist?"

Mandrag waved a mottled hand dismissively. "I'll pass."

"He's good with questions about spades," Elodin suggested.

Mandrag frowned at Elodin. "Master Archivist."

Lorren stared down at me, his long face impassive. "What are the rules of the Archives?"

I flushed at this and looked down. "Move quietly," I said. "Respect the books. Obey the scrivs. No water. No food." I swallowed. "No fire."

Lorren nodded. Nothing in his tone or demeanor indicated any sort of disapproval, but that just made it worse. His eyes moved across the table. "Master Artificer."

I cursed inwardly. Over the last span I'd read all six books Master Lorren had set aside for Re'lar to study from. Feltemi Reis' *Fall of Empire* alone took me ten hours. I wanted few things more than access to the Archives, and I'd desperately hoped to impress Master Lorren by answering whatever question he could think to ask.

But there was no help for it. I turned to face Kilvin.

"Galvanic throughput of copper," the great bearlike master rumbled through his beard.

I gave it to five places. I'd had to use it while making calculations for the deck lamps.

"Conductive coefficient of gallium."

I'd needed to know that to dope the emitters for the lamp. Was Kilvin lobbing me easy questions? I gave the answer.

"Good," Kilvin said. "Master Rhetorician."

I drew a deep breath as I turned to look at Hemme. I had gone so far as to read three of his books, though I have a sharp loathing for rhetoric and pointless philosophy.

Still, I could tamp down my distaste for two minutes' time and play the part of a good, humble student. I am one of the Ruh, I could act the part.

Hemme scowled at me, his round face like an angry moon. "Did you set fire to my rooms, you little ravel bastard?"

The raw nature of the question caught me entirely off my guard. I was ready for impossibly hard questions, or trick questions, or questions he could twist to make any answer I gave seem wrong.

But this sudden accusation caught me utterly wrong-footed. Ravel is a term I particularly despise. A welter of emotion rolled through me and brought the sudden taste of plum to my mouth. While part of me was still considering the most gracious way to respond, I found I was already speaking. "I didn't set fire to your rooms," I said honestly. "But I wish I had. And I wish you'd been in there when it started, sleeping soundly."

Hemme's expression turned from scowling to astonished.

"Re'lar Kvothe!" the Chancellor snapped. "You will keep a civil tongue in your head, or I will bring you up on charges of Conduct Unbecoming myself!"

The taste of plum disappeared as quickly as it had come, leaving me feeling slightly dizzy and sweating with fear and embarrassment. "My apologies, Chancellor," I said quickly, looking down at my feet. "I spoke in anger. Ravel is a term my people find particularly offensive. Its use makes light of the systematic slaughter of thousands of Ruh."

A curious line appeared between the Chancellor's eyebrows. "I'll admit I don't know that particular etymology," he mused. "I guess I'll make that my question."

"Hold off," Hemme interrupted. "I'm not finished."

"You are finished," the Chancellor said, his voice hard and firm. "You're as bad as the boy, Jasom, and with less excuse. You've shown you can't conduct yourself in a professional manner, so stint thy clep and consider yourself lucky I don't call for an official censure."

Hemme went white with anger, but he held his tongue.

The Chancellor turned to look at me "Master Linguist," he announced himself formally. "Re'lar Kvothe: What is the etymology of the word ravel?"

"It comes from the purges instigated by Emperor Alcyon," I said. "He issued a proclamation saying any of the *traveling rabble* on the roads were subject to fine, imprisonment, or transportation without trial. The term became shortened to 'ravel' though metaplasmic enclitization."

He raised an eyebrow at that. "Did it now?"

I nodded. "Though I also expect there is a connection to the term ravelend, referring to the ragged appearance of performing troupes that are out at the heels."

The Chancellor nodded formally. "Thank you, Re'lar Kvothe. Take a seat while we confer."

CHAPTER TEN

Being Treasured

MY TUITION WAS SET at nine talents and five. Better than the ten talents Manet had predicted, but more than I had in my purse. I had until tomorrow noon to settle up with the bursar or I would be forced to miss an entire term.

Having to postpone my studies wouldn't have been a tragedy. But only students are allowed access to University resources, such as the equipment in the Artificery. That meant if I couldn't pay my tuition, I would be barred from my work in Kilvin's shop, the only job where I could hope to earn enough money for my tuition.

I stopped at the Stocks and Jaxim smiled as I approached the open window. "Just sold your lamps this morning," he said. "We squeezed them for a little extra because they were the last ones left."

He leafed through the ledger until he found the appropriate page. "Your sixty percent comes out to four talents and eight jots. After the materials and piecework you used . . ." He ran his finger down a page. "You're left with two talents, three jots, and eight drabs."

Jaxim made a note in the ledger, then wrote me a receipt. I folded the paper carefully and tucked it into my purse. It didn't have the satisfying weight of coins, but it brought my total up to more than six talents. So much money, but still not enough.

If I hadn't lost my temper with Hemme my tuition might have been low enough. I could have studied more, or earned more money if I hadn't been forced to hide in my room for almost two whole days, weeping and raging with the taste of plum in my mouth.

A thought occurred to me. "I should start something new, I guess," I said casually. "I'll need a small crucible. Three ounces of tin. Two ounces of bronze. Four ounces of silver. A spool of fine gold wire. A copper—"

"Hold on a second," Jaxim interrupted me. He ran a finger back along my name in the ledger. "I don't have you authorized for gold or silver." He looked up at me. "Is that a mistake?"

I hesitated, not wanting to lie. "I didn't know you needed authorization," I said.

Jaxim gave me a knowing grin. "You're not the first one to try something like that," he said. "Rough tuition?"

I nodded.

He grimaced sympathetically. "Sorry. Kilvin knows Stocks could turn into a moneylender's stall if he isn't careful." He closed the ledger. "You'll have to hit the pawnshop like everyone else."

I held up my hands, showing him the fronts and backs to make a point of my lack of jewelry.

Jaxim winced. "That's rough. I know a decent moneylender on Silver Court, only charges ten percent a month. It's still like having your teeth pulled, but better than most."

I nodded and sighed. Silver Court was where the guild moneylenders had their shops. They wouldn't give me the time of day. "It's certainly better than I've gotten in the past," I said.

———

I thought things over while I walked to Imre, the familiar weight of my lute resting on one shoulder.

I was in a tight spot, but not a terrible one. No guild moneylender would lend money to an orphan Edema Ruh with no collateral, but I could borrow the money from Devi. Still, I wish it hadn't come to that. Not only was her rate of interest extortionate, but I worried what favors she might require of me if I ever defaulted my loan. I doubted they would be small. Or easy. Or entirely legal.

Such were the turnings of my thoughts as I made my way over Stone-bridge. I stopped by an apothecary, then made my way to the Grey Man.

Opening the door, I saw the Grey Man was a boarding house. There was no common room where people could gather and drink. Instead there was a small, richly-appointed parlor, complete with a well-dressed porter who eyed me with an air of disapproval, if not outright distaste.

"Can I help you, young sir?" he asked as I came in the door.

"I'm calling on a young lady," I said. "By the name of Dinael."

He nodded. "I shall go and see if she is in."

"Don't trouble yourself," I said, moving toward the stairs. "She's expecting me."

The man moved to block my way. "I'm afraid that isn't possible," he said. "But I will be glad to see if the lady is in."

He held out his hand. I looked at it.

"Your calling card?" he asked. "That I might present it to the young lady?"

"How can you give her my card if you aren't sure she is in?" I asked.

The porter gave me the smile again. It was gracious, polite, and so sharply unpleasant that I took special note of it, fixing it in my memory. A smile like that is a work of art. As someone who grew up on the stage, I could appreciate it on several levels. A smile like that is like a knife in certain social settings, and I might have need of it someday.

"Ah," the porter said. "The lady is *in*," he said with a certain emphasis. "But that does not necessarily mean she is in for *you*."

"You can tell her Kvothe has come calling," I said, more amused than offended. "I'll wait."

I didn't have to wait long. The porter came down the stairs wearing an irritated expression, as if he'd been looking forward to throwing me out. "This way," he said.

I followed him upstairs. He opened a door, and I swept past him with what I hoped was an irritating amount of dismissive aplomb.

It was a sitting room with wide windows that let in the late afternoon sun, large enough to seem spacious despite the scattered chairs and couches. A hammer dulcimer sat against the far wall, and one corner of the room was entirely occupied by a massive Modegan great harp.

Denna stood in the center of the room wearing a green velvet dress. Her hair was arranged to display her elegant neck to good effect, revealing the emerald teardrop earrings and matching necklace at her throat.

She was talking to a young man who was . . . the best word I can think of is pretty. He had a sweet, clean-shaven face with wide, dark eyes.

He had the look of a young noble who had been down on his luck too long for it to be a temporary thing. His clothing was fine but rumpled. His dark hair was cut in a style obviously meant to be curled, but it hadn't been tended to recently. His eyes were sunken, as if he hadn't been sleeping well.

Denna held out her hands to me. "Kvothe," she said. "Come meet Geoffrey."

"Pleasure to meet you, Kvothe," Geoffrey said. "Dinael has told me quite a bit about you. You're a bit of a—what is it? Wizard?" His smile was open and utterly guileless.

"Arcanist actually," I said as politely as possible. "Wizard brings too much storybook nonsense to mind. People expect us to wear dark robes and fling about the entrails of birds. And yourself?"

"Geoffrey is a poet," Denna said. "And a good one, though he'll deny it."

"I will," he admitted, then his smile faded. "I have to go. I have an appointment with folk who shouldn't be kept waiting." He gave Denna a kiss on the cheek, shook my hand warmly, and left.

Denna watched the door close behind him. "He's a sweet boy."

"You say that as if you regret it," I said.

"If he were a little less sweet, he might be able to fit two thoughts in his head at the same time. Maybe they would rub together and make a spark. Even a little smoke would be nice, then at least it would look like something was happening in there." She sighed.

"Is he really that thick?"

She shook her head. "No. He's just trusting. Hasn't got a calculating bone in his body, and he's done nothing but make bad choices since he got here a month ago."

I reached into my cloak and brought out a pair of small, cloth-wrapped bundles: one blue, one white. "I've brought you a present."

Denna reached out to take them, looking slightly puzzled.

What had seemed like such a good idea a few hours ago now seemed rather foolish. "They're for your lungs," I said, suddenly embarrassed. "I know you have trouble sometimes."

She tilted her head on one side. "And how do you know that, pray tell?"

"You mentioned it when we were in Trebon," I said. "I did some research." I pointed. "That one you can brew in a tea: featherbite, deadnettle, lohatm. . . ." I pointed to the other. "That one you boil the leaves in some water and breathe the vapor coming off the top."

Denna looked back and forth between the packages.

"I've written instructions on slips of paper inside," I said. "The blue one is the one you're supposed to boil and breathe the vapor," I said. "Blue for water, you see."

She looked up at me. "Don't you make a tea with water, too?"

I blinked at that, then flushed and started to say something, but Denna laughed and shook her head. "I'm teasing you," she said gently. "Thank you. This is the sweetest thing anyone's done for me in a long while."

Denna walked over to a chest of drawers and tucked the two bundles carefully into an ornate wooden box.

"You seem to be doing fairly well for yourself," I said, gesturing to the well-appointed room.

Denna shrugged, looking around the room indifferently. "Kellin is doing well for himself," she said. "I merely stand in his reflected light."

I nodded my understanding. "I'd thought perhaps you'd found yourself a patron."

"Nothing so formal as that. Kellin and I are walking about together, as they say in Modeg, and he is showing me my way around the harp." She nodded to where the instrument loomed hugely in the corner.

"Care to show me what you've learned?" I asked.

Denna shook her head, embarrassed. Her hair slid down around her shoulders as she did so. "I'm not very good yet."

"I will restrain my natural urge to jeer and hiss," I said graciously.

Denna laughed. "Fine. Just a bit." She walked behind the harp and drew up a tall stool to lean against. Then she lifted her hands to the strings, paused for a long moment, and began to play.

The melody was a variant of "Bell-Wether." I smiled.

Her playing was slow, almost stately. Too many people think speed is the hallmark of a good musician. It's understandable. What Marie had done at the Eolian was amazing. But how quickly you can finger notes is the smallest part of music. The real key is timing.

It's like telling a joke. Anyone can remember the words. Anyone can repeat it. But making someone laugh requires more than that. Telling a joke faster doesn't make it funnier. As with many things, hesitation is better than hurry.

This is why there are so few true musicians. A lot of folks can sing or saw out a tune on a fiddle. A music box can play a song flawlessly, again and again. But knowing the notes isn't enough. You have to know *how* to play them. Speed comes with time and practice, but timing you are born with. You have it or you don't.

Denna had it. She moved slowly through the song, but she wasn't plodding. She played it slow as a luxurious kiss. Not that I knew anything of kissing at that point in my life. But as she stood with her arms around the harp, her eyes half-lidded with concentration, her lips lightly pursed, I knew I someday wanted to be kissed with that amount of slow, deliberate care.

And she was beautiful. I suppose it should come as no surprise that I have a particular fondness for women with music running through them. But as she played I saw her for the first time that day. Before I had been distracted by the difference in her hair, the cut of her dress. But as she played, all that faded from view.

I ramble. Suffice to say she was impressive, though obviously still learning. She struck a few bad notes, but didn't flinch or cringe away from them. As they say, a jeweler knows the uncut gem. And I am. And she was. And so.

"You're a long way past 'Squirrel in the Thatch,'" I said quietly after she'd struck the final notes.

She shrugged my compliment away, not meeting my eye. "I don't have much to do but practice," she said. "And Kellin says I have a bit of a knack."

"How long have you been at it?" I asked.

"Three span?" She looked thoughtful, then nodded. "A little less than three span."

"Mother of God," I said, shaking my head. "Don't ever tell anyone how quickly you've picked it up. Other musicians will hate you for it."

"My fingers aren't used to it yet," she said, looking down at them. "I can't practice nearly as long as I like."

I reached out and took hold of one of her hands, turning it palm up so I could see her fingertips. There were fading blisters there. "You've . . ."

I looked up and realized how close she was standing. Her hand was cool in mine. She stared at me with huge, dark eyes. One eyebrow slightly raised. Not arch, or playful even, just gently curious. My stomach felt suddenly strange and weak.

"I've what?" she asked.

I realized I had no idea what I had been about to say. I thought of saying, *I have no idea what I was going to say.* Then I realized that would be a stupid thing to say. So I didn't say anything.

Denna looked down and took hold of my hand, turning it over. "Your hands are soft," she said, then touched my fingertips lightly. "I thought the calluses would be rough, but they're not. They're smooth."

Once her eyes weren't fixed on mine, I regained a small piece of my wits. "It just takes time," I said.

Denna looked up and gave a shy smile. My mind went blank as fresh paper.

After a moment, Denna let go of my hand and moved past me to the center of the room. "Would you care for something to drink?" she asked as she settled gracefully into a chair.

"That would be very kind of you," I said purely on reflex. I realized my hand was still hanging stupidly in midair, and I let it fall to my side.

She gestured to a nearby chair and I sat.

"Watch this." She picked up a small silver bell from a nearby table and rang it softly. Then she held up one hand with all five fingers extended. She folded in her thumb, then her index finger, counting downward.

Before she folded in her smallest finger, there came a knock on the door.

"Come in," Denna called, and the well-dressed porter opened the door.

"I believe I would like some drinking chocolate," she said. "And Kvothe . . ." She looked at me questioningly.

"Drinking chocolate sounds lovely," I said.

The porter nodded and disappeared, closing the door behind him.

"Sometimes I do it just to make him run," Denna admitted sheepishly, looking down at the bell. "I can't imagine how he can hear it. For a while, I was convinced he was sitting in the hallway with his ear against my door."

"Can I see the bell?" I asked.

She handed it over. It looked normal at first glance, but when I turned it upside down I saw some tiny sygaldry on the inner surface of the bell.

"He isn't eavesdropping," I said, handing it back. "There's another bell downstairs that rings in time with this one."

"How?" She asked, then answered her own question. "Magic?"

"You could call it that."

"Is that the sort of thing you do over there?" She jerked her head in the direction of the river and the University beyond. "It seems a little . . . tawdry."

"It's the most frivolous use of sygaldry I've ever seen," I said.

Denna burst out laughing. "You sound so offended," she said. Then, "It's called sygaldry?"

"Making something like that is called artificing," I said. "Sygaldry is writing or carving the runes that make it work."

Denna's eyes lit up at this. "So it's a magic where you write things down?" she asked, leaning forward in her chair. "How does it work?"

I hesitated. Not only because it was a huge question, but because the University has very specific rules about sharing Arcanum secrets. "It's rather complicated," I said.

Luckily, at that moment there was another knock on the door and our chocolate arrived in steaming cups. My mouth watered at the smell of it. The man set the tray on a nearby table and left without a word.

I sipped and smiled at the thick sweetness of it. "It's been years since I've had chocolate," I said.

Denna lifted her cup and looked around the room. "It's strange to think some people live their whole lives like this," she mused.

"It's not to your liking?" I asked, surprised.

"I like the chocolate and the harp," she said. "But I could do without the bell and a whole room just for sitting." Her mouth curved into the beginning of a frown. "And I hate knowing someone is set to guard me, like I'm a treasure someone might try to steal."

"You're not to be treasured, then?"

She narrowed her eyes over the top of her cup, as if she wasn't sure how serious I was. "I don't fancy being under lock and key," she clarified with a grim note in her voice. "I don't mind being given rooms, but they aren't really mine if I'm not free to come and go."

I raised an eyebrow at that, but before I could say anything she waved her hand dismissively. "It's not like that really," she sighed. "But I don't doubt Kellin is informed of my comings and goings. I know the porter tells him who comes calling. It rankles a bit is all." She gave a crooked smile. "I suppose that seems terribly ungrateful, doesn't it?"

"Not at all," I said. "When I was younger, my troupe traveled everywhere. But every year we would spend a few span at our patron's estate, performing for his family and his guests."

I shook my head at the memory. "Baron Greyfallow was a gracious host. We sat at his own table. He gave us gifts . . ." I trailed off, remembering a regiment of tiny lead soldiers he'd given me. I shook my head clear of the thought. "But my father hated it. Climbed the walls. He couldn't tolerate the feeling of being at someone's beck and call."

"Yes!" Denna said. "That's exactly it! If Kellin says he might pay me a visit on such and such evening, suddenly I feel I've had one foot nailed to the floor. If I leave I'm being obstinate and rude, but if I stay I feel like a dog waiting by the door."

We sat for a moment in silence. Denna twirled the ring on her finger absentmindedly, sunlight catching the pale blue stone.

"Still," I said, looking around. "They are nice rooms."

"They're nice when you're here," she said.

———

Several hours later, I climbed a narrow flight of stairs behind a butcher's shop. There was a faint, pervasive smell of rancid fat from the alley below, but I was smiling. An afternoon with Denna entirely to myself was a rare treat, and my step was surprisingly light for someone about to make a deal with a demon.

I knocked on the solid wooden door at the top of the steps and waited. No guild moneylender would trust me with a bent penny, but there are always folk willing to lend money. Poets and other romantics call them copper hawks, or sharps, but gaelet is the better term. They are dangerous people, and wise folk steer well clear of them.

The door opened a crack, then swung wide, revealing a young woman with a pixie face and strawberry-blonde hair. "Kvothe!" Devi exclaimed. "I worried I might not see you this term."

I stepped inside, and Devi bolted the door behind me. The large, windowless room smelled pleasantly of cinnas fruit and honey, a refreshing change from the alley.

One side of the room was dominated by a huge canopy bed, its dark curtains drawn. On the other side was a fireplace, a large wooden desk, and a standing bookshelf three-quarters full. I wandered over to eye the titles while Devi locked and barred the door.

"Is this copy of Malcaf new?" I asked.

"It is," she said walking over to stand beside me. "A young alchemist who couldn't settle his debt let me pick through his library in order to square things between us." Devi carefully pulled the book from the shelf, revealing *Vision and Revision* in gold leaf on the cover. She looked up at me, grinning impishly. "Have you read it?"

"I haven't," I said. I'd wanted to study it for admissions but hadn't been able to find a copy in the Stacks. "Just heard about it."

Devi looked thoughtful for a moment, then handed it to me. "When you've finished, come back and we'll discuss it. I'm woefully devoid of interesting conversation these days. If we have a decent argument, I might let you borrow another."

Once the book was in my hands, she tapped the cover lightly with a finger. "This book is worth more than you are." She said without a hint of playfulness in her voice. "If it comes back damaged, there will be an accounting."

"I'll be very careful," I said.

Devi nodded, then turned and walked past me toward the desk. "Right then, on to business." She sat down. "Cutting it a little close, aren't you?" she asked. "Tuition needs to be paid before noon tomorrow."

"I live a dangerous and exciting life," I said as I wandered over and took a seat across from her. "And delightful as I find your company, I was hoping to avoid your services this term."

"How do you like tuition as a Re'lar?" she asked knowingly. "How hard did they hit you?"

"That's a rather personal question," I said.

Devi gave me a frank look. "We are about to enter into a rather personal arrangement," she pointed out. "I hardly feel I'm overstepping myself."

"Nine and a half," I said.

She snorted derisively. "I thought you were supposed to be all manner of clever. I never got higher than seven when I was a Re'lar."

"You had access to the Archives," I pointed out.

"I had access to vast stores of intellect," she said matter-of-factly. "Plus, I am cute as a button." She gave a grin that brought out dimples in both her cheeks.

"You are shiny as a new penny," I admitted. "No man can hope to stand against you."

"Some women have trouble keeping their feet as well," she said. Her grin changed slightly, moving from adorable to impish and then well past the border into wicked.

Not having the slightest idea how to respond to that, I moved in a safer direction. "I'm afraid I need to borrow four talents." I said.

"Ah," Devi said. Suddenly businesslike, she folded her hands atop the desk. "I'm afraid I've made a few changes to my business recently," she said. "Currently, I am only extending loans of six talents or more."

I didn't bother trying to hide my dismay. "Six talents? Devi, that extra debt will be a millstone around my neck."

She gave a sigh that sounded at least slightly apologetic. "Here's the trouble. When I make a loan, I run certain risks. I risk losing my investment if my debtor dies or tries to run. I run the risk they'll attempt to report me. I run the risk of being brought up against the iron law, or worse, the moneylender's guild."

"You know I'd never try something like that, Devi."

"The fact remains," Devi continued, "my risk is the same, no matter if the loan is small or large. Why should I take those risks for small loans?"

"Small?" I asked. "I could live for a year on four talents!"

She tapped the desk with a finger, pursing her mouth. "Collateral?"

"The usual," I said, giving her my best smile. "My boundless charm."

Devi snorted indelicately. "For boundless charm and three drops of blood you can borrow six talents at my standard rate. Fifty percent interest over a two-month term."

"Devi," I said ingratiatingly. "What am I going to do with the extra money?"

"Throw a party," she suggested. "Spend a day in the Buckle. Find yourself a nice game of high-stakes faro."

"Faro," I said, "is a tax on people who can't calculate probabilities."

"Then run bank and collect the tax," she said. "Buy yourself something pretty and wear it next time you come in to see me." She looked me up and down with dangerous eyes. "Maybe then I'll be willing to cut you a deal."

"How about six talents for a month at twenty-five percent?" I asked.

Devi shook her head, not unkindly. "Kvothe, I respect the impulse to bargain, but you don't have any leverage. You're here because you're over a barrel. I'm here to capitalize on that situation." She spread her hands in a helpless gesture. "That's how I make my living. The fact that you have a sweet face doesn't really enter into it."

Devi gave me a serious look. "Conversely, if a guild moneylender would give you the time of day, I wouldn't expect you to come here simply because I'm pretty and you like the color of my hair."

"It is a lovely color," I said. "We fiery types should really stick together."

"We should," she agreed. "I propose we stick together at fifty percent interest over a two month term."

"Fine." I said, slumping back into my chair. "You win."

Devi gave me a winsome smile, dimples showing again. "I can only win if we were both actually playing." She opened a drawer in the desk, bringing out a small glass bottle and a long pin.

I reached out to take them, but instead of sliding them across the desk, she gave me a thoughtful look. "Now that I think of it, there might be another option."

"I'd love another option," I admitted.

"The last time we talked," Devi said slowly, "you implied you had a way into the Archives."

I hesitated. "I did imply that."

"That information would be worth quite a bit to me," she said over-casually. Though she tried to hide it, I could see a fierce, lean hunger in her eyes.

I looked down at my hands and didn't say anything.

"I'll give you ten talents right now," Devi said bluntly. "Not a loan. I'll buy the information outright. If I get caught in the Stacks, I never learned it from you."

I thought of everything I could do with ten talents. New clothes. A lute case that wasn't about to fall to pieces. Paper. Gloves for the coming winter.

I sighed and shook my head.

"Twenty talents," Devi said. "And guild rates on any loans you want in the future."

Twenty talents would mean half a year of worry-free tuition. I could pursue my own projects in the Fishery rather than slaving away at deck lamps. I could buy tailored clothes. Fresh fruit. I could use a laundry rather than wash my clothes myself.

I drew a reluctant breath. "I—"

"Forty talents," Devi said hungrily. "Guild rates. And I will take you to bed."

For forty talents I could buy Denna her own half-harp. I could . . .

I looked up and saw Devi staring at me from across the desk. Her lips were wet, her pale blue eyes intense. She shifted her shoulders back and forth in the slow, unconscious motion of a cat before it pounces.

I thought of Auri, safe and happy in the Underthing. What would she do if her tiny kingdom was invaded by a stranger?

"I'm sorry," I said. "I can't. Getting in is . . . complicated. It involves a friend, and I don't think they'd be willing." I decided to ignore the other part of her offer, as I hadn't the slightest idea what to say about it.

There was a long, tense moment. "Goddamn you," Devi said at last. "You sound like you're telling the truth."

"I am," I said. "It's unsettling, I know."

"Goddamn." She scowled as she pushed the bottle and pin across the desk.

I pricked the back of my hand and watched the blood well up and roll down my hand to fall into the bottle. After three drops I tipped the pin into the mouth of the bottle as well.

Devi swabbed some adhesive around the stopper and drove it angrily into the bottle. Then she reached into a drawer and pulled out a diamond stylus. "Do you trust me?" She asked as she etched a number into the glass. "Or do you want this sealed?"

"I trust you," I said. "But I'd like it sealed all the same."

She melted a daub of sealing wax onto the top of the bottle. I pressed my talent pipes into it, leaving a recognizable impression.

Reaching into another drawer, Devi brought out six talents and clattered them onto the desk. The motion might have seemed petulant if her eyes hadn't been so hard and angry.

"I'm getting in there one way or another," she said with a chill edge to her voice. "Talk to your friend. If you're the one that helps me, I'll make it worth your time."

CHAPTER ELEVEN

Haven

I RETURNED TO THE UNIVERSITY in good spirits despite the burden of my new debt. I made a few purchases, gathered up my lute, and headed out over the rooftops.

From the inside, Mains was a nightmare to navigate: a maze of irrational hallways and stairways leading nowhere. But moving across its jumbled rooftops was easy as anything. I made my way to a small courtyard that at some point in the building's construction had become completely inaccessible, trapped like a fly in amber.

Auri wasn't expecting me, but this was the first place I'd met her, and on clear nights she sometimes came out to watch the stars. I checked to make sure the classrooms overlooking the courtyard were dark and empty, then I brought out my lute and began to tune it.

I had been playing for almost an hour when I heard a rustling movement in the overgrown courtyard below. Then Auri appeared, scurrying up the overgrown apple tree and onto the roof.

She ran toward me, her bare feet skipping lightly across the tar, her hair blowing behind her. "I heard you!" she said as she came close. "I heard you all the way down in Vaults!"

"I seem to remember," I said slowly, "that I was going to play music for someone."

"Me!" She held both her hands close to her chest, grinning. She moved from foot to foot, almost dancing with her eagerness. "Play for me! I have been as patient as two stones together," she said. "You are just in time. I could not be as patient as three stones."

"Well," I said hesitantly. "I suppose it all depends on what you've brought me."

She laughed, rising up onto the balls of her feet, her hands still together, close to her chest. "What did you bring *me*?"

I knelt and began to untie my bundle. "I've brought you three things," I said.

"How traditional," she said, grinning. "You are quite the proper young gentleman tonight."

"I am." I held up a heavy dark bottle.

She took it with both hands. "Who made it?"

"Bees," I said. "And brewers in Bredon."

Auri smiled. "That's three bees," she said, and set the bottle down by her feet. I brought out a round loaf of fresh barley bread. She reached out and touched it with a finger, then nodded approvingly.

Last I brought out a whole smoked salmon. It had cost four drabs by it-self, but I worried Auri didn't get enough meat in whatever she managed to scrounge up when I wasn't around. It would be good for her.

Auri looked down at it curiously, tilting her head to look into its single staring eye. "Hello fish," she said. Then she looked back up at me. "Does it have a secret?"

I nodded. "It has a harp instead of a heart."

She looked back down at it. "No wonder it looks so surprised."

Auri took the fish out of my hands and laid it carefully on the roof. "Now stand up. I have three things for you, as is only fair."

I came to my feet and she held out something wrapped in a piece of cloth. It was a thick candle that smelled of lavender. "What's inside of it?" I asked.

"Happy dreams," she said. "I put them there for you."

I turned the candle over in my hands, a suspicion forming. "Did you make this yourself?"

She nodded and gave a delighted grin. "I did. I am terribly clever."

I tucked it carefully into one of the pockets of my cloak. "Thank you, Auri."

Auri grew serious. "Now close your eyes and bend down so I can give you your second present."

Puzzled, I closed my eyes and bent at the waist, wondering if she had made me a hat as well.

I felt her hands on either side of my face, then she gave me a tiny, delicate kiss in the middle of my forehead.

Surprised, I opened my eyes. But she was already standing several steps away, her hands clasped nervously behind her back. I couldn't think of any-thing to say.

Auri took a step forward. "You are special to me," she said seriously, her face grave. "I want you to know I will always take care of you." She reached out tentatively and wiped at my cheeks. "No. None of that tonight. This is your third present. If things are bad, you can come and stay with me in the Underthing. It is nice there, and you will be safe."

"Thank you, Auri," I said as soon as I was able. "You are special to me, too."

"Of course I am," she said matter-of-factly. "I am as lovely as the moon."

I collected myself while Auri skipped over to a piece of metal piping that jutted from a chimney and used it to pry the cap off the bottle. Then she brought it back, holding it carefully with both hands.

"Auri," I asked. "Aren't your feet cold?"

She looked down at them. "The tar is nice," she said, wriggling her toes. "It's still warm from the sun."

"Would you like a pair of shoes?"

"What would they have in them?" she asked.

"Your feet," I said. "It's going to be winter soon."

She shrugged.

"Your feet will be cold."

"I don't come out on top of things in the winter," she said. "It isn't very nice."

Before I could respond, Elodin stepped around a large brick chimney as casually as if he were out for an afternoon stroll.

The three of us stared at each other for a moment, each of us startled in our own way. Elodin and I were surprised, but out of the corner of my eye I saw Auri grow perfectly still, like a deer ready to spring away to safety.

"Master Elodin," I said in my gentlest, friendliest tones, desperately hoping he wouldn't do anything that might startle Auri into running. The last time she'd been scared back underground it had taken her a full span to re-emerge. "How nice to meet you."

"Hello there," Elodin said, matching my casual tone perfectly, as if there was nothing odd about the three of us meeting on a rooftop in the middle of the night. Though for all I knew, it might not seem odd to him.

"Master Elodin." Auri dipped one bare foot behind the other and tugged the edges of her ragged dress in a tiny curtsey.

Elodin remained in the moon-cast shadow of the tall brick chimney. He made a curiously formal bow in return. I couldn't see his face in any detail, but I could imagine his curious eyes examining the barefoot, waifish girl with the nimbus of floating hair. "And what brings the two of you out this fine night?" Elodin asked.

I tensed. Questions were dangerous with Auri.

Luckily, this one didn't seem to bother her. "Kvothe has brought me lovely things," she said. "He brought me bee beer and barley bread and a smoked fish with a harp where its heart should be."

"Ah," Elodin said, stepping away from the chimney. He patted his robes until he found something in a pocket. He held it out to her. "I'm afraid I've only brought you a cinnas fruit."

Auri took a tiny, dancer's step backward and made no motion to take it. "Have you brought anything for Kvothe?"

This seemed to catch Elodin off his stride. He stood awkwardly for a moment, arm outstretched. "I'm afraid I haven't," he said. "But I don't imagine Kvothe has brought anything for me, either."

Auri's eyes narrowed, and she gave a tiny frown, fierce with disapproval. "Kvothe has brought music," she said sternly, "which is for everyone."

Elodin paused again, and I have to admit I enjoyed seeing him discomfited by someone else's behavior for once. He turned and made a half bow in my direction. "My apologies," he said.

I made a gracious gesture. "Think nothing of it."

Elodin turned back to Auri and held out his hand a second time.

She took two small steps forward, hesitated, then took two more. She reached out slowly, paused with her hand on the small fruit, then took several scurrying steps away, bringing both hands close to her chest. "Thank you kindly," she said, making another small curtsey. "Now, you may join us if you like. And if you behave, you may stay and listen to Kvothe play afterward." She tilted her head a bit, making it a question.

Elodin hesitated, then nodded.

Auri scampered around to the other side of the roof, then down into the courtyard through the bare limbs of the apple tree.

Elodin watched her go. When he tilted his head there was just enough moonlight that I could see a thoughtful expression on his face. I felt a sudden, sharp anxiety tie knots in my stomach. "Master Elodin?"

He turned to face me. "Hmm?"

I knew from experience it would only take her three or four minutes to fetch whatever she was bringing up from the Underthing. I needed to talk fast.

"I know this looks strange," I said. "But you have to be careful. She's very nervous. Don't try to touch her. Don't make any sudden movements. It will scare her away."

Elodin expression was hidden in shadow again. "Will it now?" he said.

"Loud noises too. Even a loud laugh. And you can't ask her anything resembling a personal question. She'll just run if you do." I drew a deep breath, my mind racing. I have a good tongue in my head, and given enough time

I'm confident in my ability to persuade just about anyone of anything. But Elodin was simply too unpredictable to manipulate.

"You can't tell anyone she's here." It came out more forcefully than I'd intended, and I immediately regretted my choice of words. I was in no position to be giving orders to one of the masters, even if he was more than half mad. "What I mean," I said quickly, "is that I would take it as a great personal favor if you didn't mention her to anyone."

Elodin gave me a long, speculative look. "And why is that, Re'lar Kvothe?"

I felt myself break out in a sweat at the cool amusement in his tone. "They'll stick her in Haven," I said. "You of all people . . ." I trailed off, my throat growing dry.

Elodin stared down at me, his face little more than a shadow, but I could sense him scowling. "Of all people I what, Re'lar Kvothe? Do you presume to know my feelings toward Haven?"

I felt all my elegant, half-planned persuasion fall to tatters around my feet. And I suddenly felt like I was back on the streets of Tarbean, my stomach a hard knot of hunger, my chest full of desperate hopelessness as I clutched at the sleeves of sailors and merchants, begging for pennies, halfpennies, shims. Begging for anything so I could get something to eat.

"Please," I said to him. "Please, Master Elodin, if they chase her she'll hide, and I won't be able to find her. She isn't quite right in the head, but she's happy here. And I can take care of her. Not much, but a little. If they catch her that would be even worse. Haven would kill her. Please Master Elodin, I'll do whatever you like. Just don't tell anyone."

"Hush," Elodin said. "She's coming." He reached out to grip my shoulder, and moonlight fell across his face. His expression wasn't fierce and hard at all. There was nothing but puzzlement and concern. "Lord and lady, you're shaking. Take a breath and put your stage face on. You'll scare her if she sees you like this."

I took a deep breath and fought to relax. Elodin's concerned expression faded and he stepped back, letting go of my shoulder.

I turned in time to see Auri scurry across the roof toward us, her arms full. She stopped a short distance away, eyeing us both, before coming the rest of the way, stepping carefully as a dancer until she was back where she originally stood. Then she sat down lightly on the roof, crossing her legs beneath herself. Elodin and I sat as well, though not nearly as gracefully.

Auri unfolded a cloth, lay it carefully between the three of us, then set a large, smooth wooden platter in the middle. She brought out the cinnas fruit and sniffed it, her eyes peering over the top of it. "What is in this?" she asked Elodin.

"Sunshine," he said easily, as if he'd expected the question. "And early morning sunshine at that."

They knew each other. Of course. That was why she hadn't run away at the outset. I felt the solid bar of tension between my shoulder blades ease slightly.

Auri sniffed the fruit again and looked thoughtful for a moment. "It is lovely," she declared. "But Kvothe's things are lovelier still."

"That stands to reason," Elodin said. "I expect Kvothe is a nicer person than I am."

"That goes without saying," Auri said primly.

Auri served up dinner, sharing out the bread and fish to each of us. She also produced a squat clay jar of brined olives. It made me glad to see she could provide for herself when I wasn't around.

Auri poured beer into my familiar porcelain teacup. Elodin got a small glass jar of the sort you would use to store jam. She filled his cup for the first round but not the second. I was left wondering if he was simply out of easy reach, or if it was a subtle sign of her displeasure.

We ate without speaking. Auri delicately, taking tiny bites, her back straight. Elodin cautiously, occasionally darting a glance at me as if he were unsure how to behave. I guessed from this that he'd never shared a meal with Auri before.

When we were finished with everything else, Auri brought out a small, bright knife and divided the cinnas fruit into three parts. As soon as she broke the skin of it, I could smell it on the air, sweet and sharp. It made my mouth water. Cinnas fruit came from a long way off and was simply too expensive for people like me.

She held out my piece and I took it from her gently. "Thank you kindly, Auri."

"You are welcome kindly, Kvothe."

Elodin looked back and forth between the two of us. "Auri?"

I waited for him to finish his question, but that seemed to be all of it.

Auri understood before I did. "It's my name," she said, grinning proudly.

"Is it now?" Elodin said curiously.

Auri nodded. "Kvothe gave it to me." She beamed in my direction. "Isn't it marvelous?"

Elodin nodded. "It is a lovely name," he said politely. "And it suits you."

"It does," she agreed. "It is like having a flower in my heart." She gave Elodin a serious look. "If your name is getting too heavy, you should have Kvothe give you a new one."

Elodin nodded again and took a bite of his cinnas. As he chewed, he turned to look at me. By the light of the moon, I saw his eyes. They were cool, thoughtful, and perfectly, utterly sane.

After we finished our dinner, I sang a few songs, and we said our good-byes. Elodin and I walked away together. I knew at least a half-dozen ways to climb down from the roof of Mains, but I let him take the lead.

We made our way past a round stone observatory that stuck up from the roof and moved onto a long stretch of reasonably flat lead sheeting.

"How long have you been coming to see her?" Elodin asked.

I thought about it. "Half a year? It depends on when you start counting. It took a couple span of playing before I caught a glimpse of her, more before she trusted me enough to talk."

"You've had better luck than I have," he said. "It's been years. This is the first time she's come within ten paces of me. We barely speak a dozen words on a good day."

We climbed over a wide, low chimney and back onto a gentle slope of thick timber sealed with layers of tar. As we walked I grew more anxious. Why had he been trying to get close to her?

I thought about the time I had gone to Haven with Elodin to visit his giller, Alder Whin. I thought about Auri there. Tiny Auri, strapped to a bed with thick leather belts so she couldn't hurt herself or thrash around while she was being fed.

I stopped walking. Elodin took a few more steps before turning to look at me.

"She's my friend," I said slowly.

He nodded. "That much is obvious."

"And I don't have enough friends that I could bear to lose one," I said. "Not her. Promise me you won't tell anyone about her or bundle her off to Haven. It's not the right place for her." I swallowed against the dryness in my throat. "I need you to promise me."

Elodin tilted his head to one side. "I'm hearing an *or else*," he said, amusement in his voice. "Even though you're not actually saying it. I need to promise you *or else*. . . ." One corner of his mouth quirked up in a wry little smile.

When he smiled, I felt a flash of anger mingled with anxiety and fear. It was followed by the sudden, hot taste of plum and nutmeg in my mouth, and I became very conscious of the knife I had strapped to my thigh underneath my pants. I felt my hand slowly sliding into my pocket.

Then I saw the edge of the roof a half-dozen feet behind Elodin, and I felt my feet shift slightly, getting ready to sprint and tackle him, bearing us both off the roof and down to the hard cobblestones below.

I felt a sudden, cold sweat sweep over my body and closed my eyes. I took a deep, slow breath and the taste in my mouth faded.

I opened my eyes again. "I need you to promise me," I said. "Or else I'll probably do something stupid beyond all mortal ken." I swallowed. "And both of us will end up the worse for it."

Elodin looked at me. "What a remarkably honest threat," he said. "Normally they're much more growlish and gristly than that."

"Gristly?" I asked, emphasizing the 't.' "Don't you mean grisly?"

"Both," he said. "Usually there's a lot of, *I'll break your knees. I'll break your neck.*" He shrugged. "Makes me think of gristle, like when you're boning a chicken."

"Ah," I said. "I see."

We stared at each other for a moment.

"I'm not going to send anyone to take her in," he said at last. "Haven is the proper place for some folk. It's the only place for a lot of them. But I wouldn't wish a mad dog locked there if there were a better option."

He turned and started to walk away. When I didn't follow, he turned to look back at me.

"That's not good enough," I said. "I need you to promise."

"I swear on my mother's milk," Elodin said. "I swear on my name and my power. I swear it by the ever-moving moon."

We started walking again.

"She needs warmer clothes," I said. "And socks and shoes. And a blanket. And they need to be new. Auri won't take anything that's been worn by anyone else. I've tried."

"She won't take them from me," Elodin said. "I've left things out for her. She won't touch them." He turned to look at me. "If I give them to you, will you pass them along?"

I nodded. "In that case she also needs about twenty talents, a ruby the size of an egg, and a new set of engraving tools."

Elodin gave an honest, earthy chuckle. "Does she also need lute strings?"

I nodded. "Two pair, if you can get them."

"Why Auri?" Elodin asked.

"Because she doesn't have anyone else," I said. "And neither do I. If we don't look out for each other, who will?"

He shook his head. "No. Why did you pick that name for her?"

"Ah," I said, embarrassed. "Because she's so bright and sweet. She doesn't have any reason to be, but she is. *Auri* means sunny."

"In what language?" he asked.

I hesitated. "Siaru, I think."

Elodin shook his head. "Sunny is *leviriet* in Siaru."

I tried to think where I'd learned the word. Had I stumbled onto it in the Archives. . .?

Before I could bring it to mind, Elodin spoke. "I am preparing to teach a class," he said casually, "for those interested in the delicate and subtle art of naming." He gave me a sideways look. "It occurs to me that it might not be a complete waste of your time."

"I might be interested," I said carefully.

He nodded. "You should read Teccam's *Underlying Principles* to prepare. Not a long book, but thick, if you follow me."

"If you lend me a copy, I'd like nothing better than to read it," I said. "Otherwise, I'll have to muddle through without." He looked at me, uncomprehending. "I've been banned from the Archives."

"What, still?" Elodin asked, surprised.

"Still."

He seemed indignant. "It's been what? Half a year?"

"Three quarters of a year in three days' time," I said. "Master Lorren has made his feelings clear on the issue of letting me back inside."

"That," Elodin said with a strange protectiveness in his voice, "is utter horseshit. You're my Re'lar now."

Elodin changed directions, heading over a piece of rooftop I usually avoided because it was covered in clay roofing tiles. From there we hopped a narrow alley, made our way across the sloping roof of an inn, and stepped onto a broad roof of finished stone.

Eventually we came to a wide window with the warm glow of candlelight behind it. Elodin knocked on a pane of glass as sharply as if it were a door. Looking around, I realized we were standing atop the Masters' Hall.

After a moment, I saw the tall, thin shape of Master Lorren block the candlelight behind the window. He worked the latch and the entire window swung open on a hinge.

"Elodin, what can I do for you?" Lorren asked. If he thought anything odd about the situation, I couldn't tell from looking at his face.

Elodin jerked a thumb over his shoulder at me. "The boy here says he's still banned from the Archives. Is that so?"

Lorren's impassive eyes moved to me, then back to Elodin. "It is."

"Well let him back in," Elodin said. "He needs to read things. You've made your point."

"He's reckless," Lorren said flatly. "I'd planned to keep him out for a year and a day."

Elodin sighed. "Yes yes, very traditional. Why don't you give him a second chance? I'll vouch for him."

Lorren eyed me for a long moment. I tried to look as responsible as I could, which wasn't very, considering I was standing on a rooftop in the middle of the night.

"Very well," Lorren said. "Tomes only."

"Tombs is for feckless tits who can't chew their own food," Elodin said dismissively. "My boy's a Re'lar. He has the feck of twenty men! He needs to explore the Stacks and discover all manner of useless things."

"I am not concerned about the boy," Lorren said with unblinking calm. "My concern is for the Archives itself."

Elodin reached out and grabbed me by the shoulder, pushing me forward a bit. "How about this? If you catch him larking around again, I'll let you cut off his thumbs. That should set an example, don't you think?"

Lorren gave the two of us a slow look. Then he nodded. "Very well," he said, and closed his window.

"There you go," Elodin said expansively.

"What the hell?" I demanded, wringing my hands. "I . . . What the hell?"

Elodin looked at me, puzzled. "What? You're in. Problem solved."

"You can't offer to let him cut off my thumbs!" I said.

He raised an eyebrow. "Are you planning on breaking the rules again?" He asked pointedly.

"Wh— No. But . . ."

"Then you don't have anything to worry about," he said. He turned and continued up the slope of the roof. "Probably. I'd still step carefully if I were you. I can never tell when Lorren is kidding."

As soon as I awoke the next day, I made my way to the office of the bursar and settled accounts with Riem, the pinch-faced man who held the University's purse strings. I paid my hard-won nine talents and five, securing my place in the University for one more term.

Next I went to Ledgers and Lists where I signed up for observation in the Medica along with Physiognomy and Physic. Next was Ferrous and Cupric Metallurgy with Cammar in the Fishery. Last came Adept Sympathy with Elxa Dal.

It was only then I realized I didn't know the name of Elodin's class. I leafed through the ledger until I spotted Elodin's name, then ran my finger back to where the title of the class was listed in fresh dark ink: "Introduction to Not Being a Stupid Jackass."

I sighed and penned my name in the single blank space beneath.

CHAPTER TWELVE

The Sleeping Mind

WHEN I STIRRED AWAKE the next day, my first thought was of Elodin's class. There was an excited flutter in my stomach. After long months of trying to get Master Namer to teach me, I was finally going to get a chance to study naming. Real magic. Taborlin the Great magic.

But work came before play. Elodin's class didn't meet until noon. With Devi's debt hanging over my head, I needed to squeeze in a couple hours' work at the Fishery.

Entering Kilvin's workshop, the familiar din of a half-hundred busy hands washed over me like music. While it was a dangerous place, I found the workshop oddly relaxing. Many students resented my quick rise through the ranks of the Arcanum, but I'd earned a grudging respect from most of the other artificers.

I saw Manet working near the kilns and started to wind my way through the busy worktables toward him. Manet always knew what work paid best.

"Kvothe!"

The huge room grew quiet, and I turned to see Master Kilvin standing in the doorway of his office. He made a curt beckoning gesture and stepped back inside his office.

Sound slowly filled the room as the students returned to their work, but I could feel their eyes on me as I made my way across the room, weaving between the worktables.

As I came closer, I saw Kilvin through the wide window of his office, writing on a wall-mounted slate. He was half a foot taller than me, with a chest like a barrel. His great bristling beard and dark eyes made him look even larger than he really was.

I knocked politely on the doorframe, and Kilvin turned, setting down his chalk. "Re'lar Kvothe. Come in. Close the door."

Anxiously, I stepped into the room and pulled the door shut behind me. The clatter and din of the workshop was cut off so completely that I expected Kilvin must have some cunning sygaldry in place that muffled the noise. The result was an almost eerie quiet in the room.

Kilvin picked up a piece of paper from the corner of his worktable. "I have heard a distressing thing," he said. "Several days ago, a girl came to Stocks. She was looking for a young man who had sold her a charm." He looked me in the eye. "Do you know anything about this?"

I shook my head. "What did she want?"

"We do not know," Kilvin said. "E'lir Basil was working in Stocks at the time. He said the girl was young and seemed rather distressed. She was looking for——" He glanced down at the paper. "—a young wizard. She didn't know his name, but described him as being young, red-haired, and pretty."

Kilvin set down the piece of paper. "Basil said she grew increasingly upset as they spoke. She looked frightened, and when he tried to get her name, she ran off crying." He crossed his huge arms in front of his chest, his face severe. "So I ask you plainly. Have you been selling charms to young women?"

The question caught me by surprise. "Charms?" I asked. "Charms for what?"

"That you should tell me," Kilvin said darkly. "Charms for love, or luck. To help a woman catch with child, or to prevent the same. Amulets against demons and the like."

"Can such things be made?" I asked.

"No," Kilvin said firmly. "Which is why we do not sell them." His dark eyes settled heavily onto me. "So I ask you again: have you been selling charms to ignorant townsfolk?"

I was so unprepared for the accusation that I couldn't think of anything sensible to say in my defense. Then the ridiculousness of it struck me and I burst out laughing.

Kilvin's eyes narrowed. "This is not amusing, Re'lar Kvothe. Not only are such things expressly forbidden by the University, but a student who would sell false charms . . ." Kilvin trailed off, shaking his head. "It reveals a profound flaw of character."

"Master Kilvin, look at me," I said, plucking at my shirt. "If I was tricking gullible townsfolk out of their money, I wouldn't have to wear secondhand homespun."

Kilvin looked over, as if noticing my clothes for the first time. "True," he said. "However, one might think a student of lesser means would be more tempted to such actions."

"I've thought of it," I admitted. "With a penny's worth of iron and ten minutes easy sygaldry I could make a pendant that was cold to the touch. It wouldn't be hard to sell such a thing." I shrugged. "But I'm well aware that would fall under Fraudulent Purveyance. I wouldn't risk that."

Kilvin frowned. "A member of the Arcanum avoids such behavior because it is wrong, Re'lar Kvothe. Not because there is too much risk."

I gave him a forlorn smile. "Master Kilvin, if you had that much faith in my moral grounding we wouldn't be having this conversation."

His expression softened a little, and he gave me a small smile. "I admit, I would not expect such of you. But I have been surprised before. I would be remiss in my duty if I did not investigate such things."

"Did this girl come to complain about the charm?" I asked.

Kilvin shook his head. "No. As I said, she left no message. But I am at a loss as to why else a distressed young girl with a charm would come looking for you, knowing your description but not your name." He raised an eyebrow at me, making it a question.

I sighed. "Do you want my honest opinion, Master Kilvin?"

Kilvin raised both eyebrows at that. "Always, Re'lar Kvothe."

"I expect someone is trying to get me into trouble," I said. Compared to dosing me with an alchemical poison, spreading rumors was practically genteel behavior for Ambrose.

Kilvin nodded, absentmindedly smoothing down his beard with one hand. "Yes. I see."

He shrugged and picked up his piece of chalk. "Well then. I consider this matter resolved for the moment." He turned back to the slate and glanced over his shoulder at me. "I trust I will not be troubled by a horde of pregnant women waving iron pendants and cursing your name?"

"I'll take steps to avoid that, Master Kilvin."

I filled a few hours doing piecework in the Fishery, then made my way to the lecture hall in Mains where Elodin's class was being held. It was scheduled to begin at noon, but I was there a half hour early, the first to arrive.

The other students trickled in slowly. Seven of us in all. First came Fenton, my friendly rival from Advanced Sympathy. Then Fela arrived with Brean, a pretty girl of about twenty with sandy hair cut in the fashion of a boy's.

We chatted and introduced ourselves. Jarret was a shy Modegan I'd seen in the Medica. I recognized the young woman with bright blue eyes and honey-colored hair as Inyssa, but it took me a while to remember where I'd met her. She was one of Simmon's countless short-lived relationships. Last was Uresh, nearly thirty and a full El'the. His complexion and accent marked him as coming all the way from the Lanett.

The noon bell struck, but Elodin was nowhere to be seen.

Five minutes passed. Then ten. It wasn't until half past noon that Elodin breezed into the hall, carrying a loose armful of papers. He dropped them onto a table and began to pace back and forth directly in front of us.

"Several things should be made perfectly clear before we start," he said without any introduction or apology for his lateness. "First, you must do as I say. You must do it to the best of your ability, even when you don't see the reasons for it. Questions are fine, but in the end: I say, you do." He looked around. "Yes?"

We nodded or murmured affirmative noises.

"Second, you must believe me when I tell you certain things. Some of the things I tell you may not be true. But you must believe them anyway, until I tell you to stop." He looked at each of us, "Yes?"

I wondered vaguely if he began every lecture this way. Elodin noticed the lack of an affirmative from my direction. He glared at me, irritated. "We aren't to the hard part yet," he said.

"I'll do my best to try," I said.

"With answers like that we'll make you a barrister in no time," he said sarcastically. "Why not just do it, instead of *doing your best to try?*"

I nodded. It seemed to appease him and he turned back to the class as a whole. "There are two things you must remember. First, our names shape us, and we shape our names in turn." He stopped his pacing and looked out at us. "Second, even the simplest name is so complex that your mind could never begin to feel the boundaries of it, let alone understand it well enough for you to speak it."

There was a long stretch of quiet. Elodin waited, staring at us.

Finally Fenton took the bait. "If that's the case, how can anyone be a namer?"

"Good question," Elodin said. "The obvious answer is that it can't be done. That even the simplest of names is well beyond our reach." He held up a hand. "Remember, I am not speaking of the small names we use every day. The calling names like 'tree' and 'fire' and 'stone.' I am talking about something else entirely."

He reached into a pocket and pulled out a river stone, smooth and dark. "Describe the precise shape of this. Tell me of the weight and pressure that forged it from sand and sediment. Tell me how the light reflects from it. Tell me how the world pulls at the mass of it, how the wind cups it as it moves through the air. Tell me how the traces of its iron will feel the calling of a loden-stone. All of these things and a hundred thousand more make up the name of this stone." He held it out to us at arm's length. "This single, simple stone."

Elodin lowered his hand and looked at us. "Can you see how complex even this simple thing is? If you studied it for a long month, perhaps you would come to know it well enough to glimpse the outward edges of its name. Perhaps.

"This is the problem namers face. We must understand things that are beyond our understanding. How can it be done?"

He didn't wait for an answer and instead picked up some of the paper he'd brought in with him, handing each of us several sheets. "In fifteen minutes I will toss this stone. I will stand here," he set his feet. "Facing thus." He squared his shoulders. "I will throw it underhand with about three grip of force behind it. I want you to calculate in what manner it will move through the air so you can have your hand in the proper place to catch it when the time comes."

Elodin set the stone on a desk. "Proceed."

I set to the problem with a will. I drew triangles and arcs, I calculated, guessing at formulas I couldn't quite remember. It wasn't long before I grew frustrated at the impossibility of the task. Too much was unknown, too much was simply impossible to calculate.

After five minutes on our own, Elodin encouraged us to work as a group. That was when I first saw Uresh's talent with numbers. His calculations had outstripped mine to such a degree that I couldn't understand much of what he was doing. Fela was much the same, though she had also sketched a detailed series of parabolic arcs.

The seven of us discussed, argued, tried, failed, tried again. At the end of fifteen minutes we were frustrated. Myself especially. I hate problems I cannot solve.

Elodin looked to us as a group. "So what can you tell me?"

Some of us started to give our half-answers or best guesses, but he waved us into silence. "What can you tell me with certainty?"

After a moment Fela spoke up, "We don't know how the stone will fall."

Elodin clapped his hands approvingly. "Good! That is the right answer. Now watch."

He went to the door and stuck his head out. "Henri!" he shouted. "Yes you. Come here for a second." He stepped back from the door and ushered in one of Jamison's runners, a boy no more than eight years old.

Elodin took a half-dozen steps away and turned to face the boy. He squared his shoulders and grinned a mad grin. "Catch!" he said, lofting the stone at the boy.

Startled, the boy snatched it out of the air.

Elodin applauded wildly, then congratulated the bewildered boy before reclaiming the stone and hurrying him back out the door.

Our teacher turned to face us. "So," Elodin asked. "How did he do it? How could he calculate in a second what seven brilliant members of the Arcanum could not figure in a quarter hour? Does he know more geometry than Fela? Are his numbers quicker than Uresh's? Should we bring him back and make him a Re'lar?"

We laughed a bit, relaxing.

"My point is this. In each of us there is a mind we use for all our waking deeds. But there is another mind as well, a sleeping mind. It is so powerful that the sleeping mind of an eight-year-old can accomplish in one second what the waking minds of seven members of the Arcanum could not in fifteen minutes."

He made a sweeping gesture. "Your sleeping mind is wide and wild enough to hold the names of things. This I know because sometimes this knowledge bubbles to the surface. Inyssa has spoken the name of iron. Her waking mind does not know it, but her sleeping mind is wiser. Something deep inside Fela understands the name of the stone."

Elodin pointed at me. "Kvothe has called the wind. If we are to believe the writings of those long dead, his is the traditional path. The wind was the name aspiring namers sought and caught when things were studied here so long ago."

He went quiet for a moment, looking at us seriously, his arms folded. "I want each of you to think on what name you would like to find. It should be a small name. Something simple: iron or fire, wind or water, wood or stone. It should be something you feel an affinity toward."

Elodin strode toward the large slate mounted on the wall and began to write a list of titles. His handwriting was surprisingly tidy. "These are important books," he said. "Read one of them."

After a moment, Brean raised her hand. Then she realized it was pointless as Elodin still had his back to us. "Master Elodin?" she asked hesitantly. "Which one should we read?"

He looked over his shoulder, not pausing in his writing at all. "I don't care," he said, plainly irritated. "Pick one. The others you should skim in a desultory fashion. Look at the pictures. Smell them if nothing else." He turned back to look at the slate.

The seven of us looked at each other. The only sound in the room was the tapping of Elodin's chalk. "Which one is the most important?" I asked.

Elodin made a disgusted noise. "I don't know," he said. "I haven't read them." He wrote *En Temerant Voistra* on the board and circled it. "I don't even know if this one is in the Archives at all." He put a question mark next to it and continued to write. "I will tell you this. None of them are in Tomes. I made sure of that. You'll have to hunt for them in the Stacks. You'll have to earn them."

He finished the last title and took a step back, nodding to himself. There were twenty books in all. He drew stars next to three of them, underlined two others, and drew a sad face next to the last one on the list.

Then he left, striding out of the room without another word, leaving us thinking on the nature of names and wondering what we had gotten ourselves into.

CHAPTER THIRTEEN

The Hunt

DETERMINED TO MAKE A good showing of myself in Elodin's class, I tracked down Wilem and negotiated an exchange of future drinks for his help navigating the Archives.

We made our way through the cobbled streets of the University together, the wind gusting as the huge, windowless shape of the Archives loomed above us across the courtyard. The words *Vorfelan Rhinata Morie* were chiseled into the stone above the massive stone doors.

As we came closer, I realized my hands were sweaty. "Lord and lady, hold on for a second." I said as I stopped walking.

Wil raised an eyebrow at me.

"I'm nervous as a new whore," I said. "Just give me a moment."

"You said Lorren lifted his ban two days ago," Wilem said. "I thought you'd be inside as soon as you had permission."

"I was waiting for them to update the ledgers." I wiped my damp hands on my shirt. "I know something's going to happen," I said anxiously. "My name won't be in the book. Or Ambrose will be at the desk and I'll have some sort of relapse from that plum drug and end up kneeling on his throat and screaming."

"I'd like to see that," Wil said. "But Ambrose doesn't work today."

"That's something," I admitted, relaxing a bit. I pointed to the words above the door. "Do you know what that means?"

Wil glanced up. "The desire for knowledge shapes a man," he said. "Or something close to that."

"I like that." I took a deep breath. "Right. Let's go."

I pulled open the huge stone doors and entered a small antechamber, then Wil tugged open the inner doors and we stepped into the entry hall. In the middle of the room was a huge wooden desk with several large, leather-bound ledgers open atop it. Several imposing doors led off in different directions.

Fela sat behind the desk, her curling hair pulled back into a tail. The red light from the sympathy lamps made her look different, but no less pretty. She smiled.

"Hello Fela," I said, trying not to sound as nervous as I felt. "I heard I'm back in Lorren's good books. Could you check for me?"

She nodded and began to flip through the ledger in front of her. Her face brightened, and she pointed. Then her expression went dark.

I felt a sinking sensation in my stomach, "What is it?" I asked. "Is something wrong?"

"No," she said. "Nothing's wrong."

"You look like something's wrong," Wil grumbled. "What does it say?"

Fela hesitated, then spun the book around so we could read it: *Kvothe, Arliden's son. Red-haired. Fair complected. Young.* Written next to this in the margin in a different script were the words, *Ruh Bastard.*

I grinned at her. "Correct on all counts. Can I go in?"

She nodded. "Do you need lamps?" she asked, opening a drawer.

"I do," Wil said, already writing his name in a separate ledger.

"I've got my own," I said, pulling my small lamp from a pocket of my cloak.

Fela opened the admittance ledger and signed us in. My hand shook as I wrote, skittering the pen's nib embarrassingly, so it flicked ink across the page.

Fela blotted it away and closed the book. She smiled up at me. "Welcome back," she said.

———

I let Wilem lead the way through the Stacks and did my best to look properly amazed.

It wasn't a hard part to play. While I'd had access to the Archives for some time, I'd been forced to creep around like a thief. I had kept my lamp on its dimmest setting and avoided the main hallways for fear of accidentally running into someone.

Shelves covered every bit of the stone walls. Some hallways were broad and open with high ceilings, while others formed narrow lanes barely wide enough for two people to pass if they both turned sideways. The air was heavy with the smell of leather and dust, of old parchment and binding glue. It smelled of secrets.

Wilem led me through twisting shelves, up some stairs then through a long, wide hallway lined with books bound all in identical red leather. Finally we came to a door with dim red light showing around the edges.

"There are rooms set aside for private study," Wilem said softly. "Reading holes. Sim and I use this one a lot. Not many people know about it." Wil knocked briefly on the door before he opened it to reveal a windowless room barely larger than the table and chairs it contained.

Sim sat at the table, the red light of his sympathy lamp making his face look ruddier than usual. His eyes grew wide when he saw me. "Kvothe? What are you doing in here?" He turned to Wilem, horrified. "What is he doing in here?"

"Lorren lifted his ban," Wilem said. "Our young boy has a reading list. He's planning his first book-hunt."

"Congratulations!" Sim beamed at me. "Can I help? I'm falling asleep here." He held out his hand.

I tapped my temple. "The day I can't memorize twenty titles is the day I don't belong in the Arcanum," I said. Though that was only half the truth. The full truth was that I only owned a half-dozen precious sheets of paper. I couldn't afford to waste one on something like this.

Sim pulled a folded piece of paper out of his pocket along with a nub of pencil. "I need things written down," he said. "Not all of us memorize ballads for fun."

I shrugged and began to jot them down. "It will probably go faster if we split my list three ways," I said.

Wilem gave me a look. "You think you can just walk around and find books by yourself?" He looked at Sim, who was grinning widely.

Of course. I wasn't supposed to know anything about the layout of the Stacks. Wil and Sim didn't know I'd been sneaking in at nights for almost a month.

It's not that I didn't trust them, but Sim couldn't lie to save his life, and Wil worked as a scriv. I didn't want to force him to choose between my secret and his duty to Master Lorren.

So I decided to play dumb. "Oh, I'll muddle through," I said nonchalantly. "It can't be that hard to figure out."

"There are so many books in the Archives," Wil said slowly, "that merely reading all the titles would take you a full span." He paused, looking at me intently. "Eleven full days without pause for food or sleep."

"Really?" Sim asked. "That long?"

Wil nodded. "I worked it out a year ago. It helps stop the E'lir's mewling when they must wait for me to fetch them a book." He looked at me. "There are books without titles too. And scrolls. And clays. And many languages."

"What's a clay?" I asked.

"Clay tablet," Wil explained. "They were some of the only things to survive when Caluptena burned. Some have been transcribed, but not all."

"All that's beside the point," Sim interjected. "The problem is the organization."

"Cataloging," Wil said. "There have been many different systems over the years. Some masters prefer one, some prefer another." He frowned. "Some create their own systems for organizing the books."

I laughed. "You sound like they should be pilloried for it."

"Perhaps," Wil grumbled. "I would not weep over such a thing."

Sim looked at him. "You can't blame a master for trying to organize things in the best way possible."

"I can," Wilem said. "If the Archives were organized badly, it would be a uniform unpleasantness we could work with. But there have been so many different systems in the last fifty years. Books mislabeled. Titles mistranslated."

He ran his hands through his hair, sounding suddenly weary. "And there are always new books coming in, needing to be cataloged. Always the lazy E'lir in Tombs who want us to fetch for them. It is like trying to dig a hole in the bottom of a river."

"So what you're saying," I said slowly, "is that you find your time spent as a scriv to be both pleasant and rewarding."

Sim muffled a laugh in his hands.

"And then there are you people." Wil looked at me, his voice dangerous and low. "Students given the freedom in the Stacks. You come in, read half a book, then hide it so you can continue later at your own convenience." Wil's hands made gripping motions as if clutching at the front of someone's shirt. Or perhaps a throat. "Then you forget where you have put the book, and it is gone as surely as if you had burned it."

Wil pointed a finger at me. "If I ever discover you have done such a thing," he said, smoldering with anger, "no God will keep you safe from me."

I thought guiltily about three books I had hidden in just this way while I was studying for exams. "I promise," I said. "I won't ever do that." *Again*.

Sim stood up from the table, rubbing his hands together briskly. "Right. Simply said, it's a mess in here, but if you stick to the books they have listed in Tolem's catalog, you should be able to find what you're looking for. Tolem is the system we use now. Wil and I will show you where they keep the ledgers."

"And a few other things," Wil said. "Tolem is hardly comprehensive. Some of your books might require deeper digging." He turned to open the door.

As it turned out, only four books on my list were in the Tolem ledgers. After that, we were forced to leave the well-organized parts of the Stacks behind. Wil seemed to take the list as a personal challenge, so I learned a great deal about the Archives that day. Wil took me to the Dead Ledgers, the Backward Stair, the Bottom Wing.

Even so, at the end of four hours we'd only managed to track down the locations of seven books. Wil seemed frustrated by this, but I thanked him heartily, telling him he'd given me everything I needed to continue the search on my own.

Over the next several days, I spent almost every free moment I had in the Archives, hunting the books on Elodin's list. I wanted nothing more than to start this class with my best foot forward, and I was determined to read every book he had given us.

The first was a travelogue I found rather enjoyable. The second was some rather bad poetry, but it was short, and I forced my way through by gritting my teeth and occasionally closing one eye so as not to damage the entirety of my brain. Third was a book of rhetorical philosophy, ponderously written.

Then came a book detailing wildflowers in northern Atur. A fencing manual with some rather confusing illustrations. Another book of poetry, this one thick as a brick and even more self-indulgent than the first.

It took hours, but I read them all. I even went so far as to take notes on two of my precious pieces of paper.

Next came, as near as I could tell, the journal of a madman. While it sounds interesting, it was really only a headache pressed between covers. The man wrote in a tight script with no spaces between the words. No breaks for paragraphs. No punctuation. No consistent grammar or spelling.

That was when I began to skim. The next day when confronted with two books written in Modegan, a series of essays concerning crop rotation and a monograph on Vintish mosaics, I stopped taking notes.

The last handful of books I merely flipped through, wondering why Elodin would want us to read a two-hundred-year-old tax ledger from a barony in the Small Kingdoms, an outdated medical text, and a badly translated morality play.

While I quickly lost my fascination with reading Elodin's books, I still delighted in hunting them down. I irritated more than a few scrivs with my constant questions: Who was in charge of reshelving? Where were the Vintish dictums kept? Who had the keys to the fourth basement scroll storage? Where did the damaged books go while they were waiting to be repaired?

In the end, I found nineteen of the books. All of them except *En Temerant*

Voistra. And that one was not from lack of trying. At my best guess, the entire venture took nearly fifty hours of searching and reading.

I arrived at Elodin's next class ten minutes early, proud as a priest. I brought my two pages of careful notes, eager to impress Elodin with my dedication and thoroughness.

All seven of us showed up for class before the noon bell. The door to the lecture hall was closed, so we stood in the hallway, waiting for Elodin to arrive.

We shared stories about our search through the Archives and speculated as to why Elodin considered these books important. Fela had been a scriv for years, and she had only found seventeen of them. Nobody had found *En Temerant Voistra*, or even a mention of it.

Elodin still hadn't arrived by the time the noon bell rang, and at fifteen minutes past the hour I grew tired of standing in the hallway and tried the door to the lecture hall. At first the handle didn't move at all, but when I jiggled it in frustration, the latch turned and the door opened a crack.

"Thought it was locked," Inyssa said, frowning.

"Just stuck," I said, pushing it open.

We entered the huge, empty room and walked down the stairs to the front row of seats. On the large slate in front of us, written in Elodin's oddly tidy handwriting was a single word: "Discuss."

We settled into our seats and waited, but Elodin was nowhere to be seen. We looked at the slate, then at each other, at a loss for what exactly we were supposed to do.

From the looks on everyone's faces, I wasn't the only one who was irritated. I'd spent fifty hours digging up his damn useless books. I'd done my part. Why wasn't he doing his?

The seven of us waited for the next two hours, chatting idly, waiting for Elodin to arrive.

He didn't.

CHAPTER FOURTEEN

The Hidden City

WHILE THE HOURS I'D wasted hunting for Elodin's books left me profoundly irritated, I emerged from the experience with a solid working knowledge of the Archives. The most important thing I learned was that it was not merely a warehouse filled with books. The Archives was like a city unto itself. It had roads and winding lanes. It had alleys and shortcuts.

Just like a city, parts of the Archives teemed with activity. The Scriptorium held rows of desks where scrivs toiled over translations or copied faded texts into new books with fresh, dark ink. The Sorting Hall buzzed with activity as scrivs sifted and reshelved books.

The Buggery was not at all what I expected, thank goodness. Instead, it proved to be the place where new books were decontaminated before being added to the collection. Apparently all manner of creatures love books, some devouring parchment and leather, others with a taste for paper or glue. Bookworms were the least of them, and after listening to a few of Wilem's stories I wanted nothing more than to wash my hands.

Cataloger's Mew, the Bindery, Bolts, Palimpsest, all of them were busy as beehives, full of quiet, industrious scrivs.

But other parts of the Archives were quite the opposite of busy. The acquisitions office, for example, was tiny and perpetually dark. Through the window I could see that one entire wall of the office was nothing but a huge map with cities and roads marked in such detail that it looked like a snarled loom. The map was covered in a layer of clear alchemical lacquer, and there were notes written at various points in red grease pencil, detailing rumors of desirable books and the last known positions of the various acquisition teams.

Tomes was like a great public garden. Any student was free to come and read the books shelved there. Or they could submit a request to the scrivs, who would grudgingly head off into the Stacks to find if not the exact book you wanted, then at least something closely related.

But the Stacks comprised the vast majority of the Archives. That was where the books actually lived. And just like in any city, there were good neighborhoods and bad.

In the good neighborhoods everything was properly organized and cataloged. In these places a ledger-entry would lead you to a book as simply as a pointing finger.

Then there were the bad neighborhoods. Sections of the Archives that were forgotten, or neglected, or simply too troublesome to deal with at the moment. These were places where books were organized under old catalogs, or under no catalog at all.

There were walls of shelves like mouths with missing teeth, where long-gone scrivs had cannibalized an old catalog to bring books into whatever system was fashionable at the time. Thirty years ago two entire floors had gone from good neighborhood to bad when the Larkin ledger-books were burned by a rival faction of scrivs.

And, of course, there was the four-plate door. The secret at the heart of the city.

It was nice to go strolling in the good neighborhoods. It was pleasant to go looking for a book and find it exactly where it should be. It was easy. Comforting. Quick.

But the bad neighborhoods were fascinating. The books there were dusty and disused. When you opened one, you might read words no eyes had touched for hundreds of years. There was treasure there, among the dross.

It was in those places I searched for the Chandrian.

I looked for hours and I looked for days. A large part of the reason I had come to the University was because I wanted to discover the truth about them. Now that I finally had easy access to the Archives, I made up for lost time.

But despite my long hours of searching, I found hardly anything at all. There were several books of children's stories that featured Chandrian engaged in minor mischief like stealing pies and making milk go sour. Others had them bargaining like demons in Aturan morality plays.

Scattered through these stories were a few thin threads of fact, but nothing I didn't already know. The Chandrian were cursed. Signs showed their presence: blue flame, rot and rust, a chill in the air.

My hunt was made more difficult by the fact that I couldn't ask anyone for help. If word spread that I was spending my time reading children's stories, it would not improve my reputation.

More important, one of the few things I knew about the Chandrian was that they worked to viciously repress any knowledge of their own existence. They'd killed my troupe because my father had been writing a song about them. In Trebon they'd destroyed an entire wedding party because some of the guests had seen pictures of them on a piece of ancient pottery.

Given these facts, talking about the Chandrian didn't seem like the wisest course of action.

So I did my own searching. After days, I abandoned hope of finding anything so helpful as a book about the Chandrian, or even anything so substantial as a monograph. Still, I read on, hoping to find a scrap of truth hidden somewhere. A single fact. A hint. Anything.

But children's stories are not rich in detail, and what few details I found were obviously fanciful. Where did the Chandrian live? In the clouds. In dreams. In a castle made of candy. What were their signs? Thunder. The darkening of the moon. One story even mentioned rainbows. Who would write that? Why make a child terrified of rainbows?

Names were easier to come by, but all were obviously stolen from other sources. Almost all of these were names of demons mentioned in the *Book of the Path*, or from some play, primarily *Daeonica*. One painfully allegorical story named the Chandrian after seven well-known emperors from the days of the Aturan Empire. That, at least, gave me a brief, bitter laugh.

Eventually I discovered a slim volume called *The Book of Secrets* buried deep in the Dead Ledgers. It was an odd book: arranged like a bestiary but written like a children's primer. It had pictures of faerie-tale creatures like ogres, trow, and dennerlings. Each entry had a picture accompanied by a short, insipid poem.

Of course, the Chandrian were the only entry without a picture. Instead there was just an empty page framed in decorative scrollwork. The accompanying poem was less than useless:

> *The Chandrian move from place to place,*
> *But they never leave a trace.*
> *They hold their secrets very tight,*
> *But they never scratch and they never bite.*
> *They never fight and they never fuss.*
> *In fact they are quite nice to us.*
> *They come and they go in the blink of an eye,*
> *Like a bright bolt of lightning out of the sky.*

Irritating as it was to read something like this, it made one point abundantly clear. To the rest of the world the Chandrian were nothing more than childish faerie stories. No more real than shamble-men or unicorns.

I knew differently, of course. I had seen them with my own eyes. I had talked to black-eyed Cinder. I had seen Haliax wearing shadow all around him like a mantle.

So I continued my fruitless search. It didn't matter what the rest of the world believed. I knew the truth, and I've never been one to give up easily.

———

I settled into the rhythm of a new term. As before, I attended classes and played music at Anker's. But most of my time was spent in the Archives. I had lusted after them for so long that being able to walk through the front doors any time I wanted seemed almost unnatural.

Even my continuing failure to find anything factual about the Chandrian didn't sour the experience. As I hunted, I became increasingly distracted by other books I found. A handwritten medicinal herbal with watercolor pictures of various plants. A small quarto book of four plays I'd never heard of before. A remarkably engaging biography of Hevred the Wary.

I spent entire afternoons in the reading holes, missing meals and neglecting my friends. More than once I was the last student out of the Archives before the scrivs locked the doors for the night. I would have slept there if such things were allowed.

Some days, if my schedule was too tight for me to settle in for a long stretch of reading, I would simply walk the Stacks for a handful of minutes between classes.

I was so infatuated with my new freedoms that I did not make it over the river into Imre for many days. When I did return to the Grey Man, I brought a calling card I'd fashioned from a scrap of parchment. I thought Denna would be amused by it.

But when I arrived, the officious porter in the Grey Man's parlor told me no, he could not deliver my card. No, the young lady was no longer in residence. No, he could not take a message for her. No, he did not know where she had gone.

CHAPTER FIFTEEN

Interesting Fact

ELODIN STRODE INTO THE lecture hall almost an hour late. His clothes were covered in grass stains, and there were dried leaves tangled in his hair. He was grinning.

Today there were only six of us waiting for him. Jarret hadn't shown up for the last two classes. Given the scathing comments he'd made before disappearing, I doubted he'd be coming back.

"Now!" Elodin shouted without preamble. "Tell me things!"

This was his newest way to waste our time. At the beginning of every lecture he demanded an interesting fact he had never heard before. Of course, Elodin himself was the sole arbiter of what was interesting, and if the first fact you provided didn't measure up, or if he already knew it, he would demand another, and another, until you finally came up with something that amused him.

He pointed at Brean. "Go!"

"Spiders can breathe underwater," she said promptly.

Elodin nodded. "Good." He looked at Fenton.

"There's a river south of Vintas that flows the wrong way," Fenton said. "It's a saltwater river that runs inland from the Centhe sea."

Elodin shook his head. "Already know about that."

Fenton looked down at a piece of paper. "Emperor Ventoran once passed a law—"

"Boring," Elodin interjected, cutting him off.

"If you drink more than two quarts of seawater you'll throw up?" Fenton asked.

Elodin worked his mouth speculatively, as if he were trying to get a piece of gristle out of his teeth. Then he gave a satisfied nod. "That's a good one." He pointed to Uresh.

"You can divide infinity an infinite number of times, and the resulting pieces will still be infinitely large," Uresh said in his odd Lenatti accent. "But if you divide a non-infinite number an infinite number of times the resulting pieces are non-infinitely small. Since they are non-infinitely small, but there are an infinite number of them, if you add them back together, their sum is infinite. This implies any number is, in fact, infinite."

"Wow," Elodin said after a long pause. He leveled a serious finger at the Lenatti man. "Uresh. Your next assignment is to have sex. If you do not know how to do this, see me after class." He turned to look at Inyssa.

"The Yllish people never developed a written language," she said.

"Not true," Elodin said. "They used a system of woven knots." He made a complex motion with his hands, as if braiding something. "And they were doing it long before we started scratching pictograms on the skins of sheep."

"I didn't say they lacked recorded language," Inyssa muttered. "I said written language."

Elodin managed to convey his vast boredom in a simple shrug.

Inyssa frowned at him. "Fine. There's a type of dog in Sceria that gives birth through a vestigial penis," she said.

"Wow," Elodin said. "Okay. Yeah." He pointed to Fela.

"Eighty years back the Medica discovered how to remove cataracts from eyes," Fela said.

"I already know that," Elodin said, waving his hand dismissively.

"Let me finish," Fela said. "When they figured out how to do this, it meant they could restore sight to people who had never been able to see before. These people hadn't gone blind, they had been born blind."

Elodin cocked his head curiously.

Fela continued. "After they could see, they were shown objects. A ball, a cube, and a pyramid all sitting on a table." Fela made the shapes with her hands as she spoke. "Then the physickers asked them which one of the three objects was round."

Fela paused for effect, looking at all of us. "They couldn't tell just by looking at them. They needed to touch them first. Only after they touched the ball did they realize it was the round one."

Elodin threw his head back and laughed delightedly. "Really?" he asked her. She nodded.

"Fela wins the prize!" Elodin shouted, throwing up his hands. He reached into his pocket and brought out something brown and oblong, pressing it into her hands.

She looked at it curiously. It was a milkweed pod.

"Kvothe hasn't gone yet," Brean said.

"Doesn't matter," Elodin said in an offhand way. "Kvothe is crap at Interesting Fact."

I scowled as loudly as I could.

"Fine," Elodin said. "Tell me what you have."

"The Adem mercenaries have a secret art called the Lethani," I said. "It is the key to what makes them such fierce warriors."

Elodin cocked his head to one side. "Really?" he asked. "What is it?"

"I don't know," I said flippantly, hoping to irritate him. "Like I said, it's secret."

Elodin seemed to consider this for a moment, then shook his head. "No. Interesting, but not a fact. It's like saying the Cealdish moneylenders have a secret art called Financia that makes them such fierce bankers. There's no substance to it." He looked at me again, expectantly.

I tried to think of something else, but I couldn't. My head was full of faerie tales and dead-ended research into the Chandrian.

"See?" Elodin said to Brean. "He's crap."

"I just don't know why we're wasting our time with this," I snapped.

"Do you have better things to do?" Elodin asked.

"Yes!" I exploded angrily. "I have a thousand more important things to do! Like learning about the name of the wind!"

Elodin held up a finger, attempting to strike a sage pose and failing because of the leaves in his hair. "Small facts lead to great knowing," he intoned. "Just as small names lead to large names."

He clapped his hands and rubbed them together eagerly. "Right! Fela! Open your prize and we can give Kvothe the lesson he so greatly desires."

Fela cracked the dry husk of the milkweed pod. The white fluff of the floating seeds spilled out into her hands.

Master Namer motioned for her to toss it into the air. Fela threw it, and everyone watched the mass of white fluff sail toward the high ceiling of the lecture hall, then fall back heavily to the ground.

"Goddammit," Elodin said. He stalked over to the bundle of seeds, picked it up, and waved it around vigorously until the air was full of gently floating puffs of milkweed seed.

Then Elodin started to chase the seeds wildly around the room, trying to snatch them out of the air with his hands. He clambered over chairs, ran across the lecturer's dais, and jumped onto the table at the front of the room.

All the while he grabbed at the seeds. At first he did it one-handed, like you'd catch a ball. But he met with no success, and so he started clapping at them, the way you'd swat a fly. When this didn't work either, he tried to catch them with both hands, the way a child might cup a firefly out of the air.

But he couldn't get hold of one. The more he chased, the more frantic he became, the faster he ran, the wilder he grabbed. This went on for a full minute. Two minutes. Five minutes. Ten.

It might have gone on for the entire class period, but eventually he tripped over a chair and tumbled painfully to the stone floor, tearing open the leg of his pants and bloodying his knee.

Clutching his leg, he sat on the ground and let loose with a string of angry cursing the like of which I had never heard in my entire life. He shouted and snarled and spat. He moved through at least eight languages, and even when I couldn't understand the words he used, the sound of it made my gut clench and the hair on my arms stand up. He said things that made me sweat. He said things that made me sick. He said things I didn't know it was possible to say.

I expect this might have continued, but while drawing an angry breath, he sucked one of the floating milkweed seeds into his mouth and began to cough and choke violently.

Eventually he spat out the seed, caught his breath, got to his feet, and limped out of the lecture hall without saying another word.

This was not a particularly odd day's class under Master Elodin.

———

After Elodin's class I ate a bit of lunch at Anker's, then went to my shift in the Medica, watching more experienced El'the diagnose and treat incoming patients. After that I headed over the river with the hope of finding Denna. It was my third trip in as many days, but it was a crisp, sunny day, and after all my time in the Archives, I felt the need to stretch my legs a bit.

I stopped at the Eolian first, though it was far too early for Denna to be there. I chatted with Stanchion and Deoch before moving on to a few of the other inns I knew she occasionally frequented: Taps, Barrel and Bale, and Dog in the Wall. She wasn't at any of those either.

I wandered through a few public gardens, their trees almost entirely devoid of leaves. Then I visited all the instrument shops I could find, browsing the lutes and asking if they'd seen a pretty dark-haired woman looking at harps. They hadn't.

It was fully dark by then. So I stopped by the Eolian again and wandered slowly through the crowd. Denna was still nowhere to be seen, but I did meet up with Count Threpe. We shared a drink and listened to a few songs before I left.

I pulled my cloak more tightly around my shoulders as I started back to the University. Imre's streets were busier now than they had been during the day, and despite the chill in the air, there was a festival feel to the town. Music of a dozen different kinds poured from the doorways of inns and theaters. People crowded in and out of restaurants and exhibition halls.

Then I heard a laugh rise high and bright over the low murmuring of the crowds. I would have recognized it anywhere. It was Denna's laugh. I knew it like the backs of my own hands.

I turned around, feeling a smile spread across my face. This was always the way of it. I only seemed to be able to find her after I'd given up hope.

I scanned the faces in the milling throng and found her easily. Denna stood by the doorway of a small café, wearing a long dress of dark blue velvet.

I took a step toward her, then stopped. I watched as Denna spoke to someone standing behind the open door of a carriage. The only part of her companion I could see was the very top of his head. He was wearing a hat with a tall white plume.

A moment later, Ambrose closed the carriage door. He gave her a wide, charming smile and said something that made her laugh. Lamplight glittered on the gold brocade of his jacket, and his gloves were dyed the same dark, royal purple as his boots. The color should have looked garish on him, but it didn't.

As I stood staring, a passing two-horse fetter cart nearly knocked me flat and trampled me, which would have been fair, as I was standing in the middle of the road. The driver cursed and flicked out with his horse whip as he went past. It caught me on the back of the neck, but I didn't even feel it.

I regained my balance and looked up in time to see Ambrose kiss Denna's hand. Then, moving gracefully, he offered her his arm and they entered the café, together.

CHAPTER SIXTEEN

Unspoken Fear

AFTER SEEING AMBROSE AND Denna in Imre, I fell into a dark mood. On the walk back to the University my head spun with thoughts of them. Was Ambrose doing this purely out of spite? How had it happened? What was Denna thinking?

After a largely sleepless night, I tried not to think of it. Instead I burrowed deep into the Archives. Books are a poor substitute for female companionship, but they are easier to find. I consoled myself by hunting through the dark corners of the Archives for the Chandrian. I read until my eyes burned and my head felt thick and cramped.

Nearly a span passed, and I did little but attend classes and pillage the Archives. For my pains I gained lungs full of dust, a persistent headache from hours of reading by sympathy light, and a knot between my shoulder blades from hunching over a low table while I paged through the faded remains of the Gilean ledgers.

I also found a single mention of the Chandrian. It was in a handwritten octavo titled *A Quainte Compendium of Folke Belief.* At my best guess, the book was two hundred years old.

The book was a collection of stories and superstitions gathered by an amateur historian in Vintas. Unlike *The Mating Habits of the Common Draccus*, it made no attempt to prove or disprove these beliefs. The author had simply collected and organized the stories with occasional brief commentaries about how beliefs seemed to change from region to region.

It was an impressive volume, obviously comprising years of research. There were four chapters about demons. Three chapters for faeries: one of which was entirely devoted to tales of Felurian. There were pages on the shamblemen, rendlings, and the trow. The author recorded songs about the grey ladies and white riders. A lengthy section on barrow draugar. There were six chapters on folk magic: eight ways to cure warts, twelve ways to talk to the dead, twenty-two love charms . . .

The entire entry on the Chandrian was less than half a page:

Of the Chaendrian there is little to be said. Every Man knows of them. Every child chants their song. Yet folke tell no stories.

For the price of a small beer a Farmer will talk two hours on Dannerlings. But mention the Chaendrian and his mouth goes tight as a Spinner's Asse and he is touching iron and pushing back his chair.

Many think it bad luck to speak of the Fae, yet still folke do. What makes the Chaendrian different I knowe notte. One rather drunk Tanner in the towne of Hillesborrow said in hushed tones, "If you talk of them, they come for you." This seems the unspoken fear of these common folke.

So I write what I have gleaned, all common and inspecific. The Chaendrian are a groupe of various number. (Likely seven, given their name.) They appear and commit diverse violence for no clear reason.

There are signs which herald their Arrival, but there is no agreement as to these. Blue flame is the most common, but I have also heard of wine going sour, blindness, crops withering, unseasonable storms, miscarriage, and the sun going dark in the sky.

Altogether, I have found them a Frustrating and Profitless area of Inquirey.

I closed the book. Frustrating and profitless had a familiar ring to it.

The worst part wasn't that I already knew everything written in the entry. The worst part was that this was the best source of information I'd managed to discover in over a hundred long hours of searching.

CHAPTER SEVENTEEN

Interlude—Parts

KVOTHE HELD UP HIS hand, and Chronicler lifted his pen from the paper.

"Let's pause there for a moment," Kvothe said, nodding toward the window. "I can see Cob coming down the road."

Kvothe stood and brushed off the front of his apron. "Might I suggest the two of you take a moment to compose yourselves?" He nodded to Chronicler. "You look like you've just been doing something you shouldn't."

Kvothe walked calmly to stand behind the bar. "Nothing could be further from the truth, of course. Chronicler, you are bored, waiting for work. That is why your writing gear is out. You wish you weren't stuck without a horse in this nowhere town. But you are, and you're going to make the best of it."

Bast grinned. "Ooh! Give me something, too!"

"Play to your strengths, Bast." Kvothe said. "You're drinking with our only customer because you're a shiftless layabout nobody would ever dream of asking for help in the fields."

Bast grinned eagerly. "Am I bored too?"

"Of course you are, Bast. What else is there to be?" He folded the linen cloth and lay it on the bar. "I, on the other hand, am too busy to be bored. I am bustling about, tending to the hundred small tasks that keep the inn running smoothly."

He looked at the two of them. "Chronicler, slouch back in your chair. Bast, if you can't stop grinning, at least start telling our friend the story about the three priests and the miller's daughter."

Bast's grin widened. "That's a good one."

"Everyone have their parts?" Kvothe picked up the cloth from the bar and walked through the doorway into the kitchen, saying, "Enter Old Cob. Stage left."

There was the thump of feet on the wooden landing, then Old Cob stomped irritably into the Waystone Inn. He glanced past the table where Bast was grinning and making gestures to accompany some story, then made his way to the bar. "Hello? You in there, Kote?"

After a second the innkeeper came bustling in from the kitchen, drying his wet hands on his apron. "Hello there, Cob. What can I do for you?"

"Graham sent the little Owens boy to fetch me," Cob said, irritated. "You have any idea why I'm here instead of haulin' oats?"

Kote shook his head. "I thought he was bringing in the Murrions' wheat today."

"Damn foolishness," Cob muttered. "We're in for rain tonight, and I'm standing here with dry oats stacked in my field."

"Since you're here anyway," the innkeeper said hopefully. "Can I interest you in some cider? Pressed it fresh this morning."

Some of the irritation faded from the old man's weathered face. "Since I'm waiting anyway," he said. "Mug of cider would be proper nice."

Kote went into the back room and returned with a pottery jug. There was the sound of more feet on the landing outside and Graham came through the door with Jake, Carter, and the smith's prentice all in tow.

Cob turned to glare at them. "What's so damned important it's worth hauling me into town this time of morning?" he demanded. "Daylight's burning, a—"

There was a sudden burst of laugher from the table where Chronicler and Bast sat. Everyone turned to see Chronicler flushing a bright red, laughing and covering his mouth with one hand. Bast was laughing too, pounding at the table.

Graham led the others to the bar. "I found out Carter and the boy are helping the Orrisons take their sheep to market," he said. "Off to Baedn, wasn't it?"

Carter and the smith's prentice nodded.

"I see." Old Cob looked down at his hands. "You'll be missing his funeral then."

Carter nodded solemnly, but Aaron's expression went stricken. He looked from face to face, but everyone else was standing very still, watching the old farmer by the bar.

"Good," Cob said at last, looking up at Graham. "It's good you fetched us in." He saw the boy's face and snorted. "You look like you just killed your cat, boy. Mutton goes to market. Shep knew that. He wouldn't think one jot less of you for doing what needs doing."

He reached up to pat the smith's prentice on the back. "We'll all have a drink together to send 'im off proper. That's the important thing. What happens in the church tonight is just a bunch of priestly speechifying. We know how to say good-bye better than that." He looked behind the bar. "Bring us out some of his favorite, Kote."

The innkeeper was already moving, gathering wooden mugs and filling them with a dark brown beer from a smaller keg behind the bar.

Old Cob held up his mug and the others followed suit. "To our Shep."

Graham spoke first. "When we were kids, I broke my leg when we were out hunting," he said. "I told him to run off for help, but he wouldn't leave me. He rigged a little sled together out of pure nothing and cussedness. Dragged me the whole way back to town."

Everyone drank.

"He introduced me to my missus," Jake said. "I don't know if I ever thanked him proper for that."

Everyone drank.

"When I was sick with the croup, he came out to visit me every day," Carter said. "Not many folk did. Brought me soup his wife made, too."

Everyone drank.

"He was nice to me when I first came here," the smith's prentice said. "He would tell me jokes. And once I ruined a wagon couple he'd brought in for me to fix, and he never told Master Caleb." He swallowed hard and looked around nervously. "I really liked him."

Everyone drank.

"He was braver than all of us," Cob said. "He was the first to stick a knife to that fella last night. If the bastard had been any way normal, that would have been an end to it."

Cob's voice shook a bit, and for a moment he looked small and tired and every bit as old as he was. "But that weren't the case. These en't good days to be a brave man. But he was brave all the same. I wish I'd been brave and dead instead, and him home right now, kissing his young wife."

There was a murmur from the others, and they all drank to the bottom of their mugs. Graham coughed a bit before he set his down on the bar.

"I didn't know what to say," the smith's prentice said softly.

Graham patted him on the back, smiling. "You did fine, boy."

The innkeeper cleared his throat, and everyone's eyes turned to him. "I hope you won't think me too forward," he said. "I didn't know him as well as you. Not enough for the first toast, but maybe enough for the second."

He fidgeted with his apron strings, as if embarrassed for speaking up at all. "I know it's early, but I'd dearly like to share a tumble of whiskey with you on Shep's account."

There was a murmur of assent and the innkeeper pulled glasses from beneath the bar and began to fill them. Not with bottle whiskey either—the red-haired man tapped it from one of the massive barrels resting on the counter behind the bar. Barrel whiskey was a penny a swallow, so they raised their glasses with more earnest warmth than might have otherwise been the case.

"What's this toast going to be then?" Graham asked.

"To the end of a pisser of a year?" Jake said.

"That's no kind of toast," Old Cob grumbled at him.

"To the king?" Aaron said.

"No," the innkeeper said, his voice surprisingly firm. He held up his glass. "To old friends who deserved better than they got."

The men on the other side of the bar nodded solemnly and tossed back their drinks.

"Lord and lady, that's a lovely tumble," Old Cob said respectfully, his eyes watering slightly. "You're a gentleman, Kote. And I'm glad to know you."

The smith's prentice set his glass down only to have it tip onto its side and roll across the bar. He snatched it up before it skittered over the edge and turned it over, eyeing its rounded bottom suspiciously.

Jake laughed a loud farmer's laugh at his bewilderment while Carter made a point of setting his glass on the bar topside-down. "I don't know how they do it in Rannish," Carter said to the boy. "But round here there's a reason we call it a tumble."

The smith's prentice looked properly abashed and turned his tumble upside down to match the others on the bar. The innkeeper gave him a reassuring smile before gathering up the glasses and disappearing into the kitchen.

"Right then," Old Cob said briskly, rubbing his hands together. "We'll have a whole evening of this after the two of you get back from Baedn. But the weather won't wait on me, and I don't doubt the Orrisons are eager to be on the road."

After they filtered out of the Waystone in a loose group, Kvothe emerged from the kitchen and returned to the table where Bast and Chronicler sat.

"I liked Shep," Bast said quietly. "Cob might be a bit of a crusty old cuss, but he knows what he's talking about most of the time."

"Cob doesn't know half of what he thinks he does," Kvothe said. "You saved everyone last night. If not for you, it would have gone through the room like a farmer threshing wheat."

"That just isn't true, Reshi," Bast said, his tone plainly offended. "You would have stopped it. That's what you do."

The innkeeper shrugged the comment away, unwilling to argue. Bast's mouth formed into a hard, angry line, his eyes narrowing.

"Still," Chronicler said softly, breaking the tension before it grew too thick. "Cob was right. It was a brave thing to do. You have to respect that."

"No I don't," Kvothe said. "Cob was right about that. These aren't good times to be brave." He motioned for Chronicler to pick up his pen. "Still, I wish I'd been braver and Shep was home kissing his young wife, too."

CHAPTER EIGHTEEN

Wine and Blood

EVENTUALLY WIL AND SIM pulled me from the warm embrace of the Archives. I struggled and cursed them, but they were firm in their convictions, and the three of us braved the chill wind on the road to Imre.

We made our way to the Eolian, claiming a table near the eastern hearth where we could watch the stage and keep our backs warm. After a drink or two I felt the book-longing fade to a dull ache. The three of us talked and played cards, and eventually I began to enjoy myself despite the fact that Denna was doubtless out there somewhere, hanging on Ambrose's arm.

After several hours I sat slouched in my chair, drowsy and warm from the nearby fire while Wil and Sim bickered about whether the high king of Modeg was a true ruling monarch or merely a figurehead. I was nearly asleep when a heavy bottle knocked down hard onto our table followed by the delicate chime of wineglasses.

Denna stood next to our table. "Play along," she said under her breath. "You've been waiting for me. I'm late and you're upset."

Blearily, I struggled upright in my seat and tried to blink myself awake.

Sim leaped to the challenge. "It's been an hour," he said, scowling fiercely. He tapped the table firmly with two fingers. "Don't think buying me a drink is going to fix matters. I want an apology."

"It's not entirely my fault," Denna said, radiating embarrassment. She turned and gestured to the bar.

I looked, worried I would see Ambrose standing there, watching me smugly in his goddamn hat. But it was only a balding Cealdish man. He made a short, odd bow toward us, halfway between acknowledgment and apology.

Sim scowled at him, then turned back to Denna and made a grudging gesture to the empty chair across from me. "Fine. So are we going to play corners or what?"

Denna sank down into the chair, sitting with her back to the room. Then leaned over to kiss Simmon on the forehead. "Perfect," she said.

"I was scowling too," Wilem said.

Denna slid him the bottle. "And for that, you may pour." She set the glasses in front of each of us. "A gift from my overly persistent suitor." She gave an irritated sigh. "They always need to give you something." She eyed me specu-latively. "You're curiously mute."

I rubbed a hand over my face. "I didn't expect to see you tonight," I said. "You caught me nearly napping."

Wilem poured a pale pink wine then passed around the glasses while Denna examined the etching on the top of the bottle. "Cerbeor," she mused. "I don't even know if this is a decent vintage."

"It's not, actually," Simmon said matter-of-factly as he took his glass. "Cer-beor is Aturan. Only wines from Vintas have a vintage, technically." He took a sip.

"Really?" I asked, looking at my own glass.

Sim nodded. "It's a common misuse of the word."

Denna took a drink and nodded to herself. "Good wine, though," she said. "Is he still at the bar?"

"He is," I said without looking.

"Well then," she smiled. "It seems you're stuck with me."

"Have you ever played corners?" Sim asked hopefully.

"I'm afraid not," Denna said. "But I'm a quick study."

Sim explained the rules with help from Wil and myself. Denna asked a few pointed questions, showing she understood the gist of it. I was glad. Since she was sitting across the table from me, she was going to be my partner.

"What do you usually play for?" she asked.

"Depends," Wil said. "Sometimes we play by the hand. Sometimes by the set."

"For a set of hands then," Denna said. "How much?"

"We can do a practice set first," Sim said, brushing his hair out of his eyes. "Since you're just learning and all."

Her eyes narrowed. "I don't need any special treatment." She reached into a pocket and brought a coin up onto the table. "A jot too much for you boys?"

It was too much for me, especially with a partner who had just learned the game. "Be careful with these two," I said. "They play for blood."

"In point of fact," Wilem said. "I have no use for blood, and play for money instead." He fingered through his purse until he found a jot, which he pressed firmly onto the table. "I am willing to play a practice game, but if she finds the thought insulting, I will thrash her and take whatever she is willing to lay on the table."

Denna grinned at that. "You're my kind of guy, Wil."

The first hand went fairly well. Denna mislaid a trick, but we couldn't have won anyway, as the cards were against us. But the second hand she made a mistake in the bidding. Then, when Sim corrected her, she got flustered and bid wildly. Then she accidentally led out of turn, not a huge mistake, but she led the jack of hearts, which let everyone know exactly what sort of hand she had. She realized it too, and I heard her mutter something distinctly unlady-like under her breath.

True to their word, Wil and Sim moved in ruthlessly to take advantage of the situation. Given the weak cards in my hand, there wasn't much I could do but sit and watch as they won the next two tricks and began to close on her like hungry wolves.

Except they couldn't. She pulled a clever card force, then produced the king of hearts, which didn't make any sense as she'd tried to lead the jack before. Then she produced the ace, too.

I realized her fumbling misplay had been an act slightly before Wil and Sim. I managed to keep it off my face until I saw the dim realization creep onto their expressions. Then I started to laugh.

"Don't be smug," she said to me. "I had you fooled, too. You looked like you were going to be sick when I showed the jack." She put her hand in front of her mouth and made her eyes wide and innocent. "Oh my, I've never played corners before. Could you teach me? Is it true that sometimes people play for money?"

Denna snapped down another card onto the table and gathered in the trick. "Please. You lot should be glad I'm giving you a slap on the hand in-stead of the profound full-night fleecing you deserve."

She mopped up the rest of the hand relentlessly, and it gave us such a solid lead that the rest of the set was a forgone conclusion. Denna never missed a trick after that, and played with enough cunning flair to make Manet seem like a dray horse by comparison.

"That was instructional," Wil said as he slid his jot toward Denna. "I might need to lick my wounds a bit."

Denna lifted her glass in a salute. "To the gullibility of the well-educated."

We touched our glasses to hers and drank.

"You lot have been curiously absent," Denna said. "I've been keeping an eye out for you for almost two span."

"Why's that?" Sim asked.

Denna gave Wil and Sim a calculating look. "You two are students at the University too, aren't you? The special one that teaches magic?"

"That's us," Sim said agreeably. "We are chock full of arcane secrets."

"We tinker with dark forces better left alone," Wil said nonchalantly.

"It's called the Arcanum, by the way," I pointed out.

Denna nodded seriously as she leaned forward, her expression intent. "Between the three of you, I'm guessing you know how most of it works." She looked at us. "So tell me. How does it work?"

"It?" I asked.

"Magic," she said. "Real magic."

Wil, Sim, and I exchanged glances.

"It's complicated," I said.

Denna shrugged and leaned back in her chair. "I have all the time in the world," she said. "And I need to know how it works. Show me. Do some magic."

The three of us shifted uncomfortably in our seats. Denna laughed.

"We're not supposed to," I said.

"What?" she asked. "Does it disturb some cosmic balance?"

"It disturbs the constables," I said. "They don't take kindly to that sort of thing over here."

"The masters at the University don't care for it much either," Wil said. "They're very mindful of the University's reputation."

"Oh come now," Denna said. "I heard a story about how our man Kvothe called up some sort of demon wind." She jerked her thumb at the door behind her. "Right in the courtyard outside."

Had Ambrose told her that? "It was just a wind," I said. "No demon involved."

"They whipped him for it, too," Wil said.

Denna looked at him as if she couldn't tell if he were joking, then shrugged. "Well I wouldn't want to get anyone in trouble," she said with glaring insincerity. "But I am powerfully curious. And I have secrets I am willing to offer in trade."

Sim perked up at this. "What sort of secrets?"

"All the vast and varied secrets of womankind," she said with a smile. "I happen to know several things that can help improve your failing relations with the gentler sex."

Sim leaned closer to Wil and asked in a stage whisper. "Did she say *failing*, or *flailing*?"

Wil pointed at his own chest, then Sim's. "Me: failing. You: flailing."

Denna raised one eyebrow and cocked her head to one side, looking at the three of us expectantly.

I cleared my throat uncomfortably. "We're discouraged from sharing Arcanum secrets. It's not strictly against the laws of the University—"

"It is, actually," Simmon interrupted, giving me an apologetic look. "Several laws."

Denna gave a dramatic sigh, looking up at the high ceiling. "I thought as much," she said. "You lot just talk a good game. Admit it, you can't turn cream into butter."

"I happen to know for a fact that Sim can turn cream into butter," I said. "He just doesn't like to because he's lazy."

"I'm not asking you to *teach* me magic," Denna said. "I just need to know how it works."

Sim looked at Wil. "That wouldn't fall under Unsanctioned Divulgence, would it?"

"Illicit Revelation," Wil said grimly.

Denna leaned forward conspiratorially, resting her elbows on the table. "In that case," she said. "I am also willing to finance a night of extravagant drinking, far above and beyond the simple bottle you see before you." She turned her gaze to Wil. "One of the bartenders here has recently discovered a dusty stone bottle in the basement. Not only is it fine old scutten, drink of the kings of Cealdim, it is a Merovani as well."

Wilem's expression didn't change, but his dark eyes glittered.

I looked around the largely empty room. "Orden is a slow night. We shouldn't have any trouble if we keep things quiet." I looked at the other two.

Sim was grinning his boyish grin. "It seems reasonable. A secret for a secret."

"If it is truly a Merovani," Wilem said. "I am willing to risk offending the masters' sensibilities somewhat."

"Right then," Denna said with a wide grin. "You first."

Sim leaned forward in his chair. "Sympathy is probably the easiest to get a grip on," he said, then paused as if uncertain how to proceed.

I stepped in. "You know how a block and tackle lets you lift something too heavy for you to lift by hand?"

Denna nodded.

"Sympathy lets us do things like that," I said. "But without all the awkward rope and pulleys."

Wilem dropped a pair of iron drabs onto the table and muttered a binding. He pushed the right-hand one with a finger, and the left-hand one slid across the table at the same time, mimicking the motion.

Denna's eyes went at little wide at this, and while she didn't gasp, she did draw a long breath through her nose. It only then occurred to me that she'd probably never seen anything like this before. Given my studies, it was easy to forget that someone could live mere miles from the University without ever having any exposure to even the most basic sympathy.

To her credit, Denna recovered from her surprise without missing a beat. With only the slightest hesitation, she reached out a finger to touch one of the drabs. "This is how the bell in my room worked," she mused.

I nodded.

Wil slid his drab across the table, and Denna picked it up. The other drab rose off the table too, bobbing in midair. "It's heavy," she said, then nodded to herself. "Right, because it's like a pulley. I'm lifting both of them."

"Heat, light, and motion are all just energy," I said. "We can't create energy or make it disappear. But sympathy lets us move it around or change it from one type into another."

She put the drab back down on the table and the other followed suit. "And this is useful how?"

Wil grunted with vague amusement. "Is a waterwheel useful?" he asked. "Is a windmill?"

I reached into the pocket of my cloak. "Have you ever seen a sympathy lamp?" I asked.

She nodded.

I slid my hand lamp across the table to her. "They work under the same principle. They take a little bit of heat and turn it into light. It converts one type of energy into another."

"Like a moneychanger," Wil said.

Denna turned the lamp over in her hands curiously. "Where does it get the heat?"

"The metal itself holds heat," I explained. "If you leave it on, you'll eventually feel the metal get chilly. If it gets too cold, it won't work." I pointed. "I made that one, so it's pretty efficient. Just the heat from your hand should be enough to keep it working."

Denna flicked the switch and dull red light shone out in a narrow arc. "I can see how heat and light are related," she said thoughtfully. "The sun is bright and warm. Same with a candle." She frowned. "But motion doesn't fit into it. A fire can't push something."

"Think about friction," Sim chimed in. "When you rub something it gets hot." He demonstrated by running his hand back and forth vigorously across the fabric of his pants. "Like this."

He continued rubbing his thigh enthusiastically, unaware of the fact that, since it was happening below the level of the table, it looked more than slightly obscene. "It's all just energy. If you keep doing it, you'll feel it get hot."

Denna somehow kept a straight face. But Wilem started to laugh, covering his face with one hand, as if embarrassed to be sitting at the same table with Sim.

Simmon froze and flushed red with embarrassment.

I came to his rescue. "It's a good example. The hub of a wagon wheel will be warm to the touch. That heat comes from the motion of the wheel. A sympathist can make the energy go the other way, from heat into motion." I pointed to the lamp. "Or from heat into light."

"Fine," she said. "You're energy moneychangers. But how do you make it happen?"

"There's a special way of thinking called Alar," Wilem said. "You believe something so strongly that it becomes so." He lifted up one drab and the other followed it. "I believe these two drabs are connected, so they are." Suddenly the other drab clattered to the tabletop. "If I stop believing, it stops being so."

Denna picked up the drab. "So it's like faith?" she said skeptically.

"More like strength of will," Sim said.

She cocked her head. "Why don't you call it strength of will, then?"

"Alar sounds better," Wilem said.

I nodded. "If we didn't have impressive sounding names for things, no one would take us seriously."

Denna nodded appreciatively, a smile tugging at the corners of her lovely mouth. "And that's it then? Energy and strength of will?"

"And the sympathetic link," I said. "Wil's waterwheel analogy is a good one. The link is like a pipe leading to the waterwheel. A bad link is like a pipe full of holes."

"What makes a good link?" Denna asked.

"The more similar two objects are, the better the link. Like this." I poured an inch of the pale wine into my cup and dipped my finger into it. "Here is a perfect link to the wine," I said. "A drop of the wine itself."

I stood and walked to the nearby hearth. I murmured a binding and let a drop fall from my finger onto the hot metal andiron holding the burning logs.

I sat back down just as the wine in my glass started to steam, then boil.

"And that," Wilem said grimly, "is why you never want a sympathist to get a drop of your blood."

Denna looked at Wilem, then back to the glass, her face going pale.

"Black hands, Wil," Simmon said with a horrified look. "What a thing to say." He looked at Denna. "No sympathist would ever do something like that," he said earnestly. "It's called malfeasance, and we don't do it. Ever."

Denna managed a smile, though it was a bit strained. "If no one ever does it, why is there a name for it?"

"They used to," I said. "But not anymore. Not for a hundred years."

I let the binding go and the wine stopped boiling. Denna reached out and touched the nearby bottle. "Why doesn't this wine boil too?" she asked, puzzled. "It's the same wine."

I tapped my temple. "The Alar. My mind provides the focus and direction."

"If that's a good link," she asked, "what's a bad one?"

"Here, let me show you." I pulled out my purse, guessing coins would seem less alarming after Wilem's comment. "Sim, do you have a hard penny?"

He did, and I arranged two lines of coins on the table in front of Denna. I pointed to a pair of iron drabs and murmured a binding. "Lift it up," I said.

She picked up one drab and the other followed it.

I pointed to the second pair: a drab and my single remaining silver talent. "Now that one."

Denna picked up the second drab and the talent followed it into the air. She moved both hands up and down like the arms of a scale. "This second one's heavier."

I nodded. "Different metals. They're less similar, so you have to put more energy into it." I pointed to the drab and the silver penny and muttered a third binding.

Denna put the first two drabs into her left hand, and picked up the third in her right. The silver penny followed it into the air. She nodded to herself. "And this one's heavier still because it's a different shape *and* a different metal."

"Exactly," I said. I pointed to the fourth and final pair: a drab and a piece of chalk.

Denna almost couldn't get her fingers underneath the drab to pick it up. "It's heavier than all the others together," she said. "It's got to be three pounds!"

"Iron to chalk is a lousy link," Wilem said. "Bad transference."

"But you said energy couldn't be created or destroyed," Denna said. "If I have to struggle to lift this tiny piece of chalk, where does the extra energy go?"

"Clever," Wilem chuckled. "So clever. I went a year before I thought to ask that." He eyed her in admiration. "Some energy is lost into the air." He waved one hand. "Some goes into the objects themselves, and some goes into the body of the sympathist who is controlling the link." He frowned. "That can get dangerful."

"Danger*ous*," Simmon corrected gently.

Denna looked at me. "So right now you're believing each of these drabs is connected to each of these other things?"

I nodded.

She moved her hands around. The coins and chalk bobbed in the air. "Isn't that . . . hard?"

"It is," Wilem said. "But our Kvothe is a bit of a showoff."

"That's why I've been so quiet," Sim said. "I didn't know you could hold four bindings at once. That's impressive as hell."

"I can do five if I need to," I said. "But that's pretty much my limit."

Sim smiled at Denna. "One more thing. Watch this!" He pointed at the floating piece of chalk.

Nothing happened.

"Come on," Sim said plaintively. "I'm trying to show her something."

"Then show her," I said smugly, leaning back in my chair.

Sim took a deep breath and stared hard at the piece of chalk. It trembled.

Wil leaned close to Denna and explained. "One sympathist can oppose another's Alar," he said. "It is just a matter of firmly believing that a drab is *not* the same as a silver penny at all."

Wil pointed, and the penny clattered to the tabletop.

"Foul," I protested, laughing. "Two on one isn't fair."

"It is in this case," Simmon said, and the chalk trembled again.

"Fine," I said, taking a deep breath. "Do your worst."

The chalk dropped to the table quickly, followed by the drab. But the silver talent stayed where it was.

Sim sat back in his chair. "You're creepy," he said, shaking his head. "Fine, you win." Wilem nodded and relaxed as well.

Denna looked at me. "So your Alar is stronger than theirs put together?"

"Probably not," I said graciously. "If they had practice working together they could probably beat me."

Her eyes ranged over the scattered coins. "So that's it?" she asked, sounding slightly disappointed. "It's all just energy moneychanging?"

"There are other arts," I said. "Sim does alchemy, for example."

"While I," Wilem said, "focus on being pretty."

Denna looked us over again, her eyes serious. "Is there a type of magic that's just . . ." She wiggled her fingers vaguely. "Just sort of writing things down?"

"There's sygaldry," I said. "Like that bell in your room. It's like permanent sympathy."

"But it's still moneychanging, right?" she asked. "Just energy?"

I nodded.

Denna looked embarrassed as she asked, "What if someone told you they knew a type of magic that did more than that? A magic where you sort of wrote things down, and whatever you wrote became true?"

She looked down nervously, her fingers tracing patterns on the tabletop. "Then, if someone saw the writing, even if they couldn't read it, it would be true for them. They'd think a certain thing, or act a certain way depending on what the writing said." She looked up at us again, her expression a strange mix of curiosity, hope, and uncertainty.

The three of us looked at each other. Wilem shrugged.

"Sounds a damn sight easier than alchemy," Simmon said. "I'd rather do that than spend all day unbinding principles."

"Sounds like faerie-tale magic," I said. "Storybook stuff that doesn't really exist. I certainly never heard about anything like that at the University."

Denna looked down at the tabletop where her fingers still traced patterns against the wood. Her mouth was pursed slightly, her eyes distant.

I couldn't tell if she was disappointed or simply thoughtful. "Why do you ask?"

Denna looked up at me and her expression quickly slid into a wry smile. She shrugged away the question. "It was just something I heard," she said dismissively. "I thought it sounded too good to be true."

She looked over her shoulder. "I seem to have outlasted my overenthusiastic suitor," she said.

Wil held up the flat of his hand. "We had an arrangement," he said. "There was drink involved, and a woman's secret."

"I'll have a word with the barman before I leave," Denna said, her eyes dancing with amusement. "As for the secret: There are two ladies sitting behind you. They've been making eyes at you for most of the evening. The one in green fancies Sim, while the one with short blond hair seems to have a thing for Cealdish men who focus on being pretty."

"We have already made note of them," Wilem said without turning to look. "Unfortunately, they are already in the company of a young Modegan gentleman."

"The gentleman is not *with* them in any romantic sense," Denna said. "While the ladies have been eyeing you, the gentleman has been making it abundantly clear that he prefers redheads." She lay her hand on my arm possessively. "Unfortunately for him, I have already staked my claim."

I fought the urge to look at the table. "Are you serious?" I asked.

"Don't worry," she said to Wil and Sim. "I'll send Deoch over to distract the Modegan. That will leave the door open for the two of you."

"What's Deoch going to do?" Simmon said with a laugh. "Juggle?"

Denna gave him a frank look.

"What?" Simmon said. "Wh . . . Deoch isn't sly."

Denna blinked at him. "He and Stanchion own the Eolian together," she said. "Didn't you know that?"

"They own the place," Sim said. "They're not, you know, *together*."

Denna laughed. "Of course they are."

"But Deoch is up to his neck in women," Simmon protested. "He . . . he can't—"

Denna looked at him as if he were simple, then to Wil and myself. "The two of you knew, didn't you?"

Wilem shrugged. "I hadn't any knowledge of it. But small wonder he is a *Basha*. He is attractive enough." Wil hesitated, frowned. "*Basha*. What is a word for that here? A man who is intimate with both women and men?"

"Lucky?" Denna suggested. "Tired? Ambidextrous?"

"Ambisextrous," I corrected.

"That won't do," Denna chided me. "If we don't have impressive sounding names for things, no one will take us seriously."

Sim blinked at her, obviously unable to come to grips with the situation.

"You see," Denna said slowly, as if explaining to a child. "It's all just energy. And we can direct it in different ways." She blossomed into a brilliant smile, as if realizing the perfect way to explain the situation to him. "It's like when you do this." She began to vigorously rub her hands up and down her thighs, mimicking his earlier motion. "It's all just energy."

By this point Wilem was hiding his face in his hands, his shoulders shaking with silent laughter. Simmon's expression was still incredulous and confused, but now it was also a furious, blushing red.

I got to my feet and took Denna's elbow. "Leave the poor boy alone," I said as I steered her gently toward the door. "He's from Atur. They're laced a little tightly in those parts."

CHAPTER NINETEEN

Gentlemen and Thieves

IT WAS LATE WHEN Denna and I left the Eolian, and the streets were empty. In the distance I heard fiddle music and the hollow clopping of a horse's hooves on cobblestones.

"So what rock have you been hiding under?" she asked.

"The usual rock," I said, then a thought occurred to me. "Did you come looking for me at the University? At the big square building that smells like coal smoke?"

Denna shook her head. "I wouldn't begin to know where to find you there. It's like a maze. If I can't catch you playing at Anker's, I know I'm out of luck." She looked at me curiously. "Why?"

"Someone showed up asking for me," I said with a dismissive gesture. "She said I'd sold her a charm. I thought it might be you."

"I did come looking for you a while back," she said. "But I never mentioned your abundant charm."

The conversation lulled and silence swelled between us. I couldn't help but think of her walking arm in arm with Ambrose. I didn't want to know any more about it, but at the same time, it was the only thing in my head.

"I came to visit you at the Grey Man," I said, just to fill the air between us. "But you'd already gone."

She nodded. "Kellin and I had a bit of a falling out."

"Nothing too bad, I hope." I gestured to her throat. "I notice you still have the necklace."

Denna touched the teardrop emerald absentmindedly. "No. Nothing terrible. You can say this for Kellin, he's a traditionalist. When he gives a gift, he sticks to it. He said the color flattered me, and I should keep the earrings too." She sighed. "I'd feel better if he hadn't been so gracious. Still, they're nice to have. A safety net of sorts. They'll make my life easier if I don't hear from my patron soon."

"You're still hoping to hear from him?" I asked. "After what happened in Trebon? After he's been out of contact for more than a month with no word at all?"

Denna shrugged. "That's just his way. I told you, he's a secretive sort. It's not odd for him to be gone for long stretches of time."

"I have a friend who is trying to find me a patron," I said. "I could have him look for you too."

She looked up at me, her eyes unreadable. "It's sweet that you think I deserve better, but I really don't. I have a good voice, but that's it. Who would hire a half-trained musician without even an instrument to her name?"

"Anyone with ears to hear you," I said. "Anyone with eyes to see."

Denna looked down, her hair falling around her face like a curtain. "You're sweet," she said quietly, making an odd fidgeting gesture with her hands.

"What ended up souring things with Kellin?" I asked, steering the conversation somewhere safer.

"I spent too much time entertaining gentlemen callers," she said dryly.

"You should have explained to him that I'm nothing remotely resembling a gentleman," I said. "That might have eased his mind." But I knew I couldn't have been the problem. I'd only managed to visit once. Had it been Ambrose that had come calling? I could picture him in the lavish sitting room all too easily. That damn hat of his hanging casually off the corner of a chair as he drank chocolate and told jokes.

Denna's mouth quirked. "It was mostly Geoffrey he objected to," she said. "Apparently I was supposed to sit quiet and alone in my little box until he came to call on me."

"How is Geoffrey?" I asked to be polite. "Has he managed to get a second thought into his head yet?"

I expected to get a laugh, but Denna merely sighed. "He has, but none of them are particularly good thoughts." She shook her head. "He came to Imre to make a name for himself with his poetry, but lost his shirt gambling."

"I've heard that story before," I said. "Happens all the time over at the University."

"That was just the beginning," she said. "He figured he could win his money back, of course. First came the pawnshop. Then he borrowed money and lost that too." She made a conciliatory gesture. "Though in all fairness, he didn't gamble that away. Some bitch rooked him. Caught him with the weeping widow of all things."

I looked at her, puzzled. "The what?"

Denna looked at me sideways, then shrugged. "It's a simple rook," she said. "A young woman stands outside a pawnshop all flustered and teary, then when some rich gent walks by she explains how she came to the city to sell her wedding ring. She needs money for taxes, or to repay a moneylender."

She waved her hands impatiently. "The details don't matter. What matters is when she got to town, she asked someone else to pawn the ring for her. Because she doesn't know a thing about bargaining, of course."

Denna stopped walking in front of a pawnshop window, her face a mask of distress. "I thought I could trust him!" she said. "But he just pawned it and ran off with the money! There's the ring right there!" She pointed dramatically at the shop's window.

"But," Denna continued, holding up a finger. "Luckily, he sold the ring for a fraction of what it's worth. It's a family heirloom worth forty talents, but the pawnshop is selling it for four."

Denna stepped close and lay her hand on my chest, looking up at me with wide, imploring eyes. "If you bought the ring, we could sell it for at least twenty. I'd give you your four talents back right away."

She stepped back and shrugged. "That sort of thing."

I frowned. "How is that a rook? I'll catch on as soon as we go to the assessor."

Denna rolled her eyes. "That's not how it works. We agree to meet tomorrow at noon. But by the time I get there, you've already bought the ring yourself and run off with it."

I suddenly understood. "And you split the money with the owner of the pawnshop?"

She patted my shoulder. "I knew you'd catch on sooner or later."

It seemed fairly watertight except for one thing. "Seems you'd need a special combination of trustworthy-yet-crooked pawnshop as a partner."

"True," she admitted. "They're usually marked though." Denna pointed to the top of the nearby pawnshop's doorframe. There were a series of marks that could easily be mistaken for random scratches in the paint.

"Ah," I hesitated for half a moment before adding, "In Tarbean, markings like that meant this was a safe place to fence . . ." I groped for an appropriate euphemism. "Questionably acquired goods."

If Denna was startled by my confession she gave no sign of it. She merely shook her head and pointed more closely to the markings, moving her finger as she went. "This says, 'Reliable owner. Open to simple rooks. Even split.'" She glanced around at the rest of the doorframe and the shop's sign. "Nothing about fencing goods from uncle."

"I never knew how to read them," I admitted. I glanced sideways at her, careful to keep any judgment out of my tone. "And you know how this sort of thing works because . . .?"

"I read it in a book," she said sarcastically. "How do you think I know about it?"

She continued walking down the street. I joined her.

"I don't usually play it as a widow," Denna said, almost as an afterthought. "I'm too young for that. For me it's my mother's ring. Or grandmother's." She shrugged. "You change it to whatever feels right at the time."

"What if the gent is honest?" I ask. "What if he shows up at noon, willing to help?"

"It doesn't happen often," she with a wry twist to her mouth. "Only once for me. Caught me completely by surprise. Now I set things up in advance with the owner just in case. I'm happy to rook some greedy bastard who tries to take advantage of a young girl. But I'm not about to take money off someone who's trying to help." Her expression went hard. "Unlike the bitch who got hold of Geoffrey."

"Showed up at noon, did he?"

"Of course he did," she said. "Just gave her the money. 'No need to pay me back, miss. You go save the family farm.' " Denna ran her hands through her hair, looking up at the sky. "A farm! That doesn't even make any sense! Why would a farmer's wife have a diamond necklace?" She glanced over at me. "Why are the sweet ones such idiots with women?"

"He's noble," I said. "Can't he just write home?"

"He's never been on good terms with his family," she said. "Less so now. His last letter didn't have any money, just the news that his mother was sick."

Something in her voice caught my ear. "How sick?" I asked.

"Sick." Denna didn't look up. "Very sick. And of course he's already sold his horse and can't afford passage on a ship." She sighed again. "It's like watching one of those awful Tehlin dramas unfold. *The Path Ill-Chosen* or something of the sort."

"If that's the case, all he has to do is stumble into a church at the end of the fourth act," I said. "He'll pray, learn his lesson, and live the rest of his days a clean and virtuous boy."

"It would be different if he came to me for advice." She made a frustrated gesture. "But no, he stops by afterward to tell me what he's done. The guild moneylender cut off his credit, so what does he do?"

My stomach twisted. "He goes to a gaelet," I said.

"And he was happy when he told me!" Denna looked at me, her expression despairing. "Like he'd finally figured a way out of this mess." She shivered. "Let's go in here." She pointed to a small garden. "There's more wind tonight than I thought."

I set down my lute case and shrugged out of my cloak. "Here, I'm fine."

Denna looked like she was going to object for a moment, then drew it around herself. "And you say you're not a gentleman," she chided.

"I'm not," I said. "I just know it will smell better after you've worn it."

"Ah," she said wisely. "And then you will sell it to a perfumery and make your fortune."

"That's been my plan all along," I admitted. "A cunning and elaborate scheme. I'm more thief than a gentleman, you see."

We sat down on a bench out of the wind. "I think you've lost a buckle," she said.

I looked down at my lute case. The narrow end was gaping open, and the iron buckle was nowhere to be seen.

I sighed and absentmindedly reached for one of the inner pockets of my cloak.

Denna made a tiny noise. Nothing loud, just a startled indrawn breath as she looked suddenly up at me, her eyes wide and dark in the moonlight.

I pulled my hand back as if burned by a fire, stammering an apology.

Denna began to laugh quietly. "Well that's embarrassing," she said softly to herself.

"I'm sorry," I said quickly. "I wasn't thinking. I've got some wire in there that I can use to hold this closed for now."

"Oh," she said. "Of course." Her hands moved inside the cloak for a moment, then she held out a piece of wire.

"I'm sorry," I said again.

"I was just startled," she said. "I didn't think you were the sort to grab hold of a lady without some warning first."

I looked down at the lute, embarrassed, and made my hands busy, running the wire through a hole the buckle had left and twisting it tightly shut.

"It's a lovely lute," Denna said after a long, quiet moment. "But that case is an absolute shambles."

"I tapped myself out buying the lute itself," I said, then looked up as if suddenly struck with an idea. "I know! I'll ask Geoffrey to give me the name of his gaelet! Then I can afford two cases!"

She swatted at me playfully, and I moved to sit next to her on the bench.

Things were quiet for a moment, then Denna looked down at her hands and repeated a fidgeting gesture she'd made several times during our talk.

Only now did I realize what she was doing. "Your ring," I asked. "What happened to it?"

Denna gave me an odd look.

"You've had a ring for as long as I've known you." I explained. "Silver with a pale blue stone."

Her forehead furrowed. "I know what it looked like. How did you?"

"You wear it all the time," I said, trying to sound casual, as if I didn't know every detail of her. As if I didn't know her habit of twirling it on her finger while she was anxious or lost in thought. "What happened to it?"

Denna looked down at her hands. "A young gentleman has it," she said.

"Ah," I said. Then, because I couldn't help myself, I added. "Who?"

"I doubt you—" She paused, then looked up at me. "Actually, you might know him. He goes to the University too. Ambrose Jakis."

My stomach was suddenly filled with acid and ice.

Denna looked away. "He has a rough charm about him," she explained. "More rough than charm, really. But . . ." She trailed off into a shrug.

"I see," I said. Then, "It must be fairly serious."

Denna gave me a quizzical look, then realization spread onto her face and she burst out laughing. She shook her head, waving her hands in violent negation. "Oh no. God no. Nothing like that. He came calling a few times. We went to a play. He invited me out for dancing. He's remarkably light on his feet."

She drew a deep breath and let it out in a sigh. "The first night he was very genteel. Witty even. The second night, slightly less so." Her eyes narrowed. "On the third night he got pushy. Things went sour after that. I had to leave my rooms at the Boar's Head because he kept showing up with trinkets and poems."

A feeling of vast relief flooded me. For the first time in days I felt like I was able to take a full lungful of air. I felt a smile threatening to burst out onto my face and fought it down, fearing it would be so wide I'd look like an absolute madman.

Denna gave me a wry look. "You'd be amazed at how similar arrogance and confidence look at first glance. And he was generous, and rich, which is a nice combination." She held up her naked hand. "The fitting was loose on my ring, and he said he'd have it repaired."

"I take it he wasn't nearly so generous after things went sour?"

Her red mouth made another wry smile. "Not nearly."

"I might be able to do something," I said. "If the ring's important to you."

"It was important," Denna said, giving me a frank look. "But what would you do, exactly? Remind him, one gentleman to another, that he should treat women with dignity and respect?" She rolled her eyes. "Good luck."

I simply gave her my most charming smile. I'd already told her the truth of things: I was no gentleman. I was a thief.

CHAPTER TWENTY

The Fickle Wind

T HE NEXT EVENING FOUND me at the Golden Pony, arguably the finest inn on the University side of the river. It boasted elaborate kitchens, a fine stable, and a skilled obsequious staff. It was the sort of upscale establishment only the wealthiest students could afford.

I wasn't inside, of course. I was crouched in the deep shadows of the roof, trying not to dwell on the fact that what I was planning went well beyond the bounds of Conduct Unbecoming. If I was caught breaking into Ambrose's rooms, I would undoubtedly be expelled.

It was a clear autumn night with a strong wind. A mixed blessing. The sound of rustling leaves would cover any small noises I might make, but I worried the flapping edges of my cloak might draw attention.

Our plan was a simple one. I had slipped a sealed note under Ambrose's door. It was an unsigned, flirtatious request for a meeting in Imre. Wil had written it, as Sim and I judged he had the most feminine handwriting.

It was a goose chase, but I guessed Ambrose would take the bait. I would have preferred to have someone distract him personally, but the fewer people involved the better. I could have asked Denna to help, but I wanted it to be a surprise when I returned her ring.

Wil and Sim were my lookouts, Wil in the common room, Sim in the alley by the back door. It was their job to let me know when Ambrose left the building. More importantly, they would alert me if he came back before I'd finished searching his rooms.

I felt a sharp tug in my right-hand pocket as the oak twig gave two distinct twitches. After a moment the signal was repeated. Wilem was letting me know Ambrose had left the inn.

In my left pocket was a piece of birch. Simmon held a similar one where he stood watch over the inn's back door. It was a simple, effective signaling system if you knew enough sympathy to make it work.

I crawled down the slope of the roof, moving carefully over the heavy clay tiles. I knew from my younger days in Tarbean that they tended to crack and slide and could make you lose your footing.

I made it to the lip of the roof, fifteen feet off the ground. Hardly a dizzying height, but more than enough to break a leg or a neck. A narrow piece of roof ran beneath the long row of second-story windows. There were ten in all, and the middle four belonged to Ambrose.

I flexed my fingers a couple times to loosen them, then began to edge along the narrow strip of roof.

The secret is to concentrate on what you're doing. Don't look at the ground. Don't look over your shoulder. Ignore the world and trust it to return the favor. This was the real reason I was wearing my cloak. If I were spotted I would be nothing more than a dark shape in the night, impossible to identify. Hopefully.

The first window was dark, and the second had its curtains drawn. But the third was dimly lit. I hesitated. If you're fair-skinned like me, you never want to peer into a window at night. Your face will stand out against the dark like the full moon. Rather than risk peering in, I dug around in the pockets of my cloak until I found a piece of scrap tin from the Fishery that I'd buffed into a makeshift mirror. Then I carefully used it to peer around the corner and through the window.

Inside there were a few dim lamps and a canopy bed as big as my entire room back in Anker's. The bed was occupied. Actively occupied. What's more, there seemed to be more naked limbs than two people could account for. Unfortunately, my piece of tin was small, and I couldn't view the scene in its full complexity, otherwise I might have learned some very interesting things.

I briefly considered going back and coming at Ambrose's rooms from the other side, but the wind gusted suddenly, sending leaves skipping across the cobblestones and trying to claw me away from my narrow footing. Heart pounding, I decided to risk passing this window. I guessed the people inside had better things to do than stargazing.

I pulled the hood of my cloak down and held the edges in my teeth, covering my face while leaving my hands free. Thus blinded, I inched my way past the window, listening intently for any signs I'd been spotted. There were a few surprised noises, but they didn't seem to have anything to do with me.

The first of Ambrose's windows was elaborate stained glass. Pretty, but not designed to open. The next was perfect: a wide, double window. I pulled a thin piece of copper wire from one of the pockets of my cloak and used it to trip the simple latch holding it closed.

When the window wouldn't open, I realized that Ambrose had added a drop bar as well. That took several long minutes of tricky work, one-handed in the near-total dark. Thankfully, the wind had died down, at least for the moment.

Then, once I'd worked my way past the drop bar, the window still wouldn't budge. I began to curse Ambrose's paranoia as I searched for the third lock, hunting for nearly ten minutes before I realized the window was simply stuck shut.

I tugged on it a couple times, which isn't as easy as it sounds. They don't put handles on the outside, you realize. Eventually I got overenthusiastic and pulled too hard. The window sprang open and my weight shifted backward. I leaned off the edge of the roof, fighting every reflex that urged me to move my foot back and regain my balance, knowing there was nothing but fifteen feet of empty air behind me.

Do you know the feeling when you tip your chair too far and begin to fall backward? The sensation was something like that, mixed with self-recrimination and the fear of death. I flailed my arms, knowing it wouldn't help, my mind gone suddenly blank with panic.

The wind saved me. It gusted as I teetered on the edge of the roof, giving me just enough of a push that I could regain my balance. One of my flailing arms caught the now-open window and I scrambled desperately inside, not caring how much noise I made.

Once through the window I crouched on the floor, breathing hard. My heart was just beginning to slow when the wind caught the window and slammed it closed above my head, startling me all over again.

I brought out my sympathy lamp, thumbed the switch to a dim setting, and swept the narrow arc of light around the room. Kilvin had been right to call it a thief's lamp. It was perfect for this sort of skulking about.

It was miles to Imre and back, and I trusted Ambrose's curiosity would keep him waiting for his secret admirer for at least half an hour. Normally looking for something as small as a ring would be a full day's job. But I guessed Ambrose wouldn't even think of hiding it. In his mind, it wasn't something he'd stolen. He would consider it either a trinket or a trophy.

I set about methodically searching Ambrose's rooms. The ring wasn't on his chest of drawers or the bedside table. It wasn't in any of his desk drawers, or on his jewelry tray in his dressing room. He didn't even have a locked jewelry box, mind you, just a tray with all manner of pins, rings, and chains scattered carelessly across it.

I left everything where it was, which isn't to say I didn't think about robbing the bastard blind. Just a few pieces of his jewelry could pay my tuition for a year. But it went against my plan: get in, find the ring, and get out. So long as I left no evidence of my visit, I guessed Ambrose would simply assume he'd lost the ring if he noticed it was gone at all. It was the perfect sort of crime: no suspicion, no pursuit, no consequences.

Besides, it's notoriously difficult to fence jewelry in a town as small as Imre. It would be far too easy for someone to trace it back to me.

That said, I've never claimed to be a priest, and there were plenty of opportunities for mischief in Ambrose's rooms. So I indulged myself. While checking Ambrose's pockets, I weakened a few seams so there was a fair chance of him splitting his pants up the back the next time he sat down or mounted his horse. I loosened the handle on his chimney's flue so it would eventually fall off, and his room would fill with smoke while he scrambled to reattach it.

I was trying to think of something to do to his damned irritating plumed hat when the oak twig in my pocket twitched violently, making me jump. Then it twitched again and broke sharply in half. I cursed bitterly under my breath. Ambrose couldn't have been gone for more than twenty minutes. What had brought him back so soon?

I clicked off my sympathy lamp and stuffed it into my cloak. Then I scurried into the next room to make my escape through the window. It was irritating to go through all the trouble of getting in just to leave again, but as long as Ambrose didn't know anyone had broken into his rooms, I could simply come back another night.

But the window didn't open. I pushed harder, wondering if it had jammed itself shut when the wind had slammed it.

Then I glimpsed a thin strip of brass running along the inside of the windowsill. I couldn't read the sygaldry in the dim light, but I know wards when I see them. That explained why Ambrose was back so soon. He knew someone had broken in. What's more, the best sort of wards wouldn't just warn of an intruder, they could hold a door or window shut to seal a thief in.

I bolted for the door, hands scrabbling in the pockets of my cloak, looking for something long and slender I could use to foul the lock. Not finding anything suitable, I snatched a pen from his writing desk, jammed it into the keyhole, then jerked it hard sideways, breaking the metal head off inside the lock. A moment later I heard a grating metallic noise as Ambrose attempted to unlock the door from his side, fumbling and cursing when he couldn't get his key to fit.

By that point I was already back at the window, shining my lamp back and forth along the strip of brass and murmuring runes under my breath. It was simple enough. I could render it useless by scratching out a handful of connecting runes, then open the window and escape.

I hurried back to the sitting room and snatched the letter opener off his desk, knocking over the capped inkwell in my hurry. I was just about to begin eliding runes when I realized how stupid that would be. Any petty thief could break into Ambrose's rooms, but the number of people who knew enough sygaldry to foul a ward was much lower. I might as well sign my name on his window frame.

I took a moment to collect my thoughts, then returned the letter opener to the desk and replaced the inkwell. I returned and examined the long brass strip more closely. Breaking something is simple, understanding it is harder.

This is doubly true when you are confronted with the sounds of muttered cursing from behind a door, accompanied by the clack and rattle of someone trying to unjam a lock.

Then the hallway went quiet, which was even more unnerving. I finally managed to puzzle out the sequence of wards as I heard several sets of footsteps in the hall. I broke my mind into three pieces and focused my Alar as I pushed against the window. My hands and feet grew cold as I pulled heat from my body to counteract the ward, trying not to panic as I heard a loud thump as something heavy struck the door.

The window swung open, and I scrambled backward over the sash and onto the roof as something struck the door again and I heard the sharp crack of splintering wood. I still could have made it away safely, but when I set my right foot down on the roof, I felt a clay tile crack under my weight. As my foot slid, I grabbed the windowsill with both hands to steady myself.

Then the wind gusted, catching the open window and flinging it toward my head. I brought up my arm to protect my face, and it struck my elbow instead, smashing one of the small panes of glass. The impact pushed me sideways onto my right foot, which slid the rest of the way out from underneath me.

Then, since all my other options seemed to be exhausted, I decided it would be best if I fell off the roof.

Acting on pure instinct, my hands scrabbled madly. I dislodged a few more clay tiles, then caught hold of the lip of the roof. My grip wasn't good, but it slowed and spun me so that I didn't land on my head or my back. Instead I landed facedown, like a cat.

Except a cat's legs are all the same length. I landed on my hands and knees. My hands merely stung, but my knees striking the cobblestones hurt as badly as anything I'd ever felt in my entire young life. The pain was blinding, and I heard myself yelp like a dog that's been kicked.

A second later a hail of heavy red roofing tiles fell around me. Most shattered on the cobblestones, but one clipped the back of my head, while another caught me square on the elbow, making my entire forearm go numb.

I didn't spare it a moment's thought. A broken arm would heal, but expulsion from the University would last a lifetime. I pulled my hood up and forced myself to my feet. Using one hand to make sure the hood of my cloak stayed in place, I staggered a few steps until I was under the eaves of the Golden Pony, out of sight of the upstairs window.

Then I was running, running, running. . . .

Eventually I made my careful, limping way onto the rooftops and let myself into my room by the window. It was slow going, but I had little choice. I couldn't walk past everyone in the taproom disheveled, limping, and generally looking as if I'd just fallen off a roof.

Once I caught my breath and spent some time abusing myself for several types of blinding idiocy, I took stock of my wounds. The good news was that I hadn't broken either of my legs, but I had splendid bruises blooming just below each knee. The tile that had grazed my head had left a lump, but hadn't cut me. And while my elbow throbbed with a dull ache, my hand was no longer numb.

There was a knock at the door. I froze for a moment, then drew the birch twig from my pocket, muttered a quick binding, and jerked it back and forth.

I heard a startled noise from out in the hall, followed by Wilem's low laugh. "That's not funny," I heard Sim say. "Let us in."

I let them in. Simmon sat on the edge of the bed, and Wilem took the chair by the desk. I closed the door and sat on the other half of the bed. Even with all of us seated, the tiny room was crowded.

We eyed each other soberly for a moment, then Simmon spoke up. "Apparently Ambrose startled a thief in his rooms tonight. Fellow jumped out a window rather than get caught."

I gave a brief, humorless laugh. "Hardly. I was almost out when the window blew shut on me." I gestured awkwardly. "Knocked me off the roof."

Wilem let out a relieved sigh. "I thought I botched the binding."

I shook my head. "I had plenty of warning. I just wasn't as careful as I should have been."

"Why was he back so early?" Simmon asked, looking at Wilem. "Did you hear anything when he came in?"

"It probably occurred to him that my handwriting is not especially feminine," Wilem said.

"He had wards on his windows," I said. "Probably linked to a ring or something he carries with him. They must have tipped him off as soon as I opened the window."

"Did you get it?" Wilem asked.

I shook my head.

Simmon craned his neck to get a better look at my arm. "Are you okay?"

I followed his eyes, but didn't see anything. Then I tugged at my shirt and noticed that it was stuck to the back of my arm. With all my other pains, I hadn't noticed it.

Moving gingerly, I pulled my shirt up over my head. The elbow of the shirt was torn and speckled with blood. I cursed bitterly. I only owned four shirts, and now this one was ruined.

I tried to get a look at my the injury, and quickly realized that you couldn't get a look at the back of your own elbow, no matter how much you wanted to. Eventually I held it up for Simmon's inspection.

"It's not much," he said, holding his fingers a little more than two inches apart. "There's only one cut and it's hardly bleeding. The rest of it's just scraped up. It looks like you scuffed it hard against something."

"Clay tile from the roof fell on me," I said.

"Lucky," Wilem grunted. "Who else could fall off a roof and end up with nothing more than a few scrapes?"

"I've got bruises on my knees the size of apples," I said. "I'll be lucky if I can walk tomorrow." But deep down I knew he was right. The clay tile that had landed on my elbow could easily have broken my arm. The broken edges of the clay tiles were sometimes sharp as knives, so if it had hit me differently, it could have cut me down to the bone. I hate clay roofing tiles.

"Well, it could have been worse," Simmon said briskly as he came to his feet. "Let's go to the Medica and get you patched up."

"*Kraem* no," Wilem said. "He can't go to the Medica. They will be asking to see if anyone is hurt."

Simmon sat down again. "Of course," he said, sounding vaguely disgusted with himself. "I knew that." He looked me over. "At least you're not hurt anywhere that people can see."

I looked at Wilem. "You have a problem with blood, don't you?"

His expression grew slightly offended. "I wouldn't say . . ." His eyes darted to my elbow and his face grew a little pale despite his dark Cealdish complexion. His mouth made a thin line. "Yes."

"Fair enough." I started to cut my ruined shirt into strips of cloth. "Congratulations Sim. You've been promoted to field medic." I opened a drawer and brought out hook needle and gut, iodine, and a small pot of goose grease.

Sim looked at the needle, then back at me, eyes wide.

I gave him my best smile. "It's easy. I'll talk you through it."

———————

I sat on the floor with my arm over my head while Simmon washed, stitched, and bandaged my elbow. He surprised me by being nowhere near as squeamish as I'd expected. His hands were more careful and confident than those of many students in the Medica who did this sort of thing all the time.

"So the three of us were here, playing breath all night?" Wil asked, pointedly avoiding looking in my direction.

"Sounds good," Sim said. "Can we say I won?"

"No," I said. "People must have seen Wil at the Pony. Lie and they'll catch me for sure."

"Oh," Sim said. "What do we say then?"

"The truth." I pointed at Wil. "You were at the Pony during the excitement, then came here to tell me about it." I nodded to the small table, where a mass of gears, springs, and screws were spread in disarray. "I showed you the harmony clock I found, and you both gave me advice on how to fix it."

Sim seemed disappointed. "Not very exciting."

"Simple lies are best," I said, getting to my feet. "Thanks again, both of you. This could have gone terribly wrong without the two of you looking out for me."

Simmon got to his feet and opened the door. Wil stood as well, but didn't turn to leave. "I heard a strange rumor the other night," he said.

"Anything interesting?" I asked.

He nodded. "Very. I remember hearing that you were done antagonizing a certain powerful member of the nobility. I was surprised that you had finally decided to let sleeping dogs lie."

"Come on, Wil," Simmon said. "Ambrose isn't sleeping. He's a dog with the froth that deserves to be put down."

"He more resembles an angry bear," Wilem said. "One you seem determined to prod with a burning stick."

"How can you say that?" Sim said hotly. "In two years as a scriv has he ever called you anything other than a filthy shim? And what about that time he almost blinded me by mixing my salts? Kvothe will be working the plum bob out of his system for—"

Wil held up his hand and nodded to acknowledge Simmon's point. "I know this to be true, which is why I let myself be drawn into such foolishness. I merely wish to make a point." He looked at me. "You realize you have gone well over the hill concerning this Denna girl, don't you?"

CHAPTER TWENTY-ONE

Piecework

THE PAIN IN MY knees kept me from any sort of decent sleep that night. So when the sky outside my window started to show the first pale light of coming dawn I gave up, got dressed, and made my slow, painful way to the outskirts of town, looking for willow bark to chew. Along the way I discovered several new, exciting bruises I hadn't been aware of the night before.

The walk was pure agony, but I was glad I was making it in the early morning dark, when the streets were empty. There was bound to be a lot of talk about last night's excitement at the Golden Pony. If anyone saw me limping, it would be too easy for them to jump to the right conclusions.

Luckily, the trip loosened the stiffness in my legs and the willow bark took the edge off the pain. By the time the sun was fully up I felt well enough to appear in public. So I headed to the Fishery hoping to get in a few hours of piecework before Adept Sympathy. I needed to start earning money for next term's tuition and Devi's loan, not to mention bandages and a new shirt.

Jaxim wasn't in the Stocks when I arrived, but I recognized the student there. We had entered the University at the same time and bunked close to each other for a little while in the Mews. I liked him. He wasn't one of the nobility who drifted blithely through the school, carried by his family's name and money. His parents were wool merchants, and he worked to pay his tuition.

"Basil," I said. "I thought you made E'lir last term. What are you doing in the Stocks?"

He flushed a little, looking embarrassed. "Kilvin caught me adding water to acid."

I shook my head, giving a stern scowl. "This is contrary to proper procedure, E'lir Basil," I said dropping my voice an octave. "An artificer must move with perfect care in all things."

Basil grinned. "You've got his accent." He opened the ledger book. "What can I get you?"

"I'm not feeling up for anything more complicated than piecework right now," I said. "How about—"

"Hold on," Basil interrupted, frowning down at the ledger book.

"What?"

He spun the ledger around to face me and pointed. "There's a note next to your name."

I looked. Penciled in Kilvin's strangely childlike scrawl was: "No materials or tools to Re'lar Kvothe. Send him to me. Klvn."

Basil gave me a sympathetic look. "It's acid to water," he joked gently. "Did you forget, too?"

"I wish I had," I said. "Then I'd know what was going on."

Basil looked around nervously, then leaned forward and spoke in a low voice. "Listen, I saw that girl again."

I blinked at him stupidly. "What?"

"The girl that came in here looking for you," he prompted. "The young one that was looking for the redheaded wizard who sold her a charm?"

I closed my eyes and rubbed at my face. "She came back? This is the last thing I need right now."

Basil shook his head. "She didn't come in," he said. "At least not that I know of. But I've seen her a couple times outside. She hangs around the courtyard." He jerked his head toward the southern exit of the Fishery.

"Did you tell anyone?" I asked.

Basil looked profoundly offended. "I wouldn't do that to you," he said. "But she might have talked to someone else. You should really get rid of her. Kilvin will spit nails if he thinks you've been selling charms."

"I haven't been," I said. "I've got no idea who she is. What does she look like?"

"Young," Basil said with a shrug. "Not Cealdish. I think she had light hair. She wears a blue cloak with the hood up. I tried to walk over and talk to her, but she just ran away."

I rubbed my forehead. "Wonderful."

Basil shrugged sympathetically. "Just thought I'd warn you. If she actually comes in here and asks for you, I'll have to tell Kilvin." He grimaced apologetically. "I'm sorry, but I'm in enough trouble as it is."

"I understand," I said. "Thanks for the warning."

When I walked into the workshop, I was immediately struck by a strange quality of the light in the room. The first thing I did was look up, checking to see if Kilvin had added a new lamp to the array of glass spheres hanging up among the rafters. I hoped the change in light was due to a new lamp. Kilvin's mood was always foul when one of his lamps went unexpectedly dark.

Scanning the rafters, I didn't see any dark lamps. It took me a long moment to realize the strange quality of the light was due to actual sunlight slanting in through the low windows on the eastern wall. Normally I didn't come to work until later in the day.

The workshop was almost eerily quiet this early in the morning. The huge room seemed hollow and lifeless with only a handful of students working on projects. That combined with the odd light and the unexpected summons from Kilvin, made me rather uneasy as I crossed the room heading toward Kilvin's office.

Despite the early hour, a small forge in the corner of Kilvin's office was already well-stoked. Heat billowed past me as I stood in the open doorway. It felt good after the early winter chill outside. Kilvin stood with his back to me, working the bellows with a relentless rhythm.

I knocked loudly on the frame of the door to get his attention. "Master Kilvin? I just tried to check some materials out of Stocks. Is anything the matter?"

Kilvin glanced over in my direction. "Re'lar Kvothe. I will be a moment. Come in."

I stepped into his office and swung the heavy door closed behind me. If I was in trouble, I'd rather not have anyone listening in.

Kilvin continued to work the bellows for a long moment. It was only when he drew out a long tube that I realized it wasn't a forge he was firing, it was a small glasswork. Moving deftly, he drew out a blob of molten glass on the end of his tube, then proceeded to blow an increasingly large bubble of glass.

After a minute the glass lost its orange glow. "Bellows," Kilvin said without looking at me, putting the tube back into the mouth of the glasswork.

I scrambled to obey, working the bellows in a steady rhythm until the glass was glowing orange again. Kilvin motioned me to stop, pulled it out, and puffed at the tube for another long moment, spinning the glass until the bubble was large as a sweetmelon.

He set it back in the glasswork again, and I pumped the bellows without being asked. By the third time we repeated this, I was wringing with sweat. I wished I hadn't closed Kilvin's door, but I didn't want to leave the bellows for the time it would take for me to open it again.

Kilvin didn't seem to notice the heat. The glass bubble grew large as my head, then big as a pumpkin. But the fifth time he drew it from the heat and began to blow, it sagged on the end of the tube, deflating and falling to the floor.

"Kist, crayle, en kote," he swore furiously. He threw down the metal tube where it rang sharply against the stone floor. *"Kraemet brevetan Aerin!"*

I fought down the sudden urge to laugh. My Siaru wasn't perfect, but I was fairly certain Kilvin had said, *Shit in God's beard.*

The bearlike master stood for a long moment, looking down at the ruined glass on the floor. Then he let out a long, irritated breath through his nose, pulled off his goggles, and turned to look at me.

"Three sets of synchronized bells, brass," he said without preamble. "One tap and catch, iron. Four heat funnels, iron. Six siphons, tin. Twenty-two panes of twice-tough glass and other assorted piecework."

It was a list of all the work I had done this term in the Fishery. Simple things I could finish and sell back to Stocks for a quick profit.

Kilvin looked at me with his dark eyes. "Does this work please you, Re'lar Kvothe?"

"The projects are easy enough, Master Kilvin," I said.

"You are now a Re'lar," he said, his voice heavy with reproach. "Are you content to coast idly, making toys for the lazy rich?" he asked. "Is that what you desire from your time in the Fishery? Easy work?"

I could feel the sweat beading up in my hair and running down my back. "I am somewhat leery of venturing off on my own," I said. "You didn't particularly approve of the modifications I made to my hand lamp."

"Those are coward's words," Kilvin said. "Will you never leave the house because you were scolded once?" He looked at me. "I ask you again. Bells. Castings. Does this work please you, Re'lar Kvothe?"

"The thought of paying next term's tuition pleases me, Master Kilvin." Sweat was running down my face. I tried to wipe it away with my sleeve, but my shirt was already soaked through. I glanced at Kilvin's office door.

"And the work itself?" Kilvin prompted. There was sweat beading on the dark skin of his forehead, but he didn't seem otherwise bothered by the heat.

"Truthfully, Master Kilvin?" I asked, feeling a little light-headed.

He looked a bit offended. "I value truth in all things, Re'lar Kvothe."

"The truth is I've made eight deck lamps this last year, Master Kilvin. If I have to make another, I expect I might shit myself from pure boredom."

Kilvin huffed something that could have been a laugh, then smiled widely at me. "Good. That is how a Re'lar should feel." He pointed one thick finger at me. "You are clever, and you have good hands. I expect great things from you. Not drudgery. Make something clever and it will earn you more than a lamp. Certainly more than piecework. Leave that to the E'lir." He gestured dismissively at the window that looked out over the workshop.

"I'll do my best, Master Kilvin," I said. My voice sounded strange to my own ears, distant and tinny. "Do you mind if I open the door and get some fresh air in here?"

Kilvin grunted an agreement, and I took a step toward the door. But my legs felt loose and my head spun. I staggered and almost fell headlong onto the floor, but I managed to catch the edge of the worktable and merely went to my knees instead.

When my bruised knees hit the stone floor it was excruciating. But I didn't shout or cry out. In fact, the pain seemed to be coming from a long way off.

━━━━━━━━━━

I awoke confused, with a mouth as dry as sawdust. My eyes were gummy and my thoughts so sluggish it took me a long moment to recognize the distinctive antiseptic tang in the air. That, combined with the fact that I was lying naked under a sheet, let me know I was in the Medica.

I turned my head and saw short blond hair and the dark physicker's uniform. I relaxed back onto the pillow. "Hello Mola," I croaked.

She turned and gave me a serious look. "Kvothe," she said formally. "How do you feel?"

Still bleary, I had to think about it. "Thick," I said. Then, "Thirsty."

Mola brought me a glass and helped me drink. It was sweet and gritty. It took me a long moment to finish it, but by the time I was done, I felt halfway human again.

"What happened?" I asked.

"You fainted in the Artificery," she said. "Kilvin carried you over here himself. It was rather touching, actually. I had to shoo him away."

I felt my entire body flush with shame at the thought of being carried through the streets of the University by the huge master. I must have looked like a rag doll in his arms. "I fainted?"

"Kilvin explained you were in a hot room," Mola said. "And you'd sweat through your clothes. You were dripping wet." She gestured to where my shirt and pants lay wadded on the table.

"Heat exhaustion?" I said.

Mola held up a hand to quiet me. "That was my first diagnosis," she said. "On further examination, I've decided you're actually suffering from an acute case of jumping out of a window last night." She gave me a pointed look.

I suddenly became self-conscious. Not of my near-nakedness, but of the obvious injuries I'd received when I'd fallen off the roof of the Golden Pony. I glanced at the door and was relieved to see it was closed. Mola stood watching me, her expression carefully blank.

"Has anyone else seen?" I asked.

Mola shook her head. "We've been busy today."

I relaxed a bit. "That's something then."

Her expression was grim. "This morning, Arwyl gave orders to report any suspicious injuries. It's no secret why. Ambrose himself has offered a sizable reward to whoever helps him catch a thief who broke into his rooms and stole several valuables, including a ring his mother gave him on her deathbed."

"That bastard," I said hotly. "I didn't steal anything."

Mola raised an eyebrow. "As easy as that? No denial? No . . . anything?"

I exhaled through my nose, trying to get my temper under control. "I'm not going to insult your intelligence. It's pretty obvious I didn't fall down some stairs." I took a deep breath. "Look, Mola. If you tell anyone, they'll expel me. I didn't steal anything. I could have, but I didn't."

"Then why . . ." She hesitated, obviously uncomfortable. "What were you doing?"

I sighed. "Would you believe I was doing a favor for a friend?"

Mola gave me a shrewd look, her green eyes searching mine. "Well, you do seem to be in the favor business lately."

"I . . . what?" I asked, my thoughts moving too sluggishly to follow what she was saying.

"The last time you were here, I treated you for burns and smoke inhalation after pulling Fela out of a fire."

"Oh," I said. "That's not really a favor. Anyone would have done that."

Mola gave me a searching look. "You really believe that, don't you?" She shook her head a little, then picked up a hardback and made a few notes on it, no doubt filling out her treatment report. "Well, I consider it a favor. Fela and I bunked together back when we were both new here. Despite what you think, it's not something a lot of people would have done."

There was a knock and Sim's voice came from the hallway. "Can we come in?" Without waiting for an answer, he opened the door and led an uncomfortable looking Wilem into the room.

"We heard . . ." Sim paused and turned to look at Mola. "He's going to be okay, right?"

"He'll be fine," Mola said. "Provided his temperature levels out." She picked up a key-gauge and stuck it in my mouth. "I know this will be hard for you, but try to keep your mouth shut for a minute."

"In that case," Simmon said with a grin, "We heard Kilvin took you somewhere private and showed you something that made you faint like a little sissy girl."

I scowled at him, but kept my mouth shut.

Mola turned back to Wil and Sim. "His legs are going to hurt for a while, but there's no permanent damage. His elbow should be fine too, though the stitching's a mess. What the hell were you guys doing in Ambrose's rooms, anyway?"

Wilem simply looked at her, characteristically dark-eyed and stoic.

No such luck with Sim. "Kvothe needed to get a ring for his ladylove," he chirped cheerfully.

Mola turned to look at me, her expression furious. "You have a hell of a lot of nerve to lie right to my face," she said, her eyes flat and angry as a cat's. "Thank goodness you didn't want to insult my intelligence or anything."

I took a deep breath and reached up to take the key-gauge out of my mouth. "Goddammit Sim," I said crossly. "Some day I'm going to teach you to lie."

Sim looked back and forth between the two of us, flushed with panic and embarrassment. "Kvothe has a thing for a girl over the river," he said defensively. "Ambrose took a ring of hers and won't give it back. We just—"

Mola cut him off with a sharp gesture. "Why didn't you just tell me that?" she demanded of me, irritated. "Everyone knows what Ambrose is like with women!"

"That's why I didn't tell you," I said. "It sounded like a very convenient lie. There's also the fact that it is not one whit of your goddamn business."

Her expression hardened. "You come off pretty high and mighty for—"

"Stop. Just stop," Wilem said, startling both of us out of our argument. He turned to Mola, "When Kvothe came here unconscious, what did you do first?"

"I checked his pupils for signs of head trauma," Mola said automatically. "What the hell does that have to do with anything?"

Wilem gestured in my direction. "Look at his eyes now."

Mola looked at me. "They're dark," she said, sounding surprised. "Dark green. Like a pine bough."

Wil continued. "Don't argue with him when his eyes go dark like that. No good comes of it."

"It's like the noise a rattlesnake makes," Sim said.

"More like hackles on a dog," Wilem corrected. "It shows when he's ready to bite."

"All of you can go straight to hell," I said. "Or you can give me a mirror so I can see what you're talking about. I don't care which."

Wil ignored me. "Our little Kvothe has a flash-pan temper, but once he's had a minute to cool down, he will realize the truth." Wilem gave me a pointed look. "He's not upset because you didn't trust him, or that you tricked Sim. He's upset because you found out what asinine lengths he is willing to go to in order to impress a woman." He looked at me. "Is *asinine* the right word?"

I took a deep breath and let it out. "Pretty much," I admitted.

"I chose it because it sounded like *ass*," Wil said.

"I knew you two had to be involved," Mola said with a hint of apology in her voice. "Honestly, the three of you are thick as thieves, and I *do* mean that in all its various clever implications." She walked around the side of the bed and looked critically at my wounded elbow. "Which one of you stitched him up?"

"Me." Sim grimaced. "I know I made a mess of it."

"*Mess* would be generous." Mola said, looking it over critically. "It looks like you were trying to stitch your name onto him and kept misspelling it."

"I think he did quite well," Wil said, meeting her eye. "Considering his lack of training, and the fact that he was helping a friend under less than ideal circumstances."

Mola flushed. "I didn't mean it like that," she said quickly. "Working here, it's easy to forget that not everyone . . ." She turned to Sim. "I'm sorry."

Sim ran his hand through his sandy hair. "I suppose you could make it up to me sometime," he said, grinning boyishly. "Like maybe tomorrow afternoon? When you let me buy you lunch?" He looked at her hopefully.

Mola rolled her eyes and sighed, somewhere between amusement and exasperation. "Fine."

"My work here is done," Wil said gravely. "I'm leaving. I hate this place."

"Thanks Wil," I said.

He gave a perfunctory wave over one shoulder and closed the door behind him.

———

Mola agreed to leave mention of my suspicious injuries off her report and stuck to her original diagnosis of heat exhaustion. She also cut away Sim's stitches, then recleaned, resewed, and rebandaged my arm. Not a pleasant experience, but I knew it would heal more quickly under her experienced care.

In closing, she advised me to drink more water, get some sleep, and suggested that in the future I refrain from strenuous physical activity in a hot room the day after falling off a roof.

CHAPTER TWENTY-TWO

Slipping

UP UNTIL THIS POINT in the term, Elxa Dal had been teaching us theory in Adept Sympathy. How much light could be produced from ten thaums of continuous heat using iron? Using basalt? Using human flesh? We memorized tables of figures and learned how to calculate escalating squares, angular momentum, and compounded degradations.

Simply said, it was mind-numbing.

Don't get me wrong. I knew it was essential information. Bindings of the sort we'd shown Denna were simple. But when things grew complicated, a skilled sympathist needed to do some fairly tricky calculations.

In terms of energy, there isn't much difference between lighting a candle and melting it into a puddle of tallow. The only difference is one of focus and control. When the candle is sitting in front of you, these things are easy. You simply stare at the wick and stop pouring in heat when you see the first flicker of flame. But if the candle is a quarter mile away, or in a different room, focus and control are exponentially more difficult to maintain.

And there are worse things than melted candles waiting for a careless sympathist. The question Denna had asked in the Eolian was all-important: "Where does the extra energy go?"

As Wil had explained, some went into the air, some went into the linked items, and the rest went into the sympathist's body. The technical term for it was "thaumic overfill," but even Elxa Dal tended to refer to it as slippage.

Every year or so some careless sympathist with a strong Alar channeled enough heat through a bad link to spike his body temperature and drive himself fever-mad. Dal told us of one extreme case where a student managed to cook himself from the inside out.

I mentioned the last to Manet the day after Dal shared the story with our class. I expected him to join me in some healthy scoffing, but it turned out Manet had actually been a student back when it had happened.

"Smelled like pork," Manet said grimly. "Damnedest thing. Felt bad for him of course, but you can only feel so much pity for an idiot. A little slippage here and there, you hardly notice, but he must have slipped two hundred thousand thaums inside two seconds." Manet shook his head, not looking up from the piece of tin he was engraving. "Whole wing of Mains reeked. Nobody could use those rooms for a year."

I stared at him.

"Thermal slippage is fairly common though," Manet continued. "Now kinetic slippage . . ." He raised his eyebrows appreciatively. "Twenty years back some damn fool El'the got drunk and tried to lift a manure cart onto the roof of the Masters' Hall on a bet. Tore his own arm off at the shoulder."

Manet bent back over his piece of tin, engraving a careful rune. "Takes a special kind of stupid to do something like that."

The next day I was especially attentive to what Dal had to say.

He drilled us mercilessly. Calculations for enthaupy. Charts showing distance of decay. Equations that described the entropic curves a skilled sympathist needs to understand on an almost instinctive level.

But Dal was no fool. So before we grew bored and sloppy, he turned it into a competition.

He made us draw heat from odd sources, from red-hot irons, from blocks of ice, from our own blood. Lighting candles in distant rooms was the easiest of it. Lighting one of a dozen identical candles was harder. Lighting a candle you'd never actually seen in an unknown location . . . it was like juggling in the dark.

There were contests of precision. Contests of finesse. Contests of focus and control. After two span, I was the highest ranked student in our class of twenty-three Re'lar. Fenton nipped at my heels in second place.

As luck would have it, the day after my assault on Ambrose's rooms was the same day we began dueling in Adept Sympathy. Dueling required all the subtlety and control of our previous competitions, with the added challenge of having another student actively opposing your Alar.

So, despite my recent trip to the Medica for heat exhaustion, I melted a hole through a block of ice in a distant room. Despite two nights of scant sleep, I raised the temperature of a pint of mercury exactly ten degrees. Despite my throbbing bruises and the stinging itch of my bandaged arm, I tore the king of spades in half while leaving the other cards in the deck untouched.

All of these things I did in less than two minutes, despite the fact that Fenton set the whole of his Alar to oppose me. It is not for nothing that they came to call me Kvothe the Arcane. My Alar was like a blade of Ramston steel.

"It's rather impressive," Dal said to me after class. "It's been years since I've had a student go undefeated for so long. Will anyone even bet against you anymore?"

I shook my head. "That dried up a long time ago."

"The price of fame." Dal smiled, then looked a little more serious. "I wanted to warn you before I announce it to the class. Next span I'll probably start setting students against you in pairs."

"I'll have to go against Fenton and Brey at the same time?" I asked.

Dal shook his head. "We'll start with the two lowest ranked duelists. It will be a nice lead-in to the teamwork exercises we'll be doing later in the term." He smiled. "And it will keep you from growing complacent." Dal gave me a sharp look, his smile fading. "Are you all right?"

"Just a chill," I said unconvincingly as I shivered. "Could we go stand by the brazier?"

I stood as close as I could without pressing myself against the hot metal, spreading my hands over the glimmering bowl of hot coals. After a moment the chill passed and I noticed Dal looking at me curiously.

"I ended up in the Medica with a bit of heat exhaustion earlier today," I admitted. "My body's just a bit confused. I'm fine now."

He frowned. "You shouldn't come to class if you aren't feeling well," he said. "And you certainly shouldn't be dueling. Sympathy of this sort stresses the body and mind. You shouldn't risk compounding that with an illness."

"I felt fine when I came to class," I lied. "My body is just reminding me I owe it a good night's sleep."

"See that you give it one," he said sternly, spreading his own hands to the fire. "If you drive yourself too hard you'll pay for it later. You've been looking a little ragged lately. Ragged isn't the right word, really."

"Weary?" I guessed.

"Yes. Weary." He eyed me speculatively, smoothing his beard with a hand. "You have a gift for words. It's one of the reasons you ended up with Elodin, I expect."

I didn't say anything to that. I must have said it quite loudly too, because Dal gave me a curious look. "How are your studies progressing with Elodin?" he asked casually.

"Well enough," I hedged.

He looked at me.

"Not as well as I might hope," I admitted. "Studying with Master Elodin isn't what I expected."

Dal nodded. "He can be difficult."

A question sprang up in me. "Do you know any names, Master Dal?"

He nodded solemnly.

"What are they?" I pressed.

He stiffened slightly, then relaxed as he turned his hands back and forth over the fire. "That isn't really a polite question," he said gently. "Well, not *impolite*, it's just the sort of question you don't ask. Like asking a man how often he makes love to his wife."

"I'm sorry."

"No need to be," he said. "There's no reason for you to know. It's a hold-over from older times, I think. Back when we had more to fear from our fellow arcanists. If you knew what names your enemy knew, you could guess his strengths, his weaknesses."

We were both silent for a moment, warming ourselves by the coals. "Fire," he said after a long moment. "I know the name of fire. And one other."

"Only two?" I blurted without thinking.

"And how many do you know?" He mocked me gently. "Yes, only two. But two is a great number of names to know these days. Elodin says it was different, long ago."

"How many does Elodin know?"

"Even if I knew, it would be exceptionally bad form for me to tell you that," he said with a hint of disapproval. "But it's safe to say he knows a few."

"Could you show me something with the name of fire?" I asked. "If that's not inappropriate?"

Dal hesitated for a moment, then smiled. He looked intently into the brazier between us, closed his eyes, then gestured to the unlit brazier across the room. "Fire." He spoke the word like a commandment and the distant brazier roared up in a pillar of flame.

"Fire?" I said puzzled. "That's it? The name of fire is fire?"

Elxa Dal smiled and shook his head. "That's not what I actually said. Some part of you just filled in a familiar word."

"My sleeping mind translated it?"

"Sleeping mind?" He gave me a puzzled look.

"That's what Elodin calls the part of us that knows names," I explained.

Dal shrugged and ran a hand over his short black beard. "Call it what you will. The fact that you heard me say anything is probably a good sign."

"I don't know why I'm bothering with naming sometimes," I groused. "I could have lit that brazier with sympathy."

"Not without a link," Dal pointed out. "Without a binding, a source of energy . . ."

"It still seems pointless," I said. "I learn things every day in your class. Useful things. I don't have a thing to show for all the time I've spent on naming. Yesterday you know what Elodin lectured about?"

Dal shook his head.

"The difference between being naked and being nude," I said flatly. Dal burst into laughter. "I'm serious. I fought to be in his class, but now all I can do is think about all the time I'm wasting there, time I could be spending on more practical things."

"There are things more practical than names," Dal admitted. "But watch." He focused on the brazier in front of us again, then his eyes grew distant. He spoke again, whispering this time, then slowly lowered his hand until it was inches above the hot coals.

Then, with an intent expression on his face, Dal pressed his hand deep into the heart of the fire, nestling his spread fingers into the orange coals as if they were nothing more than loose gravel.

I realized I was holding my breath and let it out softly, not wanting to break his concentration. "How?"

"Names," Dal said firmly, and drew his hand back out of the fire. It was smudged with white ash, but perfectly unharmed. "Names reflect true understanding of a thing, and when you truly understand a thing you have power over it."

"But fire isn't a thing unto itself," I protested. "It's merely an exothermal chemical reaction. It . . ." I spluttered to a stop.

Dal drew in a breath, and for a moment it looked as if he would explain. Then he laughed instead, shrugging helplessly. "I don't have the wit to explain it to you. Ask Elodin. He's the one who claims to understand these things. I just work here."

———

After Dal's class, I made my way over the river to Imre. I didn't find Denna at the inn where she was staying, so I headed to the Eolian despite the fact that I knew it was too early to find her there.

There were barely a dozen people inside, but I did see a familiar face at the far end of the bar, talking to Stanchion. Count Threpe waved, and I walked over to join them.

"Kvothe my boy!" Threpe said enthusiastically. "I haven't seen you in a mortal age."

"Things have been rather hectic on the other side of the river," I said, setting down my lute case.

Stanchion looked me over. "You look it," he said frankly. "You look pale.

You should get more red meat. Or more sleep." He pointed to a nearby stool. "Barring that, I'll stand you a mug of metheglin."

"I'll thank you for that," I said, climbing onto a stool. It felt wonderful to take the weight off my aching legs.

"If it's meat and sleep you need," Threpe said ingratiatingly. "You should come to dinner at my estate. I promise wonderful food and conversation so dull you can drowse straight through it and not worry about missing a thing." He gave me an imploring look. "Come now. I'll beg if I must. It won't be more than ten people. I've been dying to show you off for months now."

I picked up the mug of metheglin and looked at Threpe. His velvet jacket was a royal blue, and his suede boots were dyed to match. I couldn't show up for a formal dinner at his home dressed in secondhand road clothes, which were the only sort I owned.

There was nothing ostentatious about Threpe, but he was a noble born and raised. It probably didn't even occur to him that I didn't have any fine clothes. I didn't blame him for assuming that. The vast majority of the students at the University were at least modestly wealthy. How else could they afford tuition?

The truth was, I'd like nothing better than a fine dinner and the chance to interact with some of the local nobility. I'd love to banter over drinks, repair some of the damage Ambrose had done to my reputation, and maybe catch the eye of a potential patron.

But I simply couldn't afford the price of admission. A suit of passably fine clothes would cost at least a talent and a half, even if I bought them from a fripperer. Clothes do not make the man, but you need the proper costume if you want to play the part.

Sitting behind Threpe, Stanchion made an exaggerated nodding motion with his head.

"I'd love to come to dinner," I said to Threpe. "I promise. Just as soon as things settle down a bit over at the University."

"Excellent," Threpe said enthusiastically. "I'm going to hold you to it, too. No backing out. I'll get you a patron, my boy. A proper one. I swear it."

Behind him, Stanchion nodded approvingly.

I smiled at both of them and took another drink of metheglin. I glanced at the stairway to the second tier.

Stanchion saw my look. "She's not here," he said apologetically. "Haven't seen her in a couple days, actually."

A handful of people came through the door of the Eolian and shouted something in Yllish. Stanchion waved at them and got to his feet. "Duty calls," he said, wandering off to greet them.

"Speaking of patrons," I said to Threpe. "There's something I've been wanting to ask your opinion about." I lowered my voice. "Something I'd rather you kept between the two of us."

Threpe's eyes glittered curiously as he leaned close.

I took another drink of metheglin while I gathered my thoughts. The drink was hitting me more quickly than I'd expected. It was quite nice, actually, as it dulled the ache of my many injuries. "I'm guessing you know most every potential patron within a hundred miles of here."

Threpe shrugged, not bothering with false modesty. "A fair number. Everyone who's earnest about it. Everyone with money, anyway."

"I have a friend," I said. "A musician who is just starting out. She has natural talent but not much training. Someone has approached her with an offer of help and a promise of eventual patronage. . . ." I trailed off, not sure how to explain the rest.

Threpe nodded. "You want to know if he's a legitimate sort," he said. "Reasonable concern. Some folk feel a patron has a right to more than music." He gestured to Stanchion. "If you want stories, ask him about the time Duchess Samista came here on holiday." He gave a chuckle that was almost a moan, rubbing at his eyes. "Tiny gods help me, that woman was terrifying."

"That's my worry," I said. "I don't know if he's trustworthy."

"I can ask around if you like," Threpe said. "What's his name?"

"That's part of the issue," I said. "I don't know his name. I don't think she knows it either."

Threpe frowned at this. "How can she not know his name?"

"He gave her a name," I said. "But she doesn't know if it's real. Apparently he's particular about his privacy and gave her strict instructions never to tell anyone about him," I said. "They never meet in the same place twice. Never in public. He's gone for months at a time." I looked up at Threpe. "How does that sound to you?"

"Well it's hardly ideal," Threpe said, disapproval heavy in his voice. "There's every chance this fellow isn't a proper patron at all. It sounds like he might be taking advantage of your friend."

I nodded glumly. "That was my thought too."

"Then again," Threpe said, "some patrons do work in secret. If they find someone with talent, it's not unknown for them to nurture them in private, and then . . ." He made a dramatic flourish with one hand. "It's like a magic trick. You suddenly produce a brilliant musician out of thin air."

Threpe gave me a fond smile. "I thought that's what someone had done with you," he admitted. "You came out of nowhere and got your pipes. I thought someone had been keeping you hidden away until you were ready to make your grand appearance."

"I hadn't thought of that," I said.

"It does happen," Threpe said. "But strange meeting places and the fact that she's not sure of his name?" He shook his head, frowning. "If nothing else, it's rather indecorous. Either this fellow is having a bit of fun pretending to be an outlaw, or he's genuinely dodgy."

Threpe seemed to think for a moment, tapping his fingers on the bar. "Tell your friend to be careful and keep her wits about her. It's a terrible thing when a patron takes advantage of a woman. That's a betrayal. But I've known men who did little but pose as patrons to gain a woman's trust." He frowned. "That's worse."

———————

I was halfway back to the University, with Stonebridge just beginning to loom in the distance, when I began to feel an unpleasant prickling heat run up my arm. At first I thought it was the pain of the twice-stitched cuts on my elbow, as they'd been itching and burning all day.

But instead of fading, the heat continued to spread up my arm and along the left side of my chest. I began to sweat, as if from a sudden fever.

I stripped off my cloak, letting the chill air cool me, and began to unbutton my shirt. The autumn breeze helped, and I fanned myself with my cloak. But the heat grew more intense, painful even, as if I'd spilled boiling water across my chest.

Luckily, this section of road ran parallel to a stream that fed into the nearby Omethi River. Unable to think of a better plan, I kicked off my boots, unshouldered my lute, and jumped into the water.

The chill of the stream made me gasp and sputter, but it cooled my burning skin. I stayed there, trying not to feel like an idiot while a young couple walked past, holding hands and pointedly ignoring me.

The strange heat moved through my body, like there was a fire inside me trying to find a way out. It started along my left side, then wandered down to my legs, then back up to my left arm. When it moved to my head, I ducked underwater.

It stopped after a few minutes, and I climbed out of the stream. Shivering, I wrapped myself in my cloak, glad no one else was on the road. Then, since there was nothing else to do, I shouldered my lute case and began the long walk back to the University dripping wet and terribly afraid.

CHAPTER TWENTY-THREE

Principles

"**I** DID TELL MOLA," I said as I shuffled the cards. "She said it was all in my head and pushed me out the door."

"Well, I can only guess what that feels like," Sim said bitterly.

I looked up, surprised by the uncharacteristic sharpness in his voice, but before I could ask what was the matter, Wilem caught my eye and shook his head, warning me away. Knowing Sim's history, I guessed it was another quick, painful end to another quick, painful relationship.

I kept my mouth shut and dealt another hand of breath. The three of us were killing time, waiting for the room to fill up before I started playing for my typical Felling night crowd at Anker's.

"What do you think is the matter?" Wilem asked.

I hesitated, worried that if I spoke my fears aloud it might somehow make them true. "I might have exposed myself to something dangerous in the Fishery."

Wil looked at me. "Such as?"

"Some of the compounds we use," I said. "They'll go straight through your skin and kill you in eighteen slow ways." I thought back to the day my tenten glass had cracked in the Fishery. Of the single drop of transporting agent that had landed on my shirt. It was only a tiny drop, barely larger than the head of a nail. I was so certain it hadn't touched my skin. "I hope that's not it. But I don't know what else it might be."

"It could be a lingering effect from the plum bob," Sim said grimly. "Ambrose isn't much of an alchemist. And from what I understand, one of the main ingredients is lead. If he factored it himself, some latent principles could be affecting your system. Did you eat or drink anything different today?"

I thought about it. "I had a fair bit of metheglin at the Eolian," I admitted.

"That stuff will make anyone ill," Wil said darkly.

"I like it," Sim said. "But it's practically a nostrum all by itself. There's a lot of different tincturing going on in there. Nothing alchemical, but you've got nutmeg, thyme, clove—all manner of spices. Could be that one of them triggered some of the free principles lurking in your system."

"Wonderful," I grumbled. "And how do I go about fixing that, exactly?" Sim spread his hands helplessly.

"That's what I thought," I said. "Still, it sounds better than metal poisoning."

Simmon proceeded to take four tricks in a row with a clever card force, and by the end of the hand he was smiling again. Sim was never really given to extended brooding.

Wil squared his cards away, and I pushed my chair back from the table.

"Play the one about the drunk cow and the butter churn," Sim said.

I couldn't help but crack a smile. "Maybe later," I said as I picked up my increasingly shabby lute case and made my way to the hearth amid the sound of scattered, familiar applause. It took me a long moment to open the case, untwisting the copper wire I was still using in place of a buckle.

For the next two hours I played. I sang: "Copper Bottom Pot," "Lilac Bough," and "Aunt Emme's Tub." The audience laughed and clapped and cheered. As I fingered my way through the songs, I felt my worries slough away. My music has always been the best remedy for my dark moods. As I sang, even my bruises seemed to pain me less.

Then I felt a chill, as if a strong winter wind was blowing down the chimney behind me. I fought off a shiver and finished the last verse of "Applejack," which I'd finally played to keep Sim happy. When I struck the last chord, the crowd applauded and conversation slowly welled up to fill the room again.

I looked behind me at the fireplace, but the fire was burning cheerfully with no sign of a draft. I stepped down off the hearth, hoping a little walk would chase my chill away. But as soon as I took a few steps, I realized that wasn't the case. The cold settled straight into my bones. I turned back to the fireplace, spreading my hands to warm them.

Wil and Sim appeared at my side. "What's going on?" Sim asked. "You look like you're going to be sick."

"Something like that," I said, clenching my teeth to keep them from chattering. "Go tell Anker I'm feeling ill and have to cut it short tonight. Then light a candle off this fire and bring it up to my room." I looked up at their serious faces. "Wil, can you help me get out of here? I don't want to make a scene."

Wilem nodded and gave me his arm. I leaned on him and concentrated on keeping my body from shaking as we made our way to the stairs. No one paid us much attention. I probably looked more drunk than anything. My hands were numb and heavy. My lips felt icy cold.

After the first flight of stairs, I couldn't keep my shaking under control any longer. I could still walk, but the thick muscles in my legs twitched with every step.

Wil stopped. "We should go the Medica." While he didn't sound different, his Cealdish accent was thicker, and he was starting to drop words. A sign he was genuinely worried.

I shook my head firmly and leaned forward, knowing he'd have to help me up the stairs or let me fall. Wilem put an arm around me and half-steadied, half-carried me the rest of the way.

Once in my tiny room, I staggered onto the bed. Wil wrapped a blanket around my shoulders.

There were footsteps in the hallway and Sim peered nervously around the door. He held a stub of candle, sheltering the flame with his other hand as he walked. "I've got it. What do you want it for, anyway?"

"There." I pointed to the table beside the bed. "You lit it off the fire?"

Sim's eyes were frightened. "Your lips," he said. "They're not a good color."

I pried a splinter from the rough wood of the bedside table and jabbed it hard into the back of my hand. Blood welled up and I rolled the long splinter around in it, getting it wet. "Close the door," I said.

"You are *not* doing what I think you're doing," Sim said firmly.

I jabbed the long splinter down into the soft wax of the candle alongside the burning wick. It sputtered a little bit, then the flame wrapped around it. I muttered two bindings, one right after the other, speaking slowly so my numb lips didn't slur the words.

"What are you doing?" Sim demanded. "Are you trying to cook yourself?" When I didn't answer him, he stepped forward as if he would knock the candle over.

Wil caught his arm. "His hands are like ice," he said quietly. "He's cold. Really cold."

Sim's eyes darted nervously between the two of us. He took a step back. "Just . . . just be careful."

But I was already ignoring him. I closed my eyes and bound the candle flame to the fire downstairs. Then I carefully made the second connection between the blood on the splinter and the blood in my body. It was very much like what I'd done with the drop of wine at the Eolian. With the obvious exception that I didn't want my blood to boil.

At first there was just a brief tickle of heat, not nearly enough. I concentrated harder and felt my entire body relax as warmth flooded through me. I kept my eyes closed, keeping my attention on the bindings until I could take several long, deep breaths without any shuddering or shaking.

I opened my eyes and saw my two friends looking on expectantly. I smiled at them. "I'm okay."

But before I got the words out, I began to sweat. I was suddenly too warm, nauseatingly warm. I broke both bindings as quickly as you jerk your hand away from a hot iron stove.

I took a few deep breaths, then got to my feet and walked over to the window. I opened it and leaned heavily on the sill, enjoying the chill autumn air that smelled of dead leaves and coming rain.

There was a long moment of silence.

"That looked like binder's chills," Simmon said. "Really bad binder's chills."

"It felt like the chills," I said.

"Maybe your body has lost the ability to regulate its own temperate?" Wilem suggested.

"Temperature," Sim corrected him absently.

"That wouldn't account for the burn across my chest," I said.

Sim cocked his head. "Burn?"

I was wet with sweat now, so I was glad for an excuse to unbutton my shirt and pull it off over my head. A large portion of my chest and upper arm was a bright red, a sharp contrast to my ordinarily pale skin. "Mola said it was a rash, and I was being fussy as an old woman. But it wasn't there before I jumped into the river."

Simmon leaned close to look. "I still think it's unbound principles," he said. "They can do bizarre things to a person. We had an E'lir last term that wasn't careful with his factoring. He ending up not being able to sleep or focus his eyes for almost two span."

Wilem slouched into a chair. "What makes a man cold, then hot, then cold again?"

Sim gave a halfhearted smile. "Sounds like a riddle."

"I hate riddles," I said, reaching for my shirt. Then I yelped, clutching at the bare bicep of my left arm. Blood welled out between my fingers.

Sim bolted to his feet, looking around frantically, obviously at a loss for what to do.

It felt like I'd been stabbed by an invisible knife. "God. Blackened. Damn." I gritted out between my clenched teeth. I pulled my hand away and saw the small, round wound in my arm that had come from nowhere.

Simmon's expression was horrified, his eyes wide, his hands covering his mouth. He said something, but I was too busy concentrating to listen. I already knew what he was saying, anyway: *malfeasance*. Of course. This was all malfeasance. Someone was attacking me.

I lowered myself into the Heart of Stone and brought all my Alar to bear.

But my unknown attacker wasn't wasting any time. There was a sharp pain in my chest near the shoulder. It didn't break the skin this time, but I watched a blotch of dark blue blossom under my skin.

I hardened my Alar and the next stab was little more than a pinch. Then I quickly broke my mind into three pieces and gave two of them the job of maintaining the Alar that protected me.

Only then did I let out a deep sigh. "I'm fine."

Simmon gave a laugh that choked off into a sob. His hands still covered his mouth. "How can you say that?" he demanded, plainly horrified.

I looked down at myself. Blood was still welling up through my fingers, running down the back of my hand and my arm.

"It's true," I said to him. "Honestly, Sim."

"But malfeasance," he said. "It just isn't done."

I sat down on the edge of my bed, keeping pressure on my wound. "I think we have some pretty clear proof otherwise."

Wilem sat back down. "I am with Simmon. I would never have believed this." He made an angry gesture. "Arcanists do not do this anymore. It is insane." He looked at me. "Why are you smiling?"

"I'm relieved," I said honestly. "I was worried I'd given myself cadmium poisoning, or I had some mysterious disease. This is just someone trying to kill me."

"How could someone do it?" Simmon asked. "I don't mean morally. How did someone get hold of your blood or hair?"

Wilem looked at Simmon. "What did you do with the bandages after you stitched him up?"

"I burned them," Sim said defensively. "I'm not an idiot."

Wil made a calming gesture. "I'm just narrowing our options. It probably isn't the Medica either. They're careful about that sort of thing."

Simmon stood up. "We have to tell someone." He looked at Wilem. "Would Jamison still be in his office at this time of night?"

"Sim," I said. "How about we just wait for a while?"

"What?" Simmon said. "Why?"

"The only evidence I have are my injuries," I said. "That means they'll want someone at the Medica to examine me. And when that happens . . ." With one hand still clamped over my bloody arm, I waved my bandaged elbow. "I look remarkably like someone who fell off a roof just a couple days ago."

Sim's sat back down in his chair. "It's only been three days, hasn't it?"

I nodded. "I'd be expelled. And Mola would be in trouble for not mentioning my injuries. Master Arwyl isn't forgiving about that sort of thing. The two of you would probably be implicated too. I don't want that."

We were quiet for a moment. The only sound was the distant clamor of the busy taproom below. I sat down on the bed.

"Do we even need to discuss who's doing this?" Sim asked.

"Ambrose," I said. "It's always Ambrose. He must have found some of my blood on a piece of roofing tile. I should have thought of that days ago."

"How would he know it was yours?" Simmon asked.

"Because I hate him," I said bitterly. "Of course he knows it was me."

Wil was slowly shaking his head. "No. It's not like him."

"Not like him?" Simmon demanded. "He had that woman dose Kvothe with the plum bob. That's as bad as poison. He hired those men to jump Kvothe in the alley last term."

"My point exactly," Wilem said. "Ambrose doesn't do things to Kvothe. He arranges for other people to do them. He got some woman to dose him. He paid thugs to knife you. I expect he didn't even do that, really. I'll bet someone else set it up for him."

"It's all the same," I said. "We know he's behind it."

Wilem frowned at me. "You're not thinking straight. It's not that Ambrose isn't a bastard. He is. But he's a clever bastard. He's careful to distance himself from anything he does."

Sim looked uncertain. "Wil has a point. When you were hired on as house musician at the Horse and Four, he didn't buy the place and fire you. He had Baron Petre's son-in-law do it. No connection to him at all."

"No connection here either," I said. "That's the whole point of sympathy. It's indirect."

Wil shook his head again. "If you got knifed in an alley people would be shocked. But such things happen all the time all over the world. But if you fell down in public and started gushing blood from malfeasance? People would be horrified. The masters would suspend classes. Rich merchants and nobles would hear of it and pull their children from their studies. They'd bring the constables over from Imre."

Simmon rubbed his forehead and looked up at the ceiling thoughtfully. Then he nodded to himself, first slowly, then with more certainty. "It makes sense," he said. "If Ambrose had found some blood, he could have turned it over to Jamison and had him dowse out the thief. There wouldn't have been any need to get folks in the Medica to look for suspicious injuries and such."

"Ambrose likes his revenge," I pointed out grimly. "He could have hidden the blood from Jamison. Kept it for himself."

Wilem was shaking his head.

Sim sighed. "Wil's right. There aren't that many sympathists, and everyone knows Ambrose is carrying a grudge against you. He's too careful to do something like this. It would point right to him."

"Besides," Wilem said. "How long has this been going on? Days and days. Do you honestly think Ambrose could go this long without rubbing your nose in it? Not even a little?"

"You have a point," I admitted reluctantly. "That's not like him."

I knew it had to be Ambrose. I could feel it deep in my gut. In a strange way I almost wanted it to be him. It would make things so much simpler.

But wanting something doesn't make it so. I took a deep breath and forced myself to think about it rationally.

"It would be reckless of him," I admitted at last. "And he isn't the sort to get his hands dirty." I sighed. "Fine. Wonderful. As if one person trying to ruin my life wasn't enough."

"Who could it be?" Simmon asked. "Your average person can't do this sort of thing with hair, am I right?"

"Dal could," I said. "Or Kilvin."

"It is probably safe to assume," Wilem said dryly, "that none of the masters are trying to kill you."

"Then it has to be someone with his blood," Sim said.

I tried to ignore the sinking sensation in the pit of my stomach. "There is someone with my blood," I said. "But I don't think she could be responsible."

Wil and Sim turned to look at me, and I immediately regretted saying anything. "Why would someone have your blood?" Sim asked.

I hesitated, then realized there was no way to avoid telling them at this point. "I borrowed money from Devi at the beginning of the term."

Neither one of them reacted the way I expected. Which is to say, neither one reacted at all.

"Who's Devi?" Sim asked.

I started to relax. Maybe they hadn't heard of her. That would certainly make things easier. "She's a gaelet who lives across the river," I said.

"Okay," Simmon said easily. "What's a gaelet?"

"Remember when we went to see *The Ghost and the Goosegirl*?" I asked him. "Ketler was a gaelet."

"Oh, a copper hawk," Sim said, his face brightening with realization, then darkening again as he realized the implications. "I didn't know there were any of those sort of people around here."

"Those sort of people are everywhere," I said. "The world wouldn't work without them."

"Wait," Wilem said suddenly, holding up his hand. "Did you say, your . . ." He paused, struggling to remember the appropriate word in Aturan. "Your loaner, your *gatessor* was named *Devi?*" His Cealdish accent was thick around her name, so it sounded like "David."

I nodded. This was the reaction I'd expected.

"Oh God," Simmon said, aghast. "You mean Demon Devi, don't you?"

I sighed. "So you've heard of her."

"Heard of her?" Sim said, his voice going shrill. "She was expelled during my first term! It left a real impression."

Wilem simply closed his eyes and shook his head, as if he couldn't bear to look at someone as stupid as me.

Sim threw his hands into the air. "She was expelled for malfeasance! What were you thinking?"

"No," Wilem said to Simmon. "She was expelled for Conduct Unbecoming. There was no proof of malfeasance."

"I really don't think it was her," I said. "She's quite nice, actually. Friendly. Besides, it's only a six talent loan, and I'm not late paying her back. She doesn't have any reason to do something like this."

Wilem gave me a long, steady look. "Just to explore all possibilities," he said slowly. "Would you do something for me?"

I nodded.

"Think back on your last few conversings with her," Wilem said. "Take a moment and sift them piece by piece and see if you remember doing or saying something that might have offended or upset her."

I thought back on our last conversation, playing it through in my head. "She was interested in a certain piece of information that I didn't give her."

"How interested?" Wilem's voice was slow and patient, as if he were talking to a rather dimwitted child.

"Rather interested," I said.

"Rather does not indicate a degree of intensity."

I sighed. "Fine. Extremely interested. Interested enough to—" I stopped.

Wilem arched a knowing eyebrow at me. "Yes? What have you just remembered?"

I hesitated. "She might have also offered to sleep with me," I said.

Wilem nodded calmly, as if he had expected something of the sort. "And you responded to this young woman's generous offer in what way?"

I felt my cheeks get hot. "I . . . I sort of just ignored it."

Wilem closed his eyes, his expression conveying a vast, weary dismay.

"This is so much worse than Ambrose," Sim said, putting his head in his hands. "Devi doesn't have to worry about the masters or anything. They say she could do an eight-part binding! Eight!"

"I was in a tight space," I said a little testily. "I didn't have anything to use as collateral. I'll admit it wasn't a great idea. After all this is done, we can have a symposium on how stupid I am. But for now can we just move on?" I gave them a pleading look.

Wilem rubbed at his eyes with one hand and gave a weary nod.

Simmon made an effort to get rid of his horrified expression with only marginal success. He swallowed. "Fair enough. What *are* we going to do?"

"Right now it doesn't really matter who is responsible," I said, cautiously checking to see if my arm had stopped bleeding. It had, and I peeled my bloody hand away. "I'm going to take some precautionary measures." I made a shooing motion. "You two go get some sleep."

Sim rubbed his forehead, chuckling to himself. "Body of God, you're irritating sometimes. What if you're attacked again?"

"It's already happened twice while we've been sitting here," I said easily. "It tingles a bit." I grinned at his expression. "I'm fine, Sim. Honestly. There's a reason I'm the top-ranked duelist in Dal's class. I'm perfectly safe."

"As long as you're awake," Wilem interjected, his dark eyes serious.

My grin grew stiff. "As long as I'm awake," I repeated. "Of course."

Wilem stood up and made a show of brushing himself off. "So. Clean yourself and take your precautionary measures." He gave me a pointed look. "Shall young master Simmon and I expect Dal's top-ranked duelist in my room tonight?"

I felt myself flush with embarrassment. "Why, yes. That would be greatly appreciated."

Wil gave me an exaggerated bow, then opened the door and made his way out into the hall.

Sim was wearing a wide grin by now. "It's a date then. But put on a shirt before you come. I'll watch over you tonight like the colicky infant you are, but I refuse to do it if you insist on sleeping naked."

After Wil and Sim left, I headed out the window and onto the rooftops. I left my shirt in my room, as I was a bloody mess and I didn't want to ruin it. I trusted the dark night and the lateness of the hour, hoping no one would spot me running along the University rooftops half naked and bloody.

It is relatively easy to protect yourself from sympathy if you know what you're doing. Someone trying to burn or stab me, or draw off my body heat until I lapsed into hypothermia, all those things deal with the simple, direct application of force, so they are easy to oppose. I was safe now that I knew what was happening and kept my defenses up.

My new concern was that whoever was attacking me might get discouraged and try something different. Something like dowsing out my location, then resorting to a more mundane type of attack, one I couldn't stave off with an effort of will.

Malfeasance is terrifying, but a thug with a sharp knife will kill you ten times quicker if he catches you in a dark alley. And catching someone off their guard is remarkably easy if you can track their every movement using their blood.

So I headed across the rooftops. My plan was to take a handful of autumn leaves, mark them with my blood, and send them tumbling endlessly around the House of the Wind. It was a trick I'd used before.

But as I jumped across a narrow alley, I saw lightning flicker in the clouds and smelled rain in the air. A storm was coming. Not only would the rain mat down the leaves, keeping them from moving around, but it would wash my blood away as well.

Standing there on the rooftop, feeling like I'd had twelve colors of hell beaten out of me, brought back unsettling echoes of my years in Tarbean. I watched the distant lightning for a moment and tried not to let the feeling overwhelm me. I forced myself to remember I wasn't the same helpless starving child I'd been back then.

I heard the faint, drumlike sound as a piece of tin roofing bent behind me. I stiffened, then relaxed as I heard Auri's voice, "Kvothe?"

I looked to my right and saw her small shape standing a dozen feet away. The clouds were hiding the moon, but I could hear a smile in her voice as she said, "I saw you running across the tops of things."

I turned the rest of the way around to face her, glad there wasn't much light. I didn't like to think how Auri might react to the sight of me half naked and covered in blood.

"Hello Auri," I said. "There's a storm coming. You shouldn't be up on the tops of things tonight."

She tilted her head. "You are," she said simply.

I sighed. "I am. But only—"

A great spider of lightning crawled across the sky, illuminating everything for the space of a long second. Then it was gone, leaving me flash-blind.

"Auri?" I called, worried the sight of me had scared her off.

There was another flicker of lightning, and I saw her standing closer.

She pointed at me, grinning delightedly. "You look like an Amyr," she said. "Kvothe is one of the Ciridae."

I looked down at myself and with the next lightning flicker I saw what she meant. I had dried blood running down the back of my hands from when I'd been trying to stanch my wounds. It looked like the old tattoos the Amyr had used to mark their highest ranking members.

I was so surprised by her reference that I forgot the first thing I'd learned about Auri. I forgot to be careful and asked her a question, "Auri, how do you know about the Ciridae?"

There was no response. The next flicker of lightning showed me nothing but an empty rooftop and an unforgiving sky.

CHAPTER TWENTY-FOUR

Clinks

I STOOD ON THE ROOFTOPS with the storm flickering overhead, my heart heavy in my chest. I wanted to follow Auri and apologize, but I knew it was hopeless. The wrong sort of questions made her run, and when Auri bolted, she was like a rabbit down a hole. There were a thousand places she could hide in the Underthing. I didn't have a chance of finding her.

Besides, I had vital matters to attend to. Even now someone could be dowsing out my location. I simply didn't have the time.

It took me the better part of an hour to make my way across the rooftops. The flickering light of the storm made things harder rather than easier, blinding me for long moments after every flash. Still, I eventually made my limping way to the roof of Mains where I typically met Auri.

Stiffly, I climbed down the apple tree to the enclosed courtyard. I was about to call down through the heavy metal grating that led to the Underthing when I saw a flicker of movement in the shadow of the nearby bushes.

I peered into the dark, unable to see anything but a vague shape. "Auri?" I asked gently.

"I don't like telling," she said softly, her voice thick with tears. Of all the awful things I'd been part of these last couple days, this was unquestionably the worst of it.

"I'm so sorry, Auri," I said. "I won't ask again. I promise."

There was a tiny sob from the shadows that froze my heart solid and broke off a piece of it.

"What were you doing out on top of things tonight?" I asked. I knew this was a safe question. I'd asked it many times before.

"I was looking at the lightning," she said, sniffling. Then, "I saw one that looked like a tree."

"What was in the lightning?" I asked softly.

"Galvanic ionization," she said. Then, after a pause, she added, "And river-ice. And the sway a cattail makes."

"I wish I'd seen that one," I said.

"What were you doing on top of things." She paused and gave a tiny hiccuping laugh. "All crazy and mostly nekkid?"

My heart began to thaw a bit. "I was looking for a place to put my blood," I said.

"Most people keep that inside," she said. "It's easier."

"I want to keep the rest of it inside," I explained. "But I'm worried someone might be looking for me."

"Oh," she said, as if she understood perfectly. I saw the slightly darker shadow of her move in the darkness, standing up. "You should come with me to Clinks."

"I don't think I've seen Clinks," I said. "Have you taken me there before?"

There was a motion that might have been the shaking of a head. "It's private."

I heard a metallic noise, then a rustle, then I saw a blue-green light well up from the open grate. I climbed down and met her in the tunnel underneath.

The light in her hand showed smudges across her face, probably from where she'd been rubbing away her tears. It was the first time I'd ever seen Auri dirty. Her eyes were darker than normal, and her nose was red.

Auri sniffed and rubbed her blotchy face. "You," she said gravely, "are a dreadful mess."

I looked down at my bloody hands and chest. "I am," I agreed.

Then she gave a tiny, brave smile. "I didn't run so far this time," she said tilting her chin proudly.

"I'm glad," I said. "And I'm sorry."

"No." She gave her head a tiny, firm shake. "You are my Ciridae, and thus above reproach." She reached out to touch the center of my bloody chest with a finger. *"Ivare enim euge."*

Auri led me through the maze of tunnels that comprised the Underthing. We went farther down, through Vaults, past Cricklet. Then we moved through several twisting hallways and down again, using a stone spiral staircase I'd never seen before.

I smelled damp stone and heard the low, smooth sound of running water as we descended. Every once in a while there was the gritty sound of glass on stone, or the brighter tinkling sound of glass on glass.

After about fifty steps the wide, spiraling staircase disappeared into a vast, roiling pool of black water. I wondered how far the stairs continued below the surface.

There wasn't any smell of rot or foulness. It was fresh water, and I could see ripples as it swirled in the stairwell and spread out into the dark beyond where our lights could reach. I heard the clink of glass again and saw two bottles spinning and bobbing on the surface, moving first one way, then another. One ducked under the surface and didn't come up again.

There was a burlap sack hanging from a brass torch bracket mounted into the wall. Auri reached into the bag and pulled out a heavy stoppered bottle of the sort that might have once held Bredon beer.

She handed me the bottle. "They disappear for an hour. Or a minute. Sometimes for days. Sometimes they don't come back at all." She brought another bottle out of the sack. "It's best to have at least four going at once. That way, statistically, you should always have two moving around."

I nodded, and I pulled a strand of burlap from the tattered sack and daubed it with the blood that covered my hand. I uncorked the bottle and dropped it inside.

"Hair too," Auri said.

I pulled a few from my head and threaded them through the bottle's mouth. Then I drove the cork in hard and set it floating. It rode low in the water, circling erratically.

Auri handed me another bottle and we repeated the process. When the fourth bottle was swept out into the swirling water, Auri nodded and dusted her hands briskly against each other.

"There," she said with a tone of immense satisfaction. "That's good. We're safe."

———

Hours later, washed, bandaged, and considerably less nekkid, I made my way to Wilem's room in the Mews. That night, and for many to come, Wil and Sim took turns watching over me as I slept, keeping me safe with their Alar. They were the best sort of friends. The sort everyone hopes for but no one deserves, least of all me.

CHAPTER TWENTY-FIVE

Wrongful Apprehension

DESPITE WHAT WIL AND Sim believed, I couldn't believe Devi was responsible for the malfeasance against me. While I was painfully aware that I knew next to nothing about women, she had always been friendly to me. Even sweet at times.

True, she had a grim reputation. But I knew better than anyone how quickly a handful of rumors could turn into full-blown faerie stories.

I thought it much more likely that my unknown assailant was simply a bitter student who resented my advancement in the Arcanum. Most students studied for years before they reached Re'lar, and I had managed it in less than three terms. It could even be someone who simply hated the Edema Ruh. It wouldn't be the first time that had earned me a beating.

In some ways, it really didn't matter who was responsible for the attacks. What I needed was a way to stop them. I couldn't expect Wil and Sim to watch over me for the rest of my life.

I needed a more permanent solution. I needed a gram.

A gram is a clever piece of artificery designed for just this sort of problem. It is a sort of sympathetic armor that prevents anyone from making a binding against your body. I didn't know how they worked, but I knew they existed. And I knew where to find out how to make one.

Kilvin looked up as I approached his office. I was relieved to see his glasswork was cold and dark.

"I trust you are well, Re'lar Kvothe?" he asked without getting up from the worktable. He was holding a large hemisphere of glass in one hand and a diamond stylus in the other.

"I am, Master Kilvin," I lied.

"Have you been thinking about your next project?" he asked. "Have you been dreaming clever dreams?"

"I was actually looking for a schema for a gram, Master Kilvin. But I can't find it in any of the bolt-holes or reference books."

Kilvin looked at me curiously. "And why would you be needing a gram, Re'lar Kvothe? Such a desire does not reflect good faith in your fellow arcanists."

Unsure as to whether he was joking or not, I decided to play it straight. "We've been learning about slippage in Adept Sympathy. I was thinking that if a gram works to deny outside affinities . . ."

Kilvin gave a low chuckle. "Dal has been throwing fear into you. Good. And you are correct, a gram would help protect against slippage—" His dark Cealdish eyes gave me a serious look. "To a degree. However, it seems a clever student would simply learn his lessons and avoid slippage through proper care and caution."

"I intend to, Master Kilvin," I said. "Still, a gram strikes me as a useful thing to have."

"There is truth to that," Kilvin admitted, nodding his shaggy head. "However, with repairs and the filling of our autumn orders, we are understaffed." He waved a hand toward the window that looked out into the workshop. "I cannot spare any workers to make such a thing. And even if I could, there is an issue of cost. They require delicate work, and gold is needed for the inlay."

"I'd prefer to make my own, Master Kilvin."

Kilvin shook his head. "There is reason the schema is not in the reference books. You are not far enough along to be making your own. One must be careful when meddling with sygaldry and one's own blood."

I opened my mouth to say something, but he cut me off. "More important, the sygaldry necessary for such a device is only entrusted to those who have reached the ranks of El'the. The runes for blood and bone have too great a potential for misuse."

His tone let me know there was nothing to be gained by arguing, so I shrugged it off as if I couldn't care less. "It's no matter, Master Kilvin. I have other projects to occupy my time."

Kilvin gave me a wide smile. "I am sure you do, Re'lar Kvothe. I am waiting with great eagerness to see what you will make for me."

A thought struck me. "To that purpose, Master Kilvin, could I have the use of one of the private workrooms? I'd rather not have everyone looking over my shoulder while I'm tinkering."

Kilvin's eyebrows went up at this. "Now I am doubly curious." He set down the hemisphere of glass, got to his feet, and opened a drawer in his desk. "Will one of the first floor workrooms suit you? Or is there a chance of something exploding? I will give you one on the third floor if that is the case. They are colder, but the roof is better suited for that sort of thing."

I looked at him for a moment, trying to decide if he was joking. "A first floor room will be fine, Master Kilvin. But I'll need a small smelter and a little extra room to breathe."

Kilvin muttered to himself, then brought out a key. "How much breathing will you be doing? Room twenty-seven is five hundred feet square."

"That should be plenty," I said. "I also might need permission to get precious metals from Stocks."

Kilvin chuckled at this, and nodded as he handed me the key. "I will see it is done, Re'lar Kvothe. I look forward to seeing what you will make for me."

It was galling that the schema I needed was restricted. But there are always other ways of finding information, and there are always people who know more than they are supposed to.

For example, I didn't doubt Manet knew how to make a gram. Everyone knew he was an E'lir in title only. But there was no way he would share the information with me against Kilvin's wishes. The University had been Manet's home for thirty years, and he was probably the only student who feared expulsion more than me.

This meant my options were limited. Other than a lengthy search of the Archives, I couldn't think of any way to get a schema on my own. So, after several minutes of wracking my brain for a better option, I made my way to the Bale and Barley.

The Bale was one of the more disreputable taverns this side of the river. Anker's wasn't seedy in the strictest sense, it simply lacked pretension. It was clean without smelling of flowers and inexpensive without being tawdry. People visited Anker's to eat, drink, listen to music, and occasionally have a friendly fight.

The Bale was several rungs farther down the ladder. It was grubbier, music was not a priority, and the fights were usually only recreational for one of the people involved.

Mind you, the Bale wasn't as bad as half the places in Tarbean. But it was the worst you were likely to find this close to the University. So despite being seedy, it had wooden floors and glass in the windows. And if you passed out drunk and woke up missing your purse, you could content yourself with the fact that nobody had knifed you and stolen your boots as well.

As it was still early in the day, there were a bare handful of people scattered around the common room. I was glad to see Sleat sitting in the back. I hadn't actually met him, but I knew who he was. I'd heard stories.

Sleat was one of the rare, indispensable people who have a knack for arranging things. From what I'd heard, he'd been a student on and off for the last ten years.

He was talking with a nervous-looking man at the moment, and I knew better than to interrupt. So I bought two mugs of short beer and made a pretense of drinking one while I waited.

Sleat was handsome, dark-haired and dark-eyed. Though he didn't have the characteristic beard, I expected he was at least half Cealdish. His body language screamed authority. He moved as if he were in control of everything around him.

Which wouldn't have surprised me, actually. He could own the Bale for all I knew. People like Sleat are no strangers to money.

Sleat and the anxious young man finally came to some sort of agreement. Sleat smiled warmly as they shook hands and clapped the man on the shoulder as he walked away.

I waited for a moment, then made my way over to his table. As I came closer, I noticed there was a stretch of open floor between his table and the others in the common room. It wasn't much, just enough so eavesdropping would be difficult.

Sleat looked up as I approached.

"I was wondering if we could talk," I said.

He made an expansive gesture to the empty chair. "This is a bit of a surprise," he said.

"Why's that?"

"I don't get a lot of clever folks paying me visits. I get desperate folks." He looked at the mugs. "Are those both for you?"

"You can have either or both." I nodded at the one on the right. "But I've already had my mouth on that one."

He looked at the mugs warily for a fraction of a second, then gave a wide, white smile and took the drink on the left. "From what I've heard, you're not the sort to poison a man."

"You seem to know a lot about me," I said.

His shrug was so casual I guessed he'd practiced it. "I know a lot about everyone," he said. "But I know more about you."

"Why's that?"

Sleat slouched forward, leaning on the table and speaking in a confidential tone. "Do you have any idea how boring your average student is? Half of them are rich tourists who don't care half a damn for their classes." He rolled his eyes and gestured as if throwing something over his shoulder. "The other half are bookish tits who have dreamed of this place so long they can hardly breathe once they're here. They walk on eggshells, meek as priests. Scared lest the masters cast a disapproving eye in their direction."

He sniffed disdainfully and leaned back in his seat. "Suffice to say you're a breath of fresh air. Everyone says . . ." He stopped and gave his practiced shrug again. "Well, you know."

"Actually, I don't," I admitted. "What do people say?"

Sleat gave me a sharp, beautiful smile. "Ah, that's the problem isn't it? Everyone knows a man's reputation except the man himself. For most men this isn't a bother. But some of us labor over our reputations. I have built mine brick by brick. It is a useful tool." He gave me a sly look. "I expect you understand what I am talking about."

I allowed myself a smile. "Perhaps."

"What do they say about me, then? Tell me and I'll return the favor."

"Well," I said. "You're good at finding things," I said. "You're discreet, but expensive."

He waved his hands, irritated. "Vagaries. Details are the bones of the story. Give me bones."

I thought. "I heard you managed to sell several vials of *Regim Ignaul Neratum* last term. *After* the fire in Kilvin's shop, where all of it was supposedly destroyed."

Sleat nodded, his expression giving away nothing.

"I heard you arranged to get a message to Veyane's father in Emlin despite the fact that there was a siege going on." Another nod. "You got a young prostitute working in Buttons a set of documents proving she was a distant bloodline cousin of the Baronet Gamre, allowing her to marry a certain young gentleman with minimal fuss."

Sleat smiled. "I was proud of that one."

"When you were an E'lir," I continued. "You were suspended for two terms on charges of Wrongful Apprehension. Two years later, you were fined and suspended again for Misuse of University Equipment in the Crucible. I've heard Jamison knows the sort of business you do, but he's paid to turn a blind eye. I don't believe the last one, by the way."

"Fair enough," he said easily. "Neither do I."

"Despite your extensive activities, you've only been brought up against the iron law once," I continued. "Transport of Contraband Substances, wasn't it?"

Sleat rolled his eyes. "You know the damnedest thing? I was actually innocent of that one. Heffron's boys paid off a constable to fake some evidence.

The charges were withdrawn after only two days." He scowled. "Not that the masters cared. All they gave a damn about was that I was out there besmirching the University's good name." His tone was bitter. "My tuition tripled after that."

I decided to push matters a bit. "Several months ago you poisoned a young earl's daughter with Venitasin and only gave her the antidote after she signed over the largest of the fiefdoms she stood to inherit. Then you staged it to look like she'd lost it playing a game of high-stakes faro."

He raised an eyebrow at this. "Do they say why?"

"No," I said. "I assumed she tried to default on her debt to you."

"There's some truth to that," he said. "Though it was a bit more complicated. And it wasn't Venitasin. That would be extraordinarily reckless." He looked offended and brushed at his sleeve, plainly irritated. "Anything else?"

I paused, trying to decide if I wanted to get confirmation about something I'd suspected for some time. "Only that last term you put Ambrose Jakis in touch with a pair of men who have been known to kill people for money."

Sleat's expression remained impassive, his body loose and relaxed. But I could see a slight tension in his shoulders. Very little escapes me when I'm watching closely. "They say that, do they?"

I gave a shrug that put his to shame. My shrug was so nonchalant it would make a cat jealous. "I'm a musician. I play three nights a span in a busy tavern. I hear all manner of things." I reached for my mug. "And what have you heard of me?"

"The same stories everyone else knows, of course. You convinced the masters to admit you to the University though you're just a pup, no offense. Then two days later you shame Master Hemme in his own classroom and get away bird free."

"Save for a whipping."

"Save for a whipping," he acknowledged. "During which you couldn't be bothered to cry out or bleed, even a little. I wouldn't believe that if there weren't several hundred witnesses."

"We drew a decent crowd," I said. "It was good weather for a whipping."

"I've heard some overly dramatic folk call you Kvothe the Bloodless because of it," he said. "Though I'm guessing part of that comes from the fact that you're Edema Ruh, which means you're about as far from a blooded noble as a person can be."

I smiled. "A bit of both, I expect."

He looked thoughtful. "I've heard you and Master Elodin fought in Haven. Vast and terrible magics were unleashed, and in the end he won by throwing you through a stone wall, then off the roof of the building."

"Do they say what we fought over?" I asked.

"All manner of things," he said dismissively. "An insult. A misunderstanding. You tried to steal his magic. He tried to steal your woman. Typical nonsense."

Sleat rubbed at his face. "Let me see. You play the lute passing well and are proud as a kicked cat. You are unmannerly, sharp-tongued, and show no respect for your betters, which is practically everyone given your lowly ravel birth."

I felt a flush of anger start in my face and sweep, hot and prickling, down the entire length of my body. "I am the best musician you will ever meet or see from a distance," I said with forced calm. "And I am Edema Ruh to my bones. That means my blood is red. It means I breathe the free air and walk where my feet take me. I do not cringe and fawn like a dog at a man's title. That looks like pride to people who have spent their lives cultivating supple spines."

Sleat gave a lazy smile, and I realized he'd been baiting me. "You also have a temper, so I've heard. And there's a whole boatload of other assorted nonsense floating around you as well. You only sleep an hour each night. You have demon blood. You can talk to the dead—"

I leaned forward, curious. That wasn't one of the rumors I'd started. "Really? Do I talk to spirits, or are they claiming I'm digging up bodies?"

"I'm assuming spirits," he said. "I haven't heard anyone mention grave robbing."

I nodded. "Anything else?"

"Only that you were cornered in an alley last term by two men who kill people for money. And despite the fact that they had knives and caught you quite unaware, you blinded one and beat the other senseless, calling down fire and lightning like Taborlin the Great."

We looked at each other for a long moment. It was not a comfortable silence. "Did you put Ambrose in touch with them?" I asked at last.

"That," Sleat said frankly, "is not a good question. It implies I discuss private dealings after the fact." He gave me a flat look, no hint of a smile anywhere near his mouth or eyes. "Besides, would you trust me to answer honestly?"

I frowned.

"I can say, however, that because of those stories, nobody is much interested in taking that sort of job again," Sleat said conversationally. "Not that there is much call for that sort of work around here to begin with. We're all terribly civilized."

"Not that you would know about it, even if it were going on."

His smile came back. "Exactly." He leaned forward. "Enough chatter then. What is it you're looking for?"

"I need a schema for a piece of artificing."

He set his elbows on the table. "And . . ."

"It contains sygaldry Kilvin restricts to those of El'the rank and higher."

Sleat nodded matter-of-factly. "And how quickly do you need it? Hours? Days?"

I thought about Wil and Sim staying up nights to watch over me. "Sooner is better."

Sleat looked thoughtful, his eyes unfocused. "It's going to cost, and there's no guarantee I'll be able to produce it on an exact schedule." He focused in on me. "Also, if you get caught you'll be charged with Wrongful Apprehension at the very least."

I nodded.

"And you know what the penalties are?"

"'For Wrongful Apprehension of the Arcane not leading to injury of another,'" I recited. "'The offending student may be fined no more than twenty talents, whipped no more than ten times, suspended from the Arcanum, or expelled from the University.'"

"They fined me the full twenty talents and suspended me two terms," Sleat said grimly. "And that was only some Re'lar-level alchemy. It will be worse with you if this is El'the-level stuff."

"How much?" I asked.

"To get hold of it in a few days . . ." He looked up at the ceiling for a moment. "Thirty talents."

I felt the bottom drop out of my stomach, but I kept my face composed. "Is there any room to negotiate that?"

He gave his sharp smile again, his teeth were very white. "I also deal in favors," he said. "But a thirty talent favor is going to be a big one." He looked at me thoughtfully. "We could perhaps work out something along those lines. But I feel obliged to mention that when I call a favor due, it's due. At that point, there isn't any negotiation."

I nodded calmly to show him I understood. But I felt a cold knot forming in my gut. This was a bad idea. I knew it in my bones.

"Do you owe anyone else?" Sleat asked. "And don't lie to me or I'll know."

"Six talents," I said casually. "Due at the end of the term."

He nodded. "I'm guessing you didn't manage to get it off some money-lender. Did you go to Heffron?"

I shook my head. "Devi."

For the first time in our conversation Sleat lost his composure, his charming smile fell away entirely. "Devi?" He pulled himself up in his chair, his body suddenly tense. "No. I don't think we can come to an arrangement. If you had cash it would be one thing." He shook his head. "But no. If Devi already owns a piece of you . . ."

His reaction chilled me, then I realized he was just angling for more money. "What if I were to borrow money from you so I could settle my debt with her?"

Sleat shook his head, regaining a piece of his shattered nonchalance. "That is the very definition of poaching," he said. "Devi has an ongoing interest in you. An investment." He took a drink and cleared his throat meaningfully. "She does not look kindly on other folk interfering where she's staked her claim."

I raised an eyebrow. "I guess I was taken in by your reputation," I said. "Silly of me, really."

His face creased into a frown. "What do you mean by that?"

I waved my hands dismissively. "Please, give me credit for being at least half as clever as you've heard," I said. "If you can't get what I want, just admit it. Don't waste my time by pricing things out of my reach or coming up with elaborate excuses."

Sleat seemed unsure if he should be offended. "What part of this seems elaborate to you?"

"Come now," I said. "You're willing to run against the laws of the University, risk the wrath of the masters, the constables, and the iron law of Atur. But a little slip of a girl makes your knees quivery?" I sniffed and mimicked the gesture he'd made before, pretending to ball something up and throw it away over my shoulder.

He looked at me for a moment, then burst out laughing. "Yes, that's exactly the case," he said, wiping tears of genuine amusement from his eyes. "Apparently I was fooled by your reputation too. If you think Devi is a little slip of a girl, you aren't nearly as clever as I thought."

Looking over my shoulder, Sleat nodded at someone I couldn't see and waved his hand dismissively. "Go on with you," he said. "I have business to do with rational people who know the true shape of the world. You're wasting my time."

I felt myself prickling with irritation, but forced myself to keep it off my face. "I also need a crossbow," I said.

He shook his head. "No, I've already told you. No loans or favors."

"I can offer goods in exchange."

He looked at me skeptically. "What sort of crossbow?"

"Any sort," I said. "It needn't be fancy. It just needs to work."

"Eight talents," he said.

I gave him a hard look. "Don't insult me. This is mundane contraband. I'll bet ten to a penny you can have one in two hours. If you try to gouge me, I'll just go over the river and get one from Heffron."

"Get one from Heffron and you'll have to carry it back from Imre," he said. "Constable would love seeing that."

I shrugged and began to get to my feet.

"Three talents and five," he said. "It'll be used, mind you. And a stirrup, not a crank."

I calculated in my head. "Will you accept an ounce of silver and a spool of finely drawn gold wire?" I asked, bringing them out from the pockets of my cloak.

Sleat's dark eyes unfocused slightly as he did his own internal calculations. "You drive a tight bargain." He picked up the spool of bright wire and the small ingot of silver. "There's a rain barrel behind the Grimsome Tannery. The crossbow will be there in fifteen minutes." He gave me an insulted look. "Two hours? You don't know anything about me at all."

———————

Hours later Fela emerged from the shelves in the Archives and caught me with one hand against the four-plate door. I wasn't pushing on it, exactly. Just pressing. Just checking to see if it was firmly closed. It was.

"I don't suppose they tell scrivs what's behind this?" I asked her without any hope.

"If they do, they haven't told me yet," Fela said, stepping close and reaching out to run her fingers along the grooves the letters made in the stone: *Valaritas.* "I had a dream about the door once," she said. "Valaritas was the name of an old dead king. His tomb was behind the door."

"Wow," I said. "That's better than the dreams I have about it."

"What are yours?" She asked.

"Once I dreamed I saw light through the keyholes," I said. "But mostly I'm just standing here, staring at it, trying to get in." I frowned at the door. "As if standing outside while I'm awake isn't frustrating enough, I do it while I'm asleep too."

Fela laughed softly at that, then turned away from the door to face me. "I got your note," she said. "What's the research project you were so vague about?"

"Let's go somewhere private to talk," I said. "It's a bit of a story."

We made our way to one of the reading holes, and once the door was closed I told her the whole story, embarrassments and all. Someone was practicing malfeasance against me. I couldn't go to the masters for fear of revealing I was the one who had broken into Ambrose's rooms. I needed a gram to protect myself, but I didn't know enough sygaldry to make one.

"Malfeasance," she said in a low voice, slowly shaking her head in dismay. "You're sure?"

I unbuttoned my shirt and took it down off my shoulder, revealing the dark bruise on my shoulder from the attack I'd only managed to partially stop.

She leaned in to look at it. "And you really don't know who it might be?"

"Not really," I said, trying not to think of Devi. I wanted to keep that particular bad decision to myself for now. "I'm sorry to drag you into this, but you're the only one . . ."

Fela waved her hands in negation. "None of that. I told you to ask if you ever needed a favor, and I'm glad you did."

"I'm glad you're glad," I said. "If you can get me through this, I'll owe you instead. I'm getting better at finding what I want in here, but I'm still new."

Fela nodded. "It takes years to learn your way around the Stacks. It's like a city."

I smiled. "That's how I think of it too. I haven't lived here long enough to learn all the shortcuts."

Fela grimaced a bit. "And I'm guessing you're going to need those. If Kilvin really believes the sygaldry is dangerous, most of the books you want will be in his private library."

I felt a sinking sensation in my stomach. "Private library?"

"All the masters have private libraries," Fela said matter-of-factly. "I know some alchemy so I help spot books with formulae Mandrag wouldn't want in the wrong hands. Scrivs who know sygaldry do the same for Kilvin."

"But this is pointless then," I said. "If Kilvin has all those books locked away there's no chance of finding what I'm looking for."

Fela smiled, shaking her head. "The system isn't perfect. Only about a third of the Archives are properly cataloged. What you're looking for is probably still in the Stacks somewhere. It's just a matter of finding it."

"I wouldn't even need a whole schema," I said. "If I just knew a few of the proper runes I could probably just fake the rest."

She gave me a worried look. "Is that really wise?"

"Wisdom is a luxury I can't afford," I said. "Wil and Sim have already been watching over me for two nights. They can't sleep in shifts for the next ten years."

Fela drew a deep breath then let it out slowly. "Right. We can start with the cataloged books first. Maybe what you need has slipped past the scrivs."

We collected several dozen books on sygaldry and closeted ourselves in an out-of-the-way reading hole on the fourth floor. Then we started going through them one at a time.

We began with hopes of finding a full-fledged schema for a gram, but as the hours slid by we lowered our hopes. If not a whole schema, perhaps we could find a description of one. Perhaps a reference to the sequence of runes used. The name of a single rune. A hint. A clue. A scrap. Some piece of the puzzle.

I closed the last of the books we had brought back to the reading hole. It made a solid thump as the pages settled together.

"Nothing?" she asked tiredly.

"Nothing." I rubbed my face with both hands. "So much for getting lucky."

Fela shrugged, grimacing halfway through the motion, then craned her head to one side to stretch a kink out of her neck. "It made sense to start in the most obvious places," she said. "But those will be the same places the scrivs have combed over for Kilvin. We'll just have to dig deeper."

I heard the distant sound of the belling tower and was surprised at how many times it struck. We'd been researching for over four hours. "You've missed your class," I said.

"It's just geometries," she said.

"You're a wonderful person," I said. "What's our best option now?"

"A long, slow trawl of the Stacks," she said. "But it's going to be like panning for gold. Dozens of hours, and that's with both of us working together so we don't overlap our efforts."

"I can bring in Wil and Sim to help," I said.

"Wilem works here," Fela said. "But Simmon's never been a scriv, he'll probably just get in the way."

I gave her an odd look. "Do you know Sim very well?"

"Not very," she admitted. "I've seen him around."

"You're underestimating him," I said. "People do it all the time. Sim's smart."

"Everyone here is smart," Fela said. "And Sim is nice, but . . ."

"That's the problem," I said. "He's nice. He's gentle, which people see as weak. And he's happy, which people see as stupid."

"I didn't mean it like that," Fela said.

"I know," I said, rubbing at my face. "I'm sorry. It's been a bad couple of days. I thought the University would be different than the rest of the world, but it's just like everywhere else: people cater to pompous, rude bastards like Ambrose, while the good souls like Simmon get brushed off as simpletons."

"Which one are you?" Fela said with a smile as she began to stack up the books. "Pompous bastard or good soul?"

"I'll research that later," I said. "Right now I've got more pressing concerns."

CHAPTER TWENTY-SIX

Trust

WHILE I WAS FAIRLY sure Devi wasn't behind the malfeasance, I'd have to be a fool to ignore the fact that she had my blood. So when it became clear that making a gram was going to require a great deal of time and energy, I realized the time had come to pay her a visit and make sure she wasn't responsible.

It was a miserable day: chill with a clammy wind that cut through my clothes. I didn't own gloves or a hat, and had to settle for putting up my hood and wrapping my hands in the fabric of my cloak as I pulled it more tightly around my shoulders.

As I crossed Stonebridge a new thought occurred to me: maybe someone had stolen my blood from Devi. That made better sense than anything else. I needed to make sure the bottle with my blood was safe. If she still had it, and it hadn't been tampered with, I'd know she wasn't involved.

I made my way to the western edge of Imre where I stopped at a tavern to buy a small beer and warm myself by their fire. Then I walked through the now familiar alley and up the narrow staircase behind the butcher's shop. Despite the chill and recent rain, the smell of rancid fat still hung in the air.

I took a deep breath and knocked on the door.

It opened after a minute, then Devi's face peered through a narrow crack in the door. "Well hello," she said. "Are you here for business or pleasure?"

"Business mostly," I admitted.

"Pity." She opened the door wider.

As I came into the room I tripped on the threshold, stumbling clumsily into her and resting one hand briefly on her shoulder as I steadied myself. "Sorry," I said, embarrassed.

"You look like hell," she said as she bolted the door. "I hope you're not looking for more money. I don't lend to folks who look like they're coming off a three-day drunk."

I settled wearily into a chair. "I brought back your book." I said, bringing it out from under my cloak and laying it on her desk.

She nodded at it, smiling a bit. "What did you think of good old Malcaf?"

"Dry. Wordy. Boring."

"There weren't any pictures either," she said dryly. "But that's beside the point."

"His theories about perception as an active force were interesting," I admitted. "But he writes like he's afraid someone might actually understand him."

Devi nodded, her mouth pursed. "That's about what I thought too." She reached across the desk and slid the book closer to herself. "What did you think about the chapter on proprioception?"

"He seemed to be arguing from a deep well of ignorance," I said. "I've met people in the Medica with amputated limbs. I don't think Malcaf ever has."

I watched her for some sign of guilt, some indication she'd been practicing malfeasance against me. But there was nothing. She seemed perfectly normal, cheery and sharp-tongued as ever. But I had grown up among actors. I know how many ways there are to hide your true feelings.

Devi made an exaggerated frown. "You look so serious over there. What are you thinking?"

"I had a couple of questions," I said evasively. I wasn't looking forward to this. "Not about Malcaf."

"I'm so tired of being appreciated for my intellect." She leaned back and stretched her arms over her head. "When will I be able to find a nice boy who just wants me for my body?" She gave a luxurious stretch, but stopped halfway through, giving me a puzzled look. "I'm waiting for a quip here. You're usually quicker than this."

I gave her a weak smile. "I've got a lot on my mind. I don't think I can match wits with you today."

"I never suspected you could match wits with me," she said. "But I do like a little banter now and then." She leaned forward and folded her hands on the top of the desk. "What sort of questions?"

"Did you do much sygaldry in the University?"

"Personal questions." She raised an eyebrow. "No. I didn't care for it. Too much fiddling around for my taste."

"You don't seem to be the sort of woman who'd mind a little fiddling around," I said, managing a weak smile.

"That's more like it," she said with approval. "I knew you had it in you."

"I don't suppose you have any books on advanced sygaldry?" I asked. "The sort of things they don't allow a Re'lar access to?"

Devi shook her head. "No. I've got some nice alchemical texts though. Stuff you'd never find in your precious Archives." Bitterness was thick in her voice when she said the last word.

That's when it all came together in my head. Devi wouldn't ever be so careless as to let someone steal my blood. She wouldn't sell it to turn a quick profit. She didn't need the money. She didn't have a grudge against me.

But Devi would sell her eyeteeth to get into the Archives.

"It's funny you should mention alchemy," I said as calmly as possible. "Have you ever heard of something called a plum bob?"

"I've heard of it," she said easily. "Nasty little thing. I think I have the formula." She turned in her seat a little, facing toward the shelf. "You interested in seeing it?"

Her face didn't betray her, but with enough practice, anyone can control their face. Her body language didn't give her away either. There was only the slightest tension in her shoulders, only a hint of hesitation.

It was her eyes. When I mentioned the plum bob, I saw a flicker there. Not just recognition. Guilt. Of course. She'd sold the formula to Ambrose.

And why wouldn't she? Ambrose was a high-ranking scriv. He could sneak her into the Archives. Hell, with the resources at his disposal, he might not even have to do that. Everyone knew Lorren occasionally granted non-arcanum scholars access to the Archives, especially if their patrons were willing to pave the way with a generous donation. Ambrose had once bought an entire inn just to spite me. How much more would he be willing to pay to get hold of my blood?

No. Wil and Sim had been right about that. Ambrose wasn't the sort to get his hands dirty if he could avoid it. Much simpler for him to hire Devi to do his dirty work for him. She'd already been expelled. She had nothing to lose and all the secrets of the Archives to gain.

"No thanks," I said. "I don't do much alchemy." I took a deep breath and decided to jump right to the point. "But I do need to see my blood."

Devi's cheery expression froze on her face. Her mouth still smiled, but her eyes were cold. "I beg your pardon?" It wasn't really a question.

"I need to see the blood I left here with you," I said. "I need to know it's safe."

"I'm afraid that's not possible." Her smile fell completely away, and her mouth made a thin, flat line. "That's not how I do business. Besides, do you think I'd be stupid enough to keep that sort of thing here?"

I felt a sinking sensation in my gut, still not wanting to believe it. "We can go to wherever you keep it," I said calmly. "Someone has been conducting malfeasance against me. I need to make sure it hasn't been tampered with. That's all."

"As if I would just show you where I keep that sort of thing," Devi said with scathing sarcasm. "Have you been struck in the head or something?"

"I'm afraid I must insist."

"Go ahead and be afraid," Devi said with a glare. "Go ahead and insist. It won't make any difference."

It was her. There was no other reason for her to keep it from me. "If you refuse to show me," I continued, trying to keep my voice level and calm. "I must assume you've sold my blood, or made your own mommet of me for some reason."

Devi leaned back in her chair and crossed her arms with deliberate nonchalance. "You can assume whatever stupid thing pleases you. You'll see your blood when you settle your debt with me, and not one moment sooner."

I brought out a wax doll from underneath my cloak and rested my hand on the desk so she could see it.

"Is that supposed to be me?" she said. "With hips like that?" But the words were just the shell of a joke, a reflex action. Her tone was flat and angry. Her eyes were hard.

With my other hand I brought out a short strawberry-blond hair and fixed it to the doll's head. Devi's hand went unconsciously to her own hair, her expression shocked.

"Someone has been attacking me," I said. "I need to make sure my blood is—"

This time when I mentioned my blood, I saw her eyes flicker to one of her desk's drawers. Her fingers twitched slightly.

I met her eye. "Don't," I said grimly.

Devi's hand darted to the drawer, yanking it open.

I didn't doubt for a second that the drawer held the mommet she'd made of me. I couldn't let her get hold of it. I concentrated and murmured a binding.

Devi's hand came to a jarring halt halfway to the open drawer.

I hadn't done anything to hurt her. No fire, no pain, nothing like what she'd done to me over the last several days. It was just a binding to keep her motionless. When I'd stopped at the tavern to warm myself, I'd taken a pinch of ash from their fireplace. It wasn't a great source, and it was farther away than I'd like, but it was better than nothing.

Still, I could probably only hold her like this for a few minutes before I drew so much heat from the fire that I extinguished it. But that should be enough time for me to get the truth out of her and reclaim the mommet she'd made.

Devi's eyes grew wild as she struggled to move. "How dare you!" she shouted. "How dare you!"

"How dare *you!*" I spat back angrily. "I can't believe I trusted you! I defended you to my friends—" I trailed off as the unthinkable happened. Despite my binding, Devi started to move, her hand inching its way into the open drawer.

I concentrated harder and Devi's hand came to a halt. Then, slowly, it began to creep forward again, disappearing into the drawer. I couldn't believe it.

"You think you can come in here and threaten me?" Devi hissed, her face a mask of rage. "You think I can't take care of myself? I made Re'lar before they threw me out, you little slipstick. I earned it. My Alar is like the ocean in storm." Her hand was almost completely inside the drawer now.

I felt a clammy sweat break out across my forehead and broke my mind three more times. I murmured again and each piece of my mind made a separate binding, focusing on keeping her still. I drew heat from my body, feeling the cold crawl up my arms as I bore down on her. That was five bindings in all. My outside limit.

Devi went motionless as stone, and she chuckled deep in her throat, grinning. "Oh you're *very* good. I almost believe the stories about you now. But what makes you think you can do what even Elxa Dal couldn't? Why do you think they expelled me? They feared a woman who could match a master by her second year." Sweat made her pale hair cling to her forehead. She clenched her teeth, her pixie face savage with determination. Her hand began to move again.

Then, with a sudden burst of motion she yanked her hand out of the drawer as if pulling it free from thick mud. She slammed something round and metallic down on the top of the desk, making the lamp's flame leap and stutter. It wasn't a mommet. It wasn't a bottle of my blood.

"You bastard," she said, almost chanting the words. "You think I'm not ready for this sort of thing? You think you're the first to try and take advantage of me?" She twisted the top of the grey metal sphere. It gave a distinct *click* and she drew her hand slowly away. Despite my best efforts, I couldn't keep her still.

That's when I recognized the device she'd brought out of the drawer. I'd studied them with Manet last term. Kilvin referred to them as "self-contained exothermic accelerators," but everyone else called them pocket warmers or poor-boys.

They held kerosene, or naphtha, or sugar. Once activated, a poor-boy burned the fuel inside, pouring out as much heat as a forge fire for about five minutes. Then it needed to be dismantled, cleaned, and refilled. They were messy and dangerous and tended to break easily because of the rapid heating and cooling. But for a short time, they gave a sympathist a bonfire's worth of energy.

I lowered myself into the Heart of Stone and splintered off another piece of my mind, murmuring the binding. Then I tried for a seventh and failed. I was tired, and I hurt. The cold was leeching up my arms, and I had been through so much in the last few days. But I clenched my teeth and forced myself to murmur the words under my breath.

Devi didn't even seem to notice the sixth binding. Moving as slowly as the hand of a clock, she pulled a loose thread free from her sleeve. The poor-boy made a groaning, metallic creak and heat began to roll off it in shimmering waves.

"I don't have a decent link to you right now," Devi said, as the hand holding the thread moved slowly back toward the poor-boy. "But if you don't loose your binding, I'll use this to burn every scrap of clothing off your body, and smile while you scream."

It's strange what thoughts flash into your head in these situations. The first thing I thought of wasn't being horribly burned. It was that the cloak Fela had given me would be ruined, and I'd be left with only two shirts.

My eyes darted to the top of Devi's desk where the varnish was already starting to blister in a ring around the poor-boy. I could feel the heat radiating against my face.

I know when I'm beaten. I broke the bindings, my mind reeling as the pieces slid back together.

Devi rolled her shoulders. "Let go of it," she said.

I opened my hand and the wax doll toppled drunkenly onto the desk. I sat with my hands in my lap and remained very still, not wanting to startle or threaten her in any way.

Devi stood up and leaned across the desk. She reached out and ran a hand through my hair, then made a fist, tearing some away. I yelped despite myself.

Sitting back down, Devi picked up the doll and replaced her hair with several of my own. She muttered a binding.

"Devi, you don't understand," I said. "I just needed to—"

When I had bound Devi, I had focused on her arms and legs. It's the most efficient way to restrain someone. I'd had limited heat to work with and couldn't waste energy on anything else.

But Devi had heat to spare right now, and her binding was like being shut in an iron vise. I couldn't move my arms or legs, or jaw, or tongue. I could barely breathe, only taking tiny, shallow breaths that didn't require any movement of my chest. It was horrifying, like having someone's hand around my heart.

"I trusted you." Devi's voice was low and rough, like a fine-toothed surgeon's saw cutting away an amputated leg. "I *trusted* you." She gave me a look that was pure fury and loathing. "I actually had someone come here, looking to buy your blood. Fifty-five talents. I turned him away. I denied even knowing you because you and I had a business relationship. I stick to the bargains I make."

Who? I wanted to shout. But I could only make an inarticulate *huuu huuu* sound.

Devi looked at the wax doll she held, then at the poor-boy charring a dark ring into the top of her desk. "Our business relationship is now over," she said tightly. "I am calling your debt due. You have until the end of the term to get me my money. Nine talents. If you are one half-breath late, I will sell your blood to recover my investment and wash my hands of you."

She eyed me coldly. "This is better than you deserve. I still have your blood. If you go to the masters at the University or the constable in Imre, it will end badly for you."

Smoke was curling up from the desk now, and Devi moved her hand to hold the mommet over the creaking metal of the poor-boy. She murmured, and I felt a prickle of heat wash over my whole body. It felt exactly like the sudden fevers that had been plaguing me for days.

"When I release this binding, you will say, 'I understand, Devi.' Then you will leave. At the end of the term, you will send someone with the money you owe. You will not come yourself. I do not ever want to see you again."

Devi looked at me with such contempt that I cringe to remember it. Then she spat on me, tiny flecks of saliva striking the poor-boy and hissing into steam. "If I glimpse you again, even out of the corner of my eye, it will end badly for you."

She lifted the wax mommet over her head, then brought it down sharply on the desk with her hand flat on top of it. If I'd been able to flinch or cry out in panic, I would have.

The mommet shattered, arms and legs breaking away, the head skittering off to roll across the desk and onto the floor. I felt a sudden, jarring impact, as if I'd fallen several feet and landed flat on a stone floor. It was startling, but nowhere near as bad as it could have been. Through the terror, some small part of me marveled at her precision and control.

The binding that held me fell away, and I drew a deep breath. "I understand, Devi," I said. "But can—"

"Get OUT!" she shouted.

I got out. I would like to say it was a dignified exit, but that would not be the truth.

CHAPTER TWENTY-SEVEN

Pressure

W**IL AND SIM WERE** waiting for me in the back corner of Anker's. I brought over two mugs of beer and a tray laden with fresh bread and butter, cheese and fruit, and bowls of hot soup, thick with beef and turnip.

Wilem rubbed one eye with the palm of his hand. He looked a little peaked under his dark Cealdish complexion, but other than that he didn't seem much the worse for three nights of short sleep. "What's the occasion?"

"I just want to help you two keep your energy up," I said.

"Way ahead of you," Sim said. "I had a refreshing nap during my sublimation lecture." His eyes were a little dark around the edges, but he didn't seem much the worse for wear either.

Wilem began to load up his plate. "You mentioned you had news. What sort of news?"

"It's mixed," I said. "Which do you want first, good or bad?"

"Bad news first," Simmon said.

"Kilvin won't give me the plans I need to make my own gram. It's the sygaldry involved. Runes for blood and bone and such. He feels they're too dangerous to be taught to Re'lar."

Simmon looked curious. "Did he say why?"

"He didn't," I admitted. "But I can guess. I could use them to make all manner of unpleasant things. Like a little metal disk with a hole in it. Then, if you put a drop of someone's blood in it, you could use it to burn them alive."

"God, that's awful," Sim said, setting down his spoon. "Do you ever have any nice thoughts?"

"Anyone in the Arcanum could do the same thing with basic sympathy," Wilem pointed out.

"There's a big difference," I said. "Once I made that device, *anyone* could use it. Again and again."

"That's insane," Simmon said. "Why would anyone make anything like that?"

"Money," Wilem said grimly. "People do stupid things for money all the time." He gave me a significant look. "Such as borrowing from bloodthirsty *gattesors*."

"Which brings me to my second piece of news," I said uncomfortably. "I confronted Devi."

"Alone?" Simmon said. "Are you stupid?"

"Yes," I said. "But not for the reasons you think. Things got unpleasant, but now I know she wasn't responsible for the attacks."

Wilem frowned. "If not her, then who?"

"There's only one thing that makes sense," I said. "It's Ambrose."

Wil shook his head. "We've already gone through this. Ambrose would never risk it. He—"

I held up a hand to stop him. "He'd never risk malfeasance against *me*," I agreed. "But I don't think he knows who he's attacking."

Wilem closed his mouth and looked thoughtful.

I continued. "Think about it. If Ambrose suspected it was me, he'd bring me up on charges in front of the masters. He's done it before." I rubbed my wounded arm. "They'd discover my injuries and I'd be caught."

Wil looked down at the tabletop. *"Kraem,"* he said. "It makes sense. He might suspect you of hiring a thief, but not that you'd break in yourself. He'd never do something like that."

I nodded. "He's probably trying to find the person who broke into his rooms. Or just get a little easy revenge. That explains why the attacks have been getting stronger. He probably thinks the thief ran off to Imre or Tarbean."

"We've got to go to the masters with this," Simmon said. "They can search his rooms tonight. He'll be expelled for this, and whipped." A wide, vicious grin spread over his face. "God, I'd pay ten talents if I got to hold the lash."

I chuckled at his bloodthirsty tone. It took a lot to get on Sim's bad side, but once you made it there was no going back. "We can't, Sim."

Sim gave me a look of sheer disbelief. "You can't be serious. He can't get away with this."

"I'd get expelled for breaking into his rooms in the first place. Conduct Unbecoming."

"They wouldn't expel you for that," Sim said, but his voice was far from certain.

"I'm not willing to take the risk," I said. "Hemme hates me. Brandeur follows Hemme's lead. I'm still in Lorren's bad books."

"And somehow he still finds the strength to pun," Wilem muttered.

"That's three votes against me right there."

"I think you don't give Lorren enough credit," Wilem said. "But you're right. They'd expel you. If for no other reason, they'd do it to smooth things over with Baron Jakis."

Sim looked at Wilem. "You really think so?"

Wil nodded. "It's possible they wouldn't even expel Ambrose," he said grimly. "He's Hemme's favorite, and the masters know the trouble his father could make for the University." Wil snorted. "Think of the trouble Ambrose could make when he inherits." Wilem lowered his eyes and shook his head. "I'm with Kvothe on this one, Sim."

Simmon gave a great, weary sigh. "Wonderful," he said. Then he looked up at me with narrow eyes. "I told you," he said. "I told you to leave Ambrose alone from the very beginning. Getting into a fight with him is like stepping into a bear trap."

"A bear trap?" I said thoughtfully.

He nodded firmly. "Your foot goes in easy enough, but you're never getting it out again."

"A bear trap," I repeated. "That's exactly what I need."

Wilem chuckled darkly.

"I'm serious," I said. "Where can I get a bear trap?"

Wil and Sim looked at me strangely, and I decided not to push my luck. "Just a joke," I lied, not wanting to complicate things any further. I could find one on my own.

"We need to be sure it's Ambrose," Wilem said.

I nodded. "If he's locked away in his rooms the next few times I'm attacked, that should be evidence enough."

The conversation lapsed a bit, and for a couple of minutes we ate quietly, each of us tangled in our own thoughts.

"Okay," Simmon said, seeming to have reached some conclusion. "Nothing's really changed. You still need a gram. Right?" He looked at Wil, who nodded, then back to me. "Now hurry up with the good news before I kill myself."

I smiled. "Fela has agreed to help me search the Archives for the schema." I gestured toward the two of them. "If the two of you care to join us, it will mean long, grueling hours in close contact with the most beautiful woman this side of the Omethi River."

"I might be able to spare some time," Wilem said casually.

Simmon grinned.

———————

Thus began our search of the Archives.

Surprisingly, it was fun at first, almost like a game. The four of us would scatter to different sections of the Archives then return and comb through the books as a group. We spent hours chatting and joking, enjoying the challenge and one another's company.

But as hours turned into days of fruitless searching, the excitement burned away, leaving only a grim determination. Wil and Sim continued to watch over me at night, protecting me with their Alar. Night after night they lost sleep, making them sullen and irritable. I cut my sleep down to five hours a night to make things easier for them.

Under ordinary circumstances, five hours of sleep would be a great plenty for me, but I was still recovering from my injuries. What's more, I needed to constantly maintain the Alar that kept me safe. It was mentally exhausting.

On the third day of our search I nodded off while studying my metallurgy. I only dozed for half a minute before my head lolled, startling me awake. But the icy fear followed me for the rest of the day. If Ambrose had attacked at that moment, I could have been killed.

So, even though I couldn't afford it, I began dipping into my thinning purse to buy coffee. Many of the inns and cafes near the University catered to noble tastes, so it was readily available, but coffee is never cheap. Nahlrout would have been less expensive, but it had harsher side effects that I didn't want to risk.

In between bouts of research, we set about confirming my suspicions that Ambrose was responsible for the attacks. In this, if nothing else, we were lucky. Wil watched Ambrose return to his room after his rhetoric lecture, and at the same time I was forced to stave off binder's chills. Fela watched him finish a late lunch and return to his rooms, and a quarter hour later I felt a sweaty prickle of heat along my back and arms.

Later that evening I watched him head back to his rooms in the Golden Pony after his shift in the Archives. Not long after, I felt the faint pressure in both my shoulders that let me know he was trying to stab me. After the shoulders, there followed several other prods in a more personal area.

Wil and Sim agreed that it couldn't be coincidence: it was Ambrose. Best of all, it let us know that whatever Ambrose was using against me, he kept it in his rooms.

CHAPTER TWENTY-EIGHT

Kindling

THE ATTACKS WEREN'T PARTICULARLY frequent, but they came with no warning.

On the fifth day after we started searching for the schema, when Ambrose must have been feeling particularly cussed or bored, there were eight of them: one as I was waking up in Wilem's room, two during lunch, two while I was studying physiognomy in the Medica, then three in quick succession while I was coldsmithing iron in the Fishery.

The next day there were no attacks at all. In some ways that was worse. Nothing but hours of waiting for the other shoe to drop.

So I learned to maintain an iron-hard Alar as I ate and bathed, as I attended class and had conversations with my teachers and friends. I even maintained it while dueling in Adept Sympathy. On the seventh day of our search, this distraction and my general exhaustion led to my first defeat at the hands of two of my classmates, ending my perfect string of undefeated duels.

I could say that I was too weary to care, but that wouldn't be entirely true.

———

On the ninth day of our search Wilem, Simmon, and I were combing through books in our reading hole when the door opened and Fela slipped inside. She was carrying a single book instead of her usual armload. She was breathing heavily.

"I've got it," she said, her eyes bright. Her voice so excited it was almost fierce. "I found a copy." She thrust the book out at us so we could read the gold leaf on the thick leather spine: *Facci-Moen ve Scrivani*.

We had learned about the *Scrivani* early in our search. It was an exten-sive collection of schemata by a long-dead Artificer named Surthur. Twelve thick volumes of detailed diagrams and descriptions. When we found the index, we had thought our search was nearly finished, as it listed "Diagrames Detailing the Construction of a Marvelous Five-Gramme, proven most Effectatious in the Preventing of Maleficent Sympathe." Location: volume nine, page eighty-two.

We tracked down eight versions of the *Scrivani* in the Archives, but we never found the whole set. Volumes seven, nine, and eleven were always missing, no doubt tucked away in Kilvin's private library.

We'd spent two entire days searching before finally giving up on the *Scrivani*. But now Fela had found it, not just a piece to the puzzle, but the whole thing.

"Is it the right one?" Simmon asked, his voice a mixture of excitement and disbelief.

Fela slowly removed her hand from the lower binding, revealing in bright gold: *9.*

I scrambled up out of my chair, almost knocking it over in my rush to get to her. But she smiled and held the book high over her head. "First you have to promise me dinner," she said.

I laughed and reached for the book. "Once this is over, I'll take everyone to dinner."

She sighed. "And you have to tell me I'm the best scriv ever."

"You're the best scriv ever," I said. "You're twice as good as Wil could ever be, even if he had a dozen hands and a hundred extra eyes."

"Ick." She handed me the book. "Here you go."

I hurried to the table and cracked the book open.

"The pages will be missing, or something like that," Simmon said in a low voice to Wil. "It can't be this easy after all this time. I know something's going to spike our wheel."

I stopped turning pages and rubbed my eyes. I squinted at the writing.

"I knew it," Sim said, he leaned his chair back on two legs, covering his tired eyes with his hands. "Let me guess, it's got the grey rot. Or bookworm, or both."

Fela stepped close and looked over my shoulder. "Oh no!" she said mournfully. "I didn't even look. I was so excited." She looked up at us. "Do any of you read Eld Vintic?"

"I read the chittering gibberish you people call Aturan," Wilem said sourly. "I consider myself sufficiently multilingual."

"Only a smattering," I said. "A few dozen words."

"I can," Sim said.

"Really?" I felt hope rising in my chest again. "When did you pick that up?"

Sim scooted his chair across the floor until he could look at the book. "My first term as an E'lir I heard some Eld Vintic poetry. I studied it for three terms with the Chancellor."

"I've never cared for poetry," I said.

"Your loss," Sim said absently as he turned a few pages. "Eld Vintic poetry is thunderous. It pounds at you."

"What's the meter like?" I asked, curious despite myself.

"I don't know anything about meter," Simmon said distractedly as he ran a finger down the page in front of him. "It's like this:

Sought we the Scrivani word-work of Surthur
Long-lost in ledger all hope forgotten.
Yet fast-found for friendship fair the book-bringer
Hot comes the huntress Fela, flushed with finding
Breathless her breast her high blood rising
To ripen the red-cheek rouge-bloom of beauty.

"That sort of thing," Simmon said absently, his eyes still scanning the pages in front of him.

I saw Fela turn her head to look at Simmon, almost as if she were surprised to see him sitting there.

No, it was almost as if up until that point, he'd just been occupying space around her, like a piece of furniture. But this time when she looked at him, she took all of him in. His sandy hair, the line of his jaw, the span of his shoulders beneath his shirt. This time when she looked, she actually *saw* him.

Let me say this. It was worth the whole awful, irritating time spent searching the Archives just to watch that moment happen. It was worth blood and the fear of death to see her fall in love with him. Just a little. Just the first faint breath of love, so light she probably didn't notice it herself. It wasn't dramatic, like some bolt of lightning with a crack of thunder following. It was more like when flint strikes steel and the spark fades almost too fast for you to see. But still, you know it's there, down where you can't see, kindling.

"Who read you Eld Vintic poetry?" Wil asked. Fela blinked and turned back to the book.

"Puppet," Sim said. "The first time I met him."

"Puppet!" Wil looked as if he would tear out his own hair. "God pound me, why haven't we gone to him about this? If there's an Aturan translation of this book he'll know where it is!"

"I've thought the same thing a hundred times these last few days," Simmon said. "But he hasn't been doing well lately. He wouldn't be much help."

"And Puppet knows what's on the restricted list," Fela said. "I doubt he'd just hand something like that over."

"Does everyone know this Puppet person except for me?" I asked.

"Scrivs do," Wilem said.

"I think I can piece most of this together," Simmon said, turning to look in my direction. "Does this diagram make any sense to you? It's perfect nonsense to me."

"Those are the runes." I pointed. "Clear as day. And those are metallurgical symbols." I looked closer. "The rest . . . I don't know. Maybe abbreviations. We can probably work them out as we go along."

I smiled and turned to Fela. "Congratulations, you're still the best scriv ever."

———

With Simmon's help, it took me two days to decipher the diagrams in the *Scrivani*. Rather, it took us one day to decipher and one day to double and triple check our work.

Once I knew how to construct my gram, I began to play a strange sort of hide-and-seek with Ambrose. I needed the entirety of my concentration free while I worked on the sygaldry for the gram. That meant letting my guard down. So I could only work on the gram when I was certain Ambrose was otherwise occupied.

The gram was delicate work, small engraving with no margin for error. And it didn't help that I was forced to steal the time in bits and pieces. Half an hour while Ambrose was drinking coffee with a young woman in a public café. Forty minutes when he was attending a symbolic logic lecture. A full hour and a half while he was working at the front desk in the Archives.

When I couldn't work on my gram, I labored on my pet project. In some ways I was fortunate Kilvin had charged me with making something worthy of a Re'lar. It gave me the perfect excuse for all the time I spent in the Fishery.

The rest of the time I spent lounging in the common room of the Golden Pony. I needed to establish myself as a regular customer there. Things would seem less suspicious that way.

CHAPTER TWENTY-NINE

Stolen

EVERY NIGHT I RETIRED to my tiny garret room in Anker's. Then I would lock the door, climb out the window, and slip into either Wil or Sim's room, depending on who was keeping first watch over me that night.

Bad as things were, I knew they would become infinitely worse if Ambrose realized I was the one who had broken into his rooms. While my injuries were healing, they were still more than enough to incriminate me. So I worked hard to keep up the appearance of normality.

Thus it was that late one night, I trudged into Anker's with all the nimble vigor of a shamble-man. I made a weak attempt at small talk with Anker's new serving girl, then grabbed half a loaf of bread before disappearing up the stairs.

A minute later I was back in the taproom. I was covered in a panicked sweat, my heart was thundering in my ears.

The girl looked up. "You change your mind about that drink then?" she smiled.

I shook my head so quickly my hair whipped around my face. "Did I leave my lute down here last night after I finished playing?" I asked frantically.

She shook her head. "You carried it off, same as always. Remember I asked if you needed a bit of string to hold the case together?"

I darted back up the steps, quick as a fish. Then was back again in less than a minute. "Are you sure?" I asked, breathing hard. "Could you look behind the bar, just to be sure?"

She looked, but the lute wasn't there. It wasn't in the pantry either. Or the kitchen.

I climbed the stairs and opened the door to my tiny room. There weren't many places a lute case could fit in a room that size. It wasn't under the bed. It wasn't leaning on the wall next to my small desk. It wasn't behind the door.

The lute case was too large to fit in the old trunk by the foot of the bed. But I looked anyway. It wasn't in the trunk. I looked under the bed again, just to be sure. It wasn't under the bed.

Then I looked at the window. At the simple latch I kept well-oiled so I could trip it while standing on the roof outside.

I looked behind the door again. The lute wasn't behind the door. Then I sat on the bed. If I had been weary before, then I was something else entirely now. I felt like I was made of wet paper. I felt like I could barely breathe, like someone had stolen my heart out of my chest.

CHAPTER THIRTY

More Than Salt

"TODAY," ELODIN SAID BRIGHTLY, "we will talk about things that cannot be talked about. Specifically, we will discuss why some things cannot be discussed."

I sighed and set down my pencil. Every day I hoped this class would be the one where Elodin actually taught us something. Every day I brought a hardback and one of my few precious pieces of paper, ready to take advantage of the moment of clarity. Every day some part of me expected Elodin to laugh and admit he'd just been testing our resolve with his endless nonsense.

And every day I was disappointed.

"The majority of important things cannot be said outright," Elodin said. "They cannot be made explicit. They can only be implied." He looked out at his handful of students in the otherwise empty lecture hall. "Name something that cannot be explained." He pointed at Uresh. "Go."

Uresh considered for a moment. "Humor. If you explain a joke, it isn't a joke."

Elodin nodded, then pointed at Fenton.

"Naming?" Fenton asked.

"That is a cheap answer, Re'lar," Elodin said with a hint of reproach. "But you correctly anticipate the theme of my lecture, so we will let it slide." He pointed at me.

"There isn't anything that can't be explained," I said firmly. "If something can be understood, it can be explained. A person might not be able to do a good job of explaining it. But that just means it's hard, not that it's impossible."

Elodin held up a finger. "Not hard or impossible. Merely pointless. Some things can only be inferred." He gave me an infuriating smile. "By the way, your answer should have been 'music.'"

"Music explains itself," I said. "It is the road, and it is the map that shows the road. It is both together."

"But can you explain how music works?" Elodin asked.

"Of course," I said. Though I wasn't sure of any such thing.

"Can you explain how music works without using music?"

That brought me up short. While I was trying to think of a response, Elodin turned to Fela.

"Love?" she asked.

Elodin raised an eyebrow as if mildly scandalized by this, then nodded approvingly.

"Hold on a moment," I said. "We're not done. I don't know if I could explain music without using it, but that's beside the point. That's not explanation, it's translation."

Elodin's face lit up. "That's it exactly!" he said. "Translation. All explicit knowledge is translated knowledge, and all translation is imperfect."

"So all explicit knowledge is imperfect?" I asked. "Tell Master Brandeur geometry is subjective. I'd love to watch that discussion."

"Not all knowledge," Elodin admitted. "But most."

"Prove it," I said.

"You can't prove nonexistence," Uresh interjected in a matter-of-fact way. He sounded exasperated. "Flawed logic."

I ground my teeth at that. It was flawed logic. I never would have made that mistake if I'd been better rested. "Demonstrate it then," I said.

"Fine, fine." Elodin walked over to where Fela sat. "We'll use Fela's example." He took her hand and pulled her to her feet, motioning me to follow.

I came reluctantly to my feet as well and Elodin arranged the two of us so we stood facing each other in profile to the class. "Here we have two lovely young people," he said. "Their eyes meet across the room."

Elodin pushed my shoulder and I stumbled forward half a step. "He says hello. She says hello. She smiles. He shifts uneasily from foot to foot." I stopped doing just that and there was a faint murmur of laughter from the others.

"There is something ephemeral in the air," Elodin said, moving to stand behind Fela. He put his hands on her shoulders, leaning close to her ear. "She loves the lines of him," he said softly. "She is curious about the shape of his mouth. She wonders if this could be the one, if she could unclasp the secret pieces of her heart to him." Fela looked down, her cheeks flushing a bright scarlet.

Elodin stalked around to stand behind me. "Kvothe looks at her, and for the first time he understands the impulse that first drove men to paint. To sculpt. To sing."

He circled us again, eventually standing between us like a priest about to perform a wedding. "There exists between them something tenuous and delicate. They can both feel it. Like static in the air. Faint as frost."

He looked me full in the face. His dark eyes serious. "Now. What do you do?"

I looked back at him, utterly lost. If there was one thing I knew less about than naming, it was courting women.

"There are three paths here," Elodin said to the class. He held up one finger. "First. Our young lovers can try to express what they feel. They can try to play the half-heard song their hearts are singing."

Elodin paused for effect. "This is the path of the honest fool, and it will go badly. This thing between you is too tremulous for talk. It is a spark so faint that even the most careful breath might snuff it out."

Master Namer shook his head. "Even if you are clever and have a way with words, you are doomed in this. Because while your mouths might speak the same language, your hearts do not." He looked at me intently. "This is an issue of translation."

Elodin held up two fingers. "The second path is more careful. You talk of small things. The weather. A familiar play. You spend time in company. You hold hands. In doing so you slowly learn the secret meanings of each other's words. This way, when the time comes you can speak with subtle meaning underneath your words, so there is understanding on both sides."

Elodin made a sweeping gesture toward me. "Then there is the third path. The path of Kvothe." He strode to stand shoulder to shoulder with me, facing Fela. "You sense something between you. Something wonderful and delicate."

He gave a romantic, lovelorn sigh. "And, because you desire certainty in all things, you decide to force the issue. You take the shortest route. Simplest is best, you think." Elodin extended his own hands and made wild grasping motions in Fela's direction. "So you reach out and you grab this young woman's breasts."

There was a burst of startled laughter from everyone except Fela and myself. I scowled. She crossed her arms in front of her chest and her flush spread down her neck until it was hidden by her shirt.

Elodin turned his back to her and looked me in the eye.

"Re'lar Kvothe," he said seriously. "I am trying to wake your sleeping mind to the subtle language the world is whispering. I am trying to seduce you into understanding. I am trying to *teach* you." He leaned forward until his face was almost touching mine. "Quit grabbing at my tits."

———————

I left Elodin's class in a foul mood.

Though to be honest, my mood of the last few days had been nothing but different variations of foul. I tried to hide it from my friends, but I was starting to crack under the weight of it all.

It was the loss of my lute that had done it. Everything else I'd been able to take in stride, the stinging burn across my chest, the constant ache in my knees, the lack of sleep. The persistent fear that I might let my Alar slip at the wrong moment and suddenly start vomiting blood.

I'd been coping with it all: my desperate poverty, my frustration with Elodin's class. Even the new undertow of anxiety that came from knowing Devi was waiting on the other side of the river with a heart full of rage, three drops of my blood, and an Alar like the ocean in a storm.

But the loss of my lute was too much. It wasn't just that I needed it to earn my room and board at Anker's. It wasn't just that my lute was the linchpin of my ability to make a living if I was forced out of the University.

No. The simple fact was that with my music, I could cope with the rest. My music was the glue that held me together. Only two days without it, and I was falling apart.

After Elodin's class, I couldn't bear the thought of more hours hunched over a worktable in the Fishery. My hands ached at the thought of it, and my eyes were gritty with lack of sleep.

So instead I wandered back to Anker's for an early lunch. I must have looked fairly pitiful because he brought me out a double rasher of bacon with my soup, and a short beer besides.

"How did your dinner go, if you don't mind my asking?" Anker asked, leaning against the bar.

I looked up at him. "Beg your pardon?"

"With your young lady," he said. "I'm not one to pry, but the runner just dropped it off. I had to read it to see who it was for."

I gave Anker my blankest look.

Anker gave me a puzzled look, then frowned. "Didn't Laurel give you your note?"

I shook my head and Anker cursed bitterly. "I swear, some days the light should shine straight through that girl's head." He began to rummage around behind the bar. "Runner dropped off a note for you day before yesterday. I told her to give it to you when you got in. Here it is." He held up a damp and rather draggled piece of paper and handed it to me.

It read:

Kvothe,

I am back in town and would greatly enjoy the company of a charming gentleman at dinner tonight. Sadly, there are none available. Would you care to join me at the Split Stave?

Expectantly yours,

D.

My spirits rose a little. Notes from Denna were a rare treat, and she'd never invited me to dinner before. While I was angry that I'd missed her, knowing she was back in town and eager to see me lifted my spirits considerably.

I wolfed down my lunch, and decided to skip my Siaru lecture in favor of a trip to Imre. I hadn't seen Denna in more than a span, and spending time with her was the only thing I could think of that might improve my mood.

My enthusiasm dampened a bit as I made my way over the river. It was a long walk, and my knees started to ache even before I'd made it to Stonebridge. The sun was piercingly bright, but not warm enough to fight the chill of the early winter wind. The dust off the road gusted into my eyes and made me choke.

Denna wasn't at any of the inns where she occasionally stayed. She wasn't listening to music at the Taps or Goat in the Door. Neither Deoch nor Stanchion had seen her. I worried she might have left town entirely while I was occupied. She could be gone for months. She could be gone forever.

Then I turned a corner and saw her sitting in a small public garden under a tree. She had a letter in one hand and a half-eaten pear in the other. Where had she come by a pear so late in the season?

I was halfway across the garden before I realized she was crying. I stopped where I stood, at a loss for what to do. I wanted to help, but I didn't want to intrude. Maybe it would be best . . .

"Kvothe!"

Denna tossed away the remains of the pear, hopped to her feet, and ran across the lawn toward me. She was smiling, but her eyes were rimmed with red. She wiped at her cheeks with one hand.

"Are you all right?" I asked.

Her eyes welled up with new tears, but before they could fall she screwed her eyes shut and shook her head sharply. "No," she said. "Not entirely."

"Can I help?" I asked.

Denna blotted her eyes with her shirtsleeve. "You help just by being here." She folded the letter into a small square and forced it into her pocket. Then she smiled again. It wasn't a forced smile, the sort you wear like a mask. She smiled a true smile, lovely despite the tears.

Then she tilted her head to one side and gave me a closer look, her smile fading into a look of concern. "What about you?" she asked. "You look a little peaked."

I gave a weak smile. Mine was forced and I knew it. "I've been having a rough time lately."

"I hope you don't feel as rough as you look," she said gently. "Have you been getting enough sleep?"

"I haven't," I admitted.

Denna drew a breath to speak, then paused and bit her lip. "Is it anything you'd like to talk about?" she asked. "I don't know if I could do anything to help, but . . ." She shrugged and shifted her weight slightly from one foot to another. "I don't sleep well myself. I know what it's like."

Her offer of help caught me unprepared. It made me feel . . . I cannot say exactly how it made me feel. It doesn't fit easily into words.

It wasn't the offer of help itself. My friends had been working tirelessly to help me for days. But Sim's willingness to help was different than this. His help was dependable as bread. But knowing Denna cared, that was like a swallow of warm wine on a winter night. I could feel the sweet heat of it in my chest.

I smiled at her. A real smile. The expression felt odd on my face and I wondered how long I'd been scowling without knowing it. "You're helping just by being here," I said honestly. "Just seeing you does wonders for my mood."

She rolled her eyes. "Of course. The sight of my blotchy face is a panacea."

"There isn't much to talk about," I said. "My bad luck got tangled up with my bad decisions, and I'm paying for it."

Denna gave a chuckle that hovered on the edge of being a sob. "I wouldn't know *anything* about that sort of thing," she said, her lips making a wry twist. "It's worst when it's your own stupid fault, isn't it?"

I felt my mouth curve to mimic hers. "It is," I said. "Truth be told, I'd prefer a bit of a distraction to a sympathetic ear."

"That I can provide," she said, taking hold of my arm. "Lord knows you've done the same for me often enough in the past."

I fell into step alongside her. "Have I?"

"Endlessly," she said. "It's easy to forget when you're around." She stopped walking for a moment and I had to stop too, as she'd linked her arm in mine. "That's not right. I mean to say when you're around, it's easy to forget."

"Forget what?"

"Everything," she said, and for a moment her voice wasn't quite as playful. "All the bad parts of my life. Who I am. It's nice to be able to take a vacation from myself every once in a while. You help with that. You're my safe harbor in an endless, stormy sea."

I chuckled. "Am I?"

"You are," she said easily. "You are my shady willow on a sunny day."

"You," I said, "are sweet music in a distant room."

"That's good," she said. "You are unexpected cake on a rainy afternoon."

"You're the poultice that draws the poison from my heart," I said.

"Hmm." Denna looked uncertain. "I don't know about that one. A heart full of poison isn't an appealing thought."

"Yeah," I admitted. "That sounded better before I actually said it."

"That's what happens when you mix your metaphors," she said. A pause. "Did you get my note?"

"I got it today," I said, letting all my regret pour into my voice. "Just a couple hours ago."

"Ah," she said. "That's too bad, it was a good dinner. I ate yours too."

I tried to think of something to say, but she simply smiled and shook her head. "I'm teasing. The dinner was just an excuse, actually. I have something to show you. You're a hard man to find. I thought I was going to have to wait until tomorrow when you sang at Anker's."

I felt a sharp pang in my chest, so strong even Denna's presence couldn't entirely overwhelm it. "It's lucky you caught me today," I said. "I'm not sure I'll be playing tomorrow."

She cocked her head at me. "You always sing on Felling night. Don't change that. You're hard enough for me to find."

"You're a fine one to talk," I said. "I can never catch you in the same place twice."

"Oh yes, I'm sure you're *always* looking for me," she said dismissively, then broke into an excited grin. "But that's beside the point. Come on. I'm sure this will distract you." She began to walk faster, tugging at my arm.

Her enthusiasm was infectious, and I found myself smiling as I followed her through the twisting streets of Imre.

Eventually we came to a small storefront. Denna stepped in front of me, almost bouncing with excitement. All signs of her weeping were gone and her eyes were bright. She put her cool hands over my face. "Close your eyes," she said. "It's a surprise!"

I closed my eyes, and she led me by the hand for a few steps. The inside of the shop was dim and smelled of leather. I heard a man's voice say, "Is this him, then?" followed by the hollow sound of things moving around.

"Are you ready?" Denna said into my ear. I could hear the smile in her voice. Her breath tickled the hairs on the back of my neck.

"I have no idea," I said honestly.

I felt the breath of her stifled laugh on my ear. "Okay. Open them."

I opened my eyes and saw a lean older man standing behind a long wooden counter. An empty lute case lay open like a book in front of him. Denna had bought me a present. A case for my lute. A case for my stolen lute.

I took a step closer. The empty case was long and slender, covered in smooth black leather. There were no hinges. Seven bright steel clasps circled the edge so the top lifted off like the lid of a box.

The inside was soft velvet. I reached out to touch it and found the padding soft but resilient, like a sponge. The velvet's nap was nearly half an inch thick and a deep burgundy color.

The man behind the counter gave a thin smile. "Your lady has good taste," he said. "And a serious mind about what she desires."

He lifted the lid. "The leather is oiled and waxed. There's two layers with rock maple bows beneath." He ran a finger along the bottom half of the case, then pointed at the corresponding groove on the lid. "It fits snugly enough that no air can get in or out. So you need not worry moving from a warm, wet room into an icy night."

He began to snap shut the clasps around the edge of the case. "The lady objected to brass. So these are finesteel. And once they're in place, the lid is held against a gasket. You could submerse it in a river and the velvet will stay dry inside." He shrugged. "Eventually the water would permeate the leather, of course. But there's only so much one can do."

Flipping the case over, he rapped a knuckle hard on the rounded bottom. "I have kept the maple thin, so it is not bulky or heavy, and reinforced it with bands of Glantz steel." He gestured to where Denna stood grinning. "The lady wanted Ramston steel, but I explained that while Ramston is strong, it's also rather brittle. Glantz steel is lighter and retains its shape."

He looked me up and down. "If the young master wishes, he could stand on the bowl of the case without crushing it." His mouth pursed slightly and he looked down at my feet. "Though I would prefer if you did not."

He turned the case right side up again. "I have to say, this is perhaps the finest case I have made in twenty years." He slid it across the counter toward me. "I hope you find it to your satisfaction."

I was driven speechless. A rarity. I reached out and ran a hand along the leather. It was warm and smooth. I touched the steel ring where the shoulder strap would attach. I looked at Denna, who was practically dancing with delight.

Denna stepped forward eagerly. "This is the best part," she said, flipping open the clasps with such familiar ease I could tell she'd done it before. She pulled off the lid and prodded the inside with a finger. "The padding is designed to be moved and reset. So no matter what lute you have in the future, it will still fit.

"And look!" She pressed the velvet where the neck would rest, twisted her fingers, and a lid popped up, revealing a hidden space underneath. She grinned again. "This was my idea, too. It's like a secret pocket."

"God's body, Denna," I said. "This must have cost you a fortune."

"Well, you know," she said with an air of affected modesty. "I had a little set aside."

I ran my hand along the inside, touching the velvet. "Denna, I'm serious. This case must be worth as much as my lute. . . ." I trailed off and my stomach made a nauseating twist. The lute I didn't even have anymore.

"If you don't mind my saying so, sir," the man behind the counter said. "Unless you have a lute of solid silver, I'm guessing this case is worth a damn sight more than that."

I ran my hands over the lid again, feeling increasingly sick to my stomach. I couldn't think of a word to say. How could I tell her someone had stolen my lute after she'd gone through all the work of having this beautiful gift made for me?

Denna grinned excitedly. "Let's see how your lute fits!"

She gestured, and the man behind the counter brought out my lute and set it in the case. It fit snugly as a glove.

I began to cry.

———

"God, I'm embarrassed," I said, blowing my nose.

Denna touched my arm lightly. "I'm so sorry," she repeated for the third time.

The two of us sat on the curb outside the small shop. It was bad enough bursting into tears in front of Denna. I'd wanted to compose myself without the shopkeeper staring at me too.

"I just wanted it to fit properly," Denna said, her expression stricken. "I left a note. You were supposed to come to dinner so I could surprise you. You weren't even supposed to know it was gone."

"It's okay," I said.

"It's obviously not," Denna said, her eyes starting to brim with tears. "When you didn't show up, I didn't know what to do. I looked for you everywhere last night. I knocked on your door, but you didn't answer." She looked down at her feet. "I can never find you when I go looking."

"Denna," I said. "Everything's fine."

She shook her head vigorously, refusing to look at me as tears started to spill down her cheeks. "It's not fine. I should have known. You hold it like it's your baby. If anyone in my life had ever looked at me the way you look at that lute, I'd . . ."

Denna's voice broke and she swallowed hard before words started pouring out of her again. "I knew it was the most important thing in your life. That's why I wanted to get you somewhere safe to keep it. I just didn't think it would be so . . ." She swallowed again, clenching her hands into fists. Her body was so tense she was almost trembling. "God. I'm so stupid! I never think. I always do this. I ruin everything."

Denna's hair had fallen around her face so I couldn't see her expression. "What's wrong with me?" she said, her voice low and angry. "Why am I such an idiot? Why can't I do just one thing right in my whole life?"

"Denna." I had to interrupt her, as she was barely pausing to breathe. I laid my hand on her arm and she grew stiff and still. "Denna, there's no way you could have known," I interrupted. "You've been playing for how long? A month? Have you ever even owned an instrument?"

She shook her head, her face still hidden by her hair. "I had that lyre," she said softly. "But only for a few days before the fire." She looked up at last, her expression pure misery. Her eyes and nose were red. "This happens all the time. I try to do something good, but it gets all tangled up." She gave me a wretched look. "You don't know what it's like."

I laughed. It felt amazingly good to laugh again. It boiled up from deep in my belly and burst out of my throat like notes from a golden horn. That laugh alone was worth three hot meals and twenty hours of sleep.

"I know exactly what it's like," I said, feeling the bruises on my knees and the pull of half-healed scars along my back. I considered telling her how much of a mess I'd made of retrieving her ring. Then decided it probably wouldn't help her mood if I explained how Ambrose was trying to kill me. "Denna, I am the king of good ideas gone terribly wrong."

She smiled at that, sniffing and rubbing at her eyes with a sleeve. "We're a lovely couple of weepy idiots, aren't we?"

"We are," I said.

"I'm sorry," she said again, her smile fading. "I just wanted to do something nice for you. But I'm no good at these things."

I took hold of Denna's hand in both of mine and kissed it. "Denna," I said with perfect honesty, "this is the kindest thing anyone has ever done for me."

She snorted indelicately.

"Pure truth," I said. "You are my bright penny by the roadside. You are worth more than salt or the moon on a long night of walking. You are sweet wine in my mouth, a song in my throat, and laughter in my heart."

Denna's cheeks flushed, but I rolled on, unconcerned.

"You are too good for me," I said. "You are a luxury I cannot afford. Despite this, I insist you come with me today. I will buy you dinner and spend hours waxing rhapsodic over the vast landscape of wonder that is you."

I stood and pulled her to her feet. "I will play you music. I will sing you songs. For the rest of the afternoon, the rest of the world cannot touch us." I cocked my head, making it a question.

Denna's mouth curved. "That sounds nice," she said. "I'd like to get away from the world for the space of an afternoon."

———

Hours later I walked back to the University with a spring in my step. I whistled. I sang. My lute on my shoulder was light as a kiss. The sun was warm and soothing. The breeze was cool.

My luck was beginning to change.

CHAPTER THIRTY-ONE

The Crucible

WITH MY LUTE BACK in my hands, the rest of my life slid easily back into balance. My work in the Fishery was easier. My classes breezed by. Elodin even seemed to make more sense.

It was with a light heart that I visited Simmon in the alchemy complex. He opened the door to my knocking and gestured me inside. "It worked," he said excitedly.

I eased the door shut, and he led me to a table where a series of bottles, tubes, and coal-gas burners were arranged. Sim smiled proudly and held up a short, shallow jar of the sort you use to store face paint or rouge.

"Can you show me?" I asked.

Sim lit a small coal-gas burner and the flame fanned against the bottom of a shallow iron pan. We stood quietly for a moment, listening to it hiss.

"I got new boots," Sim said conversationally, lifting up a foot so I could see.

"They're nice," I said automatically, then paused and looked closer. "Are those hobnails?" I asked incredulously.

He grinned viciously. I laughed.

The iron pan grew hot, and Sim unscrewed the jar, pressing the pad of his index finger into the translucent substance inside. Then, with a little flourish, he raised his hand and pressed the tip of his finger onto the surface of the hot iron pan.

I winced. Sim smiled smugly and stood there for the space of a long breath before pulling his finger away.

"Incredible," I said. "You guys do some crazy things over here. A heat shield."

"No," Sim said seriously. "That's absolutely the wrong way to think about it. It's not a shield. It's not an insulator. It's like an extra layer of skin that burns away before your real skin gets hot."

"Like having water on your hands," I said.

Sim shook his head again. "No, water conducts heat. This doesn't."

"So it *is* an insulator."

"Okay," Sim said, exasperated. "You need to shut up and listen. This is alchemy. You know nothing about alchemy."

I made a placating gesture. "I know. I know."

"Say it, then. Say, 'I know nothing about alchemy.' "

I glowered at him.

"Alchemy isn't just chemistry with some extra bits," he said. "That means if you don't listen to me, you'll jump to your own conclusions and be dead wrong. Dead *and* wrong."

I took a deep breath and let it out. "Okay. Tell me."

"You'll have to spread it on quickly," he said. "You'll only have about ten seconds to get it spread evenly onto your hands and lower arms." He made a gesture to his midforearm.

"It won't rub away, but you will lose a bit if you chafe at your hands too much. Don't touch your face at all. Don't rub your eyes. Don't pick your nose. Don't bite your fingernails. It's sort of poisonous."

"Sort of?" I asked.

He ignored me, holding out the finger he'd pressed onto the hot iron pan. "It's not like armor gloves. As soon as it's exposed to heat, it begins to burn away."

"Will there be any smell?" I asked. "Anything that will give it away?"

"No. It doesn't really *burn* technically. It simply breaks down."

"What does it break down into?"

"Things," Simmon said testily. "It breaks down into complicated things you can't understand because you don't know anything about alchemy."

"Is it safe to breathe?" I amended.

"Yes. I wouldn't give it to you otherwise. This is an old formula. Tried and true. Now, because it doesn't transmit heat, your hands will go straight from feeling cool to being pressed up hard against something burning hot." He gave me a pointed look. "I advise you stop touching hot things *before* it's all used up."

"How can I tell when it's about to be used up?"

"You can't," he said simply. "Which is why I advise using something other than your bare hands."

"Wonderful."

"If it mixes with alcohol it will turn acidic. Only mildly though. You'd have plenty of time to wash it off. If it mixes with a little water, like your sweat, that's fine. But if it mixes with a lot of water, say a hundred parts to one, it will turn flammable."

"And if I mix it with piss it turns into delicious candy, right?" I laughed. "Did you make a bet with Wilem about how much of this I'd swallow? Nothing becomes flammable when you mix it with water."

Sim's eyes narrowed. He picked up an empty crucible. "Fine," he said. "Fill this up then."

Still smiling, I moved to the water canister in the corner of the room. It was identical to the ones in the Fishery. Pure water is important for artificing too, especially when you're mixing clays and quenching metals you don't want contaminated.

I splashed some water into the crucible and brought it back to Sim. He dipped the tip of his finger into it, swirled it around, and poured it into the hot iron pan.

Thick orange flame roared up, burning three feet high until it flickered and died. Sim set down the empty crucible with a slight *click* and looked at me gravely. "Say it."

I looked down at my feet. "I know nothing about alchemy."

Sim nodded, seeming pleased. "Right," he said, turning back to the worktable. "Let's go over this again."

CHAPTER THIRTY-TWO

Blood and Ash

LEAVES CRUNCHED UNDERFOOT AS I made my way through the for-est to the north of the University. The pale moonlight filtering through the bare trees wasn't enough to see clearly, but I had made this trip several times in the last span and knew the way by heart. I smelled wood smoke long before I heard voices and glimpsed firelight through the trees.

It wasn't really a clearing, just a quiet space hidden behind a rocky outcrop. A few pieces of fieldstone and the trunk of a fallen tree provided makeshift seats. I had dug the fire pit myself a few days ago. It was over a foot deep and six across, lined with stones. It dwarfed the small campfire currently burning there.

Everyone else was already there. Mola and Fela shared the log-bench. Wilem was hunkered down on a stone. Sim sat cross-legged on the ground, poking at the fire with a stick.

Wil looked up as I came out of the trees. In the flickering firelight his eyes looked dark and sunken. He and Sim had been watching over me for almost two whole span. "You're late," he said.

Sim looked up to see me, cheerful as always, but there were marks of ex-haustion on his face too. "Is it finished?" he asked, excited.

I nodded. Unbuttoning my cuff, I rolled up my shirtsleeve to reveal an iron disk slightly larger than a commonwealth penny. It was covered in fine sygaldry and inlaid with gold. My newly finished gram. It was strapped flat against the inside of my forearm with a pair of leather cords.

A cheer went up from the group.

"Interesting way to wear it," Mola said. "Fashionable in a sort of barbarian raider way."

"It works best in contact with skin," I explained. "And I need to keep it out of sight, since I'm not supposed to know how to make one."

"Practical *and* stylish," Mola said.

Simmon wandered over and peered at it, reaching out to touch it with a finger. "It seems so small—aaaahh!" Sim cried out as he jumped backward, wringing his hand. "Black damn," he swore, embarrassed. "I'm sorry. It startled me is all."

"Kist and crayle," I said, my own heart racing. "What's the matter?"

"Have you ever touched one of the Arcanum guilders?" he asked. "The ones they give you when you become a full arcanist?"

I nodded. "It sort of buzzed. Made my hand go numb, like it had fallen asleep."

Sim nodded toward my gram, shaking his hand. "It feels like that. Surprised me."

"I didn't know the guilders acted as grams too," I said. "Makes sense though."

"Have you tested it?" Wilem asked.

I shook my head. "It seemed a little strange for me to test it myself," I admitted.

"You want one of us to do it?" Simmon laughed. "You're right, that's perfectly normal."

"I also thought it would be convenient to have a physicker nearby." I nodded in Mola's direction. "Just in case."

"I didn't know I was going to be needed in my professional capacity tonight," Mola protested. "I didn't bring my kit."

"It shouldn't be necessary," I said as I brought a block of sympathy wax out of my cloak and brandished it. "Who wants to do the honors?"

There was a moment of silence, then Fela held out her hand. "I'll make the doll, but I'm not sticking it with a pin."

"*Vhenata,*" Wilem said.

Simmon shrugged. "Fine, I'll do it. I guess."

I handed the block of wax to Fela, and she began warming it with her hands. "Do you want to use hair or blood?" she asked softly.

"Both," I said, trying not to let my growing anxiety show. "I need to be absolutely sure of it if I'm going to be able sleep at night." I pulled out a hatpin, pricked the back of my hand, and watched a bright bead of blood well up.

"That won't work." Fela said, still working the wax with her hands. "Blood won't mix with wax. It'll just bead up and squish out."

"And how did you come by that tidbit of information?" Simmon teased uneasily.

Fela flushed, ducking her head a little, causing her long hair to cascade off her shoulder. "Candles. When you make colored candles you can't use a water-based dye. It needs to be powder or oil. It's a solubility issue. Polar and nonpolar alignments."

"I love the University," Sim said to Wilem on the other side of the fire. "Educated women are so much more attractive."

"I'd like to say the same," Mola said dryly. "But I've never known any educated men."

I bent down and picked up a pinch of ash from the fire pit, then dusted it over the back of my hand where it absorbed the blood.

"That should work," Fela said.

"This flesh will burn. To ash all things return," Wilem intoned in a somber voice, then turned to Simmon. "Isn't that what it says in your holy book?"

"It's not *my* holy book," Simmon said. "But you're close. 'To ash all things return, so too this flesh will burn.' "

"You two are certainly enjoying yourselves," Mola observed dryly.

"I am giddy thinking of a full night's sleep," Wilem said. "An evening's entertainment is coffee after cake."

Fela held out the blob of soft wax, and I pressed the wet ash into it. She kneaded it again, then began to mold it, her fingers patting it into a man-shaped doll in a few deft motions. She held it out for the group to see.

"Kvothe's head is way bigger than that," Simmon said with his boyish grin.

"I also have genitals," I said as I took the mommet from Fela and fixed a hair to the top of its head. "But at a certain point realism becomes unproductive." I walked over to Sim and handed him both the simulacra and the long hatpin.

He took one in each hand, looking uneasily back and forth between them. "You sure about this?"

I nodded.

"Fair enough." Sim drew a deep breath and squared his shoulders. His forehead furrowed in concentration as he stared at the doll.

I doubled over, shrieking and clutching at my leg.

Fela gasped. Wilem leaped to his feet. Simmon went wide-eyed with panic, holding the doll and pin stiff-armed away from each other. He looked around wildly at everyone. "I . . . I didn't . . . ."

I straightened up, brushing at my shirt. "Just practicing," I said. "Was the scream too girly?"

Simmon went limp with relief. "Damn you," he said weakly, laughing. "That's not funny, you bastard." He continued to laugh helplessly as he wiped away the sheen of sweat from his forehead.

Wilem muttered something in Siaru and returned to his seat.

"You three are as good as a traveling troupe," Mola said.

Simmon took a deep breath and let it out slowly. He reset his shoulders and brought the doll and the pin up in front of him. His hand shook. "Tehlu anyway," he said. "You scared the hell out of me. I can't do this now."

"For the love of God." Mola stood and walked around the fire pit to stand over Simmon. She held out her hands. "Give it to me." She took the mommet and pin and turned to look me in the eye. "Are you ready?"

"Just a second." After two span of constant vigilance, letting go of the Alar that protected me felt like prying open a fist gone stiff from clutching something too long.

After a moment, I shook my head. I felt strange without the Alar. Almost naked. "Don't hold back, but hit me in the leg, just in case."

Mola paused, murmured a binding, and drove the pin through the leg of the doll.

Silence. Everyone watched me, motionless.

I didn't feel a thing. "I'm fine," I said. Everyone started to breathe again as I gave Mola a curious look. "Was that really everything you had?"

"No," Mola said frankly as she pulled the pin out of the doll's leg and knelt to hold it over the fire. "That was a gentle test run. I didn't want to listen to your girly scream again." She pulled the pin back out of the fire and stood up. "I'm going to come charging in for real this time." She poised the pin over the doll and looked at me. "You ready?"

I nodded. She closed her eyes for a moment, then murmured a binding and stabbed the hot pin through the mommet's leg. The metal of the gram went cool against the inside of my arm, and I felt a brief pressure against my calf muscle, as if someone had prodded me with a finger. I looked down to make sure Simmon wasn't getting some revenge by poking at me with a stick.

Because I wasn't watching, I missed what Mola did next, but I felt three more dull prods, one in each arm and the other in the thick muscle just above my knee. The gram grew colder.

I heard Fela gasp and looked up in time to see Mola, grim-faced and resolute, toss the mommet into the heart of the campfire, murmuring another binding.

As the wax doll arced through the air, Simmon let out a startled yelp. Wilem came to his feet again, almost lunging at Mola, but too late to stop her.

The mommet landed among the red coals with an explosion of sparks. My gram went almost painfully cold against my arm and I laughed crazily. Everyone turned to look at me, their expressions in various stages of horror and disbelief.

"I'm fine," I said. "This feels really weird though. It's flickery. Like standing in a warm, thick wind."

The gram grew icy against my arm, then the odd sensation faded as the doll melted, destroying the sympathetic link. The fire leaped up as the wax began to burn.

"Did it hurt?" Simmon asked anxiously.

"Not a bit," I said.

"And that was everything I had," Mola said. "To do any more I would have had to have a forge fire at my disposal."

"And she's El'the," Simmon said smugly. "I bet she's three times the sympathist Ambrose is."

"At least three times," I said, "But if anyone was going to go out of their way to find a forge fire, it would be Ambrose. You can overwhelm a gram if you throw enough at it."

"So we're going ahead with things tomorrow?" Mola asked.

I nodded. "I'd rather be safe than sore."

Simmon poked a stick at the spot in the fire where the doll had landed. "If Mola can do her worst and it just rolls off you, it might be enough to keep Devi off your back too. Give you some breathing room."

There was a brief moment of silence. I held my breath, hoping Fela and Mola wouldn't take any particular note of his comment.

Mola raised an eyebrow at me. "Devi?"

I glared at Simmon, and he gave me a piteous look, like a dog that knows it's going to be kicked. "I borrowed some money from a gaelet named Devi," I said, hoping she'd be satisfied with that.

Mola continued to look at me. "And?"

I sighed. Ordinarily I would have avoided the subject, but Mola tended to be insistent about this sort of thing, and I desperately needed her help for tomorrow's plan.

"Devi used to be a member of the Arcanum," I explained. "I gave her some of my blood as collateral for a loan at the beginning of the term. When Ambrose started attacking me, I jumped to the wrong conclusion and accused her of malfeasance. Our relationship went sour after that."

Mola and Fela exchanged a look. "You do go out of your way to make life exciting, don't you?" Mola said.

"I already admitted it was a mistake," I said, irritated. "What else do you want from me?"

"Are you going to be able to pay her back?" Fela interjected into the conversation before things became heated between Mola and me.

"I honestly don't know," I admitted. "With a few lucky breaks and some long nights in the Fishery, I might be able to scrape enough together by the end of the term."

I didn't mention the whole truth. While I might have a chance of earning enough to pay Devi back, I wouldn't have a chance in hell of making my tuition at the same time. I didn't want to spoil everyone's evening with the fact that Ambrose had won. By forcing me to spend so much time hunting for a gram, he'd effectively driven me out of the University.

Fela tilted her head to one side. "What happens if you can't pay her?"

"Nothing good," Wilem said darkly. "They don't call her Demon Devi for nothing."

"I'm not sure," I said. "She could sell my blood. She said she knew some-one willing to buy it."

"I'm sure she wouldn't do that," Fela said.

"I wouldn't blame her," I said. "I knew what I was getting into when I made the deal."

"But sh—"

"It's just the way the world works," I said firmly, not wanting to dwell on it any more than necessary. I wanted the evening to end on a positive note. "I, for one, am looking forward to a good night's sleep in my own bed." I looked around to see Wil and Sim nodding weary agreement. "I'll see everyone to-morrow. Don't be late."

———

Later that night, I slept in the luxury of my narrow bed in my tiny room. At some point I stirred awake, dragged into consciousness by the sensation of chill metal against my skin. I smiled, rolled over, and slid back into blissful sleep.

CHAPTER THIRTY-THREE

Fire

I PACKED MY TRAVELSACK carefully the next evening, anxious that I might forget some key piece of equipment. I was checking everything a third time when there was a knock on the door.

I opened it to see a young boy of ten or so standing there, breathing hard. His eyes darted to my hair and he looked relieved. "Are you Koath?"

"Kvothe," I said. "And yes, I am."

"Got a message for you." He reached into a pocket and pulled out a be-draggled piece of paper.

I held out my hand, and the boy took a step back, shaking his head. "The lady said you'd give me a jot for bringing it to you."

"I doubt that," I said, holding out my hand. "Let me see the note. I'll give you ha'penny if it's really for me."

The boy scowled and grudgingly handed it over.

It wasn't even sealed, just folded over twice. It was also vaguely damp. Looking at the sweat-soaked boy, I could guess why.

It read:

Kvothe,
    Your presence is graciously requested for dinner tonight. I've missed you. I have exciting news. Please meet me at the Barrel and Boar at fifth bell.
    Yours,
    Denna

Pstsrpt. I promised the boy ha'penny.

"Fifth bell?" I demanded. "God's black hands! How long did you take to get here? It's past sixth bell already."

"That en't my fault," he said, scowling fiercely. "I been lookin' all over for hours. Anchors she said. Take it to Koath at Anchors on the other side of the river. But this place en't by the docks at all. And there en't any anchors on the sign outside. How's a one supposed to find this place?"

"You ask someone!" I shouted. "Black damn boy, how thick are you?" I fought down a very real urge to strangle him and took a deep breath.

I looked out the window at the fading light. In less than half an hour my friends would be gathering around the fire pit in the woods. I didn't have time for a trip to Imre.

"Right," I said as calmly as I could manage. I dug out a stub of pencil and scratched out a note on the other side of the piece of paper.

> *Denna,*
>
>   *I'm terribly sorry. Your runner didn't find me until past sixth bell. He is unutterably thick.*
>
>   *I have missed you as well, and offer to put myself entirely at your disposal at any hour of the day or night tomorrow. Send the boy back with your response to let me know when and where.*
>
>   *Fondly,*
>   *Kvothe.*
>
> *Pstcrpt. If the boy tries to get any money off you, give him a sharp cuff round the ear. He'll get his money when he returns your note to Anker's, assuming he doesn't get confused and eat it along the way.*

I folded it over again and pressed a blob of soft candle wax over the fold.

I felt my purse. Over the last month I'd slowly burned through the extra two talents I'd borrowed from Devi. I'd squandered the money on luxuries like bandages, coffee, and the materials for tonight's plan.

As a result, all I had to my name was four pennies and a lonely shim. I shouldered my travelsack and motioned for the boy to follow me downstairs.

I nodded to Anker standing behind the bar, then turned to the boy. "Okay," I said. "You bollixed things up getting here, but I'm going to give you a chance to make it right." I pulled out three pennies and held them out for him to see. "You head back to the Barrel and Boar, find the woman who sent you, and you give her this." I held up the note. "She'll send back a reply. You bring it here and give it to him." I pointed to Anker. "And he'll give you the money."

"I en't an idiot," the boy said. "I want ha'penny first."

"I en't an idiot either," I said. "You'll get three whole pennies when you bring her note back."

He glared at me, then nodded sullenly. I handed him the note, and he ran out the door.

"Boy seemed a little addled when he came in here," Anker said.

I shook my head. "He's witless as a sheep," I said. "I wouldn't use him at all, but he knows what she looks like." I sighed and put the three pennies on the bar. "You'd be doing me a favor if you read the note to make sure the boy isn't faking."

Anker gave me a bit of an uncomfortable look. "And what if it's of an, um, personal nature?"

"Then I'll dance a merry little jig," I said. "But between the two of us, I hardly think that's likely."

———

The sun had set by the time I made it into the forest. Wilem was already there, kindling a fire in the wide pit. We worked together for a quarter hour, gathering enough wood to keep a bonfire burning for hours.

Simmon arrived a few minutes later dragging a long section of dead branch. The three of us broke it into pieces and made nervous small talk until Fela came out of the trees.

Her long hair was pinned up, leaving her elegant neck and shoulders bare. Her eyes were dark and her mouth was slightly redder than usual. Her long black gown was gathered close at her narrow waist and well-rounded hips. She was also displaying the most spectacular pair of breasts I'd ever seen at that point in my young life.

We all gaped, but Simmon gaped openly. "Wow," he said. "I mean, you were the most beautiful woman I'd ever seen before this. I didn't think there was any further for you to go." He laughed his boyish laugh and gestured at her with both hands. "Look at you. You're incredible!"

Fela flushed and looked away, obviously pleased.

"You have the hardest part tonight," I said to her. "I hate to ask, but . . ."

"But you're the only irresistibly attractive woman we know," Simmon chimed in. "Our backup plan was to stuff Wilem into a dress. Nobody wants that."

Wilem nodded. "Agreed."

"Only for you." Fela's mouth quirked into an ironic smile. "When I said I owed you a favor, I never guessed you'd ask me to go out on a date with another man." The smile went a little sour. "Especially Ambrose."

"You only need to put up with him for an hour or two. Try to get him into Imre if you can, but anywhere at least a hundred yards from the Pony will do."

Fela sighed. "At least I'll get dinner out of this." She looked at Simmon. "I like your boots."

He grinned. "They're new."

I turned at the sound of approaching footsteps. Mola was the only one of us not here, but I heard murmured voices mixed with the footsteps and gritted my teeth. It was probably a pair of young lovers out enjoying the un-seasonably warm weather.

The group of us couldn't be seen together, not tonight. It would raise too many questions. I was just about to rush out to intercept them when I recog-nized Mola's voice. "Just wait here while I explain," she said. "Please. Just wait. It will make things easier."

"Let him pitch a twelve-color fit." A familiar female voice came out of the darkness. "Let him shit out his liver for all I care."

I stopped in my tracks. I knew the second voice, but I couldn't put my finger on who it belonged to.

Mola emerged from the dark trees. At her side was a small figure with short strawberry-blond hair. Devi.

I stood stunned as Mola came closer, holding out her hands in a placating gesture and speaking quickly. "Kvothe, I know Devi from a long while ago. She showed me the ropes back when I was new here. Back before she . . . left."

"Expelled," Devi said proudly. "I'm not ashamed of it."

Mola continued hurriedly. "After what you said yesterday. It seemed like there was some misunderstanding. When I stopped in to ask her about it . . ." She shrugged. "The whole story kind of came out. She wanted to help."

"I want a piece of Ambrose," Devi said. There was a weight of cold fury in her voice when she said his name. "My help is largely incidental."

Wilem cleared his throat. "Would we be correct in assuming—"

"He beats his whores," Devi said, interrupting him abruptly. "And if I could kill the arrogant bastard and get away with it, I would have done it years ago." She stared flatly at Wilem. "And yes, we have a past. And no, it's none of your business. Is that enough reason for you?"

There was a tense silence. Wilem nodded, his face carefully blank.

Devi turned to look at me.

"Devi." I made a short bow to her. "I'm sorry."

She blinked in surprise. "Well, I'll be damned," she said, her voice sharp with sarcasm. "Maybe you do have half a brain in your head."

"I didn't think I could trust you," I said. "I was wrong, and I regret it. It wasn't the clearest thinking I've ever done."

She eyed me for a long moment. "We're not friends," she said curtly, her expression still icy. "But if you're still alive at the end of all this, we'll talk."

Devi looked past me and her expression softened. "Little Fela!" She brushed past me and gave Fela a hug. "You're all grown up!" She stepped back and held Fela at arm's length, looking her over appreciatively. "My lord, you look like a ten-stripe Modegan whore! He'll love it."

Fela smiled and spun a little so the bottom of her dress flared. "It is nice to have an excuse to dress up every once and a while."

"You should be dressing up on your own," Devi said. "And for better men than Ambrose."

"I've been busy. I'm out of practice preening. It took me an hour to remember how to do my hair. Any advice?" She held her arms out to her sides and did a slow turn.

Devi looked her up and down with a calculating eye. "You're already better than he deserves. But you're all bare. Why don't you have any sparkle on you?"

Fela looked down at her hands. "Rings won't work with the gloves," she said. "And I didn't have anything nice enough to go with the dress."

"Here then," Devi tilted her head and reached up under her hair, first on one side then the other. Then she stepped closer to Fela. "Lord you're tall, bend down."

When Fela straightened up again, she was wearing a pair of earrings that swung and caught the light of the fire.

Devi stepped back and gave an exasperated sigh. "And they look better on you, of course." She shook her head with irritation. "Good lord woman. If I had tits like yours I'd own half the world by now."

"You and me both," Sim said enthusiastically.

Wilem burst out laughing, then covered his face and stepped away from Sim, shaking his head and doing his best to look like he didn't have the slightest idea who was standing next to him.

Devi looked at Sim's unashamed, boyish grin, then back to Fela. "Who's the idiot?"

I caught Mola's eye and motioned her closer so we could talk. "You didn't need to, but thanks. It's a relief, knowing she's not out there plotting against me."

"Don't assume," Mola said grimly. "I've never seen her so angry. It just seemed a shame for the two of you to be at odds. You're a lot alike."

I darted a glance across the fire pit where Wil and Sim were cautiously approaching Devi and Fela. "I've heard a lot about you," Wilem said, looking at Devi. "I thought you'd be taller."

"How's that working out for you?" Devi asked dryly. "Thinking, I mean."

I waved my hands to get everyone's attention. "It's late," I said. "We have to get into position."

Fela nodded. "I want to be there early, just in case." She straightened her gloves nervously. "Wish me luck."

Mola walked over and gave her a quick hug. "It'll be fine. Stay somewhere public with him. He'll behave better if people are watching."

"Keep asking him about his poetry," Devi advised. "He'll talk the time away."

"If he gets impatient, compliment the wine," Mola added. "Say things like, 'Oh I'd love another glass, but I'm worried it'd go right to my head.' He'll buy a bottle and try and pour it into you."

Devi nodded. "It'll keep him off you for an extra half-hour at least." She reached out and pulled up the top of Fela's dress a bit. "Start conservative, then bring them out a little more toward the end of the dinner. Lean. Use your shoulders. If he keeps seeing more and more, he'll think he's getting somewhere. It'll keep him from getting grabby."

"This is the most terrifying thing I've ever seen," Wilem said quietly.

"Do all the women in the world secretly know each other?" Sim asked. "Because that would explain a lot."

"There's barely a hundred of us in the Arcanum," Devi said scathingly. "They confine us to a single wing of the Mews whether or not we actually want to live there. How can we *not* know each other?"

I walked over to Fela and handed her a slender oak twig. "I'll signal you when we're done. You signal me if he walks out on you."

Fela arched an eyebrow. "A woman could take that slightingly," she said, then smiled and slid the twig inside one of her long black gloves. Her earrings swung and caught the light again. They were emeralds. Smooth emerald teardrops.

"Those are lovely earrings," I said to Devi. "Where did you come by them?"

Her eyes narrowed, as if she were trying to decide whether or not to take offense. "A pretty young boy used them to settle his debt," she said. "Not that it's any of your business."

I shrugged. "Just curious."

Fela waved and walked off, but before she made it ten feet Simmon caught up with her. He smiled awkwardly, talking and making a few emphatic gestures before handing her something. She smiled and tucked it into her long black glove.

I turned to Devi. "I assume you know the plan?"

She nodded. "How far is it to his room?"

"A little more than half a mile," I said apologetically. "The slippage—"

Devi cut me off with a gesture. "I do my own calculations," she said sharply.

"Right." I gestured to where my travelsack lay near the edge of the fire pit. "There's wax and clay in there." I handed her a slim birch twig. "I'll signal you when we're in position. Start with the wax. Give it a hard half-hour, then signal and move onto the clay. Give the clay at least an hour."

Devi snorted. "With a bonfire behind me? It'll take me fifteen minutes, tops."

"It might not be tucked into his sock drawer, you realize. It might be locked away without much air."

Devi waved me away. "I know my business."

I made a half bow. "I leave it in your capable hands."

"That's it?" Mola demanded indignantly. "You lectured me for an hour! You *quizzed* me!"

"There isn't time," I said simply. "And you'll be here to coach her if need be. Besides, Devi happens to be one of the handful of people I suspect might be a better sympathist than me."

Devi gave me a dark look. "Suspect? I beat you like a red-headed stepchild. You were my little sympathy hand puppet."

"That was two span ago," I said. "I've learned a lot since then."

"Hand puppet?" Sim asked Wilem. Wil made an explanatory gesture and they both burst out laughing.

I motioned to Wilem. "Let's go."

Before we could head out, Sim handed me a small jar.

I gave it an odd look. I already had his alchemical concoction tucked away in my cloak. "What's this?"

"It's just ointment in case you get burned," he explained. "But if you mix it with piss, it turns into candy." Sim's expression was deadpan. "Delicious candy."

I nodded seriously. "Yes sir."

Mola stared in confusion. Devi pointedly ignored us and began piling wood on the fire.

———————————

An hour later, Wilem and I were playing cards at the Golden Pony. The common room was nearly full, and a harpist was doing a passable version of "Sweet Winter Rye." The room was full of murmured conversation as wealthy customers gambled, drank, and talked about whatever rich people talk about. How to properly beat the stable boy, I guessed. Or techniques for chasing the chambermaid around the estate.

The Golden Pony was not my sort of place. The clientele was too well-bred, the drinks too expensive, and the musicians more pleasing to the eye than the ear. Despite all this, I'd been coming here for nearly two span, making a show of trying to climb the social ladder. That way, no one could say it was odd I was here on this particular night.

Wilem took a drink and shuffled the cards. My own drink sat half-finished and warm. It was only a simple ale, but given the prices at the Pony I was now, quite literally, penniless.

Wil dealt another hand of breath. I picked up my cards carefully, as Simmon's alchemical concoction made my fingers ever so slightly sticky. We might as well have been playing with blank cards. I drew and threw randomly, pretending to concentrate on the game when really I was waiting, listening.

I felt a slight tickle in the corner of my eye and reached to rub it away with my fingers, catching myself at the last second with my hand upraised. Wilem stared at me from across the table, his eyes alarmed, and gave his head a small, firm shake. I went motionless for a moment, then slowly lowered my hand.

I was so busy trying to appear nonchalant that when the cry came from outside I was actually startled. It cut through the low murmur of conversation as only a shrill voice filled with panic can. "Fire! Fire!"

Everyone in the Pony froze for a moment. This always happens when people are startled and confused. They take a second to look around, smell the air, and think things like, "Did he just say fire?" or "Fire? Where? Here?"

I didn't hesitate. I leaped to my feet and made a show of looking around wildly, obviously trying to search out the fire. By the time everyone else in the common room started to move, I was already dashing for the stairs.

"Fire!" The cries continued from outside. "Oh God. Fire!"

I smiled as I listened to Basil overact his small part. I didn't know him well enough to let him in on the whole plan, but it was vital that someone notice the fire early so I could spring into action. The last thing I wanted to do was accidentally burn down half the inn.

I reached the top of the steps and looked around the upper floor of the Golden Pony. There were already footsteps pounding up the stairs behind me. A few wealthy lodgers opened their doors, peering into the hallway.

There were faint wisps of smoke curling underneath the door to Ambrose's rooms. Perfect.

"I think it's over here!" I shouted, sliding a hand into one of my cloak's pockets as I ran to the door.

In the long days we spent searching the Archives, I'd found reference to a great many interesting pieces of artificery. One of them was an elegant piece of artificery called a siege stone.

It worked on the most basic sympathetic principles. A crossbow stores energy and uses it to shoot a bolt a long distance at a great speed. A siege stone was an inscribed piece of lead that stores energy and uses it to move itself about six inches with the force of a battering ram.

Reaching the middle of the hallway, I braced myself and charged Ambrose's door with my shoulder. I also struck it with the siege stone I held concealed against the flat of my hand.

The thick-timbered door staved in like a barrel struck by an anvil hammer. There were startled gasps and exclamations from everyone in the hallway. I rushed inside, trying desperately to keep the manic grin off my face.

Ambrose's sitting room was dark, and made darker by a haze of smoke in the air. I saw flickering firelight inside, off to the left. From my previous visit I knew it was his bedroom.

"Hello?" I shouted. "Is everyone all right?" I pitched my voice carefully: Bold but concerned. No panic, of course. I was, after all, the hero of this scene.

Smoke was thick in the bedroom, catching the orange firelight and stinging my eyes. There was a massive wooden chest of drawers against the wall, big as a workbench in the Fishery. Flames licked and flickered around the edges of the drawers. Apparently Ambrose *had* been keeping the mommet in his sock drawer.

I picked up a nearby chair and used it to smash the window I'd climbed through several nights ago. "Clear the street!" I shouted down.

The bottommost left drawer seemed to be burning the hottest, and when I pulled it open the smoldering clothes inside caught the air hungrily and burst into flame. I smelled burning hair and hoped I hadn't lost my eyebrows. I didn't want to spend the next month looking constantly surprised.

After the initial flare up, I drew a deep breath, stepped forward, and pulled the heavy wooden drawer free of the bureau with my bare hands. It was full of smoldering, blackened cloth, but as I ran to the window, I could hear something hard in the bottom of the drawer rattling against the wood. It tumbled as I threw it out the window, clothes bursting into flame as the wind caught them.

Next I yanked out the top right-hand drawer. As soon as I pulled it free, smoke and flame poured out in an almost solid mass. With these two drawers gone, all the empty space inside the bureau formed a crude chimney, giving the fire all the air it wanted. As I heaved the second drawer out the window, I could actually hear the hollow rush of fire spreading through the varnished wood and the clothes inside.

Down in the street, people drawn by the commotion were doing their best to put out the flaming debris. In the middle of the small crowd, Simmon stomped about in his new hobnail boots, smashing things to flinders like a boy splashing in puddles after the first spring rain. Even if the mommet had survived the fall, it wouldn't survive that.

This was more than mere pettiness. Devi had signaled me twenty minutes ago, letting me know she'd already tried the wax mommet. Since there had been no result, it meant Ambrose had undoubtedly used my blood to make a clay mommet of me. A simple fire wasn't going to destroy it.

One by one, I grabbed the other drawers and threw them into the street as well, pausing to pull down the thick velvet curtains around Ambrose's bed to shield my hands from the heat of the fire. This also might seem petty, but it wasn't. I was terrified of burning my hands. Every talent I had revolved around them.

Petty was when I kicked the chamber pot on my way back to the bureau. It was the expensive kind, fine glazed pottery. It tipped over and rolled crazily across the floor until it struck the hearth and shattered. Suffice to say that what spilled across Ambrose's rugs was not delicious candy.

Flame flickered openly in the spaces where the drawers had been, lighting the room while the broken window let in some clear air. Eventually someone else was brave enough to make their way into the room. He used one of the blankets off Ambrose's bed to protect his hands and helped me throw the last several burning drawers out the window. It was hot, sooty work, and even with the help, I was coughing by the time the last of the drawers went tumbling onto the street.

It was over in less than three minutes. A few quick-thinking bar patrons brought in pitchers of water and doused the still-burning frame of the empty bureau. I tossed the smoldering velvet drapes out the window, shouting, "Look out down there!" so Simmon would know to retrieve my siege stone from the pile of tangled cloth.

Lamps were lit and the smoke thinned as cool night air blew in through the broken window. People filtered into the room to help, or gawk, or gossip. A cluster of amazed onlookers gathered around Ambrose's staved-in door, and I idly wondered what sort of rumors might spring out of tonight's performance.

Once the room was properly lit, I marveled at the damage the fire had done. The chest of drawers was little more than a collection of charred sticks, and the plaster wall behind it was cracked and blistered from the heat. The white ceiling was painted with a wide fan of black soot.

I caught my reflection in the dressing-room mirror and was pleased to see my eyebrows were more or less intact. I was mightily disheveled, my hair in disarray and my face smudged with sweat and dark ash. The whites of my eyes looked very bright against the black of my face.

Wilem joined me and helped bandage up my left hand. It wasn't really burned, but I knew it would look odd if I walked away entirely unscathed. Aside from a little lost hair, my worst injury was actually the holes charred in my long sleeves. Another shirt ruined. If this kept up I'd be naked by the end of the term.

I sat on the edge of the bed and watched as people brought more water to splash on the bureau. I pointed out a charred ceiling beam, and they doused it too, sending up a sharp hiss and a cloud of steam and smoke. People continued to wander in and out, looking at the wreckage and muttering to each other while shaking their heads.

Just as Wil was finishing my bandage, the sound of galloping hooves on cobblestones came through the broken window, temporarily overwhelming the noise of fiercely stomping hobnailed boots.

Less than a minute later, I heard Ambrose in the hallway. "What in the name of God is going on here? Get out! *Out!*"

Cursing and shoving people aside, Ambrose made his entrance. When he saw me sitting on his bed he pulled up short. "What are you doing in my rooms?" he demanded.

"What?" I asked, then looked around. "These are *your* rooms?" Keeping the proper amount of dismay in my tone wasn't easy, as my voice was rough with smoke. "I just burned myself saving *your* things?"

Ambrose's eyes narrowed, then went to the charred wreckage of his bureau. His eyes flicked back to me, then went wide with sudden realization. I fought the urge to grin.

"Get out of here you filthy, thieving Ruh," he spat venomously. "I swear if anything's missing, I'll bring the constable down on you. I'll have you on the iron law and see you hanged."

I drew a breath to respond, then started to cough uncontrollably and had to settle for glaring at him.

"Good job, Ambrose," Wilem said sarcastically. "You caught him. He stole your fire."

One of the onlookers chimed in, "Yeah, make him put it back!"

"Get out!" Ambrose shouted, red-faced and furious. "And take that filthy shim with you or I'll give you both the thrashing you deserve." I watched the bystanders stare at Ambrose, appalled by his behavior.

I gave him a long, proud look, playing the scene for all it was worth. "You're welcome," I said with injured dignity, and shouldered past him, jostling him roughly out of the way.

As I was leaving, a fat, florid man in a waistcoat staggered through the ruined door to Ambrose's rooms. I recognized him as the owner of the Golden Pony.

"What the devil's been going on here?" he demanded.

"Candles are dangerous things," I said. I looked over my shoulder and met Ambrose's eye. "Honestly boy," I said to him. "I don't know what you were thinking. You'd think a member of the Arcanum would have more sense."

———————

Wil, Mola, Devi, and I were sitting around what was left of the bonfire when we heard the crackle of footsteps coming through the trees. Fela was still dressed elegantly, but her hair was unpinned. Sim was making his way carefully alongside her, absentmindedly holding branches out of her way as they moved through the undergrowth.

"And just where have you two been?" Devi asked.

"I had to walk back from Imre," Fela explained. "Sim came to meet me halfway. Don't worry mother, he was a perfect gentleman."

"I hope it wasn't too bad for you," I said.

"Dinner was about what you would expect," Fela admitted. "But the second part made it all worthwhile."

"Second part?" Mola asked.

"On our way back, Sim took me to see the wreckage at the Pony. I stopped to have a word with Ambrose. I've never had so much fun." Fela's smile was wicked. "I was perfectly huffy."

"She was," Simmon said. "It was brilliant."

Fela faced Sim and set her hands on her hips. "Run off on me, will you?"

Sim screwed his face up into an exaggerated scowl and gestured wildly. "Listen to me, you daft bint!" he said in a fair imitation of Ambrose's Vintish accent. "My rooms were on fire!"

Fela turned away, throwing up her hands. "Don't lie to me! You ran off to be with some whore. I've never been so humiliated in my life! *I never want to see you again!*"

We applauded. Fela and Sim linked arms and took a bow.

"In the interest of pure accuracy," Fela said in an offhand way, "Ambrose didn't use the words 'daft bint.'" She didn't let go of Sim's arm.

Simmon looked a little embarrassed. "Yes, well. There are some things you don't call a lady, even in fun." He reluctantly let go of Fela and sat on the trunk of the fallen tree. Fela sat next to him.

Fela leaned close to him and whispered something. Sim laughed, shaking his head. "Please?" Fela asked, laying her hand on his arm. "Kvothe doesn't have his lute. Someone has to entertain us."

"Okay, Okay." Simmon said, obviously a little flustered. He closed his eyes for a moment, then spoke in a sonorous voice:

Fast came our Fela   fiery eyes flashing,
Crossing the cobbles   strength in her stride.
Came she to Ambrose   all ashes around him
Grim was his gazing   fearsome his frown.
Still Fela feared not   brave was her bo—

Simmon came to an abrupt stop before saying the word "bosom" and blushed red as a beet. Devi gave an earthy chuckle from where she sat on the other side of the fire.

Ever the good friend, Wilem stepped in with a distracting question. "What is that pause you keep doing?" he asked. "It's like you can't catch your breath."

"I asked that too," Fela said, smiling.

"It's something they use in Eld Vintic verse," Sim explained. "It's a break in the line called a caesura."

"You are dangerously well informed about poetry, Sim," I said. "I'm close to losing respect for you."

"Hush," Fela said. "I think it's lovely. You're just jealous he can do it off the cuff."

"Poetry is a song without music," I said loftily. "A song without music is like a body without a soul."

Wilem raised his hand before Simmon could respond. "Before we become mired in philosophical talk, I have a confession to make," Wilem said somberly. "I dropped a poem in the hallway outside Ambrose's rooms. It was an acrostic that spoke of his powerful affection for Master Hemme."

We all laughed, but Simmon seemed to find it particularly funny. It took him a long while to catch his breath. "It couldn't be more perfect if we planned it," he said. "I bought a few pieces of women's clothing and scattered them in with what was out on the street. Red satin. Lacy bits. A whalebone corset."

There was more laughter. Then they turned their eyes to me.

"And what did you do?" Devi prompted.

"Only what I set out to," I said somberly. "Only what was necessary to destroy the mommet so I could sleep safe at night."

"You kicked over his chamber pot," Wilem said.

"True," I admitted. "And I found this." I held up a piece of paper.

"If that's one of his poems," Devi said, "I'd suggest you burn it quickly and wash your hands."

I unfolded the slip of paper and read it aloud. "Ledger mark 4535: Ring. White gold. Blue smokestone. Remount setting and polish." I folded it carefully and put it in a pocket. "To me," I said, "This is better than a poem."

Sim sat upright. "Is that a pawnslip for your lady's ring?"

"It's a claim slip for a jeweler, if I don't miss my guess. But yes, it's for her ring," I said. "And she's not my lady, by the by."

"I'm lost," Devi said.

"That's how all this started," Wilem said. "Kvothe was trying to reclaim a bit of property for a girl he fancies."

"Someone should fill me in," Devi said. "I seem to have come in halfway through the story."

I leaned back against a piece of fieldstone, content to let my friends tell the story.

The slip of paper hadn't been in Ambrose's chest of drawers. It hadn't been on the hearth or his bedside table. It hadn't been on his jewelry tray or his writing desk.

It had, in fact, been in Ambrose's purse. I'd lifted it off him in a fit of pique half a minute after he called me a filthy, thieving Ruh. It had almost been a reflex action as I'd brushed roughly past him on my way out of his rooms at the Pony.

By strange coincidence, the purse also contained money. Almost six talents. Not a great deal of coin as far as Ambrose was concerned. Enough for an extravagant night out with a lady. But for me it was a great deal of money, so much I almost felt guilty for taking it. Almost.

CHAPTER THIRTY-FOUR

Baubles

THERE WAS NO NOTE for me from Denna when I returned to Anker's that night. Nor was there one waiting in the morning. I wondered if the boy had ever found her with my message, or if he had simply given up, or dropped it in the river, or eaten it.

The next morning I decided my mood was too good to spoil it with the inevitable madness of Elodin's class. So I shouldered my lute and headed over the river to look for Denna. It had taken longer than I'd planned, but I was eager to see the look on her face when I finally returned her ring.

———

I walked into the jeweler's and smiled at the small man standing behind a low display case. "Are you finished with the ring?"

His forehead creased. "I . . . I beg your pardon, sir?"

I sighed and dug around in my pocket, eventually producing the slip of paper.

He peered at it, then his face lit with understanding. "Ah, yes. Of course. Just a moment." He made his way through a door into the back of the shop.

I relaxed a bit. This was the third shop I'd visited. The other conversations hadn't worked out nearly this well.

The tiny man bustled out of the back room. "Here we are, sir." He held up the ring. "Right as rain again. Lovely stone too, if you don't mind my saying."

I held it to the light. It was Denna's ring. "You do good work," I said.

He smiled at this. "Thank you, sir. All told, the work came to forty-five pennies."

I gave a small, silent sigh. It had been too much to hope that Ambrose had paid for the work in advance. I juggled numbers in my head and counted a talent and six jots onto the glass top of the display case. As I did, I noticed it had the slightly oily texture of twice-tough glass. I ran my hand over it, wondering idly if it was one of the pieces I had made at the Fishery.

As the jeweler gathered up the coins, I noticed something else. Something inside the case.

"A bauble caught your eye?" he asked smoothly.

I pointed at a necklace in the center of the case.

"You have excellent taste," he said, pulling out a key and unlocking a panel in the back of the case. "This is quite an exceptional piece. Not only is the setting elegant, but the stone itself is remarkably fine. You don't often see an emerald of this quality cut in a long drop."

"Is it your work?" I asked.

The jeweler gave a dramatic sigh. "Alas, I cannot claim that distinction. A young woman brought it in several span ago. She had more need of money than adornment it seems, and we came to an arrangement."

"How much would you like for it?" I asked as casually as possible.

He told me. It was a staggering amount of money. More money than I had ever seen in one place. Enough money that a woman might live comfortably in Imre for several years. Enough money for a fine new harp. Enough for a lute of solid silver, or, if she desired, a case for such a lute.

The jeweler sighed again, shaking his head at the sad state of the world. "It is a shame," he said. "Who can tell what drives young women to such things." Then he looked up and smiled, holding the teardrop emerald to the light with an expectant expression. "Still, her loss is your gain."

Since Denna had mentioned the Barrel and Boar in her note, I decided to start looking for her there. My lute case hung heavier on my shoulder now that I knew what she'd given up to pay for it. Still, one good turn deserves another, and I hoped the return of her ring would help balance things between us.

But the Barrel and Boar wasn't an inn, merely a restaurant. Without any real hope, I asked the host if someone might have left a message for me. Nobody had. I asked if he remembered a woman who had been there the night before? Dark-haired? Lovely?

He nodded at that. "She waited for a long while," he said. "I remember thinking, 'Who would keep a woman like that waiting?'"

You would be amazed at how many inns and boarding houses there are, even in a smallish city like Imre.

CHAPTER THIRTY-FIVE

Secrets

TWO DAYS LATER I was heading off to the Fishery, hoping some honest work would clear my head and make me better able to tolerate two hours of Elodin's jackassery. I was three steps from the door, when I saw a young girl in a blue cloak hurrying across the courtyard toward me. Underneath the hood, her face was a startling mix of excitement and anxiety.

We made eye contact and she stopped moving toward me. Then, still eyeing me, she made a motion so furtive and stiff I couldn't understand what she meant until she repeated it: she wanted me to follow her.

Puzzled, I nodded. She turned and walked out of the courtyard, moving with the awkward stiffness of someone trying desperately to be nonchalant.

I followed her. Under other circumstances I would have thought she was a shill luring me into a dark alley where thugs would kick out my teeth and take my purse. But there weren't any decently dangerous alleys this close to the University, and it was a sunny afternoon besides.

Eventually she stepped into a deserted piece of road behind a glassblower and a clocksmith's shop. She looked around nervously, then turned, her face beaming under the shelter of her hood. "I finally found you!" she said breathlessly.

She was younger than I'd thought, no more than fourteen. Curls of mousy brown hair framed her pale face and fought to escape the hood. Still, I couldn't place her. . . .

"I've had a drummer of a time tracking you down," she said. "I spend so much time here my ma thinks I have a beau at the University," she said the last almost shyly, her mouth making a tiny curve.

I opened my mouth to admit I didn't have the slightest idea who she was. But before I could get a word out, she spoke again. "Don't worry," she said. "I hain't let anyone know I was coming to see you." Her bright eyes went dark with anxiety, like a pool when the sun goes behind a cloud. "I know it's safer that way."

It was only when her face went dark with worry that I recognized her. She was the young girl I'd met in Trebon when I'd gone to investigate rumors of the Chandrian.

"Nina," I said. "What are you doing here?"

"Looking for you." She thrust out her chin proudly. "I knew you must be from here cause you knew all sorts of magic." She looked around. "But it's bigger than I thought it would be. I know you didn't give anyone in Trebon your name because then they'd have power over you, but I have to say it makes you terribly hard to find."

Had I not told anyone my name in Trebon? Some of my memories of that time were vague, as I'd had a bit of a concussion. It was probably for the best I'd kept myself anonymous, given that I'd been responsible for burning down a sizable portion of the town.

"I'm sorry to put you to so much work," I said, still not sure what this was all about.

Nina took a step closer. "I had dreams after you left," she said, her voice low and confidential. "Bad dreams. I thought *they* were coming for me because of what I told you." She gave me a meaningful look. "But then I started sleeping with the amulet you gave me. I made my prayers every night, and the dreams went away." One of her hands absentmindedly fingered a piece of bright metal that hung around her neck on a leather cord.

I realized with sudden guilt that I'd inadvertently lied to Master Kilvin. I hadn't sold anyone a charm, or even made anything that would look like one. But I had given Nina an engraved piece of metal and told her it was an amulet to set her mind at ease. Before that she'd been on the edge of nervous hysteria, worried that demons were going to kill her.

"So it's been working then?" I asked, trying not to sound guilty.

She nodded. "As soon as I had it under my pillow and said my prayers, I slept like a babe at the tit. Then I started having my special dream," she said, and smiled up at me. "I dreamed about the big pot Jimmy showed me before those folks were kilt up at the Mauthen farm."

I felt hope rise in my chest. Nina was the only person alive who had seen the ancient piece of pottery. It had been covered with pictures of the Chandrian, and they are jealous of their secrets.

"You remembered something about the pot with the seven people painted on it?" I asked excitedly.

She hesitated for a moment, frowning. "There was eight of them," she said. "Not seven."

"Eight?" I asked. "Are you sure?"

She nodded earnestly. "I thought I told you before."

The rising hope in my chest suddenly fell into the pit of my stomach where it lay heavy and sour. There were seven Chandrian. It was one of the few things I knew for certain about them. If there were eight people on the painted vase Nina had seen . . .

Nina continued to chatter away, unaware of my disappointment. "I dreamed about the pot for three nights in a row," she said. "And it weren't a bad dream at all. I woke up all rested and happy every night. I knew then what God was telling me to do."

She began to root around in her pockets and brought out a length of polished horn more than a handspan long and big around as my thumb. "I remembered how you were so curious about the pot. But I couldn't tell you anything cause I'd only seen it for a moment." She handed me the piece of horn, proudly.

I looked down at the cylindrical piece of horn in my hands, not sure what I was supposed to do with it. I looked up at her, confused.

Nina gave an impatient sigh and took the horn back. She twisted it, removing the end like a cap. "My brother made this for me," she said as she carefully drew a rolled piece of parchment from inside the horn. "Don't worry. He doesn't know what it was for."

She handed me the parchment. "It's not very good," she said nervously. "My mum lets me help paint the pots, but this is different. It's harder doing people than flowers and designs. And it's hard getting something right that you can only see in your head."

I was amazed my hands weren't shaking. "This is what was painted on the vase?" I asked.

"It's one side of it," she said. "Something round like this, you can only see a third of it when you're looking at it from one side."

"So you dreamed of a different side each night?" I asked.

She shook her head. "Just this side. Three nights in a row."

I slowly unrolled the piece of paper and instantly recognized the man she had painted. His eyes were pure black. In the background there was a bare tree, and he was standing on a circle of blue with a few wavy lines on it.

"That's supposed to be water," she said, pointing. "It's hard to paint water though. And he's supposed to be standing on it. There were drifts of snow around him too, and his hair was white. But I couldn't get the white paint to work. Mixing paints for paper is harder than glazes for pots."

I nodded, not trusting myself to speak. It was Cinder, the one who had killed my parents. I could see his face in my mind without even trying. Without even closing my eyes.

I unrolled the paper further. There was a second man, or rather the shape of a man in a great hooded robe. Inside the cowl of the robe was nothing but blackness. Over his head were three moons, a full moon, a half moon, and one that was just a crescent. Next to him were two candles. One was yellow with a bright orange flame. The other candle sat underneath his outstretched hand: it was grey with a black flame, and the space around it was smudged and darkened.

"That's supposed to be shadow, I think," Nina said, pointing to the area under his hand. "It was more obvious on the pot. I had to use charcoal for that. I couldn't get it right with paint."

I nodded again. This was Haliax. The leader of the Chandrian. When I'd seen him he had been surrounded by an unnatural shadow. The fires around him had been strangely dimmed, and the cowl of his cloak had been black as the bottom of a well.

I finished unrolling the paper, revealing a third figure, larger than the other two. He wore armor and an open-faced helmet. On his chest was a bright insignia that looked like an autumn leaf, red on the outside brightening to orange near the middle, with a straight black stem.

The skin of his face was tan, but the hand he held poised upright was a bright red. His other hand was hidden by a large, round object that Nina had somehow managed to color a metallic bronze. I guessed it was his shield.

"He's the worst," Nina said, her voice subdued.

I looked down at her. Her face looked somber, and I guessed she'd taken my silence the wrong way. "You shouldn't say that," I said. "You've done a wonderful job."

Nina gave a faint smile. "That's not what I meant," she said. "He was hard to do. I got the copper pretty okay here." She touched his shield. "But this red," her finger brushed his upraised hand, "is supposed to be blood. He's got blood all over his hand." She tapped his chest. "And this was brighter, like something burning."

I recognized him then. It wasn't a leaf on his chest. It was a tower wrapped in flame. His bloody, outstretched hand wasn't demonstrating something. It was making a gesture of rebuke toward Haliax and the rest. He was holding up his hand to stop them. This man was one of the Amyr. One of the Ciridae.

The young girl shivered and pulled her cloak around herself. "I don't like looking at him even now," she said. "They were all awful to look at. But he was the worst. I can't get faces right, but his was terrible grim. He looked so angry. He looked like he was ready to burn down the whole world."

"If this is one side," I asked, "Do you remember the rest of it?"

"Not like this. I remember there was a woman with no clothes on, and a broken sword, and a fire. . . ." She looked thoughtful, then shook her head again. "Like I told you, I only saw it for a quick second when Jimmy showed me. I think an angel helped me remember this piece in a dream so I could paint it down and bring it to you."

"Nina," I said. "This is really amazing. You really have no idea how incredible this is."

Her face lit up again with a smile. "I'm glad of that. I've had a world of trouble making it."

"Where did you get the parchment?" I asked, noticing it for the first time. It was actual vellum, high-quality stuff. Far better than anything I could afford.

"I practiced on some boards at first," she said. "But I knew that wasn't going to work. Plus I knew I'd have to hide it. So I snuck into the church and cut some pages out of their book," she said the last without the faintest hint of self-consciousness.

"You cut this out of the *Book of the Path?*" I asked, somewhat aghast. I'm not particularly religious, but I do have a vestigial sense of propriety. And after so many hours in the Archives, the thought of cutting pages out of a book was horrifying to me.

Nina nodded easily. "It seemed the best thing, since an angel gave me the dream. And they can't lock the church up properly at night, since you tore off the front of the building, and killed that demon." She reached over and brushed at the paper with a finger. "It hain't that hard. All you need to do is take a knife and scrape at it a bit and all the words come off." She pointed. "I was careful never to scrape off Tehlu's name though. Or Andan's, or any of the other angels," she added piously.

I looked at it more closely and saw it was true. She'd painted the Amyr so the words *Andan* and *Ordal* rested directly on top of his shoulders, one on each side. Almost as if she were hoping the names would weigh him down, or trap him.

"Plus you said I shouldn't tell anyone what I saw," Nina said. "And painting is like telling with pictures instead of words. So I figured it would be safer to use pages from Tehlu's book, because no demon would ever look at a page of that book. Especially one with Tehlu's name still writ all over it." She looked up at me proudly.

"That was cleverly done," I said approvingly.

The belling tower began to ring the hour, and Nina's expression flared into sudden panic. "Oh no!" she said pitifully. "I should have been back at the docks by now. My mum's going to give me a birching!"

I laughed. Partly because I was utterly amazed by this unexpected piece of luck. And partly at the thought of a young girl brave enough to defy the Chandrian, but still terrified of making her mother angry. Such is the way of the world.

"Nina, you've done me a wonderful favor. If you ever need anything, or if you have another dream, you can find me at an inn called Anker's. I play music there."

Her eyes went wide. "Is it magic music?"

I laughed again. "Some people think so."

She looked around nervously. "I really have to go!" she said, then waved and took off running toward the river, the wind blowing her hood back as she went.

I carefully rerolled the piece of paper and tucked it back into the hollow piece of horn. My mind spun with what I had just learned. I thought of what I'd heard Haliax say to Cinder all those years ago: *Who keeps you safe from the Amyr, the Singers, the Sithe?*

After my months of searching, I was fairly certain the Archives held nothing more than faerie stories about the Chandrian. Nobody considered them more real than shamble-men or faeries.

But everyone knew about the Amyr. They were the bright knights of the Aturan Empire. They were the strong hand of the church for two hundred years. They were the subject of a hundred stories and songs.

I knew my history. The Amyr had been founded by the Tehlin Church in the early days of the Aturan Empire.

But the pottery Nina had seen had been much older than that.

I knew my history. The Amyr had been condemned and disbanded by the church before the empire fell.

But I knew the Chandrian were still afraid of them today.

It seemed like there was more to the story.

CHAPTER THIRTY-SIX

All This Knowing

DAYS PASSED, AND I invited Wil and Sim across the river to celebrate our successful campaign against Ambrose.

Given my taste for sounten, I was not much of a drinker, but Wil and Sim were kind enough to demonstrate the fine points of the art. We visited several different taverns, just for variety, but eventually we ended up back at the Eolian. I preferred it because of the music, Simmon because of the women, and Wilem because it served scutten.

I was moderately well-buttered when I was called up onto the stage, but it takes more than a little drink to make me fumble-fingered. Just to prove I was not drunk, I made my way through "Whither With He With the Withee," a song that's difficult enough to articulate when sober as a stone.

The audience loved it, and showed its appreciation in the appropriate way. And, since I was not drinking sounten that night, much of the evening is lost to living memory.

———

The three of us walked the long road back from the Eolian. There was a crispness to the air that spoke of winter, but the three of us were young and warmed from the inside by many drinks. A breeze pushed my cloak back and I took a full, happy breath.

Then a sudden panic seized me. "Where's my lute?" I asked more loudly than I'd intended.

"You left it with Stanchion at the Eolian," Wilem said. "He was afraid you would trip over it and break your neck."

Simmon had stopped in the middle of the road. I bumped into him, lost my balance, and tumbled to the ground. He hardly seemed to notice. "Well," he said seriously. "I certainly don't feel up to that right now."

Stonebridge rose ahead of us: two hundred feet from end to end, with a high arch that peaked five stories above the river. It was part of the Great Stone Road, straight as a nail, flat as a table, and older than God. I knew it weighed more than a mountain. I knew it had a three-foot parapet running along both its edges.

Despite all this knowing, I felt deeply uneasy at the thought of trying to cross it. I climbed unsteadily to my feet.

As the three of us examined the bridge, Wilem began to lean slowly to one side. I reached out to steady him and at the same time Simmon laid hold of my arm, though whether to help me or to brace himself I couldn't be certain.

"I certainly don't feel up to that right now," Simmon repeated.

"There's a place to sit over here," Wilem said. *"Kella trelle turen navor ka."*

Simmon and I muffled our laughter, and Wilem led us through the trees to a little clearing not fifty feet from the foot of the bridge. To my surprise a tall greystone stood at the middle of it, pointing skyward.

Wil entered the clearing with calm familiarity. I came more slowly, looking about curiously. Greystones are special to troupers, and seeing it gave rise to mixed feelings.

Simmon flopped down in the thick grass while Wilem settled his back against the trunk of a leaning birch. I moved to the greystone and touched it with my fingertips. It was warm and familiar.

"Don't push at that thing," Simmon said nervously. "You'll tip it over."

I laughed. "This stone has been here for a thousand years, Sim. I don't think my breathing on it is going to hurt it."

"Just come away from it. They're not good things."

"It's a greystone," I said, giving it a friendly pat. "They mark old roads. If anything, we're safer being next to it. Greystones mark safe places. Everyone knows that."

Sim shook his head stubbornly. "They're pagan relics."

"A jot says I'm right," I taunted.

"Ha!" Still on his back, Sim held up a hand. I stepped over to slap it, formalizing our wager.

"We can go to the Archives and settle it tomorrow," Sim said.

I sat down next to the greystone and had just started to relax when I was seized by a sudden panic. "Body of God!" I said. "My lute!" I tried to jump to my feet and failed, almost managing to knock out my brains against the greystone in the process.

Simmon tried to sit up and calm me, but the sudden motion was too much for him and he fell awkwardly onto his side and began to laugh helplessly.

"This isn't funny!" I shouted.

"It's at the Eolian," Wilem said. "You've asked about it four times since we left."

"No I haven't," I said with more conviction than I really felt. I rubbed my head where I'd knocked it against the greystone.

"There is no reason to be ashamed." Wilem waved a hand dismissively. "It is man's nature to dwell on what sits close to his heart."

"I heard Kilvin got a few in him at the Taps a couple months ago and wouldn't shut up about his new cold-sulfur lamp," Simmon said.

Wil snorted. "Lorren would rattle on about proper shelving behavior. *Grasp by the spine. Grasp by the spine.*" He growled and made clutching motions with both hands. "If I hear him say it again I will grasp *his* spine."

A flash of memory came to me. "Merciful Tehlu," I said, suddenly aghast. "Did I sing 'Tinker Tanner' at the Eolian tonight?"

"You did," Simmon said. "I didn't know it had so many verses."

I wrinkled my forehead, trying desperately to remember. "Did I sing the verse about the Tehlin and the sheep?" It was not a good verse for polite company.

"Nia," Wilem said.

"Thank God," I said.

"It was a goat," Wilem managed seriously before he bubbled up into laughter.

"'...in the Tehlin's cassock!'" Simmon sang, then joined Wilem in laughter.

"No, no," I said miserably, resting my head in my hands. "My mother used to make my dad sleep under the wagon when he sang that in public. Stanchion will beat me with a stick and take away my pipes next time I see him."

"They loved it," Simmon reassured me.

"I saw Stanchion singing along," Wilem added. "His nose was a little red by that time too."

There was a long piece of comfortable quiet.

"Kvothe?" Simmon asked.

"Yes?"

"Are you really Edema Ruh?"

The question caught me unprepared. Normally it would have set me on edge, but at the moment I didn't know how I felt about it. "Does it matter?"

"No. I was just wondering."

"Oh." I continued to watch the stars for a while. "Wondering what?"

"Nothing in particular," he said. "Ambrose called you Ruh a couple times, but he's called you other insulting things before."

"It's not an insult," I said.

"I mean he's called you things that weren't true," Sim said quickly. "You don't talk about your family, but you've said things that made me wonder." He shrugged, still flat on his back, looking up at the stars. "I've never known one of the Edema. Not well, anyway."

"What you hear isn't true," I said. "We don't steal children, or worship dark Gods or anything like that."

"I never believed any of that," he said dismissively, then added. "But some of the things they say must be true. I've never heard anyone play like you."

"That doesn't have anything to do with my being Edema Ruh," I said, then reconsidered. "Maybe a little."

"Do you dance?" Wilem asked, seemingly out of the blue.

If the comment had come from anyone else, or at a different time, it probably would have started a fight. "That's just how people picture us. Playing pipes and fiddles. Dancing around our campfires. When we aren't stealing everything that isn't nailed down, of course." A little bitterness crept into my tone when I said the last. "That's not what being Edema Ruh is about."

"What is it about?" Simmon asked.

I thought about it for a moment, but my sodden wit wasn't up to the task. "We're just people really," I said eventually. "Except we don't stay in one place very long, and everyone hates us."

The three of us watched the stars quietly.

"Did she really make him sleep under the wagon?" Simmon asked.

"What?"

"You said your mom made your dad sleep under the wagon for singing the verse about the sheep. Did she really?"

"It's mostly a figure of speech," I said. "But once she really did."

I didn't often think of my early life in my troupe, back when my parents were alive. I avoided the subject the same way a cripple learns to keep the weight off an injured leg. But Sim's question brought a memory bubbling to the surface of my mind.

"It wasn't for singing 'Tinker Tanner,' " I found myself saying. "It was a song he'd written about her. . . ."

I was quiet for a long moment. Then I said it. "Laurian."

It was the first time I'd said my mother's name in years. The first time since she'd been killed. It felt strange in my mouth.

Then, without really meaning to, I began to sing.

Dark Laurian, Arliden's wife,
Has a face like the blade of a knife
Has a voice like a pricklebrown burr
But can tally a sum like a moneylender.
My sweet Tally cannot cook.
But she keeps a tidy ledger-book
For all her faults, I do confess
It's worth my life
To make my wife
Not tally a lot less . . .

I felt oddly numb, disconnected from my own body. Strangely, while the memory was sharp, it wasn't painful.

"I can see how that might earn a man a place under the wagon," Wilem said gravely.

"It wasn't that," I heard myself saying. "She was beautiful, and they both knew it. They used to tease each other all the time. It was the meter. She hated the awful meter."

I never talked about my parents, and referring to them in the past tense felt uncomfortable. Disloyal. Wil and Sim weren't surprised by my revelation. Anyone who knew me could tell I had no family. I'd never said anything, but they were good friends. They knew.

"In Atur we sleep in the kennels when our wives are angry," Simmon said, nudging the conversation back into safer territory.

"Melosi rehu eda Stiti," Wilem muttered.

"Aturan!" Simmon shouted, his voice bubbling with amusement. "No more of your donkey talk!"

"Eda Stiti?" I repeated. "You sleep next to fire?"

Wilem nodded.

"I am officially protesting how quickly you picked up Siaru," Sim said, holding up a finger. "I studied a year before I was any good. A year! You gobble it up in a single term."

"I learned a lot growing up," I said. "I was just getting the fine points this term."

"Your accent is better," Wil said to Sim. "Kvothe sounds like some southern trader. Very low. You sound much more refined."

Sim seemed mollified by that. "Next to the fire," he repeated. "Does it seem odd that it's the men that always have to do their sleeping somewhere else?"

"It's pretty obvious women control the bed," I said.

"Not an unpleasant thought," Sim said. "Depending on the woman."

"Distrel is pretty," Sim said.

"Keh," Wil said. "Too pale. Fela."

Simmon shook his head mournfully. "Out of our league."

"She is Modegan," Wilem said, his grin so wide it was almost demonic.

"She is?" Sim asked. Wil nodded, wearing the widest smile I'd ever seen on his face. Sim sighed wretchedly. "It figures. Bad enough that she's the prettiest girl in the Commonwealth, I didn't know she was Modegan, too."

"I'll grant you prettiest girl on her side of the river," I corrected. "On this side, there's—"

"You've already gone on about your Denna," Wil interrupted. "Five times."

"Listen," Simmon said, his tone suddenly serious. "You just have to make your move. This Denna girl is obviously interested in you."

"She hasn't said anything along those lines."

"They never *say* they're interested." Simmon laughed at the absurdity of it. "There are little games. It's like a dance." He held up two hands, making them talk to each other. "'Oh, fancy meeting you here.' 'Why hello, I was just going to lunch.' 'What a happy coincidence, so was I. Can I carry your books?' "

I held up a hand to stop him. "Can we skip to the end of this puppet show, where you end up sobbing into your beer for a span of days?"

Simmon scowled at me. Wilem laughed.

"She has enough men fawning over her," I said. "They come and go like . . ." I strained to think of an analogy and failed. "I'd rather be her friend."

"You would rather be close to her heart," Wilem said without any particular inflection. "You would rather be joyfully held in the circle of her arms. But you fear she will reject you. You fear she would laugh and you would look the fool." Wilem shrugged easily. "You are hardly the first to feel this way. There is no shame in it."

That struck uncomfortably close to the mark, and for a long moment I couldn't think of anything to say in reply. "I hope," I admitted quietly. "But I don't want to assume. I've seen what happens to the men that assume too much and cling to her."

Wilem nodded solemnly.

"She bought you that lute case," Sim said helpfully. "That has to mean something."

"But what does it mean?" I said. "It seems like she's interested, but what if it's just wishful thinking on my part? All those other men must think she's interested too. But they're obviously wrong. What if I'm wrong too?"

"You'll never know unless you try," Sim said, with a bitter edge to his voice. "That's what I'd normally say. But, you know what? It doesn't work worth a damn. I chase them and they kick at me like I'm a dog at the dinner table. I'm tired of trying so hard." He gave a weary sigh, still flat on his back. "All I want is someone who likes me."

"All I want is a clear sign," I said.

"I want a magical horse that fits in my pocket," Wil said. "And a ring of red amber that gives me power over demons. And an endless supply of cake."

There was another moment of comfortable quiet. The wind brushed gently through the trees.

"They say the Ruh know all the stories in the world," Simmon said after a while.

"Probably true," I admitted.

"Tell one," he said.

I eyed him narrowly.

"Don't look at me like that," he protested. "I'm in the mood for a story, that's all."

"We are somewhat lacking for entertainment," Wilem said.

"Fine, fine. Let me think." I closed my eyes and a story with Amyr in it bubbled to the surface. Hardly surprising. They had been on my mind constantly since Nina had found me.

I sat up straight. "All right," I took a breath, then paused. "If either of you have to go piss, do it now. I don't like having to stop halfway through."

Silence.

"Okay." I cleared my throat. "There is a place not many folk have seen. A strange place called Faeriniel. If you believe the stories, there are two things that make Faeriniel unique. First, it is where all the roads in the world meet. Second, it is not a place any man has ever found by searching. It is not a place you travel to, it is the place you pass through while on your way to somewhere else.

"They say that anyone who travels long enough will come there. This is a story of that place, and of an old man on a long road, and of a long and lonely night without a moon. . . ."

CHAPTER THIRTY-SEVEN

A Piece of Fire

FAERINIEL WAS A GREAT crossroads, but there was no inn where the roads met. Instead there were clearings in the trees where travelers would set their camps and pass the night.

Once, years ago and miles away, five groups of travelers came to Faeriniel. They chose their clearings and lit their fires as the sun began to set, pausing on their way from here to there.

Later, after the sun had set and night was settled firmly in the sky, an old beggar in a tattered robe came walking down the road. He moved with slow care, leaning on a walking stick.

The old man was going from nowhere to nowhere. He had no hat for his head and no pack for his back. He had not a penny or a purse to put it in. He barely even owned his own name, and even that had been worn thin and threadbare through the years.

If you'd asked him who he was, he would have said, "Nobody." But he would have been wrong.

The old man made his way into Faeriniel. He was hungry as a dry fire and weary to his bones. All that kept him moving was the hope that someone might give him a bit of dinner and a piece of their fire.

So when the old man saw firelight flickering, he left the road and made his weary way toward it. Soon he saw four tall horses through the trees. Silver was worked into their harness and silver was mixed with the iron of their shoes. Nearby the beggar saw a dozen mules laden with goods: woolen cloth, cunning jewelry, and fine steel blades.

But what caught the beggar's attention was the side of meat above the fire, steaming and dripping fat onto the coals. He almost fainted at the sweet smell of it, for he had been walking all day with nothing to eat but a handful of acorns and a bruised apple he'd found by the side of the road.

Stepping into the clearing, the old beggar called out to the three dark-bearded men who sat around the fire. "Halloo," he said. "Can you spare a bit of meat and a piece of your fire?"

They turned, their gold chains glittering in the firelight. "Certainly," their leader said. "What do you have with you? Bits or pennies? Rings or strehlaum? Or do you have the true-ringing Cealdish coin we prize above all others?"

"I have none of these," the old beggar said, opening his hands to show they were empty.

"Then you will find no comfort here," they said, and as he watched they began to carve thick pieces from the haunch that hung by the fire.

"No offense, Wilem. It's just how the story goes."

"I didn't say anything."

"You looked like you were going to."

"I may. But it will wait until after."

The old man walked on, following the light of another fire through the trees.

"Halloo!" the old beggar called out as he stepped into the second clearing. He tried to sound cheerful, though he was weary and sore. "Can you spare a bit of meat and a piece of your fire?"

There were four travelers there, two men and two women. At the sound of his voice they rose to their feet, but none of them spoke. The old man waited politely, trying to appear pleasant and harmless. But the quiet stretched on, long as long, and still no word was spoken.

Understandably, the old man grew irritated. He was used to being shunned or shrugged aside, but these folk merely stood. They were quiet and restless, moving from foot to foot while their hands twitched nervously.

Just as he was about to sulk away, the fire flared and the beggar saw the four wore the blood-red clothes that marked them as Adem mercenaries. Then the old man understood. The Adem are called the silent folk, and they speak only rarely.

The old man knew many stories of the Adem. He'd heard that they possessed a secret craft called the Lethani. This let them wear their quiet like an armor that would turn a blade or stop an arrow in the air. This is why they seldom spoke. They saved their words, keeping them inside like coals in the belly of a furnace.

Those hoarded words filled them with so much restless energy that they could never be completely still, which is why they were always twitching and fidgeting about. Then when they fought, they used their secret craft to burn those words like fuel inside themselves. This made them strong as bears and fast as snakes.

When the beggar first heard these rumors, he thought them silly campfire stories. But years ago in Modeg, he had seen an Adem woman fight the city guard. The soldiers were armed and armored, thick of arm and chest. They had demanded to see the woman's sword in the king's name, and though hesitant, she presented it to them. As soon as they held it in their hands, they had leered and pawed at her, making lewd suggestions about what she could do to get it back.

They were tall men with bright armor and their swords were sharp. They fell like autumn wheat before her. She killed three of them, breaking their bones with her hands.

Her own wounds were minor by comparison, a dark bruise along one cheek, a slight limp, a shallow cut across one hand. Even after all the long years, the old man remembered the way she had licked the blood from the back of her hand like a cat.

This is what the old beggar thought of when he saw the Adem standing there. All thought of food and fire left him, and he backed slowly into the shelter of the surrounding trees.

Then he set off toward the next fire, hoping third time would prove lucky.

At this clearing were a number of Aturans standing around a dead donkey lying near a cart. One of them spotted the old man. "Look!" he pointed. "Grab him! We'll hitch him to the cart and make him pull!"

The old man darted back into the trees, and after running to and fro, he lost the Aturans by hiding under a pile of moldering leaves.

When the sound of the Aturans faded, the old man dragged himself from the leaves and found his walking stick. Then, with the courage of one who is poor and hungry, he set off to the fourth fire he saw in the distance.

There he might have found what he was looking for, because around the fire were traders from Vintas. Had things been different they might have welcomed him to dinner, saying, "Where six can eat, seven can eat."

But by this point the old man was quite a sight. His hair stuck from his head in wild disarray. His robe, ragged before, was now torn and dirty. His face was pale from fright, and his breathing groaned and wheezed in his chest.

Because of this, the Vints gasped and made gestures before their faces. They thought he was a barrow draug, you see, one of the unquiet dead that superstitious Vints believe walk the night.

Each of the Vints had a different thought as to how they could stop him.

Some thought fire would frighten him off, some thought salt scattered on the grass would keep him away, some thought iron would cut the strings that held the soul to his dead body.

Listening to them argue, the old beggar realized that no matter what they agreed on, he would not be the better for it. So he hurried back to the sheltering trees.

The old man found a rock to sit on and brushed the dead leaves and dirt away as best he could. After sitting for a while he thought to try one final campsite, knowing it would only take one generous traveler to fill his belly.

He was pleased to see a lone man sitting at the final fire. Coming closer, he saw a thing that left him both delighted and afraid, for though the beggar had lived many years, he had never before spoken to one of the Amyr.

Still, he knew the Amyr were a part of Tehlu's church, and—

"*They weren't part of the church,*" Wilem said.

"*What? Of course they were.*"

"*No, they were of the Aturan bureaucracy. They had . . . Vecarum—judiciary powers.*"

"*They were called the Holy Order of Amyr. They were the strong right hand of the church.*"

"*Bet a jot?*"

"*Fine. If it will keep you quiet through the rest of the story.*"

The old beggar was delighted, for he knew the Amyr were a part of Tehlu's church, and the church was sometimes generous to the poor.

The Amyr came to his feet as the old man approached. "Who goes there?" he asked. His voice was proud and powerful, but also tired. "Know I am of the Order Amyr. None should come between me and my tasks. I will act for the good of all, though Gods and men might bar my way."

"Sir," the beggar said, "I'm just hoping for a piece of fire and some charity on a long road."

The Amyr gestured the old man forward. He was armored in a suit of bright steel rings, and his sword was tall as a man. His tabard was of shining white, but from the elbows the color darkened into crimson, as if dipped in blood. In the center of his chest, he wore the symbol of the Amyr: the black tower wrapped in a crimson flame.

The old man sat near the fire and gave a sigh as the heat soaked into his bones.

After a moment, the Amyr spoke, "I'm afraid I can offer you nothing to eat. My horse eats better than I do tonight, but that does not mean that he eats well."

"Anything would be a lovely help," the old man said. "Scraps are more than what I have. I am not proud."

The Amyr sighed. "Tomorrow I must ride fifty miles to stop a trial. If I fail or falter, an innocent woman will die. This is all I have." The Amyr gestured to a piece of cloth with a crust of bread and a sliver of cheese. Both of them together would hardly be enough to dent the old man's hunger. It made a poor dinner for a man as large as the Amyr.

"Tomorrow I must ride and fight," the armored man said. "I need my strength. So I must weigh your night of hunger against this woman's life." As he spoke, the Amyr raised his hands and held them palms up, like the plates of a balancing scale.

When he made this motion, the old beggar saw the backs of the Amyr's hands, and for a second he thought the Amyr had cut himself, and that blood was running between his fingers and down his arms. Then the fire shifted and the beggar saw it was only a tattoo, though he still shivered at the bloody markings on the Amyr's hands and arms.

He would have done more than shiver had he known all that those markings meant. They showed the Amyr was trusted so completely by the Order that his actions would never be questioned. And as the Order stood behind him, no church, no court, no king could move against him. For he was one of the Ciridae, highest of the Amyr.

If he killed an unarmed man, it was not murder in the Order's eyes. If he strangled a pregnant woman in the middle of the street, none would speak against him. Should he burn a church or break an old stone bridge, the empire held him blameless, trusting all he did was in the service of the greater good.

But the beggar knew none of this, and so he tried again. "If you don't have any food to spare, could I have a penny or two?" He thought of the Cealdish camp, and how he might buy a slice of meat or bread.

The Amyr shook his head. "If I did, I would gladly give it. But three days ago I gave the last of my money to a new widower with a hungry child. I have been penniless as you are ever since." He shook his head, his expression weary and full of regret. "I wish circumstances were different. But I now must sleep, so you must go."

The old man was hardly happy about this, but there was something in the Amyr's voice that made him wary. So he creaked back onto his feet and left the fire behind.

Before the warmth of the Amyr's fire could leave him, the old man tightened his belt and made up his mind to simply walk through 'til morning. Hoping the end of his road might bring him better luck, or at least a meeting with some kinder folk.

So he walked through the center of Faeriniel, and as he did, he saw a circle of great grey stones. Inside that circle was the faint glow of firelight hidden in a well-dug pit. The old man noticed he couldn't smell a wisp of smoke either, and realized these folk were burning rennel wood, which burns hot and hard, but doesn't smoke or stink.

Then the old man saw that two of the great shapes were not stones at all. They were wagons. A handful of people huddled round a cookpot in the dim light of the fire.

But the old man didn't have a shred of hope left, so he kept walking. He was almost past the stones when a voice called out: "Ho there! Who are you, and why do you pass by so quietly at night?"

"I'm nobody," the old man said. "Just an old beggar, following my road until its end."

"Why are you out walking instead of settling down to sleep? These roads are not all safe at night," the voice replied.

"I have no bed," the old man said. "And tonight I cannot beg or borrow one for all the world."

"There is one here for you, if you would like it. And a bit of dinner if you've a mind to share. No one should walk all day and night besides." A handsome, bearded man stepped from the concealment of the tall grey stones. He took the old man's elbow and led him toward the fire, calling ahead, "We have a guest tonight!"

There was a small stir of motion ahead of them, but the night was moonless and their fire was deep in a concealing pit, so the beggar couldn't see much of what was being done. Curious, he asked, "Why do you hide your fire?"

His host sighed. "Not all folk are filled with love for us. We're safest by being out of harm's way. Besides, our fire is small tonight."

"Why is that?" the beggar asked. "With so many trees, wood should be easy to come by."

"We went gathering earlier," the bearded man explained. "But folk called us thieves and shot arrows at us." He shrugged. "So we make do, and tomorrow will take care of itself." He shook his head. "But I am talking too much. May I offer you a drink, father?"

"A bit of water, if you can spare it."

"Nonsense, you will have wine."

It had been a long time since the beggar had tasted wine, and the thought of it was enough to set his mouth all a-watering. But he knew wine was not the best thing for an empty stomach that had walked all day, so he said, "You are kind, bless you. But water is good enough for me."

The man at his elbow smiled. "Then have water and wine, each to your desire." And saying so he brought the beggar to their water barrel.

The old beggar bent and drew up a ladle of water. When it touched his lips it was cool and sweet, but as he drew up the ladle, he couldn't help but notice the barrel was very nearly empty.

In spite of this, his host urged him, "Take another and wash the dust from your hands and face. I can tell you've been on the road for a long and weary while." So the old beggar took a second dipper of water, and once his hands and face were clean, he felt much refreshed.

Then his host took his elbow again and led him to the fire. "What is your name, father?"

Again the beggar was surprised. It had been years since anyone had cared enough to ask his name. It had been so long he had to stop and think about it for a moment. "Sceop," he said at last. "I am called Sceop, and you?"

"My name is Terris," his host said as he made the old man comfortable close to the fire. "This is Silla, my wife, and Wint, our son. This is Shari and Benthum and Lil and Peter and Fent."

Then Terris brought Sceop wine. Silla gave him a heavy ladle of potato soup, a slice of warm bread, and half a golden summer squash with sweet butter in the bowl of it. It was plain, and there was not a lot, but to Sceop it seemed a feast. And as he ate, Wint kept his cup full of wine, and smiled at him, and sat by his knee and called him grandfather.

The last was too much for the old beggar, and he began to cry softly. Perhaps it was that he was old, and his day had been a long one. Perhaps it was that he was not used to kindness. Perhaps it was the wine. Whatever the reason, tears began to trickle down his face and lose themselves in his deep white beard.

Terris saw this and was quick to ask, "Father, whatever is the matter?"

"I am a silly old man," Sceop said, more to himself than to the rest of them. "You have been kinder to me than anyone in years, and I am sorry I cannot repay you."

Terris smiled and laid a hand on the old man's back. "Would you really like to pay?"

"I cannot. I have nothing to give you."

Terris's smile widened. "Sceop. We are the Edema Ruh. The thing we value most is something everyone possesses." One by one, Sceop saw the faces around the fire look up at him expectantly. Terris said, "You could tell us your story."

Not knowing what else to do, Sceop began to speak. He told how he had come to Faeriniel. How he had walked from one fire to the next, hoping for charity. At first his voice faltered and his story stumbled, for he had been alone a long time and was not used to talking. But soon his voice became stronger, his words bolder, and as the fire flickered and reflected in his bright blue eyes, his hands danced along with his old dried voice. Even the Edema Ruh, who know all the stories in the world, could do nothing but listen in wonder.

When his story came to an end the troupers stirred as if waking from a deep sleep. For a moment they did nothing but look at each other, then they looked at Sceop.

Terris knew what they were thinking. "Sceop," he asked gently. "Where were you headed, when I stopped you tonight?"

"I was going to Tinuë," said Sceop, who was a little embarrassed at how caught up in the story he had become. His face was hot and red, and he felt foolish.

"We are bound for Belenay ourselves," Terris said. "Would you consider coming with us instead?"

For a moment Sceop's face lit with hope, but then it fell. "I would be nothing but a burden. Even a beggar has his pride."

Terris laughed. "You would tell the Edema about pride? We do not ask you out of pity. We ask because you belong in our family, and we would have you tell us a dozen dozen stories in the years to come."

The beggar shook his head. "My blood is not yours. I am not a part of your family."

"What does that have to do with the price of butter?" Terris asked. "We Ruh decide who is a part of our family and who is not. You belong with us. Look around and see if I am lying."

Sceop looked up at the circle of faces and saw what Terris said was true.

And so the old man stayed, and lived with them for many years before they parted ways. Many things he saw, and many stories he told, and everyone was wiser in the end because of it.

This thing happened, though it was years and miles away. I have heard it from the mouths of the Edema Ruh, and thus I know it to be true.

CHAPTER THIRTY-EIGHT

Kernels of Truth

"IS THAT THE END?" Simmon asked after a polite pause. He was on his back, looking up at the stars.

"Yes."

"It didn't end the way I thought it would," he said.

"What did you expect?"

"I was waiting to find out who the beggar really was. I thought as soon as someone was nice to him, he would turn out to be Taborlin the Great. Then he would give them his walking stick and a sack of money and . . . I don't know. Make something magical happen."

Wilem spoke up. "He'd say, 'Whenever you are in danger knock this stick on the ground and say "stick be quick," ' and then the stick would whirl around and defend them from whoever was attacking them." Wilem was lying on his back in the tall grass, too. "I didn't think he was really an old beggar."

"Old beggars in stories are never *really* old beggars," Simmon said with hint of accusation in his voice. "They're always a witch or a prince or an angel or something."

"In real life old beggars are almost always old beggars," I pointed out. "But I know what kind of story you two are thinking about. Those are stories we tell other people to entertain them. This story is different. It's one we tell each other."

"Why tell a story if it's not entertaining?"

"To help us remember. To teach us—" I made a vague gesture. "Things."

"Like exaggerated stereotypes?" Simmon asked.

"What do you mean by that?" I asked, nettled.

" 'Tie him to the wagon and make him pull'?" Simmon made a disgusted noise. "I'd be offended if I didn't know you."

"If I didn't know *you*," I said hotly, "*I'd* be offended. Do you know Aturans used to kill people if they found them living on the road? One of your emperors declared them to be detrimental to the empire. Most were little more than beggars who had lost their homes because of the wars and taxes. Most were simply press-ganged into military service."

I tugged at the front of my shirt. "But the Edema were especially prized. They hunted us like foxes. For a hundred years Ruh-hunt was a favorite pastime among the Aturan upper crust."

A profound silence fell. My throat hurt, and I realized I'd been shouting. Simmon's voice was muffled. "I didn't know that."

I kicked myself mentally and sighed. "I'm sorry Simmon. It's a . . . It was a long time ago. And it's not your fault. It's an old story."

"It would have to be, to have a reference to the Amyr," Wilem said, obviously trying to change the subject. "They disbanded what? Three hundred years ago?"

"Still," I said. "There's some truth in most stereotypes. A seed they sprouted from."

"Basil is from Vintas," Wil said. "And he is odd about certain things. Sleeps with a penny underneath his pillow, that sort of thing."

"On my way to the University I traveled with a pair of Adem mercenaries," Simmon said. "They didn't talk to anyone except each other. And they *were* restless and fidgety."

Wilem spoke hesitantly. "I will admit to knowing many Cealdim who take great care to line their boots with silver."

"Purses," Simmon corrected him. "Boots are for putting your feet in." He wiggled a foot to illustrate.

"I know what a boot is," Wilem said crossly. "I speak this vulgar language better than you do. Boot is what we say, *Patu*. Money in your purse is for spending. Money you plan to keep is in your boot."

"Oh," Simmon said thoughtfully. "I see. Like saving it for a rainy day, I guess."

"What do you do with money when it rains?" Wilem asked, genuinely puzzled.

"And there's more to the story than you think," I interjected quickly before things digressed any further. "The story holds a kernel of truth. If you promise to keep it to yourselves, I will tell you a secret."

I felt their attention sharpen onto me. "If you ever accept the hospitality of a traveling troupe, and they offer you wine before anything else, they are Edema Ruh. That part of the story is true." I held up a finger to caution them. "But don't take the wine."

"But I like wine," Simmon said piteously.

"That doesn't matter," I said. "Your host offers you wine, but you insist on water. It might even turn into a competition of sorts, the host offering more and more grandly, the guest refusing more and more politely. When you do this, they will know you are a friend of the Edema, that you know our ways. They will treat you like family for the night, as opposed to being a mere guest."

The conversation lulled as they absorbed this piece of information. I looked up at the stars, tracing the familiar constellations in my head. Ewan the hunter, the crucible, the young-again mother, the fire-tongued fox, the broken tower. . . .

"Where would you go if you could go anywhere?" Simmon's question came out of the blue.

"Across the river," I said. "Bed."

"No no," he protested, "I mean if you could go anywhere in the world."

"Same answer," I said. "I've been a lot of places. This is where I've always wanted to go."

"But not forever," Wilem said. "You don't want to be here forever, do you?"

"That's what I meant," Simmon added. "We all want to be here. But none of us want to be here forever."

"Except Manet," Wil said.

"Where would you go?" Simmon pursued his point doggedly. "For adventure?"

I thought for a moment, quietly. "I guess I'd to go to the Tahlenwald," I said.

"Among the Tahl?" Wilem asked. "They're a primitive nomadic people, from what I've heard."

"Technically speaking, the Edema Ruh are a nomadic people," I said dryly. "I heard a story once that said the leaders of their tribes aren't great warriors, they're singers. Their songs can heal the sick and make the trees dance." I shrugged. "I'd go there and find out if it was true."

"I would go to the Faen Court," Wilem said.

Simmon laughed. "You can't pick that."

"Why not?" Wilem said with a quick anger. "If Kvothe can go to a singing tree, I can go into Faen and dance with *Embrula* . . . with Faen women."

"The Tahl is real," Simmon protested. "Faerie stories are for drunks, halfwits, and children."

"Where would you go?" I asked Simmon to keep him from antagonizing Wilem.

There was a long pause. "I don't know," he said, his voice oddly empty of any inflection. "I haven't been anywhere, really. I only came to the University because after my brothers inherit and my sister gets her dowry there isn't going to be much for me except the family name."

"You didn't want to come here?" I asked, disbelief coloring my voice.

Sim made a noncommittal shrug, and I was about to ask him something else when I was interrupted by the sound of Wilem getting noisily to his feet. "Are we feeling up to the bridge now?"

My head felt remarkably clear. I got to my feet with only a slight wobble. "Fine by me."

"Just a second." Simmon started to undo his pants as he moved toward the trees.

As soon as he was out of sight, Wilem leaned close to me. "Don't ask about his family," he said quietly. "It is not easy for him to speak about. Worse when he is drunk."

"What—"

He made a sharp motion with his hand, shaking his head. "Later."

Simmon bumbled back into the clearing, and the three of us made our silent way back to the road, then over Stonebridge and into the University.

CHAPTER THIRTY-NINE

Contradictions

LATE NEXT MORNING, WIL and I made our way to the Archives to meet up with Sim and settle our bets of the night before.

"The problem is his father," Wilem explained in low tones as we made our way between the grey buildings. "Sim's father holds a duchy in Atur. Good land, but—"

"Hold on," I interrupted. "Our little Sim's father is a duke?"

"Little Sim," Wilem said dryly, "is three years older than you and two inches taller."

"Which duchy?" I asked. "And he's not that much taller."

"Dalonir," Wilem said. "But you know how it is. Noble blood from Atur. Small wonder he does not speak of it."

"Oh come on," I chided, gesturing to the students filling the street around us. "The University has the most open-minded atmosphere since the church burned Caluptena to the ground."

"I notice you do not make any loud announcement that you're Edema Ruh."

I bristled. "Are you implying I'm embarrassed?"

"I am saying you make no loud announcement," Wil said calmly, giving me a steady look. "Neither does Simmon. I imagine you both have your reasons."

Pushing down my irritation, I nodded.

Wilem continued. "Dalonir is in the north of Aturna, so they are reasonably well off. But he has three older brothers and two sisters. The first son inherits. The father bought the second a military commission. The third was placed in the church. Simmon . . ." Wilem trailed off suggestively.

"I have a hard time imagining Sim as a priest," I admitted. "Or a soldier, come to think of it."

"And so Sim ends up at the University," Wilem finished. "His father was hoping he would become a diplomat. Then Sim discovered he liked alchemy and poetry and entered the Arcanum. His father was not entirely pleased." Wilem gave me a significant look and I gathered he was drastically understating the case.

"Being an arcanist is a remarkable thing!" I protested. "Much more impressive than being a perfumed toady in some court."

Wilem shrugged. "His tuition is paid. His allowance continues." He paused to wave at someone on the other side of the courtyard. "But Simmon does not go home. Not for even a brief visit. Sim's father likes to hunt, fight, drink, and wench. I suspect our gentle, bookish Sim was probably not given the love a clever son deserves."

———

Wil and I met up with Sim in our usual reading hole and clarified the details of our drunken wagers. Then we went our separate ways.

An hour later I returned with a modest armload of books. My search had been made considerably easier by the fact that I'd been researching the Amyr since Nina had arrived and given me her scroll.

I knocked softly on the door of the reading hole, then let myself in. Wil and Sim were already sitting at the table.

"Me first," Simmon said happily. He consulted a list, then pulled a book from his stack. "Page one hundred and fifty two." He leafed through until he found the page and then began to scan it. "Ah-ha! 'The girl then gave an account of everything. . . . *Blah blah blah* . . . And led them to the place where she stumbled onto the pagan frolic.'" He looked up, pointing at the page. "See? It says pagan right there."

I sat down. "Let's see the rest."

Sim's second book was more of the same. But the third held something of a surprise.

" 'A large preponderance of marker stones in the vicinity, suggesting this area might have been crossed with trade routes in some forgotten past. . . .'" He trailed off, then shrugged and handed the book to me. "This one seems to be on your side."

I couldn't help but laugh. "Didn't you read these before you brought them here?"

"In an hour?" He gave a laugh of his own. "Not likely, I just used a scriv."

Wilem gave him a dark look. "No you didn't. You asked Puppet, didn't you?"

Simmon assumed an innocent expression, which on his naturally innocent face only served to make him look profoundly guilty. "I might have stopped in to see him," he hedged. "And he might have happened to suggest a couple books that had information about greystones." Seeing Wilem's expression he raised a hand. "Don't get sniffy on me. It's backfired anyway."

"Puppet again," I grumbled. "Are you ever going to introduce me? The two of you are so tight-lipped about him."

Wilem shrugged. "You will understand when you meet him."

Sim's books divided into three categories. One supported his side, telling of pagan rites and animal sacrifices. The other speculated about an ancient civilization that used them as marker stones for roads, despite the fact that some were located on sheer mountainsides or river bottoms where no road could be.

His final book was interesting for other reasons:

"... a pair of matched stone monoliths with a third across the top," Simmon read. "The locals refer to it as the door-post. While spring and summer pageants involve decorating and dancing around the stone, parents forbid their children from spending time near it when the moon is full. One well-respected and otherwise reasonable old man claimed ..."

Sim broke off reading. "Whatever," he said disgustedly and moved to close the book.

"Claimed what?" Wilem asked, his curiosity piqued.

Simmon rolled his eyes and continued reading, "Claimed at certain times men could pass through the stone door into the fair land where Felurian herself abides, loving and destroying men with her embrace."

"Interesting," Wilem murmured.

"No it isn't. It's childish, superstitious bunk," Simmon said testily. "And none of this is getting us any closer to deciding who is right."

"How do you count them, Wilem?" I asked. "You're our impartial judge."

Wilem moved to the table and looked through the books. His dark eyebrows moved up and down as he considered. "Seven for Simmon. Six for Kvothe. Three contrary."

We looked briefly at the four books I had brought. Wilem ruled one of them out, which brought the tally to seven for Simmon and ten for me. "Hardly conclusive," Wilem mused.

"We could declare it a draw," I suggested magnanimously.

Simmon scowled. Good-natured or not, he hated losing a bet. "Fair enough," he said.

I turned to Wilem and gave a significant look at the pair of books still untouched on the table "It looks like our bet will be settled a little more quickly, *nia?*"

Wilem gave a predatory grin. "Very quickly." He lifted a book. "Here I have a copy of the proclamation which disbanded the Amyr." He opened to a marked page and began to read. "'Their actions will henceforth be held in account by the laws of the empire. No member of the Order shall presume to take upon themselves the right to hear a case, nor to pass judgment in court.'"

He looked up smugly. "See? If they had their adjudicating powers revoked, then they must have had some to begin with. So it stands to reason they were a part of the Aturan bureaucracy."

"Actually," I said apologetically, "The church has always had judiciary powers in Atur." I held up one of my two books. "It's funny you should bring the *Alpura Prolycia Amyr*. I brought it too. The decree itself was issued by the church."

Wilem's expression darkened. "No it wasn't. It was listed in here as Emperor Nalto's sixty-third decree."

Puzzled, we compared our two books and found them directly contradictory.

"Well I guess those cancel each other out," Sim said. "What else have you guys got?"

"This is Feltemi Reis. *The Lights of History*," Wilem grumbled. "It is definitive. I didn't think I would need any further proof."

"Doesn't this bother either of you?" I thumped the two contradictory books with a knuckle. "These shouldn't be saying different things."

"We just read twenty books saying different things," Simmon pointed out. "Why would I have a problem with two more?"

"The purpose of the greystones is speculative. There's bound to be a variety of opinions. But the *Alpura Prolycia Amyr* was an open decree. It turned thousands of the most powerful men and women in the Aturan Empire into outlaws. It was one of the primary reasons for the collapse of the empire. There's no reason for conflicting information."

"The order *has* been disbanded for over three hundred years," Simmon said. "Plenty of time for some contradictions to arise."

I shook my head, flipping through both of the books. "Contrary opinions are one thing. Contrary facts are another." I held up my book. "This is *The Fall of Empire* by Greggor the Lesser. He's a windbag and a bigot, but he's the best historian of his age." I held up Wilem's book. "Feltemi Reis isn't nearly the historian, but he's twice the scholar Greggor was, and scrupulous about his facts." I looked back and forth between the books, frowning. "This doesn't make any sense."

"So what now?" Sim said. "Another draw? That's disappointing."

"We need someone to judge," Wilem said. "A higher authority."

"Higher than Feltemi Reis?" I asked. "I doubt Lorren can be bothered to settle our bet."

Wil shook his head, then stood and brushed the wrinkles from the front of his shirt. "It means you finally get to meet Puppet."

CHAPTER FORTY

Puppet

"**THE MOST IMPORTANT THING** is to be polite," Simmon said in a hushed tone as we made our way through a narrow hallway lined with books. Our sympathy lamps shot bands of light through the shelves and made the shadows dance nervously. "But don't patronize him. He's a bit—odd, but he's not an idiot. Just treat him like you would treat anyone else."

"Except polite," I said sarcastically, tiring of this litany of advice.

"Exactly," Simmon said seriously.

"Where are we going, anyway?" I asked, mostly to stop Simmon's henpecking.

"Sub-three," Wilem said as he turned to descend a long flight of stone steps. Centuries of use had worn down the stone, making the stairs look as bowed as heavy-laden shelves. As we started down, the shadows made the steps look smooth and dark and edgeless, like an abandoned riverbed worn from the rock.

"Are you sure he's going to be there?"

Wil nodded. "I don't think he leaves his chambers very much."

"Chambers?" I asked. "He *lives* here?"

Neither of them said anything as Wilem led the way down another flight of stairs, then through a long stretch of wide hallway with a low ceiling. Finally we came to an unremarkable door tucked into a corner. If I hadn't known better I would have assumed it was one of the countless reading holes scattered throughout the Stacks.

"Just don't do anything to upset him," Simmon said nervously.

I assumed my most polite expression as Wilem rapped on the door. The handle began to turn almost immediately. The door opened a crack, then was thrown wide. Puppet stood framed in the doorway, taller than any of us.

The sleeves of his black robe billowed strikingly in the breeze of the opening door.

He stared at us haughtily for a moment, then looked puzzled and brought a hand to touch the side of his head. "Wait, I've forgotten my hood," he said, and kicked the door closed.

Odd as his brief appearance had been, I'd noticed something more disturbing. "Burned body of God," I whispered. "He's got candles in there. Does Lorren know?"

Simmon opened his mouth to answer when the door was thrown wide again. Puppet filled the doorway, his dark robe striking against the warm candlelight behind him. He was hooded now, with his arms upraised. The long sleeves of his robes caught the inrush of air and billowed impressively. The same rush of air caught his hood and blew it partway off his head.

"Damn," he said in a distracted voice. The hood settled half on, half off his head, partially covering one eye. He kicked the door shut again.

Wilem and Simmon remained straight-faced. I refrained from any comment.

There was a moment of quiet. Finally a muffled voice came from the other side of the door. "Would you mind knocking again? It doesn't seem quite right otherwise."

Obediently, Wilem stepped back up to the door and knocked. Once, twice, then the door swung open and we were confronted with a looming figure in a dark robe. His cowled hood shadowed his face, and the long sleeves of his robe stirred in the wind.

"Who calls on Taborlin the Great?" Puppet intoned, his voice resonant, but slightly muted by the deep hood. A hand pointed dramatically. "You! Simmon!" There was a pause, and his voice lost its dramatic resonance. "I've seen you already today, haven't I?"

Simmon nodded. I could sense the laughter tumbling around in him, trying to find a way out.

"How long ago?"

"About an hour."

"Hmm." The hood nodded. "Was I better this time?" He reached up to push the hood back and I noticed the robe was too big for him, the sleeves hanging down to his fingertips. When his face emerged from the hood he was grinning like a child playing dress-up in his parents' clothes.

"You weren't doing Taborlin before," Simmon admitted.

"Oh." Puppet seemed a little put out. "How was I this time? The last time, I mean. Was it a good Taborlin?"

"Pretty good," Simmon said.

Puppet looked at Wilem.

"I liked the robe," Wil said. "But I always imagined Taborlin with a gentle voice."

"Oh." He finally looked at me. "Hello."

"Hello," I said in my politest tone.

"I don't know you." A pause. "Who are you?"

"I am Kvothe."

"You seem so certain of it," he said, looking at me intently. Another pause. "They call me Puppet."

"Who is 'they?' "

"Who *are* they?" he corrected, raising a finger.

I smiled. "Who are they then?"

"Who *were* they then?"

"Who are they *now?*" I clarified, my smile growing wider.

Puppet mirrored my smile in a distracted way and made a vague gesture with one hand. "You know, them. People." He continued to stare at me the same way I might examine an interesting stone or a type of leaf I'd never seen before.

"What do you call yourself?" I asked.

He seemed a little surprised, and his eyes focused onto me in a more ordinary way. "That would be telling, I suspect," he said with a touch of reproach. He glanced at the silent Wilem and Simmon. "You should come in now." He turned and walked inside.

The room wasn't particularly large. But it seemed bizarrely out of place, nestled in the belly of the Archives. There was a deep padded chair, a large wooden table, and a pair of doorways leading into other rooms.

Books were everywhere, overflowing shelves and bookcases. They were piled on the floor, scattered across tables and stacked on chairs. A pair of drawn curtains against one wall surprised me. My mind struggled with the impression that there must be a window behind them, despite the fact that I knew we were deep underground.

The room was lit with lamps and candles, long tapers and thick dripping pillars of wax. Each tongue of flame filled me with vague anxiety as I thought of open fire in a building filled with hundreds of thousands of precious books.

And there were puppets. They hung from shelves and pegs on walls. They lay crumpled in corners and under chairs. Some were in the process of being built or repaired, scattered among tools across the tabletop. There were shelves full of figurines, each cleverly carved and painted in the shape of a person.

On his way to his table, Puppet shrugged out of the black robe and let it fall carelessly to the floor. He was dressed plainly underneath, wrinkled white shirt, wrinkled dark pants, and mismatched socks much mended in the heel. I realized he was older than I'd thought. His face was smooth and unlined, but his hair was pure white and thin on top.

Puppet cleared a chair for me, carefully removing a small string puppet from the seat and finding it a place on a nearby shelf. He then took a seat at the table, leaving Wilem and Simmon standing. To their credit, they didn't seem terribly disconcerted.

Digging a little in the clutter on the table he brought out an irregularly shaped piece of wood and a small knife. He took another long, searching look at my face, then began to methodically whittle, curls of wood falling onto the tabletop.

Oddly enough, I had no desire to ask anyone what was going on. When you ask as many questions as I do, you learn when they are appropriate.

Besides, I knew what the answers would be. Puppet was one of the talented, not-quite-sane people who had found a niche for themselves at the University.

Arcanum training does unnatural things to students' minds. The most notable of these unnatural things is the ability to do what most people call magic and we call sympathy, sygaldry, alchemy, naming, and the like.

Some minds take to it easily, others have difficulty. The worst of these go mad and end up in Haven. But most minds don't shatter when subjected to the stress of the Arcanum, they simply crack a little. Sometimes these cracks showed in small ways: facial tics, stuttering. Other students heard voices, grew forgetful, went blind, went dumb. . . . Sometimes it was only for an hour or a day. Sometimes it was forever.

I guessed Puppet was a student who had cracked years ago. Like Auri, he seemed to have found a place for himself, though I marveled at the fact that Lorren let him live down here.

"Does he always look like this?" Puppet asked Wilem and Simmon. A small drift of pale wood shavings had gathered around his hands.

"Mostly," Wilem said.

"Like what?" Simmon asked.

"Like he's just thought through his next three moves in a game of tirani and figured out how he's going to beat you." Puppet took another long look at my face and shaved another thin strip of wood away. "It's rather irritating, really."

Wilem barked a laugh. "That's his thinking face, Puppet. He wears it a lot, but not all the time."

"What's tirani?" Simmon asked.

"A thinker," Puppet mused. "What are you thinking now?"

"I'm thinking you must be a very careful watcher of people, Puppet," I said politely.

Puppet snorted without looking up. "What use is *care?* What good is watching for that matter? People are forever watching things. They should be *seeing.* I *see* the things I look at. I am a see-er."

He looked at the piece of wood in his hand, then to my face. Apparently satisfied, he folded his hands over the top of his carving, but not before I glimpsed my own profile cunningly wrought in wood. "Do you know what you have been, what you are not, and what you will be?" He asked.

It sounded like a riddle. "No."

"A see-er," he said with certainty. "Because that is what E'lir means."

"Kvothe is actually a Re'lar," Simmon said respectfully.

Puppet sniffed disparagingly. "Hardly," he said, looking at me closely. "You might be a see-er eventually, but not yet. Now you are a look-er. You'll be a true E'lir at some point. If you learn to relax." He held out the carved wooden face. "What do you see here?"

It was no longer an irregular piece of wood. My features, locked in serious contemplation, stared out of the wood grain. I leaned forward to get a closer look.

Puppet laughed and threw up his hands. "Too late!" he exclaimed, looking childlike for a moment. "You looked too hard and didn't see enough. Too much looking can get in the way of seeing, you see?"

Puppet set the carved face on the tabletop so it seemed to be staring at one of the recumbent puppets. "See little wooden Kvothe? See him looking? So intent. So dedicated. He'll look for a hundred years, but will he ever *see* what is in front of him?" Puppet settled back in his seat, his eyes wandering the room in a contented way.

"E'lir means see-er?" Simmon asked. "Do the other ranks mean things too?"

"As a student with full access to the Archives, I imagine you can find that out for yourself," Puppet said. His attention focused on a puppet on the table in front of him. He lowered it to the floor carefully to avoid tangling its strings. It was a perfect miniature of a grey-robed Tehlin priest.

"Would you have any advice as to where he could start looking?" I asked, playing a hunch.

"Renfalque's *Dictum.*" Under Puppet's direction, the Tehlin puppet raised himself from the floor and moved each of his limbs as if he were stretching after a long sleep.

"I'm not familiar with that one."

Puppet responded in a distracted voice. "It's on the second floor in the southeast corner. Second row, second rack, third shelf, right-hand side, red leather binding." The miniature Tehlin priest walked slowly around Puppet's feet. Clutched tightly in one hand was a tiny replica of the *Book of the Path,* perfectly fashioned, right down to the tiny spoked wheel painted on the cover.

The three of us watched Puppet pull the strings of the little priest, making it walk back and forth before finally coming to sit on one of Puppet's stocking-clad feet.

Wilem cleared his throat respectfully. "Puppet?"

"Yes?" Puppet replied without looking up from his feet. "You have a question. Or rather, Kvothe has a question and you're thinking of asking it for him. He is sitting slightly forward in his seat. There is a furrow between his brows and a pursing of the lips that gives it away. Let him ask me. It might do him good."

I froze in place, catching myself doing each of the things he had mentioned. Puppet continued to work the strings of his little Tehlin. It made a careful, fearful search of the area around his feet, brandishing the book in front of itself before stepping around table legs and peering into Puppet's abandoned shoes. Its movements were uncanny, and it distracted me to the point where I forgot I was uncomfortable and felt myself relax.

"I was wondering about the Amyr, actually." My eyes remained on the scene unfolding at Puppet's feet. Another marionette had joined the show, a young girl in a peasant dress. She approached the Tehlin and held out a hand as if trying to give him something. No, she was asking him a question. The Tehlin turned his back on her. She laid a timid hand on his arm. He took a haughty step away. "I was wondering who disbanded them. Emperor Nalto or the church."

"Still looking," he admonished more gently then before. "You need to go chase the wind for a while, you are too serious. It will lead you into trouble." The Tehlin suddenly turned on the girl. Trembling with rage, it menaced her with the book. She took a startled step backward and stumbled to her knees. "The church disbanded them of course. Only an edict from the pontifex had the ability to affect them." The Tehlin struck the girl with the book. Once, twice, driving her to the ground, where she lay terribly still. "Nalto couldn't have told them to cross to the other side of the street."

Some slight motion drew Puppet's eye. "Oh dear me," he said, cocking his head toward Wilem. "See what I see. The head bows slightly. The jaw clenches, but the eyes aren't fixed on anything, aiming the irritation inward. If I were the sort of person who judged by looking, I'd guess Wilem had just lost a bet. Don't you know the church frowns on gambling?" At Puppet's feet, the priest brandished the book upward at Wilem.

The Tehlin brought its hands together and turned away from the crumpled woman. It took a stately step or two away and bowed its head as if praying.

I managed to pull my attention away from the tableau and look up at our host. "Puppet?" I asked, "Have you read the *Lights of History* by Feltemi Reis?"

I saw Simmon give Wilem an anxious look, but Puppet didn't seem to find anything odd about the question. The Tehlin at his feet stood and started to dance and caper about. "Yes."

"Why would Reis say the *Apura Prolycia Amyr* was Emperor Nalto's sixty-third decree?"

"Reis wouldn't say any such thing," Puppet said without looking up from the marionette at his feet. "That's pure nonsense."

"But we found a copy of *Lights* that said exactly that," I pointed out.

Puppet shrugged, watching the Tehlin dance at his feet.

"It could be a transcription mistake," Wilem mused. "Depending on the edition of the book, the church itself might be responsible for changing that piece of information. Emperor Nalto is history's favorite whipping boy. It could be the church trying to distance itself from the Amyr. They did some terrible things toward the end."

"Clever clever," Puppet said. At his feet the Tehlin made a sweeping bow in Wilem's direction.

I was struck by a sudden idea. "Puppet," I asked. "Do you know what is behind the locked door on the floor above this one? The large stone door?"

The Tehlin stopped dancing and Puppet looked up. He gave me a long, stern look. His eyes were serious and clear. "I don't think the four-plate door should be of any concern to a student. Do you?"

I felt myself flush. "No sir." I looked away from his eyes.

The tension of the moment was broken by the distant sound of the belling tower. Simmon cursed softly. "I'm late," he said. "I'm sorry Puppet, I've got to go."

Puppet stood and hung the Tehlin on the wall. "It's time I got back to my reading, regardless," he said. He moved to the padded chair, sat, and opened a book. "Bring this one back some time." He gestured in my direction without looking up from his book. "I have some more work to do on him."

CHAPTER FORTY-ONE

The Greater Good

I LOOKED UP AT SIMMON and whispered, *"Ivare enim euge."*

Sim gave a despairing sigh. "You are *supposed* to be studying your physiognomy."

It had been a full span since we had set fire to Ambrose's rooms, and winter was finally showing its teeth, covering the University with knee-deep drifts of blowing snow. As was always the case when the weather turned inclement, the Archives were full to the brim with industrious students.

Since all the reading holes were occupied, Simmon and I had been forced to bring our books to Tomes. The high-ceilinged, windowless room was more than half full today, but still quiet as a crypt. All the dark stone and muted whispers made the place slightly eerie, making it obvious why students referred to it as Tombs.

"I am studying my physiognomy," I protested softly. "I was looking at some of Gibea's diagrams. Look what I found." I held out a book for him to see.

"Gibea?" Simmon whispered, horrified. "I swear the only reason you study with me is so you can interrupt." He pulled away from the book I was offering him.

"It's nothing grotesque," I protested. "Just . . . here. Just look at what it says here." Simmon shoved the book away, and my temper flared. "Careful!" I hissed. "This is one of his originals. I found it behind some other books, buried in Dead Ledgers. Lorren will cut off my thumbs if anything happens to it."

Sim recoiled from the book as if it were red-hot. "An original? Merciful Tehlu, it's probably written on human skin. Get it away from me!"

I almost joked about how human skin probably wouldn't take ink, but decided against it when I saw the expression on Sim's face. Still, my expression must have given me away.

"You're perverse," he spat, his voice almost rising to unacceptable levels. "God's mother, don't you know he cut apart living men to watch their organs work? I refuse to look at anything that monster was responsible for."

I set the book down. "You might as well give up studying medicine then," I said as gently as possible. "Gibea's research on the human body was the most thorough ever done. His journals are the backbone of modern physic."

Simmon's face stayed hard and he leaned forward so he could speak softly and still be heard. "When the Amyr moved against the duke, they found the bones of twenty thousand people. Great pits of bones and ashes. Women and children. Twenty thousand!" Simmon sputtered a bit before he could continue. "And those are just the ones they found."

I let him calm himself a bit before I said, "Gibea wrote twenty-three volumes concerning the machinery of the body," I pointed out as gently as I could. "When the Amyr moved against him, part of his estate burned, four of those volumes and all his notes were lost. Ask Master Arwyl what he would give to have those volumes whole again."

Simmon brought his hand down hard on the tabletop, causing several students to look in our direction. "Dammit!" he hissed. "I grew up thirty miles from Gibea! From my father's hills you can see the ruins on a cloudless day!"

That stilled me. If Sim's family lands were that close, his ancestors must have been fealty-bound to Gibea. That meant they might have been forced to help him gather subjects for his experiments. Some of his family might have ended up in the pits of bone and ash themselves.

I waited a long while before I whispered again, "I didn't know."

He regained most of his composure. "We don't talk about it," he said stiffly, brushing the hair out of his eyes.

We bent to our studies, and it was an hour before Simmon spoke again. "What did you find?" he asked too casually, as if not wanting to admit his curiosity.

"Here on the inner leaf," I whispered excitedly. I opened the cover and Sim's face twisted unconsciously as he looked down at the page, as if the book smelled of death.

". . . spilled it all over." I heard a voice as a pair of older students strolled into the hall. By their rich clothes I could tell they were both nobility, and while they weren't shouting, they weren't making any effort to be quiet, either. "Anisat made him clear up the mess before he let him wash off. He'll smell like urea for a span of days."

"What's here to see?" Simmon asked, looking down at the page. "It's just his name and the dates."

"Not the middle, look up at the top. Around the edges of the page." I pointed at the decorative scrollwork. "Right there."

"I'd wager a drab the little pug poisons himself before the term's through," the other one said, "Were we ever that stupid?"

"I still don't see anything," Simmon said softly, making a baffled gesture with both his elbows on the table. "It's pretty enough if you like that sort of thing, but I've never been a great fan of illuminated texts."

"We could head to the Twopenny." The conversation continued several tables away, drawing annoyed looks from surrounding students. "They've got a girl there who plays the pipes, I swear you've never seen anything like her before. And Linten says if you've got a bit of silver she . . ." His voice dropped conspiratorially.

"She what?" I asked, butting into their conversation as rudely as possible. I didn't need to shout. In the Tomes a normal speaking voice carries the whole room. "I'm afraid I didn't quite catch that last bit."

The two of them gave me affronted looks, but didn't reply.

"What are you doing?" Sim hissed at me, embarrassed.

"I'm trying to shut them up," I said.

"Just ignore them," he said. "Here, I'm looking at your damn book. Show me what you want me to see."

"Gibea sketched all his own journals," I said. "This is his original, so it makes sense that he did his own scrollwork too, right?" Sim nodded and brushed his hair back from his eyes. "What do you see there?" I slowly pointed from one piece of scrollwork to another. "Do you see it?"

Sim shook his head.

I pointed again, more precisely. "There," I said, "and there in the corner."

His eyes widened. "Letters! *I . . . v . . .*" he paused to puzzle them out, "*Ivare enim euge.* That's what you were rambling about." He pushed the book away. "So what's the point, aside from the fact that he was nearly illiterate in Temic?"

"It's not Temic." I pointed out. "It's Tema. An archaic usage."

"What is it even supposed to say?" He looked up from his book, his brow creasing. "Toward great good?"

I shook my head. "For *greater* good," I corrected. "Sound familiar?"

"I don't know how long she'll be there," one of the loud pair continued. "If you miss her you'll regret it."

"I told you, I can't tonight. Maybe on Felling. I'll be free on Felling."

"You should go before then," I told him. "The Twopenny's crowded Felling night."

They gave me irritated looks. "Mind your own business, slipstick," the taller one said.

That got my back up even more. "I'm sorry, weren't you talking to me?"

"Did it *look* like I was talking to you?" he said scathingly.

"It *sounded* like it," I said. "If I can hear you three tables away you must want me to be part of your conversation." I cleared my throat. "The only alternative is that you're too thick to keep your voice down in the Tomes."

His face flushed red and he probably would have replied, but his friend said something in his ear and they both gathered their books and left. There was a quiet scattering of applause as the door closed behind them. I gave my audience a smile and a wave.

"The scrivs would have taken care of that," Sim reproached softly as we leaned back over the table to talk.

"The scrivs weren't taking care of it," I pointed out. "Besides, it's quiet again, and that's what matters. Now, what does 'for greater good' remind you of?"

"The Amyr, of course," he said. "It's always the Amyr with you lately. What's your point?"

"The point," I whispered excitedly, "is that Gibea was a secret member of the order Amyr."

Sim gave me a skeptical look. "That's a bit of a stretch, but I suppose it fits. That was about fifty years before they were denounced by the church. They were pretty corrupt by then."

I wanted to point out that Gibea wasn't necessarily corrupt. He was pursuing the Amyr's purpose, the greater good. While his experiments had been horrifying, his work advanced medicine in ways it was almost impossible to comprehend. His work had probably saved ten times that many lives in the hundreds of years since.

However, I doubted Sim would appreciate my point. "Corrupt or not, he was a secret member of the Amyr. Why else would he hide their credo in the front cover of his journal?"

Simmon shrugged. "Fine, he was one of the Amyr. What does that have to do with the price of butter?"

I threw up my hands in frustration and struggled to keep my voice low. "That means the order had secret members *before* the church denounced them! That means when the pontifex disbanded them, the Amyr had hidden allies. Allies that could keep them safe. That means the Amyr could still exist today, in secret, pursuing their work in subtle ways."

I noticed a change in Simmon's face. At first I thought he was about to agree with me. Then I felt a prickle on the back of my neck and realized the truth. "Hello Master Lorren," I greeted him respectfully without turning around.

"Speaking with students at other tables is not permitted," he said from behind me. "You are suspended for five days."

I nodded and the two of us came to our feet and gathered up our things. Expressionless, Master Lorren reached out a long hand toward me.

I handed Gibea's journal over without comment and a minute later we were blinking in the chill winter sunlight outside the Archive's doors. I pulled my cloak around me and stomped the snow off my feet.

"Suspended," Simmon said. "That was clever."

I shrugged, more embarrassed than I cared to admit. I hoped one of the other students would explain I was actually trying to keep things quiet, rather than the other way around. "I was just trying to do the right thing."

Simmon laughed as we began to walk slowly in the direction of Anker's. He kicked playfully at a small drift of snow. "The world needs people like you," Simmon said in the tone of voice that let me know he was turning philosophical. "You get things done. Not always the best way, or the most sensible way, but it gets done nonetheless. You're a rare creature."

"How do you mean?" I asked, my curiosity piqued.

Sim shrugged. "Like today. Something bothers you, someone offends you, and suddenly you're off." He made a quick motion with a flat hand. "You know exactly what to do. You never hesitate, you just see and react." He was thoughtful for a moment. "I imagine that's the way the Amyr used to be. Small wonder folk were frightened of them."

"I'm not always so terribly sure of myself," I admitted.

Simmon smiled. "I find that strangely reassuring."

CHAPTER FORTY-TWO

Penance

SINCE STUDYING WASN'T AN option and winter was covering every-thing in drifts of blowing snow, I decided this was the perfect time to catch up on a few things I'd been letting fall by the wayside.

I tried to pay Auri a visit, but ice covered the rooftops and the courtyard where we usually met was full of drifted snow. I was glad I didn't see any footprints, as I didn't think Auri owned shoes, let alone a coat or hat. I would have gone searching for her in the Underthing, but the iron grate in the courtyard was locked and iced over.

I worked a few double shifts in the Medica and played an extra night at Anker's as an apology for the evening when I'd had to leave early. I worked long hours in the Fishery, calculating, running tests, and casting alloys for my project. I also made a point of catching up on a month of lost sleep.

But there is only so much sleeping one person can do, and by the fourth day of my suspension, I'd run out of excuses. As much as I didn't want to, I needed to talk to Devi.

By the time I made up my mind to go, the weather had warmed just enough so that the falling snow had turned to sheets of freezing sleet.

It was a miserable walk to Imre. I didn't have hat or gloves, and the wind-driven sleet soaked my cloak within five minutes. In ten minutes I was wet through to the skin and wishing I'd waited or spent the money on a carriage. The sleet had melted the snow on the road, and the damp slush was inches thick.

I stopped by the Eolian to warm myself a bit before heading to Devi's. But the building was locked and lightless for the first time I'd ever seen. Small wonder. What noble would come out in this weather? What musician would expose their instrument to the freezing damp?

So I slogged my way through the deserted streets, eventually coming to the alley behind the butcher's shop. It was the first time I could remember the stairway not smelling of rancid fat.

I knocked on Devi's door, alarmed by how numb my hand was. I could barely feel my knuckles hitting the door. I waited for a long moment, then knocked again, worried that she might not be in, and I'd come all this way for nothing.

The door opened just a little. Warm lamplight and a single icy blue eye peered out through the crack. Then the door opened wide.

"Tehlu's tits and teeth," Devi said. "What are you doing out in this?"

"I thought—"

"No you didn't," she said disparagingly. "Get in here."

I stepped inside, dripping, the hood of my cloak plastered to my head. She closed the door behind me, then locked and bolted it. Looking around I noticed she'd added a second bookshelf, though it was still mostly bare. I shifted my weight and a great mass of damp slush dislodged itself from my cloak and splattered wetly onto the floor.

Devi gave me a long, dispassionate looking over. I could see a fire crackling in the grate on the other side of the room near her desk, but she made no indication that I should come any farther into the room. So I remained where I was, dripping and shivering.

"You never do things the easy way, do you?" she said.

"There's an easy way?" I asked.

She didn't laugh. "If you think showing up here half-frozen and looking like a kicked dog is going to improve my disposition toward you, you're terribly . . ." She trailed off and looked at me thoughtfully for another long moment. "I'll be damned," she said, sounding surprised. "I actually do like seeing you like this. It's lifting my spirits to an almost irritating degree."

"It wasn't really my intention," I said. "But I'll take it. Would it help if I caught a terrible cold?"

Devi considered it. "It might," she admitted. "Penance does involve a certain amount of suffering."

I nodded, not having to work to look miserable. I dug into my purse with clumsy fingers and brought out a small bronze coin I'd won off Sim playing low-stakes breath several nights ago.

Devi took it. "A penance piece," she said, unimpressed. "Is this supposed to be symbolic?"

I shrugged, causing more slush to spatter to the floor. "Somewhat," I said. "I thought of going to a moneychanger and settling my entire debt with you in penance coin."

"What stopped you?" she asked.

"I realized it would just irritate you," I said. "And I wasn't looking forward to paying the moneychanger's fee." I fought the urge to looking longingly at the fireplace. "I've spent a lot of time trying to think of some gesture that might make a suitable apology to you."

"You decided it would be best to walk here during the worst weather of the year?"

"I decided it would be best if we talked," I said. "The weather was just a happy accident."

Devi scowled and turned toward the fireplace. "Come in then." She walked over to a chest of drawers near her bed and brought out a thick blue cotton robe. She handed it to me and motioned to a closed door. "Go change out of your wet clothes. Wring them out in the basin or they'll take forever to dry."

I did as she said, then brought the clothes out and hung them on the pegs in front of the fire. It felt wonderful to stand so close to the fireplace. In the light of the fire I could see that the skin under my fingernails was actually a little blue.

As much as I wanted to linger and warm myself, I joined Devi at her desk. I noticed that the top of it had been sanded down and revarnished, though it still bore a coal-black ring where the poor-boy had charred the wood.

I felt rather vulnerable sitting there wearing nothing but the robe she'd given me, but there was nothing to be done about it. "After our previous . . . meeting." I fought to avoid looking at the charred ring on her desk. "You informed me that the full amount of my loan would be due at the end of the term. Are you willing to renegotiate that?"

"Unlikely," Devi said crisply. "But rest assured that if you are unable to settle accounts in coin, I'm still in the market for certain pieces of information." She gave a sharp, hungry smile.

I nodded, she still wanted access to the Archives. "I was hoping you might be willing to reconsider, as you now know the whole story," I said. "Someone was performing malfeasance against me. I needed to know that my blood was safe."

I gave her a questioning look. Devi shrugged without taking her elbows off the desk, her expression one of vast indifference.

"What's more," I said, meeting her eye. "It is entirely possible that my irrational behavior might have been partially due to the lingering effect of an alchemical poison I was subjected to earlier this term."

Devi's expression went stiff. "What?"

She hadn't known then. That was something of a relief. "Ambrose arranged to have me dosed with the plum bob about an hour before my admissions interview," I said. "And you sold him the formula."

"You have a lot of gall!" Devi's pixie face was outraged and indignant, but it wasn't convincing. She was off balance and trying too hard.

"What I have," I said calmly, "is the lingering taste of plum and nutmeg in my mouth, and the occasional irrational desire to choke people for doing nothing more offensive than jostling me on the street."

Her false outrage fell away. "You can't prove anything," she said.

"I don't need to prove anything," I said. "I have no desire to see you in trouble with the masters or up against the iron law." I looked at her. "I just thought you might be interested in the fact that I was poisoned."

Devi sat very still. She fought to maintain her composure, but guilt was creeping onto her expression. "Was it bad?"

"It was," I said quietly.

Devi looked away and crossed her arms in front of her chest. "I didn't know it was for Ambrose," she said. "Some rich tosh came around. Made a stunningly good offer. . . ."

She looked back at me. Now that the chilly anger had left her, she looked surprisingly small. "I'd never do business with Ambrose," she said. "And I didn't know it was for you. I swear."

"You knew it was for someone," I said.

There was a long moment of silence broken only by the occasional crackling of the fire.

"Here's how I see it," I said. "Recently, we've both done something rather foolish. Something we regret." I pulled the robe more closely around my shoulders. "And while these two things certainly don't cancel each other out, it does seem to me that they establish some sort of equilibrium." I held out my hands like they were the balancing plates on a scale.

Devi gave me a small, embarrassed smile. "Perhaps I was hasty in demanding full repayment."

I returned the smile and felt myself relax. "How would you feel about sticking to the original terms of our loan?"

"That seems fair." Devi held out her hand over the desk and I shook it. The last of the tension in the room evaporated and I felt a long-standing piece of worry unknot itself in my chest.

"Your hand is freezing," Devi said. "Let's go sit by the fire."

We relocated ourselves and sat quietly for several minutes.

"Gods below," Devi said with an explosive sigh. "I was so angry with you." She shook her head. "I don't know if I've ever been that angry with anyone in my whole life."

I nodded. "I didn't really believe you'd stoop to malfeasance," I said. "I was so sure it couldn't be you. But everyone kept talking about how dangerous you were. Telling stories. Then when you wouldn't let me see my blood . . ." I trailed off, shrugging.

"Are you really still getting after-echoes from the plum bob?" she asked.

"Little flashes," I said. "And I seem to be losing my temper more easily. But that might just be the stress. Simmon says I probably have unbound principles in my system. Whatever that means."

Devi scowled. "I'm working with less than ideal equipment here," she said, gesturing to a closed door. "And I am sorry. But the fellow offered me a full set of the *Vautium Tegnostae.*" She waved to the bookshelves. "Normally I'd never make something like that, but unexpurgated copies are just impossible to find."

I turned to look at her, surprised. "You made it for him?"

"It's better than handing over the formula," Devi said defensively.

Part of me felt like I should be angry, but the majority of me was simply happy that I was warm and dry, with no threat of death hanging over me. I shrugged it off. "Simmon says you can't factor worth half a damn," I said conversationally.

Devi looked down at her hands. "I'm not proud of selling it," she admitted. Then after a moment, she looked up again, grinning. "But the *Tegnostae* has gorgeous illustrations."

I laughed. "Show me."

Hours later my clothes were dry and the sleet had changed to a gentle snow. Stonebridge would be a solid sheet of ice, but other than that, the walk home would be much more pleasant.

When I emerged from the washroom I saw Devi was sitting back at her desk. I made my way over and handed her the robe. "I won't impugn your honor by asking why you own a robe much longer and broader in the shoulder than anything a delicate young lady of your size could ever wear."

Devi snorted indelicately and rolled her eyes.

I sat down and tugged on my boots. They were delightfully warm from sitting near the fire. Then I brought out my purse and lay three heavy silver talents on the desk, pushing them toward her. Devi looked at them curiously.

"I've recently come into a little money," I said. "Not enough to settle my whole debt. But I can pay this term's interest early." I waved a hand at the coins. "A gesture of good faith."

Devi smiled and pushed the coins back across the table. "You've still got two span before the end of the term," she said. "Like I said, let's stick to our original deal. I'd feel bad about taking your money early."

Though I'd offered Devi the money as an honest peace offering, I was glad to keep my three talents for now. There is a vast difference between having some coin and no coin. There is a feeling of helplessness that comes from having an empty purse.

It's like seed grain. At the end of a long winter, if you have some grain left, you can use it for seed. You have control over your life. You can use that grain and make plans for the future. But if you have no grain for seed in the spring, you are helpless. No amount of hard work or good intention will make crops grow if you don't have the seed to start with.

So I bought clothes: three shirts, a new pair of pants, and thick woolen socks. I bought a hat and gloves and scarf to keep away the winter's chill. For Auri I bought a pouch of sea salt, a sack of dried peas, two jars of peach preserves, and a pair of warm slippers. I bought a set of lute strings, ink, and a half-dozen sheets of paper.

I also bought a sturdy brass drop-bar and screwed it to the window frame in my tiny garret room. I could circumvent it fairly easily, but it would keep my few possessions safe from even the most well-intentioned thieves.

CHAPTER FORTY-THREE

Without Word or Warning

I STARED OUT THE FRONT window of Anker's, looking at the falling snow and idly turning Denna's ring over in my fingers. Winter lay heavy over the University, and Denna had been gone for more than a month. I had three hours before class with Elodin, and I was trying to decide if the slim chance of finding Denna was worth the long, cold walk to Imre.

As I stood at the window, a Cealdish man came through the door, stomping the powdery snow from his boots and looking around curiously. It was still early in the day, and I was the only person in the common room.

He walked over to me, snowflakes melting in his beard until they were bright beads of water. "Sorry to bother you. I'm looking for a fellow." he said, surprising me with his utter lack of anything resembling a Cealdish accent. He reached inside his long coat and pulled out a thick envelope with a blood-red seal. "Ka-voth-ee." He read slowly, then turned the envelope toward me so I could see the front.

Kvothe—Anker's Inn.
University. (Two miles west of Imre.)
Belenay-Barren
Central Commonwealth.

It was Denna's handwriting. "It's Kvothe, actually," I said absentmindedly. "The e is silent."

He shrugged. "You him?"

"I am," I said.

He nodded, satisfied. "Well, I got this down in Tarbean about a span back. Bought it off a fellow for a hard penny. He said he bought it off a sailor in

Junpui for a Vintish silver bit. He couldn't remember the name of the town where the sailor had got it from, but it was inland a ways."

The man met my eye. "I'm tellin' you this so you don't think I'm trying to shim you on the deal. I paid a full hard penny, then came over myself from Imre though it was out of my way." He looked around the common room. "Though I'm guessing a fellow with a fine inn such as this won't quibble about giving a fellow his due."

I laughed. "This isn't my inn," I said. "I just have a room here."

"Oh," he said, obviously a little disappointed. "You looked kinda proprietorial standing there. Still, I'm sure you see I need to make my money off this."

"I do," I said. "How much do you think is fair?"

He looked me up and down, eyeing my clothes. "I suppose I'd be happy making my hard penny back and a soft penny besides."

I brought out my purse and fished around in it. Luckily, I'd been playing cards a few nights before, and had some Aturan currency. "Seems fair," I said as I handed over the money.

He started to go, then turned back. "Out of curiosity," he asked. "Would you have paid two hard pennies to get it?"

"Probably," I admitted.

"Kist," he swore, then headed back outside, the door banging behind him.

The envelope was heavy parchment, wrinkled and smudged with much handling. The seal showed a stag rampant standing before a barrel and a harp. I pressed it hard between my fingers, shattering it as I sat down.

The letter read:

Kvothe,

I'm sorry to leave Imre without word or warning. I sent You a message the night of my departure, but I expect you never received it.

I have gone abroad looking for greener pasture and better Opportunity. I am fond of Imre, and enjoy the pleasure of your Occasional, though Sporadic, company, but it is an expensive city in which to live, and my prospects have grown slender of late.

Yll is lovely, all rolling hills. I find the weather quite to my liking, it is warmer and the air smells of the sea. It seems I might pass an entire winter without being brought to bed by my lungs. My first in years.

I have spent some time in the Small Kingdoms and saw a skirmish between two bands of mounted men. Such a crashing and Screaming of Horses you have never heard. I have spent some time afloat as well, and learned all manner of sailor's knots, and how to spit properly. Also, my Cussing has been greatly broadened.

If you ask politely when we next meet, I may demonstrate my newfound skills.

I have seen my first Adem Mercenary. (They call them blood-shirts here.) She is hardly bigger than me, with quite the most remarkable grey eyes. She is pretty, but strange and quiet, endlessly twitching. I have not seen her fight and am not sure I wish to. Though I am curious.

I am still enamoured of the harp. And am currently housing with a skilled gentleman (whom I shall not name) for the furthurinse of my study in this.

I have drunk some wine while Writing this letter. I mention this to excuse my above spelling of the word Furtherence. Furtherance. Kist. You know what I mean.

I apologize for not writing sooner, but I have been a great deal traveling and not until now have I had Means to write a Letter. Now that I have done, I expect it might be a while longer before I find a traveler I trust to start this missive on its long road back to you.

I think of you often and fondly.

Yours,

D.

Pstscrpt. I hope your lute case is serving you well.

Elodin's class began strangely that day.

For one, Elodin was actually on time. This caught us unprepared as the six remaining students had taken to spending the first twenty or thirty minutes of the class gossiping, playing cards, and griping about how little we were learning. We didn't even notice Master Namer until he was halfway down the steps of the lecture hall, clapping his hands to get our attention.

The second odd thing was that Elodin was dressed in his formal robes. I'd seen him wear them before when occasion demanded, but always grudgingly. Even during admissions interviews they were usually rumpled and unkempt.

Today he wore them as if he meant it. They looked sharp and freshly laundered. His hair wasn't in its normal state of dishevel, either. It looked like it had been trimmed and combed.

Reaching the front of the lecture hall, he climbed onto the dais and moved to stand behind the lectern. This more than anything made everyone sit up and take notice. Elodin never used the lectern.

"Long ago," he said without any preamble, "this was a place where people came to learn secret things. Men and women came to the University to study the shape of the world."

Elodin looked out at us. "In this ancient University, there was no skill more sought after than naming. All else was base metal. Namers walked these streets like tiny Gods. They did terrible, wonderful things, and all others envied them.

"Only through skill in naming did students move through the ranks. An alchemist without any skill in naming was regarded as a sad thing, no more respected than a cook. Sympathy was invented here, but a sympathist without any naming might as well be a carriage driver. An artificer with no names behind his work was little more than a cobbler or a smith.

"They all came to learn the names of things," Elodin said, his dark eyes intense, his voice resonant and stirring. "But naming cannot be taught by rule or rote. Teaching someone to be a namer is like teaching someone to fall in love. It is hopeless. It cannot be done."

Master Namer smiled a bit then, for the first time looking like his familiar self. "Still, students tried to learn. And teachers tried to teach. And sometimes they succeeded."

Elodin pointed. "Fela!" He motioned for her to approach. "Come."

Fela stood, looking nervous as she climbed up to join him on the lecturer's dais.

"You have all chosen the name you hope to learn," Elodin said, his eyes sweeping over us. "And you have all pursued your studies with varying degrees of dedication and success."

I fought the urge to look away shamefacedly, knowing that my efforts had been halfhearted at best.

"Where you have failed, Fela has succeeded," Elodin said. "She has found the name of stone. . . ." He turned sideways to look at her. "How many times?"

"Eight times," she said looking down, her hands twisting nervously in front of her.

There was a murmur of genuine awe from all of us. She had never mentioned this in our frequent griping sessions.

Elodin nodded, as if approving of our reaction. "When naming was still taught, we namers wore our prowess proudly. A student who gained mastery over a name would wear a ring as declaration of their skill." Elodin stretched out a hand in front of Fela and opened it, revealing a river stone, smooth and dark. "And this is what Fela will do now, as proof of her ability."

Startled, Fela looked at Elodin. Her eyes flickered back and forth between him and the stone, her face growing stricken and pale.

Elodin gave her a reassuring smile. "Come now," he said gently. "You know in your secret heart you are capable of this. And more."

Fela bit her lips and took hold of the stone. It seemed bigger in her hands than it had in his. She closed her eyes for a moment and drew a long, deep breath. She let it out slowly, lifted the stone, and opened her eyes so it was the first thing she would see.

Fela stared at the stone and there was a long moment's silence. The tension in the room built until it was tight as a harp string. The air vibrated with it.

A long minute passed. Two long minutes. Three terribly long minutes.

Elodin sighed gustily, breaking the tension. "No no no," he said, snapping his fingers near her face to get her attention. He pressed a hand over her eyes like a blindfold. "You're looking at it. Don't look at it. *Look* at it!" He pulled his hand away.

Fela lifted the stone and opened her eyes. At the same moment Elodin gave her a sharp slap on the back of the head with the flat of his hand.

She turned to him, her expression outraged. But Elodin merely pointed at the stone she still held in her hand. "Look!" he said excitedly.

Fela's eyes went to the stone, and she smiled as if seeing an old friend. She covered it with a hand and brought it close to her mouth. Her lips moved.

There was a sudden, sharp cracking sound, as if a speck of water had been dropped into a pan of hot grease. There followed dozens more, so sharp and quick they sounded like an old man popping his knuckles, or a storm of hailstones hitting a hard slate roof.

Fela opened her hand and a scattering of sand and gravel spilled out. With two fingers she reached into the jumble of loose stone and pulled out a ring of sheer black stone. It was round as a cup and smooth as polished glass.

Elodin laughed in triumph before sweeping Fela into an enthusiastic hug. Fela threw her arms around him wildly in return. They took several quick steps together that were half stagger, half dance.

Still grinning, Elodin held out his hand. Fela gave him the ring, and he looked it over carefully before nodding.

"Fela," he said seriously. "I hereby promote you to the rank of Re'lar." He held up the ring. "Your hand."

Almost shyly, Fela held out her hand. But Elodin shook his head. "Left hand," he said firmly. "The right means something else entirely. None of you are anywhere near ready for that."

Fela held out her other hand, and Elodin slid the ring of stone easily onto her finger. The rest of the class broke into applause, rushing close to get a look at what she had done.

Fela gave a radiant smile and held out her hand for all of us to see. The ring wasn't smooth as I'd first thought. It was covered in a thousand tiny, flat facets. They circled each other in a subtle, swirling pattern unlike anything I'd ever seen before.

CHAPTER FORTY-FOUR

The Catch

DESPITE THE TROUBLE WITH Ambrose, my obsession with the Archives, and my countless fruitless trips to Imre hunting Denna, I managed to finish my project in the Fishery.

I would have liked another span of days to run a few more tests and tinker with it. But I was simply out of time. The admissions lottery was coming up soon, and my tuition would be due not long after. Before I could put my project up for sale, I needed Kilvin to approve my design.

So it was with no small amount of trepidation that I knocked on the door of Kilvin's office.

The Master Artificer was hunched over his personal worktable, carefully removing the screws from the bronze casing of a compression pump. He didn't look up as he spoke, "Yes, Re'lar Kvothe?"

"I'm finished, Master Kilvin," I said simply.

He looked up at me, blinking. "Are you now?"

"Yes, I was hoping to make an appointment so I might demonstrate it to you."

Kilvin set the screws in a tray and brushed his hands together. "For this I am available now."

I nodded and led the way through the busy workshop, past Stocks, to the private workroom Kilvin had assigned me. I brought out the key and unlocked the heavy timber door.

It was large as workrooms go, with its own fire well, anvil, fume hood, drench, and other assorted staples of the artificing trade. I'd pushed the worktable aside to leave half of the room empty except for several thick bales of straw stacked against the wall.

Hanging from the ceiling in front of the bales was a crude scarecrow. I'd dressed it in my burned shirt and a pair of sackcloth pants. Part of me wished

I'd run a few more tests in the time it had taken to sew the pants and stuff the straw man. But at the end of the day, I am a trouper first and all else second. As such, I couldn't ignore the chance for a little showmanship.

I closed the door behind us while Kilvin looked around the room curiously. Deciding to let my work speak for itself, I brought out the crossbow and handed it to him.

The huge master's expression went dark. "Re'lar Kvothe," he said, his voice heavy with disapproval. "Tell me you have not squandered the labor of your hands on the improvement of such a beastly thing."

"Trust me, Master Kilvin," I said, holding it out to him.

He gave me a long look, then took the crossbow and began to examine it with the meticulous care of a man who spent every day working with deadly equipment. He fingered the tightly woven string and eyed the curved metal arm of the bow.

After several long minutes he nodded, put one foot through the stirrup, and cocked it without any noticeable effort. Idly, I wondered how strong Kilvin was. My shoulders ached and my hands were blistered from struggling with the unwieldy thing over the last several days.

I handed him the heavy bolt and he examined it as well. I could see him looking increasingly perplexed. I knew why. The bow didn't have any obvious modifications or sygaldry. Neither did the bolt.

Kilvin slotted the bolt into the crossbow and raised an eyebrow at me.

I made an expansive gesture to the straw man, trying to look more confident than I felt. My hands were sweating and my stomach was full of doves. Tests were fine and good. Tests were important. Tests were like rehearsal. But all that really matters is what happens when the audience is watching. This is a truth all troupers know.

Kilvin shrugged and raised the crossbow. It looked small braced against his broad shoulder, and he took a moment to carefully sight along the top of it. I was surprised to see him calmly draw half a breath, then exhale slowly as he pulled the trigger.

The crossbow jerked, the string twanged, the bolt blurred.

There was a harsh, metallic *clank*, and the bolt stopped midair as if it had struck an invisible wall. It clattered to the stone floor in the middle of the room, fifteen feet away from the straw man.

Unable to help myself, I laughed and threw my arms triumphantly into the air.

Kilvin raised his eyebrows and looked at me. I grinned a manic grin.

The master retrieved the bolt from the floor and examined it again. Then he recocked the crossbow, sighted, and pulled the trigger.

Clank. The bolt dropped to the floor a second time, skittering slightly to one side.

This time Kilvin spotted the source of the noise. Hanging from the ceiling in the far corner of the room was a metal object the size of a large lantern. It was rocking back and forth and spinning slightly, as if someone had just struck it a glancing blow.

I took it off its hook and brought it back to where Master Kilvin waited at the worktable. "What is this thing, Re'lar Kvothe?" he said curiously.

I set it down on the table with a heavy clunk. "In general terms, Master Kilvin, it's an automatically triggered kinetic opposition device." I beamed proudly. "More specifically, it stops arrows."

Kilvin bent to look at it, but there was nothing to see except for featureless plates of dark iron. My creation looked like nothing so much as a large, eight-sided lantern made entirely of metal.

"And what do you call it?"

That was the one part of my invention I hadn't managed to finish. I'd thought of a hundred names, but none of them seemed to fit. Arrow-trap was pedestrian. The Traveler's Friend was prosaic. Banditbane was ridiculously melodramatic. I could never have looked Kilvin in the eye again if I'd tried to call it that.

"I'm having some trouble with the name," I admitted. "But for now I'm calling it an arrowcatch."

"Hmmph," Kilvin grunted. "It does not catch the arrow, precisely."

"I know," I said, exasperated. "But it was either that or call it a 'clank.' "

Kilvin looked at me sideways, his eyes smiling a little. "One would think a student of Elodin's would prove more facile with his naming, Re'lar Kvothe."

"Delivari had it easy, Master Kilvin," I said. "He just made a better axle and stuck his name on it. I can't very well call this 'the Kvothe.' "

Kilvin chuckled. "True." He turned back to the arrowcatch, eyeing it curiously. "How does it work?"

I grinned and brought out a large roll of paper covered in diagrams, complicated sygaldry, metallurgical symbols, and painstaking formulae for kinetic conversion.

"There are two main parts," I said. "The first is the sygaldry that automatically forms a sympathetic link with any thin, fast-moving piece of metal within twenty feet. I don't mind telling you that took me a long couple of days to figure out."

I tapped the appropriate runes on the piece of paper. "At first I thought that might be enough by itself. I hoped if I bound an incoming arrowhead to a stationary piece of iron, it would absorb the arrow's momentum and make it harmless."

Kilvin shook his head. "It has been tried before."

"I should have realized before I even tried," I said. "At best it only absorbs a third of the arrow's momentum, and anyone two-thirds arrowshot is still going to be in a bad way."

I gestured to a different diagram. "What I really needed was something that could push back against the arrow. And it had to push very fast and very hard. I ended up using the spring steel from a bear trap. Modified, of course."

I picked up a spare arrowhead from the worktable and pretended it was moving toward the arrowcatch. "First, the arrow comes close and establishes the binding. Second, the incoming arrow's momentum sets off the trigger, just like stepping on a trap." I snapped my fingers sharply. "Then the spring's stored energy pushes back at the arrow, stopping it or even knocking it backward."

Kilvin was nodding along. "If it needs to be reset after each use, how did it stop my second bolt?"

I pointed to the central diagram. "This wouldn't be of much use if it only stopped one arrow," I said. "Or if it only stopped arrows coming from one direction. I designed it to have eight springs in a circle. It should be able to stop arrows from several directions at once." I shrugged apologetically. "In theory. I haven't been able to test that."

Kilvin looked back at the straw man. "Both of my shots came from the same direction," he said. "How was the second one stopped if that spring had already been triggered?"

I picked up the arrowcatch by the ring I'd set into the top and showed how it could rotate freely. "It hangs on a pivot ring," I said. "The shock of the first arrow set it spinning slightly, which brought a new spring into alignment. Even if it hadn't, the energy of the incoming arrow tends to swing it around to the nearest untriggered spring, like a weathervane points into the wind."

I hadn't actually planned the last. It had been a lucky accident, but I didn't see any reason to tell Kilvin that.

I touched the red dots visible on two of the eight iron faces of the arrowcatch. "These show which springs have been triggered."

Kilvin took it from me and turned it in his hands. "How do you reset the springs?"

I slid a metal device out from under the worktable, little more than a piece of iron with a long lever attached. Then I showed Kilvin the eight-sided hole in the bottom of the arrowcatch. I fit the arrowcatch onto the device and pressed down on the lever with my foot until I heard a sharp *click*. Then I rotated the arrowcatch and repeated the process.

Kilvin bent to pick it up and turned it over in his huge hands. "Heavy," he commented.

"It needed to be sturdy," I said. "A crossbow bolt can punch through a two-inch oak plank. I needed the spring to snap back with at least three times that much force to stop the arrow."

Kilvin shook the arrowcatch idly, holding it to the side of his head. It didn't make any noise. "And what if the arrowheads are not made of metal?" he asked. "Vi Sembi raiders are said to use arrows of flint or obsidian."

I looked down at my hands and sighed. "Well . . ." I said slowly. "If the arrowheads aren't some sort of iron, the arrowcatch wouldn't trigger when they came within twenty feet."

Kilvin gave a noncommittal grunt and set the arrowcatch back down on the table with a thump.

"But," I said brightly. "When it came within fifteen feet, any piece of sharp stone or glass would trigger a different set of bindings." I tapped my schema. I was proud of it, as I'd also had the foresight to inscribe the inset pieces of obsidian with the sygaldry for twice-tough glass. That way they wouldn't shatter under the impact.

Kilvin glanced at the schema, then grinned proudly and chuckled deep in his chest. "Good. Good. What if the arrow has a head of bone or ivory?"

"The runes for bone aren't trusted to a lowly Re'lar like myself," I said.

"And if they were?" Kilvin asked.

"Then I still wouldn't use them," I said. "Lest some child doing a cartwheel trigger the arrowcatch with a thin, quickly moving piece of their skull."

Kilvin nodded his approval. "I was thinking of a galloping horse," he said. "But you show your wisdom in this. You show you have the careful mind of an artificer."

I turned back to the schema and pointed. "That said, Master Kilvin, at ten feet a fast-moving cylindrical piece of wood will trigger the arrowcatch." I sighed. "It's not a good link, but it's enough to stop the arrow, or at least deflect it."

Kilvin bent to examine the schema more closely, his eyes wandering the crowded page for a long couple of minutes. "All iron?" he asked.

"Closer to steel, Master Kilvin. I worried iron would be too brittle in the long term."

"And each of these eighteen bindings are inscribed on each of the springs?" he asked, gesturing.

I nodded.

"That is a great duplication of effort," Kilvin said, his tone more conversational than accusatory. "Some might say such a thing is overbuilt."

"I care very little what other people think, Master Kilvin," I said. "Only what you think."

He grunted, then looked up from the paper and turned to face me. "I have four questions."

I nodded expectantly.

"First, of all things, why make this?" he asked.

"No one should ever die from ambush on the road," I said firmly.

Kilvin waited, but I had nothing more to say on the matter. After a moment he shrugged and gestured to the other side of the room. "Second, where did you get the . . ." His brow furrowed slightly. "*Tevetbem.* The flatbow?"

My stomach clenched at the question. I'd held the vain hope that Kilvin, being Cealdish, wouldn't know such things were illegal here in the Commonwealth. Barring that, I'd hoped he simply wouldn't ask.

"I . . . procured it, Master Kilvin," I said evasively. "I needed it to test the arrowcatch."

"Why not use a simple hunter's bow?" Kilvin said sternly. "And thereby avoid the need of illegal procurement?"

"It would be too weak, Master Kilvin. I needed to be sure my design would stop any arrow, and a crossbow fires a bolt harder than any other."

"A Modegan longbow is equal of a flatbow," Kilvin said.

"But the use of one is beyond my skill," I said. "And the purchase of a Modegan bow is far beyond my means."

Kilvin let out a deep sigh. "Before, when you made your thief's lamp, you made a bad thing in a good way. That I do not like." He looked down at the schema. "This time you have made a good thing in a bad way. That is better, but not entirely. Best is to make a good thing in a good way. Agreed?"

I nodded.

He lay one massive hand on the crossbow. "Did anyone see you with it?"

I shook my head.

"Then we will say it is mine, and you procured it under my advisement. It will join the equipment in Stocks." He gave me a hard look. "And in the future you will come to me if you need such things."

That stung a bit, as I'd been planning on selling it back to Sleat. Still, it could have been worse. The last thing I wanted was to run afoul of the iron law.

"Third, I see no mention of gold wire or silver in your schema," he said. "Nor can I imagine any use they could be put to in such a device as yours. Explain why you have checked these materials out of Stocks."

I was suddenly pointedly aware of the cool metal of my gram against the inside of my arm. Its inlay was gold, but I could hardly tell him that. "I was short on money, Master Kilvin. And I needed materials I couldn't get in Stocks."

"Such as your flatbow."

I nodded. "And the straw and the bear traps."

"Wrong follows wrong," Kilvin said disapprovingly. "The Stocks are not a moneylender's stall and should not be used as such. I am rescinding your precious metals authorization."

I bowed my head, hoping I looked appropriately chastised.

"You will also work twenty hours in Stocks as your punishment. If anyone asks, you will tell them what you did. And explain that as a punishment you were forced to repay the value of the metals plus an additional twenty percent. If you use Stocks as a moneylender, you will be charged interest like a moneylender."

I winced at that. "Yes, Master Kilvin."

"Last," Kilvin said, turning to lay one huge hand on the arrowcatch. "What do you imagine such a thing would sell for, Re'lar Kvothe?"

My heart rose in my chest. "Does that mean you approve it for sale, Master Kilvin?"

The great bearlike artificer gave me a puzzled look. "Of course I approve it, Re'lar Kvothe. It is a wondrous thing. It is an improvement to the world. Every time a person sees such a thing, they will see how artificery is used to keep men safe. They will think well of all artificers for the making of such a thing."

He looked down at the arrowcatch, frowning thoughtfully. "But if we are to sell it, it must have a price. What do you suggest?"

I'd been wondering on this question for six span. The simple truth was I hoped it would bring me enough money to pay for my tuition and my interest on Devi's loan. Enough to keep me in the University for one more term.

"I honestly don't know, Master Kilvin," I said. "How much would you pay to avoid having a long yard of ash arrow shot through your lung?"

He chuckled. "My lung is quite valuable," he said. "But let us think in other terms. Materials come to . . ." He glanced at the schema. "Roughly nine jots, am I correct?"

Uncannily correct. I nodded.

"How many hours did it take you to make?"

"About a hundred," I said. "Maybe a hundred and twenty. But a lot of that was experimentation and testing. I could probably make another in fifty or sixty hours. Less if moldings are made."

Kilvin nodded. "I suggest twenty-five talents. Does that seem reasonable to you?"

The sum took my breath away. Even after I repaid Stocks for materials and the workshop took its forty percent commission, it was six times more than I'd earn working on deck lamps. An almost ridiculous amount of money.

I began to agree enthusiastically, then a thought occurred to me. Though it pained me, I slowly shook my head. "Honestly, Master Kilvin. I'd prefer to sell them more cheaply than that."

He raised an eyebrow. "They will pay it," he reassured me. "I have seen people pay more for less useful things."

I shrugged. "Twenty-five talents is a lot of money," I said. "Safety and peace of mind shouldn't only be available to those with heavy purses. I think eight would be a great plenty."

Kilvin looked at me for a long moment, then nodded. "As you say. Eight talents." He ran his hand over the top of the arrowcatch, almost petting it. "However, as this is the first and only one in existence, I will pay you twenty-five for it. It will go in my personal collection." He cocked his head at me. *"Lhinsatva?"*

"Lhin," I said gratefully, feeling a great weight of anxiety lifting off my shoulders.

Kilvin smiled and nodded toward the table. "I would also like to examine the schema at my leisure. Would you like to make me a copy?"

"For twenty-five talents," I said, smiling as I slid the paper across the table, "you can have the original."

———

Kilvin wrote me a receipt and left, clutching the arrowcatch like a child with a new favorite toy.

I hurried to Stocks with my slip of paper. I had to settle my debt for materials, including the gold wire and silver ingots. But even after the workshop took its commission I was left with almost eleven talents.

I went through the remainder of the day grinning and whistling like an idiot. It is as they say: a heavy purse makes for a light heart.

CHAPTER FORTY-FIVE

Consortation

I SAT ON THE HEARTH at Anker's with my lute in my lap. The room was warm and quiet, full of people who had come to hear me play.

Felling was my regular night at Anker's, and it was always busy. Even in the worst weather there weren't enough chairs, and those who came late were forced to cluster around the bar and lean against walls. Lately, Anker had needed to bring in an extra girl on Felling night just to hurry drinks around the room.

Outside the inn, winter was still clutching at the University, but inside the air was warm and sweet with the smell of beer and bread and broth. Over the months I had slowly trained my audience to be properly attentive while I played, so the room was hushed as I fingered my way through the second verse of "Violet Bide."

I was in fine form that night. My audience had bought me half a dozen drinks, and in a fit of generosity, a tipsy scriv had tossed a hard penny into my lute case where it lay shining among the dull iron and copper. I'd made Simmon cry twice, and Anker's new serving girl was smiling and blushing at me with such frequency that even I couldn't miss the signal. She had beautiful eyes.

For the first time I could remember, I actually felt like I had some control over my life. There was money in my purse. My studies were going well. I had access to the Archives, and despite the fact that I was forced to work in Stocks, everyone knew Kilvin was terribly pleased with me.

The only thing missing was Denna.

I looked down at my hands as I entered into the final chorus of "Violet Bide." I'd had a few more drinks than I was used to, and I didn't want to fumble. As I watched my fingers, I heard the door of the taproom open and felt a chill wind curl around the room. The fire swayed and danced beside me as I heard boots moving across the wooden floor.

The room was quiet as I sang:

She sits by her window.
She sips at her tea.
She waits for her love,
To return from the sea.
Her suitors come calling.
She watches the tides,
And all the while Violet bides.

I hit the final chord but instead of the thunderous applause I expected, there was only an echoing quiet. I looked up and saw four tall men standing in front of the hearth. The shoulders of their heavy cloaks were wet with melted snow. Their faces were grim.

Three of them wore the dark round caps that marked them as constables. And if that weren't clue enough as to their business, each of them carried a long oak cudgel bound in iron. They watched me like hard-eyed hawks.

The fourth man stood aside from the others. He didn't wear a constable's cap and wasn't nearly so tall or broad across the shoulders. Despite that, he carried himself with undeniable authority. His face was lean and grim as he drew out a piece of heavy parchment decorated with several black, official-looking seals.

"Kvothe, Arliden's son," he read aloud to the room, his voice clear and strong. "In the sight of these witnesses I bind you to stand to your own account before the iron law. You are charged with Consortation with Demonic Powers, Malicious Use of Unnatural Arts, Unprovoked Assault, and Malfeasance."

Needless to say, I was caught completely flat-footed. "What?" I said stupidly. As I said, I'd had more than a few drinks.

The grim man ignored me and turned to one of the constables. "Bind him."

One of the constables drew out a length of clattering iron chain. Up until now I'd been too startled to be properly afraid, but the sight of this grim-faced man pulling a pair of dark iron manacles out of a sack filled me with a fear that turned my bones to water.

Simmon appeared next to the hearth, pushing his way past the constables to stand in front of the fourth man.

"What exactly is going on here?" Sim demanded, his voice hard and angry.

It was the only time I'd ever heard him sound like the son of a duke. "Explain yourself."

The man holding the parchment eyed Simmon calmly, then reached inside his cloak and brought out a stout iron rod with a band of gold around each end. Sim paled a bit as the grim man held it up for everyone in the room to see. Not only was it every bit as threatening as the constable's cudgels, the rod was an unmistakable symbol of his authority. The man was a sumner for the Commonwealth courts. Not just a regular sumner either, the gold bands meant he could order anyone to stand before the iron law: priests, government officials, even members of the nobility up to the rank of baron.

At this point Anker made his way through the crowd as well. He and Sim looked over the sumner's document and found it to be very legitimate and official. It was signed and sealed by all manner of important people in Imre. There was nothing to be done. I was going to be brought up against the iron law.

Everyone at Anker's watched as I was bound hand and foot in chains. Some of them looked shocked, some confused, but most of them simply looked frightened. When the constables dragged me through the crowd toward the door, barely a handful of my audience were willing to meet my eye.

They marched me the long way back to Imre. Over Stonebridge and down the flat expanse of the great stone road. All the way the winter wind chilled the iron around my hands and feet until it burned and bit and froze my skin.

———

The next morning Sim arrived with Elxa Dal and matters slowly became clear. It had been months since I had called the name of the wind in Imre after Ambrose broke my lute. The masters had brought me up on charges of malfeasance and had me publicly whipped at the University. It had been so long ago that the lash marks on my back were nothing more than pale silver scars. I had thought the matter resolved.

Apparently not. Since the incident had occurred in Imre, it fell under the jurisdiction of the Commonwealth courts.

We live in a civilized age, and few places are more civilized than the University and its immediate environs. But parts of the iron law are left over from darker times. It had been a hundred years since anyone had been burned for Consortation or Unnatural Arts, but the laws were still there. The ink was faded, but the words were clear.

Ambrose wasn't directly involved, of course. He was much too clever for that. This sort of trial was bad for the University's reputation. If Ambrose had brought this case against me it would have infuriated the masters. They worked hard to protect the good name of the University in general and of the Arcanum in particular.

So Ambrose was in no way connected with the charges. Instead, the case was brought before Imre's courts by a handful of Imre's influential nobles. Oh, certainly they *knew* Ambrose, but that wasn't incriminating. Ambrose knew everyone with power, blood, or money on either side of the river, after all.

Thus was I brought up against the iron law. For the space of six days it was a source of extraordinary irritation and anxiety to me. It disrupted my studies, brought my work in the Fishery to a standstill, and drove the final nail into the coffin I used to bury my hopes of ever finding a local patron.

What started as a terrifying experience quickly became a tedious process filled with pomp and ritual. More than forty letters of testimony were read aloud, confirmed, and copied into the official records. There were days filled with nothing but long speeches. Quotations from the iron law. Points of procedure. Formal modes of address. Old men reading out of old books.

I defended myself to the best of my ability, first in the Commonwealth court, then in church courts as well. Arwyl and Elxa Dal spoke on my behalf. Or rather, they wrote letters, then read them aloud to the court.

In the end, I was cleared of any wrongdoing. I thought I was vindicated. I thought I had won. . . .

But I was still terribly naive in many ways.

CHAPTER FORTY-SIX

Interlude—A Bit of Fiddle

KVOTHE CAME SLOWLY TO his feet and gave a quick stretch. "Let's pause there for now," he said. "I expect we'll see more than the usual number of people for lunch today. I need to check on the soup and get a few things ready." He nodded to Chronicler. "You might want to do the same."

Chronicler remained seated. "Wait a minute," he said. "This was your trial in Imre?" He looked down at the page, dismayed. "That's it?"

"That's it," Kvothe said. "Not much to it, really."

"But that's the first story I ever heard about you when I came to the University," Chronicler protested. "How you learned Tema in a day. How you spoke your entire defense in verse and they applauded afterward. How you . . ."

"A lot of nonsense, I expect," Kvothe said dismissively as he walked back to the bar. "You've got the bones of it."

Chronicler looked down at the page. "You seem to be giving it pretty short shrift."

"If you're desperate for the full account, you can find it elsewhere," Kvothe said. "Dozens of people saw the trial. There are already two full written accounts. I see no need to add a third."

Chronicler was taken aback. "You've already spoken to a historian about this?"

Kvothe chuckled deep in his throat. "You sound like a jilted lover." He began to bring out stacks of bowls and plates from beneath the bar. "Rest assured, you're the first to get my story."

"You said there were written accounts," Chronicler said. Then his eyes widened. "Are you telling me you've written a memoir?" There was a strange note in the scribe's voice, something almost like hunger.

Kvothe frowned. "No, not really." He gave a gusty sigh. "I started something of the sort, but I gave it up as a bad idea."

"You wrote all the way to your trial in Imre?" Chronicler said, looking at
the paper in front of him. Only then did he realize he was still holding his
pen poised above the page. He began to unscrew and clean the brass nib of
the pen on a cloth with an air of vast irritation. "If you already had all this
written down, you could have saved me cramping my hand for the last day
and a half."

Kvothe's forehead creased in confusion. "What?"

Chronicler rubbed the nib briskly with a cloth, every motion screaming
with affronted dignity. "I should have known," he said. "It all fit together too
smoothly." He glared up. "Do you know how much this paper cost me?" He
made an angry gesture to the satchel that held the finished pages.

Kvothe simply stared at him for a moment, then laughed with sudden
understanding. "You misunderstand. I gave up the memoir after a day or so. I
wrote a handful of pages. Not even that."

The irritation faded from Chronicler's face, leaving a sheepish expression.
"Oh."

"You *are* like a wounded lover," Kvothe said, amused. "Good lord, calm
yourself. My story is virginal. Yours are the first hands to touch it." He shook
his head. "There's something different about writing a story down. I don't
seem to have the knack for it. It came out all wrong."

"I'd love to see what you wrote," Chronicler said, leaning forward in his
chair. "Even if it's just a few pages."

"It was quite a while ago," Kvothe said. "I don't know if I remember
where the pages are."

"They're up in your room, Reshi," Bast said brightly. "On your desk."

Kvothe gave a deep sigh. "I was trying to be gracious, Bast. The truth is,
there's nothing on them worth showing to anyone. If I'd written anything
worth reading, I would have kept writing it." He walked into the kitchen and
there were muted, bustling sounds from the back room.

"Good try," Bast said softly. "But it's a lost cause. I've tried."

"Don't coach me," Chronicler said testily. "I know how to get a story out
of a person."

There was more bumping from the back room, a splash of water, the
sound of a door closing.

Chronicler looked at Bast. "Shouldn't you go help him?"

Bast shrugged, lounging further back into his chair.

After a moment, Kvothe emerged from the back room carrying a cutting
board and a bowl full of freshly scrubbed vegetables.

"I'm afraid I'm still confused," Chronicler said. "How can there already be two written accounts if you never wrote it yourself or talked to a historian?"

"Never been brought to trial, have you?" Kvothe said, amused. "The Commonwealth courts keep painstaking records, and the church is even more obsessive. If you have a desperate desire for the details, you can dig around in their deposition ledgers and act books respectively."

"That might be the case," Chronicler said. "But your account of the trial . . ."

"Would be tedious," Kvothe said. He finished paring the carrots, and began to cut them. "Endless formal speeches and readings from the *Book of the Path*. It was tedious to live through, and it would be tedious to repeat."

He brushed the sliced carrots from the board into a nearby bowl. "I've probably kept us at the University too long, anyway," he said. "We'll need the time for other things. Things no one has ever seen or heard."

"Reshi no!" Bast shouted in alarm, sitting bolt upright in his chair. His expression was plaintive as he pointed to the bar. "Beets?"

Kvothe looked down at the dark red root on the cutting board as if surprised to see it there.

"Don't put beets in the soup, Reshi," Bast said. "They're foul."

"A lot of people like beets, Bast," Kvothe said. "And they're healthful. Good for the blood."

"I hate beets," Bast said piteously.

"Well," Kvothe said calmly, "since I'm finishing the soup, I get to pick what goes into it."

Bast came to his feet and stomped toward the bar. "I'll take care of it then," he said impatiently, making a shooing motion. "You go get some sausage and one of those veiny cheeses." He pushed Kvothe toward the basement steps before storming into the kitchen, muttering. Soon there was the sound of rattling and thumping from the back room.

Kvothe looked over at Chronicler and gave a wide, lazy smile.

———

People began to trickle into the Waystone Inn. They came in twos and threes, smelling of sweat and horses and freshly mown wheat. They laughed and talked and tracked chaff across the clean wooden floors.

Chronicler did a brisk business. Folk sat leaning forward in their chairs, sometimes gesturing with their hands, sometimes speaking with slow deliberation. The scribe's face was impassive as his pen scratched across the page, occasionally darting back for ink.

Bast and the man who called himself Kote worked together as a comfortable team. They served up soup and bread. Apples, cheese, and sausage. Beer and ale and cool water from the pump out back. There was roasted mutton too, for those who wanted it, and fresh apple pie.

Men and women smiled and relaxed, glad to be off their feet and sitting in the shade. The room was full of the gentle buzz of conversation as folk gossiped with neighbors they had known their whole lives. Familiar insults, soft and harmless as butter, were traded back and forth, and friends had comfortable arguments about whose turn it was to buy the beer.

But underneath it all, there was a tension in the room. A stranger would never have noticed it, but it was there, dark and silent as an undertow. No one spoke of taxes, or armies, or how they had begun to lock their doors at night. No one spoke of what had happened in the inn the night before. No one eyed the stretch of well-scrubbed wooden floor that didn't show a trace of blood.

Instead there were jokes and stories. A young wife kissed her husband, drawing whistles and hoots from the rest of the room. Old Man Benton tried to lift up the hem of the Widow Creel's skirt with his cane, cackling when she swatted him. A pair of little girls chased each other around the tables, shrieking and laughing while everyone watched and smiled fond smiles. It helped a bit. It was all that you could do.

The inn's door banged open. Old Cob, Graham, and Jake trudged in out of the brilliant midday sunlight.

"Hullo Kote!" Old Cob called, looking around at the handful of people spread around the inn. "You've got a bit of a crowd in here today!"

"You missed the bigger part of it," Bast said. "We were downright frantic for a while."

"Anything left for the stragglers?" Graham asked as he sank onto his stool.

Before he could reply, a bull-shouldered man clattered an empty plate onto the bar and set a fork down gently beside it. "That," he said in a booming voice, "was a damn fine pie."

A thin woman with a pinched face stood next to him. "Don't you cuss, Elias," she said sharply. "There's no call for that."

"Oh honey," the big man said. "Don't get yourself in a twit. Damfine is a kind of apple, innit?" He grinned around at the folks sitting at the bar. "Sort of foreign apple from off in Atur? They named it after Baron Damfine if I remember correct."

Graham grinned back at him. "I think I heard that."

The woman glared at all of them.

"I got these from the Bentons," the innkeeper said meekly.

"Oh," the big farmer said with a smile. "That's my mistake then." He picked up a crumb of crust from the plate and chewed it speculatively. "I'd swear it was a Damfine pie for all that. Maybe the Bentons got them some Damfine apples and don't know it."

His wife sniffed, then saw Chronicler sitting idle at his table and pulled her husband away.

Old Cob watched them go, shaking his head. "I don't know what that woman needs in her life to make her a little happy," he said. "But I hope she finds it before she pecks old Eli bloody."

Jake and Graham made vague grumbles of agreement.

"Nice to see folks filling up the place." Old Cob looked at the red-haired man behind the bar. "You're a fine cook, Kote. And you've got the best beer in twenty miles. All folk need is a bit of an excuse to stop by."

Old Cob tapped the side of his nose speculatively. "You know," he said to the innkeeper. "You should bring in a singer or sommat on nights. Hell, even the Orrison boy can play a bit of his daddy's fiddle. I bet he'd be glad to come in for the price of a couple drinks." He looked around at the inn. "A little music is just what this place needs."

The innkeeper nodded. His expression was so easy and amiable it almost wasn't an expression at all. "I expect you're right," Kote said. His voice was perfectly calm. It was a perfectly normal voice. It was colorless and clear as window glass.

Old Cob opened his mouth, but before he could say anything else Bast rapped one knuckle hard on the bar. "Drinks?" he asked the men sitting at the bar. "I'm guessing you'd all like a little something before we bring you out a bite to eat."

They did, and Bast bustled around behind the bar, pulling beer into mugs and pressing them into waiting hands. After a slow moment, the innkeeper swung silently into motion alongside his assistant, heading into the kitchen to fetch soup. And bread with butter. And cheese. And apples.

CHAPTER FORTY-SEVEN

Interlude—The Hempen Verse

CHRONICLER SMILED AS HE made his way to the bar. "That's a solid hour's work," he said proudly as he took a seat. "I don't suppose there's anything left in the kitchen for me?"

"Or any of that pie Eli mentioned?" Jake asked hopefully.

"I want pie too," Bast said, sitting next to Jake, nursing a drink of his own.

The innkeeper smiled, wiping his hands on his apron. "I think I might have remembered to set one by, just in case you three came in later than the rest."

Old Cob rubbed his hands together. "Can't remember last time I had warm apple pie," he said.

The innkeeper went back into the kitchen. He pulled the pie from the oven, sliced it, and laid the pieces neatly onto plates. By the time he carried them out toward the taproom he could hear raised voices in the other room.

"It was too a demon, Jake," Old Cob was saying angrily. "I told you last night, and I'll tell you again a hundred times. I'm not a one to change my mind like other folk change their socks." He held up a finger. "He called up a demon and it bit this fellow and sucked out his juice like a plum. I heard it from a fella who knew a woman that seen it herself. That's why the constable and the deputies came and hauled him off. Meddling with dark forces is against the law over in Amary."

"I still say folk just thought it was a demon," Jake persisted. "You know how folk are."

"I know folk." Old Cob scowled. "I've been around longer than you Jacob. And I know my own story too."

There was a long moment of tense silence at the bar before Jake looked away. "I was just sayin'," he muttered.

The innkeeper slid a bowl of soup toward Chronicler. "What's this then?"

The scribe gave the innkeeper a sly look. "Cob's telling us about Kvothe's trial in Imre," he said, a hint of smugness in his voice. "Don't you remember? He started the story last night but only made it halfway through."

"Now." Cob glared around, as if daring them to interrupt. "It was a tight spot. Kvothe knew if he was found guilty they'd string him up and let him hang." Cob made a gesture to one side of his neck like he was holding a noose, tilting his head to the side.

"But Kvothe had read a great many books when he was at the University, and he knew himself a trick." Old Cob stopped to take a forkful of pie and closed his eyes for a moment as he chewed. "Oh lord and lady," he said to himself. "That's a proper pie. I swear it's better than me mam used to make. She always skint on the sugar." He took another bite, a blissful expression spreading over his weathered face.

"So Kvothe knew a trick?" Chronicler prompted.

"What? Oh." Cob seemed to remember himself. "Right. You see, there's two lines in the *Book of the Path*, and if you can read them out loud in the old Tema only priests know, then the iron law says you get treated like a priest. That means a Commonwealth judge can't do a damn thing to you. If you read those lines, your case has to be decided by the church courts."

Old Cob took another bite of pie and chewed it slowly before swallowing. "Those two lines are called the hempen verse, because if you know them, you can keep yourself from getting strung up. The church courts can't hang a man, you see."

"What are the lines?" Bast asked.

"I dearly wish I knew," Old Cob said mournfully. "But I don't speak Tema. Kvothe didn't know it himself. But he memorized the verse ahead of time. Then he pretended to read it and the Commonwealth court had to let him go.

"Kvothe knew he had two days until a Tehlin Justice could make it all the way to Amary. So he set about learning Tema. He read books and practiced for a whole day and a whole night. And he was so powerful smart that at the end of his studying he could speak Tema better than most folk who been doing it their whole lives.

"Then, on the second day before the Justice showed up, Kvothe mixed himself a potion. It was made out of honey, and a special stone you find in a snake's brain, and a plant that only grows at the bottom of the sea. When he drank the potion, it made his voice so sweet anyone who listened couldn't help but agree with anything he said.

"So when the Justice finally showed up, the whole trial only took fifteen minutes," Cob said, chuckling. "Kvothe gave a fine speech in perfect Tema, everyone agreed with him, and they all went home."

"And he lived happily ever after," the red-haired man said softly from behind the bar.

Things were quiet at the bar. Outside the air was dry and hot, full of dust and the smell of chaff. The sunlight was hard and bright as a bar of gold.

Inside the Waystone it was dim and cool. The men had just finished the last slow bites of their pie, and there was still a little beer in their mugs. So they sat for a little while longer, slouching at the bar with the guilty air of men too proud to be properly lazy.

"I never much cared for Kvothe stories myself," the innkeeper said matter-of-factly as he gathered up everyone's plates.

Old Cob looked up from his beer. "That so?"

The innkeeper shrugged. "If I'm going to have a story with magic, I'd like it to have a proper wizard in it. Someone like Taborlin the Great, or Serapha, or The Chronicler."

At the end of the bar, the scribe didn't choke or startle. He did pause for half a second though, before lowering his spoon back into his second bowl of soup.

The room went comfortably quiet again as the innkeeper gathered up the last of the empty plates and turned toward the kitchen. But before he could get through the doorway, Graham spoke up. "The Chronicler?" he said. "I haven't ever heard of him."

The innkeeper turned back, surprised. "You haven't?"

Graham shook his head.

"I'm sure you have," the innkeeper said. "He carries around a great book, and whatever he writes down in that book comes true." He looked at all of them expectantly. Jake shook his head too.

The innkeeper turned to the scribe at the end of the bar, who was keeping his attention on his food. "You've heard of him, I'm sure," Kote said. "They call him Lord of Stories, and if he learns one of your secrets he can write whatever he wants about you in his book." He looked at the scribe. "Haven't you ever heard of him?"

Chronicler dropped his eyes and shook his head. He dipped the crust of his bread in his soup and ate it without speaking.

The innkeeper looked surprised. "When I was growing up, I liked The Chronicler more than Taborlin or any of the rest. He's got a bit of Faerie blood in him, and it's made him sharper than a normal man. He can see for a hundred miles on a cloudy day and hear a whisper through a thick oak door. He can track a mouse through a forest on a moonless night."

"I've heard of him," Bast said eagerly. "His sword is named Sheave, and the blade is made of a single piece of paper. It's light as a feather, but so sharp that if he cuts you, you see the blood before you even feel it."

The innkeeper nodded. "And if he learns your name, he can write it on the blade of the sword and use it to kill you from a thousand miles away."

"But he's got to write it in his own blood," Bast added. "And there's only so much space on the sword. He's already written seventeen names on it, so there's not that much room left."

"He used to be a member of the high king's court in Modeg," Kote said. "But he fell in love with the high king's daughter."

Graham and Old Cob were nodding now. This was familiar territory.

Kote continued, "When Chronicler asked to marry her, the high king was angry. So he gave Chronicler a task to prove he was worthy. . . ." The innkeeper paused dramatically. "Chronicler can only marry her if he finds something more precious than the princess and brings it back to the high king."

Graham made an appreciative noise. "That's a pisser of a task. What's a man to do? You can't bring something back and say, 'Here, this is worth more than your little girl. . . .' "

The innkeeper gave a grave nod. "So Chronicler wanders the world looking for ancient treasures and old magics, hoping to find something he can bring back to the king."

"Why doesn't he just write about the king in his magic book?" Jake asked. "Why doesn't he write down, 'And then the king stopped being a bastard and let us get married already.' "

"Because he doesn't know any of the king's secrets," the innkeeper explained. "And the high king of Modeg knows some magic and can protect himself. Most importantly, he knows Chronicler's weaknesses. He knows if you trick Chronicler into drinking ink, he has to do the next three favors you ask of him. And more important, he knows Chronicler can't control you if you have your name hidden away somewhere safe. The high king's name is written in a book of glass, hidden in a box of copper. And that box is locked away in a great iron chest where nobody can touch it."

There was a moment's pause as everyone considered this. Then Old Cob began nodding thoughtfully. "That last bit tickled my memory," he said slowly. "I seem to remember a story about this Chronicler fellow going to look for a magic fruit. Whoever ate the fruit would suddenly know the names of all things, and he'd have powers like Taborlin the Great."

The innkeeper rubbed his chin, nodding slowly. "I think I heard that one too," he said. "But it was a long time ago, and I can't say as I remember all the details...."

"Ah well," Old Cob said as he drank the last of his beer and knocked down his mug. "Nothing to be 'shamed of, Kote. Some folk are good at remembering and some ain't. You make a fine pie, but we all know who the storyteller is around here."

Old Cob climbed stiffly down off his stool and motioned to Graham and Jake. "Come on then, we can walk together as far as Byres' place. I'll tell you two all about it. Now this Chronicler, he's tall and pale, and thin as a rail, with hair as black as ink—"

The door of the Waystone Inn banged closed.

"What in God's name was that all about?" Chronicler demanded.

Kvothe looked sideways at Chronicler. He smiled a small, sharp smile. "How does it feel," he asked, "knowing people out there are telling stories about you?"

"They're not telling stories about me!" Chronicler said. "They're just a bunch of nonsense."

"Not nonsense," Kvothe said, seeming a little bit offended. "It might not be true, but that doesn't mean it's nonsense." He looked at Bast. "I liked the paper sword."

Bast beamed. "The king's task was a nice touch, Reshi. I don't know about the Faerie blood though."

"Demon blood would have been too sinister," Kvothe said. "He needed a twist."

"At least I won't have to hear him tell it," Chronicler said sullenly, prodding a bit of potato with his spoon.

Kvothe looked up, then chuckled darkly. "You don't understand, do you? A fresh story like that on a harvest day? They'll be at it like a child with a new toy. Old Cob will talk about Chronicler to a dozen people while they're bucking hay and drinking water in the shade. Tonight at Shep's wake, folk from ten towns will hear about the Lord of Stories. It will spread like a fire in a field."

Chronicler looked back and forth between the two of them, his expression vaguely horrified. "Why?"

"It's a gift," Kvothe said.

"You think I want this?" Chronicler said incredulously. "Fame?"

"Not fame," Kvothe said grimly. "Perspective. You go rummaging around in other people's lives. You hear rumors and go digging for the painful truth beneath the lovely lies. You believe you have a right to these things. But you don't." He looked hard at the scribe. "When someone tells you a piece of their life, they're giving you a gift, not granting you your due."

Kvothe wiped his hands on the clean linen cloth. "I'm giving you my story with all the grubby truths intact. All my mistakes and idiocies laid out naked in the light. If I decide to pass over some small piece because it bores me, I'm well within my rights. I won't be goaded into changing my mind by some farmer's tale. I'm not an idiot."

Chronicler looked down at his soup. "It was a little heavy-handed, wasn't it?"

"It was," Kvothe said.

Chronicler looked up with a sigh and gave a small, embarrassed smile. "Well. You can't blame me for trying."

"I can, actually," Kvothe said. "But I believe I've made my point. And for what it's worth, I'm sorry for any trouble that might cause you." He gestured to the door and the departed farmers. "I might have overreacted a bit. I've never responded well to manipulation."

Kvothe stepped out from behind the bar, heading to the table near the hearth. "Come on now, both of you. The trial itself was tedious business. But it had important repercussions."

CHAPTER FORTY-EIGHT

A Significant Absence

I WENT THROUGH THE ADMISSIONS lottery and was lucky enough to draw a late slot. I was glad for the extra time, as my trial had left me little opportunity to study for my exams.

Still, I wasn't terribly worried. I had time to study and free access to the Archives. What's more, for the first time since I'd come to the University, I wasn't a pauper. I had thirteen talents in my purse. Even after I paid Devi the interest on her loan, I would easily have enough for tuition.

Best of all, the long hours spent searching for the gram had taught me a great deal about the Archives. While I might not know as much as an experienced scriv, I was familiar with many of her hidden corners and quiet secrets. So while I studied, I also allowed myself the freedom to do other reading while I prepared for admissions.

I closed the book I'd been poring over. A well-written, comprehensive history of the Aturan church. It was as useless as all the rest.

Wilem looked up as my book thumped shut. "Nothing?" he asked.

"Less than nothing," I said.

The two of us were studying in one of the fourth-floor reading holes, much smaller than our customary place on the third floor, but given how close we were to admissions, we'd been lucky to find a private room at all.

"Why don't you let it go?" Wil suggested. "You've been beating this Amyr thing like a dead horse for what, two span?"

I nodded, not wanting to admit my research into the Amyr had actually started long before our bet had taken us to Puppet.

"And what have you found so far?"

"Shelves of books," I said. "Dozens of stories. Mentions in a hundred histories."

He gave me a level look. "And this wealth of information irritates you."

"No," I said. "The *lack* of information troubles me. There isn't any solid information about the Amyr in any of these books."

"None?" Wilem said skeptically.

"Oh, every historian in the last three hundred years *talks* about them," I said. "They speculate on how the Amyr influenced the decline of the empire. Philosophers talk about the ethical ramifications of their actions." I gestured to the books. "That tells me what people think about the Amyr. It doesn't tell me anything about the Amyr themselves."

Wilem frowned at my stack of books. "It can't all be historians and philosophers."

"There are stories too," I said. "Early on there are stories about the great wrongs they righted. Later you get stories about the terrible things they did. An Amyr in Renere kills a corrupt judge. Another in Junpui puts down a peasant uprising. A third in Melithi poisons half the town's nobility."

"And that isn't solid information?" Wilem asked.

"They're soft stories," I said. "Second- or third-hand. Three-quarters of them are simply hearsay. I can't find corroborating evidence for them anywhere. Why can't I find any mention of the corrupt judge in the church records? His name should be recorded in every case he tried. What was the date of this peasant uprising, and why can't I find it mentioned in any of the other histories?"

"It was three hundred years ago," Wilem said reproachfully. "You can't expect all those little details to survive."

"I expect *some* of the little details to survive. You know how obsessive the Tehlins are about their records," I said. "We have a thousand years of court documents from a hundred different cities squirreled away down in sub-two. Whole rooms full . . ."

I waved my hands dismissively. "But fine, let's abandon the small details. There are huge questions I can't find any answers for. When was the Order Amyr founded? How many Amyr were there? Who paid them, and how much? Where did that money come from? Where were they trained? How did they come to be a part of the Tehlin church?"

"Feltemi Reis answered that," Wilem said. "They grew out of the tradition of the mendicant judges."

I picked up a book at random and thumped it onto the table in front of him. "Find me one bit of proof to support that theory. Find me one record that shows a mendicant judge being promoted into the ranks of the Amyr.

Show me one record of an Amyr being employed by a court. Find me one church document that shows an Amyr presiding over a case." I crossed my arms in front of my chest belligerently. "Go on, I'll wait."

Wilem ignored the book. "Maybe there weren't as many Amyr as people assume. Perhaps there were only a few of them and their reputation grew out of their control." He gave me a pointed look. "You should understand how that works."

"No," I said. "This is a significant absence. Sometimes finding nothing can be finding something."

"You're starting to sound like Elodin," Wilem said.

I frowned at him but decided not to rise to the bait. "No, listen for a minute. Why would there be so little factual information about the Amyr? There are only three possibilities."

I held up fingers to mark them off. "One: nothing was written down. I think we can safely discard that. They were too important to be so entirely neglected by historians, clerks, and the obsessive documentation of the church." I tucked that finger away.

"Two. By an odd chance, copies of the books that do have this information have simply never made their way here to the Archives. But that's ridiculous. It's impossible to think that over all the years nothing on the subject has ended up in the largest library in the world." I folded down the second finger.

"Three." I pointed with the remaining finger. "Someone has removed this information, altered it, or destroyed it."

Wilem frowned. "Who would do that?"

"Who indeed?" I said, "Who would benefit most from the destruction of the information of the Amyr?" I hesitated, letting the tension build. "Who else but the Amyr themselves?"

I had expected him to dismiss my idea, but he didn't. "An interesting thought," Wilem said. "But why assume the Amyr are behind it? It is much more sensible to think the church itself is responsible. Certainly the Tehlins would like nothing better than to quietly erase the Amyr's atrocities."

"True," I admitted. "But the church isn't very strong here in the Commonwealth. And these books come from all over the world. A Cealdish historian wouldn't have any compunctions about writing a history of the Amyr."

"A Cealdish historian would have very little interest in writing the history of a heretic branch of a pagan church," Wilem pointed out. "Besides, how could a discredited handful of Amyr do something the church itself could not achieve?"

I leaned forward. "I think the Amyr are far older than the Tehlin church," I said. "During the time of the Aturan Empire, a great deal of their public strength was with the church, but they were more than just a group of wandering justices."

"And what leads you to this belief?" Wil said. From his expression I could see I was losing Wilem's support rather than gaining it.

A piece of ancient pottery, I thought. *A story I heard from an old man in Tarbean. I know it because of something the Chandrian let slip after they killed everyone I ever knew.*

I sighed and shook my head, knowing how crazy I would sound if I told the truth. That was why I scoured the Archives. I needed some tangible evidence to support my theory, something that wouldn't make me a laughingstock.

"I found copies of the court documents from the time the Amyr were denounced," I said. "Do you know how many Amyr they put on trial in Tarbean?"

Wil shrugged.

I held up a single finger. "One. One Amyr in all of Tarbean. And the clerk writing the transcript of the trial made it clear the man they put on trial was a simpleton who didn't understand what was going on."

I still saw doubt on Wilem's face. "Just think on it," I pleaded. "The scraps I've found suggest there were at least three thousand Amyr in the empire before they were disbanded. Three thousand highly trained, heavily armed, wealthy men and women *absolutely* devoted to the greater good.

"Then one day the church denounces them, disbands their entire order, and confiscates their property." I snapped my fingers. "And three thousand deadly, justice-obsessed fanatics just disappear? They roll over and decide to let someone else take care of the greater good for a while? No protest? No resistance? Nothing?"

I gave him a hard look and shook my head firmly. "No. That goes against human nature. Besides, I haven't found one record of a member of the Amyr being brought before the church's justice. Not one. Is it so outrageous to think they might have decided to go underground, to continue their work in a more secret way?

"And if that's reasonable," I continued before he could interrupt. "Doesn't it also make sense they might try to preserve their secrecy by carefully pruning histories over the last three hundred years?"

There was a long pause.

Wilem didn't dismiss it out of hand. "An interesting theory," he said slowly. "But it leads me to one last question." He eyed me seriously. "Have you been drinking?"

I slumped in my chair. "No."

He came to his feet. "Then you should start. You have been spending too much time with all these books. You need to wash the dust from your brains."

So we went for a drink, but I still harbored my suspicions. I bounced the idea off Simmon when I next had the chance. He accepted it more easily than Wilem had. Which isn't to say he believed me, just that he accepted the possibility. He said I should mention it to Lorren.

I didn't. The blank-faced Master Archivist still made me nervous, and I avoided him at every opportunity for fear I might give him some excuse to ban me from the Archives. The last thing I wanted to do was suggest his precious Archives had been slowly pruned over the last three hundred years.

CHAPTER FORTY-NINE

The Ignorant Edema

I SAW ELXA DAL RAISE a hand in greeting from across the courtyard. "Kvothe!" He smiled warmly. "The very fellow I was hoping to see! Could I borrow a moment of your time?"

"Of course," I said. While I liked Master Dal, we hadn't had much contact together outside the lecture hall. "Could I buy you a drink, or a bite of lunch? I've been meaning to thank you more properly for speaking on my behalf at the trial, but I've been busy. . . ."

"As have I," Dal said. "I've actually been meaning to talk to you for days, but time keeps getting away from me." He looked around. "I wouldn't turn down a bit of lunch, but I should probably forego the drink. I have admissions to oversee in less than an hour."

We stepped into the White Hart. I'd barely even seen the inside of the place, as it was far too rich for the likes of me.

Elxa Dal was recognizable in his dark master's robes, and the host fawned a bit as he led the two of us to a private table. Dal seemed perfectly at his ease as he took a seat, but I was increasingly nervous. I couldn't imagine why the Master Sympathist would seek me out for a conversation.

"What can I bring you?" asked the tall, thin man as soon as we were in our chairs. "Drinks? A selection of cheeses? We have a delightful lemoned trout as well."

"The trout and cheeses would do nicely," Dal said.

The host turned to me. "And yourself?"

"I'll try the trout as well," I said.

"Wonderful," he said, rubbing his hands together in anticipation. "And to drink?"

"Cider," I said.

"Do you have any Fallows red?" Dal asked hesitantly.

"We do," said the host. "And it's a lovely year, too, if I do say so myself."

"I'll have a cup," Dal said, glancing at me. "One cup shouldn't alter my judgment too badly."

The host hurried away, leaving me alone at the table with Elxa Dal. It felt odd sitting across the table from him. I shifted nervously in my seat.

"So how are things with you?" Dal asked conversationally.

"Passing fair," I said. "It was a good term with the exception of . . ." I made a gesture toward Imre.

Dal gave a humorless chuckle. "That was a brush with the old days, wasn't it?" He shook his head. "Consortation with Demons. Good lord."

The host returned with our drinks and left without a word.

Master Dal picked up his wide clay cup and held it in the air. "To not getting burned alive by superstitious folk," he said.

I smiled despite my discomfiture and raised my wooden mug. "A fine tradition."

We both drank, Dal sighing appreciatively at the wine.

Dal looked at me across the table. "So tell me," he said. "Have you ever considered what you're going to do with yourself when you're done here? After you have your guilder, I mean."

"I haven't thought of it that much," I admitted honestly. "It seems such a long way off."

"At the rate you're rising through the ranks it might not be so long at that. Already a Re'lar at . . . how old are you again?"

"Seventeen," I lied smoothly. I was sensitive about my age. Many students were nearly twenty before they enrolled in the University, let alone joined the Arcanum.

"Seventeen," Dal mused softly. "It's so easy to forget that. You carry yourself so tall." His eyes got a faraway look in them. "Lord and lady, I was a mess at seventeen. My studies, trying to sort out my place in the world. Women . . ." He shook his head slowly. "It gets better, you know. Give it three or four years and everything settles down a bit."

He raised his clay cup to me briefly before taking another drink. "Not that you seem to be having much trouble. Re'lar at seventeen. Quite a mark of distinction."

I flushed a bit, not knowing what to say.

The host returned and began laying dishes on the table. A small board with an array of different sliced cheeses. A bowl with small, toasted pieces of bread. A bowl of strawberry preserves. A bowl of blueberry jam. A small dish of shelled walnuts.

Dal picked up a small piece of bread and a slice of crumbling white cheese. "You're quite the sympathist," he said. "There are any number of opportunities out there for a person as skilled as yourself."

I spread a bit of strawberry across a piece of cheese and toast, then put it into my mouth to give myself time to think. Was Dal implying he wanted me to focus more on my study of sympathy? Was he implying he wanted to sponsor me to El'the?

Elodin had sponsored my elevation to Re'lar, but I knew these things changed. Masters occasionally fought over particularly promising students. Mola, for example, had been a scriv before Arwyl stole her away into the Medica.

"I do enjoy my study of sympathy quite a bit," I said carefully.

"That's abundantly clear," Dal said with a smile. "Some of your classmates wish you enjoyed it a little less, I can assure you of that." He ate another piece of cheese, then continued, "That said, it is possible to overdo it. Didn't Teccam say 'Too much study harms the student?'"

"Ertram the Wiser, actually." I said. It had been in one of the books Master Lorren had set aside for Re'lar to study this term.

"It's true at any rate," he said. "You might want to consider taking a term off to relax a bit. Travel a little, get some sun." He took another drink. "It's not good to see one of the Edema Ruh without a tan."

I didn't know what to say to that. The thought of taking a holiday from the University had never occurred to me. Where would I possibly go?

The host arrived with plates of fish, steaming and smelling of lemon and butter. For a while both of us concentrated on our food. I was glad for an excuse not to talk. Why would Dal compliment me on my studies, then encourage me to leave?

After a while Elxa Dal gave a contented sigh and pushed back his plate. "Let me tell you a little story," he said. "A story I like to call 'The Ignorant Edema.'"

I looked up at that, slowly chewing my mouthful of fish. I kept my expression carefully composed.

He arched an eyebrow, as if waiting to see if I had anything to say.

When I didn't, he continued. "Once there was a learned arcanist. He knew all of sympathy and sygaldry and alchemy. He had ten dozen names tucked neatly into his head, spoke eight languages, and had exemplary penmanship. Really, the only thing that kept him from being a master was poor timing and a certain lack of social grace."

Dal took a sip of wine. "So this fellow went chasing the wind for a while, hoping to find his fortune out in the wide world. And while he was on the road to Tinuë, he came to a lake he needed to cross."

Dal smiled broadly. "Luckily, there was an Edema boatman who offered to ferry him to the other side. The arcanist, seeing the trip would take several hours, tried to start a conversation.

" 'What do you think,' he asked the boatman, 'about Teccam's theory of energy as an elemental substance rather than a material property?'

"The boatman replied he'd never thought on it at all. What's more, he had no plans to.

" 'Surely your education included Teccam's *Theophany?*' the arcanist asked.

" 'I never had what you might call an education, y'honor,' the boatman said. 'And I wouldn't know this Teccam of yours if he showed up selling needles to m'wife.'

"Curious, the arcanist asked a few questions and the Edema admitted he didn't know who Feltemi Reis was, or what a gearwin did. The arcanist continued for a long hour, first out of curiosity, then with dismay. The final straw came when he discovered the boatman couldn't even read or write.

" 'Really sir,' the arcanist said, appalled. 'It is every man's job to improve himself. A man without the benefits of education is hardly more than an animal.' "

Dal grinned. "Well, as you can guess, the conversation didn't go very far after that. They rode for the next hour in a tense silence, but just as the far shore was coming into sight a storm blew up. Waves started to lash the little boat, making the timbers creak and groan.

"The Edema took a hard look at the clouds and said, 'It'll be true bad in five minutes, then sommat worse afore it clears. This boat of mine won't hold together through it all. We're gonnta have to swim the last little bit.' And with this the ferryman takes off his shirt and begins to tie it around his waist.

" 'But I don't know how to swim,' says the arcanist."

Dal drank off the last of his wine, turned the cup upside down, and set it firmly on the tabletop. There was a moment of expectant silence as he watched me, a vaguely self-satisfied expression on his face.

"Not a bad story," I admitted. "The Ruh's accent was a little over the top."

Dal bent at the waist in a quick, mocking bow. "I will take it under consideration," he said, then raised one finger and gave me a conspiratorial look. "Not only is my story designed to delight and entertain, but there is a kernel of truth hidden within, where only the cleverest student might find it." His expression turned mysterious. "All the truth in the world is held in stories, you know."

———————

Later that evening, I related the encounter to my friends while playing cards at Anker's.

"He's giving you a hint, thickwit," Manet said irritably. The cards had been against us all night, and we were five hands behind. "You just refuse to hear it."

"He's hinting I should leave off studying sympathy for a term?" I asked.

"No," Manet snapped. "He's telling you what I've told you twice already. You're a king-high idiot if you go through admissions this term."

"What?" I asked. "Why?"

Manet set his cards down with profound calm. "Kvothe. You're a clever boy, but you have a world of trouble listening to things you don't want to hear." He looked left then right at Wilem and Simmon. "Can you try telling him?"

"Take a term off," Wilem said without looking up from his cards. Then added, "Thickwit."

"You really have to," Sim said earnestly. "Everyone's still talking about the trial. It's all anyone is talking about."

"The trial?" I laughed. "That was more than a span ago. They're talking about how I was found completely innocent. Exonerated in the eyes of the iron law and merciful Tehlu himself."

Manet snorted loudly, lowering his cards. "It would have been better if you'd been guilty in a quiet way, rather than be innocent so loud." He looked at me. "Do you know how long it's been since an arcanist was brought up on charges of Consortation?"

"No," I admitted.

"Neither do I," he said. "Which means it's been a long, long while. You're innocent. Lovely for you. But the trial has given the University a great shining black eye. It's reminded folk that while *you* might not deserve burning, some arcanists might." He shook his head. "You can be certain the masters are uniformly wet-cat-mad about that."

"Some students aren't too pleased either," Wil added darkly.

"It isn't my fault there was a trial!" I protested, then backed up a bit. "Not entirely. Ambrose stirred this up. He was backstage during the whole thing, laughing up his sleeve."

"Even so," Wil said. "Ambrose is sensible enough to avoid admissions this term."

"What?" I asked, surprised. "He's not going through admissions?"

"He is not," Wilem said. "He left for home two days ago."

"But there was nothing to connect him to the trial," I said. "Why would he leave?"

"Because the masters are not idiots," Manet said. "The two of you have been snapping at each other like mad dogs since you first met." He tapped his lips thoughtfully, his expression full of exaggerated innocence. "Say, that reminds me. Whatever were you doing at the Golden Pony the night Ambrose's room caught fire?"

"Playing cards," I said.

"Of course you were," Manet said, his tone thick with sarcasm. "The two of you have been throwing rocks at each other for a full year, and one of them has finally hit the hornet's nest. The only sensible thing to do is run off to a safe distance and wait 'til the buzzing stops."

Simmon cleared his throat timidly. "I hate to join the chorus," he said apologetically. "But rumor has gotten around you were seen having lunch with Sleat." He grimaced. "And Fela told me she'd heard you were . . . um . . . courting Devi."

"You know that's not true about Devi," I said. "I've just been visiting her in order to keep the peace. She was half an inch away from wanting to eat my liver for a while there. And I only had one conversation with Sleat. It was barely fifteen minutes long."

"Devi?" Manet exclaimed with dismay. "Devi and Sleat? One expelled and the other the next best thing?" He threw down his cards. "Why would you be seen with those people? Why am I even being seen with you?"

"Oh come now." I looked back and forth between Wil and Sim. "It's that bad?"

Wilem set down his cards. "I predict," he said calmly, "that if you go through admissions, you will receive a tuition of at least thirty-five talents." He looked back and forth between Sim and Manet. "I will wager a full gold mark to this effect. Does anyone care to take my bet?"

Neither of them took him up on his offer.

I felt a desperate sinking in my stomach. "But this can't . . ." I said. "This . . ."

Sim put his cards down as well, the grim expression out of place on his friendly face. "Kvothe," he said formally. "I am telling you three times. Take a term away."

———

Eventually I realized my friends were telling me the truth. Unfortunately, this left me entirely at loose ends. I had no exams to study for, and starting another project in the Fishery would be nothing but foolishness. Even the thought of searching the Archives for information on the Chandrian or the Amyr had little appeal. I had searched so long and found so little.

I toyed with the idea of searching elsewhere. There are other libraries, of

course. Every noble house has at least a modest collection containing household accounts and histories of their lands and family. Most churches had extensive records going back hundreds of years, detailing trials, marriages, and
dispositions. The same was true of any sizable city. The Amyr couldn't have
destroyed every trace of their existence.

The research itself wouldn't be the hard part. The hard part would be gaining access to the libraries in the first place. I could hardly show up in Renere
dressed in rags and road dust, asking to thumb through the palace archives.

This was another instance in which a patron would have been invaluable.
A patron could write me a letter of introduction that would open all manner
of doors for me. What's more, with a patron's backing, I could make a decent
living for myself as I traveled. Many small towns wouldn't even let you play
at the local inn without a writ of patronage.

The University had been the center of my life for a solid year. Now, confronted with the necessity of leaving, I was utterly at sea, with no idea of what
I could do with myself.

CHAPTER FIFTY

Chasing the Wind

I GAVE MY ADMISSIONS TILE to Fela, telling her I hoped it brought her luck. And so the winter term came to an end.

Suddenly three-quarters of my life simply disappeared. I had no classes to occupy my time, no shifts in the Medica to fill. I could no longer check out materials from Stocks, use tools in the Fishery, or enter the Archives.

At first it wasn't so bad. The midwinter pageantry was wonderfully distracting, and without the worry of work and study I was free to enjoy myself and spend time in the company of my friends.

Then spring term started. My friends were still there, but they were busy with their own studies. I found myself crossing the river more and more. Denna was still nowhere to be found, but Deoch and Stanchion were always willing to share a drink and some idle gossip.

Threpe was there too, and while he occasionally pressed me to attend a dinner at his house, I could tell his heart wasn't in it. My trial hadn't pleased people on this side of the river either, and they were still telling stories about it. I wouldn't be welcome in any respectable social circle for a great long time, if ever.

I toyed with the idea of leaving the University. I knew people would forget about the trial more quickly if I wasn't around. But where would I go? The only thought that came to mind was heading off to Yll with the vain hope of finding Denna. But I knew that was nothing but foolishness.

Since I didn't need to save money for tuition, I went to repay Devi. But for the first time ever, I wasn't able to find her. Over the course of several days I grew increasingly nervous. I even slid several apologetic notes under her door until I heard from Mola that she was taking a holiday and would be returning soon.

Days passed. And I sat idle as winter slowly withdrew from the University. Frost left the corners of windowpanes, drifts of snow dwindled, and trees began to show their first greening buds. Eventually Simmon caught his first glimpse of bare leg beneath a flowing dress and declared spring had officially arrived.

One afternoon as I sat drinking metheglin with Stanchion, Threpe came through the door practically bubbling with excitement. He whisked me off to a private table on the second tier, looking ready to burst with whatever news he was carrying.

Threpe folded his hands on the tabletop. "Since we haven't had much luck finding you a local patron, I started casting my nets farther afield. It's nice to have a local patron. But if you have the support of a properly influential lord, it hardly matters where he lives."

I nodded. My troupe had ranged all over the four corners under the protection of Lord Greyfallow's name.

Threpe grinned. "Have you ever been to Vintas?"

"Possibly," I said. Then seeing his puzzled look, I explained, "I traveled quite a bit when I was young. I can't remember if we ever made it that far east."

He nodded. "Do you know who the Maer Alveron is?"

I did, but I could tell Threpe was bursting to tell me himself. "I seem to remember something . . ." I said vaguely.

Threpe grinned. "You know the expression 'rich as the King of Vint?' "

I nodded.

"Well, that's him. His great-great-grandfathers *were* the kings of Vint, back before the empire stomped in, converting everyone to the iron law and the *Book of the Path*. If not for a few quirks of fate a dozen generations back, Alveron would be the royal family of Vintas, not the Calanthis, and my friend the Maer would be the king."

"Your friend?" I said appreciatively. "You know Maer Alveron?"

Threpe made a vacillating gesture. "*Friend* may be stretching things a little," he admitted. "We've been corresponding for some years, exchanging news from our different corners of the world, doing each other a favor or two. It would be more appropriate to say we're *acquainted*."

"An impressive acquaintance. What is he like?"

"His letters are quite polite. Never a bit snobby even though he does stand quite a good rank above me," Threpe said modestly. "He's every bit a king except for the title and crown, you know. When Vintas formed, his family refused to surrender any of their plenary powers. That means the Maer has the authority to do most anything King Roderic himself can do: grant titles, raise an army, coin money, levy taxes—"

Threpe shook his head sharply. "Ah, I forget what I'm doing," he said as he began to search his pockets. "I received a letter from him only yesterday." He produced a piece of paper, unfolded it, then cleared his throat and read:

> *I know you are knee-deep in poets and musicians out there, and I am rather in need of a young man who is good with words. I cannot find anyone to suit me here in Severen. And, everything said, I would prefer the best.*
>
> *He should be good with words above all, perhaps a musician of some sort. After that, I would desire him to be clever, well-spoken, mannerly, educated, and discreet. On reading this list you may see why I have had no luck finding such a one for myself. If you happen to know a man of this rare sort, encourage him to call on me.*
>
> *I would tell you what use I intend to put him to, but the matter is of a private nature. . . .*

Threpe studied the letter for a moment or two. "It goes on for a bit. Then he says, 'As to the matter I mentioned before, I am in some haste. If there is no one suitable in Imre, please send me a letter by post. If you happen to send someone my way, encourage him to make speed.'" Threpe's eyes scanned the paper for a moment more, his lips moving silently. "That's all of it," he said finally, and tucked it back into a pocket. "What do you think?"

"You do me a great —"

"Yes, yes." He waved a hand impatiently. "You're flattered. Skip all that." He leaned forward seriously. "Will you do it? Will your studies," he made a dismissive gesture westward, toward the University, "permit an absence of a season or so?"

I cleared my throat. "I've actually been considering taking my studies abroad for a time."

The count burst into a wide grin and thumped the arm of his chair. "Good!" he laughed. "I thought I was going to have to pry you out of your precious University like a penny from a dead shim's fist! This is a wonderful opportunity, you realize. Once in a lifetime, really." He gave me a sly wink. "Besides, a young man like yourself would be hard-pressed to find a better patron than a man who's richer than the king of Vint."

"There's some truth to that," I admitted aloud. Silently, I thought, *Could I hope for better assistance in my search for the Amyr?*

"There's *much* truth to that," he chuckled. "How soon can you be ready to leave?"

I shrugged. "Tomorrow?"

Threpe raised an eyebrow. "You don't give much time for the dust to settle, do you?"

"He said he was in haste, and I'd rather be early than late."

"True. True." He drew a silver gear-watch from his pocket, looked at it, then sighed as he clicked it closed. "I'll have to miss some sleep tonight drafting a letter of introduction for you."

I glanced at the window. "It's not even dark yet," I said. "How long do you expect it to take?"

"Hush," he said crossly. "I write slowly, especially when I'm sending a letter to someone as important as the Maer. Plus I have to describe you, no easy task by itself."

"Let me help you then," I said. "No sense losing sleep on my account." I smiled. "Besides, if there's one thing I'm well-versed in it's my own good qualities."

The next day I made a round of hasty good-byes to everyone I knew at the University. I received heartfelt handshakes from Wilem and Simmon and a cheerful wave from Auri.

Kilvin grunted without looking up from his engraving and told me to write down any ideas I might have for the ever-burning lamp while I was away. Arwyl gave me a long, penetrating look through his spectacles and told me there would be a place for me in the Medica when I returned.

Elxa Dal was refreshing after the other masters' reserved responses. He laughed and admitted he was a little jealous of my freedom. He advised me to take full advantage of every reckless opportunity that presented itself. If a thousand miles wasn't enough to keep my escapades secret, he said, then nothing would.

I had no luck finding Elodin, and settled for sliding a note under the door of his office. Though since he never seemed to use the place, it might be months before he found it.

I bought a new travelsack and a few other things a sympathist should never be without: wax, string and wire, hook-needle and gut. My clothes were easy to pack, as I didn't own many.

As I loaded my pack, I slowly realized I couldn't take everything with me. This came as something of a shock. For so many years I'd been able to carry everything I've owned, usually with a hand to spare.

But since I'd moved into this small garret room, I'd begun gathering odd-ments and half-finished projects. I now had the luxury of two blankets. There were pages of notes, a circular piece of half-inscribed tin from the Fishery, a broken gear-clock I'd taken to pieces to see if I could put it back together again.

I finished loading my travelsack, then packed everything else into the trunk that sat at the foot of my bed. A few worn tools, a broken piece of slate I used for ciphering, a small wooden box with the handful of small treasures Auri had given me....

Then I went downstairs and asked Anker if he would mind stowing my possessions in the basement until I returned. He admitted a little guiltily that before I'd started sleeping there, the tiny, slant-ceilinged room had been empty for years, and only used for storage. He was willing to leave it unrented if I promised to continue our current room-for-music arrangement after I returned. I gladly agreed, and swinging my lute case onto my shoulder I headed out the door.

———

I wasn't entirely surprised to find Elodin on Stonebridge. Very little about the Master Namer surprised me these days. He sat on the waist-high stone lip of the bridge, swinging his bare feet over the hundred-foot drop to the river below.

"Hello Kvothe," he said without turning his eyes from the churning water.

"Hello Master Elodin," I said. "I'm afraid I'm going to be leaving the University for a term or two."

"Are you really afraid?" I noticed a whisper of amusement in his quiet, resonant voice.

It took me a moment to realize what he was referring to. "It's just a figure of speech."

"The figures of our speaking are like pictures of names. Vague, weak names, but names nonetheless. Be mindful of them." He looked up at me. "Sit with me for a moment."

I started to excuse myself, then hesitated. He was my sponsor, after all. I set down my lute and travelsack on the flat stone of the bridge. A fond smile came over Elodin's boyish face and he slapped the stone parapet next to him-self with the flat of his hand, offering me a seat.

I looked over the edge with a hint of anxiety. "I'd rather not, Master Elodin."

He gave me a reproachful look. "Caution suits an arcanist. Assurance suits a namer. Fear does not suit either. It does not suit you." He slapped the stone again, more firmly this time.

I carefully climbed onto the parapet and swung my feet over the edge. The view was spectacular, exhilarating.

"Can you see the wind?"

I tried. For a moment it seemed as if . . . No. It was nothing. I shook my head.

Elodin shrugged nonchalantly, though I sensed a hint of disappointment. "This is a good place for a namer. Tell me why."

I looked around. "Wide wind, strong water, old stone."

"Good answer." I heard genuine pleasure in his voice. "But there is another reason. Stone, water, and wind are other places too. What makes this different?"

I thought for a moment, looked around, shook my head. "I don't know."

"Another good answer. Remember it."

I waited for him to continue. When he didn't, I asked, "What makes this a good place?"

He looked out over the water for a long time before he answered. "It is an edge," he said at last. "It is a high place with a chance of falling. Things are more easily seen from edges. Danger rouses the sleeping mind. It makes some things clear. Seeing things is a part of being a namer."

"What about falling?" I asked.

"If you fall, you fall," Elodin shrugged. "Sometimes falling teaches us things too. In dreams you often fall before you wake."

We were both silent in our thoughts for a while. I closed my eyes and tried to listen for the name of the wind. I heard the water below, felt the stone of the bridge beneath my palms. Nothing.

"Do you know what they used to say when a student left the University for a term?" Elodin asked.

I shook my head.

"They said he was chasing the wind," he chuckled.

"I've heard the expression."

"Have you? What did it seem to mean?"

I took a moment to choose my words. "It had a frivolous flavor. As if students were running around to no good purpose."

Elodin nodded. "Most students leave for frivolous reasons, or to pursue frivolous things." He leaned forward to look straight down at the river below. "But that was not always the meaning of it."

"No?"

"No." He sat back up again. "Long ago, when all students aspired to be namers, things were different." He licked a finger and held it to the air. "The name most fledgling namers were encouraged to find was that of the wind.

After they found that name, their sleeping minds were roused and finding other names was easier.

"But some students had trouble finding the name of the wind. There were too few edges here, too little risk. So they would go off into the wild, uneducated lands. They would seek their fortunes, have adventures, hunt for secrets and treasure. . . ." He looked at me. "But they were really looking for the name of the wind."

Our conversation paused as someone came onto the bridge. It was a man with dark hair and a pinched face. He watched us from the corner of his eye without turning his head, and as he walked behind us I tried not to think how easy it would be for him to push me off the bridge.

Then he was past us. Elodin gave a weary sigh and continued. "Things have changed. There are even fewer edges now than there were before. The world is less wild. There are fewer magics, more secrets, and only a handful of people who know the name of the wind."

"You know it, don't you?" I asked.

Elodin nodded. "It changes from place to place, but I know how to listen for its changing shape." He laughed and clapped me on the shoulder. "You should go. Chase the wind. Do not be afraid of the occasional risk." He smiled. "In moderation."

I swung my legs around, hopped off the thick wall, and resettled my lute and travelsack over my shoulder. But as I started toward Imre, Elodin's voice stopped me. "Kvothe."

I turned and saw Elodin lean forward over the side of the bridge. He grinned like a schoolboy. "Spit for luck."

Devi opened the door for me and widened her eyes in shock. "My goodness," she said, pressing a piece of paper dramatically to her chest. I recognized it as one of the notes I left under her door. "It's my secret admirer."

"I was trying to pay off my loan," I said. "I made four trips."

"The walk is good for you," she said with a cheerful lack of sympathy as she motioned me inside, bolting the door behind me. The room smelled of . . .

I sniffed. "What is that?" I asked.

Her expression went rueful. "It was supposed to be pear."

I lay down my lute case and travelsack and took a seat at her desk. Despite my best intentions, my eyes were drawn to the charred black ring.

Devi tossed her strawberry-blonde hair and met my eye. "Care for a rematch?" she asked, her mouth curving. "I can still take you, gram or no gram. I can take you while I'm dead asleep."

"I'll admit to being curious," I said. "But I should tend to business instead."

"Very well," she said. "Are you really going to pay me off entire? Have you finally found yourself a patron?"

I shook my head. "However, I have had a remarkable opportunity arise. The chance to get a fine patron indeed." I paused. "In Vintas."

She raised an eyebrow. "That's a long ways off," she said pointedly. "I'm glad you stopped to settle your debt before jaunting off to the other side of the world. Who knows when you'll be back."

"Indeed," I said. "However. I find myself in a bit of an odd place, financially speaking."

Devi was already shaking her head before I finished speaking. "Absolutely not. You're already into me for nine talents. I am not loaning you more money the day you leave town."

I held up my hands defensively. "You misunderstand," I said. I opened my purse and spilled talents and jots onto the table. Denna's ring tumbled out too, and I stopped it before it could roll off the edge of the table.

I gestured to the pile of coins in front of me, slightly more than thirteen talents. "This is all the money I have in the world," I said. "With it, I need to get myself to Severen with fair speed. A thousand miles with some to spare. That means passage on at least one ship. Food. Lodging. Money for coaches or the use of a post note."

As I listed each of these things, I slid an appropriate amount of money from one side of the desk to the other. "When I finally arrive in Severen, I will need to buy myself clothes that will allow me to move among the court without looking like the ragged musician I am." I slid more coins.

I pointed at the few straggling coins remaining. "This does not leave me enough to settle my debt with you."

Devi watched me over her steepled fingers. "I see," she said seriously. "We must discover some alternate method for you to square your debt."

"My thought is this," I said. "I can leave you with collateral against my eventual return."

Her eyes flickered down to the slender, dark shape of my lute case.

"Not my lute," I said quickly. "I need that."

"What then?" she asked. "You've always said you have no collateral."

"I have a few things," I said, rummaging around in my travelsack and brought up a book.

Devi's eyes lit up. Then she read the spine. *"Rhetoric and Logic?"* She made a face.

"I feel the same way," I said. "But it's worth something. Especially to me. Also . . ." I reached into the pocket of my cloak and brought out my hand lamp. "I have this. A sympathy lamp of my own design. It has a focused beam and a graded switch."

Devi picked it up off the desk, nodding to herself. "I remember this," she said. "Before, you said you couldn't give it up because of a promise you'd made to Kilvin. Has that changed?"

I gave a bright smile that was two-thirds lie. "That promise is actually what makes that lamp the perfect piece of collateral," I said. "If you take this lamp to Kilvin, I have every confidence he will pay a lavish sum just to get it out of . . ." I cleared my throat. "Unsavory hands."

Devi flicked the switch idly with her thumb, spinning it from dim to bright and back again. "And I imagine this would be a stipulation you require? That I return it to Kilvin?"

"You know me so well," I said. "It's almost embarrassing."

Devi set the lamp back on the table next to my book and took a slow breath through her nose. "A book that's only valuable to you," she said. "And a lamp that's only valuable to Kilvin." She shook her head. "This is not an appealing offer."

I felt a pang as I reached to my shoulder and unclasped my talent pipes and slid them onto the table as well. "Those are silver," I said. "And hard to come by. They'll get you into the Eolian free, too."

"I know what they are." Devi picked them up and looked them over with a sharp eye. Then she pointed. "You had a ring."

I froze. "That's not mine to give."

Devi laughed. "It's in your pocket, isn't it?" She snapped her fingers. "Come now. Let me see it."

I brought it out of my pocket, but I didn't hand it over. "I went through a lot of trouble for this," I said. "It's the ring Ambrose took from a friend of mine. I'm just waiting to return it to her."

Devi sat silently, her hand outstretched. After a moment I put the ring onto her palm.

She held it close to the lamp and leaned forward, squinting one eye closed on her pixie face. "That's a nice stone," she said appreciatively.

"The setting's new," I said miserably.

Devi set the ring carefully on top of the book next to my pipes and hand lamp. "Here is the deal," she said. "I will keep these items as collateral against your current debt of nine talents. This will last for the space of one year."

"A year and a day," I said.

A smile curved the corner of her mouth. "How storybook of you. Very well. This will postpone your repayment for a year and a day. If you have not repaid me by the end of that time, these items will be forfeit, and our debt will be cleared." Her smile went sharp. "Though I may be persuaded to re-turn them in exchange for certain information."

I heard the belling tower in the distance and gave a deep sigh. I didn't have much time for bargaining, as I was already late for my meeting with Threpe. "Fine," I said, irritated. "But the ring will be kept somewhere safe. You can't wear it until I've defaulted."

Devi frowned. "You don't—"

"I am not movable on this point," I said seriously. "It belongs to a friend. It is precious to her. I would not have her see it on someone else's hand. Not after everything I did to get it back from Ambrose."

Devi said nothing, her pixie face set in a grim expression. I put on my own grim expression and met her eye. I do a good grim expression when I need to.

A long moment of silence stretched between us.

"Fine!" she said at last.

We shook hands. "A year and a day," I said.

CHAPTER FIFTY-ONE

All Wise Men Fear

I STOPPED BY THE EOLIAN where Threpe was waiting for me, practically dancing with impatience. He had, he told me, found a boat heading downriver in less than an hour. What's more, he had already paid my way as far as Tarbean, where I should easily be able to find passage east.

The two of us hurried to the docks, arriving just as the ship was going through its final preparations. Threpe, red-faced and puffing from our brisk walk, hurried to give me a lifetime's worth of advice in the space of three minutes.

"The Maer is old, old blood," he said. "Not like most of the little nobility around these parts who can't tell you who their great-grandfathers are. So treat him with respect."

I rolled my eyes. Why did everyone always expect me to behave so poorly?

"And remember," he said. "If you look like you're chasing money, they'll see you as provincial. As soon as that happens no one will take you seriously. You're there to curry favor. That's the high-stakes game. Besides, fortune follows favor, as they say. If you get one, you'll have the other. It's like what Teccam wrote, 'The cost of a loaf is a simple thing, and so a loaf is often sought . . .' "

" '. . . but some things are past valuing: laughter, land, and love are never bought.' " I finished. It was actually a quote from Gregan the Lesser, but I didn't bother correcting him.

"Hoy there!" a tan, bearded man shouted to us from the deck of the ship. "We got one straggler we're waitin' on, and Captain's angry as an ugly whore. He swears he'll leave if he ain't here in two minutes. You'd do well to be aboard by then." He wandered off without waiting for a reply.

"Address him as your grace," Threpe continued as if we hadn't been inter-

rupted. "And remember: speak least if you would be most often heard. Oh!"
He drew a sealed letter from his breast pocket. "Here's your letter of introduction. I may send another copy by post, just so he knows to expect you."

I gave him a broad smile and gripped his arm. "Thank you, Denn," I said
earnestly. "For everything. I appreciate all of this more than you know."

Threpe waved the comment aside. "I know you'll do splendidly. You're a
clever boy. Mind that you find a good tailor when you get there. The fashions
will be different. As they say: know a lady by her manner, a man by his cloth."

I knelt and opened up my lute case. Moving the lute aside, I pressed the
lid of the secret compartment and twisted it open. I slid Threpe's sealed letter
inside, where it joined the hollow horn with Nina's drawing and a small sack
of dried apple I had stowed there. There was nothing special about the dried
apple, but in my opinion if you have a secret compartment in your lute case
and don't use it to hide things, there is something terribly, terribly wrong
with you.

I snapped the clasps closed, refastening the lid, then stood and gathered up
my belongings, ready to board the ship.

Threpe gripped my shoulder suddenly. "I almost forgot! Alveron mentioned in one of his letters that the young people in his court gamble. He
thinks it's a deplorable habit, so stay clear of it. And remember, small thaws
make great floods, so be twice wary of a slowly changing season."

I saw someone running down the dock toward us. It was the pinch-faced
man who had passed Elodin and me on Stonebridge earlier. He carried a
cloth-wrapped package close under one arm.

"I'm guessing that's their missing sailor," I said quickly. "I'd better get
aboard." I gave Threpe a quick embrace and tried to get away before he could
give me any more advice.

But he caught my sleeve as I turned. "Be careful on your way there," he
said, his expression anxious. "Remember: There are three things all wise men
fear: the sea in storm, a night with no moon, and the anger of a gentle man."

The sailor passed us and hit the gangplank running, unmindful of how the
board jounced and clattered under his feet. I gave Threpe a reassuring smile
and followed close on his heels. Two leathery men hauled up the plank, and
I returned Threpe's final wave.

Orders were shouted, men scrambled, and the ship began to move. I turned
to face downriver, toward Tarbean, toward the sea.

CHAPTER FIFTY-TWO

A Brief Journey

MY ROUTE WAS A simple one. I would head downriver to Tarbean, through the Refting Strait, down the coast toward Junpui, then up the Arrand River. It was more roundabout than going overland, but better in the long run. Even if I were to purchase a post letter and change horses at every opportunity, it would still take me almost three span to reach Severen overland. And most of that time would be in southern Atur and the Small Kingdoms. Only priests and fools expected the roads in that part of the world to be safe.

The water route added several hundred miles to the distance traveled, but ships at sea need not mind the twistings and turnings of a road. And while a good horse can set a better pace than a ship, you can't ride a horse day and night without stopping to rest. The water route would take about a dozen days, depending on the weather.

My curiosity was also glad to take the sea route. I had never been on any water larger than a river. My only real concern was that I might become bored with nothing but wind, waves, and sailors for company.

Several unfortunate complications arose during the trip.

In brief, there was a storm, piracy, treachery, and shipwreck, although not in that order. It also goes without saying that I did a great many things, some heroic, some ill-advised, some clever and audacious.

Over the course of my trip I was robbed, drowned, and left penniless on the streets of Junpui. In order to survive I begged for crusts, stole a man's shoes, and recited poetry. The last should demonstrate more than all the rest how truly desperate my situation became.

However, as these events have little to do with the heart of the story, I must pass them over in favor of more important things. Simply said, it took me sixteen days to reach Severen. A bit longer than I had planned, but at no point during my journey was I ever bored.

CHAPTER FIFTY-THREE

The Sheer

I LIMPED THROUGH THE GATES of Severen ragged, penniless, and hungry. I am no stranger to hunger. I know the countless hollow shapes it takes inside you. This particular hunger wasn't a terrible one. I'd eaten two apples and some salt pork a day ago, so this hunger was merely painful. It wasn't the bad hunger that leaves you weak and trembling. I was safe from that for at least eight hours or so.

Over the last two span everything I owned had been lost, destroyed, stolen, or abandoned. The only exception was my lute. Denna's marvelous case had paid for itself ten times during my trip. In addition to saving my life on one occasion, it had protected my lute, Threpe's letter of introduction, and Nina's invaluable drawing of the Chandrian.

You may notice I don't include any clothing on my list of possessions. There are two good reasons for this. The first is that you couldn't really call the grubby rags I wore clothing without stretching the truth to its breaking point. Secondly, I had stolen them, so it doesn't seem right to claim them as my own.

The most irritating was the loss of Fela's cloak. I'd been forced to tear it up and use it for bandages in Junpui. Nearly as bad was the fact that my hard-won gram now lay somewhere deep below the cold, dark waters of the Centhe Sea.

The city of Severen was split into two unequal portions by a tall, white cliff. The majority of the living business of the city took place in the larger portion of the city at the foot of this cliff, aptly named the Sheer.

Atop the Sheer was a much smaller piece of the city. It consisted mostly of estates and manor houses belonging to aristocracy and wealthy merchants. Also present were the attendant number of tailors, liveries, theaters, and brothels necessary to provide for the needs of the upper class.

The stark cliff of white stone looked as if it had been thrust skyward to give the nobility a better view of the countryside. As it wandered off to the northeast and south, it lost height and stature, but where it bisected Severen, it was two hundred feet tall and steep as a garden wall.

In the center of the city, a wide peninsula of cliff jutted out from the Sheer. Perched on this outthrust piece of cliff was Maer Alveron's estate. Its pale stone walls were visible from anywhere in the city below. The effect was daunting, as if the Maer's ancestral home was peering down on you.

Seeing it without a coin in my pocket or a decent set of clothes on my back was rather intimidating. I'd planned to take Threpe's letter straight to the Maer despite my disheveled state, but looking up at the tall stone walls, I realized I probably wouldn't be let through the front door. I looked like a filthy beggar.

I had few resources and even fewer options to choose from. With the exception of Ambrose some miles to the south in his father's barony, I didn't know a single soul in all of Vintas.

I've begged before, and I've stolen. But only when I've had no other options available to me. They are dangerous occupations and only a complete fool attempts them in an unfamiliar city, let alone an entirely new country. Here in Vintas, I didn't even know what laws I might be breaking.

So I gritted my teeth and took the only option available to me. I wandered barefoot through the cobblestone streets of Severen-Low until I found a pawn shop in one of the better parts of the city.

I stood across the street for the better part of an hour, watching the people come and go, trying to think of some better option. But I simply didn't have one. So I removed Threpe's letter and Nina's painting from the secret compartment in my lute case, crossed the street, and pawned my lute and case for eight silver nobles and a span note.

If you've led the sort of easy life that's never taken you to the pawners, let me explain. The note was a receipt of sorts, and with it, I could buy my lute back for the same amount of money, so long as I did it within eleven days. On the twelfth day it became the property of the pawnbroker who would undoubtedly turn around and sell it for ten times that amount.

Back on the street, I hefted the coins. They seemed thin and insubstantial compared to Cealdish currency or the heavy Commonwealth pennies I was familiar with. Still, money spends the same the world round, and seven nobles bought me a fine suit of clothes of the sort a gentleman might wear, along with a pair of soft leather boots. What remained bought a haircut, shave, bath, and my first solid meal in three days. After that I was coin-poor again, but feeling much more sure of myself.

Still, I knew it would be difficult to make my way to the Maer. Men with his degree of power live within layers of protection. There are customary, graceful ways to navigate these layers: introductions and audiences, messages and rings, calling cards and ass-kissing.

But with only eleven days to get my lute out of pawn, my time was too precious for that. I needed to make contact with Alveron quickly.

So I made my way to the foot of the Sheer and found a small café that catered to a genteel clientele. I used one of my precious few remaining coins to buy a mug of chocolate and a seat with a view of the haberdasher's across the street.

Over the next several hours I listened to the gossip that flows through such places. Even better, I won the trust of the clever young boy who worked at the café, waiting to refill my mug if I so desired. With his help and some casual eavesdropping, I learned a great deal about the Maer's court in a short amount of time.

Eventually the shadows grew longer, and I decided it was time to move. I called the boy over and pointed across the street. "Do you see that gentleman? The one in the red vest?"

"Yes, sir."

"Do you know who it is?"

"The Esquire Bergon, if'n it please you."

I needed someone more important than that. "How about the cross-looking fellow in the awful yellow hat?"

The boy hid a smile. "That's Baronet Pettur."

Perfect. I stood and clapped Jim on the back. "You'll do well for yourself with a memory like that. Keep well." I gave him ha'penny and strolled to where the baronet stood, fingering a bolt of deep green velvet.

It goes without saying that in terms of social rank, there are none lower than the Edema Ruh. Even leaving aside my heritage, I was a landless commoner. This meant in terms of social standing the baronet was so high above me that if he were a star, I would not be able to see him with the naked eye. A person of my position should address him as "my lord," avoid eye contact, and bow deeply and humbly.

Truth be told, a person of my social standing shouldn't speak to him at all.

Things were different in the Commonwealth, of course. And the University itself was particularly egalitarian. But even there, nobility were still rich and powerful and well-connected. People like Ambrose would always run roughshod over folk like myself. And if things got difficult, he could always hush things up or bribe a judge to get himself out of trouble.

But I was in Vintas now. Here Ambrose wouldn't need to bribe the judge. If I'd accidentally jostled the Baronet Pettur in the street while I was still barefoot and muddy, he could have horsewhipped me bloody, then called the constable to arrest me for being a public nuisance. The constable would have done it too, with a smile and a nod.

Let me try to say this more succinctly. In the Commonwealth, the gentry are people with power and money. In Vintas, the gentry have power and money and *privilege*. Many rules simply do not apply to them.

That meant in Vintas, social rank was of utmost importance.

That meant if the baronet knew I was below him, he would lord it over me, quite literally.

On the other hand . . .

As I walked across the street toward the baronet, I straightened my shoulders and raised my chin a bit. I stiffened my neck and narrowed my eyes slightly. I looked around as if I owned the entire street, and it was currently something of a disappointment.

"Baronet Pettur?" I said briskly.

The man looked up, smiling vaguely, as if he couldn't decide if he recognized me or not. "Yes?"

I made a curt gesture toward the Sheer. "You would be doing the Maer a great service if you would escort me to his estate as quickly as possible." I kept my expression stern, almost angry.

"Well, certainly." He sounded anything but certain. I could sense the questions, the excuses beginning to bubble up in him. "W—"

I fixed the baronet with my haughtiest stare. The Edema might be on the lowest rung of the social ladder, but there are no finer actors breathing. I had been raised on the stage, and my father could play a king so regal I'd seen audiences doff their hats when he made his entrance.

I made my eyes as hard as agates and looked the florid man up and down as if he were a horse I wasn't sure I cared to bet on. "If the matter were not urgent, I would never impose on you this way." I hesitated, then added a stiff, reluctant, "Sir."

Baronet Pettur looked me in the eye. He was slightly off balance, but not nearly as much as I'd hoped. Like most nobility, he was self-centered as a gyroscope, and the only thing keeping him from sniffing and looking down his nose at me was his uncertainty. He eyed me, trying to decide if he could risk offending me by asking my name and how we were acquainted.

But I still had a final trick to play. I brought out the thin, sharp smile the porter at the Grey Man had used when I had come calling on Denna all those months ago. As I'd said, it was a good smile: gracious, polite, and more patronizing than if I'd reached out and patted the man on the head like a dog.

The Baronet Pettur bore up under the weight of the smile for almost a full second. Then he cracked like an egg, his shoulders rounding a bit, and his manner becoming ever so slightly obsequious. "Any service I can lend the Maer is a service I am glad to render," he said. "Please, allow me." He took the lead, heading toward the foot of the cliff.

Following behind, I smiled.

CHAPTER FIFTY-FOUR

The Messenger

I MANAGED TO BLUFF AND fast-talk my way through the majority of the Maer's defenses. The Baronet Pettur helped me simply by his presence. Being escorted by a recognizable member of the nobility was enough to get me deep inside Alveron's estate. After that, he soon outlived his usefulness and I left him behind.

Once he was out of sight I put on my most impatient face, asked a busy servant for directions, and made it all the way to the outer doors of the Maer's audience chamber before I was stopped by an unassuming man in his middle years. He was portly, with a round face, and despite his fine clothes he looked like a grocer to me.

If not for the several hours I'd spent gathering information in Severen-Low I might have made a terrible mistake and tried to bluff my way past this man, thinking him nothing more than a well-dressed servant.

But this was actually the person I was looking for: the Maer's manservant, Stapes. Though he looked like a grocer, he had the aura of true authority about him. His manner was quiet and certain, unlike the overbearing, brash one I had used to bully the baronet.

"How can I help you?" Stapes asked. His tone was perfectly polite, but there were other questions lurking beneath the surface of his words. *Who are you? What are you doing here?*

I brought out Count Threpe's letter and handed it over with a slight bow. "You would be doing me a great service if you would convey this to the Maer," I said. "He is expecting me."

Stapes gave me a cool look, making it perfectly clear that if the Maer had been expecting me, he would have known about it ten days ago. He rubbed his chin as he looked me over, and I saw he wore a dull iron ring with gold letters scrolling across the surface.

Despite his obvious misgivings, Stapes took the letter and disappeared through a set of double doors. I stood in the hallway for a nervous minute before he returned and ushered me inside, his manner still vaguely disapproving.

We moved through a short hallway, then came to a second set of doors flanked by armored guards. These weren't ceremonial guards of the sort you sometimes see in public, standing stiffly at attention, holding halberds. They wore the Maer's colors but beneath their sapphire and ivory were functional breastplates with steel rings and leather. Each man wore a long sword and a long knife. They eyed me seriously as I approached.

The Maer's manservant nodded to me, and one of the guards manhandled me in a quick, competent way, sliding his hands along my arms and legs and around my chest, searching for hidden weapons. I was suddenly very glad for some of the misfortunes on my trip, specifically the ones that had ended with me losing the pair of slender knives I'd grown accustomed to wearing underneath my clothes.

The guard stepped back and nodded. Then Stapes gave me another irritated look and opened the inner door.

Inside, two men sat at a map-strewn table. One was tall and bald with the hard, weathered look of a veteran soldier. Next to him sat the Maer.

Alveron was older than I had expected. He had a serious face, proud around the mouth and eyes. His well-trimmed salt-and-pepper beard had very little black left to it, but his hair was still full and thick. His eyes too, seemed to belie his age. They were clear grey, clever and piercing. They were not the eyes of an old man.

The Maer turned those eyes on me as I entered the room. He held Threpe's letter in one hand.

I made a standard number three bow. "The Messenger" as my father called it. Low and formal, as fitting the Maer's high station. Deferential, but not obsequious. Just because I tread heavily on propriety's toes doesn't mean I can't play the game when it's of use to me.

The Maer's eyes flickered down to the letter, then back up. "Kvothe, is it? You travel swiftly to arrive in such good time. I'd not expected even a reply from the count so soon."

"I made all possible speed to put myself at your disposal, your grace."

"Indeed." He looked me over carefully. "And you seem to vindicate the count's opinion of your wit by making it all the way to my door with nothing but a sealed letter in your hand."

"I thought it best to present myself as soon as possible, your grace," I said neutrally. "Your letter implied you were in some haste."

"And an impressive job you did of it too," Alveron said, glancing at the tall man sitting at the table next to him. "Wouldn't you say, Dagon?"

"Yes, your grace." Dagon looked at me with dark, dispassionate eyes. His face was hard and sharp and emotionless. I suppressed a shiver.

Alveron glanced down at the letter again. "Threpe certainly has some flattering things to say about you here," he said. "Well-spoken. Charming. Most talented musician he's met in ten years. . . ."

The Maer continued reading, then looked back up, his eyes shrewd. "You seem a bit young," he said hesitantly. "You're barely past twenty, aren't you?"

I was a month past my sixteenth birthday. A fact I'd pointedly omitted from the letter. "I am young, your grace," I admitted, sidestepping the actual lie. "But I've been making music since I was four." I spoke with quiet confidence, doubly glad of my new clothes. In my rags, I couldn't have helped but look like a starving urchin. As it was, I was well-dressed and tanned from my days at sea, and the lean lines of my face added years to my appearance.

Alveron eyed me for a long, speculative moment, then nodded, apparently satisfied. "Very well," he said. "Unfortunately, I am rather busy at present. Would tomorrow be convenient for you?" It wasn't really a question. "Have you found lodgings in the city?"

"I have not made any arrangements as of yet, your grace."

"You will stay here," he said evenly. "Stapes?" He called in a voice hardly louder than his normal speaking tone, and the portly, grocer-looking fellow appeared almost instantly. "Set our new guest somewhere in the south wing, near the gardens." He turned back to me. "Will your luggage be following?"

"I fear all my luggage was lost on the way, your grace. Shipwreck."

Alveron raised an eyebrow briefly. "Stapes will see you are properly outfitted." He folded Threpe's letter and made a gesture of dismissal. "Good evening."

I made a quick bow and followed Stapes from the room.

———

The rooms were the most opulent I'd ever seen, let alone lived in, full of old wood and polished stone. The bed had a feather mattress a foot thick, and when I drew its curtains and lay inside, it seemed as big as my entire room back at Anker's.

My rooms were so pleasant it took me almost a full day to realize how much I hated them.

Again you have to think in terms of shoes. You don't want the biggest pair. You want a pair that fits. If your shoes are too big, your feet chafe and blister.

In a similar way, my rooms chafed at me. There was an immense empty wardrobe, empty chests of drawers, and bare bookshelves. My room in Anker's had been tiny, but here I felt like a dried pea rattling around inside an empty jewelry box.

But while the rooms were too large for my nonexistent possessions, they were too small for me. I was obliged to remain there, waiting for the Maer to summon me. Since I had no idea when this might happen, I was effectively trapped.

In defense of the Maer's hospitality, I should mention a few positive things. The food was excellent, if somewhat cold by the time it made its way from the kitchens. There was also a wonderful copper bathing basin. Servants brought the hot water, but it drained away through a series of pipes. I had not expected to find such conveniences so far from the civilizing influence of the University.

I was visited by one of the Maer's tailors, an excitable little man who measured me six dozen different ways while chattering about the court gossip. The next day, a runner boy delivered two elaborate suits of clothing in colors that flattered me.

In a way, I was fortunate I'd met with trouble at sea. The clothing Alveron's tailors supplied was much better than anything I could have afforded, even with Threpe's help. As a result, I cut quite a striking figure during my stay in Severen.

Best of all, while checking the fit of my clothes the chatty tailor mentioned cloaks were in fashion. I took the opportunity to exaggerate somewhat about the cloak Fela had given me, bemoaning the loss of it.

The result was a richly colored burgundy cloak. It wouldn't keep the rain off worth a damn, but I was quite fond of it. Not only did it make me look rather dashing, but it was full of clever little pockets, of course.

So I was dressed, fed, and boarded in luxury. But despite this largess, by noon of the next day I was prowling my rooms like a cat in a crate. I itched to be outside, to have my lute out of pawn, to discover why the Maer needed the service of someone clever, well-spoken, and above all, discreet.

CHAPTER FIFTY-FIVE

Grace

I PEERED AT THE MAER through a gap in the hedge. He was sitting on a stone bench under a shade tree in his gardens, looking every bit the gentleman in his loose sleeves and waistcoat. He wore the house colors of Alveron: sapphire and ivory. But while his clothes were fine, they weren't ostentatious. He wore a gold signet ring, but no other jewelry. Compared to many others in his court, the Maer was almost plainly dressed.

At first this seemed to imply that Alveron disdained the fashions of the court. But after a moment, I saw the truth of it. The ivory of his shirt was creamy and flawless, the sapphire of his waistcoat vibrant. I would have bet my thumbs they hadn't been worn more than a half-dozen times.

As a display of wealth, it was subtle and staggering. It was one thing to be able to afford fine clothes, but how much would it cost to maintain a wardrobe that never showed the slightest hint of wear? I thought of what Count Threpe had said about Alveron: *Rich as the King of Vint.*

The Maer himself looked much the same as before. Tall and thin. Greying and immaculately groomed. I took in the tired lines of his face, the slight tremble of his hands, his posture. *He looks old*, I thought to myself, *but he's not.*

The belling tower began to strike the hour. I stepped back from the hedge and strolled around the corner to meet the Maer.

Alveron nodded, his cool eyes looking me over carefully. "Kvothe, I was rather hoping you would come."

I gave a semi-formal bow. "I was pleased to receive your invitation, your grace."

Alveron made no gesture for me to seat myself, so I remained standing. I guessed he was testing my manners. "I hope you do not mind our meeting outside. Have you seen the gardens yet?"

"I haven't had the opportunity, your grace." I'd been trapped in my damned rooms until he had sent for me.

"You must allow me to show you around." He took hold of a polished walking stick that rested against the shade tree. "I've always found that taking some air is good for whatever troubles a body, though others disagree." He leaned forward as if he would stand, but a shadow of pain crossed his face and he drew a shallow, painful breath between his teeth. *Sick.* I realized. *Not old, sick.*

I was at his side in a twinkling and offered him my arm. "Allow me, your grace."

The Maer gave a stiff smile. "If I were younger, I'd make light of your offer," he sighed. "But pride is the luxury of the strong." He laid a thin hand on my arm and used my support to gain his feet. "I must settle for being gracious instead."

"Graciousness is the luxury of the wise," I said easily. "So it can be noted that your wisdom lends you grace."

Alveron gave a wry chuckle and patted my arm. "That makes it a bit easier to bear, I suppose."

"Would you like your stick, your grace?" I asked. "Or shall we walk together?"

He made the same dry chuckle. " 'Walk together.' That's delicately put." He took the stick in his right hand while his left held my arm in a surprisingly strong grip.

"Lord and lady," he swore under his breath. "I hate to be seen doddering about. But it's less galling to lean on a young man's arm than hobble around on my own. It's a horrible thing to have your body fail you. You never think about it when you're young."

We began to walk, and our conversation lulled as we listened to the sound of water splashing in the fountains and birds singing in the hedges. Occasionally the Maer would point out a particular piece of statuary and tell which of his ancestors had commissioned it, made it, or (he spoke of these in a quieter, apologetic tone) plundered it from foreign lands in times of war.

We walked about the gardens for the better part of an hour. Alveron's weight on my arm gradually lessened and soon he was using me more for balance than support. We passed several gentlefolk who bowed or nodded to the Maer. After they were out of earshot he would mention who they were, how they ranked in court, and a snippet or two of amusing gossip.

"They're wondering who you are," he said after one such couple had passed behind a hedge. "By tonight it will be all the talk. Are you an ambassador from Renere? A young noble looking for a rich fief and a wife to go along? Perhaps you are my long-lost son, a remnant from my wilder youth." He chuckled to himself and patted my arm. He might have continued, but he stumbled on a protruding flagstone and almost fell. I steadied him quickly, and eased him onto a stone bench beside the path.

"Damn and bother," he cursed, obviously embarrassed. "How would that have looked, the Maer scrabbling about like a beetle on its back?" He looked around crossly, but we seemed to be alone. "Would you do an old man a favor?"

"I am at your disposal, your grace."

Alveron gave me a shrewd look. "Are you indeed? Well, it's a little thing. Keep secretive about who you are and what your business is. It'll do wonders for your reputation. The less you tell them, the more everyone will be wanting to get from you."

"I'll keep close about myself, your grace. But I would have better luck avoiding the subject of why I'm here if I knew what it was. . . ."

Alveron's expression went sly. "True. But this is too public a place. You've shown good patience so far. Exercise it while longer." He looked up at me. "Would you be so kind as to walk me to my rooms?"

I held out my arm. "Certainly, your grace."

After returning to my rooms, I removed my embroidered jacket and hung it in the carved rosewood wardrobe. The huge piece of furniture was lined with cedar and sandalwood, scenting the air. Large, flawless mirrors hung on the insides of the doors.

I walked across the polished marble floor and sat on a red velvet lounging couch. I idly wondered how exactly one was supposed to lounge. I couldn't remember ever doing it myself. After a moment's consideration, I decided lounging was probably similar to relaxing, but with more money in your pocket.

Restless, I got to my feet and moved around the room. There were paintings on the walls, portraits and pastoral scenes done skillfully in oil. One wall held a huge tapestry that showed a vast naval battle in intricate detail. That occupied my attention for almost half an hour.

I missed my lute.

It had been terribly hard to pawn it, like cutting off my hand. I'd fully expected to spend the next ten days sick with worry, anxious that I wouldn't be able to buy it back.

But without meaning to, the Maer himself had set my mind at ease. In my wardrobe hung six suits of clothing, fine enough for any lord. When they had been delivered to my room, I'd felt myself relax. My first thought on seeing them wasn't that I could now mingle comfortably with court society. I thought that if worse came to worst, I could steal them, sell them to a fripperer, and easily have enough money to reclaim my lute.

Of course if I did such a thing, I would burn all my bridges with the Maer. It would render my entire trip to Severen pointless, and would embarrass Threpe so profoundly that he might never speak to me again. Nevertheless, knowing I had that option gave me a thin thread of control over the situation. It was enough so I could keep from going absolutely mad with worry.

I missed my lute, but if I could gain the Maer's patronage, my life's road would grow suddenly smooth and straight. The Maer had money enough for me to continue my education at the University. His connections could help me continue my research into the Amyr.

Perhaps most important was the power of his name. If the Maer were my patron, I would be under his protection. Ambrose's father might be the most powerful baron in all of Vintas, a dozen steps from royalty. But Alveron was practically a king in his own right. How much simpler would my life become without Ambrose endlessly spiking my wheel? It was a giddy thought.

I missed my lute, but all things have their price. For a chance of having the Maer as a patron, I was willing to grit my teeth and spend a span bored and anxious, without music.

Alveron turned out to be right about the curious nature of his attendant court. After he called me to his study that evening, rumor exploded like a brushfire around me. I could understand why the Maer enjoyed this sort of thing. It was like watching stories being born.

CHAPTER FIFTY-SIX

Power

ALVERON SENT FOR ME again the next day, and soon the two of us were strolling along the garden paths again, his hand resting lightly on my arm. "Let's head toward the south side." The Maer pointed with his walking stick. "I hear the selas will reach full bloom soon."

We took the left turning of the path and he drew a breath. "There are two types of power: inherent and granted," Alveron said, letting me know the topic of today's conversation. "Inherent power you possess as a part of yourself. Granted power is lent or given by other people." He looked sideways at me. I nodded.

Seeing my agreement, the Maer continued. "Inherent power is an obvious thing. Strength of body." He patted my supporting arm. "Strength of mind. Strength of personality. All these things lie within a person. They define us. They determine our limits."

"Not entirely, your grace," I protested gently. "A man can always improve himself."

"They limit us," the Maer said firmly. "A man with one hand will never wrestle in the roundings. A man with one leg will never run as quickly as a man with two."

"An Adem warrior with only one hand might be more deadly than a common warrior with two, your grace." I pointed out. "Despite his deficiency."

"True, true," the Maer said crossly. "We can improve ourselves, exercise our bodies, educate our minds, groom ourselves carefully." He ran a hand down his immaculate salt-and-pepper beard. "For even appearance is a type of power. But there are always limits. While a one-handed man might become a passable warrior, he could not play a lute."

I nodded slowly. "You make a good point, your grace. Our power has limits we can extend, but not indefinitely."

Alveron held up a finger. "But that is only the first type of power. We are only limited if we rely upon the power we ourselves possess. There is still the type of power that is given. Do you understand what I mean by granted power?"

I thought a moment. "Taxes?"

"Hmm," the Maer said, surprised. "That's a rather good example, actually. Have you put much thought into this sort of thing before?"

"A bit," I admitted. "But never in these terms."

"It is a difficult thing," he said, sounding pleased by my response. "Which do you think is the greater type of power?"

I only had to think for a second. "The inherent, your grace."

"Interesting. Why do you say that?"

"Because a power you possess yourself cannot be taken away, your grace."

"Ah." He raised a long finger as if to caution me. "But we've already agreed that type of power is severely limited. Granted power has no limits."

"*No* limits, your grace?"

Alveron nodded his head in concession. "Very few limits, then."

I still didn't agree. The Maer must have seen it on my face because he leaned toward me to explain. "Let's say I have an enemy, young and strong. Let's say he has stolen something of mine, some money. Are you with me?"

I nodded.

"No manner of training will make me the match of a quarrelsome twenty-year-old. So what do I do? I get one of my young, strong friends to go and box his ears. With that strength I can accomplish a feat which would be otherwise impossible."

"Your enemy could box your friend's ears instead," I pointed out as we rounded a corner. An arching trellis turned the path ahead of us into a shaded tunnel, thick with deep green leaves.

"Let's say I got three friends together," the Maer amended. "Suddenly I've been granted the strength of three men! My enemy, even if he were very strong, could never be as strong as that. Look to the selas. Terribly difficult to cultivate, they tell me."

We entered the shadow of the trellis tunnel where hundreds of deep red petals blossomed in the shade of leaf and arch. The smell was sweet and tremulous. I brushed a hand across one of the deep red blooms. It was unspeakably soft. I thought of Denna.

The Maer returned to our discussion. "You're missing the point, anyway.

The lending of strength is just a small example. Some types of power can *only* be given."

He made a subtle gesture to a corner of the garden. "Do you see Compte Farlend over there? If you asked him about his title, he would say he possesses it. He would claim it is a part of him as much as his own blood. A *part* of his blood, in fact. Almost any noble would say the same thing. They would argue their lineage imbued them with the right to rule."

The Maer looked up at me, his eyes glittering in amusement. "But they're wrong. It is not inherent power. It is granted. I could take away his lands and leave him a pauper on the street."

Alveron motioned me closer, and I leaned a bit. "Here is a great secret. Even *my* title, my riches, my control over people and the land. It is only granted power. It belongs to me no more than does the strength of your arm." He patted my hand and smiled at me. "But *I* know the difference, and that is why I am always in control."

He straightened and spoke in normal tones. "Good afternoon, Compte. Lovely day to be out in the sun, wouldn't you say?"

"Indeed, your grace. The selas are quite breathtaking." The Compte was a heavy man with jowls and a thick mustache. "My compliments."

After the compte had passed us by, Alveron continued. "You notice he complimented *me* on the selas? I have never touched a trowel in my life." He looked sideways at me, his expression slightly smug. "Do you still think inherent power is the better of the two?"

"You make a compelling point, your grace," I said. "However—"

"You're a hard one to convince. One last example, then. Can we agree that I will never be able to give birth to a child?"

"I think that is safe to say, your grace."

"Yet if a woman grants me the right to wed her, I can give birth to a son. Through granted power, a man can make himself as fast as a horse, as strong as an ox. Can inherent power do this for you?"

I couldn't argue that. "I bow to your argument, your grace."

"I bow to your wisdom in accepting it." He chuckled, and at the same time the faint ringing of the hour moved through the garden. "Oh bother," the Maer said, his expression souring. "I must go take that dreadful nostrum of mine or Caudicus will be completely unmanageable for a span of days." I gave him a quizzical look and he explained. "He somehow discovered that I poured yesterday's dose in the chamber pot."

"Your grace should be mindful of your health."

Alveron scowled. "You overstep yourself," he snapped.

I flushed in embarrassment, but before I could apologize he waved me into silence. "You're right, of course. I know my duty. But you sound just like him. One Caudicus is enough for me."

He paused to nod toward an approaching couple. The man was tall and handsome, a few years older than myself. The woman was perhaps thirty, with dark eyes and an elegant, wicked mouth. "Good evening, Lady Hesua. I trust your father is continuing to improve?"

"Oh yes," she said. "The surgeon says he should be up before the span is through." She caught my eye and held it briefly, her red mouth curving into a knowing smile.

Then she was past us. I found myself sweating a bit.

If the Maer noticed, he ignored it. "Terrible woman. New man every span of days. Her father was wounded in a duel with Esquire Higton over an 'inappropriate' remark. A true remark, but that doesn't count for much once the swords are out."

"What of the squire?"

"Died the day after. Pity too. He was a good man, just didn't know enough to mind his tongue." He sighed and looked up at the belling tower. "As I was saying. One physician is quite enough for me. Caudicus clucks over me like a mother hen. I hate taking medicine when I am already on the mend."

The Maer did seem better today. He hadn't really needed the support of my arm during our walk. I sensed he only leaned on me to give us an excuse to be talking so close together. "Your improving health seems proof enough that his ministrations work to heal you," I said.

"Yes, yes. His potives drive away my illness for a span of days. Sometimes for months." He sighed bitterly. "But they always come back. Shall I be drinking potions the rest of my life?"

"Perhaps the need for them will pass, your grace."

"I had hoped the same thing myself. In his recent travels Caudicus gathered some herbs that worked wondrous well. His last treatment left me hale for nearly a year. I thought I was finally free of it." The Maer scowled down at his walking stick. "Yet here I am."

"If I could aid you in any way, your grace, I would."

Alveron turned his head to look me in the eye. After a moment he nodded to himself. "I do believe you would," he said. "How extraordinary."

Several conversations of a similar sort followed. I could tell the Maer was trying to get a feel for me. With all the skill learned in forty years of courtly intrigue, he steered the conversation in subtle ways, learning my opinions, determining whether or not I was worthy of his trust.

While I didn't have the Maer's experience, I was a fair conversationalist myself. I was always careful with my answers, always courteous. After a few days, a mutual respect began to grow between us. Not a friendship such as I had with Count Threpe. The Maer never encouraged me to disregard his title or sit in his presence, but we were growing closer. While Threpe was a friend, the Maer was like a distant grandfather: kind but older, serious, and reserved.

I got the impression the Maer was a lonely man, forced to remain aloof from his subjects and the members of his court. I almost suspected he might have sent to Threpe for a companion. Someone clever but removed from the politics of court so he could have an honest conversation once in a while.

At first I dismissed such an idea as unlikely, but the days continued to pass and still the Maer avoided any mention of what use he planned to put me to.

If I'd had my lute I could have passed the time pleasantly, but it still lay in Severen-Low, seven days away from belonging to the pawnshop. So there was no music, just my echoing rooms and my damnable useless idleness.

As rumors about me spread, various members of the court came to visit. Some made a pretense of welcoming me. Others made a show of wanting to gossip. I even suspected there were a few attempts at seduction, but at that point in my life I knew so little of women that I was immune to those games. One gentleman even tried to borrow money from me, and I was hard pressed not to laugh in his face.

They told different stories and used different degrees of subtlety, but they were all there for the same reason: to glean information from me. However, since I was under the Maer's instructions to be tight-lipped about myself, all the conversations were brief and unsatisfying.

All but one, I should say. The exception proves the rule.

CHAPTER FIFTY-SEVEN

A Handful of Iron

I MET BREDON ON MY fourth day in Severen. It was early, but I was already pacing my rooms, nearly insane with boredom. I'd had my breakfast, and it was hours before lunch.

So far today I'd dealt with three courtiers come to pry at me. I dealt with them deftly, running our conversations aground at every opportunity. *So where are you from, my boy?* Oh, you know how it is. One travels so. *And your parents?* Yes actually. I had them. Two in fact. *What brings you to Severen?* A coach and four, for the most part. Though I walked a bit as well. Good for the lungs, you know. *And what are you doing here?* Enjoying good conversation, of course. Meeting interesting people. *Really? Who?* Why all sorts. Including you, Lord Praevek. You are quite the fascinating fellow. . . .

And so on. It wasn't long before even the most tenacious rumormonger grew weary and left.

Worst of all, these brief exchanges would be the most interesting part of my day if the Maer didn't call for me. So far we'd conversed over a light lunch, three times during brief walks in the garden, and once late at night when most sensible people would be abed. Twice Alveron's runner woke me from a sound sleep before the sky began to color with the blue beginning of dawn's light.

I know when I am being tested. Alveron wanted to see if I was truly willing to make myself available to him at any unreasonable hour of the day or night. He was watching to see if I would become impatient or irritated by his casual use of me.

So I played the game. I was charming and unfailingly polite. I came when he called and left as soon as he was through with me. I asked no impertinent questions, made no demands on him, and spent the remainder of my day

grinding my teeth, pacing my overlarge rooms, and trying not to think about
how many days I had left before the span note on my lute expired.

Small wonder that a knock on that fourth day sent me scrambling for the
door. I hoped it was a summons from the Maer, but at this point, any distraction would be welcome.

I opened the door to reveal an older man, a gentleman down to his bones.
His clothes gave him away, certainly, but more important was the fact that he
wore his wealth with the comfortable indifference of someone born into it.
New-made nobles, pretenders, and rich merchants simply don't carry themselves the same way.

Alveron's manservant, for example, had finer clothes than half the gentry,
but despite the self-assurance Stapes possessed, he looked like a baker wearing
his holiday best.

Thanks to Alveron's tailors, I was dressed as well as anyone. The colors
were good on me, leaf green, black, and burgundy, with silver workings on
the cuff and collar. However, unlike Stapes, I wore the clothes with the casual
ease of nobility. True, the brocade itched. True, the buttons, buckles, and endless layers made every outfit stiff and awkward as a suit of mercenary's leathers. But I lounged in it as easily as if it were a second skin. It was a costume,
you see, and I played my part as only a trouper can.

As I was saying, I opened the door to see an older gentleman standing in
the hall.

"So you're Kvothe, are you?" he asked.

I nodded, caught slightly off my stride. The custom in northern Vintas
was to send a servant ahead to request a meeting. The runner brought a note
and a ring with the noble's name inscribed. You sent a gold ring to request
a meeting with a noble of higher rank than yourself, silver for someone of
roughly the same rank, and iron for someone beneath you.

I didn't have any rank, of course. No title, no lands, no family, and no
blood. I was lowborn as they come, but no one here knew that. Everyone assumed the mysterious red-haired man spending time with Alveron was some
flavor of nobility, and my origin and standing was a much-debated topic.

The important thing was that I had not been officially introduced to the
court. As such, I had no *official* ranking. That meant all the rings sent to me
were iron. And one does not typically refuse a request sent with an iron ring,
lest one offend one's betters.

So it was rather surprising to find this older gentleman standing outside
the door. Obviously noble, but unannounced and uninvited.

"You may call me Bredon," he said, looking me in the eye. "Do you know
how to play tak?"

I shook my head, unsure what to make of this.

He gave a small, disappointed sigh. "Ah well, I can teach you." He thrust a black velvet sack toward me and I took hold of it with both hands. It felt as if it were full of small, smooth stones.

Bredon gestured behind him, and a pair of young men bustled into my room carrying a small table. I stepped out of their way, and Bredon swept through the door in their wake. "Set it by the window," he directed them, pointing with his walking stick. "And bring some chairs— No, the rail-back chairs."

In a short moment everything was arranged to his satisfaction. The two servants left, and Bredon turned to me with an apologetic look on his face. "You'll forgive an old man a dramatic entrance, I hope?"

"Of course," I said graciously. "Please have a seat." I gestured toward the new table by the window.

"Such aplomb," he chuckled, leaning his walking stick against the window sill. The sunlight caught on the polished silver handle wrought in the shape of a snarling wolf's head.

Bredon was older. Not elderly by any means, but what I consider grandfather old. His colors weren't colors at all, merely ash grey and a dark charcoal. His hair and beard were pure white, and all cut to the same length, making a frame for his face. As he sat there, peering at me with his lively brown eyes, he reminded me of an owl.

I took a seat across from him and wondered idly how he was going to attempt to wheedle information out of me. He'd obviously brought a game. Perhaps he'd try to gamble it out of me. That would be a new approach at least.

He smiled at me. An honest smile I found myself returning before I realized what I was doing. "You must have a fair collection of rings by this point," he said.

I nodded.

He leaned forward curiously. "Would you mind terribly if I looked them over?"

"Not at all." I went into the other room and brought back a handful of rings, spilling them onto the table.

He looked them over, nodding to himself. "You've had all our best gossipmongers descend on you. Veston, Praevek, and Temenlovy have all taken a crack." His eyebrows went up as he saw the name on another ring. "Praevek twice. And none of them got a shred of anything out of you. Nothing half as solid as a whisper."

Bredon glanced up at me. "That tells me you are keeping your tongue tightly between your teeth, and you are good at it. Rest assured, I'm not here in some vain attempt to pry at your secrets."

I didn't entirely believe him, but it was nice to hear. "I'll admit that's a relief."

"As a brief aside," he mentioned casually. "I'll mention the rings are traditionally left in the sitting room near the door. They are displayed as a mark of status."

I hadn't known that, but I didn't want to admit to it. If I was unfamiliar with the customs of the local court, it would let him know I was either a foreigner or not one of the gentry. "There's no real status in a handful of iron," I said dismissively. Count Threpe had explained the basics of the rings to me before I left Imre. But he wasn't from Vintas, and obviously hadn't known the fine points.

"There's some truth to that," Bredon said easily. "But not the truth entire. Gold rings imply those below you are working to curry your favor. Silver indicates a healthy working relationship with your peers." He laid the rings in a row on the table. "However, iron means you have the attention of your betters. It indicates you are desirable."

I nodded slowly. "Of course," I said. "Any ring the Maer sends will be an iron one."

"Exactly." Bredon nodded. "To have a ring from the Maer is a mark of great favor." He pushed the rings toward me across the top of the smooth marble table. "But there is no such ring here, and that itself is meaningful."

"It seems you're no stranger to courtly politics yourself," I pointed out.

Bredon closed his eyes and nodded a weary agreement. "I was quite fond of it when I was young. I was even something of a power, as these things go. But at present, I have no machinations to advance. That takes the spice from such maneuverings." He looked at me again, meeting my eyes directly. "I have simpler tastes now. I travel. I enjoy wines and conversation with interesting people. I've even been learning how to dance."

He smiled again, warmly, and rapped a knuckle on the board. "More than anything, however, I enjoy playing tak. However, I know few people with time or wit enough to play the game properly." He raised an eyebrow at me.

I hesitated. "One might assume that someone well-skilled in the subtle art of conversation could use long stretches of idle chatter to glean information from an unsuspecting victim."

Bredon smiled. "By the names on these rings, I can tell you've seen nothing but the most gaudy and grasping of us. You're understandably skittish regarding your secrets, whatever they may be." He leaned forward. "Consider this instead. Those who have approached you are like magpies. They caw and flap around you, hoping to snatch something bright to carry home with them." He rolled his eyes disdainfully. "What gain is there in that? Some small notoriety, I suppose. Some brief elevation among one's gaudy, gossipy peers."

Bredon ran a hand over his white beard. "I am no magpie. I need nothing shiny, nor do I care what gossipmongers think. I play a longer, more subtle game." He began to work the drawstring loose on the black velvet bag. "You are a man of some wit. I know this as the Maer does not waste his time with fools. I know you either stand in the Maer's good grace, or you have a chance to gain that grace. So here is my plan." He smiled his warm smile again. "Would you like to hear my plan?"

I found myself smiling back without meaning to, as I had before. "That would be unusually kind of you."

"My plan is to insinuate myself into your favor now. I will make myself useful and entertaining. I will provide conversation and a way to pass the time." He spilled a set of round stones out onto the marble tabletop. "Then, when your star grows ascendant in the Maer's sky, I may find myself in possession of an unexpectedly useful friend." He began to sort the stones into their different colors. "And should your star fail to rise, I am still richer by several games of tak."

"I also imagine it won't hurt your reputation to spend several hours alone with me," I mentioned. "Given that all my other conversations have been barren things not likely to last a quarter hour."

"There is some truth to that as well," he said as he began to arrange the stones. His curious brown eyes smiled at me again. "Oh yes, I think I'm going to have quite a bit of fun playing with you."

My next several hours were spent learning how to play tak. Even if I had not been nearly mad with idleness, I would have enjoyed it. Tak is the best sort of game: simple in its rules, complex in its strategy. Bredon beat me handily in all five games we played, but I am proud to say that he never beat me the same way twice.

After the fifth game he leaned back with a satisfied sigh. "That was approaching a good game. You got clever in the corner here." He wiggled his fingers at the edge of the board.

"Not clever enough."

"Clever nonetheless. What you attempted is called a brooker's fall, just so you know."

"And what's the name for the way you got away from it?"

"I call it Bredon's defense," he said, smiling rakishly. "But that's what I call any maneuver when I get out of a tight corner by being uncommonly clever."

I laughed and began to separate the stones again. "Another?"

Bredon sighed. "Alas, I have an unavoidable appointment. I needn't hurry out the door, but I don't have enough time for another game. Not a proper one."

His brown eyes looked me over as he began to gather the stones into the velvet bag. "I won't insult you by asking if you're familiar with the local customs," Bredon said. "However, I thought I might give a few general pieces of advice, on the off chance they might be helpful." He smiled at me. "It would be best to listen, of course. If you refuse, you reveal your knowledge of these things."

"Of course," I said with a straight face.

Bredon slid open the table's drawer and pulled out the handful of iron rings we had swept aside to clear the board for our game. "The presentation of the rings implies a great deal. If they are jumbled in a bowl for example, it implies disinterest in the social aspects of the court."

He arranged the rings with their engraved names facing me. "Laid out in careful display, they show you are proud of your connections." He looked up and smiled. "Either way, a new arrival is usually left alone in the sitting room on some pretext. This gives them a chance to paw through your collection in order to satisfy their curiosity."

Shrugging, Bredon pushed the rings toward me. "You have, of course, always made a point of offering to return the rings to their owners." He was careful not to make it into a question.

"Of course," I said honestly. Threpe had known that much.

"It is the most polite thing to do." He looked up at me, his brown eyes peering owlishly from the halo of his white hair and beard. "Have you worn any of them in public?"

I held up my bare hands.

"Wearing a ring can indicate a debt, or that you are attempting to curry favor." He looked at me. "If the Maer ever declines to take his ring back from you, it would be an indication he was willing to make your connection somewhat more formal."

"And not wearing the ring would be viewed as a slight," I said.

Bredon smiled. "Perhaps. It is one thing to display a ring in your sitting room, quite another to display it on your hand. Wearing the ring of one's better can be viewed as quite presumptuous. Also, if you wore another noble's ring while visiting the Maer, he might take it amiss. As if someone had poached you from his forest."

He leaned back in his chair. "I mention these things as general talking points," he said, "suspecting this information is already well known to you, and you are politely letting an old man ramble."

"Perhaps I am still reeling from a series of numbing defeats at tak," I said.

He waved my comment away, and I noticed he wore no rings of any sort on his fingers. "You took to it quickly, like a baron at a brothel, as they say. I expect you'll prove a decent challenge after a month or so."

"Wait and see," I said. "I'll beat you the next time we play."

Bredon chuckled. "I like to hear that." He reached into his pocket and pulled out a smaller velvet bag. "I have also brought you a small gift."

"I couldn't possibly," I said reflexively. "You've already provided me with an afternoon's entertainment."

"Please," he said, pushing the bag across the table. "I must insist. These are yours without obligation, let, or lien. A freely given gift."

I upended the bag and three rings chimed into my palm. Gold, silver, and iron. Each of them had my name etched into the metal: *Kvothe*.

"I heard a rumor your luggage was lost," Bredon said. "And thought these might prove useful." He smiled. "Especially if you desire another game of tak."

I rolled the rings around in my hand, idly wondering if the gold ring was solid or simply plated. "And what ring would I send my new acquaintance if I desired his company?"

"Well," Bredon said slowly. "That *is* complicated. By my rash and unseemly barging into your rooms, I have neglected a proper introduction and failed to inform you as to my title and rank." His brown eyes looked into mine seriously.

"And it would be terribly rude of me to inquire about such things," I said slowly, not quite sure what he was playing at.

He nodded. "So for now, you must assume I am without either title or rank. That puts us on a curious footing: you unannounced to the court, and myself unannounced to you. As such, it would be fitting for you to send me a silver ring if, in the future, you would like to share a lunch or graciously lose another game of tak."

I rolled the silver ring around in my fingers. If I sent it to him, rumor would get around that I was claiming a rank roughly equal to his, and I had no idea what rank that was. "What will people say?"

His eyes danced a bit. "What indeed?"

So the days continued to pass. The Maer summoned me for urbane chatter. Magpie nobles sent their cards and rings and were met with polite conversational rebuffment.

Bredon alone kept me from growing mad with caged boredom. The next day I sent him my new silver ring with a card saying, "At your leisure. My rooms." Five minutes later he arrived with his tak table and bag of stones. He offered my ring back to me and I accepted it as graciously as possible. I wouldn't have minded him keeping it. But as he knew, I only had the one.

Our fifth game was interrupted when I was summoned by the Maer, his ring of iron sitting darkly on the runner's polished silver tray. I made my apologies to Bredon and hurried off to the gardens.

Later that night Bredon sent me his own silver ring and a card saying, "After supper. Your rooms." I wrote "Delighted" on the card and sent it back.

When he arrived, I offered to return his ring. He politely declined and it joined the rest in the bowl by my door. It sat there for everyone to see, bright silver glittering among the handful of iron.

CHAPTER FIFTY-EIGHT

Courting

THE MAER HAD NOT called on me for two days.

I was trapped in my rooms, and near mad with boredom and irritation. Worst was the fact that I didn't know why the Maer wasn't calling on me. Was he busy? Had I offended him? I thought of sending him a card along with the gold ring Bredon had given me. But if Alveron were testing my patience, that could be a grave mistake.

But I *was* impatient. I had come here to gain a patron, or at least some assistance in my pursuit of the Amyr. So far, all I had to show for my time in the Maer's service was a profoundly flattened ass. If it hadn't been for Bredon, I swear I would have gone frothing mad.

Worse, my lute and Denna's lovely case were only two days away from becoming someone else's property. I had hoped by this point to have gained enough of the Maer's favor that I could ask him for the money I needed to get it out of pawn. I'd wanted him to be indebted to me, not the other way around. Once you owe something to a member of the nobility, it is notoriously difficult to work your way free of their debt.

But if Alveron's lack of summons was any indication, I seemed to be far from his good graces. I racked my memory, trying to think of what I might have said during our last conversation that could have offended him.

I'd pulled a card from the drawer and was trying to think of a politic way of asking the Maer for money when a knock came at the door. Thinking it was my lunch come early, I called for the boy to leave it on the table.

There was a significant pause that roused me from my reverie. I hurried to the door and was startled to see the Maer's manservant, Stapes, standing outside. Alveron's summons had always been delivered by runner before.

"The Maer would like to see you," he said. I noticed the manservant

looked worn around the edges. His eyes were weary, as if he hadn't been
sleeping enough.

"In the garden?"

"In his rooms," Stapes said. "I will take you there."

If the gossiping courtiers were to be believed, Alveron rarely received visitors in his rooms. As I fell into step behind Stapes, I couldn't help but feel
relief. Anything was better than waiting.

Alveron was propped upright in his great feather bed. He seemed paler and
thinner than when I'd seen him last. His eyes were still clear and sharp, but
today they held something else, some hard emotion.

He gestured to a nearby chair. "Kvothe. Come in. Sit down." His voice was
weaker too, but it still carried the weight of command. I sat at his bedside,
sensing the time was not appropriate for thanking him for the privilege.

"Do you know how old I am, Kvothe?" he said without preamble.

"No, your grace."

"What would your guess be? How old do I seem?" I caught the hard emotion in his eyes again: anger. A slow, smoldering anger, like hot coals beneath
a thin layer of ash.

My mind raced, trying to decide what the best answer might be. I didn't
want to risk giving offense, but flattery irritated the Maer unless it was done
with consummate subtlety and skill.

My last resort then. Honesty. "Fifty-one, your grace. Perhaps fifty-two."

He nodded slowly, his anger seeming to fade like thunder in the distance.
"Never ask a young man your age. I am forty, with a birthday next span.
You're right though, I look fifty years if I look a day. Some might even say
you were being generous." His hands smoothed the bedcovers absently. "It's a
terrible thing, growing old before your time."

He stiffened in pain, grimacing. After a moment it passed, and he drew a
deep breath. A faint sheen of sweat covered his face. "I don't know how long
I'll be able to speak with you. I don't seem to be doing very well today."

I stood. "Should I fetch Caudicus, your grace?"

"No," he spat. "Sit down."

I did.

"This damnable sickness has crept on me this last month, adding years and
making me feel them. I have spent my life tending to my lands, but I have
been lax in one regard. I have no family, no heir."

"Do you mean to take a wife, your grace?"

He sagged against his pillows. "The rumor has finally gotten around, has it?"

"No, your grace. I guessed it from what you've said in some of our conversations."

He gave me a penetrating look. "Truthfully? A guess and not from a rumor?"

"Truthfully, your grace. There are rumors, a whole courtload, if you'll excuse the expression."

" 'Courtload.' That's good." He smiled a thin whisper of a smile.

"But most of it concerns some mysterious visitor from the west." I performed a small seated bow. "There's nothing of marriage. Everyone sees you as the world's first bachelor."

"Ah," he said, his face showing his relief. "That used to be the case. My father tried to marry me off when I was younger. I was rather strong-headed about not taking a wife at the time. That's another problem with power. If you possess too much, people don't dare point out your mistakes. Power can be a terrible thing."

"I imagine so, your grace."

"It takes away your choices," he said. "It gives a man opportunities, but at the same time it takes others away. My situation is difficult, to say the least."

Over the course of my life I've been hungry too many times to feel much empathy for the nobility. But the Maer looked so pale and weak as he lay there that I felt a flicker of sympathy. "What situation is that, your grace?"

Alveron struggled to sit upright against his pillows. "If I am to be married, it must be to someone suitable. Someone from a family well-positioned as my own. Not only that, but this cannot be a marriage of alliance. The girl must be young enough to—" He cleared his throat, a papery noise. "Produce an heir. Several if possible." He looked up at me. "Do you begin to see my problem?"

I nodded slowly. "Just the bare shape of it, your grace. How many such daughters are there?"

"A bare handful," Alveron said, a hint of the old fire coming back to his voice. "But it can't be one of the young women the king has under his control. Bargaining chips and treaty sealers. My family has fought to hold our plenary powers since the founding of Vintas. I won't negotiate with that bastard Roderic for a wife. I won't remit a grain of power to him."

"How many women are beyond the king's control, your grace?"

"One." The word fell like a lead weight. "And that is not the worst of it. The woman is perfect in every way. Her family is respectable. She is educated. Young. Beautiful." The last word seemed to come hard to him.

"She is pursued by a flock of love-struck courtiers, strong young men with honey on their tongues. They want her for every reason, her name, her land, her wit." He gave a long pause. "How will she respond to the courting of a sick old man who walks with a stick when he can walk at all?" His mouth twisted, as if the words were bitter.

"But surely your position . . ." I began.

He lifted a hand and looked me squarely in the eye. "Would you marry a woman you had bought?"

I looked down. "No, your grace."

"Neither will I. The thought of using my position to persuade this girl to marry me is . . . distasteful."

We were quiet for a moment. Outside the window I watched two squirrels chase each other around the tall trunk of an ash tree. "Your grace, if I am going to help you pay court to this lady . . ." I felt the heat of the Maer's anger before I turned to see it. "I beg pardon, your grace. I've overstepped myself."

"Is this another one of your guesses then?"

"Yes, your grace."

He seemed to struggle with himself for a moment. Then he sighed, and the tension in the room faded. "I must ask *your* pardon. This clawing pain wears my temper thin, and it is not my custom to discuss personal matters with strangers, much less have them guessed from underneath me. Tell me the rest of what you guess. Be bold, if you must."

I breathed a little easier. "I guess you want to marry this woman. To suit your duty, primarily, but also because you love her."

There was another pause, not so bad as the last one, but tense nonetheless. "Love," he said slowly, "is a word the foolish use too often. She is worthy of love, that is certain. And I have a fondness for her." He looked uncomfortable. "That is all I will say." He turned to look at me. "Can I count on your discretion?"

"Of course, your grace. But why so secretive about it?"

"I prefer to move at a time of my own choosing. Rumor forces us to act before we are ready, or ruins a situation before it becomes fully ripe."

"I understand. What is the lady's name?"

"Meluan Lackless," he said her name carefully. "Now, I have discovered for myself that you are charming and well-mannered. What's more, Count Threpe assures me you are a great maker and player of songs. These things are exactly what I need. Will you enter my service in this regard?"

I hesitated. "How exactly will your grace be putting me to use?"

He gave me a skeptical look. "I would think it rather obvious for so excellent a guesser as yourself."

"I know you hope to court the lady, your grace. But I don't know *how*. Do you want me to compose a letter or two? Write her songs? Will I climb balconies by moonlight to leave flowers on her windowsill? Dance with her wearing a mask, claiming your name as my own?" I gave him a wan smile. "I'm not much of a dancer, your grace."

Alveron gave a deep, honest laugh, but even through the joyful sound of it, I could tell the act of laughing pained him. "I was thinking more of the first two," he admitted, sinking back into the pillows, his eyes heavy.

I nodded. "I'll need to know more about her, your grace. Trying to court a woman without knowing her would be worse than foolish."

Alveron nodded tiredly. "Caudicus can lay the groundwork for you. He knows a great deal about the history of the families. Family is the foundation upon which a man stands. You'll need to know where she comes from if you're to court her." He motioned me closer and held out an iron ring, his arm trembling with the effort of staying in the air. "Show this to Caudicus and he will know you are on my business."

I took it quickly. "Does he know you plan to marry?"

"No!" Alveron's eyes flew open. "Do not speak of this to anyone! Invent some reason for your inquiries. Fetch my medicine."

He lay back, closing his eyes. As I left I heard him speaking faintly: "Sometimes they don't give it knowingly, sometimes they don't give it willingly. Nevertheless . . . all power."

"Yes, your grace," I said, but he had already fallen into a fitful sleep before I left the room.

CHAPTER FIFTY-NINE

Purpose

AS I LEFT THE Maer's rooms, I considered sending a runner with my card and ring ahead to Caudicus. Then I dismissed the thought. I was on an errand for the Maer. Surely that would excuse a slight breach of etiquette.

From the rumor mill, I knew Alveron's arcanist had been a permanent part of the Maer's court for more than a dozen years. But other than the fact that he lived in one of the estate's southern towers, I had no idea what to expect from the man.

I knocked on the thick-timbered door.

"Hold on then," the voice came faintly. There was the sound of a bolt being drawn back, and the door opened to reveal a thin man with a long, hawkish nose and curling black hair. He wore a long, dark garment vaguely reminiscent of a master's robe. "Yes?"

"I was wondering if I might borrow a moment of your time, sir?" I said, my nervousness only half-feigned.

He looked me over, taking in my fine clothes. "I don't do love potions. You can find that sort of thing down in Severen-Low." The heavy door began to inch closed. "Though you'd be better off with a little dancing and some roses if you ask me."

"I'm here for something else," I said quickly. "Two things actually. One for the Maer and one for myself." I lifted my hand, revealing the iron ring on my palm, Alveron's name blazed in bright gold across the face of it.

The door stopped closing. "You'd best come in, then," Caudicus said.

The room looked like a small University contained in a single room. Lit with the familiar red glow of sympathy lamps, there were shelves of books, tables full of twisted glassware, and far in the back, half concealed by the curving wall of the tower, I thought I could see a small furnace or kiln.

"Good God!" I exclaimed, covering my mouth with one hand. "Is that a dragon?" I pointed to a huge stuffed crocodile that hung from one of the ceiling beams.

You have to understand, some arcanists are more territorial than sharks, especially those who have managed to acquire luxurious court positions such as this. I had no idea how Caudicus might react to a young arcanist-in-training arriving in his territory, so I decided it was safer to play the part of a pleasantly dim, nonthreatening lordling.

Caudicus closed the door behind me, chuckling. "No. It's an alligator. Quite harmless I assure you."

"It gave me a bit of a start," I said. "What is the use of such a thing?"

"Honestly?" He looked up at it. "I don't rightly know. It belonged to the arcanist who lived here before me. It seemed a shame to throw it away. Impressive specimen, don't you think?"

I gave it a nervous look. "Quite."

"What is this business you mentioned?" He gestured to a large, cushioned chair and settled himself into a similar chair across from me. "I'm afraid I only have a few minutes before I will be otherwise occupied. Until then my time is yours . . ." He trailed off questioningly.

I could see he knew quite well who I was: the mysterious young man the Maer had been meeting with. I guessed he was eager as the rest to find out why I was in Severen.

"Kvothe," I said. "Actually, the Maer's medicine is half my business." I saw a faint, irritated line appear between his eyebrows and hurried to correct whatever he might be thinking. "I was speaking with the Maer earlier." I gave the barest pause, as if I was unreasonably proud of this. "And he asked me if I might bring him his medicine after I had finished speaking with you."

The line disappeared. "Certainly," Caudicus said easily. "It would save me the trip to his rooms. But what is the matter you wished to speak about?"

"Well," I leaned forward excitedly. "I'm doing research into the histories of the noble families in Vintas. I am thinking of writing a book, you see."

"A genealogy?" I saw boredom begin to fog his eyes.

"Oh no. There are genealogies aplenty. I was thinking of a collection of stories related to the great families." I was rather proud of this lie. Not only did it explain my curiosity about Meluan's family, it gave a reason for why I was spending so much time with the Maer. "History tends to be rather dry, but everyone enjoys a story."

Caudicus nodded to himself. "Clever idea. That could be an interesting book."

"I'll be writing a brief historical preface for each family, as an introduction to the stories that follow. The Maer mentioned you were quite the authority on the old families, and said he would be pleased if I called on you."

The compliment had its desired effect, and Caudicus puffed himself up ever so slightly. "I don't know if I'd consider myself an *authority*," he said with false modesty. "But I am a bit of a historian." He raised an eyebrow at me. "You must realize the families themselves would probably be a superior source of information."

"One would *think* that," I said with a sideways look. "But families tend to be reluctant to share their most interesting stories."

Caudicus gave a wide grin. "I imagine so." The grin faded just as quickly. "But I'm certain I don't know any stories of that sort regarding the Maer's family," he said seriously.

"Oh no no no!" I waved my hands in violent negation. "The Maer is a special case. I wouldn't dream . . ." I trailed off, swallowing visibly. "I was hoping you might be able to enlighten me regarding the Lackless family. I'm rather in the dark about them."

"Really?" he said, surprised. "They've fallen from what they once were, but they're a treasure trove of stories." His eyes focused far away and he tapped his lips with his fingers distractedly. "How about this, I'll brush up on their history, and you can come back tomorrow for a longer talk. It's nearly time for the Maer's medicine, and it shouldn't be delayed."

He got to his feet and began to roll up his sleeves. "There's one thing I can remember off the top of my head, if you don't mind my rambling while I prepare the Maer's medicine."

"I've never seen a potion being made," I said enthusiastically. "If you wouldn't find it too distracting . . ."

"Not at all. I could prepare it in my sleep." He moved behind a worktable and lit a pair of blueflame candles. I took care to look suitably impressed even though I knew they were just for show.

Caudicus shook a portion of dried leaf onto a small hand scale and weighed it. "Do you have any trouble accepting rumor into your research?"

"Not if it's interesting."

He was silent while he carefully measured a small amount of clear liquid from a glass-stoppered bottle. "From what I understand, the Lackless family has an heirloom. Well, not an heirloom *exactly*, but an ancient thing that dates back to the beginning of their line."

"There's not much odd with that. Old families are rife with heirlooms."

"Hush," he said testily. "There's more to it than that." He poured the liquid into a flat lead bowl with some crude symbols carved along the outside. It bubbled and hissed, filling the air with a faint, acrid smell.

He decanted the liquid into the pan over the candles. From there he added the dry leaf, a pinch of something, and a measure of white powder. He added a splash of fluid I assumed was simply water, stirred, and poured the result through a filter and into a clear glass vial, stoppering it with a cork.

He held the result up for me to see: a clear amber liquid with a slight greenish tint. "There you go. Remind him to drink it all."

I took the warm vial. "What was this heirloom?"

Caudicus rinsed his hands in a porcelain bowl and shook them dry. "I've heard that on the oldest parts of the Lackless lands, in the oldest part of their ancestral estate, there is a secret door. A door without a handle or hinges." He watched me to make sure I was paying attention. "There's no way of opening it. It is locked, but at the same time, lockless. No one knows what's on the other side."

He nodded toward the vial in my hand. "Now get that to the Maer. It'll be best if he drinks it while it's warm." He escorted me to the door. "Do come back tomorrow." he smirked a bit. "I know a story about the Menebras that will turn your red hair white."

"Oh, I only work on one family at a time," I said, not wanting to risk getting bogged down in endless court gossip. "Two is the absolute most. Right now I'm working on Alveron and Lackless. I couldn't bring myself to start a third as well." I gave an insipid smile. "I'd put myself all in a muddle."

"That's a shame," Caudicus said. "I travel quite a bit, you see. Many of the noble houses are eager to host the Maer's own arcanist." He gave me a sly look. "This makes me privy to some rather interesting facts." He opened the door. "Think on it. And do stop back tomorrow. I'll have more on the Lacklesses at any rate."

I was at the doors to the Maer's rooms before the vial had a chance to cool. Stapes opened the door to my knocking and led me to the Maer's inner rooms.

The Maer Alveron was sleeping in the same position I had left him in. As Stapes shut the door behind me, one of the Maer's eyes opened and he beckoned to me feebly. "You took your sweet time."

"Your grace, I—"

He motioned me forward again, more sharply this time. "Give me my medicine," he said thickly. "Then leave. I'm tired."

"I'm afraid it's rather important, your grace."

Both eyes opened, and the smoldering anger was there again. "What?" he snapped.

I moved to the side of the bed and leaned close. Before he could protest my impropriety, I whispered, "Your grace, Caudicus is poisoning you."

CHAPTER SIXTY

Wisdom's Tool

THE MAER'S EYES WENT wide at my words, then narrowed again. Even in the midst of his infirmity, Alveron's wit was sharp. "You were right to speak that close and soft," he said. "You are treading dangerous ground. But speak, I will hear you."

"Your grace, I suspect Threpe did not mention in his letter that I am a student at the University as well as a musician."

The Maer's eyes showed no glimmer of recognition. "Which university?" he asked.

"*The* University, your grace," I said. "I am a member of the Arcanum."

Alveron frowned. "You're far too young to make such a claim. And why would Threpe neglect to mention this?"

"You were not looking for an arcanist, your grace. And there is a certain stigma attached to that sort of study this far east." It was the closest I could come to speaking the truth: that Vints are superstitious to the point of idiocy.

The Maer blinked slowly, his expression hardening. "Very well," he said. "Perform some work of magic if you are what you say."

"I am only an arcanist in training, your grace. But if you would like to see a bit of magic . . ." I looked at the three lamps lining the walls, licked my fingers, concentrated, and pinched the wick of the candle sitting on his bedside table.

The room went dark and I heard his startled intake of breath. I brought out my silver ring, and after a moment it began to shine with a silver-blue light. My hands grew cold, as I had no source of heat other than my own body.

"That will do," the Maer said. If he was at all unnerved, there was no hint of it in his voice.

I stepped across the room and opened the shuttered windows. Sunlight flooded the room. There was a hint of selas flower, a trill of birdsong. "I've always found that taking in some air is good for whatever troubles a body, though others disagree." I smiled at him.

He didn't return it. "Yes, yes. You're very clever. Come here and sit." I did so, taking a chair near his bedside. "Now explain yourself."

"I told Caudicus I was compiling a collection of stories from the noble houses," I said. "A handy excuse, as it also explains why I have been spending time with you."

The Maer's expression remained grim. I saw pain blur his eyes like a cloud passing in front of the sun. "Proof that you are a skilled liar hardly gains you my trust."

A cold knot began to form in my stomach. I had assumed the Maer would accept the truth more easily than this. "Just so, your grace. I lied to *him* and I am telling *you* the truth. Since he thought me nothing more than an idle lordling, he let me watch while he made your medicine." I held up the amber flask. The sunlight broke itself into rainbows on the glass.

Alveron remained unmoved. His normally clear eyes fogged with confusion and pain. "I ask for proof and you tell me a story. Caudicus has been a faithful servant for a dozen years. Nevertheless, I will consider what you've said." His tone implied it would be a short, unkind consideration. He held out his hand for the vial.

I felt a small flame of anger strike up inside me. It helped to ease the cold fear settling in my gut. "Your grace wants proof?"

"I want my medicine!" he snapped. "And I want to sleep. Please do—"

"Your grace, I can—"

"How *dare* you interrupt me?" Alveron struggled to sit upright in his bed, his voice furious. "You go too far! Leave now and I may still consider retaining your services." He was trembling with rage, his hand still reaching for the vial.

There was a moment of silence. I held out the vial, but before he could grasp it, I said, "You have vomited recently. It was milky and white."

The tension in the room rose sharply, but the Maer went motionless when he heard what I said. "Your tongue feels thick and heavy. Your mouth is dry and filled with an odd, sharp taste. You have had a craving for sweets, for sugar. You wake in the night and find you cannot move, cannot speak. You are struck with palsy, with colic and unreasoning panic."

As I spoke the Maer's hand slowly drew away from the vial. His expression was no longer livid and angry. His eyes seemed unsure, almost frightened, but they were clear again, as if the fear had awakened some sleeping caution.

"Caudicus told you," the Maer said, but he sounded far from certain.

"Would Caudicus discuss the details of your illness with a stranger?" I asked pointedly. "My concern is for your life, your grace. If I must bruise propriety to save it, I will do so. Give me two minutes to speak and I will give you proof."

Alveron gave a slow nod.

"I'm not going to claim to know exactly what this is." I gestured with the vial. "But most of what is poisoning you is lead. This accounts for the palsy, the pain in your muscles and viscera. The vomiting and paralysis."

"I've had no paralysis."

"Hmmm." I looked him over with a critical eye. "That's fortunate. But there is more than simply lead in this. I'm guessing this contains a goodly amount of ophalum, which isn't exactly poisonous."

"What is it then?"

"It's more of a medicine, or a drug."

"Which is it then?" he snapped. "Poison or medicine?"

"Has your grace ever taken laudanum?"

"Once when I was younger, to help me sleep through the pain of a broken leg."

"Ophalum is a similar drug, but it is usually avoided as it is highly addictive." I paused. "It is also called denner resin."

The Maer grew paler at this, and in that moment his eyes grew almost perfectly clear. Everyone knew about the sweet-eaters.

"I suspect he added it because you had been irregular about taking your medicine," I said. "The ophalum would make you crave it while easing your pain at the same time. It would also account for your sugar craving, your sweats, and any odd dreams you've been having. What else did he put in here?" I mused to myself. "Probably stitchroot or mannum to keep you from vomiting too much. Clever. Horrible and clever."

"Not so clever." The Maer gave a rictus smile. "He didn't manage to kill me."

I hesitated, then decided to tell him the truth. "Killing you would have been simple, your grace. He could easily dissolve enough lead in this vial to kill you." I held it up to the light. "Getting enough to make you sick without killing or paralyzing you, *that* is difficult."

"Why? Why poison me if not to kill me?"

"Your grace would have better luck solving that riddle. You know more about the politics involved."

"Why poison me at all?" The Maer sounded genuinely puzzled. "I pay him lavishly. He is a member of the court in high regard. He has the freedom to pursue his own projects and travel when he wishes. He has lived here a dozen years. Why now?" He shook his head. "I tell you it doesn't make sense."

"Money?" I suggested. "They say every man has a price."

Maer continued to shake his head. Then he looked up suddenly. "No. I've just remembered. I fell ill long before Caudicus began to treat me." He stopped to think. "Yes, that's right. I approached him to see if he could treat my illness. The symptoms you mentioned didn't appear until months after he started treating me. It *couldn't* have been him."

"Lead works slowly in small doses, your grace. If he were going to poison you, he would hardly want you vomiting blood ten minutes after you drank his medicine." I suddenly remembered who I was talking to. "That was poorly said, your grace. I apologize."

He nodded a stiff acceptance. "Too much of what you say is too close to the mark for me to ignore. Yet still, I can't believe Caudicus would do such a thing."

"We can put it to the test, your grace."

He looked up at me. "How is that?"

"Order a half-dozen birds brought to your rooms. Sipquicks would be ideal."

"Sipquicks?"

"Tiny, bright things, yellow and red," I held up my fingers about two inches apart. "They're thick in your gardens. They drink the nectar from your selas flowers."

"Oh. We call them flits."

"We will mix your medicine with their nectar and see what happens."

His expression grew bleak. "If lead works slowly, as you say, this would take months. I'll not go without my medicine for months on some poorly supported fancy of yours." I saw his temper burning close to the surface of his voice.

"They weigh much less than you, your grace, and their metabolisms are much faster. We should see results within a day or two at most." *I hoped.*

He seemed to consider this. "Very well," he said, lifting a bell from his bedside table.

I spoke quickly before he could ring it. "Might I ask your grace to invent some reason for needing these birds? A little caution would serve us well."

"I have known Stapes forever," the Maer said firmly, his eyes as clear and sharp as I had ever seen them. "I trust him with my lands, my lockbox, and my life. I do not ever wish to hear you imply he is anything other than perfectly trustworthy." There was unshakable belief in his voice.

I dropped my eyes. "Yes, your grace."

He rang the bell, and it was barely two seconds before the portly manservant opened the door. "Yes sir?"

"Stapes, I miss being able to walk in the gardens. Could you find me a half-dozen flits?"

"Flits, sir?"

"Yes," the Maer said as if it he were ordering lunch. "They're pretty things. I think the sound of them will help me sleep."

"I'll see what I can do, sir." Before he closed the door, Stapes scowled at me.

After the door was shut, I looked at the Maer. "Might I ask your grace why?"

"To save him the trouble of lying. He hasn't the knack for it. And there is wisdom in what you said. Caution is always wisdom's tool." I saw a thin layer of perspiration covering his face.

"If I am correct, your grace, tonight will be difficult for you."

"All my nights are difficult of late," he said bitterly. "What will make this one any worse than the last?"

"The ophalum, your grace. Your body is craving it. In two days you should be through the worst of it, but until then you will be in considerable . . . discomfort."

"Speak plainly."

"There will be aching in your jaw and head, sweating, nausea, cramps and spasms, especially in your legs and lower back. You may lose control of your bowels and there will be alternating periods of intense thirst and vomiting." I looked down at my hands. "I am sorry, your grace."

Alveron's expression was rather pinched by the end of my description, but he nodded graciously. "I would rather know."

"There are a few things that will make it slightly more tolerable, your grace."

He brightened a bit. "Such as?"

"Laudanum for one. Just a bit, to ease your body's craving. And a few other things. Their names are unimportant. I can mix them into a tea for you. Another problem is that you still have a goodly deal of lead in your body that isn't going to go away on its own."

This seemed to alarm him more than anything I'd said so far. "Won't I simply pass it?"

I shook my head. "Metals are insidious poisons. They become trapped in your body. Only by a special effort can we leach the lead away."

Maer scowled. "Damn and bother. I hate leeches."

"A figure of speech, your grace. Only imbeciles and toad-eaters use leeches in this day and age. The lead needs to be *drawn* out of you." I thought about telling him the truth, that he would most likely never be rid of all of it, but decided to keep that bit of information to myself.

"Can you do it?"

I thought for a long moment. "I am probably your best option, your grace. We are a long way from the University. I wager not one in ten physicians here have any respectable training, and I don't know who among them might know Caudicus." I thought for a moment longer then shook my head. "I can think of fifty people better suited to the job, but they are a thousand miles away."

"I appreciate your honesty."

"Most of what I need I can find down in Severen-Low. However . . ." I trailed off, hoping the Maer would understand my meaning and save me the embarrassment of asking for money.

He stared at me blankly. "However?"

"I will need money, your grace. The things you will need are not easy to come by."

"Oh, of course." He produced a purse and passed it to me. I was a little surprised to find the Maer had at least one well-stocked purse within easy arm's reach of his bed. Unbidden, I remembered my tirade to a tailor in Tarbean years ago. What had I said to him? *A gentleman is never far from his purse?* I fought down an inappropriate fit of laughter.

Stapes returned shortly after that. In a surprising display of resourcefulness, he produced a dozen sipquicks in a wheeled cage the size of a wardrobe.

"My word, Stapes," the Maer exclaimed as his manservant rolled the fine mesh cage through the doorway. "You've outdone yourself."

"Where would it suit you best, sir?"

"Just leave it there for now. I'll have Kvothe move it for me."

Stapes looked a trifle wounded. "It's no trouble."

"I know you'd be glad to do it, Stapes. But I was hoping you would fetch me a fresh pitcher of appledraw instead. I think it might settle my stomach."

"Certainly." He hurried out again, closing the door behind him.

As soon as the door was closed, I moved to the cage. The little gemlike birds darted from perch to perch with a blurring speed. "Pretty things," I heard the Maer muse. "I was fascinated with them as a child. I remember thinking how wonderful it must be to eat nothing but sugar all day."

There were three feeders wired to the outside of the cage, glass tubes filled with sugar-water. Two of them had spouts shaped like tiny selas blooms, while the third was a stylized iris. The perfect pet for nobility. Who else could afford to feed their pet sugar every day?

I unscrewed the tops of the feeders and poured a third of the Maer's medicine into each. I held out the empty vial to Alveron. "What do you normally do with these?"

He set it on the table near his bed.

I watched the cage until I saw one of the birds fly to a feeder and drink. "If you tell Stapes you want to feed them yourself, will it keep him from meddling with their food?"

"Yes. He always does exactly as I tell him."

"Good. Let them drain the feeders before you refill them. They'll get a better dose that way, and we'll see results faster. Where do you want me to put the cage?"

He looked around the room, his eyes moving sluggishly. "Next to the chest of drawers in the sitting room," he said finally. "I should be able to see the cage from here."

I carefully rolled the cage into the next room. When I returned, I found Stapes pouring the Maer a glass of appledraw.

I made a bow to Alveron. "With your permission, your grace."

He made a gesture of dismissal. "Stapes, Kvothe will be returning later this afternoon. Let him in, even if I happen to be sleeping."

Stapes nodded stiffly and gave me another disapproving look.

"He may be bringing me a few things as well. Please don't mention it to anyone."

"If there is anything you require . . ."

Alveron gave a tired smile. "I know you would, Stapes. I am simply putting the boy to use. I would rather have you close at hand." Alveron patted his manservant's arm, and Stapes looked mollified. I let myself out.

My trip to Severen-Low took hours longer than it needed to. Though I chafed at the delay, it was a necessary one. As I walked the streets, I caught glimpses of folk dogging along behind me.

I wasn't surprised. From what I had seen of the rumor-driven nature of the Maer's court, I expected to have a servant or two watching my errands in Severen-Low. As I've said, the Maer's court was rather curious about me at this point, and you have no idea what lengths bored nobility will go to in order to nose about in other people's business.

While the rumors themselves were of no concern to me, their effects could be catastrophic. If Caudicus heard I had gone shopping through apothecaries after visiting the Maer, what steps would he take? Anyone willing to poison the Maer wouldn't hesitate to snuff me like a candle.

So, to avoid suspicion, the first thing I did when I came to Severen was buy dinner. Good, hot stew and rough bread. I was sick to death of elegant food that was milk-warm by the time it made its way to my rooms.

Afterward I bought two tippling flasks, the sort normally used for brandy. Then I spent a relaxing half-hour watching a small traveling troupe perform the end of *The Ghost and the Goosegirl* on a street corner. They weren't Edema Ruh, but they did a good job of it. The Maer's purse was generous to them when they passed the hat.

Eventually I found my way to a well-stocked apothecary. I bought several things in a nervous, haphazard manner. After I had everything I needed and a few things I didn't, I awkwardly made inquiries with the owner about what a man might take if he was . . . having certain troubles . . . in the bedroom.

The chemist nodded seriously and recommended several things with a perfectly straight face. I bought a little of each, then made a bumbling attempt to threaten and bribe him into silence. By the time I finally left, he was insulted and thoroughly irritated. If anyone asked, he would be quick to tell the story of a rude gentleman interested in impotence cures. It was hardly something I was eager to add to my reputation, but at least there wouldn't be any stories making their way back to Caudicus about my purchasing laudanum, deadnettle, bitefew, and other equally suspicious drugs.

Lastly, I bought my lute back from the pawner with an entire day to spare. It nearly emptied the Maer's purse, but it was my final errand. The sun was setting by the time I made my way back to the foot of the Sheer.

There were only a handful of options for making your way between Severen-High and Severen-Low. The most ordinary were the two narrow staircases that cut back and forth up the face of the Sheer. They were old, crumbling, and narrow in places, but they were free, and therefore the usual choice for the common folk who lived in Severen-Low.

For those who didn't relish the thought of climbing two hundred feet of narrow stairway, there were other options. The freight lifts were run by a pair of former University students. Not full arcanists, but clever men who knew enough sympathy and engineering to manage the rather mundane task of hauling wagons and horses up and down the Sheer on a large wooden platform.

For passengers, the freights cost a penny going up and a halfpenny going · down, though you'd occasionally have to wait for some merchant to finish loading or unloading his goods before the lift could make its trip.

Nobility didn't use the freights. The Vintic suspicion of all things remotely arcane took them to the horse lifts. These were drawn by a team of twenty horses hitched to a complex series of pulleys. This meant the horse lifts were a little faster and cost a full silver eighth-bit to ride. Best of all, every month or so some drunk lordling would fall to his death from them, adding to their popularity by showing the breeding of the clientele.

Since the money in my purse wasn't my own, I decided to use the horse lifts.

I joined the four gentlemen and one lady who were already in line, waited for the lift to lower itself, then handed over my thin silver bit and stepped aboard.

It was no more than an open-sided box with a brass rail running around the edge. Thick hempen ropes connected to the corners, giving it some stability, but any extreme motion set the thing swaying in a most disturbing fashion. A smartly dressed boy rode up and down with each load of passengers, opening the gate and signaling the horse drivers at the top when to begin their pull.

It is the custom of the nobility to put their backs to Severen as they ride the lifts. Gawking was something common folk did. Not particularly caring what the nobles thought of me, I stood at the front rail. My stomach did peculiar things as we rose from the ground.

I watched Severen spread out below. It was an old city, and proud. The high stone wall circling it spoke of troubled times long past. It said much of the Maer that even in these peaceful times the fortifications were kept in excellent repair. All three of the gates were guarded, and they were closed at sundown every night.

As the lift continued I could see the different sections of Severen as clearly as if I were looking down on a map. There was a rich neighborhood, spaced with gardens and parks, the buildings all of brick and old stone. There was the poor quarter, the streets narrow and twisting, where all the roofs were tar and wooden shingles. At the foot of the cliff a black scar marked where a fire had cut through the city at some point in the past, leaving little more than the charred bones of buildings.

Too soon the ride was over. I let the other gentles disembark as I leaned against the railing, looking out over the city far below.

"Sir?" the boy who rode the lift prompted wearily. "All off."

I turned, stepped off the lift, and saw Denna standing in the front of the line.

Before I had time to do anything other than stare in wonder, she turned and met my eyes. Her face lit. She cried my name, ran at me, and was nestled in my arms before I knew what was happening. I settled my arms around her and rested my cheek against her ear. We came together easily, as if we were dancers. As if we'd practiced it a thousand times. She was warm and soft.

"What are you doing here?" she asked. Her heart was racing, and I felt it thrilling against my chest.

I stood mutely as she stepped back from me. Only then did I notice an old bruise fading to yellow high on her cheek. Even so, she was the most beautiful thing I had seen in two months and a thousand miles. "What are *you* doing here?" I asked.

She laughed her silver laugh and reached out to touch my arm. Then her eyes flicked over my shoulder and her face fell. "Hold on!" she cried to the boy who was closing the gate to the lift. "I have to catch this one or I'll be late," she said, her face full of pained apology as she stepped past me onto the lift. "Come find me."

The boy closed the gate behind her and my heart fell as the lift began to drop from sight. "Where should I look?" I stepped closer to the edge of the Sheer, watching her fall away.

She was looking up, her face white against the darkness, her hair a shadow in the night. "The second street north of Main: Tinnery Street."

Shadow took her, and suddenly I was alone. I stood, the smell of her still in the air around me, the warmth of her just fading from my hands. I could still feel the tremor of her heart, like a caged bird beating against my chest.

CHAPTER SIXTY-ONE

Deadnettle

AFTER MY TRIP TO Severen, I deposited my lute case in my room and made my way to Alveron's private rooms as quickly as possible. Stapes was not pleased to see me, but he showed me in with the same bustling efficiency as always.

Alveron lay in a sweaty stupor, his bedclothes twisted around him. It was only then I noticed how thin he had grown. His arms and legs were stringy and his complexion had faded from pale to grey. He glowered at me as I entered the room.

Stapes arranged the Maer's covers in a more modest fashion and helped him into a seated position, propping him up with pillows. The Maer endured these ministrations stoically, then said, "Thank you, Stapes," in a tone of dismissal. The manservant left slowly, giving me a decidedly uncivil stare.

I approached the Maer's bed and brought several items from the pockets of my cloak. "I found everything I needed, your grace. Though not everything I hoped for. How do you feel?"

He gave me a look that spoke volumes. "It took you a damn long time getting back. Caudicus came while you were away."

I fought down a wave of anxiety. "What happened?"

"He asked me how I was feeling, and I told him the truth. He looked in my eyes and down my throat and asked me if I had thrown up. I told him yes, and that I wanted more medicine and to be left alone. He left and sent some over."

I felt a panic rise in me. "Did you drink it?"

"If you'd been gone much longer I would have, and to hell with your faerie stories." He brought another vial from beneath his pillow. "I can't see what harm it could do. I can feel myself dying already." He thrust it toward me angrily.

"I should be able to improve matters, your grace. Remember, tonight will be the most difficult. Tomorrow will be bad. After that, all should be well."

"If I live so long as that," he groused.

It was just the petulant grumble of a sick man, but it mirrored my thoughts so precisely that ice ran down my back. Earlier, I hadn't considered that the Maer might die despite my intervention. But when I looked at him now, frail and grey and trembling, I realized the truth: he might not live through the night.

"First, there's this, your grace." I took out the tippling flask.

"Brandy?" he said with muted anticipation. I shook my head and opened it. He wrinkled his nose at the smell and sank back onto the pillows. "God's teeth. As if my dying wasn't bad enough. Cod liver oil?"

I nodded seriously. "Take two good swallows, your grace. This is part of your cure."

He made no move to take it. "I've never been able to stomach the stuff, and lately I even vomit up my tea. I won't put myself through the hell of drinking it only to sick it back up."

I nodded and restoppered the flask. "I'll give you something to stop that." There was a pot of water on the bedside table, and I began to mix him a cup of tea.

He craned weakly to see what I was doing. "What are you putting in that?"

"Something to keep you from being sick, and something to help you pass the poison out of your system. A bit of laudanum to ease your craving. And tea. Does your grace take sugar?"

"Normally, no. But I'm guessing it will taste like stumpwater without it." I added a spoonful, stirred, and handed him the cup.

"You first," Alveron said. Pale and grim, he watched me with his sharp grey eyes. He smiled a terrible smile.

I hesitated, but only for a moment. "To your grace's health." I said, and took a good swallow. I grimaced and added another spoonful of sugar. "Your grace predicted it quite well. Stumpwater it is."

He took the cup with both hands and began to drink it in a number of quick, determined sips. "Dreadful," he said simply. "But better than nothing. Do you know what a hell it is to be thirsty but not be able to drink for fear of throwing up? I wouldn't wish it on a dog."

"Wait a bit to finish it," I cautioned. "That should settle your stomach in a few minutes."

I went into the other room and added the new vial of medicine to the flit's feeders. I was relieved to see they were still sipping at the medicated nectar. I had worried they might avoid it due to a change in flavor or some natural instinct for self-preservation.

I also worried that lead might not be poisonous to sipquicks. I worried they might take a span to show any ill effects, not mere days I worried at the Maer's rising temper. I worried at his illness. I worried at the possibility I might be wrong about everything I'd guessed.

I returned to the Maer's bedside and found him cradling the empty cup in his lap. I mixed a second cup similar to the first, and he drank it quickly. Then we sat in silence for the space of fifteen minutes or so.

"How do you feel, your grace?"

"Better," he admitted grudgingly. I detected a slight dullness to his speech. "Much better."

"That is probably the laudanum," I commented. "But your stomach should be settled by now." I picked up the flask of cod liver oil. "Two good swallows, your grace."

"Is this really the only thing that will do?" he asked distastefully.

"If I had access to the apothecaries near the University, I could find something more palatable, but at the moment this is the only thing that can be done."

"Get me another cup of tea to wash it down with." He picked up the flask, took two sips, and handed it back, his mouth turned down in a ghastly expression.

I sighed internally. "If you are going to sip it, we will be here all evening. Two solid swallows, the kind sailors use to drink cheap whiskey."

He scowled. "Don't speak to me as if I were a child."

"Then act the part of a man," I said harshly, stunning him to silence. "Two swallows every four hours. That whole flask should be finished by tomorrow."

His grey eyes narrowed dangerously. "I would remind you who you are speaking to."

"I am speaking to a sick man who will not take his medicine," I said levelly.

Anger smoldered behind his laudanum-dulled eyes. "A pint of fish oil is not medicine," he hissed. "It is a malicious and unreasonable request. It can't be done."

I fixed him with my best withering stare and took the flask out of his hand. Without looking away, I drank the whole thing down. Swallow after swallow of the oil passed my gullet as I held the Maer's eye. I watched his face shift from angry to disgusted, then finally settle into an expression of muted, sickened awe. I upended the flask, ran my finger around the inside of it and licked it clean.

I pulled out a second flask from a pocket of my cloak. "This was going to be your dose for tomorrow, but you will need to use it tonight. If you find it easier, one swallow every two hours should suffice." I held it out to him, still holding his eyes with mine.

He took it mutely, drank two good swallows, and stoppered the flask with a grim determination. Pride is always a better lever against the nobility than reason.

I fished in one of the pockets of my rich burgundy cloak and brought out the Maer's ring. "I forgot to return this to you before, your grace." I held it out to him.

He began to reach out for it, then stopped. "Keep it for now," he said. "You've earned that much, I imagine."

"Thank you, your grace," I said, careful to keep my expression composed. He wasn't inviting me to wear the ring, but allowing me to keep it was a tangible step forward in our relationship. No matter how his courtship of the Lady Lackless went, I had made an impression on him today.

I poured him more tea and decided to finish his instructions while I had his attention. "You should drink the rest of this potful tonight, your grace. But remember, it's all you'll have until tomorrow. When you send for me, I'll brew you some more. You should try to drink as many fluids as you can tonight. Milk would be best. Put some honey in it and it will go down easier."

He agreed and seemed to be easing toward sleep. Knowing how difficult his night would be, I let him nod off. I gathered my things before letting myself out.

Stapes was waiting in the outer rooms. I mentioned to him that the Maer was sleeping, and told him not to toss out the tea in the pot, as his grace would be wanting it when he woke up.

As I left, the look Stapes gave me was not merely chilly, as it had been before. It was hateful, practically venomous. Only after he closed the door behind me did I realize what this must look like to him. He assumed I was taking advantage of the Maer in his time of weakness.

There are a great many such people in the world, traveling physicians with no qualms about preying on the fears of the desperately ill. The best example of this is Deadnettle, the potion seller in *Three Pennies for Wishing*. Easily one of the most despised characters in all drama, there's no audience that doesn't cheer when Deadnettle gets pilloried in the fourth act.

With that in mind, I began to dwell on how fragile and grey the Maer had looked. Living in Tarbean, I had seen healthy young men killed by ophalum withdrawal, and the Maer was neither young nor healthy.

If he did die, who would be blamed? Certainly not Caudicus, trusted advisor. Certainly not Stapes, beloved manservant. . . .

Me. They would blame me. His condition *had* worsened soon after I arrived. I didn't doubt Stapes would quickly bring to light the fact that I'd been spending time alone with the Maer in his rooms. That I'd brewed him a pot of tea right before he had a very traumatic night.

At best I would look like a young Deadnettle. At worst, an assassin.

Such was the turning of my thoughts as I made my way through the Maer's estate back to my rooms, pausing only to lean out one of the windows overlooking Severen-Low and vomit up a pint of cod liver oil.

CHAPTER SIXTY-TWO

Crisis

THE NEXT MORNING I made my way to Severen-Low before the sun was up. I ate a hot breakfast of eggs and potatoes while I waited for an apothecary to open. When I was finished, I bought two more pints of cod liver oil and a few other oddments I hadn't thought of the day before.

Then I walked the entire length of Tinnery Street, hoping to stumble onto Denna despite the fact that it was far too early in the morning for her to be up and about. Wagons and farmers' carts vied for space on the cobbled streets. Ambitious beggars were laying claim to the busiest corners while shopkeepers hung out their shingles and threw wide their shutters.

I counted twenty-three inns and boarding houses on Tinnery Street. After making note of the ones Denna would probably find appealing, I forced myself back to the Maer's estates. This time I took the freight lifts, partly to confuse anyone following me, but also because the purse the Maer had given me was nearly empty.

Since I needed to keep a normal face on things, I remained in my rooms, waiting for the Maer to send for me. I sent my card and ring to Bredon, and soon he was sitting across from me, thrashing me at tak and telling stories.

"...so the Maer had him hung in a gibbet. Right alongside the eastern gate. Hung here for days, howling and cursing. Saying he was innocent. Saying it wasn't right and how he wanted a trial."

I couldn't quite bring myself to believe it. "A gibbet?"

Bredon nodded seriously. "An actual iron gibbet. Who knows where he managed to find one in this day and age. It was like something out of a play."

I searched for something relatively noncommittal to say. While it did sound grotesque, I also knew better than to openly criticize the Maer. "Well," I said, "banditry *is* a terrible thing."

Bredon began to place a stone on the board, then reconsidered. "Quite a few folks thought the whole thing was in rather . . ." He cleared his throat. "Bad taste. But nobody said so very loudly, if you catch my meaning. It was a grisly thing. But it got the point across."

He finally chose the placement of his stone, and we played quietly for a time.

"It's a strange thing," I said. "I ran into someone the other day who didn't know where Caudicus would rank in the overall scheme of things."

"That's not terribly surprising," Bredon gestured to the board. "The giving and receiving of rings is a lot like tak. On the face of it, the rules are simple. In execution they become quite complicated." He clicked down a stone, his dark eyes crinkling with amusement. "In fact, the other day I was explaining the intricacies of the custom to a foreigner not familiar with such things."

"That was kind of you," I said.

Bredon gave a gracious nod. "It seems simple at first glance," he said. "A baron ranks above a baronet. But sometimes young money is worth more than old blood. Sometimes control of a river is more important than how many soldiers you can put to field. Sometimes a person is actually more than one person, technically speaking. The Earl of Svanis is, by strange inheritance, also the Viscount of Tevn. One man, but two different political entities."

I smiled. "My mother once told me she knew a man who owed fealty to himself," I said. "Owed himself a share of his own taxes every year, and if he were ever threatened, there were treaties in place demanding he provide himself with prompt and loyal military support."

Bredon nodded. "It happens more often than folk realize," he said. "Especially with the older families. Stapes, for example, exists in several separate capacities."

"Stapes?" I asked. "But he's just a manservant, isn't he?"

"Well," Bredon said slowly. "He is that. But he's hardly *just* a manservant. His family is quite old, but he has no title of his own. Technically, he ranks no higher than a cook. But he owns substantial lands. He has money. And he is the *Maer's* manservant. They've known each other since they were boys. Everyone knows he has Alveron's ear."

Bredon's dark eyes peered at me. "Who would dare insult such a man with an iron ring? Go to his room and you will see the truth: there is nothing in his bowl but gold."

———

Bredon excused himself shortly after our game, claiming a prior engagement. Luckily, I now had my lute to occupy my time. I set about retuning it, checking the frets, and fussing over the tuning peg that was constantly coming loose. We had been away from each other for a long while, and it takes time to get reacquainted.

Hours passed. I discovered myself absentmindedly playing "Deadnettle's Lament" and forced myself to stop. Noon came and went. Lunch was delivered and cleared away. I retuned my lute and ran some scales. Before I knew it I found myself playing "Leave the Town, Tinker." Only then did I realize what my hands were trying to tell me. If the Maer was still alive, he would have called for me by now.

I let the lute fall silent and began to think very quickly. I needed to leave. Now. Stapes had seen me bring medicine to the Maer. I could even be accused of tampering with the vial I had brought from Caudicus' rooms.

Slow fear began to knot my gut as I realized the helplessness of my situation. I didn't know the Maer's estates well enough to attempt a clever escape. On my way to Severen-Low this morning, I'd gotten turned around and had to stop to ask directions.

The knock on the door was louder than usual, more forceful than that of the errand boy who normally came to deliver the Maer's invitation. Guards. I froze in my seat. Would it be best to answer the door and tell the truth? Or duck out the window into the garden and somehow try to make a run for it?

The knock came again, louder. "Sir? Sir?"

The voice was muffled by the door, but it was not a guard's voice. I opened the door and saw a young boy carrying a tray with the Maer's iron ring and card.

I picked them up. The card had a single word written in a shaky hand: *Immediately.*

Stapes looked uncharacteristically ragged around the edges and greeted me with an icy stare. Yesterday he'd looked as if he wanted me dead and buried. Today his look implied that simply buried would be good enough.

The Maer's bedroom was generously decorated with selas flowers. Their delicate smell was almost enough to cover the odors they'd been brought in to conceal. Combined with Stapes' appearance, I knew my predictions of the night's unpleasantness had been close to the truth.

Alveron was propped into a sitting position in his bed. He looked as well as could be expected, which is to say exhausted, but no longer sweating and racked with pain. As a matter of fact, he looked almost angelic. A rectangle of sunlight washed over him, lending his skin a frail translucency and making his disarrayed hair shine like a silver crown around his head.

As I stepped closer he opened his eyes, breaking the beatific illusion. No angel ever had eyes as clever as Alveron's.

"I trust I find your grace well?" I asked politely.

"Passing fair," he responded. But it was mere social noise, telling me nothing.

"How do you *feel?*" I asked in a more serious tone.

He gave me a long look that let me know he did not approve of my addressing him so casually, then said. "Old. I feel old and weak." He took a deep breath. "But for all that, I feel better than I have in several days. A little pain, and I am mightily tired. But I feel . . . clean. I think I've passed the crisis."

I did not ask about last night. "Would you like me to mix you another pot of tea?"

"Please." His tone was measured and polite. Unable to guess his mood, I hurried through the preparations and handed him his cup.

He looked up at me after sampling it. "This tastes different."

"There is less laudanum in it," I explained. "Too much would be harmful to your grace. Your body would begin to depend on it as surely as it craved the ophalum."

He nodded. "You'll note my birds are doing well," he said in an overly casual tone.

I looked through the doorway and saw the sipquicks darting about in their gilded cage, lively as ever. I felt a chill at the implication of his comment. He still didn't believe Caudicus was poisoning him.

I was too stunned to make a quick reply, but after a breath or two I managed to say, "Their health does not concern me nearly so much as your own. You *do* feel better, don't you, your grace?"

"That is the nature of my illness. It comes and goes." The Maer set down his cup of tea, still three-quarters full. "Eventually it fades entirely, and Caudicus is free to go off gallivanting for months at a time, gathering ingredients for his charms and potives. Speaking of," he said, folding his hands in his lap. "Would you do me the favor of fetching my medicine from Caudicus?"

"Certainly, your grace." I stretched a smile over my face, trying to ignore the unease settling in my chest. I cleaned up the clutter I had created while fixing his tea, tucking packages and bundles of herbs back into the pockets of my burgundy cloak.

The Maer nodded graciously, then closed his eyes and seemed to lapse back into his tranquil, sunlit nap.

"Our fledgling historian!" Caudicus said as he gestured me inside and offered me a seat. "If you'll excuse me for a moment, I'll be right back."

I sank into the padded chair and only then noticed the array of rings on the nearby table. Caudicus had gone so far as to have a rack built for them. Each was displayed with the name facing outward. There were a great many of them, silver, iron, and gold.

Both my gold ring and Alveron's iron one sat on a small tray on the table. I reclaimed them, taking note of this rather graceful way of wordlessly offering the return of a ring.

I looked around the large tower room with muted curiosity. What possible motive could he have for poisoning the Maer? Barring access to the University itself, this place was every arcanist's dream.

Curious, I got to my feet and wandered to his bookshelves. Caudicus had a respectable library, with nearly a hundred books crowding for space. I recognized many of the titles. Some were chemical references. Some were alchemical. Others dealt with the natural sciences, herbology, physiology, bestiology. The vast majority seemed to be historical in nature.

A thought occurred to me. Perhaps I could get the native Vintish superstition to work to my advantage. If Caudicus was a serious scholar and even half as superstitious as a native Vint, he might know something about the Chandrian. Best of all, since I was playing the dimwitted lordling, I didn't need to worry about damaging my reputation.

Caudicus came around the corner and seemed somewhat taken aback when he saw me standing by the bookshelves. But he rallied quickly and gave me a polite smile. "See anything you're interested in?"

I turned, shaking my head. "Not particularly," I said. "Do you know anything about the Chandrian?"

Caudicus looked at me blankly for a moment, then burst out laughing. "I know they're not going to come into your room at night and steal you out of your bed," he said, wiggling his fingers at me, the way you'd tease a child.

"You don't study mythology then?" I asked, fighting down a wave of disappointment at his reaction. I tried to console myself with the fact that this would firmly solidify me as a half-wit lordling in his mind.

Caudicus sniffed. "That's hardly *mythology*," he said dismissively. "One could barely even stoop to calling it folklore. It's superstitious bunk, and I don't waste my time with it. No serious scholar would."

He began to putter around the room, restoppering bottles and tucking them into cabinets, straightening up stacks of papers, and returning books to their shelves. "Speaking of serious scholarship, if I remember correctly, you were curious about the Lackless family?"

I simply stared at him for a moment. With everything that had happened since, I'd all but forgotten the pretense of the anecdotal genealogy I'd invented yesterday.

"If it wouldn't be any trouble," I said quickly. "As I've said, I know practically nothing of them."

Caudicus nodded seriously. "In that case you might be well-served in considering their name." He adjusted an alcohol lamp underneath a simmering glass alembic in the midst of an impressive array of copper tubing. Whatever he was distilling, I guessed it wasn't peach brandy. "You see, names can tell you a great deal about a thing."

I grinned at that, then fought to smother the expression. "You don't say?"

He turned back to face me just as I got my mouth under control. "Oh yes," he said. "You see, names are sometimes based on other, older names. The older the name, the closer it lies to the truth. *Lackless* is a relatively new name for the family, not much more than six hundred years old."

For once I didn't have to feign amazement. "Six hundred years is new?"

"The Lackless family is *old*." He stopped his pacing and settled down into a threadbare armchair. "Much older than the house of Alveron. A thousand years ago the Lackless family enjoyed a power at least as great as Alveron's. Pieces of what are now Vintas, Modeg, and a large portion of the small kingdoms were all Lackless lands at one point."

"What was their name before that?" I asked.

He pulled down a thick book and flipped its pages impatiently. "Here it is. The family was called Loeclos or Loklos, or Loeloes. They all translate the same, Lockless. Spelling was rather less important in those days."

"What days were those?" I asked.

He consulted the book again. "About nine hundred years ago, but I've seen other histories that mention the Loeclos a thousand years before the fall of Atur."

I boggled at the thought of a family older than empires. "So the Lockless family became the Lackless family? What reason could a family have for changing its name?"

"There are historians who would cut off their own right hands to answer that," Caudicus said. "It's generally accepted that there was some sort of falling out that splintered the family. Each piece took on a separate name. In Atur they became the Lack-key family. They were numerous, but fell on hard times. That's where the word 'lackey' comes from, you know. All those paupered nobility forced to scrape and bow to make ends meet.

"In the south they became the Lacliths, who slowly spiraled into obscurity. The same with the Kaepcaen in Modeg. The largest piece of the family was here in Vintas, except Vintas didn't exist back then." He closed the book and held it out to me. "You can borrow this if you'd like."

"Thank you." I took the book. "You're too kind."

There was the distant sound of a belling tower. "I'm too long-winded," he said. "I've talked away our time and haven't given you anything of use."

"Just the history makes a great difference," I said gratefully.

"Are you sure I can't interest you in a few stories from other families?" he asked, walking over to a worktable. "I wintered with the Jakis family not long ago. The baron is a widower you know. Quite wealthy and somewhat eccentric." He raised both eyebrows at me, his eyes wide with implied scandal. "I'm sure I could remember a few interesting things if I were assured of my anonymity."

I was tempted to break character for that, but instead I shook my head. "Perhaps when I'm done working on the Lackless section," I said with all the self-importance of someone devoted to a truly useless project. "My research is quite delicate. I don't want to get tangled up in my head."

Caudicus frowned a bit, then shrugged it away as he rolled up his sleeves and began to make the Maer's medicine.

I watched him go through his preparations again. It wasn't alchemy. I knew that from watching Simmon work. This was barely even chemistry. Mixing a medicine like this was closer to following a recipe than anything. But what were the ingredients?

I watched him move through it step by step. The dried leaf was probably bitefew. The liquid from the stoppered jar was no doubt muratum or aqua fortis, some sort of acid at any rate. When it bubbled and steamed in the lead bowl it dissolved a small amount of lead, maybe only a quarter-scruple. The white powder was probably the ophalum.

He added a pinch of the final ingredient. I couldn't even guess what that was. It looked like salt, but then again, most everything looks like salt.

As he went through the motions, Caudicus nattered on about court gossip. DeFerre's eldest son had broken his leg jumping out a brothel window. Lady Hesua's most recent lover was Yllish and didn't speak a word of Aturan. There was a rumor of highwaymen on the king's road to the north, but there are always rumors of bandits, so that was nothing new.

I don't care one whit for gossip, but I can fake interest when I must. All the while I watched Caudicus for some telltale sign. Some whisper of nervousness, a bead of sweat, a moment's hesitation. But there was nothing. Not the slightest indication he was preparing a poison for the Maer. He was perfectly comfortable, utterly at ease.

Was it possible he was poisoning the Maer by accident? Impossible. Any arcanist worth his guilder knew enough chemistry to . . .

Then it dawned on me. Maybe Caudicus wasn't an arcanist at all. Maybe he was simply a man in a dark robe who didn't know the difference between an alligator and a crocodile. Maybe he was just a clever pretender who happened to be poisoning the Maer out of simple ignorance.

Maybe that *was* peach brandy in his distillery.

He tamped the cork into the vial of amber liquid and handed it to me. "There you are," he said. "Make sure you take it to him straightaway. It'll be best if he gets it while it's still warm."

The temperature of a medicine doesn't make one whit of difference. Any physicker knows that.

I took the vial and pointed to his chest as if I'd just noticed something. "My word, is that an amulet?"

He seemed confused at first, then and drew out the leather cord from underneath his robes. "Of sorts," he said with a tolerant smile. At a casual glance, the piece of lead he wore around his neck looked very much like an Arcanum guilder.

"Does it protect you from spirits?" I asked in a hushed voice.

"Oh yes," he said flippantly. "All sorts."

I swallowed nervously. "May I touch it?"

He shrugged and leaned forward, holding it out to me.

I took it timidly with my thumb and forefinger, then jumped back a step. "It bit me!" I said, pitching my voice somewhere between indignation and anxiety as I wrung my hand.

I saw him fighting down a smile. "Ah, yes. I need to feed it, I suspect." He tucked it back inside his robes. "Go on now." He made a shooing motion toward the door.

I made my way back to the Maer's rooms, trying to massage some feeling back into my numb fingers. It was a genuine Arcanum guilder. He was a real arcanist. He knew exactly what he was doing.

―――――――――――

I returned to the Maer's rooms and engaged in five minutes of painfully formal small talk while I refilled the flit's feeders with the still-warm medicine. The birds were unnervingly energetic, humming and chirruping sweetly.

The Maer sipped a cup of tea as we talked, his eyes following me quietly from the bed. When my work with the birds was finished I made my goodbyes and left as quickly as propriety allowed.

Though our conversation hadn't touched on anything more serious than the weather, I could read his underlying message as plainly as if he'd written it for me to read. He was in control. He was keeping his options open. He didn't trust me.

CHAPTER SIXTY-THREE

The Gilded Cage

AFTER MY BRIEF TASTE of freedom, I was trapped in my rooms again. Though I hoped the Maer was through the worst of his recovery, I still needed to be at hand should his condition worsen and he call on me. I couldn't justify even a brief trip to Severen-Low, no matter how desperately I wanted to head back to Tinnery Street with the hope of meeting up with Denna.

So I called on Bredon and spent a pleasant afternoon playing tak. We played game after game, and I lost each one in new and exciting ways. This time when we parted ways, he left the game table with me, claiming his servants were tired of carrying it back and forth between our rooms.

In addition to tak with Bredon and my music, I had a new distraction, albeit an irritating one. Caudicus was every bit the gossip he seemed to be, and word had spread about my story genealogy. So now in addition to courtiers trying to pry information out of me, I was deluged with a steady flow of people eager to air everyone else's dirty laundry.

I dissuaded those I could, and encouraged the especially rabid to write their stories down and send them to me. A surprising number of them took time to do this, and a stack of slanderous stories began to accumulate on a desk in one of my unused rooms.

The next day when the Maer summoned me, I arrived to find Alveron sitting in a chair near his bed, reading a copy of Fyoren's *Claim of Kings* in the original Eld Vintic. His color was remarkably good and I saw no trembling in his hands as he turned a page. He didn't look up as I entered the room.

Without speaking, I prepared a new pot of tea with the hot water waiting at the Maer's bedside table. I poured a cup and set it at the table by his elbow.

I checked the gilded cage in his sitting room. The flits darted back and forth to the feeders, playing dizzying aerial games which made them difficult to count. Still, I was reasonably certain there were twelve of them. They seemed none the worse despite three days of poisonous diet. I resisted an urge to knock the cage about a bit.

Finally I replaced the Maer's flask of cod liver oil and found it was still three-quarters full. Yet another sign of my fading credibility.

Wordlessly I gathered up my things and prepared to leave, but before I made it to the door, the Maer turned his eyes up from his book. "Kvothe?"

"Yes, your grace?"

"It seems I am not as thirsty as I thought. Would you mind finishing this for me?" He gestured to the untasted cup of tea that sat on the table.

"To your grace's health," I said, and drank a sip. I made a face and added a spoon of sugar, stirred, and drained the rest of it with the Maer watching me. His eyes were calm, clever, and too knowing to be wholly good.

Caudicus let me in and ushered me into the same seat as before. "You'll excuse me for a moment," he said. "I have an experiment I must attend to, or I fear it will be ruined." He hurried up a set of steps that led to a different part of the tower.

With nothing else to occupy my attention, I eyed his display of rings again, realizing that a person could make a fair guess at his position in the court by using the rings themselves as triangulation points.

Caudicus returned just as I was idly considering stealing one of his gold rings.

"I was not sure if you wanted your rings back," Caudicus said, gesturing.

I looked back at the table and saw them resting on a tray. It seemed odd I hadn't noticed them before. I picked them up and slid them into an inner pocket of my cloak. "Thank you kindly," I said.

"And will you be taking the Maer his medicine again today?" he asked.

I nodded, puffing myself up proudly.

When I nodded, the motion of my head made me dizzy. It was only then I realized the trouble: I'd drunk a full cup of the Maer's tea. There hadn't been much laudanum in it. Or rather, not much laudanum if you were in pain and being slowly weaned away from a budding addiction to ophalum.

However, it was quite a bit of laudanum for someone like myself. I could feel the effects of it slowly creeping over me, a warm lassitude running through my bones. Everything seemed to be moving a little more slowly than normal.

"The Maer seemed eager for his medicine today," I said, taking extra care to speak clearly. "I'm afraid I don't have much time to chat." I was in no condition to play the half-wit gentry for any length of time.

Caudicus nodded seriously and retreated to his worktable. I followed him as I always did, wearing my best curious expression.

I watched with half an eye as Caudicus mixed the medicine. But my wits were fuddled by the laudanum, and what remained were focused on other matters. The Maer was hardly speaking to me. Stapes hadn't trusted me from the beginning, and the flits were healthy as ever. Worst of all, I was trapped in my rooms while Denna waited down on Tinnery Street, no doubt wondering why I hadn't come to visit.

I looked up, aware that Caudicus had asked me a question. "Beg your pardon?"

"Could you pass me the acid?" Caudicus repeated as he finished measuring out a portion of leaf into his mortar and pestle.

I picked up the glass decanter and began to hand it to him before I remembered I was just an ignorant lordling. I couldn't tell salt from sulfur. I didn't even know what an acid was.

I did not flush or stumble. I didn't sweat or stutter. I am Edema Ruh born, and even drugged and fuddled I am a performer down to the marrow of my bones. I met his eyes and asked, "This one, right? The clear bottle comes next."

Caudicus gave me a long, speculative look.

I flashed him a brilliant grin. "I've got a good eye for detail," I said smugly. "I've watched you go through this twice now. I bet I could mix the Maer's medicine myself if I wanted to."

I pitched my voice with all the ignorant self-confidence I could muster. This is the true mark of nobility. The unshakable belief that they can do anything: tan leather, shoe a horse, spin pottery, plow a field . . . if they really wanted to.

Caudicus looked at me a moment longer, then began to measure out the acid. "I daresay you could, young sir."

Three minutes later I was walking down the hall with the warm vial of medicine in my sweaty palm. It almost didn't matter whether I'd fooled him or not. What mattered was that for some reason, Caudicus was suspicious of me.

Stapes stared daggers into my back as he let me into the Maer's rooms, and Alveron ignored me as I poured the new dose of poison into the flit's feeders. The pretty things hummed about their cage with infuriating energy.

I took the long way back to my rooms, trying to get a better feel for the layout of the Maer's estate. I already had my escape route half planned, but Caudicus' suspicion encouraged me to put the finishing touches on it. If the flits didn't start dying tomorrow, it would probably be in my best interest to disappear from Severen as quickly and quietly as possible.

———

Late that night, when I was reasonably sure the Maer wouldn't call on me, I slipped out the window of my room and made a thorough exploration of the gardens. There were no guards this late at night, but I did have to avoid a half-dozen couples taking moonlight strolls. There were two others sitting in close, romantic conversation, one in a bower, the other in a gazebo. The last couple I nearly trod on while cutting through a hedgerow. They were neither strolling nor conversing in any conventional sense, but their activities were romantic. They didn't notice me.

Eventually I found my way onto the roof. From there I could see the grounds surrounding the estate. The western edge was out of the question, of course, as it was pressed up against the edge of the Sheer, but I knew there had to be other opportunities for escape.

While exploring the southern end of the estate, I saw lights burning brightly in one of the towers. What's more, they had the distinctive, red tint of sympathy lamps. Caudicus was still awake.

I made my way over and risked a look inside, peering down into the tower. Caudicus was not simply working late. He was talking to someone. I craned my neck, but I couldn't see who he was speaking to. What's more, the window was leaded shut and I couldn't hear anything.

I was about to move to a different window when Caudicus stood and began to walk to the door. The other person came into view, and even from this steep angle I could recognize the portly, unassuming figure of Stapes.

Stapes was clearly worked up about something. He made an emphatic gesture with one hand, his face deathly serious. Caudicus nodded several times in agreement before opening the door to let the manservant out.

I noted Stapes wasn't carrying anything when he left. He hadn't stopped by for medicine. He hadn't stopped by to borrow a book. Stapes had stopped by in the middle of the night to have a private conversation with the man who was trying to kill the Maer.

CHAPTER SIXTY-FOUR

Flight

*Though no family can boast a truly peaceful past, the Lacklesses have been espe-
cially ripe with misfortune. Some from without: assassination, invasion, peasant
revolt, and theft. More telling is misfortune that comes from within: how can a
family thrive when the eldest heir forsakes all family duty? Small wonder they
are often called the "Luckless" by their detractors.*

*It seems a testament to the strength of their blood that they have survived so
much for so long. Indeed, if not for the burning of Caluptena, we might possess
records tracing the Lackless family back far enough for them to rival the royal line
of Modeg in its antiquity. . . .*

I tossed the book onto the table in a way that would have made Master Lorren spit blood. If the Maer thought this sort of information was enough to
woo a woman, he was in worse need of my help than he thought.

But as things currently stood, I doubted the Maer would be asking me
for any help with anything, least of all something as sensitive as his courting.
Yesterday he hadn't summoned me to his rooms at all.

I was clearly out of favor, and I sensed Stapes had a hand in it. Given what
I had seen two nights ago in Caudicus' tower, it was fairly obvious Stapes was
part of the conspiracy to poison the Maer.

Though it meant spending all day trapped in my rooms, I stayed where I
was. I knew better than to jeopardize Alveron's already low opinion of me by
approaching him without being summoned first.

An hour before lunch Viscount Guermen stopped by my rooms with a
few pages of handwritten gossip. He also brought a deck of cards, apparently
thinking to take a page from Bredon's book. He offered to teach me how to

play thrush, and, as I was just learning the game, agreed to play for the pittance of a single silver bit per hand.

He made the mistake of letting me deal, and left in a bit of huff after I won eighteen hands in a row. I suppose I could have been more subtle. I could have played him like a fish on a line and bilked him for half his estate, but I was in no mood for it. My thoughts were not pleasant, and I preferred to be alone with them.

———

An hour after lunch, I decided I was no longer interested in currying favor with the Maer. If Alveron wished to trust his treacherous manservant, that was his business. I'd be damned if I would spend one more minute sitting idle in my room, waiting by the door like a whipped dog.

I threw on my cloak, grabbed my lute case, and decided to take a walk down Tinnery Street. If the Maer needed me while I was away, he could damn well leave a note.

I was halfway into the hall when I saw the guard standing at attention outside my door. He was one of Alveron's own, clad in sapphire and ivory.

We stood for a moment, motionless. There was no sense in asking if he was there on my account. Mine was the only door for twenty feet in any direction. I met his eye. "And you are?"

"Jayes, sir."

At least I still rated a "sir." That was worth something. "And you're here because . . . ?"

"I'm to accompany you if you leave your room. Sir."

"Right." I stepped back into my room and closed the door behind me. Were his orders from Alveron or Stapes? It didn't really matter.

I went out my window, into the garden, over the little streamlet, behind a hedgerow, and up a section of decorative stone wall. My burgundy cloak was not the best color for sneaking around in the garden, but it worked quite nicely against the red of the roofing tiles.

After that I made my way onto the roof of the stables, through a hayloft, and out the back door of a disused barn. From there it was just a matter of jumping a fence and I was off the Maer's estate. Simple.

I stopped at twelve inns on Tinnery Street before I found the one where Denna was staying. She wasn't there, so I continued along the street, keeping my eyes open and trusting to my luck.

I spotted her an hour later. She was standing at the edge of a crowd, watching a street corner a production of, believe it or not, *Three Pennies for Wishing*.

Her skin was darker than when I'd seen her last at the University, tanned from travel, and she wore a high-necked dress after the local fashion. Her dark hair fell in a straight sheaf across her back, all except a single slender braid that hung close to her face.

I caught her eye just as Deadnettle shouted out his first line in the play:

I've cures for what ails you!
My wares never fails you!
I've potions for pennies, results guaranteed!
So if you've got a dicky heart,
Or can't get her legs apart,
Come straightaway to my cart,
You'll find what you need!

Denna smiled when she saw me. We might have stayed for the play, but I already knew the ending.

———————————

Hours later, Denna and I were eating sweet Vintish grapes in the shadow of the Sheer. Some industrious stonemason had carved a shallow niche into the white stone of the cliff, making smooth seats of stone. It was a cozy place we had discovered while walking aimlessly through the city. We were alone, and I felt myself to be the luckiest man in the world.

My only regret was that I didn't have her ring with me. It would have been the perfect unexpected gift to go with our unexpected meeting. Worse yet, I couldn't even tell Denna about it. If I did, I'd be forced to admit I'd used it as collateral for my loan with Devi.

"You seem to be doing fairly well for yourself," Denna said, rubbing the edge of my burgundy cloak between her fingers. "Have you given up the bookish life?"

"Taking a vacation," I hedged. "Right now I'm assisting the Maer Alveron with a thing or two."

Her eyes widened appreciatively. "Do tell."

I looked away uncomfortably. "I'm afraid I can't. Delicate matters and all that." I cleared my throat and tried to change the subject. "What of you? You seem to be doing fairly well yourself." I brushed two fingers across the embroidery that decorated the high neck of her dress.

"Well I'm not rubbing elbows with the Maer," she said, making an exaggerated deferential gesture in my direction. "But as I mentioned in my letters, I—"

"Letters?" I asked. "You sent more than one?"

She nodded. "Three since I left," she said. "I was about to start a fourth, but you've saved me the trouble."

"I only got the one," I said.

Denna shrugged. "I'd rather tell you in person, anyway." She paused dramatically. "I finally have my formal patronage."

"You have?" I said, delighted. "Denna, that's wonderful news!"

Denna grinned proudly. Her teeth were white against the light nut color of her travel-tanned face. Her lips, as always, were red without the aid of any paint.

"Is he part of the court here in Severen?" I asked. "What's his name?"

Denna's grin faded into a serious look, a confused smile playing around her mouth. "You know I can't tell you that," she chided. "You know how closely he guards his privacy."

My excitement fell away, leaving me cold. "Oh no. Denna. It's not the same fellow as before, is it? The one who sent you to play for that wedding in Trebon?"

Denna looked puzzled. "Of course it is. I can't tell you his real name. What was it you called him before? Master Elm?"

"Master Ash," I said, and it felt like a mouthful of ashes when I said it. "Do *you* at least know his real name? Did he tell you that much before you signed up?"

"I expect I know his real name," she shrugged, running a hand through her hair. When her fingers touched the braid she seemed surprised to find it there and quickly began to unravel it, her deft fingers smoothing it away. "Even if I don't, what does it matter? Everyone has secrets, Kvothe. I don't particularly care what his are so long as he continues to deal square with me. He's been very generous."

"He's not just secretive, Denna," I protested. "From the way you've described him, I'd say he's either paranoid or tangled up in dangerous business."

"I don't know why you're carrying such a grudge against him."

I couldn't believe she could say that. "Denna, he beat you senseless."

She went very still. "No." Her hand went to the fading bruise on her cheek. "No he didn't. I told you. I fell while I was out riding. The stupid horse couldn't tell a stick from a snake."

I shook my head. "I'm talking about last fall in Trebon."

Denna's hand fell back to her lap where it made an absentminded fidgeting gesture, trying to toy with a ring that wasn't there. She looked at me, her expression blank. "How did you know about that?"

"You told me yourself. That night on the hill, waiting for the draccus to come."

She looked down, blinking. "I . . . I don't remember saying that."

"You were a little addled at the time," I said gently. "But you did. You told me all about it. Denna, you shouldn't have to stay with someone like that. Anyone who could do that to you . . ."

"He did it for my own good," she said, her dark eyes beginning to flicker with anger. "Did I tell you that? There I was without a scratch on me and everyone else at the wedding dead as leather. You know what small towns are like. Even after they found me unconscious they thought I might have had something to do with it. You remember."

I put my head down and shook it like an ox worrying its yoke. "I don't believe it. There had to be another way around the situation. I would have found another way."

"Well I guess we can't all be as clever as you," she said.

"Clever doesn't have anything to do with it!" I came close to shouting. "He could have taken you away with him! He could have come forward and vouched for you!"

"He couldn't let anyone know he was there," Denna said. "He said—"

"He beat you." And as I spoke the words I felt a terrible anger come together inside me. It wasn't hot and furious, as some of my flashes of temper tend to be. This was different, slow and cold. And as soon as I felt it, I realized it had been there inside me for a long while, crystallizing, like a pond slowly freezing solid over a long winter night.

"He beat you," I said again, and I could feel it inside, a solid block of icy anger. "Nothing you can say will change that. And if I ever see him, I'll likely stick a knife in him rather than shake his hand."

Denna looked up at me then, the irritation fading from her face. She gave me a look that was all sweet fondness and mingled pity. It was the sort of look you give a puppy when it growls, thinking itself terribly fierce. She put her hand gently on the side of my face, and I felt myself flush hot and hard, suddenly embarrassed by my own melodrama.

"Can we not argue about it?" she asked. "Please? Not today? It's been so long since I've seen you. . . ."

I decided to let it go rather than risk driving her away. I knew what happened when men pressed her too hard. "Fair enough," I said. "For today. Can you at least tell me what sort of thing your patron brought you out here for?"

Denna leaned back in her seat, smiling a wide smile. "Sorry, delicate matters and all that," she mimicked.

"Don't be that way," I protested. "I'd tell you if I could, but the Maer values his privacy very highly."

Denna leaned forward again to lay her hand over mine. "Poor Kvothe, it's not out of spite. My patron is at *least* as private as the Maer. He made it very clear that things would go badly if I ever made our relationship public. He was quite emphatic about it." Her expression had gone serious. "He's a powerful man." She seemed as if she would say more, then stopped herself.

Though I didn't want to, I understood. My recent brush with the Maer's anger had taught me caution. "What *can* you tell me about him?"

Denna tapped a finger against her lips thoughtfully. "He's a surprisingly good dancer. I think I can say that without betraying anything. He's quite graceful," she said, then laughed at my expression. "I'm doing some research for him, looking into old genealogies and histories. He's helping me write a couple songs so I can make a name for myself. . . ." She hesitated, then shook her head. "I think that's all I can say."

"Will I get to hear the songs after you're done?"

She gave a shy smile. "I think that can be arranged." She leapt to her feet and grabbed my arm to pull me to my feet. "Enough talking. Come and walk with me!"

I smiled, her enthusiasm as infectious as a child's. But when she pulled at my hand, she let out a tiny yelp, flinching and pressing one of her hands to her side.

I was standing next to her in a second. "What's the matter?"

Denna shrugged and gave me a brittle smile, holding her arm close to her ribs. "My fall," she said. "That stupid horse. I get a twinge when I forget and move too quickly."

"Has anyone looked at it?"

"It's just a bruise," she said. "And the sort of doctor I can afford, I wouldn't trust to touch me."

"What of your patron?" I asked. "Certainly he could arrange something."

She slowly straightened. "It's really not a problem." She lifted her arms above her head and made a quick, clever dance step, then laughed at my serious expression. "No more talk of secret things for now. Come walk with me. Tell me dark and lurid gossip from the Maer's court."

"Very well," I said as we began to walk. "I've heard the Maer is marvelously recovered from a long-standing illness."

"You're a poor rumormonger," she said. "Everyone knows that."

"The Baronet Bramston played a disastrous deck of faro last night."

Denna rolled her eyes. "Boring."

"The Comptess DeFerre lost her virginity while attending a performance of *Daeonica*."

"Oh," Denna raised her hand to her mouth, stifling a laugh. "Did she really?"

"She certainly didn't have it with her after the intermission," I said in a hushed voice. "But it turns out she had just left it behind in her rooms. So it was merely misplaced, not really lost. The servants found it two days later when they were cleaning up. Turns out, it had rolled underneath a chest of drawers."

Denna's expression turned indignant. "I can't believe I believed you!" She swatted at me, then grimaced again, sucking a sharp breath through her teeth.

"You know," I said softly. "I've been trained at the University. I'm not a physicker, but the medicine I know is good. I could take a look at it for you."

She gave me a long look, as if she wasn't quite sure what to make of my offer. "I think," she said at last, "that might be the most circumspect route anyone has ever tried for getting me out of my clothes."

"I . . ." I felt myself blush furiously. "I didn't mean . . ."

Denna laughed at my discomfiture. "If I let anyone play doctor with me, it would be you, my Kvothe," she said. "But I'll tend to it for now." She linked arms with me and we continued our walk down the street. "I know enough to take care of myself."

I returned to the Maer's estate hours later, taking the direct route rather than come in over the rooftops. When I arrived in the hallway leading to my room, I found two guards standing there instead of the single one that had been waiting before. I guessed they had discovered my escape.

Even this couldn't dampen my spirits overmuch, as the time I'd spent with Denna had left me feeling twelve feet tall. Better yet, I was meeting with her tomorrow to go riding. Having a specific time and place to meet was an unexpected treat where Denna was concerned.

"Good evening, gentlemen," I said as I came down the hall. "Anything interesting happen while I was out?"

"You're to be confined to your rooms," Jayes said grimly. I noticed he left off the "sir" this time.

I paused with my hand on the doorknob. "Beg pardon?"

"You're to remain in your rooms until we get further orders," he said. "And one of us is to stay with you at all times."

I felt my temper flare up. "And does Alveron know about this?" I asked sharply.

They looked at each other uncertainly.

It *was* Stapes giving the orders then. That uncertainty would be enough to keep them from laying hands on me. "Let's get this sorted out straightaway," I said, and started down the hall at a brisk walk, leaving the guards to catch up with me, their armor clattering.

My temper fanned itself hotter as I made my way through the halls. If my credibility with the Maer was truly ruined, I preferred to have done with it now. If I couldn't have the Maer's good will, I would at least have my freedom and the ability to see Denna when I wished.

I turned the corner just in time to see the Maer emerging from his rooms. He looked as healthy as I had ever seen him, carrying a sheaf of papers under one arm.

As I approached, irritation flashed across his face and I thought he might simply have the guards carry me away. Nevertheless, I approached him as boldly as if I had a written invitation. "Your grace," I said with cheery cordiality. "Might we talk for a moment?"

"Certainly," he replied in a similar tone as he swung open the door he had been about to close behind himself. "Do come in." I watched his eyes and saw an anger as hot as mine. A small, sensible part of me quailed, but my temper had the bit in its teeth and was galloping madly ahead.

We left the bemused guards in the antechamber, and Alveron led me through the second set of doors into his personal rooms. Silence hung dangerous in the air, like the calm before a sudden summer storm.

"I cannot believe your impudence," the Maer hissed once the doors were closed. "Your wild accusations. Your ridiculous claims. I mislike public unpleasantness so we will deal with this later." He made an imperious gesture. "Return to your rooms and do not leave until I decide how best to deal with you."

"Your grace—"

I could tell by the set of his shoulders that he was ready to call the guards. "I do not hear you," he said flatly.

He met my gaze then. His eyes were hard as flint and I saw how angry he truly was. This wasn't the anger of a patron or employer. It wasn't someone irritated by my failure to respect the social order. This was a man who had ruled everything around him from the age of sixteen. This man thought nothing of hanging someone from an iron gibbet to make a point. This was a man who, but for a twist of history, would now be king of all Vintas.

My temper sputtered and went out like a snuffed candle, leaving me chilled. I realized then that I had misjudged my situation badly.

When I was a child, homeless on the streets of Tarbean, I'd learned to deal with dangerous people: drunken dockworkers, guardsmen, even a homeless child with a bottle-glass knife can kill you.

The key to staying safe was knowing the rules of the situation. A guard wouldn't beat you in the middle of the street. A dockworker wouldn't chase you if you ran.

Now, with sudden clarity, I realized my mistake. The Maer was not bound by any rules. He could order me killed then hang my body over the city gates. He could throw me in jail and forget about me. He could leave me there while I grew starved and sickly. I had no position, no friends to intercede on my behalf. I was helpless as a child with a willow-switch sword.

I realized this in a flash and felt a gnawing fear settle in my belly. I should have stayed in Severen-Low while I had the chance. I never should have come here in the first place and meddled in the affairs of powerful folk such as this.

It was just then that Stapes bustled in from the Maer's dressing room. Seeing us, his normally placid expression flickered briefly into panic and surprise. He recovered quickly. "I beg your pardon, sirs," he said, and hurried back the way he came.

"Stapes," the Maer called out before he could leave. "Come here."

Stapes slunk back into the room. He wrung his hands nervously. His face had the stricken look of a guilty man, a man caught in the midst of something dishonest.

Alveron's voice was stern. "Stapes, what do you have there?" Looking closer, I saw the manservant wasn't wringing his hands, he was clutching something.

"It's nothing—"

"Stapes!" the Maer barked. "How *dare* you lie to me! Show me at once!"

Numbly, the portly manservant opened his hands. A tiny gem-bright bird lay lifeless on his palm. His face had lost all hint of color.

Never in the history of the world has the death of a lovely thing brought such relief and joy. I had been certain of Stapes' betrayal for days now, and here was the unquestionable proof of it.

Nevertheless, I kept quiet. The Maer had to see this with his own eyes.

"What is the meaning of this?" the Maer asked slowly.

"It's not good to think of such things, sir," the manservant said quickly, "and worse to dwell on them. I'll just fetch another one. It'll sing just as sweet."

There was a long pause. I could see Alveron struggling to contain the rage he'd been ready to unleash on me. The silence continued to stretch.

"Stapes," I said slowly. "How many birds have you replaced these last few days?"

Stapes turned to me, his expression indignant.

Before he could speak, the Maer broke in. "Answer him, Stapes." His voice sounded almost choked. "Has there been more than this one?"

Stapes gave the Maer a stricken look. "Oh Rand, I didn't want to trouble you. You were so bad for a time. Then you asked for the birds and had that terrible night. Then the next day one of them died."

Looking down at the tiny bird in his hand, his words came faster and faster, almost tumbling over each other. Too clumsy to be anything but sincere. "I didn't want to fill your head with talk of dying things. So I snuck it out and brought a new one in. Then you kept getting better and they started falling four or five a day. Every time I looked there would be another one lying in the bottom of the cage like a little cut flower. But you were doing so well. I didn't want to mention it."

Stapes covered the dead sipquick with a cupped hand. "It's like they were giving up their little souls to make you well again." Something inside the man suddenly gave way, and he began to cry. The deep, hopeless sobs of an honest man who has been frightened and helpless for a long time, watching the slow death of a well-loved friend.

Alveron stood motionless for a stunned moment, all the anger spilling out of him. Then he moved to put his arms gently around his manservant. "Oh Stapes," he said softly. "They were, in a way. You haven't done anything you can be blamed for."

I quietly left the room and busied myself removing the feeders from the gilded cage.

An hour later the three of us were eating a quiet supper together in the Maer's rooms. Alveron and I told Stapes what had been happening over the last several days. Stapes was almost giddy, both at his master's health and at the knowledge it would continue to improve.

As for myself, after suffering a few days under Alveron's displeasure, being so suddenly in his good graces again was a relief. Nevertheless, I was shaken by how close to disaster I had been.

I was honest with the Maer about my misguided suspicion of Stapes, and I offered the manservant my sincere apology. Stapes in turn admitted his doubts about me. In the end we shook hands and thought much better of each other.

As we were chatting over the last bites of supper Stapes perked up, excused himself, and hurried out.

"My outer door," the Maer explained. "He has ears like a dog. It's uncanny."

Stapes opened the door to admit the tall man with the shaven head who had been looking over maps with Alveron when I'd first arrived, Commander Dagon.

As Dagon stepped into the room his eyes flicked to each of the corners, to the window, to the other door, briefly over me, then back to the Maer. When his eyes touched me, all the deep feral instincts that had kept me alive on the streets of Tarbean told me to run. Hide. Do anything so long as it took me far away from this man.

"Ah, Dagon!" the Maer said cheerily. "Are you well this fine day?"

"Yes, your grace." He stood attentively, not quite meeting the Maer's eye.

"Would you be good enough to arrest Caudicus for treason?"

There was a half-heartbeat pause. "Yes, your grace."

"Eight men should be sufficient, providing they're not likely to panic in a complicated situation."

"Yes, your grace." I began to sense subtle differences in Dagon's responses.

"Alive," Alveron responded, as if answering a question. "But you needn't be gentle."

"Yes, your grace." With that, Dagon turned to leave.

I spoke up quickly. "Your grace, if he's truly an arcanist you ought to take certain precautions." I regretted the word "ought" as soon as I had said it, "ought" was presumptuous. I should have said, *You may wish to consider taking certain precautions.*

Alveron seemed to take no notice of my misstep. "Yes, of course. Set a thief to catch a thief. Dagon, before you settle him downstairs, bind him hand and foot with good iron chain. Pure iron, mind you. Gag and blindfold him. . . ." He thought for a brief moment, tapping his lips with a finger "And cut off his thumbs."

"Yes, your grace."

Alveron looked at me. "Do you think that should be sufficient?"

I fought down a wave of nausea and forced myself not to wring my hands in my lap. I didn't know which I found more unsettling, the cheerful tone with which Alveron delivered the commands, or the flat emotionless one with which Dagon accepted them. A full arcanist was nothing to trifle with, but I found the thought of crippling the man's hands more horrifying than killing him outright.

Dagon left, and after the door closed Stapes shuddered. "Good lord, Rand, he's like cold water down the back of my neck. I wish you'd get rid of him."

The Maer laughed. "So someone else could have him? No, Stapes. I want him right here. My mad dog on a short leash."

Stapes frowned. But before he could make anything more of it, his eyes were drawn through the doorway into the sitting room. "Oh, there's another one." He walked to the cage and returned with another dead flit, holding its tiny body tenderly as he carried it out of the chambers. "I know you needed to test the medicine on something," he said from the other room. "But it's a little rough on the poor little calanthis."

"Beg pardon?" I asked.

"Our Stapes is old-fashioned," Alveron explained with a smile. "And more educated than he cares to admit. Calanthis is the Eld Vintic name for them."

"I could swear I've heard that word somewhere else."

"It's also the surname of the royal line of Vintas," Alveron said chidingly. "For someone who knows so much, you're curiously blind in places."

Stapes craned his neck to look toward the cage again. "I know you had to do it," he said, "But why not use mice, or Comptess DeFerre's nasty little dog?"

Before I could answer, there was a thump from the outer rooms and a guard burst through the inner door before Stapes could come to his feet.

"Your grace," the man said breathlessly as he jumped to the room's only window and slammed the shutters. Next he ran to the sitting room and did the same with the window in there. There followed other, similar noises from rooms farther back I had never seen. There was a faint sound of furniture being moved.

Stapes looked puzzled and half rose to his feet, but the Maer shook his head and motioned for him to sit down. "Lieutenant?" he called out, a tinge of irritation in his voice.

"Beg pardon, your grace," the guard said as he reentered the room, breathing heavily. "Dagon's orders. I was to secure your rooms straightaway."

"I take it all is not well," Alveron said dryly.

"There was no answer from the tower when we knocked. Dagon had us force the door. There was . . . I know not what it was, your grace. Some malignant spirit. Anders is dead, your grace. Caudicus is nowhere in his rooms, but Dagon is after him."

Alveron's expression darkened. "Damn!" he thundered, striking the arm of his chair with a fist. His brow furrowed and he let out an explosive sigh. "Very well." He waved the guard away.

The guard stood stiffly. "Sir. Dagon said I'm not to leave you unguarded."

Alveron gave him a dangerous look. "Very well, but stand over there." He pointed to the corner of the room.

The guard appeared perfectly happy to fade into the background. Alveron leaned forward, pressing the tips of his fingers to his forehead. "How in the name of God did he suspect?"

The question seemed rhetorical, but it set the wheels of my mind spinning. "Did your grace pick up his medicine yesterday?"

"Yes, yes. I did everything the same as I had done in days past."

Except you didn't send me to get your medicine, I thought to myself. "Do you still have the vial?" I asked.

He did. Stapes brought it to me. I uncorked it and ran a finger along the inside of the glass. "How does your grace's medicine taste?"

"I've told you. Brackish, bitter." I watched the Maer's eyes go wide as I brought my finger to my mouth and touched it lightly to the tip of my tongue. "Are you mad?" Alveron said incredulously.

"Sweet," I said simply. Then I rinsed my mouth with water and spat it as delicately as possible into an empty glass. I took a small folded packet of paper from a pocket in my vest, shook a small amount into my hand and ate it, grimacing.

"What's that?" Stapes asked.

"Liguellen," I lied, knowing the real answer, charcoal, would only provoke more questions. I took a mouthful of water and spat it out as well. This time it was black, and Alveron and Stapes stared at it, startled.

I bulled ahead. "Something must have made him suspect you were not taking your medicine, your grace. If it suddenly tasted different, you would have asked him."

The Maer nodded. "I saw him yesterday evening. He asked after my health." He beat his fist softly onto the arm of his chair. "All the cursed luck. If he has any wit, he's been gone half a day. We'll never catch him."

I thought about reminding him that if he had believed me from the first, none of this would have happened, then thought better of it. "I'd advise your men to stay out of his tower, your grace. He's had time to prepare a great deal of mischief in there, traps and the like."

The Maer nodded and passed his hand in front of his eyes. "Yes. Of course. See to it, Stapes. I believe I'll take a bit of rest. This business may take a while to sort out."

I gathered myself to leave. But the Maer gestured me back into my seat. "Kvothe, stay a moment and make me a pot of tea before you go."

Stapes rang for servants. While clearing the remains of our lunch away, they glanced at me curiously. Not only sitting in the Maer's presence, I was sharing a meal with him in his private chambers. This news would be rumored through the estate in under ten minutes.

After the servants left, I made the Maer another pot of tea. I was preparing to leave when he spoke over the top of his cup, too softly for the guard to overhear.

"Kvothe, you have proved perfectly trustworthy and I regret any doubts I briefly entertained about you." He sipped and swallowed before continuing. "Unfortunately, I cannot allow news of a poisoning to spread. Especially with the poisoner escaped." He gave me a significant look. "It would interfere with the matter we discussed before."

I nodded. Widespread knowledge that his own arcanist had nearly killed him would hardly help Alveron win the hand of the woman he hoped to marry.

He continued. "Unfortunately this need for silence also precludes my giving you a reward you all too richly deserve. Were the situation different, I would consider the gift of lands mere token thanks. I would grant you title too. This power my family still retains, free from the controlment of the king."

My head reeled at the implication of what the Maer was saying as he continued. "However, if I were to do such a thing, there would be need of explanation. And an explanation is the one thing I cannot afford."

Alveron extended his hand, and it took me a moment to realize he intended me to shake it. One does not typically shake hands with the Maer Alveron. I immediately regretted that the only person present to see it was the guard. I hoped he was a gossip.

I took his hand solemnly, and Alveron continued, "I owe you a great debt. If you ever find yourself in need, you shall have at your command all the help a grateful lord can lend."

I nodded graciously, trying to keep a calm demeanor despite my excitement. This was exactly what I had been hoping for. With the Maer's resources, I could make a concerted search for the Amyr. He could get me access to monastery archives, private libraries, places where important documents hadn't been pruned and edited as they had in the University.

But I knew this wasn't the proper time to ask. Alveron had promised his help. I could simply bide my time and choose what type of help I wanted most.

As I stepped outside the Maer's rooms, Stapes surprised me with a sudden, wordless embrace. The expression on his face couldn't have been more grateful if I'd pulled his family from a burning building. "Young sir, I doubt you understand how much I'm in your debt. If there's anything you ever need, just make me wise of it."

He gripped my hand, pumping it up and down enthusiastically. At the same time I felt him press something into my palm.

Then I was standing in the hallway. I opened my hand and saw a fine silver ring with Stapes' name etched across the face. Alongside it was a second ring that wasn't metal at all. It was smooth and white, and also had the manservant's name carved in rough letters across the surface of it. I had no idea what such a thing might signify.

I made my way back to my rooms, almost dizzy with my sudden fortune.

CHAPTER SIXTY-FIVE

A Beautiful Game

THE NEXT DAY MY meager belongings were moved to rooms the Maer deemed more suitable for someone firmly in his favor. There were five of them in all, three with windows overlooking the garden.

It was a nice gesture, but I couldn't help but think that these rooms were even farther from the kitchens. My food would be cold as a stone by the time it made its way to me.

I'd barely been there an hour before a runner arrived bearing Bredon's silver ring and a card that read: "Your glorious new rooms. When?"

I turned the card over, wrote: "As soon as you like," and sent the boy on his way.

I placed his silver ring on a tray in my sitting room. The bowl next to it now had two silver rings glittering among the iron.

I opened the door to see Bredon's dark eyes peering owlishly out at me from the halo of his white beard and hair. He smiled and bowed, his walking stick tucked under one arm. I offered him a seat, then excused myself politely and left him alone in the sitting room for a moment, as was the gracious thing to do.

I was barely through the doorway before I heard his rich laugh coming from the other room, "Ho ho!" he said. "Now there's a thing!"

When I returned, Bredon was sitting by the tak board holding the two rings I had recently received from Stapes. "This is certainly a turn for the books," he said. "Apparently I misjudged things yesterday when my runner was turned away from your door by an altogether surly guard."

I grinned at him. "It's been an exciting couple of days," I said.

Bredon tucked his chin and chuckled, looking even more owlish than usual. "I daresay," he said, holding up the silver ring. "This tells quite a story.

But this . . ." He gestured to the white ring with his walking stick. "This is something else entirely. . . ."

I pulled up a seat across from him. "I'll be frank with you," I said. "I can only guess what it's made of, let alone what it signifies."

Bredon raised an eyebrow. "That's remarkably forthright of you."

I shrugged. "I feel somewhat more secure in my position here," I admitted. "Enough that I can be a little less guarded with the people who have been kind to me."

He chuckled again as he lay the silver ring on the board. "Secure," he said. "I daresay you are at that." He picked up the white ring. "Still, it's not odd that you wouldn't know about this."

"I thought there were just three types of rings," I said.

"That's true for the most part," Bredon said. "But the giving of rings goes back quite a ways. The common folk were doing it long before it became a game for the gentry. And while Stapes may breathe the rarified air with the rest of us, his family is undeniably common."

Bredon set the white ring back onto the board and folded his hands over it. "Those rings were made of things ordinary folk might find easily at hand. A young lover might give a ring of new green grass to someone he was courting. A ring of leather promises service. And so on."

"And a ring of horn?"

"A ring of horn shows enmity," Bredon said. "Powerful and lasting enmity."

"Ah," I said, somewhat taken aback. "I see."

Bredon smiled and held the pale ring up to the light. "But this," he said, "is not horn. The grain is wrong, and Stapes would never give a horn ring alongside a silver one." He shook his head. "No. Unless I miss my guess, this is a ring of bone." He handed it to me.

"Wonderful," I said glumly, turning it over in my hands. "And that means what? That he'll stab me in the liver and push me down a dry well?"

Bredon gave me his wide, warm smile. "A ring of bone indicates a profound and lasting debt."

"I see." I rubbed it between my fingers. "I have to say I prefer being owed a favor."

"Not just a favor," Bredon said. "Traditionally, a ring such as this is carved from the bone of a deceased family member." He raised an eyebrow. "And while I doubt that is currently the case, it does get the point across."

I looked up, still slightly dazed by it all. "And that is. . . ?"

"That these things are not given lightly. It's not a part of games the gentry play, and not the sort of ring you should display." He gave me a look. "If I were you, I'd tuck it safe away."

I put it carefully into my pocket. "You've been such help," I said. "I wish I could repay—"

He held up a hand, cutting me off midsentence. Then, moving with solemn care, he pointed one finger downward, made a fist, and rapped a knuckle on the surface of the tak board.

I smiled and brought out the stones.

———

"I think I'm finally getting my teeth into the game," I said an hour later after losing by the narrowest of margins.

Bredon pushed his chair away from the table with an expression of distaste. "No," he said. "Quite the opposite. You have the basics, but you're missing the whole point."

I began to sort out the stones. "The point is that I'm finally close to beating you after all this time."

"No," Bredon said. "That's not it at all. Tak is a subtle game. That's the reason I have such trouble finding people who can play it. Right now you are stomping about like a thug. If anything you're worse than you were two days ago."

"Admit it," I said. "I nearly had you that last time."

He merely scowled and pointed imperiously to the table.

I set to it with a will, smiling and humming, sure that today I would finally beat him.

But nothing could be further from the truth. Bredon set his stones ruthlessly, not a breath of hesitation between his moves. He tore me apart as easily as you rip a sheet of paper in half.

The game was over so quickly it left me breathless.

"Again," Bredon said, a note of command in his voice I'd never heard before.

I tried to rally, but the next game was worse. I felt like a puppy fighting a wolf. No. I was a mouse at the mercy of an owl. There was not even the pretence of a fight. All I could do was run.

But I couldn't run fast enough. This game was over sooner than the last.

"Again," he demanded.

And we played again. This time, I was not even a living thing. Bredon was calm and dispassionate as a butcher with a boning knife. The game lasted about the length of time it takes to gut and bone a chicken.

At the end of it Bredon frowned and shook his hands briskly to both sides of the board, as if he had just washed them and was trying to flick them dry.

"Fine," I said, leaning back in my chair. "I take your point. You've been going easy on me."

"No," Bredon said with a grim look. "That is far gone from the point I am trying to make."

"What then?"

"I am trying to make you understand the game," he said. "The entire game, not just the fiddling about with stones. The point is not to play as tight as you can. The point is to be bold. To be dangerous. Be elegant."

He tapped the board with two fingers. "Any man that's half awake can spot a trap that's laid for him. But to stride in boldly with a plan to turn it on its ear, that is a marvelous thing." He smiled without any of the grimness leaving his face. "To set a trap and know someone will come in wary, ready with a trick of their own, then beat them. That is twice marvelous."

Bredon's expression softened, and his voice became almost like an entreaty. "Tak reflects the subtle turning of the world. It is a mirror we hold to life. No one wins a dance, boy. The point of dancing is the motion that a body makes. A well-played game of tak reveals the moving of a mind. There is a beauty to these things for those with eyes to see it."

He gestured at the brief and brutal lay of stones between us. "Look at that. Why would I ever want to win a game such as this?"

I looked down at the board. "The point isn't to win?" I asked.

"The point," Bredon said grandly, "is to play a beautiful game." He lifted his hands and shrugged, his face breaking into a beatific smile. "Why would I want to win anything other than a beautiful game?"

CHAPTER SIXTY-SIX

Within Easy Reach

LATER THAT EVENING I sat alone in what I guessed might be my drawing room. Or perhaps my sitting room. Honestly, I wasn't entirely sure what the difference was.

I was surprised to find I liked my new rooms quite a lot. Not for the extra space. Not because they had a better view of the garden. Not because the inlay in the marble floor was more pleasing to the eye. Not even because the room had its own exceptionally well-stocked wine cabinet, though that was quite pleasant.

No. My new rooms were preferable because they had several cushioned, armless chairs that were perfect for playing my lute. It's uncomfortable to play for any length of time in a chair with armrests. In my previous room, I'd usually ended up sitting on the floor.

I decided to dub the room with the good chairs my lutery. Or perhaps my performatory. I would need a while to come up with something suitably pretentious.

Needless to say, I was pleased by the recent turn of events. By way of celebration, I opened a bottle of fine, dark Feloran wine, relaxed, and brought out my lute.

I started quick and tripping, playing my way through "Tintatatornin" to limber up my fingers. Then I played sweet and easy for a time, slowly growing reacquainted with my lute. By the time I'd played for about half a bottle, I had my feet up and my music was mellow and content as a cat in a sunbeam.

That's when I heard the noise behind me. I stopped in a jangle of notes and sprang to my feet, expecting Caudicus, or the guards, or some other deadly trouble.

What I found was the Maer, smiling an embarrassed smile, like a child that's just played a joke. "I trust your new rooms are to your satisfaction?"

I collected myself and made a small bow. "It's rather much for the likes of me, your grace."

"It's rather little, considering my debt to you," Alveron said. He sat on a nearby couch and made a gracious gesture indicating I should feel free to take a seat myself. "What was that you were playing just now?"

I returned to my chair. "It wasn't really a proper song, your grace. I was just playing."

The Maer raised an eyebrow. "It was of your own devising?" I nodded, and he motioned to me. "I'm sorry to have interrupted you. Please, continue."

"What would you like to hear, your grace?"

"I have it on good report that Meluan Lackless is fond of music and sweet words," he said. "Something along those lines."

"There are many types of sweet, your grace," I said. I played the opening to "Violet Bide." The notes rang out light and sweet and sad. Then I changed to "The Lay of Savien," my fingers moving quickly through the complex chording, making it sound every bit as hard as it was.

Alveron nodded to himself, his expression growing more satisfied as he listened. "And you can compose as well?"

I nodded easily. "I can, your grace. Though it takes time to do such things properly."

"How much time?"

I shrugged. "A day or two, or three. Depending on the sort of song you desire. Letters are easier."

The Maer leaned forward. "It pleases me that Threpe's praise was not exaggerated," he said. "I will admit I moved you to these rooms with more than gratitude in mind. A passage connects them to my own rooms. We will need to meet frequently in order to discuss my courting."

"It should prove most convenient, your grace," I said, then chose my next words carefully. "I've learned her family's history, but that will only go so far toward courting a woman."

Alveron chuckled. "You must take me for a fool," he said gently. "I know you'll need to meet her. She will be here in two days, visiting with a host of other nobility. I have declared a month of festivities to celebrate the passing of my long illness."

"Clever," I complimented him.

He shrugged. "I'll arrange something to bring the two of you together early on. Is there anything you require for the practice of your art?"

"A goodly amount of paper should suffice, your grace. Ink and pens."

"Nothing more than that? I've heard tell of poets who need certain extravagancies to aid them in their composition." He made an inarticulate gesture. "A specific type of drink or scenery? I've heard of a poet, quite famous in Renere, who has a trunk of rotting apples he keeps close at hand. Whenever his inspiration fails him, he opens it and breathes the fumes they emit."

I laughed. "I am a *musician*, your grace. Leave the poets to their superstitious bone rattling. All I need is my instrument, two good hands, and a knowledge of my subject."

The idea seemed to trouble Alveron. "Nothing to aid your inspiration?"

"I would have your leave to freely wander the estates and Severen-Low according to my will, your grace."

"Of course."

I gave an easy shrug. "In that case, I have everything I need for inspiration within easy reach."

I had barely set foot on Tinnery Street when I saw her. With all the fruitless searching I had done over the last several months, it seemed odd that I should find her so easily now.

Denna moved through the crowd with slow grace. Not the stiffness that passes for grace in courtly settings, but a natural leisure of movement. A cat does not think of stretching, it stretches. But a tree does not even do this. A tree simply sways without the effort of moving itself. That is how she moved.

I caught up to her as quickly as I could without attracting her attention. "Excuse me, miss?"

She turned. Her face brightened at the sight of me. "Yes?"

"I would never normally approach a woman in this way, but I couldn't help but notice that you have the eyes of a lady I was once desperately in love with."

"What a shame to love only once," she said, showing her white teeth in a wicked smile. "I've heard some men can manage twice or even more."

I ignored her gibe. "I am only a fool once. Never will I love again."

Her expression turned soft and she laid her hand lightly on my arm. "You poor man! She must have hurt you terribly."

"'Struth, she wounded me more ways than one."

"But such things are to be expected," she said matter-of-factly. "How could a woman help but love a man so striking as yourself?"

"I know not," I said modestly. "But I think she must not, for she caught me with an easy smile, then stole away without a word. Like dew in dawn's pale light."

"Like a dream upon waking," Denna added with a smile.

"Like a faerie maiden slipping through the trees."

Denna was silent for a moment. "She must have been wondrous indeed, to catch you so entire," she said, looking at me with serious eyes.

"She was beyond compare."

"Oh come now." Her manner changed to jovial. "We all know that when the lights are out all women are the same height!" She gave a rough chuckle and ribbed me knowingly with an elbow.

"Not true," I said with firm conviction.

"Well," she said slowly. "I guess I'll have to take your word for it." She looked back up at me. "Perhaps in time you can convince me."

I looked into the deep brown of her eyes. "That has ever been my hope."

Denna smiled and my heart stepped sideways in my chest. "Maintain it." She slid her arm inside the curve of mine and fell into step beside me. "For without hope what do any of us have?"

CHAPTER SIXTY-SEVEN

Telling Faces

I SPENT A FAIR PORTION of the next two days under Stapes' tutelage, ensuring I knew the proper etiquette for a formal dinner. I was already familiar with a great deal of it from my early childhood, but I was glad for the review. Customs differ from place to place and year to year, and even small missteps can lead to great embarrassment.

So Stapes conducted a dinner for just the two of us, then informed me of a dozen small but important mistakes I had made. Setting down a dirty utensil was considered crude, for example. That meant it was perfectly acceptable to lick one's knife clean. In fact, if you didn't want to dirty your napkin it was the only seemly thing to do.

It was improper to eat the entirety of a piece of bread. Some portion should always be left on the plate, preferably more than crust. The same was true of milk: the final swallow should always remain in the glass.

The next day Stapes staged another dinner and I made more mistakes. Commenting on the food wasn't rude, but it was rustic. The same was true of smelling the wine. And, apparently, the small soft cheese I'd been served possessed a rind. A rind any civilized person would have recognized as inedible and meant to be pared away.

Barbarian that I am, I had eaten all of it. It had tasted quite nice too. Still, I took note of this fact and resigned myself to throw away half of a perfectly good cheese if it was set in front of me. Such is the price of civilization.

I arrived for the banquet wearing a suit of clothes tailored just for the occasion. The colors were good for me, leaf green and black. There was too much brocade for my taste, but tonight I made a grudging bow to fashion as I would be seated to the left of Meluan Lackless.

Stapes had staged six formal dinners for me in the last three days, and I felt prepared for anything. When I arrived outside the banquet hall, I expected the hardest part of the evening would be feigning interest in the food.

But while I might have been prepared for the meal, I was not prepared for the sight of Meluan Lackless herself. Luckily, my stage training took hold and I moved smoothly through the ritual motion of smiling and offering my arm. She nodded courteously and we made our procession to the table together.

There were tall candelabra with dozens of candles. Engraved silver pitchers held hot water for handbowls and cold water for drinking glasses. Old vases with elaborate floral arrangements sweetened the air. Cornucopia overflowed with polished fruit. Personally, I found it gaudy. But it was traditional, a show-case for the wealth of the host.

I walked the Lady Lackless to the table and held out her chair. I had avoided looking in her direction as we walked the length of the room, but as I helped her into her seat, her profile struck me with such a strong resemblance that I couldn't help but stare. I knew her, I was certain of it. But I couldn't for the life of me remember where we might have met. . . .

As I took my seat, I tried to guess where I might have seen her before. If the Lackless lands weren't a thousand miles away, I would have thought I knew her from the University. But that was ridiculous. The Lackless heir wouldn't study so far from home.

My eyes wandered over maddeningly familiar features. Might I have met her at the Eolian? That didn't seem likely. I would have remembered. She was strikingly lovely, with a strong jaw and dark brown eyes. I'm sure if I'd seen her there . . .

"Do you see aught that interests you?" she asked without turning to look at me. Her tone was pleasant, but accusation lay not far beneath the surface.

I had been staring. Hardly a minute at table and I was already putting my elbow in the butter. "I beg your pardon. But I am a keen observer of faces, and yours struck me."

Meluan turned to look at me, her irritation fading a bit. "Are you a turagior?"

Turagiors claimed to be able to tell your personality or future from your face, eyes, and the shape of your head. Pure-blooded Vintic superstition. "I dabble a bit, m'lady."

"Really? What does my face tell you then?" She looked up and away from me.

I made a show of looking over Meluan's features, taking note of her pale skin and artfully curled chestnut hair. Her mouth was full and red without the benefit of any paint. The line of her neck was proud and graceful.

I nodded. "I can see a piece of your future in it, m'lady."

One of her eyebrows went up a bit. "Do tell."

"You will be receiving an apology shortly. Forgive my eyes, they flit like the calanthis, place to place. I could not keep them from your fair flower face."

Meluan smiled, but did not blush. Not immune to flattery, but no stranger to it either. I tucked that bit of information away. "That was a fairly easy fortune to tell," she said. "See you anything else?"

I took another moment to search her face. "Two other things, m'lady. It tells me you are Meluan Lackless, and that I am at your service."

She smiled and gave me her hand to kiss. I took hold of it and bowed my head over it. I didn't actually kiss it, as would have been proper back in the Commonwealth, instead I pressed my lips briefly onto my own thumb that held her hand. Actually kissing her hand would have been terribly forward in this part of the world.

Our banter was stalled by the arrival of the soups, forty servants placing them before forty guests all at once. I tasted mine. Why in God's name would anyone make a sweet soup?

I ate another spoonful and pretended to enjoy it. From the corner of my eye, I watched my neighbor, a tiny, older man I knew to be the Viceroy of Bannis. His face and hands were wrinkled and spotted, his hair a disarrayed tousle of grey. I watched him put a finger into his soup without a hint of self-consciousness, taste it, then push the bowl aside.

He rummaged in his pockets and opened his hand to show me what he'd found. "I always bring a pocket full of candy almonds to these things," he said in a conspiratorial whisper, his eyes as cunning as a child's. "You never know what they'll try to feed you." He held his hand out. "You can have one if you like."

I took one, thanked him, and faded from his awareness for the rest of the evening. When I glanced back several minutes later, he was eating unabashedly from his pocket and bickering with his wife about whether or not the peasantry could make bread from acorns. From the sound of it, I guessed it was a small piece of a larger argument that they had been having their entire lives.

To Meluan's right there was a Yllish couple, chatting away in their own lilting language. Combined with strategically placed decorations that made it difficult to see the guests on the other side of the table, Meluan and I were more alone than if we had been walking together in the gardens. The Maer had arranged his seating well.

The soup was taken away and replaced with a piece of meat I assumed was pheasant covered in a thick cream sauce. I was surprised to find it quite to my taste.

"So how do you think we came to be paired?" Meluan asked conversationally. "Mister . . ."

"Kvothe." I made a small seated bow. "It could be because the Maer wished you to be entertained, and I am at times entertaining."

"Quite."

"Or it could be I paid the steward an incredible sum of money." Her smile flickered again as she took a drink of water. *Enjoys boldness*, I thought to myself.

I wiped my fingers and almost set the napkin on the table, which would have been a terrible mistake. That was a signal to remove whatever course was currently being served. Done too soon, it implied a silent but scathing criticism of the host's hospitality. I felt a bead of sweat begin to trickle down my back between my shoulder blades as I deliberately folded the napkin and laid it on my lap.

"So how do you occupy yourself, Mr. Kvothe?"

She hadn't asked as to my employment, which meant she assumed I was a member of the nobility. Luckily, I'd already laid the groundwork for this. "I write a bit. Genealogies. A play or two. Do you enjoy the theater?"

"Occasionally. Depending."

"Depending on the play?"

"Depending on the performers," she said, an odd tension touching her voice.

I wouldn't have noticed it if I hadn't been watching her so closely. I decided to change the subject to safer ground.

"How did you find the roads on your way to Severen?" I asked. Everyone loves to complain about the roads. It's as safe a topic as the weather. "I heard there has been some difficulty with bandits to the north." I hoped to excite the conversation a little. The more she talked, the better I could get to know her.

"The roads are always thick with Ruh bandits this time of year," Meluan said coldly.

Not just bandits, *Ruh* bandits. She said the word with such a weight of cold loathing in her voice that I was chilled to hear it. She hated the Ruh. Not the simple distaste most people feel for us, but a true, sharp hate with teeth in it.

I was saved from making a response by the arrival of chilled fruit pastries.

To my left the viceroy argued acorns to his wife. To my right, Meluan slowly tore a strawberry pastry in half, her face pale as an ivory mask. Watching her flawless polished nails tear the pastry into pieces, I knew her thoughts were dwelling on the Ruh.

Aside from her brief mention of the Edema Ruh, the evening went quite well. I slowly set Meluan at her ease, talking casually of small things. The elaborate dinner lasted two hours, giving us ample time for discussion. I found her to be everything Alveron had suggested: intelligent, attractive, and well-spoken. Even the knowledge that she loathed the Ruh could not entirely keep me from enjoying her company.

I returned to my room immediately after dinner and began to write. By the time the Maer came to call I had three drafts of a letter, an outline of a song, and five sheets filled with notes and phrases I hoped to use later.

"Come in, your grace." I glanced up as he entered. He hardly seemed the same sickly, doddering man I'd nursed back to health. He'd put on some weight and looked five years younger.

"What did you think of her?" Alveron said. "Did she mention any suitors when you spoke?"

"No, your grace," I said, handing him a folded piece of paper. "Here is the first letter you will want to send to her. I trust you can find a way of delivering it to her secretly?"

He unfolded it and began to read, his lips moving silently. I labored out another line of song, scratching out the chording alongside the words.

Eventually the Maer looked up. "Don't you think this is a little much?" he said uncomfortably.

"No." I paused in my writing long enough to gesture with my pen toward a different piece of paper. "*That* one is too much. The one in your hand is just enough. She's got a streak of romance in her. She wants to be swept from her feet, though she'd probably deny it."

The Maer's expression was still doubtful so I pushed myself away from the table and set down my quill. "Your grace, you were right. She is a woman well worthy of pursuit. In a handful of days there will be a dozen men in the estates who would gladly take her to wife, am I right?"

"There are already a dozen here," he said grimly. "Soon there will be three dozen."

"Add another dozen she will meet at dinner or walking in the garden. Then another dozen who will court her merely for the chase. Of those dozens, how many will write her letters and poems? They will send her flowers, trinkets, tokens of affection. Soon she will be receiving a deluge of attention. You have one, best hope."

I pointed to the letter. "Act quickly. That letter will catch her imagination, her curiosity. In a day or two, when the other notes are cluttering her desk, she will already be awaiting the second one of ours."

He seemed to hesitate a moment, then his shoulders bowed. "Are you sure?"

I shook my head. "There are no certainties in this, your grace. Only hopes. That is the best one I can give you."

Alveron hesitated. "I know nothing of this," he said with a hint of petulance. "I wish there were some book of rules a man could follow." For a moment he looked very much like an ordinary man and very little like the Maer Alveron at all.

Truthfully, I was more than slightly concerned myself. What I personally knew about courting women could comfortably fit into a thimble without taking it off your finger first.

On the other hand, I had a vast wealth of secondary knowledge. Ten thousand romantic songs, plays, and stories taken all together had to be worth something. And on the negative side, I'd seen Simmon pursue nearly every woman within three miles of the University with the doomed enthusiasm of a child trying to fly. What's more, I had watched a hundred men dash themselves to pieces against Denna like ships attempting to ignore the tide.

Alveron looked at me, his face still showing honest concern. "Will a month be enough time, do you think?"

When I spoke, I was surprised by the confidence in my own voice. "Your grace, if I cannot help you catch her in the space of a month, then it cannot be done."

CHAPTER SIXTY-EIGHT

The Cost of a Loaf

THE DAYS THAT FOLLOWED were pleasant ones. My sunlight hours were spent with Denna in Severen-Low, exploring the city and surrounding countryside. We spent time riding, swimming, singing, or simply talking the afternoons away. I flattered her outrageously and without hope, because only a fool would hope to catch her.

Then I would return to my rooms and pen the letter that had been building inside me all day. Or I would pour out a torrent of song to her. And in that letter or song I said all the things I hadn't dared to tell Denna during the day. Things I knew would only frighten her away.

After I finished the letter or the song, I would write it again. I would dull its edges a little, remove an honesty or two. I slowly smoothed and stitched until it fit Meluan Lackless as snugly as a calfskin glove.

It was idyllic. I had better luck finding Denna in Severen than I ever had in Imre. We met for hours at a stretch, sometimes more than once a day, sometimes three or four days in a row.

Though, in the interest of honesty, things were not perfect. There were a few burrs in the blanket, as my father used to say.

The first was a young gentleman named Gerred who accompanied Denna on one of our early meetings down in Severen-Low. He didn't know her as Denna, of course. He called her Alora, and so did I for the rest of the day.

Gerred's face held the doomed expression I had come to know very well. He had known Denna long enough to fall for her, and he was just beginning to realize his time was drawing to an end.

I watched as he made the same mistakes I'd seen others make before him. He put his arm around her possessively. He gave her the gift of a ring. As we strolled the city, if her eye focused on anything for more than three seconds he offered to buy it for her. He tried to pin her down with a promise of some future meeting. A dance at the DeFerre's manse? Dinner at the Golden Board? *The Tenpenny King* was being performed tomorrow by Count Abelard's men. . . ?

Individually, any of these things would have been fine. Perhaps even charming. But taken together they showed themselves as pure, white-knuckled desperation. He clutched at Denna as if he were a drowning man and she a plank of wood.

He glared at me when she wasn't watching, and when Denna bid the two of us good-bye that evening, his face was drawn and white as if he were already two days dead.

The second burr was worse. After I'd been helping the Maer court his lady for almost two span, Denna disappeared. No trace or word of warning. No note of farewell or apology. I waited for three hours at the livery where we'd agreed to meet. After that I went to her inn, only to find that she had left with all her things the night before.

I went to the park where we had taken lunch the previous day, then to a dozen other places where we'd made a habit of each other's company. It was near midnight by the time I took the lifts back to the top of the Sheer. Even then some foolish part of me hoped she would greet me at the top, rushing into my arms again with her wild enthusiasm.

But she wasn't there. That night I wrote no letter or song for Meluan.

The second day I ghosted through Severen-Low for hours, worried and wounded. Later that night in my rooms, I sweat and cursed and crumpled my way through twenty sheets of paper before I arrived at three brief, half-tolerable paragraphs which I gave to the Maer to do with as he wished.

The third day my heart sat like a stone in my chest. I tried to finish the song I'd been writing for the Maer, but nothing worthwhile came of my efforts. For the first hour the notes I played were leaden and lifeless. The second hour they grew discordant and faltering. I pressed on until every sound my lute made grated like a knife against teeth.

I finally let my poor, tortured lute fall silent, remembering something my father had said long ago: "Songs choose their hour and their own season. When your tune's tin, there is a reason. The tone of a tune is your heart's mettle, and there's no clear water from a muddy well. All you can do is let the silt settle, or you'll sound sour as a broken bell."

I lowered my lute into its case, knowing the truth of it. I needed a few days before I could productively return to courting Meluan on the Maer's behalf. The work was too delicate to force or fake.

On the other hand, I knew the Maer would not be pleased with a delay.

I needed a diversion, and since the Maer was too clever by half, it needed to be at least halfway legitimate.

———————

I heard the telltale sigh of air that signaled the Maer's secret passage opening in my dressing room. I made sure I was pacing anxiously by the time he came through the doorway.

Alveron had continued to put on weight in the last two span, and his face was no longer hollow and drawn. He cut quite a figure in his finery, a creamy ivory shirt and stiff jacket of deep sapphire blue. "I got your message," he said brusquely. "Have you finished the song then?"

I turned to face him. "No, your grace. Something more important than the song has come to my attention."

"As far as you are concerned, there is nothing more important than the song," the Maer said firmly, tugging the cuff of his shirt to straighten it. "I've heard from several people that Meluan was greatly pleased with the first two. You should focus the whole of your efforts in that direction."

"Your grace, I am well aware that—"

"Out with it," Alveron said impatiently, glancing at the face of the tall gear-clock that stood in the corner of the room. "I have appointments to keep."

"Your life is in further danger from Caudicus."

I'll give this to the Maer, he could have made his living on the stage. The only break in his composure was a brief hesitation as he tugged his other cuff into place. "And how is that?" he asked, apparently unconcerned.

"There are ways for him to harm you other than poison. Things that can be done from a distance."

"A spell, you mean," Alveron said. "He means to conjure up a sending and set it to bedevil me?"

Tehlu anyway, spells and sendings. It was easy to forget this intelligent, subtle, and otherwise educated man was little better than a child when it came to arcane matters. He probably believed in faeries and the walking dead. Poor fool.

However, attempting to reeducate him would be tiresome and counterproductive. "There is a chance of that, your grace. As well as other, more direct threats."

He dropped some of his unconcerned pose and looked me in the eye. "What could be more direct than a sending?"

The Maer was not the sort of man to be moved through words alone, so I picked up an apple from a bowl of fruit and polished it on my sleeve before handing it to him. "Would you hold this for a moment, your grace?"

He took it, suspiciously. "What's this about then?"

I walked over to where my lovely burgundy cloak hung on the wall, and retrieved a needle from one of its many pockets. "I'm showing you the sort of thing Caudicus is capable of, your grace." I held out my hand for the apple.

He gave it back and I looked it over. Holding it at an angle to the light, I saw what I'd hoped for, smudged onto the glossy skin of the apple. I muttered a binding, focused my Alar, and pushed the needle into the center of the blurry imprint his forefinger had made on the apple's skin.

Alveron twitched and made an inarticulate noise of surprise, staring at his hand as if it had been unexpectedly, say, pricked with a pin.

I'd half-expected him to rebuke me, but he did nothing of the sort. His eyes went wide, his face pale. Then his expression grew thoughtful as he watched the bead of blood swell on the pad of his finger.

He licked his lips and slowly put his finger into his mouth. "I see," he said quietly. "Such things can be guarded against?" It wasn't really a question.

I nodded, keeping my expression grave. "Somewhat, your grace. I believe I can create a . . . a charm to protect you. I only regret I didn't think of this sooner, but with one thing and another—"

"Yes, yes." The Maer waved me into silence. "And what will you require for such a charm?"

It was a layered question. On the surface he was asking what materials I would need. But the Maer was a practical man. He was asking me my price as well.

"The workshop in Caudicus' tower should have the equipment I need, your grace. What materials he doesn't have on hand, I should be able to find in Severen, given time."

Then I paused, considering the second portion of his question, thinking of the hundred things the Maer could grant me: money enough to swim in, a newly crafted lute of the sort only kings could afford. I felt a shock run through me at the thought. An Antressor lute. I'd never even seen one, but my father had. He'd played one once in Anilin, and sometimes when he'd had a cup of wine he would talk about it, his hands making gentle shapes in the air.

The Maer could arrange this sort of thing in the blink of an eye.

All that and more, of course. Alveron could arrange access to a hundred private libraries. A formal patronage would be no small thing either, coming from him. The Maer's name would open doors as quickly as the king's.

"There are a few things," I said slowly. "That I have been hoping to discuss with your grace. I have a project I need assistance to pursue properly. And I have a friend, a talented musician, who could use a well-placed patron. . . ." I trailed off meaningfully.

Alveron nodded, his grey eyes showing he understood. The Maer was no fool. He knew the cost of a loaf. "I'll have Stapes get you the keys to Caudicus' tower," he said. "How long will this charm take to produce?"

I paused as if considering. "At least four days, your grace." That would give me time for the muddy waters of my creative well to clear. Or time for Denna to return from whatever errand had pulled her suddenly away. "If I was sure of his equipment, it could be sooner, but I will have to move carefully. I don't know what Caudicus might have done to foul things before he fled."

Alveron frowned at this. "Will you be able to continue your current projects as well?"

"No your grace. It will be rather exhausting and time-consuming. Especially since I'm assuming you'd prefer I be circumspect while gathering my materials in Severen-Low?"

"Yes of course." He exhaled hard through his nose. "Damn and bother, things were going so well. Who can I bring in to write letters while you're occupied?" He said the last musingly, mostly to himself.

I needed to nip that thought in the bud. I did not want to share credit for Meluan's courtship with anyone. "I don't think that will be necessary, your grace. Seven or eight days ago, perhaps. But now, as you say, we have her interest. She is excited, eager for the next contact. If a few days pass with nothing from us, she will be disappointed. But more importantly, she will be anxious for the return of your attention."

The Maer smoothed his beard with one hand, his expression pensive. I considered making a comparison to playing a fish on a line, but I doubted the Maer had ever engaged in anything so rustic as fishing. "Not to presume, your grace. But in your younger days, did you ever attempt to win the affection of a young lady?"

Alveron smiled at my careful phrasing. "You may presume."

"Which did you find more interesting? The ones who leapt to your arms straightaway, or those who were more difficult, reluctant, even indifferent to your pursuit?" The Maer's eyes were far away with remembering. "The same is true of women. Some cannot bear it when a man clings to them. And they all appreciate space to make their own choices. It's hard to long for something that is always there."

Alveron nodded. "There is some truth in that. Absence feeds affection." He nodded more firmly. "Very well. Three days." He glanced at the gear clock again. "And now I must be—"

"One final thing, your grace," I said quickly. "The charm I will make must be tuned specifically to you. It will require some of your cooperation."

I cleared my throat. "More precisely, some of your . . ." I cleared my throat. "Substance."

"Speak plainly."

"A small amount of blood, saliva, skin, hair, and urine." I sighed internally, knowing that to someone of the superstitious Vintic mind-set, this would sound like a recipe for a sending or some other equally ridiculous thing.

As I'd expected, the Maer's eyes narrowed at the list. "While I am no expert," he said slowly, "those seem to be the very things I should avoid parting with. How can I trust you?"

I could have protested my loyalty, pointed out my past service, or brought to his attention that I'd already saved his life. But over the last month I'd come to know how the Maer's mind worked.

I gave him my best knowing smile. "You are an intelligent man, your grace. I'm sure you know the answer without my telling you."

He returned my smile. "Humor me, then."

I shrugged. "You're of no use to me if you're dead, your grace."

His grey eyes searched mine for a moment, then nodded, satisfied. "Very true. Send a message when you need those things." He turned to leave. "Three days."

CHAPTER SIXTY-NINE

Such Madness

I MADE SEVERAL TRIPS TO Severen-Low to gather materials for Alveron's gram. Raw gold. Nickel and iron. Coal and etching acids. I acquired the money for these purchases by selling off various pieces of equipment from Caudicus' workshop. I could have asked the Maer for money, but I'd rather he thought of me as independently resourceful rather than an ongoing financial drain.

Quite by coincidence, in the course of this buying and selling, I visited many of the places Denna and I had spent time together.

I'd grown so accustomed to finding her that now I caught glimpses of her when she wasn't there. Every day my hopeful heart rose at the sight of her turning a corner, stepping into a cobbler's, raising her hand to wave from across a courtyard. But it was never truly her, and I returned to the Maer's estate each evening more desolate than the day before.

Making things worse was the fact that Bredon had left Severen several days ago to visit some nearby relatives. I didn't realize how much I'd come to depend on him until he was gone.

As I've already said, a gram is not particularly difficult to make if you have the proper equipment, a schema, and an Alar like a blade of Ramston steel. The metalworking tools in Caudicus' tower were serviceable, though nowhere near as nice as those in the Fishery. The schema was no difficulty either, as I have a good memory for such things.

While I was working on the Maer's gram, I started a second one to replace the one I'd lost. Unfortunately, given the relatively crude nature of the equipment I was working with, I didn't have time to finish it properly.

I finished the Maer's gram three days after talking to the Maer, six days after Denna's sudden disappearance. The following day I abandoned my pointless searching and planted myself in one of the open air-cafés where I drank coffee and tried to find inspiration for the song I owed the Maer. Ten hours I spent there, and the only act of creation I accomplished was to magically transform nearly a gallon of coffee into marvelous, aromatic piss.

That night I drank an unwise amount of scutten and fell asleep at my writing desk. Meluan's song was still unfinished. The Maer was less than pleased.

Denna reappeared on the seventh day as I wandered our haunts in Severen-Low. Despite all my searching, she saw me first and ran laughing to my side, excited to tell me about a song she'd heard the day before. We spent the day together as easily as if she'd never left.

I didn't ask her about her unexplained disappearance. I'd known Denna for more than a year now, and I understood a few of the hidden turnings of her heart. I knew she valued her privacy. I knew she had secrets.

That night, we were in a small garden that ran along the very edge of the Sheer. We sat on a wooden bench looking out over the dark city below: a messy splay of lamplight, streetlight, gaslight, with a few rare sharp points of sympathy light scattered throughout.

"I am sorry, you know," she said softly.

We'd been sitting, quietly watching the lights of the city for nearly a quarter hour. If she was continuing some previous conversation, I couldn't remember what it was. "Beg pardon?"

When Denna didn't say anything immediately, I turned to look at her. There was no moon, and the night was dark. Her face was dimly illuminated by the thousand lights below.

"Sometimes I leave," she said at last. "Quick and quiet in the night."

Denna didn't look at me as she spoke, keeping her dark eyes fixed on the city below. "It's what I do," she continued, her voice quiet. "I leave. No word or warning first. No explanation after. Sometimes it's the only thing that I can do."

She turned to meet my eyes then, her face serious in the dim light. "I hope you know without my telling you," she said. "I hope I don't need to say it. . . ."

Denna turned back to look at the glimmering lights below. "But for what it's worth, I am sorry."

We sat for a while then, enjoying a comfortable silence. I wanted to say something. I wanted to say it didn't bother me, but that would be a lie. I wanted to tell her all that really mattered to me was that she came back, but I was worried that might be too much truth.

So rather that risk saying the wrong thing, I said nothing. I knew what happened to the men who clung to her too tightly. That was the difference between me and the others. I did not clutch at her, try to own her. I did not slip my arm around her, murmur in her ear, or kiss her unsuspecting cheek.

Certainly, I thought of it. I still remembered the warmth of her when she had thrown her arms around me near the horse lift. There were times I would have given my right hand to hold her again.

But then I thought of the faces of the other men when they realized Denna was leaving them. I thought of all the others who had tried to tie her to the ground and failed. So I resisted showing her the songs and poems I had written, knowing that too much truth can ruin a thing.

And if that meant she wasn't entirely mine, what of it? I would be the one she could always return to without fear of recrimination or question. So I did not try to win her and contented myself with playing a beautiful game.

But there was always a part of me that hoped for more, and so there was a part of me that was always a fool.

———

Days passed, and Denna and I explored the streets of Severen. We lounged in cafés, attended plays, went riding. We climbed the face of the Sheer using the low road just to say we'd done it. We visited the dock markets, a traveling menagerie, and several curiosity cabinets.

Some days we did nothing but sit and talk, and on those days, nothing filled our conversations as much as music.

We spent countless hours discussing the craft of it. How songs fit together. How chorus and verse play against each other, about tone and mode and meter.

These were things I'd learned at an early age and thought about often. And though Denna was new to this study, in some ways that worked to her advantage. I'd learned about music since before I could talk. I knew ten thousand rules of melody and verse better than I knew the backs of my own hands.

Denna didn't. In some ways this hampered her, but in other ways it made her music strange and marvelous. . . .

I'm doing a poor job of explaining this. Think of music as being a great snarl of a city like Tarbean. In the years I spent living there, I came to know its streets. Not just the main streets. Not just the alleys. I knew shortcuts and rooftops and parts of the sewers. Because of this, I could move through the city like a rabbit in a bramble. I was quick and cunning and clever.

Denna, on the other hand, had never been trained. She knew nothing of shortcuts. You'd think she'd be forced to wander the city, lost and helpless, trapped in a twisting maze of mortared stone.

But instead, she simply walked through the walls. She didn't know any better. Nobody had ever told her she couldn't. Because of this, she moved through the city like some faerie creature. She walked roads no one else could see, and it made her music wild and strange and free.

———

In the end it took twenty-three letters, six songs, and, though it shames me to say it, one poem.

There was more to it than that, of course. Letters alone cannot win a woman's heart. Alveron did a fair piece of his own courting. And after he revealed himself as Meluan's anonymous suitor, he did the lion's share of the work, slowly wooing Meluan to his side with the gentle reverence he felt for her.

But my letters caught her attention. My songs brought her close enough for Alveron to work his slow, garrulous charm.

Even so, I can take only a small piece of credit for the letters and songs. And as for the poem, there is only one thing in the world that could move me to such madness.

CHAPTER SEVENTY

Clinging

I MET DENNA OUTSIDE HER inn on Chalker's Lane, a little place called the Four Tapers. As I turned the corner and saw her standing in the light cast by a lantern hanging above the front door, I felt an upwelling of joy at the simple pleasure of being able to find her when I went looking.

"I got your note," I said. "Imagine my delight."

Denna smiled and made a one-handed curtsey. She was wearing a skirt, not a complicated dress of the sort a noblewoman would wear, but a simple sweep of fabric you could wear while bucking hay or going to a barn dance. "I wasn't sure you would be able to make it," she said. "It being past the hour most civilized folk have taken to their beds."

"I'll admit I was surprised," I said. "If I was the sort of man to pry, I would wonder what kept you occupied until this most unseemly hour."

"Business," she said with a dramatic sigh. "A meeting with my patron."

"He's in town again?" I asked.

She nodded.

"And he wanted to meet you at midnight?" I asked. "That's . . . odd."

Denna stepped out from under the inn's sign and we began to walk down the street together. "The hand that holds the purse . . ." she said, giving a helpless shrug. "Odd times and inconvenient places are the rule with Master Ash. Some part of me suspects he might simply be some lonely noble, bored with ordinary patronage. I wonder if it adds some spice for him, pretending he's meshed in some dark intrigue instead of just commissioning some songs from me."

"So what do you have planned for tonight?" I asked.

"Only to pass time in your lovely company," Denna said, reaching out and linking her arm with mine.

"In that case," I said, "I have something to show you. It's a surprise. You'll have to trust me."

"I've heard each of those a dozen times." Denna's dark eyes glittered wickedly. "But never all together, and never from you." She smiled. "I'll give you the benefit of the doubt and save my world-weary gibes for later. Take me where you will."

So we made our way to Severen-High by way of the horse lifts, where we both gawked at the lights of the nighttime city below like the lowborn cretins we were. I took her on a long stroll through cobblestone streets, past shops and small gardens. Then we left the buildings behind, climbed over a low wooden fence, and moved toward the dark shape of an empty barn.

At this, Denna was no longer able to keep quiet. "Well, you've done it," she said. "You've surprised me."

I grinned at her and continued to lead the way into the dark of the barn. It was full of the smell of hay and absent animals. I led her to a ladder that disappeared into the dark above our heads.

"A hayloft?" she demanded, her voice incredulous. She stopped walking and gave me an odd, curious look. "You obviously have me mistaken for a fourteen-year-old farm girl named . . ." Her mouth worked soundlessly for a moment. "Something rustic."

"Gretta," I suggested.

"Yes," she said. "You obviously have me mistaken for a low-bodiced farm girl named Gretta."

"Rest assured," I said. "If I were going to try to seduce you, this isn't the way I would go about it."

"Is that so?" she said, running her hand through her hair. Her fingers began to idly twine her hair into a braid, then she stopped and brushed it out. "In that case, what are we doing here?"

"You mentioned how much you enjoyed gardens," I said. "And Alveron's gardens are particularly fine. I thought you might enjoy a turn about the place."

"In the middle of the night," Denna said.

"A charming moonlit stroll," I corrected.

"There's no moon tonight," she pointed out. "Or if there is, it's barely a slender sliver."

"Be that as it may," I said, refusing to be daunted. "How much moonlight does one actually need to enjoy the smell of gently blooming jasmine?"

"In the hayloft," Denna said, her voice thick with disbelief.

"The hayloft is the easiest way onto the roof," I said. "Thence into the Maer's estates. Thence to the garden."

"If you're in the Maer's employ," she said, "why not simply ask him to let you in?"

"Ah," I said dramatically, holding up a finger. "Therein lies the adventure. There are a hundred men who could simply *take* you strolling in the Maer's the gardens. But there is only one who can sneak you in." I smiled at her. "What I'm offering you, Denna, is a singular opportunity."

She grinned at me. "You know my secret heart so well."

I extended my hand as if I were about to assist her into a carriage. "M'lady."

Denna took my hand, then stopped as soon as she put her foot onto the first rung of the ladder. "Hold on, you aren't being genteel. You're trying to get a look up my dress."

I gave her my best offended look, pressing my hand to my chest. "Lady, as a gentleman I assure you—"

She swatted at me. "You've already told me you're not a gentleman," she said. "You're a thief, and you're trying to steal a look." She stepped back and made a parody of my courtly gesture of a moment before. "M'lord . . ."

We made our way through the hayloft, onto the roof, and into the garden. The sharp sliver of moon above us was thin as a whisper, so pale that it did nothing to dim the light of the stars.

The gardens were surprisingly quiet for such a warm and lovely night. Ordinarily even at this late hour couples would be strolling the paths, or murmuring to each other on the bower benches. I wondered if some ball or courtly function had pulled them all away.

The Maer's gardens were vast, with curving paths and cunningly placed hedges making them seem larger still. Denna and I walked side by side, listening to the sigh of the wind through the leaves. It was like we were the only people in the world.

"I don't know if you remember," I said softly, not wanting to intrude upon the silence. "A conversation we had some time ago. We talked of flowers."

"I remember," she said just as softly.

"You said you thought all men had got their lessons in courting from the same worn book."

Denna laughed quietly, more a motion than a sound. She put her hand to her mouth. "Oh. I'd forgotten. I did say that, didn't I? "

I nodded. "You said they all brought you roses."

"They still do," she said. "I wish they would find a new book."

"You made me pick a flower that would suit you better," I said.

She smiled up at me shyly. "I remember, I was testing you." Then she frowned. "But you got the better of me by picking one I'd never heard of, let alone seen."

We turned a corner and the path led toward the dark green tunnel of an arching bower. "I don't know if you've seen them yet," I said. "But here is your selas flower."

There were only stars lighting our way. The moon so slender it was almost no moon at all. Under the trellis it was dark as Denna's hair.

Our eyes were wide and stretching to the dark, and where the starlight slanted through the leaves, they showed hundreds of selas blossoms yawning open in the night. If the scent of selas were not so delicate, it would have been overpowering.

"Oh," Denna sighed, looking around with wide eyes. Under the bower, her skin was brighter than the moon. She reached out her hands to both sides. "They're so soft!"

We walked in silence. All around us selas vines wove themselves around the trellis, clinging to the wood and wire, hiding their faces from the night-time sky. When eventually we came out the other side, it seemed as bright as daylight.

The silence stretched until I started to grow uncomfortable. "So now you know your flower," I said. "It seemed a shame you'd never seen one. They're rather difficult to cultivate, from what I've heard."

"Perhaps they do suit me then," Denna said softly, looking down. "I don't take root easily."

We continued walking until the path turned and hid the bower behind us.

"You treat me better than I deserve," Denna said at last.

I laughed at the ridiculousness of that. Only respect for the silence of the garden kept it from rolling out of me in a great booming laugh. Instead I stifled it as much as possible, though the effort threw me off my stride and made me stumble.

Denna watched me from a step away, a smile spreading across her mouth.

Eventually I caught my breath. "You who sang with me the night I won my pipes. You who have given me the finest gift I ever did receive." A thought occurred to me. "Did you know," I said, "that your lute case saved my life?"

The smile spread and grew, wide as a flower. "Did it now?"

"It did," I said. "I cannot ever hope to treat you as well as you deserve. Given what I owe you, this is but the smallest payment."

"Well, I think it is a lovely start." She looked up at the sky and drew a long, deep breath. "I've always liked moonless nights best. It's easier to say things in the dark. It's easier to be yourself."

She began walking again and I fell into step beside her. We passed a fountain, a pool, a wall of pale jasmine open to the night. We crossed a small stone bridge that led us back among the shelter of the hedges.

"You could put your arm around me, you know," she said matter-of-factly. "We are walking in the gardens, alone. In the moonlight, such as it is." Denna looked sideways at me, the side of her mouth quirking upward. "Such things are permitted, you realize."

Her sudden change in manner caught me off my guard. Since we had met in Severen I had courted her with wild, hopeless pageantry, and she had matched me without missing a beat. Each flattery, each witticism, each piece of playful banter she returned to me, not in an echo but a harmony. Our back-and-forth had been like a duet.

But this was different. Her tone was less playful and more plain. It was so sudden a change that I was at a loss for words.

"Four days ago I turned my foot on that loose flagstone," she said softly. "Remember? We were walking on Mincet Lane. My foot slipped and you caught me almost before I knew that I was stumbling. It made me wonder how closely you must be watching me to see something like that."

We turned a corner in the path, and Denna continued to speak without looking up at me. Her voice was soft and musing, almost as if she were talking to herself. "You had your hands on me then, sure as anything, steadying me. You almost had your arm around me. It would have been so easy for you then. A matter of inches. But when I got my feet beneath me, you took your hands away. No hesitation. No lingering. Nothing I might take amiss."

She started to turn her face to me, then stopped and looked down again. "It's quite a thing," she said. "There are so many men, all endlessly attempting to sweep me off my feet. And there is one of you, trying just the opposite. Making sure my feet are firm beneath me, lest I fall."

Almost shyly, she reached out. "When I move to take your arm, you accept it easily. You even lay your hand on mine, as if to keep it there." She explained my movement exactly as I was making it, and I fought to keep the gesture from becoming suddenly awkward. "But that's all. You never presume. You never push. Do you know how strange that is to me?"

We looked at each other for a moment, there, in the silent moonlight garden. I could feel the heat of her standing close to me, her hand clinging to my arm.

Inexperienced as I was with women, even I could read this cue. I tried to think of what to say, but I could only wonder at her lips. How could they be so red as this? Even the selas was dark in the faint moonlight. How were her lips so red?

Then Denna froze. Not that we were moving much, but in a moment she went from motionless to still, cocking her head like a deer straining to catch a half-heard sound. "Someone's coming," she said. "Come *on*." Clinging to my arm, she pulled me off the path, over a stone bench, and through a low, narrow gap in the hedges.

We finally came to rest in the center of some thick bushes. There was a convenient hollow where we both had room to crouch. Thanks to the work of the gardeners there was no undergrowth to speak of, no dry leaves or twigs to crackle or snap under our hands and knees. In fact, the grass in this sheltered place was thick and soft as any lawn.

"There are a thousand girls who could walk with you along the moonlit garden paths," Denna said breathlessly. "But there's only one who'll hide in the shrubbery with you." She grinned at me, her voice bubbling with amusement.

Denna peered out of the hedge toward the path, and I looked at her. Her hair fell like a curtain down the side of her head, and the tip of her ear was peeking out through it. It was, at that moment, the most lovely thing that I had ever seen.

Then I heard the faint grit of footsteps on the path. The soft sound of voices came sifting through the hedge, a man and a woman. After a moment they came walking around the corner, arm in arm. I recognized them immediately.

I turned and leaned close, breathing softly into Denna's ear. "That's the Maer," I said. "And his young ladylove."

Denna shivered, and I shrugged out of my burgundy cloak, draping it over her shoulders.

I peered back out at the two of them. As I watched, Meluan laughed at something he said and rested her hand atop his on her arm. I doubted he'd have much more need of my services if they were already on such familiar terms as that.

"Not for you, my dear," I heard the Maer say clearly as they passed near us. "You shall have nothing but roses."

Denna turned to look at me, her eyes wide. She pressed both her hands against her mouth to stifle her laugher.

In another moment they were past us, strolling slowly along, walking in step. Denna removed her hands and took several deep, shuddering breaths. "He has a copy of the same worn book," she said, her eyes dancing.

I couldn't help but smile. "Apparently."

"So that's the Maer," she said quietly, her dark eyes peering between the leaves. "He's shorter than I imagined."

"Would you like to meet him?" I asked. "I could introduce you."

"Oh that would be lovely," she said with a gentle edge of mockery. She chuckled, but when I didn't join her laughter, she looked up at me and stopped. "You're serious?" She cocked her head to one side, her expression trapped between amusement and confusion.

"We probably shouldn't burst out of the hedge at him," I admitted. "But we could come out on the other side and loop around to meet him." I gestured with my hand at the route we could take. "I'm not saying he'll invite us to dinner or anything. But we can make a polite nod as we pass him on the path."

Denna continued to stare at me, her eyebrows furrowing in the faint beginning of a frown. "You're serious," she repeated.

"What do you . . ." I stopped as I realized what her expression meant. "You thought I was lying about working for the Maer," I said. "You thought I was lying about being able to invite you in here."

"Men tell stories," she said dismissively. "They like to brag a bit. I didn't think any less of you for telling me a bit of a tall tale."

"I wouldn't lie to you," I said, then reconsidered. "No, that's not the truth. I would. You're worth lying for. But I wasn't. You're worth telling the truth for too."

Denna gave me fond smile. "That's harder to come by anyway."

"So would you like to?" I asked. "Meet him, I mean?"

She looked out of the hedge toward the path. "No." When she shook her head her hair moved like drifting shadows. "I believe you. There's no need." She looked down. "Besides, I've got grass stains on my dress. What would he think?"

"I've got leaves in my hair," I admitted. "I know exactly what he would think."

We stepped out from the hedge. I picked the leaves out of my hair and Denna brushed her hands down the front of her skirt, wincing a bit as she moved over the grass stains.

We made our way back onto the path and started walking again. I thought of putting my arm around her, but didn't. I was no good judge of these things, but it seemed the moment had passed.

Denna looked up as we passed a statue of a woman picking a flower. She sighed. "It was more exciting when I didn't know I had permission," she admitted with a little regret in her voice.

"It always is," I agreed.

CHAPTER SEVENTY-ONE

Interlude—The Thrice-locked Chest

KVOTHE RAISED HIS HAND, motioning Chronicler to stop. The scribe wiped the nib of his pen on a nearby cloth and rolled his shoulder stiffly. Wordlessly, Kvothe brought out a worn deck of cards and began to deal them around the table. Bast picked up his cards and looked them over curiously.

Chronicler frowned. "What—"

Footsteps sounded on the wooden landing outside, and the door to the Waystone Inn opened, revealing a bald, thick-bodied man wearing an embroidered jacket.

"Mayor Lant!" the innkeeper said, putting down his cards and getting to his feet. "What can I do for you? A drink? A bite to eat?"

"A glass of wine would be quite welcome," the mayor said as he moved into the room. "Do you have any red Gremsby in?"

The innkeeper shook his head. "I'm afraid not," he said. "The roads, you know. It's hard to keep things in stock."

The mayor nodded. "I'll take anything red then," he said. "But I won't pay more than a penny for it, mind you."

"Of course not, sir," the innkeeper said solicitously, wringing his hands a bit. "Anything to eat?"

"No," the bald man said. "I'm actually here to make use of the scribe. I thought I'd wait until things quieted down a bit, so we could have some privacy." He looked around the empty room. "I don't imagine you'd mind my borrowing the place for half an hour, would you?"

"Not at all." The innkeeper smiled ingratiatingly. He made a shooing motion to Bast.

"But I had a full board!" Bast protested, waving his cards.

The innkeeper frowned at his assistant, then headed back into the kitchen.

The mayor removed his jacket and laid it across the back of a chair while Bast gathered up the rest of the cards, grumbling.

The innkeeper brought out a glass of red wine, then locked the front door with a large brass key. "I'll take the boy upstairs with me," he said to the mayor, "to give you some privacy."

"That's exceedingly kind of you," the mayor said as he sat across from Chronicler. "I'll give a shout when I'm finished."

The innkeeper nodded and herded Bast out of the common room and up the stairs. Kvothe opened the door to his room and gestured Bast inside.

"I wonder what old Lant wants to keep secret," Kvothe said as soon as the door was closed behind them. "I hope he's not too long about it."

"He's got two children by the Widow Creel," Bast said matter-of-factly.

Kvothe raised an eyebrow at that. "Really?"

Bast shrugged. "Everyone in town knows."

Kvothe *humphed* at this as he settled down into a large upholstered chair. "What are we going to do with ourselves for half an hour?" he asked.

"It's been ages since we've had lessons." Bast pulled a wooden chair away from the small desk and sat on the edge of it. "You could teach me something."

"Lessons," Kvothe mused. "You could read *Celum Tinture*."

"Reshi," Bast said imploringly. "It's so *boring*. I don't mind lessons, but do they need to be book lessons?"

Bast's tone wrung a smile from Kvothe. "A puzzle lesson then?" Bast's face broke into a grin. "Very well, let me think for a second." He tapped his fingers against his lips and let his eyes wander the room. It wasn't long before they were drawn to the foot of the bed where the dark chest lay.

He made a casual gesture. "How would you open my chest if you had a mind to?"

Bast's expression grew slightly apprehensive. "Your thrice-locked chest, Reshi?"

Kvothe looked at his student, then laughter bubbled up out of him. "My what?" he asked incredulously.

Bast blushed and looked down. "That's just how I think of it," he mumbled.

"As names go . . ." Kvothe hesitated, a smile playing around his mouth. "Well, it's a little storybook, don't you think?"

"You're the one who made the thing, Reshi," Bast said sullenly. "Three locks and fancy wood and all that. It's not my fault if it sounds storybook."

Kvothe leaned forward and rested an apologetic hand on Bast's knee. "It's a fine name, Bast. Just caught me off my guard is all." He leaned back again. "So. How would you attempt to plunder the thrice-locked chest of Kvothe the Bloodless?"

Bast smiled. "You sound like a pirate when you say it that way, Reshi." He gave the chest a speculative look from across the room. "I suppose asking you for the keys is out of the question?" he asked at last.

"Correct," Kvothe said. "For our purposes, assume I have lost the keys. Better yet, assume I am dead, and you are now free to pry into all my secret things."

"That's a little grim, Reshi," Bast reproached gently.

"Life is a little grim, Bast," Kvothe said without any hint of laughter in his voice. "You'd best start getting used to it." He waved a hand toward the chest. "Go on, I'm curious to see how you go about cracking this little chestnut."

Bast gave him a flat look. "Puns are worse than book lessons, Reshi," he said, walking over to the chest. He nudged it idly with his foot, then bent and looked at the two separate lock plates, one dark iron, the other bright copper. Bast prodded the rounded lid with a finger, wrinkling his nose. "I can't say as I care for this wood, Reshi. And the iron lock is positively unfair."

"What a useful lesson this has already been," Kvothe said dryly. "You've deduced a universal truth: *things are usually unfair.*"

"There aren't any hinges, either!" Bast exclaimed, looking at the back of the chest. "How can you have a lid without any hinges?"

"That did take me a while to work out," Kvothe admitted with a touch of pride.

Bast got down on his hands and knees and looked into the copper keyhole. He lifted one hand and pressed it flat against the copper plate. Then he closed his eyes and went very still, as if he were listening.

After a moment of this, he leaned forward and breathed against the lock. When nothing happened, his mouth began to move. While his words were spoken too softly to hear, they carried an undeniable tone of entreaty.

After a long moment of this, Bast sat back on his haunches, frowning. Then he grinned playfully, reached out with a hand, and knocked on the lid of the chest. It made barely any noise at all, as if he were rapping his knuckle against a stone.

"Out of curiosity," Kvothe asked. "What would you do if something knocked back?"

Bast came to his feet, left the room, and returned a moment later with an assortment of tools. He got to one knee and, using a piece of bent wire, fiddled with the copper lock for several long minutes. Eventually he began to curse under his breath. When he shifted position to get a different angle, his hand brushed the dull iron faceplate of the lock and he jerked back, hissing and spitting.

Getting back to his feet, Bast threw down the wire and brought out a long prybar of bright metal. He tried to work the thin end of it under the lid, but couldn't gain any purchase in the hair-thin seam. After a few minutes he abandoned this as well.

Next, Bast tried to tip the chest on its side to examine the bottom, but his best efforts only managed to slide it an inch or so across the floor. "How much does this weigh, Reshi?" Bast exclaimed, looking rather exasperated. "Three hundred pounds?"

"Over four hundred when it's empty," Kvothe said. "Remember the trouble we had getting it up the stairs?"

Sighing, Bast examined the chest for another long moment, his expression fierce. Then he extracted a hatchet from his bundle of tools. It wasn't the rough, wedge-headed hatchet they used to cut kindling behind the inn. It was slender and menacing, all forged of a single piece of metal. The shape of its blade was vaguely reminiscent of a leaf.

He tossed the weapon lightly in his palm, as if testing its weight. "This is where I would go next, Reshi. If I were genuinely interested in getting inside." He gave his teacher a curious look. "But if you'd rather I not. . . ."

Kvothe made a helpless gesture. "Don't look to me, Bast. I'm dead. Do as you will."

Bast grinned and brought the hatchet down on the rounded peak of the chest. There was a strange, soft, ringing noise, like a padded bell being struck in a distant room.

Bast paused, then rained a flurry of angry blows down on the top of the chest. First swinging wildly with one hand, then using both hands in great overhand chopping motions, as if he were splitting wood.

The bright, leaf-shaped blade refused to bite into the wood, each blow turning aside as if Bast were attempting to chop apart a great, seamless block of stone.

Eventually Bast stopped, breathing hard, and bent to look at the top of the chest, running his hand over the surface before turning his attention to the hatchet's blade. He sighed. "You do good work, Reshi."

Kvothe smiled and tipped an imaginary hat.

Bast gave the chest a long look. "I'd try to set fire to it, but I know Roah doesn't burn. I'd have better luck getting it hot enough so the copper lock would melt. But to do that, I'd need to get the whole thing to sit face down in a forge fire." He looked at the chest, large as a gentleman's traveling trunk. "But it would have to be a bigger forge than the one we have here in town. And I don't even know how hot copper needs to be in order to melt."

"Information such as that," Kvothe said, "would doubtless be the subject of a book lesson."

"And I expect you've taken precautions against that sort of thing."

"I have," Kvothe admitted. "But it was a good idea. It shows lateral thinking."

"And acid?" Bast said. "I know we have some potent stuff downstairs. . . ."

"Formic is useless against Roah." Kvothe said. "As is the muriatic. You might have some luck with Aqua Regius. But the wood is quite thick, and we don't have much on hand."

"I wasn't thinking of the wood, Reshi. I was thinking of the locks again. With enough acid I could eat clean through them."

"You're assuming they are copper and iron all the way through," Kvothe said. "Even if they were, it would take a great deal of acid, and you would have to worry about the acid itself spilling into the chest, ruining whatever's inside. The same is true with the fire, of course."

Bast looked at the chest for another long moment, stroking his lips thoughtfully. "That's all I have, Reshi. I'll need to think on it some more."

Kvothe nodded. Looking somewhat disheartened, Bast gathered up his tools and carried them away. When he returned, he pushed the chest from the other side, sliding it back a fraction of an inch until it was square with the foot of the bed again.

"It was a good attempt, Bast," Kvothe reassured him. "Very methodical. You went about it just as I would have."

"Hullo?" the mayor's voice came hollowly up from the room below. "I'm finished."

Bast hopped up and hurried to the door, pushing his chair back under the desk. The sudden motion disturbed one of the crumpled sheets of paper resting there, causing it to tumble to the floor where it bounced and rolled beneath the chair.

Bast paused, then bent to pick it up.

"No," Kvothe said grimly. "Leave it." Bast stopped with his hand outstretched, then stood and left the room.

Kvothe followed, closing the door behind them.

CHAPTER SEVENTY-TWO

Horses

SEVERAL DAYS AFTER DENNA and I had our moonlit stroll in the garden, I finished a song for Meluan called "Nothing but Roses." The Maer specifically requested it, and I had leapt to the project with a will, knowing that Denna would laugh herself sick when I played it for her.

I slid the Maer's song into an envelope and looked at the clock. I'd thought I'd be busy the entire night finishing it, but it had come with surprising ease. Consequently, I had the rest of the evening free. It was late, but not terribly late. Not late for Cendling night in a lively city like Severen. Perhaps not too late to find Denna.

I threw on a set of fresh clothes and hurried out of the estates. Since the money in my purse came from selling pieces of Caudicus' equipment and playing cards with nobles who knew more about fashion than statistics, I paid the full bit for the horse lifts, then jogged the half-mile to Newell Street. I slowed to a walk for the last several blocks. Enthusiasm is flattering, but I didn't want to arrive at Denna's inn panting and sweating like a lathered horse.

I wasn't surprised when I didn't find her at the Four Tapers. Denna wasn't the sort to sit and twiddle her thumbs just because I was busy. But the two of us had spent the better part of a month exploring the city together, and I had a few good guesses as to where I might find her.

Five minutes later I spotted her. She was moving through the crowded street with a definite purpose, walking as if she had somewhere important to be.

I started to make my way toward her, then hesitated. Where would she be going so purposefully, alone, so late at night?

She was going to meet her patron.

I wish I could say I agonized before I decided to follow her, but I really didn't. The temptation of finally learning the identity of her patron was simply too strong.

So I put up the hood of my cloak and began to ghost through the crowd behind Denna. It's remarkably easy if you have a little practice. I used to make a game of it in Tarbean, seeing how far I could follow someone without being seen. It helped that Denna wasn't a fool and stayed in the good parts of the city where the streets were busy, and in the dim light my cloak looked a nondescript black.

I followed her for half an hour. We passed cart vendors selling chestnuts and greasy meat pies. Guards mingled with the crowd, and the streets were bright with scattered streetlights and lanterns hung outside the doors of inns. An occasional out-at-the-heels musician played with his hat in front of him, and once we passed a troupe of mummers acting out a play in a small cobblestone square.

Then Denna turned and left the better streets behind. Soon there were fewer lights and tipsy revelers. The musicians gave way to beggars who called out or clutched at your clothes as you walked by. Lamplight still poured through the windows of nearby pubs and inns, but the street was no longer bustling. People clustered in twos or threes, women wearing corsets and men with hard eyes.

These streets weren't dangerous, strictly speaking. Or rather, they were dangerous in a broken glass sort of way. Broken glass won't go out of its way to hurt you. You can even touch it if you're careful. Some streets are dangerous as frothing dogs, where no amount of care will keep you safe.

I was beginning to get nervous when I saw Denna stop suddenly at the mouth of a shadowed alley. She craned her neck for a moment, as if listening to something. Then, after peering into the dark, she darted inside.

Was *this* where she was meeting her patron? Was she taking a shortcut to a different street? Or was she simply following her paranoid patron's instructions to make sure no one followed her?

I began to curse under my breath. If I followed her into the alley and she saw me, it would be obvious I'd been trailing her. But if I didn't follow her, I'd lose her. And while this wasn't a truly dangerous part of the city, I didn't want to leave her walking alone so late at night.

So I scanned the nearby buildings and spotted one fronted with crumbling fieldstone. After a quick glance around, I climbed the face of it quick as a squirrel, another useful skill from my misspent youth.

Once I was on the roof, it was a simple matter to run over the tops of several other buildings, then slink into the shadow of a chimney before peering down into the alley. There was a sliver of moon overhead, and I expected to see Denna striding quickly along her shortcut, or having a hushed and hidden meeting with her dodgy patron.

But what I saw was nothing of the sort. Dim lamplight from an upstairs window showed a woman splayed out motionless on the ground. My heart thudded hard for several beats until I realized it wasn't Denna. Denna was dressed in shirt and pants. This woman's white dress was crumpled around her, her bare legs pale against the dark stone of the street.

My eyes darted around until I saw Denna outside the window's light. She stood close to a broad-shouldered man with moonlight shining on his bald head. Was she embracing him? Was this her patron?

Finally my eyes adjusted enough that I could see the truth: the two were standing very close and still, but she wasn't holding him. She had one hand hard against his neck, and I saw white moonlight glitter on metal there, like a distant star.

The woman on the ground started to stir, and Denna called out to her. The woman climbed unsteadily to her feet, staggering a bit as she stepped on her own dress, then edged slowly past them, keeping close to the wall as she made her way to the mouth of the alley.

Once the woman was behind her, Denna said something else. I was too far away to make out any of the words, but her voice was hard and angry enough to raise the hair on the back of my arms.

Denna stepped away from the man and he backed away, one hand going to the side of his throat. He began to curse her viciously, spitting and making grasping motions with his free hand. His voice was louder than hers, but slurred enough that I couldn't make out much of what he said, though I did identify the word "whore" several times.

But for all his talk, he didn't come anywhere close to within arm's reach of her. Denna simply stood facing him, her feet set squarely on the ground. She held the knife low in front of her, tilted at an angle. Her posture was almost casual. Almost.

After cursing for a minute or so, the man took half a shuffling step forward, shaking a fist. Denna said something and made a short, sharp gesture with the knife towards the man's groin. Silence filled the alley and the man's shoulders shifted a bit. Denna made the gesture again, and the man began to curse more softly, turning away and walking down the alley, his hand still pressed to the side of his neck.

Denna watched him go, then relaxed and slid the knife carefully into her pocket. She turned and walked to the mouth of the alleyway.

I scurried to the front of the building. On the street below I saw Denna and the other woman standing under a streetlamp. In the better light I saw the woman was much younger than I'd thought, just a slip of a girl, her shoulders heaving with sobs. Denna rubbed her back in small circles, and the girl slowly calmed down. After a moment they began walking down the street.

I hurried back to the alley where I had spotted an old iron drainpipe, a relatively easy way to get back down onto the street. But even so it cost me two long minutes and most of the skin off my knuckles to get cobblestones back under my feet.

Only through a pure effort of will did I keep myself from running out of the alley to catch up with Denna and the girl. The last thing I wanted was for Denna to discover I'd been following her.

Luckily, they weren't moving very fast, and I caught sight of them easily. Denna led the girl back to the nicer part of the city, then took her into a respectable-looking inn with a painted rooster on the sign.

I stood outside for a minute, peering at the layout of the inn through one of the windows. Then I settled my hood more firmly over my face, walked casually around the back portion of the inn, and slid into a seat on the other side of a dividing wall, just around the corner from Denna and the young girl. If I'd wanted to, I could have leaned forward to peer at their table, but as it was, neither one of us could see the other.

The taproom was mostly empty, and a serving girl came up to me almost as soon as I took my seat. She eyed the rich fabric of my cloak and smiled. "What can I get you?"

I eyed the impressive array of polished glass behind the bar. I motioned the serving girl closer and spoke softly, with a rasp in my throat, as if I were recovering from the croup cough. "I'll take a tumble of your best whiskey," I said. "And a glass of fine Feloran red."

She nodded and left.

I turned my finely tuned eavesdroppers' ears to the next table.

". . . your accent," I heard Denna say. "Where are you from?"

There was a pause and a murmur as the girl spoke. Since she was facing away from me, I couldn't hear what she said.

"That's in the western farrel isn't it?" Denna asked. "You're a long way from home."

There was murmuring from the girl. Then a long pause where I couldn't hear anything. I couldn't tell if she'd stopped talking, or if she was speaking too quietly for me to hear. I fought the urge to lean forward and peer at their table.

Then the murmuring came back, very soft.

"I know he said he loved you," Denna said, her voice gentle. "They all say that."

The serving girl set a tall wineglass in front of me and handed me my tumble. "Two bits."

Merciful Tehlu. With prices like that, no wonder the place was nearly empty.

I tossed back the whiskey in a single swallow, fighting the urge to cough as it burned down my throat. Then I drew a full silver round out of my purse, set the heavy coin on the table, and put the empty tumble down over the top of it.

I motioned the serving girl close again. "I have a proposal for you," I said quietly. "Right now I want nothing more than to sit here quietly, drink my wine, and think my thoughts."

I tapped the overturned tumble with the coin underneath. "If I am allowed to do this without interruption, all of this, less the cost of my drinks, is yours." Her eyes went a little wide at that, darting down to the coin again. "But if anyone comes over to bother me, even in a helpful way, even to ask if I would like anything to drink, I will simply pay and leave." I looked up at her. "Can you help me get a little privacy tonight?"

She nodded eagerly.

"Thank you," I said.

She hurried away and went immediately to another woman standing behind the bar, making a few gestures in my direction. I relaxed a bit, reasonably certain they wouldn't be drawing any attention to me.

I sipped my wine and listened.

"...does your father do?" Denna asked. I recognized the pitch of her voice. It was the same low, gentle tone my father had used when talking to skittish animals. A tone designed to calm someone and set them at their ease.

The girl murmured, and Denna responded. "That's a fine job. What are you doing here then?"

Another murmur.

"Got handsy, did he?" Denna said matter-of-factly. "Well that's the nature of eldest sons."

The girl spoke up again, this time with some fire in her voice, though I still couldn't make out any of the words.

I buffed the surface of my wineglass a little with the edge of my cloak, then tipped it out and away from me a bit. The wine was so deep a red that it was almost black. It made the side of the glass act like a mirror. Not a wonderful mirror, but I could see tiny shapes at the table around the corner.

I heard Denna sigh, cutting off the low murmur of the girl's voice. "Let me guess," Denna said, sounding exasperated. "You stole the silver, or something similar, then ran off to the city."

The small reflection of the girl just sat there.

"But it wasn't like you thought it would be, was it?" Denna said, more gently this time.

I could see the girl's shoulders begin to shake and heard a series of faint, heartbreaking sobs. I looked away from the wineglass and set it back on the table.

"Here." There was the sound of a glass being knocked onto the table. "Drink that," Denna said. "It will help a bit. Not a lot. But a bit."

The sobbing stopped. The girl gave a surprised cough, choking a little.

"You poor, silly thing," Denna said softly. "Meeting you is worse than looking in a mirror."

For the first time, the girl spoke loudly enough for me to hear her. "I thought, if he's going to take me anyway and get it for free, I might as well go somewhere I can pick and choose and get paid for it. . . ."

Her voice trailed off until I couldn't make out any words, leaving only the low rise and fall of her muffled voice.

"*The Tenpenny King?*" Denna interrupted incredulously. Her tone more venomous than anything I'd ever heard from her before. "Kist and crayle, I hate that Goddamn play. Modegan faerie-story trash. The world doesn't work like that."

"But . . ." the girl began.

Denna cut her off. "There's no young prince out there, dressed in rags and waiting to save you. Even if there were, where would you be? You'd be like a dog he'd found in the gutter. He'd own you. After he took you home, who would save you from him?"

A piece of silence. The girl coughed again, but only a little.

"So what are we going to do with you?" Denna said.

The girl sniffed and said something.

"If you could take care of yourself we wouldn't be sitting here," Denna said.

A murmur.

"It's an option," Denna said. "They'll take half of what you make, but that's better than getting nothing and having your throat slit on top of it. I'm guessing you figured that out yourself tonight."

There was the sound of cloth on cloth. I tipped my wineglass to get a look, but all I saw was Denna making some indistinct motion. "Let's see what we have here," she said. Then there came the familiar clatter of coins on a table.

The girl made an awed murmur.

"No, I'm not," Denna said. "It's not so much when it's all your money in the world. You should know by now how expensive it is to make your own way in the city."

A murmur that rose at the end. A question.

I heard Denna draw a breath, then let it out again slowly. "Because someone helped me once when I needed it," she said. "And because if you don't get some help you'll be dead in a span of days. Take it from someone who's made her own share of bad decisions."

There was the sound of coins sliding on the table. "Okay," Denna said. "First option. We get you apprenticed up. You're a little old, and it will cost, but we could do it. Nothing fancy. Weaving. Cobbling. They'll work you hard, but you'd have your room and board, and you'd learn a trade."

A questioning murmur.

"With your accent?" Denna asked archly. "Can you curl a lady's hair? Paint her face? Mend her dress? Tat lace?" A pause. "No, you don't have the training to be a maidservant, and I wouldn't know who to bribe."

The sound of coins being gathered together. "Option two," Denna said. "We get you a room until that bruise is gone." Coins sliding. "Then buy you a seat on a coach back home." More coins. "You've been gone a month. That's the perfect amount of time for some serious worry to set in. When you come home they'll just be happy you're alive."

Murmur.

"Tell them whatever you like," Denna said. "But if you've got half a brain in your head you'll make it sensible. Nobody's going to believe you met some prince who sent you home."

A murmur so soft I could hardly hear it.

"Of course it will be hard, you silly little bint," Denna said sharply. "They'll hold it over your head for the rest of your life. Folk will whisper when you walk by on the street. It will be hard to find a husband. You'll lose friends. But that's the price you'll have to pay if you want to have anything like your normal life back again."

The coins clinked as they were gathered together again. "Third option. If you're certain you want to make a go of whoring, we can arrange it so you don't end up dead in a ditch. You've got a nice face, but you'll need proper clothes." Coins sliding. "And someone to teach you manners." More coins. "And someone else to get rid of that accent of yours." Coins again.

Murmur.

"Because it's the only sensible way to do it," Denna said flatly.

Another murmur.

Denna gave a tight, irritated sigh. "Okay. Your father's stable master, right? Think about the different horses the baron owns: plow horses, carriage horses, hunting horses. . . ."

Excited murmur.

"Exactly," Denna said. "So if you had to pick, what sort of horse would you want to be? A plow horse works hard, but does it get the best stall? The best feed?"

Murmur.

"That's right. That goes to the fancy horses. They get petted and fed and only have to work when there's a parade or someone goes hunting."

Denna continued, "So if you're going to be a whore, you do it smart. You don't want to be some dockside drab, you want to be a duchess. You want men to court you. Send you gifts."

Murmur.

"Yes, gifts. If they pay, they'll feel like they own you. You saw how that turned out tonight. You can keep your accent and that low bodice and have sailors paw you for ha'penny a throw. Or you can learn some manners, get your hair done, and start entertaining gentlemen callers. If you're interesting, and pretty, and you know how to listen, men will desire your company. They'll want to take you dancing as much as take you to bed. Then *you* have the control. Nobody makes a duchess pay for her room in advance. Nobody bends a duchess over a barrel in an alley then kicks out her teeth once he's had his fun."

Murmur.

"No." Denna said, her voice grim. There was the sound of coins being clinked softly into a purse. "Don't lie to yourself. Even the fanciest horse is still a horse. That means sooner or later, you're going to get ridden."

A questioning murmur.

"Then you leave," Denna said. "If they want more than you're willing to give, that's the only way. You leave, quick and quiet in the night. But if you do, you'll burn your bridges. That's the price you pay."

A hesitant murmur.

"I can't tell you that," Denna said. "You need to decide what you want for yourself. You want to go home? There's a price. You want control over your life? There's a price. You want the freedom to say no? There's a price. There's *always* a price."

There was the sound of a chair being pushed away from a table, and I pressed myself back against the wall as I heard the two of them stand up. "It's something everyone has to figure out on their own," Denna said, her voice growing more distant. "What do you want more than anything else? What do you want so badly you'll pay anything to get it?"

I sat for a long time after they left, trying to drink my wine.

CHAPTER SEVENTY-THREE

Blood and Ink

IN THE *THEOPHANY*, Teccam writes of secrets, calling them painful treasures of the mind. He explains that what most people think of as secrets are really nothing of the sort. Mysteries, for example, are not secrets. Neither are little-known facts or forgotten truths. A secret, Teccam explains, is true knowledge actively concealed.

Philosophers have quibbled over his definition for centuries. They point out the logical problems with it, the loopholes, the exceptions. But in all this time none of them has managed to come up with a better definition. That, perhaps, tells us more than all the quibbling combined.

In a later chapter, less argued over and less well-known, Teccam explains that there are two types of secrets. There are secrets of the mouth and secrets of the heart.

Most secrets are secrets of the mouth. Gossip shared and small scandals whispered. These secrets long to be let loose upon the world. A secret of the mouth is like a stone in your boot. At first you're barely aware of it. Then it grows irritating, then intolerable. Secrets of the mouth grow larger the longer you keep them, swelling until they press against your lips. They fight to be let free.

Secrets of the heart are different. They are private and painful, and we want nothing more than to hide them from the world. They do not swell and press against the mouth. They live in the heart, and the longer they are kept, the heavier they become.

Teccam claims it is better to have a mouthful of poison than a secret of the heart. Any fool will spit out poison, he says, but we hoard these painful treasures. We swallow hard against them every day, forcing them deep inside us. There they sit, growing heavier, festering. Given enough time, they cannot help but crush the heart that holds them.

Modern philosophers scorn Teccam, but they are vultures picking at the bones of a giant. Quibble all you like, Teccam understood the shape of the world.

———————

The day after I'd followed Denna through the city, she sent me a note, and I met her outside the Four Tapers. We'd met there dozens of times in the last several span, but today something was different. Today Denna wore a long, elegant dress, not layered and high necked in the current fashion, but close fitting and open at the throat. It was a deep blue, and when she took a step I could glimpse a long stretch of her bare leg beneath.

Her harp case leaned against the wall behind her, and she had an expectant look in her eye. Her dark hair was lustrous in the sunlight, unadorned except for three narrow braids tied with blue string. She was barefoot, and her feet were grass-stained. She smiled.

"It's done," she said, excitement thrumming through her voice like distant thunder. "Done enough to play you a piece at any rate. Would you like to hear it?" I caught a bit of well-hidden shyness in her voice.

As we were both working for patrons who valued their privacy, Denna and I didn't often discuss our work. We compared our ink-stained fingers and bemoaned our difficulties, but only in vague ways.

"I'd like nothing better than to hear it," I said as Denna picked up her harp case and started down the street. I fell into step beside her. "But won't your patron mind?"

Denna gave a too-casual shrug. "He says he wants my first song to be something that men will sing for a hundred years, so I doubt he'll want me to keep it bottled up forever." She gave me a sideways look. "We'll go somewhere private and I'll let you hear. So long as you don't go shouting it from rooftops, I should be safe."

We started walking to the western gate by unspoken agreement. "I'd have brought my lute," I said, "but I finally found a luthier I trust. I'm having that loose peg mended."

"You'll serve me best as audience today," she said. "Sit rapt in admiration as I play. Tomorrow I'll watch you, all dewy-eyed with wonder. I'll marvel at your skill and wit and charm." She moved her harp to her other shoulder and grinned at me. "Provided you aren't having them mended at the shop."

"I'm always up for a duet," I suggested. "Harp and lute is rare but not unheard of."

"That's delicately phrased." She glanced sideways at me. "I'll think on it."

As I had a dozen times before, I fought the urge to tell her I'd reclaimed her ring from Ambrose. I wanted to tell her the story of it, mistakes and all. But I was fairly certain the romantic impact of my gesture would be diminished by the end of the story, where I'd effectively pawned the ring before I left Imre. Better to keep it a secret for now, I thought, and surprise her with the ring itself.

"So what would you think," I asked, "of having Maer Alveron for your patron?"

Denna stopped walking and turned to look at me. "What?"

"I'm currently in his good graces," I said. "And he owes me a favor or two. I know you've been looking for a patron."

"I have a patron," she said firmly. "One I've earned on my own."

"You have half a patron," I protested. "Where's your writ of patronage? Your Master Ash might be able to give you some financial support, but the more important half of a patron is their name. It's like armor. It's like a key that opens—"

"I know how a patronage works," Denna said, cutting me off.

"Then you know yours is shortchanging you," I said. "If the Maer had been your patron when things went wrong at that wedding, no one in that shabby little town would have dared to raise their voice to you, let alone their hand. Even from a thousand miles away the Maer's name would have protected you. He would have kept you safe."

"A patron can offer more than a name and money," Denna said with an edge to her voice. "I'm fine without the shelter of a title, and honestly, I'd be irritated if some man wanted to dress me in his colors. My patron gives me other things. He knows things I need to know." She gave me an irritated look as she flicked her hair over her shoulder. "I've told you all this before. I'm content with him for now."

"Why not have both?" I suggested. "The Maer in public and your Master Ash in secret. Surely he couldn't object to that. Alveron could probably even look into this other fellow for you, make sure he's not trying to win you with false—"

Denna gave me a horrified look. "No. God no." She turned to me, her expression earnest. "Promise me you won't try to find out anything about him. It could ruin everything. You're the only one I've told in all the wide world, but he'd be furious if he knew I'd mentioned him to anyone."

I felt a bizarre glow of pride at this. "If you'd really rather I not . . ."

Denna stopped walking and set her harp case down on the cobblestones where it made a hollow thump. Her expression was deadly serious. "Promise me."

I probably wouldn't have agreed if I hadn't spent half the previous night following her around the city with the hope of discovering this very thing. But I had. Then I'd eavesdropped on her, too. So today I was practically sweating with guilt.

"I promise," I said. When her anxious look didn't evaporate I added, "Don't you trust me? I'll swear it, if that will set your mind at ease."

"What would you swear it on?" she asked, beginning to smile again. "What's important enough that it will hold you to your word?"

"My name and my power?" I said.

"You are many things," she said dryly. "But you are not Taborlin the Great."

"My good right hand?" I suggested.

"Only one hand?" she asked, playfulness creeping back into her tone. She reached out and took both of my hands in her own, turning them over and making a show of inspecting them closely. "I like the left one better," she decided. "Swear by that one."

"My good *left* hand?" I asked dubiously.

"Fine," she said. "The right. You're such a traditionalist."

"I swear I won't attempt to uncover your patron," I said bitterly. "I swear it on my name and my power. I swear it by my good left hand. I swear it by the ever-moving moon."

Denna peered at me closely, as if she wasn't sure if I was mocking her. "Fine," she said with a shrug, picking up her harp. "Consider me reassured."

We started walking again, moving through the western gates and into the countryside. The silence between us stretched, starting to grow uncomfortable.

Worried things would grow awkward, I said the first thing that came to mind. "So, are there any new men in your life?"

Denna chuckled low in her throat. "Now you sound like Master Ash. He's always asking after them. He doesn't think any of my suitors are good enough for me."

I couldn't agree more, but decided it wouldn't be prudent to say so. "And what does he think of me?"

"What?" she asked, confused. "Oh. He doesn't know about you," she said. "Why would he?"

I tried to give a nonchalant shrug, but I couldn't have been very convincing as she burst out laughing. "Poor Kvothe. I'm teasing you. I only tell him about the ones that come prowling around, panting and sniffing like dogs. You're not like them. You've always been different."

"I've always prided myself on my lack of panting and sniffing."

Denna turned her shoulder and let her swinging harp bump me playfully. "You know what I mean. They come and go with little gain or loss. You are the gold behind the windblown dross. Master Ash might think he has a right to know about my personal affairs, my comings and goings." She scowled a bit. "But he doesn't. I'm willing to concede some of that, for now. . . ."

She reached out and took hold of my upper arm possessively. "But you are not part of the bargain," she said, her voice almost fierce. "You are mine. Mine alone. I don't intend to share you."

The momentary tension passed, and we walked the wide west road away from Severen, laughing and talking of small things. Half a mile past the city's last inn was a quiet patch of trees with a single tall greystone nestled in its center. We had found it while searching for wild strawberries, and it had become one of our favorite places to escape the noise and stink of the city.

Denna sat at the base of the greystone and put her back against it. Then she brought her harp out of its case and pulled it close to her chest, causing her dress to gather and expose a scandalous amount of leg. She arched an eyebrow at me and smirked as if she knew exactly what I was thinking.

"Nice harp," I said casually.

She snorted indelicately.

I sat where I was, sprawling comfortably on the long, cool grass. I tugged a few strands of it out of the ground and idly began to twist them together into a braid.

Honestly, I was nervous. While we had spent a great deal of time together over the last month, I'd never heard Denna play anything of her own creation. We had sung together, and I knew she had a voice like honey on warm bread. I knew her fingers were sure, and she had a musician's timing. . . .

But writing a song isn't the same as playing one. What if hers wasn't any good? What would I say?

Denna spread her fingers to the strings, and my worries faded to the background. I've always found something powerfully erotic about the way a woman puts her hands to a harp. She began a rolling gliss down the strings from high to low. The sound of it was like hammers on bells, like water over stones, like birdsong through the air.

She stopped and tuned a string. Plucked, tuned. She struck a sharp chord, a hard chord, a lingering chord, then turned to look at me, flexing her fingers nervously. "Are you ready?"

"You're incredible," I said.

I saw her flush a little, then brush her hair back to hide her reaction. "Fool. I haven't played you anything yet."

"You're incredible all the same."

"Hush." She struck a hard chord and let it fade into a quiet melody. As it rose and fell, she spoke the introduction to her song. I was surprised at such a traditional opening. Surprised but pleased. Old ways are best.

Gather round and listen well,
For I've a tale of tragedy to tell.
I sing of subtle shadow spread
Across a land, and of the man
Who turned his hand toward a purpose few could bear.
Fair Lanre: stripped of wife, of life, of pride
Still never from his purpose swayed.
Who fought the tide, and fell, and was betrayed.

At first it was her voice that caught my breath, then it was the music.

But before ten lines had passed her lips I was stunned for different reasons. She sang the story of Myr Tariniel's fall. Of Lanre's betrayal. It was the story I had heard from Skarpi in Tarbean.

But Denna's version was different. In her song, Lanre was painted in tragic tones, a hero wrongly used. Selitos' words were cruel and biting, Myr Tariniel a warren that was better for the purifying fire. Lanre was no traitor, but a fallen hero.

So much depends upon where you stop a story, and hers ended when Lanre was cursed by Selitos. It was the perfect ending for a tragedy. In her story Lanre was wronged, misunderstood. Selitos was a tyrant, an insane monster who tore out his own eye in fury at Lanre's clever trickery. It was dreadfully, painfully wrong.

Despite this, it had the first glimmers of beauty to it. The chords well-chosen. The rhyme subtle and strong. The song was very fresh, and there were rough patches aplenty, but I could feel the shape of it. I saw what it could become. It would turn men's minds. They would sing it for a hundred years.

You've probably heard it, in fact. Most folk have. She ended up calling it "The Song of Seven Sorrows." Yes. Denna composed it, and I was the first person to hear it played entire.

As the last notes faded in the air, Denna lowered her hands, unwilling to meet my eye.

I sat, still and silent on the grass.

For this to make sense, you need to understand something every musician knows. Singing a new song is a nervous thing. More than that. It's terrifying. It's like undressing for the first time in front of a new lover. It's a delicate moment.

I needed to say something. A compliment. A comment. A joke. A lie. Anything was better than silence.

But I couldn't have been more stunned if she had written a hymn praising the Duke of Gibea. The shock was simply too much for me. I felt raw as reused parchment, as if every note of her song had been another flick of a knife, scraping until I was entirely blank and wordless.

I looked down dumbly at my hands. They still held the half-formed circle of green grass I'd been weaving when the song began. It was a broad, flat plait already beginning to curve into the shape of a ring.

Still looking down, I heard the rustle of Denna's skirts as she moved. I needed to say something. I'd already waited too long. There was too much silence in the air.

"The city's name wasn't Mirinitel," I said without looking up. It was not the worst thing I could have said. But it wasn't the right thing to say.

There was a pause. "What?"

"Not Mirinitel," I repeated. "The city Lanre burned was Myr Tariniel. Sorry to tell you that. Changing a name is hard work. It will wreck the meter in a third of your verses." I was surprised at how quiet my voice was, how flat and dead it sounded in my own ears.

I heard her draw a surprised breath. "You've heard the story before?"

I looked up at Denna, her expression excited. I nodded, still feeling oddly blank. Empty. Hollow as a dried gourd. "What made you pick this for a song?" I asked her.

It wasn't the right thing to say either. I can't help but feel that if I'd said the right thing at that moment, everything would have turned out differently. But even now, after years of thinking, I can't imagine what I could have said that might have made things right.

Her excitement faded slightly. "I found a version of it in an old book when I was doing genealogical research for my patron," she said. "Hardly anyone remembers it, so it's perfect for a song. It's not like the world needs another story about Oren Velciter. I'll never make my mark repeating what other musicians have already hashed over a hundred times before."

Denna gave me a curious look. "I thought I was going to be able to surprise you with something new. I never would have guessed you'd heard of Lanre."

"I heard it years ago," I said numbly. "From an old storyteller in Tarbean."

"If I had half your luck . . ." Denna shook her head in dismay. "I had to piece it together out of a hundred little scraps." She made a conciliatory gesture. "Me and my patron, I should say. He's helped."

"Your patron," I said. I felt a spark of emotion when she mentioned him. Hollow as I was, it was surprising how quickly the bitterness spread through my gut, as if someone had kindled a fire inside me.

Denna nodded. "He fancies himself a bit of a historian," she said. "I think he's angling for a court appointment. He wouldn't be the first to ingratiate himself by shining a light on someone's long-lost heroic ancestor. Or maybe he's trying to invent a heroic ancestor for himself. That would explain the research we've been doing in old genealogies."

She hesitated for a moment, biting her lips. "The truth is," she said, as if confessing something. "I half suspect the song is for Alveron himself. Master Ash has implied he's had dealings with the Maer." She gave a mischievous grin. "Who knows? Running in the circles you do, you might have already met my patron and not even known it."

My mind flickered over the hundreds of nobles and courtiers I'd met in passing over the last month, but it was hard to focus on their faces. The fire in my gut was spreading until my whole chest was full of it.

"But enough of this," Denna said, waving her hands impatiently. She pushed her harp away and folded her legs to sit cross-legged on the grass. "You're teasing me. What did you think of it?"

I looked down at my hands and idly fingered the flat braid of green grass I'd woven. It was smooth and cool between my fingers. I couldn't remember how I'd planned to join the ends together to form a ring.

"I know it's got some rough patches," I heard Denna say, her voice brimming with nervous excitement. "I'll have to fix that name you mentioned, if you're sure it's the right one. The beginning is rough, and the seventh verse is a shambles, I know. I need to expand the battles and his relationship with Lyra. The ending needs tightening. But overall, what did you think?"

Once she smoothed it out, it would be brilliant. As good a song as my parents might have written, but that just made it worse.

My hands were shaking, and I was amazed at how hard it was to make them stop. I looked away from them, up at Denna. Her nervous excitement faded when she saw my face.

"You're going to have to rework more than just the name." I tried to keep my voice calm. "Lanre wasn't a hero."

She looked at me oddly, as if she couldn't tell if I was making a joke. "What?"

"You've got the whole thing wrong," I said. "Lanre was a monster. A traitor. You need to change it."

Denna tossed back her head and laughed. When I didn't join her, she cocked her head, puzzled. "You're serious?"

I nodded.

Denna's face went stiff. Her eyes narrowed and her mouth made a thin line. "You have to be kidding." Her mouth worked silently for a moment, then she shook her head. "It wouldn't make any sense. The whole story falls apart if Lanre isn't the hero."

"It's not about what makes a good story," I said. "It's about what's true."

"True?" She looked at me incredulously. "This is just some old folk story. None of the places are real. None of the people are real. You might as well get offended at me for coming up with a new verse for 'Tinker Tanner.' "

I could feel words rising in my throat, hot as a chimney fire. I swallowed down hard against them. "Some stories are just stories," I agreed. "But not this one. It's not your fault. There's no way you could have—"

"Oh well, *thank* you," she said bitingly. "I'm so glad this isn't my fault."

"Fine," I said sharply. "It *is* your fault. You should have done more research."

"What do you know about the research I did?" she demanded. "You haven't the slightest idea! I've been all over the world digging up pieces of this story!"

It was the same thing my father had done. He'd started writing a song about Lanre, but his research led him to the Chandrian. He'd spent years chasing down half-forgotten stories and digging up rumors. He wanted his song to tell the truth about them, and they had killed my entire troupe to put an end to it.

I looked down at the grass and thought about the secret I had kept for so long. I thought of the smell of blood and burning hair. I thought of rust and blue fire and the broken bodies of my parents. How could I explain something so huge and horrible? Where would I even begin? I could feel the secret deep inside me, huge and heavy as a stone.

"In the version of the story I heard," I said, touching the far edge of the secret. "Lanre became one of the Chandrian. You should be careful. Some stories are dangerous."

Denna stared at me for a long moment. "The Chandrian?" she said incredulously. Then she laughed. It was not her usual delighted laugh. This was sharp and full of derision. "What kind of a child are you?"

I knew exactly how childish it made me sound. I felt myself flush hot with embarrassment, my whole body suddenly prickling with sweat. I opened my mouth to speak, and it felt like cracking open the door of a furnace. "*I'm* like a child?" I spat. "What do you know about anything, you stupid . . ." I almost bit off the end of my tongue to keep from shouting the word *whore*.

"You think you know everything, don't you?" she demanded. "You've been to the University so you think the rest of us are—"

"Quit looking for excuses to be upset and listen to me!" I snapped. The words poured out of me like molten iron. "You're having a snit like a spoiled little girl!"

"Don't you dare." She jabbed a finger at me. "Don't talk to me like I'm some sort of witless farm girl. I know things they don't teach at your precious University! Secret things! I'm not an idiot!"

"You're acting like an idiot!" I shouted so loudly the words hurt my throat. "You won't shut up long enough to listen to me! I'm trying to help you!"

Denna sat in the center of a chilly silence. Her eyes were hard and flat. "That's what it's all about, isn't it?" she said coldly. Her fingers moved in her hair, every flick of her fingers stiff with irritation. She untied her braids, smoothed them out, then absentmindedly retied them in a different pattern. "You hate that I won't take your help. You can't stand that I won't let you fix every little thing in my life, is that it?"

"Well maybe someone needs to fix your life," I snapped. "You've made a fair mess of it so far, haven't you?"

She continued to sit very still, her eyes furious. "What makes you think you know *anything* about my life?"

"I know you're so afraid of anyone getting close that you can't stay in the same bed four days in a row," I said, hardly knowing what I was saying anymore. Angry words poured out of me like blood from a wound. "I know you live your whole life burning bridges behind you. I know you solve your problems by running—"

"What makes you think your advice is worth one thin sliver of a damn, anyway?" Denna burst out. "Half a year ago you had one foot in the gutter. Hair all shaggy and only three raggedy shirts. There isn't a noble in a hundred miles of Imre that would piss on you if you were on fire. You had to run a thousand miles to have a chance of a patron."

My face burned with shame at her mention of my three shirts, and I felt my temper flare hot again. "You're right of course," I said scathingly. "You're much better off. I'm sure your patron would be perfectly happy to piss on you—"

"Now we get to the heart of it," she said, throwing her hands up in the air. "You don't like my patron because you could get me a better one. You don't like my song because it's different from the one you know." She reached for her harp case, her movements stiff and angry. "You're just like all the rest."

"I'm trying to help you!"

"You're trying to fix me," Denna said crisply as she put away her harp. "You're trying to buy me. To arrange my life. You want to keep me like I'm your pet. Like I'm your faithful dog."

"I'd never think of you as a dog," I said, giving her a bright and brittle smile. "A dog knows how to listen. A dog has sense enough not to bite a hand that's trying to help."

Our conversation spiraled downward from there.

At this point in the story I'm tempted to lie. To say I spoke these things in an uncontrollable rage. That I was overwhelmed with grief at the memory of my murdered family. I'm tempted to say I tasted plum and nutmeg. Then I would have some excuse. . . .

But they were my words. In the end, I was the one who said those things. Only me.

Denna responded in kind, hurt and furious and sharp-tongued as myself. We were both proud and angry and filled with the unshakable certainty of youth. We said things we never would have said otherwise, and when we left, we did not leave together.

My temper was hot and bitter as a bar of molten iron. It seared at me as I walked all the way back to Severen. It burned as I made my way through the city and waited for the freight lifts. It smoldered as I stalked through the Maer's estates and slammed the door to my rooms behind me.

It was only hours later that I cooled enough to regret my words. I thought of what I might have said to Denna. I thought of telling her of how my troupe was killed, about the Chandrian.

I decided I would write her a letter. I would explain it all, no matter how foolish or unbelievable it seemed. I brought out pen and ink and laid a sheet of fine white paper on the writing desk.

I dipped the pen and tried to think of where I could begin.

My parents had been killed when I was eleven. It was an event so huge and horrifying it had driven me nearly mad. In the years since, I had never told a soul of those events. I had never so much as whispered them in an empty room. It was a secret I had clutched so tightly for so long that when I dared think of it, it lay so heavy in my chest that I could barely breathe.

I dipped the pen again, but no words came. I opened a bottle of wine, thinking it might loosen the secret inside me. Give me some fingerhold I could use to pry it up. I drank until the room spun and the nib of the pen was crusted with dry ink.

Hours later the blank sheet still stared at me, and I beat my fist against the desk in fury and frustration, striking it so hard my hand bled. That is how heavy a secret can become. It can make blood flow easier than ink.

CHAPTER SEVENTY-FOUR

Rumors

THE DAY AFTER I fought with Denna, I woke late in the afternoon, feeling miserable for all the obvious reasons. I ate and bathed, but pride kept me from heading down to Severen-Low to look for Denna. I sent a ring to Bredon, but the runner returned with the news that he was still away from the estate.

So I opened a bottle of wine and began to leaf through the pile of stories that had been slowly accumulating in my room. The majority of these were scandalous, spiteful things. But their petty meanness suited my mood and helped distract me from my own misery.

Thus I learned the previous Compte Banbride hadn't died of consumption, but of syphilis contracted from an amorous stable hand. Lord Veston was addicted to Denner resin, and money intended for the maintenance of the king's road was paying for his habit.

Baron Jakis had paid several officials to avoid scandal when his youngest daughter was discovered in a brothel. There were two versions of that story, one where she was selling, and another where she was buying. I filed that information away for future use.

I'd started a second bottle of wine by the time I read that young Netalia Lackless had run away with a troupe of traveling performers. Her parents had disowned her, of course, leaving Meluan the only heir to the Lackless lands. That explained Meluan's hatred of the Ruh, and made me doubly glad I hadn't made my Edema blood public here in Severen.

There were three separate stories of how the Duke of Cormisant flew into rages while in his cups, beating whoever happened to be nearby, including his wife, his son, and several dinner guests. There was a brief speculative account of how the king and queen held depraved orgies in their private gardens, hidden from the eyes of the royal court.

Even Bredon made an appearance. He was said to conduct pagan rituals in the secluded woods outside his northern estates. They were described with such extravagant and meticulous detail that I wondered if they weren't copied directly from the pages of some old Aturan romance.

I read well into the evening, and was only halfway through the stack of stories when I finished the bottle of wine. I was just about to send a runner for another when I heard the soft hush of air from the other room that announced Alveron's entrance into my chambers through his secret passage.

I pretended to look surprised when he entered the room. "Good afternoon, your grace," I said as I came to my feet.

"Sit if you wish," he said shortly.

I remained standing out of deference, as I'd learned it was better to err on the side of formality with the Maer. "How are things progressing with your lady?" I asked. From Stapes' excited gossip, I knew matters were rapidly coming to a close.

"We pledged a formal troth today," he said distractedly. "Signed papers and all. It's done."

"If you'll forgive me for saying so, your grace, you don't seem very pleased."

He gave a sour smile. "I suppose you've heard about the trouble on the roads of late?"

"Only rumors, your grace."

He snorted. "Rumors I have been trying to keep quiet. Someone has been waylaying my tax collectors on the north road."

That was serious. "Collectors, your grace?" I asked, stressing the plural. "How much have they managed to take?"

The Maer gave me a stern look that let me know the impropriety of my question. "Enough. More than enough. This is the fourth I've had go missing. Over half of my northern taxes taken by highwaymen." He gave me a serious look. "The Lackless lands are in the north, you know."

"You think the Lacklesses are waylaying your collectors?"

He gave me a stunned look. "What? No, no. It's bandits in the Eld."

I blushed a little in embarrassment. "Have you sent out patrols, your grace?"

"Of course I've sent out patrols," he snapped. "I've sent a dozen. They haven't found so much as a campfire." He paused and looked at me. "I suspect someone in my guard is in league with them." His expression was grave.

"I assume your grace has given your collectors escorts?"

"Two apiece," he said. "Do you know how much it costs to replace a dozen guardsmen? Armor, weapons, horses?" He sighed. "On top of it all, only part of the stolen taxes are mine, the rest belong to the king."

I nodded an understanding. "I don't imagine he's very pleased."

Alveron waved a hand dismissively. "Oh, Roderic will have his money regardless. He holds me personally responsible for his tithe. So I am forced to send the collectors around again to gather his majesty's share a second time."

"I don't imagine that sits very well with most people," I said.

"It does not." He sat in an overstuffed chair and rubbed his face tiredly. "I'm at my wit's end over the matter. How will it look to Meluan if I cannot keep my own roads safe?

I took a seat as well, facing him. "What of Dagon?" I asked. "Couldn't he find them?"

Alveron gave a short, humorless bark of a laugh. "Oh, Dagon would find them. He'd have their heads on poles inside ten days."

"Then why not send him?" I asked, puzzled.

"Because Dagon is a man of straight lines. He would raze a dozen villages and set fire to a thousand acres of the Eld to find them." He shook his head seriously. "Even if I thought him suited to this task, he is tracking down Caudicus at the moment. Besides, I believe there may be magic at work in the Eld, and that is outside Dagon's ken."

I suspected the only magic at work was half a dozen sturdy Modegan longbows. But it's the nature of people to cry magic whenever they're faced with something they cannot easily explain, especially in Vintas.

Alveron leaned forward in his seat. "Might I rely on your help in this?"

There was only one response to that. "Of course, your grace."

"Do you know much woodcraft?"

"I studied under a yeoman when I was younger," I exaggerated, guessing he was looking for someone to help devise a better defense for his collectors. "I know enough to track a man and hide myself."

Alveron raised an eyebrow at that. "Really? You are possessed of quite the diverse education, aren't you?"

"I've led an interesting life, your grace." The bottle of wine I'd drunk made me bolder than usual, and I added. "I've got an idea or two you might find helpful in dealing with your bandit problem."

He leaned forward in his chair. "Do tell."

"I could devise some arcane protection for your men." I made a flourish with the long fingers of my right hand, hoping it looked sufficiently mystical. I juggled numbers in my head and wondered how long it would take to create an arrowcatch using only the equipment in Caudicus' tower.

Alveron nodded thoughtfully. "That might suffice if I was only concerned for the safety of my collectors. But this is the king's road, a major artery of trade. I need to be rid of the bandits themselves."

"In that case," I said, "I would assemble a small group who know how to make their way quietly in a forest. They shouldn't have too much difficulty locating your bandits. When they do, it should be a simple matter to send your guard out to catch them."

"Easier yet to set an ambush and kill them, wouldn't you say?" Alveron said slowly, as if looking to gauge my reaction.

"Or that," I admitted. "Your grace is the arm of the law."

"Death is the penalty for banditry. Especially on the king's road," Alveron said firmly. "Does that seem harsh to you?"

"Not in the least," I said, looking him squarely in the eye. "Safe roads are the bones of civilization."

Alveron surprised me with a sudden smile. "Your plan is the very image of my own. I have gathered a handful of mercenaries to do just as you've suggested. I've had to move secretly, as I don't know who might be sending these bandits their warnings. But I've got four good men ready to leave tomorrow: a tracker, two mercenaries with some skill in the forest, and an Adem mercenary. The last did not come cheaply, either."

I gave him a congratulatory nod. "You've already planned it better than I could, your grace. It hardly seems as if you need my help at all."

"Quite the contrary," he said, "I still need someone with a little sense to lead them." He looked at me meaningfully. "Someone who understands magic. Someone I can trust."

I felt a sudden sinking sensation.

Alveron got to his feet, smiling warmly. "Twice now you have served me beyond all expectations. Are you familiar with the expression 'third time pays for all'?"

Again, there was only one reasonable answer to that question. "Yes, your grace."

Alveron took me to his rooms, and we looked over maps of the countryside where his men had been lost. It was a long stretch of the king's highway running through a piece of the Eld that had been old when Vintas was nothing more than a handful of squabbling sea kings. It was a little more than eighty miles away. We could be there in four days of hard walking.

Stapes provided me with a new travelsack, and I packed it as well as I was able. I took a few of the more practical clothes from my wardrobe, though they were still more suited for a ballroom than the road. I packed away a few items I'd quietly pilfered from Caudicus' lab over the last span, and gave Stapes a list of a few essential items I was lacking, and he produced them all more quickly than a grocer in a store.

Finally, at the hour when all but the most desperate and dishonest persons are abed, Alveron gave me a purse containing a hundred silver bits. "This is a messy way of handling it," Alveron said. "Normally I would give you a writ charging citizens to provide you with assistance and aid." He sighed. "But using something like that as you travel would be as good as blowing a trumpet announcing your arrival."

I nodded. "If they're clever enough to have a spy among your guard, it's safe to assume they have connections with the local populace as well, your grace."

"They might *be* the local populace," he said darkly.

Stapes led me out of the estate through the same secret passage the Maer used to enter my rooms. Carrying a hooded thief's lamp, he took me through several twisting passages, then down a long, dark stairway that bored deep into the stone of the Sheer.

Thus I found myself standing alone in the chill cellar of an abandoned shop in Severen-Low. It was in the section of the city that had been ravaged by fire some years ago, and the building's few remaining roof beams stretched like dark bones against the first pale light of dawn.

I stepped from the burned shell of the building. Above, the Maer's estates perched on the edge of the Sheer like some predatory bird.

I spat, none too pleased with my situation, press-ganged into mercenary service. My eyes were gritty from my sleepless night and my long journey through the twisting stone passages in the Sheer. The wine I'd drunk wasn't improving anything either. For the last few hours I could feel myself growing less drunk and more hungover by slow degrees. I'd never been awake through the entire process before, and it was not pleasant. I'd managed to keep up appearances in front of Alveron and Stapes, but the fact of the matter was that my gut was sour and my thoughts were thick and sluggish.

The cool, predawn air cleared my head a little, and within a hundred steps I began thinking of things I'd forgotten to include on the list I'd given Stapes. The wine had done me no favors there. I had no tinderbox, no salt, no knife. . . .

My lute. I hadn't picked it up from the luthier after having its loose peg fixed. Who knew how long I might be hunting bandits for the Maer. How long would it sit unclaimed before the man decided it had been abandoned?

I went two miles out of my way, but found the luthier's shop dark and lifeless. I hammered on the door to no avail. Then, after a moment's indecision,

I broke in and stole it. Though it hardly seemed to be stealing, since the lute was mine to begin with, and I'd already paid for the repairs.

I had to climb a wall, force a window, and trip two locks. It was fairly simple stuff, but given my sleepless wine-sodden head, I'm probably lucky I didn't fall off the roof and break my neck. But aside from a loose piece of slate that set my heart racing, things went smoothly and I was back on my way in twenty minutes.

The four mercenaries Alveron had assembled were waiting in a tavern two miles north of Severen. We made brief introductions and left immediately, heading north on the king's highway.

My thoughts were so sluggish that I was miles north of Severen before I began to reconsider a few things. Only then did it occur to me that the Maer might have been less than completely honest in everything he had told me the night before.

Was I truly the best person to lead a handful of trackers into an unfamiliar forest to kill a band of highwaymen? Did the Maer really think so much of me?

No. Of course not. It was flattering, but simply not true. The Maer had access to better resources than that. The truth was, he probably wanted his sweet-tongued assistant out of the way now that he had the Lady Lackless well in hand. I was foolish for not realizing it sooner.

So he sent me on a fool's errand to get me out from underfoot. He expected me to spend a month chasing his wild goose in the deep forest of the Eld then come back empty-handed. The purse made better sense, too. A hundred bits would keep us provisioned for a month or so. Then, when I ran out of money I'd be forced to return to Severen where the Maer would cluck his tongue in disappointment and use my failure as an excuse to ignore some of the favor I'd accumulated so far.

On the other hand, if I got lucky and found the bandits, all the better. It was exactly the sort of plan I'd credit to the Maer. No matter what happened, he got something he wanted.

It was irritating. But I could hardly go back to Severen and confront him. Now that I'd committed myself, there was nothing to do but make the best of the situation.

As I walked north, my head throbbing and my mouth gritty, I decided I would surprise the Maer again. I'd hunt down his bandits.

Then third time would pay for all, and Maer Alveron would be well and truly in my debt.

CHAPTER SEVENTY-FIVE

The Players

OVER THE NEXT FEW hours of walking, I did my best to get to know the men Alveron had saddled me with. I speak figuratively, of course, as one of them was a woman, and we were all five of us afoot.

Tempi caught my eye first and held it the longest, as he was the first Adem mercenary I'd ever met. Far from being the imposing, hard-eyed killer I'd expected, Tempi was rather nondescript, neither particularly tall nor heavily built. He was fair-skinned with light hair and pale grey eyes. His expression was blank as fresh paper. Strangely blank. *Studiously* blank.

I knew Adem mercenaries wore blood-red clothing as a sort of badge. But Tempi's outfit was different than I'd expected. His shirt was held tight against his body with a dozen soft leather straps. His pants, too, were belted tightly at the thigh and calf and knee. Everything was dyed the same bright and bloody red, and it fit him snugly as a gentleman's glove.

As the day grew warm, I saw him begin to sweat. After living in the cool, thin air of the Stormwal, the weather must have seemed disproportionately hot to him. An hour before noon, he loosened the leather straps of his shirt and peeled it away, using it to wipe the sweat from his face and arms. He didn't seem even slightly self-conscious about walking the king's highway naked to the waist.

Tempi's skin was so pale it was almost the color of cream, and his body was lean and sleek as a coursing hound, his muscles shifting under his skin with an animal grace. I tried not to stare, but my eyes couldn't help but pick out the thin, pale scars that crossed his arms and chest and back.

He never offered a word of complaint about the heat. Words of any sort seemed rare from him, and he responded to most questions with a nod or a shake of the head. He carried a travelsack like mine, and his sword, far from being intimidating, seemed rather short and unimpressive.

Dedan was as different from Tempi as one man can be from another. He was tall, wide, and thick around the chest and neck. He carried a heavy sword, a long knife, and wore a mismatched set of boiled leather armor, hard enough to knock on and often mended. If you have ever seen a caravan guard, then you have seen Dedan, or at least someone cut from the same bolt of cloth.

He ate most, complained most, swore most, and had a stubborn streak thicker than a broad oak plank. But to be fair, he also had a friendly manner and an easy laugh. I was tempted to think of him as stupid due to his manners and his size, but Dedan had a quick wit when he bothered using it.

Hespe was a female mercenary. Not as rare a creature as some folk think. In appearance and equipage she was a near-mirror of Dedan. The leather, the heavy sword, the slightly weatherworn and world-wise attitude. She had broad shoulders, strong hands, and a proud face with a jaw like a cinder-brick. Her hair was blonde and fine, but cut short, in the fashion of a man's.

But to see her as a female version of Dedan was a mistake. She was reserved where Dedan was all bravado. And while Dedan had an easy manner when his temper wasn't up, Hespe had a vague hardness about her, as if she were constantly expecting someone to give her trouble.

Marten was the oldest of us, our tracker. He wore a little leather, softer and better cared for than Dedan's or Hespe's. He carried a long knife, a short knife, and a hunter's bow.

Marten had worked as a huntsman before falling out of favor with the baronet whose forests he had tended. Mercenary work was a poor job by comparison, but it kept him fed. His skill with a bow made him valuable despite the fact that he wasn't nearly as physically imposing as either Dedan or Hespe.

The three of them had formed a loose partnership some months ago and had been selling their services as a group ever since. Marten told me they'd done other jobs for the Maer, the most recent of which involved scouting some of the lands around Tinuë.

It took me about ten minutes to realize Marten should be the leader of this expedition. He had more woodcraft than all the rest of us put together and had even hunted men for bounty once or twice. When I mentioned this to him, he shook his head and smiled, telling me that being able to do something and wanting to do it were two very different things indeed.

Last was me: their fearless leader. The Maer's letter of introduction had described me as, "a discerning young man of good education and diverse useful qualities." While this was perfectly true, it also made me sound like the most wretchedly useless court dandy in existence.

Not helping matters was the fact that I was younger than any of them by years and wearing clothes more suited for a dinner party than the road. I carried my lute and the Maer's purse. I wore no sword, no armor, no knife.

I daresay they didn't quite know what to make of me.

———

The sun was about an hour from setting when we passed a tinker on the road. He wore the traditional brown robe, belted with a length of rope. He didn't have a cart, but led a single donkey so loaded with bundles of oddments that it looked like a mushroom.

He made his slow way toward us, singing:

If you need no mending, and nothing needs tending
A wise man will still see the right time for spending.
Enjoy the sunshine,
But though you might feel fine,
If you don't stop now, you'll be filled with regret.
It's better to simply pay,
And prepare for a rainy day
Than think of the tinker when you're dripping wet.

I laughed and applauded. Proper traveling tinkers are a rare breed of people, and I am always glad to see one. My mother told me they were lucky, and my father had valued them for their news. The fact that I was in desperate need of a few items made this meeting three times welcome.

"Ho, Tinker," Dedan said, smiling. "I need fire and a pint. How long before we hit an inn?"

The tinker pointed back the way he had come. "Not twenty minutes' walk." He eyed Dedan. "But you can't tell me there's nothing you need," he admonished. "Everyone needs something."

Dedan shook his head politely. "I beg your pardon, Tinker. My purse is too thin."

"How about you?" The tinker eyed me up and down. "You've the look of a lad who's wanting something."

"I do need a few things," I admitted. Seeing the others look longingly down the road, I motioned them on. "Go ahead," I told them. "I'll be a few minutes."

As they headed off, the tinker rubbed his hands together, grinning. "Well now, what is it you're looking for?"

"Some salt to begin with."

"And a box to put it in," he said as he began to rummage around in his donkey's packs.

"I could use a knife too, if you have one that's not too hard to come by."

"Especially if you're heading north," he said without missing a beat. "Dangerous road that way. Wouldn't do to be without a knife."

"Did you have any trouble?" I asked, hoping he might know something that could help us find the bandits.

"Oh no," he said as he dug through his packs. "Things aren't so bad that anyone would dream of laying hands on a tinker. Still, it's a bad stretch of road." He produced a long, narrow knife in a leather sheath and handed it to me. "Ramston steel."

I drew it out of its sheath, and gave the blade a close look. It was Ramston steel. "I don't need anything that fine," I said, handing it back. "I'll be putting it to everyday use, eating mostly."

"Ramston's fine for everyday use," the tinker said pushing it back into my hands. "You can use it to trim kindling, then shave with it if you like. Keeps an edge forever."

"I might have to put it to hard use," I clarified. "And Ramston's brittle."

"There is that," the tinker admitted easily. "As my father always used to say, 'the best knife you'll ever have until it breaks.' But the same could be said of any knife. And truth be told, that's the only knife I have."

I sighed. I know when I'm being skinned. "And a tinderbox."

He held one out almost before I finished saying it. "I couldn't help but notice you've got a little ink about the fingers." He gestured at my hands. "I've got some paper here, good quality. Pen and ink too. Nothing worse than having an idea for a song and not being able to write it down." He held out a leather parcel of paper, pens, and ink.

I shook my head, knowing that the Maer's purse would only stretch so far. "I think I'm done with song writing for a while, Tinker."

He shrugged, still holding it out. "Letter writing then. I know a fellow who had to open a vein once to write a note to his ladylove. Dramatic, true. Symbolic, certainly. But also painful, unsanitary, and more than slightly macabre. Now he carries pen and ink with him wherever he goes."

I felt the color drain from my face as the tinker's words reminded me of something else I'd forgotten in my rush to leave Severen: Denna. All thought of her had been forced out of my mind by the Maer's talk of bandits, two bottles of strong wine, and a night with no sleep. I had left without a word after our terrible fight. What would she think if I spoke so cruelly to her, then simply disappeared?

I was already a full day's journey from Severen. I couldn't go back just to tell her I was leaving, could I? I considered it for a moment. No. Besides, Denna herself had disappeared for days without a word of warning. Surely she would understand if I did the same. . . .

Stupid. Stupid. Stupid. My thoughts spun in circles as I tried to decide among my several unpleasant options.

The harsh *hee haa* of the tinker's donkey startled a thought into me. "Are you headed to Severen, Tinker?"

"More through than to," he said. "But yes."

"I just remembered a letter I need to send. If I gave it to you, could you deliver it to a certain inn?"

He nodded slowly. "I could," he said. "Given that you'll be needing paper and ink. . . ." He smiled, waving the package again.

I grimaced. "I will, Tinker. But how much will the lot of this cost me?"

He looked at the accumulated items. "Salt and box: four bits. Knife: fifteen bits. Paper, pens, and ink: eighteen bits. Tinderbox: three bits."

"And the delivery," I said.

"An *urgent* delivery," the tinker said with a bit of a smile. "To a lady, unless I mistake the look on your face."

I nodded.

"Right," he rubbed his chin. "Ordinarily, I'd push for about thirty-five then have a nice leisurely dicker where you bargain me down to thirty."

The price was reasonable, especially considering how hard it was to find good paper. Still, it was a full third of the money the Maer had given me. We would need that money for food, lodging, and other supplies.

But before I could say anything, the tinker continued. "Now I can tell that's too much for your comfort," he said. "And I hope you don't think me too forward in saying this, but that is a rather fine cloak you're wearing. I'm always willing to make a fellow a trade."

I pulled my lovely burgundy cloak around me self-consciously. "I suppose I'd be willing to give it up," I said, not having to fake the regret in my voice. "But that will leave me with no cloak at all. What will I do when it rains?"

"No trouble there," the tinker said. He pulled a bundle of cloth out of a pack and held it up for me to see. It had been black once upon a time, but long use and many washings had faded it to a dark greenish color.

"It's a little tatty," I said, reaching out to finger a fraying seam.

"It's just broken in, that's all," he said easily, spreading it across my shoulders. "Good fit. Good color for you, brings out your eyes. Besides, you don't want to be looking too well-off, what with those bandits on the road."

I sighed. "What will you give me in trade?" I asked, handing my beautiful cloak over to him. "That cloak's not a month old, mind you, and it's never even seen a drop of rain."

The tinker ran his hands over my beautiful cloak. "It's got all sorts of little pockets!" he said admiringly. "That's just lovely!"

I fingered the thinning cloth of the tinker's cloak. "If you'll throw in needle and thread, I'll trade you my cloak for the lot of it," I said with sudden inspiration. "Plus I'll give you an iron penny, a copper penny, and a silver penny."

I grinned. It was a pittance. But that's what tinkers in stories ask for when they trade some fabulous piece of magic to an unsuspecting widow's son when he's off to make his fortune in the world.

The tinker threw his head back and laughed. "I was about to suggest that very thing," he said. Then he tossed my cloak over his arm and shook my hand firmly.

I fished around in my purse and handed over an iron drab, two Vintish half-pennies, and, much to my pleasant surprise, an Aturan hard penny. The last was lucky for me as it was only worth a fraction of a Vintish silver round. I emptied the dozen pockets of my burgundy cloak into my travelsack and collected my new possessions from the tinker.

Then I wrote a quick letter to Denna, explaining that my patron had sent me away unexpectedly. I apologized for the rash things I'd said, and told her I would meet with her as soon as I was back in Severen. I would have liked more time to compose it. I would have liked to give a more subtle apology, a more detailed explanation, but the tinker had finished packing away my beautiful cloak and was obviously eager to be on his way again.

Not having any sealing wax to secure the letter, I used a trick I'd invented while writing notes on the Maer's behalf. I folded the piece of paper against itself, then tucked it together in such a way that it would be necessary to tear the paper in order to unfold it again.

I handed it to the tinker. "It goes to a pretty, dark-haired woman by the name of Denna. She's staying at the Four Tapers in Severen-Low."

"That reminds me," he exclaimed as he tucked my letter into a pocket. "Candles." He reached into a saddlebag and pulled out a handful of fat tallow tapers. "Everyone needs candles."

Funny thing was, I *could* use some, though not for the reasons he thought.

"I've also got some rubbing wax for your boots," he continued, rooting through his bundles. "We get fierce rain this time of year."

I held up my hands, laughing. "I'll give you a bit for four candles, but I can't afford any more. If this keeps up I'll have to buy your donkey just to carry the lot with me."

"Suit yourself," he said with an easy shrug. "Pleasure doing business with you, young sir."

CHAPTER SEVENTY-SIX

Tinder

THE SUN WAS STARTING to set by the time we found a good place to camp on the second night. Dedan went foraging for firewood. Marten began cutting up carrots and potatoes and sent Hespe to fill the cookpot with water. I used Marten's small spade to dig a pit for our fire.

Without being asked, Tempi picked up a branch and used his sword to shave thin strips of dry wood to use for tinder. Unsheathed, his sword still didn't seem terribly impressive. But given how easily it was peeling away paper-thin strips of wood, it must have been sharp as a shaving razor.

I finished lining the pit with stones. Wordlessly, Tempi handed me a handful of tinder.

I nodded. "Would you like to use my knife?" I asked, hoping to draw him into a bit of a conversation. I'd barely shared a dozen words with him in the last two days.

Tempi's pale grey eyes looked at the knife on my belt, then back at his sword. He shook his head, fidgeting nervously.

"Isn't it bad for the edge?" I asked.

The mercenary shrugged, avoiding my eye.

I began to lay the fire, and that was when I made my first mistake. As I've said, there was a chill in the air, and we were all of us tired. So rather than spend half an hour slowly nursing a spark into a decent campfire, I arranged twigs around Tempi's tinder, then stacked progressively bigger sticks around it, making a tightly packed cluster of wood.

Dedan returned with another armload of firewood just as I was finishing. "Lovely," he groused, quiet enough he could pretend he was just talking to himself, but loud enough so everyone could hear. "And you're in charge. Wonderful."

"What's stuck in your teeth now?" Marten asked, tiredly.

"Boy's making a little wooden fort, not a fire." Dedan sighed dramatically, then assumed a tone he probably thought was fatherly, but came across as profoundly condescending. "Here, I'll help you out. A spark will never catch on that. Do you have flint and steel? I'll show you how to use them."

No one enjoys being talked down to, but I have a particular aversion to it. Dedan had been making it clear for two days that he thought I was an idiot.

I gave a tired sigh. My oldest, most world-weary sigh. That was how I needed to play it. He thought of me as young and useless. I needed to drive home the point that I was nothing of the sort. "Dedan," I asked, "what do you know about me?"

He gave me a blank look.

"You know one thing about me," I said calmly. "You know the Maer put me in charge." I looked him in the eye. "Is the Maer an idiot?"

Dedan made a dismissive gesture. "Of course not, I was just sayin'. . ."

I stood up and regretted it, as it just brought into sharp contrast how much taller he was. "Would the Maer have put me in charge if I were an idiot?"

He gave an insincere smile, trying to pass off two days' worth of derogatory muttering as some sort of misunderstanding. "Now don't get all twisted up over—"

I held up my hand. "This isn't your fault. You just don't know anything about me. But let's not waste time on it tonight. We're all tired. For now, rest assured that I'm not some rich tit's son, out for a lark."

I pinched a thin piece of Tempi's tinder between my fingers and concentrated. I pulled more heat than I needed and felt my arm go chilly all the way to the shoulder. "And rest assured I know how to start a fire."

The shaved pieces of wood caught fire, flaring up hot and sudden, catching the rest of the tinder and making flames leap up almost instantly.

I'd meant it to be a dramatic gesture so Dedan would stop thinking of me as some useless boy. But the time I spent at the University had made me jaded. Starting a fire like this was as simple as putting on your boots for a member of the Arcanum.

Dedan, on the other hand, had never met an arcanist, and probably hadn't ever been within five hundred miles of the University. Everything he knew about magic was from campfire stories.

So when the fire flared up, he went pale as a sheet and took several sudden steps back. He looked for all the world as if I'd suddenly called up a roaring sheet of fire like Taborlin the Great.

Then I saw Marten and Hespe wearing the same expression, native Vintish superstition written clearly on their faces. Their eyes went to the flickering fire, then back to me. I was one of *those*. I meddled with dark powers. I summoned demons. I ate the entire little cheese, including the rind.

Looking at their stunned faces, I realized nothing I said would set them at ease. Not right now. So instead I sighed and began to set up my sleeping roll for the night.

While there wasn't much cheerful conversation around the fire that night, there wasn't any muttering from Dedan either. I'd like respect, but failing that, a little healthy fear can go a long way to making things run smoothly.

———

Two days with no further dramatics on my part helped everyone relax. Dedan was still all bluff and bravado, but he had quit calling me "boy" and was only complaining about half as much, so I considered it a victory.

Flushed with this lukewarm success, I decided to make an active attempt to draw Tempi into a conversation. If I was going to be in charge of this little group, I needed to know more about him. Most importantly, I needed to know if he could speak more than five words in a row.

So I approached the Adem mercenary when we stopped for our midday meal. He was sitting slightly apart from the rest of us. He wasn't standoffish. It's just that the rest of us would sit and talk while we ate. Tempi, on the other hand, simply ate.

But today I made a point of sitting down next to him with my lunch: a chunk of hard sausage and some cold potatoes. "Hello, Tempi."

He looked up and nodded. For a second I caught a glimpse of his pale grey eyes. Then he looked away, shifting restlessly. He ran his hand through his hair, and for a second he reminded me of Simmon. They both had the same slender build and sandy hair. Simmon wasn't this quiet though. Sometimes I could barely get a word in edgewise with Sim.

I'd tried to talk to Tempi before, of course. Ordinary small talk: the weather, sore feet after a long day's walk, the food. These had all come to nothing. At best a word or two. More often a nod or a shrug. But most common was a blank look followed by fidgeting and a stubborn refusal to do so much as look me in the eye.

So today I had a conversational gambit. "I have heard stories about the Lethani," I said. "I would like to know more. Would you tell me about it?"

Tempi's pale eyes touched mine briefly, his expression still blank. Then he looked away again. He tugged one of the red leather straps that held his shirt close to his body and fidgeted with his sleeve. "No. I will not speak on Lethani. It is not for you. Do not ask."

He looked away from me again, down at the ground.

I counted in my head. Sixteen words. That answered one of my questions at least.

CHAPTER SEVENTY-SEVEN

Pennysworth

TWILIGHT WAS SETTLING IN as we rounded a curve in the road. I
heard clapping and stomping mingled with music, shouting, and roars
of laughter. After ten hours of walking, the sound lifted my spirits to an almost cheerful level.

Located at the last major crossroad south of the Eld, the Pennysworth
Inn was enormous. Built of rough-hewn timber, it had two full stories and
a scattering of gables that hinted at a smaller, third floor above that. Through
the windows I caught glimpses of men and women dancing while an unseen
fiddler sawed out a mad and breathless tune.

Dedan took a deep breath. "Can you smell that? I tell you, there's a woman
in this place could cook a stone and make me beg for more. Sweet Peg. By
these hands, I hope she's still around." He made a curving gesture, showing
the double meaning of his words as he nudged Marten with an elbow.

Hespe's eyes narrowed as she stared at the back of Dedan's head.

Oblivious, Dedan continued, "Tonight I'll sleep with a bellyful of lamb
and brandy. Although a little less sleeping might prove a little more entertaining, if my last trip here was any indication."

I saw the storm brewing on Hespe's face and spoke up quickly. "Whatever's in the pot and a bunk for each of us," I said firmly. "Anything else comes
out of your own pocket."

Dedan looked as if he couldn't quite believe his ears. "Come off it. We've
been sleeping rough for days. Besides, 'taint your money, don't be a stingy
shim with it."

"We haven't done our job yet," I said calmly. "Not even a piece of it. I
don't know how long we may be out here, but I know I'm not rich. If we run
through the Maer's purse too quickly we're going to have to hunt for what

we eat." I looked around at everyone. "Unless someone else has enough coin to keep us fed and cares to share?"

Marten smiled ruefully at the suggestion. Hespe's eyes were for Dedan, who continued glowering in my direction.

Tempi fidgeted, his expression unreadable as ever. Avoiding my eyes, he glanced at everyone in turn, his expression blank. His eyes moved, not from face to face, but at Dedan's hands, then Dedan's feet. Then Marten's feet, then Hespe's, then mine. He shifted his weight and moved a half-step closer to Dedan.

Hoping to dispel the tension, I softened my tone and said, "After everything is done we'll split what's left of the purse. That way each of us will have a little extra in our pocket before we even get back to Severen. We can each spend our lots as we want to. Then."

I could tell Dedan wasn't pleased and waited to see if he would press the point.

Instead it was Marten who spoke up. "After a day of long walking," he said in a musing voice, as if talking to himself. "A drink *would* go down nice."

Dedan looked to his friend, then back to me expectantly.

"I think the purse can stand a round of drinks," I conceded with a smile. "I don't think the Maer is trying to make priests of us, do you?"

This got a throaty laugh from Hespe, while Marten and Dedan cracked smiles. Tempi glanced at me with his pale eyes, fidgeted, and looked away.

———

A few minutes of relaxed haggling got the five of us common bunks, a simple supper, and a round of drinks for a single silver bit. After that was done, I found a table in a quieter corner of the room and tucked my lute out of harm's way under my bench. Then I sat down, bone weary and wondering what I could do to get Dedan to stop acting like such a little swaggercock.

Such was the distracted turning of my thoughts when my dinner thumped onto the table in front of me. I looked up to see a woman's face and well-advertised bosom framed by a tumble of bright red curls. Her skin was white as cream with just the barest hint of freckle. Her lips a pale, dangerous pink. Her eyes a bright, dangerous green.

"Thank you," I said, somewhat belatedly.

"You're welcome, love." She smiled playfully with her eyes and brushed her hair back from her bare shoulder. "It looked like you were almost a-sleeping in your seat."

"I nearly was. A long day and a long road."

"That's a shame indeed," she said with playful regret as she rubbed the back of her neck. "If I thought you'd still be on your feet in an hour, I'd take you off them." She reached out and twined her fingers lightly through the hair on the back of my head. "The two of us would be enough to start a fire."

I froze like a startled deer. I cannot say why, except perhaps that I was tired from several days on the road. Perhaps it was that I'd never been approached in such a forthright manner before. Perhaps—

Perhaps I was young and woefully inexperienced. Let us leave it at that.

I scrambled desperately for something to say, but by the time I found my tongue she'd taken a half step away and given me a shrewd look. I felt my face grow hot, embarrassing me further. Without thinking, I looked down at the table and the dinner she'd brought. *Potato soup*, I thought numbly.

She gave a small, quiet laugh and touched my shoulder kindly. "I'm sorry lad. You looked like you were a little more—" She broke off, as if reconsidering her words, then started again. "I liked the fresh look of you, but I didn't think you were *that* young."

Though she spoke gently, I could hear the smile in her voice. It made my face burn even hotter, all the way to my ears. Finally, seeming to realize that anything she said would just embarrass me further, she took her hand off my shoulder. "I'll be back to see if you need anything later."

I nodded dumbly and watched her go. Her retreat was pleasing, but I was distracted by the sounds of scattered laughter. I looked around to see amusement on the faces of the men sitting at the long tables around me. One group raised their mugs in a silent, mocking salute. Another fellow leaned over to pat my back consolingly, saying, "Don't take it personal, boy, she's turned all of us away."

Feeling as if everyone in the room was watching me, I kept my eyes low and began to eat my dinner. As I tore off pieces of bread and dipped them in my soup, I composed a mental catalog of the extent of my idiocy. Surreptitiously, I watched the red-haired serving girl entertain and rebuff the ploys of a dozen men as she carried drinks from table to table.

I had regained a bit of my composure by the time Marten slid into a chair next to me. "You did a good job with Dedan out there," he said without preamble.

My spirits lifted a bit. "Did I?"

Marten nodded slightly as his sharp eyes wandered over the crowd that filled the room. "Most folk try to bully him, make him feel stupid. He'd have paid you back ten times the trouble if you'd done it that way."

"He *was* being stupid," I pointed out. "And when you come right down to it, I *did* bully him."

It was his turn to shrug. "But you did it smart, so he'll still listen to you."

He took a drink and paused, changing the subject. "Hespe offered to share a room with him tonight," he said casually.

"Really?" I said, more than slightly surprised. "She's getting bolder."

He gave a slow nod.

"And?" I prompted.

"And nothing. Dedan said he'd be damned before he spent money on a room he should have for free." He slid his eyes to me and raised an eyebrow.

"You're not serious," I said flatly. "He has to know. He's just playing the simpleton because he doesn't like her."

"I don't think so," Marten said, turning toward me and lowering his voice a bit. "Three span ago we finished a caravan job from Ralien. It was a long haul, and Dedan and me had a pocket full of coin and nothing in particular to do with it, so by the end of the night we're sitting in this grubby little dockside tavern, too drunk to stand up and leave. And he starts talking about her."

Marten shook his head slowly. "He went on for an hour, and you wouldn't have recognized the woman he was describing as our hard-eyed Hespe. He practically sang about her." He sighed. "He thinks she's too good for him. *And* he's convinced if he so much as looked at her sideways he'd end up with his arm broken in three places."

"Why didn't you tell him?"

"Tell him what? That was before she started going all cow-eyed over him. I thought his worries were fairly sensible at the time. What do you think Hespe would do to you if you were to give her a friendly pat on any of her friendlier parts?"

I looked over to where Hespe stood at the bar. One foot tapped roughly in time to the rhythm of the fiddle. Other than that, the set of her shoulders, her eyes, the line of her jaw were all hard, almost belligerent. There was a small but noticeable gap between her and the men standing on either side of her at the bar.

"I probably wouldn't risk my arm either," I admitted. "But he *has* to know by now. He isn't blind."

"He's no worse off than the rest of us."

I started to protest, then glanced at the red-haired serving girl. "We could tell him," I said. "*You* could. He trusts you."

Marten sucked at his teeth with his tongue. "Nah," he said, setting his drink down firmly. "It would just make things muddier. Either he'll see it or he won't. In his own time, in his own way." He shrugged. "Or not, and the sun will still rise in the morning."

Neither of us spoke for a long while. Marten watched the buzzing room over the top of his mug, his eyes growing distant. I let the noise of the place fade to a low comforting purr as I leaned against the wall, drowsing.

And as my thoughts untended tend to do, they wandered to Denna. I thought about the smell of her, the arch of her neck near her ear, the way her hands moved when she talked. I wondered where she was tonight, if she was well. I wondered just a bit if her thoughts ever wandered into warm musings of me. . . .

———

". . . hunting bandits shouldn't be hard. Besides, it'll be nice to get the jump on them for a change, lawless damn ravel bastards."

The words drew me out of my warm drowse like a fish yanked from a pool. The fiddler had stopped playing to have a drink, and in the relative quiet of the room Dedan's voice was loud as a donkey's bray. I opened my eyes and saw Marten was looking around in mild alarm too, no doubt roused by the same words that had caught my ear.

It only took me a second to spot Dedan. He was sitting two tables away, having a drunken conversation with a grey-haired farmer.

Marten was already getting to his feet. Not wanting to draw attention to the situation, I hissed, "Get him," and forced myself back into my seat.

I gritted my teeth as Marten threaded quickly through the tables, tapped Dedan on the shoulder, and jerked a thumb toward the table where I sat. Dedan grumbled something I'm glad I didn't hear and grudgingly pushed himself to his feet.

I forced my eyes to wander around the room rather than follow Dedan. Tempi was easy to spot in his mercenary reds. He was facing the hearth, watching the fiddler tune his instrument. There were several empty glasses on the table in front of him, and he had loosened the leather straps of his shirt. He eyed the fiddler with a strange intensity.

As I watched, a serving girl brought him another drink. He looked her over, his pale eyes moving pointedly up and down her body. She said something, and he kissed the back of her hand as smoothly as a courtier. She blushed and pushed at his shoulder playfully. One of his hands moved smoothly to the curve of her waist and rested there. She didn't seem to mind.

Dedan stepped close to my table, eclipsing my view of Tempi just as the fiddler lifted his bow and began to saw out a jig. A dozen people came to their feet, eager to dance.

"What?" Dedan demanded as he came to stand in front of my table. "Have ye called me over here to tell me it's gettin' late? That I've got a busy day tomorrow and I should tuck my little self into bed?" He leaned forward onto the table, putting his eyes more on level with mine. I caught a sour smell on his breath: dreg. A cheap, repulsive liquor you can start fires with.

I laughed dismissively. "Hell, I'm not your mum." Actually I had been about to say that very thing and scrambled mentally for something else to distract him with. My eye lighted on the redhead that had served me my dinner earlier that evening, and I leaned forward in my seat. "I was wondering if you could tell me something," I said in my best conspiratorial tone.

His scowl gave way to curiosity, and I lowered my voice a little more. "You've been here before, right?" He nodded, leaning a little closer. "Do you know what that girl's name is?" I nodded my head in the redhead's direction.

Dedan took an over-careful look over his shoulder that surely would have drawn her attention if she hadn't been facing away from us. "The blonde one the Adem's pawin' at?" Dedan asked.

"Redhead."

Dedan's broad forehead wrinkled as he squinted the far side of the room into focus. "Losine?" He asked softly. He turned to me, still squinting. "Little Losi?"

I shrugged and began to regret my choice of diversionary tactic.

An explosive laugh burst out of the big man and he half fell, half slid onto the bench across from me.

"Losi," he chuckled a little more loudly than I liked. "Kvothe, I had you all wrong." He slapped the table with the flat of his hand and laughed again, nearly tipping himself over backward on the bench. "Ah, you've got a good eye, boy, but you haven't got a damn chance."

My battered pride pricked up at this. "Why not? Isn't she, well—" I trailed off, making an inarticulate gesture.

He somehow managed to gather my meaning. "A whore?" he asked incredulously. "God boy, no. There's a couple around." He made a sweeping gesture over his head, then lowered his voice to a more private level. "Not really whores, mind you. Just girls who don't mind a little extra at night." He paused, blinked. "Money. Extra money. *And* extra other things." He chortled.

"I just thought . . ." I began weakly.

"Ay, any man who ever had eyes and balls thought that." He leaned a little closer. "She's a lusty little one. She'll trip a man who catches her eye, but she can't be talked or bought into bed. If she could, she'd be rich as the king of Vint." He looked in her direction. "How much's a roll with that worth? I'd give—"

He squinted in her direction, his lips moving as if going through some silent, complex arithmetic. After a moment he shrugged. "More than I've got." He looked back to me, shrugged again. "Still, it's no good wishing. Save yourself the trouble. If ye want, I know a lady here who's no shame to look at. Might be willing to brighten up your evening." He started to look around the room.

"No!" I put my hand on his arm to stop him. "I was just curious, that's all." I sounded insincere and I knew it. "Thanks for filling me in."

"Nothin' to it." He carefully got to his feet.

"Oh," I said, as if a thought had just occurred to me. "Could you do me a favor?" He nodded and I gestured him closer. "I'm worried Hespe might end up talking about our job for the Maer. If the bandits hear we're hunting them, things will get ten times harder." A guilty look flashed across his face. "I'm pretty sure she wouldn't mention it, but you know how women like to talk."

"I understand," he said quickly as he stood up. "I'll talk to her. Better to be careful."

The hawk-faced fiddler finished his jig, and everyone clapped and stomped and pounded empty mugs on their tables. I sighed and rubbed my face into my hands. When I looked up I saw Marten at the table next to mine. He touched his fingers to his forehead and nodded a small salute. I gave a slight, seated bow. It's always nice to have an appreciative audience.

CHAPTER SEVENTY-EIGHT

Another Road, Another Forest

I TOOK A CERTAIN DARK pleasure in seeing a rather hungover Dedan on the road before the sun was fully in the sky the next morning. The large man carried himself delicately, but to give him due credit, he didn't offer a word of complaint, unless the occasional low moan can be counted as a word.

Now that I was watching more closely, I spotted the marks of infatuation on Dedan. The way he said Hespe's name. The coarse jokes he made when talking to her. Every few minutes he would find an excuse to glance in her direction. Always under some pretext: a stretch, an idle glance at the road, a gesture to the trees around us.

Despite this, Dedan remained oblivious to the sporadic courtship Hespe was paying him in return. At times it was amusing to watch, like a well-orchestrated Modegan tragedy. At times I wanted to strangle them both.

Tempi traveled wordlessly among us like a mute, well-behaved puppy. He watched everything: the trees, the road, the clouds. If it weren't for the un-questionably intelligent look in his eyes, I'd have thought him a simpleton by this point. The few questions I put to him were still met with awkward fidgeting, nods, shrugs, or shakes of the head.

All the while my curiosity nagged at me. I knew the Lethani was just a piece of storybook nonsense, but part of me couldn't help but wonder. Was he really saving his words? Could he really use his quiet like armor? Move fast as a snake? The truth was, after catching glimpses of what Elxa Dal and Fela could do by calling on the names of fire and stone, the thought of someone storing up words to burn as fuel didn't seem nearly as foolish as it used to.

The five of us got to know each other in dribs and drabs, growing familiar with each other's quirks. Dedan carefully groomed the ground where he lay his bedroll, not just removing twigs and stones, but stomping flat every tuft of grass or lump of dirt.

Hespe whistled tunelessly when she thought no one was listening and picked her teeth methodically after every meal. Marten wouldn't eat meat that had the barest bit of pink to it or drink water that hadn't been boiled or mixed with wine. He told the rest of us at least twice a day that we were fools for not doing the same.

But in terms of odd behavior, Tempi was the prize winner of the lot. He wouldn't look me in the eye. Didn't smile. Didn't frown. Didn't speak.

Since we left the Pennysworth, he had made only one comment of his own free will. "Rain would make this road another road, this forest another forest." He said each word distinctly, as if he had been deliberating on the statement all day. For all I knew, he had.

He washed himself obsessively. The rest of us would take advantage of a bathhouse when we stopped at an inn, but Tempi bathed every day. If there was a stream handy, he would bathe both at night and then again when he woke. Otherwise, he would wash himself using a cloth and some of his drinking water.

And twice a day without fail, he performed an elaborate ritual stretch, his hands making careful shapes and patterns in the air. It reminded me of the slow court dances they perform in Modeg.

It obviously kept him limber, but it was strange to watch. Hespe made jokes about how if the bandits asked us to dance, our sweet-smelling mercenary would be a wonderful help. But she said it quietly, when Tempi was out of earshot.

In terms of quirks, I suppose I was in no position to throw stones. I played my lute most evenings, when I wasn't too weary from walking. I daresay it didn't improve the others' opinion of me as a tactical leader or arcanist.

As we neared our destination, I grew increasingly anxious. Marten was the only one of us truly suited to this work. Dedan and Hespe would be good in a fight, but they were troublesome to work with. Dedan was argumentative and stubborn. Hespe was lazy. She rarely helped prepare meals or clean up afterward unless she was asked, and even then her help was so grudging it was barely any help at all.

And then there was Tempi, a hired killer who wouldn't look me in the eye or hold a conversation. A mercenary I firmly believed could look forward to a decent career in the Modegan theater....

Five days after leaving Severen, we came to the area where the attacks had been made. A twenty-mile stretch of twisting road that ran through the Eld: no towns, no inns, not even an abandoned farm. An utterly isolated stretch of the king's highway in the middle of an endless ancient wood. The natural habitat of bears, mad hermits, and poachers. A highwayman's paradise.

Marten went scouting while the rest of us set up camp. An hour later he emerged from the trees, winded but in good spirits. He reassured us he hadn't found sign of anyone else nearby.

"I can't believe I'm defending tax collectors," Dedan muttered disgustedly. Hespe gave a throaty laugh.

"You're defending civilization," I corrected. "And you're keeping the roads safe. Besides, Maer Alveron does important things with those taxes." I grinned. "Like pay us."

"That's what *I'm* fighting for," Marten said.

After dinner, I outlined the only strategy I'd been able to come up with in five long days of thinking. I drew a curving line on the ground with a stick. "Okay. Here's the road, about twenty miles of it."

"Mieles." The soft voice was Tempi's.

"Excuse me?" I asked. This was the first thing I had heard him say in a day and a half.

"Miils?" His accent was so thick around the unfamiliar word that it took me a second to understand he was saying "miles."

"Miles." I said distinctly. I pointed in the direction of the road and held up one finger. "From here to the road is one mile. Today we walked fifteen miles."

He nodded once.

I turned back to my drawing. "It's safe to assume the bandits are within ten miles of the road." I drew a box around my crude sketch of the road. "That gives us four hundred square miles of forest to search."

There was a moment of silence as everyone absorbed that piece of information. Finally, Tempi spoke, "That is large."

I nodded seriously. "It would take us months to search that much territory, but we shouldn't have to." I added a couple more lines to my drawing. "Every day Marten will scout ahead for us." I looked up to him. "How much ground can you safely cover in a day?"

He thought for a second, looking around at the trees surrounding us. "This forest? With this much underscrub? About a square mile."

"How many if you're being careful?"

He smiled. "I'm always careful."

I nodded and drew a line parallel to the road. "Marten will scout a strip about a half mile wide, about a mile back from the road. He'll keep an eye out for their camp or their sentries so the rest of us don't stumble into them accidentally."

Hespe shook her head. "That's no good. They won't be that close to the road. If they're looking to stay hid, they'll be farther back. At least two or three miles."

Dedan nodded. "I'd make sure I was at least four miles from the road before I hunkered down and made a habit of killing folk."

"I think so too," I agreed. "But they have to make their way to the road sooner or later. They have to post lookouts and travel back and forth for ambushes. They need to reprovision themselves. Since they've been here several months, odds are they've worn some sort of trail."

I added a little detail to my dirt map with my stick. "After Marten has scouted, two of us will go in and make a careful search behind him. We'll cover a thin strip of forest, searching it for any sign of their trail. The other two will keep an eye on the camp.

"We can cover about two miles a day. We'll start on the north side of the road and search from west to east. If we don't find a trail, we'll cross to the south side of the road and work our way back from east to west." I finished drawing in the dirt and stood back. "We'll find their trail in a span of days. Maybe two, depending on our luck." I leaned back and drove my stick into the ground.

Dedan stared bleakly at the rough map. "We'll need more supplies."

I nodded. "We'll move camp every fifth day. Two of us will walk back to Crosson to get supplies. The other two will move the camp. Marten will rest."

Marten spoke up. "We'll have to be careful with our fires from now on, too," he said. "The smell of smoke will give us away if we're upwind of them."

I nodded. "We'll need a fire pit every night, and we'll want to keep an eye out for rennel trees." I looked at Marten. "You know what a rennel looks like, don't you?" His expression was surprised.

Hespe looked back and forth between us. "What's rennel?" she asked.

"It's a tree," Marten said. "Good for firewood. It burns clean and hot. No smoke to speak of, and hardly any stink of smoke either."

"Even when the wood is green," I said. "Same with the leaves. It's useful stuff. It doesn't grow everywhere, but I've seen some around."

"How does a city boy like you know something like that?" Dedan asked.

"Knowing things is what I do," I said seriously. "And what in the world makes you think I grew up in a city?"

Dedan shrugged, looking away.

"That should be the only wood we burn from here on out," I said. "If it's in short supply, we'll save it for a cookfire. If we don't have any, we'll have to eat cold. So keep an eye out."

Everyone nodded, Tempi slightly later than the rest.

"Lastly, we'd better have our stories straight in case they stumble onto us while we're looking for them." I pointed to Marten. "What are you going to say if someone catches you while you're out scouting?"

He looked surprised, but hardly hesitated in his response. "I'm a poacher." He pointed to his unstrung bow leaning against a tree. "It won't be far from the truth."

"And you're from?"

There was a flicker of hesitation. "Crosson, just a day west of here."

"And your name is?"

"M-Meris," he said awkwardly. Dedan laughed.

I cracked a smile. "Don't lie about your name. It's hard to do convincingly. If they catch you and let you go, fine. Just don't lead them back to our camp. If they want to take you back with them, make the best of it. Pretend you'd like to join up. Don't try to run."

Marten looked uneasy. "I just stay with them?"

I nodded. "They'll expect you to run on the first night if they think you're stupid. If they think you're clever, they'll expect you to run on the second night. But by the third night they should trust you a bit. Wait until midnight, then start some sort of disturbance. Light a couple of tents on fire or something. We'll be waiting for the confusion and take them apart from the outside."

I looked around at the other three. "The plan is the same for any of you. Wait until the third night."

"How will you find their camp?" Marten asked, a thin layer of sweat on his forehead. I didn't blame him. This was a dangerous game we were playing. "If they catch me, I won't be there to help track you down."

"I won't be finding *them*," I said. "I'll be finding you. I can find any of you in the forest."

I looked around the fire, expecting at least a grumble from Dedan, but none of them seemed to doubt my arcane abilities. Idly, I wondered how much they thought I was capable of.

The truth was I'd surreptitiously collected a hair from each of them in the last few days. So I could easily could create a makeshift dowsing pendulum for anyone in the group in less than a minute. Given Vintish superstition, I doubted they'd be happy knowing the specific details.

"What should our stories be?" Hespe tapped Dedan on the chest with the back of her hand, her knuckles making a hollow noise on his hard leather vest.

"Do you think you could convince them you were disgruntled caravan guards who had decided to turn bandit?"

Dedan snorted. "Hell, I've thought about it once or twice." At a look from Hespe he snorted. "Don't tell me you haven't done the same. Span after span of walking in the rain, eating beans, sleeping on the ground. All for penny a day?" He shrugged. "God's teeth. I'm surprised half of us don't take to the trees."

I smiled. "You'll do just fine."

"What about him?" Hespe jerked her thumb at Tempi. "Nobody is going to believe he's gone wild. Adem make ten times what we do for a day's work."

"Twenty times," Dedan grumbled.

I'd been thinking the same thing. "Tempi, what will you do if you are found by the bandits?"

Tempi fidgeted a little, but didn't say anything. He looked at me briefly, then broke eye contact, glancing down and to the side. I couldn't tell if he was thinking, or merely confused.

"If it weren't for his Adem reds, he wouldn't look like anything special," Marten said. "Even the sword doesn't look like much."

"Doesn't look like twenty times as much as me, that's for sure," Dedan's voice was low, but not so low that everyone couldn't hear.

I was worried about Tempi's outfit too. I'd tried to draw the Adem into a conversation several times with the hope of discussing the problem with him, but it was like trying to have a chat with a cat.

But the fact that he hadn't known the word "miles" made me realize something I should have thought of long before. Aturan wasn't his native language. Having recently struggled to make myself fluent in Siaru at the University, I could understand the impulse to keep quiet rather than speak and make a fool of myself.

"He could try to play along, same as us," Hespe said dubiously.

"It's hard to lie convincingly when you're not good with the language," I said.

Tempi's pale eyes darted to each of us as we spoke, but he didn't offer any comment.

"Folk underestimate a person who can't speak well," Hespe said. "Maybe he could sort of just . . . play dumb? Act confused like he was lost?"

"Wouldn't have to play dumb," Dedan continued under his breath. "Could just *be* dumb."

Tempi looked at Dedan, still expressionless, but with more intensity than before. He drew a slow, deliberate breath before speaking. "Quiet is not stupid," he said, his voice flat. "You? Always talk. *Chek chek chek chek chek.*" He made a motion with one hand, like a mouth opening and closing. "Always. Like dog all night barking at tree. Try to be big. No. Just noise. Just dog."

I shouldn't have laughed, but it caught me completely off guard. Partly because I thought of Tempi as so quiet and passive, and partly because he was absolutely right. If Dedan were a dog, he would be a dog that barked endlessly at nothing. Barking just to hear himself bark.

Still, I shouldn't have laughed. But I did. Hespe laughed too and tried to hide it, which was worse.

Dedan's face went dark with anger and he got to his feet. "You come here and say that."

Still expressionless, Tempi stood and walked around the fire until he stood next to Dedan. Well . . . if I say he stood *next* to him, you will take the wrong impression. Most people stand two or three feet away when talking to you. But Tempi walked until he was less than a foot away from Dedan. To get any closer, he would have had to give him a hug or climb him.

I could lie and say this happened too quickly for me to intervene, but that wouldn't be true. The simple truth was that I couldn't think of an easy way to break up the situation. But the more complicated truth was that I was pretty fed up with Dedan myself by this point.

What's more, this was the most I'd ever heard Tempi speak. For the first time since I'd met him, he was behaving like a person, not just some mute, ambulatory doll.

And I was curious to see him fight. I'd heard a lot about the legendary Adem prowess, and I was hoping to see it thump some of the sullen mutter out of Dedan's thick head.

Tempi walked up to Dedan, standing close enough to put his arms around him. Dedan stood a full head taller, broader across the shoulders, and thicker in the chest. Tempi looked up at him without a trace of anything you might expect to see on his face. No bravado. No mocking smile. Nothing.

"Just dog," Tempi said softly, with no particular inflection. "Big noise dog." He lifted up his hand and made a mouth of it again. *"Chek. Chek. Chek."*

Dedan lifted a hand and shoved hard against Tempi's chest. I'd seen this sort of thing countless times in the taverns near the University. It was the sort of shove that sends a man staggering backward, off balance and prone to stagger and trip.

Except Tempi didn't stagger. He just . . . stepped away. Then he reached out casually and cuffed Dedan along one side of his head, the way a parent might swat an unruly child in the market. It wasn't even hard enough to move

Dedan's head, but we could all hear a soft *paff* sound, and Dedan's hair puffed out like a milkweed pod someone had blown against.

Dedan stood still for a moment, as if he couldn't quite understand what had happened. Then he frowned and brought both hands up to give Tempi a more violent shove. Tempi stepped away from this too, then swatted Dedan on the other side of his head.

Dedan scowled, grunted, and brought his hands up, making fists. He was a big man, and his mercenary leathers creaked and strained at the shoulders as he lifted his arms. He waited a moment, obviously hoping Tempi would make the first move, then he stomped forward, drew his arm back, and threw a punch, hard and heavy as a farmhand swinging an axe.

Tempi saw it coming and stepped away a third time. But halfway through his clumsy swing, everything about Dedan changed. He raised himself up on the balls of his feet and his ponderous haymaker punch evaporated. Suddenly, he no longer looked like a lumbering bull, and instead, he darted forward and snapped out three quick punches, fast as a bird's wing flapping.

Tempi sidestepped one, slapped the other aside, but the third caught him high on the shoulder, spinning him partway around and knocking him backward. He took two quick steps out of Dedan's reach, regained his balance, and shook himself slightly. Then he laughed, high and delighted.

The sound softened the expression on Dedan's face, and he grinned in return, though he didn't lower his hands or move off the balls of his feet. Despite this, Tempi stepped up, avoided another jab, and struck Dedan in the face with the flat of his hand. Not across the cheek, as if they were squabbling lovers onstage. Tempi's hand came down from above and struck Dedan across the front of his face, from his forehead down to his chin.

"Arrhhgh!" Dedan shouted. "Black damn!" He staggered away, clutching at his nose. "What's wrong with you? Did you just slap me?" He peered out at Tempi from behind his hand. "You fight like a woman."

For a moment, Tempi looked as if he might object. Then he gave the first smile I had ever seen from him and gave a small nod and shrug instead. "Yes. I fight like a woman."

Dedan hesitated, then laughed and clapped Tempi roughly on the shoulder. I half expected Tempi to dart away from his touch, but instead the Adem returned the gesture, even to the point of gripping Dedan's shoulder and jostling him around playfully.

The display struck me as odd coming from someone who had been so reserved over the last several days, but I decided not to look a gift horse in the mouth. Anything other than fidgety silence from the Adem was a blessing.

Even better, I now had a measure of Tempi's fighting ability. Whether or not Dedan wanted to admit it, Tempi obviously had the better of him. I guessed the Adem reputation was more than just empty air.

Marten watched Tempi return to his seat. "Those clothes are still a problem," the woodsman said, as if nothing much had happened. He eyed Tempi's blood-red shirt and pants. "Might as well run around waving a flag as wear that in the trees."

"I'll talk with him about it," I told the others. If Tempi was self-conscious about his Aturan, I guessed our conversation would go more smoothly without an audience. "And I'll work out what he'll do if he runs into them. You three can go settle in and get dinner started."

The three of them scattered off, looking to claim the prime places for their bedrolls. Tempi watched them go, then turned back to look at me. He glanced down at the ground and took a small, shuffling step away.

"Tempi?"

He cocked his head and looked at me.

"We need to talk about your clothing."

It happened again as soon as I started to talk. His attention slowly slid away from me, his eyes drifting down and to the side. As if he couldn't be bothered to actually listen. As if he were a sulky child.

I don't need to tell you how infuriating it is to try and have a discussion with a person who won't look you in the eye. Still, I didn't have the luxury of taking offense or putting off this talk. I'd already delayed this conversation too long.

"Tempi." I fought the urge to snap my fingers in order to draw his attention back to me. "Your clothes are red," I said, trying to keep it as simple as possible. "Easy to see. Dangerous."

He gave no response for a long moment. Then his pale eyes darted up to mine and he nodded, a simple bob of the head.

I began to have a horrible suspicion that he might not actually understand what it was we were doing out here in the Eld. "Tempi, you know what we are doing out here, in the forest?"

Tempi's eyes moved to my rough sketch in the dirt, then back up at me. He shrugged and made a vague gesture with both hands. "What is many but not all?"

At first I thought he was asking some strange philosophical question, then I realized he was asking for a word. I held up my hand and grabbed two of my fingers. "Some?" I grabbed three fingers. "Most?"

Tempi watched my hands intently, nodding. "Most," he said, fidgeting. "I know most. Talk is fast."

"We are looking for men." His eyes slid away as soon as I started to speak, and I fought the urge to sigh. "We are trying to find men."

Nod. "Yes. *Hunt* men." He stressed the word. "Hunt *visantha*."

At least he knew why we were here. "Red?" I reached out and touched the red leather strap that held the fabric of his shirt tight to his body. It was surprisingly soft. "For hunting? Do you have other clothes? Not red?"

Tempi looked down at his outfit, fidgeting. Then he nodded and went over to his pack and drew out a shirt of plain grey homespun. He held it up for me. "For hunting. But not fighting."

I wasn't sure what his distinction meant, but I was willing to let it go for now. "What will you do if *visantha* find you in the forest?" I asked. "Talk or fight?"

He seemed to think about it for a moment. "Not good at talk," he admitted. "*Visantha?* Fight."

I nodded. "One bandit, fight. Two, talk."

He shrugged. "Can fight two."

"Fight and win?"

He gave another nonchalant shrug and pointed to where Dedan was carefully picking twigs out of the sod. "Like him? Three or four." He held out his hand, palm up, as if offering me something. "If three bandit, I fight. If four, I try best talk. I wait until three night. Then . . ." he made an odd, elaborate gesture with both hands. "Fire in tents."

I relaxed, glad he had followed our earlier discussion. "Yes. Good. Thank you."

The five of us had a quiet dinner of soup, bread, and a rather unimpressive gummy cheese we'd bought in Crosson. Dedan and Hespe bickered in a friendly way, and I speculated with Marten about what sort of weather we might expect over the next few days.

Other than that, there wasn't much chatter. Two of us had already come to blows. We'd come a hundred miles since Severen, and we were all aware of the grim work ahead of us.

"Hold on," Marten said. "What if they catch *you?*" He looked up at me. "We all have a plan if the bandits find us. We head back with them and you'll track us down on the third day."

I nodded. "And don't forget the distraction."

Marten looked anxious. "But what if they catch you? I don't have any magic. I can't guarantee I'll be able to track them down by that third night. Probably, sure. But tracking isn't a certain thing. . . ."

"I'm just a harmless musician," I reassured him. "I got in some trouble with the Baronet Banbride's niece and thought it would be best if I legged it into the forest for a while." I grinned. "They might rob me, but as I don't have much, they'll probably just let me go. I'm a persuasive fellow, and I don't look like much of a threat."

Dedan muttered something under his breath I was glad I couldn't hear.

"But what if?" Hespe pressed. "Marten's got a point. What if they take you back with them?"

That was something I hadn't figured out yet, but rather than end the evening on a sour note, I smiled my most confident smile. "If they take me back to their camp, I should be able to kill them off myself without much trouble." I shrugged with exaggerated nonchalance. "I'll meet you back at camp after the job is done." I thumped the ground beside me, grinning.

I had intended it as a joke, sure Marten at least would chuckle at my flippant response. But I'd underestimated how deep Vintic superstition tends to run, and my comment was met with an uncomfortable silence.

There was little conversation after that. We drew lots for the watch, doused the fire, and one by one we drifted off to sleep.

CHAPTER SEVENTY-NINE

Signs

AFTER BREAKFAST, MARTEN BEGAN teaching Tempi and me how to search for the bandits' trail.

Anyone can spot a piece of torn shirt hanging from a branch or a footprint gouged into the dirt, but those things never happen in real life. They make for convenient plot devices in plays, but really, when have you ever torn your clothing so seriously that you've left a piece of it behind?

Never. The people we were hunting were clever, so we couldn't count on them making any obvious mistakes. That meant Marten was the only one among us who had any idea what we were really looking for.

"Any broken twig," he said. "They'll mostly be where things are thick and tangled: waist high or ankle high." He gestured as if kicking through thick scrub and pushing things aside with his hands. "Seeing the actual break is hard, so look at the leaves instead." He gestured to a nearby bush. "What do you see there?"

Tempi pointed at a lower branch. He wore his plain grey homespun today, and without his mercenary reds, he looked even less imposing.

I looked where Tempi was pointing and saw the branch had been snapped, but not badly enough to break off.

"So someone has been through here?" I asked

Marten shrugged his bow higher up on his shoulder. "I was. I did this last night." He looked at us. "See how even the leaves that aren't hanging strange are starting to wilt?

I nodded.

"That means someone has been by this way within a day or so. If it's been two or three days, the leaves will brown out and die. You see both close to each other . . ." He looked at me.

"It means you have someone moving through the area more than once, days apart."

He nodded. "Since I'm scouting and keeping an eye out for bandits, you'll be the ones with your noses to the ground. When you find something like this, call me."

"Call?" Tempi cupped his hands around his mouth and turned his head in different directions. He made a wide gesture to the surrounding trees and put his hand to his ear, pretending to listen.

Marten frowned. "You're right. You can't just go shouting for me." He rubbed the back of his neck in frustration. "Damn, we didn't think this all the way through."

I smiled at him. "I thought it through," I said, and brought out a rough wooden whistle I'd carved last night. It only had two notes, but that was all we needed. I put it to my mouth and blew. *Ta-ta DEE. Ta-ta DEE.*

Marten grinned. "That's a Will's Widow, isn't it? The pitch is dead on."

I nodded. "That's what I do."

He cleared his throat. "Unfortunately, Will's Widow is also called a night-jar." He grimaced apologetically. "*Night*-jar, mind you. That'll catch at the ear of any experienced woodsman like a fishhook if you go blowing it every time you want me to come take a look at something."

I looked down at the whistle. "Black hands," I swore. "I should have thought of that."

"It's a good idea," he said. "We just need one for a daytime bird. Maybe a gold piper." He whistled two notes. "That should be simple enough."

"I'll carve a different one tonight," I said, then reached down for a twig. I snapped it and handed half to Marten. "This will do if I need to signal you today."

He looked at the stick oddly. "How exactly will this help?"

"When we need your opinion on something we've found, I'll do this." I concentrated, muttered a binding, and moved my half of the stick.

Marten jumped two feet up and five feet back, dropping the stick. To his credit, he didn't shout. "What in ten hells was that?" he hissed, wringing his hand.

His reaction had startled me, and my own heart was racing. "Marten, I'm sorry. It's just a little sympathy." I saw a wrinkle in between his eyebrows and changed my tack. "Just a small magic. It's like a bit of magic string I use to tie two things together."

I imagined Elxa Dal swallowing his tongue at this description, but pressed ahead. "I can tie these things together, so when I tug on mine . . ." I moved to stand over where his half of the twig lay on the ground. I raised my half, and the half on the ground lifted into the air.

My display had the desired effect. Moving together, the two twigs looked like the crudest, saddest string puppet in the world. Nothing to be frightened of. "It's just like invisible string, except it won't get tangled or caught on anything."

"How hard will it pull at me?" he asked warily. "I don't want it yanking me out of a tree when I'm scouting."

"It's just me on the other end of the string," I said. "I'll just jiggle it a bit. Like the float on a fishing line."

Marten stopped wringing his hand and relaxed a little. "Startled me is all," he said.

"That's my fault," I said. "I should have warned you." I picked up the stick, handling it with a deliberate casualness. As if it were nothing more than an ordinary stick. Of course it *was* nothing more than an ordinary stick, but Marten needed to be reassured as to that point. It's like Teccam said, nothing in the world is harder than convincing someone of an unfamiliar truth.

Marten showed us how to see when leaves or needles had been disturbed, how to spot when stones had been walked across, how to tell if moss or lichen had been damaged by someone's passing.

The old huntsman was a surprisingly good teacher. He didn't belabor his points, didn't talk down to us, and didn't mind questions. Even Tempi's trouble with the language didn't frustrate him.

Even so, it took hours. A full half day. Then, when I thought we were finally finished, Marten turned us around and started leading us back toward the camp.

"We've already been that way," I said. "If we're going to practice, let's practice in the right direction."

Marten ignored me and kept walking. "Tell me what you see."

Twenty paces later, Tempi pointed. "Moss," he said. "My foot. I walked."

Realization dawned, and I began to see all the marks Tempi and I had made. For the next three hours, Marten walked us step by humiliating step back through the trees, showing us everything we had done to betray our presence there: a scuff against the lichen on a tree trunk, a piece of freshly broken rock, the discoloration of overturned pine needles.

Worst of all were a half-dozen bright green leaves that lay shredded on the ground in a tidy semicircle. Marten raised an eyebrow, and I blushed. I had plucked them from a nearby bush, idly shredding them while listening to Marten.

"Think twice and step carefully," Marten said. "And keep an eye on each other." He looked back and forth between Tempi and me. "We're playing a dangerous game here."

Then Marten showed us how to cover our tracks. It quickly became clear that a poorly concealed sign was often more obvious than one simply left alone. So over the next two hours we learned how to hide our mistakes and spot mistakes that others had tried to hide.

Only then, as afternoon was turning to evening, did Tempi and I begin searching this swath of forest bigger than most baronies. We walked close together, zigzagging back and forth, looking for any sign of the bandits' trail.

I thought about the long days stretching out ahead of us. I'd thought searching the Archives had been tedious. But looking for a broken twig in this much forest made hunting for the gram seem like going to the baker for a bun.

In the Archives I had the chance to make accidental discoveries. In the Archives I'd had my friends: conversation, jokes, affection. Looking sideways at Tempi, I realized I could count the words he had said today: twenty-four, and the number of times he had met my eye: three.

How long would this take? Ten days? Twenty? Merciful Tehlu, could I spend a month out here without going mad?

With thoughts like this, when I saw some bark chipped off a tree and a tuft of grass bent the wrong way, I was flooded with relief.

Not wanting to get my hopes up, I motioned to Tempi. "Do you see anything here?" He nodded, fidgeting with the collar of his shirt, then pointed to the grass I'd spotted. Then he pointed to a scuffed bit of exposed root I hadn't noticed.

Almost light-headed with excitement, I pulled out the oak twig and signaled Marten. I twitched it very gently, not wanting to send him into another panic.

It was only two minutes before Marten came out of the trees, but in that time, I had already formed three plans as to how to track and kill the bandits, composed five apologetic soliloquies to Denna, and decided that when I got back to Severen, I would donate money to the Tehlin church as thanks for this tangible miracle.

I expected Marten to be irritated that we'd called him back so soon. But his expression was purely matter-of-fact as he came to stand next to us.

I pointed out the grass, the bark, and the root. "Tempi spotted the last." I said, giving credit where credit is due.

"Good," he said seriously. "Good job. There's also a bent branch over there." He gestured a few paces off to the right.

I turned to face the direction the trail seemed to indicate. "Odds are they're going to be north of here," I said. "Farther from the road. Do you think it would be better to scout things out a bit now, or wait until tomorrow when we're fresh?"

Marten squinted at me. "Good lord, boy. These aren't real trail signs. So obvious, all so close together." He gave me a long look. "*I* left them. I needed to make sure you weren't going to glaze over after a few minutes of looking."

My elation fell from some place in my chest and landed around my feet, shattering like a glass jar tipped from a high shelf. My expression must have been pitiful, as Marten gave me an apologetic smile. "I'm sorry. I should have told you. I'll be doing it off and on every day. It's the only chance we have to stay alert. This isn't my first time hunting through haystacks, you know."

———

The third time we called Martin back, he suggested we make a standing wager. Tempi and I would win a ha'penny for every sign we found, and he'd win a silver bit for every one we missed. I jumped at the offer. Not only would it help keep us on our toes, but five-to-one odds seemed rather generous.

This made the rest of the day pass quickly. Tempi and I missed a few signs: a log shifted out of place, some scattered leaves, and a broken spiderweb. I thought this last one was a bit unfair, but even so, by the time we headed back to camp that evening, Tempi and I were two pennies ahead.

Over supper, Marten told a story about a young widow's son who left home to make his fortune. A tinker sold him a pair of magic boots that helped him rescue a princess from a tower high in the mountains.

Dedan nodded along while he ate, smiling as if he'd heard it before. Hespe laughed in places, gasped in others, the perfect audience. Tempi sat perfectly still with his hands folded in his lap, showing none of the nervous restlessness I'd come to expect from him. He stayed that way through the entire story, listening while his dinner grew cold.

The story was a good one. There was a hungry giant and a riddle game. But the widow's son was clever, and in the end he brought the princess back and married her. It was a familiar story, and listening to it reminded me of days long gone, back when I had a home, a family.

CHAPTER EIGHTY

Tone

THE NEXT DAY MARTEN left with Hespe and Dedan while Tempi and I remained behind to keep an eye on the camp.

With nothing else to occupy my time, I started gathering extra firewood. Then I searched for useful herbs in the undergrowth and brought water from the nearby spring. Then I busied myself by unpacking, sorting, and rearranging everything in my travelsack.

Tempi disassembled his sword, meticulously cleaning and oiling all the pieces. He didn't look bored, but then again, he never looked like anything.

By midday I was nearly mad with boredom. I would have read, but I hadn't brought a book. I would have sewn pockets into my threadbare cloak, but I didn't have any spare cloth. I would have played my lute, but a trouper's lute is designed to carry music through a noisy taproom. Out here, the sound of it could carry for miles.

I would have chatted with Tempi, but trying to have a conversation with him was like playing catch with a well.

Still, it seemed to be my only option. I walked over to where Tempi sat. He had finished cleaning his sword and was making small adjustments to the leather grip. "Tempi?"

Tempi lay aside his sword and came to his feet. He stood uncomfortably close to me, with barely more than eight inches of space between us. Then he hesitated and frowned. It wasn't much of a frown, barely a thinning of the lips and a slight line between his eyebrows, but on Tempi's blank sheet of a face, it stood out like a word written in red ink.

He backed away from me by two good paces, then eyed the ground between us and stepped forward slightly.

Understanding dawned on me. "Tempi, how close do Adem stand?"

Tempi looked at me blankly for a second, then burst out laughing. A shy smile flickered onto his face, making him look very young. It left his mouth quickly, but lingered around his eyes. "Smart. Yes. Different in Adem. For you, close." He stepped uncomfortably close, then backed away.

"For me?" I asked. "Is it different for different people?"

He nodded. "Yes."

"How close for Dedan?"

He fidgeted. "Complicated."

I felt a familiar curiosity flicker up inside me. "Tempi," I asked. "Would you teach me these things? Teach me your language?"

"Yes," he said. And though his face betrayed none of it, I could hear a great weight of relief in his voice. "Yes. Please. Yes."

———————

By the end of the afternoon, I had learned a wild, useless scattering of Ademic words. The grammar was still a mystery, but that is how it always begins. Luckily, languages are like musical instruments: the more you know, the easier it is to pick up new ones. Ademic was my fourth.

Our major problem was that Tempi's Aturan was not very good, which gave us little common ground. So we drew in the dirt, pointed, and waved our hands quite a bit. Several times, when mere gestures were not enough, we ended up performing something close to pantomime or little mummer's plays in order to get our meaning across. It was more entertaining than I had expected.

There was one stumbling block the first day. I had learned a dozen words and thought of another that would be useful. I made a fist and pretended to throw a punch at Tempi.

"*Freaht,*" he said.

"*Freaht,*" I repeated.

He shook his head. "No. *Freaht.*"

"*Freaht,*" I said carefully.

"No," he said firmly. "*Freaht* is . . ." He bared his teeth and worked his jaw as if he were biting something. "*Freaht.*" He punched his fist into his palm.

"*Freaht,*" I said.

"No." I was amazed at the weight of condescension in his voice. "Freaht."

My face got hot. "That's what I'm saying. *Freaht! Freaht! Fre—*"

Tempi reached out and smacked me in the side of the head with the flat of his hand. It was the same way he had struck Dedan last night, the way my father had cuffed me when I was being troublesome in public. It wasn't hard enough to hurt, it was just startling. No one had done that to me in years.

Even more startling was that I hardly saw it. The motion was smooth and lazy and faster than snapping your fingers. He didn't seem to mean anything insulting by it. He was merely getting my attention.

He lifted his sandy hair and pointed to his ear. "Hear," he said firmly. *"Freaht."* He bared his teeth again, making a biting motion. *"Freaht."* Raised fist. *"Freaht.* Freaht."

And I did hear it. It wasn't the sound of the word itself, it was the cadence of the word. *"Freaht?"* I said.

He favored me with a small, rare smile. "Yes. Good."

Then I had to go back and relearn all the words, making note of their rhythm. I hadn't really heard it before, just mimicked it. Slowly, I discovered each word could have several different meanings depending on cadence of the sound that composed them.

I learned the all-important phrases "What does that mean?" and "Explain that more slowly," in addition to a couple dozen words: Fight. Look. Sword. Hand. Dance. The dumbshow I had to perform to get him to understand the last of these left both of us laughing.

It was fascinating. The differing cadences of each word meant the language itself had a sort of music to it. I couldn't help but wonder . . .

"Tempi?" I asked. "What are your songs like?" He looked at me blankly for a moment, and I thought he might not understand the abstract question. "Could you sing me an Adem song?"

"What is song?" he asked. In the last hour, Tempi had learned twice as many words as I had.

I cleared my throat and sang:

Little Jenny no-shoes went a-walking with the wind.
She was looking for a bonny boy to laugh and make her grin.
Upon her head a feather cap, upon her lips a whistle.
Her lips were wet and honey sweet. Her tongue was sharp as thistle.

Tempi's eyes went wide as I sang. He practically gaped.

"You?" I prompted, pointing to his chest. "Can you sing an Adem song?"

His face flushed a burning red, and a dozen emotions ran wild and un-disguised over his face: astonishment, horror, embarrassment, shock, disgust. He got to his feet, turning away and chattering something in Ademic far too quickly for me to follow. He looked for all the world as if I'd just asked him to strip naked and dance for me.

"No," he said, managing to collect himself somewhat. His face was com-posed again, but his fair skin was still flushed a violent red. "No." Looking down at the ground, he touched his chest, shaking his head. "No song. No Adem song."

I got to my feet as well, not knowing what I'd done wrong. "Tempi. I'm sorry."

Tempi shook his head. "No. Nothing sorry." He drew a deep breath and shook his head as he turned and started to walk away. "Complicated."

CHAPTER EIGHTY-ONE

The Jealous Moon

THAT EVENING MARTEN SHOT a trio of fat rabbits. I dug roots and picked a few herbs, and before the sun was down the five of us sat down to a meal made perfect by the addition of two large loaves of fresh bread, butter, and a crumbly cheese too local to have any specific name.

Spirits were high after a day of good weather, and so with dinner came more stories.

Hespe told a surprisingly romantic tale of a queen who loved a serving boy. She told her story with a gentle passion. And if her telling didn't show a tender heart, the looks she gave Dedan as she spoke of the queen's love did.

Dedan, however, failed to see the marks of love on her. And with a folly I have rarely seen equaled, he began to tell a story he'd heard at the Pennysworth Inn. A tale of Felurian.

"The boy who told me this was hardly as old as Kvothe here," Dedan said. "And if you'd heard him talk you'd have seen he wasn't the sort who could invent such a tale." The mercenary tapped his temple meaningfully. "But listen and judge for yourself if it's worth believing."

As I've said, Dedan had a good tongue in his head, and a sharper wit than you'd guess, when he decided to use it. Unfortunately, this was one of the times that the former was working and the latter was not.

"For time out of mind, men have been wary of this stretch of woods. Not for fear of lawless men or becoming lost." He shook his head. "No. They say the fair folk make their homes here.

"Cloven-hoofed pucks that dance when the moon is full. Dark things with long fingers that steal babes from cribs. Many's the woman, old wife or new, who leaves out bread and milk at night. And many's the man who makes well sure he builds his house with all his doors in a row.

"Some might call these folk superstitious, but they know the truth. The safest thing is to avoid the Fae, but barring that, you want to keep in their good graces.

"This is a story of Felurian. Lady of Twilight. Lady of the First Quiet. Felurian, who is death to men. But a glad death, and one they go to willingly."

Tempi drew a breath. It was a small motion, but it was eye-catching as he'd continued his habit of sitting perfectly still through the evening's stories. Now this made better sense to me. He was being quiet.

"Felurian," Tempi asked. "Death to men. She is—" he paused. "She is *sentin?*" He lifted his hands in front of himself and made a sort of gripping gesture. He eyed us expectantly. Then, seeing we didn't understand, he touched his sword where it lay at his side.

I understood. "No," I said. "She's not one of the Adem."

Tempi shook his head and pointed at Marten's bow.

I shook my head. "No. She's not a fighter at all. She . . ." I trailed off, unable to think of how I would explain how Felurian killed men, especially if we were forced to resort to gestures. Desperate, I looked to Dedan for help.

Dedan didn't hesitate. "Sex," he said frankly. "Do you know sex?"

Tempi blinked, then threw back his head and laughed. Dedan looked as if he were trying to decide whether or not to be offended. After a moment Tempi caught his breath. "Yes," he said simply. "Yes. I know sex."

Dedan smiled. "That's how she kills men."

For a moment, Tempi looked more blank than usual, then a slow horror spread across his face. No, not horror, it was raw disgust and revulsion, made all the worse by the fact that his face was usually so blank. His hand clenched into several unfamiliar gestures at his side. "How?" he choked out the word.

Dedan started to say something, then stopped. Then he started to make a gesture and stopped that as well, looking self-consciously at Hespe.

Hespe chuckled low in her throat and turned to Tempi. She thought for a moment, then made a gesture as if holding someone in her arms, kissing them. Then she began to tap her chest rhythmically, mimicking a heartbeat. She beat faster and faster, then stopped, clenching her hand into a fist and making her eyes wide. She tensed her whole body, then went limp, lolling her head to one side.

Dedan laughed and clapped at her performance. "That's it. But sometimes . . ." He tapped his temple, then snapped his fingers, crossing his eyes and sticking out his tongue. "Crazy."

Tempi relaxed. "Oh," he said, plainly relieved. "Good. Yes."

Dedan nodded and settled back into his story. "Right. Felurian. Fondest desire of all men. Beauty beyond compare." For Tempi's benefit, he made a gesture as if he were brushing out long hair.

"Twenty years ago, this boy's father and uncle were out hunting in this very stretch of forest as the sun began to set. They stayed out later than they should, then decided to make their way home by cutting straight through the forest instead of using the road like sensible folk.

"They hadn't been walking very long when they heard singing in the distance. They made their way toward it, thinking they were close to the road, but instead they found themselves at the edge of a small clearing. And there stood Felurian singing softly to herself:

> *Cae-Lanion Luhial*
> *di mari Felanua*
> *Kreata Tu ciar*
> *tu alaran di*
> *Dirella. Amauen.*
> *Loesi an delan*
> *tu nia vor ruhlan*
> *Felurian thae."*

Though Dedan made rough work of the tune, I shivered at the sound of it. The melody was eerie, compelling, and utterly unfamiliar. I didn't recognize the language, either. Not a bit of it.

Dedan nodded as he saw my reaction. "More than anything, that song gives the boy's story the ring of truth. I can't put a bit of sense to those words, but they stuck right in my head even though he only sang it once.

"So the two brothers are huddled at the edge of the clearing. And thanks to the moon they could see like it was noon instead of night. She wan't wearing a stitch, and though her hair was almost to her waist, it were real obvious she was as naked as the moon."

I have always enjoyed stories about Felurian, but as I glanced at Hespe my anticipation cooled. She was watching Dedan, and as he spoke, her eyes narrowed.

Dedan failed to see this. "She was tall with long graceful legs. Her waist was slender, her hips curved as if begging for the touch of a hand. Her stomach was perfect and smooth, like a flawless piece of birch bark, and the dimple of her navel seemed made for kissing."

Hespe's eyes were dangerous slits by this point. But even more telling was her mouth, which had formed a thin, straight line. A word of advice to you.

Should you ever see that look on a woman's face, leave off talking at once and sit on both your hands. It may not mend matters, but it will at least keep you from making them any worse.

Unfortunately Dedan continued, his thick hands gesturing in the firelight. "Her breasts were full and round, like peaches waiting to be taken from the tree. Even the jealous moon which steals the color from all things couldn't hide the rosy—"

Hespe made a disgusted noise and pushed herself to her feet. "I'll just leave then," she said. Her voice held such a chill even Dedan couldn't miss it.

"What?" He looked up to her, still holding his hands in front of himself, frozen in the act of cupping an imagined pair of breasts.

She stormed away, muttering under her breath.

Dedan let his hands drop heavily into his lap. His expression moved from confused to injured to angry in the space of a breath. After a second he got to his feet, roughly brushing bits of leaf and twig from his pants and muttering to himself. Gathering up his blankets, he started toward the other side of our little clearing.

"Did it end with both brothers chasing after her, and the boy's father falling behind?" I asked.

Dedan looked back at me. "You've already heard it then. You could have stopped me if you didn't—"

"I'm just guessing," I said quickly. "I hate not hearing the ending of a story."

"Father put his foot in a rabbit hole," Dedan said shortly. "Sprained his ankle. Nobody saw the uncle again." He stalked out of the circle of firelight, his expression grim.

I cast an imploring look at Marten, who shook his head. "No," he said softly. "I won't have any part of it. Not for the world. Trying to help right now would be like trying to put out a fire with my hands. Painful, and with no real results."

Tempi began to make up his bed. Marten made a circular gesture with one finger and gave me a questioning look, asking if I wanted the first watch. I nodded, and he gathered up his bedroll, saying, "Attractive as some things are, you have to weigh your risks. How badly do you want it, how badly are you willing to be burned?"

I spread the fire and soon the deep dark of night settled into the clearing. I lay on my back, looked at the stars, and thought of Denna.

CHAPTER EIGHTY-TWO

Barbarians

THE NEXT DAY, TEMPI and I moved camp while Dedan and Hespe walked back to Crosson for supplies. Marten scouted out an isolated piece of flat ground close to water. Then we packed and moved everything, dug the privy, built the firepit, and generally got everything settled.

Tempi was willing to talk as we worked, but I was nervous. I had offended him by asking about the Lethani early on, so I knew to avoid that subject. But if he was upset by a simple question about singing, how could I begin to guess what might offend him?

Again, his blank expression and refusal to make eye contact were the main problems. How could I make intelligent conversation with a person when I had no idea how he felt? It was like trying to walk blindfolded through an unfamiliar house.

So I took the safer road and simply asked for more words as we worked. Objects, for the most part, as we were both too busy with our hands to pantomime.

Best of all, Tempi got to practice his Aturan while I built up my Ademic vocabulary. I noticed the more mistakes I made in his language, the more comfortable he grew in his own attempts at expressing himself.

This meant, of course, that I made many mistakes. In fact, I was occasionally so thickheaded that Tempi was forced to explain himself several times in several different ways. All in Aturan of course.

We finished setting up camp around noon. Marten left to go hunting and Tempi stretched and began to move through his slow dance. He did it twice in a row, and I began to suspect he was somewhat bored himself. By the time he finished he was covered in a sheen of sweat and told me he was going to bathe.

With the camp to myself, I melted down the tinker's candles to make two small wax simulacra. I'd been wanting to do this for days, but even at the University creating a mommet was questionable behavior. Here in Vintas . . . suffice to say I thought it best to be discreet.

It wasn't elegant work. Tallow isn't nearly as convenient as sympathy wax, but even the crudest mommet can be a devastating thing. Once I had them tucked into my travelsack, I felt much better prepared.

I was cleaning the last of the tallow off my fingers when Tempi returned from his bath, naked as a new baby. Years of stage training allowed me to keep a calm expression, but just barely.

After spreading his wet clothing over a nearby branch to dry, Tempi walked over to me without showing the least embarrassment or modesty.

He held out his right hand, thumb and forefinger pinched together. "What is this?" He spread his fingers slightly for me to see.

I looked closely, glad to have something to focus my attention on. "That's a tick."

This close, I couldn't help but notice his scars again, faint lines crossing his arms and chest. I could read scars from my time in the Medica, and his didn't show the wide, puckered pink that would indicate a deep wound cutting through the layers of skin, fat, and muscle underneath. These were shallow wounds. Dozens of them. I couldn't help but wonder how long he had been a mercenary to have scars so old. He didn't look much older than twenty.

Oblivious to my scrutiny, Tempi stared at the thing between his fingers. "It bites. On me. Bites and *stays*." His expression was blank as always, but his tone was tinged with disgust. His left hand fidgeted.

"There are no ticks in Ademre?"

"No." He made a point of trying to pinch it between his fingers. "It not break."

I gestured, showing him how to crush it between his fingernails, which he did with a certain amount of relish. He threw it away and stalked back to his bedroll. Then, still naked, he proceeded to pull out all of his clothing and give it a vigorous shaking.

I kept my eyes averted, knowing deep down in my heart that this would be the moment Dedan and Hespe would return from Crosson.

Thankfully they didn't. After a quarter hour or so, Tempi put on a pair of dry pants, carefully inspecting them first.

Shirtless, he walked back to where I sat. "I hate tick," he declared.

When he spoke, his left hand made a sharp gesture, as if he were brushing crumbs off the front of his shirt near his hip. Except he wasn't wearing a shirt, and there was nothing on his bare skin to brush away. What's more, I realized he'd made the same gesture earlier.

In fact, now that I thought of it, I'd seen him make that gesture a half-dozen times in the last several days, though never so violently.

I had a sudden suspicion. "Tempi? What does this mean?" I mimicked the brushing away gesture.

He nodded. "It is this." He scrunched his face up in an exaggerated expression of disgust.

My mind went spinning back over the last span of days, thinking of how many times I had seen Tempi fidgeting restlessly while we talked. I reeled at the thought of it.

"Tempi," I asked. "Is all of this?" I made a gesture to my face, then smiled, frowned, rolled my eyes. "Does all this happen with hands in Ademic?"

He nodded and made a gesture at the same time.

"That!" I pointed at his hand. "What is that?"

He hesitated, then gave a forced, awkward-looking smile.

I copied the gesture, splaying my hand slightly and pressing my thumb to the inside of my middle finger.

"No," he said. "Other hand. Left."

"Why?"

He reached out and thumped on my chest, just left of the breastbone: *Tum-tump. Tum-tump.* Then he ran a finger down to my left hand. I nodded to show I understood. It was closest to the heart. He held up his right hand and made a fist. "This hand is strong." He held up his left. "This hand is clever."

It made sense. That is why most lutists chord with the left hand and strum with their right. The left hand is more nimble, as a rule.

I made the gesture with my left hand, fingers splayed. Tempi shook his head. "That is this." He quirked half of his mouth up into a smirk.

The expression seemed so out of place on his face that it was all I could do to keep from gawking. I looked more closely at his hand and adjusted the position of my fingers slightly.

He nodded approval. His face was expressionless, but for the first time I understood why.

In the hours that followed, I learned that Ademic hand gestures did not actually represent facial expressions. It was nothing so simple as that. For example a smile can mean you're amused, happy, grateful, or satisfied. You can smile to comfort someone. You can smile because you're content or because you're in love. A grimace or a grin look similar to a smile, but they mean entirely different things.

Imagine trying to teach someone how to smile. Imagine trying to describe what different smiles mean and when, precisely, to use them in conversation. It's harder than learning to walk.

Suddenly so many things made sense. Of course Tempi wouldn't look me in the eye. There was nothing to be gained by looking at the face of the person you were talking to. You listen to the voice, but you watch the hand.

I spent the next several hours attempting to learn the basics, but it was maddeningly difficult. Words are fairly simple things. You can point to a stone. You can act out running or jumping. But have you ever tried to pantomime compliance? Respect? Sarcasm? I doubt even my father could have accomplished such a thing.

Because of this my progress was frustratingly slow, but I couldn't help but be fascinated. It was like suddenly being given a second tongue.

And it was a secret thing, of sorts. I have always had a weakness for secrets.

It took three hours to learn a handful of gestures, if you'll pardon the pun. My progress felt glacial, but when I finally learned the hand-speak for "understatement" I felt a glow of pride that can barely be described.

I think Tempi felt it too. "Good," he said with a flattening of the hand I was fairly certain indicated approval. He rolled his shoulders and got to his feet, stretching. He glanced at the sun through the branches overhead. "Food now?"

"Soon." There was one question that had been bothering me. "Tempi, why make all this work?" I asked. "A smile is easy. Why smile with your hands?"

"With hands is easy too. Better. More . . ." He made a slightly modified version of the shirt-brushing gesture he'd used earlier. Not disgust, *irritation?* "What is the word for people living together. Roads. Right things." He ran his thumb along his collarbone, was that *frustration?* "What is word for good together living? Nobody shits in the well."

I laughed. "Civilization?"

He nodded, splaying his fingers: *amusement.* "Yes," he said. "Speaking with hands is civilization."

"But smiling is natural," I protested. "Everyone smiles."

"Natural is not civilization," Tempi said. "Cooking meat is civilization. Washing off stink is civilization."

"So in Ademre you always smile with hands?" I wished I knew the gesture for dismay.

"No. Smiling with face good with family. Good with some friend."

"Why only family?"

Tempi repeated his thumb-on-collarbone gesture again. "When you make this." He pressed his palm to the side of his face and blew air into it, making a great flatulent noise. "That is natural, but you do not make it near others. Rude. With family . . ." He shrugged. *Amusement.* ". . . civilization not important. More natural with family."

"What about laughing?" I asked. "I have seen you laugh." I made a *ha-ha* sound so he knew what I was talking about.

He shrugged. "Laughing is."

I waited for a moment, but he didn't seem inclined to continue. I tried again. "Why not laugh with hands?"

Tempi shook his head. "No. Laugh is different." He stepped close and used two fingers to tap my chest over my heart. "Smile?" He ran his finger down my left arm. "Angry?" He tapped my heart again. He made a scared expression, a confused one, and poked his lip out in a ridiculous pout. Each time he tapped my chest.

"But laugh?" He pressed the flat of his hand against my stomach. "Here lives laugh." He ran his finger straight up to my mouth and spread his fingers. "Push back laugh is not good. Not healthy."

"Also cry?" I asked. I traced an imaginary tear down my cheek with one finger.

"Also cry." He put his hand on his own belly. "Ha ha ha," he said, pressing in with his hand to show me the motion of his stomach. Then his expression changed to sad. "Huh huh huh," he heaved with exaggerated sobs, pressing his stomach again. "Same place. Not healthy to push down."

I nodded slowly, trying to imagine what it must be like for Tempi, constantly assaulted by people too rude to keep their expressions to themselves. People whose hands constantly made gestures that were nonsense. "It must be very hard for you, out here."

"Not so hard." *Understatement.* "When I leave Ademre, I know this. Not civilization. Barbarians are rude."

"Barbarians?"

He made a wide gesture, encompassing our clearing, the forest, all of Vintas. "Everyone here like dogs." He made a grotesquely exaggerated expression of rage, showing all his teeth, snarling and rolling his eyes madly. "That is all you know." He shrugged nonchalant acceptance, as if to say he didn't hold it against us.

"What of children?" I asked. "Children smile before they talk. Is that wrong?"

Tempi shook his head. "All children barbarians. All smile with face. All children rude. But they go old. Watch. Learn." He paused thoughtfully. Choosing his words. "Barbarians have no woman to teach them civilization. Barbarians cannot learn."

I could tell he didn't mean any offense, but it made me more determined than ever to learn the particulars of the Adem hand-talk.

Tempi stood and began limbering up with a number of stretches similar to those the tumblers used in my troupe when I was young. After fifteen minutes of twisting himself this way and that, he began his slow, dancelike pantomime. Though I didn't know it at the time, it was called the Ketan.

Still nettled about Tempi's "barbarians cannot learn" comment, I decided I would follow along. After all, I didn't have anything better to do.

As I tried to mimic him, I became aware of how devilishly complex it was: keeping the hands cupped just so, the feet correctly positioned. Despite the fact that Tempi moved with almost glacial slowness, I found it impossible to imitate his smooth grace. Tempi never paused or looked in my direction. He never offered a word of encouragement or advice.

It was exhausting, and I was glad when it was over. Then I started the fire and lashed together a tripod. Wordlessly, Tempi brought out a hard sausage and several potatoes that he began to peel carefully using his sword.

I was surprised by this, as Tempi fussed over his sword much the same way I did with my lute. Once when Dedan had picked it up, the Adem had responded with a rather dramatic emotional outburst. Dramatic for Tempi, that is. He'd spoken two full sentences and frowned a bit.

Tempi saw me watching him and cocked his head curiously.

I pointed. "Sword?" I asked. "For cutting potatoes?"

Tempi looked down at the half-peeled potato in one hand, his sword in another. "Is sharp." He shrugged. "Is clean."

I returned the shrug, not wanting to make an issue of it. While working together, I learned the words for iron, knot, leaf, spark, and salt.

Waiting for the water to boil, Tempi stood, shook himself, and began his limbering stretches a second time. I followed him again. It was harder this time. The muscles of my arms and legs were loose and shaky from my previous effort. Toward the end I had to fight to keep myself from trembling, but I gleaned a few more secrets.

Tempi continued to ignore me, but I didn't mind. I've always been drawn to a challenge.

CHAPTER EIGHTY-THREE

Lack of Sight

"...SO TABORLIN WAS PRISONED deep underground," Marten said. "They had left him with nothing but the clothes upon his back and an inch of guttering candle to push away the darkness.

"The sorcerer-king planned to leave Taborlin trapped until hunger and thirst weakened his will. Scyphus knew if Taborlin swore to help him, the wizard would abide by his promise, because Taborlin never broke his word.

"Worst of all, Scyphus had taken Taborlin's staff and sword, and without them his power was all dim and guttery. He'd even taken Taborlin's cloak of no particular color, but he *ware*—sorry. But—*achhm*. Hespe, would you be a darling and pass me the skin?"

Hespe tossed Marten the waterskin and he took a deep drink. "That's better." He cleared his throat. "Where was I again?"

We had been in the Eld for twelve days, and things had fallen into a steady rhythm. Marten had changed our standing wager to reflect our growing skill. First to ten to one, then fifteen to one, which was the same arrangement he had with Dedan and Hespe.

My understanding of the Adem hand-language was growing, and as a result, Tempi was becoming something other than a frustrating blank page of a man. As I learned to read his body language, he was slowly being colored in around the edges.

He was thoughtful and gentle. Dedan rubbed him the wrong way. He loved jokes, though many of mine fell flat, and the ones he tried to tell invariably made no sense in translation.

This isn't to say things were perfect between us. I still offended Tempi occasionally, making social gaffes I couldn't understand even after the fact.

Every day I continued to follow him in his strange dance, and every day he pointedly ignored me.

"Now Taborlin needed to escape," Marten said, continuing his story. "But when he looked around his cave, he saw no door. No windows. All around him was nothing but smooth, hard stone.

"But Taborlin the Great knew the names of all things, so all things were his to command. He said to the stone: *'break!'* and the stone broke. The wall tore like a piece of paper, and through that hole Taborlin could see the sky and breathe the sweet spring air.

"Taborlin made his way out of the caves, into the castle, and finally to the doors of the royal hall itself. The doors were barred against him, so he said, *'burn!'* and they burst into flame and were soon nothing more than fine grey ash.

"Taborlin stepped into the hall and saw King Scyphus sitting there with fifty guards. The king said, 'Capture him!' But the guards had just seen the doors burn to ash, so they moved closer, but none of them came *too* close, if you know what I mean.

"King Scyphus said, 'Cowards! I will battle Taborlin with wizardry and best him!' He was afraid of Taborlin too, but he hid it well. Besides, Scyphus had his staff, and Taborlin had none.

"Then Taborlin said, 'If you're so brave, give me my staff before we duel.'

" 'Certainly,' Scyphus said, even though he didn't really mean to give it back, you see. 'It's right next to you in that chest there.' "

Marten looked around at us conspiratorially. "You see, Scyphus knew the chest was locked and had only one key. And that key was right in his pocket. So Taborlin went over to the chest, but it was locked. Then Scyphus laughed and so did a few of the guards.

"That made Taborlin angry. And before any of them could do anything he struck the top of the chest with his hand and shouted, *'Edro!'* The chest sprung open and he grabbed his cloak of no particular color, wrapping it around himself."

Marten cleared his throat again. "Excuse me," he said, and paused to take another long drink.

Hespe turned to Dedan. "What color do you think Taborlin's cloak was?"

Dedan's forehead creased a bit, almost like the beginning of a scowl. "What do you mean? It's no particular color, just like it says."

Hespe's mouth went flat. "I *know* that. But when you think of it in your head, what does it look like? You have to picture it as looking like something, don't you?"

Dedan looked thoughtful for a moment. "I always pictured it as kind of shimmery," he said. "Like the cobblestones outside a tallow-works after a hard rain."

"I always thought of it as a dirty grey," she said. "Sort of washed out from his being on the road all the time."

"That makes good sense," Dedan said, and I watched Hespe's face go gentle again.

"White," Tempi volunteered. "I think white. No color."

"I always thought of it as kind of a pale sky-blue," Marten admitted, shrugging. "I know that doesn't make any sense. That's just how I picture it."

Everyone turned to look at me.

"Sometimes I think of it like a quilt," I said. "Made entirely out of patchwork, a bunch of different colored rags and scraps. But most of the time I think of it as dark. Like it really is a color, but it's too dark for anyone to see."

When I was younger, stories of Taborlin had left me wide-eyed with wonder. Now that I knew the truth about magic, I enjoyed them on a different level, somewhere between nostalgia and amusement.

But I held a special place in my heart for Taborlin's cloak of no particular color. His staff held much of his power. His sword was deadly. His key, coin, and candle were valuable tools. But the cloak was at the heart of Taborlin. It was a disguise when he needed it, helped him hide when he was in trouble. It protected him. From rain. From arrows. From fire.

He could hide things in it, and it had many pockets full of wonderful things. A knife. A toy for a child. A flower for a lady. Whatever Taborlin needed was somewhere in his cloak of no particular color. These stories are what made me beg my mother for my first cloak when I was young. . . .

I drew my own cloak around me. My nasty, tatty, faded cloak the tinker had traded me. On one of our trips into Crosson for supplies, I'd picked up some spare cloth and sewn a few clumsy pockets into the inside. But it was still a poor replacement for my rich burgundy cloak, or the lovely black and green one Fela had made for me.

Marten cleared his throat again and launched back into his story. "So Taborlin struck the trunk with his hand and shouted. *'Edro!'* The lid of the chest popped open, and he grabbed his cloak of no particular color and his staff. He called forth great barbs of lightning and killed twenty guards. Then he called forth a sheet of fire and killed another twenty. Those that were left threw down their swords and cried for mercy.

"Then Taborlin gathered up the rest of his things from the chest. He took out his key and coin and tucked them safe away. Lastly he brought out his copper sword, Skyaldrin, and belted—"

"What?" Dedan interrupted, laughing. "You tit. Taborlin's sword wasn't copper."

"Shut up, Den," Marten snapped, nettled at the interruption. "It was so copper."

"You shut up," Dedan replied. "Who's ever heard of a copper sword? Copper wouldn't hold an edge. It'd be like trying to kill someone with a big penny."

Hespe laughed at that. "It was probably a silver sword, don't you think, Marten?"

"It was a copper sword," Marten insisted.

"Maybe it was early on in his career," Dedan said in a loud whisper to Hespe. "All he could afford was a copper sword."

Marten shot the two of them an angry look. "Copper, damn you. If you don't like it, you can just guess at the ending." He folded his arms in front of himself.

"Fine," Dedan said. "Kvothe can give us one. He might be a pup, but he knows how to tell a proper story. Copper sword my ass."

"Actually," I said, "I'd like to hear the end of Marten's."

"Oh go ahead," the old tracker said bitterly. "I'm in no mood to finish now. And I'd rather listen to you than hear that donkey *he-yaw* his way through one of his."

Nightly stories had been one of the few times we could sit as a group without falling into petty bickering. Now, even they were becoming tense. What's more, the others were beginning to count on me for the evening's entertainment. Hoping to put an end to the trend, I'd put a lot of thought into what story I was going to tell tonight.

"Once upon a time," I began. "There was a little boy born in a little town. He was perfect, or so his mother thought. But one thing was different about him. He had a gold screw in his belly button. Just the head of it peeping out.

"Now his mother was simply glad he had all his fingers and toes to count with. But as the boy grew up he realized not everyone had screws in their belly buttons, let alone gold ones. He asked his mother what it was for, but she didn't know. Next he asked his father, but his father didn't know. He asked his grandparents, but they didn't know either.

"That settled it for a while, but it kept nagging him. Finally, when he was old enough, he packed a bag and set out, hoping he could find someone who knew the truth of it.

"He went from place to place, asking everyone who claimed to know something about anything. He asked midwives and physickers, but they couldn't make heads or tails of it. The boy asked arcanists, tinkers, and old hermits living in the woods, but no one had ever seen anything like it.

"He went to ask the Cealdim merchants, thinking if anyone would know about gold, it would be them. But the Cealdim merchants didn't know. He went to the arcanists at the University, thinking if anyone would know about screws and their workings, they would. But the arcanists didn't know. The boy followed the road over the Stormwal to ask the witch women of the Tahl, but none of them could give him an answer.

"Eventually he went to the King of Vint, the richest king in the world. But the king didn't know. He went to the Emperor of Atur, but even with all his power, the emperor didn't know. He went to each of the small kingdoms, one by one, but no one could tell him anything.

"Finally the boy went to the High King of Modeg, the wisest of all the kings in the world. The high king looked closely at the head of the golden screw peeping from the boy's belly button. Then the high king made a gesture, and his seneschal brought out a pillow of golden silk. On that pillow was a golden box. The high king took a golden key from around his neck, opened the box, and inside was a golden screwdriver.

"The high king took the screwdriver and motioned the boy to come closer. Trembling with excitement, the boy did. Then the high king took the golden screwdriver and put it in the boy's belly button."

I paused to take a long drink of water. I could feel my small audience leaning toward me. "Then the high king carefully turned the golden screw. Once: Nothing. Twice: Nothing. Then he turned it the third time, and the boy's ass fell off."

There was a moment of stunned silence.

"What?" Hespe asked incredulously.

"His ass fell off," I repeated with an absolutely straight face.

There was a long silence. Everyone's eyes were fixed on me. The fire snapped, sending a red ember floating upward.

"And then what happened?" Hespe finally asked.

"Nothing," I said. "That's it. The end."

"What?" she said again, more loudly. "What kind of story is that?"

I was about to respond when Tempi burst out laughing. And he kept laughing; great shaking laughs that left him breathless. Soon I began to laugh as well, partly at Tempi's display, and partly because I'd always considered it an oddly funny story myself.

Hespe's expression turned dangerous, as if she were the butt of the joke.

Dedan was the first to speak. "I don't understand. Why did . . .?" he trailed off.

"Did they get the boy's ass back on?" Hespe interjected.

I shrugged. "That's not part of the story."

Dedan gestured wildly, his expression frustrated. "What's the point of it?"

I put on an innocent face. "I thought we were just telling stories."

The big man scowled at me. "Sensible stories! Stories with endings. Not stories that just have a boy's ass . . ." He shook his head. "This is ridiculous. I'm going to sleep." He moved off to make his bed. Hespe stalked off in her own direction.

I smiled, reasonably sure neither one of them would be troubling me for any more stories than I cared to tell.

Tempi got to his feet as well. Then, as he walked past me he smiled and gave me a sudden hug. A span of days ago this would have shocked me, but now I knew that physical contact was not particularly odd among the Adem.

Still, I was surprised he did it in front of the others. I returned his hug as best I could, feeling his chest still shaking with laughter. "His ass off," he said quietly, then made his way to bed.

Marten's eyes followed Tempi, then he gave me a long, speculative look. "Where did you hear that one?" he asked.

"My father told it to me when I was young," I said honestly.

"Odd story to tell a child."

"I was an odd child," I said. "When I was older he confessed he made the stories up to keep me quiet. I used to pepper him with questions. Hour after hour. He said the only thing that would keep me quiet was some sort of puzzle. But I cracked riddles like walnuts, and he ran out of those."

I shrugged and started to lay out my bed. "So he made up stories that seemed like puzzles and asked me if I understood what they meant." I smiled a little wistfully. "I remember thinking about that boy with the screw in his belly button for days and days, trying to find the sense in it."

Marten frowned. "That's a cruel trick to play on a boy."

The comment surprised me. "What do you mean?"

"Tricking you just to get a little peace and quiet. It's a shabby thing to do."

I was taken aback. "It wasn't done in meanness. I enjoyed it. It gave me something to think about."

"But it was pointless. Impossible."

"Not pointless." I protested. "It's the questions we can't answer that teach us the most. They teach us how to think. If you give a man an answer, all he gains is a little fact. But give him a question and he'll look for his own answers."

I spread my blanket on the ground and folded over the threadbare tinker's cloak to wrap myself in. "That way, when he finds the answers, they'll be precious to him. The harder the question, the harder we hunt. The harder we hunt, the more we learn. An impossible question . . ."

I trailed off as realization burst onto me. Elodin. That is what Elodin had been doing. Everything he'd done in his class. The games, the hints, the cryptic riddling. They were all questions of a sort.

Marten shook his head and wandered off, but I was lost in my thoughts and hardly noticed. I had wanted answers, and in spite of all I had thought, Elodin had been trying to give them to me. What I had taken as a malicious crypticism on his part was actually a persistent urging toward the truth. I sat there, silent and stunned by the scope of his instruction. By my lack of understanding. My lack of sight.

CHAPTER EIGHTY-FOUR

The Edge of the Map

WE CONTINUED TO INCH our way through the Eld. Every day began with the hope of finding traces of a trail. Every night ended with disappointment.

The shine was definitely off the apple, and our group was slowly being overtaken by irritation and backbiting. Any fear Dedan once felt for me had worn paper-thin, and he pushed at me constantly. He wanted to buy a bottle of brand using the Maer's purse. I refused. He thought we didn't need to keep nightly watches, merely set up a tripline. I disagreed.

Every small battle I won made him resent me more. And his low grumbling steadily increased as our search wore on. It was never anything so bold as a direct confrontation, just a sporadic peppering of snide comments and sulky insubordination.

On the other hand, Tempi and I were slowly moving toward something like friendship. His Aturan was becoming better, and my Ademic had progressed to the point where I could actually be considered inarticulate, as opposed to just confusing.

I continued to mimic Tempi as he performed his dance, and he continued to ignore me. Now that I'd been doing it for a while, I recognized a hint of martial flavor to it. A slow motion with one arm gave the impression of a punch, a glacial raising of the foot resembled a kick. My arms and legs no longer shook from the effort of moving slowly along with him, but I was still irritated by how clumsy I was. I hate nothing so much as doing a thing badly.

For example, there was a portion halfway through that looked easy as breathing. Tempi turned, circled his arms, and took a small step. But whenever I tried to do the same, I inevitably found myself stumbling. I had tried a half-dozen different ways of placing my feet, but nothing made any difference.

But the day after I told my "loose screw" story, as Dedan eventually came to refer to it, Tempi stopped ignoring me. This time after I stumbled, he stopped and faced me. His fingers flicked: *Disapproval, irritation.* "Go back," he said settling into the dance position that came before my stumble.

I went into the same position and tried to mimic him. I lost my balance again, and had to shuffle my feet to keep from stumbling. "My feet are stupid," I muttered in Ademic, curling the fingers on my left hand: *Embarrassment.*

"No." Tempi grabbed my hips in his hands and twisted them. Then he pushed my shoulders back, and slapped at my knee, making me bend it. "Yes."

I tried moving forward again, and felt the difference. I still lost my balance, but only a little.

"No," he said again. "Watch." He tapped his shoulder. "This." He stood directly in front of me, barely a foot away, and repeated the motion. He turned, his hands made a circle to the side, and his shoulder pushed into my chest. It was the same motion you would make if you were trying to push open a door with your shoulder.

Tempi wasn't moving very quickly, but his shoulder pushed me firmly aside. It wasn't rough or sudden, but the force of it was irresistible, like when a horse brushes up against you on a crowded street.

I moved through it again, focusing on my shoulder. I didn't stumble.

Since we were the only ones at the camp, I kept the smile from my face and gestured: *Happiness.* "Thank you." *Understatement.*

Tempi said nothing. His face was blank, his hands still. He merely went back to where he had stood before and began his dance again from the beginning, facing away from me.

I tried to remain stoic about the exchange, but I took this as a great compliment. Had I known more about the Adem, I would have realized it was far more than that.

———

Tempi and I came over a rise to find Marten waiting for us. It was too early for lunch, so hope rose in my chest as I thought that finally, after all these long days of searching, he might have caught the bandits' trail.

"I wanted to show you this," Marten said, gesturing to a tall, sprawling, fernlike plant that stood a dozen feet away. "A bit of a rare thing. Been years since I've seen one."

"What is it?"

"It's called An's blade," he said proudly, looking it over. "You'll need to keep an eye out. Not many folk know about them so it might give us a clue if there are any more of them about."

Marten looked back and forth between us eagerly. "Well?" he said at last.

"What's so special about it?" I asked dutifully.

Marten smiled. "The An's blade is interesting because it can't tolerate folk," he said. "If any part of it touches your skin, it'll turn red as fall leaves in a couple hours. Redder than that. Bright as your mercenary reds," Marten gestured to Tempi. "And then that whole plant will dry up and die."

"Really?" I asked, no longer having to feign interest.

Marten nodded. "A drop of sweat will kill it just the same. Which means most times it will die just from touching a person's clothes. Armor too. Or a stick you've been holding. Or a sword." He gestured to Tempi's hip. "Some people say it will die if you so much as breathe on it," Marten said. "But I don't know if that's the truth."

Marten turned to lead us away from the An's blade. "This is an old, old piece of forest. You don't see the blade anywhere near where folk have settled. We're off the edge of the map here."

"We're hardly on the edge of the map," I said. "We know exactly where we are."

Marten snorted. "Maps don't just have outside edges. They have inside edges. Holes. Folk like to pretend they know everything about the world. Rich folk especially. Maps are great for that. On this side of the line is Baron Taxtwice's field, on that side is Count Uptemuny's land."

Marten spat. "You can't have blanks on your maps, so the folks who draw them shade in a piece and write, 'The Eld.' " He shook his head. "You might as well burn a hole right through the map for what good that does. This forest is big as Vintas. Nobody owns it. You head off in the wrong direction in here, you'll walk a hundred miles and never see a road, let alone a house or plowed field. There are places around here that have never felt the press of a man's foot or heard the sound of his voice."

I looked around. "It looks the same as most other forests I've seen."

"A wolf looks like a dog," Marten said simply. "But it's not. A dog is . . ." He paused. "What's that word for animals that are around people all the time? Cows and sheep and such."

"Domesticated?"

"That's it," he said, looking around. "A farm is domesticated. A garden. A park. Most forests too. Folks hunt mushrooms, or cut firewood, or take their sweethearts for a little rub and cuddle."

He shook his head and reached out to touch the rough bark of a nearby tree. The gesture was oddly gentle, almost loving. "Not this place. This place is old and wild. It doesn't care one thin sliver of a damn about us. If these folk we're hunting get the jump on us, they won't even have to bury our bodies.

We'll lie on the ground for a hundred years and no one will come close to stumbling on our bones."

I turned where I stood, looking at the rise and fall of the land. The worn rocks, the endless ranks of trees. I tried not to think about how the Maer had sent me here, like moving a stone on a tak board. He had sent me to a hole in the map. A place where no one would ever find my bones.

CHAPTER EIGHTY-FIVE

Interlude—Fences

K VOTHE SAT UPRIGHT IN his seat, craning his neck to get a better look out the window. He was just holding his hand up to Chronicler when they heard a quick, light tapping on the wooden landing outside. Too fast and soft to be the heavy boots of farmers, it was followed by a high peal of childish laughter.

Chronicler quickly blotted the page he was writing, then tucked it under a stack of blank paper as Kvothe got to his feet and walked toward the bar. Bast leaned back, tipping his chair onto two legs.

After a moment, the door opened and a young man with broad shoulders and a thin beard stepped into the inn, carefully ushering a little blonde girl through the doorway ahead of him. Behind him a young woman carried a baby boy sitting on her arm.

The innkeeper smiled, raising a hand. "Mary! Hap!"

The young couple exchanged a brief word before the tall farmer walked over to Chronicler, still gently ushering the little girl in front of him. Bast got to his feet and offered up his chair to Hap.

Mary approached the bar, casually untangling one of the little boy's hands from her hair. She was young and pretty, with a smiling mouth and tired eyes. "Hello Kote."

"I haven't seen you two in a long while," the innkeeper said. "Can I get you some cider? I pressed it fresh this morning."

She nodded, and the innkeeper poured three mugs. Bast carried two over to Hap and his daughter. Hap took his, but the little girl hid behind her father, peering shyly around his shoulder.

"Would young master Ben like his own cup?" Kote asked.

"He would," Mary said, smiling at the boy as he chewed on his fingers.

"But I wouldn't give it to him unless you're eager to clean the floors." She reached into her pocket.

Kote shook his head firmly, holding up a hand. "I won't hear of it," he said. "Hap didn't take half of what the work was worth when he fixed my fences out back."

Mary smiled a tired, anxious smile and picked up her mug. "Thank you kindly, Kote." She walked over to where her husband sat, talking to Chronicler. She spoke to the scribe, swaying gently back and forth, bouncing the baby on one hip. Her husband nodded along, occasionally interjecting a word or two. Chronicler dipped his pen and began to write.

Bast moved back to the bar and leaned against it, eyeing the far table curiously. "I still don't understand all of this," he said. "I know for a fact Mary can write. She's sent me letters."

Kvothe looked curiously at his student, then shrugged. "I expect he's writing wills and dispositions, not letters. You want that sort of thing done in a clear hand, spelled properly and with no confusion." He motioned to where Chronicler was pressing a heavy seal onto a sheet of paper. "See? That shows he's a court official. Everything he witnesses has legal weight."

"But the priest does that," Bast said. "Abbe Grimes is all sorts of official. He writes the marriage records and the deed when someone buys a plot of land. You said yourself, they love their records."

Kvothe nodded. "True, but a priest likes it when you leave money to the church. If he writes up your will and you don't give the church as much as a bent penny . . ." He shrugged. "That can make life hard in a little town like this. And if you can't read . . . well, then the priest can write down whatever he wants, can't he? And who's to argue with him after you're dead?"

Bast looked shocked. "Abbe Grimes wouldn't do something like that!"

"He probably wouldn't," Kvothe conceded. "Grimes is a decent sort for a priest. But maybe you want to leave a piece of land to the young widow down the lane and some money to her second son?" Kvothe raised an eyebrow meaningfully. "That's the sort of thing a fellow doesn't care to have his priest writing down. Better to have that news come out after you're dead and buried deep."

Understanding came into Bast's eyes and he looked at the young couple as if trying to guess what secrets they were trying to hide.

Kvothe pulled out a white cloth and began to polish the bar absentmindedly. "Most times it's simpler than that. Some folk just want to leave Ellie the music box and not hear the other sisters wail about it for the next ten years."

"Like when the Widow Graden died?"

"Exactly like when Widow Graden died. You saw how that family tore itself up fighting over her things. Half of them still aren't on speaking terms."

Across the room, the little girl stepped close to her mother and tugged insistently on her dress. A moment later Mary came over to the bar with the little girl in tow. "Little Syl has to tend to her necessary," she said apologetically. "Could we . . . ?"

Kote nodded and pointed to the door near the stairway.

Mary turned and held out the little boy to Bast. "Would you mind?"

Moving mostly on reflex, Bast reached out with both hands to take hold of the boy, then stood there awkwardly as Mary escorted her daughter away.

The little boy looked around brightly, not sure what to make of this new situation. Bast turned to face Kvothe, the baby held stiffly in front of himself. The child's expression slowly shifted from curious to uncertain to unhappy. Finally he began to make a soft, anxious noise. He looked as if he were thinking about whether or not he wanted to cry, and was slowly starting to realize that, yes, as a matter of fact, he probably did.

"Oh for goodness sake, Bast," Kvothe said in an exasperated voice. "Here." He stepped forward and took hold of the boy, sitting him on top of the bar and holding him steady with both hands.

The boy seemed happier there. He rubbed a curious hand on the smooth top of the bar, leaving a smudge. He looked at Bast and smiled. "Dog," he said.

"Charming," Bast said, his voice dry.

Little Ben began to chew on his fingers and looked around again, more purposefully this time. "Mam," he said. "Mamamama." Then he began to look concerned and make the same, low anxious noise as before.

"Hold him up," Kvothe said, moving to stand directly in front of the little boy. Once Bast was steadying him, the innkeeper grabbed hold of the boy's feet and began a singsong chant.

> Cobbler, cobbler, measure my feet.
> Farmer, farmer, plant some wheat.
> Baker, baker, bake me bread.
> Tailor, make a hat for my head.

The little boy watched as Kvothe made a different hand motion for each line, pretending to plant wheat and knead bread. By the final line the little boy was laughing a delighted, burbling laugh as he clapped his hands to his own head along with the red-haired man.

Miller, keep your thumb off the scale.
Milkmaid, milkmaid, fill your pail
Potter, potter, spin a jug,
Baby, give your daddy a hug!

Kvothe made no gesture for the last line, instead he tilted his head, eyeing Bast expectantly.

Bast merely stood there, confused. Then realization dawned on his face. "Reshi, how could you think that?" he asked, his voice slightly offended. He pointed at the little boy. "He's blonde!"

Looking back and forth between the two men, the boy decided that he would, actually, like to have a bit of a cry. His face clouded over, and he began to wail.

"This is your fault," Bast said flatly.

Kvothe picked the little boy up off the bar and jiggled him in a marginally successful attempt to calm him. A moment later when Mary came back into the taproom, the baby howled even louder and leaned toward her, reaching with both hands.

"Sorry," Kvothe said, sounding abashed.

Mary took him back and he went instantly quiet, tears still standing in his eyes. "None of yours," she said. "He's just mother-hungry lately." She touched her nose to his, smiling, and the baby gave another delighted, burbling laugh.

"How much did you charge them?" Kvothe asked as he walked back to Chronicler's table.

Chronicler shrugged. "Penny and a half."

Kvothe paused in the act of sitting down. His eyes narrowed. "That won't cover the cost of your paper."

Chronicler asked. "I have ears, don't I? The smith's prentice mentioned the Bentleys are on hard times. Even if he hadn't, I still have eyes. Fellow's got seams on both knees and boots worn nearly through. Little girl's dress is too short for her and half patches besides."

Kvothe nodded, his expression grim. "Their south field's been flooded out two years running. And they had both their goats die this spring. Even if these were good times it would be a bad year for them. With their new little boy . . ." He drew a long breath and let it out in a long, pensive sigh. "It's the levy taxes. Two this year already."

"Do you want me to wreck the fence again, Reshi?" Bast said eagerly.

"Hush about that, Bast." A smile flickered around the edges of Kvothe's mouth. "We'll need something different this time." His smile faded. "Before the next levy."

"Maybe there won't be another," Chronicler said.

Kvothe shook his head. "It won't come until after the harvest, but it'll come. Regular taxmen are bad enough, but they know enough to occasionally look the other way. They know they'll be back next year, and the year after. But the bleeders . . ."

Chronicler nodded. "They're different," he said grimly. Then recited, "'If they could, they'd take the rain. If they can't get gold, they'll take the grain.'"

Kvothe gave a thin smile and continued.

If you've got no grain, they'll take your goat.
They'll take your firewood and your coat.
If you've a cat, they'll take your mouse.
And in the end, they'll take your house.

"Everyone hates the bleeders," Chronicler agreed darkly. "If anything, the nobles hate them twice as much."

"I find that hard to believe," Kvothe said. "You should hear the talk around here. If the last one hadn't had a full armed guard, I don't think he would have made it out of town alive."

Chronicler gave a bent smile. "You should have heard the things my father used to call them," he said. "And he'd only had two levies in twenty years. He said he'd rather have locusts followed by a fire than the king's bleeder moving through his lands." Chronicler glanced at the door of the inn. "They're too proud to ask for help?"

"Prouder than that," Kvothe said. "The poorer you are, the more your pride is worth. I know the feeling. I never could have asked a friend for money. I would have starved first."

"A loan?" Chronicler asked.

"Who has money to lend these days?" Kvothe asked grimly. "It's already going to be a hungry winter for most folk. But after a third levy tax the Bentleys will be sharing blankets and eating their seed grain before the snow thaws. That's if they don't lose their house as well. . . ."

The innkeeper looked down at his hands on the table and seemed surprised that one of them was curled into a fist. He opened it slowly and spread both hands flat against the tabletop. Then he looked up at Chronicler, a rueful smile on his face. "Did you know I never paid taxes before I came here? The Edema don't own property, as a rule." He gestured at the inn. "I never understood how galling it was. Some smug bastard with a ledger comes into town, makes you pay for the privilege of owning something."

Kvothe gestured for Chronicler to pick up his pen. "Now, of course, I understand the truth of things. I know what sort of dark desires lead a group of men to wait beside the road, killing tax collectors in open defiance of the king."

CHAPTER EIGHTY-SIX

The Broken Road

WE FINISHED SEARCHING THE north side of the king's highway and started on the southern half. Often the only thing that marked one day from the next were the stories we told around the fire at night. Stories of Oren Velciter, Laniel Young-Again, and Illien. Stories of helpful swineherds and the luck of tinker's sons. Stories of demons and faeries, of riddle games and barrow draugs.

The Edema Ruh know all the stories in the world, and I am Edema down to the center of my bones. My parents told stories around the fire every night while I was young. I grew up watching stories in dumbshow, listening to them in songs, and acting them out on stage.

Given this, it was hardly surprising that I already knew the stories Dedan, Hespe, and Marten told at night. Not every detail, but I knew the bones of them. I knew their shapes and how they would end.

Don't mistake me. I still enjoyed them. Stories don't need to be new to bring you joy. Some stories are like familiar friends. Some are dependable as bread.

Still, a story I haven't heard before is a rare and precious thing. And after twenty days of searching the Eld, I was rewarded with one of those.

———

"Once, long ago and far from here," Hespe said as we sat around the fire after dinner, "there was a boy named Jax, and he fell in love with the moon.

"Jax was a strange boy. A thoughtful boy. A lonely boy. He lived in an old house at the end of a broken road. He—"

Dedan interrupted. "Did you say a *broken* road?"

Hespe's mouth went firm. She didn't scowl exactly, but it looked like she was getting all the pieces of a scowl together in one place, just in case she needed them in a hurry. "I did. A broken road. That's how my mother told this story a hundred times when I was little."

For a minute it looked like Dedan was going to ask another question. But instead he showed a rare foresight and simply nodded.

Hespe reluctantly put the pieces of her scowl away. Then she looked down at her hands, frowning. Her mouth moved silently for a moment, then she nodded to herself and continued.

———

Everyone who saw Jax could tell there was something different about him. He didn't play. He didn't run around getting into trouble. And he never laughed.

Some folk said, "What can you expect of a boy who lives alone in a broken house at the end of a broken road?" Some said the problem was that he never had any parents. Some said he had a drop of faerie blood in him and that kept his heart from ever knowing joy.

He was an unlucky boy. There was no denying that. When he got a new shirt, he would tear a hole in it. If you gave him a sweet, he would drop it in the road.

Some said the boy was born under a bad star, that he was cursed, that he had a demon riding his shadow. Other folks simply felt bad for him, but not so bad that they cared to help.

One day, a tinker came down the road to Jax's house. This was something of a surprise, because the road was broken, so nobody ever used it.

"Hoy there, boy!" the tinker shouted, leaning on his stick. "Can you give an old man a drink?"

Jax brought out some water in a cracked clay mug. The tinker drank and looked down at the boy. "You don't look happy, son. What's the matter?"

"Nothing is the matter," Jax said. "It seems to me a person needs something to be happy about, and I don't have any such thing."

Jax said this in a tone so flat and resigned that it broke the tinker's heart. "I'm betting I have something in my pack that will make you happy," he said to the boy. "What do you say to that?"

"I'd say that if you make me happy, I'll be grateful indeed," Jax said. "But I haven't got any money to spend, not a penny to borrow to beg or to lend."

"Well that is a problem," said the tinker. "I am in business, you see."

"If you can find something in your pack that will make me happy," Jax said. "I will give you my house. It's old and broken, but it's worth something."

The tinker looked up at the huge old house, one short step away from being a mansion. "It is at that," he said.

Then Jax looked up at the tinker, his small face serious. "And if you can't make me happy, what then? Will you give me the packs off your back, the stick in your hand, and the hat off your head?"

Now the tinker was fond of a wager, and he knew a good bet when he heard one. Besides, his packs were bulging with treasures from all over the Four Corners, and he was confident he could impress a small boy. So he agreed, and the two of them shook hands.

First the tinker brought out a bag of marbles all the colors of sunlight. But they didn't make Jax happy. The tinker brought out a ball and cup. But that didn't make Jax happy.

"Ball and cup doesn't make anyone happy," Marten muttered. *"That's the worst toy ever. Nobody in their right mind enjoys ball and cup."*

The tinker went through his first pack. It was full of ordinary things that would have pleased an ordinary boy: dice, puppets, a folding knife, a rubber ball. But nothing made Jax happy.

So the tinker moved on to his second pack. It held rarer things. A gear sol-dier that marched if you wound him. A bright set of paints with four different brushes. A book of secrets. A piece of iron that fell from the sky. . . .

This went on all day and late into the night, and eventually the tinker began to worry. He wasn't worried about losing his stick. But his packs were how he made his living, and he was rather fond of his hat.

Eventually, he realized he was going to have to open his third pack. It was small, and it only had three items in it. But they were things he only showed to his wealthiest customers. Each was worth much more than a broken house. But still, he thought, better to lose one than to lose everything and his hat besides.

Just as the tinker was reaching for his third pack, Jax pointed. "What is that?"

"Those are spectacles," the tinker said. "They're a second pair of eyes that help a person see better." He picked them up and settled them onto Jax's face.

Jax looked around. "Things look the same," he said. Then he looked up. "What are those?"

"Those are stars," the tinker said.

"I've never seen them before." He turned, still looking up. Then he stopped stock still. "What is that?"

"That is the moon," the tinker said.

"I think that would make me happy," Jax said.

"Well there you go," the tinker said, relieved. "You have your spectacles. . . ."

"Looking at it doesn't make me happy," Jax said. "No more than looking at my dinner makes me full. I want it. I want to have it for my own."

"I can't give you the moon," the tinker said. "She doesn't belong to me. She belongs only to herself."

"Only the moon will do," Jax said.

"Well I can't help you with that," the tinker said with a heavy sigh. "My packs and everything in them are yours."

Jax nodded, unsmiling.

"And here's my stick. A good sturdy one it is, too."

Jax took it in his hand.

"I don't suppose," the tinker said reluctantly, "that you'd mind leaving me with my hat? I'm rather fond of it. . . ."

"It's mine by right," Jax said. "If you were fond of it, you shouldn't have gambled it away." The tinker scowled as he handed over his hat.

Tempi made a low noise in his throat and shook his head. Hespe smiled and nodded. Apparently even the Adem know it's bad luck to be rude to a tinker.

So Jax settled the hat on his head, took the stick in his hand, and gathered up the tinker's packs. When he found the third one, still unopened, he asked, "What's in here?"

"Something for you to choke on," the tinker spat.

"No need to get tetchy over a hat," the boy said. "I have greater need of it than you. I have a long way to walk if I'm to find the moon and make her mine."

"But for the taking of my hat, you could have had my help in catching her," the tinker said.

"I will leave you with the broken house," Jax said. "That is something. Though it will be up to you to mend it."

Jax put the spectacles on his face and started walking down the road in the direction of the moon. He walked all night, only stopping when she went out of sight behind the mountains.

So Jax walked day after day, endlessly searching—

———

Dedan snorted. "Doesn't that sound just a little too familiar?" he muttered loud enough for everyone to hear. "I wonder if he was pissing his time up a tree like we are?"

Hespe glared at him, the muscles in her jaw clenching.

I gave a quiet sigh.

"Are you done?" Hespe asked pointedly, glaring at Dedan for a long moment.

"What?" Dedan asked.

"Shut up while I'm telling my story is what," Hespe said.

"Everyone else had their say!" Dedan climbed to his feet, indignant. "Even the mute chimed in." He waved a hand at Tempi. "How come I'm the only one you get hissy at?"

Hespe seethed for a moment, then said. "You're trying to pick a fight half-way through my story is why."

"Tellin' the truth isn't picking a fight," Dedan grumbled. "Someone needs to speak some sense around here."

Hespe threw her hands up in the air, "You're still doing it! Can't you set it down for one evening? Every chance you get you have to bitch and minge on!"

"At least when I don't agree I speak my mind," Dedan said. "I don't take the coward's way out."

Hespe's eyes flashed, and despite my better judgment, I decided to jump in. "Fine," I interrupted, looking at Dedan. "If you've got a better idea for finding these folk, let's hear it. Let's talk it over like adults."

My interjection didn't slow Dedan down the least bit. It just pointed him in my direction. "What would you know about adults?" he said. "I'm sick and tired of being talked down to by some boy who probably doesn't even have hair on his balls yet."

"I'm sure if the Maer had known how hairy your balls were, he would have put you in charge," I said with what I hoped was infuriating calmness. "Unfortunately, it seems he missed that fact and decided on me instead."

Dedan drew a breath, but Tempi broke in before he could start. "Balls," the Adem said curiously. "What is balls?"

All the air went out of Dedan in a rush, and he turned to look at Tempi, half irritated, half amused. The big mercenary chuckled and made a very clear motion between his legs with a cupped hand. "You know. Balls," he said without a trace of self-consciousness.

Behind his back, Hespe rolled her eyes, shaking her head.

"Ah," Tempi said, nodding to show his understanding. "Why is the Maer looking at hairy balls?"

A pause, then a storm of laughter rolled through our camp, exploding with all the force of the pent-up tension that had been ready to boil into a fight. Hespe laughed herself breathless, clutching at her stomach. Marten wiped tears from his eyes. Dedan laughed so hard he couldn't stand upright and ended up crouching with one hand on the ground to steady himself.

By the end of it, everyone was sitting around the fire, breathing hard and grinning like silly idiots. The tension that had been thick as winter fog was gone for the first time in days. It was only then that Tempi briefly caught my eye. His thumb and forefinger rubbed together gently. *Gladness?* No. *Satisfaction.* Realization dawned on me as I met his eye again, his expression was blank as always. Studiously blank. So blank it was almost smug.

"Can we get back to your story, love?" Dedan asked Hespe. "I'd like to know how this boy gets the moon into bed."

Hespe smiled at him, the first honest smile I'd seen her give Dedan in a handful of days. "I've lost my place," she said. "There's a rhythm to it, like a song. I can tell it from the beginning, but if I start halfway through I'll get it all tangled up in my head."

"Will you start over tomorrow if I promise to keep my mouth shut?"

"I will," she agreed, "if you promise."

CHAPTER EIGHTY-SEVEN

The Lethani

THE NEXT DAY TEMPI and I went to Crosson for supplies. It meant a long day of walking, but not having to look for trail sign every step of the way made it feel like we were flying down the road.

As we walked, Tempi and I traded words back and forth. I learned the word for dream, and smell, and bone. I learned there were different words in Ademic for iron and sword–iron.

Then we had a long hour's worth of fruitless conversation as he tried to help me understand what it meant when he rubbed his fingers over his eyebrow. It almost seemed to be the same thing as a shrug, but he made it clear it wasn't the same. Was it indifference? Ambiguity?

"Is it the feeling you have when someone offers you a choice?" I tried again. "Someone offers you an apple or a plum?" I held up both hands in front of myself. "But you like both the same." I pressed my fingers together and smoothed them over my eyebrow twice. "This feeling?"

Tempi shook his head. "No." He stopped walking for a moment, then resumed. At his side, his left hand said: *Dishonesty.* "What is plum?" *Attentive.*

Confused, I looked at him. "What?"

"What does plum mean?" He gestured again: *Profoundly serious. Attentive.*

I turned my attention to the trees and immediately heard it: movement in the undergrowth.

The noise came from the south side of the road. The side we hadn't searched yet. The bandits. Excitement and fear swelled in my chest. Would they attack us? In my tatty cloak I doubted I looked like much of a target, but I was carrying my lute in its dark, expensive case.

Tempi had changed back to his tight mercenary reds for the trip into town. Would that discourage a man with a longbow? Or would it seem I was a minstrel rich enough to hire an Adem bodyguard? We might look like fruit ripe for the picking.

I thought longingly of the arrowcatch I'd sold to Kilvin, and realized he'd been right. People would pay dearly for them. I'd give every penny in my pocket for one right now.

I gestured to Tempi: *Acceptance. Dishonesty. Agreement.* "A plum is a sweet fruit," I said, straining my ears for telltale sounds from the surrounding trees.

Should we run to the trees for cover, or would it be better to pretend we were unaware of them? What could I do if they attacked? I had the knife I'd bought from the tinker on my belt, but I had no idea how to use it. I was suddenly aware of how terribly unprepared I was. What in God's name was I doing out here? I didn't belong in this situation. Why had the Maer sent me?

Just as I was starting to sweat in earnest, I heard a sudden snap and rustle in the underbrush. A horned hart burst from the trees and was across the road in three easy bounds. A moment later, two hinds followed. One paused in the center of the road and turned to look at us curiously, her long ear twitching. Then she was off and lost among the trees.

My heart was racing, and I let out a low, nervous laugh. I turned to look at Tempi, only to find him with his sword drawn. The fingers of his left hand curled into *embarrassment*, then made several quick gestures I couldn't identify.

He sheathed the sword without a flourish of any sort. A gesture as casual as putting your hand in your pocket. *Frustration.*

I nodded. Glad as I was to not be sprouting arrows from my back, an ambush would at least have given us a clue as to where the bandits were. *Agreement. Understatement.*

We silently continued our walk toward Crosson.

———

Crosson wasn't much as far as towns go. Twenty or thirty buildings with thick forest on every side. If it hadn't been on the king's highway, it probably wouldn't even have warranted a name.

But since it was on the king's highway, there was a reasonably stocked general goods store that supplied travelers and the scattering of nearby farms. There was a small post station that was also a livery and a farrier, and a small church that was also a brewery.

And an inn, of course. While the Laughing Moon was barely a third the size of the Pennysworth, it was still several steps above what you'd expect for a town like this. It was two stories tall, with three private rooms and a bathhouse. A large handpainted sign showed a gibbous moon wearing a waistcoat, holding its belly while it rocked with laughter.

I'd brought my lute that morning, hoping I might be able to play in exchange for a bit of lunch. But that was just an excuse. I was desperate for any excuse to play. My enforced silence was wearing on me as much as Dedan's muttering. I hadn't gone so long without my music since I'd been homeless on the streets of Tarbean.

Tempi and I dropped off our list of supplies with the elderly woman who ran the store. Four large loaves of trail bread, a half-pound of butter, quarter-pound of salt, flour, dried apple, sausages, a side of bacon, a sack of turnips, six eggs, two buttons, feathers for refletching Marten's hunting arrows, bootlaces, soap, and a new whetstone to replace one Dedan had broken. All told, it would come to eight silver bits from the Maer's rapidly thinning purse.

Tempi and I made our way over to the inn for lunch, knowing it would be an hour or two before our order was ready. Surprisingly, I could hear noise from the taproom from across the street. Places like this were usually busy in the evening when travelers stopped for the night, not in the middle of the day when everyone was in the fields or on the road.

The room quieted when we opened the door. At first I hoped the customers were glad to see a musician, then I saw their eyes were all for Tempi in his tight mercenary reds.

There were fifteen or twenty people idling in the taproom. Some hunched at the bar, others clustered around tables. It wasn't so crowded we couldn't find a table to sit, but it did take a couple minutes before the single harassed-looking serving girl came to our table.

"What'll it be then?" she asked, brushing a sweaty strand of hair away from her face. "We've got pea soup with bacon in, and a bread pudding."

"Sounds lovely," I said. "Can we get some apples and cheese too?"

"Drink?"

"Soft cider for me," I said.

"Beer," Tempi said, then made a gesture with two fingers on the tabletop. "Small whiskey. Good whiskey."

She nodded. "I'll need to see your money."

I raised an eyebrow. "You've had trouble lately?"

She sighed and rolled her eyes.

I handed her three halfpennies, and she hurried off. By then I was sure I wasn't imagining it: the men in the room were giving Tempi dark looks.

I turned to a man at the table next to us, quietly eating his bowl of soup. "Is this a market day or something?"

He looked at me like I was an idiot, and I saw he had a bruise going purple on his jaw. "There's no market day in Crosson. There's no market."

"I came through here a while back and things were quiet. What's everyone doing here?"

"Same thing as always," he said. "Looking for work. Crosson is the last stop before the Eld gets good and thick. A smart caravan'll pick up an extra guard or two." He took a drink. "But too many folk been gettin' feathered off in the trees lately. Caravans aren't coming through so often."

I looked around the room. They weren't wearing any armor, but now that I was looking I could see the marks of mercenary life on most of them. They were rougher looking than ordinary townsfolk. More scars, more broken noses, more knives, more swagger.

The man dropped his spoon into his empty bowl and got to his feet. "You can have the place for all I care," he said, "I've been here six days and only seen four wagons come through. Besides, only an idiot would head north as a pay-a-day."

He picked up a large pack and slipped it over his shoulders. "And with all the folk gone missing, only an idiot would take on extra help in a place like this. I'll tell you this for free, half of these reeking bastards would probably cut your throat the first night on the road."

A broad-shouldered man with a wild black beard let loose a mocking laugh from where he stood at the bar. "Just because ych can't roll dice dinna make me a criminal, souee," he said with a thick northern accent. "Yeh say sommat like that agin and I'll give'e twice as much as yeh got last night. Plus intrest."

The fellow I'd been talking to made a gesture you didn't have to be Adem to understand and headed out the door. The bearded man laughed.

Our drinks showed up just then. Tempi drank off half his whiskey in a single swallow and let out a long, satisfied sigh, slouching down in his seat. I sipped my cider. I'd been hoping to play for an hour or two in exchange for our meal. But I wasn't fool enough to play to a room composed entirely of frustrated mercenaries.

I could have done it, mind you. In an hour, I could have them laughing and singing. In two hours I could have them crying into their beer and apologizing to the serving girl. But not for the price of a meal. Not unless I had no better options. This room reeked of trouble. It was a fight waiting to happen. No trouper worth his salt could fail to recognize that.

The broad-shouldered man picked up a wooden mug and sauntered with theatrical casualness over to our table where he pulled out a chair for himself.

He smiled a wide, insincere smile through his thick black beard and stuck his hand out in Tempi's direction. "Hullo there," he said loud enough for everyone in the bar to hear. "M' name's Tam. Yussef?"

Tempi reached out and shook, his own hand looking small and pale gripped in the other man's huge hairy one. "Tempi."

Tam grinned at him. "And what're yeh doin' in town?"

"We're just passing through," I said. "We met up on the road and he was nice enough to walk with me."

Tam looked me up and down dismissively. "I wan't talkin' to you, boy," he growled. "Mind yer betters."

Tempi remained silent, watching the big man with the same placid, attentive expression he always wore. I watched his left hand come up to his ear in a gesture I didn't recognize.

Tam took a drink, watching Tempi all the while. When he lowered his mug, the dark hair around his mouth was wet, and he wiped his forearm across his face to dry it. "I've always wonnert," he said, loud enough for it to carry through the whole room. "Yeh Adem. How much does one of yeh fancy lads make?"

Tempi turned to look at me, his head tilted slightly to one side. I realized he probably couldn't understand the man's thick accent.

"He wants to know how much money you earn," I explained.

Tempi made a wavering motion with one hand. "Complicated."

Tam leaned over the table. "Wha if yeh were hired to guard a caravan? How much would'ee charge a day?"

"Two jots." Tempi shrugged. "Three."

Tam gave a showy laugh, loud enough that I could smell his breath. I'd expected it to stink, but it didn't. It smelled like cider, sweet with mulling spices. "Yeh hear that boys?" He shouted over his shoulder. "Three jots a day. And he canna hardly talk!"

Most everyone was already watching and listening, and this piece of information brought a low, irritated murmur from the room.

Tam turned back to the table. "Most of us get penny a day, when we get work at all. I get two, 'cause I'm good with horses and can lift up the back of a wagon if I need to." He rolled his broad shoulders. "Are yeh worth twenny men in a fight?"

I don't know how much of it Tempi understood, but he seemed to follow the last question fairly well. "Twenty?" he looked around appraisingly. "No. Four." He wavered his spread hand back and forth uncertainly. "Five."

This did nothing to improve the atmosphere in the room. Tam shook his head in exaggerated bemusement. "Even if I believed yeh for a second," he said, "that means yeh should make four or five pennies a day. Not twenny. Wh—"

I put on my most ingratiating smile and leaned into the conversation. "Listen, I—"

Tam's mug knocked hard against the tabletop, sending a splash of cider leaping up into the air. He gave me a dangerous look that didn't hold any of the false playfulness he'd been showing Tempi. "Boy," he said. "Yeh innerupt me again, and I'll knock yer teeth right out." He said it without any particular emphasis, as if he were letting me know that if I jumped into the river, I was bound to get wet.

Tam turned back to Tempi. "What makes you think you're worth three jots a day?"

"Who buys me, buys this." Tempi held up his hand. "And this." He pointed to the hilt of his sword. "And this." He tapped a leather strap that bound his distinctive Adem reds tightly to his chest.

The big man slapped the table hard with the flat of his hand. "So tha's the secret!" he said. "I need to get me a red shirt!" This brought a chuckle from the room.

Tempi shook his head. "No."

Tam leaned forward, and flicked at one of the straps near Tempi's shoulder with a thick finger. "Are yeh saying I'm not good enough to wear a fancy red shirt like yours?" He flicked the strap again.

Tempi nodded easily. "Yes. You are not good enough."

Tam grinned madly. "What if I said yer mother was a whore?"

The room grew quiet. Tempi turned to look at me. *Curiosity.* "What is whore?"

Unsurprisingly, that hadn't been one of the words we had shared over the last span of days. For half a moment I considered lying, but there was no way I could manage it. "He says your mother is a person men pay money to have sex with."

Tempi turned back to the mercenary and nodded graciously. "You are very kind. I thank you."

Tam's expression darkened, as if he suspected he was being mocked. "Yeh coward. For a bent penny I'd give yeh such a kickin' you'd be wearing your pecker backwards."

Tempi turned to me again. "I do not understand this man," he said. "Is he attempting to buy sex with me? Or does he wish to fight?"

Laughter roared through the room, and Tam's face grew red as blood under his beard.

"I'm pretty sure he wants to fight," I said, trying to keep from laughing myself.

"Ah," Tempi said. "Why does he not say? Why all of this . . ." He flicked his fingers back and forth and gave me a quizzical look.

"Pauncing around?" I suggested. Tempi's confidence was having a relaxing effect on me, and I wasn't above getting a little dig of my own in. After seeing how easily the Adem had dealt with Dedan, I was looking forward to seeing him thump some of the arrogance out of this horse's ass.

Tempi looked back toward the big man. "If you wish to fight, now stop pauncing around." The Adem made a broad gesture to the rest of the room. "Go find others to fight with you. Bring enough women to feel safe. Good?" My brief moment of relaxation evaporated as Tempi turned back to me, exasperation thick in his voice. "You people are always talk."

Tam stomped back to the table where his friends sat throwing dice. "Arright now. Yeh heard him. The little gripshit says he's worth four of us, so let's show him the sort of damage four of us can do. Brenden, Ven, Jane, you in?"

A bald man and a tall woman came to their feet, smiling. But the third waved his hand dismissively. "I'm too drunk to fight proper, Tam. But that's not half as drunk as I'd need to be to go up against a bloodshirt. They's bastards in a fight. I's seen it."

I was no stranger to bar fights. You'd think they'd be rare in a place like the University, but liquor is the great leveler. After six or seven solid drinks, there is very little difference between a miller on the outs with his wife and a young alchemist who's done poorly on his exams. They're both equally eager to skin their knuckles on someone else's teeth.

Even the Eolian, genteel as it was, saw its share of scuffles. If you stayed late enough you had a decent chance of seeing two of the embroidered nobility slapping away at each other.

My point is, when you're a musician you see a lot of fights. Some people go to the bars to drink. Some go to play dice. Some folk go looking for a fight, and others go hoping to watch a fight.

Folk don't get hurt as much as you'd expect. Bruises and split lips are usually the worst of it. If you're unlucky you might lose a tooth or break an arm, but there's a vast difference between a friendly bar fight and a back-alley koshing. A bar fight has rules and a host of unofficial judges standing around to enforce them. If things start to get vicious spectators are quick to leap in and break things up, because that's what you'd want someone to do for you.

There are exceptions, of course. Accidents happen, and I knew all too well from my time at the Medica how easy it was to sprain a wrist or dislocate a finger. Those might be minor injuries to a cattle drover or an innkeeper, but to me, with so much of my livelihood relying on my clever hands, the thought of a broken thumb was terrifying.

My stomach knotted as I watched Tempi take another swallow of whiskey and get to his feet. The problem was that we were strangers here. If things got ugly, could I count on the irritated mercenaries to step in and put a stop to things? Three against one was nothing close to a fair fight, and if it got ugly it would get ugly fast.

Tempi took a mouthful of beer and looked at me calmly. "Watch my back," he said, then turned to walk to where the other mercenaries stood.

For a moment I was simply impressed by his good use of Aturan. Since I'd known him, he'd gone from practically mute to using idiomatic speech. But that pride quickly faded as I tried to think of something I could do to stop the fight if things got out of control.

I couldn't think of a blessed thing. I hadn't seen this coming, and I had no clever tricks up my sleeve. For lack of any better options, I drew my knife out of its sheath and held it out of sight below the level of the table. The last thing I'd want to do is stab someone, but I could at least menace them with it and buy us enough time to get out the door.

Tempi gave the three mercenaries an appraising look. Tam was inches taller than he, with shoulders like an ox. There was a bald fellow with a scarred face and a wicked grin. Last was the blonde woman who stood a full hand taller than Tempi.

"There is only one woman," Tempi said, looking Tam in the eye. "Is enough? You may bring one more."

The female mercenary bristled. "You swaggercock," she spat. "I'll show you what a woman can do in a fight."

Tempi nodded politely.

His continuing lack of concern began to relax me. I had heard the stories, of course, a single Adem mercenary defeating a dozen regular soldiers. Could Tempi really fight off these three at the same time? He certainly seemed to think so. . . .

Tempi looked at them. "This is my first fight of this sort. How does begin?"

My palm started to sweat where I gripped the knife.

Tam stepped up so their chests were only inches apart. He loomed over Tempi. "We'll start by whipping you bloody. Then we'll give you a kicking. Then we'll come round and do it agin to make sure we didn't miss anything." As he said the last, he slammed his forehead down into Tempi's face.

My breath caught in my chest, and before I could get it back, the fight was over.

When the bearded mercenary snapped his head forward, I had expected to see Tempi reel backward, nose broken and gushing blood. But Tam was the one who staggered backward, howling and clutching at his face, blood spurting from beneath his hands.

Tempi stepped forward, got his hand on the back of the big man's neck, and spun him effortlessly into the ground where he landed in a messy tangle of arms and legs.

Without a hint of hesitation, Tempi turned and kicked the blonde woman squarely in the hip, making her stagger. While she was reeling, Tempi punched her sharply in the side of the head, and she folded bonelessly to the ground.

That's when the bald man stepped in, arms spread like a wrestler. Quick as a snake, he got one hand on Tempi's shoulder and the other on his neck.

I honestly can't say what happened next. There was a flurry of movement, and Tempi was left gripping the man's wrist and shoulder. The bald man snarled and struggled. But Tempi simply twisted the man's arm until he was bent over, staring at the floor. Then Tempi kicked the man's leg out from under him, sending him tumbling to the ground.

All in less time than it takes to tell it. If I hadn't been so stunned, I would have burst into applause.

Tam and the woman lay with the dead stillness of those deeply unconscious. But the bald man snarled something and began to make his way unsteadily back to his feet. Tempi stepped close, struck him in the head with casual precision, then watched the man slump limply to the ground.

It was, I thought idly, the most polite punch I'd ever seen. It was the careful blow of a skilled carpenter pounding a nail: hard enough to drive it fully home, but not so hard as to bruise the wood around it.

The room was very quiet in the aftermath. Then the tall man who had refused to fight raised his mug in salute, spilling a little. "Good on you!" he said loudly to Tempi, laughing. "Nobody will think less of you if you show Tam a bit of your boot while he's down there. Lord knows he's done it enough in his day."

Tempi looked down as if considering it, then shook his head and walked quietly back to our table. All eyes were still watching him, but the looks weren't nearly as dark as before.

Tempi came back to the table. "Did you watch my back?"

I looked up at him blankly, then nodded.

"What did you see?"

Only then did I understand what he really meant. "Your back was very straight."

Approval. "Your back is not straight." He held up a flat hand, tilted to one side. "That is why you stumble in the Ketan. It is . . ." Looking down, he trailed off, having noticed my knife half-concealed in my tatty cloak. He frowned. Actually frowned with his face. It was the first time I'd seen him do it, and it was amazingly intimidating.

"We will speak on this later," he said. At his side, he gestured: *Vast disapproval.*

Feeling more chastised than if I'd spent an hour on the horns, I ducked my head and put the knife away.

We had been walking quietly for hours, our packs heavy with supplies, when Tempi finally spoke. "There is a thing I must teach you." *Serious.*

"I am always glad to learn," I said, making the gesture I hoped meant *earnest.*

Tempi walked to the side of the road, set down his heavy pack, and sat on the grass. "We must speak of the Lethani."

It took all my control to not burst out into a sudden, giddy smile. I had been wanting to bring up the subject for a long while, as we were much closer than when I'd first asked him. But I hadn't wanted to risk offending him again.

I sat quietly for a moment, partly to maintain my composure, but also to let Tempi know I was treating this subject with respect. "The Lethani," I repeated carefully. "You said I must not ask of it."

"You must not then. Now perhaps, I ." *Uncertain.* "I am pulled many ways. But now asking is."

I waited for another moment to see if he would continue on his own. When he didn't, I asked the obvious question. "What is the Lethani?"

Serious. Tempi looked at me for a long moment, then suddenly burst out laughing. "I do not know. And I cannot tell you." He laughed again. *Understatement.* "Still we must speak of it."

I hesitated, wondering if this was one of his strange jokes that I could never seem to understand.

"Is complicated," he said. "Hard in my own language. Yours?" *Frustration.* "Tell me what you know of the Lethani."

I tried to think of how I could describe what I'd heard of the Lethani using only the words he knew. "I heard the Lethani is a secret thing that makes the Adem strong."

Tempi nodded. "Yes. This is true."

"They say if you know the Lethani, you cannot lose a fight."

Another nod.

I shook my head, knowing I wasn't getting my point across. "They say the Lethani is a secret power. Adem keep their words inside." I made a gesture as if gathering things close to my body and hoarding them. "Then those words are like wood in a fire. This word fire makes the Adem very strong. Very fast. Skin like iron. This is why you can fight many men and win."

Tempi looked at me intently. He made a gesture I didn't recognize. "That is mad talking," he said at last. "Is that the correct word? Mad?" He stuck out his tongue and rolled his eyes, wiggling his fingers at the side of his head.

I couldn't help but laugh nervously at the display. "Yes. Mad is the word. Also crazy."

"Then what you have said is mad talking and also crazy."

"But what I saw today," I said. "Your nose did not break when struck with a man's head. That is no natural thing."

Tempi shook his head as he climbed to his feet. "Come. Stand."

I stood, and Tempi stepped close to me. "Striking with the head is clever. It is quick. Can startle if opponent is not ready. But I am not not ready."

He stepped closer still, until we were almost touching chests. "You are the loud man," he said. "Your head is hard. My nose is soft." He reached out and took hold of my head with both his hands. "You want this." He brought my head down, slowly, until my forehead pressed his nose.

Tempi let go of my head. "Striking with the head is quick. For me, little time. Can I move?" He moved my head down as he pulled away, and this time my forehead came into contact with his mouth instead, as if he were giving me a kiss. "This is not good. The mouth is soft."

He tipped my head back again. "If I am very fast . . ." He took a full step back and brought my head down farther, until my forehead touched his chest. He let me go and I stood back up. "This is still not good. My chest is not soft. But this man has a head harder than many." His eyes twinkled a little, and I chuckled, realizing he had made a joke.

"So." Tempi said, stepping back to where we were before. "What can Tempi do?" He motioned. "Strike with the head. Slow. I show."

Vaguely nervous, I brought my head down slowly, as if trying to break his nose.

Matching my slow speed, Tempi leaned forward and tucked his chin a bit. It wasn't much of a change, but this time as I brought my head down, my nose met the top of his head.

Tempi stepped back. "See? Cleverness. Not mad-thinking word fire."

"It was very fast," I said, feeling slightly embarrassed. "I could not see."

"Yes. Fighting is fast. Train to be fast. Train, not word fire."

He gestured *earnest* and met my eye, a rarity for him. "I tell this because you are the leader. You need the knowing. If you think I have secret ways and iron skin . . ." He looked away, shaking his head. *Dangerous.*

We both sat back down next to our packs.

"I heard it in a story," I said by way of explanation. "A story like we tell around the fire at night."

"But you," he pointed to me. "You have fire in your hands. You have . . ." He snapped his fingers, then made a gesture like a fire roaring up suddenly. "You have the doing of this, and you think the Adem have word fires inside?"

I shrugged. "That is why I ask of the Lethani. It seems mad, but I have seen mad things be true, and I am curious." I hesitated before asking my other question. "You said who knows the Lethani cannot lose a fight."

"Yes. But not with word fires. The Lethani is a type of knowing." Tempi paused, obviously considering his words carefully. "Lethani is most important thing. All Adem learn. Mercenary learn twice. Shehyn learn three times. Most important. But complicated. Lethani is . . . many things. But nothing touched or pointed to. Adem spend whole lives thinking on the Lethani. Very hard.

"Problem," he said. "It is not my place to teach my leader. But you are my student in language. Women teach the Lethani. I am not such. It is part of civilization and you are a barbarian." *Gentle sorrow.* "But you want to be civilization. And you have need of the Lethani."

"Explain it," I said. "I will try to understand."

He nodded. "The Lethani is doing right things."

I waited patiently for him to continue. After a minute, he gestured, *frustration.* "Now you ask questions." He took a deep breath and repeated. "The Lethani is doing right things."

I tried to think of an archetypical example of something good. "So the Lethani is giving a hungry child food to eat."

He made the wavering motion that meant, *yes and no.* "The Lethani is not doing a thing. Lethani is the thing that shows us."

"Lethani means rules? Laws?"

Tempi shook his head. "No." He gestured to the forest around us. "Law is from outside, controlling. It is the . . . the horse mouth metal. And the head strings." *Questioning.*

"Bridle and bit?" I suggested. Motioning as if pulling a horse's head about with a pair of reins.

"Yes. Law is bridle and bit. It controls from outside. The Lethani . . ." He pointed between his eyes, then at his chest. ". . . lives inside. Lethani helps decide. Law is made because many have no understanding of Lethani."

"So with the Lethani a person does not need to follow the law."

Pause. "Perhaps." *Frustration.* He drew out his sword and held it parallel to the ground, its edge pointing up. "If you were small, walking this sword would be like the Lethani."

"Painful for feet?" I asked, trying to lighten the mood a bit. *Amusement. Anger. Disapproval.* "No. Difficult to walk. Easy to fall on one side. Difficult to stay."

"The Lethani is very straight?"

"No." Pause. "What is it called when there is many mountain and one place for walking?"

"A path? A pass?"

"Pass." Tempi nodded. "The Lethani is like a pass in the mountains. Bends. Complicated. Pass is easy way through. Only way through. But not easy to see. Path that is easy much times not go through mountains. Sometimes goes nowhere. Starve. Fall onto hole."

"So the Lethani is the right way through the mountains."

Partial agreement. Excitement. "It is the right way through the mountains. But the Lethani is also knowing the right way. Both. And mountains are not just mountains. Mountains are everything."

"So the Lethani is civilization."

Pause. *Yes and no.* Tempi shook his head. *Frustrated.*

I thought back to what he had said about mercenaries having to learn the Lethani twice. "Is the Lethani fighting?" I asked.

"No."

He said this with such absolute certainty that I had to ask the opposite to make sure. "Is the Lethani *not* fighting?"

"No. One who knows the Lethani knows when to fight and not fight." *Very important.*

I decided to change directions. "Was it of the Lethani for you to fight today?"

"Yes. To show Adem is not afraid. We know with barbarians, not fighting is coward. Coward is weak. Not good for them to think. So with many watching, fight. Also, to show one Adem is worth many."

"What if they had won?"

"Then barbarians know Tempi is not worth many." *Slight amusement.*

"If they had won, would today's fight be not of the Lethani?"

"No. If you fall and break a leg in mountain pass, it is still the pass. If I fail while following the Lethani, it is still the Lethani." *Serious.* "This is why we are talking now. Today. With your knife. That was not the Lethani. It was not a right thing."

"I was afraid you would be hurt."

"The Lethani does not put down roots in fear," he said, sounding as if he were reciting.

"Would it be the Lethani to let you be hurt?"

A shrug. "Perhaps."

"Would it be of the Lethani to let you be . . ." *Extreme emphasis.* "Hurt?"

"Perhaps no. But they did not. To be first with the knife is not of the Lethani. If you win and are first with the knife, you do not win." *Vast disapproval.*

I couldn't puzzle out what he meant by the last. "I don't understand," I said.

"The Lethani is right action. Right way. Right time." Tempi's face suddenly lit up. "The old trader man," he said with visible enthusiasm. "In the stories with the packs. What is the word?"

"Tinker?"

"Yes. The tinker. How you must treat such men?"

I knew, but I wanted to see what the Adem thought. "How?"

He looked at me, his fingers pressing together *irritation.* "You must be kind, and help them. And speak well. Always polite. *Always.*"

I nodded. "And if they offer something, you must consider buying it."

Tempi made a triumphant gesture. "Yes! You can do many things when meeting tinker. But there is only one right thing." He calmed himself a little. *Caution.* "But only doing is not the Lethani. First knowing, then doing. That is the Lethani."

I thought on this for a moment. "So being polite is the Lethani?"

"Not polite. Not kind. Not good. Not duty. The Lethani is none of these. Each moment. Each choice. All different." He gave me a penetrating look. "Do you understand?"

"No."

Happiness. Approval. Tempi got to his feet, nodding. "It is good you know you do not. Good that you say. That is also of the Lethani."

CHAPTER EIGHTY-EIGHT

Listening

T EMPI AND I RETURNED to find the camp surprisingly cheerful. Dedan and Hespe were smiling at each other and Marten had managed to shoot a wild turkey for dinner.

So we ate and joked. And after the washing up was done, Hespe told her story about the boy who loved the moon, starting again at the beginning. Dedan kept his mouth miraculously shut, and I dared to hope our little group was finally, finally starting to become a team.

Jax had no trouble following the moon because in those days the moon was always full. She hung in the sky, round as a cup, bright as a candle, all unchanging.

Jax walked for days and days until his feet grew sore. He walked for months and months and his back grew tired beneath his packs. He walked for years and years and grew up tall and lean and hard and hungry.

When he needed food, he traded out of the tinker's packs. When his shoes wore thin he did the same. Jax made his own way, and he grew up clever and sly.

Through it all, Jax thought about the moon. When he began to think he couldn't go another step, he'd put on his spectacles and look up at her, round-bellied in the sky. And when he saw her he would feel a slow stirring in his chest. And in time he came to think he was in love.

Eventually the road Jax followed passed through Tinuë, as all roads do. Still he walked, following the great stone road east toward the mountains.

The road climbed and climbed. He ate the last of his bread and the last of his cheese. He drank the last of his water and the last of his wine. He walked for days without either, the moon growing larger in the night sky above him.

Just as his strength was failing, Jax climbed over a rise and found an old man sitting in the mouth of a cave. He had a long grey beard and a long grey robe. He had no hair on the top of his head, or shoes on the bottom of his feet. His eyes were open and his mouth was closed.

His face lit up when he saw Jax. He came to his feet and smiled. "Hello, hello," he said, his voice bright and rich. "You're a long way from anywhere. How is the road to Tinuë?"

"It's long," Jax said. "And hard and weary."

The old man invited Jax to sit. He brought him water and goat's milk and fruit to eat. Jax ate hungrily, then offered the man a pair of shoes from his pack in trade.

"No need, no need," the old man said happily, wiggling his toes. "But thanks for offering all the same."

Jax shrugged. "As you will. But what are you doing here, so far from everything?"

"I found this cave when I was out chasing the wind," the old man said. "I decided to stay because this place is perfect for what I do."

"And what is that?" Jax asked.

"I am a listener," the old man said. "I listen to things to see what they have to say."

"Ah," Jax said carefully. "And this is a good place for that?"

"Quite good. Quite excellent good," the old man said. "You need to get a long ways away from people before you can learn to listen properly." He smiled. "What brings you out to my little corner of the sky?"

"I am trying to find the moon."

"That's easy enough," the old man said, gesturing to the sky. "We see her most every night, weather permitting."

"No. I'm trying to catch her. If I could be with her, I think I could be happy."

The old man looked at him seriously. "You want to catch her, do you? How long have you been chasing?"

"More years and miles than I can count."

The old man closed his eyes for a moment, then nodded to himself. "I can hear it in your voice. This is no passing fancy." He leaned close and pressed his ear to Jax's chest. He closed his eyes for another long moment and was very still. "Oh," he said softly. "How sad. Your heart is broken and you've never even had a chance to use it."

Jax moved around, a little uncomfortable. "If you don't mind my asking," Jax said, "What's your name?"

"I don't mind you asking," the old man said. "So long as you don't mind me not telling. If you had my name, I'd be under your power, wouldn't I?"

"Would you?" Jax asked.

"Of course." The old man frowned. "That is the way of things. Though you don't seem to be much for listening, it's best to be careful. If you managed to catch hold of even just a piece of my name, you'd have all manner of power over me."

Jax wondered if this man might be able to help him. While he didn't seem to be terribly ordinary, Jax knew he was on no ordinary errand. If he'd been trying to catch a cow, he would ask a farmer's help. But to catch the moon, perhaps he needed the help of an odd old man. "You said you used to chase the wind," Jax said. "Did you ever catch it?"

"In some ways yes," the old man said. "And in other ways, no. There are many ways of looking at that question, you see."

"Could you help me catch the moon?"

"I might be able to give you some advice," the old man said reluctantly. "But first you should think this over, boy. When you love something, you have to make sure it loves you back, or you'll bring about no end of trouble chasing it."

Hespe didn't look at Dedan as she said this. She looked everywhere in the world but at him. Because of this, she didn't see the stricken, helpless look on his face.

"How can I find out if she loves me?" Jax asked.

"You could try listening," the old man said, almost shyly. "It works wonders, you know. I could teach you how."

"How long would that take?"

"A couple years," the old man said. "Give or take. It depends on if you have a knack for it. It's tricky, proper listening. But once you have it, you'll know the moon down to the bottoms of her feet."

Jax shook his head. "Too long. If I can catch her, I can talk with her. I can make—"

"Well that's part of your problem right there," the old man said. "You don't really want to catch her. Not really. Will you trail her through the sky? Of course not. You want to *meet* her. That means you need the moon to come to you."

"How can I do that?" he said.

The old man smiled. "Well that's the question, isn't it? What do you have that the moon might want? What do you have to offer the moon?"

"Only what I have in these packs."

"That's not quite what I meant," the old man muttered. "But we might as well take a look at what you've brought, too."

The old hermit looked through the first pack and found many practical things. The contents of the second pack were more expensive and rare, but no more useful.

Then the old man saw the third pack. "And what do you have in there?"

"I've never been able to get it open," Jax said. "The knot is too much for me."

The hermit closed his eyes for a moment, listening. Then he opened his eyes and frowned at Jax. "The knot says you tore at it. Pricked it with a knife. Bit it with your teeth."

Jax was surprised. "I did," he admitted. "I told you, I tried everything to get it open."

"Hardly everything," the hermit said scornfully. He lifted the pack until the knotted cord was in front of his face. "I'm terribly sorry," he said. "But would you open up?" He paused. "Yes. I apologize. He won't do it again."

The knot unraveled and the hermit opened the pack. Looking inside, his eyes widened and he let out a low whistle.

But when the old man spread the pack open on the ground, Jax's shoulders slumped. He had been hoping for money, or gems, some treasure he could give the moon as a gift. But all the pack held was a bent piece of wood, a stone flute, and a small iron box.

Of these, only the flute caught Jax's attention. It was made of a pale green stone. "I had a flute when I was younger," Jax said. "But it broke and I could never make it right again."

"They're all quite impressive," the hermit said.

"The flute is nice enough," Jax said with a shrug. "But what use is a piece of wood and a box too small for anything practical?"

The hermit shook his head. "Can't you hear them? Most things whisper. These things shout." He pointed at the piece of crooked wood. "That is a folding house unless I miss my guess. Quite a nice one too."

"What's a folding house?"

"You know how you can fold a piece of paper on itself, and each time it gets smaller?" the old man gestured at the piece of crooked wood. "A folding house is like that. Except it's a house, of course."

Jax took hold of the piece of crooked wood and tried to straighten it. Suddenly he was holding two pieces of wood that resembled the beginning of a doorframe.

"Don't unfold it here!" the old man shouted. "I don't want a house outside my cave, blocking my sunlight!"

Jax tried to push the two pieces of wood, back together. "Why can't I fold it back up?"

"Because you don't know how, I expect," the old man said plainly. "I suggest you wait until you know where you want it before you unfold it the rest of the way."

Jax set the wood down carefully, then picked up the flute. "Is this special too?" He put it to his lips and blew a simple trill like a Will's Widow.

Hespe smiled teasingly, lifted a familiar wooden whistle to her lips, and blew: Ta-ta DEE. Ta-ta DEE.

Now everyone knows the Will's Widow is also called a nightjar. So it isn't out when the sun is shining. Despite this, a dozen nightjars flew down and landed all around Jax, looking at him curiously and blinking in the bright sunlight.

"It seems to be more than the usual flute," the old man said.

"And the box?" Jax reached out and picked it up. It was dark, and cold, and small enough that he could close his hand around it.

The old man shivered and looked away from the box. "It's empty."

"How can you tell without seeing inside?"

"By listening," he said. "I'm amazed you can't hear it yourself. It's the emptiest thing I've ever heard. It echoes. It's meant for keeping things inside."

"All boxes are meant for keeping things inside."

"And all flutes are meant to play beguiling music," the old man pointed out. "But this flute is moreso. The same is true with this box."

Jax looked at the box for a moment, then set it down carefully and began to tie up the third pack with the three treasures inside it. "I think I'll be moving on," Jax said.

"Are you sure you won't consider staying for a month or two?" the old man said. "You could learn to listen just a bit more closely. Useful thing, listening."

"You've given me some things to think about," Jax said. "And I think you're right, I shouldn't be chasing the moon. I should make the moon come to me."

"That's not what I actually said," the old man murmured. But he did so in a resigned way. Skilled listener that he was, he knew he wasn't being heard.

Jax set off the next morning, following the moon higher into the mountains. Eventually he found a large, flat piece of ground nestled high among the tallest peaks.

Jax brought out the crooked piece of wood and, piece by piece, began to unfold the house. With the whole night in front of him, he was hoping to have it finished well before the moon began to rise.

But the house was much larger than he had guessed, more a mansion than a simple cottage. What's more, unfolding it was more complicated than he had expected. By the time the moon reached the top of the sky, he was still far from being finished.

Perhaps Jax hurried because of this. Perhaps he was reckless. Or perhaps it was just that Jax was unlucky as ever.

In the end the result was the same: the mansion was magnificent, huge and sprawling. But it didn't fit together properly. There were stairways that led sideways instead of up. Some rooms had too few walls, or too many. Many rooms had no ceiling, and high above they showed a strange sky full of unfamiliar stars.

Everything about the place was slightly skewed. In one room you could look out the window at the springtime flowers, while across the hall the windows were filmed with winter's frost. It could be time for breakfast in the ballroom, while twilight filled a nearby bedroom.

Because nothing in the house was true, none of the doors or windows fit tight. They could be closed, even locked, but never made fast. And as big as it was, the mansion had a great many doors and windows, so there were a great many ways both in and out.

Jax paid no mind to any of this. Instead, he raced to the top of the highest tower and put the flute to his lips.

He poured out a sweet song into the clear night sky. No simple bird trill, this was a song that came from his broken heart. It was strong and sad. It fluttered like a bird with a broken wing.

Hearing it, the moon came down to the tower. Pale and round and beautiful, she stood before Jax in all her glory, and for the first time in his life he felt a single breath of joy.

They spoke then, on the top of the tower. Jax telling her of his life, his wager, and his long, lonely journey. The moon listened, and laughed, and smiled.

But eventually she looked longingly toward the sky.

Jax knew what this foretold. "Stay with me," he pleaded. "I can only be happy if you're mine."

"I must go," she said. "The sky is my home."

"I have made a home for you," Jax said, gesturing to the vast mansion below them. "There is sky enough for you here. An empty sky that is all for you."

"I must go," she said. "I have been away too long."

He raised his hand as if to grab her, then stopped himself. "Time is what we make it here," he said. "Your bedroom can be winter or spring, all according to your desire."

"I must go," she said, looking upward. "But I will return. I am always and unchanging. And if you play your flute for me, I will visit you again."

"I have given you three things," he said. "A song, a home, and my heart. If you must go, will you not give me three things in return?"

She laughed, holding her hands out to her sides. She was naked as the moon. "What do I have that I can leave with you? But if it is mine to give, ask and I will give it."

Jax found his mouth was dry. "First I would ask for a touch of your hand."

"One hand clasps another, and I grant you your request." She reached out to him, her hand smooth and strong. At first it seemed cool, then marvelously warm. Gooseflesh ran all up and down Jax's arms.

"Second, I would beg a kiss," he said.

"One mouth tastes another, and I grant you your request." She leaned in close to him. Her breath was sweet, her lips firm as fruit. The kiss pulled the breath out of Jax, and for the first time in his life, his mouth curved into the beginning of a smile.

"And what is the third thing?" the moon asked. Her eyes were dark and wise, her smile was full and knowing.

"Your name," Jax breathed. "That I might call you by it."

"One body . . ." the moon began, stepping forward eagerly. Then she paused. "Only my name?" she asked, sliding her hand around his waist.

Jax nodded.

She leaned close and spoke warmly against his ear, *"Ludis."*

And Jax brought out the black iron box, closing the lid and catching her name inside.

"Now I have your name," he said firmly. "So I have mastery over you. And I say you must stay with me forever, so I can be happy."

And so it was. The box was no longer cold in his hand. It was warm, and inside he could feel her name, fluttering like a moth against a windowpane.

Perhaps Jax had been too slow in closing the box. Perhaps he fumbled with the clasp. Or perhaps he was simply unlucky in all things. But in the end he only managed to catch a piece of the moon's name, not the thing entire.

So Jax could keep her for a while, but she always slips away from him. Out from his broken mansion, back to our world. But still, he has a piece of her name, and so she always must return.

———————

Hespe looked around at us, smiling. "And that is why the moon is always changing. And that is where Jax keeps her when she is not in our sky. He caught her and he keeps her still. But whether or not he is happy is only for him to know."

There was a long moment of silence.

"That," Dedan said, "is one hell of a story."

Hespe looked down, and though the firelight made it difficult to tell, I would have bet a penny she was blushing. Hard Hespe, who I wouldn't have guessed had a drop of blushing in her. "It took me a long time to remember all of it," she said, "My mother used to tell it to me when I was a little girl. Every night, always the same. Said she learned it from her mother."

"Well you'll need to make sure you tell your daughters, too," Dedan said. "A story like that is too good to let fall by the roadside."

Hespe smiled.

———

Unfortunately, that peaceful evening was like the lull that comes in the center of a storm. The next day Hespe made a comment that sent Dedan off in a huff, and for two hours they could barely look at each other without hissing like angry cats.

Dedan tried to convince everyone we should give up our search and instead sign up as caravan guards, hoping the bandits would attack us. Marten said that made as much sense as trying to find a bear trap by putting your foot in it. Marten was right, but that didn't keep Dedan and the tracker from snapping at each other over the next couple days.

Two days later, Hespe gave a surprisingly girlish shriek of alarm while bathing. We ran to her assistance, expecting bandits, and instead found Tempi naked, knee-deep in the stream. Hespe stood half-dressed and dripping wet on the shore. Marten thought it was hilarious. Hespe did not. And the only thing that kept Dedan from flying into a rage and attacking Tempi was the fact that he couldn't figure out how to attack a naked man without looking in his direction or actually touching him.

The day after that, the weather grew foggy and damp, souring everyone's mood and slowing our search even further.

Then it began to rain.

CHAPTER EIGHTY-NINE

Losing the Light

THE LAST FOUR DAYS had been endlessly overcast and raining. At first the trees had given us some shelter, but we soon discovered that the leaves overhead merely held the rain, and the slightest stir of wind sent down showers of heavy drops that had been gathering for hours. This meant that whether or not it was currently raining, we were constantly dripped upon and damp.

Stories after supper had stopped. Marten caught a cold, and as it worsened he grew sullen and sarcastic. And two days ago the bread had gotten wet. This might sound like a small thing, but if you've ever tried to eat a piece of wet bread after a day of walking in the rain, you know what sort of mood it puts you in.

Dedan had grown truly unmanageable. He balked and complained at the simplest of tasks. The last time he had gone into town for supplies, he had bought a bottle of dreg instead of potatoes, butter, and bowstrings. Hespe left him behind at Crosson and he didn't get back to camp until nearly midnight, stinking drunk and singing loud enough to make the dead cover their ears.

I didn't bother telling him off. Sharp as my trouper's tongue was, he was obviously immune to it. Instead I waited until he passed out, poured the remaining dreg on the fire, and left the bottle sitting in the coals for him to see. After that, he stopped his constant derogatory muttering about me and settled into chilly silence. While the quiet was nice, I knew it was a bad sign.

Given everyone's rising temper, I'd decided each of us would search for trail sign on our own. This was partly because walking in someone's footsteps over wet turf was a sure way to tear up the ground and leave a trail. But the other reason is that I knew if I sent Dedan and Hespe out together, their eventual argument would alert any bandit within ten miles.

I came back to camp dripping wet and miserable. It turns out the boots I'd bought in Severen didn't have a lick of waterproofing, so they drank rainwater like sponges. In the evening I could dry them out using the heat of the fire and a little careful sympathy. But as soon as I took three steps they were soaked through again. So on top of everything my feet had been cold and damp for days.

It was our twenty-ninth day in the Eld, and when I came over the tiny ridge that hid our latest camp, I saw Dedan and Hespe sitting on opposite sides of the fire, ignoring each other. Hespe was oiling her sword. Dedan was idly jabbing the ground in front of him with a pointed stick.

I wasn't in much mood for conversation myself. Hoping the silence held, I went wordlessly to the fire.

Except there was no fire.

"What happened to the fire?" I asked stupidly. What had happened was rather obvious. It had been left to burn down to charred sticks and damp ashes.

"It's not my turn to get wood," Hespe said pointedly.

Dedan poked at the dirt with his stick. I noticed the beginnings of a bruise high on his cheek.

All I wanted in the world was a little something hot to eat and ten minutes with dry feet. It wouldn't make me happy, but it would bring me closer to happy than I'd been all day. "I'm surprised the two of you can piss without help," I spat.

Dedan glared up at me. "Just what do you mean by that?"

"When Alveron asked me to do this job for him, he implied I would have adults helping me, not a handful of schoolchildren."

Dedan's snapped. "You don't know what she—"

I cut him off. "I don't care. I don't care what you're bickering about. I don't care what she threw at you. I care that the fire is out. Tehlu above, a trained dog would be more help!"

Dedan's expression firmed into a familiar belligerence. "Maybe if—"

"Shut up," I said. "I would rather listen to a jackass braying than waste my time with whatever you're saying. When I come back to camp I expect fire and a meal. If this is beyond you, I'll arrange to have some five-year-old come out from Crosson and babysit the both of you."

Dedan stood. The wind gusted in the trees above us, sending down heavy drops to patter on the ground. "You're on your way to a meal you won't be able to stomach, boy."

His hands clenched into fists, and I reached into my pocket to grip the mommet I had made of him two days ago. I felt my stomach clench in fear and fury. "Dedan, if you take a single step toward me, I will lay such pain on you that you will scream for me to kill you." I stared him square in the eye. "Right now I am irritated. Do not even think of making me angry."

He paused, and I could almost hear him thinking of every story he had ever heard about Taborlin the Great. Fire and lightning. There was a moment of long silence as the two of us stared at each other, unblinking.

Luckily, at this point Tempi returned to camp, breaking the tension. Feeling a little foolish, I went to the embers of the fire to see if I could rekindle it. Dedan stomped into the trees, hopefully in search of wood. At this point I didn't care if it was rennel or not.

Tempi sat by the side of the dead fire. Perhaps if I hadn't been busy I might have noticed something odd in his movement. Then again, perhaps not. Even for a semieducated barbarian such as myself, the moods of the Adem are difficult to read.

As I coaxed the fire slowly back to life, I began to regret how I had handled things. That thought alone kept me from lashing out at Dedan when he returned with an armload of wet wood and dropped it at the edge of my newly rebuilt fire, scattering it.

Marten came back shortly after I had rebuilt the fire a second time. He settled at the edge of it and spread his hands. His eyes were sunken and dark.

"Feeling any better?" I asked him.

"Loads." His voice rasped wetly in his chest, sounding worse than it had this morning. I worried about the sound of his breathing, about pneumonia, about fever.

"I can mix you a tea that will make your throat a little easier," I suggested without much hope. He'd rejected all my offers of help over the last several days.

He hesitated, then nodded. As I was heating the water he had a fit of violent coughing that lasted nearly a minute. If the rain didn't stop tonight we would have to head into town and wait for him to recover. I couldn't risk him catching pneumonia or giving away our position to bandit sentries with a coughing fit.

I handed him his tea, and Tempi stirred in his seat by the edge of the fire. "I killed two men today," he said.

There was a long moment of stunned silence. Rain pattered on the ground around us. The fire hissed and spat.

"What?" I asked incredulously.

"I was attack by two men behind trees," Tempi said calmly.

I rubbed the back of my neck. "Dammit Tempi, why didn't you say something before?"

He gave me a level look and his fingers made an unfamiliar circle. "It is not easy to kill two men," he said.

"Are you hurt?" Hespe asked.

Tempi turned his cool look on her next. *Offended.* I'd misunderstood his previous comment. It wasn't the fight itself he had found difficult. It was the fact that he had killed two men. "I have needed this time to settle my thought. Also, I wait to when all are here."

I tried to remember the gesture for *apology*, but had to settle for *sorrow* instead. "What happened?" I asked calmly as I fingered the frayed ends of my patience.

Tempi paused to choose his words. "I was trying to find trail when two men jump out from trees."

"What did they look like?" Dedan asked, beating me to the question.

Another pause. "One your size, his arms longer than mine, stronger than me but slow. Slower than you." Dedan's expression darkened, as if he couldn't decide if he had been insulted. "The other was smaller and quicker. Both their swords were broad and thick. Edged on both sides. This long." He held his hands perhaps three feet apart.

I thought the description revealed more about Tempi than the men he fought. "Where did it happen? How long ago?"

He pointed in the direction we had been searching. "Less than one mile. Less than one hour."

"Do you think they were waiting for you?"

"They weren't there when I came through," Marten said defensively. He gave a wet, tearing cough deep in his chest and spat something thick onto the ground. "If they were waiting, they couldn't have been waiting long."

Tempi gave an eloquent shrug.

"What sort of armor did they have?" Dedan asked.

Tempi was quiet for a moment, then reached out to tap my boot. "This?"

"Leather?" I suggested.

He nodded. "Leather. Hard, and with some metal."

Dedan relaxed a bit. "That's something at least." He mused, then looked up sharply at Hespe, "What? What was that look you just gave me?"

"I wasn't looking at you," Hespe said frostily.

"You were so. You rolled your eyes." He looked at Marten. "You saw her roll her eyes, didn't you?"

"Shut. Up." I snarled at the two of them. Surprisingly, things grew quiet. I pressed the heels of my hands to my eyes and gave our situation a moment of uninterrupted thought. "Marten, how much light do we have left?"

He looked up at the slate-colored sky. "About another hour and a half like this," he rasped. "Enough to track in. Then maybe a quarter hour of bad light after that. The sun will go down quick behind these clouds."

"Do you feel up to a little more running around today?" I asked.

His grin surprised me. "If we can find these bastards tonight, let's do it. They've kept me tramping around this God-forsaken place long enough."

I nodded, reached out, and took a pinch of damp ash from the pitifully small fire. I rubbed it between my fingers thoughtfully, then wiped it onto a small rag and tucked it into my cloak. It wouldn't be a good source of heat, but anything was better than nothing.

"Alright," I said. "Tempi will lead us to the bodies, then we'll see if we can trail them back to their camp." I stood up.

"Whoa!" Dedan said, holding out his hands. "What about us?"

"You and Hespe stay here and guard the camp." I bit my tongue to keep from adding, *and try to keep the fire from going out.*

"Why? Let's all go. We can take care of them tonight!" He got to his feet.

"And what if there's a dozen of them?" I asked in my best scathing tones.

He paused, but didn't back down. "We'll have the element of surprise."

"We *won't* have the element of surprise if all five of us go tramping around," I said hotly.

"Why are *you* going then?" Dedan demanded. "It could just be Tempi and Marten."

"*I'm* going because *I* need to see what we're up against. *I'm* the one that is going to be making the plan that will get us through this alive."

"Why should greenwood like you be making the plan at all?"

"We're losing the light," Marten interjected wearily.

"Blessed Tehlu, a voice of reason speaks." I looked at Dedan. "We are going. You are staying. That is an order."

"An order?" Dedan echoed with dark incredulity.

We eyed each other dangerously for a moment, then I turned and followed Tempi into the trees. Thunder growled through the sky above us. A wind moved through the trees, clearing away the endless drizzle. In its place a steady rain began to fall.

CHAPTER NINETY

To Sing a Song About

TEMPI LIFTED THE PINE boughs that covered the two men. Laid carefully on their backs, they looked as if they were sleeping. I knelt at the side of the larger one, but before I could get a better look, I felt a hand on my shoulder. Looking back I saw Tempi shaking his head.

"What?" I asked. We had less than an hour of light left. Hunting down the bandits' camp without getting caught was going to be difficult enough. Doing it in a pitch-black storm would be a nightmare.

"You should not," he said. *Firm. Serious.* "Troubling the dead is not of the Lethani."

"I need to know about our enemies. I can learn things from them that will help us."

His mouth almost frowned, *disapproval.* "Magic?"

I shook my head. "Looking only." I pointed to my eyes then tapped my temple. "Thinking."

Tempi nodded. But as I turned back to the bodies, I felt his hand on my shoulder again. "You must ask. They are my dead."

"You already agreed," I pointed out.

"Asking is the right thing," he said.

I took a deep breath. "May I look at your dead, Tempi?"

He nodded once, formally.

I looked over to where Marten was giving his bowstring a careful inspection under a nearby tree. "Do you want to see if you can find their trail?" He nodded and pushed himself away from the tree. "I'd start over there." I pointed to the south between two ridges.

"I know my business," he said as he walked off, shouldering his bow.

Tempi took a couple steps away, and I turned my attention to the bodies.

One was actually quite a bit larger than Dedan, a great bull of a man. They were older than I had expected, and their hands had the calluses that mark long years of working with weapons. These were not disgruntled farm boys. These were veterans.

"I've got their trail," Marten said, startling me. I hadn't heard the sound of him approaching over the low susurrus of the falling rain. "It's clear as day. A drunk priest could follow it." There was a flicker of lightning across the sky and an accompanying grumble of thunder. The rain started to come down harder. I frowned and pulled the tinker's sodden cloak tighter around my shoulders.

Marten tilted his head up and let the rain fall full on his face. "I'm glad this weather is finally doing us some good," he said. "The more it rains the easier it will be for us to sneak in and away from their camp." He wiped his hands on his dripping shirt and shrugged. "Besides, it's not like we can get any wetter than we already are."

"You have a point," I said, standing.

Tempi covered the bodies with the branches, and Marten led us away to the south.

Marten knelt to examine something on the ground, and I took the opportunity to catch up with him.

"We're being followed," I said, not bothering to whisper it. They were at least seventy feet behind us, and the rain was rolling through the trees with a noise like waves against the shore.

He nodded and pretended to point at something on the ground. "I didn't think you'd seen them."

I smiled and stripped water from my face with a wet hand. "You're not the only one here with eyes. How many do you think there are?"

"Two, maybe three."

Tempi drew close to us. "Two," he said with certainty in his voice.

"I only saw one," I admitted. "How close are we to their camp?"

"No guess. Could be over the next hill. Could be miles off. There are still just these two sets of tracks, and I can't smell any fires." He stood up and started to follow the trail again without looking back.

I pushed a low branch aside as Tempi walked past and caught a glimpse of movement behind us that had nothing to do with wind or rain. "Let's go over this next ridge and set a little trap."

"Sounds like the very thing," Marten agreed.

Gesturing for us to wait, Marten crouched low and edged his way up to the top of the small rise. I fought the urge to look behind us while he peered over the lip of the ridge, then scampered over.

There was a bright flash as lightning struck nearby. The thunder was like a fist in my chest. I startled. Tempi stood.

"This is like of home," he said smiling faintly. He made no attempt to keep the water from his face.

Marten waved, and we stalked over the top of the ridge. Once we were out of sight of whoever was following us, I looked around quickly. "Keep following the tracks up to that twisted spruce, then circle back." I gestured. "Tempi hides there. Marten behind that fallen tree. I'll go behind that stone. Marten will make the first move. Use your judgment, but it would probably be best if you waited until they were past that broken stump. Try to leave one of them alive if possible, but we can't have them getting away or making too much noise."

"What will you be doing?" Marten asked as we hurried to lay down a clear set of tracks as far as the twisted spruce tree.

"I'll be staying out of the way. The two of you are better equipped for this sort of thing. But I have a trick or two if it comes to that." We reached the tree. "Ready?"

Marten seemed a little startled by my sudden barrage of orders, but they both nodded and went quickly to their places.

I circled around and settled behind a lumpish upcrop of stone. From my vantage I could see our muddy footprints mingling with the trail we followed. Past that I saw Tempi position himself behind the trunk of a thick burl oak. To his right, Marten nocked an arrow, drew the string back to his shoulder, and waited, motionless as a statue.

I brought out the rag that held the pinch of ash and a slender piece of iron, holding them ready in my hand. My stomach churned as I thought about what we had been sent here to do: hunt and kill men. True, they were outlaws and murderers, but men nonetheless. I deepened my breathing and tried to relax.

The surface of the stone was chill and gritty against my cheek. I strained my ears but couldn't hear anything over the steady drumming of the rain. I fought the urge to lean farther around the edge of the stone and broaden my field of vision. Lightning flashed again, and I was counting the seconds until the thunder when I saw a pair of figures slink into view.

I felt a sullen heat flare up in my chest. "Shoot them, Marten," I said loudly.

Dedan whirled around and was facing me with his sword drawn by the time I stepped from my hiding place. Hespe was a little more restrained and stopped with her sword halfway out of its scabbard.

I put my knife away and walked to within a half-dozen steps of Dedan. The thunder rolled over us as I caught and held his eyes. His expression was defiant, and I did not bother to disguise my anger. After a long minute of silence he looked away, pretending he needed to brush the water from his eyes.

"Put that away." I nodded to his sword. After a second's hesitation he did so. Only then did I slide the thin piece of brittle steel I held back into the lining of my cloak. "If we were bandits you would already be dead." I moved my gaze from Dedan to Hespe and back again. "Go back to camp."

Dedan's expression twisted. "I'm sick of you talking to me like I'm a kid." He jabbed a finger toward me. "I've been in this world a lot longer than you. I'm not stupid."

I bit down several angry responses that couldn't help but make matters worse. "I don't have time to argue with you. We're losing the light, and you're putting us in danger. Go back to camp."

"We should take care of this tonight," he said. "We've already knackered off two of them, there's probably only five or six left. We'll surprise them in the dark, in the middle of the storm. Wham. Bam. We'll be back in Crosson tomorrow for lunch."

"And what if there's a dozen of them? What if there's twenty? What if they're holed up in a farmhouse? What if they find our camp while no one's there? All our supplies, our food, and *my lute* could be gone, and a trap waiting for us when we come back. All because you couldn't sit still for an hour." His face reddened dangerously, and I turned away. "Go back to camp. We'll talk about this tonight."

"No, dammit. I'm coming, and there's not a damn thing you can do to stop me."

I ground my teeth. The worst part was that it was true. I had no way of enforcing my authority. There was nothing I could do short of subduing him with the wax simulacra I'd made. And I knew that to be the worst possible option. Not only would it turn Dedan into an outright enemy, it would undoubtedly turn Hespe and Marten against me too.

I looked to Hespe. "Why are you here?"

She darted a quick look at Dedan. "He was going to go alone. I thought it was better if we stayed together. And we did think it through. Nobody's going to stumble onto the camp. We hid our gear and doused the fire before we left."

I gave a tight sigh and tucked the useless pinch of ash into a pocket of my cloak. Of course they did.

"But I agree," she said. "We should try to finish it tonight."

I looked to Marten.

He gave me an apologetic look. "I'd be lying if I said I didn't want this over," he said, then added quickly, "If we can do it smart." He might have said more, but the words caught in his throat and he began to cough.

I looked at Tempi. Tempi looked back.

The worst thing was, my gut agreed with Dedan. I wanted this done. I wanted a warm bed and a decent meal. I wanted to get Marten somewhere dry. I wanted to go back to Severen where I could bask in Alveron's gratitude. I wanted to find Denna, apologize, and explain why I had left without a word.

Only a fool fights the tide. "Fine." I looked up at Dedan. "If one of your friends dies because of this, it will be your fault." I saw a flicker of uncertainty cross his face, then disappear as he set his jaw. He had said too much for his pride to let him back down.

I leveled a long finger at him. "But from now on each of you must do as I say. I'll listen to your suggestions, but I give the orders." I looked around. Marten and Tempi nodded right away, with Hespe following only a second after. Dedan gave a slow nod.

I looked at him. "Swear it." His eyes narrowed. "If you pull another stunt like this when we're attacking tonight, you could get us killed. I don't trust you. I'd rather leave tonight than go into this with someone I can't trust."

There was another tense moment, but before it stretched too long Marten chimed in, "C'mon Den. The boy's actually got a fair bit on the ball. He set up this little ambush in about four seconds." His tone turned jocular. "Besides, he's not as bad as that bastard Brenwe, and the money for *that* little privy-dance wasn't half as good."

Dedan cracked a smile. "Yeah, I suppose you're right. So long as it's over tonight."

I didn't doubt for a second Dedan would still go his own way if it suited him. "Swear you'll follow my orders."

He shrugged and looked away. "Yeah. I swear."

Not enough. "Swear it on your name."

He wiped the rain from his face and looked back at me, confused. "What?"

I faced him and spoke formally. "Dedan. Will you do as I say tonight, without questioning or hesitation? Dedan. Do you swear it on your name?"

He shifted from foot to foot for a moment, then straightened a little. "I swear it on my name."

I stepped closer to him and said "Dedan" very softly. At the same time I fed a small, tiny burst of heat through the wax simulacra in my pocket. Not enough to do anything, but enough that he could feel it, just for a moment.

I saw his eyes widen, and I gave him my best Taborlin the Great smile. The smile was full of secrets, wide and confident, and more than slightly smug. It was a smile that told an entire story all by itself.

"*I have your name now*," I said softly. "*I have mastery over you.*"

The look on his face was almost worth a month of his grumbling. I stepped back and let the smile disappear, quick as a flicker of lightning. Easy as taking off a mask. Which, of course, would leave him wondering which expression was the real one, the young boy or the half-glimpsed Taborlin?

I turned away before I lost the moment. "Marten will scout ahead. Tempi and I will follow five minutes behind. That will give him time to spot their lookouts and come back to warn us. You two follow ten minutes behind us."

I gave Dedan a pointed look and held up both hands with my fingers splayed. "Ten full minutes. It'll be slower this way. But it's safest. Any suggestions?" Nobody said anything. "All right. Marten, it's your show. Come back if you run into trouble."

"Count on it," he said, and soon passed from our sight, lost in the blurry green and brown of leaf and bark and rock and rain.

The rain continued to pelt down, and the light was beginning to fail as Tempi and I followed the trail, slinking from one hiding place to another. Noise, at least, was not a concern as the thunder made a near constant grumbling overhead.

Marten appeared with no warning from the underbrush and motioned us to the marginal shelter of a leaning maple. "Their camp is right up ahead," he said. "There's tracks all over the place, and I saw light from their fire."

"How many of them?"

Marten shook his head. "I didn't get that close. As soon as I saw different sets of footprints I came back. I didn't want you following the wrong tracks and getting lost."

"How far?"

"About a minute's creep. You could see their fire from here, but their camp's on the other side of a rise."

I looked at the faces of my two companions in the dimming light. Neither of them seemed nervous. They were suited for this sort of work, trained for it. Marten had his abilities as a tracker and a bowman. Tempi had the legendary skill of the Adem.

I might have felt calm too, if I had had the opportunity to prepare some plan, some trick of sympathy that could tip things in our favor. But Dedan had ruined all hopes of that by insisting we attack tonight. I had nothing, not even a bad link to a distant fire.

I stopped that line of thinking before it could turn from anxiety to panic. "Let's go then," I said, pleased at the calm timbre of my voice.

The three of us crept forward as the last of the light slowly bled from the sky. In the grey, Marten and Tempi were difficult to see, which reassured me. If it was hard for me, it would be near impossible for sentries to spot us from a distance.

Soon I spied firelight reflecting off the undersides of high branches ahead. Crouching, I followed Marten and Tempi up the side of a steep bank, made slippery by the rain. I thought I saw a stir of movement ahead of us.

Then lightning struck. In the near dark it was enough to blind me, but not before the muddy bank was highlighted in dazzling white.

A tall man stood on the ridge with a drawn bow. Tempi crouched a few feet up the bank, frozen in the act of carefully placing his feet. Above him was Marten. The old tracker had gone to one knee and drawn his bow as well. The lightning showed me all of this in a great flash, then left me blind. The thunder came an instant after, deafening me as well. I dropped to the ground and rolled, wet leaves and dirt clinging to my face.

When I opened my eyes all I could see were the blue ghosts the lightning had left dancing in front of my eyes. There was no outcry. If the sentry had made one it had been covered by the thunder. I lay very still until my eyes adjusted. It took me a long, breathless second to find Tempi. He was up the bank some fifteen feet, kneeling over a dark shape. The sentry.

I approached him, scrabbling through the wet fern and muddy leaves. Lightning flickered again above us, more gently this time, and I saw the shaft of one of Marten's arrows protruding at an angle from the sentry's chest. The fletching had come loose and it fluttered in the wind like a tiny, sodden flag.

"Dead," Tempi said when Marten and I were close enough to hear.

I doubted it. Even a deep chest wound won't kill a man as quickly as that. But as I moved closer I saw the angle of the arrow. It was a heart shot. I looked at Marten with amazement. "That's a shot to sing a song about," I said quietly.

"Luck." He dismissed it and turned his attention to the top of the ridge a few feet above us. "Let's hope I have some left," he said as he began to crawl.

As I crawled after him I caught a glimpse of Tempi still kneeling over the fallen man. He leaned close, as if whispering to the body.

Then I saw the camp, and all vague curiosity about the Adem's peculiarity was pushed from my mind.

CHAPTER NINETY-ONE

Flame, Thunder, Broken Tree

THE RIDGE WE CROUCHED on made a wide half-circle, holding the bandits' camp in the center of a protective crescent. The result was that the camp sat at the bottom of a large, shallow bowl. From our position I could see the open portion of the bowl was bordered by a stream that curved in and away.

The trunk of a towering oak tree rose like a pillar in the center of the bowl, sheltering the camp with its huge branches. Two fires burned sullenly on either side of the great oak. Both would have been big as bonfires if not for the weather. As it was, they merely shed enough light to reveal the camp.

Camp is a misleading term, "encampment" would be better. There were six field tents, short and sloping, mostly intended for sleeping and storing equipment. The seventh tent was almost a small pavilion, rectangular and large enough for several men to stand upright.

Six men sat huddled close to the fires on makeshift benches. They were bundled up against the rain, all of them with the hard-eyed, long-suffering look of experienced soldiers.

I ducked back below the ridgeline and was surprised to feel no fear at all. I turned to Marten, and saw his eyes were a little wild. "How many do you think there are?" I asked.

His eyes flickered thoughtfully. "At least two to a tent. If their leader keeps to the big tent that makes thirteen, and we've killed three. So ten. Ten at the very least." He licked his lips nervously. "But they could be sleeping as many as four to a tent, and the big tent could sleep five more in addition to the leader. That makes thirty, less three."

"So at best we're outnumbered two to one," I said. "Do you like those odds?"

His eyes moved to the ridgeline, then back to me. "I'd take two to one. We've got surprise, we're right up close." He paused and coughed into his sleeve. He spat. "But there's twenty of them down there. I can feel it in my balls."

"Can you convince Dedan?"

He nodded. "He'll believe me. He's not half the ass he seems most of the time."

"Good." I considered briefly. Things had been happening more quickly than I can tell them aloud. So despite everything that had happened, Dedan and Hespe were still five or six minutes behind us. "Go turn the two of them around," I told Marten. "Then come back for Tempi and me."

He looked uncertain. "You sure you don't want to come now? We don't know when their guard might change."

"I'll have Tempi with me. Besides, it should only take you a couple minutes. I want to see if I can get a better count of how many there are."

Marten hurried off, and Tempi and I edged our way back up to the top of the ridge. After a moment he edged closer until the left side of his body was pressed up against my right.

I noticed something I'd missed earlier. There were wooden poles the size of tall fenceposts scattered throughout the camp.

"Posts?" I asked Tempi, driving my finger into the ground to illustrate what I mean.

He nodded to show he understood, then shrugged.

I guessed they might be tethers for horses, or drying poles for sodden clothes. I pushed it from my mind in favor of more pressing matters. "What do you think we should do?"

Tempi was silent for a long moment. "Kill some. Leave. Wait. Others come. We . . ." He gave the characteristic pause that meant he was lacking the word he wanted to use. "Jump behind trees?"

"Surprise."

He nodded. "We surprise. Wait. Hunt rest. Tell Maer."

I nodded. Not the quick resolution we had hoped for, but the only sane option against this number of men. When Marten came back the three of us would take our first sting at them. I guessed with surprise on our side, Marten could mark as many as three or four with his bow before we were forced to flee. Odds were he wouldn't kill all of them, but any man arrowshot would be less of a threat to us in the days to come. "Any other way?"

A long pause. "No way that is of the Lethani," he said.

Having seen enough, I carefully slid down several feet until I was out of sight. I shivered as the rain continued to pelt down. It felt colder than it had a couple minutes ago, and I began to worry that I'd caught Marten's cold. That was the last thing I needed right now.

I caught sight of Marten approaching and was about to explain our plan when I saw his panicked expression.

"I can't find them!" he hissed frantically. "I trailed back to where they should have been. But they weren't there. So either they already turned back, which they wouldn't do, or they were too close behind us and ended up following the wrong set of tracks in this bad light."

I felt a chill that had nothing to do with the constant rain. "Can't you track them down?"

"If I could, I would have. But all the prints look the same in the dark. What are we going to do?" He clutched at my arm, I could tell by his eyes that he was on the verge of panic. "They won't be careful. They'll think we've scouted everything ahead of them. What should we do?"

I reached into the pocket that held Dedan's simulacra. "I can find them."

But before I could do anything, there was an outcry from the eastern edge of the camp. It was followed a second later by a furious shout and a string of cursing.

"Is that Dedan?" I asked.

Marten nodded. From over the ridge came the sound of frantic movement. The three of us moved as quickly as we dared, peering over the top.

Men were swarming from the low tents like hornets from a nest. There were at least a dozen of them now, and I saw four with strung bows. Long sections of planking appeared from nowhere and were leaned against the posts, making crude walls about four feet high. Within seconds the vulnerable, wide-open camp became a veritable fortress. I counted at least sixteen men, but now whole sections of the camp were cut off from view. The light was worse as well, as the makeshift walls blocked the fires and cast deep shadows against the night.

Marten was swearing a steady stream, understandably, as his bow wasn't nearly as useful now. He nocked an arrow quick as winking and might have fired it just as fast if I hadn't laid a hand on his arm. "Wait."

He frowned, then nodded, knowing they would have half a dozen arrows for every one of his. Tempi was suddenly useless as well. He would be riddled with arrows long before he came close to the camp.

The only bright facet was that their attention wasn't directed toward us. They were focused off to the east where we had heard the sentry's cry and Dedan's cursing. The three of us might escape before we were discovered, but that would mean leaving Dedan and Hespe behind.

This was the time when a skilled arcanist should be able to tip the scales, if not to give us an advantage, then at least to make escape possible. But I had no fire, no link. I was clever enough to make do without one of those, but without both I was nearly helpless.

Rain began to pour down more heavily. Thunder grumbled. It was only a matter of time before the bandits figured out there were only two of them and rushed over the ridge to make short work of our companions. If the three of us drew their attention we would be overrun just as quickly.

There was a concert of gentle hums, and a flight of arrows leapt over the eastern ridge. Marten stopped swearing and held his breath. He looked at me. "What are we going to do?" he said urgently. There was a questioning shout from the camp, and when no answer was forthcoming another flight of arrows hummed over the eastern ridge, finding the range of their target.

"What are we going to do?" Marten repeated. "What if they're hurt?"

What if they're dead? I closed my eyes and slid down below the ridgeline, trying to gain a moment of clear thought. My foot bumped something soft and solid. The dead sentry. A dark thought occurred. I drew a deep breath and threw myself into the Heart of Stone. Deep. Deeper than I had ever been before. All fear left me, all hesitation.

I took hold of the body by its wrist and began to drag it up toward the lip of the ridge. He was a heavy man, but I hardly noticed. "Marten, may I use your dead?" I asked absently. The words were in a pleasant baritone, the calmest voice I had ever heard.

Without waiting for an answer, I looked over the ridgeline toward the camp. I saw one of the men behind the wall bending his bow for another shot. I drew my long, slender knife of good Ramston steel and fixed the image of the bowman in my mind. I set my teeth and stabbed the dead sentry in the kidney. The knife went in slowly, as if I were stabbing heavy clay instead of flesh.

A scream rose above the sound of the thunder. The man fell, his bow flying wildly out of his hands. Another mercenary stooped to look at his companion. I refocused and stabbed the sentry in his other kidney, using both hands this time. There was a second scream, shriller than the first. *More a keen than a scream*, I thought in an odd separate corner of my mind.

"Don't shoot yet," I cautioned Marten calmly, not looking away from the camp. "They still don't know where we are." I drew the knife out, refocused, and drove it coolly into the sentry's eye. A man stood upright behind the wooden wall, blood pouring down his face from underneath his clutching hands. Two of his comrades rose, trying to get him back below the wooden parapet. My knife rose and fell and one of them toppled to the ground even as his hands rose to his own bleeding face.

"Holy God," Marten choked. "Dear holy God."

I set the knife against the sentry's throat and surveyed the camp. Their military efficiency was falling apart as they began to panic. One of the wounded men continued to scream, high and piercing over the grumbling thunder.

I saw one of the bowmen searching the ridgeline with hard eyes. I drew the knife across the sentry's throat, but nothing seemed to happen. Then the bowman looked puzzled and raised his hand to touch his own throat. It came away lightly smeared with blood. His eyes grew wide and he began to shout. Dropping his bow he ran to the other side of the low wall, then back, trying to escape but not knowing where to run.

Then he regained his composure and began desperately searching the ridgeline all around the camp. He showed no signs of falling. I frowned, set the knife against the dead sentry's neck again and leaned against it hard. My arms trembled, but the knife began to move again, slowly, as if I were trying to cut a block of ice. The bowman's hands flew to his neck and blood poured over them. He staggered, stumbled, and fell into one of the fires. He thrashed wildly, scattering burning coals everywhere, adding to the confusion.

I was deciding where to strike next when lightning lit the sky, showing me a clear, stark picture of the body. The rain had mingled with the blood, and it was everywhere. My hands were dark with it.

Unwilling to maim his hands, I rolled him over onto his stomach and struggled to remove his boots. Then I refocused myself and sawed through the thick tendons above the ankles and behind the knees. It crippled two more men. But the knife was moving more and more slowly, and my arms ached with the strain of it. The corpse was an excellent link, but the only energy I had was the strength of my body. Under these conditions, it felt more like I was cutting wood than flesh.

It had been scarcely more than a minute or two since the camp had been alerted. I spat water and took a moment's rest for my trembling arms and exhausted mind. I eyed the camp below, watching the confusion and panic build.

A man emerged from the large tent at the base of the tree. He was dressed differently than the others, wearing a hauberk of bright chainmail that came nearly to his knees with a coif covering his head. He stepped into the chaos with a fearless grace, taking everything in at a glance. He snapped orders I couldn't hear over the sound of rain and thunder. His men calmed, settled back into their positions, and took up their bows and swords.

As I watched him stride across the encampment I was reminded of . . . something. He stood in plain view, not bothering to crouch behind one of the protective walls. He gestured to his men, and something in that motion was terribly familiar. . . .

"Kvothe," Marten hissed. I looked up to see the tracker with his bow drawn tight to his ear. "I've got the shot on their boss."

"Take it."

His bow hummed and the man sprouted an arrow from his upper thigh, piercing the chain mail, the leg itself, and the armor behind it. From the corner of my eye I saw Marten draw another arrow and put it to the string in a fluid motion, but before he could shoot it, I saw their leader bend. Not a deep bending at the waist as if he were doubling over in pain. He bent at the neck to look down at the arrow that had pierced his leg.

After a second's scrutiny he grasped the arrow in a fist and snapped off the fletching. Then he reached behind himself and pulled the arrow from his leg. I froze as he looked straight toward us and pointed to our position with the hand that held the broken arrow. He spoke a brief word of command to his men, tossed the arrow into the fire, and stalked gracefully to the other side of the camp.

"Great Tehlu overroll me with your wings," Marten said, his hand falling away from his bowstring. "Protect me from demons and creatures that walk in the night."

Only the fact that I was deep in the Heart of Stone kept me from a similar reaction. I turned back to the camp in time to see a small forest of bows being bent in our direction. I ducked my head and aimed a kick at the stupefied tracker, knocking him over as the arrows hummed past. He tumbled over, his quiver of arrows scattering down the muddy bank.

"Tempi?" I called.

"Here," he replied from off to my left. "*Aesh*. No arrow."

More arrows sang overhead, a few of them sticking into trees. Soon they would get the range and start arcing the arrows overhead so they fell on us from above. A thought came to me as calmly as a bubble rising to the surface of a pond. "Tempi, bring me this man's bow."

"*Ia.*"

I heard Marten muttering something, his voice low, urgent, and indistinct. At first I thought he'd been shot, then I realized he was praying. "Tehlu shelter me from iron and anger," he murmured softly. "Tehlu keep me safe from demons in the night."

Tempi pushed the bow into my hand. I took a deep breath and broke my mind into two pieces, then three, then four. In each piece of my mind I held the bowstring. I forced myself to relax and broke my mind again, five. I tried again and failed. Tired, wet and cold, I had reached my limit. I heard bowstrings thrum again and arrows hit the ground around us like a heavy rain. I felt a tug on the outside of my arm near my shoulder as one of the arrows grazed me before burying itself in the dirt. There was a stinging, then a burning pain.

I pushed the pain away and set my teeth. Five would have to be enough. I drew my knife lightly across the back of my own arm, just enough to draw a little blood, then mouthed the proper bindings and drew the blade across the bowstring, hard.

The string held for a terrifying moment, then parted. The bow jerked in my hand, jolting my wounded arm before it flew out of my grasp. Cries of pain and dismay came over the ridge, letting me know I'd been at least partly successful. Hopefully all five strings had been severed, leaving us with only one or two bowmen to deal with.

But as soon as the bow flung itself out of my grasp, I felt the cold leech into me. Not just my arms, but all the way through me: stomach, chest, and throat. I had known I couldn't trust the strength of my arm alone to make it through five bowstrings at once. So I had used the only fire that is always with an arcanist, the heat of my blood. Binder's chills would have me soon. If I didn't find a way to get warm, I would lapse into shock, then hypothermia, then death.

I fell out of the Heart of Stone and let the pieces of my mind slide back together, reeling a bit in confusion. Chill, wet, and dizzy, I clawed my way back to the top of the ridgeline. The rain felt cold as sleet on my skin.

I saw only one bowman. Unfortunately, he had kept his wits about him, and as soon as my face appeared over the top of the ridge, he drew and let fly in a smooth motion.

A gust of wind saved me. His arrow struck harsh yellow sparks from a stone outcrop not two feet from my head. Rain pelted my face and lightning spidered across the sky. I pushed myself back down out of sight and stabbed the sentry's body over and over in a delirious rage.

Finally, I struck a buckle and the blade snapped. Panting, I dropped the broken knife. I came back to my senses with the sound of Marten's forlorn praying in my ears. My limbs felt cold as lead, heavy and awkward.

Worse than that, I could feel the numb sluggishness of hypothermia creeping through me. I realized I wasn't shivering, and knew it was a bad sign. I was soaking wet with no fire nearby to call my own.

Lightning etched the sky again. I had an idea. I laughed a terrible laugh.

I looked over the top of the ridge and was pleased to see no bowmen. But the leader was barking new orders and I didn't doubt new bows would be found or strings replaced. Worse, they might simply abandon their shelter and overrun us with sheer numbers. There were easily a dozen men still standing.

Marten still lay praying on the bank. "Tehlu who the fire could not kill, watch over me in fire."

I kicked at him. "Get up here damn you, or we're all dead." He paused in his praying and looked up. I shouted something incomprehensible and leaned over to drag him upward by the scruff of his shirt. I shook him hard and thrust his bow at him with my other hand, not knowing how it had come to be there.

Lightning flashed again and showed me what he saw. My hands and arms were covered with the sentry's blood. The pelting rain made it streak and run, but hadn't washed it away. It looked black in the brief, glaring light.

Marten took his bow numbly. "Shoot the tree," I shouted over the thunder. He looked at me as if I had gone mad. "Shoot it!"

Something in my expression must have convinced him, but his arrows were scattered, and he took up his litany again as he searched the muddy bank for one. "Tehlu who held Encanis to the wheel, watch over me in darkness."

After a long moment of searching he found an arrow and fumbled to fit it to his string with trembling hands, praying all the while. I turned my attention back to the camp. Their leader had brought them back under control. I could see his mouth shouting orders, but all I could hear was the sound of Marten's trembling voice:

Tehlu, whose eyes are true,
Watch over me.

Suddenly the leader paused and cocked his head. He held himself perfectly still as if listening to something. Marten continued praying:

Tehlu, son of yourself,
Watch over me.

Their leader looked quickly to the left and right, as if he had heard something that disturbed him. He cocked his head again. "He can hear you!" I shouted madly at Marten. "Shoot! He's getting them ready to do something!"

Marten took aim at the tree in the center of the camp. Wind buffeted him as he continued to pray.

Tehlu who was Menda who you were.
Watch over me in Menda's name,
In Perial's name

In Ordal's name
In Andan's name
Watch over me.

Their leader turned his head as if to search the sky for something. Something about the motion seemed terribly familiar, but my thoughts were growing muddy as binder's chills tightened their grip. The bandit leader turned and bounded for the tent, disappearing inside. "Shoot the tree!" I screamed.

He let the arrow fly, and I saw it wedge firmly into the trunk of the massive oak that loomed in the center of the bandit's camp. I scrabbled in the mud for one of Marten's scattered arrows and began to laugh at what I was going to attempt. It might do nothing. It might kill me. The slippage alone . . . But it didn't matter. I was dead already unless I found a way to get warm and dry. I would go into shock soon. Perhaps I was already there.

My hand closed on an arrow. I broke my mind six ways and shouted my bindings as I drove it deep into the sodden ground. "As above, so below!" I shouted, making a joke only someone from the University could hope to understand.

A second passed. The wind faded.

There was a whiteness. A brightness. A noise. I was falling.

Then nothing.

CHAPTER NINETY-TWO

Taborlin the Great

I WOKE. I WAS WARM and dry. It was dark.

I heard a familiar voice questioning.

Marten's voice, "It was all him. He did it."

Questioning.

"I won't never say, Den. I swear to God I won't. I don't want to think of it. Get him to tell you if you want."

Questioning.

"You'd know if you'd seen. Then you wouldn't want to know no more. Don't cross him. I've seen him angry. That's all I'll say. Don't cross him."

Questioning.

"Leave off, Den. He was killing them one by one. Then he went a little crazy. He . . . No. All I'll say is this. I think he called the lighting down. Like God himself."

Like Taborlin the Great, I thought. And smiled. And slept.

CHAPTER NINETY-THREE

Mercenaries All

AFTER FOURTEEN HOURS OF sleep I was fit as a fiddle. My compan-ions seemed surprised by this, as they'd found me unconscious, cold to the touch, and covered in blood. They had stripped me, rubbed my limbs a bit, then rolled me in blankets and put me inside the bandits' single surviv-ing tent. The other five had been either burned, buried, or lost when a great white pillar of lightning blasted the tall oak that stood at the center of the bandits' camp.

The next day was overcast but blessedly free of rain. First we tended to our hurts. Hespe had taken an arrow in the leg when the sentry had surprised them. Dedan had a deep gash along one of his shoulders, which was fairly lucky, considering he'd rushed the sentry bare-handed. When I asked him about it, he said he simply hadn't had time to draw his sword.

Marten had an angry red lump on his forehead above one eyebrow, either from when I had kicked him over or dragged him around. It was tender to the touch, but he claimed he had gotten worse a dozen times in tavern brawls.

After I recovered from the chills I was fine. I could tell my companions were surprised by my sudden return from the doors of death and decided to leave them to their amazement. A little mystery wouldn't hurt my reputation.

I bandaged the ragged cut where the arrow had grazed my shoulder and tended to a few bruises and scrapes I didn't remember receiving. I also had the long, shallow cut I had made on the top of my arm, but it was barely worth stitches.

Tempi was unhurt, unruffled, unreadable.

Our second order of business was to tend to the dead. While I had been unconscious the rest of the group had pulled most of the burned, lifeless bod-ies to one side of the clearing. They tallied thus:

One sentry, killed by Dedan.

Two who had surprised Tempi in the forest.

Three who had survived the lightning and tried to escape. Marten brought one down, Tempi claimed the other two.

Seventeen burned, broken, or otherwise ravaged by the lightning. Of those, eight had been dead, or wounded unto death, beforehand.

We found tracks of one sentry who had watched the whole incident from the northeast piece of the ridge. His tracks were a day old before we found them, and none of us felt the slightest desire to hunt him down. Dedan pointed out he might be worth more alive if he spread word of this spectacular defeat to others who were thinking of banditry as a way of life. For once we agreed on something.

The leader's body was not among those gathered. The large tent he had ducked into had been crushed beneath large sections of the huge oak's blasted trunk. Having more than enough to occupy us for the time being, we left his remains alone for now.

Rather than try to dig twenty-three graves, or even a mass grave large enough for twenty-three bodies, we built a pyre and kindled it while the surrounding forest was still wet with rain. I used my skills to ensure it burned hot and hard.

But there was one other: the sentry Marten had shot and I had put to use. While my companions were busy collecting wood for the pyre I went over the south side of the ridge and found where Tempi had hidden him away, covered with a fir branch.

I looked at the body for a long time before I carried it away to the south. I found a quiet place under a willow and built a cairn of stones. Then I crept into the underbrush and was quietly, violently sick.

The lightning? Well, the lightning is difficult to explain. A storm overhead. A galvanic binding with two similar arrows. An attempt to ground the tree more strongly than any lightning rod. Honestly, I don't know if I can take credit for the lightning striking when and where it did. But as far as stories go, I called the lightning and it came.

From the stories the others told, when the lightning struck it wasn't a single startling bolt, but several in quick succession. Dedan described it as "a pillar of white fire," and said it shook the ground hard enough to knock him off his feet.

Regardless of why, the towering oak was reduced to a charred stump about the height of a greystone. Huge pieces of it lay scattered about. Smaller trees and shrubs had caught fire and been doused by the rain. Most of the long planks the bandits had used for their fortifications had exploded into pieces no bigger than the tip of your finger or burned to charcoal. Streaking out from the base of the tree were great tracks of churned-up earth, making the clearing look as if it had been plowed by a madman or raked by the claws of some huge beast.

Despite this, we stayed at the bandit's camp for three days following our victory. The stream provided easy water, and what remained of the bandits' provisions were superior to our own. What's more, after we salvaged some lumber and canvas, each of us had the luxury of a tent or lean-to.

With our job completed, the tensions plaguing our group faded. The rain stopped, and we didn't need to be bashful about our fires anymore, and as a result Marten's cough was improving. Dedan and Hespe were civil to each other, and Dedan stopped about three-quarters of his incessant jackassery toward me.

But despite the relief at our job being done, things weren't entirely comfortable. There were no stories at night, and Marten distanced himself from me whenever he could. I could hardly blame him, considering what he had seen.

With that in mind, I took the first chance I had to privately destroy the wax mommets I had made. I had no use for them now, and I feared what might happen if one of my companions discovered them in my travelsack.

Tempi made no comment on what I'd done with the bandit's body, and from what I could tell, he didn't seem to hold it against me. Looking back, I realize how little I truly understood the Adem. But at the time, all I noticed was that Tempi spent less time helping me practice the Ketan, and more time practicing our language and discussing the ever-confusing concept of the Lethani.

We fetched our equipment from our previous camp on the second day. I was relieved to have my lute back, and doubly glad to find Denna's marvelous case had stayed dry and tight despite the endless rain.

And, since we were no longer slinking about, I played. For a solid day I did little else. It had been nearly a month since I had made any music, and I'd missed it more than you can imagine.

At first I thought Tempi didn't care for my music. Aside from the fact that I'd somehow insulted him by singing early on, he always left camp when I brought out my lute. Then I began to catch glimpses of him watching me, though always from a distance and usually at least partly hidden from sight. Once I knew to look for him, I discovered he was always listening while I played. Wide-eyed as an owl. Motionless as a stone.

On the third day, Hespe decided her leg could stand a little walking. So we had to decide what was going to come with us, and what would get left behind.

It wasn't going to be as difficult as it might have been. Most of the bandits' equipment had been destroyed by the lightning, the falling tree, or exposure to the storm. But there were still valuables to be salvaged from the ruined camp.

We had been prevented from making a good search of the leader's tent, as it had been crushed beneath one of the huge branches of the fallen oak. Over two feet thick, the fallen limb was larger than most trees in its own right. However, on the third day we finally managed to hatchet enough of it away so we could roll it off the wreckage of the tent.

I was anxious to get a closer look at the leader's body, as something about him had been nagging my memory ever since I saw him step from the tent. And, in a more worldly vein, I knew his chain mail was worth at least a dozen talents.

But we didn't find any sign of the leader at all. It gave us a bit of a puzzle. Marten had only found one set of tracks leading away from the camp, those of the escaped sentry. None of us could guess where the leader had gone.

To me it was a puzzle and an annoyance, as I had been wanting to get a clearer look at his face. Dedan and Hespe believed he'd simply escaped in the chaos following the lighting, maybe using the stream to avoid leaving tracks.

Marten, however, grew distinctly uneasy when we didn't find his body. He murmured something about demons and refused to go near the wreckage. I thought he was being a superstitious fool, but I won't deny that I found the missing body more than slightly unnerving as well.

Inside the ruined tent we found a table, a cot, a desk, and a pair of chairs, all shattered and useless. In the ruined desk there were some papers I would have given a good deal to read, but they had spent too long in the wet, and the ink had run. There was also a heavy hardwood box slightly smaller than a loaf of bread. Alveron's family crest was enameled on the cover, and it was locked tight.

Both Hespe and Marten admitted they had a little skill at opening locks, and, since I was curious about what was inside, I let them have a go so long as they didn't damage the lock. Each of them took a long turn at it, but neither met with any success.

After about twenty minutes of careful fiddling, Marten threw up his hands. "I can't find the trick for it," he said as he stretched, pressing his hands against the small of his back.

"I might as well have a try myself," I said. I'd hoped one of them would trick it open. Picking locks is not the sort of skill an arcanist should pride himself on. It didn't fit with the reputation I was hoping to build for myself.

"Will you now?" Hespe said, raising an eyebrow at me. "You really are a young Taborlin."

I thought back to the story Marten had told days before. "Of course," I laughed, then shouted, *"Edro!"* in my best Taborlin the Great voice and struck the top of the box with my hand.

The lid sprung open.

I was surprised as everyone else, but I hid it better. What had obviously happened is that one of them had actually tripped the lock, but the lid had been stuck. Probably the wood had swollen as it lay for days in the damp. When I'd struck it, it had simply come loose.

But they didn't know that. From the looks on their faces you would think I had just transmuted gold in front of them. Even Tempi raised an eyebrow.

"Nice trick, Taborlin," Hespe said, as if she weren't sure if I were playing a joke on them.

I decided to hold my tongue and slid my set of makeshift lockpicks back into the pocket of my cloak. If I was going to be an arcanist, I might as well be a famous arcanist.

Doing my best to radiate an air of solemn power, I lifted the lid and looked inside. The first thing I saw was a thick, folded piece of paper. I pulled it out.

"What's that?" Dedan asked.

I held it for all of them to see. It was a careful map of the surrounding area, featuring not only an accurate depiction of the curving highway, but the locations of nearby farms and streams. Crosson, Fenhill, and the Pennysworth Inn were marked and labeled on the western road.

"What's that?" Dedan asked, gesturing with a thick finger to an unlabeled X deep in the forest on the south side of the road.

"I think it's this camp," Marten said, pointing. "Right next to that stream."

I nodded. "If this is right, we're closer to Crosson than I thought. We could just head southeast from here, and save ourselves more than a day's walking." I looked at Marten. "Does that seem right to you?"

"Here. Let me see." I handed him the map and he looked it over. "It looks like it," he agreed. "I didn't think we had come that far south. We'd save at least two dozen miles going that way."

"That's no small blessing," Hespe said, rubbing at her bandaged leg. "That is, unless one of you gentlemen would like to carry me."

I turned my attention back to the lockbox. It was full of tightly wrapped cloth packages. Lifting one out, I saw the glint of gold.

There was a murmur from everyone present. I checked the rest of the small, heavy bundles and was greeted with more coins, all gold. At a rough count, there were over two hundred royals. While I'd never actually held one, I knew a single gold royal was worth eighty bits, almost as much as the Maer had given me to finance this entire trip. No wonder the Maer had been eager to stop the waylaying of his tax collectors.

I juggled numbers in my head, converting the contents of the box to a more familiar currency and came up with more than five hundred silver talents. Enough money to buy a good-sized roadside inn, or an entire farmstead with all the livestock and equipage included. With that much money you could buy yourself a minor title, a court appointment, or an officer's position in the military.

I saw everyone else making their own calculations. "How about we share a little bit of that around?" Dedan said without much hope.

I hesitated, then reached into the box. "Does a royal each seem fair to everyone?"

Everyone was silent as I unwrapped one of the bundles. Dedan looked at me incredulously. "Are you serious?"

I handed him a heavy coin. "The way I see it, less scrupulous people might forget to tell Alveron about this. Or they'd never go back to Alveron at all. I think a royal each is a good reward for us being such honest folk." I tossed Marten and Hespe a bright gold coin each.

"Besides," I added, tossing a royal to Tempi. "I was hired to find a group of bandits, not destroy a minor military encampment." I held up my royal. "This is our bonus for services beyond the call of duty." I slid it into my pocket and patted it. "Alveron need never know about it."

Dedan laughed and clapped me on the back. "You're not so much different from the rest of us after all," he said.

I returned his smile and pressed the lid of the box closed, hearing the lock click tightly into place.

I didn't mention the two other reasons for what I did. First, I was effectively buying their loyalty. They couldn't help but realize how easy it would be to simply grab the box and disappear. The thought had crossed my mind, too. Five hundred talents would pay my way through the University for the next ten years with plenty to spare.

Now, however, they were considerably richer, and they got to feel honest about it. A heavy piece of gold would keep their minds off the money I was carrying. Though I still planned on sleeping with the locked box under my pillow at night.

Second, I could use the money. Both the royal I had tucked openly into my pocket, and the other three I'd palmed when handing out coins to the others. As I said, Alveron would never know the difference, and four royals would cover a full term's tuition at the University.

———

After I secured the Maer's lockbox in the bottom of my travelsack, each of us decided what we would scavenge from the bandits' equipment.

The tents we left for the same reason we hadn't brought our own in the first place. They were too bulky to carry. We took as much of their food as we could stow, knowing the more we carried, the less we would have to buy.

I decided to take one of the bandits' swords. I wouldn't have wasted the money to buy one, since I didn't know how to use it, but if they were free for the taking. . . .

As I was looking over the assorted weapons, Tempi came over and gave a few words of advice. After we had narrowed my options to two swords, Tempi finally spoke his mind. "You cannot use a sword." *Questioning. Embarrassment.*

I got the impression that to him, the thought of someone not being able to use a sword was more than slightly shameful. Like not knowing how to eat using a knife and fork. "No," I said slowly. "But I was hoping you could show me."

Tempi stood very still and quiet. I might have taken it for a refusal if I had not come to know him so well. This type of stillness meant he was thinking.

Pauses are a key part of Ademic conversation, so I waited patiently. The two of us stood quietly for a minute, then two. Then five. Then ten. I fought to stay still and quiet. Perhaps this *was* a polite refusal.

I thought myself terribly savvy, you see. I had known Tempi for nearly a month, learned a thousand words and fifty pieces of the Adem hand-speech. I knew the Adem were not bashful about nudity, or touching, and I was beginning to grasp the mystery that was the Lethani.

Oh yes, I thought I was terribly clever. Had I truly known anything about the Adem, I never would have dared to ask Tempi such a question.

"Will you teach me that?" He pointed across the camp to where my lute case lay, leaning against a tree.

I was caught off guard by the question. I had never tried to teach anyone how to play the lute before. Perhaps Tempi knew this and was implying something similar about himself. I knew he was prone to subtly layered speaking.

A fair offer. I nodded. "I will try."

Tempi nodded and pointed to one of the swords we had been considering. "Wear it. But no fighting." With that he turned and left. At the time I took this for his natural brevity.

The scavenging continued throughout the day. Marten took a good number of arrows and all the bowstrings he could find. Then, after checking to see no one wanted any of them, he decided to take the four longbows that had survived the lightning. They made an awkward bundle, but he claimed they'd be worth a heavy penny when he sold them in Crosson.

Dedan grabbed a pair of boots and an armored vest nicer than the one he was wearing. He also laid claim to a deck of cards and a set of ivory dice.

Hespe took a slender set of shepherd's pipes and tucked almost a dozen knives into the bottom of her pack with the hope of selling them later.

Even Tempi found some things he fancied: a whetstone, a brass saltbox, and a pair of linen pants he took down to the stream and dyed a familiar blood-red.

I took less than the rest of them. A small knife to replace the one I'd broken and a small shaving razor with a horn handle. I didn't need to shave that often, but I'd gotten into the habit while in the Maer's court. I might have followed Hespe's example and taken a few knives as well, but my travelsack was already unpleasantly heavy with the weight of the Maer's lockbox.

This may seem a little ghoulish, but it is simply the way of the world. Looters become looted, while time and tide make us mercenaries all.

CHAPTER NINETY-FOUR

Over Rock and Root

WE DECIDED TO TRUST the map we'd found and cut straight west through the forest, heading toward Crosson. Even if we missed the town, we couldn't help but hit the road and save ourselves long miles of walking.

Hespe's wounded leg made the going slow, and we only put six or seven miles behind us that first day. It was during one of our many breaks that Tempi began my true instruction in the Ketan.

Fool that I was, I'd assumed he had already been teaching me. The truth was, he had merely been correcting my more horrifying mistakes because they irritated him. Much the same way I'd be tempted to tune someone's lute if they were playing off-key in the same room.

This instruction was a different thing entirely. We started at the beginning of the Ketan and he corrected my mistakes. All my mistakes. He found eighteen in the first motion alone, and there are more than a hundred motions in the Ketan. I quickly began to have doubts about this apprenticeship.

I also began to teach Tempi the lute. I played notes as we walked, and taught him their names, then showed him some chords. It seemed as good a place as any to begin.

We hoped to make it to Crosson by noon of the next day. But near mid-morning we encountered a stretch of dreary, reeking swamp that hadn't been marked on the map.

Thus began a truly miserable day. We had to test our footing with every step, and our progress slowed to a crawl. At one point Dedan startled and fell, thrashing about and spattering the rest of us with brackish water. He said he'd seen a mosquito bigger than his thumb with a sucker like a woman's hairpin.

I suggested it might have been a sipquick. He suggested several unpleasant, unsanitary things I could do to myself at my earliest convenience.

As the afternoon wore on, we gave up on making it back to the road and focused on more immediate things, such as finding a piece of dry ground where we could sit without sinking. But all we found was more marsh, sink-holes, and clouds of keening mosquitoes and biting flies.

The sun began to set before we finally made our way out of the swamp, and the weather quickly turned from hot and muggy to chill and damp. We trudged until the ground finally began to slope upward. And though we were all weary and wet, we unanimously decided to press on and put a little distance between ourselves and the insects and smell of rotting plants.

The moon was full, giving us more than enough light to pick our way through the trees. Despite the miserable day, our spirits began to rise. Hespe had grown tired enough to lean on Dedan, and as the mud-covered mercenary put an arm around her she told him he hadn't smelled this good in months. He replied that he would have to bow to the judgment of a woman of such obvious grace.

I tensed, waiting for their banter to turn sour and sarcastic. But as I plodded along behind them I noticed how gently he had his arm around her. Hespe leaned on him almost tenderly, hardly favoring her wounded leg at all. I glanced at Marten, and the old tracker smiled, his teeth white in the moonlight.

Before long we found a clear stream and washed the worst of the smell and mud away. We rinsed out our clothes and donned dry ones. I unpacked my tatty, threadbare cloak and fastened it across my chest, vainly hoping it might keep away the evening's chill.

As we were finishing up, we heard the faint sound of singing upstream. Each of us pricked up our ears, but the chattering sound of the stream made it difficult to hear with any clarity.

But singing meant people, and people meant we were almost to Crosson, or perhaps even the Pennysworth if the swamp had turned us too far south. Even a farmhouse would be better than another night in the rough.

So, despite the fact that we were tired and aching, the hope of soft beds, warm meals, and cool drinks gave us energy to gather up our packs and press on.

We followed the stream, Dedan and Hespe still walking as a pair. The sound of singing came and went. The recent rains meant the stream was running high, and the noise of it tumbling over rock and root was sometimes enough to drown out even the sound of our own footsteps.

Eventually the stream grew broad and still as the heavy brush thinned and opened into a wide clearing.

There was no singing any longer. Nor did we see a road, inn, or any flicker of firelight. Just a wide clearing well-lit by moonlight. The stream broadened out, forming a bright pool. And sitting on a smooth rock by the side of the pool. . . .

"Lord Tehlu protect me from the demons of the night," Marten said woodenly. But he sounded more reverent than afraid. And he did not look away.

"That's . . ." Dedan said weakly. "That's . . ."

"I do not believe in faeries," I tried to say, but it came out as barely a whisper. It was Felurian.

CHAPTER NINETY-FIVE

Chased

THE FIVE OF US stood frozen for a moment. The slow rippling of the pool reflected onto the fair form of Felurian. Naked in the moonlight, she sang:

cae-lanion luhial
di mari felanua
kreata tu ciar
tu alaran di.
dirella. amauen.
loesi an delian
tu nia vor ruhlan
Felurian thae.

The sound of her voice was strange. It was soft and gentle, far too quiet for us to hear across the entire length of the clearing. Far too faint for us to hear over the sound of moving water and stirring leaves. Despite this, I *could* hear it. Her words were clear and sweet as the rising and falling notes of a distant flute. It reminded me of something I could not press my finger to.

The tune was the same Dedan had sung in his story. I did not understand a word of it save her name in the final line. Nevertheless I felt the draw of it, inexplicable and insistent. As if an unseen hand had reached into my chest and tried to pull me into the clearing by my heart.

I resisted. I looked away and set one hand against a nearby tree to steady myself.

Behind me I heard Marten murmuring, "No no no," in a low voice as if he were trying to convince himself. "No no no no no. Not for all the money in the world."

I looked over my shoulder. The tracker's eyes were fixed feverishly on the clearing in front of him, but he seemed more afraid than aroused. Tempi stood, surprise plain on his normally impassive face. Dedan stood rigidly to one side, his face drawn while Hespe's eyes darted back and forth between him and the clearing.

Then Felurian began to sing again. It felt like the promise of a warm hearth on a cold night. It was like a young girl's smile. I found myself thinking of Losi at the Pennysworth, her red curls like a tumble of fire. I remembered the swell of her breasts and the way her hand had felt running through my hair.

Felurian sang, and I felt the pull of it. It was strong, but not so strong that I couldn't hold myself back. I looked into the clearing again and saw her, skin silver-white under the evening sky. She bent to dip one hand in the water of the pool, more graceful than a dancer.

A sudden clarity of thought came over me. What was I afraid of? A faerie story? There was magic here, real magic. What's more, it was a magic of singing. If I missed this opportunity I would never forgive myself.

I looked back again at my companions. Marten was shaking visibly. Tempi was backing slowly away. Dedan's hands made fists at his sides. Was I going to be like them, superstitious and afraid? No. Never. I was of the Arcanum. I was a namer. I was one of the Edema Ruh.

I felt wild laughter boil up in me. "I will meet you at the Pennysworth in three days' time," I said, and stepped into the clearing.

I felt Felurian's pull more strongly now. Her skin was bright in the moonlight. Her long hair fell like a shadow all around her.

"Sod this," I heard Dedan say behind me. "If he's going, then I'm g—" There was a short scuffle ending with the sound of something hitting the ground. I glanced behind me and saw him facedown on the low grass. Hespe had her knee on the small of his back and one of his arms pulled up tight behind him. He was struggling weakly and cursing strongly.

Tempi watched them impassively, as if scoring a wrestling bout. Marten was gesturing frantically in my direction. "Kid," he hissed urgently. "Get back here! Kid! Come back!"

I turned back to the stream. Felurian was watching me. Even from a hundred feet away, I could see her eyes, dark and curious. Her mouth spread into a wide, dangerous smile. She laughed a wild laugh. It was bright and delighted. It was no human sound.

Then she darted across the clearing, swift as a sparrow, graceful as a deer. I leapt to the chase, and despite the weight of my travelsack and the sword at my hip, I moved so quickly my cloak flared like a flag behind me. Never have I run like that before, and never since. It was the way a child runs, light and quick, without the least fear of falling.

Felurian ahead of me. Into the scrub. I dimly remember trees, the smell of earth, the grey of moonlit stone. She laughs. She dodges, dances, pulls ahead. She waits till I am almost close enough to touch, then skips away. She shines in the light of the moon. There are clutching branches, a spray of water, a warm wind . . .

And I have hold of her. Her hands are tangled in my hair, pulling me close. Her mouth eager. Her tongue shy and darting. Her breath in my mouth, filling my head. The hot tips of her breasts brush my chest. The smell of her like clover, like musk, like ripe apples fallen to the ground . . .

And there is no hesitation. No doubt. I know exactly what to do. My hands are on the back of her neck. Brushing her face. Tangled in her hair. Sliding along the smooth length of her thigh. Grabbing her hard by the flank. Circling her narrow waist. Lifting her. Laying her down . . .

And she writhes beneath me, lithe and languorous. Slow and sighing. Her legs around me. Her back arches. Her hot hands clutch my shoulders, my arms, pressing the small of my back . . .

And she is astride me. Her movements wild. Her long hair trails across my skin. She tosses her head, trembling and shaking, crying out in a language I do not know. Her sharp nails digging into the flat muscles of my chest . . .

And there is music to it. The wordless cries she makes, rising and falling. Her sigh. My racing heart. Her motion slows. I clutch her hips in frantic counterpoint. Our rhythm is like a silent song. Like sudden thunder. Like the half-heard thrumming of a distant drum . . .

And everything stops. All of me arches. I am taut as a lute string. Trembling. Aching. I am tuned too tight, and I am breaking. . . .

CHAPTER NINETY-SIX

The Fire Itself

I WOKE WITH SOMETHING BRUSHING at the edges of my memory. I opened my eyes and saw trees stretched against a twilight sky. There were silken pillows all around me, while a few feet away Felurian lay, her naked body loosely splayed in sleep.

She looked smooth and perfect as a sculpture. She sighed in her sleep, and I chided myself for the thought. I knew she was nothing like cold stone. She was warm and supple, the smoothest marble grindstone by comparison.

My hand reached out to touch her, but I stopped myself, not wanting to disturb the perfect scene before me. A distant thought began to nag at me, but I brushed it away like an irritating fly.

Felurian's lips parted and sighed, making a sound like a dove. I remembered the touch of those lips. I ached, and forced myself to look away from her soft, flower-petal mouth.

Her closed eyelids were patterned like a butterfly's wings, swept in whorls of deep purple and black with traceries of pale gold that blended to the color of her skin. As her eyes moved gently in sleep, the pattern shifted, as if the butterfly fanned its wings. That sight alone was probably worth the price all men must pay for seeing it.

I ate her with my eyes, knowing all the songs and stories I had heard were nothing. She is what men dream of. All the places I have been, all the women I have seen, I have met her equal only once.

Something in my mind screamed at me, but I was bemused by the motion of her eyes beneath her lids, the shape her mouth made, as if she would kiss me even while she slept. I swatted the thought away again, irritated.

I was going to go mad, or die.

The idea finally fought its way through to my conscious mind, and I felt every hair on my body stand suddenly on end. I had a moment of perfect, clear lucidity that resembled coming up for air and quickly closed my eyes, trying to lower myself into the Heart of Stone.

It didn't come. For the first time in my life, that cool taciturn state escaped me. Behind my eyes, Felurian distracted me. The sweet breath. The soft breast. The urgent half-despairing sighs that slipped through hungry, petal-tender lips. . . .

Stone. I kept my eyes closed and wrapped the calm rationality of Heart of Stone around me like a mantle before I dared even think of her again.

What did I know? I brought to mind a hundred stories of Felurian and plucked out the recurring themes. Felurian was beautiful. She charmed mortal men. They followed her into the Fae and died in her embrace.

How did they die? It was fairly simple to guess: extreme physical stress. Things *had* been rather rigorous, and the sedentary or frail might not have fared so well as I. Now that I stopped to notice, my entire body felt like a well-wrung rag. My shoulders ached, my knees burned, and my neck bore the sweet bruising of love bites from my right ear, down my chest, and. . . .

My body flushed and I struggled deeper into the Heart of Stone until my pulse slowed and I could force the thought of her from the front of my mind.

I could remember four stories where men had come back from the Fae alive, all of them cracked as the potter's cobbles. What manner of madness did they exhibit? Obsessive behavior, accidental death due to separation from reality, and wasting away from extreme melancholy. Three died within a span of days. The fourth story told of the man lasting nearly half a year.

But something didn't make sense. Admittedly, Felurian was lovely. Skilled? Without a doubt. But to the extent that every man died or went insane? No. It simply wasn't likely.

I don't mean to belittle the experience. I don't doubt for a second that it had, quite naturally, deprived men of their faculties in the past. I, however, knew myself to be quite sane.

I briefly entertained the notion that I was insane and didn't know it. Then I considered the possibility that I had always been insane, acknowledged it as more likely than the former, then pushed both thoughts from my mind.

Eyes still closed, I lay there, enjoying a quiet languor of a sort I'd never felt before. I savored the moment, then opened my eyes and prepared to make my escape.

I looked around the pavilion at silken draperies and scattered cushions. These were only ornaments for Felurian. She lay in the middle of it all, all rounded hip and slender leg and lithe muscle shifting underneath her skin.

She was watching me.

If she was beautiful at rest she was doubly so awake. Asleep she was a painting of a fire. Awake she was the fire itself.

It may seem strange to you that at this point I felt fear. It may seem strange that only an arm's length from the most attractive woman in the world, I was suddenly reminded of my own mortality.

She smiled like a knife in velvet and stretched like a cat in the sun.

Her body was built to stretch, the arch of her back, the smooth expanse of her belly going taut. The round fullness of her breasts was lifted by the motion of her arms, and suddenly I felt like a stag in rut. My body reacted to her, and I felt as if someone were hammering at the cool impassivity of Heart of Stone with a hot poker. My control slipped for a moment, and a less disciplined piece of my mind started composing a song to her.

I couldn't spare the attention to rein that piece of myself back in. So I focused on staying safe in the Heart of Stone, ignoring both her body and that nattering part of my mind forming rhyming couplets somewhere in the back of my head.

It wasn't the easiest thing to do. As a matter of fact, it made the ordinary rigors of sympathy seem simple as skipping. If not for the training I'd received at the University, I would have been a broken, pitiful thing, only able to concentrate on my own captivation.

Felurian slowly relaxed out of her stretch and looked at me with ancient eyes. Eyes unlike anything I had ever seen. They were a striking color . . .

The summer dusk was in her eyes

. . . a sort of twilight blue. They were fascinating. In fact . . .

With lids of winged butterflies

. . . there wasn't any white to them at all. . . .

Her lips the shade of sunset skies

I clenched my jaw, split that chattering piece of myself away, and walled it off in a distant corner of my mind, letting it sing to itself.

Felurian tilted her head to one side. Her eyes were as intent and expressionless as a bird's. "why are you so quiet, flame lover? have I quenched you?"

Her voice was odd to my ear. It had no rough edges to it at all. It was all quiet smoothness, like a piece of perfectly polished glass. Despite its odd softness, Felurian's voice ran down my spine, making me feel like a cat that's just been stroked down to the tip of its tail.

I retreated further into the Heart of Stone, felt it cool and reassuring around me. However, while the majority of my attention was focused on self-control, the small, mad, lyric part of my mind leapt to the fore and said: "Never quenched. Though I am doused in you, I burn. The motion of your turning head is like a song. Is like a spark. Is like a breath that billows me and fans to flame a fire that cannot help but spread and roar your name."

Felurian's face lit up. "a poet! I should have known you for a poet by how your body moved."

The gentle hush of her voice caught me unprepared again. It wasn't that her words were breathy, or husky, or sultry. It was nothing so tawdry or affected as that. But when she spoke, I couldn't help but be aware of the fact that her breath was pressed from her breast, past the soft sweetness of her throat, then shaped by the careful play of lips and teeth and tongue.

She came closer, moving on her hands and knees through the pillows. "you looked like a poet, fiery and fair." Her voice was no louder than a breath as she cupped my face with her hands. "poets are gentler. they say nice things."

There was only one person I'd ever heard whose voice was similar to this. Elodin. On rare occasions his voice would fill the air as if the world itself were listening.

Felurian's voice was not resonant. It did not fill the forest glade. Hers was the hush before a sudden summer storm. It was soft as a brushing feather. It made my heart step sideways in my chest.

Speaking thus, when she called me a poet, it did not raise my hackles or make me grit my teeth. From her, it sounded like the sweetest thing a man was ever called. Such was the power of her voice.

Felurian brushed her fingertips across my lips. "poet kisses are best. you kiss me like a candle flame." She brought one of her hands back to touch her mouth, her eyes bright at the memory.

I took her hand and pressed it tenderly. My hands have always seemed graceful, but next to hers, they looked brutish and crude. I breathed against her palm as I spoke. "Your kisses are like sunlight on my lips."

She lowered her eyes, butterfly wings dancing. I felt my mindless need for her slacken and began to understand. This was magic, but nothing like what I knew. Not sympathy or sygaldry. Felurian made men mad with desire the same way I gave off body heat. It was natural for her, but she could control it.

Her gaze wandered over my tangle of clothes and belongings strewn messily at one corner of the glade. They looked oddly out of place amid the silks and soft colors. I saw her eyes settle on my lute case. She froze.

"is my flame a *sweet* poet? does he sing?" Her voice trembled and I could feel a tenseness in her body as she waited for an answer. She looked back at me. I smiled.

Felurian scampered off and brought back my lute case like a child with a new toy. As I took it, I saw her eyes were wide and . . . wet?

I looked into her eyes, and in a flash of understanding I realized what her life must be like. A thousand years old, and lonely from time to time. If she wanted companionship she had to seduce and lure. And for what? An evening of company? An hour? How long could an average man last before his will broke and he became as mindless as a fawning dog? Not long.

And who would she meet in the forest? Farmers and hunters? What entertainment could they provide, slaved to her passions? I felt a moment of pity for her. I know what loneliness is like.

I took the lute from its case and began to tune it. I struck an experimental chord and carefully tuned it again. What to play for the most beautiful woman in the world?

It wasn't hard to decide, actually. My father had taught me to judge an audience. I struck up "Sisters Flin." If you've never heard of it, I'm not surprised. It's a bright and lively song about two sisters gossiping while they argue over the price of butter.

Most people want to hear stories of legendary adventure and romance. But what do you play for someone out of legend? What do you sing for a woman who has been the object of romance for a mortal age? You play her songs of ordinary people. So I hoped.

She clapped delightedly at the end of it. "more! more?" She smiled hopefully, cocking her head to make it a request. Her eyes were wide and eager and adoring.

I played her "Larm and His Alepot." I played her "Blacksmith's Daughters." I played her a ridiculous song about a priest chasing a cow that I'd written when I was ten and never even named.

Felurian laughed and applauded. She covered her mouth in shock and her eyes in embarrassment. The more I played, the more she reminded me of a young country wife attending her first fair, full of pure joy, face shining with innocent delight, eyes wide in amazement at everything she sees.

And lovely, of course. I concentrated on my fingering so as not to think about it.

After each song she rewarded me with a kiss that made it difficult to decide what to play next. Not that I minded horribly. I'd come to realize rather quickly that I preferred kisses to coins.

I played her "Tinker Tanner." Let me tell you, the image of Felurian, her quiet, fluting voice singing the chorus of my favorite drinking song is something that will never, never leave me. Not until I die.

All the while I felt the charm she had on me slacken, bit by bit. It gave me room to breathe. I relaxed and let myself slide a little farther out of the Heart of Stone. Dispassionate calm can be a useful frame of mind, but it does not make for a compelling performance.

I played for hours, and by the end of it I felt like myself again. By which I mean I could look at Felurian with no more reaction than you might normally feel, looking at the most beautiful woman in the world.

I can still remember her, sitting naked among the cushions, twilight-colored butterflies dancing in the air between us. I wouldn't have been alive had I not been aroused. But my mind seemed to be my own again, and I was grateful for that.

She made a disappointed noise of protest as I set the lute back into its case. "are you weary?" she asked with a hint of a smile. "I would not have tired you, sweet poet, had I known."

I gave my best apologetic smile. "I'm sorry, but it seems to be getting late." Actually, the sky still showed the same purple hint of twilight it had since I first woke, but I pushed on. "I'll need to be moving quickly if I'm to meet . . ."

My mind went numb as quickly as if I'd been struck a blow to the back of my head. I felt the passion, fierce and insatiable. I felt the need to have her, to crush her body to mine, to taste the savage sweetness of her mouth.

Only because of my arcane training did I hold onto any concept of my own identity at all. Even so, I only held it with my barest fingertips.

Felurian sat cross-legged on the cushions across from me, her face angry and terrible, her eyes cold and hard as distant stars. With a deliberate calm she brushed a slowly fanning butterfly from her shoulder. There was such a weight of fury in her simple gesture that my stomach clenched and I realized this fact:

No one *ever* left Felurian. Ever. She kept men until their bodies and minds broke beneath the strain of loving her. She kept them until she tired of them, and when she sent them away it was the leaving that drove men mad.

I was powerless. I was a novelty. I was a toy, favorite because it was newest. It might be a long while before she tired of me, but the time would come. And when she finally set me free my mind would tear itself apart with wanting her.

CHAPTER NINETY-SEVEN

Blood and Bitter Rue

As I sat among the silks with my control slipping away, I felt a wave of cold sweat sweep over my body. I clenched my jaw and felt a small anger flare up. Over the course of my life my mind has been the only thing I've always been able to rely on, the only thing that has always been entirely mine.

I could feel my resolve melting as my natural desires were replaced by some animal thing unable to think beyond its own lust.

The part of me that was still Kvothe raged, but I felt my body respond to her presence. With a horrible fascination I felt myself crawl through the cushions toward her. One arm found her slender waist, and I bent to kiss her with a terrible hunger.

I howled inside my own mind. I have been beaten and whipped, starved and stabbed. But my mind is my own, no matter what becomes of this body or the world around. I threw myself against the bars of an intangible cage made of moonlight and desire.

And, somehow, I held myself away from her. My breath tore out of my throat as if racing to escape.

Felurian reclined on the cushions, her head tilted up toward me. Her lips were pale and perfect. Her eyes half-lidded and hungry.

I forced myself to look away from her face, but there was nowhere safe to look. Her throat was smooth and delicate, trembling with her rapid pulse. One breast stood round and full, while the other angled slightly to one side, following the downward slope of her body. They rose and fell with her breath, moving gently, making candle-cast shadows on her skin. I glimpsed the perfect whiteness of her teeth behind the pale pink of her parted lips. . . .

I closed my eyes, but somehow that only made it worse. The heat of her body was like standing near a fire. The skin of her waist was soft beneath my hand. She moved beneath me, and her breast brushed softly against my chest. I felt her breath against my neck. I shivered and began to sweat.

I opened my eyes again and saw her staring at me. Her expression was innocent, almost hurt, as if she couldn't understand being refused. I nursed my small flame of anger. No one did this to me. No one. I held myself away from her. A slight line of a frown touched her forehead, as if she were annoyed, or angry, or concentrating.

Felurian reached up to touch my face, her eyes intent as if trying to read something written deep inside me. I tried to pull back, remembering her touch, but my body simply shook. Beads of sweat fell from my skin to patter gently on the silk cushions and the flat plane of her stomach below.

She touched my cheek softly. Softly, I bent to kiss her, and something broke in my mind.

I felt the snap as four years of my life slid away. Suddenly I was back on the streets of Tarbean. Three boys, bigger than me with greasy hair and piggish eyes had dragged me from the broken crate where I'd been sleeping. Two of them held me down, pinning my arms. I lay in a stagnant puddle that was bitterly cold. It was early in the morning and the stars were out.

One of them had his hand over my mouth. It didn't matter. I had been in the city for months. I knew better than to yell for help. At best no one would come. At worst someone would, and then there would be more of them.

Two of them held me down. The third cut my clothes off my body. He cut me. They told me what they were going to do. Their breath was horribly warm against my face. They laughed.

There in Tarbean, half-naked and helpless, I felt something well up inside me. I bit two fingers off the hand over my mouth. I heard a scream and swearing as one of them staggered away. I strained and strained against the one who was still on top of me. I heard my own arm break, and his grip loosened. I started to howl.

I threw him off. Still screaming I stood, my clothes hanging in rags around me. I knocked one of them to the ground. My scrabbling hand found a loose cobblestone and I used it to break one of his legs. I remember the noise it made. I flailed until his arms were broken, then I broke his head.

When I looked up, I saw the one who had cut me was gone. The third huddled against a wall. He clutched his bloody hand to his chest. His eyes were white and wild. Then I heard footsteps approaching, and I dropped the stone and ran and ran and ran. . . .

Suddenly, years later, I was that feral boy again. I jerked my head back and snarled inside my mind. I felt something deep inside myself. I reached for it.

A tense stillness settled inside of me, the sort of silence that comes before a thunderclap. I felt the air begin to crystallize around me.

I felt cold. Detachedly, I gathered up the pieces of my mind and fit them all together. I was Kvothe the trouper, Edema Ruh born. I was Kvothe the student, Re'lar under Elodin. I was Kvothe the musician. I was Kvothe.

I stood above Felurian.

I felt as if this was the only time in my life I had been fully awake. Everything looked clear and sharp, as if I was seeing with a new set of eyes. As if I wasn't bothering with my eyes at all, and was looking at the world directly with my mind.

The sleeping mind, some piece of me realized faintly. *No longer sleeping*, I thought and smiled.

I looked at Felurian, and in that moment I understood her down to the bottoms of her feet. She was of the Fae. She did not worry over right or wrong. She was a creature of pure desire, much like a child. A child does not concern itself with consequence, neither does a sudden storm. Felurian resembled both, and neither. She was ancient and innocent and powerful and proud.

Was this the way Elodin saw the world? Was this the magic he spoke of? Not secrets or tricks, but Taborlin the Great magic. Always there, but beyond my seeing until now?

It was beautiful.

I met Felurian's eyes and the world grew slow and sluggish. I felt as if I had been thrust underwater, as if my breath had been pressed from my body. For that tiny moment I was stunned and numb as if I had been struck by lightning.

The moment passed and things began to move again. But now, looking into Felurian's twilight eyes, I understood her far beyond the bottoms of her feet. Now I knew her to the marrow of her bones. Her eyes were like four lines of music, clearly penned. My mind was filled with the sudden song of her. I drew a breath and sang it out in four hard notes.

Felurian sat upright. She passed her hand before her eyes and spoke a word as sharp as shattered glass. There was a pain like thunder in my head. Darkness flickered at the edges of my sight. I tasted blood and bitter rue.

The world snapped back into focus, and I caught myself before I fell.

Felurian frowned. Straightened. Stood. Her face intent, she took a step.

Standing, she was not tall or terrible. Her head was barely level with my chin. Her dark hair hung, a sheaf of shadow, straight as a knife until it brushed against her curving hip. She was slight, and pale, and perfect. Never have I seen a face so sweet, a mouth so made for kissing. She was no longer frowning. Not smiling either. Her lips were soft and slightly parted.

She took another step. The simple motion of her moving leg was like a dance, the unexaggerated shifting of her hip entrancing as a fire. The arch of her bare foot said more of sex than anything I'd seen in my young life.

Another step. Her smile was fierce and full. She was as lovely as the moon. Her power hung about her like a mantle. It shook the air. It spread behind her like a pair of vast and unseen wings.

Close enough to touch, I felt her power thrumming in the air. Desire rose around me like the sea in storm. She raised her hand. She touched my chest. I shook.

She met my eyes, and in the twilight written there I saw again the four clear lines of song.

I sang them out. They burst from me like birds into the open air.

Suddenly my mind was clear again. I drew a breath and held her eyes in mine. I sang again, and this time I was full of rage. I shouted out the four hard notes of song. I sang them tight and white and hard as iron. And at the sound of them, I felt her power shake then shatter, leaving nothing in the empty air but ache and anger.

Felurian gave a startled cry and sat so suddenly that it was almost like a fall. She curled her knees toward herself and huddled, watching me with wide and frightened eyes.

Looking around, I saw the wind. Not the way you might see smoke or fog, I saw the ever-changing wind itself. It was familiar as the face of a forgotten friend. I laughed and spread my arms, marveling at its shifting shape.

I cupped my hands and breathed a sigh into the hollow space within. I spoke a name. I moved my hands and wove my breath gossamer-thin. It billowed out, engulfing her, then burst into a silver flame that trapped her tight inside its changing name.

I held her there above the ground. She watched me with an air of fear and disbelief, her dark hair dancing like a second flame inside the first.

I knew then that I could kill her. It would be as simple as throwing a sheet of paper to the wind. But the thought sickened me, and I was reminded of ripping the wings from a butterfly. Killing her would be destroying something strange and wonderful. A world without Felurian was a poorer world. A world I would like a little less. It would be like breaking Illien's lute. It would be like burning down a library in addition to ending a life.

On the other hand, my safety and sanity were at stake. I believed the world was more interesting with Kvothe in it as well.

But I couldn't kill her. Not like this. Not wielding my newfound magic like a dissecting knife.

I spoke again, and the wind brought her down among the pillows. I made a tearing motion and the silver flame that once had been my breath became three notes of broken song and went to play among the trees.

I sat. She reclined. We looked each other over for several long minutes. Her eyes flashed from fear to caution to curiosity. I saw myself reflected in her eyes, naked among the cushions. My power rode like a white star on my brow.

Then I began to feel a fading. A forgetting. I realized the name of the wind no longer filled my mouth, and when I looked around I saw nothing but empty air. I tried to remain outwardly calm, but as these things left me I felt like a lute whose strings were being cut. My heart clenched with a loss I hadn't felt since my parents died.

I could see a slight shimmer in the air around Felurian, some shred of her power returning. I ignored it as I struggled frantically to keep some part of what I had learned. But it was like trying to hold a handful of sand. If you have ever dreamed of flying, then come awake, dismayed to realize you had lost the trick of it, you have some inkling how I felt.

Piece by piece it faded until there was nothing left. I felt hollow inside and ached as badly as if I'd discovered my family never loved me. I swallowed against the lump in my throat.

Felurian looked at me curiously. I could still see myself reflected in her eyes, the star on my forehead no more than a pinprick of light. Then even the perfect vision of my sleeping mind began to fade. I looked desperately at the world around me. I tried to memorize the sight of it, unblinking.

Then it was gone. I bowed my head, half in grief and half to hide the tears.

CHAPTER NINETY-EIGHT

The Lay of Felurian

ALONG MOMENT PASSED BEFORE I regained enough of my composure to look up. There was a hesitancy in the air, as if we were young
lovers who didn't know what was expected of us next, who didn't know
what parts we were supposed to play.

I picked up my lute and brought it close to my chest. The motion was
instinctive, like clutching a wounded hand. I struck a chord out of habit, then
made it minor so the lute seemed to be saying *sad*.

Without thinking or looking up I began to play one of the songs I had
written in the months after my parents died. It was called Sitting by the Water
Remembering. My fingers strummed sorrow into the evening air. It was
several minutes before I realized what I was doing, and several more before I
stopped. I wasn't done with the song. I don't know if it really has an ending.

I felt better, not *good* by any means, but better. Less empty. My music always
helped. As long as I had my music, no burden was ever too heavy to bear.

I looked up and saw tears on Felurian's face. It made me less ashamed of
my own.

I also felt myself wanting her. The emotion was damped by the ache in my
chest, but that touch of desire focused my attention on my most immediate
concern. Survival. Escape.

Felurian seemed to reach a decision and started through the cushions
toward me. Moving in a cautious crawl, she stopped several feet away and
looked at me.

"does my tender poet have a name?" Her voice was so gentle it startled me.

I opened my mouth to speak, then stopped. I thought of the moon, caught
by her own name, and a thousand faerie stories I had heard as a child. If you
believed Elodin, names were the bones of the world. I hesitated for about

half a second before I decided I had given Felurian a damn sight more than my name already.

"I am Kvothe." The sound of it seemed to ground me, to put me inside myself again.

"kvothe." She spoke it softly, and it reminded me of a bird calling. "would you sing sweet for me again?" She reached out slowly, as if afraid of being burned, and laid her hand lightly on my arm. "please? your songs are like a caress, my kvothe."

She pronounced my name like the beginning of a song. It was lovely. However, I wasn't entirely comfortable with the way she referred to me as *her* Kvothe.

I smiled and nodded. Mostly because I didn't have a better idea. I struck a couple of tuning chords, then paused, thinking.

Then I started to play "In the Forest Fae," a song about, of all things, Felurian herself. It wasn't particularly good. It used about three chords and two dozen words. But it had the effect I was looking for.

Felurian brightened at the mention of her name. There was no false modesty in her. She knew she was most beautiful, most skilled. She knew men told stories, and she knew her reputation. No man could resist her, no man could endure her. By the end of the song, pride had her sitting straighter.

I finished the song. "Would you like to hear another?" I asked.

She nodded and grinned eagerly. She sat among the cushions, back straight, as regal as a queen.

I moved into a second song, similar to the first. It was called "Lady Fae" or something of the sort. I didn't know who had written it, but they had an appalling habit of sticking extra syllables into their lines. It wasn't bad enough to get anything thrown at me in a tavern, but it was close.

I watched Felurian closely as I played. She was flattered, but I could read a slight dissatisfaction growing. As if she was irritated, but she couldn't decide why. Perfect.

Last I played a song written for Queen Serule. I guarantee you haven't heard it, but I'm sure you know the type. Written by some toadying minstrel looking for a patronage, my father had taught it to me as an example of certain things to avoid when writing a song. It was a numbing example of mediocrity. You could tell the writer was either truly inept, had never met Serule, or that he simply didn't find her attractive at all.

While singing it, I simply exchanged the name Felurian for Serule. I also replaced some of the better phrases with less poetic ones. By the time I was through with it, the song was truly wretched, and Felurian wore an expression of naked dismay upon her face.

I sat for a long moment, as if deeply considering something. When I finally did speak, my voice was hushed and hesitant. "Lady, might I write a song for you?" I gave her a sheepish smile.

Her smile was like the moon through the clouds. She clapped her hands and threw herself onto me with a kittenish delight, peppering me with kisses. Only fear that my lute might be broken kept me from properly enjoying the experience.

Felurian pulled away and sat very still. I tried a couple of chord combinations, then stilled my hands and looked up at her. "I will call it 'The Lay of Felurian.'" She blushed a bit and looked at me through lowered eyes, her expression bashful and brazen.

All immodest boasting aside, I write a fine song when I set my hand to it, and my skills had recently been sharpened in the Maer's employ. I am not the best, but I am one of the best. Given enough time, a worthy subject, and the proper motivation I daresay I could write a song nearly as well as Illien. Nearly.

Closing my eyes, I coaxed sweet strains from my lute. My fingers flew, and I captured the music of wind in the branches, of rustling leaves.

Then I looked to the back of my mind where the mad, chattering part of me had been composing a song to Felurian all this while. I brushed the strings more lightly and began to sing.

> *Flashing moon silver, midnight blue her eyes*
> *The lids were subtle-colored butterflies.*
> *Her hair swayed, a dark scythe swinging*
> *Through the trees with the wind singing.*
> *Felurian! O Lady Fair,*
> *Blessed be your forest glade.*
> *Your breath is light upon the air.*
> *Your hair is shadow-dappled shade.*

Felurian grew still as I sang. Toward the end of the chorus I could hardly tell if she was breathing. A few of the butterflies that had been frightened away by our earlier conflict came dancing back to us. One of them landed on Felurian's hand, brushing its wings once, twice, as if curious why its mistress was so sudden still. I turned my eyes to my lute again and chose notes like raindrops licking the leaves of trees.

> *She danced in dancing shadows candle cast*
> *She held my eyes, my face, my form, full fast.*

Her smile a snare ten times as strong
As legendary faerie song.
O Lady Fair! Felurian,
Your kiss is honeysuckle sweet.
I pity any other man
Unknown to you and incomplete.

I watched her from the corner of my eye. She sat as if listening with her entire body. Her eyes were wide. She'd raised one hand to her mouth, upsetting the butterfly resting there, while the other pressed against her chest as she drew a slow breath. This is what I had wanted, but I regretted it nonetheless.

I bent over my lute and danced my fingers across the strings. I wove chords like water over river stones, like a soft breath against the ear. Then I steeled myself and sang:

Her eyes were of the bluest black
Like night sky with the clouds blown back
Her skills in love—

I stuttered my fingers on the strings, pausing for just a moment as if unsure of something. I saw Felurian wake halfway from her reverie and continued:

Her skills in love they do suffice
In close embrace men find her nice.
Felurian! O Mistress Bright,
Your touch more sought than silver
I br—

"what?" Even though I was expecting the interruption, the ice in her voice startled me into a jangle of notes and sent several butterflies into flight. I took a breath, assumed my most innocent expression, and looked up.

Her expression was a storm of rage and disbelief. "nice?" I felt the blood drain from my face at her tone. Her voice was still round and gentle as a distant flute. But that meant nothing. Distant thunder doesn't drub the ears, you feel it prowling through your chest. The quiet of her voice moved through me in that distant-thunder way. *"nice?"*

"It *was* nice," I said to mollify her, my air of innocence only half affected.

She opened her mouth as if she would speak, then closed her mouth. Her eyes flashed pure fury.

"I'm sorry," I said. "I should have known better than to try." I pitched my voice somewhere between broken spirit and beaten child. I lowered my hands from the lute strings.

Some of the fire left her, but when she found her voice it was tight and dangerous. "my skills *'suffice'?*" She hardly seemed able to force out the last word. Her mouth formed a thin, outraged line.

I exploded, my voice a roll of thunder. "How the hell am I supposed to know? It's not like I've ever done this sort of thing before!"

She reeled back at the vehemence of my words, some of the anger draining out of her. "what is it you mean?" she trailed off, confused.

"This!" I gestured awkwardly at myself, at her, at the cushions and the pavilion around us, as if that explained everything.

The last of the anger left her as I saw realization begin to dawn, "you . . ."

"No," I looked down, my face growing hot. "I have never been with a woman." Then I straightened and looked her in the eye as if challenging her to make an issue out of it.

Felurian was still for a moment, then her mouth turned up into a wry smile. "you tell me a faerie story, my kvothe."

I felt my face go grim. I don't mind being called a liar. I am. I am a marvelous liar. But I hate being called a liar when I'm telling the perfect truth.

Regardless of its motivation, my expression seemed to convince her. "but you were like a gentle summer storm." She made a fluttering gesture with a hand. "you were a dancer fresh upon the field." Her eyes glittered wickedly.

I tucked that comment away for later ego-polishing purposes. My reply was slightly wounded, "Please, I'm not a complete rube. I've read several books—"

Felurian giggled like a brook. "you learned from books." She looked at me as if she couldn't decide whether or not to take me seriously. She laughed, stopped, then laughed again. I didn't know if I should be offended.

"You were rather good too," I said hurriedly, knowing I sounded like the last dinner guest to compliment her on a salad. "As a matter of fact, I've read—"

"books? books! you compare me with books!" Her anger crashed over me. Then without even pausing for breath, Felurian laughed again, high and delighted. Her laugh was wild as a fox's cry, clear and sharp as morning birdsong. It was no human sound.

I put on my innocent face. "Isn't it always like this?" I kept my expression calm while inwardly I braced myself for another outburst.

She simply sat. "I am Felurian."

It wasn't a simple stating of a name. It was a declaration. It was a proud flag flying.

I held her eyes for a moment, then sighed and dropped my gaze to my lute. "I'm sorry about the song. I didn't mean to offend you."

"it was more lovely than the setting sun," she protested, sounding close to tears. "but.... *nice?*" The word seemed bitter to her.

I set my lute back into its case. "I'm sorry, I can't fix it without some basis for comparison...." I sighed. "Pity, it was a good song. They would have sung it for a thousand years." My voice was thick with regret.

Felurian's expression brightened as if with an idea, then her eyes narrowed into slits. She looked at me as if she was trying to read something written on the inside of my skull.

She knew. She knew I was holding the unfinished song as ransom. The unspoken messages were clear: Unless I leave I can never finish the song. Unless I leave no one will ever hear these beautiful words I have made for you. Unless I leave and taste the fruits mortal women have to offer, I'll never know how skilled you truly are.

There, amid the cushions, under the eternal twilight sky, Felurian and I stared at each other. She held a butterfly, and my hand rested on the smooth wood of my lute. Two armored knights eyeing each other across a bloody field could not have matched the intensity of our stare.

Felurian spoke slowly, gauging my response. "if you go, will you finish it?" I tried to look surprised, but I wasn't fooling her. I nodded. "will you come back to me and sing it?"

My surprise became genuine. I hadn't considered her asking for that. I knew there would be no leaving the second time. I hesitated, but only for a barest moment. Half a loaf is better than none. I nodded.

"promise?" I nodded again. "promise with kisses?" She closed her eyes and tilted her head back, like a flower basking in the sun.

Life is too short to refuse offers like that. I moved toward her, drew her naked body toward my own, and kissed her as well as my limited practice would allow. It seemed to be good enough.

As I pulled away she looked up at me and sighed. "your kisses are like snowflakes on my lips." She lay back on the cushions, head resting on her arm. Her free hand brushed my cheek.

To say she was lovely is such an understatement I cannot begin to repair it. I realized that over the last several minutes she hadn't been trying to make me desire her, at least not in any supernatural sense.

She brushed her lips lightly over the palm of my hand and released it. Then she lay still, watching me intently.

I was flattered. To this day I know of only one answer to a question so politely phrased. I bent to kiss her. And laughing, she took me in her arms.

CHAPTER NINETY-NINE

Magic of a Different Kind

BY THIS POINT IN my life, I'd earned myself a modest reputation.
No, that's not entirely true. It's better to say that I had *built* myself a reputation. I'd crafted it deliberately. I'd cultivated it.

Three-quarters of the stories folk told about me at the University were ridiculous rumors I'd started myself. I spoke eight languages. I could see in the dark. When I was three days old, my mother hung me in a basket from a rowan tree by the light of the full moon. That night a faerie laid a powerful charm on me to always keep me safe. It turned my eyes from blue to leafy green.

I knew how stories worked, you see. Nobody believed that I'd traded a cupped handful of my own fresh blood to a demon in exchange for an Alar like a blade of Ramston steel. But still, I *was* the highest ranked duelist in Dal's class. On a good day, I could beat any two of them together.

That thread of truth wove through the story, gave it strength. So even though you might not believe it, you might tell it to a wide-eyed first term student with a drink in him, just to watch his face, just for fun. And if you'd had a drink or three yourself, you might begin to wonder. . . .

And so the stories spread. And so, around the University at least, my tiny reputation grew.

There were a few true stories as well. Pieces of my reputation I'd honestly earned. I had rescued Fela from a blazing inferno. I had been whipped in front of a crowd and refused to bleed. I'd called the wind and broken Ambrose's arm. . . .

Still, I knew my reputation was a coat spun out of cobweb. It was storybook nonsense. There were no demons out there, bargaining for blood. There were no helpful faeries granting magic charms. And though I might pretend, I knew I was no Taborlin the Great.

These were my thoughts when I woke, tangled in Felurian's arms. I lay quietly among the cushions for a time, her head resting lightly on my chest, her leg thrown loosely over mine. Looking up through the trees at the twilight sky, I realized I could not recognize the stars. They were brighter than those in the mortal sky, their patterns unfamiliar.

It was only then that I realized my life had taken a step in a new direction. Up until now, I had been playing at being a young Taborlin. I had spun lies around myself, pretending to be a storybook hero.

But now there was no sense pretending. What I'd done was truly worth a story, every bit as odd and wonderful as any tale of Taborlin himself. I'd followed Felurian into the Fae, then bested her with magics I couldn't explain, let alone control.

I felt different now. More solid somehow. Not older, exactly. Not wiser. But I knew things that I'd never known before. I knew the Fae were real. I knew their magic was real. Felurian could break a man's mind with a kiss. Her voice could tug me like a puppet by its strings. There were things I could learn here. Strange things. Powerful things. Secret things. Things I might never ever have a chance to learn again.

I gently freed myself from Felurian's sleeping embrace and walked down to the nearby pool. I splashed water on my face and scooped up several handfuls to drink.

I looked through the plants that grew at the water's edge. I picked some leaves and chewed them as I considered how I might approach the subject with Felurian. The mint sweetened my breath.

When I returned to the pavilion, Felurian was standing there, brushing pale fingers through her long dark hair.

I handed her a violet, its color dark as her eyes. She smiled at me and ate it.

I decided to approach the subject gently, lest I offend her. "I was wondering," I said carefully, "if you would be willing to teach me."

She reached out to touch the side of my face gently. "foolish sweet," she said fondly. "have not I already begun?"

I felt excitement rise in my chest, amazed that it could be so simple. "Am I ready for my next lesson?" I asked.

Her smile grew wider and she looked me up and down, her eyes going half-lidded and mysterious. "are you?"

I nodded.

"it is good you are eager," Felurian said, her fluting voice tinged with amusement. "you have some cleverness and natural skill. but there is much to learn." She looked into my eyes, her delicate face gravely serious. "when you leave to walk among the mortal, I will not have you shame me."

Felurian took my hand and drew me into the pavilion. She pointed. "sit."

I sat on a cushion, placing my head level with the smooth expanse of her stomach. Her navel was terribly distracting.

She looked down at me, her expression proud and regal as a queen. *"amouen,"* she said, spreading the fingers of one hand and making a deliberate gesture. "this we call the hushed hart. an easy lesson to begin, and one I expect you will enjoy."

Felurian smiled at me then, her eyes old and knowing. And even before she pushed me back against the cushions and began to bite the side of my neck, I realized that she did not intend to teach me magic. Or if she did, it was magic of a different kind.

While it was not the subject I'd hoped to study under her, it's fair to say that I was not entirely disappointed. Learning lover's arts from Felurian far outstripped any curriculum offered at the University.

I am not referring to the vigorous sweaty wrestling most men—and alas, most women—think of as love. While sweat and vigor are pleasant parts of it, Felurian brought to my attention the subtler pieces. If I were to go into the world, she said, I would not embarrass her by being an incompetent lover, and so she took care to show me a great many things.

A few of them in her words: The pinioned wrist. The sigh toward the ear. Devouring the neck. Drawing the lips. The kissing of the throat, the navel, and—as Felurian phrased it—the woman's flower. The breathing kiss. The feather kiss. The climbing kiss. So many different types of kissing. Too many to remember. Almost.

There was drawing water from the well. The fluttering hand. Birdsong at morning. Circling the moon. Playing ivy. The harrowed hare. Just the names would fill a book. But this, I suppose, is not the place for such things. Alas then for the world.

I don't mean to give the impression that all our hours were spent in dalliance. I was young and Felurian was immortal, but there is only so much two bodies can endure. The rest of the time we amused ourselves in other ways. We swam and ate. I played songs for Felurian, and she danced for me.

I asked Felurian a few careful questions about magic, not wanting to offend her by prying at her secrets. Unfortunately, her answers were not particularly enlightening. Her magic came as naturally as breathing. I might as well have asked a farmer how seeds sprouted. When her answers weren't hopelessly nonchalant, they were puzzlingly cryptic.

Still, I continued to ask, and she answered as best she could. And occasionally I felt a small spark of understanding.

But most of our time was spent telling stories. We had so little in common that stories were all that we could share.

You might think Felurian and I would be unevenly matched in this regard. She was older than the sky, while I was not yet seventeen.

But Felurian was not the narrative treasure trove you would think. Powerful and clever? Certainly. Energetic and lovely? Absolutely. But storytelling was not among her many gifts.

I, on the other hand, was of the Edema Ruh, and we know all the stories in the world.

So I told her "The Ghost and the Goosegirl." I told her "Tam and the Tinker's Spade." I told her stories of woodcutters and widow's daughters and the cleverness of orphan boys.

In exchange, Felurian told me manling stories: "The Hand at the Heart of the Pearl," "The Boy Who Ran Between." The Fae have their own cast of legendary characters: Mavin the Manshaped, Alavin Allface. Surprisingly, Felurian had never heard of Taborlin the Great or Oren Velciter, but she did know who Illien was. It made me proud that one of the Edema Ruh had gained a place in the stories the Fae tell each other.

I wasn't blind to the fact that Felurian herself might have the information I was looking for about the Amyr and the Chandrian. How much more enjoyable would it be to learn the truth from her, rather than rooting endlessly through ancient books in dusty rooms?

Unfortunately, Felurian wasn't the mine of information I'd hoped. She knew stories of the Amyr, but they were thousands of years old.

When I asked her about the more recent Amyr, asking about church knights and the Ciridae with their bloody tattoos, she merely laughed. "there were never any human amyr," she said, dismissing the idea out of hand. "those you speak of sound like children dressing in their parents' clothes."

While I might expect that reaction from others, getting it from Felurian was particularly disheartening. Still, it was nice to know I had been right about the Amyr existing long before they became knights of the Tehlin church.

Then, since the Amyr were a lost cause, I tried to steer her in the direction of the Chandrian.

"no," she said, looking me squarely in the eye, her back straight. "I will not speak of the seven." Her soft voice held no lilting whimsy. No playfulness. No room for discussion or negotiation.

For the first time since our initial conflict, I felt a trickle of icy fear sweep over me. She was so slight and lovely, it was so easy to forget what she truly was.

Still, I couldn't let the subject go so easily. This was, quite literally, a once in a lifetime opportunity. If Felurian could be persuaded to tell me even a piece of what she knew, I could learn things no one else in the world might know.

I gave her my most charming smile and drew a breath to speak, but before I could get the first word out, Felurian leaned forward and kissed me full upon the mouth. Her lips were plush and warm. Her tongue brushed mine and she bit the swell of my lower lip playfully.

When she pulled her mouth from mine, it left me breathless with a racing heart. She looked at me, her dark eyes full of tender sweetness. She laid her hand along my face, brushing my cheek as gently as a flower.

"my sweet love," she said. "if you ask of the seven again in this place, I will drive you from it. no matter if your asking be firm or gentle, honest or slantways. if you ask, I will whip you forth from here with a lash of brambles and snakes. I will drive you before me, bloody and weeping, and will not stop until you are dead or fled from fae."

She didn't look away from me as she spoke. And though I hadn't looked away or seen them change, her eyes were no longer soft with adoration. They were dark as storm clouds, hard as ice.

"I do not jest," she said. "I swear this by my flower and the ever-moving moon. I swear it by salt and stone and sky. I swear this singing and laughing, by the sound of my own name." She kissed me again, pressing her lips to mine tenderly. "I will do this thing."

And that was the end of it. I might be a fool, but I am not that much of a fool.

———

Felurian was more than willing to talk about the Fae realm itself. And many of her stories detailed the fractious politics of the faen courts: the Tain Mael, the Daendan, the Gorse Court. These stories were difficult for me to follow as I didn't know anything about the factions involved, let alone the web of alliances, false friendships, open secrets, and old grudges that bound Fae society together.

This was complicated by the fact that Felurian took it for granted that I understood certain things. If I were telling you a story, for example, I wouldn't bother mentioning that most moneylenders are Cealdish, or that there is no royalty older than the Modegan royal line. Who doesn't know such things?

Felurian left similar details out of her stories. Who wouldn't know, for example, that the Gorse Court had meddled in the Berentaltha between the Mael and the House of Fine?

And why was this important? Well of course that would lead to members of the Gorse being scorned by those on the dayward side of things. And what was the Berentaltha? A sort of dance. And why was this dance important?

After a handful of questions such as this, Felurian's eyes would narrow. I quickly learned it was better to follow along, quiet and confused, rather than try to winkle out every detail and risk her irritation.

Still, I learned things from these stories: a thousand small, scattered facts about the Fae. The names of the courts, old battles, and notable persons. I learned you must never look at one of the Thiana with both eyes at once, and that the gift of a single cinnas fruit is considered a terrible insult if given to one of the Beladari.

You might think these thousand facts gave me some insight into the Fae. That I somehow fit them together like puzzle pieces and discovered the true shape of things. A thousand facts is quite a lot, after all....

But no. A thousand seems like a lot, but there are more stars than that in the sky, and they make neither a map nor a mural. All I knew for certain after hearing Felurian's stories is that I had no desire to ever entangle myself in even the kindest corner of the faen court. With my luck I'd whistle while walking under a willow and thereby insult God's barber, or something of the sort.

Here is the one thing I learned from these stories: the Fae are not like us. This is endlessly easy to forget, because many of them look as we do. They speak our language. They have two eyes. They have hands, and their mouths make familiar shapes when they smile. But these things are only seemings. We are not the same.

I have heard people say that men and the Fae are as different as dogs and wolves. While this is an easy analogy, it is far from true. Wolves and dogs are only separated by a minor shade of blood. Both howl at night. If beaten, both will bite.

No. Our people and theirs are as different as water and alcohol. In equal glasses they look the same. Both liquid. Both clear. Both wet, after a fashion. But one will burn, the other will not. This has nothing to do with temperament or timing. These two things behave differently because they are profoundly, fundamentally not the same.

The same is true with humans and the Fae. We forget it at our peril.

CHAPTER ONE HUNDRED

Shaed

I SHOULD, PERHAPS, EXPLAIN a few peculiarities of the Fae.

At first glance, Felurian's forest glade did not seem particularly odd. In most ways it resembled an ancient, untouched piece of forest. If not for the unfamiliar stars above, I might have suspected I was still in an isolated piece of the Eld.

But there were differences. Since I had left my mercenary companions I had slept perhaps a dozen times. Despite this, the sky above Felurian's pavilion remained the deep purpling blue of summer dusk and showed no signs of changing.

I had only the roughest guess as to how long I had been in the Fae. More importantly, I had no idea how much time might have been passing in the mortal world. Stories are full of boys who fall asleep in faerie circles only to wake as old men. Young girls wander into the woods and return years later, looking no older and claiming only minutes have passed.

For all I knew, years could pass each time I slept in Felurian's arms. I could return to find a century had passed, or no time at all.

I did my best not to think about it. Only a fool worries over what he can't control.

The other difference in the Fae realm was much more subtle and difficult to describe. . . .

In the Medica, I had spent a fair amount of time around unconscious patients. I mention this to make a point: there is a great difference between being in a room that is empty and being in a room where someone is sleeping. A sleeping person is a presence in a room. They are aware of you, even if it is only a dim, vague awareness.

That is what the Fae was like. It was such an odd, intangible thing that I didn't notice it for a long while. Then, once I became aware of it, it took me much longer to lay my finger on what the difference was.

It felt as if I had moved from an empty room into a room where someone was asleep. Except, of course, that there was no one there. It was as if everything around me was deeply asleep: the trees, the stones, the rippling stream that widened into Felurian's pool. All these things felt more solid, more present than I was used to, as if they were ever so slightly aware of me.

———————

The thought that I would eventually leave the Fae alive and unbroken was an unfamiliar one for Felurian, and I could tell it troubled her. Often, while in the midst of an unrelated conversation, she would change direction and make me promise, *promise*, to return to her.

I reassured her as best I could, but there are only so many ways you can say the same thing. After perhaps three dozen times I said, "I will do my best to keep myself safe so I can come back to you."

I saw her face change, becoming first anxious, then grim, then thoughtful. For a moment I worried she had decided to keep me as a pet mortal after all, and I began to berate myself for not fleeing the Fae when I had the chance. . . .

But before I could begin to grow genuinely concerned, Felurian cocked her head to one side and seemed to change the subject, "would my sweet flame like a coat? a cloak?"

"I have one," I said, gesturing to where my possessions lay scattered at the edge of the pavilion. Only then did I notice that the tatty old tinker's cloak *wasn't* there. I saw my clothes, my boots, and my travelsack still bulging with the Maer's lockbox. But my cloak and sword were gone. The fact that I hadn't noticed their absence was understandable, as I hadn't bothered dressing since I first woke next to Felurian.

She looked me over slowly, her expression intent. Her eyes lingering on my knee, my lower arm, my upper arm. It was only when she took hold of my shoulder, and turned me so she could examine my back, that I realized she was looking at my scars.

Felurian took hold of my hand and traced a pale line that ran along my forearm. "you are not good at keeping yourself safe, my kvothe."

I was a little offended, especially as there was more than a little truth to what she said. "I do fairly well," I said stiffly. "Considering the trouble that I find."

Felurian turned over my hand and examined my palm and fingers closely. "you are not a fighter," she mused softly to herself. "yet you are all iron-bitten. you are a sweet bird that cannot fly. no bow. no knife. no chain."

Her hand moved to my foot, running thoughtfully along the calluses and scars from my years on the streets of Tarbean. "you are a long walker. you find me in the wild at night. you are a deep knower. and bold. and young. and trouble finds you."

She looked up at me, her face intent. "would my sweet poet like a *shaed?*"

"A what?"

She paused as if considering her words. "a shadow."

I smiled. "I already have one." Then I checked to make sure. I was in the Fae after all.

Felurian frowned, shaking her head at my lack of understanding. "another I would give a shield, and it would keep him safe from harm. another I would gift with amber, bind a scabbard tight with glamour, or craft a crown so men might look on you with love."

She shook her head solemnly. "but not for you. you are a night walker. a moon follower. you must be safe from iron, from cold, from spite. you must be quiet. you must be light. you must move softly in the night. you must be quick and unafraid." She nodded to herself. "this means I must make you a shaed."

She stood and started walking toward the forest. "come," she said.

Felurian had a way of making requests that took some getting used to. I'd discovered that unless I was steeling myself to resist, I'd find myself automatically doing whatever it was she asked of me.

It wasn't that she spoke with authority. Her voice was too soft and edgeless to carry the weight of command. She did not demand or cajole. When she spoke, it was matter-of-fact. As if she couldn't imagine a world in which you didn't want to do exactly as she said.

Because of this, when Felurian told me to follow her, I jumped like a puppet with its strings pulled. Soon I was padding along beside her, deep in the twilight shadows of the ancient forest, naked as a jaybird.

I almost went back to grab my clothes, then decided to follow some advice my father had given me when I was young. "Everyone eats a different part of the pig," he'd said. "You want to fit in, you'll do the same." Different places, different decorums.

So I followed, naked and unprepared. Felurian struck out at a good pace, the moss muffling the sound of our bare feet.

As we walked the forest grew darker. At first I thought it was simply the branches of the trees arching over our heads. Then I realized the truth. Above us, the twilight sky was slowly growing darker. Eventually, the last hint of purple was gone, leaving the sky a perfect velvet black, flecked with unfamiliar stars.

Felurian kept walking, I could see her pale skin in the starlight and the shapes of trees around us, but nothing more. Thinking myself clever, I made a sympathetic binding for light and held my hand above my head as if it were a torch. I was more than slightly proud of this, as the motion-to-light binding is rather difficult without a piece of metal to use as a focus.

Light swelled and I caught a moment's glimpse of our surroundings. Dark trunks of trees rose like massive pillars as far as the eye could see. There were no low-hanging branches, no undergrowth, no grass. Only dark moss underfoot and the arch of dark branches overhead. I was reminded of a vast, empty cathedral swathed in sooty velvet.

"ciar nalias!" Felurian snapped.

Understanding her tone if not her words, I broke the binding and let the darkness rush back over us. An instant later Felurian leapt at me and bore me to the ground, her lithe, naked body pressed against mine. It was not an entirely uncommon occurrence, but this time the experience was not particularly erotic as the back of my head struck a knuckle of protruding root.

Because of this I was half dazed and nine-tenths blind when the earth shuddered slightly beneath us. Something vast and almost perfectly silent stirred the air above us and slightly off to one side of where we lay.

Poised atop me, one leg on either side, Felurian's body was as taut as a harp string. The muscles of her thighs were tense and quivering. Her long hair fell over us, covering us like a silk sheet. Her breasts pressed against my chest as she drew a shallow, silent breath.

Her body thrummed with the rhythm of her racing heart, and I felt her mouth move where it rested near the hollow of my throat. Softer than a whisper, Felurian spoke a gentle, edgeless word. I felt it press against my skin, sending silent ripples through the air the same way a thrown stone makes circles on the surface of a pond.

There was a soft sound of movement above us, as if someone was folding a huge piece of velvet around a piece of broken glass. Saying that I realize it makes no sense, but still, that is the best way I can describe the sound. It was a soft noise, the half-heard sound of deliberate movement. I cannot tell you why it made me think of something terrible and sharp, but it did. My forehead prickled with sweat, and I was filled with a sudden pure and breathless terror.

Felurian went perfectly still, as if she were a startled deer or a cat about to pounce. Quietly, she drew a breath, then spoke a second word. Her breath brushed hot against my throat, and at the half-heard word my body thrummed as if I were a drumhead soundly struck.

Felurian turned her head a bare degree, as if straining to listen. This movement pulled a thousand strands of her splayed hair slowly over the entire left half of my naked body, covering me in gooseflesh. Even in the grip of my nameless terror, I shivered and gave a soft, involuntary gasp.

There was a stirring in the air directly above us.

The sharp nails of Felurian's left hand dug hard into the muscle of my shoulder. She shifted her hips, and slowly slid her naked body up along my own until her face was even with mine. Her tongue flicked against my lips, and without even thinking I tilted my head, reaching for the kiss.

Her mouth met mine, and she drew a long slow breath, pulling the air out of me. I felt my head grow light. Then, her lips still tight against mine, Felurian pushed her breath hard into me, filling my lungs. It was softer than silent. It tasted of honeysuckle. The ground shivered beneath me and everything was still. For an endless moment my heart ceased beating in my chest.

A subtle tension left the air above us.

Felurian pulled her mouth from mine and my heart thumped again, sudden and hard. A second beat. A third. I pulled in a deep, shaking breath.

Only then did Felurian relax. She lay atop me, loose and supple, her naked body flowing over mine like water. Her head nestled into the curve of my neck and she gave a sweet, contented sigh.

A languid moment passed, then she laughed, her body shaking with it. It was wild and delighted, as if she had just played the most marvelous joke. She sat up and kissed my mouth fiercely, then nipped at my ear before climbing off me and pulling me to my feet.

I opened my mouth. Then closed it, deciding this was probably not the right time for questions. Half of seeming clever is keeping your mouth shut at the right times.

So we continued in darkness. Eventually my eyes adjusted, and through the branches above I could see the stars, differently patterned and brighter than those in the mortal sky. Their light was barely enough to give an impression of the ground and surrounding trees. Felurian's slender form was a silver shadow in the darkness.

We kept walking, and the trees grew taller and thicker, blocking out the pale starlight bit by bit. Then it became truly dark. Felurian was little more than a piece of pale darkness ahead of me. She stopped walking before I lost sight of her entirely and cupped her hands around her mouth as if she were about to shout.

I cringed at the thought of a loud noise invading the warm quiet of this place. But instead of a shout there was nothing. No. Not nothing. It was like a low, slow purr. Not anything so loud and rough as a cat's purr. It was closer to the sound a heavy snowfall makes, a muffled hush that almost makes less noise than no noise at all.

Felurian did this several times. Then she took me by the hand and led me farther into the dark where she repeated the odd, almost inaudible noise. After she had done this three times it was so dark I could no longer see even the faintest shape of her.

After the final pause, Felurian stepped close to me in the dark, pressing her body to mine. She gave me a long and thorough kiss that I expected to become something more involved when she pulled away and spoke softly into my ear. "quietly," she breathed. "they come."

For several minutes I strained my eyes and ears to no avail. Then I saw something luminous in the distance. It disappeared quickly, and I thought my light-starved eyes were playing tricks on me. Then I saw another flicker. Two more. Ten. A hundred pale lights danced toward us through the trees, faint as foxfire.

I'd heard of fool's fire before, but never seen it. And given that we were in the Fae, I doubted this was anything so mundane. I thought of a hundred faerie stories and wondered which of those creatures could be responsible for these dim, madly dancing lights. Tom-Sparks? Will o' wisps? Dennerlings with lanterns full of corpselight?

Then they were all around us, startling me. The lights were smaller than I'd thought, and closer. I heard the hushed snowfall sound again, this time from all around me. I still couldn't guess what they might be until one of them brushed my arm as lightly as a feather. They were moths of some sort. Moths with luminescent patches on their wings.

They shone with a pale, silvery light too weak to illuminate anything around them. But hundreds of them, dancing between the boles of trees, showed the silhouette of our surroundings. Some of them lit on trees or the ground. A few landed on Felurian, and though I still could not see more than a few inches of her pale skin, I could use the moving light of them to follow her.

We walked a long while after that, Felurian leading between the trunks of ancient trees. Once I felt grass soft beneath my bare feet instead of moss, then there was soft soil, as if we were crossing a farmer's fresh-tilled field. For a time we followed a twisting path of smooth paved stone that led us over the arch of a high bridge. All the while the moths followed us, giving me only the dimmest impression of our surroundings.

Eventually Felurian stopped. By now the darkness was so thick I could almost feel it like a warm blanket around me. I could tell by the sound of the wind in the trees and the motion of the moths that we were standing in an open space.

There were no stars above us. If we were in a clearing, the trees must be vast for their branches to meet overhead. But for all I knew we could just as easily be deep underground. Or perhaps the sky was black and empty in this portion of the Fae. It was a strangely unsettling thought.

The subtle feeling of sleeping alertness was stronger here. If the rest of the Fae felt like it was sleeping, this place felt like it had stirred half a moment ago and hovered on the verge of waking. It was disconcerting.

Felurian gently pressed the flat of her hand against my chest, then a finger against my lips. I watched as she moved away from me, softly humming a little snatch of the song I had made for her. But even this piece of flattery couldn't distract me from the fact that I was in the center of the Fae realm, blind, stark naked, and without the slightest idea of what was going on.

A handful of moths had landed on Felurian, resting on her wrist, hip, shoulder and thigh. Watching them gave me a vague impression of her movements. If I had to guess, I would have said she was picking things out of the trees, from behind or beneath bushes or stones. A warm breeze sighed through the clearing, and I felt strangely comforted as it brushed my bare skin.

After about ten minutes, Felurian came back and kissed me. She held something soft and warm in her arms.

We walked back the way we had come. The moths gradually lost interest in us, leaving us with less and less of an impression of our surroundings. After what seemed an interminable amount of time I saw light filtering through a break in the trees ahead. It was only faint starlight, but at that moment it seemed bright as a curtain of burning diamonds.

I started to walk through it, but Felurian took hold of my arm to stop me. Without a word she sat me down where the first faint beams of starlight lanced through the trees to touch the ground.

Carefully she stepped between the rays of starlight, avoiding them as if they might burn her. When she stood in the center of them, she lowered herself to the ground and sat cross-legged, facing me. She held whatever she had collected in her lap, but other than the fact that it was shapeless and dark I could tell nothing about it.

Then Felurian reached out a hand, took hold of one of the thin beams of starlight, and pulled it toward the dark shape in her lap.

I might have been more surprised if Felurian's manner hadn't been so casual. In the dim light, I saw her hands make a familiar motion. A second later she reached out again, almost absentmindedly, and grasped another narrow strand of starlight between her thumb and forefinger.

She drew it in as easily as the first and manipulated it in the same way. Again the motion struck me as familiar, but it was nothing I could press my finger to.

Felurian started to hum quietly to herself as she gathered in the next beam of starlight, brightening things an imperceptible amount. The shape in her lap looked like thick, dark cloth. Seeing this I realized what she reminded me of: my father sewing. Was she sewing by starlight?

Sewing with starlight. Realization came to me in a flood. Shaed meant shadow. She had somehow brought back an armful of shadow and was sewing it with starlight. Sewing me a cloak of shadow.

Sound absurd? It did to me. But regardless of my ignorant opinion, Felurian took hold of another strand of starlight and brought it to her lap. I brushed any doubt aside. Only a fool disbelieves what he sees with his own eyes.

Besides, the stars above me were bright and strange. I was sitting next to a creature out of a storybook. She had been young and beautiful for a thousand years. She could stop my heart with a kiss and talk to butterflies. Was I going to start quibbling now?

After a while I moved closer so I could watch more carefully. She smiled as I sat next to her, favoring me with a hasty kiss.

I asked a couple questions, but her answers either made no sense or were hopelessly nonchalant. She didn't know the first thing about the laws of sympathy, or sygaldry, or the Alar. She simply didn't think there was anything odd about sitting in the forest holding a handful of shadow. First I was offended, then I was terribly jealous.

I remembered when I'd found the name of the wind in her pavilion. It had felt as if I were truly awake for the first time, true knowledge running like ice in my blood.

The memory exhilarated me for a moment, then left me with a broken chord of loss. My sleeping mind was slumbering again. I turned my attention back to Felurian and tried to understand.

Before too long, Felurian stood in a fluid motion and helped me to my feet. She hummed happily and took my arm as we strolled back the way we had come, chatting of little things. She held the dark shape of the shaed draped easily over her arm.

Then, just as the first faint hint of twilight began to touch the sky, she hung it invisibly in the dark branches of a nearby tree. "sometimes slow seduction is the only way," she said. "the gentle shadow fears the candleflame. how could your fledgling shaed not feel the same?"

CHAPTER ONE HUNDRED ONE

Close Enough to Touch

AFTER OUR SHADOW-GATHERING EXPEDITION, I asked more pointed questions about Felurian's magic. Most of her answers continued to be hopelessly matter-of-fact. How do you take hold of a shadow? She motioned with one hand, as if reaching for a piece of fruit. That was how, apparently.

Other answers were nearly incomprehensible, filled with Fae words I didn't understand. When she tried to describe those terms, our conversations became hopeless rhetorical tangles. At times I felt like I'd found myself a quieter, more attractive version of Elodin.

Still, I learned a few scraps. What she was doing with the shadow was called grammarie. When I asked, she said it was "the art of making things be." This was distinct from glamourie, which was "the art of making things seem."

I also learned that there aren't directions of the usual sort in the Fae. Your trifoil compass is useless as a tin codpiece there. North does not exist. And when the sky is endless twilight, you cannot watch the sun rise in the east.

But if you look closely at the sky, one piece of the horizon will be a shade brighter, in the opposite direction a shade darker. If you walk toward the brighter horizon, eventually it will become daytime. The other way leads to darker night. If you keep walking in one direction long enough, you will eventually see a whole "day" pass and end up in the same place you began. That's the theory, at any rate.

Felurian described those two points of the Fae compass as Day and Night. The other two points she referred to at different times as Dark and Light, Summer and Winter, or Forward and Backward. Once she even referred to them as Grimward and Grinning, but something about the way she said it made me suspect it was a joke.

I have a good memory. That, perhaps more than anything else, sits in the center of what I am. It is the talent upon which so many of my other skills depend.

I can only guess how I came by my memory. My early stage training, perhaps. The games my parents used to help me remember my lines. Perhaps it was the mental exercises Abenthy taught me to prepare me for the University.

Wherever it came from, my memory has always served me well. Sometimes it works much better than I'd like.

That said, my memory is strangely patchy when I think of my time in the Fae. My conversations with Felurian are clear as glass. Her lessons may as well be written on my skin. The sight of her. The taste of her mouth. They are all fresh as yesterday.

But other things I cannot bring to mind at all.

For example, I remember Felurian in the purpling twilight. It dappled her through the trees, making her look as if she were underwater. I remember her in flickering candlelight, the teasing shadows of it concealing more than it revealed. And I remember her in the full, rich amber of lamplight. She basked in it like a cat, her skin warm and glowing.

But I do not remember lamps. Or candles. There is a great deal of fuss when dealing with such things, but I cannot remember a single moment spent trimming a wick or wiping soot from the glass hood of a lamp. I do not remember the smell of oil or smoke or wax.

I remember eating. Fruit and bread and honey. Felurian ate flowers. Fresh orchids. Wild trillium. Lush selas. I tried some myself. The violets were my favorite.

I don't mean to imply she ate only flowers. She enjoyed bread and butter and honey. She liked blackberries especially. And there was meat, too. Not with every meal, but sometimes. Wild venison. Pheasant. Bear. Felurian ate hers so rare that it was almost raw.

She was not a fastidious eater, either. Not prim or courtly. We ate with our hands and teeth, and afterward, if we were sticky with honey or pulp or the blood of bears, we would wash ourselves in the nearby pool.

I can see her even now, naked, laughing, blood running down her chin. She was regal as a queen. Eager as a child. Proud as a cat. And she was like none of those things. Nothing like them. Not in the least little bit.

My point is this: I can remember our eating. What I cannot remember is where the food came from. Did someone bring it? Did she gather it herself? I cannot bring it to mind to save my life. The thought of servants intruding on the privacy of her twilight glade seems impossible to me, but so is the thought of Felurian baking her own bread.

The deer, on the other hand, I could understand. I had not the least doubt she could run one to ground and kill it with her hands if she desired. Or I could picture a shy hart venturing into the quiet of her twilight glade. I can imagine Felurian sitting, patient and calm, waiting until it came close enough to touch. . . .

The Ever-Moving Moon

FELURIAN AND I WERE walking down to the pool when I noticed a subtle difference in the quality of light. Looking up, I was surprised to see the pale curve of the moon peering through the trees above us.

Even though it was only the slenderest crescent, I recognized it as the same moon I had known my whole life. Seeing it in this strange place was like meeting a long-lost friend far from home.

"Look!" I said, pointing. "The moon!"

Felurian smiled indulgently. "you are my precious newborn lamb. look! there hangs a cloud as well! *amouen!* dance for joy!" She laughed.

I flushed, embarrassed. "It's just that I haven't seen it in . . ." I trailed off, having no way to gauge my time. "A long while. Besides, you have different stars. I thought perhaps you had a different moon as well."

Felurian ran her fingers gently through my hair. "foolish sweet, there is only one moon. we have been waiting on her. she will help us *enbighten* your shaed." She slipped into the water, sleek as an otter. When she surfaced her hair slicked her shoulders like ink.

I sat on a stone by the edge of a pool and dangled my feet. The water was warm as a bath. "How can the moon be here," I asked, "if this is a different sky?"

"there is only one slender slip of her here," Felurian said. "she is still mostly in the mortal now."

"But how?" I asked.

Felurian stopped swimming and floated on her back, looking up at the sky. "oh moon," she said forlornly. "I perish for kisses. why have you brought me an owl when I desired a man?" She sighed, then softly hooted into the night: *how? how? how?*

I slid into the water, not as lithe as an otter perhaps, but somewhat better at kissing.

A while later we lay in the shallows on a broad sheet of stone worn water-smooth. "thank you moon," Felurian said, looking up at the sky contentedly. "for this sweet and lusty manling."

There were luminous fishes in the pool. No larger than your hand, each with a stripe or spot of gently glowing color. I watched them emerge from whatever hiding places they had scattered to, startled by the recent turbulence. They were orange as glowing coals, yellow as buttercups, blue as noontime sky.

Felurian slid back into the water, then tugged at my leg. "come, my kissing owl," she said. "and I will show to you the workings of the moon."

I followed her into the pool until we stood shoulder deep. The fish came to explore, the braver ones coming close enough to swim between us. Their motion revealed the hidden silhouette of Felurian's body beneath the water. Despite the fact that I had explored her nakedness in great detail, I suddenly found myself fascinated by the suggested shape of her.

The fish came closer still. One brushed me, and I felt a gentle nip against my ribs. I jumped, though its tiny bite was soft as a tapping finger. I watched as more of the fish circled round, occasionally nibbling at us.

"even the fish delight in kissing you," Felurian said, stepping closer to press her wet body against mine.

"I think they must like the salt on my skin," I said, looking down at them.

She pushed me away, irritated. "mayhap they like the taste of owl."

Before I could make an appropriate reply, she assumed a serious expression, flattened her hand, and lowered it into the water between us.

"there is only one moon," Felurian said. "she moves between your mortal sky and mine." She pressed her palm against my chest, then brought it back and pressed it to her own. "she sways between. back and forth." She stopped, frowning at me. "be mindful of my words."

"I am," I lied.

"no. you are mindful of my breasts."

It was true. They flirted with the surface of the water. "They are well worth minding," I said. "To not attend to them would be a terrible insult."

"I speak of important things. knowings you must have if you are to return safe to me." She gave an exasperated sigh. "if I let you touch one, will you attend to my words?"

"Yes."

She took hold of my hand and pulled it close to cup her breast. "make waves upon lilies."

"You haven't shown me waves upon lilies yet."

"that will come later, then." She put her flat hand back in the water between us, then sighed softly, her eyes going halfway closed. "ah," she said. "oh."

Eventually the fish emerged from their hiding places again.

"my most distractible owl," Felurian said, not unkindly. She dove to the bottom of the pool and returned holding a smooth, round stone. "attend you now to what I say. you are the mortal, I the fae."

"here is the moon," she said, tucking the stone between our palms and lacing our fingers together to hold it. "she's tethered tight to both the fae and mortal night."

Felurian stepped forward and pressed the stone against my chest. "thus moves the moon," she said, tightening her fingers around mine. "now when I look above, there is no glimmer of the light I love. instead, all like a flower unfurled, her face shines on your mortal world."

She stepped back so our arms were straight with our clasped hands between us. Then she pulled the stone toward her chest, dragging me through the water by my hand. "now all your mortal maidens sigh, for she is fully in my sky."

I nodded, understanding. "Beloved by both the Fae and men. Our moon's a merry wanderer then?"

Felurian shook her head. "not so. a traveler, yes. a wanderer, no. she moves but cannot freely go."

"I heard a story once," I said. "About a man who stole the moon."

Felurian's expression went solemn. She unlaced her fingers from mine and looked down at the stone in her hand. "that was the end of it all." She sighed. "until he stole the moon there was some hope for peace."

I was stunned by the matter-of-fact tone in her voice. "What?" I asked dumbly.

"the stealing of the moon." She cocked her head at me, puzzled. "you said you knew of it."

"I said I'd heard a story," I said. "But it was a silly thing. Not a story of what truly was. It was a f . . . It was the sort of story that you tell a child."

She smiled again. "you may call them faerie stories. I know of them. they are fancies. we tell our children manling tales betimes."

"But the moon was truly stolen?" I asked. "That was no fancy?"

Felurian scowled. "this I have been showing you!" she said, bringing her hand down in an angry splash.

I found myself making the Adem gesture for *apology* below the surface of the water before realizing it was doubly pointless. "I'm sorry," I said. "But without the truth of this story I am lost. I beg of you to tell me it."

"it is an old story, and a sad one." She gave me a long look. "what then will you trade me?"

"The hushed hart," I said.

"in that you give a gift that is a gift to you," she said archly. "what else?"

"I will also make thousand hands," I said, watching her expression soften. "And I will show you something new I have thought of all myself. I call it swaying against the wind."

She crossed her arms and looked away, making a great show of indifference. "new perhaps to you. I doubtless know it by a different name."

"Perhaps," I said. "But if you will not trade you cannot know."

"very well," she conceded with a sigh. "but only because you are quite good at thousand hands."

Felurian looked up at the slender moon for a moment, then said. "long before the cities of man. before men. before fae. there were those who walked with their eyes open. they knew all the deep names of things." She paused and looked at me. "do you know what this means?"

"When you know the name of a thing you have mastery over it," I said.

"no," she said, startling me with the weight of rebuke in her voice. "mastery was *not* given. they had the deep knowing of things. not mastery. to swim is not mastery over the water. to eat an apple is not mastery of the apple." She gave me a sharp look. "do you understand?"

I didn't. But I nodded anyway, not wanting to upset her or sidetrack the story.

"these old name-knowers moved smoothly through the world. they knew the fox and they knew the hare, and they knew the space between the two."

She drew a deep breath and let it out in a sigh. "then came those who saw a thing and thought of changing it. *they* thought in terms of mastery.

"they were shapers. proud dreamers." She made a conciliatory gesture. "and it was not all bad at first. there were wonders." Her face lit with memory and her fingers gripped my arm excitedly. "once, sitting on the walls of murella, I ate fruit from a silver tree. it shone, and in the dark you could mark the mouth and eyes of all those who had tasted it!"

"Was Murella in the Fae?"

Felurian frowned. "no. I have said. this was before. there was but one sky. one moon. one world, and in it was murella. and the fruit. and myself, eating it, eyes shining in the dark."

"How long ago was this?"

She gave a small shrug. "long ago."

Long ago. Longer than any book of history I had ever seen or even heard of. The Archives had copies of Caluptenian histories that went back two millennia, and none of them held the barest whisper of the things Felurian spoke of.

"Forgive my interruption," I said as politely as possible, and made as much of a bow to her as I could without going entirely underwater.

Mollified, she continued, "the fruit was but the first of it. the early toddlings of a child. they grew bolder, braver, wild. the old knowers said 'stop,' but the shapers refused. they quarreled and fought and forbade the shapers. they argued against mastery of this sort." Her eyes brightened. "but oh," she sighed, "the things they made!"

This from a woman weaving me a cloak out of shadow. I couldn't guess what she might marvel at. "What did they make?"

She gestured widely around us.

"Trees?" I asked, awestruck.

She laughed at my tone. "no. the faen realm." she waved widely. "wrought according to their will. the greatest of them sewed it from whole cloth. a place where they could do as they desired. and at the end of all their work, each shaper wrought a star to fill their new and empty sky."

Felurian smiled at me. "*then* there were two worlds. two skies. two sets of stars." She held up the smooth stone. "but still one moon. and it all round and cozy in the mortal sky."

Her smile faded. "but one shaper was greater than the rest. for him the making of a star was not enough. he stretched his will across the world and pulled her from her home."

Lifting the smooth stone to the sky, Felurian carefully closed one eye. She tilted her head as if trying to fit the curve of the stone into the empty arms of the crescent moon above us. "that was the breaking point. the old knowers realized no talk would ever stop the shapers." Her hand dropped back into the water. "he stole the moon and with it came the war."

"Who was it?" I asked.

Her mouth curved into a tiny smile. She hooted: *"who? who?"*

"Was he of the faen courts?" I prompted gently.

Felurian shook her head, amused. "no. as I said, this was before the fae. the first and greatest of the shapers."

"What was his name?"

She shook her head. "no calling of names here. I will not speak of that one, though he is shut beyond the doors of stone."

Before I could ask more questions, Felurian took my hand and nestled the stone between our palms again. "this shaper of the dark and changing eye stretched out his hand against the pure black sky. he pulled the moon, but could not make her stay. so now she moves 'twixt mortal and the fae."

She gave me a solemn look, so rare a thing on her fair face. "you have your tale. your *who* and *how*. there is a final secret now. so all your owlish listening lend." She brought our joined hands back to the surface of the water. "this is the part on which you must attend."

Felurian's eyes were black in the dim light. "the moon has our two worlds beguiled, like parents clutching at a child, pulling at her, to and fro, neither willing to let go."

She stepped away, and we stood as far apart as we could, the stone gripped in our hands. "when she is torn, half in your sky, you see how far apart we lie." Felurian reached toward me with her free hand making futile grasping gestures in the empty water. "no matter how we long to kiss, the space between us is not ripe for this."

Felurian stepped forward and pressed the stone close to my chest. "and when your moon is waxing full, all of faerie feels the pull. she draws us close to you, so bright. and now a visit for a night is easier than walking through a door or stepping off a ship that's near the shore." She smiled at me. " 'twas thus while wandering in the wild, you found Felurian, manling child."

The thought of an entire world of fae creatures drawn close by the swelling moon was troubling. "And this is true of any fae?"

She shrugged and nodded. "have they the will, and know the way. there are a thousand half-cracked doors that lead between my world and yours."

"How have I never heard of this? It seems it would be hard to miss, Fae dancing on the mortal grass. . . ."

She laughed. "but has not just this come to pass? the world is wide and time is long, but still you say you heard my song before you saw me singing there, brushing moonlight through my hair."

I frowned. "Still, it seems I should have seen more signs of those who walk between."

Felurian shrugged. "most fae are sly and subtle folk who step as soft as chimney smoke. some go among your kind enshaedn, glamoured as a pack mule laden, or wearing gowns to fit a queen." She gave me a frank look. "we know enough to not be seen."

She took my hand again. "many of the darker sort would love to use you for their sport. what keeps these from moonlit trespass? iron, fire, mirror-glass. elm and ash and copper knives, solid-hearted farmer's wives who know the rules of games we play and give us bread to keep away. but worst of all, my people dread the portion of our power we shed when we set foot on mortal earth."

"We *are* more trouble than we're worth," I admitted, smiling.

Felurian reached out and touched a finger to my mouth. "while she is full you may still laugh, but know there is a darker half." She spun away to arm's length, pulling me through the water in a slow spiral. "a clever mortal fears the night without a hint of sweet moonlight."

She began to draw my hand to her chest, dragging me through the water toward her as she spun. "on such a night, each step you take might catch you in the dark moon's wake, and pull you all unwitting into fae." She stopped and gave me a grim look. "where you will have no choice but stay."

Felurian took a step backward in the water, tugging at me. "and on such unfamiliar ground, how can a mortal help but drown?"

I took another step toward her and found nothing beneath my feet. Felurian's hand was suddenly no longer clasping mine, and black water closed over my head. Blind and choking, I began to thrash desperately, trying to find my way back to the surface.

After a long, terrifying moment, Felurian's hands caught me and dragged me into the air as if I weighed no more than a kitten. She brought me close to her face, her dark eyes hard and glittering.

When she spoke her voice was clear. "I do this so you cannot help but hear. a wise man views a moonless night with fear."

CHAPTER ONE HUNDRED THREE

Close Enough to Touch

TIME PASSED. FELURIAN TOOK me Dayward to a piece of forest even older and grander than the one that surrounded her twilight glade. There we climbed trees as tall and broad as mountains. In the highest branches, you could feel the vast tree swaying in the wind like a ship on the swelling sea. There, with nothing but the blue sky around us and the slow motion of the tree beneath, Felurian taught me ivy on the oak.

I tried to teach Felurian tak, only to discover she already knew it. She beat me handily, and played a game so lovely Bredon would have wept to look on it.

I learned a bit of the Fae tongue. A small bit. A scattering.

Actually, in the interest of pure honesty, I will admit that I failed miserably in my attempt to learn the Fae language. Felurian was a less than patient teacher, and the language bafflingly complex. My failure went beyond mere incompetence to the point where Felurian actually forbade me from attempting to speak it in her presence.

Overall, I gained a few phrases and a great dollop of humility. Useful things.

Felurian taught me several faen songs. They were harder for me to remember than mortal songs, their melodies slippery and twisting. When I tried to play them on my lute the strings felt strange beneath my fingers, making me fumble and stutter as if I was some country boy who'd never held a lute before. I learned their lyrics by rote, without the least inkling what the words might mean.

Through it all, we continued to work on my shaed. Rather, Felurian worked on it. I asked questions, watched, and tried to avoid feeling like a curious child underfoot in the kitchen. As we grew more comfortable with each other, my questions became more insistent. . . .

"But how?" I asked for the tenth time. "Light hasn't any weight, any substance. It behaves like a wave. You shouldn't be able to touch it."

Felurian had worked her way up from starlight and was wefting moonlight into the shaed. She didn't look up from her work when she replied, "so many thoughts, my kvothe. you know too much to be happy."

That sounded uncomfortably like something Elodin would say. I brushed the evasion aside. "You shouldn't be able—"

She nudged me with her elbow and I saw both her hands were full. "sweet flame," she said, "bring that to me." She nodded to a moonbeam that pierced the trees above and touched the ground beside me.

Her voice bore the familiar, subtle tone of command, and without thinking I grabbed the moonbeam as if it were a hanging vine. For a second I felt it against my fingers, cool and ephemeral. Startled, I froze, and suddenly it was an ordinary moonbeam again. I passed my hand through it several times to no effect.

Smiling, Felurian reached out and took hold of it as if it were the most natural thing in the world. She touched my cheek with her free hand, then turned her attention to her lap and worked the strand of moonlight into the folds of shadow.

The Cthaeh

AFTER FELURIAN HELPED ME discover what I was capable of, I took a more active hand in the creation of my shaed. Felurian seemed pleased at my progress, but I was frustrated. There were no rules to follow, no facts to remember. Because of this, my quick wit and trouper's memory were of little use to me, and my progress seemed irritatingly slow.

Eventually, I could touch my shaed without fear of damaging it and change its shape according to my desire. With some practice I could turn it from a short cape to a full hooded mourning cloak or anything in between.

Still, it would be unfair for me to take even a hair of the credit for its creation. Felurian was the one who gathered the shadow, wove it with moon and fire and daylight. My major contribution was the suggestion that it should have numerous little pockets.

After we took the shaed all the way into daylight, I thought our work was done. My suspicions seemed confirmed when we spent a long stretch of time swimming, singing, and otherwise enjoying each other's company.

But Felurian avoided the topic of the shaed whenever I brought it up. I didn't mind, as her evasions on the subject were always delightful. Because of this, I had the impression some part of it was left unfinished.

One morning we awoke in an embrace, spent perhaps an hour kissing to arouse our appetites, then fell to our breakfast of fruit and fine white bread with honeycomb and olives.

Then Felurian grew serious and asked me for a piece of iron.

Her request surprised me. Some time ago I had thought to resume a few of my mundane habits. Using the surface of the pool as a mirror, I used my small razor to shave. At first Felurian had seemed pleased by my smooth cheeks and chin, but when I moved to kiss her she pushed me to arm's length, snorting as if to clear her nose. She told me I reeked of iron and sent me into the forest telling me not to return until I got the bitter stink of it from my face.

So it was with no small amount of curiosity that I dug a piece of broken iron buckle out of my travelsack. I held it out to her nervously. The way you might hand a child a sharp knife. "Why do you need it?" I asked, trying to appear unconcerned.

Felurian said nothing. She held it tightly between her thumb and two forefingers, as if it were a snake struggling to twist around and bite her. Her mouth made a thin line, and her eyes began to brighten from their customary twilight purple to a deep-water blue.

"Can I help?" I asked.

She laughed. Not the light, chiming laugh I had heard so often, but a wild, fierce laugh. "do you want to help truly?" she asked. The hand holding the shard of iron trembled slightly.

I nodded, a little frightened.

"then go." Her eyes were still changing, brightening to a bluish-white. "I do not need flame now, or songs, or questions." When I didn't move she made a shooing motion. "go to the forest. do not wander far, but do not trouble me for the time it takes to love four times." Her voice had changed slightly too. Though still soft, it had taken on a brittle edge that alarmed me.

I was about to protest when she gave me a terrible look that sent me scampering mindlessly for the trees.

I wandered aimlessly for a while, trying to regain my composure. This was difficult, as I was baby-naked and had been shooed away from the presence of serious magic the way a mother sends a bothersome child away from the cookfire.

Still, I knew I wouldn't be welcome back in the clearing for some time. So I pointed my face Dayward and set off to explore.

I can't say why I wandered so far afield that day. Felurian had warned me to stay close, and I knew it to be good advice. Any of a hundred stories from my childhood told me the danger of wandering in the Fae. Even discounting them, the stories Felurian herself had told should have been enough to keep me close to the safety of her twilight grove.

My natural curiosity must take some of the blame, I suppose. But most of it belongs to my bruised pride. Pride and folly, they go together like two tightly grasping hands.

I walked for the better part of an hour as the sky above me slowly brightened into full daylight. I found a path of sorts, but saw nothing living aside from the occasional butterfly or leaping squirrel.

With every step I took, my mood teetered between boredom and anxiety.

I was in the Fae, after all. I should be seeing marvelous things. Castles of glass. Burning fountains. Bloodthirsty trow. Barefoot old men, eager to give me advice . . .

The trees gave way to a great grassy plain. All the parts of the Fae Felurian had shown me had been forested. So this seemed a clear sign I was well outside the bounds of where I ought to be.

Still I continued, enjoying the feel of sunlight on my skin after so long in the dim twilight of Felurian's glade. The trail I followed seemed to be leading to a lone tree standing in the grassy field. I decided I would go as far as that tree, then head back.

However, after walking for a long while I didn't seem to be coming much closer to the tree. At first I thought this was another oddity of the Fae, but as I continued to make my stubborn way along the path, the truth became clear. The tree was simply larger than I had thought. Much larger and much farther away.

The path did not ultimately lead to the tree. In fact, it curved away from it, avoiding it by more than half a mile. I was considering turning back when a bright flutter of color under the tree's canopy caught my eye. After a brief struggle, my curiosity won out and I stepped off the path into the long grass.

It was no type of tree I had ever seen before, and I approached it slowly. It resembled a vast spreading willow, with broader leaves of a darker green. The tree had deep, hanging foliage scattered with pale, powder-blue blossoms.

The wind shifted, and as the leaves stirred I smelled a strange, sweet smell. It was like smoke and spice and leather and lemon. It was a compelling smell. Not in the same way that food smells appealing. It didn't make my mouth water or my stomach growl. Despite this, if I'd seen something sitting on a table that smelled this way, even if it were a lump of stone or a piece of wood, I would have felt compelled to put it in my mouth. Not out of hunger, but from sheer curiosity, much like a child might.

As I stepped closer I was struck with the beauty of the scene: the deep green of the leaves contrasted with the butterflies flitting from branch to branch, sipping from the pale blossoms of the tree. What I had taken at first to be a bed of flowers beneath the tree turned out to be a carpet of butterflies almost completely covering the ground. The scene was so breathtaking I stopped several dozen feet away from the tree's canopy, not wanting to startle them into flight.

Many of the butterflies flitting among the flowers were purple and black, or blue and black, like those in Felurian's clearing. Others were a solid, vibrant green, or grey and yellow, or silver and blue. But my eye was caught by a single large red one, crimson shot through with a faint tracery of metallic gold. Its wings were bigger than my spread hand, and as I watched it fluttered deeper into the foliage in search of a fresh flower to light upon.

Suddenly, its wings were no longer moving in concert. They tumbled apart and fluttered separately to the ground like falling autumn leaves.

It was only after my eyes followed them to the base of the tree that I saw the truth. The ground below was not a resting place for butterflies . . . it was strewn with lifeless wings. Thousands of them littered the grass beneath the tree's canopy, like a blanket of gemstones.

"The red ones offend my aesthetic," claimed a cool, dry voice from the tree.

I took a step back, trying to peer through the thick canopy of hanging leaves.

"What manners," chided the dry voice. "No introduction? Staring?"

"My apologies, sir," I said earnestly. Then, remembering the tree's flowers, I amended, "Ma'am. But I have never spoken with a tree before and find myself at something of a loss."

"I daresay you are. I am no tree. No more than is a man a chair. I am the Cthaeh. You are fortunate to find me. Many would envy you your chance."

"Chance?" I echoed, trying to catch a glimpse of whatever was speaking to me from among the branches of the tree. A piece of an old story tickled my memory, some scrap of folklore I'd read while searching for the Chandrian. "You're an oracle," I said.

"Oracle. How quaint. Do not try to pin me with small names. I am Cthaeh. I am. I see. I know." Two iridescent blue-black wings fluttered separately where there had been a butterfly before. "At times I speak."

"I thought the red ones offended you?"

"There are no red ones left." The voice was nonchalant. "And the blue ones are ever so slightly sweet." I saw a flicker of movement, and another pair of sapphire wings began spinning slowly to the ground. "You're Felurian's new manling, aren't you?" I hesitated, but the dry voice continued as if I'd answered. "I thought as much. I can smell the iron on you. Just a hint. Still, one has to wonder how she stands it."

A pause. A blur. A slight disturbance of a dozen leaves. Two more wings twitched, then fluttered downward. "Come now," the voice continued, now coming from a different part of the tree, though still hidden by the hanging leaves. "Surely a curious boy is bound to have a question or two. Come. Ask. Your silence much offends me."

I hesitated, then said, "I suppose I might have a question or two."

"*Ahhhh*," the sound was slow and satisfied. "I thought you might."

"What can you tell me of the Amyr?"

"*Kyxxs*," the Cthaeh spat an irritated noise. "What is this? Why so guarded? Why the games? Ask me of the Chandrian and have done."

I stood, stunned and silent.

"Surprised? Why should you be? Goodness boy, you're like a clear pool. I can see ten feet through you, and you're barely three feet deep." There was another blur of motion and two pairs of wings went spinning to the ground, one blue, one purple.

I thought I saw a sinuous motion among the branches, but it was hidden by the endless, wind-brushed swaying of the tree. "Why the purple one?" I asked, simply to have something to say.

"Pure spite," the Cthaeh said. "I envied its innocence, its lack of care. Besides, too much sweetness cloys me. As does willful ignorance." A pause. "You wish to ask me of the Chandrian, do you not?"

I could do nothing but nod.

"Not much to say really," the Cthaeh remarked flippantly. "You would do better to call them the Seven though. 'Chandrian' has so much folklore hanging off it after all these years. The names used to be interchangeable, but nowadays if you say Chandrian people think of ogres and rendlings and scaven. Such silliness."

There was a long pause. I stood motionless until I realized the creature was waiting for a response. "Tell me more," I said. My voice sounded terribly thin to my own ears.

"Why?" I thought I detected a playful note in the voice.

"Because I need to know," I said, trying to force some strength back into my voice.

"Need?" Cthaeh asked skeptically. "Why this sudden need? The masters at the University might know the answers you're looking for. But they wouldn't tell you even if you did ask, which you won't. You're too proud for that. Too clever to ask for help. Too mindful of your reputation."

I tried to speak, but my throat did nothing but make a dry clicking sound. I swallowed and tried again. "Please, I need to know. They killed my parents."

"Are you going to try to kill the Chandrian?" The voice sounded fascinated, almost taken aback. "Track and kill them all yourself? My word, how will you manage it? Haliax has been alive five thousand years. Five thousand years and not one second's sleep.

"Clever to go looking for the Amyr, I suppose. Even one proud as you can recognize the need for help. The Order might give it to you. Trouble is they're as hard to find as the Seven themselves. Oh dear, oh dear. Whatever is a brave young boy to do?"

"Tell me!" I meant to shout it, but it came out pleading.

"It would be frustrating, I suppose," the Cthaeh continued calmly. "The few people who believe in the Chandrian are too afraid to talk, and everyone else will just laugh at you for asking." There was a dramatic sigh that seemed to come from several places in the foliage at once. "That's the price you pay for civilization though."

"What price?" I asked.

"Arrogance," the Cthaeh said. "You assume you know everything. You laughed at faeries until you saw one. Small wonder all your civilized neighbors dismiss the Chandrian as well. You'd have to leave your precious corners far behind before you found someone who might take you seriously. You wouldn't have a hope until you made it to the Stormwal."

There was a pause, then another pair of purple wings went drifting to the ground. I swallowed against the dryness in my throat, trying to think of what question I could ask to get more information.

"Not many folk will take your search for the Amyr seriously, you realize," the Cthaeh continued calmly. "The Maer, however, is quite the extraordinary man. He's already come close to them, though he doesn't realize it. Stick by the Maer and he will lead you to their door."

The Cthaeh gave a thin, dry chuckle. "Blood, bracken, and bone, I wish you creatures had the wit to appreciate me. Whatever else you might forget, remember what I just said. Eventually you'll get the joke. I guarantee. You'll laugh when the time comes."

"What can you tell me about the Chandrian?" I asked.

"Since you ask so sweetly, Cinder is the one you want. Remember him? White hair? Dark eyes? Did things to your mother, you know. Terrible. She held up well though. Laurian was always a trouper, if you'll pardon the expression. Much better than your father, with all his begging and blubbering."

My mind flashed pictures of things I had tried to forget for years. My mother, her hair wet with blood, her arms unnaturally twisted, broken at the wrist, the elbow. My father, his belly cut open, had left a trail of blood for twenty feet. He'd crawled to be closer to her. I tried to speak, but my mouth was dry. "Why?" I managed to croak.

"Why?" the Cthaeh echoed. "What a good question. I know so many whys. Why did they do such nasty things to your poor family? Why, because they wanted to, and because they could, and because they had a reason.

"Why did they leave you alive? Why, because they were sloppy, and because you were lucky, and because something scared them away."

What scared them away? I thought numbly. But it was all too much. The memories, the things the voice said. My mouth worked silently, questioning.

"What?" the Cthaeh asked. "Are you looking for a different why? Are you wondering why I tell you these things? What good comes of it? Maybe this Cinder did me a bad turn once. Maybe it amuses me to set a young pup like you snapping at his heels. Maybe the soft creaking of your tendons as you clench your fists is like a sweet symphony to me. Oh yes it is. And you can be sure.

"Why can't you find this Cinder? Well, that's an interesting why. You'd think a man with coal-black eyes would make an impression when he stops to buy a drink. How can it be that you haven't managed to catch wind of him in all this time?"

I shook my head, trying to clear it of the smell of blood and burning hair.

The Cthaeh seemed to take it as a signal. "That's right, I suppose you don't need me to tell you what he looks like. You've seen him just a day or three ago."

Realization thundered into me. The leader of the bandits. The graceful man in chain mail. Cinder. He was the one who had spoken to me when I was a child. The man with the terrible smile and the sword like winter ice.

"Pity he got away," the Cthaeh continued. "Still, you must admit you've had quite a piece of luck. I'd say it was a twice-in-a-lifetime-opportunity meeting up with him again. Pity you wasted it. Don't feel bad you didn't recognize him. They have a lot of experience hiding those telltale signs. Not your fault at all. It's been a long time. Years. Besides, you've been busy: currying favor, rolling around in the cushions with some piksie, sating your base desires."

Three green butterflies twitched all at once. Their wings looked like leaves as they spun to the ground.

"Speaking of desires, what would your Denna think? My my. Imagine her, seeing you here. You and the piksie all tangled up, at it like rabbits. He beats her, you know. Her patron. Not all the time, but often. Sometimes in a temper, but mostly it's a game to him. How far can he go before she cries? How far can he push before she tries to leave and he has to lure her back again? It's nothing grotesque, mind you. No burns. Nothing that will leave a scar. Not yet.

"Two days ago he used his walking stick. That was new. Welts the size of your thumb under her clothes. Bruises down to the bone. She's trembling on the floor with blood in her mouth and you know what she thinks before the black? You. She thinks of you. You thought of her too, I'm guessing. In between the swimming and strawberries and the rest."

The Cthaeh made a sound like a sigh. "Poor girl, she's tied to him so tight. Thinks that's all she's good for. Wouldn't leave him even if you asked. Which you won't. You, so careful. So scared of startling her away. And well you should be too. She's a runner, that one. Now that she's left Severen, how can you hope to find her?

"It is a shame you left without a word, you know. She was just beginning to trust you before that. Before you got angry. Before you ran off. Just like every other man in her life. Just like every other man. Lusting after her, full of sweet words, then just walking away. Leaving her alone. Good thing she's used to it by now, isn't it? Otherwise you might have hurt her. Otherwise you just might have broken that poor girl's heart."

It was all too much. I turned and ran, pelting madly back the way I had come. Back to the quiet twilight of Felurian's clearing. Away. Away. Away.

And as I ran I could hear Cthaeh speaking behind me. Its dry, quiet voice followed me longer than I would have thought possible. "Come back. Come back. I've more to say. I've so much more to tell you, won't you stay?"

———————

It was hours before I came back to Felurian's clearing. I'm not sure how I found my way. I only remember being surprised at the sight of her pavilion through the trees. The sight of it slowed the mad spinning of my thoughts until I could begin to think again.

I went to the pool and took a long, deep drink, splashing water on my face to clear my head and hide the signs of tears. After a moment or two of quiet reflection, I stood and walked to the pavilion. It was only then that I noticed a curious lack of butterflies. There were usually at least a handful flitting around, but now there were none.

Felurian was there, but the sight of her only unsettled me further. It was the only time I had ever seen her look less than perfectly beautiful. She lay among the cushions, drawn and weary. As if I had been gone for days instead of hours, and she had not eaten or slept all the while.

She lifted her head tiredly when she heard me approach. "it is done," she said, but when she looked at me her eyes widened with surprise.

I looked down and saw that I was bramble-torn and bloody. I was spattered with mud and grass stained along my entire left side. I must have fallen during my mindless flight away from the Cthaeh.

Felurian sat upright. "what has come of you?"

I brushed absently at a bit of dried blood on my elbow. "I might ask the same of you." My voice sounded thick and coarse, as if I had been shouting. When I looked up I saw real concern in her eyes. "I went walking Dayward. I found something in a tree. It called itself a Cthaeh."

Felurian went motionless when I spoke its name. "the Cthaeh? did you speak?"

I nodded.

"did you ask of it?" But before I could answer she gave a quiet, despairing cry and rushed to me. She began to run her hands over my body, as if searching for wounds. After a minute of this she took my face in her hands and looked into my eyes as if frightened of what she might find there. "are you well?"

Her concern brought a faint smile to my lips. I began to assure her that I was fine—then I remembered the things the Cthaeh had said. I remembered the fires and the man with ink-black eyes. I thought of Denna sprawled on the floor with a mouthful of blood. Tears came to my eyes and I choked. I turned away and shook my head, eyes clenched shut and unable to speak.

She stroked the back of my neck and said, "all is well. the hurt will go. it has not bit you, and your eyes are clear, so all is well."

I pulled away from her enough to look her in the face. "My eyes?"

"the things the Cthaeh says can leave men broken in their heads. but I would see if it were so. you are still my kvothe, still my sweet poet." She leaned forward, oddly hesitant, then gave me a gentle kiss on my forehead.

"It lies to men and drives them mad?"

She shook her head slowly, "the Cthaeh does not lie. it has the gift of seeing, but it only tells things to hurt men. only a dennerling would speak to the Cthaeh." She touched the side of my neck to soften her words.

I nodded, knowing it to be the truth. And I began to cry.

CHAPTER ONE HUNDRED FIVE

Interlude—A Certain Sweetness

KVOTHE MOTIONED FOR CHRONICLER to stop writing. "Are you all right, Bast?" He gave his student a look of concern. "You look like you've swallowed a lump of iron."

Bast did look stricken. His face was pale, almost waxy. His normally cheerful expression was aghast. "Reshi," he said, his voice as dry as autumn leaves. "You never told me you spoke with the Cthaeh."

"There's a lot of things I've never told you, Bast," Kvothe said flippantly. "That's why you find the sordid details of my life so enthralling."

Bast gave a sickly smile, shoulders sagging with relief. "You didn't really, then. Talk with it, I mean? It's something you just added to make things a little more colorful?"

"Please, Bast," Kvothe said, obviously offended. "My story has quite enough color without my adding to it."

"Don't lie to me!" Bast shouted suddenly, coming halfway out of his seat with the force of it. "Don't you lie to me about this! Don't you *dare!*" Bast struck the table with one hand, toppling his mug and sending Chronicler's inkwell skittering across the table.

Quick as blinking, Chronicler snatched up the half-covered sheet of paper and pushed his chair back from the table with his feet, saving the sheet from the sudden spray of ink and beer.

Bast leaned forward, his face livid as he stabbed a finger at Kvothe. "I don't care what other shit you spin into gold here! But you don't lie about this, Reshi! Not to me!"

Kvothe gestured to where Chronicler sat, holding the pristine sheet of paper in the air with both hands. "Bast," he said. "This is my chance to tell the full and honest story of my life. Everything is—"

Bast closed his eyes and pounded the table like a child in the grip of a tantrum. "Shut up. Shut up! *SHUT UP!*"

Bast pointed at Chronicler. "I don't give a fiddler's fuck what you tell him, Reshi. He'll write what I say or I'll eat his heart in the market square!" He turned the finger back to the innkeeper and shook it furiously. "But you'll tell *me* the truth and you'll tell me *now!*"

Kvothe looked up at his student, the amusement bleeding out of his face. "Bast, we both know I'm not above the occasional embellishment. But this story is different. This is my chance to get the truth of matters recorded. It's the truth behind the stories."

The dark young man hunched forward in his chair and covered his eyes with one hand.

Kvothe looked at him, his face full of concern. "Are you alright?"

Bast shook his head, still covering his eyes.

"Bast," Kvothe said gently. "Your hand is bleeding." He waited a long moment before asking, "Bast, what's the matter?"

"That's just it!" Bast burst out, throwing his arms wide, his voice high and hysterical. "I think I finally understand what the matter is!"

Bast laughed then, but it was loud and strained, and choked off into something that sounded like a sob. He looked up at the rafters of the taproom, his eyes bright. He blinked, as if fighting back tears.

Kvothe leaned forward to lay his hand on the young man's shoulder. "Bast, please . . ."

"It's just that you know so many things," Bast said. "You know all sorts of things you're not supposed to. You know about the Berentaltha. You know about the white sisters and the laughing-way. How can you not know about the Cthaeh? It's . . . it's a monster."

Kvothe relaxed visibly. "Good Lord, Bast, is that all? You had me all in a sweat. I've faced down things far worse than—"

"There isn't anything worse than the Cthaeh!" Bast shouted, bringing his clenched fist down on the tabletop again. This time there was the sharp sound of tearing wood as one of the thick timbers bowed and cracked. "Reshi, shut up and listen. Really listen." Bast looked down for a moment, choosing his words carefully. "You know who the Sithe are?"

Kvothe shrugged. "They're a faction among the Fae. Powerful, with good intentions—"

Bast waved his hands. "You don't understand them if you use the term 'good intentions.' But if any of the Fae can be said to work for the good, it's them. Their oldest and most important charge is to keep the Cthaeh from having any contact with anyone. With *anyone.*"

"I didn't see any guards," Kvothe said in the tones a man might use to soothe a skittish animal.

Bast ran his hands through his hair, leaving it in disarray. "I can't for all the salt in me guess how you slipped past them, Reshi. If anyone manages to come in contact with the Cthaeh, the Sithe kill them. They kill them from a half-mile off with their long horn bows. Then they leave the body to rot. If a crow so much as lands on the body, they kill it too."

Chronicler cleared his throat gently, then spoke up. "If what you're saying is true," he asked, "why would anyone go to the Cthaeh?"

Bast looked for a moment as if he would snap at the scribe, then gave a bitter sigh instead. "In all fairness, my people are not known for making good decisions," he said. "Every Fae girl and boy knows the Cthaeh's nature, but there's always someone eager to seek it out. Folk go to it for answers or a glimpse of the future. Or they hope to come away with a flower."

"A flower?" Kvothe asked.

Bast gave him another startled look. "The Rhinna?" Not seeing any recognition in the innkeeper's face he shook his head in dismay. "The flowers are a panacea, Reshi. They can heal any illness. Cure any poison. Mend any wound."

Kvothe raised his eyebrows at that. "Ah," he said, looking down at his folded hands on the tabletop. "I see. I can understand how that might draw a person in, though they knew better."

The innkeeper looked up. "I have to admit I don't see the trouble," he said apologetically. "I've seen monsters, Bast. The Cthaeh falls short of that."

"That was the wrong word for me to use, Reshi," Bast admitted. "But I can't think of a better one. If there was a word that meant poisonous and hateful and contagious, I'd use that."

Bast drew a deep breath and leaned forward in his chair. "Reshi, the Cthaeh can see the future. Not in some vague, oracular way. It sees *all* the future. Clearly. Perfectly. Everything that can possibly come to pass, branching out endlessly from the current moment."

Kvothe raised an eyebrow. "It can, can it?"

"It can," Bast said gravely. "And it is purely, perfectly malicious. This isn't a problem for the most part, as it can't leave the tree. But when someone comes to visit . . ."

Kvothe's eyes went distant as he nodded to himself. "If it knows the future perfectly," he said slowly, "then it must know exactly how a person will react to anything it says."

Bast nodded. "And it is vicious, Reshi."

Kvothe continued in a musing tone. "That means anyone influenced by the Cthaeh would be like an arrow shot into the future."

"An arrow only hits one person, Reshi." Bast's dark eyes were hollow and hopeless. "Anyone influenced by the Cthaeh is like a plague ship sailing for a harbor." Bast pointed at the half-filled sheet Chronicler held in his lap. "If the Sithe knew that existed, they would spare no effort to destroy it. They would kill us for having heard what the Cthaeh said."

"Because anything carrying the Cthaeh's influence away from the tree . . ." Kvothe said, looking down at his hands. He sat silently for a long moment, nodding thoughtfully. "So a young man seeking his fortune goes to the Cthaeh and takes away a flower. The daughter of the king is deathly ill, and he takes the flower to heal her. They fall in love despite the fact that she's betrothed to the neighboring prince . . ."

Bast stared at Kvothe, watching blankly as he spoke.

"They attempt a daring moonlight escape," Kvothe continued. "But he falls from the rooftops and they're caught. The princess is married against her will and stabs the neighboring prince on their wedding night. The prince dies. Civil war. Fields burned and salted. Famine. Plague . . ."

"That's the story of the Fastingsway War," Bast said faintly.

Kvothe nodded. "It's one of the stories Felurian told. I never understood the part about the flower until now. She never mentioned the Cthaeh."

"She wouldn't have, Reshi. It's considered bad luck." He shook his head. "No, not bad luck. It's like spitting poison in someone's ear. It simply isn't done."

Chronicler recovered some of his composure and slid his chair back toward the table, still holding the sheet carefully. He frowned at the table, broken and streaked with beer and ink. "It seems like this creature has quite a reputation," he said. "But I find it hard to believe it's quite as dangerous as all that. . . ."

Bast looked at Chronicler incredulously. "Iron and bile," he said, his voice quiet. "Do you think I'm a child? You think I don't know the difference between a campfire story and the truth?"

Chronicler made a mollifying gesture with one hand. "That's not what I . . ."

Without taking his eyes from Chronicler, Bast laid his bloody palm flat on the table. The wood groaned and the broken timbers snapped back into place with a sudden crackling sound. Bast lifted his hand, then brought it down sharply on the table, and the dark runnels of ink and beer suddenly twisted and shaped themselves into a jet-black crow that burst into flight, circling the taproom once.

Bast caught it with both hands and tore the bird carelessly in half, casting the pieces into the air where they exploded into great washes of flame the color of blood.

It all happened in the space of a single breath. "Everything you know about the Fae could fit inside a thimble," Bast said, looking at the scribe with no expression at all, his voice flat and even. "How dare you doubt me? You have no idea who I am."

Chronicler sat very still, but he did not look away.

"I swear it by my tongue and teeth," Bast said crisply. "I swear it on the doors of stone. I am telling you three thousand times. There is nothing in my world or yours more dangerous than the Cthaeh."

"There's no need for that, Bast," Kvothe said softly. "I believe you."

Bast turned to look at Kvothe, then sagged miserably in his chair. "I wish you didn't, Reshi."

Kvothe gave a wry smile. "So after a person meets the Cthaeh, all their choices will be the wrong ones."

Bast shook his head, his face pale and drawn. "Not wrong, Reshi, catastrophic. Iax spoke to the Cthaeh before he stole the moon, and that sparked the entire creation war. Lanre spoke to the Cthaeh before he orchestrated the betrayal of Myr Tariniel. The creation of the Nameless. The Scaendyne. They can all be traced back to the Cthaeh."

Kvothe's expression went blank. "Well, that certainly puts me in interesting company, doesn't it?" he said dryly.

"It does more than that, Reshi," Bast said. "In our plays, if the Cthaeh's tree is shown in the distance in the backdrop, you know the story is going to be the worst kind of tragedy. It's put there so the audience knows what to expect. So they know everything will go terribly wrong in the end."

Kvothe looked at Bast for a long moment. "Oh Bast," he said softly to his student. His smile was gentle and sad. "I know what sort of story I'm telling. This is no comedy."

Bast looked up at him with hollow, hopeless eyes. "But Reshi . . ." His mouth moved, trying to find words and failing.

The red-haired innkeeper gestured at the empty taproom. "This is the end of the story, Bast. We all know that." Kvothe's voice was matter-of-fact, as casual as if he were describing yesterday's weather. "I have led an interesting life, and this reminiscence has a certain sweetness to it. But . . ."

Kvothe drew a deep breath and let it out gently. ". . . but this is not a dashing romance. This is no fable where folk come back from the dead. It's not a rousing epic meant to stir the blood. No. We all know what kind of story this is."

It seemed for a moment that he would continue, but instead his eyes wandered idly around the empty taproom. His face was calm, without a trace of anger or bitterness.

Bast darted a look at Chronicler, but this time there was no fire in it. No anger. No fury or command. Bast's eyes were desperate, pleading.

"It's not over if you're still here," Chronicler said. "It's not a tragedy if you're still alive."

Bast nodded eagerly at this, looking back at Kvothe.

Kvothe looked at both of them for a moment, then smiled and chuckled low in his chest. "Oh," he said fondly. "You're both so young."

CHAPTER ONE HUNDRED SIX

Returning

AFTER MY ENCOUNTER WITH the Cthaeh, it was a long time before I was my right self again.

I slept a great deal, but only fitfully as I was endlessly set upon by terrible dreams. Some of them were vivid and impossible to forget. These were mostly of my mother, my father, my troupe. Worse were the ones where I woke weeping with no memory of what I'd dreamed, only an aching chest and an emptiness in my head like the bloody gap left by a missing tooth.

The first time I awoke like this, Felurian was there, watching me. Her expression was so gentle and worried that I expected her to murmur softly to me and stroke my hair, as Auri had done in my room months ago.

But Felurian did nothing of the sort. "are you well?" she asked.

I had no answer for this. I was blurry with memory, confusion, and grief. Not trusting myself to speak without bursting into tears again, I merely shook my head.

Felurian bent down and kissed me on the corner of my mouth, looked at me for a long moment, and sat back up. Then she went to the pool and brought me back a drink of water in her cupped hands.

Over the following days Felurian did not press me with questions or try to draw me out. She occasionally tried to tell me stories, but I couldn't focus on them, so they made less sense than ever. Some parts made me weep uncontrollably, though the stories themselves had nothing in them that was sad.

Once I woke to find her gone, only to have her return hours later carrying a strange green fruit bigger than my head. She smiled shyly and handed it to me, showing me how to peel off the thin leathery skin to reveal the orange meat inside. Pulpy and tangy-sweet, it pulled apart in spiraling segments.

We ate these silently, until nothing was left but a round, hard, slippery seed.

It was dark brown and so big I could not close my hand around it. With a slight flourish, Felurian cracked this open against a rock and showed me that the inside was dry, like a roasted nut. We ate this too. It tasted dark and peppery, vaguely reminiscent of smoked salmon.

Nestled inside that was another seed, white as bone and the size of a marble. This Felurian gave to me. It was candy-sweet and slightly gummy, like a caramel.

One time she left me alone for endless hours, only to return with two brown birds, one carefully cupped in each hand. They were smaller than sparrows, with striking, leaf-green eyes. She set them down next to where I lay on the cushions, and when she whistled, they began to sing. Not snippets of birdsong, they sang an actual song. Four verses with a chorus between. First they sang together, then in a simple harmony.

Once I woke and she gave me a drink in a leather cup. It smelled of violets and tasted of nothing at all, but it was clear and warm and clean in my mouth, like I was drinking summer sunlight.

Another time she gave me a smooth red stone that was warm in my hand. After several hours it hatched like an egg, revealing a creature like a tiny squirrel that chittered angrily at me before running away.

Once I woke and she was not nearby. Looking around I saw her sitting on the edge of the water, arms wrapped around her knees. I could barely hear the gentle song of her sobbing quietly to herself.

I slept and I woke. She gave me a ring made from a leaf, a cluster of golden berries, a flower that opened and closed at the stroking of a finger. . . .

And once, when I startled awake with my face wet and my chest aching, she reached out to lay her hand on top of mine. The gesture was so tentative, her expression so anxious, you would think she had never touched a man before. As if she was worried I might break or burn or bite. Her cool hand lay on mine for a moment, gentle as a moth. She squeezed my hand softly, waited, then pulled away.

It struck me as odd at the time. But I was too clouded with confusion and grief to think clearly. Only now, looking back, do I realize the truth of things. With all the awkwardness of a young lover, she was trying to comfort me, and she didn't have the slightest idea how.

———————

Still, all things mend with time. My dreams receded. My appetite returned. I grew clearheaded enough to banter with Felurian a bit. Shortly after that, I recovered enough to flirt. When this happened, her relief was palpable, as if she couldn't relate to a creature that did not want to kiss her.

Last came my curiosity, the surest sign I was my own true self again. "I never asked you how went your final workings with the shaed," I said.

Her face lit. "it is done!" I could see the pride in her eyes. She took my hand and pulled me to the edge of the pavilion. "the iron was not an easy thing, but it is done." She started forward, then stopped herself. "can you find it?"

I took a long, careful look around. Even though she'd taught me what to look for, it was a long moment before I spotted a subtle depth in the darkness of a nearby tree. I reached out and drew my shaed from the concealing shadow.

Felurian skipped to my side, laughing as if I had just won a game. She caught me around the neck and kissed me with the wildness of a dozen children.

She had never let me wear the shaed before, and I marveled as she spread it over my naked shoulders. It was nearly weightless and softer than the richest velvet. It felt like wearing a warm breeze, the same breeze that had brushed me in the darkened forest glade where Felurian had taken me to gather the shadows.

I thought of going to the forest pool to see how I looked in the water's reflection, but Felurian threw herself onto me. Bearing me to the ground, she landed astride me, my shaed spread beneath us like a thick blanket. She gathered the edges of it around us, then kissed my chest, my neck. Her tongue was hot against my skin.

"this way," she said against my ear, "whenever your shaed wraps you, you will think of me. when it touches you it will seem like my touch." She moved slowly against me, rubbing the length of her naked body along mine. "through all the other women you will remember Felurian, and you will return."

———

After that I knew my time in the Fae was drawing to a close. The Cthaeh's words stuck in my mind like burrs, goading me out into the world. The fact that I had been within a stone's throw of the man who had killed my parents and not realized it left a bitter taste in my mouth that even Felurian's kisses could not erase. And what the Cthaeh had said of Denna kept playing over and over in my head.

Eventually I awoke and knew the time had come. I rose, put my travelsack in order, and dressed for the first time in ages. The feeling of clothes against my skin felt odd after all this time. How long had I been gone? I brushed my fingers through my beard and shrugged the thought away. Guessing was pointless when I would know the answer soon enough.

Turning, I saw Felurian standing in the center of the pavilion, her expression sad. For a moment I thought she might protest my leaving, but she did nothing of the sort. Moving to my side, she fastened the shaed around my shoulders, reminding me of a mother dressing her child against the cold. Even the butterflies that followed her seemed melancholy.

She led me through the forest for hours until we came to a pair of tall greystones. She drew up the hood of my shaed and bid me close my eyes. Then she led me in a brief circle and I felt a subtle change in the air. When I opened my eyes I could tell this forest was not the same one I had been walking through a moment before. The strange tension in the air was gone. This was the mortal world.

I turned to Felurian. "My lady," I said. "I have nothing to give you before I go."

"except your promise to return." Her voice was lily soft, with a whisper of a warning.

I smiled. "I mean I have nothing to leave you with, lady."

"except remembrance." She leaned close.

Closing my eyes, I bid her farewell with few words and many kisses.

Then I left. I would like to say I did not look back, but that would not be the truth. The sight of her almost broke my heart. She seemed so very small beside the huge grey stones. I almost went back to give one final kiss, one last good-bye.

But I knew if I went back, I would never manage to leave again. Somehow I kept walking.

When I looked back the second time, she was gone.

Fire

I CAME TO THE PENNYSWORTH Inn long after the sun had set. The huge inn's windows swelled with lamplight and there were a dozen horses tethered outside, champing into their feed bags. The door was open, casting a slant square of light into the dark street.

But something was wrong. There was none of the pleasant rousing clamor that should be coming from a busy inn at night. Not a whisper. Not a word.

Anxious, I crept closer. Every faerie tale I'd ever heard was running through my head. Had I been gone years? Decades?

Or was it more ordinary trouble? Had there been more bandits than we thought? Had they returned to find their camp destroyed, then come here to make trouble?

I slid close to a window, peered inside, and saw the truth.

There were forty or fifty people in the inn. They sat at tables and benches and lined up at the bar. Every eye was pointed at the hearth.

Marten sat there, taking a long drink. "I couldn't look away," he continued. "I didn't want to. Then Kvothe stepped in front of me, blocking the sight of her, and for a second I was free of her spell. I was covered in a sweat so thick and cold it felt like someone had thrown a bucket of water over me. I tried to pull him back, but he shook me off and ran to her." Marten's expression was lined with regret.

"How come she didn't get the Adem and the big one too?" asked a man with a hawkish face sitting nearby on the corner of the hearth. He drummed his fingers on a battered fiddle case. "If you'd *really* seen her, you all would have run off after her."

There was a murmur of agreement from the room.

Tempi spoke up from a nearby table, his blood-red shirt making him easy to spot. "When I was growing, I train to have control." He held up a hand and made a tight fist to illustrate his point. "Hurt. Hungry. Thirsty. Tired." He shook his fist after each of these to show his mastery over it. "Women." The faintest of smiles touched his face and he shook his fist again, but with none of the firmness he had used before. A murmur of laughter ran through the room. "I say this. If Kvothe did not go, I may."

Marten nodded. "As for our other friend . . ." He cleared his throat and gestured across the room. "Hespe convinced him to stay." There was more laughter at this. After a moment of searching I spied where Dedan and Hespe sat. Dedan seemed to be fighting down a furious blush. Hespe rested a hand possessively on his leg. She smiled a private, satisfied smile.

"The next day we looked for him," Marten said, regaining the room's attention. "We followed his trail through the woods. We found his sword half a mile from the pool. No doubt he lost it in his haste to catch her. His cloak hung from a branch not far from there."

Marten lifted up the threadbare cloak I had bought from the tinker. It looked like it had been savaged by a mad dog. "It was caught on a branch. He must have torn free rather than lose sight of her." He idly fingered the ripped edges. "If it had been made of stronger stuff he might still be with us here tonight."

I know my cue when I hear it. I stepped through the doorway and felt everyone turn to look at me. "I have found a better cloak since," I said. "Made by Felurian's own hand. And I have a story too. One you will be telling your children's children." I smiled.

There was a moment of silence, then an uproar as everyone began to speak at once.

My companions stared at me in stunned disbelief. Dedan was the first to recover, and after making his way to where I stood, surprised me with a rough, one-armed embrace. Only then did I notice one of his arms was hanging from his neck in a splint.

I gave it a questioning look. "Did you run into trouble?" I asked while the room buzzed chaotically around us.

Dedan shook his head. "Hespe," he said simply. "She didn't take too kindly to the thought of me running off after that faerie woman. She sort of . . . convinced me to stay."

"She broke your arm?" I remembered my parting glimpse of Hespe holding him to the ground.

The big man looked down at his feet. "A bit. She sort of held onto it while I tried to twist away." He gave a slightly sheepish smile. "I guess you could say we broke it together."

I clapped him on his good shoulder and laughed. "That's sweet. Truly touching." I would have continued, but the room had quieted. Everyone was watching us, watching me.

As I looked at the crowd of people, I felt suddenly disoriented. How can I explain. . . ?

I've already told you I don't know how much time I spent in the Fae. But it had been a long, long while. I had lived there so long, that the strangeness of it had faded. I'd grown comfortable there.

Now that I was back in the mortal world, this crowded taproom seemed strange to me. How odd to be indoors, rather than under the naked sky. The thick-timbered wooden benches and tables looked so primitive and rough. The lamplight seemed unnaturally bright and harsh to my eyes.

I'd had no company but Felurian for ages, and the people around me seemed strange by comparison. The whites of their eyes were startling. They smelled like sweat and horses and bitter iron. Their voices were hard and sharp. Their postures stiff and awkward.

But that only scratches the bare surface of it. I felt out of place in my own skin. It was profoundly irritating to be wearing clothes again, and I wanted nothing more than to be comfortably naked. My boots felt like a prison. On my long walk to the Pennysworth, I'd had to constantly fight the urge to remove them.

Looking at the faces around me, I saw a young woman of no more than twenty. She had a sweet face and clear blue eyes. She had a perfect mouth for kissing. I took half a step towards her, fully intending to catch her up in my arms and . . .

I stopped suddenly, just as I began to reach out with one hand to caress the side of her neck, and my head spun with something very close to vertigo. Things were different here. The man sitting beside the woman was obviously her husband. That was important, wasn't it? It seemed a very vague and distant fact. Why wasn't I already kissing this woman? Why wasn't I naked, eating violets, and playing music underneath the open sky?

Looking around the room again, everything seemed terribly ridiculous. These people sitting on their benches, wearing layers on layers of clothing, eating with knives and forks. It all struck me as so pointless and contrived. It was incredibly funny. It was like they were playing a game and didn't even realize it. It was like a joke I'd never understood before.

And so I laughed. It wasn't loud or particularly long, but it was high and wild and full of strange delight. It was no human laugh, and it moved through the crowd like wind among the wheat. Those near enough to hear it shifted in their seats, some looking at me with curiosity, some with fear. Some shivered and refused to meet my eye.

Seeing their reaction shook me, and I made an effort to get a grip on myself. I drew a deep breath and closed my eyes. The moment of strange disorientation passed, though my boots still felt hard and heavy on my feet.

When I opened my eyes again, I saw Hespe looking up at me. She spoke hesitantly. "Kvothe," she said hesitantly. "You look . . . well."

I smiled wide. "I am."

"We thought you were . . . lost."

"You thought I was gone," I corrected gently as I made my way to the fireplace where Marten stood. "Dead in Felurian's arms or wandering the forest, mad and broken with desire." I looked at them each in turn. "Isn't that right?"

I felt the whole room's eyes on me and decided to make the most of the situation. "Come now, I am Kvothe. I am Edema Ruh born. I have studied at the University and can call down lightning like Taborlin the Great. Did you really think Felurian would be the death of me?"

"She would be," said a rough voice from the edge of the hearth. "If you had ever so much as seen her shadow."

I turned to see the hawk-faced fiddler. "I beg your pardon, sir?"

"You should beg the pardon of everyone here," he said, his voice dripping with disdain. "I don't know what you hope to gain from this, but I don't believe the lot of you saw Felurian, not for a second."

I met his eyes. "I did more than see her, friend."

"If that were true, then you'd be mad now, or dead. And while I'll admit you might be mad, it's not from any faerie charm." The room chuckled at this. "No one has seen her in a score of years. The fair folk have left this place behind, and you're no Taborlin, no matter what your friends say. I'm guessin' you're just a clever storyteller hopin' to make a name for himself."

That struck uncomfortably close to the mark, and I could see some of the crowd eyeing me skeptically.

Before I could say anything Dedan burst in. "What about his beard then? When he ran off three nights ago his face was smooth as a baby's ass."

"So *you* say," the fiddler replied. "I was going to keep quiet even though I didn't believe half what you told us about those bandits or him calling the lightning. But I thought to myself, 'Their friend probably died and they want folks to remember him with a proud story or two.'"

He looked down his broken nose to where Dedan sat. "But *really*, this has gone too far. It's not wise to tell lies about the fair folk. I don't appreciate strangers coming here and spinning my friends' heads full of nonsense. Be quiet, the lot of you. We've heard enough out of you tonight."

Having said his piece, the fiddler opened the battered case that sat next to him and drew out his instrument. The mood of the room had grown vaguely hostile by this point, and more than a few people eyed me resentfully.

Dedan sputtered angrily. "Now listen h—" Hespe said something and tried to pull him down into his seat, but Dedan shook her off. "No. I won't be called a liar. We were sent here by Alveron himself because of them bandits. And we did our job. We're not expecting a parade, but I'll be damned before I let you call me a liar. We killed those bastards. And afterward we did see Felurian. And Kvothe there did take off after her."

Dedan glared around the room belligerently, mostly in the direction of the fiddler. "That's the truth and I swear it by my good right hand. If anyone wants to call me a liar we can have it out right now."

The fiddler picked up his bow and met Dedan's eye. He drew a screaming note across the strings. "Liar."

Dedan nearly leapt across the room as people pushed their chairs back to make a clear space for the fight. The fiddler came to his feet slowly. He was taller than I'd expected, with short grey hair and scarred knuckles that told me he knew his way around a fistfight.

I managed to get in front of Dedan and leaned against him, speaking low in his ear, "Do you really want to brawl with a broken arm? If he gets hold of it, you'll just scream and piss yourself in front of Hespe." I felt him relax a bit and gave him a gentle push back toward his seat. He went, but he wasn't happy.

". . . something here." I heard a woman say behind me. "If you want to have a scuff with someone you take it outside and don't bother coming back. You don't get paid to fight the customers. You hear?"

"Now Penny," the fiddler said soothingly. "I was just showin' some teeth to him. He's the one took it all personal. You can't blame me for makin' fun with the sort of stories they come in with."

I turned around and saw the fiddler explaining himself to an angry woman in her middle years. She was a full foot shorter than him, and had to reach up to jab his chest with a finger.

That's when I heard a voice exclaim to one side of me, "God's mother, Seb. You see that? Look at it! It's movin' by itself."

"You're blind drunk. It's just a breeze."

"There ain't no wind in tonight. It's moving itself. Look again!"

It was my shaed, of course. By now several people had noticed it blowing gently in a breeze that wasn't there. I thought the effect was rather nice, but

I could tell by their wide eyes that folk were becoming alarmed. One or two slid their chairs away from me uneasily.

Penny's eyes were fixed on my gently flowing shaed, and she walked over to stand in front of me. "What is it?" she asked, her voice showing just a hint of fear.

"Nothing to worry over," I said easily, holding out a fold of it for her inspection. "It is my shadow cloak. Felurian made it for me."

The fiddler made a disgusted noise.

Penny shot him a look and hesitantly brushed my cloak with a hand. "It's soft," she murmured, looking up at me. When our eyes met she looked surprised for a moment, then exclaimed, "You're Losi's boy!"

Before I could ask what she meant, I heard a woman's voice say, "What?" I turned to see a red-haired serving girl moving toward us. The same one who had embarrassed me so badly on our first visit to the Pennysworth.

Penny nodded toward me. "It's your fresh-faced fiery boy from about three span back! You remember pointing him out to me? I didn't recognize him with the beard."

Losi came to stand in front of me. Bright red curls tumbled over the bare, pale skin of her shoulders. Her dangerous green eyes swept over my shaed and made their slow way up to my face. "It's him all right," she said sideways to Penny. "Beard or no."

She took a step closer, almost pressing against me. "Boys are always wearing beards and hoping it will make them men." Her bright emerald eyes settled boldly onto mine as if expecting me to blush and fumble about as I had before.

I thought of everything I'd learned at the hands of Felurian, and felt the strange, wild laughter welling up in me again. I fought it down as best I could, but I could feel it tumbling around inside me as I met her eye and smiled.

Losi took a startled half-step back, her pale skin blushing to a furious red.

Penny held out a hand to steady her. "Lord girl, what's the matter with you?"

Losi tore her eyes away from me. "Look at him Penny, really look at him. He's got a fae look about him. Look at his eyes."

Penny looked curiously at my face, then flushed a bit herself and crossed her arms in front of her chest, as if I had seen her naked. "Merciful lord," she said breathlessly. "It's all true, then. Isn't it?"

"Every word," I said.

"How did you get away from her?" Penny asked.

"Oh come on, Penny!" the fiddler cried out in disbelief. "You aren't buyin' this pup's story, are ya?"

Losi turned and spoke hotly. "There's a look a man has when he knows his way around a woman, Ben Crayton. Not that you would know. When this one was here a couple span ago I liked his face and thought I'd have a roll with him. But when I tried to trip him . . ." She trailed off, seemingly at a loss for words.

"I remember that," a man at the bar called out. "Funniest damn thing. I thought he was gonna piss himself. He couldn't say a word to her."

The fiddler shrugged. "So he found some farmer's daughter since then. It don't mean . . ."

"Hush Ben," Penny said with quiet authority. "There's more changed here than a bit of beard can account for." Her eyes searched my face. "Lord but you're right, girl. There is a fae look about him." The fiddler started to speak again but Penny shot him a sharp look. "Hush or get out. I don't want any fights in here tonight."

The fiddler looked around the room and saw the tide had turned against him. Red-faced and scowling, he gathered up his fiddle and stormed out.

Losi stepped close to me again, brushing her hair back. "Was she really as beautiful as they say?" Her chin went up proudly. "More beautiful than me?"

I hesitated, then spoke softly. "She was Felurian, most beautiful of all." I reached out to brush the side of her neck where her red hair began its curling tumble downward, then leaned forward and whispered seven words into her ear. "For all that, she lacked your fire." And she loved me for those seven words, and her pride was safe.

Penny spoke up. "How did you manage to get away?"

I looked around the room and felt everyone's attention settle onto me. The wild, fae laughter tumbled around inside me. I smiled a lazy smile. My shaed billowed.

Then I moved to the front of the room, sat on the hearth, and told them the story.

Or rather, I told them *a* story. If I'd told them the entire truth they wouldn't have believed it. Felurian let me go because I was holding a song hostage? It simply didn't fit the classic lines.

So what I told them was closer to the story they expected to hear. In that story, I chased Felurian into the Fae. Our bodies tangled together in her twilight glade. Then, as we rested, I played her music light enough to make her laugh, music dark enough to make her gasp, music sweet enough to make her weep.

But when I tried to leave the Fae, she would not let me. She was too fond of my . . . artistry.

I shouldn't be coy, I suppose. I implied rather strongly that Felurian thought quite highly of me as a lover. I offer no apology for this behavior except to say that I was a young man of sixteen, proud of my newfound skills, and not above a little bragging.

I told them how Felurian had tried to trap me in the Fae, how we fought with magic. For this I borrowed a little from Taborlin the Great. There was fire and lightning.

At the end I bested Felurian but spared her life. In her gratitude she wove me a faerie cloak, taught me secret magics, and gave me a silver leaf as a token of her favor. The leaf was pure fabrication, of course. But it wouldn't have been a proper story if she hadn't given me three gifts.

All in all, it was a good story. And if it wasn't entirely true . . . well, at least it had some truth mixed in. In my defense, I could have dispensed with the truth entirely and told a much better story. Lies are simpler, and most of the time they make better sense.

Losi watched me all through the telling, and seemed to take the whole thing as something of a challenge to the prowess of mortal women. After the story was over, she laid claim to me and led me to her small room on the topmost floor of the Pennysworth.

I managed very little sleep that night, and Losi came closer to killing me than Felurian ever had. She was a delightful partner, every bit as wonderful as Felurian had been.

But how could that be? I hear you ask. How could any mortal woman compare with Felurian?

It is easier to understand if you think of it in terms of music. Sometimes a man enjoys a symphony. Elsetimes he finds a jig more suited to his taste. The same holds true for lovemaking. One type is suited to the deep cushions of a twilight forest glade. Another comes quite naturally tangled in the sheets of narrow beds upstairs in inns. Each woman is like an instrument, waiting to be learned, loved, and finely played, to have at last her own true music made.

Some might take offense at this way of seeing things, not understanding how a trouper views his music. They might think I degrade women. They might consider me callous, or boorish, or crude.

But those people do not understand love, or music, or me.

Quick

WE SPENT A FEW days at the Pennysworth while our welcome was warm. We had our own rooms and all our meals for free. Fewer bandits meant safer roads and more customers, and Penny knew our presence at the inn would draw a better crowd than fiddle playing any night.

We put the time to good use, enjoying hot meals and soft beds. All of us could use the time to mend. Hespe was still nursing her arrow-shot leg, Dedan his broken arm. My own minor injuries from the fight with the bandits were long since gone, but I had newer ones, mostly consisting of a heavily scratched back.

I taught Tempi the basics of the lute, and he resumed teaching me how to fight. My training consisted of short, terse discussions concerning the Lethani and long, strenuous periods of practicing the Ketan.

I also pieced together a song about my Felurian experience. I originally called it "In Twilight Versed," which you have to admit wasn't a very good title. Luckily, the name didn't stick and these days most folk know it as "The Song Half-Sung."

It wasn't my best work, but it was easy to remember. The customers at the inn seemed to enjoy it, and when I heard Losi whistling it as she served drinks, I knew it would spread like a fire in a seam of coal.

Since folk kept asking for stories, I shared a few other interesting events from my life. I told them how I'd managed to get admitted into the University when I was barely fifteen years old. I told them how I'd gained entry to the Arcanum in a mere three days' time. I told them how I had called the name of the wind in a furious rage after Ambrose broke my lute.

Unfortunately, by the third night, I was out of true stories. And, since my audience was still hungry for more, I simply stole a story about Illien and put myself in his place instead, stealing a few pieces from Taborlin while I was at it.

I'm not proud of that, and in my defense, I'd like to say I'd had quite a bit to drink. What's more, there were a few pretty women in my audience. There is something powerfully beguiling about the excited eyes of a young woman. They can pull all manner of nonsense out of a foolish young man, and I was no exception to this rule.

Meanwhile, Dedan and Hespe occupied the small exclusive world new lovers make for themselves. They were a delight to watch. Dedan was gentler, quieter. Hespe's face lost much of its hardness. They spent a great deal of time in their room. Catching up on their sleep, no doubt.

Marten flirted outrageously with Penny, drank enough to drown a fish, and generally enjoyed himself enough for any three men.

We left the Pennysworth after three days, not wanting to wear our welcome thin. I for one was glad to go. Between Tempi's training and Losi's attentions I was nearly dead from exhaustion.

We made slow time on the road back to Severen. Part of this was out of concern for Hespe's injured leg, but some of it was because we knew our time together was drawing to an end. Despite our difficulties, we had become close, and it is hard to leave such things behind.

News of our adventures had run ahead of us on the road. So when we stopped for the night our meals and beds were easy to come by, if not free.

On our third day out of the Pennysworth, we ran across a small troupe of performers. They weren't Edema Ruh and looked rather out at the heels. There were just four of them: an older fellow, two men in their twenties, and a boy of eight or nine. They were packing up their rickety cart just as we were stopping to give Hespe's leg a bit of a rest.

"Hello the troupers," I called out.

They looked up nervously, then relaxed as they saw the lute across my back. "Hello the bard."

I laughed and shook their hands. "No bard here, just a bit of a singer."

"Hello the same," the older man said, smiling. "Which way are you heading?"

"North to south. Yourself?"

They relaxed further once they knew I was heading in a different direction. "East to west," he said.

"How's your luck been?"

He shrugged. "Poor enough lately. But we've heard tell of a Lady Chalker who lives two days off. They say she never turns a man away if he can fiddle a bit or mum a play. We hope to come off with a penny or two."

"Things were better when we had the bear," one of the younger men said. "Folk'll pay to see a bear-bait."

"Went sick of a dog bite," the other man explained to me. "Died near a year ago."

"That's a shame," I said. "Bear's hard to come by." They nodded a silent agreement. "I've got a new song for you. What will you trade me for it?"

He eyed me warily. "Well now, new to you isn't exactly new to us," he pointed out. "And a new song ain't necessarily a good song, if you know what I mean."

"Judge for yourself," I said as I uncased my lute. I'd written it to be easy to remember and simple to sing, but I still had to repeat it twice before he caught all of it. As I've said, they weren't Edema Ruh.

"A good enough song," he admitted grudgingly. "Everyone likes Felurian, but I don't know what we can trade you for it."

The young boy piped up, "I made up a verse to 'Tinker Tanner.' "

The others tried to hush him, but I smiled. "I'd love to hear it."

The boy puffed himself up and sang out in a piping voice:

I once saw a fair farmer's daughter
On the riverbank far from all men
She was taking a bath when I saw her
Said she didn't feel right
If a man caught a sight
So she soaped herself slowly all over again.

I laughed. "That's good," I complimented him, "But how about this?

I once saw a fair farmer's daughter
On the riverbank far from all men.
She confessed to me once when I caught her
That she didn't feel clean
If her bathing was seen
So she washed herself over again.

The boy thought about it. "I like mine better," he said after a moment's consideration.

I patted him on the back. "It's a good man that sticks to his own verse." I turned back to the leader of the little troupe. "Any gossip?"

He thought for a moment. "Bandits north of here in the Eld."

I nodded. "They've been cleared out now, so I've heard."

He thought some more. "I heard Alveron's getting married to the Lackless woman."

"I know a poem about Lackless!" The young boy chimed in again, and began:

Seven things stand before
The entrance to the Lackless door—

"Hush." The older man cuffed the boy gently along side of his head. He looked up apologetically. "Boy's got a good ear, but not one lick of manners."

"Actually," I said. "I'd like to hear it."

He shrugged and let go of the boy, who glared at him before reciting:

Seven things stand before
The entrance to the Lackless door.
One of them a ring unworn
One a word that is forsworn
One a time that must be right
One a candle without light
One a son who brings the blood
One a door that holds the flood
One a thing tight-held in keeping
Then comes that which comes with sleeping.

"It's one of those riddle rhymes," the father said apologetically. "Lord knows where he hears them, but he knows better than to go spouting every lewd thing he hears."

"Where did you hear it?" I asked.

The boy thought for a moment, then shrugged and began to scratch himself behind his knee. "Dunno. Kids."

"We should be getting on," the older man said, looking up at the sky. I dug into my purse, and handed him a silver noble. "What's this then?" he asked, eyeing it suspiciously.

"To help with a new bear," I said. "I've been through some tight times too, but I'm flush now."

They left after thanking me profusely. Poor fellows. No self-respecting Ruh troupe would ever stoop to bearbaiting. There was no skill involved, no pride in the performance.

But they could hardly be blamed for the the their lack of Ruh blood, and we troupers have to watch out for each other. No one else does.

———————

Tempi and I used our walking hours to discuss the Lethani and evenings to practice the Ketan. It was becoming easier for me, and I could sometimes make it as far as Catching Rain before Tempi caught some minuscule mistake and made me start over.

The two of us had found a halfway secluded place beside the inn where we had stopped for the day. Dedan, Hespe, and Marten were inside drinking. I worked my way carefully through the Ketan while Tempi sat with his back to a tree, practicing a basic fingering drill I had taught him with relentless determination. Over and over. Over and over.

I had just made it through Circling Hands when I caught a flicker of movement from the corner of my eye. I did not pause, as Tempi had taught me to avoid distraction while performing the Ketan. If I turned to look I would have to start over again.

Moving with painful slowness I began Dance Backwards. But as soon as I placed my heel, I could tell my balance was wrong. I waited for Tempi to call out, but he didn't.

I stopped the Ketan and turned to see a group of four Adem mercenaries walking toward us with a prowling grace. Tempi was already on his feet and walking toward them. My lute was back in its case and leaning up against the side of the tree.

Soon the five of them were standing in a tight group, close enough that their shoulders almost touched. Close enough that I couldn't hear the barest whisper of what they were saying or even see their hands. But I could tell from the angle of Tempi's shoulders that he was uncomfortable, defensive.

I knew calling out to Tempi would be considered rude, so I walked over. But before I came close enough to hear, one of the unfamiliar mercenaries stretched out a hand and pushed me away, his spread fingers pressing firmly against the center of my chest.

Without thinking, I made Break Lion, taking hold of his thumb and turning his wrist away from me. He loosed his hand from mine without any apparent effort and moved to trip me with Chasing Stone. I made Dance Backwards and got the balance right this time, but his other hand struck me in the temple just enough to dizzy me for half a second, not hard enough to even hurt.

My pride stung though. It was the same way Tempi struck me in silent rebuke for sloppy performance of the Ketan.

"Quick," the mercenary said softly in Aturan. It was only when I heard her voice that I realized she was a woman. Not that she was particularly masculine, it was simply that she seemed so similar to Tempi. She had the same sandy hair, pale grey eyes, calm expression, blood-red clothes. She was taller than Tempi by a few inches, and her shoulders were broader than his. But while she was whipcord thin, the tightness of her mercenary reds still revealed the lean curves of hip and breast.

Looking more closely, I could easily see three of the four mercenaries were women. The broad-shouldered one facing me had a thin scar cutting through her eyebrow and another close to her jaw. They were the same pale silver scars Tempi had on his arms and chest. And while they were far from gruesome, they made her expressionless face look oddly grim.

"Quick" she had said. On the surface it seemed to be a compliment, but I've been mocked enough in my life to recognize it, regardless of the language.

Even worse, her right hand slid all the way around to rest in the small of her back, palm facing out. Even with my rudimentary knowledge of Adem hand-talk I knew what that meant. Her hand was as far as it could possibly get from the hilt of her sword. At the same time, she turned her shoulder to me and looked away. I wasn't just being declared unthreatening, this was insultingly dismissive.

I fought to keep my face calm, guessing any expression would only further lower her opinion of me.

Tempi pointed back where I had come from. "Go," he said. *Serious. Formal.*

I reluctantly obeyed, not wanting to make a scene.

The Adem stood in a close knot a quarter hour as I practiced the Ketan. Though I didn't hear a whisper of their conversation, it was obvious they were arguing. Their gestures were sharp and angry, the placement of their feet aggressive.

Eventually the four unfamiliar Adem left, walking back toward the road. Tempi returned to where I was trying to work my way through Threshing Wheat.

"Too wide." *Irritation.* He tapped my back leg and pushed my shoulder to show my balance was lacking.

I moved my foot and tried again. "Who were they, Tempi?"

"Adem," he said simply, sitting himself back down at the foot of the tree.

"Did you know them?"

"Yes." Tempi looked around, then brought my lute out of its case. With his hands occupied, he was doubly mute. I went back to practicing the Ketan, knowing that trying to pry answers out of him would be like pulling teeth.

Two hours passed, and the sun began to sink behind the western trees.

"Tomorrow I leave," he said. With both his hands still on the lute, I could only guess at his mood.

"Where?"

"To Haert. To Shehyn."

"Are those cities?"

"Haert is city. Shehyn is my teacher."

I had given some thought to what might be the matter. "Are you in trouble for teaching me?"

He set the lute back in the case and pressed the lid back in place. "Perhaps." *Yes.*

"Is it forbidden?"

"It is most forbidden," he said.

Tempi stood and began the Ketan. I followed him, and both of us were quiet for a while.

"How much trouble?" I asked eventually.

"Most trouble," he said, and I heard an uncharacteristic shred of emotion in his voice, anxiety. "It was perhaps unwise."

Together we moved as slowly as the setting sun.

I thought of what the Cthaeh had said. The one shred of potentially useful information it had let slip in our conversation. *You laughed at faeries until you saw one. Small wonder all your civilized neighbors dismiss the Chandrian as well. You'd have to leave your precious corners far behind before you found someone who might take you seriously. You wouldn't have a hope until you made it to the Stormwal.*

Felurian had said the Cthaeh only spoke the truth.

"Could I accompany you?" I asked.

"Accompany?" Tempi asked, his hands moving in a graceful circle intended to break the long bones of the arm.

"Travel with. Follow. To Haert."

"Yes."

"Would it help your trouble?"

"Yes."

"I will come."

"I thank you."

Barbarians and Madmen

TRUTHFULLY, I WANTED NOTHING more than to make my way back to Severen. I wanted to sleep in a bed again and take advantage of the Maer's favor while it was still fresh in his mind. I wanted to find Denna and make things right between us.

But Tempi was in trouble for teaching me. I couldn't simply run off and leave him to face that by himself. What's more, the Cthaeh had told me Denna had already left Severen behind. Though I hardly needed a prophetic faerie to tell me that. I'd been gone for a month, and Denna was never the sort to let grass grow under her feet.

So the next morning our group parted ways. Dedan, Hespe, and Marten were going south to Severen to report to the Maer and collect their pay. Tempi and I were heading northeast toward the Stormwal and Ademre.

"You sure you don't want me to take him the box?" Dedan asked for the fifth time.

"I promised the Maer I'd return any monies to him personally," I lied. "But I do need you to give him this." I handed the big mercenary the letter I'd written the night before. "It explains why I had to make you the leader of the group." I grinned. "You might get a bonus out of it."

Dedan puffed up importantly as he took hold of the letter.

Standing nearby, Marten made a noise that could have been a cough.

As Tempi and I traveled, I managed to coax a few details from the mercenary. Eventually I learned it was customary for someone of his social standing to gain permission before he took a student of his own.

Complicating matters was the fact that I was an outsider. A barbarian. In teaching a person like me, it seems like Tempi had done more than violate a custom. He had broken a trust with his teacher and his people.

"Will there be a trial of some sort?" I asked.

He shook his head. "No trial. Shehyn will ask me questions. I will say, 'I saw in Kvothe good iron waiting. He is of Lethani. He needs Lethani to guide him.' "

Tempi nodded at me. "Shehyn will ask you of the Lethani to see if I were right in my seeing. Shehyn will decide if you are iron worth striking." His hand circled, making the gesture for *uneasy*.

"And what will happen if I am not?" I asked.

"For you?" *Uncertainty.* "For me? I will be cut away."

"Cut away?" I asked, hoping I misunderstood.

He held up a hand and wiggled his fingers. "Adem." He made a tight fist and shook it. "Ademre." Then he opened his hand and touched his little finger. "Tempi." He touched the other fingers. "Friend. Brother. Mother." He touched the thumb. "Shehyn." Then he made a gesture as if paring off his little finger and throwing it away. "Cut away," he said.

Not killed then, but exiled. I started to breathe easier until I looked in Tempi's pale eyes. For just a moment there was a crack in his perfect, placid mask, and behind it I saw the truth. Death would be a kinder punishment than being cut away. He was terrified, as frightened as anyone I had ever seen.

We agreed our best hope was for me to put myself entirely in Tempi's hands during the trip to Haert. I had approximately fifteen days to polish what I knew to a bright shine. The hope being that when I met Tempi's superiors, I could make a good impression.

Before we began that first day, Tempi instructed me to put my shaed away. Reluctantly, I did so. It folded down into a surprisingly small bundle that stowed easily into my travelsack.

The pace Tempi set was grueling. First the two of us moved through the dancer's stretch I had watched many times before. Then, instead of our usual brisk walk, we ran for an hour. Then we performed the Ketan with Tempi correcting my endless mistakes. Then we walked a mile.

Finally, we sat and discussed the Lethani. The fact that these discussions were in Ademic did not make matters easier, but we agreed I should immerse myself in the language so when I reached Haert I could speak as a civilized person.

"What is the purpose of the Lethani?" Tempi asked.

"To give us a path to follow?" I replied.

"No," Tempi said sternly. "The Lethani is not a path."

"What is the purpose of the Lethani, Tempi?"

"To guide us in our actions. By following the Lethani, you act rightly."

"Is this not a path?"

"No. The Lethani is what helps us choose a path."

Then we would begin the cycle again. Run an hour, perform the Ketan, walk a mile, discuss the Lethani. It took about two hours, and after our brief discussion was finished, we began again.

At one point in our discussion of the Lethani I began to make the gesture for *understatement*. But Tempi lay his hand on top of mine, stopping me.

"When we are having talk about the Lethani, you are to make none of this." His left hand moved quickly through *excitement, negation,* and several others gestures I didn't recognize.

"Why?"

Tempi thought for a moment. "When you speak of Lethani, it should not come from here," he tapped on my head. "Or here." He tapped on my chest over my heart and ran his fingers down to my left hand. "True knowing of the Lethani lives deeper. Lives here." He prodded me in the stomach, below my navel. "You must speak from here, without thinking."

As we continued, I slowly came to understand the unspoken rules to our discussions. Not only was it intended to teach me the Lethani, it was supposed to reveal how deeply rooted understanding of the Lethani had become within me.

That meant questions were to be answered quickly, with none of the deliberate pauses that usually marked Ademic conversation. You were not supposed to give a thoughtful answer, you were supposed to give an earnest one. If you truly understood the Lethani, that knowledge would become obvious in your answers.

Run. Ketan. Walk. Discuss. We completed the cycle three times before our midday break. Six hours. I was covered in sweat and half-convinced I would die. After an hour to rest and eat, we were off again. We finished another three cycles before we stopped for the night.

We made camp by the side of the road. I chewed my supper half-asleep, spread my blanket, and wrapped myself in my shaed. In my exhausted state it seemed soft and warm as a down eider.

In the middle of the night, Tempi shook me awake. Though some deep animal part of me hated him, I knew it was necessary as soon as I stirred. My body was stiff and aching, but the slow, familiar movements of the Ketan helped loosen my tight muscles. He made me stretch and drink water, then I slept like a stone for the remainder of the night.

The second day was worse. Even strapped tightly to my back, my lute became a miserable burden. The sword I couldn't even use dragged at my hip.
My travelsack felt heavy as a millstone, and I regretted not letting Dedan take
the Maer's box. My muscles were rubbery and disloyal, and when we ran my
breath burned in my throat.

The moments when Tempi and I spoke of Lethani were the only real rest,
but they were disappointingly brief. My mind spun with exhaustion, and
it took all my concentration to pull my thoughts into order, trying to give
proper answers. Even so, my responses only irritated him. Time after time he
shook his head, explaining how I was wrong.

Eventually I gave up trying to be right. Too weary to care, I quit pulling
my exhausted thoughts into order, and simply enjoyed sitting down for a
few minutes. I was too weary to remember what I said half the time, but,
surprisingly, Tempi found those answers more to his liking. That was a blessing. When my answers pleased him, our discussions lasted longer, and I could
spend more time resting.

I felt considerably better the third day. My muscles no longer ached as
badly. My breath came easier. My head felt clear and light, like a leaf floating
on the wind. In this frame of mind, answers to Tempi's questions tripped easily off the tip of my tongue, simple as singing.

Run. Ketan. Walk. Discuss. Three cycles. Then, as we moved through the
Ketan on the side of the road, I collapsed.

Tempi had been watching closely and caught me before I hit the ground.
My world spun dizzily for a few minutes before I realized I was in the shade
of a tree at the side of the road. Tempi must have carried me there.

He held out my waterskin. "Drink."

The thought of water was not appealing, but I took a mouthful anyway.
"I am sorry, Tempi."

He shook his head. "You came far before falling. You did not complain.
You showed your mind is stronger than your body. That is good. When the
mind controls the body, that is of the Lethani. But knowing your limit is also
of the Lethani. It is better to stop when you must than run until you fall."

"Unless falling is what the Lethani requires," I said without thinking. My
head still felt light as a windblown leaf.

He gave me a rare smile. "Yes. You are beginning to see."

I returned his smile. "Your Aturan is coming very well, Tempi."

Tempi blinked. *Worry.* "We are speaking my language, not yours."

"I'm not speaking . . ." I started to protest, but as I did I listened to the
words I was using. *Sceopa teyas.* My head reeled for a moment.

"Drink again," Tempi said, and though his face and voice were carefully controlled, I could tell he was concerned.

I took another sip to pacify him. Then, as if my body suddenly realized it needed the water, I became very thirsty and took several large swallows. I stopped before I drank too much and cramped my stomach. Tempi nodded, *approval.*

"Am I speaking well then?" I said to distract myself from my thirst.

"You are speaking well for a child. Very well for a barbarian."

"Only well? Am I making the words wrong?"

"You touch eyes too much." He widened his eyes and stared pointedly into my own, unblinking. "Also, your words are good, but simple."

"You must teach me more words then."

He shook his head. *Serious.* "You already know too many words."

"Too many? Tempi, I know very few."

"It is not the words, it is their use. In Adem there is an art to speaking. There are those who can say many things in one thing. My Shehyn is such. They say a thing in one breath and others will find meaning in it for a year." *Gentle reproach.* "Too often you say more than you need. You should not speak in Ademic as you sing in Aturan. A hundred words to praise a woman. Too many. Our talk is smaller."

"So when I meet a woman, I should simply say, 'You are beautiful?' "

Tempi shook his head. "No. You would say simply 'beautiful,' and let the woman decide the rest of what you mean."

"Isn't that . . ." I didn't know the words for "vague" or "unspecific" and had to start again to get my point across. "Doesn't that lead to confusion?"

"It leads to thoughtfulness," he said firmly. "It is delicate. That should always be the concern when one is speaking. To be too much talking." He shook his head. *Disapproval.* "It is . . ." He stalled, searching for a word.

"Rude?"

Negation. Frustration. "I go to Severen, and there are people who stink. There are people who do not. Both are people, but those who do not stink are people of quality." He tapped my chest firmly with two fingers. "You are not a goatherd. You are a student of the Lethani. My student. You should speak as a person of quality."

"But what about clarity? What if you were building a bridge? There are many pieces to that. All of them must be said clearly."

"Of course," Tempi said. *Agreement.* "Sometimes. But in most things, important things, delicate is better. Small is better."

Tempi reached out and gripped my shoulder firmly. Then he looked up, met my eye and held it for a brief moment. Such a rarity for him. He gave a small, quiet smile.

"Proud," he said.

The remainder of the day was spent in recovery. We would walk a few miles, perform the Ketan, discuss the Lethani, then walk again. We stopped at a roadside inn that evening where I ate enough for three men and fell into bed before the sun had left the sky.

The next day we went back to the cycles, but only two before midday and two after. My body burned and ached, but I was no longer delirious with exhaustion. Fortunately, with a little mental effort, I could slide back into that strange anticipatory clear-headedness I'd used to answer Tempi's questions the day before.

Over the next couple of days I came to think of that odd mental state as Spinning Leaf.

It seemed like a distant cousin to Heart of Stone, the mental exercise I'd learned so long ago. That said, there was little similarity between the two. Heart of Stone was practical: it stripped away emotion and focused my mind. It made it easier to break my mind into separate pieces or maintain the all-important Alar.

On the other hand, Spinning Leaf seemed largely useless. It was relaxing to let my mind grow clear and empty, then float and tumble lightly from one thing to the next. But aside from helping me draw answers to Tempi's questions out of thin air, it seemed to have no practical value. It was the mental equivalent of a card trick.

By the eighth day on the road, my body no longer ached constantly. That was when Tempi added something new. After performing the Ketan the two of us would fight. It was hard, as that was when I was the most weary. But after the fighting we would always sit, rest, and discuss the Lethani.

"Why did you smile as we fought today?" Tempi would say.

"Because I was happy."

"Did you enjoy the fighting?"

"Yes."

Tempi radiated displeasure. "That is not of the Lethani."

I thought a moment on my next question. "Should a man take pleasure in the fight?"

"No. You take pleasure in acting rightly and following the Lethani."

"What if following the Lethani requires me to fight? Should I not take pleasure in it?"

"No. You should take pleasure in following the Lethani. If you fight well, you should take pride in doing a thing well. For the fighting itself you should feel only duty and sorrow. Only barbarians and madmen take pleasure in combat. Whoever loves the fight itself has left the Lethani behind."

———

On the eleventh day, Tempi showed me how to incorporate my sword into the Ketan. The first thing I learned was how quickly a sword becomes lead-heavy when held at arm's length.

With our sparring and the addition of the sword, each cycle took nearly two and a half hours. Still we kept to our schedule every day. Three cycles before noon, three cycles after. Fifteen hours in all. I could feel my body hardening, becoming quick and lean like Tempi's.

So we ran, and I learned, and Haert drew ever closer.

CHAPTER ONE HUNDRED TEN

Beauty and Branch

A S WE TRAVELED, WE moved quickly through towns, stopping only for food and water. The countryside was a blur. My mind was focused on the Ketan, the Lethani, and the language I was learning.

The road became narrower as we made our way into the foothills of the Stormwal. The land grew rocky and jagged and the road began to snake back and forth as it avoided box valleys, bluffs, and jumbles of broken rock. The air changed, growing cooler than I expected in summer.

We finished the trip in fifteen days. At my best guess, we covered almost three hundred miles in that time.

Haert was the first Adem town I'd ever seen, and to my inexperienced eye it hardly seemed a town at all. There was no central street lined with houses and shops. What buildings I did see were widely spaced, oddly shaped, and built to fit closely with the natural shape of the land, as if they were trying to keep out of sight.

I didn't know that the powerful storms that gave the mountain range its name were common here. Their sudden, changing winds would tear apart anything so upthrust and angular as the square timber houses common in the lands below.

Instead the Adem built sensibly, hiding their buildings from the weather. Homes were built into the sides of hills, or outward from the leeward walls of sheltering cliffs. Some were dug downward. Others were carved into the stony sides of bluffs. Some you could hardly see unless you were standing next to them.

The exception was a group of low stone buildings clustered close together some distance from the road.

We stopped outside the largest of these. Tempi turned to face me, tugging nervously at the leather straps holding his mercenary reds tight to his arms. "I must go and make my introductions to Shehyn. It may be some time." *Anxiety. Regret.* "You must wait here. Perhaps long." His body language told me more than his words. *I cannot take you inside, as you are a barbarian.*

"I will wait," I reassured him.

He nodded and went inside, glancing back at me before closing the door behind himself.

I looked around, watching a few people quietly going about their business: a woman carrying a basket, a young boy leading a goat by a piece of rope. The buildings were made of the same rough stone as the landscape, blending into their surroundings. The sky was overcast, adding another shade of grey.

The wind blew over everything, snapping around corners and making patterns in the grass. I thought briefly of pulling on my shaed, but decided against it. The air was thinner here, and cooler. But it was still summer, and the sun was warm.

It felt oddly peaceful here, with none of the clamor and stink of a larger town. No clatter of hooves on cobblestones. No cart vendors singing out their wares. I could imagine someone like Tempi growing up in a place like this, soaking in the quiet until he was full of it, then taking it with him when he left.

With little else to look at, I turned to the nearby building. It was made from uneven pieces of stone pieced together like a jigsaw. Looking closer, I was puzzled by the lack of mortar. I tapped it with a knuckle, wondering briefly if it might be a single piece of stone carved to look like many stones fit together.

Behind me, I heard a voice say in Ademic, "What do you think of our wall?"

I turned to see an older woman with the characteristic pale grey eyes of the Adem. Her face was impassive, but her features were kind and motherly. She wore a yellow woolen cap pulled down over her ears. It was roughly knitted, and the sandy hair that stuck out from underneath was starting to go white. After all this time traveling with Tempi, it was odd to see an Adem who wasn't strapped into tight mercenary reds and wearing a sword. This woman wore a loose-fitting white shirt and linen pants.

"Is it fascinating, our wall?" she asked, gesturing *gentle amusement, curiosity* with one hand. "What do you think of it?"

"I think it is beautiful," I responded in Ademic, careful to make only brief eye contact.

Her hand tilted in an unfamiliar gesture. "Beautiful?"

I gave the barest of shrugs. "There is beauty that belongs to simple things of function."

"Perhaps you are mistaking a word," she said. *Gentle apology.* "Beauty is a flower or a woman or a gem. Perhaps you mean to say 'utility.' A wall is useful."

"Useful, but beautiful as well."

"Perhaps a thing gains beauty being used."

"Perhaps a thing is used according to its beauty," I countered, wondering if this was the Adem equivalent of small talk. If it was, I preferred it to the insipid gossip of the Maer's court.

"What of my hat?" she asked, touching it with a hand. "Is it beautiful because it is used?"

It was knitted from a thick homespun wool and dyed a bright cornsilk yellow. It was slightly lopsided, and its stitching was uneven in places. "It seems very warm," I said carefully.

She gestured *small amusement,* and her eyes twinkled ever so slightly. "It is that," she said. "And to me it is beautiful, as it was made for me by my daughter's daughter."

"Then it is beautiful as well." *Agreement.*

The woman hand-smiled at me. Her hand tilted differently than Tempi's when she made the gesture, and I decided to take it as a fond, motherly smile. Keeping my face blank, I gestured a smile in return, doing my best to make it both warm and polite.

"You speak well for a barbarian," she said and reached out to grip my arms in a friendly gesture. "Visitors are rare, especially those so courteous. Come with me and I will show you beauty, and you will speak to me of what its use might be."

I looked down. *Regret.* "I cannot. I am waiting."

"For one inside?"

I nodded.

"If they have gone inside, I suspect you will be waiting some time. Certainly they would be pleased if you came with me. I may prove more entertaining than a wall." The old woman lifted her arm and caught the attention of a young boy. He trotted over and looked up at her expectantly, his eyes darting briefly to my hair.

She made several gestures to the boy, but I only understood *quietly.* "Tell those inside I am taking this man for a walk so he need not stand alone in the wind. I will return him shortly."

She tapped my lute case, then did the same to my travelsack and the sword on my hip. "Give these to the boy and he will take them inside for you."

Without waiting for me to reply, she began to tug my travelsack off my shoulder, and I couldn't think of a graceful way of disengaging myself without seeming terribly impolite. Every culture is different, but one thing is always true: the surest way to give offense is to refuse the hospitality of your host.

The boy scurried off with my things and the old woman took my arm, leading me away. I resigned myself somewhat gratefully to her company, and we walked quietly until we came to a deep valley that opened suddenly in front of us. It was green, with a stream at the bottom, and sheltered from the persistent wind.

"What would you say of such a thing?" she asked, gesturing to the hidden valley.

"It is much like Ademre."

She patted my arm affectionately. "You have the gift of saying without saying. That is rare for one as you are." She began to make her way down into the valley, keeping one hand on my arm for support as she stepped carefully along a narrow rocky path that twisted along the valley wall. I spotted a young boy with a herd of sheep not too far off. He waved to us, but did not call out.

We made our way to the valley bottom where the stream rolled white over stones. It made clear pools where I could see the ripples of fish stirring in the water.

"Would you call this beautiful?" she asked after we had looked a while.

"Yes."

"Why?"

Uncertainty. "Perhaps its movement."

"The stone moved not at all, and you called it beautiful as well." *Questioning.*

"It is not the nature of stone to move. Perhaps it is beauty to move according to your nature."

She nodded as if my answer pleased her. We continued to watch the water.

"Have you heard of the Latantha?" she asked.

"No." *Regret.* "But perhaps I simply do not know the word."

She turned and we made our way along the valley floor until we came to a wider spot with the carefully groomed look of a garden. In the center of it was a tall tree the like of which I had never seen before.

We stopped at the edge of the clearing. "This is the sword tree," she said, and made a gesture I did not recognize, brushing the back of her hand against her cheek. "The Latantha. Would you say it is beautiful?"

I watched it for a moment. *Curiosity.* "I would enjoy seeing it more closely."

"That is not allowed." *Emphatic.*

I nodded and watched it as well as I could from this distance. It had high, arching branches like an oak, but its leaves were broad, flat, and spun in odd circles when they caught the wind. "Yes." I answered after a long while.

"Why did it take you so long to decide?"

"I was considering the reason for its beauty," I admitted.

"And?"

"I could say it both moves and doesn't move according to its nature, and that grants it beauty. But I do not think that is the reason."

"Why then?"

I watched it for a long time. "I do not know. What do you consider the reason?"

"It simply is," she said. "That is enough."

I nodded, feeling slightly foolish about the elaborate answers I had given before.

"Do you know of the Ketan?" she asked, surprising me.

I now had an inkling of how important such things were to the Adem. So I hesitated to give an open answer. However I did not want to lie either. "Perhaps." *Apology.*

She nodded. "You are cautious."

"Yes. Are you Shehyn?"

Shehyn nodded. "When did you suspect me of being who I am?"

"When you asked of the Ketan," I said. "When did you suspect me of knowing more than a barbarian should?"

"When I saw you set your feet."

Another silence.

"Shehyn, why do you not wear the red like other mercenaries?"

She made a pair of unfamiliar gestures. "Has your teacher told you why they wear the red?"

"I did not think to ask," I said, not wanting to imply Tempi had neglected my training.

"I ask you then."

I thought a moment. "So their enemies will not see them bleed?"

Approval. "Why then do I wear white?"

The only answer I could think of chilled me. "Because you do not bleed."

She gave a partial nod. "Also because if an enemy draws my blood, she should see it as her fair reward."

I fretted silently, doing my best to mimic proper Adem composure. After an appropriately polite pause, I asked. "What will become of Tempi?"

"That remains to be seen." She gestured something close to irritation, then asked, "Are you not concerned for yourself?"

"I am more concerned for Tempi."

The sword tree spun patterns on the wind. It was almost hypnotic.

"How far have you come in your training?" Shehyn asked.

"I have studied the Ketan for a month."

She turned to face me and raised her hands. "Are you ready?"

I could not help but think that she was shorter than me by six inches and old enough to be my grandmother. Her lopsided yellow hat didn't make her look terribly intimidating either. "Perhaps," I said, and raised my hands as well.

Shehyn came toward me slowly, making Hands like Knives. I countered with Catching Rain. Then I made Climbing Iron and Fast Inward, but could not touch her. She quickened slightly, made Turning Breath and Striking Forward at the same time. I stopped one with Fan Water, but couldn't escape the other. She touched me below my ribs then on my temple, softly as you would press a finger to someone's lips.

Nothing I tried had any effect on her. I made Thrown Lighting, but she simply stepped away, not even bothering to counter. Once or twice I felt the brush of cloth against my hands as I came close enough to touch her white shirt, but that was all. It was like trying to strike a piece of hanging string.

I set my teeth and made Threshing Wheat, Pressing Cider, and Mother at the Stream, moving seamlessly from one to the other in a flurry of blows.

She moved like nothing I had ever seen. It wasn't that she was fast, though she was fast, but that was not the heart of it. Shehyn moved perfectly, never taking two steps when one would do. Never moving four inches when she only needed three. She moved like something out of a story, more fluid and graceful than Felurian dancing.

Hoping to catch her by surprise and prove myself, I moved as fast as I dared. I made Maiden Dancing, Catching Sparrows, Fifteen Wolves . . .

Shehyn took one single, perfect step.

"Why do you weep?" Shehyn asked as she made Heron Falling. "Are you ashamed? Are you in fear?"

I blinked my eyes to clear them. My voice was harsh from the exertion and emotion. "You are beautiful, Shehyn. For in you is the stone of the wall, the water of the stream, and the motion of the tree in one."

Shehyn blinked, and in her moment of surprise I found myself firmly gripping her shoulder and arm. I made Thunder Upward, but instead of being thrown, Shehyn stood still and solid as a stone.

Almost absentmindedly, she freed herself with Break Lion and made Threshing Wheat. I flew six feet and hit the ground.

I was up quickly with no harm done. It was a gentle throw on soft turf, and Tempi had taught me how to fall without hurting myself. But before I could advance again Shehyn stopped me with a gesture.

"Tempi has both taught you and not taught you," she said, her expression unreadable. I forced my eyes away from her face again. So hard to break that lifetime's worth of habit. "Which is both bad and good. Come." She turned and walked closer to the tree.

It was bigger than I had thought. The smaller branches moved in wild, curving patterns as the wind tossed them about.

Shehyn picked up a fallen leaf and handed it to me. It was broad and flat, the size of a small plate, and surprisingly heavy. My hand stung and I saw a thin line of blood trailing down my thumb.

I examined the edge of the leaf and saw it was rigid, its edge as sharp as a blade of grass. Sword tree indeed. I looked up at the spinning leaves. Anyone standing near the tree when the wind was high would be cut to ribbons.

Shehyn said, "If you were to attack this tree, what would you do? Would you strike the root? No. Too strong. Would you strike the leaf? No. Too fast. Where then?"

"The branch."

"The branch." *Agreement.* She turned to me. "That is what Tempi has not taught you. It would have been wrong for him to teach you that. Nevertheless, you have suffered for it."

"I don't understand."

She gestured for me to begin the Ketan. Automatically I fell into Catch Sparrows.

"Stop." I froze in position. "If I am to attack you, where should it be? Here, at the root?" She pushed my leg and found it unyielding. "Here at the leaf?" She pushed at my upheld hand, moving it easily, but accomplishing little else. "Here. The branch." She pushed gently against one of my shoulders, moving me easily. "And here." She added pressure to my hip, spinning me around. "Do you see? You find the place to spend your strength, or it is wasted. Wasting strength is not of the Lethani."

"Yes, Shehyn."

She raised her hands, falling into the position where I had caught her before, midway through Heron Falling. "Make Thunder Upward. Where is my root?"

I pointed to her solidly planted feet.

"Where is the leaf?"

I pointed to her hands.

"No. From here to here is the leaf." She indicated her whole arm and demonstrated how she could freely strike with her hands, elbows or shoulders. "Where is the branch?"

I thought for a long moment, then tapped her knee.

Though she gave no sign of it, I sensed her surprise. "And?"

I tapped her opposite side under her armpit, then her shoulder.
"Show me."

I came in close to her, set one leg close against her knee, and made Thunder Upward, throwing her to the side. I was surprised at how little force was required.

However, instead of being thrown into the air to tumble to the ground, Shehyn gripped my forearm. I felt a jolt run up my arm and was pulled one staggering step to the side. Rather than being thrown Shehyn used her grip as leverage so her feet came down beneath her. She took a single perfect step and had her balance again.

Shehyn looked me straight in the eye for a long, speculative moment, then turned to leave, gesturing for me to follow.

A Liar and a Thief

SHEHYN AND I RETURNED to the complex of stone buildings to find Tempi standing outside, shifting nervously from foot to foot. That confirmed my suspicion. He hadn't sent Shehyn to test me. She had found me on her own.

When we came close enough, Tempi held his sword out in his right hand, point down. His left hand gestured *elaborate respect*. "Shehyn," he said, "I—"

Shehyn motioned for him to follow as she entered the low stone building. She motioned to a young boy. "Fetch Carceret." The boy took off running.

Curiosity. I gestured to Tempi.

He didn't look at me. *Profound seriousness. Attend*. It didn't reassure me that these were the same gestures he had made on the road to Crosson when he thought we were walking into an ambush. His hands, I noticed, were shaking slightly.

Shehyn led us to an open doorway where a woman in mercenary reds joined us. I recognized the thin scars on her eyebrow and jaw. This was Carceret, the mercenary we had met while heading to Severen, the one who had pushed me.

Shehyn motioned the two mercenaries inside, but held up a hand to me. "Wait here. What Tempi has done is not good. I will listen. Then I will decide what is to be done with you."

I nodded, and she closed the door behind her.

———

I waited for an hour, then two. I strained my ears, but I couldn't hear anything from the other side of the door. A few people walked past in the hallway:

two in mercenary reds, and another in simple grey homespun. Each of them looked at my hair, though none of them stared.

Instead of smiling and nodding as would have been sociable among barbarians, I kept my face blank, returned their small gestures of greeting, and avoided touching eyes.

Somewhere past the third hour, the door opened and Shehyn waved me inside.

It was a well-lit room with walls of finished stone. It was the size of a large bedroom at an inn, but seemed even larger due to the lack of any significant furniture. There was a small iron stove radiating gentle heat near one wall, and four chairs facing each other in a rough circle. Tempi, Shehyn, and Carceret filled three of them. At a gesture from Shehyn, I took the fourth.

"How many have you killed?" Shehyn asked. Her tone was different than before. Peremptory. It was the same tone Tempi used during our discussions of the Lethani.

"Many." I responded without any hesitation. I might be thick at times, but I know when I'm being tested.

"How many is many?" Not a request for clarification. It was a new question.

"In killing men, one is many."

She nodded slightly. "Have you killed men outside of the Lethani?"

"Perhaps."

"Why do you not say yes or no?"

"Because the Lethani has not always been clear to me."

"And why is that?"

"Because the Lethani is not always clear."

"What makes the Lethani clear?"

I hesitated, though I knew it wasn't the right thing to do. "The words of a teacher."

"Can one teach the Lethani?"

I began to gesture *uncertainty*, then remembered hand-talk wasn't appropriate. "Perhaps," I said. "I cannot."

Tempi shifted slightly in his chair. This wasn't going well. For lack of any other ideas, I took a deep breath, relaxed, and tipped my mind gently into Spinning Leaf.

"Who knows the Lethani?" Shehyn asked.

"The windblown leaf," I responded, though I cannot honestly say what I meant by it.

"Where does the Lethani come from?"

"The same place as laughing."

Shehyn hesitated slightly, then said, "How do you follow the Lethani?"

"How do you follow the moon?"

My time with Tempi had taught me to appreciate the different sorts of pauses that can punctuate a conversation. Ademic is a language that says as much with silence as with words. There is a pregnant pause. A polite pause. A confused pause. There is a pause that implies much, a pause that apologizes, a pause that adds emphasis. . . .

This pause was a sudden gape in the conversation. It was the empty space of an indrawn breath. I sensed I had said something very clever or something very stupid.

Shehyn shifted in her seat, and the air of formality evaporated. Sensing we were moving on, I let my mind settle out of Spinning Leaf.

Shehyn turned to look at Carceret. "What do you say?"

Carceret had sat like a statue through all of this, expressionless and still. "I say as I have said before. Tempi has *netinad* us all. He should be cut away. This is the reason we have laws. To ignore a law is to erase it."

"To blindly follow law is to be a slave," Tempi said quickly.

Shehyn gestured *sharp rebuke*, and Tempi flushed with embarrassment.

"As for this." Carceret gestured at me. *Dismissal.* "He is not of Ademre. At best he is a fool. At worst a liar and a thief."

"And what he said today?" Shehyn asked.

"A dog can bark three times without counting."

Shehyn turned to Tempi. "By speaking out of turn you refuse your turn to speak." Tempi flushed again, his lips growing pale as he struggled to maintain his composure.

Shehyn drew a deep breath and let it out slowly. "The Ketan and the Lethani are what make us Ademre," she said. "There is no way a barbarian can know of the Ketan." Both Tempi and Carceret stirred, but she held up a hand. "At the same time, to destroy one who has understanding of the Lethani is not correct. The Lethani does not destroy itself."

She said "destroy" very casually. I hoped I might be mistaken as to the true meaning of the Ademic word.

Shehyn continued. "There are those who might say, 'This one has enough. Do not teach him the Lethani, because whoever has knowledge of the Lethani overcomes all things.' "

Shehyn gave a severe look to Carceret. "But I am not one who would say that. I think the world would be better if more were of the Lethani. For while it brings power, the Lethani also brings wisdom in the use of power."

There was a long pause. My stomach knotted itself as I tried to maintain a calm appearance. "I think," Shehyn said at last, "it is possible Tempi did not make a mistake."

This seemed a long way from a ringing endorsement, but from the sudden stiffness in Carceret's back and Tempi's slow, relieved exhalation, I guessed it was the news we were hoping for.

"I will give him to Vashet," Shehyn said.

Tempi went motionless. Carceret made a gesture of *approval* wide as a madman's smile.

Tempi's voice was strained. "You will give him to the Hammer?" His hand flickered. *Respect. Negation. Respect.*

Shehyn got to her feet, signaling an end to the discussion. "Who better? The Hammer will show if he is iron worth striking."

With this, Shehyn pulled Tempi aside and spoke to him for a brief moment. Her hands brushed his arms lightly. Her voice was too soft for even my finely tuned eavesdropper's ears.

I stood politely near my chair. All the fight seemed to have left Tempi, and his gestures were a steady rhythm of *agreement* and *respect.*

Carceret stood apart from them as well, staring at me. Her expression was composed, but her eyes were angry. At her side, out of sight of the other two, she made several small gestures. The only one I understood was *disgust*, but I could guess the general meaning of the others.

In return, I made a gesture that was not Ademic. By the narrowing of her eyes, I suspected she managed to glean my meaning fairly well.

There was the high sound of a bell ringing three times. A moment later, Tempi kissed Shehyn's hands, the peak of her forehead, and her mouth. Then he turned and motioned for me to follow.

Together we walked to a large, low-ceilinged room filled with people and the smell of food. It was a dining hall, full of long tables and dark wooden benches worn smooth with time.

I followed Tempi, gathering food onto a wide wooden plate. Only then did I realize how terribly hungry I was.

Despite my expectations, this dining hall didn't resemble the Mess at the University in the least. It was quieter for one thing, and the food was far better. There was fresh milk and lean tender meat that I suspected was goat. There was hard, sharp cheese and soft, creamy cheese and two kinds of bread still warm from the oven. There were apples and strawberries for the taking. Saltboxes sat open on all the tables, and everyone could take as much as they liked.

It was strange being in a room full of Adem talking. They spoke so softly I couldn't make out any words, but I could see their hands flickering. I could only understand one gesture in ten, but it was odd being able to see all the flickering emotions around me: *Amusement. Anger. Embarrassment. Negation.*

Disgust. I wondered how much of it was about me, the barbarian among them.

There were more women than I'd expected, and more young children. There were a handful of the familiar blood-red mercenaries, but more wore the simple grey I'd seen during my walk with Shehyn. I saw a white shirt as well, and was surprised to see it was Shehyn herself, eating elbow to elbow with the rest of us.

None of them stared at me, but they were looking. A lot of attention was being paid to my hair, which was understandable. There were fifty sandy heads in the room, a few darker, a few lighter or grey with age. I stood out like a single burning candle.

I tried to draw Tempi into a conversation, but he would have none of it and focused on his food instead. He hadn't loaded his plate nearly as full as mine and ate only a fraction of what he took.

With no conversation to slow things, I finished quickly. When my plate was empty, Tempi quit pretending to eat and led us away. I could feel dozens of eyes on my back as we left the room.

He took me down a series of passages until we came to a door. Tempi opened it, revealing a small room with a window and a bed. My lute and travelsack were there. My sword was not.

"You are to have another teacher," Tempi spoke at last. "Do your best. Be civilized. Your teacher will decide much." *Regret.* "You will not see me."

He was obviously troubled, but I couldn't think of anything to say that might reassure him. Instead I gave him a comforting hug, which he seemed to appreciate. Then he turned and left without another word.

Inside my room, I undressed and lay on the bed. It seems like I should say I tossed and turned, nervous about what was to come. But the simple truth is that I was exhausted and slept like a happy baby at his mother's breast.

The Hammer

I SAT IN A TINY park composed of nothing more than two smooth stone benches, a handful of trees, and a small path running through the long grass. You could walk from one edge to the other in a minute. There were cliffs close on two sides, sheltering it from the wind. Not out of the wind, mind you. There didn't seem to be anywhere in all of Haert entirely out of the wind.

As Vashet approached, the first thing I noticed was that she didn't wear her sword on her hip. Instead she slung it over her shoulder, just as I carried my lute. She walked with the most subtle, solid confidence I have over seen, as if she knew she ought to swagger, but couldn't quite be bothered.

She had the same moderate build I'd come to expect from the Adem along with the pale, creamy complexion and grey eyes. Her hair was lighter than Tempi's by a fine shade, and she wore it pulled back into a horsetail. When she came closer, I could see her nose had been broken at some point, and while it wasn't crooked, the slight crimp looked strangely incongruous on her otherwise delicate face.

Vashet smiled at me, a wide pink smile that showed her white teeth. "So," she said in flawless Aturan. "You are mine now."

"You speak Aturan," I said stupidly.

"Most of us do," she said. There were a few lines around the mouth and the corners of her eyes, so I guessed she was perhaps ten years older than me. "It's hard to make your way in the world if you don't have a good grip on the language. Hard to do business."

I remembered myself too late. *Formal. Respect.* "Am I correct in assuming you are Vashet?"

The smile tugged back onto her mouth. Vashet returned my gesture broadly, exaggerating it so I couldn't help but feel I was being mocked. "I am. I am to be your teacher."

"What of Shehyn? I understood she was the teacher here."

Vashet arched an eyebrow at me, the extravagant expression startling on an Adem face. "In a general sense that is true. But in a more practical sense, Shehyn is far too important to be spending her time with someone like you."

I gestured, *polite*. "I was quite happy with Tempi," I said.

"And if your happiness were our goal, that might matter," she said. "However, Tempi is closer to being a sailboat than a teacher."

I bristled a little at that. "He is my friend, you realize."

Her eyes narrowed. "Then as his friend you may fail to realize his faults. He is a competent fighter, but no more than that. He barely speaks your language, has little experience with the real world, and, to be completely frank, he is not terribly bright."

"I'm sorry," I said. *Regret.* "I didn't mean to offend you."

"Don't show me humility unless you mean it," she said, still looking me over with narrow eyes. "Even when you make your face a mask, your eyes are like glittering windows."

"I am sorry," I said earnestly. *Apology.* "I'd hoped to make a good first impression."

"Why?" she asked.

"I would rather you thought well of me."

"I would rather have reason to think well of you."

I decided to take another tack, hoping to steer the conversation into safer water. "Tempi called you the Hammer. Why is that?"

"That is my name. Vashet. The Hammer. The Clay. The Spinning Wheel." She pronounced her name three separate ways, each with its own cadence. "I am that which shapes and sharpens, or destroys."

"Why the clay?"

"That is also what I am," Vashet said. "Only that which bends can teach."

I felt a growing excitement as she spoke, "I will admit," I said. "It will be pleasant to share a language with my teacher. There are a thousand questions I have not asked because I knew Tempi could not understand. Or even if he did, I wouldn't be able to make sense of his answers."

Vashet nodded and sat down on one of the benches. "Knowing how to communicate is also the way of a teacher," she said. "Now, go find a long piece of wood and bring it back to me. Then we will begin the lesson."

I headed off into the trees. Her request had a ritual air about it, so I didn't want to run back with any odd branch I found on the ground. Eventually I found a willow tree and snapped off a supple branch longer than my arm and big around as my little finger.

I returned to where Vashet sat on the bench. I handed her the willow branch, and she pulled her sword over her shoulder and began to trim the smaller nubs of the remaining branches away.

"You said *only that which bends can teach*," I said. "So I thought this would be appropriate."

"It will serve for today's lesson," she said as she stripped the last of the bark away, leaving nothing but a slender white rod. She wiped her sword on her shirt, sheathed it, and came to her feet.

Holding the willow branch in one hand, Vashet swung it back and forth, making a low *whop whop* noise as it skimmed through the air.

Now that she was closer to me, I noticed that while Vashet wore the familiar mercenary reds, unlike Tempi and many of the others, her clothes weren't held tight with leather straps. Her shirt and pants were bound snugly to her arms and legs and chest by bands of blood-red silk instead.

She met my eye. "I am going to hit you now," she said seriously. "Stand still."

Vashet began to walk around me in a slow circle, still swinging the willow rod. *Whop whop.* She moved behind me, and not being able to see her was worse. *Whop whop.* She swung the rod faster and the noise changed. *Viiiip. Viiiip.* I didn't flinch.

She circled again, moved behind me, then hit me twice. Once on each arm just below the shoulder. *Viiiip. Viiiip.* At first it merely felt like she'd tapped me, then pain blossomed across my arms, blazing like fire.

Then, before I could react, she struck me across the back so hard I felt the impact in my teeth. The only reason the rod didn't break is because it was supple green willow.

I didn't cry out, but only because she had caught me between breaths. I gasped though, sucking in air so quickly I choked and coughed. My back screamed with pain as if it had been set afire.

She came around to the front of me again, giving me that same serious look. "Here is your lesson," she said matter-of-factly. "I do not think well of you. You are a barbarian. You are not clever. You are not welcome. You do not belong here. You are a thief of our secrets. Your presence is an embarrassment and a complication this school does not need."

Vashet contemplated the end of the willow rod, then turned her eyes back to me. "We will meet here again, an hour after lunch. You will pick another stick, and I will try to teach you this lesson again." She gave me a pointed look. "If the stick you bring me does not please me, I will choose my own.

"We will do the same after dinner. Then the same the next day. This is the only lesson I have to teach you. When you learn it, you will leave Haert and never return." She looked at me, her face cool. "Do you understand?"

"What will—" Her hand flicked out, and the tip of the rod caught me on the cheek. This time I had the breath for it, and I gave a high, startled yelp.

Vashet looked at me. I'd never thought anything so simple as eye contact could be so intimidating. But her pale grey eyes were hard as ice. "Say to me, 'Yes, Vashet. I understand.'"

I glared. "Yes, Vashet. I understand." The right side of my upper lip felt huge and unwieldy as I spoke.

She searched my face, as if trying to decide something, then shrugged and tossed the stick aside.

Only then did I risk speaking again. "What would happen to Tempi if I were to leave?"

"*When* you leave," she said, stressing the first word. "The few that doubt it will know he was wrong to teach you. Doubly wrong to bring you here."

"And what will . . ." I paused and backtracked. "What would become of him in that case?"

She shrugged and turned away. "That is not for me to decide," she said, and walked away.

I touched my cheek and lip, then looked at my hand. No blood, but I could feel the red welt rising on my skin, plain as a brand for anyone to see.

———————

Not sure what else I should do, I returned to the school for lunch. After making my way to the dining hall, I looked around but didn't see Tempi among the blood-red mercenaries there. I was glad for that. As much as I would have enjoyed some friendly company, I couldn't bear the thought of him knowing how badly things had gone. I wouldn't even need to tell him. The mark on my face said it plainly for everyone in the room to see.

I kept my face impassive and my eyes low as I moved through the line and filled my plate. Then I chose an empty section of table, not wanting to force my company on anyone.

I have been alone for most of my life. But rarely have I felt it so much as at that moment. I knew one person within four hundred miles, and he'd been ordered to keep away from me. I was unfamiliar with the culture, barely competent with the language, and the burning all across my back and face was a constant reminder of how much I was unwelcome.

The food was good though. Roasted chicken, crisp longbeans, and a slice of sweet molasses pudding. Better fare than I could usually afford for myself at the University, and hotter than the food at the Maer's estate. I wasn't particularly hungry, but I've been hungry enough in my life that I have a hard time walking away from an easy meal.

There was a shadow of movement on the edge of my vision as someone sat down across the table from me. I felt my mood lighten. At least one person was brave enough to visit the barbarian. Someone was kind enough to comfort me, or at least curious enough to come and talk.

Lifting my head I saw Carceret's lean, scarred face. She set her wide wooden plate down across from me.

"How do you like our town?" she said quietly, her left hand resting on the surface of the table. Her gestures were different, as we were sitting, but I could still recognize *curious* and *polite*. To anyone watching, it would seem like we were having a pleasant conversation. "How do you like your new teacher? She thinks as I think. That you do not belong."

I chewed another mouthful of chicken and swallowed mechanically, not looking up.

Concern. "I heard you cry out," she continued softly. She spoke slower now, as if talking to a child. I wasn't sure if it was meant as an insult, or to ensure I understood her. "It was like a tiny bird."

I took a drink of warm goat's milk and wiped my mouth. The motion of my arm pulled my shirt across the welt on my back, stinging like a hundred wasps.

"Was it a cry of love?" she asked, making a gesture I didn't recognize. "Did Vashet embrace you? Does your cheek bear the mark of her tongue?"

I took a bit of pudding. It wasn't as sweet as I remembered.

Carceret took a bite of her own pudding. "Everyone gambles on when you will leave," she continued, still speaking slow and low, for my ears only. "I have two talents wagered that you will not last a second day. If you leave in the night, as I hope, I win silver. If I am wrong and you stay, I win in bruises and listening to your cries." *Entreaty.* "Stay."

I looked up at her. "You speak as a dog barks," I said. "With no end. With no sense."

I spoke quietly enough to be polite. But not so quietly that my voice didn't reach the ears of everyone sitting close to us. I know how to make a soft voice carry. We Ruh invented the stage whisper.

I saw her face flush, making the pale scars on her jaw and eyebrow stand out.

I looked down and continued to eat, the very picture of calm unconcern. It's tricky, insulting someone from a different culture. But I'd chosen my words carefully, based on things I'd heard Tempi say. If she responded in any way, it would only seem to prove my point.

I finished the rest of my meal slowly and methodically, imagining I could feel the rage rolling off her like waves of heat. This small battle, at least, I could win. It was a hollow victory, of course. But sometimes you have to take what you can get.

———

When Vashet returned to the small park, I was already sitting on one of the stone benches, waiting for her.

She stood before me and sighed gustily. "Lovely. A slow learner," she said in her perfect Aturan. "Go fetch your stick then. We'll see if I can make my point more clearly this time."

"I've already found my stick," I said. I reached behind the bench and brought out a wooden training sword I'd borrowed from the school.

It was old, oiled wood, worn smooth by countless hands, hard and heavy as a bar of iron. If she used this to strike my shoulders as she had with the willow rod, it would break bones. If she struck my face, it would shatter my jaw.

I set it on the bench beside me. The wood didn't clatter against the stone. It was so hard it almost rang like a bell.

After I set down the training sword, I began to pull my shirt up over my head, sucking a breath through my teeth when it dragged against the hot welt on my back.

"Are you hoping to sway me with the offer of your tender young body?" Vashet asked. "You're pretty, but not so pretty as that."

I laid my shirt carefully on the bench. "I just thought it would be best if I showed you something." I turned so she could see my back.

"You've been whipped," she said. "I cannot say I'm surprised. I already knew you to be a thief."

"These are not from thieving," I said. "These are from the University. I was brought up on charges and sentenced to be whipped. When this happens, many students simply leave and take their education elsewhere. I decided to stay. It was only three lashes, after all."

I waited, still facing away. After a moment she took the bait. "There are more scars here than three lashes can account for."

"Some time after that," I said, "I was brought up on charges again. Six lashes this time. Still I stayed." I turned back to face her. "I stayed because there was no other place I could learn what I desired. Mere whipping could not keep me away from it."

I picked up the heavy wooden sword from the bench. "I thought it only fair that you should know this. I cannot be frightened away with the threat of pain. I will not abandon Tempi after the trust he has shown me. There are things I desire to learn, and I can only learn them here."

I handed her the hard, dark piece of wood. "If you want me to leave, you must do worse than welts."

I stepped back and let my hands hang at my sides. I closed my eyes.

Barbarian Tongue

I'D LIKE TO SAY I kept my eyes closed, but that wouldn't be the truth. I heard the gritty sound of dirt beneath the soles of Vashet's shoes and couldn't help but open them.

I didn't peek. That would only make me seem childish. I simply opened my eyes and looked at her. She stared back, making more eye contact than I would get from Tempi in a span of days. Her pale grey eyes were hard in her delicate face. Her broken nose no longer looked out of place. It was a grim warning to the world.

The wind swirled between us, raising gooseflesh on my naked arms.

Vashet drew a resigned breath and shrugged, then flipped the wooden rod to grip the handle end. She hefted it thoughtfully with both hands, getting a feel for its weight. Then she brought it up to her shoulder and swung.

Except she didn't.

"Fine!" she said, exasperated, throwing up her hands. "You twiggy little skeeth. Fine! Shit and onions. Put your shirt back on. You're making me cold."

I sank down until I was sitting on the bench. "Thank God," I said. I started to put my shirt back on, but it was difficult, as my hands were shaking. It wasn't from the cold.

Vashet saw. "I knew it!" she said triumphantly, pointing a finger at me. "You standing there like you're ready to be hanged. I knew you were ready to run like a rabbit!" She stamped her foot in frustration. "I knew I should have taken a swing at you!"

"I'm glad you didn't," I said. I managed to get my shirt on, then realized it was inside out. I decided to leave it rather than drag it across my stinging back again.

"What gave me away?" she demanded.

"Nothing," I said. "It was a masterful performance."

"Then how'd you know I wasn't going to crack your skull open?"

"I thought it through," I said. "If Shehyn had really wanted me driven off, she could have just sent me packing. If she wanted me dead, she could have done that too."

I rubbed my sweaty hands on my pants. "That meant you were really meant to be my teacher. So there were only three sensible options." I held up a finger. "This was a ritual initiation." A second finger. "It was test of my resolve . . ."

"Or I was really trying to run you off," Vashet finished as she sat on the bench opposite me. "What if I'd been telling the truth and thumped you bloody?"

I shrugged. "At least I'd have known. But it seemed like long odds that Shehyn would choose someone like that. If she'd wanted me beaten she could have let Carceret do it." I cocked my head. "Out of curiosity, which was it? Initiation or test of resolve? Does everyone go through this?"

She shook her head. "Resolve. I needed to make sure of you. I wasn't going to waste my time teaching a coward or someone afraid of a little smack or two. I also needed to know you were dedicated."

I nodded. "That seemed the most likely. I thought I'd save myself several days of welts and force the issue."

Vashet gave me a long look, curiosity plain on her face. "I will admit, I've never had a student offer himself up for a vicious beating in order to prove he's worth my time."

"This was nothing," I said nonchalantly. "Once I jumped off a roof."

———

We spent an hour talking about small things, letting the tension between us slowly bleed away. She asked how exactly I'd come to be whipped, and I gave her the bones of the story, glad to have the chance to explain myself. I didn't want her thinking of me as a criminal.

Vashet examined my scars more closely afterward. "Whoever tended to you certainly knew their physic," she said admiringly. "This is very clean work. As good as any I've ever seen."

"I'll pass along your compliments," I said.

Her hand brushed gently along the edge of the hot welt that ran across the whole length of my back. "I'm sorry for this, by the way."

"It hurts worse than the whipping ever did, I'll tell you that for free."

"It'll be gone in a day or two," she said. "Which isn't to say you won't be sleeping on your stomach tonight." She helped me settle my shirt, then moved back to the other bench, facing me.

I hesitated before saying, "No offense, Vashet. But you seem different from the other Adem I've met. Not that I've met many, mind you."

"You're just hungry for familiar body language," she said.

"There is that," I said. "But you seem more . . . expressive than the other Adem I've seen." I pointed at my face.

Vashet shrugged. "Where I'm from, we grow up speaking your language. And I spent four years as bodyguard and captain for a poet in the Small Kingdoms who also happened to be a king. I probably speak Aturan better than anyone in Haert. Including you."

I ignored the last. "You didn't grow up here?"

She shook her head. "I'm from Feant, a town farther north. We're more . . . cosmopolitan. Haert only has the one school, and everyone is tied very tightly to it. The sword tree is one of the old paths, too. Rather formal. I grew up following the path of joy."

"There are other schools?"

Vashet nodded. "This is one of the many schools that follow the Latantha, the path of the sword tree. It's one of the oldest, behind the Aethe and Aratan. There are other paths, maybe three dozen. But some of those are very small, with only one or two schools teaching their Ketan."

"Is that why your sword is different?" I asked. "Did you bring it from your other school?"

Vashet gave me a narrow look. "What do you know of my sword?"

"You brought it out to trim the willow switch," I said. "Tempi's sword was well-made, but yours is different. The handle is worn, but the blade looks new."

She gave me a curious look. "Well you certainly have your eyes open, don't you?"

I shrugged.

"Strictly speaking, it's not my sword," Vashet said. "It's merely in my keeping. It is an old sword, and the blade is the oldest part of it. It was given to me by Shehyn herself."

"Is that why you came to this school?"

Vashet shook her head. "No. Shehyn gave me the sword much later." She reached back and touched the hilt fondly. "No. I came here because while the Latantha might be rather formal, they excel in the use of the sword. I had learned as much as I could from the path of joy. Three other schools refused me before Shehyn brought me in. She is a clever woman and realized there was something to be gained in teaching me."

"I guess we're both lucky she has an open mind," I said.

"You more than me," Vashet said. "There's a certain amount of one-upsmanship among the different paths. When I joined the Latantha, it was a bit of a feather in Shehyn's cap."

"It must have been hard," I said. "Coming here and being the stranger to everyone."

Vashet shrugged, making her sword rise and fall on her shoulder. "At first," she admitted. "But they recognize talent, and I have that to spare. Among those who study the path of joy, I was viewed as rather stiff and stodgy. But here I'm seen as somewhat wild." She grinned. "It's pleasant, like having a new set of clothes to wear."

"Does the path of joy also teach the Lethani?" I asked.

Vashet laughed. "That is a matter of some considerable debate. The simple answer is yes. All Adem study the Lethani to some degree. Those in the schools especially. That said, the Lethani is open to a broad interpretation. What some schools cling to, others spurn."

She gave me a thoughtful look. "Is it true you said the Lethani comes from the same place as laughing?"

I nodded.

"That is a good answer," she said. "My teacher in the path of joy once said that very thing to me." Vashet frowned. "You look pensive when I say that. Why?"

"I'd tell you," I said. "But I don't want you to think less of me."

"I think less of you for keeping something from your teacher," she said seriously. "There must be trust between us."

I sighed. "I am glad you like my answer. But honestly, I don't know what it means."

"I didn't ask you what it means," she said easily.

"It's just a nonsense answer," I said. "I know you all place great stock in the Lethani, but I don't really understand it. I've just found a way to fake it."

Vashet smiled indulgently. "There is no pretending to understand the Lethani," she said confidently. "It is like swimming. It is obvious to anyone watching if you really know the way of it."

"A person can pretend to swim too," I pointed out. "I've simply been moving my arms and walking on the bottom of the river."

She gave me a curious look. "Very well then. How have you managed to fool us?"

I explained Spinning Leaf to her. How I had learned to tip my thoughts into a light, empty, floating place where the answers to their questions came easily.

"So you have stolen the answers from yourself," she said with mock seriousness. "You have cleverly fooled us by pulling the answers from your own mind."

"You don't understand," I said, growing irritated. "I don't have the slightest idea what the Lethani really is! It's not a path, but it helps choose a path. It's the simplest way, but it is not easy to see. Honestly, you people sound like drunk cartographers."

I regretted saying it as soon as it was out of my mouth, but Vashet merely laughed. "There are many drunks who are quite conversant with the Lethani," she said. "Several legendarily so."

Seeing I was still agitated, she made a motion to calm me. "I don't understand the Lethani either, not in a way that can be explained to another. The teaching of the Lethani is an art I do not possess. If Tempi has managed to instill the Lethani in you, it is a great mark in his favor."

Vashet leaned forward seriously. "Part of the problem is with your language," she said. "Aturan is very explicit. It is very precise and direct. Our language is rich with implication, so it is easier for us to accept the existence of things that cannot be explained. The Lethani is the greatest of these."

"Can you give me an example of one other than the Lethani?" I asked. "And please don't say 'blue,' or I might go absolutely mad right here on this bench."

She thought for a moment. "Love is such a thing. You have knowledge of what it is, but it defies careful explication."

"Love is a subtle concept," I admitted. "It's elusive, like justice, but it can be defined."

Her eyes sparkled. "Do so then, my clever student. Tell me of love."

I thought for a quick moment, then for a long moment.

Vashet grinned. "You see how easy it will be for me to pick holes in any definition you give."

"Love is the willingness to do anything for someone," I said. "Even at detriment to yourself."

"In that case," she said. "How is love different from duty or loyalty?"

"It is also combined with a physical attraction," I said.

"Even a mother's love?" Vashet asked.

"Combined with an extreme fondness then," I amended.

"And what exactly do you mean by 'fondness'?" she asked with a maddening calm.

"It is . . ." I trailed off, racking my brain to think how I could describe love without resorting to other, equally abstract terms.

"This is the nature of love." Vashet said. "To attempt to describe it will drive a woman mad. That is what keeps poets scribbling endlessly away. If one could pin it to the paper all complete, the others would lay down their pens. But it cannot be done."

She held up a finger. "But only a fool claims there is no such thing as love. When you see two young ones staring at each other with dewy eyes, there it is. So thick you can spread it on your bread and eat it. When you see a mother with her child, you see love. When you feel it roil in your belly, you know what it is. Even if you cannot give voice to it in words."

Vashet made a triumphant gesture. "Thus also is the Lethani. But as it is greater, it is more difficult to point toward. That is the purpose of the questions. Asking them is like asking a young girl about the boy she fancies. Her answers may not use the word, but they reveal love or the lack of it within her heart."

"How can my answers reveal a knowledge of the Lethani when I don't truly know what it is?" I asked.

"You obviously understand the Lethani," she said. "It is rooted deep inside you. Too deep for you to see. Sometimes it is the same with love."

Vashet reached out and tapped me on the forehead. "As for this Spinning Leaf. I have heard of similar things practiced by other paths. There is no Aturan word for it that I know. It is like a Ketan for your mind. A motion you make with your thoughts, to train them."

She made a dismissive gesture. "Either way, it is not cheating. It is a way of revealing that which is hidden in the deep waters of your mind. The fact that you found it on your own is quite remarkable."

I nodded to her. "I bow to your wisdom, Vashet."

"You bow to the fact that I am unarguably correct."

She clapped her hands together. "Now, I have much to teach you. However, as you are still welted and flinching, let us forbear the Ketan. Show me your Ademic instead. I want to hear you wound my lovely language with your rough barbarian tongue."

I learned a great deal about Ademic over the next several hours. It was refreshing to be able to ask detailed questions and receive clear, specific answers in return. After a month of dancing about and drawing in the dirt, learning from Vashet was so easy it felt dishonest.

On the other hand, Vashet made it clear that my hand-language was embarrassingly crude. I could get my point across, but what I was doing was, at best, baby talk. At worst, it resembled the rantings of a deranged maniac.

"Right now you speak like this." She got to her feet, waved both hands over her head, and pointed to herself with both thumbs. "I want to make good fight." She gave a wide, insipid grin. "With sword!" She thumped her chest with both fists, then jumped into the air like an excited child.

"Come now," I said, embarrassed. "I'm not that bad."

"You are close," Vashet said seriously as she sat back down on the bench. "If you were my son, I would not let you leave the house. As my student, it is only tolerable because you are a barbarian. It's as if Tempi brought home a dog that can whistle. The fact that you are out of tune stands quite beside the point."

Vashet made as if she would get to her feet. "That said, if you are happy speaking like a simpleton, just say the word and we can move to other things. . . ."

I reassured her I wanted to learn.

"First, you say too much, and you speak too loudly," she said. "The heart of Adem is stillness and silence. Our language reflects this.

"Second, you must be much more careful with your gestures," she said. "With their placement and timing. They modify specific words and thoughts. They do not always reinforce what you say, sometimes they run purposely counter to your surface meaning."

She made seven or eight different gestures in quick succession. All of them said *amusement*, but each of them was slightly different. "You must also come to understand the fine shades of meaning. The difference between slim and slender, as my poet king used to say. Right now you only have one smile, and that cannot help but make a person look a fool."

We worked for several hours, and Vashet made clear something Tempi could only hint at. Aturan was like a wide, shallow pool; it had many words, all very specific and precise. Ademic was like a deep well. There were fewer words, but they each had many meanings. A well-spoken sentence in Aturan is a straight line pointing. A well-spoken sentence in Adem is like a spider-web, each strand with a meaning of its own, a piece of something greater, more complex.

I arrived in the dining hall for supper in a considerably better mood than before. My welts still stung, but my fingers told me the swelling on my cheek was much reduced. I still sat alone, but I didn't keep my head down as I had before. Instead I watched the hands of everyone around me, trying to note the subtle shades of difference between *excitement* and *interest*, between *denial* and *refusal*.

After supper, Vashet brought a small pot of salve which she smeared liberally across my back and upper arms, then more sparingly on my face. It tingled at first, then burned, then settled down to a dull, numb heat. Only after the pain along my back faded did I realize how tense my entire body had been.

"There," Vashet said, twisting the stopper back into the bottle. "How is that?"

"I could kiss you," I said gratefully.

"You could," she said. "But your lip is swollen, and you would doubtless make a mess of it. Instead, show me your Ketan."

I hadn't stretched, but not wanting to make excuses, I fell into Open Hands and began to move slowly through the rest.

As I've already mentioned, Tempi usually stopped me when I made the slightest mistake in the Ketan. So when I reached the twelfth position without interruption, I felt rather smug. Then I misplaced my foot badly in Grandmother Gathers. When Vashet said nothing, I realized she was merely watching and withholding judgment until the end. I began to sweat, and didn't stop until I reached the end of the Ketan ten minutes later.

After I'd finished, Vashet stood stroking her chin. "Well," she said slowly. "It certainly could be worse . . ." I felt a flicker of pride until she continued. "You could, for instance, be missing a leg."

Then she walked in a circle around me, looking me up and down. She reached out to prod at my chest and stomach. She gripped at my upper arm and the thick muscle above my leg. I felt like a suckling pig brought to market.

Lastly she took hold of my hands, turning them over to examine them. She looked pleasantly surprised. "You never fought before Tempi taught you?" she asked.

I shook my head.

"You have good hands," she said, her fingers running up my forearms, feeling at the muscles there. "Half of you barbarians have soft, weak hands from doing nothing. The other half have strong, stiff hands from cutting wood or working behind a plow." She turned my hands over in her own. "But you have strong, clever hands with good motion in your wrists." She looked up at me questioningly. "What do you do for a living?"

"I am a student at the University where I work with fine tools, shaping metal and stone." I explained. "But I'm also a musician. I play the lute."

Vashet looked startled, then burst into laughter. She let my hands fall and shook her head in dismay. "A musician on top of everything else," she said. "Perfect. Does anyone else know?"

"What does it matter?" I said. "I'm not ashamed of who I am."

"No," she said. "Of course you're not. That's part of the problem." She drew in a deep breath and let it out again. "Okay. You should know about this as soon as possible. It will save us both trouble in the long run." She looked me in the eye. "You're a whore."

I blinked. "I beg your pardon?"

"Pay attention for a moment. You're not thick. You must have realized there are huge cultural differences between here and where you grew up in ..."

"The Commonwealth," I said. "And you're right. The cultural divide between Tempi and myself was huge compared to the other mercenaries from Vintas."

She nodded. "Part of that is because Tempi has fewer wits than tits," she said. "And he is as fresh as a baby chick when it comes to making his way in the world." She waved a hand. "All that aside, you're right. There are huge differences."

"I noticed," I said. "You don't seem to have a nudity taboo for one thing. Either that or Tempi is a bit of an exhibitionist."

"I'd be curious how you found that out," she chuckled. "But you're right. Strange as it may seem to you, we have no particular fear of a naked body."

Vashet looked thoughtful for a moment, then seemed to reach some kind of decision. "Here. It will be simpler to show you. Watch."

I watched the familiar Adem impassivity slide over her face, leaving her face blank as new paper. Her voice lost most of its inflection at the same time, shedding its emotional content. "Tell me what I mean when I do this," she said.

Vashet stepped close, making no eye contact. Her hand said, *respect.* "You fight like a tiger." Her face was expressionless, her voice flat and calm. She grabbed hold of the top of my shoulder with one hand, and gripped my arm with the other, giving it a squeeze.

"It's a compliment," I said.

Vashet nodded and stepped back. Then she changed. Her face grew animated. She smiled and met my eyes. She stepped close to me. "You fight like a tiger," she said, her voice glowing with admiration. One of her hands rested on the top of my shoulder while the other slipped around my biceps. She squeezed.

I was suddenly embarrassed at how close we were standing. "It's a sexual advance," I said.

Vashet stepped away and nodded. "Your folk view certain things as intimate. Naked skin. Physical contact. The nearness of a body. Loveplay. To the Adem, these are nothing remarkable."

She looked me in the eye. "Can you think of a single time you have heard one of us shout? Raise our voice? Or even speak loudly enough we can be overheard?"

I thought for a moment, then shook my head.

"That is because for us, speaking is private. Intimate. Facial expression too. And this . . ." She pressed her fingers to her throat. "The warmth a voice can make. The emotion it reveals. That is a very private thing."

"And nothing carries more emotion than music," I said, understanding. It was a thought too strange for me to cope with all at once.

Vashet nodded gravely. "A family might sing together if they are close. A mother might sing to her child. A woman might sing to her man." A slight flush rose on Vashet's cheeks as she said this. "But only if they are very much in love, and very much alone.

"But you?" She gestured to me. "A musician? You do this to a whole room full of people. All at once. And for what? A few pennies? The price of a meal?" She gave me a grave look. "And you do it again and again. Night after night. With *anyone*."

Vashet shook her head in dismay and shuddered a bit, while her left hand unconsciously clenched in rough gestures: *Horror, disgust, rebuke.* It was rather intimidating getting both sets of emotional signals from her at the same time.

I fought off the mental image of standing naked on the stage of the Eolian, then moving through the crowd, pressing my body to everyone there. Young and old. Fat and thin. Rich noble and penniless commoner. It was a sobering thought.

"But Play Lute is the thirty-eighth position in the Ketan," I protested. I was grasping at straws and I knew it.

"And Sleeping Bear is twelfth." She shrugged. "But you will find no bears here, or lions, or lutes. Some names reveal. The names in the Ketan are meant to hide the truth, that we may speak of it without spilling its secrets to the open air."

"I understand," I said at last. "But many of you have been out in the world. You yourself speak Aturan beautifully and with much warmth in your voice. Surely you know there is nothing inherently wrong with a person singing."

"You have been out in the world as well," she said calmly. "And surely you know there is nothing inherently wrong with having sex with three people in a row on the broad hearth of a busy inn." She looked me in the eye pointedly.

"I imagine the stone would be rather rough. . . ." I said.

She chuckled. "Very well, assume they had use of a blanket too. What would you call that person?"

If she'd asked me two span ago, when I'd been fresh out of the Fae, I might not have understood her. If I'd stayed with Felurian any longer, it's entirely possible that having sex on the hearth wouldn't have seemed odd to me. But I'd been back in the mortal world for a while now. . . .

A whore, I thought silently to myself. And a cheap and shameless whore to boot. I was glad I hadn't mentioned Tempi's desire to learn the lute to anyone. How ashamed he must have felt for such an innocent impulse. I thought of a young Tempi wanting to make music but never telling anyone because he knew it was dirty. It broke my heart.

My face must have given away quite a bit, because Vashet reached out to grip my hand gently. "I know this is hard for you folk to understand. So much harder because you have never even entertained the possibility of thinking otherwise." *Caution.*

I struggled with everything this implied. "How do you get your news?" I asked. "With no troupers wandering from town to town, how do you keep in touch with the outside world?"

Vashet smirked a bit at this, and made a gesture to the windswept land-scape. "Does this seem to be a place that concerns itself overmuch with the turning of the world?" She dropped her arm. "But it is not so bad as you think. Traveling peddlers are more welcome here than in most places. Tinkers doubly so. And we ourselves travel quite a bit. Those who take the red come and go, bringing news with them."

She laid a reassuring hand on my shoulder. "And, occasionally, a rare singer or musician will travel through. But they do not play for a whole town at once. They will visit a single family. Even then, they perform while sitting be-hind a screen so they cannot be seen. You can tell an Adem musician because when they travel they carry their tall screens on their backs." Her mouth pursed a bit. "But even these are not viewed in an entirely favorable light. It is a valuable occupation, but not a respectable one."

I relaxed a bit. The thought of a place where no performer was welcome struck me as profoundly wrong, sick even. But a place with strange customs I could understand. Adapting to fit your audience is common as changing costumes to the Edema Ruh.

Vashet continued. "This is the way of things, and you would do well to accept it sooner rather than later. I say this as a well-traveled woman. I have spent eight years among the barbarians. I have even listened to music in a group of people." She said this proudly, with a defiant tilt to her head. "I have done it more than once."

"Have you ever sung in public?" I asked.

Vashet's face went stony. "That is not a polite question to ask," she said, stiffly. "And you will make no friends with it here."

"All I mean," I said quickly, "is that if you tried it, you might find it is nothing shameful. It is a great joy to everyone."

Vashet gave me a severe look and made a hard gesture of *refusal* and *finality.*

"Kvothe, I have traveled much and seen much. Many of the Adem here are worldly. We know of musicians. And, to be completely forthright, many of us have a secret, guilty fascination with them. Much the same way your folk are enamored with the skill of the Modegan courtesans."

She gave me a hard look. "But for all that, I would not want my daughter to bring one home, if you catch my meaning. Neither would it improve anyone's opinion of Tempi if others knew he had shared the Ketan with such as you. Keep it to yourself. You have enough to overcome without all Ademre knowing you are a musician on top of everything."

His Sharp and Single Arrow

RELUCTANTLY, I TOOK VASHET'S advice. And though my fingers itched for it, I did not bring out my lute that night and fill my small corner of the school with music. I even went so far as to slide my lute case underneath my bed, lest the mere sight of it fill the school with rumor.

For several days I did little but study under Vashet. I ate alone and made no attempt to speak with anyone, as I was suddenly self-conscious of my language. Carceret kept her distance, but she was always there, watching me, her eyes flat and angry as a snake's.

I took advantage of Vashet's excellent Aturan and asked a thousand questions that would have been too subtle for Tempi to understand.

I waited three entire days until I asked her the question that had been slowly smoldering inside me since I'd climbed the foothill of the Stormwal. Personally, I thought this showed exceptional restraint.

"Vashet," I asked. "Do your people have stories of the Chandrian?"

She looked at me, her normally expressive face gone suddenly impassive. "And what does this have to do with your hand-talk?" Her hand flickered through several different variations of the gesture that indicated disapproval and reproach.

"Nothing," I said.

"Does it have something to do with your fighting, then?" she asked.

"No," I admitted. "But—"

"Surely it relates to the Ketan?" Vashet said. "Or to the Lethani? Or perhaps it touches on some subtle shade of meaning you have difficulty grasping in Ademic."

"I am merely curious."

Vashet sighed. "Can I persuade you to focus your curiosity on more pressing matters?" She asked, gesturing *exasperated*. *Firm rebuke.*

I quickly let the matter drop. Not only was Vashet my teacher, she was my only companion. The last thing I wanted to do was irritate her, or give the impression that I was less than attentive to her lessons.

With that one disappointing exception, Vashet was a sparkling font of information. She answered my endless questions quickly and clearly. As a result, I couldn't help but feel that my skill in speaking and fighting was progressing in great leaps and bounds.

Vashet did not share my enthusiasm, and was not bashful about saying so. Eloquently. In two languages.

Vashet and I were down in the hidden valley that contained the sword tree. We had been practicing our hand fighting for about an hour, and were now sitting in the long grass, catching our breath.

Rather, *I* was catching *my* breath. Vashet was not winded at all. Fighting me was nothing to her, and there was no time when she couldn't chide me for sloppiness by reaching lazily past my defenses to cuff me on the side of the head.

"Vashet," I said, mustering the courage to ask a question that had been bothering me for some time. "May I ask a question that is perhaps presumptuous?"

"I prefer a presumptuous student," she said. "I had hoped we were beyond the point of worrying about such things."

"What is the purpose of all of this?" I gestured between the two of us.

"The purpose of this," she mimicked my gesture, "is to teach you enough so that you no longer fight like a little boy, drunk on his mother's wine."

Today her sandy hair was tied in two short braids that hung down her back on either side of her neck. This made her look oddly girlish, and had not done wonders for my self-esteem over the last hour as she had repeatedly thrown me to the ground, forced me into submission, and struck me with countless solid but generously pulled punches and kicks.

And once, laughing, she had stepped easily behind me and slapped me firmly on the ass, as if she were a lecherous taproom drunk and I some low-bodiced serving girl.

"But why?" I asked. "To what purpose are you teaching me? If Tempi was wrong to teach me, why continue to teach me more?"

Vashet nodded approvingly. "I've been wondering how long it would take you to ask that," she said. "It should have been one of your first questions."

"I've been told I ask too many questions," I said. "I've been trying to step a little more carefully here."

Vashet sat forward, suddenly businesslike. "You know things you should not. Shehyn does not mind that you know of the Lethani, though others feel differently. But there is agreement on the subject of our Ketan. It is not for barbarians. It is only for the Adem, and only for those who follow the path of the sword tree."

Vashet continued, "Shehyn's thought is thus. If you were part of the school, you would be part of Ademre. If you are part of Ademre, you are no longer a barbarian. And if you are no longer a barbarian, it would not be wrong for you to know these things."

It had a certain convoluted logic to it. "That also means Tempi would not be wrong for teaching me."

She nodded. "Exactly. Instead of bringing home an unwanted puppy, it would be as if he had returned a lost lamb to the fold."

"Must I be a lamb or a puppy?" I sighed. "It's undignified."

"You fight as a puppy fights," she said. "Eager and clumsy."

"But aren't I already part of the school?" I asked. "You are teaching me, after all."

Vashet shook her head. "You sleep in the school and eat our food, but that does not make you a student. Many children study the Ketan with hopes of entering the school and someday wearing the red. They live and study with us. They are *in* the school, but not *of* the school, if you follow me."

"It seems odd to me that so many want to become mercenaries," I said as gently as possible.

"You seem eager enough," she said with an edge to her voice.

"I am eager to learn," I said, "not take the life of a mercenary. I mean no offense."

Vashet stretched her neck, working out some stiffness. "It is your language getting in the way. In the barbarian lands, mercenaries are the lowest rung of society. No matter how thick or useless a man might be, he can carry a cudgel and earn a ha'penny a day guarding a caravan. Am I right?"

"The lifestyle does tend to attract a rough sort of person," I said.

"We are not mercenaries of that kind. We are paid, but we choose which jobs we take." She paused. "If you fight for your purse, you are a mercenary. What are you called if you fight out of duty for your country?"

"A soldier."

"If you fight for the law?"

"A constable or a bailiff."

"If you fight for your reputation?"

I had to think a bit on that one. "A duelist, perhaps?"

"If you fight for the good of others?"

"An Amyr," I said without thinking.

She cocked her head at me. "That is an interesting choice," she said.

Vashet held up her arm, displaying the red sleeve proudly. "We Adem are paid to guard, to hunt, to protect. We fight for our land and our school and our reputations. And we fight for the Lethani. With the Lethani. In the Lethani. All of these things together. The Adem word for one who takes the red is *Cethan*." She looked up at me. "And it is a very proud thing."

"So becoming a mercenary is quite high on the Adem social ladder," I said.

She nodded. "But barbarians do not know this word, and wouldn't understand even if they did. So 'mercenary' must suffice."

Vashet pulled two long strands of grass from the ground and began to twist them together into a cord. "This is why Shehyn's decision is not an easy one to make. She must balance what is right against what is best for her school. All the while taking into consideration the good of the entire path of the sword tree. Rather than make a rash decision, she is playing a more patient game. Personally, I think she's hoping the problem will take care of itself."

"How would this take care of itself?" I asked.

"You could have run off," she said simply. "Many assumed you would. If I'd decided you were not worth teaching, that would have taken it out of her hands as well. Or you could die during your training, or become crippled."

I stared at her.

She shrugged. "Accidents happen. Not often, but sometimes. If Carceret had been your teacher . . ."

I grimaced. "So how does one officially become a member of the school? Is there some sort of test?"

She shook her head, "First, someone must stand on your behalf, saying you are worthy of joining the school."

"Tempi?" I asked.

"Someone of consequence," she clarified.

"So that would be you," I said slowly.

Vashet grinned, tapping the side of her crimped nose, then pointing at me. "Only took you two guesses. If you ever progress to the point I feel you won't embarrass me, I'll stand on your behalf and you can take the test."

She continued to twist the blades of grass together, her hands moving in a steady, complicated pattern. I'd never seen another Adem idly toy with something like this while talking. They couldn't, of course. They needed one hand free to talk. "If you pass this test, you are no longer a barbarian. Tempi is vindicated, and everyone goes home happy. Except for those who aren't, of course."

"And if I don't pass this test?" I asked. "Or what if you decide I'm not good enough to take it?"

"Then things grow complicated." She came to her feet. "Come, Shehyn has asked to speak with you today. It would not be polite of us to be late."

———

Vashet led the way back to the small cluster of low stone buildings. When I'd first seen them I'd assumed they were the town itself. Now I knew they composed the school. The group of buildings was like a tiny University, except there was none of the scheduled regimen I was used to.

There was no formal ranking system, either. Those with their reds were treated with deference, and Shehyn was obviously in charge. Other than that, all I had was a vague impression of a social pecking order. Tempi was obviously rather low and not well-thought-of. Vashet was rather high and respected.

When we arrived for our meeting, Shehyn was midway through performing the Ketan. I watched silently as she moved at the speed of honey spreading on a tabletop. The Ketan grows more difficult the slower it is done, but she performed it flawlessly.

It took her half an hour to finish, after which she opened a window. A curl of wind brought in the sweet smell of summer grass and the sound of leaves.

Shehyn sat. She wasn't breathing hard, though a sheen of sweat covered her skin. "Did Tempi tell you of the nine-and-ninety tales?" she asked without preamble. "Of Aethe and the beginning of the Adem?"

I shook my head.

"Good," Shehyn said. "It is not his place to do such a thing, and he could not do it properly." She looked at Vashet. "How is language coming?"

"Quickly, as these things go," she said. *However.*

"Very well," Shehyn said, switching to precise, slightly accented Aturan. "I will tell it like this, so there will be less interruption, and less room for misunderstanding."

I did my best to gesture *respectful gratitude.*

"This is a story of years ago," Shehyn said formally. "Before this school. Before the path of the sword tree. Before any Adem knew of the Lethani. This is a story of the beginning of such things.

"The first Adem school was not a school that taught sword-work. Surprisingly, it was founded by a man named Aethe who sought mastery over the arrow and the bow."

Shehyn paused in her tale and gave a word of explanation. "You should know that in those days, use of the bow was very common. The skill of it was much prized. We were shepherds, and much set on by our enemies, and the bow was the best tool we had to defend ourselves."

Shehyn leaned back in her chair and continued. "Aethe did not set out to found a school. There were no schools in those days. He merely sought to improve his skill. All his will he bent upon this, until he could shoot an apple from a tree one hundred feet away. Then he strove until he could shoot the wick of a burning candle. Soon the only target that challenged him was a piece of hanging silk blowing in the wind. Aethe strove until he could anticipate the turning of the wind, and once he had mastered this thing, he could not miss.

"Stories of his talent spread, and others came to him. Among them was a young woman named Rethe. At first Aethe doubted she possessed the strength to draw the bow. But she was soon regarded as his finest student.

"As I have said, this was long years and distant miles from where we sit. In those days, the Adem did not have the Lethani to guide us, and so it was a rough and bloody time. In those days it was not uncommon for one Adem to kill another out of pride, or from an argument, or as a proof of skill.

"Since Aethe was the greatest of archers, many challenged him. But a body is nothing of a target when one can strike silk blowing in the wind. Aethe slew them easily as cutting wheat. He took only a single arrow with him to a duel, and claimed if that single arrow was not enough, he deserved to be struck down.

"Aethe grew older, and his fame spread. He put down roots and began the first of the Adem schools. Years passed, and he trained many Adem to be deadly as knives. It became well known that if you gave Aethe's students three arrows and three coins, your three worst enemies would never bother you again.

"So the school grew rich and famous and proud. And so did Aethe.

"It was then that Rethe came to him. Rethe, his best student. Rethe who stood nearest his ear and closest to his heart.

"Rethe spoke to Aethe, and they disagreed. Then they argued. Then they shouted loud enough that all the school could hear it through the thick stone walls.

"And at the end of it, Rethe challenged Aethe to a duel. Aethe accepted, and it was known that the winner would control the school from that day forth.

"As the challenged, Aethe chose his place first. He chose to stand among a grove of young and swaying trees that gave him shifting cover. Normally he would not bother with precautions such as this, but Rethe was his finest student, and she could read the wind just as well as he. He took with him his bow of horn. He took with him his sharp and single arrow.

"Then Rethe chose her place to stand. She walked to the top of a high hill, her outline clear against the naked sky. She carried neither bow nor arrow. And when she reached the top of the hill, she sat calmly on the ground. This was perhaps the oddest thing of all, as Aethe was known to sometimes strike a foe through the leg rather than kill them.

"Aethe saw his student do this, and he was filled with anger. Aethe took his single arrow and fitted it to his bow. Aethe drew the string against his ear. The string Rethe had made for him, woven from the long, strong strands of her own hair."

Shehyn met my eye. "Full of anger, Aethe shot his arrow. It struck Rethe like a thunderbolt. Here." She pointed with two fingers at the inner curve of her left breast.

"Still seated, arrow sprouting from her chest, Rethe drew a long ribbon of white silk from beneath her shirt. She took a white feather from the arrow's fletching, dipped it in her blood, and wrote four lines of poetry.

"Then Rethe held the ribbon aloft for a long moment, waiting as the wind pulled first one way, then another. Then Rethe loosed it, the silk twisting through the air, rising and falling on the breeze. The ribbon twisted in the wind, wove its way through the trees, and pressed itself firmly against Aethe's chest.

"It read:

Aethe, near my heart.
Without vanity, the ribbon.
Without duty, the wind.
Without blood, the victory.

I heard a low noise and looked over to see Vashet weeping quietly to herself. Her head was lowered, and tears ran down her face to drip deeper spots of red onto the front of her shirt.

Shehyn continued. "Only after Aethe read these lines did he recognize the deep wisdom his student possessed. He hurried to tend Rethe's wounds, but the head of the arrow was lodged too close to her heart to be removed.

"Rethe lived only three days after that, with the grief-stricken Aethe tending her. He gave her control of the school, and listened to her words, all the while the head of the arrow riding close to her heart.

"During those days, Rethe dictated nine-and-ninety stories, and Aethe wrote them down. These tales were the beginning of our understanding of the Lethani. They are the root of all Ademre.

"Late in the third day Rethe finished telling the ninety-ninth story to Aethe, who now held himself to be his student's student. After Aethe finished writing, Rethe said to him, 'There is one final story, more important than all the rest, and that one shall be known when I awake.'

"Then Rethe closed her eyes and slept. And sleeping, she died.

"Aethe lived forty years after that, and it is said he never killed again. In the years that followed, he was often heard to say, 'I won the only duel I ever lost.'

"He continued to run the school and train his students to be masters of the bow. But now he also trained them to be wise. He told them the nine-and-ninety tales, and thus it was the Lethani first came to be known by all Ademre. And that is how we came to be that which we are."

There was a long pause.

"I thank you, Shehyn," I said doing my best to gesture *respectful gratitude*. "I would very much like to hear these nine-and-ninety stories."

"They are not for barbarians," she said. But she didn't seem offended at my request, gesturing a combination of *reproach* and *regret*. She changed the subject. "How is your Ketan coming?"

"I struggle to improve, Shehyn."

She turned to Vashet. "Does he?"

"There is certainly struggle," Vashet said, her eyes still red with tears. *Wry amusement*. "But there is improvement, too."

Shehyn nodded. *Reserved approval.* "Several of us will be fighting tomorrow. Perhaps you could bring him to watch."

Vashet made an elegant motion that made me appreciate how little I knew of the subtleties of hand-language: *Gracious thankful slightly submissive acceptance.*

"You should be flattered," Vashet said cheerfully. "A conversation with Shehyn and an invitation to watch her fight."

We were making our way back to a sheltered box valley where we typically practiced the Ketan and our hand fighting.

However, my mind kept spinning back to several unavoidable and unpleasant thoughts. I was thinking about secrets and how people longed to keep them. I wondered what Kilvin would do if I brought someone into the Fishery and showed them the sygaldry for blood and bone and hair.

The thought of the big artificer's anger was enough to make me shiver. I knew the sort of trouble I would face. That was clearly laid out in the University's laws. But what would he do to the person I had taught these things to?

Vashet slapped my chest with the back of her hand to get my attention. "I said you should be flattered," she repeated.

"I am," I said.

She took hold of my shoulder, turning me to face her. "You've gone all pensive on me."

"What will be done with Tempi if all of this ends badly?" I asked bluntly.

Her cheerful expression faded. "His reds will be taken away, and his sword, and his name, and he will be cut away from the Latantha." She drew a slow breath. "It is unlikely any other school would take him after such a thing, so this would effectively exile him from all Ademre."

"But exile won't work for me," I said. "Forcing me back into the world would only make the problem worse, wouldn't it?"

Vashet didn't say anything.

"When all of this started," I said. "You encouraged me to leave. If I had run, would I have been allowed to go?"

There was a long silence that told me the truth of it. But she said it aloud, too. "No."

I appreciated not being lied to about it. "And what is my punishment to be?" I asked. "Imprisonment?" I shook my head. "No. It's not practical to keep me locked up here for years." I looked up at her. "So what?"

"Punishment is not our concern," she said. "You are a barbarian, after all. You did not know you were doing anything wrong. The main concern is to prevent you from teaching others what you have stolen, to keep you from using it to your own profit."

She hadn't answered my question. I gave her a long look.

"Some say killing you would be the best way," she said frankly. "But most believe killing is not in keeping with the Lethani. Shehyn is among these. As am I."

I relaxed slightly, that was something at least. "And I don't suppose a promise on my part would reassure anyone?"

She gave me a sympathetic smile. "It speaks well of you that you came back with Tempi. And you stayed when I tried to drive you away. But the promise of a barbarian amounts for little in this."

"What then?" I asked, suspecting the answer and knowing I wasn't going to like it.

She took a deep breath. "You could be prevented from teaching by removing your tongue or putting out your eyes," she said frankly. "To keep you from using the Ketan you might be hobbled. Your ankle tendon cut, or the knee of your favored leg lamed." She shrugged. "But one can still be a good fighter even with a damaged leg. So it would be more effective to remove the two smallest fingers from your right hand. This would be . . ."

Vashet kept speaking in her matter-of-fact tone. I think she intended it to be reassuring, calming. But it had the opposite effect. All I could think of was her cutting off my fingers as calmly as you would pare away a piece of apple. Everything grew bright around the edges of my vision, and the vivid mental picture made my stomach roll over. I thought for a moment I might be sick.

The light-headedness and nausea passed. As I came to my senses, I realized Vashet had finished talking and was staring at me.

Before I could say anything, she waved a hand dismissively. "I see I will get no more use of you today. Take the rest of the evening for yourself. Get your thoughts in order or practice the Ketan. Go watch the sword tree. Tomorrow we will continue."

———

I walked aimlessly for a while, trying not to think about my fingers being cut away. Then, coming over a hill, I stumbled almost literally onto a naked Adem couple tucked away in a grove of trees.

They didn't scramble for their clothes when I burst out of the trees, and rather than try to apologize with my poor language and fuddled wits, I simply turned and left, face burning with embarrassment.

I tried to practice the Ketan but couldn't keep my mind on it. I went to watch the sword tree, and for a while the sight of it moving gracefully in the wind calmed me. Then my mind drifted and I was confronted with the image of Vashet paring off my fingers again.

I heard the three high bells and went to dinner. I was standing in line, half stupid with the mental effort of not thinking of someone maiming my hands, when I noticed the Adem standing nearby were staring at me. A young girl of about ten wore an expression of open amazement on her face, and a man in his mercenary reds looked at me as if he had just seen me wipe my ass with a piece of bread and eat it.

Only then did I realize I was humming. Not loud, exactly, but loud enough for those nearby to hear. I couldn't have been doing it for long, as I was only six lines into "Leave the Town, Tinker."

I stopped, then lowered my eyes, took my food, and spent ten minutes trying to eat. I managed a few bites, but that was all. Eventually I gave up and headed to my room.

I lay in bed, running through the options in my mind. How far could I run? Could I lose myself in the surrounding countryside? Could I steal a horse? Had I even seen a horse since I'd been in Haert?

I brought out my lute and practiced my chording a bit, all five of my clever fingers flicking up and down the long neck of the lute. But my right hand ached to strum and pick notes from the strings. It was as frustrating as trying to kiss someone using only one lip, and I soon gave up.

At last I brought out my shaed and wrapped it around myself. It was warm and comforting. I drew the hood over my head as far as it would go and thought of the dark piece of Fae where Felurian had gathered its shadows.

I thought of the University, of Wil and Sim. Of Auri and Devi and Fela. I had never been popular at the University, and my circle of friends had never seemed particularly large. But the truth was I'd simply forgotten what it was like to be truly alone.

I thought of my family then. I thought of the Chandrian, of Cinder. His fluid grace. His sword held easy in his hand like a piece of winter ice. I thought of killing him.

I thought of Denna and what the Cthaeh had told me. I thought of her patron and the things I had said during our fight. I thought about the time she had slipped on the road and I had caught her, how the gentle curve above her hip had felt against my hand. I thought about the shape of her mouth, the sound of her voice, the smell of her hair.

And, eventually, I stepped softly through the doors of sleep.

Storm and Stone

I WOKE THE NEXT MORNING knowing the truth. My only way out of this situation was through the school. I needed to prove myself. That meant I needed everything Vashet could teach me as quickly as possible.

So the next morning I rose in the pale blue light of dawn. And when Vashet emerged from her small stone house I was waiting for her. I was not particularly bright-eyed or bushy-tailed, as my sleep had been filled with troubling dreams, but I was ready to learn.

———

I realize now that I may have given an inaccurate impression of Haert.

It was no thriving metropolis, obviously. And it couldn't be considered a city by any stretch of the imagination. In some ways it was barely a town.

I do not say this disparagingly. I spent the majority of my young life traveling with my troupe, moving from small town to small town. Half the world is made of tiny communities that have grown up around nothing more than a crossroads market, or a good clay pit, or a bend of river strong enough to turn a mill wheel.

Sometimes these towns are prosperous. Some have rich soil and generous weather. Some thrive on the trade moving through them. The wealth of these places is obvious. The houses are large and well-mended. People are friendly and generous. The children are fat and happy. There are luxuries for sale: pepper and cinnamon and chocolate. There is coffee and good wine and music at the local inn.

Then there are the other sort of towns. Towns where the soil is thin and tired. Towns where the mill burned down, or the clay was mined out years ago. In these places the houses are small and badly patched. The people are lean and suspicious, and wealth is measured in small, practical ways. Cords of firewood. A second pig. Five jars of blackberry preserve.

At first glance, Haert seemed to be this sort of town. It was little more than tiny homes, broken stone, and the occasional penned goat.

In most parts of the Commonwealth, or anywhere in the Four Corners for that matter, a family living in a small cottage with only a few sticks of furniture would be viewed as unfortunate. One step away from paupers.

But while most of the Adem homes I had seen were relatively small, they weren't the same sort you would find in a desperate Aturan town, made of sod and logs chinked with mud.

The Adem homes were all snug stone, fit together as cunningly as anything I had ever seen. There were no cracks letting in the endless wind. No leaking roofs. No cracking leather hinges on the doors. The windows weren't oiled sheepskin or empty holes with wooden shutters. They were fitted glass, tight as any you'd find in a banker's manor.

I never saw a fireplace in all my time in Haert. Don't get me wrong, fireplaces are better than freezing to death by a long step. But most of the rough ones folk can build for themselves out of loose fieldstone or cinder-brick are drafty, dirty, and inefficient. They fill your house with soot and your lungs with smoke.

Instead of fireplaces, each Adem home had its own iron stove. The sort of stove that weighs hundreds of pounds. The sort of stove made of thick drop-iron so you can stoke it until it glows with heat. The sort of stove that lasts a century and costs more than a farmer earns from an entire year of hard harvesting. Some of these stoves were small, good for heating and cooking. But I saw more than a few that were larger and could be used for baking too. One of these treasures was tucked away in a low stone house of only three rooms.

The rugs on the Adem floors were mostly simple, but they were of thick, soft wool, deeply dyed. The floors beneath those rugs were smooth-sanded wood, not dirt. There were no guttering tallow tapers or reedlights. There were beeswax candles or lamps that burned a clean white oil. And once, through a distant window, I recognized the unwavering red light of a sympathy lamp.

It was this last that made me realize the truth. This was not a scattered handful of desperate folk, scratching out a lean existence on the bare mountainside. They were not living hand-to-mouth, eating cabbage soup and living in fear of winter. This community was comfortably, quietly prosperous.

More than that. Despite the lack of glittering banquet halls and fancy gowns, despite the absence of servants and statuary, each of these homes was like a tiny manor house. They were each of them wealthy in a quiet, practical way.

"What did you think?" Vashet said, laughing at me. "That a handful of us win our reds and run off to lives of mad luxury while our families drink their own bathwater and die of scurvy?"

"I hadn't though of it at all, really," I said, looking around. Vashet was beginning to show me how to use a sword. We had been at it for two hours, and she had done little more than explain the different ways of holding it. As if it were a baby and not a piece of steel.

Now that I knew what to look for, I could see dozens of the Adem houses worked cunningly into the landscape. Heavy wooden doors were dug into bluffs. Others looked like little more than tumbles of stone. Some had grass growing on their roofs and could only be recognized by the stovepipes peeping out. A fat nanny goat grazed atop one of these, her udder swinging as she stretched out her neck to crop a mouthful of grass.

"Look at the land around you," she said, spinning in a slow circle to take in the landscape. "The ground is too thin for the plow, too jagged for horses. The summer too wet for wheat, too harsh for fruit. Some mountains hold iron, or coal, or gold. But not these mountains. In winter the snow will pile higher than your head. In spring the storms will push you from your feet."

She looked back at me. "This is our land because no one else wants it." She shrugged. "Or rather, it became ours for that reason."

Vashet adjusted her sword on her shoulder, then eyed me speculatively. "Sit and listen," she said formally. "And I will tell a story of a time long gone."

I sat on the grass, and Vashet took her place on a nearby stone. "Long ago," she said, "the Adem were upheaved from our rightful place. Something we cannot remember drove us out. Someone stole our land, or ruined it, or made us flee in fear. We were forced to wander endlessly. Our whole nation mendicant, like beggars. We would find a place, and settle, and rest our flocks. Then those who lived nearby would drive us off.

"The Adem were fierce back then. If we had not been fierce, there would be none of us left today. But we were few, so we were always driven forth. Finally we found this thin and windy place, unwanted by the world. We dug our roots deep into the stone and made it ours."

Vashet's eyes wandered the landscape. "But this land had little to give us, a place for our flocks to graze, stone, and endless wind. We could not find a way to sell the wind, so we sold our fierceness to the world. So we lived, and slowly we sharpened ourselves into the thing we are today. No longer only fierce, but dangerous and proud. Unceasing as the wind and strong as stone."

I waited a moment to make sure she was finished. "My people are wanderers too," I said. "It is our way. Nowhere and everywhere is where we live."

She shrugged, smiling. "It is a story, mind you. And an old one. Take from it what you will."

"I am fond of stories," I said.

"A story is like a nut," Vashet said. "A fool will swallow it whole and choke. A fool will throw it away, thinking it of little worth." She smiled. "But a wise woman finds a way to crack the shell and eat the meat inside."

I got to my feet and walked to where she was sitting. I kissed her hands and her forehead and her mouth. "Vashet," I said. "I am glad Shehyn gave me to you."

"You are a foolish boy." She looked down, but I could see a faint blush rising on her face as she spoke. "Come. We should go. You do not want to miss the chance to see Shehyn fight."

Vashet led me to an unmarked piece of meadow where the thick grass had been grazed close to the ground. A few other Adem already stood nearby, waiting. Some folk had brought small stools or rolled pieces of log to use as benches. Vashet simply sat on the ground. I joined her.

A crowd slowly gathered. Only thirty people or so, but it was the most Adem I'd ever seen together other than in the dining hall. They gathered in twos and threes, moving from one conversation to another. Rarely did a group of five coalesce for any length of time.

Though there were a dozen conversations all within a stone's throw of me, I couldn't hear more than a murmur. The speakers stood close enough to touch, and the wind in the grass made more noise than their voices.

But I could tell the tone of each conversation from where I sat. Two months ago this gathering would have seemed eerily subdued. A gathering of fidgety, emotionless, near-mutes. But now I could plainly see one pair of Adem were teacher and student by how far apart they stood, by the deference in the younger woman's hands. The cluster of three red-shirted men were friends, easy and joking as they jostled at each other. That man and woman were fighting. She was angry. He was trying to explain.

I suddenly wondered how I ever could have thought of these people as restless or fidgety. Every motion was to a purpose. Every shifting of the feet implied a change in attitude. Every gesture spoke volumes.

Vashet and I sat close to each other and kept our voices low, continuing our discussion in Aturan. She explained how each school had standing accounts with the Cealdish moneylenders. That meant far-flung mercenaries could deposit the school's share of their earnings anywhere people used Cealdish currency, which meant anywhere in the entire civilized world. That money was then tallied to the appropriate account so the school could make use of it.

"How much does a mercenary send back to the school?" I asked, curious.

"Eighty percent," she said.

"Eight percent?" I asked, holding up all my fingers but two, sure I had misheard.

"Eighty," Vashet said firmly. "That is the proper amount, though many pride themselves on giving more. The same would be true for you," she said dismissively, "if you stood a fiddler's chance in hell of ever wearing the red."

Seeing my astonishment, she explained. "It is not so much, when you think of it. For years, the school feeds and clothes you. It gives you a place to sleep. It gives you your sword, your training. After this investment, the mercenary supports the school. The school supports the village. The village produces children who hope to someday take the red." She made a circle with her finger. "Thus all Ademre thrives."

Vashet gave me a grave look. "Knowing this, perhaps you can begin to understand what you have stolen," she said. "Not just a secret but the major export of the Adem. You have stolen the key to this entire town's survival."

It was a sobering thought. Suddenly Carceret's anger made much better sense.

I caught a glimpse of Shehyn's white shirt and roughly knitted yellow cap through the crowd. The scattered conversations grew still, and everyone began to gather into a large, loose circle.

It wasn't just Shehyn fighting today, apparently. The first to fight were two boys a few years younger than myself, neither of them wearing red. They circled each other warily, then fell on each other in a flurry of blows.

It was too fast for my eye to follow, and I saw a dozen half-formed pieces of the Ketan scattered and discarded. It finally ended when one boy caught the other's wrist and shoulder in Sleeping Bear. It was only when I saw the boy twist his opponent's arm and force him to the ground that I recognized it as the grip Tempi had used in the bar fight in Crosson.

The boys separated, and two red-shirted mercenaries came out to talk to them, presumably their teachers.

Vashet leaned her head close to mine. "What do you think?"

"They're very quick," I said.

She looked at me. "But . . ."

"They seem rather sloppy," I said, being careful to speak quietly. "Not at first, but after they started." I pointed at one. "His feet were too close together. And the other kept leaning forward so his balance was off. That's how he got caught in Sleeping Bear."

Vashet nodded, pleased. "They fight like puppies. They are young, and boys. They are full of anger and impatience. Women have less trouble with these things. It's part of what makes us better fighters."

I was more than slightly surprised to hear her say that. "Women are better fighters?" I asked carefully, not wanting to contradict her.

"Generally speaking," she said matter-of-factly. "There are exceptions, of course, but as a whole women are better."

"But men are stronger," I said. "Taller. They have better reach."

She turned to look at me, slightly amused. "Are you stronger and taller than me then?"

I smiled. "Obviously not. But as a whole, you have to admit, men are bigger and stronger."

Vashet shrugged. "And that would matter if fighting were the same as splitting wood or hauling hay. That is like saying a sword is better the longer and heavier it is. Foolishness. Perhaps for thugs this is true. But after taking the red, the key is knowing *when* to fight. Men are full of anger, so they have trouble with this. Women less so."

I opened my mouth, then thought of Dedan and closed it.

A shadow fell over us, and I looked up to see a tall man in his reds standing at a polite distance. He held his hand poised near the hilt of his sword. *Invitation.*

Vashet gestured back. *Gentle regret and refusal.*

I watched as he walked away. "Won't they think less of you for not fighting?"

Vashet sniffed disdainfully. "He didn't want to fight," she said. "It would only embarrass him and waste my time. He merely wanted to show he was brave enough to fight me." She sighed and gave me a pointed look. "It is that sort of foolishness that leads men from the Lethani."

The next match was between two red-shirted mercenaries, and the difference was obvious. Everything was much cleaner and crisper. The two boys had been frantic as sparrows flapping in the dust, but the fights that followed were elegant as dances.

Many of the bouts were hand fighting. These lasted until one person submitted or was visibly stunned by a blow.

One fight stopped immediately when a man bloodied his opponent's nose. Vashet rolled her eyes at this, though I couldn't tell if she thought less of the woman for allowing herself to be struck, or the man for being reckless enough to hurt her.

There were several bouts with wooden swords, too. These tended to go more quickly, as even a light touch was considered enough for a victory.

"Who won that one?" I asked. After a quick exchange of clacking sword-play ended with both women scoring hits at the same time.

"Neither," she said, frowning.

"Why don't they fight again if it was a tie?" I asked.

Vashet frowned at me. "It wasn't a tie, strictly speaking. Drenn would have died in minutes, struck through the lung. Lasrel would have died in days when the wound in her gut soured."

"So Lasrel won?"

Vashet gave me a look of withering contempt and turned her attention back to the next fight.

The tall Adem man who had asked Vashet to fight was bouting with a thin whip of a woman. Strangely, he used a wooden sword while she was barehanded. He won by a narrow margin after catching two solid kicks to the ribs.

"Who won there?" Vashet asked me.

I could tell she wasn't looking for the obvious answer. "It's not much of a victory," I said. "She didn't even have a sword."

"She is of the third stone and far outstrips him as a fighter. It was the only way for things to be balanced between them unless he were to bring a companion to fight by his side," Vashet pointed out. "So I ask again. Who won?"

"He won the bout," I said. "But he'll have some impressive bruises tomorrow. Also, his swings seemed somewhat reckless."

Vashet turned to look at me. "So who won?"

I thought about it for a moment. "Neither," I decided.

She nodded. *Formal approval.* The gesture warmed me, as everyone facing us could see it.

At long last, Shehyn stepped into the circle. She had removed her lopsided yellow hat, and her greying hair swirled about in the wind. Seeing her among the other Adem, I realized how small she was. She carried herself with such confidence that I had come to think of her as taller, but she barely came up to the shoulder of some of the taller Adem.

She carried a straight wooden sword with her. Nothing ornate, but it was carved to have the shape of a hilt and blade. Many of the other practice swords I had seen were barely more than smoothed sticks that gave the impression of being swords. Her white shirt and pants were tied tightly to her body with thin white chords.

Alongside Shehyn came a much younger woman. She was shorter than Shehyn by an inch or so. Her frame was more delicate, too, her small face and shoulders making her look almost childlike. But the pronounced curve of her high breasts and round hips beneath her tight mercenary reds made it obvious she was no child.

Her wooden sword was also carved. It was curved slightly, unlike most of the others I had seen. Her sandy hair was braided into a long, narrow plait that hung down to the small of her back.

The two of them raised their swords and began to circle each other.

The young woman was amazing. She struck so fast I could barely see the motion of her hand, let alone the blade of her sword. But Shehyn brushed it away casually with Drifting Snow, taking half a step in retreat. Then, before Shehyn could respond with an attack of her own, the young woman spun away, her long braid swinging.

"Who is she?" I asked.

"Penthe," Vashet said admiringly. "She is a fury, is she not? Like one of our old ancestors."

Penthe closed with Shehyn again, feinting and thrusting. She darted in, low to the ground. Impossibly low. Her back leg thrust out for balance, not even touching the ground. Her sword arm licked out in front of her, her knee bent so deeply that her entire body was below the level of my head, even though I was sitting cross-legged on the ground.

Penthe unfurled all this sinuous motion as quickly you can snap your fingers. The tip of her sword came in low under Shehyn's guard and angled up toward her knee.

"What is that?" I asked softly, not even expecting an answer. "You never showed me that." But it was just astonished noise. Never in a hundred years could my body do that.

But Shehyn somehow avoided the attack. Not leaping away with any sudden motion. Not darting out of reach. She was quick, but that was not the heart of how she moved. Instead she was deliberate and perfect. She was already halfway gone before Penthe's sword had begun to flick toward her leg. The tip of Penthe's sword must have come within an inch of her knee. But it was not a close thing. Shehyn had only moved as much as was needed, no more.

This time Shehyn did manage to counterattack, stepping forward with Sparrow Strikes the Hawk. Penthe rolled sideways, touched the grass briefly, then pushed herself up off the ground. No, she *threw* herself away from the ground using only her left hand. Her body snapped like a steel spring, arcing away while her sword licked out twice, driving Shehyn back.

Penthe was full of passion and fury. Shehyn was calm and steady. Penthe was a storm. Shehyn a stone. Penthe was a tiger and Shehyn a bird. Penthe danced and wove madly. Shehyn turned and took one single perfect step.

Penthe slashed and spun and whirled and struck and struck and struck. . . .

And then they stopped, the tip of Penthe's wooden sword pressed to Shehyn's white shirt.

I gasped, though not loudly enough to draw any attention. Only then did I realize my heart was racing. My entire body was covered in sweat.

Shehyn lowered her sword, gesturing *irritation, admiration*, and a mingling of other things I couldn't identify. She bared her teeth a little in a grimace and used her hand to chafe roughly at her ribs where Penthe had struck her. The same way you rub your shin when you bark it against a chair.

Horrified, I turned to Vashet. "Will she be the new leader of the school?" I asked.

Vashet looked at me, puzzled.

I gestured to the open circle in front of us where the two women stood talking. "This Penthe. She's beaten Shehyn . . ."

Vashet looked at me for a moment, uncomprehending, then burst out in a long, delighted laugh. "Shehyn is *old*," she said. "She is a grandmother. You cannot expect her to always win against a limber young thing like Penthe, all full of fire and fresh wind."

"Ah," I said. "I see. I thought . . ."

Vashet was kind enough not to laugh at me again. "Shehyn is not the head of the school because no one can beat her. What an odd notion. What chaos that would be, everything tipping this way and that, changing with the luck of one fight or another."

She shook her head. "Shehyn is the head because she is a marvelous teacher, and because her understanding of the Lethani is deep. She is the head because she is wise in the ways of the world, and because she is clever at dealing with troublesome problems." She tapped me pointedly on the chest with two fingers.

Then Vashet made a conciliatory gesture. "She is also an excellent fighter, of course. We would not have a leader who could not fight. Shehyn's Ketan is without equal. But a leader is not a muscle. A leader is a mind."

I looked up in time to see Shehyn approaching. One of the cords holding her sleeve in place had come loose during the fight, and the cloth was fluttering in the wind like a luffing sail. She had donned her lopsided yellow cap again and gestured *formal greeting* to both of us.

Then Shehyn turned to me. "At the end," she asked. "Why was I struck?" *Curiosity*.

Frantically, I thought back to the final moments of the fight, looking them over in my mind's eye.

I tried to gesture with the subtlety Vashet had been teaching me: *respectful uncertainty*. "You misplaced your heel slightly," I said. "Your left heel."

Shehyn nodded. "Good." She gestured *pleased approval* widely enough so anyone who happened to be watching could see it. And, of course, everyone was.

Giddy with praise, but conscious of the fact I was being watched, I kept my face locked in the proper impassivity as Shehyn walked away with Penthe in tow.

I leaned my head close to Vashet's. "I like Shehyn's little hat," I said.

Vashet shook her head and sighed. "Come." She jostled my shoulder with her own and got to her feet. "We should leave before you spoil the good impression you have made today."

———

That night at supper, I sat in my customary place at the corner of one table by the wall farthest from the food. Since no one was willing to sit within ten feet of me, there was no sense my taking up space where people might actually want to sit.

My good mood still buoyed me, so I was not surprised when I saw a flicker of red slide into the seat across from me. Carceret again. Once or twice a day she made a point to come close enough to hiss a few words at me. She was overdue.

But looking up, I was surprised. Vashet sat across from me. She nodded, her impassive face staring into my astonished one. Then I composed myself, nodded back, and we ate for a while in companionable silence. After we were finished eating, we passed some time pleasantly, speaking softly of small things.

We left the dining hall together, and when we stepped into the evening air, I switched back into Aturan so I could properly articulate something I'd been thinking for several hours.

"Vashet," I said. "It occurs to me it would be nice to fight someone whose ability is somewhat closer to my own."

Vashet laughed, shaking her head. "That is like throwing two virgins into a bed. Enthusiasm, passion, and ignorance are not a good combination. Someone is likely to get hurt."

"I hardly think it's fair to call my fighting *virginal*," I said. "I'm not near your level, but you yourself said my Ketan is remarkably good."

"I said your Ketan was remarkably good considering the amount of time you have been studying," she corrected me. "Which is less than two months. Which is no time at all."

"It's frustrating," I admitted. "If I strike a blow against you, it's because you let me. There is no substance to it. You've given it to me. I haven't earned it for myself."

"Any strike or throw you make against me is earned," she said. "Even if I offer it to you. But I understand. There is something to be said for honest competition."

I started to say something else, but she put her hand over my mouth. "I've said I understand. Stop fighting after you have won." Hand still over my mouth, she tapped a finger thoughtfully. "Very well. Continue your progress and I will find you someone at your own level to fight."

Height

I WAS ALMOST BEGINNING TO feel comfortable in Haert. My language was improving and I felt less isolated now that I was able to exchange brief pleasantries with others. Vashet occasionally shared meals with me, helping me feel like slightly less of a pariah.

We had done sword-work this morning, which meant an easy start to the day. Vashet was still showing me how the sword was incorporated into the Ketan, and the moments we fought were few and far between. After a few hours of this, we worked on my Ademic, then more sword-work.

After lunch, we moved on to hand fighting. I couldn't help but feel that here, at least, I was progressing well. After half an hour, not only was Vashet breathing harder, but she began to sweat a bit. I was still no sort of challenge to her, of course, but after days of humiliating nonchalance on her part, she was finally having to put forth a shred of effort to keep ahead of me.

So we continued to fight, and I noticed that— How can I say this delicately? She smelled wonderful. Not like perfume or flowers or anything like that. She smelled like clean sweat and oiled metal and crushed grass from when I'd thrown her to the ground some time before. It was a good smell. She . . .

I can't describe this delicately, I suppose. What I mean to say is that she smelled like sex. Not as if she'd been having it, as if she was made of it. When she came in close to grapple me, the smell of her combined with her body pressing against mine . . . For a second it was like someone had thrown a switch in my head. All I could think of was kissing her mouth, biting the soft skin of her neck, tearing at her clothes and licking the sweat off her—

I did none of these things, of course. But at the moment I wanted nothing more. This is embarrassing to look back on, but I will not bother defending myself except to point out that I was in the full flower of my youth, fit and healthy. And she was quite an attractive woman, though ten years my senior.

Add to this the simple fact that I had gone from the loving arms of Felurian, to the eager arms of Losine, and from thence to a long, barren stretch of training with Tempi as we traveled to Haert. That meant for three span, I had been constantly exhausted, anxious, confused, and terrified by turns.

Now I was none of these things. Vashet was a good teacher and made sure I was well-rested and relaxed as possible. I was growing more confident in my abilities and more comfortable around her.

Given all of this, it's no great surprise I had the reaction I did.

At the time, however, I was startled and embarrassed as only a young man can be. I stepped away from Vashet, blushing and fumbling an apology. I tried to hide my obvious arousal, and in doing so only drew more attention to it.

Vashet looked down at what my hands were trying vainly to conceal. "Well then, I suppose I will take that as a compliment and not a curious new avenue of attack."

If a person could die from shame, I would have.

"Would you like to take care of it yourself?" Vashet asked easily. "Or would you prefer a partner?"

"I beg your pardon?" I said stupidly.

"Come now." She gestured to my hands. "Even if you could keep your mind away from that, it would doubtless throw your balance off." She gave a low, throaty chuckle. "You'll need to tend to it before we continue your lessons. I can leave you to it, or we can find a soft spot and see who can pin the other best two of three."

The casual tone of her voice convinced me I'd misunderstood her. Then she gave me a knowing smirk, and I realized I'd understood her perfectly well.

"Where I come from, a teacher and a student would never . . ." I stumbled, trying to think of a polite way to defuse the situation.

Vashet rolled her eyes at me, the exasperated expression looking odd on an Adem face. "Do your teachers and students also never fight? Never talk? Never eat together?"

"But this," I said, "This . . ."

She sighed. "Kvothe, you need to remember. You come from a barbarous place. Much of what you grew up thinking is quite wrongheaded and foolish. None of it as much as the strange customs you barbarians have built around your sexplay."

"Vashet," I said. "I . . ."

She cut me off with a sharp gesture. "Whatever you are about to say, I have doubtless heard before from my poet king. But there are only so many hours of light in the day. So I ask you this: are you desirous of sex?"

I gave a helpless shrug, knowing it would be pointless to deny it.

"Would you like to have sex with me?"

I could still smell her. At that moment, I wanted it more than anything. "Yes."

"Are you free of disease?" she asked seriously.

I nodded, too off balance to be startled by the frankness of the question.

"Very well then. If I remember correctly, there is a nice patch of moss out of the wind not too far from here." She began to walk up a nearby hill, her fingers working the buckle that fastened her sword's scabbard over her shoulder. "Come with me."

Her memory did serve her well. Two trees arched their branches over a thick bed of soft moss that was snugged up against a small stony bluff, sheltered from the wind by some convenient bushes.

It quickly became obvious that what Vashet had in mind was not an afternoon of twining idly in the shade. To say she was businesslike would be a great disservice to her, as Vashet's laughter always ran very close to the surface. But she was not flirtatious or coy.

She stripped off her mercenary reds without the least fanfare or teasing, revealing a few scars, and a body hard and lean and corded with muscle. Which isn't to say that she wasn't also round and soft as well. Then she teased me for staring as if I'd never seen a naked woman before, when the truth was I'd simply never seen one standing full naked in the sunlight.

When I didn't undress fast enough to suit her, Vashet laughed and mocked my bashfulness. Stepping close, she stripped me naked as a plucked chicken, then kissed me on the mouth, her warm skin pressing against the entire front of my body.

"I've never kissed a woman my own height before," I mused when we stopped for a breath. "It's a different experience."

"See how I continue to be your teacher in all things?" she said. "Your next lesson is this: all women are the same height lying down. The same cannot be said for your sort, of course. Too much depends on a man's mood and his natural gifts."

Vashet took my hand and brought us both to lie on the soft moss. "There," she said. "As I suspected. Now you are taller than me. Does this set you at your ease?"

It did.

———

I was prepared for things to be awkward after Vashet and I returned from the bushes, and was surprised to find they were nothing of the sort. She did not suddenly grow flirtatious, which I wouldn't have known how to cope with. Neither did she feel obliged to treat me with any newfound tenderness. This became clear somewhere around the fifth time she managed to lure me off my guard, catch me with Thunder Upward, and throw me roughly to the ground.

In all, she acted as if nothing odd at all had happened. Which meant either nothing odd had happened or something very odd had happened and she was pointedly ignoring it.

Which meant that everything was lovely, or everything was going terribly wrong.

Later, as I ate supper alone, I rolled what I knew of the Adem around in my head. No nudity taboo. They didn't consider physical contact particularly intimate. Vashet had been very casual both before, during, and after our encounter.

I thought back to the naked couple I had stumbled onto several days ago. They had been startled, but not embarrassed.

Sex was viewed differently here, obviously. But I didn't know any of the specific differences. That meant I didn't have the first idea of how to conduct myself properly. And *that* meant what I was doing was dangerous as walking around blind. More like running blind, really.

Normally if I had a question about the Adem culture, I asked Vashet. She was my touchstone. But I could imagine too many ways for that conversation to go astray, and her goodwill was all that stood between me and the loss of my fingers.

By the time I finished eating, I'd decided it would be best to simply follow Vashet's lead. She was my teacher, after all.

Barbarian Cunning

THE DAYS PASSED QUICKLY, as days tend to do when there is much to
fill them. Vashet continued to teach me, and I turned the whole of my
attention toward being a clever and attentive student.

Our amorous encounters continued, punctuating my training. I never ini-
tiated them directly, but Vashet could tell when I was unproductively distracted and was quick to pull me down into the bushes. "In order to clear
your foolish barbarian head," as she said.

Before and afterward I still found these encounters troubling. During,
however, I was far from anxious. Vashet seemed to enjoy herself as well.

That said, she didn't seem the least interested in much of what I had
learned from Felurian. She had no interest in playing ivy, and while she did
enjoy thousand hands, she had little patience for it, and it usually ended up
being more like seventy-five hands. Generally speaking, as soon as we had
caught our breath, Vashet was tying on her mercenary reds and reminding me
that if I kept forgetting to turn my heel out, I would never be able to hit any
harder than a boy of six.

Not all my time was spent training with Vashet. When she was busy, she set
me to practice the Ketan, consider the Lethani, or watch the other students
spar.

There were a few afternoons or evenings when Vashet simply sent me on
my way. So I explored the surrounding town and discovered Haert was much
larger than I'd originally assumed. The difference was that all its houses and
shops weren't huddled together in a knot. They were scattered over several
square miles of rocky hillside.

I found the baths early on. By which I mean, I was pointedly directed there by Vashet with instructions to wash off my barbarian stink.

They were a marvel. A sprawling stone building built on the top of what I guessed was either a natural hot spring or some marvelously engineered plumbing. There were large rooms full of water and small rooms full of steam. Rooms with deep pools for soaking, and rooms with great brass tubs for scrubbing. There was even one room with a pool big enough for swimming.

All through the building, the Adem mingled without any regard for age, gender, or state of undress. This didn't surprise me nearly as much as it would have a month ago, but it still took a great deal of getting used to.

At first I found it hard not to stare at the breasts of the naked women. Then, when some of that novelty faded, I found it hard not to stare at the scars that crossed the bodies of mercenaries. It was easy to tell who had taken the red even when their clothes were off.

Rather than fight my urge to gawk, I found it easier to go early in the morning or late at night when the baths were largely empty. Coming and going at odd hours wasn't difficult, as there was no lock on the door. It was open at all hours for anyone to use. Soap and candles and towels were available for the taking. The baths, Vashet told me, were maintained by the school.

I found the smithy by following the noise of ringing iron. The man working there was pleasantly talkative. He was glad to show me his tools and tell me the names for them in Ademic.

Once I knew to look, I saw there were signs above the doors of the stores. Pieces of wood carved or painted to show what was sold inside: bread, herbs, barrel staves. . . . None of the signs had words, which was fortunate for me, as I had no idea how to read Ademic.

I visited an apothecary where I was told I was not welcome, and a tailor where I was greeted warmly. I spent some of the three royals I'd stolen to buy two new sets of clothes, as those I had with me were showing their miles. I bought shirts and pants in muted colors after the local fashion, hoping they might help me fit in just a little better.

I also spent many hours watching the sword tree. At first I did this under Vashet's direction, but before long I found myself drawn back when I had time of my own to spend. Its motions were hypnotic, comforting. At times it seemed the branches wrote against the sky, spelling the name of the wind.

———————

True to her word, Vashet found me a sparring partner.

"Her name is Celean," Vashet told me over breakfast. "Your first meeting will be at the sword tree at midday. You should take this morning to prepare yourself however you think is best."

At last. A chance to prove myself. A chance to match wits with someone at my own level of skill. A real contest.

I was at the sword tree early, of course, and when I first saw them approaching, I had a moment of confused panic when I thought the small figure at Vashet's side was Penthe, the woman who had beaten Shehyn.

Then I realized it couldn't be Penthe. The figure approaching with Vashet was short, but the wind revealed a straight, lean body with none of Penthe's curves. What's more, the figure wore a shirt of bright cornsilk yellow, not mercenary red.

I fought down a stab of disappointment, even though I knew it was foolish. Vashet had said she had found a fair fight for me. Obviously it couldn't be someone who had already taken the red.

They came closer still, and my excitement guttered and died.

It was a little girl. Not even a young girl of fourteen or so. It was a *little* girl, no more than ten by my best guess. She was skinny as a twig and so short her head barely made it up to my breastbone. Her grey eyes were huge in her tiny face.

I was humiliated. The only thing that kept me from crying out in protest was the fact that I knew Vashet would find it unspeakably rude.

"Celean, this is Kvothe," Vashet said in Ademic.

This young girl looked me up and down appraisingly, then took an unconscious half-step closer. A compliment. She considered me enough of a threat that she wanted to be close enough to strike at me if necessary. It was closer than an adult would have stood, because she was shorter.

Polite greeting, I gestured.

Celean returned my gesture. It might have been my imagination, but it seemed the angle of her hands implied *polite nonsubordinate greeting*.

If Vashet saw it, she made no comment. "It is my desire that the two of you fight."

Celean looked me over again, her narrow face set in the typical Adem impassivity. The wind blew at her hair, and I could see a half-healed cut running from above her eyebrow up into her hairline.

"Why?" the girl asked calmly. She didn't seem afraid. It sounded more as if she couldn't think of the least reason she would want to fight me.

"Because there are things you can learn from each other," Vashet said. "And because I say you will."

Vashet gestured to me: *Attend*. "Celean's Ketan is quite exceptional. She has years of experience, and is easily the match of any two girls her size."

Vashet tapped Celean on the shoulder twice. *Caution.* "Kvothe, on the other hand, is new to the Ketan and has much to learn. But he is stronger than you, and taller, with a better reach. He also possesses a barbarian's cunning."

I looked at Vashet, unsure if she were poking fun at me or not.

"Also," Vashet continued to Celean, "you will very likely have your mother's height when you are grown, so you should practice fighting those larger than yourself." *Attend.* "Lastly, he is new to our language, and for this you will not mock him."

The girl nodded. I noticed Vashet hadn't specified I couldn't be mocked for other reasons.

Vashet straightened and spoke formally. "Nothing with the intention to injure." She held up fingers, marking the rules she had taught me when we started hand fighting. "You may strike hard, but not viciously. Be careful of the head and neck, and nothing at all toward the eyes. You are each responsible for the other's safety. If one of you gains a solid submission against the other, do not attempt to break it. Signal fairly and count it the end of the bout."

"I know this," Celean said. *Irritation.*

"It bears repeating," Vashet said. *Stern rebuke.* "Losing a fight is forgivable. Losing your temper is not. This is why I have brought you here instead of some little boy. Did I choose wrongly?"

Celean looked down. *Apologetic regret. Embarrassed acceptance.*

Vashet addressed us both. "Injuring another through carelessness is not of the Lethani."

I couldn't see how my beating up a ten-year-old girl was of the Lethani either, but I knew better than to say so.

And with that, Vashet left us alone, walking to a stone bench some forty feet away where another woman in mercenary reds was sitting. Celean made a complicated gesture I didn't recognize toward Vashet's back.

Then the young girl turned to face me, looking me up and down. "You are the first barbarian I have fought," she said after a long moment. "Are you all red?" She lifted her hand to her own hair to clarify her meaning.

I shook my head. "Not many of us."

She hesitated, then reached out her hand. "Can I touch it?"

I almost smiled at this, but caught myself. I ducked my head a bit and bent down so she could reach.

Celean ran her hand through my hair, then rubbed some between her thumb and forefinger. "It's soft." She gave a little laugh. "But it looks like metal."

She let go of my hair and stepped back to a formal distance again. She gestured *polite thanks*, then brought up her hands. "Are you ready?"

I nodded uncertainly, bringing up my own hands.

I wasn't ready. Celean darted forward, catching me flat-footed. Her arm drove out in a punch straight toward my groin. Raw instinct made me crouch so it struck my stomach instead.

Luckily, by this point I knew how to take a punch, and a month of hard training had made my stomach a sheet of muscle. Still, it felt like someone had thrown a rock at me, and I knew I'd have a bruise by dinner.

I got my feet under me and flicked an exploratory kick at her. I wanted to see how skittish she was, and hoped to make her back away so I could get my balance settled and make better use of my longer reach.

It turned out Celean wasn't skittish at all. She didn't back away. Instead she slipped alongside my leg and struck me squarely in the thick knot of muscle directly above the knee.

Because of this I couldn't help but stagger when my foot came back down, leaving me off balance with Celean close enough to climb me if she wanted. She set her hands together, braced her feet, and struck me with Threshing Wheat. The force of it knocked me over backward.

Given the thick grass, it wasn't a hard landing. I rolled to get some distance and came back to my feet. Celean chased me and made Thrown Lightning. She was fast, but I had longer legs, and managed to back away or block everything she threw. She faked a kick and I fell for it, giving her the opportunity to hit me right above the knee in the same place as before.

It hurt, but I didn't stagger this time, instead stepping sideways and away. Still she followed me, relentless and overeager. And in her haste she left an opening.

But despite the bruises and the fall she'd already given me, I couldn't bring myself to throw a punch at such a tiny girl. I knew how solidly I could hit Tempi or Vashet. But Celean was such a tiny twig of a thing. I worried I would hurt her. Hadn't Vashet said we were responsible for each other's safety?

So instead I grabbed her with Climbing Iron. My left hand missed, but the long, strong fingers of my right hand wrapped all the way around her slender wrist. I didn't have her in the proper submission, but now it was a game of strength, and I couldn't help but win. I already had her wrist, all that remained was to grip her shoulder and I'd have her in Sleeping Bear before—

Celean made Break Lion. But it wasn't the version I had learned. Hers used both hands, striking and twisting so quickly that my hand was stinging and empty before I could think. Then she grabbed my wrist and pulled, lashing out to kick my leg in a fluid motion. I leaned, buckled, and she stretched me out flat above the ground.

This landing wasn't soft, more a jarring flop onto the grass. It didn't completely stun me, but that didn't matter because Celean simply reached out and tapped my head twice. Signaling that if she'd wanted to, she could easily have knocked me unconscious.

I rolled into a sitting position, aching in several places and with a sprained pride. It wasn't badly sprained though. My time with Tempi and Vashet had taught me to appreciate skill, and Celean's Ketan truly was excellent.

"I've never seen that version of Break Lion before," I said.

Celean grinned. It was only a small grin, but it still showed a glimpse of her white teeth. In the world of Adem impassivity, it was like the sun coming from behind a cloud. "That is mine," she said. *Extreme pride.* "I made it. I am not strong enough to use regular Break Lion against my mother or anyone your size."

"Would you show it to me?" I asked.

Celean hesitated, then nodded and stepped forward, holding out her hand. "Grab my wrist."

I took hold of it, gripping firmly but not fiercely.

She did it again, like a magic trick. Both of her hands moved in a flurry of motion, and I was left with a stinging, empty hand.

I reached out again. *Amusement.* "I have slow barbarian eyes. Could you make it again so I can learn it?"

Celean stepped back, shrugging. *Indifference.* "Am I your teacher? Should I give something of mine to a barbarian who cannot even strike me in a fight?" She lifted her chin and looked off toward the spinning sword tree, but her eyes darted back to me, playfully.

I chuckled and came to my feet, bringing up my hands again.

She laughed and turned to face me. "Go!"

This time I was ready, and I knew what Celean was capable of. She was no sort of delicate flower. She was quick and fearless and aggressive.

So I went on the offensive, taking advantage of my long arms and legs. I struck out with Dancing Maiden, but she skipped away. No. It would be better to say she slid away from me, never compromising her balance in the least, her feet weaving smoothly through the long grass.

Then she changed directions suddenly, catching me between steps and slightly off my stride. She feigned a punch at my groin, then pushed me slightly off balance with Turning Millstone. I staggered but managed to keep my feet beneath me.

I tried to regain my balance, but she brushed me again with Turning Millstone, then again. And again. Each time only shoving me a few inches, but it kept me in a helpless stumbling retreat until she managed to plant her foot behind mine, tripping me and sending me flat onto my back.

Before I'd finished striking the ground she already had hold of my wrist, and soon had my arm tangled firmly in Ivy on the Oak. This pressed my face into the grass while putting uncomfortable pressure against my wrist and shoulder.

For a second I considered trying to struggle free, but only for a second. I was stronger than she was, but the whole point of positions like Ivy on the Oak and Sleeping Bear is to put pressure on the fragile parts of the body. You did not need a great deal of strength to attack the branch.

"I submit," I said. This is easier to say in Ademic: *Veh.* An easy noise to make when you are winded, tired, or in pain. I'd become rather used to saying it lately.

Celean let go of me and stepped away, watching as I sat up.

"You really aren't very good," she said with brutal honesty.

"I am not used to striking young girls," I said.

"How could you become used to it?" She laughed. "To grow used to a thing, you must do it over and again. I expect you have never struck a woman even once."

Celean extended a hand. I took it in what I hoped was a gracious manner, and she helped pull me to my feet. "I mean where I come from, it is not right to fight with women."

"I do not understand," she said. "Do they not let the men fight in the same place as the women?"

"I mean, for the most part, our women do not fight," I explained.

Celean rolled her wrist over, opening and closing her hand as if there were some dirt on the palm and she was absentmindedly trying to rub it off. It was the hand-talk equivalent of *puzzlement*, a confused frown of sorts. "How do they improve their Ketan if they do not practice?" she asked.

"Where I come from, the women have no Ketan at all."

Her eyes narrowed, then brightened. "You mean to say they have a *secret* Ketan," she said, using the Aturan word for "secret." Though her face was composed, her body vibrated with excitement. "A Ketan only they know, that the men are not allowed to see."

Celean pointed over to the bench where our teachers sat ignoring us. "Vashet has such a thing. I have asked her to show it to me many times, but she will not."

"Vashet knows another Ketan?" I asked.

Celean nodded. "She was schooled in the path of joy before she came to us." She looked over at her, her face serious, as if she would pull the secret out of the other woman by sheer force of will. "Someday I will go there and learn it. I will go everywhere, and I will learn all the Ketans there are. I will learn the hidden ways of the ribbon and the chain and of the moving pool. I will learn the paths of joy and passion and restraint. I will have *all* of them."

When she spoke, Celean didn't say this in a tone of childish fancy, as if she were daydreaming of eating an entire cake. Neither was she boastful, as if she were describing a plan she had put together on her own and thought very clever.

Celean said it with a quiet intensity. It was almost as if she were simply explaining who she was. Not to me. She was telling herself.

She turned back to look at me. "I will go to your land too," she said. *Absolute*. "And I will learn the barbarian Ketan your women keep secret from you."

"You will be disappointed," I said. "I did not misspeak. I know the word for secret. What I meant to say is that where I come from, many women do not fight."

Celean rolled her wrist again in puzzlement, and I knew I had to be more clear. "Where I come from, most women spend their whole lives without holding a sword. Most grow up not knowing how to strike another with a fist or the blade of their hand. They know nothing of any sort of Ketan. They do not fight at all." I stressed the last two words with *strong negation*.

That finally seemed to get the point across to her. I had half expected her to look horrified, but instead she simply stood there blankly, hands motionless, as if at a loss for what to think. It was as if I'd just explained to her that the women where I came from didn't have any heads.

"They do not fight?" she asked dubiously. "Not with the men or with each other or with anyone at all?"

I nodded.

There was a long, long pause. Her brow furrowed and I could actually see her struggling to come to grips with this idea. *Confusion. Dismay.* "Then what do they do?" she said at last.

I thought of the women I knew: Mola, Fela, Devi. "Many things," I said, having to improvise around the words I didn't know. "They make pictures out of stones. They buy and sell money. They write in books."

Celean seemed to relax as I recited this list, as if relieved to hear these foreign women, empty of any Ketan, weren't strewn around the countryside like boneless corpses.

"They heal the sick and mend wounds. They play . . ." I almost said *play music and sing songs*, but caught myself in time. "They play games and plant wheat and make bread."

Celean thought for a long moment. "I would rather do those things and fight as well," she said decisively.

"Some women do, but for many it is considered not of the Lethani." I used the phrase "of the Lethani" because I could not think of how to say "proper behavior" in Ademic.

Celean gestured *sharp disdain and reproach*. I was amazed how much more it stung coming from this young girl in her bright yellow shirt than it ever had from Tempi or Vashet. "The Lethani is the same everywhere," she said firmly. "It is not like the wind, changing from place to place."

"The Lethani is like water," I responded without thinking. "It is itself unchanging, but it shapes itself to fit all places. It is both the river and the rain."

She glared at me. It was not a furious glare, but coming from one of the Adem, it had the same effect. "Who are you to say the Lethani is like one thing and not another?"

"Who are you to do the same?"

Celean looked at me for a moment, the hint of a serious line between her pale eyebrows. Then she laughed brightly and brought up her hands. "I am Celean," she proclaimed. "My mother is of the third stone. I am Adem born, and I am the one who will throw you to the ground."

She was as good as her word.

CHAPTER ONE HUNDRED EIGHTEEN

Purpose

VASHET AND I FOUGHT, moving back and forth across the foothills of Ademre.

After all this time, I barely noticed the wind anymore. It was as much a part of the landscape as the uneven ground beneath my feet. Some days it was gentle, and did little more than make patterns in the grass or flick my hair into my eyes. Other days it was strong enough to make the loose fabric of my clothes crack and snap against my skin. It could come at you from un-expected directions without a moment's warning, pushing you as firmly as a hand between your shoulder blades.

"Why do we spend so much time on my hand fighting?" I asked Vashet as I made Picking Clover.

"Because your hand fighting is sloppy," Vashet said, blocking me with Fan Water. "Because you embarrass me every time we fight. And because three times of four you lose to a child half your size."

"But my sword fighting is even worse," I said as I circled, looking for an opening.

"It is worse," she acknowledged. "That is why I do not let you fight any-one but me. You are too wild. You could hurt someone."

I smiled. "I thought that was the point of this."

Vashet frowned, then reached out casually to grip my wrist and shoulder, twisting me into Sleeping Bear. Her right hand held my wrist over my head, stretching my arm at an awkward angle, while her left pressed firmly against my shoulder. Helpless, I was forced to bend at the waist, staring at the ground.

"Veh," I said in submission.

But Vashet didn't release me. She twisted, and the pressure against my shoulder increased. The small bones of my wrist began to ache.

"Veh," I said a little louder, thinking she hadn't heard me. But still she held me, twisting a little harder at my wrist. "Vashet?" I tried to turn my head to look at her, but from this angle all I could see was her leg.

"If the point of this is to hurt someone," she said, "why should I let you go?"

"That's not what I meant . . ." Vashet pushed down harder, and I stopped talking.

"What is the purpose of Sleeping Bear?" she asked calmly.

"To incapacitate your opponent," I said.

"Very well." Vashet began to bear down with the slow, relentless force of a glacier. Dull pain began to build in my shoulder as well as my wrist. "Soon your arm will be twisted from the cup of your shoulder. Your tendons will stretch and pull free of the bone. Your muscles will tear and your arm will hang like a wet rag at your side. Then will Sleeping Bear have served its purpose?"

I struggled a bit out of pure animal instinct. But it only turned the burning pain into something sharper, and I stopped. Over the course of my training, I had been put into inescapable positions before. Every time I had been helpless, but this was the first time I had truly felt that way.

"The purpose of Sleeping Bear is control," Vashet said calmly. "Right now, you are mine to do with as I wish. I can move you, or break you, or let you free."

"I would prefer free," I said, trying to sound more hopeful than desperate.

There was a pause. Then she asked, calmly, "What is the purpose of Sleeping Bear?"

"Control."

I felt her hands release me, and I stood, slowly rolling my shoulder to ease the ache.

Vashet stood there, frowning at me. "The point of all of this is control. First you must have control of yourself. Then you can gain control of your surroundings. Then you gain control of whoever stands against you. This is the Lethani."

———

After the better part of a month in Haert, I could not help but feel that things were going well. Vashet acknowledged that my language was improving, congratulating me by saying I sounded like a child, rather than just an imbecile.

I continued to meet with Celean in the grassy field next to the sword tree. I looked forward to these encounters despite the fact that she thrashed me with cheerful ruthlessness every time we fought. It took three days before I finally managed to beat her.

That's an interesting verse to add to the long story of my life, isn't it?

Come listen all, and I will tell
A tale of brave and daring deeds.
Of wonders Kvothe the Bloodless wrought,
And of the time he bravely fought
A twigling girl no more than ten.
And listen how it came to pass,
The mighty blow he bravely dealt
That knocked her sprawling to the grass,
And of the glow of joy he felt.

Awful as it might sound, I was proud. And justifiably so. Celean herself congratulated me when it happened, seeming more than a little surprised that I had managed it. There, in the long shadow of the sword tree, she showed me her two-handed variant of Breaking Lion as a reward, flattering me with the familiarity of an impish grin.

That same day we finished our prescribed number of bouts early. I went to sit on a nearby lump of stone that had been smoothed into a comfortable seat. I nursed my dozen small hurts from the fight and prepared to watch the sword tree until Vashet returned to fetch me.

Celean, however, was not the sort to sit and wait. She skipped over to the sword tree, standing only a few feet from where the longest branches bobbed and danced in the wind, sending the round, razor-sharp leaves turning in wild circles.

Then she lowered her shoulders and darted under the canopy, in among the thousand madly spinning leaves.

I was too startled to cry out, but I did come halfway to my feet before I heard her laughing. I watched as she darted and jigged and spun, her tiny body dodging out of the way of the wind-tossed leaves as if she were playing tag. She made it halfway to the trunk and stopped. She ducked her head, reached out, and swatted away a leaf that otherwise would have cut her.

No. She didn't just lash out. She used Drifting Snow. Then I watched her move even closer to the trunk, weaving back and forth and protecting herself. First she used Maiden Combs Her Hair, then Dance Backwards.

Then she skipped to one side, the Ketan abandoned. She crouched and sprinted through a gap in the leaves and made her way to the trunk of the tree, slapping it with one hand.

And she was back among the leaves. She made Pressing Cider, ducked and spun and ran until she was clear of the canopy. She didn't shout out in triumph as a Commonwealth child might have, but she jumped into the air, hands raised in victory. Then, still laughing, she did a cartwheel.

Breathless, I watched Celean play her game again and again, moving in and out of the tree's dancing leaves. She didn't always make it to the trunk. Twice she scampered back out of the reach of the leaves without making it, and it was obvious even from where I sat that she was angry. Once she slipped and was forced to crawl out under the reach of the leaves.

But she made it to the trunk and back four times, each time celebrating her escape with upraised hands, laughter, and a single perfect cartwheel.

She only stopped when Vashet returned. I watched from a distance as Vashet stormed over and gave the girl a stern telling off. I couldn't hear what was said, but their body language spoke volumes. Celean looked down and shuffled her feet. Vashet shook a finger and cuffed the young girl on the side of her head. It was the same scolding any child receives. Stay out of the neighbor's garden. Don't tease the Bentons' sheep. Don't play tag among the thousand spinning knives of your people's sacred tree.

Hands

ONCE VASHET JUDGED MY language only moderately embarrassing, she arranged for me to talk with an odd handful of people scattered around Haert.

There was a garrulous old man who spun silk thread while chattering endlessly, telling strange, pointless, half-delirious stories. There was a story of a boy who put shoes on his head to keep a cat from being killed, another where a family swore to eat a mountain stone by stone. I could never make any sense of them, but I listened politely and drank the sweet beer he offered me.

I met with twin sisters who made candles and showed me the steps of strange dances. I spent an afternoon with a woodcutter who spoke for hours of nothing but splitting wood.

At first I thought these were important members of the community. I thought Vashet might be parading me in front of them in order to show how civilized I had become.

It wasn't until I spent the morning with Two-fingers that I realized she sent me to each of these people with the hope I would learn something.

Two-fingers was not his real name. I'd merely come to think of him as that. He was a cook at the school, and I saw him at every meal. His left hand was whole, but his right was viciously crippled, with only his thumb and forefinger remaining.

Vashet sent me to him in the morning, and together we prepared lunch and talked. His name was Naden. He told me he had spent ten years among the barbarians. What's more, he had brought more than two hundred and thirty silver talents back into the school before he was injured and could no longer fight. He mentioned the last several times, and I could tell that it was a particular point of pride with him.

The bells rang and folk filtered into the dining hall. Naden ladled up the stew we'd made, hot and thick with chunks of beef and carrot. I cut slices of warm white bread for those who wanted it. I exchanged nods and occasional polite gestures with those who moved through the line. I was careful to make only the briefest eye contact, and tried to convince myself it was just a coincidence so few people seemed interested in bread today.

Carceret made a show of her feelings for everyone to see. First she made it to the front of the line, then made a widely visible gesture of *abhorrent disgust* before walking away, leaving her wooden plate behind.

Later Naden and I tended to the washing up. "Vashet tells me your swordplay is progressing poorly," he said without preamble. "She says you fear too much for your hands, and this makes you hesitant." *Firm reproach.*

I froze at the abruptness of it, fighting the urge to stare at his ruined hand. I nodded, not trusting myself to speak.

He turned from the iron pot he was scrubbing and held out his hand in front of him. It was a defiant gesture, and his face was hard. I looked then, as ignoring it would be rude. Only his thumb and forefinger remained, enough to grip at things, but not enough for any delicate work. The half of his hand that remained was a mass of puckered scar.

I kept my face even, but it was hard. In some ways I was looking at my worst fear. I felt very self-conscious of my uninjured hands and fought the urge to make a fist or hide them behind my back.

"It has been a dozen years since this hand held a sword," Naden said. *Proud anger. Regret.* "I have thought long on that fight where my fingers were lost. I did not even lose them to a skilled opponent. They fell to some barbarian whose hands were better suited to a shovel than the sword."

He flexed his two fingers. In some ways, he was lucky. There were other Adem in Haert who were missing entire hands, or eyes, or limbs to the elbow or knee.

"I have thought a long time. How could I have saved my hand? I have thought about my contract, protecting a baron whose lands were in rebellion. I think: What if I had not taken that contract? I think: What if I had lost my left hand? I could not talk, but I could hold a sword." He let his hand drop to his side. "But holding a sword is not enough. A proper mercenary requires two hands. I could never make Lover out the Window or Sleeping Bear with only one. . . ."

He shrugged. "It is the luxury of looking backward. You can do it forever, and it is useless. I took the red proudly. I brought over two hundred and thirty talents to the school. I was of the second stone, and I would have made the third in time."

Naden held up his ruined hand again. "I could have gained none of these things if I had lived in fear of losing my hand. If I flinched and cringed, I would never have been accepted into the Latantha. Never made the second stone. I would be whole, but I would be less than I am now."

He turned back and began to scrub the pots again. After a moment I joined him.

"Is it bad?" I asked quietly, unable to help myself.

Naden didn't answer for a long moment. "When it first happened, I thought to myself it was not so bad. Others have had worse wounds. Others have died. I was luckier than them."

He drew in a deep breath, then let it out slowly. "I tried to think it was not bad. My life would continue on. But no. Life stops. Much is lost. Everything is lost."

Then he said, "When I dream, I have two hands."

We finished the dishes together, sharing silence between us. Sometimes that is all you can share.

———————

Celean had a lesson of her own to teach me. Namely that there are opponents who will not hesitate to punch, kick, or elbow a man directly in his genitals.

Never hard enough to permanently injure me, mind you. She'd been fighting her entire young life and had the control Vashet valued so highly. But that meant she knew exactly how hard to strike to leave me stunned and reeling, making her victory utterly unquestionable.

So I sat on the grass, feeling grey and nauseous. After incapacitating me, Celean had given me a comforting pat on the shoulder before skipping blithely away. No doubt going to dance among the wind-tossed branches of the sword tree again.

"You were doing well until the end," Vashet said, lowering herself onto the ground across from me.

I said nothing. Like a child playing find-and-catch, it was my sincere hope that if I closed my eyes and remained perfectly still, the pain wouldn't be able to find me.

"Come now, I saw her kick," Vashet said dismissively. "It was not so hard as that." I heard her sigh. "Still, if you need someone to look at them and make sure they are still intact. . . ."

I chuckled slightly. It was a mistake. Unbelievable pain uncoiled in my groin, radiating down to my knee and up to my sternum. Nausea rolled over me, and I opened my eyes to steady myself.

"She will grow out of it," Vashet said.

"I should hope so," I said through gritted teeth. "It's a noxious habit."

"That is not what I meant," Vashet said. "I mean she will grow taller. Hopefully then she will distribute her attentions more evenly across the body. Right now she attacks the groin too regularly. It makes her easy to predict and defend against." She gave me a pointed look. "To anyone with a shred of wit."

I closed my eyes again. "No lessons right now, Vashet," I begged. "I'm ready to vomit up yesterday's breakfast."

She climbed to her feet. "It sounds like the perfect time for a lesson. Stand up. You should learn how to fight while wounded. This is an invaluable skill Celean has given you the chance to practice. You should thank her."

Knowing it was pointless to argue, I climbed to my feet and began to walk gingerly toward my training sword.

Vashet caught me by the shoulder. "No. Hands only."

I sighed. "Must we, Vashet?"

She raised an eyebrow at me. "Must we what?"

"Must we focus always on hand fighting?" I said. "My swordplay is falling farther and farther behind."

"Am I not your teacher?" she asked. "Who are you to say what is best?"

"I am the one who will have to use these skills out in the world," I said pointedly. "And out in the world, I would rather fight with a sword than a fist."

Vashet lowered her hands, her expression blank. "And why is that?"

"Because other people have swords," I said. "And if I'm in a fight, I intend to win."

"Is winning a fight easier with a sword?" she asked.

Vashet's outward calm should have warned me I was stepping onto thin conversational ice, but I was distracted by the nauseating pain radiating from my groin. Though honestly, even if I hadn't been distracted, it's possible I wouldn't have noticed. I had grown comfortable with Vashet, too comfortable to be properly careful.

"Of course," I said. "Why else carry a sword?"

"That is a good question," she said. "Why does one carry a sword?"

"Why do you carry anything? So you can use it."

Vashet gave me a look of raw disgust. "Why do we bother to work on your language, then?" She asked angrily, reaching out to grab my jaw, pinching my cheeks and forcing my mouth open as if I were a patient in the Medica refusing my medicine. "Why do you need this tongue if a sword will do? Tell me that?"

I tried to pull away, but she was stronger than me. I tried to push her away, but she shrugged my flailing hands away as if I were a child.

Vashet let go of my face, then caught my wrist, jerking my hand up in front of my face. "Why do you have hands at all and not knives at the ends of your arms?"

Then she let go of my wrist and struck me hard across the face with the flat of her hand.

If I say she slapped me, you will take the wrong impression. This wasn't the dramatic slap of the sort you see on a stage. Neither was it the offended, stinging slap a lady-in-waiting makes against the smooth skin of a too-familiar nobleman. It wasn't even the more professional slap of a serving girl defending herself from the unwelcome attention of a grabby drunk.

No. This was hardly any sort of slap at all. A slap is made with the fingers or the palm. It stings or startles. Vashet struck me with her open hand, but behind that was the strength of her arm. Behind that was her shoulder. Behind that was the complex machinery of her pivoting hips, her strong legs braced against the ground, and the ground itself beneath her. It was like the whole of creation striking me through the flat of her hand, and the only reason it didn't cripple me is that even in the middle of her fury, Vashet was always perfectly in control.

Because she was in control, Vashet didn't dislocate my jaw or knock me unconscious. But it made my teeth rattle and my ears ring. It made my eyes roll in my head and my legs go loose and shaky. I would have fallen if Vashet hadn't gripped me by the shoulder.

"Do you think I am teaching you the secrets of the sword so you can go out and use them?" she demanded. I dimly realized she was shouting. It was the first time I had ever heard one of the Adem raise their voice. "Is that what you think we are doing here?"

As I lolled in her grip, stupefied, she struck me again. This time her hand caught more of my nose. The pain of it was amazing, as if someone had driven a sliver of ice directly into my brain. It jolted me out of my daze so I was fully alert when she hit me the third time.

Vashet held me for a moment while the world spun, then let go. I took one unsteady step and crumpled to the ground like a puppet with its strings cut. Not unconscious, but profoundly dazed.

It took me a long time to collect myself. When I was finally able to sit up, my body felt loose and unwieldy, as if it had been taken apart and put back together again in a slightly different way.

By the time I gathered my wits enough to look around, I was alone.

Kindness

TWO HOURS LATER I sat alone in the dining hall. My head ached, and the side of my face was hot and swollen. I'd bitten my tongue at some point, so it hurt to eat and everything tasted of blood. My mood was exactly what you might imagine, except worse.

When I saw a red form slide onto the bench across from me, I dreaded looking up. If it was Carceret, it would be bad. But Vashet would be even worse. I had waited until the dining hall was almost empty before coming to eat, hoping to avoid them both.

But glancing up, I saw it was Penthe, the fierce young woman who had beaten Shehyn.

"Hello," she said in lightly accented Aturan.

I gestured, *polite formal greeting*. Considering the way my day was going, I thought it best to be as careful as possible. Vashet's comments led me to believe Penthe was a high-ranking and well-respected member of the school.

For all that, she wasn't very old. Perhaps it was her small frame or her heart-shaped face, but she didn't look much more than twenty.

"Could we speak your language?" she asked in Aturan. "It would be a kindness. I am in need of practice with my talking."

"I will gladly join you," I said in Aturan. "You speak very well. I am jealous. When I speak Ademic, I feel I am a great bear of a man, stomping around in heavy boots."

Penthe gave a small, shy smile, then covered her mouth with her hand, blushing slightly. "Is that correct, to smile?"

"It is correct, and polite. A smile such as that shows a small amusement. Which is perfect, as mine was a very small joke."

Penthe removed her hand and repeated the shy smile. She was charming as spring flowers. It eased my heart to look at her.

"Normally," I said, "I would smile in answer to yours. But here, I worry others would view it as impolite."

"Please," she said, making a series of gestures wide enough for anyone to see. *Bold invitation. Imploring entreaty. Familiar welcome.* "I must practice."

I smiled, though not quite as widely as I would have ordinarily. Partly out of caution, and partly because my face hurt. "It feels good to smile again," I said.

"I have anxiousness about my smiling." She started to gesture and stopped herself. Her expression shifted, her eyes narrowing a bit, as if she were irritated.

"This?" I asked, gesturing *mild worry*.

She nodded. "How do you make that with the face?"

"It is like this," I drew my brows together slightly. "Also, as a woman, you would do this," I pursed my lips slightly. "I would do this, as I am a man." I drew my lips down into a small frown instead.

Penthe looked at me blankly. *Aghast.* "It is different for men and women?" she asked, disbelief creeping into her tone.

"Only some," I reassured her. "And only small things."

"There is so much," she said, allowing a note of despair into her voice. "With one's family one knows what every small movement of face means. You grow up watching. You know the all of what is in them. Those friends you are young with, before you know better than to grin at everything. It is easy with them. But this . . ." She shook her head. "How can one possibly remember when to correctly show one's teeth? How often am I supposed to touch eyes?"

"I understand," I said. "I am very good at speaking in my language. I can make the cleverest meanings. But here that is useless." I sighed. "Keeping my face still is very hard. I feel I am always holding my breath."

"Not always," she said. "We are not always still of the face. When you are with . . ." She trailed off, then quickly gestured, *apology*.

"I have none I am close to," I said. *Gentle regret.* "I had hoped I was growing close to Vashet, but I fear I ruined that today."

Penthe nodded. "I saw." She reached out and ran her thumb along the side of my face. It felt cool against the swelling. "You must have angered her very."

"I can tell that by the ringing of my ears," I said.

Penthe shook her head. "No. Your marks." She gestured to her own face this time. "With another, it might be a mistake, but Vashet would not leave such if she did not wish everyone to see."

The bottom dropped out of my stomach and my hand went unconsciously to my face. Of course. This wasn't mere punishment. It was a message to all of Ademre.

"Fool that I am," I said softly. "I did not realize this until now."

We ate quietly for several minutes, before I asked, "Why did you come to sit with me today?"

"When I saw you today, I thought I had heard many people speak about you. But I knew nothing of you from personal knowing." A pause.

"And what do others say?" I said with a small, wry smile.

She reached out to touch the corner of my mouth with her fingertips. "That," she said. "What is the bent smile?"

Gentle mocking, I gestured in explanation. "But of myself, not you. I can guess what they say."

"Not all is bad," she said gently.

Penthe looked up at me and met my eyes then. They were huge in her small face, slightly darker grey than usual. They were so bright and clear that when she smiled, the sight of it almost broke my heart. I felt tears well up in my eyes and I quickly looked down, embarrassed.

"Oh!" she said softly, and gestured a hurried *distressed apology*. "No. I am wrong with my smiling and eye touching. I meant this." *Kind encouragement*.

"You are right with your smiling," I said without looking up, blinking furiously in an attempt to clear the tears away. "It is an unexpected kindness on a day when I do not deserve such a thing. You are the first to speak with me from your own desire. And there is a sweetness in your face that hurts my heart." I made *gratitude* with my left hand, glad that I didn't need to meet her eyes to show her how I felt.

Her left hand crossed the table and caught hold of mine. Then she turned my hand face up and pressed *comfort* softly into my palm.

I looked up and gave her what I hoped was a reassuring smile.

She mirrored it almost exactly, then covered her mouth again. "I maintain anxiousness about my smiling."

"You should not. You have the perfect mouth for smiling."

Penthe looked up at me again, her eyes meeting mine for a heartbeat before darting away. "True?"

I nodded. "In my own language, it is a mouth I would write a—" I brought myself up short, sweating a bit when I realized I'd almost said "song."

"Poem?" she suggested helpfully.

"Yes," I said quickly. "It is a smile worthy of a poem."

"Make one then," she said. "In my language."

"No," I said quickly. "It would be a bear's poem. Too clumsy for you."

This just seemed to spur her on, and her eyes grew eager. "Do. If it is clumsy, it will make me feel better of my own stumbling."

"If I do," I threatened, "you must, too. In my language."

I'd thought this would scare her away, but after only a moment's hesitation she nodded.

I thought of the only Ademic poetry I had heard: a few snippets from the old silk spinner and the piece from the story Shehyn had told about the archer. It wasn't much to go on.

I thought of the words I knew, the sounds of them. I felt the absence of my lute sharply here. This is why we have music, after all. Words cannot always do the work we need them to. Music is there for when words fail us.

Finally I looked around nervously, glad there were only a scattered handful of people left in the dining hall. I leaned toward her and said:

Double-weaponed Penthe
No sword in hand,
Her flower-mouth curves,
And cuts a heart a dozen steps away.

She gave the smile again, and it was just as I said. I felt the sharpness of it in my chest. Felurian had had a beautiful smile, but it was old and knowing. Penthe's smile was bright as a new penny. It was like cool water on my dry, tired heart.

The sweet smile of a young woman. There is nothing better in the world. It is worth more than salt. Something in us sickens and dies without it. I am sure of this. Such a simple thing. How strange. How wonderful and strange.

Penthe closed her eyes for a moment, her mouth moving silently as she chose the words of her own poem.

Then she opened her eyes and spoke in Aturan.

Burning as a branch,
Kvothe speaks.
But the mouth that threatens boots
reveals a dancing bear.

I smiled wide enough to make my face hurt. "It is lovely," I said honestly. "It is the first poem anyone has ever made for me."

After my conversation with Penthe, I felt considerably better. I was uncertain as to whether or not we had been flirting, but that hardly mattered. It was enough for me to know there was at least one person in Haert who didn't want me dead.

I walked to Vashet's house as I usually did after meals. Half of me hoped she would greet me, smiling and sarcastic, the morning's unpleasantness put wordlessly behind us. The other half of me feared she would refuse to speak with me at all.

As I came over the rise, I saw her sitting on a wooden bench outside her door. She leaned against the rough stone wall of her house, as if she were merely enjoying the afternoon sun. I drew a deep breath and let it out, feeling myself relax.

But as I came closer, I saw her face. She was not smiling. Neither did she wear the impassive Adem mask. She watched me approach, her expression hangman grim.

I spoke as soon as I came close enough. "Vashet," I said earnestly. "I'm—"

Still sitting, Vashet held up her hand, and I stopped speaking as quickly as if she had struck me across the mouth. "Apology now is of little consequence," she said, her voice flat and chill as slate. "Anything you say at this point cannot be trusted. You know I am well and truly angry, so you are in the grip of fear.

"This means I cannot trust any word you say, as it comes from fear. You are clever, and charming, and a liar. I know you can bend the world with your words. So I will not listen."

She shifted her position on the bench, then continued. "Early on I noticed a gentleness in you. It is a rare thing in one so young, and it was a large piece of what convinced me you were worth teaching. But as the days pass, I glimpse something else. Some other face that is far from gentle. I have dismissed these as flickers of false light, thinking them the brags of a young man or the odd jokes of a barbarian.

"But today as you spoke, it came to me that the gentleness was the mask. And this other half-seen face, this dark and ruthless thing, that is the true face hiding underneath."

Vashet gave me a long look. "There is something troubling inside you. Shehyn has seen it in your conversations. It is not a lack of the Lethani. But this makes my unease more, not less. That means there is something in you deeper than the Lethani. Something the Lethani cannot mend."

She met my eye. "If this is the case, then I have been wrong to teach you. If you have been clever enough to show me a false face for so long, then you are a danger to more than just the school. If this is the case, then Carceret is right, and you should be killed swiftly for the safety of everyone involved."

Vashet came to her feet, moving as if she were very tired. "This I have thought today. And I will continue to think for long hours tonight. Tomorrow I will have decided. Take this time to order your thoughts and make whatever preparations seem best to you."

Then, without meeting my eye, she turned and went into her house, closing the door silently behind her.

For a while, I wandered aimlessly. I went to watch the sword tree, hoping I might find Celean there, but she was nowhere to be seen. Watching the tree itself did nothing to soothe me. Not today.

So I went to the baths, where I soaked myself joylessly. Afterward, in one of the mirrors scattered through the smaller rooms, I caught the first glimpse of my face since Vashet had struck me. Half my face was red and swollen, with bruises beginning to mottle blue and yellow around my temple and the line of my jaw. I also had the raw beginnings of a profoundly blackened eye.

As I stared at myself in the mirror I felt a low anger flicker to life deep in my belly. I was, I decided, tired of waiting helplessly while others decided whether I could come or go. I had played their game, learned their language, been unfailingly polite, and in return I had been treated like a dog. I had been beaten, sneered at, and threatened with death and worse. I was finished with it.

So I made my way slowly around Haert. I visited the twin sisters, the talkative smithy, and the tailor where I had bought my clothes. I chatted amiably, passing the time, asking questions, and pretending I didn't look as if someone had beaten me unconscious a handful of hours ago.

My preparations took a long time. I missed dinner, and the sky was growing dark by the time I came back to the school. I went straight to my room and closed the door behind me.

Then I emptied the contents of my pockets onto my bed, some purchased, some stolen. Two fine, soft beeswax candles. A long shard of brittle steel from a poorly forged sword. A spool of blood-red thread. A small stoppered bottle of water from the baths.

I closed my fist tightly around the last. Most people don't understand how much heat water holds inside it. That is why it takes so long to boil. Despite the fact that the scalding-hot pool I had pulled this from was more than half a mile away, what I held in my hand was of better use to a sympathist than a glowing coal. This water had fire in it.

I thought of Penthe with a twinge of regret. Then I picked up a candle and began to turn it in my hands, warming it with my skin, softening the wax and beginning to shape a doll of it.

I sat in my room, thinking dark thoughts as the last of the light faded from the sky. I looked over the tools I had gathered and knew deep in my gut that sometimes a situation grows so tangled that words are useless. What other option did I have, now that words had failed me?

What do any of us have when words fail us?

When Words Fail

IT WAS WELL INTO the dark hours of night when I approached Vashet's house, but there was candlelight flickering in her window. I didn't doubt she would have me killed or crippled for the good of all Ademre, but Vashet was nothing if not careful. She would give it a long night's thought beforehand.

Empty-handed, I knocked softly on her door. After a moment, she opened it. She still wore her mercenary reds, but she had removed most of the silk ties that held it tight to her body. Her eyes were tired.

Her mouth thinned when she saw me standing there, and I knew if I spoke she would refuse to listen. So I gestured *entreaty* and stepped backward, out of the candlelight and into the dark. I knew her well enough by this point to be sure of her curiosity. Her eyes narrowed suspiciously as I stepped away, but after a moment's hesitation she followed me. She did not bring her sword.

It was a clear night, and we had a piece of moon to light our way. I led us up into the hills, away from the school, away from the scattered houses and shops of Haert.

We walked more than a mile before we came to the place I had chosen. A small grove of trees where a tall jumble of stone would keep any noise from carrying back toward the sleeping town.

The moonlight slanted in through the trees, revealing dark shapes in a tiny clear space tucked among the stones. There were two small wooden benches here. I took gentle hold of Vashet's arm and guided her to sit.

Moving slowly, I reached into the deep leeward shadow of a nearby tree and brought out my shaed. I draped it carefully over a low-hanging branch so it hung like a dark curtain between us.

Then I sat on the other bench, bent, and worked the clasps on my lute

case. As each of them snapped open, the lute within made a familiar har-
monic thrum, as if eager to be free.

I brought it out and gently began to play.

I had tucked a piece of cloth inside the bowl of the lute to soften the
sound, not wanting it to carry over the rocky hills. And I had woven some
of the red thread between the strings. Partly to keep them from ringing too
brightly, and partly out of a desperate hope that it might bring me luck.

I began with "In the Village Smithy." I did not sing, worried Vashet would
be offended if I went that far. But even without the words, it is a song that
sounds like weeping. It is music that speaks of empty rooms and a chill bed
and the loss of love.

Without pausing, I moved on to "Violet Bide," then "Home Westward
Wind." The last had been a favorite of my mother's, and as I played it I
thought of her and began to cry.

Then I played the song that hides in the center of me. That wordless music
that moves through the secret places in my heart. I played it carefully, strum-
ming it slow and low into the dark stillness of the night. I would like to say
it is a happy song, that it is sweet and bright, but it is not.

And, eventually, I stopped. The tips of my fingers burned and ached. It had
been a month since I had played for any length of time, and they had lost
their calluses.

Looking up, I saw Vashet had pulled my shaed aside and was watching me.
The moon hung behind her, and I could not see the expression on her face.

"This is why I do not have knives instead of hands, Vashet," I said quietly.
"This is what I am."

CHAPTER ONE HUNDRED TWENTY-TWO

Leaving

THE NEXT MORNING I woke early, ate quickly, and was back in my room before most of the school was stirring in their beds.

I shouldered my lute and travelsack. I wrapped my shaed around me, checking that everything I needed was properly stowed in my pockets: red string, wax mommet, brittle iron, vial of water. Then I drew up the hood of my shaed and left the school, making my way to Vashet's house.

Vashet opened the door between my second and third knock. She was shirtless, and stood bare-breasted in the doorway. She eyed me pointedly, taking note of my cloak, my travelsack, my lute.

"It is a morning for visitors," she said. "Come in. The wind is chill this early."

I stepped inside and tripped on the threshold, stumbling so that I had to rest my hand on Vashet's shoulder to steady myself. My hand caught clumsily in her hair as I did so.

Vashet shook her head as she closed the door behind me. Unconcerned with her near-nakedness, she reached both her hands behind her head and began to plait half of her hanging hair into a short, tight braid.

"The sun was barely in the sky this morning when Penthe knocked on my door," she said conversationally. "She knew I was angry with you. And though she did not know what you had done, she spoke on your behalf."

Holding the braid with one hand, Vashet reached for a piece of red string and tied it off. "Then, almost before my door had time to close, Carceret paid me a visit. She congratulated me on finally giving you the treatment you deserve."

She reached back to braid the other side of her hair, her fingers twisting nimbly. "Both of them irritated me. They had no place speaking to me about my student."

Vashet tied off the second braid. "Then I thought to myself, whose opinion do I respect more?" She looked at me, making it a question for me to answer.

"You respect your own opinion more," I said.

Vashet smiled widely. "You are exactly right. But Penthe is not entirely a fool either. And Carceret can be angry as a man when the mood is on her."

She picked up a long piece of dark silk and wound it around her torso, over her shoulders and across her naked breasts, supporting and holding them close to her chest. Then she tucked the end of the cloth into itself and it somehow remained tightly secured. I had seen her do this several times before, but how it actually worked was still a mystery to me.

"And what have you decided?" I asked.

She shrugged her blood-red shirt over her head. "You are still a puzzle," she said. "Gentle and troubling and clever and foolish." Her head emerged from the shirt and she gave me a serious look. "But someone who breaks a puzzle because they cannot solve it has left the Lethani. I am not such a one."

"I am glad," I said. "I would not have enjoyed leaving Haert."

Vashet raised an eyebrow at that. "I daresay you would not." She gestured at the lute case that hung over my shoulder. "Leave that here, or people will talk. Leave your bag too. You can take them back to your room later."

She looked at me speculatively. "But bring the cloak. I will show you how to fight while wearing it. Such things can be useful, but only if you can avoid tripping over them."

———

I went back to my training almost as if nothing had happened. Vashet showed me how to avoid tripping over my own cloak. How it could be used to bind a weapon or disarm the unwary. She commented on it being very fine, strong, and durable, but never seemed to note anything unusual about it.

Days passed. I continued to spar with Celean and eventually learned to protect my precious manhood from all forms of uncouth attack. Slowly, I grew skilled enough that we were nearly even in our bouts, trading victories back and forth.

There were even a handful of conversations with Penthe at mealtimes, and I was glad to have one other person willing to occasionally smile in my direction.

But I was no longer at my ease in Haert. I had come too close to disaster.

Whenever I spoke to Vashet I thought twice about every word. Some words I thought about three times.

And while Vashet seemed to return to her familiar wry and smiling self, I would catch her watching me from time to time, her face grim, her eyes intent.

As the days passed, the tension between us gradually wore away, fading as slowly as the bruises on my face. I like to think eventually it would have disappeared entirely. But we were not given enough time for that.

———————

It came like lightning from the clear blue sky.

Vashet opened her door to my knock. But instead of coming outside, she stood in the doorway. "Tomorrow is your test," she said.

For a second, I didn't understand what she was talking about. I had been focusing so intently on my sword practice, my sparring with Celean, the language, the Lethani. I had almost forgotten the purpose of it all.

I felt a rush of excitement in my chest, followed by a chill knot in my stomach. "Tomorrow?" I said stupidly.

She nodded, smiling faintly at my expression.

Her subdued response did little to set me at my ease. "So soon?"

"Shehyn feels it would be best. If we wait another month, there could be early snow, keeping you from going freely on your way."

I hesitated, then said, "You aren't telling me the whole truth, Vashet."

Another faint smile and a small shrug. "You're right in that, though Shehyn does think waiting is unwise. You are charming, in your clumsy barbarian way. The longer you are here, the more folk will come to feel kindly toward you. . . ."

I felt the chill settle deeper into my gut. "And if I am to be mutilated, it would be better if it were done before more folk realize I'm actually a real person and not some faceless barbarian," I said harshly, though not as harshly as I wanted to.

Vashet looked down, then nodded. "You would not have heard. But Penthe blackened Carceret's eye two days ago in an argument about you. Celean too, has grown fond of you, and talks to the other children. They watch you from the trees while you train." She was still for a moment. "And there are others."

I knew enough after all this time to read Vashet's small silence for what it really meant. Suddenly her muted mood, her stillness made much better sense.

"Shehyn must attend to the best interests of the school," Vashet said. "She must decide according to what is right. She cannot allow herself to be swayed by the fact that some few are fond of you. At the same time, if she makes a correct decision and many in the school resent it, that is not good either." Another shrug. "So."

"Am I ready?"

Vashet was quiet for a long time. "That's not an easy question," she said. "Being invited to the school isn't merely a matter of skill. It is a test of fit, of suitability. If one of us fails, we can try again. Tempi took his test four times before he was admitted. For you there will only be one chance." She looked up at me. "And ready or not, it is time."

CHAPTER ONE HUNDRED TWENTY-THREE

The Spinning Leaf

THE NEXT MORNING VASHET came to collect me just as I was finishing my breakfast. "Come," she said. "Carceret has been praying for a storm all night, but it's only gusting."

I didn't know what that meant, but I didn't feel like asking either. I returned my wooden plate and turned around to find Penthe standing there, a slight yellowing bruise along her jawline.

Penthe didn't say anything, merely gripped my arms in an open show of support. Then she hugged me tightly. I was surprised when her head only came up to my chest. I'd forgotten how small she was. The dining room was even more quiet than normal, and while no one was staring, everyone was watching.

Vashet walked me to the tiny park where we had first met and began our usual limbering stretch. The routine of it relaxed me, lulling my anxiety to a dull rumble. When we were finished, Vashet led me down into the hidden valley of the sword tree. I wasn't surprised. Where else would the test take place?

There were a dozen people scattered in the open field around the tree. Most of them were dressed in mercenary reds, but I saw three wearing lighter clothes. I guessed they were important members of the community, or perhaps retired mercenaries still involved with the school.

Vashet pointed toward the tree. At first I thought she was drawing my attention to the motion of it. It was, as she had said, a rather blustery day, and the branches lashed wildly at the empty air. Then I saw a glint of metal against its trunk. Looking more closely, I could see a sword there, tied to the trunk of the tree.

I thought of Celean dancing among the sharp leaves to slap the trunk of the tree. Of course.

"There are several items around the base of the tree," Vashet said. "Your test is to go in, choose one, and bring it out again."

"This is the test?" I demanded. It came out a little sharper than I'd planned. "Why didn't you tell me?"

"Why didn't you ask?" she countered dryly, then laid her hand gently on my arm. "I would have," she said. "Eventually. But I knew if I told you too soon, you would try your hand at it and hurt yourself."

"Well thank God we saved that for today," I said, then sighed. *Resigned apology*. "What happens if I go in there and get cut to ribbons?"

"Getting cut is usually a given," she said and pulled aside the neck of her shirt, revealing a pair of familiar pale, thin scars on her shoulder. "The question is how much, and where, and how you behave." She shrugged her shirt back into place. "The leaves will not cut deep, but be careful of your face and neck. The places where vessels and tendons are close to the surface. A cut on your chest or arm can be mended easily. Less so a severed ear."

I watched the tree as it caught a gust of wind, branches flailing madly. "What keeps a person from crawling there on hands and knees?"

"Pride," she said, her eyes searching my face. "Will you be known as the one who crawled during his test?"

I nodded. This was an issue for me especially. As a barbarian, I had twice as much to prove.

I looked at the tree again. It was thirty feet from the edge of the lashing branches to the trunk. I thought back to the scars I'd seen on Tempi's body, on Carceret's face. "So this is a test of nerve," I said. "A test of pride."

"It is a test of many things," Vashet said. "Your behavior signifies a great deal. You could throw your arms over your face and rush ahead. The straightest line is quickest, after all. But what does that reveal of you? Are you a bull that charges blindly? Are you an animal without subtlety or grace?" She shook her head, frowning. "I expect better from a student of mine."

I squinted my eyes, trying to see what other items were gathered around the tree. "I suppose I'm not allowed to ask what the proper choice is."

"There are many proper choices, and many more improper ones. It is different for everyone. The item you bring back reveals much. What you do with the item afterward reveals much. How you comport yourself reveals much." She shrugged. "All these things Shehyn will consider before deciding if you are to be admitted into the school."

"If Shehyn is the one to decide, why are all these others here?"

Vashet forced a smile, and I saw anxiety lurking deep in her eyes. "Shehyn does not embody the entire school herself." She gestured to the distant Adem standing around the sword tree. "Less does she represent the entirety of the path of the Latantha."

I looked around and realized the handful of non-red shirts were not light, but white. These were the heads of other schools. They had traveled here to see the barbarian take his test.

"Is this usual?" I asked.

Vashet shook her head. "I could feign ignorance. But I suspect Carceret spread word."

"Can they overrule Shehyn's decision?" I asked.

Vashet shook her head. "No. It is her school, her decision. No one would dispute her right to make it." At her side, her hand flicked. *However.*

"Very well," I said.

Vashet reached out and gripped my hand in both of hers, squeezed it, then let it fall.

I walked to the sword tree. For a moment the wind eased, and the thick canopy of hanging branches reminded me of the tree where I had met the Cthaeh. It was not a comforting thought.

I watched the spinning leaves, trying not to think of how sharp they were. How they would slice into the meat of me. How they could glide through the thin skin of my hands and slice through the delicate tendons underneath.

From the edge of the canopy to the safety of the trunk couldn't be more than thirty feet. In some ways, not very far at all. . . .

I thought of Celean darting wildly through the leaves. I thought of her, jumping and swatting branches away. If she could do it, then certainly so could I.

But even as I thought it, I knew it simply wasn't true. Celean had played here all her life. She was skinny as a twig, quick as a cricket, and half my size. Compared to her, I was a lumbering bear.

I saw a handful of Adem mercenaries on the far side of the tree. Two of the more intimidating white shirts were there as well. I could feel their eyes on me, and in a strange way, I was glad.

When you're alone, it's easy to be afraid. It's easy to focus on what might be lurking in the dark at the bottom of the cellar steps. It's easy to obsess on unproductive things, like the madness of stepping into a storm of spinning knives. When you're alone it's easy to sweat, panic, fall apart . . .

But I wasn't alone. And it wasn't just Vashet and Shehyn watching me. There were a dozen mercenaries and the heads of other schools besides. I had an audience. I was onstage. And there is nowhere in the world I am more comfortable than on a stage.

I waited just outside the reach of the longest branches, watching for a break in their motion. I hoped their random spinning would, just for a moment, open into a path I could dart through, striking away any leaves that came too close. I could use Fan Water to keep them away from my face.

I stood at the edge of the canopy and watched, waiting for an opening, trying to anticipate the pattern. The motion of the tree lulled me like it had so many times before. It was beautiful, all circles and arcs.

As I watched, gently dazed by the motion of the tree, I felt my mind slip lightly into the clear, empty float of Spinning Leaf. I realized the motion of the tree wasn't random at all, really. It was actually a pattern made of endless changing patterns.

And then, my mind open and empty, I saw the wind spread out before me. It was like frost forming on a blank sheet of window glass. One moment, nothing. The next, I could see the name of the wind as clearly as the back of my own hand.

I looked around for a moment, marveling in it. I tasted the shape of it on my tongue and knew if desired I could stir it to a storm. I could hush it to a whisper, leaving the sword tree hanging empty and still.

But that seemed wrong. Instead I simply opened my eyes wide to the wind, watching where it would choose to push the branches. Watching where it would flick the leaves.

Then I stepped under the canopy, calmly as you would walk through your own front door. I took two steps, then stopped as a pair of leaves sliced through the air in front of me. I stepped sideways and forward as the wind spun another branch through the space behind me.

I moved through the dancing branches of the sword tree. Not running, not frantically batting them away with my hands. I stepped carefully, deliberately. It was, I realized, the way Shehyn moved when she fought. Not quickly, though sometimes she was quick. She moved perfectly, always where she needed to be.

Almost before I realized it, I was standing on the dark earth that circled the wide trunk of the sword tree. The spinning leaves could not reach here. Safe for the moment, I relaxed and focused on what was waiting there for me.

The sword I had seen from the edge of the clearing was bound to the tree with a white silk cord that ran around the trunk. The sword was half-drawn from its sheath, and I could see the blade was similar to Vashet's sword. The metal was an odd, burnished grey without mark or blemish.

Next to the tree on a small table sat a familiar red shirt, folded neatly in half. There was an arrow with stark white fletching and a polished wooden cylinder of the sort that would hold a scroll.

A bright glitter caught my eye, and I turned to see a thick gold bar nestled in the dark earth among the roots of the tree. Was it truly gold? I bent and touched it. It was chill under my fingers, and was too heavy for my single hand to pry up from the ground. How much did it weigh? Forty pounds? Fifty? Enough gold for me to stay at the University forever, no matter how viciously they raised my tuition.

I slowly made my way around the trunk of the sword tree and saw a fluttering piece of silk hanging from a low branch. There was another sword of a more ordinary sort, hanging from the same white cord. There were three blue flowers tied with a blue ribbon. There was a tarnished Vintish halfpenny. There was a long, flat whetstone, dark with oil.

Then I came to the other side of the tree and saw my lute case leaning casually against the trunk.

Seeing it there, knowing someone had gone into my room and taken it from under my bed, filled me with a sudden, terrible rage. It was all the worse knowing what the Adem thought of musicians. It meant they knew I wasn't merely a barbarian, but a cheap and tawdry whore as well. It had been left there to taunt me.

I had called the name of the wind in the grip of a terrible anger before, in Imre after Ambrose had broken my lute. And I had called it in terror and fury to defend myself against Felurian. But this time the knowledge of it hadn't come to me borne on the back of some strong emotion. I had slipped into it gently, the way you must reach out to catch a gently floating thistle seed.

So when I saw my lute, the welter of hot emotion brought me crashing out of Spinning Leaf like a sparrow struck with a stone. The name of the wind tattered to shreds, leaving me empty and blind. Looking around at the madly dancing leaves, I could see no pattern at all, only a thousand wind-blown razors slicing at the air.

I finished my slow circuit of the tree with a knot of worry tightening my stomach. The presence of my lute made one thing clear. Any of these objects could be a trap someone had left for me.

Vashet had said the test was more than what I brought back from the tree. It was also how I brought it, and what I did with it afterward. If I brought out the heavy bar of gold and gave it to Shehyn, would that show I was willing to bring money back to the school? Or it would signify that I would cling greedily to something heavy and unwieldy despite the fact that it put me in danger?

The same was true of any of these things. If I took the red shirt, I could be seen as either nobly striving for the right to wear it, or arrogantly presuming I was good enough to join their ranks. This was doubly true of the ancient sword that hung there. I didn't doubt that it was as precious to the Adem as a child.

I made another slow circuit of the tree, pretending to consider my choices, but really just stalling for time. I nervously looked over the items a second time. There was a small book with a brass lock. There was a spindle of grey woolen thread. There was a smooth round stone sitting on a clean white cloth.

As I looked at them all, I realized any choice I made could be interpreted so many ways. I didn't know nearly enough about Adem culture to guess what my item might signify.

Even if I did, without the name of the wind to guide me back through the canopy, I would be cut to ribbons leaving the tree. Probably not enough to maim me, but enough to make it clear I was a clumsy barbarian who obviously didn't belong.

I looked at the gold bar again. If I chose that, at least the weight of it would give me an excuse for being awkward on my way out. Perhaps I could still make a good showing of it . . .

Nervously I made a third circuit of the tree. I felt the wind pick up, gusting and making the branches flail about more wildly than before. It pulled the sweat from my body, chilling me and making me shiver.

In the middle of that anxious moment, I was suddenly aware of nothing as much as the sudden, urgent pressure of my bladder. My biology cared nothing for the gravity of my situation, and I was seized with a powerful need to relieve myself.

Thus it was that in the center of a storm of knives, in the midst of my test that was also my trial, that I thought of urinating up against the side of the sacred sword tree while two dozen proud and deadly mercenaries watched me do it.

It was such a horrifying and inappropriate thought that I burst out laughing. And when the laugh rolled out of me, the tension knotting my stomach and clawing at the muscles of my back melted away. Whatever choice I made, it would have to be better than pissing on the Latantha.

At that moment, no longer boiling with anger, no longer gripped with fear, I looked at the moving leaves around me. Always before when the name of the wind had left me, it had faded like a dream on waking: irretrievable as an echo or a fading sigh.

But this time it was different, I had spent hours watching the patterns of these moving leaves. I looked out through the branches of the tree and thought of Celean jumping and spinning, laughing and running.

And there it was. Like the name of an old friend that had simply slipped my mind for a moment. I looked out among the branches and I saw the wind. I spoke the long name of it gently, and the wind grew gentle. I breathed it out as a whisper, and for the first time since I had come to Haert the wind went quiet and utterly still.

In this place of endless wind, it seemed as if the world were suddenly holding its breath. The unceasing dance of the sword tree slowed, then stopped. As if it were resting. As if it had decided to let me go.

I stepped away from the tree and began to walk slowly toward Shehyn, bringing nothing with me. As I walked, I raised my left hand and drew my open palm across the razor edge of a hanging leaf.

I came to stand before Shehyn, stopping the polite distance from her. I stood, my face an impassive mask. I stood, utterly silent, perfectly still.

I extended my left hand, bloody palm up, and closed it into a fist. The gesture meant *willing*. There was more blood than I'd expected, and it pressed between my fingers to run down the back of my hand.

After a long moment, Shehyn nodded. I relaxed, and only then did the wind return.

Of Names

"YOU," VASHET SAID AS we walked through the hills, "are one great gaudy showboating bastard, you know that?"

I inclined my head slightly to her, gracefully gesturing *subordinate acceptance*.

She cuffed me on the side of the head. "Get over yourself, you melodramatic ass. You can fool them, but not me."

Vashet held her hand to her chest as if gossiping. "Did you hear what Kvothe brought back from the sword tree? The things a barbarian cannot understand: silence and stillness. The heart of Ademre. What did he offer to Shehyn? Willingness to bleed for the school."

She looked at me, her expression trapped between disgust and amusement. "Seriously, it's like you stepped out of a storybook."

I gestured: *Gracious flattering understated affectionate acceptance.*

Vashet reached out and flicked my ear hard with a finger.

"Ow!" I burst out laughing. "Fine. But don't you dare accuse me of melodrama. You people are one great unending dramatic gesture. The quiet. The blood-red clothes. The hidden language. Secrets and mysteries. It's like your lives are one giant dumbshow." I met her eye. "And I do mean that in all its various clever implications."

"Well, you impressed Shehyn," she said. "Which is the most important thing. And you did it in such a way that the heads of the other schools won't be able to grumble too much. Which is the other most important thing."

We reached our destination, a low building of three rooms next to a small split-timber goat pen. "Here is the one who will tend to your hand," she said.

"What of the apothecary?" I asked.

"The apothecary is close friends with Carceret's mother," Vashet said.

"And I would not have her looking after your hands for a weight of gold." She nodded her head at the nearby house. "Daeln, on the other hand, is who I would come to if I needed mending."

She knocked on the door. "You may be a member of the school, but do not forget that I am still your teacher. In all things, I know what is best."

———

Later, my hand tightly bandaged, Vashet and I sat with Shehyn. We were in a room I'd never seen before, smaller than the rooms where we had discussed the Lethani. There was a small, messy writing desk, some flowers in a vase, and several comfortably cushioned chairs. Along one wall was a picture of three birds in flight against a sunset sky, not painted, but composed of thousands of pieces of bright enameled tile. I suspected we might be in the equivalent of Shehyn's study.

"How is your hand?" Shehyn said.

"Fine," I said. "It is a shallow cut. Daeln has the smallest stitches I have ever seen. He is quite remarkable."

She nodded. *Approval.*

I held up my left hand, wrapped in clean white linen. "The hard part will be keeping this hand idle for four days. I already feel as if it were my tongue that were cut, and not my hand."

Shehyn gave a slight smile at this, startling me. The familiarity of the expression was a great compliment. "You performed quite well today. Everyone is speaking of it."

"I expect the few that saw have better things to speak about," I said modestly.

Amused disbelief. "That may be true, but those who watched from hiding will doubtless say what they have seen. Celean herself will have already told a hundred people unless I miss my guess. By tomorrow everyone will expect your stride to shake the ground as if you were Aethe himself come back to visit us."

I couldn't think of anything to say, so I kept quiet. A rarity for me. But as I've said, I had been learning.

"There is something I have been waiting to speak to you about," Shehyn said. *Guarded curiosity.* "After Tempi brought you here, he told me the long story of your time together," she said. "Of your search for the bandits."

I nodded.

"Is it true that you made blood magic to destroy some men, then called lightning to destroy the rest?"

Vashet looked up at this, glancing back and forth between us. I had grown so used to speaking Aturan with her that it was odd to see the expressionless Adem impassivity covering her face. Still, I could tell she was surprised. She hadn't known.

I thought of trying to offer an explanation for my actions, then decided against it. "Yes."

"You are powerful then."

I had never thought of it in those terms before. "I have some power. Others are more powerful."

"Is that why you seek the Ketan? To gain power?"

"No. I seek from curiosity. I seek the knowing of things."

"Knowing is a type of power," Shehyn pointed out, then seemed to change the subject. "Tempi told me there was a Rhinta among the bandits as their leader."

"Rhinta?" I asked respectfully.

"A bad thing. A man who is more than a man, yet less than a man."

"A demon?" I asked, using the Aturan word without thinking.

"Not a demon," Shehyn said, switching easily to Aturan. "There are no such things as demons. Your priests tell stories of demons to frighten you." She met my eye briefly, gesturing a graceful: *Apologetic honesty* and *serious import*. "But there are bad things in the world. Old things in the shape of men. And there are a handful worse than all the rest. They walk the world freely and do terrible things."

I felt hope rising within me. "I have also heard them called the Chandrian," I said.

Shehyn nodded. "I have heard this too. But Rhinta is a better word." Shehyn gave me a long look and fell back into Ademic. "Given what Tempi has told me of your reaction, I think that you have met such a one before."

"Yes."

"Will you meet such a one again?"

"Yes." The certainty in my own voice surprised me.

"With purpose?"

"Yes."

"What purpose?"

"To kill him."

"Such things are not easily killed."

I nodded.

"Will you use what Tempi has taught you to do this?"

"I will use all things to that purpose." I unconsciously began to gesture *absolute*, but the bandage on my hand stopped me. I frowned at it.

"That is good," Shehyn said. "Your Ketan will not be enough. It is poor for one as old as you are. Good for a barbarian. Good for one with as little training as you have had, but still poor overall."

I fought hard to keep the eagerness out of my voice, wishing I could use my hand to indicate how important the question was to me. "Shehyn, I have a great desire to know more of these Rhinta."

Shehyn was quiet for a long moment. "I will consider this," she said at last, making a gesture I thought might be *trepidation*. "Such things are not spoken of lightly."

I kept my face impassive, and forced my bandaged hand to say *profound respectful desire*. "I thank you for considering it, Shehyn. Anything you could tell me of them I would value more than a weight of gold."

Vashet gestured *firm discomfort*, then *polite desire, difference*. Two span ago I couldn't have understood, but now I realized she wanted to move the conversation onto a different subject.

So I bit my tongue and let it go. I knew enough about the Adem by this point to realize that pushing the issue was the worst thing to do if I wanted to learn more. In the Commonwealth I could have pressed the point, teased and wheedled it out of the person I was talking to. That wouldn't work here. Stillness and silence were the only things that would work. I had to be patient and let Shehyn return to the subject in her own time.

"I was saying," Shehyn continued. *Reluctant confession*, "Your Ketan is poor. But were you to train yourself in proper fashion for a year, you would be Tempi's equal."

"You flatter me."

"I do not. I tell you your weaknesses. You learn quickly. That leads to rash behavior, and rashness is not of the Lethani. Vashet is not alone in thinking there is something troubling about your spirit."

Shehyn gave me a long look. For over a minute she stared at me. Then she gave an eloquent shrug and glanced at Vashet, favoring the younger woman with a ghost of a smile. "Still," *Whimsical musing*. "if I have ever met someone without a single shadow on their heart, it was surely a child too young for speaking." She pushed herself out of her chair and brushed off her shirt with both hands. "Come. Let us go and have a name for you."

———

Shehyn led the three of us up the side of a steep, rocky hill.

None of us had spoken since we had left the school. I didn't know what was about to happen, but it didn't seem proper to ask. It would have seemed irreverent, like a groom blurting out, "What comes next?" halfway through his own wedding.

We came to a grassy ledge with a leaning tree clutching tight to the bare face of a cliff. Beside the tree was a thick wooden door, one of the hidden Adem homes.

Shehyn knocked and opened the door herself. Inside it wasn't cavelike at all. The stone walls were finished, and the floor was smooth wood. It was much larger than I'd expected, too, with a high ceiling and six doors leading deeper into the stone of the cliff.

A woman sat at a low table, copying something from one book into another. Her hair was white, her face wrinkled as an old apple. It occurred to me then that this was the first person I'd seen reading or writing in all my time in Haert.

The old woman nodded a greeting at Shehyn, then turned to Vashet and her eyes crinkled around the edges. *Gladness.* "Vashet," she said. "I did not know you were returned."

"We are come for a name, Magwyn," Shehyn said. *Polite formal entreaty.*

"A name?" Magwyn asked, puzzled. She looked from Shehyn to Vashet, then her eyes moved to where I stood behind them. To my bright red hair and my bandaged hand. "Ah," she said, growing suddenly somber.

Magwyn closed her books and came to her feet. Her back was bent, and she took small, shuffling steps. She motioned me forward and walked a slow circle around me, looking me carefully up and down. She avoided looking at my face, but took hold of my unbandaged hand, turning it over to look at the palm and the fingertips.

"I would hear you say something," she said, still looking intently at my hand.

"As you will, honored shaper of names," I said.

Magwyn looked up at Shehyn. "Does he mock me?"

"I think not."

Magwyn made another circle of me, running her hands over my shoulders, my arms, the back of my neck. She moved her fingers through my hair, then stopped in front of me and looked me fully in the eye.

Her eyes were like Elodin's. Not in any of the details. Elodin's eyes were green, sharp, and mocking. Magwyn's were the familiar Adem grey, slightly watery and red around the edges. No, the similarity was in how she looked at me. Elodin was the only other person I had met who could look at you like that, as if you were a book he was idly thumbing through.

When Magwyn met my eyes for the first time, I felt like all the air had been sucked out of me. For the barest of moments I thought she might be startled by what she saw, but that was probably just my anxiety. I had come to the edge of disaster too often lately, and despite how well my recent test had gone, part of me was still waiting for the other shoe to drop.

"Maedre," she said, her eyes still fixed on mine. She looked down and made her way back to her book.

"Maedre?" Vashet said, a hint of dismay in her voice. She might have said more, but Shehyn reached out and cuffed her sharply on the side of the head.

It was exactly the same motion Vashet had used to chastise me a thousand times in the last month. I couldn't help myself. I laughed.

Vashet and Shehyn glared at me. Actually glared.

Magwyn turned to look at me. She didn't seem upset. "Do you laugh at the name I have given you?"

"Never, Magwyn," I said trying my best to gesture *respect* with my bandaged hand. "Names are important things."

She continued to eye me. "And what would a barbarian know of names?"

"Some," I said, fumbling with my bandaged hand again. I couldn't add fine shades of meaning to my words without it. "Far away, I have made a study of such things. I know more than many, but still only just a little."

Magwyn looked at me for a long time. "Then you will know you should not speak of your new name to anyone," she said. "It is a private thing, and dangerous to share."

I nodded.

Magwyn looked satisfied at this, and settled back onto her chair, opening a book. "Vashet, my little rabbit, you should come and visit me soon." *Gentle chiding fondness.*

"I will, grandmother," Vashet said.

"Thank you, Magwyn," Shehyn said. *Deferential gratitude.*

The old woman nodded a distracted dismissal, and Shehyn led us from the cave.

Later that evening, I walked back to Vashet's house. She was sitting on the bench out front, watching the sky as the sun began to set.

She tapped the bench beside her, and I took a seat. "How does it feel to no longer be a barbarian?" she asked.

"Mostly the same," I said. "Slightly drunker."

After dinner Penthe had pulled me away to her house, where there was a party of sorts. Call it a gathering, rather, as there was no music or dancing. Still, I was flattered that Penthe had gone to the effort of finding five other Adem who were willing to celebrate my admittance to the school.

I was pleased to learn the Adem impassivity dissolved quite easily after a few drinks, and we were all grinning like barbarians in no time. It relaxed me, especially as much of my own clumsiness with the language could now be blamed on my bandaged hand.

"Earlier today," I said carefully, "Shehyn said she knew a story about the Rhinta."

Vashet turned to look at me, her face expressionless. *Hesitant.*

"I have searched all over the world for such a thing," I said. "There are few things I would value more." *Utter sincerity.* "And I worry that I did a poor job of letting Shehyn know this." *Questioning. Intense entreaty.*

Vashet looked at me for a moment, as if waiting for me to continue. Then she gestured *reluctance.* "I will mention it to her," she said. *Reassurance. Finished.*

I nodded and let the subject drop.

Vashet and I sat for a while in companionable silence as the sun slowly sank into the horizon. She drew a deep breath and sighed expansively. I realized that, with the exception of waiting for me to catch my breath or recover from a fall, we had never done anything like this before. Up until this point, every moment we had spent together had been focused on my training.

"Tonight," I said at last. "Penthe told me she thought I had a fine anger, and that she'd like to share it with me."

Vashet chuckled. "That didn't take very long." She gave me a knowing look. "What happened?"

I blushed a bit. "Ah. She . . . reminded me the Adem do not consider physical contact particularly intimate."

Vashet's smile grew practically lecherous. "Grabbed hold of you, did she?"

"Almost," I said. "I move more quickly than I did a month ago."

"I doubt you move quickly enough to keep away from Penthe," Vashet said. "All she is looking for is sexplay. There is no harm in it."

"That is why I was asking you," I said slowly. "To see if there was any harm in it."

Vashet she raised an eyebrow, at the same time gesturing *vague puzzlement.*

"Penthe is quite lovely," I said carefully. "However, you and I have . . ." I looked for an appropriate term. "Been intimate."

Realization washed over Vashet's face and she laughed again. "What you mean is that we have been sexual. The intimacy between a teacher and student is greater by far than that."

"Ah," I said, relaxing. "I'd suspected something of the sort. But it is nice to know for certain."

Vashet shook her head. "I had forgotten what it is like with you barbarians," she said, her voice heavy with fond indulgence. "It has been so many years since I had to explain such things to my poet king."

"So you would not be offended if I were to . . ." I made an inarticulate gesture with my bandaged hand.

"You are young and energetic," she said. "It is a healthy thing for you to do. Why would I be offended? Do I suddenly own your sex, that I should be worried about you giving it away?"

Vashet stopped as if something had just occurred to her. She turned to look at me. "Are *you* offended that I have been having sex with others all this while?" She watched my face intently. "I see you are startled by it."

"I am startled," I admitted. Then I did a mental inventory and was surprised to discover I wasn't sure how I felt. "I feel I ought to be offended," I said at last. "But I don't think I am."

Vashet nodded approvingly. "That is a good sign. It shows you are becoming civilized. The other feeling is what you were brought up to think. It is like an old shirt that no longer fits you. And now, when you look at it closely, you can see it was ugly to begin with."

I hesitated for a moment. "Out of curiosity," I said, "how many others have you been with since we have been together?"

Vashet seemed surprised by the question. She pursed her mouth and looked up at the sky for a long moment before shrugging. "How many people have I spoken with since then? How many have I sparred with? How many times have I eaten, or practiced my Ketan? Who counts such things?"

"And most Adem think this way?" I asked, glad to finally have the chance to ask these questions. "That sex is not an intimate thing?"

"Of course it is intimate," Vashet said. "Anything that brings two people close together is intimate. A conversation, a kiss, a whisper. Even fighting is intimate. But we are not strange about our sex. We do not feel shame about it. We do not feel it important to keep someone else's sex all to ourselves, like a miser hoarding gold." She shook her head. "More than any other, this strangeness in your thinking sets you barbarians apart."

"But what of romance then?" I asked, slightly indignant. "What of love?"

Vashet laughed again then, loud and long and vastly amused. Half of Haert must have heard it, and it echoed back to us from the distant hills.

"You barbarians," she said, wiping moisture from her eyes. "I had forgotten how backward you are. My poet king was the same way. It took him a long, miserable time before he realized the truth of things: There is a great deal of difference between a penis and a heart."

CHAPTER ONE HUNDRED TWENTY-FIVE

Caesura

THE NEXT DAY I woke somewhat blearily. I hadn't drunk that much, but my body was no longer used to such things, and so I felt each drink three times that morning. I straggled to the baths, dunked myself in the hottest pool I could stand, then scrubbed the vaguely gritty feeling away as best I could.

I was heading back to the dining hall when Vashet and Shehyn found me in the hallway. Vashet gestured for me to follow, and I fell in step behind them. I hardly felt up for training or a formal conversation, but refusing didn't seem like a realistic option.

We wound our way through several hallways, eventually emerging near the center of the school. Passing through a courtyard we approached a small, square building that Shehyn unlocked with a small iron key: the first locked door I had seen in all of Haert.

The three of us moved into a small windowless entryway. Vashet closed the outside door and the room grew black as pitch, cutting off the sound of the persistent wind. Then Shehyn opened the inner door. Warm light from a half-dozen candles greeted us. At first it seemed odd they had been left to burn in an empty room. . . .

Then I saw what hung on the walls. Swords gleamed in the candlelight, dozens of them covering the walls. They were all of them naked, their scabbards hanging underneath them.

There were no ritual trappings of the sort you might find in a Tehlin church. No tapestries or paintings. Just the swords themselves. Still, it was obvious that this was an important place. There was a tension in the air of the sort you might feel in the Archives or an old graveyard.

Shehyn turned to Vashet. "Choose."

Vashet looked startled by this, almost stricken. She started to make a gesture, but Shehyn held up a hand before she could protest.

"He is your student," Shehyn said. *Refusal.* "You have brought him into the school. It is your choice."

Vashet looked from Shehyn, to me, to the dozens of gleaming swords. They were all slender and deadly, each subtly different from the others. Some were curved, some longer or thicker than others. Some showed signs of much use, while some few resembled Vashet's, with worn hilts and unmarked blades of grey burnished metal.

Slowly, Vashet moved to the right-hand wall. She picked up a sword, hefted it, and put it back. Then she lifted a different one, gripped it, and held it out to me.

I took hold of it. It was light and thin as a whisper.

"Maiden Combs Her Hair," Vashet said.

I obeyed, feeling somewhat self-conscious, as Shehyn was watching. But before I made it halfway through the sweeping movement, Vashet was already shaking her head. She took the sword back from me and returned it to the wall.

After another minute she handed me a second sword. It had worn etching running down the blade, like a crawling ivy. At Vashet's request, I made Heron Falling. I swept high and lunged low, sword flickering. Vashet raised an eyebrow to me, questioning.

I shook my head. "The point is too heavy for me."

Vashet didn't seem particularly surprised and returned that sword to the wall as well.

So things continued. Vashet hefted swords and rejected most without a word. She set three more in my hands, asked for various pieces of the Ketan, then returned them to the wall without asking my opinion.

Vashet moved more slowly as she made her way along the second wall. She handed me a sword slightly curved like Penthe's, and my breath caught when I saw the blade was the same flawless, burnished grey as Vashet's. I took it carefully, but the grip wasn't right for my fingers. When I handed it back, I saw relief written plainly on her face.

As she progressed along the wall, occasionally Vashet would steal a glance at Shehyn. At those moments, she looked very little like my confident, swaggering teacher and very much like a young woman desperately hoping for a word of advice. Shehyn remained impassive.

Eventually Vashet came to the third wall, moving slower and slower. She handled almost every sword now, taking a long time before setting them back in their places.

Then, slowly, she laid her hand on another sword with a blade of burnished grey. She lifted it off the wall, gripped it, and seemed to age ten years.

Vashet avoided looking at Shehyn, and handed me the sword. The guard of this one extended out slightly, curving to give a hint of protection to the hand. It was nothing like a full hand guard. Anything that bulky would render half the Ketan useless. But it looked as if it would give my fingers an extra bit of shelter, and that was appealing to me.

The warm grip settled into my palm as smoothly as the neck of my lute.

Before she could ask, I made Maiden Combs Her Hair. It felt like stretching after a long stiff sleep. I eased into Twelve Stones, and for the smallest of moments I felt graceful as Penthe looked when she fought. I made Heron Falling and it was sweet and simple as a kiss.

Vashet held out her hand to take it back from me. I didn't want to give it up, but I did. I knew this was the worst possible time and place for me to make a scene.

Holding the sword, Vashet turned to Shehyn. "This is the one for him," she said. And for the first time since I'd known my teacher, it was as if all the laughing had been pressed out of her. Her voice was thin and dry.

Shehyn nodded. "I agree. You have done well to find it."

Vashet's relief was palpable, though her face still looked somewhat stricken. "It will perhaps offset his name," she said. She held the sword out to Shehyn.

Shehyn gestured: *Refusal*. "No. Your student. Your choice. Your responsibility."

Vashet took the scabbard from the wall and sheathed the sword. Then she turned and held it out to me. "This is named Saicere."

"Caesura?" I asked, startled by the name. Wasn't that what Sim had called the break in the line of Eld Vintic verse? Was I being given a poet's sword?

"Saicere," she said softly, as if it were the name of God. She stepped back, and I felt the weight of it settle back into my hands.

Sensing something was expected of me, I drew it from its sheath. The faint ring of leather and metal seemed a whisper of its name: *Saicere*. It felt light in my hand. The blade was flawless. I slid it back into its sheath and the sound was different. It sounded like the breaking of a line. It said: *Caesura*.

Shehyn opened the inner door, and we left as we came. Silently and with respect.

———

The rest of the day was quite the opposite of exciting. With a dogged and humorless persistence, Vashet taught me how to care for my sword. How to clean and oil my sword. How to dismantle and reassemble my sword. How to strap the scabbard to my shoulder or hip. How the slightly enlarged guard would alter a few of the grips and motions of the Ketan.

The sword was not mine. The sword belonged to the school. To Ademre. I would return it when I was no longer able to fight.

While I normally have little tolerance for hearing the same thing over and over again, I let Vashet ramble. The least I could do was let her repeat herself a bit when she was plainly anxious and trying to settle her mind.

Around the fifteenth repetition, I asked what I should do if the sword broke. Not the hilt or the guard, but the blade itself. Should I still bring it back?

Vashet gave me a look of dismay so raw it verged on horror. She didn't answer, and I made a point of not asking any more questions for the rest of the morning.

After lunch Vashet took me back to Magwyn's cave. My teacher's mood seemed somewhat improved, but she was still far from her regular gregarious self.

"Magwyn will be giving you Saicere's story," she said. "You must memorize it."

"Its story?" I asked.

Vashet shrugged. "In Ademic it is *Atas*. It is the history of your sword. Everyone who has carried it. What they have done. It is something you must know."

We reached the top of the path and stood before Magwyn's door. Vashet gave me a serious look. "You must be on your best behavior and be very polite."

"I will," I said.

"Magwyn is an important person, and you must attend closely to what she says."

"I will," I said.

Vashet knocked on the door and escorted me in.

Magwyn sat at the same table as before. For all I could tell, she was copying the same book. She smiled when she saw Vashet, then noticed me and let her face slide into the familiar Adem impassivity.

"Magwyn," Vashet said. *Profoundly polite entreaty.* "This one needs the *Atas* of his sword."

"Which sword did you find for him?" Magwyn asked, her face wrinkling even further as she squinted to see.

"Saicere," Vashet said.

Magwyn gave a laugh that was almost a cackle. She got down off her chair. "I can't say I'm surprised," she said, and disappeared through a door that led back into the cliff.

Vashet let herself out, and I stood there feeling awkward, like one of those terrible dreams when you're on stage and can't remember what to say, or even what part you were meaning to play.

Magwyn returned, carrying a thick book bound in brown leather. At a gesture from her, we took seats in chairs facing each other. Hers was a deeply cushioned leather chair. Mine was not. I sat with Caesura across my knees. Partly because it seemed appropriate, and partly because I was fond of the feel of it beneath my hand.

She opened the book, the binding crackling as she spread it open on her lap. She flipped pages for a moment until she found the place she was looking for. "First came Chael," she read. "Who shaped me in fire for an unknown purpose. He carried me then cast me aside."

Magwyn looked up, unable to gesture as her hands were both occupied by the large book. "Well?" she demanded.

"What would you like me to do?" I asked politely. I couldn't gesture due to my bandages. We made a fine pair of half-mutes.

"Repeat it back," she said, irritated. "You need to learn them all."

"First came Chael," I said. "Who shaped me in fire for an unknown purpose. He carried me then cast me aside."

She nodded and continued. "Next came Etaine . . ."

I repeated it. We continued this way for perhaps a half hour. Owner after owner. Name after name. Loyalties declaimed and enemies killed.

At first the names and places were tantalizing. Then, as it continued, the list began to depress me, as nearly each piece ended with the death of the owner. They were not peaceful deaths either. Some died in wars, some in duels. Many were merely "killed by" or "slain by," giving no clue as to the circumstances. After thirty of these, I had heard nothing resembling, "Passed from this world peacefully in his sleep, surrounded by fat grandchildren."

Then the list stopped being depressing and became simply boring instead.

"Next came Finol of the clear and shining eye," I repeated attentively. "Much beloved of Dulcen. She herself slew two daruna, then was killed by gremmen at the Drossen Tor."

I cleared my throat before Magwyn could recite another passage. "If I may ask," I said. "How many have carried Caesura over the years?"

"Saicere," she corrected me sharply. "Do not presume to meddle with her name. It means to break, to catch, and to fly."

I looked down at the sheathed sword across my lap. I felt the weight of it, the chill of the metal under my fingers. A small sliver of the smooth grey blade was visible above the top of the sheath.

How can I say this so you can understand? Saicere was a fine name. It was thin and bright and dangerous. It fit the sword like a glove fits a hand.

But it wasn't the perfect name. This sword's name was Caesura. This sword was the jarring break in a line of perfect verse. It was the broken breath. It was smooth and swift and sharp and deadly. The name didn't fit like a glove. It fit like skin. More than that. It was bone and muscle and movement. Those things *are* the hand. And Caesura was the sword. It was the both the name and the thing itself.

I can't tell you how I knew this. But I knew it.

Besides, if I was to be a namer, I decided I could damn well choose the name of my own sword.

I looked up at Magwyn. "It is a good name," I agreed politely, deciding to keep my opinion to myself until I was well gone from Ademre. "I am only wondering how many owners there have been entirely. That is something I should know as well."

Magwyn gave me a sour look that said she knew I was patronizing her. But she flipped ahead several pages in her book. Then a few more.

Then a few more.

"Two hundred and thirty-six," she said. "You will be the two hundred thirty-seventh." She flipped back to the beginning of the list. "Let us begin again." She drew a breath and said. "First came Chael, who shaped me in fire for an unknown purpose. He carried me then cast me aside."

I fought down the urge to sigh. Even with my trouper's knack for learning lines it would take long, weary days setting them all to memory.

Then I realized what this truly meant. If each owner had kept Caesura for ten years, and it had never sat idle for longer than a day or two, that meant Caesura was, at a very conservative estimate, more than two thousand years old.

I received my next surprise three hours later when I tried to excuse myself for supper. As I stood to leave Magwyn explained I was to remain with her until I learned all of Caesura's story by heart. Someone would bring us our meals, and there was a room nearby where I could sleep.

First came Chael . . .

The First Stone

I SPENT THE NEXT THREE days with Magwyn. It wasn't bad, especially considering my left hand was still healing, so my ability to talk and fight was rather limited.

I like to think I did rather well. It would have been easier for me to memorize an entire play than this. A play fits together like a jigsaw. Dialogue moves back and forth. There is a shape to a story.

But what I learned from Magwyn was merely a long string of unfamiliar names and unconnected events. It was a laundry list masquerading as a story.

Still, I learned it all by heart. It was late in the evening of the third day when I recited it back flawlessly to Magwyn. The hardest part was not singing it as I recited. Music carries words over miles and into hearts and memories. Committing Caesura's history to memory had been much easier when I'd started fitting it to the tune of an old Vintish ballad in my head.

The next morning Magwyn demanded I recite it again. After I made it through a second time, she scribbled a note to Shehyn, sealed it in wax, and shooed me out of her cave.

"We had not expected Magwyn to be finished with you for several days yet," Shehyn said, reading the note. "Vashet took a trip to Feant and will not be back for at least two days."

That meant I had memorized the *Atas* twice as quickly as their best estimate. I felt more than a little pride in that.

Shehyn glanced at my left hand and gave the barest frown. "When did you have your dressings removed?" she asked.

"I could not find you at first," I said. "So I went to visit Daeln. He said it has healed quite nicely." I flexed my newly unbandaged left hand and gestured *joyful relief*. "There is hardly any stiffness in the skin, and he reassures me even that will fade soon with proper care."

I looked at Shehyn, expecting to see some gesture of approval or satisfaction. Instead I saw *exasperated irritation*.

"Have I done something wrong?" I asked. *Confused regret. Apology.*

Shehyn motioned to my hand. "It could have been a convenient excuse to postpone your stone trial," she said. *Irritated resignation.* "Now we must go ahead with it today, Vashet or no."

I felt a familiar anxiety settle back onto me, like a dark bird clenching its claws deep into the muscles of my neck and shoulders. I'd thought the tedium of memorization had been the last of it, but apparently the final shoe was yet to drop. I didn't like the sound of the term "stone trial," either.

"Return here after midday meal." Shehyn said. *Dismissal.* "Go. I have much to prepare before then."

I went looking for Penthe. With Vashet gone, she was the only one I knew well enough to ask about the upcoming trial.

But she wasn't in her house, the school, or the baths. Eventually I gave up, stretched, and rehearsed my Ketan, first with Caesura, then without. Then I made my way to the baths and scrubbed away three days of sitting and doing nothing.

Shehyn was waiting for me when I returned after lunch, holding her carved wooden sword. She looked at my empty hands and made an exasperated gesture. "Where is your dueling sword?"

"In my room," I said. "I did not know I would need it."

"Run fetch it," she said. "Then meet me at the stone hill."

"Shehyn," I said. *Urgent imploring.* "I don't know where that is. I don't know anything about the stone trial."

Surprise. "Vashet never told you?" *Disbelief.*

I shook my head. *Sincere apology.* "We were focused on other things."

Exasperation. "It is simple enough," she said. "First you will recite Saicere's *Atas* for all gathered. Then you will climb the hill. At the first stone, you will fight one from the school who is ranked of the first stone. If you win, you will continue to climb and fight someone of the second stone."

Shehyn looked at me. "In your case, this is a formality. Occasionally a student enters the school with exceptional talent. Vashet was one such as this, and she gained the second stone at her first trial." *Blunt honesty.* "You are not such a one. Your Ketan is still poor, and you cannot expect to gain even the first stone. The stone hill is east of the baths." She flicked her hand at me: *Hurry.*

There was a crowd gathered at the foot of the stone hill by the time I arrived, more than a hundred people. Grey homespun and muted colors vastly out-numbered mercenary red, and the low murmur of the crowd's conversation was audible from a distance.

The hill itself wasn't particularly high, nor was it steep. But the path to the top cut back and forth in a series of switchbacks. At each corner there was a wide, flat space with a large block of grey stone. There were four corners, four stones, and four red-shirted mercenaries. At the top of the hill stood a tall greystone, familiar as a friend. Beside that stood a small figure in blinding white.

As I came closer, I caught a smell drifting on the breeze: toasted chestnuts. Only then did I relax. This was pageantry of a sort. While "stone trial" had an intimidating sound to it, I doubted very much that I was going to be brutal-ized in front of a milling audience while someone sold roasted nuts.

I entered the crowd and approached the hill. I could see it was Shehyn next to the greystone. I also recognized the heart-shaped face and long, hang-ing braid of Penthe at the third stone.

The crowd parted gently as I walked to the foot of the hill. Out of the cor-ner of my eye I saw a blood-red figure rushing toward me. Alarmed, I turned and saw it was none other than Tempi. He hurried toward me, gesturing a broad *enthusiastic greeting*.

I fought the urge to smile and shout his name, settling instead on a gesture of *joyful excitement*.

He came to stand directly in front of me, gripping me by my shoulder and jostling me around playfully, as if congratulating me. But his eyes were intense. Close to his chest his hand said, *deception* where only I could see. "Lis-ten," he spoke quickly under his breath. "You cannot win this fight."

"Don't worry." *Reassurance.* "Shehyn thinks the same, but I might surprise you."

Tempi's grip on my shoulder grew painfully tight. "Listen," he hissed. "Look who is at the first stone."

I looked over his shoulder. It was Carceret. Her eyes were like knives.

"She is full of rage," Tempi said quietly, gesturing *fond affection* for the crowd to see. "As if your admittance to the school was not enough, you have been given her mother's sword."

That piece of news knocked the wind out of me. My mind flickered to the final piece of the *Atas.* "Larel was Carceret's mother?" I asked.

Tempi ran his right hand affectionately through my hair. "Yes. She is enraged past reason. I fear she would gladly cripple you, even if it means being thrown from the school."

I nodded seriously.

"She will try to disarm you. Be wary of it. Do not grapple. If she catches you with Sleeping Bear or Circling Hands, submit quickly. Shout it if you must. If you hesitate or try to break away, she will shatter your arm or pull it from your shoulder. I heard her say this to her sister not an hour ago."

Suddenly, Tempi stepped away from me and gestured *deferential respect*.

I felt a tapping at my arm and turned to see Magwyn's wrinkled face. "Come," she said with quiet authority. "It is time."

I fell into step behind her. As we walked, everyone in the crowd gestured some manner of respect toward her. Magwyn led me to the beginning of the path. There was a block of grey stone, slightly taller than my knee and identical to the others at each corner of the path.

The old woman gestured for me to climb up onto the stone. I looked out over the group of Adem and had an unprecedented moment of stage fright.

Bending a bit, I spoke softly to Magwyn. "Is it appropriate for me to raise my voice when reciting this?" I asked her nervously. "I do not mean to be offensive, but if I do not, those in the back will not be able to hear."

Magwyn smiled at me for the first time, her wrinkled face suddenly sweet. She patted my hand. "No one will be offended at a loud voice here," she said, gesturing *considerate moderation*. "Give."

I unbuckled Saicere and handed it over. Then Magwyn urged me onto the stone.

I recited the *Atas* while Magwyn watched. Though I was confident of my memory, it was still nerve-wracking. I wondered what would happen if I skipped an owner or misplaced a name.

It took the better part of an hour before I was done, the audience of Adem listening with an almost eerie quiet. When I finished, Magwyn offered her hand, helping me down from the stone as if I were a lady descending from a carriage. Then she gestured up the hill.

I wiped the sweat from my hand and gripped the wooden hilt of my dueling sword as I started up the path. Carceret's reds were strapped tightly across her long arms and broad shoulders. The leather straps she used were wider and thicker than Tempi's. They looked to be a brighter red, too, and I wonder if she had dyed them especially for today. As I came closer, I saw she had the fading remains of a black eye.

Once she saw I was watching, Carceret tossed her wooden sword away in a slow, deliberate motion. She gestured *disdain* broadly enough so they could see it in the ha'penny seats at the back of the crowd.

There was a murmur from the crowd and I stopped walking, uncertain what to do. After a moment's thought, I lay my own training sword down by the side of the path and continued to walk.

Carceret waited in the center of a flat, grassy circle about thirty feet across. The ground was soft here, so I wouldn't ordinarily worry about being thrown. Ordinarily. Vashet had taught me the difference between throwing someone to the ground and throwing someone *at* the ground. The first was what you did during a polite bout. The second was what you would use in a true fight where the intention was to maim or kill your opponent.

Before I came too close, I fell into the now-familiar fighter's crouch. I raised my hands, bent my knees, and fought the urge to rise up onto the balls of my feet, knowing I would feel quicker, and ruin my balance as a result. I took a deep, steadying breath and slowly moved toward her.

Carceret fell into a similar crouch, and just as I was coming to the outside limits of her reach, she made a feint toward me. It was only a slight twitch of the hand and shoulder, but, anxious as I was, I fell for it wholeheartedly and skittered away like a startled rabbit.

Carceret lowered her hands and stood up straight, abandoning her fighting crouch. *Amusement*, she gestured broadly, *invitation*. Then she beckoned with both hands. I heard a few pieces of laughter drift up from the crowd below.

Humiliating as her attitude was, I was eager to take advantage of her lowered guard. I moved forward and made a cautious attempt at Hands like Knives. Too cautious, and she stepped away from it without even needing to lift her hands.

I knew I was outclassed as a fighter. That meant my only hope was to play on her already hot emotions. If I could infuriate her, she might make mistakes. If she made mistakes, I might be able to win. "First came Chael," I said, giving her my widest, most barbaric smile.

Carceret took a half step closer. "I am going to crush your pretty hands," she hissed in perfect Aturan. As she spoke she reached out and made a vicious gripping motion at me.

She was trying to scare me, make me recoil and lose my balance. And honestly, the raw venom in her voice made me want to do just that.

But I was ready. I resisted my reflex to pull back. In doing so I froze for a moment, neither retreating nor advancing.

Of course, this is what Carceret was truly waiting for, a half-moment's hesitation as I fought the urge to flee. She closed on me in a single easy step and caught my wrist, her hand tight as a band of iron.

Without thinking, I used Celean's curious two-handed version of Break

Lion. Perfect for a small girl struggling against a grown man, or a hopelessly outclassed musician trying to escape an Adem mercenary.

I regained control of my hand, and the unorthodox movement startled Carceret ever so slightly. I took advantage of it and struck out quickly with Sowing Barley, snapping my knuckles hard against the meat of her inner bicep.

It wasn't a hard punch, I was too close for that. But if I managed to hit the nerve properly, the blow would numb her hand. This wouldn't just make her weak on her left side, but it would make all the two-handed motions of the Ketan more difficult. A significant advantage.

Since I was still so close, I immediately followed Sowing Barley with Turn Millstone, giving her a short, firm push to knock her off balance. I managed to get both hands on her, and even pushed her backward by perhaps four inches, but Carceret came nowhere near to losing her balance.

Then I saw her eyes. I'd thought she'd been angry before, but it was nothing compared to now. Now I'd managed to actually strike her. Not just once, but twice. A barbarian with less than two months of training had struck her twice, while everyone in the school looked on.

I cannot describe how she looked. And even if I could, it would not impress upon you the truth of things, as her face was still almost entirely impassive. Instead let me say this. I have never seen anyone so furious in my entire life. Not Ambrose. Not Hemme. Not Denna when I criticized her song or the Maer when I defied him. Those angers were pale candles compared to the forge fire burning in Carceret's eyes.

But even in the full flower of her fury, Carceret was perfectly in control. She didn't lash out wildly or snarl at me. She kept her words inside her, burning them like fuel.

I couldn't win this fight. But my hands moved automatically, trained by hundreds of hours of practice to take advantage of her nearness. I stepped forward and tried to grab hold of her for Thunder Upward. Her hands snapped out, brushing the attack away. Then she lashed out with Bargeman at the Dock.

I don't think she expected it to connect. A more competent opponent would have avoided or blocked it. But I had let myself get slightly wrong-footed, so I was off balance, so I was slow, so her foot caught me in the stomach and *pushed*.

Bargeman at the Dock isn't a quick kick meant to break bones. It is a kick that shoves the opponent off balance. As I was already off balance, it pushed me right off my feet. I landed jarringly on my back, then rolled to a stop in a messy tangle of limbs.

Now some might say that I had taken a bad fall and was obviously too stupefied to find my feet and continue the fight. Others might say that while it was messy, the fall wasn't quite as hard as all that, and I had certainly found my feet after worse.

Personally, I think the line between being stupefied and being wise is sometimes very thin. How thin, I suppose, I will leave to you to decide.

CHAPTER ONE HUNDRED TWENTY-SEVEN

Anger

"**W**HAT WERE YOU THINKING?" Tempi demanded. *Disappointment. Fierce chastisement.* "What fool sets his sword aside?"

"She threw her sword away first!" I protested.

"Only to lure you in," Tempi said. "Only as a trap."

I was buckling Caesura's scabbard so the hilt hung over my shoulder. There hadn't been any particular ceremony after I had lost. Magwyn simply returned my sword and smiled at me, patting my hand in a comforting way.

I watched the crowd slowly dispersing below, and gestured *polite disbelief* to Tempi. "Should I have kept my sword when she was unarmed?"

"Yes!" *Absolute agreement.* "She is five times the fighter you are. You might have had a chance if you had kept your sword!"

"Tempi is right," I heard Shehyn's voice behind me. "Knowing your enemy is in keeping with the Lethani. Once a fight is inevitable, a clever fighter takes any advantage." I turned and saw her coming down the path. Penthe walked beside her.

I gestured *polite certainty.* "If I had kept my sword and won, people would have thought Carceret was a fool and resented me for gaining a rank I did not deserve. And if I had kept my sword and lost, it would have been humiliating. Neither reflects well on me." I looked back and forth between Shehyn and Tempi. "Am I wrong in this?"

"You are not wrong in this." Shehyn said. "But neither is Tempi wrong."

"Victory is always to be sought," Tempi said. *Firm.*

Shehyn turned to face him. "Success is key," she said. "Victory is not always needed to succeed."

Tempi gestured *respectful disagreement* and opened his mouth to respond, but Penthe spoke first, cutting him off. "Kvothe, are you hurt from your fall?"

"Not badly," I said, moving my back gingerly. "A few bruises, perhaps."

"Do you have anything to put on them?"

I shook my head.

Penthe stepped forward and took hold of my arm. "I have things at my house. We will leave these two to discuss the Lethani. Someone should tend to your hurts." She held my arm with her left hand, making her statement curiously empty of any emotional content.

"Of course," Shehyn said after a moment, and Tempi gestured a hasty *agreement*. But Penthe was already leading me firmly down the hill.

We walked for a quarter mile or so, Penthe holding my arm lightly.

Eventually she spoke in her lightly accented Aturan. "Are you bruised badly enough to need a salve?" she asked.

"Not really," I admitted.

"I thought not," she said. "But after I have lost a fight, I rarely wish to have people tell me how I lost it." She flashed me a small, secret smile.

I smiled back.

We continued to walk, and Penthe kept hold of my arm, subtly guiding us through a grove of trees, then up a steep path carved through a small bluff. Eventually we came to a secluded dell that had a carpet of wild papavler-flower blossoming among the grass. Their loose, blood-red petals were almost exactly the same color as Penthe's mercenary reds.

"Vashet told me barbarians have strange rituals with your sex," Penthe said. "She told me if I wanted to bed you, I should bring you to some flowers." She gestured around. "These are the best I could find in this season." She looked up at me expectantly.

"Ah," I said. "I expect Vashet was having a bit of a joke with you. Or perhaps a joke with me." Penthe frowned and I hurried to continue. "But it is true that among the barbarians there are many rituals that lead up to sex. It is somewhat more complicated there."

Penthe gestured *sullen irritation*. "I should not be surprised," she said. "Everyone tells stories about the barbarians. Some of it is training, so I can move well among you." *Wry however*. "Since I have not been out among them yet, they also tell stories to tease me."

"What sort of stories?" I asked, thinking of what I had heard about the Adem and the Lethani before I had met Tempi.

She shrugged, *slight embarrassment*. "It is foolishness. They say all the barbarian men are huge." She gestured far above her head, showing a height of more than seven feet. "Naden told me he went to a town where the barbarians ate a soup made of dirt. They say the barbarians never bathe. They say barbarians drink their own urine, believing it will help them live longer." She shook her head, laughing and gesturing *horrified amusement.*

"Are you saying," I asked slowly, "that you don't drink yours?"

Penthe froze midlaugh and looked at me, her face and hands showing a confused, apologetic mix of embarrassment, disgust, and disbelief. It was such a bizarre tangle of emotions I couldn't help but laugh, and I saw her relax when she realized the joke.

"I understand," I said. "We tell similar stories about the Adem."

Her eyes lit up. "You must tell me as I told you. It is fair."

Given Tempi's reaction when I'd told him of the word-fire and Lethani, I decided to share something else. "They say those who take the red never have sex. They say you take that energy and put it into your Ketan, and that is why you are such good fighters."

Penthe laughed hard at that. "I would have never made the third stone if that were the case," she said. *Wry amusement.* "If keeping from sex gave me my fighting, there would be days I could not make even a fist."

I felt my pulse quicken a bit at that.

"Still," she said. "I can see where that story comes from. They must think we have no sex because no Adem would bed a barbarian."

"Ah," I said, somewhat disappointed. "Why have you brought me to the flowers then?"

"You are now of Ademre," she said easily. "I expect many will approach you now. You have a sweet face, and it is hard not to be curious about your anger."

Penthe paused and glanced significantly downward. "That is unless you are diseased?"

I blushed at this. "What? No! Of course not!"

"Are you certain?"

"I have studied at the Medica," I said somewhat stiffly. "The greatest school of medicine in all the world. I know all about the diseases a person might catch, how to spot them and how to treat them."

Penthe gave me a skeptical look. "I do not question you in particular. But it is well known that barbarians are quite frequently diseased in their sex."

I shook my head. "This is just another foolish story. I assure you the barbarians are no more diseased than the Adem. In fact, I expect we may be less."

She shook her head, her eyes serious. "No. You are wrong in this. Of a hundred barbarians, how many would you say were so afflicted?"

It was an easy statistic I knew from the Medica. "Out of every hundred? Perhaps five. More among those who work in brothels or frequent such places, of course."

Penthe's face showed obvious disgust and she shivered. "Of one hundred Adem, none are so afflicted," she said firmly. *Absolute.*

"Oh come now." I held up my hand, making a circle with my fingers. "None?"

"None," she said with grim certainty. "The only place we could catch such a thing is from a barbarian, and those who travel are warned."

"What if you caught a disease from another Adem who had not been careful while traveling?" I asked.

Penthe's tiny heart-shaped face went grim, her nostrils flaring. "From one of my own?" *Vast anger.* "If one of Ademre were to give me a disease, I would be furious. I would shout from the top of a cliff what they had done. I would make their life as painful as a broken bone."

She gestured *disgust*, brushing at the front of her shirt in the first piece of Adem hand-talk I had ever learned from Tempi. "Then I would make the long trek over the mountains into the Tahl to be cured of it. Even if the trip should take two years and bring no money to the school. And none would think the less of me for that."

I nodded to myself. It made sense. Given their attitudes about sex, if it were any other way, disease would run rampant through the population.

I saw Penthe looking at me expectantly. "Thank you for the flowers," I said.

She nodded and stepped closer, looking up at me. Her eyes were excited as she smiled her shy smile. Then her face grew serious. "Is it enough to satisfy your barbarian rituals, or is there more that must be done?"

I reached down and ran my hand along the smooth skin of her neck, sliding my fingertips under the long braid so they brushed the back of her neck. She closed her eyes and tipped her face up toward mine.

"They are lovely, and more than enough," I said, and bent to kiss her.

———

"I was right," Penthe said with a contented sigh as we lay naked among the flowers. "You have a fine anger." I lay on my back, her small body curled under my arm, her heart-shaped face resting gently on my chest.

"What do you mean by that?" I asked. "I think anger might be the wrong word."

"I mean *Vaevin*," she said, using the Ademic term. "Is that the same?"

"I don't know that word," I admitted.

"I think anger is the right word," she said. "I have spoken with Vashet in your language, and she did not correct me."

"What do you mean by anger, then?" I asked. "I certainly don't feel angry."

Penthe lifted her head from my chest and gave me a lazy, satisfied smile. "Of course not," she said. "I have taken your anger. How could you feel such a way?"

"Are . . . are you angry then?" I asked, sure I was missing the point entirely.

Penthe laughed and shook her head. She had undone her long braid and her honey-colored hair hung down the side of her face. It made her look like an entirely different person. That and the lack of the mercenary reds, I supposed. "It is not that kind of anger. I am glad to have it."

"I still do not understand," I said. "This could be something barbarians do not know. Explain it to me as if I were a child."

She looked at me for a moment, her eyes serious, then she rolled over onto her stomach so she could face me more easily. "This anger is not a feeling. It is . . ." She hesitated, frowning prettily. "It is a desire. It is a making. It is a wanting of life."

Penthe looked around, then focused on the grass around us. "Anger is what makes the grass press up through the ground to reach the sun," she said. "All things that live have anger. It is the fire in them that makes them want to move and grow and do and make." She cocked her head. "Does that make sense to you?"

"I think so," I said. "And women take the anger from men in sex?"

She smiled, nodding. "That is why afterward a man is so weary. He gives a piece of himself. He collapses. He sleeps." She glanced down. "Or a part of him sleeps."

"Not for long," I said.

"That is because you have a fine, strong anger," she said proudly. "As I have already said. I can tell because I have taken a piece of it. I can tell there is more waiting."

"There is," I admitted. "But what do women do with the anger?"

"We use it," Penthe said simply. "That is why, afterward, a woman does not always sleep as a man does. She feels more awake. Full of the need to move. Often full of desire for more of what brought her the anger in the first place." She lowered her head to my chest and bit me playfully, wriggling her naked body against me.

It was pleasantly distracting. "Does this mean women have no anger of their own?"

She laughed again. "No. All things have anger. But women have many uses for their anger. And men have more anger than they can use, too much for their own good."

"How can one have too much of the desire to live and grow and make?" I asked. "It seems more would be better."

Penthe shook her head, brushing her hair back with one hand. "No. It is like food. One meal is good. Two meals is not better." She frowned again. "No. It is more like wine. One cup of wine is good, two is sometimes better, but ten . . ." She nodded seriously. "That is very much like anger. A man who grows full of it, it is like a poison in him. He wants too many things. He wants all things. He becomes strange and wrong in his head, violent."

She nodded to herself. "Yes. That is why anger is the right word, I think. You can tell a man who has been keeping all his anger to himself. It goes sour in him. It turns against itself and drives him to breaking rather than making."

"I can think of men like that," I said. "But I can think of women too."

"All things have anger," she repeated with a shrug. "A stone does not have much compared to a budding tree. It is the same with people. Some have more, or less. Some use it wisely. Some do not." She gave me a wide smile. "I have a great deal, which is why I am so fond of sex and fierce in my fighting." She bit at my chest again, less playfully this time, and began to work her way up to my neck.

"But if you take the anger from a man in sex," I said, struggling to concentrate, "doesn't that mean the more sex you have, the more you want?"

"It is like the water one uses to prime a pump," she said hotly against my ear. "Come now, I will have all of it, even if it takes us all day and half the night."

————————

We eventually moved from the grassy field to the baths, and then to Penthe's house of two snug rooms built against the side of a bluff. The moon was in the sky and had been watching us for some time through the window, though I doubt we showed her anything she hadn't seen before.

"Is that enough for you?" I said breathlessly. We were side by side in her pleasantly capacious bed, the sweat drying off our bodies. "If you take much more of it, I might not have enough anger left to speak or breathe."

My hand lay on the flat plane of her belly. Her skin was soft and smooth, but when she laughed I could feel the muscles of her stomach jump, going hard as sheets of steel.

"It is enough for now," she said, exhaustion plain in her voice. "It would upset Vashet if I left you empty as a fruit with all the juice pressed out."

Despite my long day, I was oddly wakeful, my thoughts bright and clear. I remembered something she had said earlier. "You mentioned that a woman has many uses for her anger. What use does a woman have for it that a man does not?"

"We teach," she said. "We give names. We track the days and tend to the smooth turning of things. We plant. We make babies." She shrugged. "Many things."

"A man can do those things as well," I said.

Penthe chuckled. "You have the wrong word," she said, rubbing at my chin. "A beard is what a man makes. A baby is something different, and that you have no part of."

"We don't carry the baby," I said, slightly offended. "But still, we play our part in making it."

Penthe turned to look at me, smiling as if I had made a joke. Then her smile faded. She propped herself up on her elbow and looked at me for another long moment. "Are you in serious?"

Seeing my perplexed expression, her eyes grew wide with amazement and she sat upright on the bed. "It is true!" she said. "You believe in manmothers!" She giggled, covering the bottom half of her face with both hands. "I never believed it was true!" She lowered her left hand, revealing an excited grin as she gestured *amazed delight.*

I felt I should be irritated, but I couldn't quite muster the energy. Perhaps some of what she said about men giving away their anger had some truth to it. "What is a man–mother?" I asked.

"Are you not making a joke?" she asked, one hand still half-covering her smile. "Do you truly believe a man puts a baby in a woman?"

"Well . . . yes," I said a little awkwardly. "In a manner of speaking. It takes a man and a woman to make a baby. A mother and a father."

"You have a word for it!" she said, delighted. "They told me this too. With the stories of dirt soup. But I never thought it a real story!"

I sat up myself at this point, growing concerned. "You do know how babies are made, don't you?" I asked, gesturing *serious earnestness.* "What we have been doing for most of the day is what makes a baby."

She looked at me for a moment in stunned silence, then dissolved helplessly into laughter, trying to speak several times only to have it overwhelm her again when she looked up at the expression on my face.

Penthe put her hands on her belly, prodding it as if puzzled. "Where is my baby?" She looked down at her flat belly. "Perhaps I have been sexing wrong these years." When she laughed, the muscles across her stomach flickered, making a pattern like a turtle's shell. "I should have a hundred babies if what you say is true. Five hundred babies!"

"It does not happen every time there is sex," I said. "There are only certain times when a woman is ripe for a baby."

"And have you done this?" she asked, looking at me with mock seriousness while a smile tugged at her mouth. "Have you made a baby with a woman?"

"I have been careful not to do such a thing," I said. "There is an herb called silphium. I chew it every day, and it keeps me from putting a baby in a woman."

Penthe shook her head. "This is more of your barbarian sex rituals," she said. "Does bringing a man to the flowers also make a baby where you come from?"

I decided to take a different tack. "If men do not help with making babies, how do you explain that babies look like their fathers?"

"Babies look like angry old men," Penthe said. "All bald and with . . ." She hesitated, touching her cheek. ". . . with face lines. Perhaps the old men are the only ones making babies then?" She smirked.

"What about kittens?" I asked. "You have seen a litter of kittens. When a white cat and a black cat have sex, you get kittens both white and black. And kittens of both colors."

"Always?" she asked.

"Not always." I admitted. "But most times."

"What if there is a yellow kitten?" she asked.

Before I could put together an answer, she waved the question away. "Kittens have little to do with this," she said. "We are not like animals. We do not go into season. We do not lay eggs. We do not make cocoons, or fruit, or seeds. We are not dogs or frogs or trees."

Penthe gave me a serious look. "You are committing a false thinking. You could as easily say two stones make baby stones by banging against each other until a piece breaks off. Therefore two people make baby peoples in the same way."

I fumed, but she was right. I was committing a fallacy of analogy. It was faulty logic.

Our conversation continued along this vein for some time. I asked her if she had ever known a woman to get pregnant who had not had sex in the previous months. She said she didn't know of any woman who would willingly go three months without sex, except those who were traveling among the barbarians, or very ill, or very old.

Eventually Penthe waved a hand to stop me, gesturing exasperation. "Do you hear your own excuses? Sex makes babies, but not always. Babies look like man-mothers, but not always. The sex must be at the right time, but not always. There are plants that make it more likely, or less likely." She shook her head. "You must realize what you say is thin as a net. You keep sewing new threads, hoping it will hold water. But hoping does not make it true."

Seeing me frown, she took my hand and gestured *comfort* into it as she had before in the dining hall, all the laughter gone out of her face. "I can see you think this truly. I can understand why barbarian men would want to believe it. It must be comforting to think you are important in this way. But it is simply not."

Penthe looked at me with something close to pity. "Sometimes a woman ripens. It is a natural thing, and men have no part in it. That is why more women ripen in the fall, like fruit. That is why more women ripen here in Haert, where it is better to have a child."

I tried to think of some other convincing argument, but none would come to mind. It was frustrating.

Seeing my expression, Penthe squeezed my hand and gestured *concession*. "Perhaps it is different for barbarian women," she said.

"You are only saying that to make me feel better," I said sullenly and was overcome with a jaw-popping yawn.

"I am," she admitted. Then she gave me a gentle kiss and pushed at my shoulders, encouraging me to lie back down on the bed.

I did, and she nestled into the crook of my arm again, resting her head on my shoulder. "It must be hard to be a man," she said softly. "A woman knows she is part of the world. We are full of life. A woman is the flower and the fruit. We move through time as part of our children. But a man . . ." She turned her head and looked up at me with gentle pity in her eyes. "You are an empty branch. You know when you die, you will leave nothing of any import behind."

Penthe stroked my chest fondly. "I think that is why you are so full of anger. Maybe you do not have more than women. Maybe the anger in you simply has no place to go. Maybe it is desperate to leave some mark. It hammers at the world. It drives you to rash action. To bickering. To rage. You paint and build and fight and tell stories that are bigger than the truth."

She gave a contented sigh and rested her head on my shoulder, snugging herself firmly into the circle of my arm. "I am sorry to tell you this thing. You are a good man, and a pretty thing. But still, you are only a man. All you have to offer the world is your anger."

CHAPTER ONE HUNDRED TWENTY-EIGHT

Names

IT WAS THE DAY that I would either stay or leave. I sat with Vashet on a green hill, watching the sun rise out of the clouds to the east.

"Saicere means to fly, to catch, to break," Vashet said softly, repeating herself for the hundredth time. "You must remember all the hands that have held her. Many hands, all following the Lethani. You must never use her in an improper way."

"I promise," I said for the hundredth time, then hesitated before bringing up something that had been bothering me. "But Vashet, you used your sword to trim the willow branch you beat me with. I saw you use it to hold your window open once. You pare your nails with it . . ."

Vashet gave me a blank look. "Yes?"

"Isn't that improper?" I asked.

She cocked her head, then laughed. "You mean I should only use it for fighting?"

I gestured *obvious implication*.

"A sword is sharp," she said. "It is a tool. I carry it constantly, how is using it improper?"

"It seems *disrespectful*," I clarified.

"You respect a thing by putting it to good use," she said. "It may be years before I return to the barbarian lands and fight. How does it harm my sword if it cuts kindling and carrots in the meantime?" Vashet's eyes grew serious. "To carry a sword your whole life, knowing it was only for killing . . ." She shook her head. "What would that do to a person's mind? It would be a horrible thing."

Vashet had returned to Haert last night, dismayed that she had missed my stone trial. She said I was right to lay aside my sword when Carceret did, and that I had made her proud.

Yesterday, Shehyn had formally invited me to stay and train at the school. In theory, I already had earned that right, but everyone knew that was more of a political fiction than anything. Her offer was a flattering one, an opportunity I knew I would likely never have again.

We watched a boy herd a flock of goats down the side of a hill. "Vashet, is it true that the Adem have no concept of fatherhood?"

Vashet nodded easily, then paused. "Tell me you did not embarrass both of us by talking about this with everyone while I was gone," she said with a sigh.

"Only with Penthe," I said. "She thought it was the funniest thing she had heard in ten months' time."

"It is fairly amusing at that," Vashet said, her mouth curving a little.

"It's true then?" I asked. "Even you believe this? You've . . ."

Vashet held up a hand and I trailed off. "Peace," she said. "Think whatever you wish about your man-mothers. It is all the same to me." She gave a soft smile of remembrance. "My poet king actually believed a woman was nothing more than the ground in which a man might plant a baby."

Vashet made an amused huffing sound that wasn't quite a laugh. "He was so sure he was right. Nothing could sway him. Years ago I decided arguing such things with a barbarian is a long, weary waste of my time." She shrugged. "Think what you want about making babies. Believe in demons. Pray to a goat. So long as it doesn't bruise me, why should I bother myself?"

I chewed it over for a moment. "There's wisdom in that," I said.

She nodded.

"But either a man helps with a baby or he does not," I pointed out. "There can be many opinions on a thing, but there is only one truth."

Vashet smiled lazily. "And if the pursuit of truth was my goal, that would concern me." She gave a long yawn, stretching like a happy cat. "Instead I will focus on the joy in my heart, the prosperity of the school, and understanding the Lethani. If I have time left after that, I will put it toward worrying on the truth."

We watched the sunrise for a while longer in silence. It occurred to me Vashet was quite a different person when she wasn't struggling to cram the Ketan and all of Ademic into my head as quickly as possible.

"That said," Vashet added, "if you persist in clinging to your barbarian beliefs about man-mothers, you would do well to keep quiet about it. Amusement is the best you can hope for. Most will simply assume you an idiot for thinking such things."

I nodded. After a long moment, I decided to finally ask the question I had been holding off for days. "Magwyn called me Maedre. What does it mean?"

"It is your name," she said. "Speak of it to no one."

"It is a secret thing?" I asked.

She nodded. "It is a thing for you and your teachers and Magwyn. It would be dangerous to let others know what it is."

"How could it be dangerous?"

Vashet looked at me as if I were daft. "When you know a name you have power over it. Surely you know this?"

"But I know your name, and Shehyn's and Tempi's. What danger is in that?"

She waved a hand. "Not those names. Deep names. Tempi is not the name he was given by Magwyn. Just as Kvothe is not yours. Deep names have meanings."

I already knew what Vashet's name meant. "What does Tempi mean?"

"Tempi means 'little iron.' Tempa means iron, and it means to strike iron, and it means angry. Shehyn gave him that name years ago. He was a most troublesome student."

"In Aturan temper means angry." I pointed it out rather excitedly, amazed at the coincidence. "And it is also something you do with iron when forging it into steel."

Vashet shrugged, unimpressed. "That is the way of names. Tempi is a small name, and still it holds much. That is why you should not speak of yours, even to me."

"But I do not know your language well enough to tell what it means myself," I protested. "A man should know the meaning of his own name."

Vashet hesitated, then relented. "It means flame, and thunder, and broken tree."

I thought for a while and decided I liked it. "When Magwyn gave it to me, you seemed surprised. Why is that?"

"It is not proper for me to comment on another's name." *Absolute refusal.* Her gesture was so sharp it almost hurt to look at. She came to her feet, then brushed her hands against her pants. "Come, it is time you gave your answer to Shehyn."

Shehyn motioned for us to sit as we entered her room. Then she took a seat herself, startling me by showing the smallest of smiles. It was a terribly flattering gesture of familiarity. "Have you decided?" she asked.

I nodded. "I thank you, Shehyn, but I cannot stay. I must return to Severen to speak with the Maer. Tempi fulfilled his obligation when the road was made safe, but I am bound to return and explain everything that happened." I thought of Denna as well, but didn't mention her.

Shehyn gestured an elegant mingling of *approval* and *regret*. "Fulfilling one's duty is of the Lethani." She gave me a serious look. "Remember, you have a sword and a name, but you must not hire yourself out as if you had taken the red."

"Vashet has explained everything to me," I said. *Reassurance.* "I will make arrangements for my sword to be returned to Haert if I am killed. I will not teach the Ketan or wear the red." *Carefully attentive curiosity.* "But I am permitted to tell others I have studied fighting with you?"

Reserved agreement. "You may say you have studied with us. But not that you are one of us."

"Of course," I said. "And not that I am equal to you."

Shehyn gestured *content satisfaction.* Then her hands shifted and she made a small gesture of *embarrassed admission.* "This is not entirely a gift," she said. "You will be a better fighter than many barbarians. If you fight and win, the barbarians will think: Kvothe studied only slightly the Adem's arts, and still he is formidable. How much more skilled must they themselves be?" *However.* "If you fight and lose, they will think: He only learned a piece of what the Adem know."

The old woman's eyes twinkled ever so slightly. She gestured *amusement.* "No matter what, our reputation thrives. This serves Ademre."

I nodded. *Willing acceptance.* "It will not hurt my reputation either," I said. *Understatement.*

There was a pause in the conversation, then Shehyn gestured *solemn importance.* "When we spoke before, you asked me of the Rhinta. Do you remember?" Shehyn asked. From the corner of my eye I saw Vashet shift uncomfortably in her seat.

Suddenly excited, I nodded.

"I have remembered a story of such. Would you like to hear it?"

I gestured *extreme eager interest.*

"It is an old story, old as Ademre. It is always told the same. Are you ready to hear it?" *Profound formality.* There was a hint of ritual in her voice.

I nodded again. *Pleading entreaty.*

"As with all things, there are rules. I will tell this story once. After, you may not speak of it. After, you may not ask questions." Shehyn looked back and forth between Vashet and myself. *Grave seriousness.* "Not until you have slept one thousand nights may you speak on this. Not until you have traveled one thousand miles may you ask questions. Knowing this, are you willing to hear it?"

I nodded a third time, my excitement rising in me.

Shehyn spoke with great formality. "Once there was a great realm peopled by great people. They were not Ademre. They were what Ademre was before we became ourselves.

"But at this time they were themselves, the women and men fair and strong. They sang songs of power and fought as well as Ademre do.

"These people had a great empire. The name of the empire is forgotten. It is not important as the empire has fallen, and since that time the land has broken and the sky changed.

"In the empire there were seven cities and one city. The names of the seven cities are forgotten, for they are fallen to treachery and destroyed by time. The one city was destroyed as well, but its name remains. It was called Tariniel.

"The empire had an enemy, as strength must have. But the enemy was not great enough to pull it down. Not by pulling or pushing was the enemy strong enough to drag it down. The enemy's name is remembered, but it will wait.

"Since not by strength could the enemy win, he moved like a worm in fruit. The enemy was not of the Lethani. He poisoned seven others against the empire, and they forgot the Lethani. Six of them betrayed the cities that trusted them. Six cities fell and their names are forgotten.

"One remembered the Lethani, and did not betray a city. That city did not fall. One of them remembered the Lethani and the empire was left with hope. With one unfallen city. But even the name of that city is forgotten, buried in time.

"But seven names are remembered. The name of the one and of the six who follow him. Seven names have been carried through the crumbling of empire, through the broken land and changing sky. Seven names are remembered through the long wandering of Ademre. Seven names have been remembered, the names of the seven traitors. Remember them and know them by their seven signs:

Cyphus bears the blue flame.
Stercus is in thrall of iron.
Ferule chill and dark of eye.
Usnea lives in nothing but decay.
Grey Dalcenti never speaks.
Pale Alenta brings the blight.
Last there is the lord of seven:
Hated. Hopeless. Sleepless. Sane.
Alaxel bears the shadow's hame.

CHAPTER ONE HUNDRED TWENTY-NINE

Interlude—Din of Whispering

"RESHI!" BAST CRIED OUT, his face stricken. "No! Stop!" He held out his hands as if he would press them against the innkeeper's mouth. "You shouldn't say such things!"

Kvothe smiled in a humorless way. "Bast, who taught you your name lore in the first place?"

"Not you, Reshi." Bast shook his head. "There are things every Fae child knows. It's never good to speak such things aloud. Not ever."

"And why is that?" Kvothe prompted in his best teacher's voice.

"Because some things can tell when their names are spoken," Bast swallowed. "They can tell *where* they're spoken."

Kvothe gave a somewhat exasperated sigh. "There's small harm in saying a name once, Bast." He sat back in his chair. "Why do you think the Adem have their traditions surrounding that particular story? Only once and no questions after?"

Bast's eyes narrowed thoughtfully, and Kvothe gave him a small, tight smile. "Exactly. Trying to find someone who speaks your name once is like tracking a man through a forest from a single footprint."

Chronicler spoke up hesitantly, as if afraid of interrupting. "Can such a thing really be done?" he asked. "Truthfully?"

Kvothe nodded grimly. "I expect that's how they found my troupe when I was young."

Chronicler looked around nervously, then frowned and made an obvious effort to stop. The result was that he sat very still, looking every bit as nervous as before. "Does that mean they might come here? You've certainly been talking about them enough. . . ."

Kvothe made a dismissive gesture. "No. Names are the key. Real names.

Deep names. And I have been avoiding them for just that reason. My father was a great one for details. He had been asking questions and digging up old stories about the Chandrian for years. I expect he stumbled onto a few of their old names and worked them into his song...."

Understanding washed over Chronicler's face. " ... and then rehearsed it again and again."

The innkeeper gave a faint, fond smile. "Endlessly, if I knew him at all. I have no doubt he and my mother did their solid best to work every tiny burr out of their song before they made it public. They were perfectionists." He gave a tired sigh. "To the Chandrian, it must have been like someone constantly lighting a signal fire. I expect the only thing that kept them safe for so long was that we were constantly traveling."

Bast broke in again. "Which is why you shouldn't say such things, Reshi."

Kvothe frowned. "I have slept my thousand nights and traveled several thousand miles since then, Bast. It is safe to say them once. With all the hell that's breaking loose in the world these days you can believe people are telling old stories more often. If the Chandrian are listening for names, I don't doubt they've got a slow din of whispering from Arueh to the Circle Sea."

Bast's expression made it clear he was less than reassured.

"Besides," Kvothe said with a bit of a weary sigh. "It's good to have them written down. They may prove useful to someone someday."

"Still Reshi, you should be more careful."

"What have I been these last years except for careful, Bast?" Kvothe said, his irritation finally bubbling to the surface. "What good has it done me? Besides, if what you say about the Cthaeh is true, then things will end in tears no matter what I do. Isn't that right?"

Bast opened his mouth, then closed it, obviously at a loss. Then he darted a look toward Chronicler, his eyes pleading for support.

Seeing this, Kvothe turned to look at Chronicler as well, raising an eyebrow curiously.

"I'm sure I don't know in the least," Chronicler said, looking down as he opened his satchel and brought out an ink-stained piece of cloth. "Both of you have seen the full extent of my naming prowess: Iron. And that is a fluke by all accounts. Master Namer declared me an utter waste of his time."

"That sounds familiar," Kvothe murmured.

Chronicler shrugged. "In my case I took him at his word."

"Can you remember the excuse he gave you?"

"He had many specific criticisms: I knew too many words. I'd never been hungry. I was too soft...." Chronicler's hands were busy cleaning the nib of his pen. "I felt he made his overall position clear when he said, 'Who would have thought a papery little scriv like you could have any iron in him at all?'"

Kvothe's mouth quirked into a sympathetic smile. "Did he really?"

Chronicler shrugged. "He called me a twat, actually. I was trying not to offend the innocent ears of our young friend here." He nodded at Bast. "From what I can tell, he's had a rough day."

Kvothe smiled in full now. "It's a shame we weren't ever at the University at the same time."

Chronicler gave the nib one last rub against the soft cloth and held it up to the fading light from the inn's window. "Not really," he said. "You wouldn't have liked me. I *was* a papery little twat. And spoiled. And full of myself."

"And what's changed since then?" Kvothe asked.

Chronicler blew air through his nose dismissively. "Not much, depending who you ask. But I like to think I've had my eyes opened a bit." He screwed the nib carefully back into his pen.

"And how did that happen, exactly?" Kvothe asked.

Chronicler looked across the table, seeming surprised at the question. "Exactly?" he asked. "*Telling* a story isn't what I'm here for." He tucked the cloth back into his satchel. "In brief, I had a snit and left the University looking for greener pasture. Best thing I ever did. I learned more from a month on the road than I had in three years of classes."

Kvothe nodded. "Teccam said the same thing: No man is brave that has never walked a hundred miles. If you want to know the truth of who you are, walk until not a person knows your name. Travel is the great leveler, the great teacher, bitter as medicine, crueler than mirror-glass. A long stretch of road will teach you more about yourself than a hundred years of quiet introspection."

CHAPTER ONE HUNDRED THIRTY

Wine and Water

SAYING MY FAREWELLS IN Haert took an entire day. I shared a meal with Vashet and Tempi and let both of them give me more advice than I needed or desired. Celean cried a bit, and told me she would come visit me when she finally took the red. We bouted one final time, and I suspect she let me win.

Lastly, I spent a pleasant evening with Penthe that turned into a pleasant night and, eventually, into a pleasant late night. I did manage to catch a few hours of sleep in the pale hours before dawn.

I grew up among the Ruh, so I am endlessly amazed how quickly a person can put down roots in a place. Though I had been in Haert less than two months, it was hard to leave.

Still, it felt good to be back on the road again, heading toward Alveron and Denna. It was time I collected my reward for a job well done and delivered an earnest and rather belated apology.

———

Five days later I was walking one of those long, lonely stretches of road you only find in the low hills of eastern Vintas. I was, as my father used to say, on the edge of the map.

I had only passed one or two travelers all day and not a single inn. The thought of sleeping outdoors wasn't particularly troubling, but I had been eating from my pockets for a couple days, and a warm meal would have been a welcome thing.

Night had nearly fallen, and I had given up hope of something decent in my stomach when I spotted a line of white smoke trailing into the twilight sky ahead of me. I took it for a farmhouse at first. Then I heard a faint strain of music and my hopes for a bed and a hearth-hot meal began to rise.

But as I came around a curve in the road, I, found a surprise better than any roadside inn. Through the trees I saw a tall campfire flickering between two achingly familiar wagons. Men and women lounged about, talking. One strummed a lute, while another tapped a small tabor idly against his leg. Others were pitching a tent between two trees while an older woman set a tripod over the fire.

Troupers. What's better, I recognized familiar markings on the side of one of the wagons. To me they stood out more brightly than the fire. Those signs meant these were true troupers. My family, the Edema Ruh.

As I stepped from the trees, one of the men gave a shout, and before I could draw breath to speak there were three swords pointing at me. The sudden stillness after the music and chatter was more than slightly unnerving.

A handsome man with a black beard and a silver earring took a slow step forward, never taking the tip of his sword off my eye. "Otto!" he shouted into the woods behind me. "If you're napping I swear on my mother's milk I'll gut you. Who the hell are you?"

The last was directed at me. But before I could respond, a voice came out of the trees. "I'm right here, Alleg, as . . . Who's that? How in the God's name did he get past me?"

When they'd drawn their swords on me, I'd raised my hands. It's a good habit to have when anyone points something sharp at you. Nevertheless I was smiling as I spoke. "Sorry to startle you, Alleg."

"Save it," he said coldly. "You have one breath left to tell me why you were sneaking around our camp."

I had no need to talk, and instead turned so everyone by the fire could see the lute case slung across my back.

The change in Alleg's attitude was immediate. He relaxed and sheathed his sword. The others followed suit as he smiled and approached me, laughing.

I laughed too. "One family."

"One family." He shook my hand and turned toward the fire, shouting, "Best behavior everyone. We have a guest tonight!" There was a low cheer, and everyone went busily back to whatever they had been doing before I arrived.

A thick-bodied man wearing a sword stomped out of the trees. "I'll be damned if he came past me, Alleg. He's probably from . . ."

"He's from our family," Alleg interjected smoothly.

"Oh," Otto said, obviously taken aback. He looked at my lute. "Welcome then."

"I didn't go past, actually," I lied. When it was dark, my shaed made me very difficult to see. But that wasn't his fault, and I didn't want to get him in trouble. "I heard the music and circled around. I thought you might be a different troupe, and I was going to surprise them."

Otto gave Alleg a pointed look, then turned and stomped back into the woods.

Alleg put his arm around my shoulders. "Might I offer you a drink?"

"A little water, if you can spare it."

"No guest drinks water by our fire," he protested. "Only our best wine will touch your lips."

"The water of the Edema is sweeter than wine to those who have been upon the road." I smiled at him.

"Then have water and wine, each to your desire." He led me to one of the wagons, where there was a water barrel.

Following a tradition older than time, I drank a ladle of water and used a second to wash my hands and face. Patting my face dry with the sleeve of my shirt, I looked up at him and smiled. "It's good to be home again."

He clapped me on the back. "Come. Let me introduce you to the rest of your family."

First were two men of about twenty, both with scruffy beards. "Fren and Josh are our two best singers, excepting myself of course." I shook their hands.

Next were the two men playing instruments around the fire. "Gaskin plays lute. Laren does pipes and tabor." They smiled at me. Laren struck the head of the tabor with his thumb, and the drum made a mellow *tum*.

"There's Tim." Alleg pointed across the fire to a tall, grim man oiling a sword. "And you've already met Otto. They keep us from falling into danger on the road." Tim nodded, looking up briefly from his sword.

"This is Anne." Alleg gestured to an older woman with a pinched expression and grey hair pulled back in a bun. "She keeps us fed and plays mother to us all." Anne continued to cut carrots, ignoring both of us.

"And far from last is our own sweet Kete, who holds the key to all our hearts." Kete had hard eyes and a mouth like a thin line, but her expression softened a little when I kissed her hand.

"And that's everyone," Alleg said with a smile and a little bow. "Your name is?"

"Kvothe."

"Welcome, Kvothe. Rest yourself and be at your ease. Is there anything we can do for you?"

"A bit of that wine you mentioned earlier?" I smiled.

He touched the heel of his hand to his forehead. "Of course! Or would you prefer ale?"

I nodded, and he fetched me a mug.

"Excellent," I said after tasting it, seating myself on a convenient stump.

He tipped an imaginary hat. "Thank you. We were lucky enough to nick it on our way through Levinshir a couple days ago. How has the road been treating you of late?"

I stretched backward and sighed. "Not bad for a lone minstrel." I shrugged. "I take advantage of what opportunities present themselves. I have to be careful since I'm alone."

Alleg nodded wisely. "The only safety we have is in numbers," he admitted, then nodded to my lute. "Would you favor us with a bit of a song while we're waiting for Anne to finish dinner?"

"Certainly," I said, setting down my drink. "What would you like to hear?"

"Can you play 'Leave the Town, Tinker'?"

"Can I? You tell me." I lifted my lute from its case and began to play. By the chorus, everyone had stopped what they were doing to listen. I even caught sight of Otto near the edge of the trees as he left his lookout to peer toward the fire.

When I was done, everyone applauded enthusiastically. "You can play it," Alleg laughed. Then his expression became serious, and he tapped a finger to his mouth. "How would you like to walk the road with us for a while?" he asked after a moment. "We could use another player."

I took a moment to consider it. "Which way are you heading?"

"Easterly," he said.

"I'm bound for Severen," I said.

Alleg shrugged. "We can make it to Severen," he said. "So long as you don't mind taking the long way around."

"I have been away from the family for a long time," I admitted, looking at the familiar sights around the fire.

"One is a bad number for an Edema on the road," Alleg said persuasively, running a finger along the edge of his dark beard.

I sighed. "Ask me again in the morning."

He slapped my knee, grinning. "Good! That means we have all night to convince you."

I replaced my lute and excused myself for a call of nature. Coming back, I knelt next to Anne where she sat near the fire. "What are you making for us, mother?" I asked.

"Stew," she said shortly.

I smiled. "What's in it?"

Anne squinted at me. "Lamb," she said, as if daring me to challenge the fact.

"It's been a long while since I've had lamb, mother. Could I have a taste?"

"You'll wait, same as everyone else," she said sharply.

"Not even a small taste?" I wheedled, giving her my best ingratiating smile.

The old woman drew a breath, then shrugged it away. "Fine," she said. "But it won't be my fault if your stomach sets to aching."

I laughed. "No, mother. It won't be your fault." I reached for the long-handled wooden spoon and drew it out. After blowing on it, I took a bite. "Mother!" I exclaimed. "This is the best thing to touch my lips in a full year."

"Hmph," she said, squinting at me.

"It's the first truth, mother," I said earnestly. "Anyone who does not enjoy this fine stew is hardly one of the Ruh in my opinion."

Anne turned back to stir the pot and shooed me away, but her expression wasn't as sharp as it had been before.

After stopping by the keg to refill my mug, I returned to my seat. Gaskin leaned forward. "You've given us a song. Is there anything you'd like to hear?"

"How about 'Piper Wit'?" I asked.

His brow furrowed. "I don't recognize that one."

"It's about a clever Ruh who outwits a farmer."

Gaskin shook his head. "I'm afraid not."

I bent to pick up my lute. "Let me. It's a song every one of us should know."

"Pick something else," Laren protested. "I'll play you something on the pipes. You've played for us once already tonight."

I smiled at him. "I forgot you piped. You'll like this one," I assured him, "Piper's the hero. Besides, you're feeding my belly, I'll feed your ears." Before they could raise any more objections, I started to play, quick and light.

They laughed through the whole thing. From the beginning when Piper kills the farmer, to the end when he seduces the dead man's wife and daughter. I left off the last two verses where the townsfolk kill Piper.

Laren wiped his eyes after I was done. "Heh. You're right, Kvothe. I'm better off knowing that one. Besides . . ." He shot a look at Kete where she sat across the fire. "It's an honest song. Women can't keep their hands off a piper."

Kete snorted derisively and rolled her eyes.

We talked of small things until Anne announced the stew was done. Everyone fell to, breaking the silence only to compliment Anne on her cooking.

"Honestly, Anne," Alleg asked after his second bowl. "Did you lift a little pepper back in Levinshir?"

Anne looked smug. "We all need our secrets, dear," she said. "Don't press a lady."

I asked Alleg, "Have times been good for you and yours?"

"Oh certainly," he said between mouthfuls. "Three days ago Levinshir was especially good to us." He winked. "You'll see how good later."

"I'm glad to hear it."

"In fact." He leaned forward conspiratorially. "We've done so well that I feel quite generous. Generous enough to offer you anything you'd like. Anything at all. Ask and it is yours." He leaned closer and said in a stage whisper, "I want you to know this is a blatant attempt to bribe you into staying on with us. We would make a thick purse off that lovely voice of yours."

"Not to mention the songs he could teach us," Gaskin chimed in.

Alleg gave a mock snarl. "Don't help him bargain, boy. I have the feeling this is going to be hard enough as it is."

I gave it a little thought. "I suppose I could stay...." I let myself trail off uncertainly.

Alleg gave a knowing smile. "But . . ."

"But I would ask for three things."

"Hmm, three things." He looked me up and down. "Just like in one of the stories."

"It only seems right," I urged.

He gave a hesitant nod. "I suppose it does. And how long would you travel with us?"

"Until no one objects to my leaving."

"Does anyone have any problem with this?" Alleg looked around.

"What if he asks for one of the wagons?" Tim asked. His voice startled me, harsh and rasping like two bricks grating together.

"It won't matter, as he'll be traveling with us," Alleg argued. "They belong to all of us anyway. And since he can't leave unless we say so...."

There were no objections. Alleg and I shook hands and there was a small cheer.

Kete held up her mug. "To Kvothe and his songs!" she said. "I have a feeling he'll be worth whatever he costs us."

Everyone drank, and I held up my own glass. "I swear on my mother's milk, none of you will ever make a better deal than the one you made with me tonight." This evoked a more enthusiastic cheer and everyone drank again.

Wiping his mouth, Alleg looked me in the eye. "So, what is the first thing you want from us?"

I lowered my head. "It's a little thing really. I don't have a tent of my own. If I'm going to be traveling with my family . . ."

"Say no more!" Alleg waved his wooden mug like a king granting a boon. "You'll have my own tent, piled with furs and blankets a foot deep!" He made a gesture over the fire to where Fren and Josh sat. "Go set it up for him."

"That's all right," I protested. "I can manage it myself."

"Hush, it's good for them. Makes them feel useful. Speaking of which . . ." He made another gesture at Tim. "Bring them out, would you?"

Tim stood and pressed a hand to his stomach. "I'll do it in a quick minute. I'll be right back." He turned to walk off into the woods. "I don't feel very good."

"That's what you get for eatin' like you're at a trough!" Otto called after him. He turned back to the rest of us. "Someday he'll realize he can't eat more'n me and not feel sick afterward."

"Since Tim's busy painting a tree, I'll go get them," Laren said with thinly veiled eagerness.

"I'm on guard tonight," Otto said. "I'll do it."

"*I'll* get them," Kete said, exasperated. She stared the other two back into their seats and walked behind the wagon on my left.

Josh and Fren came out of the other wagon with a tent, ropes, and stakes. "Where do you want it?" Josh asked.

"That's not a question you usually have to ask a man, is it, Josh?" Fren joked, nudging his friend with an elbow.

"I tend to snore," I warned them. "You'll probably want me a little away from everyone else." I pointed. "Over between those two trees would be fine."

"I mean, with a man, you normally know where they want it, don't you, Josh?" Fren continued as they wandered off and began to string up the tent.

Kete returned a minute later, leading a pair of lovely young girls. One had a lean body and face, with straight, black hair cut short like a boy's. The other was more generously rounded, with curling golden hair. Both wore hopeless expressions and looked to be about sixteen.

"Meet Krin and Ellie," Kete said, gesturing to the girls.

Alleg smiled. "They are one of the ways in which Levinshir was generous to us. Tonight, one of them will be keeping you warm. My gift to you, as the new member in our family." He made a show of looking them over. "Which one would you like?"

I looked from one to the other. "That's a hard choice. Let me think on it a little while."

Kete sat them near the edge of the fire and put a bowl of stew in each of their hands. The girl with the golden hair, Ellie, ate woodenly for a few bites, then slowed to a stop like a toy winding down. Her eyes looked almost blind, as if she were watching something none of us could see. Krin's eyes, on the other hand, were focused fiercely into the fire. She sat stiffly with her bowl in her lap.

"Girls," Alleg chided. "Don't you know that things will get better as soon as you start cooperating?" Ellie took another slow bite, then stopped. Krin stared into the fire, her back stiff, her expression hard.

From where she sat by the fire, Anne prodded at them with her wooden spoon. "Eat!" The response was the same as before. One slow bite. One tense rebellion. Scowling, Anne leaned closer and gripped the dark-haired girl firmly by the chin, her other hand reaching for the bowl of stew.

"Don't," I urged. "They'll eat when they get hungry enough." Alleg looked up at me curiously. "I know what I'm talking about. Give them something to drink instead."

The old woman looked for a moment as if she might continue anyway, then shrugged and let go of Krin's jaw. "Fine. I'm sick of force-feeding this one anyway. She's been nothing but trouble."

Kete sniffed in agreement. "Little bitch came at me when I untied her for her bath," she said, brushing her hair away from the side of her face to reveal scratch marks. "Almost took out my damn eye."

"Did a runner, too," Anne said, still scowling. "I've had to start doping her at night." She made a disgusted gesture. "Let her starve if she wants."

Laren came back to the fire with two mugs, setting them in the girl's un-resisting hands.

"Water?" I asked.

"Ale," he said. "It'll be better for them if they aren't eating."

I stifled my protest. Ellie drank in the same vacant manner in which she had eaten. Krin moved her eyes from the fire, to the cup, to me. I felt an almost physical shock at her resemblance to Denna. Still looking at me, she drank. Her hard eyes gave away nothing of what was happening inside her head.

"Bring them over to sit by me," I said. "It might help me to make up my mind."

Kete brought them over. Ellie was docile. Krin was stiff.

"Be careful with this one," Kete said, nodding to the dark-haired girl. "She's a scratcher."

Tim came back looking a little pale. He sat by the fire where Otto nudged him with an elbow. "Want some more stew?" he asked maliciously.

"Sod off," Tim rasped weakly.

"A little ale might settle your stomach," I advised.

He nodded, seeming eager for anything that might help him. Kete fetched him a fresh mugful.

By this time the girls were sitting on either side of me, facing the fire. Closer, I saw things I had missed before. There was a dark bruise on the back of Krin's neck. The blonde girl's wrists were merely chafed from being tied, but Krin's were raw and scabbed. For all that, they smelled clean. Their hair was brushed and their clothes had been washed recently. Kete had been tending to them.

They were also much more lovely up close. I reached out to touch their shoulders. Krin flinched, then stiffened. Ellie didn't react at all.

From off in the direction of the trees Fren called out, "It's done. Do you want us to light a lamp for you?"

"Yes, please," I called back. I looked from one girl to the other and then to Alleg. "I cannot decide between the two," I told him honestly. "So I will have both."

Alleg laughed incredulously. Then, seeing I was serious, he protested, "Oh come now. That's hardly fair to the rest of us. Besides, you can't possibly. . . ."

I gave him a frank look.

"Well," he hedged, "Even if you can, it . . ."

"This is the second thing I ask for," I said formally. "Both of them."

Otto made a cry of protest that was echoed in the expressions of Gaskin and Laren.

I smiled reassuringly at them. "Only for tonight."

Fren and Josh came back from setting up my tent. "Be thankful he didn't ask for you, Otto," Fren said to the big man. "That's what Josh would have asked for, isn't it Josh?"

"Shut your hole, Fren," Otto said, exasperated. "Now *I* feel ill."

I stood and slung my lute over one shoulder. Then I led both lovely girls, one golden and one dark, toward my tent.

Black by Moonlight

FREN AND JOSH HAD done a good job with the tent. It was tall enough to stand in the center, but still crowded with me and both girls standing. I gave the golden-haired one, Ellie, a gentle push toward the bed of thick blankets. "Sit down," I said gently.

When she didn't respond, I took her by the shoulders and eased her into a sitting position. She let herself be moved, but her blue eyes were wide and vacant. I checked her head for any signs of a wound. Not finding any, I guessed she was in deep shock.

I took a moment and dug through my travel sack, then shook some powdered leaf into my traveling cup and added some water from my waterskin. I set the cup into Ellie's hands, and she took hold of it absently. "Drink it," I encouraged, trying to capture the tone of voice Felurian had used to gain my thoughtless compliance from time to time.

It may have worked, or perhaps she was just thirsty. Whatever the reason, Ellie drained the cup to the bottom. Her eyes still held the same faraway look they had before.

I shook another measure of the powdered leaf into the cup, refilled it with water, and held it out for the dark-haired girl to drink.

We stayed there for several minutes, my arm outstretched, her arms motionless at her sides. Finally she blinked, her eyes focusing on me. "What did you give her?" she asked.

"Crushed velia," I said gently. "It's a countertoxin. There was poison in the stew."

Her eyes told me she didn't believe me. "I didn't eat any of the stew."

"It was in the ale too. I saw you drink that."

"Good," she said. "I want to die."

I gave a deep sigh. "It won't kill you. It'll just make you miserable. You'll throw up and be weak with muscle cramps for a day or two." I raised the cup, offering it to her.

"Why do you care if they kill me?" she asked tonelessly. "If they don't do it now they'll do it later. I'd rather die. . . ." She clenched her teeth before she finished the sentence.

"They didn't poison you. I poisoned them and you happened to get some of it. I'm sorry, but this will help you over the worst of it."

Krin's gaze wavered for a second, then became iron hard again. She looked at the cup, then fixed her gaze on me. "If it's harmless, you drink it."

"I can't," I explained. "It would put me to sleep, and I have things to do tonight."

Krin's eyes darted to the bed of furs laid out on the floor of the tent.

I smiled my gentlest, saddest smile. "Not those sorts of things."

She still didn't move. We stood there for a long while. I heard a muted retching sound from off in the woods. I sighed and lowered the cup. Looking down, I saw Ellie had already curled up and gone to sleep. Her face looked almost peaceful.

I took a deep breath and looked back up at Krin. "You don't have any reason to trust me," I said, looking straight into her eyes. "Not after what has happened to you. But I hope you will." I held out the cup again.

She met my eyes without blinking, then reached for the cup. She drank it off in one swallow, choked a little, and sat down. Her eyes stayed hard as marble as she stared at the wall of the tent. I sat down, slightly apart from her.

In fifteen minutes she was asleep. I covered the two of them with a blanket and watched their faces. In sleep they were even more beautiful than before. I reached out to brush a strand of hair from Krin's cheek. To my surprise, she opened her eyes and stared at me. Not the marble stare she had given me before, she looked at me with the dark eyes of a young Denna.

I froze with my hand on her cheek. We watched each other for a second. Then her eyes drew closed again. I couldn't tell if it was the drug pulling her under, or her own will surrendering to sleep.

I settled myself at the entrance of the tent and lay Caesura across my knees. I felt rage like a fire inside me, and the sight of the two sleeping girls was like a wind fanning the coals. I set my teeth and forced myself to think of what had happened here, letting the fire burn fiercely, letting the heat of it fill me. I drew deep breaths, tempering myself for what was to come.

I waited for three hours, listening to the sounds of the camp. Muted conversation drifted toward me, shapes of sentences with no individual words. They faded, mixing with cursing and sounds of people being ill. I took long, slow breaths as Vashet had shown me, relaxing my body, slowly counting my exhalations.

Then, opening my eyes, I looked at the stars and judged the time to be right. I slowly unfolded myself from my sitting position and made a long, slow stretch. There was a solid crescent of moon hanging in the sky, and everything seemed very bright.

I approached the campfire slowly. It had fallen to sullen coals that did little to light the space between the two wagons. Otto was there, his huge body slumped against one of the wheels. I smelled vomit. "Is that you, Kvothe?" he asked blurrily.

"Yes," I continued my slow walk toward him.

"That bitch Anne didn't let the lamb cook through," he moaned. "I swear to holy God I've never been this sick before." He looked up at me. "Are you all right?"

Caesura leapt, caught the moonlight briefly on her blade, and tore his throat. He staggered to one knee, then toppled to his side, his hands staining black as they clutched his neck. I left him bleeding darkly in the moonlight, unable to cry out, dying but not dead.

I tossed a piece of brittle iron into the coals of the fire and headed toward the other tents.

Laren startled me as I came around the wagon. He made a surprised noise as he saw me walk around the corner with my naked sword. But the poison had made him sluggish, and he had barely managed to raise his hands before Caesura took him in the chest. He choked a scream as he fell backward, writhing on the ground.

None of them had been sleeping soundly due to the poison, so Laren's cry set them pouring from the wagons and tents, staggering and looking around wildly. Two indistinct shapes that I knew must be Josh and Fren leapt from the open back of the wagon closest to me. I struck one in the eye before he hit the ground and tore the belly from the other.

Everyone saw, and now there were screams in earnest. Most of them began to run drunkenly into the trees, some falling as they went. But the tall shape of Tim hurled itself at me. The heavy sword he had been sharpening all evening glinted silver in the moonlight.

But I was ready. I slid a second long, brittle piece of sword-iron into my hand and muttered a binding. Then, just as he came close enough to strike I snapped the iron sharply between my fingers. His sword shattered with the sound of a broken bell, and the pieces tumbled and disappeared in the dark grass.

Tim was more experienced than me, stronger, and with longer reach. Even poisoned and with half a sword he made a good showing of himself. It took me nearly half a minute before I snuck past his guard with Lover Out the Window and severed his hand at the wrist.

He fell to his knees, letting out a raspy howl and clutching at the stump. I struck him high in the chest and headed for the trees. The fight hadn't taken long, but every second was vital, as the others were already scattering into the woods.

I hurried in the direction I'd seen one of the dark shapes stagger. I was careless, so when Alleg threw himself on me from the shadow of a tree he caught me unaware. He didn't have a sword, only a small knife flashing in the moonlight as he dove for me. But a knife is enough to kill a man. He stabbed me in the stomach as we rolled to the ground. I struck the side of my head against a root and tasted blood.

I fought my way to my feet before he did and cut the hamstring on his leg. Then I stabbed him in the stomach and left him cursing on the ground as I went to hunt the others. I held one hand tight across my stomach. I knew the pain would hit me soon, and after that I might not have long to live.

It was a long night, and I will not trouble you with any further details. I found all the rest of them as they made their way through the forest. Anne had broken her leg in her reckless flight, and Tim made it nearly half a mile despite the loss of his hand and the wound in his chest. They shouted and cursed and begged for mercy as I stalked them through the forest, but nothing they said could appease me.

It was a terrible night, but I found them all. There was no honor to it, no glory. But there was justice of a sort, and blood, and in the end I brought their bodies back.

I came back to my tent as the sky was beginning to color to a familiar blue. A sharp, hot line of pain burned a few inches below my navel, and I could tell from the unpleasant tugging when I moved that dried blood had matted my shirt to the wound. I ignored the feeling as best I could, knowing I could do nothing for myself with my hands shaking and no decent light to see by. I'd have to wait for dawn to see how badly I was hurt.

I tried not to dwell on what I knew from my work in the Medica. Any deep wound to the gut promises a long, painful trip to the grave. A skilled physicker with the right equipment could make a difference, but I couldn't be farther from civilization. I might as well wish for a piece of the moon.

I wiped my sword, sat in the wet grass in front of the tent, and began to think.

The Broken Circle

I HAD BEEN BUSY FOR more than an hour when the sun finally peered over the tops of the trees and began to burn the dew from the grass. I had found a flat rock and was using it as a makeshift anvil to hammer a spare horseshoe into a different shape. Above the fire a pot of oats was boiling.

I was just putting the finishing touches on the horseshoe when I saw a flicker of movement from the corner of my eye. It was Krin peeking around the corner of the wagon. I guessed I'd woken her with the sound of hammering iron.

"Oh my God." Her hand went to her mouth and she took a couple stunned steps out from behind the wagon. "You killed them."

"Yes," I said simply, my voice sounding dead in my ears.

Krin's eyes ran up and down my body, staring at my torn and bloody shirt. "Are . . ." Her voice caught in her throat, and she swallowed. "Are you alright?"

I nodded silently. When I'd finally worked up the courage to examine my wound, I'd discovered that Felurian's cloak had saved my life. Instead of spilling open my guts, Alleg's knife had merely given me a long, shallow cut across my belly. He had also ruined a perfectly good shirt, but I had a hard time feeling bad about that, all things considered.

I examined the horseshoe, then used a damp leather strap to tie it firmly to one end of a long, straight branch. I pulled the kettle of oats off the fire and thrust the horseshoe into the coals.

Seeming to recover from some of her shock, Krin slowly approached, eyeing the row of bodies on the other side of the fire. I had done nothing other than lay them out in a rough line. It wasn't tidy. Blood stained the bodies, and their wounds gaped openly. Krin stared as if she were afraid they might start to move again.

"What are you doing?" she asked finally.

In answer, I pulled the now-hot horseshoe from the coals of the fire and approached the nearest body. It was Tim. I pressed the hot iron against the back of his remaining hand. The skin smoked and hissed and stuck to the metal. After a moment I pulled it away, leaving a black burn against his white skin. A broken circle. I moved back to the fire and began to heat the iron again.

Krin stood mutely, too stunned to react normally. Not that there could be a normal way to react in a situation like this, I suppose. But she didn't scream or run off as I thought she might. She simply looked at the broken circle and repeated, "What are you doing?"

When I finally spoke, my voice sounded strange to my own ears. "All of the Edema Ruh are one family," I explained. "Like a closed circle. It doesn't matter if some of us are strangers to others, we are still family, still close. We have to be this way, because we are always strangers wherever we go. We are scattered, and people hate us.

"We have laws. Rules we follow. When one of us does a thing that cannot be forgiven or mended, if he jeopardizes the safety or the honor of the Edema Ruh, he is killed and branded with the broken circle to show he is no longer one of us. It is rarely done. There is rarely a need."

I pulled the iron from the fire and walked to the next body. Otto. I pressed it to the back of his hand and listened to it hiss. "These were *not* Edema Ruh. But they made themselves out to be. They did things no Edema would do, so I am making sure the world knows they were not part of our family. The Ruh do not do the sort of things that these men did."

"But the wagons," she protested. "The instruments."

"They were not Edema Ruh," I said firmly. "They probably weren't even real troupers, just a group of thieves who killed a band of Ruh and tried to take their place."

Krin stared at the bodies, then back at me. "So you killed them for pretending to be Edema Ruh?"

"For pretending to be Ruh? No." I put the iron back in the fire. "For killing a Ruh troupe and stealing their wagons? Yes. For what they did to you? Yes."

"But if they aren't Ruh . . ." Krin looked at the brightly painted wagons. "How?"

"I am curious about that myself," I said. Pulling the broken circle from the fire again, I moved to Alleg and pressed it onto his palm.

The false trouper jerked and screamed himself awake.

"He isn't dead!" Krin exclaimed shrilly.

I had examined the wound earlier. "He's dead," I said coldly. "He just hasn't stopped moving yet." I turned to look him in the eye. "How about it, Alleg? How did you come by a pair of Edema wagons?"

"Ruh bastard," he cursed at me with blurry defiance.

"Yes," I said, "I am. And you are not. So how did you learn my family's signs and customs?"

"How did you know?" he asked. "We knew the words, the handshake. We knew water and wine and songs before supper. How did you know?"

"You thought you could fool me?" I said, feeling my anger coiling inside me again like a spring. "This is my family! How could I not know? Ruh don't do what you did. Ruh don't steal, don't kidnap girls."

Alleg shook his head with a mocking smile. There was blood on his teeth. "Everyone knows what you people do."

My temper exploded. "Everyone thinks they know! They think rumor is the truth! Ruh don't do this!" I gestured wildly around me. "People only think those things because of people like you!" My anger flared even hotter and I found myself screaming. "Now tell me what I want to know or God will weep when he hears what I've done to you!"

Alleg paled and had to swallow before he found his voice. "There was an old man and his wife and a couple other players. I traveled guard with them for half a year. Eventually they took me in." He ran out of breath and gasped a bit as he tried to get it back.

He'd said enough. "So you killed them."

Alleg shook his head vigorously. "No . . . were attacked on the road." He gestured weakly to the other bodies. "They surprised us. The other players were killed, but I was just . . . knocked out."

I looked over the line of bodies and felt the rage flare up, even though I'd already known. There was no other way these people could have come by a pair of Edema wagons with their markings intact.

Alleg was talking again. "I showed them afterward . . . How to act like a troupe." He swallowed against the pain. "Good life."

I turned away, disgusted. He was one of us, in a way. One of our adopted family. It made everything ten times worse knowing that. I pushed the horseshoe into the coals of the fire again, then looked to the girl as it heated. Her eyes had gone to flint as she watched Alleg.

Not sure if it was the right thing to do, I offered her the brand. Her face went hard and she took it.

Alleg didn't seem to understand what was about to happen until she had the hot iron against his chest. He shrieked and twisted but lacked the strength to get away as she pressed it hard against him. She grimaced as he struggled weakly against the iron, her eyes brimming with angry tears.

After a long minute she pulled the iron away and stood, crying quietly. I let her be.

Alleg looked up at her and somehow managed to find his voice. "Ah girl, we had some good times, didn't we?" She stopped crying and looked at him. "Don't—"

I kicked him sharply in the side before he could say anything else. He stiffened in mute pain and then spat blood at me. I landed another kick, and he went limp.

Not knowing what else to do, I took back the brand and began heating it again.

There was a long silence. "Is Ellie still asleep?" I asked.

Krin nodded.

"Do you think it would help for her to see this?"

She thought about it, wiping at her face with a hand. "I don't think so," she said finally. "I don't think she *could* see it right now. She's not right in her head."

"The two of you are from Levinshir?" I asked to keep the silence at arm's length.

"My family farms just north of Levinshir," Krin said. "Ellie's father is mayor."

"When did these come into your town?" I asked as I set the brand to the back of another hand. The sweet smell of charred flesh was becoming thick in the air.

"What day is it?"

I counted in my head. "Felling."

"They came into town on Theden." She paused. "Five days ago?" Her voice was tinged with disbelief. "We were glad to have the chance to see a play and hear the news. Hear some music." She looked down. "They were camped on the east edge of town. When I came to get my fortune read they told me to come back that night. They seemed so friendly, so exciting."

Krin looked at the wagons. "When I showed up, they were all sitting around the fire. They sang me songs. The old woman gave me some tea. I didn't even think . . . I mean . . . she looked like my gran." Her eyes strayed to the body of the old woman, then away. "Then I don't remember what happened. I woke up in the dark, in one of the wagons. I was tied up and I . . ." Her voice broke a little, and she rubbed absentmindedly at her wrists. She glanced back at the tent. "I guess Ellie got an invitation too."

I finished branding the backs of their hands. I had been planning to do their faces too, but the iron was slow to heat in the fire, and I was quickly growing sick of the work. I hadn't slept at all, and the anger that had burned so hot for so long was in its final flicker, leaving me feeling cold and numb.

I made a gesture to the pot of oats I'd pulled off the fire. "Are you hungry?"

"Yes," she said, then darted a look toward the bodies. "No."

"Me neither. Go wake up Ellie and we can get you home."

Krin hurried off to the tent. After she disappeared inside, I turned to the line of bodies. "Does anyone object to my leaving the troupe?" I asked.

None of them did. So I left.

Dreams

IT WAS AN HOUR'S work to drive the wagons into a thick piece of forest and hide them. I destroyed their Edema markings and unhitched the horses. There was only one saddle, so I loaded the other two horses with food and whatever other portable valuables I could find.

When I returned with the horses, Krin and Ellie were waiting for me. More precisely, Krin was waiting. Ellie was merely standing nearby, her expression vacant, her eyes empty.

"Do you know how to ride?" I asked Krin.

She nodded and I handed her the reins to the saddled horse. She got one foot in the stirrup and stopped, shaking her head. She brought her foot back down slowly. "I'll walk."

"Do you think Ellie would stay on a horse?"

Krin looked over to where the blonde girl was standing. One of the horses nuzzled her curiously and got no response. "Probably. But I don't think it would be good for her. After . . ."

I nodded in understanding. "We'll all walk then."

———

"What is the heart of the Lethani?" I asked Vashet.

"Success and right action."

"Which is the more important, success or rightness?"

"They are the same. If you act rightly success follows."

"But others may succeed by doing wrong things," I pointed out.

"Wrong things never lead to success," Vashet said firmly. "If a man acts wrongly and succeeds, that is not the way. Without the Lethani there is no true success."

Sir? A voice called. "Sir?"

My eyes focused on Krin. Her hair was windblown, her young face tired.
She looked at me timidly. "Sir? It's getting dark."

I looked around and saw twilight creeping in from the east. I was bone weary
and had fallen into a walking doze after we had stopped for lunch at midday.

"Just call me Kvothe, Krin. Thanks for jogging my elbow. My mind was
somewhere else."

Krin gathered wood and started a fire. I unsaddled the horses, then fed and
rubbed them down. I took a few minutes to set up the tent, too. Normally I
don't bother with such things, but there had been room for it on the horses,
and I guessed the girls weren't used to sleeping out of doors.

After I finished with the tent, I realized I'd only brought one extra blanket
from the troupe's supplies. There would be a chill tonight too, if I was any
judge of such things.

"Dinner's ready," I heard Krin call. I tossed my blanket and the spare one
into the tent and headed back to where she was finishing up. She'd done a
good job with what was available. Potato soup with bacon and toasted bread.
There was a green summer squash nestled into the coals as well.

Ellie worried me. She had been the same all day, walking listlessly, never
speaking or responding to anything Krin or I said to her. Her eyes would follow things, but there was no thought behind them. Krin and I had discovered
the hard way that if left to herself she would stop walking, or wander off the
road if something caught her eye.

Krin handed me a bowl and spoon as I sat down. "It smells good." I complimented her.

She half-smiled and dished a second bowl for herself. She started to fill a
third bowl, then hesitated, realizing Ellie couldn't feed herself.

"Would you like some soup, Ellie?" I asked in normal tones. "It smells good."
She sat blankly by the fire, staring into nothing.

"Do you want to share mine?" I asked as if it were the most natural thing
in the world. I moved closer to her and blew on a spoonful to cool it. "Here
you go."

Ellie ate it mechanically, turning her head slightly in my direction, toward
the spoon. Her eyes reflected the dancing patterns of the fire. They were like
the windows of an empty house.

I blew on another spoonful and held it out to the blonde girl. She opened
her mouth only when the spoon touched her lips. I moved my head, trying
to see past the dancing firelight in her eyes, desperately hoping to see something behind them. Anything.

"I bet you're an Ell, aren't you?" I said conversationally. I looked at Krin.
"Short for Ellie?"

Krin shrugged helplessly. "We weren't friends, really. She's just Ellie Anwater. The mayor's daughter."

"It sure was a long walk today," I continued speaking in the same easy tone. "How do your feet feel, Krin?"

Krin continued to watch me with her serious dark eyes. "A little sore."

"Mine too. I can't wait to get my shoes off. Are your feet sore, Ell?"

No response. I fed her another bite.

"It was pretty hot too. It should cool off tonight, though. Good sleeping weather. Won't that be nice, Ell?"

No response. Krin continued to watch me from the other side of the fire. I took a bite of soup for myself. "This is truly fine, Krin," I said earnestly, then turned back to the vacant girl. "It's a good thing we have Krin to cook for us, Ell. Everything I cook tastes like horseshit."

On her side of the fire, Krin tried to laugh with a mouthful of soup with predictable results. I thought I saw a flicker in Ell's eyes. "If I had some horse apples I could make us a horse apple pie for dessert," I offered. "I could make some tonight if you want . . ." I trailed off, making it a question.

Ell gave the slightest frown, a small wrinkle creased her forehead.

"You're probably right," I said. "It wouldn't be very good. Would you like more soup instead?"

The barest nod. I gave her a spoonful.

"It's a little salty, though. You probably want some water."

Another nod. I handed her the waterskin and she lifted it to her own lips. She drank for a long, long minute. She was probably parched from our long walk today. I would have to watch her more closely tomorrow to make sure she drank enough.

"Would you like a drink, Krin?"

"Yes please," Krin said, her eyes fixed on Ell's face.

Moving automatically, Ell held the waterskin out toward Krin, holding it directly over the fire with the shoulder strap dragging in the coals. Krin grabbed it quickly, then added a belated, "Thank you, Ell."

I kept the slow stream of conversation going through the whole meal. Ell fed herself toward the end of it, and though her eyes were clearer, it was as if she were looking at the world through a sheet of frosted glass, seeing but not seeing. Still, it was an improvement.

After she ate two bowls of soup and half a loaf of bread, her eyes began to bob closed. "Would you like to go to sleep, Ell?" I asked.

A more definite nod.

"Should I carry you to the tent?"

Her eyes snapped open at this and she shook her head firmly.

"Maybe Krin would help you get ready for bed if you asked her."

Ell turned to look in Krin's direction. Her mouth moved in a vague way. Krin darted a glance at me and I nodded.

"Let's go and get tucked in then," Krin said, sounding every bit the older sister. She came over and took Ell's hand, helping her to her feet. As they went into the tent, I finished off the soup and ate a piece of bread that had been too badly burnt for either of the girls.

Before too long Krin came back to the fire. "Is she sleeping?" I asked.

"Before she hit the pillow. Do you think she will be all right?"

She was in deep shock. Her mind had stepped through the doors of madness to protect itself from what was happening. "It's probably just a matter of time," I said tiredly, hoping it was the truth. "The young heal quickly." I chuckled humorlessly as I realized she was probably only about a year younger than me. I felt every year twice tonight, some of them three times.

Despite the fact that I felt covered in lead, I forced myself to my feet and helped Krin clean the dishes. I sensed her growing unease as we finished cleaning up and repicketing the horses to a fresh piece of grazing. The tension grew worse as we approached the tent. I stopped and held the flap open for her. "I'll sleep out here tonight."

Her relief was tangible. "Are you sure?"

I nodded. She slipped inside, and I let the flap fall closed behind her. Her head poked back out almost immediately, followed by a hand holding a blanket.

I shook my head. "You'll need them both. There'll be a chill tonight." I pulled my shaed around me and lay directly in front of the tent. I didn't want Ell wandering out during the night and getting lost or hurt.

"Won't you be cold?"

"I'll be fine," I said. I was tired enough to sleep on a running horse. I was tired enough to sleep *under* a running horse.

Krin ducked her head back into the tent. Soon I heard her nestling into the blankets. Then everything was quiet.

I remembered the startled look on Otto's face as I cut his throat. I heard Alleg struggle weakly and curse me as I dragged him back to the wagons. I remembered the blood. The way it had felt against my hands. The thickness of it.

I had never killed anyone like that before. Not coldly, not close up. I remembered how warm their blood had been. I remembered the way Kete had cried as I stalked her through the woods. "It was them or me!" she had screamed hysterically. "I didn't have a choice. It was them or me!"

I lay awake a long while. When I finally slept, the dreams were worse.

CHAPTER ONE HUNDRED THIRTY-FOUR

The Road to Levinshir

WE MADE POOR TIME the next day, as Krin and I were forced to lead the three horses and Ell besides. Luckily, the horses were well-behaved, as Edema-trained horses tend to be. If they had been as wayward-witted as the poor mayor's daughter, we might never have made it to Levinshir at all.

Even so, the horses were almost more trouble than they were worth. The glossy roan in particular liked to wander off into the underbrush, foraging. Three times now I'd had to drag him out, and we were irritated with each other. I'd named him Burrback for obvious reasons.

The fourth time I had to pull him back onto the road, I seriously considered cutting him loose to save myself the trouble. I didn't, of course. A good horse is the same as money in your pocket. And it would be quicker to ride back to Severen than walk the whole way.

Krin and I did our best to keep Ell engaged in conversation as we walked. It seemed to help a bit. And by the time our noon meal came around she seemed almost aware of what was going on around her. Almost.

I had an idea as we were getting ready to set out again after lunch. I led our dappled grey mare over to where Ell stood. Her golden hair was one great tangle and she was trying to run one of her hands through it while her eyes wandered around in a distracted way, as if she didn't quite understand where she was.

"Ell." She turned to look. "Have you met Greytail?" I gestured to the mare. A faint, confused shake of the head.

"I need your help leading her. Have you led a horse before?"

A nod.

"She needs someone to take care of her. Can you do it?" Greytail looked at me with one large eye, as if to let me know she needed leading as much as I needed wheels to walk. But then she lowered her head a bit and nuzzled Ell in a motherly way. The girl reached out a hand to pet her nose almost automatically, then took the reins from me.

"Do you think that's a good idea?" Krin asked when I came back to pack the other horses.

"Greytail is gentle as a lamb."

"Just because Ell is witless as a sheep," Krin said archly, "doesn't make them a good pairing."

I cracked a smile at that. "We'll watch them close for an hour or so. If it doesn't work, it doesn't. But sometimes the best help a person can find is helping someone else."

———————

Since I had slept poorly I was twice weary today. My stomach was sour, and I felt gritty, like someone had sanded the first two layers of my skin away. I was almost tempted to doze in the saddle, but I couldn't bring myself to ride while the girls walked.

So I plodded along, leading my horse and nodding on my feet. But today I couldn't fall into the comfortable half-sleep I tend to use when walking. I was plagued with thoughts of Alleg, wondering if he was still alive.

I knew from my time in the Medica that the gut wound I'd given him was fatal. I also knew it was a slow death. Slow and painful. With proper care it might be a full span of days before he died. Even alone in the middle of nowhere he could live for days with such a wound.

Not pleasant days. He would grow delirious with fever as the infection set in. Every movement would tear the wound open again. He couldn't walk on his hamstrung leg, either. So if he wanted to move he'd have to crawl. He would be cramped with hunger and burning with thirst by now.

But not dead from thirst. No. I had left a full waterskin nearby. I had laid it at his side before we had left. Not out of kindness. Not to make his last hours more bearable. I had left it because I knew that with water he would live longer, suffer more.

Leaving him that waterskin was the most terrible thing I'd ever done, and now that my anger had cooled to ashes I regretted it. I wondered how much longer he would live because of it. A day? Two? Certainly no more than two. I tried not to think of what those two days would be like.

But even when I forced thoughts of Alleg from my mind, I had other demons to fight. I remembered bits and pieces of that night, the things the false troupers had said as I cut them down. The sounds my sword had made as it dug into them. The smell of their skin as I had branded them. I had killed two women. What would Vashet think of my actions? What would anyone think?

Exhausted from worry and lack of sleep, my thoughts spun in these circles for the remainder of the day. I set up camp from force of habit and kept up a conversation with Ell through an effort of sheer will. The time for sleep came before I was ready, and I found myself rolled in my shaed, in the front of the girls' tent. I was dimly aware that Krin had started giving me the same worried look she'd been giving Ell for the past two days.

I lay wide-eyed for an hour before falling asleep, wondering about Alleg.

When I slept I dreamed of killing them. In my dream I stalked the forest like grim death, unwavering.

But it was different this time. I killed Otto, his blood spattering my hands like hot grease. Then I killed Laren and Josh and Tim. They moaned and screamed, twisting on the ground. Their wounds were horrible, but I could not look away.

Then the faces changed. I was killing Taren, the bearded ex-mercenary in my troupe. Then I killed Trip. Then I was chasing Shandi through the forest, my sword naked in my hand. She was crying out, weeping in fear. When I finally caught her she clutched at me, knocking me to the ground, burying her face in my chest, sobbing. "No no no," she begged. "No no no."

I came awake. I lay on my back, terrified and not knowing where my dream ended and the world began. After a brief moment I realized the truth. Ell had crawled from the tent and lay curled against me. Her face pressed against my chest, her hand grasping desperately at my arm.

"No no," she choked out. "No no no no no." Her body shook with helpless sobs when she couldn't say it anymore. My shirt was wet with hot tears. My arm was bleeding where she clutched it.

I made consoling noises and brushed at her hair with my hand. After a long while she quieted and eventually fell into an exhausted sleep, still clinging tightly to my chest.

I lay very still, not wanting to wake her by moving. My teeth were clenched. I thought of Alleg and Otto and all the rest. I remembered the blood and screaming and the smell of burning skin. I remembered it all and dreamed of worse things I could have done to them.

I never had the nightmares again. Sometimes I think of Alleg and I smile.

We made it to Levinshir the next day. Ell had come to her senses, but remained quiet and withdrawn. Still, things went more quickly now, especially as the girls decided they had recovered enough to take turns riding Greytail.

We covered six miles before we stopped at midday, with the girls becoming increasingly excited as they began to recognize parts of the countryside. The shape of hills in the distance. A crooked tree by the road.

But as we grew closer to Levinshir they grew quiet.

"It's just over the rise there," Krin said, getting down off the roan. "You ride from here, Ell."

Ell looked from her, to me, to her feet. She shook her head.

I watched them. "Are the two of you okay?"

"My father's going to kill me." Krin's voice was barely a whisper, her face full of serious fear.

"Your father will be one of the happiest men in the world tonight," I said, then thought it best to be honest. "He might be angry too. But that's only because he's been scared out of his mind for the last eight days."

Krin seemed slightly reassured, but Ell burst out crying. Krin put her arms around her, making gentle sounds.

"No one will marry me," Ell sobbed. "I was going to marry Jason Waterson and help him run his store. He won't marry me now. No one will."

I looked up to Krin and saw the same fear reflected in her wet eyes. But Krin's eyes were angry while Ell's held nothing but despair.

"Any man who thinks that way is a fool," I said, weighting my voice with all the conviction I could bring to bear. "And the two of you are too clever and too beautiful to be marrying fools."

It seemed to calm Ell somewhat, her eyes turning up at me as if looking for something to believe.

"It's the truth," I said. "And none of this was your fault. Make sure you remember that for these next couple days."

"I hate them!" Ell spat, surprising me with her sudden rage. "I hate men!" Her knuckles were white as she gripped Greytail's reins. Her face twisted into a mask of anger. Krin put her arms around Ell, but when she looked at me I saw the sentiment reflected quietly in her dark eyes.

"You have every right to hate them," I said, feeling more anger and helplessness than ever before in my life. "But I'm a man too. Not all of us are like that."

We stayed there for a while, not more than a half-mile from town. We had a drink of water and a small bite to settle our nerves. And then I took them home.

CHAPTER ONE HUNDRED THIRTY-FIVE

Homecoming

LEVINSHIR WASN'T A BIG town. Two hundred people lived there, maybe three if you counted the outlying farms. It was mealtime when we rode in, and the dirt road that split the town in half was empty and quiet. Ell told me her house was on the far side of town. I hoped to get the girls there without being seen. They were worn down and distraught. The last thing they needed was to face a mob of gossipy neighbors.

But it wasn't meant to be. We were halfway through the town when I saw a flicker of movement in a window. A woman's voice cried out, *"Ell!"* and in ten seconds people began to spill from every doorway in sight.

The women were the quickest, and inside a minute a dozen of them had formed a protective knot around the two girls, talking and crying and hugging each other. The girls didn't seem to mind. Perhaps it was better this way. A warm welcome might do a lot to heal them.

The men held back, knowing they were useless in situations like this. Most watched from doorways or porches. Six or eight came down onto the street, moving slowly and eyeing up the situation. These were cautious men, farmers and friends of farmers. They knew the names of everyone within ten miles of their homes. There were no strangers in a town like Levinshir, except for me.

None of the men were close relatives to the girls. Even if they were, they knew they wouldn't get near them for at least an hour, maybe as much as a day. So they let their wives and sisters take care of things. With nothing else to occupy them, their attention wandered briefly past the horses and settled onto me.

I motioned over a boy of ten or so. "Go tell the mayor his daughter's back. Run!" He tore off in a cloud of road dust, his bare feet flying.

The men moved slowly closer to me, their natural suspicion of strangers made ten times worse by recent events. A boy of twelve or so wasn't as cautious as the rest and came right up to me, eyeing my sword, my cloak.

"What's your name?" I asked him.

"Pete."

"Can you ride a horse, Pete?"

He looked insulted. "S'nuf."

"Do you know where the Walker farm is?"

He nodded. "'Bout north two miles by the millway."

I stepped sideways and handed him the reins to the roan. "Go tell them their daughter's home. Then let them use the horse to come back to town."

He had a leg over the horse before I could offer him a hand up. I kept a hand on the reins long enough to shorten the stirrups so he wouldn't kill himself on the way there.

"If you make it there and back without breaking your head or my horse's leg, I'll give you a penny," I said.

"You'll give me two," he said.

I laughed. He wheeled the horse around and was gone.

The men had wandered closer in the meantime, gathering around me in a loose circle.

A tall, balding fellow with a scowl and a grizzled beard seemed to appoint himself leader. "So who're you?" he asked, his tone speaking more clearly than his words, *Who the hell are you?*

"Kvothe," I answered pleasantly. "And yourself?"

"Don't know as that's any of your business," he growled. "What are you doing here?" *What the hell are you doing here with our two girls?*

"God's mother, Seth," an older man said to him. "You don't have the sense God gave a dog. That's no way to talk to the . . ."

"Don't give me any of your lip, Benjamin," the scowling man bristled back. "We got a good right to know who he is." He turned to me and took a few steps in front of everyone else. "You one of those trouper bastards what came through here?"

I shook my head and attempted to look harmless. "No."

"I think you are. I think you look kinda like one of them Ruh. You got them eyes." The men around him craned to get a better look at my face.

"God, Seth," the old fellow chimed in again. "None of them had red hair. You remember hair like that. He ain't one of 'em."

"Why would I bring them back if I'd been one of the men who took them?" I pointed out.

His expression grew darker and he continued his slow advance. "You gettin' smart with me, boy? Maybe you think all of us are stupid here? You think if you bring 'em back you'll get a reward or maybe we won't send anyone else out after you?" He was almost within arm's reach of me now, scowling furiously.

I looked around and saw the same anger lurking in the faces of all the men who stood there. It was the sort of anger that comes to a slow boil inside the hearts of good men who want justice, and finding it out of their grasp, decide vengeance is the next best thing.

I tried to think of a way to calm the situation, but before I could do anything I heard Krin's voice lash out from behind me. "Seth, you get away from him!"

Seth paused, his hands half raised against me. "Now . . ."

Krin was already stepping toward him. The knot of women loosened to release her, but stayed close. "He saved us, Seth," she shouted furiously. "You stupid shit-eater, *he* saved us. Where the hell were all of you? Why didn't you come get us?"

He backed away from me as anger and shame fought their way across his face. Anger won. "We came," he shouted back. "After we found out what happened we went after 'em. They shot out Bil's horse from under him, and he got his leg crushed. Jim got his arm stabbed, and old Cupper still ain't waked up from the thumping they give him. They almost killed us."

I looked again and saw anger on the men's faces. Saw the real reason for it. The helplessness they had felt, unable to defend their town from the false troupe's rough handling. Their failure to reclaim the daughters of their friends and neighbors had shamed them.

"Well it wasn't good enough!" Krin shouted back hotly, her eyes burning. "He came and got us because he's a real man. Not like the rest of you who left us to die!"

The anger leapt out of a young man to my left, a farm boy, about seventeen. "None of this would have happened if you hadn't been running around like some Ruh whore!"

I broke his arm before I quite realized what I was doing. He screamed as he fell to the ground.

I pulled him to his feet by the scruff of his neck. "What's your name?" I snarled into his face.

"My arm!" He gasped, his eyes showing me their whites.

I shook him like a rag doll. "Name!"

"Jason," he blurted. "God's mother, my arm . . ."

I took his chin in my free hand and turned his face toward Krin and Ell. "Jason," I hissed quietly in his ear. "I want you to look at those girls. And I want you to think about the hell they've been through in these past days, tied hand

and foot in the back of a wagon. And I want you to ask yourself what's worse. A broken arm, or getting kidnapped by a stranger and raped four times a night?"

Then I turned his face toward me and spoke so quiet that even an inch away it was hardly a whisper. "After you've thought of that, I want you to pray to God to forgive you for what you just said. And if you mean it, Tehlu grant your arm heal straight and true." His eyes were terrified and wet. "After that, if you ever think an unkind thought about either of them, your arm will ache like there's hot iron in the bone. And if you ever say an unkind word, it will go to fever and slow rot and they'll have to cut it off to save your life." I tightened my grip on him, watching his eyes widen. "And if you ever do anything to either of them, I'll know. I will come here, and kill you, and leave your body hanging in a tree."

There were tears on his face now, although whether from shame or fear or pain I couldn't guess. "Now you tell her you're sorry for what you said." I let go of him after making sure he had his feet under him and pointed him in the direction of Krin and Ell. The women stood around them like a protective cocoon.

He clutched his arm weakly. "I shouldn'ta said that, Ellie," he sobbed, sounding more wretched and repentant than I would have thought possible, broken arm or no. "It was a demon talkin' out of me. I swear though, I been sick worryin'. We all been. And we did try to come get you, but they was a lot of them and they jumped us on the road, then we had to bring Bil home or he would've died from his leg."

Something tickled my memory about the boy's name. Jason? I suddenly suspected I had just broken Ell's boyfriend's arm. Somehow I couldn't feel bad for it just now. Best thing for him, really.

Looking around I saw the anger bleed out of the faces of the men around me, as if I'd used up the whole town's supply in a sudden, furious flash. Instead they watched Jason, looking slightly embarrassed, as if the boy were apologizing for the lot of them.

Then I saw a big, healthy-looking man running down the street followed by a dozen other townsfolk. From the look on his face I guessed it was Ell's father, the mayor. He forced his way into the knot of women, gathered his daughter up in his arms, and swung her around.

You find two types of mayor in small towns like this. The first type are balding, older men of considerable girth who are good with money and tend to wring their hands a great deal when anything unexpected happens. The second type are tall, broad-shouldered men whose families have grown slowly prosperous because they had worked like angry bastards behind a plow for twenty generations. Ell's father was the second sort.

He walked over to me, keeping one arm around his daughter's shoulders. "I understand I have you to thank for bringing our girls back." He reached out to shake my hand and I saw his arm was bandaged. His grip was solid in spite of it. He smiled the widest smile I'd seen since I left Simmon at the University.

"How's the arm?" I asked, not realizing how it would sound. His smile faded a little, and I was quick to add, "I've had some training as a physicker. And I know that those sort of things can be tricky to deal with when you're away from home." *When you're living in a country that thinks mercury is medicine,* I thought to myself.

His smile came back, and he flexed his fingers. "It's stiff, but that's all. Just a little meat. They caught us by surprise. I got my hands on one of them, but he stuck me and got away. How did you end up getting the girls away from those godless Ruh bastards?" He spat.

"They weren't Edema Ruh," I said, my voice sounding more strained than I would have liked. "They weren't even real troupers."

His smile began to fade again. "What do you mean?"

"They weren't Edema Ruh. We don't do the things they did."

"Listen," the mayor said plainly, his temper starting to rise a bit. "I know damn well what they do and don't do. They came in all sweet and nice, played a little music, made a penny or two. Then they started to make trouble around town. When we told them to leave they took my girl." He almost breathed fire as he said the last words.

"We?" I heard someone say faintly behind me. "Jim, he said *we.*"

Seth scowled around the side of the mayor to get a look at me again. "I told you he looked like one," he said triumphantly. "I know 'em. You can always tell by them eyes."

"Hold on," the mayor said with slow incredulity. "Are you telling me you're one of *them?*" His expression grew dangerous.

Before I could explain myself. Ell had grabbed his arm. "Oh, don't make him mad, Daddy," she said quickly, holding onto his good arm as if to pull him away from me. "Don't say anything to get him angry. He's not with them. He brought me back, he saved me."

The mayor seemed somewhat mollified by this, but his congeniality was gone. "Explain yourself," he said grimly.

I sighed inside, realizing what a mess I'd made of this. "They weren't troupers, and they certainly weren't Edema Ruh. They were bandits who killed some of my family and stole their wagons. They were only pretending to be performers."

"Why would anyone pretend to be Ruh?" the mayor asked, as if the thought were incomprehensible.

"So they could do what they did," I snapped. "You let them into your town and they abused that trust. That's something no Edema Ruh would ever do."

"You never did answer my question," he said. "How did you get the girls away?"

"I took care of things," I said simply.

"He killed them," Krin said loudly enough for everyone to hear. "He killed them all."

I could feel everyone looking at me. Half of them were thinking, *All of them? He killed seven men?* The other half were thinking, *There were two women with them, did he kill them too?*

"Well, then." The mayor looked down at me for a long moment. "Good," he said as if he had just made up his mind. "That's good. The world's a better place for it."

I felt everyone relax slightly. "These are their horses." I pointed to the two horses that had been carrying our baggage. "They belong to the girls now. About forty miles east you'll find the wagons. Krin can show you where they're hidden. They belong to the girls too."

"They'll fetch a good price off in Temsford," the mayor mused.

"Together with the instruments and clothes and such, they'll fetch a heavy penny," I agreed. "Split two ways, it'll make a fine dowry," I said firmly.

He met my eyes, nodded slowly in understanding. "That it will."

"What about the things they stole from us?" a stout man in an apron protested. "They smashed up my place and stole two barrels of my best ale!"

"Do you have any daughters?" I asked him calmly. The sudden, stricken look on his face told me he did. I met his eye, held it. "Then I think you came away from this pretty well."

The mayor finally noticed Jason clutching his broken arm. "What happened to you?"

Jason looked at his feet, and Seth spoke up for him, "He said some things he shouldn't."

The mayor looked around and saw that getting more of an answer would involve an ordeal. He shrugged and let it go.

"I could splint it for you," I said easily.

"No!" Jason said too quickly, then backpedaled. "I'd rather go to Gran."

I gave a sideways look to the mayor. "Gran?"

He gave a fond smile. "When we scrape our knees Gran patches us back up again."

"Would Bil be there?" I asked. "The man with the crushed leg?"

He nodded. "She won't let him out of her sight for another span of days if I know her."

"I'll walk you over," I said to the sweating boy who was carefully cradling his arm. "I'd like to watch her work."

As far from civilization as we were, I expected Gran to be a hunched old woman who treated her patients with leeches and wood alcohol.

That opinion changed when I saw the inside of her house. Her walls were covered with bundles of dry herbs and shelves lined with small, carefully labeled bottles. There was a small desk with three heavy leather books on it. One of them lay open, and I recognized it as *The Heroborica*. I could see handwritten notes scrawled in the margins, while some of the entries had been edited or crossed out entirely.

Gran wasn't as old as I'd thought she'd be, though she did have her share of grey hair. She wasn't hunched either, and actually stood taller than me, with broad shoulders and a round, smiling face.

She swung a copper kettle over the fire, humming to herself. Then she brought out a pair of shears and sat Jason down, prodding his arm gently. Pale and sweating, the boy kept up a constant stream of nervous chatter while she methodically cut his shirt away. In the space of a few minutes, without her even asking, he'd given her an accurate if somewhat disjointed version of Ell and Krin's homecoming.

"It's a nice clean break," she said at last, interrupting him. "How'd it happen?"

Jason's wild eyes darted to me, then away. "Nothin'," he said quickly. Then realized he hadn't answered the question. "I mean . . ."

"I broke it," I said. "Figured the least I could do was come along and see if there's anything I could do to help set it right again."

Gran looked back at me. "Have you dealt with this sort of thing before?"

"I've studied medicine at the University," I said.

She shrugged. "Then I guess you can hold the splints while I wrap 'em. I have a girl who helps me, but she run off when she heard the commotion up the street."

Jason eyed me nervously as I held the wood tight to his arm, but it took Gran less than three minutes to bind up the splint with an air of bored competence. Watching her work, I decided she was worth more than half the students I could name in the Medica.

After we'd finished she looked down at Jason. "You're lucky," she said. "It didn't need to be set. You hold off using it for a month, it should heal up just fine."

Jason left as quickly as he was able, and after a small amount of persuasion Gran let me see Bil, who was laid up in her back room.

If Jason's arm was a clean break, then Bil's was messy as a break can be. Both the bones in his lower leg had broken in several places. I couldn't see under the bandages, but his leg was hugely swollen. The skin above the bandages was bruised and mottled, stretched as tight as an overstuffed sausage.

Bil was pale but alert, and it looked like he would probably keep the leg. How much use it would be was another matter. He might come away with nothing more than a heavy limp, but I wouldn't bet on him ever running again.

"What sort of folk shoot a man's horse?" he asked indignantly, his face covered in a sheen of sweat. "It ain't right."

It had been his own horse, of course. And this wasn't the sort of town where folk had horses to spare. Bil was a young man with a new wife and his own small farm, and he might never walk again because he'd tried to do the right thing. It hurt to think about.

Gran gave him two spoonfuls of something from a brown bottle, and it dragged his eyes shut. She ushered us out of the room and closed the door behind her.

"Did the bone break the skin?" I asked once the door was closed.

She nodded as she put the bottle back on the shelf.

"What have you been using to keep it from going septic?"

"Sour, you mean?" she asked. "Ramsburr."

"Really?" I asked. "Not arrowroot?"

"Arrowroot," she snorted as she added wood to the fire and swung the now-steaming kettle off of it. "You ever tried to keep something from going sour with arrowroot?"

"No," I admitted.

"Let me save you the trouble of killing someone, then." She brought out a pair of wooden cups. "Arrowroot is useless. You can eat it if you like, but that's about it."

"But a paste of arrowroot and bessamy is supposed to be ideal for this."

"Bessamy might be worth half a damn," she admitted. "But ramsburr is better. I'd rather have some redblade, but we can't always have what we want. A paste of motherleaf and ramsburr is what I use, and you can see he's doing just fine. Arrowroot is easy for folk to find, and it pulps smooth, but it hain't got any worthwhile properties."

She shook her head. "Arrowroot and camphor. Arrowroot and bessamy.

Arrowroot and saltbine. Arrowroot hain't a palliative of any sort. It's just good at carrying around what works."

I opened my mouth to protest, then looked around her house, at her heavily annotated copy of *The Heroborica*. I closed my mouth.

Gran poured hot water from the kettle into two cups. "Sit yourself down for a bit," she said. "You look like you're on your last leg."

I looked longingly at the chair. "I should probably be getting back," I said.

"You've got time for a cup," she said, taking my arm and setting me firmly into the chair. "And a quick bite. You're pale as a dry bone, and I have a bit of sweet pudding here that hain't got anybody to give it a home."

I tried to remember if I'd eaten any lunch today. I remembered feeding the girls. . . . "I don't want to put you to any more trouble," I said. "I've already made more work for you."

"About time somebody broke that boy's arm," she said conversationally. "Has a mouth on him like you wouldn't believe." She handed me one of the wooden cups. "Drink that down and I'll get you some of that pudding."

The steam coming off the cup smelled wonderful. "What's in it?" I asked.

"Rosehip. And some apple brandy I still up my own self." She gave a wide smile that crinkled the edges of her eyes. "If you like, I can put in some arrowroot, too."

I smiled and sipped. The warmth of it spread through my chest, and I felt myself relax a bit. Which was odd, as I hadn't realized I'd been tense before.

Gran bustled about a bit before setting two plates on the table and easing herself down into a nearby chair.

"You really kill those folk?" she asked plainly. There wasn't any accusation in her voice. It was just a question.

I nodded.

"You probably shouldn't have told anyone," she said. "There's bound to be a fuss. They'll want a trial and have to bring in the azzie from Temsford."

"I didn't tell them," I said. "Krin did."

"Ah," she said.

The conversation lulled. I drank the last swallow out of my cup, but when I tried to set it on the table my hands were shaking so badly that it knocked against the wood, making a sound like an impatient visitor at the door.

Gran sipped calmly from her cup.

"I don't care to talk about it," I said at last. "It wasn't a good thing."

"Some folk might argue that," she said gently. "I think you done the right thing."

Her words brought a sudden hot ache behind my eyes, as if I were about to burst into tears. "I'm not so sure about that," I said, my voice sounding strange in my own ears. My hands were shaking worse now.

Gran didn't seem surprised by this. "You've had the bit in your teeth for a couple days now, haven't you?" Her tone made it clear it wasn't really a question. "I know the look. You've been keeping busy. Looking after the girls. Not sleeping. Probably not eating much." She picked up the plate. "Eat your pudding. It will help to get some food in you."

I ate the pudding. Halfway through, I began to cry, choking a bit as it stuck in my throat.

Gran refilled my cup with more tea and poured another dollop of brandy in on top of it. "Drink that down," she repeated.

I took a swallow. I didn't mean to say anything, but I found myself talking anyway. "I think there might be something wrong with me," I said quietly. "A normal person doesn't have it in him to do the things I do. A normal person would never kill people like this."

"That may be," she admitted, sipping from her own cup. "But what would you say if I told you Bil's leg had gone a bit green and sweet smelling under that bandage?"

I looked up, startled. "He's got the rot?"

She shook her head. "No. I told you he's fine. But what if?"

"We'd have to cut the leg off," I said.

Gran nodded seriously. "That's right. And we'd have to do it quick. Today. No dithering about and hoping he'd fight his way through on his own. That wouldn't do a thing but kill him." She took a sip, watching me over the top of her cup, making it a question of sorts.

I nodded. I knew it was true.

"You've got some medicine," she said. "You know that proper doctoring means hard choices." She gave me an unflinching look. "We hain't like other folk. You burn a man with an iron to stop his bleeding. You save the mother and lose the babe. It's hard, and nobody ever thanks you for it. But we're the ones that have to choose."

She took another slow drink of tea. "The first few times are the worst. You'll get the shakes and lose some sleep. But that's the price of doing what needs to be done."

"There were women too," I said, the words catching in my throat.

Gran's eyes flashed. "They earned it twice as much," she said, and the sudden, furious anger in her sweet face caught me so completely by surprise that I felt prickling fear crawl over my body. "A man who would do that to a girl is like a mad dog. He hain't hardly a person, just an animal needs to be put down. But a woman who helps him do it? That's worse. She knows what she's doing. She knows what it means."

Gran put her cup down gently on the table, her expression composed again. "If a leg goes bad, you cut it off." She made a firm gesture with the flat of her hand, then picked up her slice of pudding and began to eat it with her fingers. "And some folk need killing. That's all there is to it."

———

By the time I got myself under control and made it back outside, the crowd in the street had swelled. The local tavern keeper had rolled a barrel onto his front landing and the air was sweet with the smell of beer.

Krin's father and mother had ridden back into town on the roan. Pete was there too, having run back. He offered up his unbroken head for my inspection and demanded his two pennies for services rendered.

I was warmly thanked by Krin's parents. They seemed to be good people. Most people are if given the chance. I caught hold of the roan's reins, and using him as a sort of portable wall I managed to get a moment of relatively private conversation with Krin.

Her dark eyes were a little red around the edges, but her face was bright and happy. "Make sure you get Lady Ghost," I said, nodding to one of the horses. "She's yours." The mayor's daughter would have a fair dowry no matter what, so I'd loaded Krin's horse with the more valuable goods, as well as most of the false troupers' money.

Her expression grew serious as she met my eyes, and again she reminded me of a young Denna. "You're leaving," she said.

I guess I was. She didn't try to convince me to stay, and instead surprised me with a sudden embrace. After kissing me on the cheek she whispered in my ear, "Thank you."

We stepped away from each other, knowing propriety would only allow so much. "Don't sell yourself short and marry some fool," I said, feeling as if I should say something.

"Don't you either," she said, her dark eyes mocking me gently.

I took Greytail's reins and led her over to where the mayor stood, watching the crowd in a proprietary way. He nodded as I approached.

I drew a deep breath. "Is the constable about?"

He raised an eyebrow at this, then shrugged and pointed off into the crowd. "That's him there. He was three-quarters drunk even before you brought our girls home, though. Don't know how much use he'll be to you now."

"Well," I said hesitantly. "I'm guessing someone is going to need to lock me up until you can get word to the azzie off in Temsford." I nodded to the small stone building in the center of town.

The mayor looked sideways at me, frowning a bit. "You *want* to be locked up?"

"Not particularly," I admitted.

"You can come and go as you please then," he said.

"The azzie won't be happy when he hears," I said. "I'd rather not have anyone else go up against the iron law because of something I've done. Aiding in the escape of a murderer can be a hanging offense."

The big man gave me a long looking over. His eyes lingered a bit on my sword, the worn leather of my boots. I could almost feel him noticing the lack of any serious wounds despite the fact that I'd just killed half a dozen armed men.

"So you'd let us just lock you up?" he asked. "Easy as that?"

I shrugged.

He frowned again, then shook his head as if he couldn't make sense of me. "Well aren't you just as gentle as a lamb?" he said wonderingly. "But no. I won't lock you up. You haven't done anything less than proper."

"I broke that boy's arm," I said.

"Hmm," he rumbled darkly. "Forgot about that." He reached into his pocket and brought out ha'penny. He handed it to me. "Much obliged."

I laughed as I put it in my pocket.

"Here's my thought," he said. "I'll head over and see if I can find the constable. Then I'll explain to him we've got to lock you up. If you've slipped off in the middle of this confusion, we wouldn't hardly be aiding in the escape, would we?"

"It would be negligence in maintenance of the law," I said. "He might take a few lashes for it, or lose his post."

"Shouldn't come to that," the mayor said. "But if it does, he'll be happy to do it. He's Ellie's uncle." He looked out at the crowd on the street. "Will fifteen minutes be enough for you to slip off in all the confusion?"

"If it's all the same to you," I said. "Could you say I disappeared in a strange and mysterious way when your back was turned?"

He laughed at this. "Don't see why not. You need more than fifteen minutes on account of it being mysterious and all?"

"Ten should be a great plenty," I said as I unpacked my lute case and travelsack from Greytail and handed the mayor the reins. "You'd be doing me a favor if you took care of him until Bil is up and about," I said.

"You leaving your horse?" he asked.

"He's just lost his." I shrugged. "And we Ruh are used to walking. I wouldn't know what to do with a horse, anyway," I said half-honestly.

The big man gripped the reins and gave me a long look, as if he wasn't quite sure what to make of me. "Is there anything we can do for you?" he asked at last.

"Remember it was bandits who took them," I said as I turned to leave. "And remember it was one of the Edema Ruh who brought them back."

Interlude—Close to Forgetting

KVOTHE HELD UP A hand to Chronicler. "Let's take a moment, shall we?" He looked around the dark inn. "I've let myself get a little caught up in the story. I should tend to a few things before it gets any later."

The innkeeper came stiffly to his feet and stretched. He lit a candle at the fireplace and moved around the inn, lighting the lamps one by one, driving back the dark by slow degrees.

"I was focused rather closely myself," Chronicler said, standing up and stretching. "What time is it?"

"Late," Bast said. "I'm hungry."

Chronicler looked out the dark window into the street. "I'd have thought you'd have had at least a few folks in for dinner by now. You pulled a good crowd for lunch."

Kvothe nodded. "We would've seen a few of my regulars if not for Shep's funeral."

"Ah." Chronicler looked down. "I'd forgotten. Is that something I've kept you two from attending?"

Kvothe lit the last lamp behind the bar and blew out his candle. "Not really," he said. "Bast and I aren't from around these parts. And they're practical folk. They know I have a business to run, such as it is."

"And you don't get along with Abbe Leodin," Bast said.

"And I don't get along with the local priest," Kvothe admitted. "But you should make an appearance, Bast. It will seem odd if you don't."

Bast's eyes darted around nervously. "I don't want to leave, Reshi."

Kvothe smiled warmly at him. "You should, Bast. Shep was a good man, go have a drink to send him off. In fact . . ." He bent and rummaged around under the bar for a moment before coming up with a bottle. "Here. A fine old bottle of brand. Better stuff than anyone around here asks for. Go share it around." He set it on the bar with a solid sound.

Bast took an involuntary step forward, his face conflicted. "But Reshi, I . . ."

"Pretty girls dancing, Bast," Kvothe said, his voice low and soothing. "Someone on the fiddle and all of them just glad to be alive. Kicking up their skirts to the music. Laughing and a little tipsy. Their cheeks all rosy and ready to be kissed. . . ." He gave the heavy brown bottle a nudge, and it slid down the bar toward his student. "You're my ambassador to the town. I may be stuck minding the shop, but you can be there and make my apologies."

Bast closed his hand around the neck of the bottle. "I'll have one drink," he said, his voice thick with resolve. "And one dance. And one kiss with Katie Miller. And maybe another with the Widow Creel. But that's all." He looked Kvothe in the eye. "I'll only be gone half an hour. . . ."

Kvothe gave a warm smile. "I have things to tend to, Bast. I'll cobble together dinner and we'll give our friend's hand a bit of a rest."

Bast grinned and picked up the bottle. "Two dances then!" He bolted for the door, and when he opened it the wind gusted around him, swirling his hair wildly. "Save me something to eat!" He shouted over his shoulder.

The door banged shut.

Chronicler gave the innkeeper a curious look.

Kvothe gave a small shrug. "He was getting too tangled up in the story. He can't feel a thing halfway. A little time away will give him some perspective. Besides, I do have dinner to prepare, even if it's only for three."

The scribe brought a grimy piece of cloth out of his leather satchel and looked at it with some distaste. "I don't suppose I could trouble you for a clean rag?" he asked.

Kvothe nodded and brought out a white linen cloth from beneath the bar. "Is there anything else you need?"

Chronicler stood and walked over to the bar. "If you had some strong spirits it would be a great help," he said, sounding slightly embarrassed. "I hate to ask, but when I was robbed . . ."

Kvothe waved the comment away. "Don't be ridiculous," he said. "I should have asked you yesterday if there was anything you needed." He moved out from behind the bar toward the basement stairs. "I'm assuming wood alcohol would work best?"

Chronicler nodded, and Kvothe disappeared into the basement. The scribe picked up the crisply folded square of linen and rubbed it idly between his fingers. Then his eyes wandered up to the sword hanging high on the wall behind the bar. The grey metal of the blade was striking against the dark wood of the mounting board.

Kvothe came back up the steps carrying a small clear bottle. "Is there any-thing else you need? I have a good stock of paper and ink here too."

"It may come to that by tomorrow," Chronicler said. "I've used up most of my paper. But I can grind more ink tonight."

"Don't put yourself to the trouble," Kvothe said easily. "I have several bot-tles of fine Aruean ink."

"True Aruean ink?" Chronicler asked, surprised.

Kvothe gave a broad smile and nodded.

"That's terribly kind of you," Chronicler said, relaxing a bit. "I'll admit I wasn't looking forward to spending an hour grinding tonight." He gathered up the clear bottle and cloth, then paused. "Would you mind if I asked you a question? Unofficially, as it were?"

A smirk curled the corner of Kvothe's mouth. "Very well then, unofficially."

"I can't help notice that your description of Caesura doesn't . . ." Chronicler hesitated. "Well, it doesn't quite seem to match the actual sword itself." His eyes flicked to the sword behind the bar. "The hand guard isn't what you described."

Kvothe gave a wide grin. "Well you're just sharp as anything, aren't you?"

"I don't mean to imply—" Chronicler said quickly, looking embarrassed.

Kvothe laughed a rich warm laugh. The sound of it tumbled around the room, and for a moment the inn didn't feel empty at all. "No. You're abso-lutely right." He turned to look at the sword. "This isn't . . . what did the boy call it this morning?" His eyes went distant for a moment, then he smiled again. "Kaysera. The poet killer."

"I was just curious," Chronicler said apologetically.

"Am I supposed to be offended that you're paying attention?" Kvothe laughed again. "What fun is there in telling a story if nobody's listening?" He rubbed his hands together eagerly. "Right then. Dinner. What would you like? Hot or cold? Soup or stew? I'm a dab hand at pudding too."

They settled on something simple to avoid restoking the stove in the kitchen. Kvothe moved briskly around the inn, gathering what was needed. He hummed to himself as he fetched cold mutton and half a hard, sharp cheese from the basement.

"These will be a nice surprise for Bast." Kvothe grinned at Chronicler as he brought out a jar of brined olives from the pantry. "He can't know we have them or he'd have eaten them already." He untied his apron, pulling it off over his head. "I think we have a few tomatoes left in the garden too."

Kvothe returned after several minutes with his apron wrapped into a bun-dle. He was spattered with rain and his hair was in wild disarray. He wore a boyish grin, and at that moment he looked very little like the somber, slow-moving innkeeper.

"It can't quite decide if it wants to storm," he said as he set his apron on the bar, carefully removing the tomatoes. "But if it makes up its mind, we're in for a wagon-tipper tonight." He began to hum absentmindedly while he cut and arranged everything on a broad wooden platter.

The door of the Waystone opened and a sudden gust of wind made the lamplight flicker. Two soldiers came in, hunched against the weather, their swords sticking out like tails behind them. Dark spatters of rain spotted the fabric of their blue and white tabards.

They dropped their heavy packs, and the shorter of the two pressed his shoulder to the door, forcing it closed against the wind.

"God's teeth," said the taller one, straightening his clothes. "It's a bad night to be caught in the open." He was bald on top, with a thick black beard that was flat as a spade. He looked at Kvothe, "Ho boy!" he said cheerfully. "We were glad to see your light. Run and fetch the owner, would you? We need to have a word with him."

Kvothe picked his apron up off the bar and ducked his head into it. "That would be me," he said, clearing his throat as he tied the strings around his waist. He ran his hands through his tousled hair, smoothing it down.

The bearded soldier peered at him, then shrugged. "Fair enough. Any chance of us getting a spot of dinner?"

The innkeeper gestured to the empty room. "It didn't seem worth putting the kettle on tonight," he said. "But we've got what you see here."

The two soldiers strode to the bar. The blonde one ran his hands through his curly hair, shaking a few drops of rain out of it. "This town looks deader than ditchwater," he said. "We didn't see a single light but this."

"Long harvest day," the innkeeper said. "And there's a wake tonight at one of the nearby farms. The four of us are probably the only folk in town right now." He rubbed his hands together briskly. "Can I interest you fine folk in a drink to take off the chill?" He brought out a bottle of wine and sat it on the bar with a solid, satisfying sound.

"Well that's a difficulty," the blonde soldier said with a bit of an embarrassed smile. "I'd dearly love a drink, but my friend and I just took the king's coin." He reached into his pocket and brought out a bright gold coin. "This is all the money I have on me. I don't suppose you have enough to break a whole royal, would you?"

"I'm stuck with mine too," the bearded soldier groused. "Most money I've ever had, but it don't spend well in a lump. Most of the towns we've been through could barely make change for ha'penny." He chuckled at his own joke.

"I should be able to help you out with that," the innkeeper said easily.

The two soldiers exchanged a look. The blonde one nodded.

"Right then." The blonde soldier put the coin back in his pocket. "Here's the truth. We aren't really going to be stopping for the night." He picked up a piece of cheese off the bar and took a bite. "And we aren't going to be paying for anything either."

"Ah," the innkeeper said. "I see."

"And if you've got enough money in your purse to change out two gold royals," the bearded one said eagerly, "then we'll have that off you as well."

The blonde soldier spread his hands in a calming gesture. "Now this don't need to be any sort of ugly thing. We aren't bad folk. You pass over your purse and we go on our way. No folk get hurt, and nothing gets wrecked. It's bound to sting a bit." He raised an eyebrow at the innkeeper. "But a little sting beats hell out of getting yourself killed. Am I right?"

The bearded soldier looked over at where Chronicler sat near the hearth. "This hain't got nothing to do with you, either," he said grimly, his beard waggling as he spoke. "We don't want anything of yours. You just stay sat where you're at and don't get feisty on us."

Chronicler shot a glance to the man behind the bar, but the innkeeper's eyes were fixed on the two soldiers.

The blonde one took another bite of cheese while his eyes wandered around the inn. "Young man like you is doing pretty well for himself. You'll be doing just as well after we're gone. But if you start trouble, we'll feed you your teeth, wreck up the place, and you'll still be out your purse." He dropped the rest of the cheese on the bar and clapped his hands together briskly. He smiled. "So, are we all going to be civilized folk?"

"That seems reasonable," Kvothe said as he walked out from behind the bar. He moved slowly and carefully, the way you would approach a skittish horse. "I'm certainly no barbarian." Kvothe reached down and removed his purse from his pocket. He held it out in one hand.

The blonde soldier walked over to him, swaggering just a bit. He took hold of the purse and hefted it appreciatively. He turned to smile at his friend. "You see, I told—"

In a smooth motion, Kvothe stepped forward and struck the man hard in the jaw. The soldier staggered and fell to one knee. The purse arced through the air and hit the floorboards with a solid metallic thud.

Before the soldier could do more than shake his head, Kvothe stepped forward and calmly kicked him in the shoulder. Not a sharp kick of the sort that breaks bones, but a hard kick that sent him sprawling backward. The man landed hard on the floor, rolling to a stop in a messy tangle of arms and legs.

The other soldier stepped past his friend, grinning wide under his beard.

He was taller than Kvothe, and his fists were broad knots of scar and knuckle. "Right cully," he said, dark satisfaction in his voice. "You're gettin' a kickin' now."

He snapped out a quick punch, but Kvothe stepped aside and kicked out sharply, hitting the soldier just above the knee. The bearded man grunted in surprise, stumbling slightly. Then Kvothe stepped close, caught the bearded man's shoulder, gripped his wrist, and twisted his outstretched arm at an awkward angle.

The big man was forced to bend over, grimacing in pain. Then he jerked his arm roughly out of the innkeeper's grip. Kvothe had half a moment to look startled before the soldier's elbow caught him in the temple.

The innkeeper staggered backward, trying to gain a little distance and a moment to clear his head. But the soldier followed close after him, fists raised, waiting for an opening.

Before Kvothe could regain his balance, the soldier stepped close and drove a fist hard into his gut. The innkeeper let out a pained huff of air, and as he started to double over the soldier swung his other fist into the side of the innkeeper's face, snapping Kvothe's head to the side and sending him reeling.

Kvothe managed to keep his feet by grabbing a nearby table for support. Blinking, he threw a wild punch to keep the bearded man at a distance. But the soldier merely brushed it aside and caught hold of the innkeeper's wrist in one huge hand, easy as a father might grab hold of a wayward child in the street.

Blood running down the side of his face, Kvothe struggled to free his wrist. Dazed, he made a quick motion with both hands, then repeated it, trying to pull away. His eyes half-focused and dull with confusion, he looked down at his wrist and made the motion again, but his hands merely scrabbled uselessly at the soldier's scarred fist.

The bearded soldier eyed the stupefied innkeeper with amused curiosity, then reached out and slapped him hard on the side of the head. "You're almost a bit of a scrapper, boy," he said. "You actually stuck one on me."

Behind them, the blonde soldier was slowly getting to his feet. "Little bastard sucker-punched me."

The big soldier yanked the innkeeper's wrist so he stumbled forward. "Say you're sorry, cully."

The innkeeper blinked blearily, opened his mouth as if he were about to speak, then staggered. Or rather, he seemed to stagger. Halfway through the stumbling motion became deliberate, and the innkeeper stomped down hard with the heel of his foot, aiming at the soldier's boot. At the same time he snapped his forehead down at the bearded man's nose.

But the big man merely laughed, moving his head to the side as he jerked the innkeeper off balance again by his wrist. "None of that," he chided, back-handing Kvothe across the face.

The innkeeper let out a yelp and lifted a hand to his bleeding nose. The soldier grinned and casually drove a knee hard into the innkeeper's groin.

Kvothe doubled over, first gasping soundlessly, then making a series of choked retching noises.

Moving casually, the soldier let go of Kvothe's wrist, then reached out and picked up the bottle of wine from the bar. Gripping it by the neck, he swung it like a club. When it hit the side of the innkeeper's head, it made a solid, almost metallic sound.

Kvothe crumpled bonelessly to the floor.

The big man looked at the bottle of wine curiously before setting it back on the bar. Then he bent, grabbed the innkeeper's shirt, and dragged his limp body out onto the open floor. He nudged the unconscious body with a foot until it stirred sluggishly.

"Said I'd give you a kickin', boy," the soldier grunted, and drove his foot hard into Kvothe's side.

The blonde soldier walked over, rubbing at the side of his face. "Had to get all clever, didn't you?" he said, spitting on the floor. He drew back his boot and landed a hard kick of his own. The innkeeper drew a sharp, hissing breath, but made no other sound.

"And you . . ." The bearded soldier pointed a thick finger at Chronicler. "I've got more than one boot. Would you like to see the other? I've already skint my knuckles. It's no bother to me if you want to lose a couple teeth."

Chronicler looked around and seemed genuinely surprised to find himself standing. He lowered himself slowly back into his chair.

The blonde soldier limped off to reclaim the purse from where it had fallen, while the big bearded man remained standing over Kvothe. "I suppose you figured you had to try," he said to the crumpled body, giving him another solid kick in the side. "Damn fool. Pasty little innkeep against two of the king's own." He shook his head and spat again. "Honestly, who do you think you are?"

Curled on the floor, Kvothe began to make a low, rhythmic sound. It was a dry, quiet noise that scratched around the edges of the room. Kvothe paused as he drew a painful breath.

The bearded soldier frowned and kicked him again. "I asked you a question, cully . . ."

The innkeeper made the same noise again, louder than before. Only then did it become obvious that he was laughing. Each low, broken chuckle sounded like he was coughing up a piece of shattered glass. Despite that, it was a laugh, full of dark amusement, as if the red-haired man had heard a joke that only he could understand.

It went on for some time. The bearded soldier shrugged and drew back his foot again.

Chronicler cleared his throat and the two men turned to look at him. "In the interest of keeping things civilized," he said. "I feel I should mention that the innkeeper sent his assistant out on an errand. He should be back soon. . . ."

The bearded soldier slapped his companion on the chest with the back of his hand. "He's right. Let's get out of here."

"Wait a moment," the blonde soldier said. He hurried back to the bar and snatched the bottle of wine. "Right, let's go."

The bearded soldier grinned and went behind the bar, stepping on the innkeeper's body rather than over it. He grabbed a random bottle, knocking over half a dozen others as he did so. They rolled and spun on the counter between the two huge barrels, a tall, sapphire-colored one slowly toppling over the edge to shatter on the floor.

In less than a minute the men had gathered up their packs and were out the door.

Chronicler hurried over to where Kvothe lay on the wooden floor. The red-haired man was already struggling into a sitting position.

"Well that was embarrassing," Kvothe said. He touched his bloody face and looked at his fingers. He chuckled again, a jagged, joyless sound. "Forgot who I was there for a minute."

"Are you alright?" Chronicler asked.

Kvothe touched his scalp speculatively. "I'll need a stitch or two, I suspect."

"What can I do to help?" Chronicler asked, shifting his weight from foot to foot.

"Don't hover over me." Kvothe pushed himself awkwardly to his feet, then slumped into one of the tall stools at the bar. "If you want, you can fetch me a glass of water. And maybe a wet cloth."

Chronicler scurried back into the kitchen. There was the sound of frantic rummaging followed by several things falling to the ground.

Kvothe closed his eyes and leaned heavily against the bar.

"Why is the door open?" Bast called as he stepped through the doorway. "It's cold as a witch's tit in here." He froze, his expression stricken. "Reshi! What happened? What . . . I . . . What happened?"

"Ah Bast," Kvothe said. "Close the door, would you?"

Bast hurried over, a numb expression on his face. Kvothe sat in a stool at the bar, his face swollen and bloody. Chronicler stood next to him, dabbing awkwardly at the innkeeper's scalp with a damp cloth.

"I might need to prevail on you for a few stitches, Bast," Kvothe said. "If it wouldn't be too much trouble."

"Reshi," Bast repeated. "What happened?"

"Devan and I got into a bit of an argument," Kvothe said, nodding at the scribe, "about the proper use of the subjunctive mood. It got a little heated toward the end."

Chronicler looked up at Bast, then blanched and took several quick steps backward. "He's joking!" he said quickly, holding up his hands. "It was soldiers!"

Kvothe chuckled painfully to himself. There was blood on his teeth.

Bast looked around the empty taproom. "What did you do with them?"

"Not much, Bast," the innkeeper said. "They're probably miles away by now."

"Was there something wrong with them, Reshi? Like the one last night?" Bast asked.

"Just soldiers, Bast," Kvothe said. "Just two of the king's own."

Bast's face went ashen. "What?" he asked. "Reshi, why did you let them do this?"

Kvothe gave Bast an incredulous look. He gave a brief, bitter laugh, then stopped with a wince, sucking air through his teeth. "Well they seemed like such clean and virtuous boys," he said, his voice mocking. "I thought, why not let these nice fellows rob me then beat me to a pulp?"

Bast expression was full of dismay. "But you—"

Kvothe wiped away the blood that was threatening to run into his eye, then looked at Bast as if he were the stupidest creature drawing breath in the entire world. "What?" he demanded. "What do you want me to say?"

"Two soldiers, Reshi?"

"Yes!" Kvothe shouted. "Not even two! Apparently one thick-fisted thug is all it takes to beat me half to death!" He glared furiously at Bast, throwing up his arms. "What is it going to take to shut you up? Do you want a story? Do you want to hear the details?"

Bast took a step backward at the outburst. His face went even paler, his expression panicked.

Kvothe let his arms fall heavily to his sides. "Quit expecting me to be something I'm not," he said, still breathing hard. He hunched his shoulders and rubbed at his eyes, smearing blood across his face. He let his head sag wearily. "God's mother, why can't you just leave me alone?"

Bast stood as still as a startled hart, his eyes wide.

Silence flooded the room, thick and bitter as a lungful of smoke.

Kvothe drew a slow breath, the only motion in the room. "I'm sorry Bast," he said without looking up. "I'm just in a little pain right now. It got the better of me. Give me a moment and I'll have it sorted out."

Still looking down, Kvothe closed his eyes and drew several slow, shallow breaths. When he looked up, his expression was chagrined. "I'm sorry Bast," he said. "I didn't mean to snap at you."

A touch of the color returned to Bast's cheeks, and some of the tension left his shoulders as he gave a nervous smile.

Kvothe took the damp cloth from Chronicler and wiped the blood away from his eye again. "I'm sorry I interrupted you before, Bast. What is it you were about ask me?"

Bast hesitated, then said. "You killed five scrael not three days ago, Reshi." He waved toward the door. "What's some thug compared to that?"

"I picked the time and place for the scrael rather carefully, Bast," Kvothe said. "And I didn't exactly dance away unscathed, either."

Chronicler looked up, surprised. "You were hurt?" he asked. "I didn't know. You didn't look it. . . ."

A small, wry smile twisted the corner of Kvothe's mouth. "Old habits die hard," he said. "I do have a reputation to maintain. Besides, we heroes are only hurt in properly dramatic ways. It rather ruins the story if you find out Bast had to knit about ten feet of stitches into me after the fight."

Realization broke over Bast's face like a sunrise. "Of course!" he said, his voice thick with relief. "I forgot. You're still hurt from the scrael. I knew it had to be something like that."

Kvothe looked at the floor, every line of his body sagging and weary. "Bast . . ." he began.

"I knew it, Reshi," Bast said emphatically. "There's no way some thug could get the better of you."

Kvothe drew a shallow breath, then let it out in a rush. "I'm sure that's it, Bast," he said easily. "I expect I could have taken them both if I'd been fresh."

Bast's expression grew uncertain again. He turned to face Chronicler. "How could you let this happen?" he demanded.

"It's not his fault, Bast," Kvothe said absentmindedly. "I started the fight." He put a few fingers into his mouth and felt around gingerly. His fingers came out of his mouth bright with blood. "I expect I'm going to lose this tooth," he mused.

"You will not lose your tooth, Reshi," Bast said fiercely. "You will *not*."

Kvothe made a slight motion with his shoulders, as if trying to shrug without moving any more of his body than he needed to. "It doesn't matter much in the grand scheme of things, Bast." He pressed the cloth to his scalp then looked at it. "I probably won't need those stitches, either." He pushed himself upright on the stool. "Let's have our dinner and get back to the story." He raised an eyebrow at Chronicler. "If you're still up for it, of course."

Chronicler stared at him blankly.

"Reshi," Bast said, worried. "You're a mess." He reached out. "Let me look at your eyes."

"I'm not concussed, Bast," Kvothe said, irritated. "I've got four broken ribs, a ringing in my ears, and a loose tooth. I have a few minor scalp wounds that look more serious than they really are. My nose is bloody but not broken, and tomorrow I will be a vast tapestry of bruises."

Kvothe gave the faint shrug again. "Still, I've had worse. Besides, they reminded me of something I was close to forgetting. I should probably thank them for that." He prodded at his jaw speculatively and worked his tongue around in his mouth. "Perhaps not a terribly warm thanks."

"Reshi, you need stitches," Bast said. "And you need to let me do something about that tooth."

Kvothe climbed off the stool. "I'll just chew on the other side for a few days."

Bast took hold of Kvothe's arm. His eyes were hard and dark. "Sit down Reshi." It was nothing like a request. His voice was low and sudden, like a throb of distant thunder. "Sit. Down."

Kvothe sat.

Chronicler nodded approvingly and turned to Bast. "What can I do to help?"

"Stay out of my way," Bast said brusquely. "And keep him in this chair until I get back." He strode upstairs.

There was a moment of silence.

"So," Chronicler said. "Subjunctive mood."

"At best," Kvothe said, "it is a pointless thing. It needlessly complicates the language. It offends me."

"Oh come now," Chronicler said, sounding slightly offended. "The subjunctive is the heart of the hypothetical. In the right hands . . ." He broke off as Bast stormed back into the room, scowling and carrying a small wooden box.

"Bring me water," Bast said imperiously to Chronicler. "Fresh from the rain barrel, not from the pump. Then I need milk from the icebox, some warmed honey, and a broad bowl. Then clean up this mess and stay out of my way."

Bast washed the cut on Kvothe's scalp, then threaded one of his own hairs through a bone needle and laced four tight stitches through the innkeeper's skin more smoothly than a seamstress.

"Open your mouth," Bast said, then peered inside, frowning while he prodded one of the back teeth with a finger. He nodded to himself.

Bast handed Kvothe the glass of water. "Rinse out your mouth, Reshi. Do it a couple times and spit the water back into the cup."

Kvothe did. When he finished the water was red as wine.

Chronicler returned with a bottle of milk. Bast sniffed it, then poured a splash into a wide pottery bowl. He added a dollop of honey and swirled it around to mix it. Finally, he dipped his finger into the glass of bloody water, drew it out, and let a single drop fall into the bowl.

Bast swirled it again and handed Kvothe the bowl. "Take a mouthful of this," he said. "Don't swallow it. Hold it in your mouth until I tell you."

His expression curious, Kvothe tipped the bowl and took a mouthful of the milk.

Bast took a mouthful as well. Then he closed his eyes for a long moment, a look of intense concentration on his face. Then he opened his eyes. He brought the bowl close to Kvothe's mouth and pointed into it.

Kvothe spat out his mouthful of milk. It was a perfect, creamy white.

Bast brought the bowl to his own mouth and spat. It was a frothy pink.

Kvothe's eyes widened. "Bast," he said. "You shouldn't—"

Bast made a sharp gesture with one hand, his eyes still hard. "I did not ask for your opinion, Reshi."

The innkeeper looked down, uncomfortable. "It's more than you should do, Bast."

The dark young man reached out and laid a gentle hand on the side of his master's face. For a moment he looked tired, weary through to the bone. Bast shook his head slowly, wearing an expression of bemused dismay. "You are an idiot, Reshi."

Bast drew his hand back, and the weariness was gone. He pointed across the bar where Chronicler stood watching. "Bring the food." He pointed at Kvothe. "Tell the story."

Then he spun on his heel, walked back to his chair by the hearth, and lowered himself into it as if it were a throne. He clapped his hands twice, sharply. "Entertain me!" he said with a wide, mad smile. And even from where the others stood near the bar, they could see the blood on his teeth.

CHAPTER ONE HUNDRED THIRTY-SEVEN

Questions

WHILE THE MAYOR OF Levinshir seemed to approve of how I'd handled the false troupers, I knew matters weren't as simple as that. According to the iron law, I was guilty of at least three egregious crimes, any one of which would be enough to see me hanged.

Unfortunately, everyone in Levinshir knew my name and description, and I worried the story might run ahead of me on the road. If that happened, I could easily come to a town where the local constables would do their duty and lock me up until a traveling magistrate arrived to judge my case.

So I made my best speed toward Severen. I put in two days of hard walking, then paid for a seat on a coach heading south. Rumor travels fast, but you can keep ahead of it if you're willing to ride hard and lose a little sleep.

After three days of bone-jarring ride, I arrived in Severen. The coach entered the city by the eastern gate, and for the first time I saw the gibbet Bredon had told me about. The sight of the bleached bones in the iron cage did not ease my anxieties. The Maer had put a man in there for simple banditry. What might he do to someone who had slaughtered nine traveling players on the road?

I was sorely tempted to head straight to the Four Tapers, where I hoped to find Denna despite what the Cthaeh had said. But I was covered in several days of grime and sweat. I needed a bath and a brush before I spoke with anyone.

As soon as I was inside the Maer's estate I sent a ring and note to Stapes, knowing it would be the quickest way to get in touch with the Maer for a private conversation. I made it back to my room with little delay, though it meant brushing roughly past a few courtiers in the halls. I had just set down my travelsack and sent runners for hot water when Stapes appeared in the doorway.

"Young Master Kvothe!" he beamed, grabbing my hand to shake it. "It's good to have you back. Lord and lady, but I've been worried about you."

His enthusiasm wrung a tired smile from me. "It's good to be back, Stapes. Have I missed much?"

"Much?" He laughed. "The wedding for one."

"Wedding?" I asked, but I knew the answer as soon as I said it. "The Maer's wedding?"

Stapes nodded excitedly. "Oh, it was a grand thing. It's a shame you had to be gone for it, considering." He gave a knowing look, but didn't say anything else. Stapes was always very discreet.

"They didn't waste much time, did they?"

"It's been two months since the betrothal," Stapes said with a hint of reproach. "Not a bit less than proper." I saw him relax a bit, and he gave me a wink. "Which isn't to say they weren't both a bit eager."

I chuckled as runner boys came through the open door with buckets of steaming water. The splashing as they began to fill the bath was like sweet music.

The manservant watched them leave, then leaned close and said in a quieter voice, "You'll be glad to hear our other unresolved matter has been tended to properly."

I looked at him blankly, searching through my memory for what he might be referring to. So much had happened since I'd left. . . .

Stapes saw my expression. "Caudicus," he said, his mouth twisting bitterly around the name. "Dagon brought him back only two days after you left. He'd gone to ground not ten miles from the city."

"So close?" I asked, surprised.

Stapes nodded grimly. "He was tucked away in a farmhouse like a badger in a burrow. He killed four of the Maer's personal guard and cost Dagon an eye. In the end they only caught him by setting fire to the place."

"And what happened then?" I asked. "Not a trial, certainly."

"The matter was tended to," Stapes repeated. "Properly." He said the last with a great weight of grim finality. His normally kind eyes were narrow with hate. In that moment the round-faced little man looked very little like a grocer at all.

I remembered Alveron calmly saying, "take off his thumbs." Given what I knew of Alveron's swift and decisive anger, I doubted anyone would ever see Caudicus again.

"Did the Maer manage to uncover why?" Even though I spoke softly, I left the rest unsaid, knowing Stapes would not approve of my mentioning the poisoning openly.

"It's not my place to say," Stapes said carefully. His tone was slightly offended, as if I should know better than to ask him such things.

I let the subject go, knowing that I wouldn't be able to get anything else out of Stapes. "You'd be doing me a favor if you could deliver something to the Maer for me," I said, walking to where I'd dropped my worn travelsack. I rooted through it until I found the Maer's lockbox down near the bottom.

I held it out to Stapes. "I'm not sure what's in it," I said. "But it's got his crest on the top. And it's heavy. I hope it might be some of the taxes that were stolen." I smiled. "Tell him it's a wedding present."

Stapes took hold of the box, smiling. "I'm sure he'll be delighted."

Three more runners appeared, but only two of them ran past with steaming buckets. The third went to Stapes and handed him a note. There was more splashing in the other room, and all three of the boys left again, stealing glances at me

Stapes skimmed the note then looked up at me. "The Maer is hoping it would be convenient for you to meet him in the garden at fifth bell," he said.

The garden meant polite conversation. If the Maer had wanted a serious discussion he would have summoned me to his rooms, or paid me a call through the secret passage that connected his rooms with mine.

I looked at the clock on the wall. It wasn't a sympathy clock of the sort I was used to at the University. This was a harmony clock, swinging pendulum and all. Beautiful machinery, but not nearly as accurate. Its hands showed a quarter to the hour.

"Is that clock fast, Stapes?" I asked hopefully. Fifteen minutes was barely enough time for me to strip out of my road clothes and lace myself into some sufficiently decorous court finery. But given the layers of dirt and sour sweat that covered me, that would be as pointless as tying a silk ribbon around a steaming cowpat.

Stapes looked over my shoulder, then checked a small gear watch he kept in his pocket. "It looks about five minutes slow, actually."

I rubbed my face, considering my options. I wasn't simply mussed from a day's travel. I was filthy. I had walked hard under the summer sun, then spent days trapped in a stifling-hot carriage. While the Maer was not one to judge things entirely by appearances, he did value propriety. I would not make a good impression if I showed up reeking and filthy.

Unbidden, the memory of the iron gibbet rose up in my mind, and I decided I couldn't risk making a bad impression. Not with the news I brought. "Stapes, I won't be ready for at least an hour. I could meet with him at sixth bell if he would like."

Stapes' expression turned stiff and affronted. Its message was clear. You simply didn't request a different meeting time with the Maer Alveron. He asked. You came. That was the way of things.

"Stapes," I said as gently as I could. "Look at me. *Smell* me. I've come three hundred miles in the last span of days. I'm not going to go strolling in the garden covered in road dust and reeking like a barbarian."

Stapes' mouth firmed into a frown. "I'll tell him you're otherwise occupied."

More steaming buckets arrived. "Tell him the truth, Stapes," I said as I began to unbutton my shirt. "I'm sure he'll understand."

After I was scrubbed, brushed, and properly dressed, I sent the Maer my golden ring and a card that said, "Private conversation at your earliest convenience."

Within an hour a runner returned with a card from the Maer saying, "Await my summons."

I waited. I sent a runner to fetch dinner, then waited the rest of the evening. The following day passed without any further message. And, because I didn't know when Alveron's summons might come, I was effectively trapped in my rooms again, waiting for his ring.

It was nice to have time to catch up on my sleep and have a second bath. But I was worried about the news from Levinshir catching up with me. The fact that I couldn't make my way down to Severen-Low to look for Denna was a vast irritation as well.

It was the sort of silent rebuke all too common in courtly settings. The Maer's message was clear: *When I call, you come. My terms or not at all.*

It was childish in the way only the nobility can be. Still, there was nothing to be done. So I sent my silver ring to Bredon. He arrived in time to share supper with me and caught me up on the season's worth of gossip I'd missed. Court rumor can be terribly insipid stuff, but Bredon skimmed the cream off the top for me.

Most of it centered around the Maer's whirlwind courtship and marriage to the Lackless heir. They were besotted with each other, apparently. Many suspected a child might already be on the way. The royal court in Renere was busy too. The Prince Regent Alaitis had been killed in a duel, sending much of the southern farrel into chaos as various nobility did their best to capitalize on the death of such a highly ranked member of the court.

There were rumors too. The Maer's men had taken care of some bandits off in a remote piece of the Eld. They'd been waylaying tax collectors, apparently. There was grumbling in the north, where folk had to suffer a second visit from the Maer's collectors. But at least the roads were clear again, and those responsible were dead.

Bredon also mentioned an interesting rumor of a young man who had gone to visit Felurian and come back more or less intact, though slightly fae around the edges. It wasn't a court rumor, exactly. More the sort of thing you heard in a taproom. A low sort of rumor no highborn person would ever deign to lend an ear to. His dark, owlish eyes glittered merrily as he spoke.

I agreed that such stories were indeed quite low, and beneath the notice of fine persons such as ourselves. My cloak? It was rather fine, was it not? I couldn't remember where exactly I'd had it tailored. Somewhere exotic. By the way, I'd heard quite an interesting song the other day on the subject of Felurian. Would he like to hear it?

We also played tak, of course. Despite the fact that I had spent a long time away from the board, Bredon said my playing was much improved. It seemed I was learning how to play a beautiful game.

Needless to say, when Alveron sent his next summons, I came. I was tempted to arrive a few minutes late, but I resisted, knowing no good could come of it.

The Maer was walking about on his own when I met him in the garden. He stood straight and tall, looking for all the world as if he'd never needed to lean on my arm or use a walking stick.

"Kvothe," he smiled warmly. "I'm glad you could find time to visit me."

"Always my pleasure, your grace."

"Shall we walk?" he asked. "The view is pleasant from the south bridge this time of day."

I fell into step beside him, and we began to wind our way among the carefully tended hedges.

"I could not help but notice that you are armed," he remarked, disapproval heavy on his voice.

My hand went unconsciously to Caesura. It was at my hip now, rather than over my shoulder. "Is there aught amiss with that, your grace? I have understood that all men keep the right to gird themselves in Vintas."

"It is hardly *proper*." He stressed the word.

"I understand that in the king's court in Renere, there's not a gentleman would dare be seen without a sword."

"Well-spoken as you are, you are no gentleman," Alveron pointed out coolly, "as you would do well to remember."

I said nothing.

"Besides, it is a barbarian custom, and one that will bring the king to grief in time. No matter what the custom in Renere, in my city, my house, and my garden, you will not come before me armed." He turned to look at me with hard eyes.

"I apologize if I have given any offense, your grace." I stopped and offered him a more earnest bow than the one I'd given before.

My show of submission seemed to appease him. He smiled and laid a hand on my shoulder. "There's no need for all that. Come, look at the mourning-fire. The leaves will be turning soon."

We walked for a piece of an hour, chatting amiably about small nothings. I was unfailingly polite and Alveron's mood continued to improve. If catering to his ego kept me in his good graces, it was a small price to pay for his patronage.

"I must say that marriage suits your grace."

"Thank you." He nodded graciously. "I have found it much to my liking."

"And your health continues well?" I asked, pressing the boundaries of public conversation.

"Exceeding well," he said. "Another benefit of married life, no doubt." He gave me a look that told me he would not appreciate further inquiry, at least not in so public a place as this.

We continued our walk, nodding to the nobles we passed. The Maer chatted on about trivialities, rumors in the court. I played along, filling my part in the conversation. But the truth was, I needed to have done with this so we could have an earnest conversation in private.

But I also knew Alveron could not be rushed into a discussion. Our talks had a ritual pattern. If I violated that, I would do nothing but annoy him. So I bided my time, smelled the flowers, and pretended interest in the gossip of the court.

After a quarter hour, there was a characteristic pause in the conversation. Next we would engage in an argument. After that we could go somewhere private enough to speak of important matters.

"I have always thought," Alveron said at last, introducing the topic of our discussion, "that everyone has a question that rests in the center of who they are."

"How do you mean, your grace?"

"I believe everyone has some question that drives them. A question that keeps them awake nights. A question they worry like a dog with an old bone. If you understand a man's question, it brings you closer to understanding the man himself." He looked sideways at me, half-smiling. "Or so I have always believed."

I thought on it for a moment. "I would have to agree with you, your grace."

Alveron raised an eyebrow at this. "As easy as that?" He sounded slightly disappointed. "I was expecting a bit of a struggle from you."

I shook my head, glad for the easy opportunity to introduce a topic of my own. "I've been worrying at a question for some years now, and I expect I will worry it some few years more. So what you say makes a perfect sense to me."

"Really?" he said hungrily. "What is it?"

I considered telling him the truth. About my search for the Chandrian and the death of my troupe. But there was no real chance of that. That secret still sat in my heart, heavy as a great smooth stone. It was too personal a thing to tell someone as clever as the Maer. What's more, it would reveal my Edema Ruh blood, something I had not made public knowledge in the Maer's court. The Maer knew I wasn't nobility, but he didn't know my blood was quite so low as that.

"It must be a heavy question for you to take so long in weighing it," Alveron joked as I hesitated. "Come, I insist. In fact I will offer you a trade, a question for a question. Mayhap we will help each other to an answer."

I could hardly hope for better encouragement than that. I thought for a moment, choosing my words carefully. "Where are the Amyr?"

"The bloody-handed Amyr," Alveron mused softly to himself. He glanced sideways at me. "I assume you are not asking where their bodies are bestowed?"

"No, your grace," I said somberly.

His face turned thoughtful. "Interesting." I drew a relieved breath. I had half expected him to give a flip response, to tell me the Amyr were centuries dead. Instead he said, "I studied the Amyr a great deal when I was younger, you know."

"Truly, your grace?" I said, surprised by my own good luck.

He looked at me, a ghost of a smile touching his lips. "Not *that* surprising. I wanted to *be* one of the Amyr when I was a boy." He looked ever so slightly embarrassed. "Not all the stories are dark, you know. They did important things. They made hard choices that no one else was willing to. That sort of thing frightens people, but I believe they were a great force for good."

"I've always thought so too," I admitted. "Out of curiosity, which was your favorite story?"

"Atreyon," Alveron said a little wistfully. "I haven't thought of that in years. I could probably recite the Eight Oaths of Atreyon from memory." He shook his head and glanced in my direction. "And you?"

"Atreyon is a bit bloody for me," I admitted.

Alveron looked amused. "They weren't called the bloody-handed Amyr for nothing," he said. "The tattoos of the Ciradae were hardly decorative."

"True," I admitted. "Still, I prefer Sir Savien."

"Of course," he said, nodding. "You're a romantic."

We walked in silence for a moment, turning a corner and strolling past a fountain. "I was enamored with them as a child," Alveron said at last, as if confessing something slightly embarassing. "Men and women with all the power of the church behind them. And that was at a time when all the power of Atur stood behind the church." He smiled. "Brave, fierce, and answerable to no one save themselves and God."

"And other Amyr," I added.

"And, ultimately, the pontifex," he finished. "I assume you've read his proclamation declaiming them?"

"Yes."

We came to a small arching bridge of wood and stone, then stopped at the top of the arch and looked out over the water, watching the swans maneuver slowly on the current. "Do you know what I found when I was younger?" the Maer asked.

I shook my head.

"Once I'd grown too old for children's stories of the Amyr, I started wondering more specific things. How many Amyr were there? How many were gentry? How many horse could they put to field for an armed action?" He turned slightly to gauge my reaction. "I was in Felton at the time. They have an old Aturan mendary where they keep church records for the whole of the northern farrel. I looked through their books for two days. Do you know what I found?"

"Nothing," I said. "You didn't find anything."

Alveron turned to look at me. His expression held a carefully controlled surprise.

"I found the same thing at the University," I said. "It seemed as if someone had removed information about the Amyr from the Archives there. Not everything, of course. But there were scarce few solid details."

I could see the Maer's own conclusions sparking to life behind his clever grey eyes. "And who would do such a thing?" he prompted.

"Who would have better reason than the Amyr themselves?" I said. "Which means they are still around, somewhere."

"Thus your question." Alveron started walking again, slower than before. "Where are the Amyr?"

We left the bridge and began to walk the path around the pond, the Maer's face full of serious thought. "Would you believe I had the same thought after searching in the mendary?" he asked me. "I thought the Amyr might have avoided being brought to trial. Gone into hiding. I thought there might even be Amyr in the world after all this while, acting in secret for the greater good."

I could feel the excitement bubbling in my chest. "What did you discover?" I asked eagerly.

"Discover?" Alveron looked surprised. "Nothing. My father died that year and I became Maer. I dismissed it as a boyish fancy." He looked out over the water and the gently gliding swans. "But if you found this same thing half a world away. . . ." He trailed off.

"*And* I drew the same conclusion, your grace."

Alveron nodded slowly. "It is disturbing that there might be a secret this important." He looked around the garden at the walls of his estate. "And in my own lands. I don't like that." He turned back to me, his eyes sharp and clear. "How do you propose to search them out?"

I smiled ruefully. "As your grace pointed out, no matter how well-spoken or well-educated I am, I will never be nobility. I lack the connections and the resources to research this as thoroughly as I would like. But with your name to open doors, I could make a search of many private libraries. I could access archives and records too private or too hidden to be pruned. . . ."

Alveron nodded, his eyes not leaving mine. "I think I understand you. I, for one, would give a great deal to know the truth of this matter."

He looked away as the sound of laughter drifted upward, mixing with the footsteps of a group of approaching nobles. "You've given me a great deal to think about," he said in softer tones. "We will discuss this further in more privacy."

"What time would be convenient for you to meet, your grace?"

Alveron gave me a long, speculative look. "Come to my rooms this evening. And since I cannot give you an answer, let me offer you a question of my own instead."

"I value questions near as much, your grace."

CHAPTER ONE HUNDRED THIRTY-EIGHT

Notes

WITH NEARLY FIVE HOURS until my meeting with the Maer, I was finally free to go about my business in Severen-Low. From the horse lifts, the sky was so clear and blue it could break your heart to look at it. With that in mind, I made my way to the Four Tapers inn.

The taproom wasn't busy, so it isn't surprising that the innkeeper spotted me heading toward the back stairs. "Stop you!" he called out in broken Aturan. "Pay! Room only for paying men!"

Not wanting a scene, I approached the bar. The innkeeper was a thin, greasy man with a thick Lenatti accent. I smiled at him. "I was just visiting a friend. The woman in room three. Long dark hair." I gestured to show how long. "Is she still here?"

"Ah," he said, giving me a knowing look. "The girl. Her name Dinay?"

I nodded, knowing Denna changed her name as often as some other women changed their hair.

The greasy man nodded again. "Yes. The pretty dark eyes? She gone for long."

My heart fell, despite the fact that I'd known better than to hope she would still be here after all this time. "Do you know where she might have gone?"

He barked a short laugh. "No. You and all the other wolves come sniffing after her. I could have sold knowing to you all to made a thick purse. But no, I haen't idea."

"Might she have left a message for me?" I asked without real hope. I hadn't found any letter or note waiting for me at Alveron's estate. "She was expecting me to find her here."

"Was she?" he said mockingly, then seemed to remember something. "I think there a note found. Might be. Not much a reader me. You would like it?" He smiled.

I nodded, my heart lifting a little.

"She left without payment in her room," he said. "Seventeen and a half pennies."

I brought out a silver round and showed it to him. He reached for it, but I set it on the table and held it there with two fingers.

He scurried off into a back room and was gone for a long five minutes. He finally returned with a tightly folded piece of paper clutched in one hand. "I am find it," he said triumphantly, waving it in my direction. "Not much good for paper here but kindling."

I looked at the piece of paper and felt my spirits lift. It was folded against itself in the same fashion as the letter I'd had the tinker deliver. If she'd copied that trick, it meant she must have read my letter and left this note for me. Hopefully it would tell me where she had gone. How to find her. I slid the coin toward the innkeeper and took the note.

Once outside, I hurried to the shadow of a recessed doorway, knowing it was the closest thing to privacy I would find on the busy street. I tore the note open carefully, unfolded it, and edged into the light. It read:

Denna,

I have been forced to leave town on an errand for my patron. I will be away some time, perhaps several span. It was sudden and unavoidable, else I would have made a point to see you before I left.

I regret many of the things I said when we last spoke and wish I could apologize for them in person.

I will find you when I return.

Yours,

Kvothe

At eighth bell I made my way to the Maer's rooms, leaving Caesura behind. I felt oddly naked without it. It's strange how quickly we become accustomed to such things.

Stapes showed me into the Maer's sitting room, and Alveron sent his manservant to invite Meluan to join us at her convenience. I wondered idly what would happen if she decided not to come? Would he ignore her for three days in silent rebuke?

Alveron settled onto a couch and gave me a speculative look. "I've heard some rumors surrounding your recent excursion," he said. "Some rather fantastic things I'm not given to believing. Perhaps you'd like to tell me what *really* happened."

For a moment I wondered how he'd managed to hear about my activities near Levinshir so quickly. Then I realized he wanted to know the details of our bandit hunt in the Eld. I breathed a mental sigh of relief. "I trust Dedan found you easily enough?" I asked.

Alveron nodded.

"I regretted having to send him in my stead, your grace. He is not a subtle creature."

He shrugged. "No real harm was done. By the time he came to me the need for secrecy was past."

"He did deliver my letter then?"

"Ah yes, the letter." Alveron pulled it out of a nearby drawer. "I assumed it was some sort of odd joke."

"Your grace?"

He gave me a frank stare, then looked down at my letter. "*Twenty-seven men,*" he read aloud. "*Experienced mercenaries by their actions and appearance . . . A well-established camp with rudimentary fortifications.*" He looked up again, "You can't expect me to believe this as the truth. The five of you couldn't possibly succeed against so many."

"We surprised them, your grace," I said with a certain smug understatement.

The Maer's expression soured. "Come now, all provincial humor aside, I consider this to be in extremely poor taste. Simply tell me the truth and have done."

"I have told you the truth, your grace. Had I known you would require proof I would have let Dedan bring you a sackful of thumbs. It took a full hour of arguing to drive the notion out of his head."

This didn't set the Maer back as I expected. "Perhaps you should have let him," he said.

The humor of the situation was rapidly fading for me. "Your grace, if I were to lie to you, I would choose a more convincing tale." I let him consider this for a moment. "Besides, if all you want is proof, simply send someone out to verify it. We burned the bodies, but the skulls will still be there. I'll mark their camp for you on a map."

The Maer took a different tack. "What of this other part? Their leader. The man who didn't mind being shot through the leg? The one who stepped into his tent and 'disappeared'?"

"True, your grace."

Alveron eyed me for a long moment, then sighed. "Then I believe you," he said. "But still, it's strange and bitter news," he muttered, almost to himself.

"Indeed, your grace."

He gave me an oddly calculating look. "What do you make of it?"

Before I could answer, there was the sound of a female voice from the outer rooms. Alveron's scowl vanished and he sat up straighter in his chair. I hid a smile behind my hand.

"It's Meluan," Alveron said. "If I am correct, she is bringing us the question I mentioned earlier." He gave me a sly smile. "I think you will enjoy it, a puzzling thing indeed."

Lockless

STAPES ESCORTED MELUAN INTO the room while Alveron and I rose to our feet. She was dressed in grey and lavender, and her curling chestnut hair was pulled back to reveal her elegant neck.

Meluan was followed by two serving boys carrying a wooden chest. The Maer moved to take his wife's elbow, while Stapes directed the boys to set the chest to one side of her chair. Alveron's manservant hurried them outside and gave me a conspiratorial wink before he closed the door behind himself.

Still standing, I turned to Meluan and made my bows. "I am pleased to have the chance to meet with you again . . . my lady?" I made the last a question as I wasn't sure how to address her. The Lackless lands used to be a full earldom, but that was before the bloodless rebellion, when they still controlled Tinüe. Her marriage to the Alveron complicated things too, as I wasn't sure if there was a female counterpart to the title of Maershon.

Meluan waved her hand easily, dismissing the issue entirely. "Lady is well enough between us two, at least when we are closeted. I've no need for formality from one to whom I owe so great a debt." She took hold of Alveron's hand. "Please sit if you've a mind."

I made another bow and took my seat, eyeing the chest as casually as possible. It was about the size of a large drum, made of well-jointed birch and bound in brass.

I knew the proper thing to do was engage in polite small talk until the matter of the chest was broached by one of the two of them. However, my curiosity got the better of me. "I was told you were bringing a question with you. It must be a weighty one for you to keep it so tightly bound." I made a nod toward the chest.

Meluan looked at Alveron and laughed as if he had told a joke. "My husband said you weren't the type to let a puzzle sit for very long."

I gave a slightly shamefaced smile. "It goes against my nature, lady."

"I would not have you battle your nature on my account." She smiled. "Would you be so good as to bring it round in front of me?"

I managed to lift the chest without hurting myself, but if it weighed less than ten stone then I'm a poet.

Meluan sat forward in her chair, leaning over the chest. "Lerand has told me of the part you played in bringing us together. For that, my thanks. I hold myself in debt to you." Her dark brown eyes were gravely serious. "However, I also consider the greater piece of that debt repaid by what I am about to show you. I can count on both hands the people who have seen this. Debt or no, I would never have considered showing you had not my husband vouchsafed me your full discretion." She gave me a pointed look.

"By my hand, I will not speak of what I see to anyone," I assured her, trying not to seem as eager as I was.

Meluan nodded. Then, rather than drawing out a key as I'd expected, she pressed her hands to the sides of the chest and slid two panels slightly. There was a soft click and the lid sprang slightly ajar.

Lockless, I thought to myself.

The open lid revealed another chest, smaller and flatter. It was the size of a bread box, and its flat brass lockplate held a keyhole that was not keyhole shaped, but a simple circle instead. Meluan drew something from a chain around her neck.

"May I see that?" I asked.

Meluan seemed surprised. "I beg your pardon?"

"That key. May I see it for a moment?"

"God's bother," Alveron exclaimed. "We haven't come to the interesting bit yet. I offer you the mystery of an age and you admire the wrapping paper!"

Meluan handed me the key, and I gave it a quick but thorough examination, turning it in my hands. "I like to take my mysteries layer by layer," I explained.

"Like an onion?" He snorted.

"Like a flower," I countered, handing the key back to Meluan. "Thank you."

Meluan fit the key and opened the lid of the inner chest. She slid the chain back around her neck, tucked it underneath her clothes, and rearranged her clothes and hair, repairing any damage done to her appearance. This seemed to take an hour or so.

Finally she reached forward and lifted something out of the chest with both hands. Holding it just out of my sight behind the open lid, she looked up at me and took a deep breath. "This has been . . ." she began.

"Just let him see it, dear," Alveron interjected gently. "I'm curious to see what he thinks on his own." He chuckled. "Besides, I fear the boy will have a fit if you keep him waiting any longer."

Reverently, Meluan handed me a piece of dark wood the size of a thick book. I took it with both hands.

The box was unnaturally heavy for its size, the wood of it smooth as polished stone under my fingers. As I ran my hands over it, I found the sides were carved. Not dramatically enough to attract the attention of the eyes, but so subtly my fingers could barely feel a gentle pattern of risings and fallings in the wood. I brushed my hands over the top and felt a similar pattern.

"You were right," Meluan said softly. "He's like a child with a midwinter's gift."

"You haven't seen the best of it yet," Alveron replied. "Wait until he starts. The boy has a mind like an iron hammer."

"How do you open it?" I asked. I turned it in my hands and felt something shift inside. There were no obvious hinges or lid, not even a seam where a lid might be. It looked for all the world like a single piece of dark and weighty wood. But I knew it was a box of some sort. It *felt* like a box. It wanted to be opened.

"We don't know," Meluan said. She might have continued, but her husband hushed her gently.

"What's inside?" I tilted it again, feeling the contents shift.

"We don't know," she repeated.

The wood itself was interesting. It was dark enough to be roah, but it had a deep red grain. What's more, it seemed to be a spicewood. It smelled faintly of . . . something. A familiar smell I couldn't quite put my finger on. I lowered my face to its surface and breathed in deeply through my nose, something almost like lemon. It was maddeningly familiar. "What sort of wood is this?"

Their silence was answer enough.

I looked up and met their eyes. "You don't give a body much to work with, do you?" I smiled to soften any offense the words might bring.

Alveron sat forward in his chair. "You must admit," he said with thinly veiled excitement, "this is a most excellent question. You've shown me your gift at guessing before." His eyes glittered grey. "So what can you guess about this?"

"It's an heirloom," I said easily. "Very old—"

"How old would you think?" Alveron interjected hungrily.

"Perhaps three thousand years," I said. "Give or take." Meluan stiffened in surprise. "I am close to your own guesses I take it?"

She nodded mutely.

"The carving has no doubt been eroded over the long years of handling."

"Carving?" Alveron asked, leaning forward in his chair.

"It's very faint," I said, closing my eyes. "But I can feel it."

"I felt no such thing."

"Nor I," said Meluan. She seemed slightly offended.

"I have exceptionally sensitive hands," I said honestly. "They're necessary for my work."

"Your magic?" she asked with a well-hidden hint of childlike awe.

"And music," I said. "If you'll allow me?" She nodded. So I took her hand in my own, and pressed it to the top of the box. "There. Can you feel it?"

She furrowed her forehead in concentration. "Perhaps, just a bit." She took her hand away. "Are you sure it's a carving?"

"It's too regular to be an accident. How can it be you haven't noticed it before? Isn't it mentioned in any of your histories?"

Meluan was taken aback. "No one would think of writing down anything regarding the Loeclos Box. Haven't I said this is the most secret of secrets?"

"Show me," Alveron said. I guided his fingers over the pattern. He frowned. "Nothing. My fingers must be too old. Could it be letters?"

I shook my head. "It's a flowing pattern, like scrollwork. But it doesn't repeat, it changes . . ." A thought struck me. "It might be a Yllish story knot."

"Can you read it?" Alveron asked.

I ran my fingers over it. "I don't know enough Yllish to read a simple knot if I had the string between my fingers." I shook my head. "Besides, the knots would have changed in the last three thousand years. I know a few people who might be able to translate it at the University."

Alveron looked to Meluan, but she shook her head firmly. "I will not have this spoken of to strangers."

The Maer seemed disappointed by this answer, but didn't press the point. Instead he turned back to me. "Let me ask you your own questions back again. What sort of wood is it?"

"It's lasted three thousand years," I mused aloud. "It's heavy despite being hollow. So it has to be a slow wood, like hornbeam or rennel. Its color and weight make me think it has a good deal of metal in it too, like roah. Probably iron and copper." I shrugged. "That's the best I can do."

"What's inside it?"

I thought for a long moment before saying anything. "Something smaller than a saltbox. . . ." I began. Meluan smiled, but Alveron gave the barest of frowns so I hurried on. "Something metal, by the way the weight shifts when I tilt it." I closed my eyes and listened to the padded thump of its contents moving in the box. "No. By the weight of it, perhaps something made of glass or stone."

"Something precious," Alveron said.

I opened my eyes. "Not necessarily. It has *become* precious because it is old, and because it has been with a family for so long. It is also precious because it is a mystery. But was it precious to begin with?" I shrugged. "Who can say?"

"But you lock up precious things," Alveron pointed out.

"Precisely." I held up the box, displaying its smooth face. "This isn't locked up. In fact, it might be locked away. It may be something dangerous."

"Why would you say that?" Alveron asked curiously.

"Why go through this trouble?" Meluan protested. "Why save something dangerous? If something is dangerous, you destroy it." She seemed to answer her own question as soon as she had voiced it. "Unless it was precious as well as dangerous."

"Perhaps it was too useful to destroy," Alveron suggested.

"Perhaps it couldn't be destroyed," I said.

"Last and best," Alveron said, leaning forward even further in his seat. "How do you open it?"

I gave the box a long look, turned it in my hands, pressed the sides. I ran my fingers over the patterns, feeling for a seam my eyes could not detect. I shook it gently, tasted the air around it, held it to the light.

"I have no idea," I admitted.

Alveron slumped a little. "It was too much to expect, I suppose. Perhaps some piece of magic?"

I hesitated to tell him that sort of magic only existed in stories. "None I have at my command."

"Have you ever considered simply cutting it open?" Alveron asked his wife.

Meluan looked every bit as horrified as I felt at the suggestion. "Never!" She said as soon as she caught her breath. "It is the very root of our family. I would sooner think of salting every acre of our lands."

"And hard as this wood is," I hurried to say, "you would most likely ruin whatever was inside. Especially if it is delicate."

"It was only a thought." Alveron reassured his wife.

"An ill-considered one," Meluan said sharply, then seemed to regret her words. "I'm sorry, but the very thought . . ." She trailed off, obviously distraught.

He patted her hand. "I understand, my dear. You're right, it was ill-considered."

"Might I put it away now?" Meluan asked him.

I reluctantly handed the box back to Meluan. "If there were a lock I could attempt to circumvent it, but I can't even make a guess at where the hinge might be, or the seam for the lid." *In a box, no lid or locks/ Lackless keeps her husband's rocks.* The child's skipping rhyme ran madly through my head and I only barely managed to turn my laugh into a cough.

Alveron didn't seem to notice. "As always, I trust to your discretion." He got to his feet. "Unfortunately, I fear I have used up the better portion of our time. I'm certain you have other matters to attend to. Shall we meet tomorrow to discuss the Amyr? Second bell?"

I had risen to my feet with the Maer. "If it please your grace, I have another matter that warrants some discussion."

He gave me a serious look. "I trust this is an important matter."

"Most urgent, your grace," I said nervously. "It should not wait another day. I would have mentioned it sooner, had we both privacy and time."

"Very well," he sat back down. "What presses you so direly?"

"Lerand," Meluan said with slight reproach. "It is past the hour. Hayanis will be waiting."

"Let him wait," he said. "Kvothe has served me well in all regards. He does nothing lightly, and I ignore him only to my detriment."

"You flatter me, your grace. This matter is a grave one." I glanced at Meluan. "And somewhat delicate as well. If your lady desires to leave, it might be for the best."

"If the matter is important, should I not stay?" she asked archly.

I gave the Maer a questioning look.

"Anything you wish to say to me you can tell my lady wife," he said.

I hesitated. I needed to tell Alveron about the false troupers soon. I was sure if he heard my version of events first, I could present them in a way that cast me in a favorable light. If word came through official channels first he might not be willing to overlook the bald facts of the situation, that I had slaughtered nine travelers of my own free will.

Despite that, the last thing I wanted was Meluan present for the conversation. It couldn't help but complicate the situation. I tried one final time. "It is a matter most dark, your grace."

Alveron shook his head, frowning slightly. "We have no secrets."

I fought down a resigned sigh and drew a thick piece of folded parchment from an inner pocket of my shaed. "Is this one of the writs of patronage your grace has granted?"

His grey eyes flickered over it, showing some surprise. "Yes. How did you come by it?"

"Oh, Lerand," Meluan said. "I knew you let the beggars travel in your lands, but I never thought you would stoop to patronizing them as well."

"Only a handful of troupes," he said. "As befitting my rank. Every respectable household has at least a few players."

"Mine," Meluan said firmly, "does not."

"It is convenient to have one's own troupe," Alveron said gently. "And more convenient to have several. Then one can choose the proper entertainment to accompany whatever event you might be hosting. Where do you think the musicians at our wedding came from?"

When Meluan's expression did not soften, Alveron continued. "They're not permitted to perform anything bawdy or heathen, dear. I keep them under most close controlment. And rest assured, no town in my lands would let a troupe perform unless they had a noble's writ with them."

Alveron turned back to me. "Which brings us back to the matter at hand. How did you come to have their writ? The troupe must be doing poorly without it."

I hesitated. With Meluan here, I was unsure as to the best way to approach the subject. I'd planned on speaking to the Maer alone. "They are, your grace. They were killed."

The Maer showed no surprise. "I thought as much. Such things are unfortunate, but they happen from time to time."

Meluan's eyes flashed. "I'd give a great deal to see them happen more often."

"Have you any idea who killed them?" the Maer asked.

"In a certain manner of speaking, your grace."

He raised his eyebrows expectantly. "Well then?"

"I did."

"You did what?"

I sighed. "I killed the men carrying that writ, your grace."

He stiffened in his seat. "What?"

"They had kidnapped a pair of girls from a town they passed through." I paused, looking for a delicate way of saying it in front of Meluan. "They were young girls, your grace, and the men were not kind to them."

Meluan's expression, already hard, grew cold as ice at this. But before she could speak, Alveron demanded incredulously, "And you took it on yourself to kill them? An entire troupe of performers I had given license to?" He rubbed his forehead. "How many were there?"

"Nine."

"Good lord . . ."

"I think he did right," Meluan said hotly. "I say you give him a score of guards and let him do the same to every ravel band of Ruh he finds within your lands."

"My dear," Alveron said with a touch of sternness. "I don't care for them much more than you, but law is law. When . . ."

"Law is what *you* make it," she interjected. "This man has done you a noble service. You should grant him fief and title and set him on your council."

"He killed nine of my subjects," Alveron pointed out sternly. "When men step outside the rule of law, anarchy results. If I heard of this in passing, I would hang him for a bandit."

"He killed nine Ruh rapists. Nine murdering ravel thieves. Nine fewer Edema men in the world is a service to us all." Meluan looked at me. "Sir. I think you did nothing but what was right and proper."

Her misdirected praise did nothing but fan the fire beneath my temper. "Not all of them were men, my lady," I said to her.

Meluan paled a bit at that remark.

Alveron rubbed his face with a hand. "Good lord, man. Your honesty is like a felling axe."

"And I should mention," I said seriously, "begging both your pardons, that those I killed were not Edema Ruh. They were not even a real troupe."

Alveron shook his head tiredly and tapped the writ in front of him. "It says here otherwise. Edema Ruh and troupers both."

"The writ was stolen goods, your grace. The folk I met on the road had killed a troupe of Ruh and taken up their place."

He gave me a curious look. "You seem rather certain of it."

"One of them told me so, your grace. He admitted they were merely impersonating a troupe. They were pretending to be Ruh."

Meluan looked as if she couldn't decide whether she was confused or sickened by the thought. "Who would pretend such a thing?"

Alveron nodded. "My wife makes a point," he said. "It seems more likely that they lied to you. Who wouldn't deny such a thing? Who would willingly admit to being one of the Edema Ruh?"

I felt myself flush hot at this, suddenly ashamed that I had concealed my Edema Ruh blood for all this time. "I don't doubt your original troupe were Edema Ruh, your grace. But the men I killed were not. No Ruh would do the things they did."

Meluan's eyes flashed furiously. "You do not know them."

I met her eyes. "My lady, I think I know them rather well."

"But why?" Alveron asked. "Who in their right mind would try to pass themselves off as Edema Ruh?"

"For ease of travel," I said. "And the protection your name offers."

He shrugged my explanation away. "They were probably Ruh that tired of honest work and took up thieving instead."

"No, your grace," I insisted. "They were not Edema Ruh."

Alveron gave me a reproachful look. "Come now. Who can tell the difference between bandits and a band of Ruh?"

"There is no difference," Meluan said crisply.

"Your grace, I would know the difference," I said hotly. "*I* am Edema Ruh."

Silence. Meluan's expression turned from blank shock, to disbelief, to rage, to disgust. She came to her feet, looked for a moment as if she would spit on me, then walked stiffly out the door. There was a clatter as her personal guard came to attention and followed her out of the outer rooms.

Alveron continued to look at me, his face severe. "If this is a joke, it is a poor one."

"It is none, your grace," I said, wrestling with my temper.

"And why have you found it necessary to hide this from me?"

"I have not hidden it, your grace. You yourself have mentioned several times that I am far from gentle birth."

He struck the arm of his chair angrily. "You know what I mean! Why did you never mention that you are one of the Ruh?"

"I think the reason rather obvious, your grace," I said stiffly, trying to keep from spitting out the words. "The words 'Edema Ruh' have too strong a smell for many gentle noses. Your wife has found her perfume cannot cover it."

"My lady has had unfortunate dealings with the Ruh in the past," he said by way of explanation. "You would do well to note."

"I know of her sister. Her family's tragic shame. Run off and love a trouper. How terrible," I said scathingly, my entire body prickling with hot rage. "Her sister's sense does credit to her family; less so the actions of your lady wife. My blood is worth as much as any man's, and more than most. And even were it not, she has no leave to treat me as she did."

Alveron's expression hardened. "I rather think that she has leave to treat you as she will," he said. "She was simply startled by your sudden proclamation. Given her feelings about you ravel, I think she showed remarkable restraint."

"I think she rues the truth. A trouper's tongue has gotten her to bed more quickly than her sister."

As soon as I said it, I knew I had gone too far. I clenched my teeth to keep from saying anything worse.

"That will be all," Alveron said with cold formality, his eyes flat and angry.

I left with all the angry dignity I could muster. Not because I had nothing else to say, but because if I had stayed one moment longer he would have called for guards, and that is not how I wished to make my exit.

CHAPTER ONE HUNDRED FORTY

Just Rewards

I WAS IN THE MIDDLE of dressing the following morning when an errand boy arrived bearing a thick envelope with Alveron's seal. I took a seat by the window and discovered several letters inside. The outermost one read:

> *Kvothe,*
>
> *I have thought a while and decided your blood matters but little in light of the services you have rendered me.*
>
> *However, my soul is bound to another whose comfort I hold more dearly than my own. Though I had hoped to retain your services, I cannot. What's more, as your presence is the cause of my wife's considerable distress, I must ask you to return my ring and leave Severen at your earliest convenience.*

I stopped reading, got to my feet, and opened the door to my rooms. A pair of Alveron's guards were standing at attention in the hallway.

"Sir?" one of them said, eyeing my half-dressed state.

"Just checking," I said, closing the door.

I returned to my seat and picked up the letter again.

> *As to the matter that precipitated this unfortunate circumstance, I believe you have acted in the best interest of myself and Vintas as a whole. In fact, I have received report just this morning that two girls were returned to their families in Levinshir by a red-haired "gentleman" named Kvothe.*
>
> *As reward for your many services I offer the following:*
>
> *First, a full pardon for those you killed near Levinshir.*
>
> *Second, a letter of credit enabling you to draw on my coffers for the payment of your tuition at the University.*

Third, a writ granting you the right to travel, play, and perform wherever you
will within my lands.
    Lastly, my thanks.
    Maershon Lerand Alveron

I sat for a few long minutes, watching the birds flit in the garden outside
my window. The contents of the envelope were just as Alveron had said. The
letter of credit was a work of art, signed and sealed in four places by Alveron
and his chief exchequer.

The writ was, if anything, even more lovely. It was drawn on a thick sheet
of creamy vellum, signed by the Maer's own hand and fixed with both his
family's seal and that of Alveron himself.

But it was not a writ of patronage. I read through it carefully. By omission
it made it clear that neither was I in the Maer's service, nor were we bound
to each other. Still, it granted free travel and the right to perform under his
name. It was an odd compromise of a document.

I'd just finished dressing when there came another knock on the door.
I sighed, half expecting more guards coming to roust me out of my rooms.

But opening the door revealed another runner boy. He carried a silver tray
bearing another letter. This one had the Lackless seal upon the top. Beside it
lay a ring. I picked it up and turned it over in my hands, puzzled. It wasn't
iron, as I'd expected, but pale wood. Meluan's name was burned crudely into
the side of it.

I noticed the runner boy's wide eyes darting back and forth between the
ring and myself. More importantly, I noticed the guards were not staring at
it. Pointedly not staring. The sort of not-staring you only engage in when
something very interesting has come to your attention.

I handed the boy my silver ring. "Take this to Bredon," I said. "And don't
dawdle."

Bredon was looking up at the guards as I opened the door. "Keep up the good
work, my boys," he said, playfully tapping one of them on the chest with his
walking stick. The silver wolf's head chimed lightly against the guard's breast-
plate, and Bredon smiled like a jolly uncle. "We all feel safer for your vigilance."

He closed the door behind himself and raised an eyebrow at me. "Lord's
mercy boy, you're up the ladder by leaps and bounds. I knew you sat solid in
the Maer's good grace, but to have him assign you two of his personal guard?"
He pressed his hand to his heart and sighed dramatically. "Soon you will be
too busy for the likes of poor old useless Bredon."

I gave him a weak smile. "I think it's more complicated than that." I held up the wooden ring for him to see. "I need you to tell me what this means."

Bredon's jovial cheer evaporated more quickly than if I'd pulled out a bloody knife. "Lord and lady," he said. "Tell me you got that from some old-fashioned farmer."

I shook my head and handed it to him.

He turned the ring over in his hands. "Meluan?" he asked quietly. Handing it back, he sank into a nearby chair, his walking stick across his knees. His face had gone slightly grey. "The Maer's new lady wife sent you this? As a summons?"

"It's about as far from a summons as anything can be," I said. "She sent a charming letter, too." I held it up with my other hand.

Bredon held out his hand. "Can I see it?" he asked, then drew his hand back quickly. "I'm sorry. That's terribly rude of me to ask—"

"You could do me no greater favor than reading it," I said, pressing it into his hands. "I am in desperate need of your opinion."

Bredon took the letter and began to read, his lips moving slightly. His expression grew paler as he made his way down the page.

"The lady has a gift for well-turned phrase," I said.

"That cannot be denied," he said. "She might as well have written this in blood."

"I think she would have liked to," I said. "But she would have had to kill herself to fill the second page." I held it out to him.

Bredon took it and continued to read, his face growing even paler. "Gods all around us," he said. "Is 'excrescence' even a word?" he asked.

"It is," I said.

Bredon finished the second page, then went back to the beginning and slowly read it through a second time. Finally he looked up at me. "If there were a woman," he said, "who loved me with one-tenth the passion this lady feels for you, I would count myself the luckiest of men."

"What does this mean?" I asked, holding up the ring. I could smell smoke on it. She must have burned her name into it just this morning.

"From a farmer?" he shrugged. "Many things, depending on the wood. But here? From one of the nobility?" He shook his head, obviously at a loss for words.

"I thought there were only three types of courtly rings," I said.

"Only three a person would use," he said. "Only three that are sent and displayed. It used to be you sent wooden rings to summon servants. Those too low for iron. But that was a long while back. Eventually it became a terrible snub to send someone in the court a wooden ring."

"A snub I can live with," I said, relieved. "I've been snubbed by better folk than her."

"That was a hundred years ago," Bredon said. "Things have changed. The problem was, once the wooden rings were seen as a snub, some servants would be offended by them. You don't want to offend the master of your stables, so you don't send him a wooden ring. But if he doesn't get a wooden ring, then your tailor might be offended by one."

I nodded my understanding. "And so on. Eventually anyone was offended by a wooden ring."

Bredon nodded. "A wise man is careful to stay on the good side of his servants," he said. "Even the boy that brings your dinner can carry a grudge, and there are a thousand invisible revenges available to the lowest of them. Wooden rings aren't used at all anymore. They probably would have fallen out of memory entirely if they weren't used as a plot device in a handful of plays."

I looked at the ring. "So I'm lower than the boy who collects the slops."

Bredon cleared his throat self-consciously. "More than that, actually." He pointed. "That means to her, you aren't even a person. You aren't worth recognizing as a human being."

"Ah," I said. "I see."

I slid the wooden ring onto my finger and made a fist. It was quite a good fit, actually.

"It's not the sort of ring you wear," Bredon said uncomfortably. "It's quite the other sort of ring, actually." He gave me a curious look. "I don't suppose you still have Alveron's ring?"

"He's asked for it back, actually." I picked the Maer's letter off the table and handed it to Bredon as well.

"At your earliest convenience," Bredon quoted with a dry chuckle. "That says quite a bit more than it seems." He set the letter down. "Still, it's probably better this way. If he left you with his favor you'd be a battleground for them: a peppercorn between her mortar and his pestle. They would crush you with their bickering."

His eyes flickered back to the wooden ring on my hand. "I don't suppose she gave it to you personally?" he asked hopefully.

"She sent it with a runner." I let out a low sigh. "The guards saw it too."

There was a knock on the door. I answered it, and a runner boy handed me a letter.

I closed the door and looked at the seal. "Lord Praevek," I said.

Bredon shook his head. "I swear that man spends every waking moment with his ear against a keyhole or his tongue up someone's ass."

Chuckling, I cracked the letter open and scanned it quickly. "He's asking for his ring back," I said. "It's smudged too, he didn't even wait for the ink to dry."

Bredon nodded. "Word is undoubtedly spreading. It wouldn't be so bad if she wasn't sitting strong at Alveron's right hand. But she is, and she's made her opinion clear. Anyone who treats you better than a dog will doubtless share the scorn she feels for you." He fluttered her letter. "And scorn such as this, there's plenty to go around without worry of it spreading thin."

Bredon gestured to the bowl of rings and gave a dry, mirthless chuckle. "Just when you were getting some silver, too."

I walked over to the bowl, dug out his ring, and held it out to him. "You should take this back," I said.

Bredon's expression looked pained, but he made no move to take the ring.

"I'm going to be leaving soon," I said. "And I'd hate for you to be tarnished by your contact with me. There's no way I can thank you for the help you've given me. The least I can do is help minimize the damage to your reputation."

Bredon hesitated, then closed his eyes and sighed. He took the ring with a defeated shrug.

"Oh," I said, suddenly remembering something else. I went to the stack of slanderous stories and pulled out the pages that described his pagan frolics. "You might find this amusing," I said as I handed it to him. "Now you should probably go. Simply being here can't be good for you."

Bredon sighed and nodded. "I'm sorry it didn't work out better for you, my boy. If you're ever back in these parts don't hesitate to call on me. These things do blow over eventually." His eyes kept drifting back to the wooden ring on my finger. "You really shouldn't keep wearing that."

After he was gone, I fished Stapes' gold ring out of the bowl and Alveron's iron one as well. Then I stepped out into the hallway.

"I'm going to pay a call on Stapes," I said politely to the guards. "Would the two of you care to accompany me?"

The taller one glanced at the ring on my finger, then looked at his companion before murmuring an agreement. I turned on my heel and set off, my escort keeping pace behind me.

———

Stapes ushered me inside his sitting room and closed the door behind me. His rooms were even finer than my own and considerably more lived in. I also saw a large bowl of rings on a nearby table. All of them were gold. The only iron ring in sight was Alveron's, and that was on his finger.

He might look like a grocer, but Stapes had a sharp set of eyes. He spotted the ring on my finger straightaway. "She did it then," he said, shaking his head. "You really shouldn't wear it."

"I'm not ashamed of what I am," I said. "If this is the ring of an Edema Ruh, I'll wear it."

Stapes sighed. "It's more complicated than that."

"I know," I said. "I didn't come here to make your life difficult. Could you return this to the Maer for me?" I handed him Alveron's ring.

Stapes put it in his pocket.

"I also wanted to return these." I handed him the two rings he had given me. One bright gold, one white bone. "I don't want to make trouble between you and your master's new wife."

Stapes nodded, holding up the gold ring. "It would make trouble if you kept it," he said. "I am in the Maer's service. As such, I need to be mindful of the games of the court."

Then he reached out and took my hand, pressing the bone ring back into it. "But this lies outside my duty to the Maer. It is a debt between two men. The games of the court have no sway over such things." Stapes met my eye. "And I insist you keep it."

———

I ate a late supper alone in my rooms. The guards were still waiting patiently outside as I read the Maer's letter for the fifth time. Each time I hoped to find some clement sentiment hidden in his phrasing. But it simply wasn't there.

On the table sat the various papers the Maer had sent. I emptied my purse beside them. I had two gold royals, four silver nobles, eight and a half pennies, and, inexplicably, a single Modegan strelum, though I couldn't for the life of me remember where I'd come by it.

Altogether they equaled slightly less than eight talents. I stacked them next to Alveron's papers. Eight talents, a pardon, a player's writ, and my tuition paid at the University. It was not an inconsiderable reward.

Still, I couldn't help but feel rather shorted. I had saved Alveron from a poisoning, uncovered a traitor in his court, won him a wife, and rid his roads of more dangerous folk than I cared to count.

Despite all that, I was still left without a patron. Worse, his letter had made no mention of the Amyr, no mention of the support he had promised to lend me in my search for them.

But there was nothing to be gained by making a fuss, and much that I could lose. I refilled my purse and tucked Alveron's letters into the secret compartment in my lute case.

I also nicked three books I'd brought from Caudicus' library, since no one knew I had them, and tipped the bowlful of rings into a small sack. The wardrobe held two dozen finely tailored outfits. They were worth a heavy penny, but weren't very portable. I took two of the nicer outfits and left the rest hanging.

Lastly I belted on Caesura and worked my shaed into a long cape. Those two items reassured me that my time in Vintas had not been entirely wasted, though I'd earned them on my own, not through any help of Alveron's.

I locked the door, snuffed the lamps, and climbed out a window into the garden. Then I used a piece of bent wire to lock the window and close the shutters behind me.

Petty mischief? Perhaps, but I'd be damned if I'd be escorted from the estates by the Maer's guard. Besides, the thought of them puzzling over my escape made me chuckle, and laughter is good for the digestion.

———

I made my way out of the estates without anyone seeing me. My shaed was well suited to sneaking about in the dark. After an hour of searching I found a greasy bookbinder in Severen-Low.

He was an unsavory fellow with the morals of a feral dog, but he *was* interested in the stack of slanderous stories the nobility had been sending to my rooms. He offered me four reels for the lot of them, plus the promise of ten pennies for every volume of the book he sold after they were printed. I bargained him up to six reels and six pennies per copy and we shook hands. I left his shop, burned the contract, and washed my hands twice. I did keep the money, however.

After that I sold both suits of fine clothing and all of Caudicus' books except for one. With the money I'd accumulated, I spent the next several hours on the docks and found a ship leaving the next day for Junpui.

As night settled onto the city, I wandered the high parts of Severen, hoping I might run into Denna. I didn't, of course. I could tell she was long gone. A city feels different when Denna is somewhere inside it, and Severen felt as hollow as an empty egg.

At the end of several hours of fruitless searching, I stopped by a dockside brothel and spent some time drinking in the taproom. It was a slow night, and the ladies were bored. So I bought drinks for everyone, and we talked. I told a few stories and they listened. I played a few songs and they applauded. Then I asked a favor, and they laughed and laughed and laughed.

So I poured the sackful of rings into a bowl and left them on the bar. Soon the ladies were trying them on and arguing over who would get the silver ones. I bought another round of drinks and left, my mood somewhat improved.

I wandered aimlessly after that, eventually finding a small public garden near the lip of the Sheer looking out over Severen-Low. The lamps below were burning orange, while here or there a gaslight or sympathy lamp flickered greenish blue and crimson. It was as breathtaking as the first time I had seen it.

I had been watching for some time before I realized I wasn't alone. An older man leaned against a tree several feet away, looking down at the lights much as I had been. A faint and not unpleasant aroma of beer wafted from him.

"She's a pretty thing, innit she?" he said, his accent marking him as a dockworker.

I agreed. We watched the twinkling fires silently for a time. I unscrewed the wooden ring from my finger and considered throwing it off the cliff. Now that someone was watching, I couldn't help but feel the gesture was somewhat childish.

"They say a nobleman can piss on half o' Severen from up here," the dockman said conversationally.

I tucked the ring into a pocket of my shaed. A memento then. "Those are the lazy ones," I replied. "The ones I've met can piss a lot farther than that."

CHAPTER ONE HUNDRED FORTY-ONE

A Journey to Return

FATE FAVORED ME ON the way back to the University. We had a good wind and everything was delightfully uneventful. The sailors had heard of my encounter with Felurian, so I enjoyed a modest fame for the duration of the trip. I played them the song I'd written about it, and told them the story about half as often as they asked me to.

I also told them about my trip to the Adem. They didn't believe a piece of it at first, but then I showed them the sword and threw their best wrestler three times. They showed me a different sort of respect after that, and a rougher, more honest sort of friendship.

I learned a goodly bit from them on my journey home. They told me sea stories and the names of stars. They talked about wind and water and wimmin, sorry, women. They tried to teach me sailor's knots, but I didn't have a knack for it, though I proved to be a dab hand at untying them.

Altogether it was very pleasant. The friendship of the sailors, the song of the wind in the rigging, the smell of sweat and salt and tar. Over the long days, these things slowly eased the bitterness I felt toward my ill treatment at the hands of Maer Alveron and his loving lady wife.

CHAPTER ONE HUNDRED FORTY-TWO

Home

EVENTUALLY WE DOCKED IN Tarbean, where the sailors helped me find a cheap berth on a billow boat heading upstream toward Anilin. I got off two days later in Imre and walked to the University just as the first blue light of dawn was coloring the sky.

I've never in my life had anything like a home. As a young child I grew up on the road, endlessly traveling with my troupe. Home wasn't a place. It was people and wagons. Later in Tarbean I had had a secret place where three roofs came together and gave me shelter from the rain. I slept there and hid a few precious things, but it wasn't anything like a home.

Because of this, I'd never in my life enjoyed the feeling of coming home after a journey. I felt it for the first time that day as I crossed the Omethi, the stones of the bridge familiar underneath my feet. As I came to the tallest part of its broad arch I could see the grey shape of the Archives rising out of the trees ahead of me.

The streets of the University were comforting under my feet. I'd been gone for three-quarters of a year. In some ways it seemed much longer, but at the same time everything here felt so familiar that it felt like hardly any time at all had passed.

It was still early when I got to Anker's, and the front door was locked. I briefly considered climbing up to my window, then thought better of it, given that I was carrying my lute case and travelsack, and wearing Caesura as well.

Instead I made my way to the Mews and knocked on Simmon's door. It was early, and I knew I'd be waking him, but I was hungry for a familiar face. After waiting a short minute and hearing nothing, I knocked again, louder, and practiced my best jaunty smile.

Sim opened the door, his hair in disarray, his eyes red from too little sleep. He looked blearily out at me. For the space of a breath his expression was blank, then he hurled himself at me with a crushing hug.

"Blackened body of God," he said, using stronger language than I'd ever heard from him before. "Kvothe. You're alive."

———

Sim had a bit of a cry, then shouted at me for a while, and then we laughed and sorted matters out. It seems Threpe had been keeping closer tabs on my travels than I'd thought. Consequently, when my ship had gone missing, he'd assumed the worst.

A letter would have cleared things up, but I'd never thought to send one. The thought of writing home was utterly alien to me.

"The ship was reported as all hands lost," Sim said. "Word spread around the Eolian and guess who heard the news."

"Stanchion?" I asked, knowing he was a terrible gossip.

Sim shook his head grimly. "Ambrose."

"Oh lovely," I observed dryly.

"It would have been bad coming from anyone," Sim said. "But it was worst from him. I was half convinced he'd somehow arranged to sink your ship." He gave a sickly smile. "He waited until right before admissions before he broke the news to me. Needless to say, I pissed all over myself during my exam and spent another term as an E'lir."

"Spent?" I said. "You made Re'lar?"

He grinned. "Just yesterday. I was sleeping off the celebration when you woke me up this morning."

"How's Wil?" I asked. "Did he take the news hard?"

"Even-keeled as always," Sim said. "But for all that, yeah, pretty hard." He grimaced. "Ambrose has been making his life difficult in the Archives, too. Wil got fed up with it and went home for a term. He should be back today."

"How's everyone else?" I asked.

A thought seemed to strike Sim all of a sudden. He stood up. "Oh God, Fela!" Then he sat down hard, as if his legs had been cut from underneath him. "Oh God, Fela," he said in a completely different tone.

"What?" I asked. "Did something happen to her?"

"She didn't take the news well either." He gave me a shaky smile. "It turns out she had quite a thing for you."

"Fela?" I said stupidly.

"Don't you remember? Wil and I thought she liked you?"

It seemed like years ago. "I remember."

Sim seemed uncomfortable. "Well, you see. While you were gone, Wil and I started spending a lot of time with her. And . . ." He made an inarticulate gesture, his expression was stuck between sheepish and grinning.

Realization struck. "You and Fela? Sim, that's great!" I felt a grin spread across my face, then saw his expression. "Oh." My grin fell away. "Sim, I wouldn't get in the way of that."

"I know you wouldn't." He smiled a sickly smile. "I trust you."

I rubbed my eyes. "This is a hell of a homecoming. I haven't even been through admissions yet."

"Today's the last day," Sim pointed out.

"I know," I said, getting to my feet. "I have an errand to run first."

I left my baggage in Simmon's room and paid a visit to the bursar in the basement of Hollows. Riem was a balding, pinch-faced man who had disliked me ever since the masters had assigned me a negative tuition in my first term. He wasn't in the habit of giving money out, and the entire experience had rubbed him the wrong way.

I showed him my open letter of credit to Alveron's coffers. As I've said, it was an impressive document. Signed by the Maer's own hand. Wax seals. Fine vellum. Excellent penmanship.

I drew the bursar's attention to the fact that the Maer's letter would allow the University to draw any amount needed to cover my tuition. Any amount.

The bursar read it over and agreed that that seemed to be the case.

It's too bad my tuition was always so low, I mused aloud. Never more than ten talents. It was a bit of a missed opportunity for the University. The Maer was richer than the King of Vint, after all. And he would pay *any* tuition. . . .

Riem was a savvy man, and he understood what I was hinting at immediately. There followed a brief bout of negotiation, after which we shook hands and I saw him smile for the first time.

I grabbed a bite of lunch, then waited in line with the rest of the students who didn't have admissions tiles. Most of them were new students, but a few were applying for readmission like myself. It was a long line, and everyone was visibly nervous to some degree. I whistled to pass the time and bought a meat pie and a mug of hot cider from a man with a cart.

I caused a bit of a stir when I stepped into the circle of light in front of the masters' table. They had heard the news and were surprised to see me alive, most of them pleasantly so. Kilvin demanded I report to the workshop soon, while Mandrag, Dal, and Arwyl argued over which courses of study I would pursue. Elodin merely waved at me, the only one apparently unimpressed by my miraculous return from the dead.

After a minute of congenial chaos, the Chancellor got things back under control and started my interview. I answered Dal's questions easily enough, and Kilvin's. But I fumbled my cipher with Brandeur, then had to admit I simply didn't know the answer to Mandrag's question about sublimation.

Elodin shrugged away his opportunity to question me, yawning hugely. Lorren asked a surprisingly easy question about the Mender heresies, and I managed a quick and clever answer for him. I had to think for a long moment before answering Arwyl's question about lacillium.

That left only Hemme, who had been scowling furiously since I'd first stepped up to the masters' table. My lackluster performance and slow answers had brought a smug curve to his lips by this point. His eyes gleamed whenever I gave a wrong answer.

"Well well," he said, shuffling through the sheaf of papers in front of him. "I didn't think we'd have to deal with your type of trouble again." He gave me an insincere smile. "I'd heard you were dead."

"I heard you wear a red lace corset," I said matter-of-factly. "But I don't believe every bit of nonsense that gets rumored about."

Some shouting followed, and I was quickly brought up on charges of Improper Address of a Master. I was sentenced to compose a letter of apology and fined a single silver talent. Money well spent.

It was bad behavior though, and poorly timed, especially after my otherwise lackluster performance. As a result, I was assigned a tuition of twenty-four talents. Needless to say, I was terribly embarrassed.

Afterward I returned to the bursar's office. I officially presented Alveron's letter of credit to Riem and unofficially collected my agreed-upon cut: half of everything over ten talents. I put the seven talents in my purse and wondered idly if anyone had ever been paid so well for insolence and ignorance.

I headed to Anker's, where I was pleased to discover no one had informed the owner of my death. The key to my room was somewhere at the bottom of the Centhe Sea, but Anker had a spare. I went upstairs and felt myself relax at the familiar sight of the sloping ceiling and narrow bed. Everything was covered in a thin layer of dust.

You might think my tiny room with its sloped ceiling and narrow bed would feel cramped after my grand suite in Alveron's estate. But nothing could be further from the truth. I busied myself unpacking my travelsack and getting cobwebs out of corners.

After an hour, I'd managed to pick the lock on the trunk at the foot of my bed and unpack the things I'd stored away. I rediscovered my half-dismantled harmony clock and tinkered with it idly, trying to remember whether I'd been in the middle of taking it apart or putting it back together.

Then, since I had no other pressing engagements, I made my way back across the river. I stopped at the Eolian, where Deoch greeted me with an enthusiastic bear hug that lifted me from the ground. After so long on the road, so much time spent among strangers and enemies, I'd forgotten what it was like to be surrounded by the warmth of friendly faces. Deoch, Stanchion, and I shared drinks and traded stories until it started to get dark outside, and I left them to tend to their business.

I prowled the city for a while, going to a few familiar boarding houses and taverns. Two or three public gardens. A bench beneath a tree in a courtyard. Deoch told me he hadn't so much as glimpsed Denna's shadow in a year. But even looking for her and not finding her was comforting in a way. In some ways that seemed to be the heart of our relationship.

———

Later that night I climbed onto Mains and made my way through the familiar maze of chimneys and mismatched slate and clay and tin. I came around a corner and saw Auri sitting on a chimney, her long, fine hair floating around her head as if she were underwater. She was staring up at the moon and swinging her bare feet.

I cleared my throat softly, and Auri turned to look. She hopped off the chimney and came scampering across the roof, pulling up a few steps short of me. Her grin was brighter than the moon. "There is a whole family of hedgehogs living in Cricklet!" she said excitedly.

Auri took two more steps and grabbed my hand with both of hers. "There are babies tiny as acorns!" She tugged at me gently. "Will you come see?"

I nodded, and Auri led me across the roof to the apple tree we could use to climb down into the courtyard. When we finally got there, she looked at the tree, then down to where she still held my long, tan hand with both of her tiny white ones. Her grip wasn't tight, but it was firm, and she didn't give any sign of letting go.

"I missed you," she said softly without looking up. "Don't go away again."

"I don't ever plan on leaving," I said gently. "I have too much to do here."

Auri tilted her head sideways to peek up at me through the cloud of her hair. "Like visit me?"

"Like visit you," I agreed.

CHAPTER ONE HUNDRED FORTY-THREE

Bloodless

THERE WAS ONE FINAL surprise waiting for me on my return to the University.

I'd been back for a handful of days before I returned to my work in the Fishery. While I was no longer in desperate need of money, I missed the work. There is something deeply satisfying in shaping something with your hands. Proper artificing is like a song made solid. It is an act of creation.

So I went to Stocks, thinking to start with something simple, as I was out of practice. As I approached the window, I saw a familiar face. "Hello Basil," I said. "What did you do to get stuck here this time?"

He looked down. "Improper handling of reagents," he muttered.

I laughed. "That's not so bad. You'll be out in a span or so."

"Yeah." He looked up and gave a shamefaced grin. "I heard you were back. You come for your credit?"

I stopped halfway through my mental list of everything I'd need to make a heat funnel. "I beg your pardon?"

Basil cocked his head to the side. "Your credit," he repeated. "For the Bloodless." He looked at me for a moment, then realization dawned on his face. "That's right, you wouldn't know. . . ." He stepped away from the window for a moment, and returned with something that looked like an eight-sided lamp made entirely of iron.

It was different than the arrowcatch I'd made. The one I'd constructed was built from scratch and rather rough around the edges. This one was smooth and sleek. All the pieces fit together snugly, and it was covered in a thin layer of clear alchemical enamel that would protect it from rain and rust. Clever, I should have included that in my original design.

While part of me was flattered that someone had liked my design enough to copy it, a larger part of me was irritated to see an arrowcatch so much more polished than my original. I noticed a telltale uniformity in the pieces. "Someone made a set of moldings?" I asked.

Basil nodded. "Oh yes. Ages ago. Two sets." He smiled. "I've got to say, it's clever stuff. Took me a long while to get my head around how the inertial trigger worked, but now that I've got it . . ." He tapped his forehead. "I've made two myself. Good money for the time they take. Beats the hell out of deck lamps."

That wrung a smile out of me. "Anything is better than deck lamps," I agreed, picking it up. "Is this one of yours?"

He shook his head. "Mine sold a month back. They don't sit long. Clever of you to price them so low."

I turned it over in my hands and saw a word grooved into the metal. The blocky letters went deep into the iron, so I knew they were part of the mold. They read, "Bloodless."

I looked up at Basil. He smiled. "You took off without giving it a proper name," he said. "Then Kilvin formalized the schema and added it to the records. We needed to call it something before we started to sell it." His smile faded a bit. "But that was around the same time word came back you'd been lost at sea. So Kilvin brought in Master Elodin. . . ."

"To give it a proper name," I said, still turning it in my hands. "Of course."

"Kilvin grumbled a bit," Basil said. "Called it dramatic nonsense. But it stuck." He shrugged and ducked down and rummaged a bit before bringing up a book. "Anyway, you want your credit?" He started flipping pages. "You've got to have a chunk of it built up by now. Lot of folk have been making them."

He found the page he wanted and ran his finger along the ledger line. "There we are. Sold twenty-eight so far . . ."

"Basil," I said. "I really don't understand what you're talking about. Kilvin already paid me for the first one I made."

Basil furrowed his brow. "Your commission," he said matter-of-factly. Then, seeing my blank look, he continued. "Every time Stocks sells something, the Fishery gets a thirty percent commission and whoever owns the schema gets ten percent."

"I thought Stocks kept the whole forty," I said, shocked.

He lifted one shoulder in a shrug. "Most times it does. Stocks owns most of the old schemas. Most things have already been invented. But for something new . . ."

"Manet never mentioned that," I said.

Basil gave an apologetic grimace. "Old Manet is a workhorse," he said politely. "But he's not the most innovative fellow around. He's been here, what, thirty years? I don't think he has a single schema to his name." He flipped through the book a bit, scanning the pages. "Most serious artificers have at least one just as a point of pride, even if it's something fairly useless."

Numbers spun in my head. "So ten percent of eight talents each," I murmured, then looked up. "I've got twenty-two talents waiting for me?"

Basil nodded, looking at the entry in the book. "Twenty-two and four," he said, bringing out a pencil and a piece of paper. "You want all of it?"

I grinned.

When I set out for Imre my purse was so heavy I feared I might develop a limp. I stopped by Anker's and picked up my travelsack, resting it on my opposite shoulder to balance things out.

I wandered through town, idly passing by all the places Denna and I had frequented in the past. I wondered where in the world she might be.

After my ritual search was complete, I made my way to a back alley that smelled of rancid fat and climbed a set of narrow stairs. I knocked briskly on Devi's door, waited for a long minute, then knocked again, louder.

There was the sound of a bolt being thrown and a lock turning. The door cracked open and a single pale blue eye peered out at me. I grinned.

The door swung open slowly. Devi stood in the doorway, staring blankly at me, her arms at her sides.

I raised an eyebrow at her. "What?" I said. "No witty banter?"

"I don't do business on the landing," she said automatically. Her voice was absolutely without inflection. "You'll have to come inside."

I waited, but she didn't step out of the doorway. I could smell cinnamon and honey wafting out from the room behind her.

"Devi?" I asked. "Are you okay?"

"You're a . . ." She trailed off, still staring at me. Her voice was flat and emotionless. "You're supposed to be dead."

"In this and many other things, I aim to disappoint," I said.

"I was sure he'd done it," Devi continued. "His father's barony is called the Pirate Isles. I was sure he'd done it because we'd set fire to his rooms. I was the one that actually set the fire, but he couldn't know that. You were the only one he saw. You and that Cealdish fellow."

Devi looked up at me, blinking in the light. The pixie-faced gaelet had always been fair-skinned, but this was the first time I'd ever seen her look pale. "You're taller," she said. "I'd almost forgotten how tall you are."

"I almost forgot how pretty you are," I said. "But I couldn't quite manage it."

Devi continued to stand in the doorway, pale and staring. Concerned, I stepped forward and laid my hand lightly on her arm. She didn't pull away as I half-expected. She simply looked down at my hand.

"I'm waiting for a quip here," I teased gently. "You're usually quicker than this."

"I don't think I can match wits with you right now," she said.

"I never suspected you could match wits with me," I said. "But I do like a little banter now and then."

Devi gave a ghost of a smile, a little color coming back to her cheeks. "You're a horse's ass," she said.

"That's more like it," I said encouragingly as I drew her out of the doorway into the bright autumn afternoon. "I knew you had it in you."

The two of us walked to a nearby inn, and with the help of a short beer and long lunch, Devi recovered from the shock of seeing me alive. Soon she was her usual sharp-tongued self again, and we bantered back and forth over mugs of spiced cider.

Afterward we strolled back to her rooms behind the butcher shop, where Devi discovered she'd forgotten to lock her door.

"Merciful Tehlu," she said, once we were inside, looking around frantically. "That's a first."

Looking around, I saw that little had changed in her rooms since I'd last seen them, though her second set of bookshelves was almost half full. I looked over the titles as Devi searched the other rooms to make sure nothing was missing.

"Anything you'd like to borrow?" she asked, as she came back into the room.

"Actually," I said, "I have something for you."

I set my travelsack on her desk and rooted around until I found a flat rectangular package wrapped in oilskin and tied with twine. I moved my travelsack onto the floor and put the package on the desk, nudging it toward her.

Devi approached the desk wearing a dubious expression, then sat down and unwrapped the parcel. Inside was the copy of *Celum Tinture* I'd stolen from Caudicus' library. Not a particularly rare book, but a useful resource for an alchemist exiled from the Archives. Not that I knew anything about alchemy, of course.

Devi looked down at it. "And what's this for?" she asked.

I laughed. "It's a present."

She eyed me narrowly. "If you think this will get you an extension on your loan. . . ."

I shook my head. "I just thought you'd like it," I said. "As for the loan . . ." I brought out my purse and counted nine thick talents onto her desk.

"Well then," Devi said, mildly surprised. "It looks like someone had a profitable trip." She looked up at me. "Are you sure you don't want to wait until after you've paid tuition?"

"Already taken care of," I said.

Devi made no move to take the money. "I wouldn't want to leave you penniless at the start of the new term," she said.

I hefted my purse in one hand. It clinked with a delightful fullness that was almost musical.

Devi brought out a key and unlocked a drawer at the bottom of her desk. One by one she brought out my copy of *Rhetoric and Logic*, my talent pipes, my sympathy lamp, and Denna's ring.

She piled them neatly on her desk, but still didn't reach for the coins. "You still have two months before your year and a day is up," she said. "Are you sure you wouldn't prefer to wait?"

Puzzled, I looked down at the money on the table, then around at Devi's rooms. Realization came to me like a flower unfurling in my head. "This isn't about the money at all, is it?" I said, amazed it had taken me this long to figure it out.

Devi cocked her head to the side.

I gestured at the bookshelves, the large velvet-curtained bed, at Devi herself. I'd never noticed before, but while her clothes weren't fancy, the cut and cloth were fine as any noble's.

"This doesn't have anything to do with money," I repeated. I looked at her books. Her collection had to be worth five hundred talents if it was worth a penny. "You use the money as bait. You lend it out to desperate folks who might be useful to you, then hope they can't pay you back. Your real business is favors."

Devi chuckled a bit. "Money is nice," she said, her eyes glittering. "But the world is full of things that people would never sell. Favors and obligation are worth far, far more."

I looked down at the nine talents gleaming on her desk. "You don't have a minimum loan amount, do you?" I asked, already knowing the answer. "You just told me that so I'd be forced to borrow more. You were hoping I'd dig myself a hole too deep and not be able to pay you back."

Devi smiled brightly. "Welcome to the game," she said as she began to pick up the coins. "Thanks for playing."

Sword and Shaed

WITH MY PURSE FULL to bursting and Alveron's letter of credit assuring my tuition, my winter term was carefree as a walk in the garden.

It was strange not having to live like a miser. I had clothes that fit me and could afford to have them laundered. I could have coffee or chocolate whenever I wanted. I no longer needed to toil endlessly in the Fishery and could spend time tinkering simply to satisfy my curiosity or pursue projects simply for the joy of it.

After almost a year away, it took me a while to settle back into the University. It felt odd not wearing a sword after all this time. But such things were frowned on here, and I knew it would cause more trouble than it was worth.

At first I left Caesura in my rooms. But I knew better than anyone how easy it would be to break in and steal it. The drop bar would only keep away a very genteel thief. A more pragmatic one could simply break my window and be gone in less than a minute. Since the sword was quite literally irreplaceable, and I'd made promises to keep it safe, it wasn't long before I moved it to a hiding place in the Underthing.

My shaed was easier to keep at hand, as I was able to change its shape with a little work. These days it only rarely billowed on its own. More commonly it refused to move as much as the gusting wind seemed to demand. You'd think people would notice such things, but they didn't. Even Wilem and Simmon, who teased me about my fondness for it, never marked my cloak as anything more than an exceptionally versatile piece of clothing.

In fact, Elodin was the only one to notice anything out of the ordinary about it. "What's this?" he exclaimed when we crossed paths in a small courtyard outside Mains. "How did you come to be enshaedn?"

"I beg your pardon?" I asked.

"Your cloak, boy. Your turning cape. How in God's sweet grace did you tumble onto a shaed?" He mistook my surprise for ignorance. "Don't you know what you're wearing?"

"I know what it is," I said. "I'm just surprised that you do."

He gave me an insulted look. "I wouldn't be much of a namer if I couldn't spot a faerie cloak a dozen feet away." He took a corner of it between his fingers. "Oh, that's just lovely. Here's a piece of old magic man rarely lays a finger on."

"It's new magic, actually," I said.

"What do you mean?" he asked.

When it became obvious my explanation involved a long story, Elodin led us into a small, cozy pub I'd never seen before. I hesitate to call it a pub at all, actually. It wasn't full of chattering students and the smell of beer. It was dim and quiet with a low ceiling and scattered clusters of deep, comfortable chairs. It smelled of leather and old wine.

We sat near a warm radiator and sipped mulled cider while I told him the whole story of my unintentional trip into the Fae. It was a wonderful relief. I hadn't been able to tell anyone yet for fear of being laughed out of the University.

Elodin proved to be a surprisingly attentive audience and was especially interested in the fight Felurian and I had had when she had tried to bend me to her will. After I'd finished the story, he peppered me with questions. Could I remember what I'd said to call the wind? How had it felt? The strange wakefulness I described, was it more like being drunk, or more like going into shock?

I answered as best I could, and eventually he leaned back in his chair, nodding to himself. "It's a good sign when a student goes chasing the wind and catches it," he said approvingly. "That's twice you've called it now. It can only get easier."

"Three times, actually," I said. "I found it again when I was off in Ademre."

He laughed. "You chased it to the edge of the map!" he said, making a broad motion with his splayed left hand. Stunned, I realized it was Adem hand-talk for *amazed respect*. "How did it feel? Do you think you could find its name again if you had need of it?"

I concentrated, trying to nudge my mind into Spinning Leaf. It had been a month and a thousand miles since I'd tried, and it was hard to tip my mind into that strange, tumbling emptiness.

Eventually I managed it. I looked around the small room, hoping to see the name of the wind like a familiar friend. But there was nothing there except dust motes swirling in a beam of sunlight that slanted through a window.

"Well?" Elodin asked. "Could you call it if you needed to?"

I hesitated. "Maybe."

Elodin nodded as if he understood. "But probably not if someone were to ask you to?"

I nodded, more than a little disappointed.

"Don't be discouraged. It will give us something to work toward." He grinned happily and clapped me on the back. "But I think there's more to your story than you realize. You called more than the wind. From what you've said, I believe you called Felurian's name itself."

I thought back. My memories of my time in the Fae were oddly patchy, none more than my confrontation with Felurian, which had an odd, almost dreamlike quality to it. When I tried to remember it in detail, it almost seemed as if it had happened to another person. "I suppose it's possible."

"It's more than possible," he assured me. "I doubt a creature as old and powerful as Felurian could be subdued with nothing more than wind. Not to belittle your accomplishment," he hurried to add. "Calling the wind is more than one student in a thousand ever manages. But calling the name of a living thing, let alone one of the Fae . . ." He raised his eyebrows at me. "That's a horse of a different color."

"Why would a person's name be so much different?" I asked, then answered my own question. "The complexity."

"Exactly," he said. My understanding seemed to excite him. "To name a thing you must understand it entire. A stone or a piece of wind is difficult enough. A person . . ." He trailed off significantly.

"I couldn't claim to understand Felurian," I said.

"Some part of you did," he insisted. "Your sleeping mind. A rare thing indeed. If you'd known how difficult it was, you never would have stood a chance of doing it."

Since poverty no longer forced me to work endless hours in the Fishery, I was free to study more broadly than ever before. I continued my usual classes in sympathy, medicine, and artificing, then added chemistry, herbology, and comparative female anatomy.

My curiosity had been pricked by my encounter with the Lockless box, and I attempted to learn something about Yllish story knots. But I quickly discovered most books on Yll were historical, not linguistic, and gave no information as to how I might actually read a knot.

So I scoured the Dead Ledgers and discovered a single shelf of disused books concerning Yll in one of the unpleasant, low-ceilinged sections of the lower basements. Then, while looking for a place to sit and read, I discovered a small room tucked behind a piece of jutting shelving.

It wasn't a reading hole as I suspected. Inside were hundreds of large wooden spools wound about with knotted string. They weren't books, precisely, but they were the Yllish equivalent. A thin layer of dust covered everything, and I doubted anyone had been in the room for decades.

I have a vast weakness for secret things. But I quickly found that reading the knots was impossible without first understanding Yllish. There were no classes on the subject, and asking around revealed none of Master Linguist's gillers knew more than a scattering of words.

I wasn't terribly surprised, considering Yll had been nearly ground to dust under the iron boots of the Aturan Empire. The piece that remained today was populated mostly by sheep. And if you stood in the middle of the country, you could throw a stone across the border. Still, it was a disappointing end to my search.

Then, several days later, Master Linguist summoned me to his office. He'd heard that I'd been making inquiries, and he happened to speak Yllish rather well. He offered to tutor me personally, and I gladly took him up on his offer.

Since I'd come to the University, I'd only seen Master Linguist during admissions interviews and when I was brought up on the horns for disciplinary reasons. Acting as Chancellor, he was rather grim and formal. But when he wasn't sitting in the Chancellor's chair, Master Herma was a surprisingly deft and gentle teacher. He was witty with a surprisingly irreverent sense of humor. The first time he told me a dirty joke, you could have knocked me over with a feather.

Elodin wasn't teaching a class this term, but I began to study naming privately under his direction. It went more smoothly now that I understood there was a method to his madness.

Count Threpe was overjoyed to find me alive and threw a resurrection party where I was proudly displayed to the local nobility. I had a suit of clothes tailored specifically for the event, and in a fit of nostalgia I chose to have them done in the colors my old troupe had worn: the green and grey of Lord Greyfallow's men.

After the party, over a bottle of wine in his sitting room, I told Threpe of my adventures. I left off the story of Felurian, as I knew he wouldn't believe it. And I couldn't tell him half of what I'd done in the Maer's service. Consequently, Threpe thought Alveron had been quite generous in rewarding me. I didn't argue the point.

CHAPTER ONE HUNDRED FORTY-FIVE

Stories

AMBROSE HAD BEEN BLESSEDLY absent during the winter term, but when spring arrived he came back to roost like some sort of hateful, migratory bird. By no coincidence, the day after he returned, I skipped all my classes and spent the entire day making myself a new gram.

As soon as the snow melted and the ground grew firm again, I resumed my practice of the Ketan. Remembering how odd it had looked when I'd first seen it, I did this in the privacy of the forest north of the University.

With spring term came a new round of admissions. I showed up for my interview with a profound hangover and fumbled a few questions. My tuition was set at eighteen talents and five, earning me four talents and change from the Bursar.

Sales of the Bloodless had slackened over the winter, as there were fewer merchants visiting the University. But once snows melted and roads grew dry, the handful that had accumulated in the Stocks sold quickly, bringing me another six talents.

I was unused to having so much money at my disposal, and I'll admit I went a little mad with it. I owned six suits of clothes that fit me and had all the paper I could use. I bought fine, dark ink from Arueh and purchased my own set of engraving tools. I had two pairs of shoes. *Two*.

I found an ancient, ragged Yllish dictum buried in a bookstore in Imre. Full of drawings of knots, the bookstore owner thought it was a sailor's journal and I bought it for a mere talent and a half. Not long after I bought a copy of *The Heroborica*, then added a copy of *Termigus Techina* I could use as a reference while designing schema in the privacy of my own room.

I bought dinner for my friends. Auri had new dresses and bright ribbons for her hair. All this and still money in my purse. How odd. How wonderful.

———————

Toward the middle of the term I began to hear familiar stories. Stories about a certain red-haired adventurer who had spent the night with Felurian. Stories of a dashing young arcanist with all the powers of Taborlin the Great. It had taken months, but my exploits in Vintas had finally passed their way from mouth to ear all the long miles back to the University.

It may be true that when I finally became aware of these stories I lengthened my shaed a bit and wore it more often than before. It might also be the case that I spent a shameful amount of time in alehouses over the next several span, lurking quietly, listening to stories. I might even have gone so far as to offer a suggestion or two.

I was young, after all, and it was only natural for me to delight in my notoriety. I thought it would fade in time. Why shouldn't I revel a bit in the sidelong glances my fellow students made? Why not enjoy it while it lasted?

Many of the stories centered around me hunting bandits and rescuing young girls. But none of them came terribly close to the truth. No story can move a thousand miles by word of mouth and keep its shape.

While the details differed, most of them followed a familiar thread: young women were in need of rescuing. Sometimes a nobleman hired me. Sometimes it was a concerned father, a distraught mayor, or a bumbling constable.

Most of the time I saved a pair of girls. Sometimes only one, sometimes there were three. They were best friends. They were mother and daughter. I heard one story where there were seven of them, all sisters, all beautiful princesses, all virgins. You know that sort of story.

There was a great deal of variety as to who exactly I was rescuing the girls from. Bandits were fairly common, but there were also wicked uncles, stepmothers, and shamble-men. One story, in an odd twist, had me rescuing them from Adem mercenaries. There was even an ogre or two.

While I did occasionally rescue the girls from a troupe of traveling players, I'm proud to say I never heard a story where they were kidnapped by the Edema Ruh.

The story generally had one of two endings. In the first I leapt to the battle like Prince Gallant and fought sword on sword until everyone was dead, fled, or appropriately repentant. The second ending was more popular. It involved me calling down fire and lightning from the sky after the fashion of Taborlin the Great.

In my favorite version of the story, I met a helpful tinker on the road. I shared my dinner, and he told me of two children stolen from a nearby farm.

Before I left, he sold me an egg, three iron nails, and a shabby cloak that could render me invisible. I used the items and my considerable wit to save the children from the clutches of a cunning, hungry trow.

But while there were many versions of that tale, the story of Felurian was more popular by far. The song I'd written had made the journey west as well. And since songs hold their shape better than stories, the details about my encounter with Felurian were moderately close to the truth.

When Wil and Sim pressed me for details, I told them the whole story. It took me a while to convince them I was telling the truth. Rather, it took me a while to convince Sim. For some reason, Wil was perfectly willing to accept the existence of the Fae.

I didn't blame Sim. Until I saw her, I would have bet solid money Felurian didn't exist. It's one thing to enjoy a story, but it's quite another to take it for the truth.

"The real question," Sim said thoughtfully, "is how old you really are."

"I know that one," Wilem said with the somber pride of someone desperately pretending to not be drunk. "Seventeen."

"Ahhhh . . ." Sim held up a finger dramatically. "You'd think so, wouldn't you?"

"What are you talking about?" I asked.

Sim leaned forward in his chair. "You went into the Fae, spent some time there, then came out to discover only three days had passed," Sim said. "Does that mean you're only three days older? Or did you age while you were there?"

I was quiet for a moment. "I hadn't thought of that," I admitted.

"In stories," Wilem said, "boys go into Fae and return as men. That implies one grows older."

"If you're going to go by stories," Sim said.

"What else?" Wil asked. "Will you consult *Marlock's Compendium of Fae Phenomenon?* Find me such a book, and I will reference it."

Sim gave an agreeable shrug.

"So," Wil said, turning to me. "How long were you there?"

"That's hard to figure," I said. "There wasn't any day or night. And my memories are a bit odd." I thought for a long moment. "We talked, swam, ate dozens upon dozens of times, explored a bit. And, well . . ." I paused to clear my throat meaningfully.

"Cavorted," suggested Wil.

"Thank you. And cavorted quite a bit as well." I counted the skills Felurian had taught me, and then figured she couldn't have taught me more than two or three a day. . . .

"It was at least a couple months," I said. "I shaved once, or was it twice? Time enough for me to grow a bit of a beard."

Wil rolled his eyes at this, running his hand over his own dark Cealdish beard.

"Nothing like your marvelous facebear," I said. "Still, mine grew out at least two or three times."

"So at least two months," Sim said. "But how long could it have been?"

"Three months?" How many stories had we shared? "Four or five months?" I thought of how slowly we'd had to move my shaed from starlight to moonlight to firelight. "A year?" I thought about the wretched time I'd spent recovering from my encounter with the Cthaeh. "I'm sure it couldn't have been more than a year. . . ." My voice didn't sound nearly as convincing as I would have liked.

Wilem raised an eyebrow. "Well then, happy birthday." He lifted his glass to me. "Or birthdays, depending."

Failures

DURING SPRING TERM I experienced several failures.
The first of these was mostly a failure in my own eyes. I had expected that picking up Yllish would be relatively easy. But nothing could have been further from the truth.

In a handful of days I had learned enough Tema to defend myself in court. But Tema was a very orderly language, and I'd already known a little bit from my studies. Perhaps most importantly, there was a great deal of overlap between Tema and Aturan. They used the same characters for writing, and many words are related.

Yllish shared nothing with Aturan or Shaldish, or even with Ademic for that matter. It was an irrational, tangled mess. Fourteen indicative verb tenses. Bizarre formal inflections of address.

You couldn't merely say "the Chancellor's socks." Oh no. Too simple. All ownership was oddly dual: as if the Chancellor owned his socks, but at the same time the socks somehow also gained ownership of the Chancellor. This altered the use of both words in complex grammatical ways. As if the simple act of owning socks somehow fundamentally changed the nature of a person.

So even after months of study with the Chancellor, Yllish grammar was still a muddy jumble to me. All I had to show for my work was a messy smattering of vocabulary. My understanding of the story knots was even worse. I tried to improve matters by practicing with Deoch. But he wasn't much of a teacher and admitted the only person he'd ever known who could read story knots had been his grandmother who had died when he was very young.

Second came my failure in advanced chemistry, taken under Mandrag's giller, Anisat. While the material fascinated me, I did not get along with Anisat himself.

I loved the discovery chemistry offered. I loved the thrill of experiment, the challenge of trial and retrial. I loved the puzzle of it. I also will admit a somewhat foolish fondness toward the apparatus involved. The bottles and tubes. The acids and salts. The mercury and flame. There is something primal in chemistry, something that defies explication. Either you feel it or you don't.

Anisat didn't feel it. For him chemistry was written journals and carefully penned rows of numbers. He would make me perform the same titration four times simply because my notation was incorrect. Why write a number down? Why should I take ten minutes to write what my hands could finish in five?

So we argued. Gently at first, but neither of us were willing to back down. As a result, barely two span into the term we ended up shouting at each other in the middle of the Crucible while thirty students looked on, openmouthed with dismay.

He told me to leave his class, calling me an irreverent dennerling with no respect for authority. I called him a pompous slipstick who had missed his true calling as a counting-house scribe. In all fairness, we both had some valid points.

My other failure came in mathematics. After listening to Fela chatter excitedly for months about what she was learning under Master Brandeur, I set out to further my number lore.

Unfortunately the loftier peaks of mathematics did not delight me. I am no poet. I do not love words for the sake of words. I love words for what they can accomplish. Similarly, I am no arithmetician. Numbers that speak only of numbers are of little interest to me.

Due to my abandonment of chemistry and arithmetic, I had a great deal of free time on my hands. Some of this I spent in the Fishery, making a Bloodless of my own that sold practically before it hit the shelves. I also spent a fair amount of time in the Archives and the Medica, doing research for an essay titled "On the Non-Efficacy of Arrowroot." Arwyl was skeptical, but agreed my initial research warranted attention.

I also spent some of my time romantically. It was a new experience for me, as I had never caught the eye of women before. Or if I had, I hadn't known what to do with the attention.

But I was older now, and wiser to some degree. And because of the stories circulating, women on both sides of the river were beginning to show an interest in me.

My romances were all pleasant and brief. I cannot say why brief, except to state the obvious: that I do not have much in me that might encourage a woman to make long habit of my company. Simmon, for example, had a great deal to offer. He was a gemstone in the rough. Not stunning at first glance, but with a great deal of worth beneath the surface. Sim was tender, kind, and attentive as any woman could care for. He made Fela deliriously happy. Sim was a prince.

By contrast, what did I have to offer? Nothing really. Less now. I was more like a curious stone that is picked up, carried a while, and finally dropped again with the realization that for all its interesting look, it is nothing more than hardened earth.

"Master Kilvin," I asked. "Can you think of a metal that will stand hard use for two thousand years and remain relatively unworn or unblemished?"

The huge artificer looked up from the brass gear he was inscribing and eyed me standing in the doorway of his office. "And what manner of project are you planning now, Re'lar Kvothe?"

In the last three months, I'd been trying to create another schema as successful as my Bloodless. Partly for the money, but also because I'd learned that Kilvin was much more likely to promote students with three or four impressive schema to their credit.

Unfortunately, I had met with a string of failures here, too. I'd had more than a dozen clever ideas, none of which had led to a finished design.

Most of the ideas were struck down by Kilvin himself. Eight of my clever ideas had already been created, some of them more than a hundred years ago. Five of them, Kilvin informed me, would require the use of runes that were forbidden to Re'lar. Three of them were mathematically unsound, and he quickly sketched out how they were doomed to failure, saving me dozens of hours of wasted time.

One of my ideas, he rejected as "utterly inappropriate for a responsible artificer." I argued that a mechanism that would cut the time needed to reload a ballista would help ships defend against piracy. It would help defend towns against attack by Vi Sembi raiders. . . .

But Kilvin would hear none of it. When his face began to grow dark as a storm cloud, I quickly abandoned my carefully planned arguments.

In the end, only two of my ideas were sound, acceptable, and original. But after weeks of work, I was forced to abandon them as well, unable to get them to work.

Kilvin set down his stylus and half-inscribed brass gear, turning to face me. "I admire a student who thinks in terms of durability, Re'lar Kvothe. But a thousand years is a great deal to ask of stone, let alone metal. To say nothing of metal put to heavy use."

I was asking about Caesura, of course. But I hesitated to tell Kilvin the full truth. I knew all too well that the Master Artificer did not approve of artificery being used in conjunction with any sort of weapon. While he might appreciate the craftsmanship of such a sword, he would not think well of me for owning such a thing.

I smiled. "It isn't for a project," I said. "I was just curious. During my travels I was shown a sword that was quite serviceable and sharp. Despite this, there seemed to be proof that it was over two thousand years old. Do you know of any metal that could avoid breaking for so long as that? Let alone keep an edge?"

"Ah." Kilvin nodded, his expression not particularly surprised. "There are such things. Old magics, one could say. Or old arts now lost to us. These things are scattered through the world. Marvelous devices. Mysteries. There are many reliable sources that speak of the ever-burning lamp." He gestured with a broad hand at the hemispheres of glass laid out on his worktable. "We even possess a handful of these things here at the University."

I felt my curiosity flare up. "What sort of things?" I asked.

Kilvin tugged his beard idly with one hand. "I have a device devoid of any sygaldry that seems to do nothing but consume angular momentum. I have four ingots of white metal, lighter than water, that I can neither melt nor mar in any way. A sheet of black glass, one side of which lacks any frictive properties at all. A piece of oddly shaped stone that maintains a temperate slightly above freezing, no matter what the heat around it." His massive shoulders shrugged. "These things are mysteries."

I opened my mouth, then hesitated. "Would it be inappropriate for me to ask to see some of these things?"

Kilvin's smile was very white against the dark of his skin and his beard. "It is never inappropriate to ask, Re'lar Kvothe," he said. "A student should be curious. I would be troubled if you were indifferent to such things."

The big artificer went to his large wooden desk, so strewn with halffinished projects that the surface was barely visible. He unlocked a drawer with a key from his pocket and drew out two dull metal cubes, slightly larger than dice.

"Many of these old things we cannot fathom or make use of," he said. "But some possess remarkable utility." He rattled the two metal cubes as if they were dice, and they rang together sweetly in his hand. "We call these warding stones."

He bent and set them on the floor, spaced several feet apart from each other. He touched them and spoke very softly under his breath, too quietly for me to hear.

I felt a subtle change in the air. At first I thought that the room was growing colder, but then I realized the truth: I couldn't feel the radiant heat of the smoldering forge at the other end of Kilvin's office.

Kilvin casually picked up the bar of iron used to stir the forge and swung it hard at my head. His gesture was so casual that it caught me completely off my guard, and I didn't even have time to cower or flinch away.

The bar stopped two feet away from me, as if striking some unseen obstruction. There was no sound as if it had struck something, neither did it rebound in Kilvin's grip.

I reached out my hand cautiously and it butted up against . . . nothing. It was as if the intangible air in front of me was suddenly made solid.

Kilvin grinned at me. "The warding stones are of particular use when performing dangerous experiments or testing certain equipment," he said. "They somehow produce a thaumic and kinetic barrier."

I continued to run my hand along the unseen barrier. It wasn't hard, or even solid. It gave way slightly when I pushed at it and felt slippery as buttered glass.

Kilvin watched me, his expression faintly amused. "Truthfully, Re'lar Kvothe, until Elodin made his suggestion, I was thinking of calling your arrow-arresting device the Minor Ward." He frowned slightly. "Not entirely accurate, of course, but more so than Elodin's dramatic nonsense."

I leaned hard against the unseen barrier. It was solid as a stone wall. Now that I was looking more closely, I could see a subtle distortion in the air, as if I were looking through a slightly imperfect sheet of glass. "This is far superior to my arrowcatch, Master Kilvin."

"True." Kilvin gave a conciliatory nod and bent to pick up the stones, muttering again under his breath. I staggered a little when the barrier disappeared. "But your cleverness we can repeat endlessly. This mystery we cannot."

Kilvin held up the two cubes of metal on the palm of his huge hand. "These are useful, but never forget: cleverness and caution profit the artificer. We do our work in the realm of the real." He closed his fingers over the warding stones. "Leave mystery to poets, priests, and fools."

Despite my other failures, my study with Master Elodin was progressing rather well. He claimed all I needed to improve myself as a namer was time and dedication. I gave him both, and he put them to use in odd ways.

We spent hours riddling. He made me drink a pint of applejack, then read Teccam's *Theophany* from cover to cover. He made me wear a blindfold for three days straight, which didn't improve my performance in my other classes, but amused Wil and Sim to no end.

He encouraged me to see how long I could stay awake. And since I could afford all the coffee I liked, I managed nearly five days. Though by the end I was rather manic and starting to hear voices.

And there was the incident on the roof of the Archives. Everyone has heard about that in one version or another, it seems.

There was a great beast of a thunderstorm rolling in, and Elodin decided it would do me good to spend some time in the middle of it. The closer the better, he said. He knew Lorren would never allow us access to the roof of the Archives, so Elodin simply stole the key.

Unfortunately, that meant when the key went tumbling off the roof, no one knew we were trapped up there. As a result the two of us were forced to spend the entire night on the bare stone rooftop, caught in the teeth of the furious storm.

It wasn't until midmorning that the weather calmed enough for us to call down to the courtyard for help. Then, as there didn't seem to be a second key, Lorren took the straightest course and had several burly scrivs simply batter down the door leading to the roof.

None of this would have been a particular problem if, just as it had started to rain, Elodin hadn't insisted that we strip ourselves naked, wrap our clothes in an oilskin, and weigh them down with a brick. According to Elodin, it would help me experience the storm to the fullest degree possible.

The winds were stronger than he'd expected, and they had snatched both the brick and our bundled clothes, hurling them into the sky like a handful of leaves. That was how we lost the key, you see. It had been in the pocket of Elodin's pants.

Because of this, Master Lorren, Lorren's giller Distrel, and three brawny scrivs found Elodin and me stark naked and wet as drowned rats on the roof of the Archives. Within fifteen minutes, everyone in the University had heard the story. Elodin laughed his head off at the whole thing, and though I can see the humor of it now, at the time I was far from amused.

I won't burden you with the entire list of our activities. Suffice to say that Elodin went to great lengths to wake my sleeping mind. Ridiculous lengths, really.

And much to my surprise, our work paid dividends. I called the name of the wind three times that term.

The first time I stilled the wind for the space of a long breath while standing on Stonebridge in the middle of the night. Elodin was there, coaching me. By which I mean he was prodding me with a riding crop. I was also barefoot and more than slightly drunk.

The second time came on me unexpectedly while I was studying in

Tomes. I was reading a book of Yllish history when suddenly the air in the cavernous room whispered to me. I listened as Elodin had taught me, then spoke it gently. Just as gently the hidden wind stirred into a breeze, startling the students and sending the scrivs into a panic.

The name faded from my mind some minutes later, but while it lasted I held the certain knowledge that should I wish it, I could stir a storm or start a thunderclap with equal ease. The knowledge itself had to be enough for me. If I had called the wind's name strongly in the Archives, Lorren would have hung me by my thumbs above the outer doors.

You may not think these terribly impressive feats of naming, and I suppose you are right. But I called the wind a third time that spring, and third time pays for all.

CHAPTER ONE HUNDRED FORTY-SEVEN

Debts

SINCE I HAD A great deal of free time on my hands, midway through the term I hired the use of a two horse fetter-cart and headed to Tarbean on a bit of a lark.

It took me all of Reaving to get there, and I spent most of Cendling visiting old haunts and paying old debts: a cobbler who had been kind to a shoeless boy, an innkeeper who had let me sleep on his hearth some nights, a tailor I had terrorized.

Parts of Waterside were strikingly familiar, while other pieces I didn't recognize at all. That didn't particularly surprise me. A city as busy as Tarbean is constantly changing. What did surprise me was the strange nostalgia I felt for this place that had been so cruel to me.

I had been gone for two years. For all practical purposes it was a lifetime ago.

It had been a span of days since the last rain, and the city was dry as a bone. The shuffling feet of a hundred thousand people kicked up a cloud of fine dust that filled the city streets. It covered my clothes and got in my hair and eyes, making them itch. I tried not to dwell on the fact that it was mostly pulverized horseshit, with an assortment of dead fish, coal smoke, and urine thrown in for flavor.

If I breathed through my nose, I was assaulted with the smell. But if I breathed through my mouth, I could taste it, and the dust filled my lungs making me cough. I didn't remember it being as bad as this. Had it always been so dirty here? Had it always smelled this bad?

After half an hour of searching, I finally found the burned-out building with a basement underneath. I made my way down the stairs and through the long hallway to a damp room. Trapis was still there, barefoot and wearing the same tattered robe, tending to his hopeless children in the cool dark below the city streets.

He recognized me. Not as other people would, not as a budding hero out of stories. Trapis had no time for such things. He remembered me as the smudgy, starveling boy who fell down his stairs fever-sick and crying one winter night. You could say I loved him even more for that.

I gave him as much money as he would take: five talents. I tried to give him more, but he refused. If he spent too much money, he said, it would attract the wrong sort of attention. He and his children were safest if nobody noticed them.

I bowed to his wisdom and spent the remainder of the day helping him. I pumped water and fetched bread. I made a quick examination of the children, then took a trip to an apothecary and brought back a few things that would help.

Lastly I tended to Trapis himself, at least as much as he would allow. I rubbed his poor, swollen feet with camphor and mother's leaf, then made him a gift of tight-fitting stockings and a good pair of shoes so he wouldn't have to go barefoot in the damp of the basement anymore.

As the afternoon faded into evening, ragged children began to arrive in the basement. They came looking for a bit of food, or because they were hurt or hoping for a safe place to sleep. They all eyed me suspiciously. My clothes were new and clean. I didn't belong there. I wasn't welcome.

If I stayed there would be trouble. At the very least, my presence would make some of the starveling children so uncomfortable they wouldn't stay the night. So I said good-bye to Trapis and left. Sometimes leaving is the only thing you can do.

Since I had a few hours before the taverns started to fill up, I bought a single piece of creamy writing paper and a matching envelope of heavy parchment. They were extremely fine quality, much nicer than anything I'd ever owned before.

Next I found a quiet café and ordered drinking chocolate with a glass of water. I arranged the paper on the table and brought out pen and ink from my shaed. Then I wrote in an elegant, fluid script:

Ambrose,
The child is yours. You know it is true and so do I.
I fear my family will disown me. If you do not behave as a gentleman and see to your obligations, I will go to your father and tell him everything.
Do not test me in this, I am resolved.

I didn't sign a name, merely wrote a single initial which could have been an ornate R or perhaps a shaky B.

Then, dipping my finger into my glass of water, I let several drops fall onto the page. They swelled the paper a bit and smeared the ink slightly before I blotted them away. They made a fair approximation of teardrops.

I let one final heavy drop fall onto the initial I'd signed, obscuring it even more. Now the letter looked as if it could also be an F or a P or an E. Perhaps even a K. It could be anything, really.

I folded the paper carefully, then walked over to one of the room's lamps and melted a generous blob of sealing wax onto the fold. On the outside of the envelope I wrote:

Ambrose Jakis
University (Two miles west of Imre)
Belenay-Barren
Central Commonwealth

I paid for my drink and headed to Drover's Lot. When I was just a few streets away I removed my shaed and tucked it into my travelsack. Then I dropped the letter in the street and stepped on it, scuffing it around with my foot a bit before picking it up and brushing it off.

I was almost to the square when I saw the final thing I needed. "Hoy there," I said to an old, whiskery man sitting against a building. "I'll give you ha'penny if you let me borrow your hat."

The old man pulled the draggled thing off and looked at it. His head was very bald and very pale underneath. He squinted a bit in the late afternoon sunlight. "My hat?" he asked, his voice rough. "You can have it for a whole penny, and my blessing too." He gave a hopeful grin as he held out a thin, shaky hand.

I gave him a penny. "Could you hold this for a second?" I passed him the envelope, then used both hands to screw the old, shapeless hat down over my ears. I used a nearby shop window to make sure every scrap of my red hair was tucked away underneath.

"Suits you," the old man said, giving a phlegmy cough. I reclaimed the letter and eyed the smudgy fingerprints he'd left.

From there it was a quick step to Drover's Square. I slouched a bit and narrowed my eyes as I wandered through the milling throng. After a couple minutes my ear caught the distinctive sound of a southern Vintish accent, and I walked over to a handful of men loading a wagon with burlap sacks.

"Hoy," I said, putting on the same accent. "You folk heading up Imre-way?"

One of the men heaved his sack into the wagon and walked over, dusting off his hands. "Headin' through there," he said. "You looking for a ride?"

I shook my head and brought the letter out of my travelsack. "I've got a letter for up that way. I was going to take it myself but my ship sails tomorrow. I bought it from a sailor off in Gannery for a full quater bit," I said. "He had it himself off some noble gel for a single bit." I winked. "She was quite urgent that it get to him, I hear."

"Yeh paid quater bit?" the man said, already shaking his head. "Yeh grummer. En't nobody going to pay that much for a letter."

"Heh," I said, holding up a finger. "Yeh en't seen who's it for yet." I held it up for him to see.

He squinted. "Jakis?" he said slowly, then his face lit with recognition. "Is that Baron Jakis' boy, then?"

I nodded smugly. "The eldest himself. Boy rich as that should pay a fair piece for a letter from his lady. Much as whole noble, I figure."

He eyed the letter. "Could be," he said cautiously. "But look. It en't got anything on it other than University. I been up that way. That en't a small place."

"Baron Jakis' boy en't going to sleep in a tin shack," I said crossly. "Ask someone what the fanciest place is, that's where he'll be."

The man nodded to himself, his hand creeping unconsciously toward his purse. "I suppose I could take it off your hands," he said grudgingly. "But only at a quater bit. I'm taking a risk anyways at that."

"Have a heart, now!" I protested pitifully. "I brought it eight hundred miles! That's worth better'n nothing!"

"Fine," he said, pulling coins out of his purse. "I'll give you three bits then."

"I'd take half a round," I grumbled.

"You'll take three bits," he said, holding out a grubby hand.

I handed him the letter. "Remember to tell him it's from a noble lady," I said as I turned to leave. "Rich tosh. Get whatever yeh can off him, that's what I say."

I left the square, then straightened my shoulders and took off the hat. I pulled my shaed back out of my travelsack and swirled it easily around my shoulders. I started to whistle, and as I passed the bald old beggar, I returned his hat and gave him the three bits besides.

———————

When I first heard the stories people were telling about me at the University, I'd expected them to be short-lived. I thought they would flare up, then die just as quickly, like a fire exhausting its fuel.

But that hadn't been the case. The tales of Kvothe rescuing girls and bedding Felurian mixed and mingled with scraps of truth and the ridiculous lies I'd spread to bolster my reputation. There was fuel aplenty, so the stories swirled and spread like a brushfire with the wind blowing hard behind it.

Honestly, I didn't know if I should be amused or alarmed. When I went to Imre, people would point at me and whisper to each other. My notoriety spread until it was impossible for me to casually cross the river and eavesdrop on the stories people told.

Tarbean, on the other hand, was forty miles away.

After I left Drover's Lot behind, I returned to the room I'd rented in one of the nicer parts of Tarbean. In this part of the city, the wind off the ocean brushed away the stink and the dust, leaving the air feeling sharp and clear. I called up water for a bath, and in a fit of lavish spending that would have left my younger self dizzy, I paid three pennies to have the porter take my clothes to the nearest Cealdish laundry.

Then, clean and sweet smelling again, I went down to the taproom.

I'd picked the inn carefully. It wasn't fancy, but wasn't seedy either. The taproom was low-ceilinged and intimate. It sat at the corner of two of Tarbean's most well-traveled roads, and I could see Cealdish traders rubbing elbows with Yllish sailors and Vintish wagoneers. It was the perfect place for stories.

It wasn't long before I was lurking at the end of the bar, listening to how I had killed the Black Beast of Trebon. I was stunned. I had actually killed a rampaging draccus in Trebon, but when Nina had come to visit me a year ago, she hadn't known my name. My growing reputation had somehow swept through the town of Trebon and gathered up that story in its wake.

There at the bar, I learned many things. Apparently, I owned a ring of amber which could force demons to obey me. I could drink all night and never be the worse for it. Locks opened at the barest touch of my hand, and I had a cloak made all out of cobwebs and shadows.

That was also the first time I heard anyone call me Kvothe the Arcane. It was not a new name, apparently. The cluster of men listening to the story simply nodded along when they heard it.

I learned that Kvothe the Arcane knew a word that would stop arrows dead in the air. Kvothe the Arcane only bled if the knife that cut him was made of raw, untempered iron.

The young clerk was building to the dramatic finish of the story, and I was genuinely curious as to how I was going to stop the demon beast with my ring shattered and my cloak of shadows nearly burned away. But just as I forced my way into Trebon's church, shattering the door with a magic word and a single blow of my bare hand, the door of the inn burst open, startling everyone as it banged hard against the wall.

A young couple stood there. The woman was young and beautiful, dark-haired and dark-eyed. The man was richly dressed and pale with panic. "I don't know what's the matter!" he cried, looking about wildly. "We were just walking and then she couldn't breathe!"

I was at her side before anyone else in the room had time to stand. She had half-collapsed onto an empty bench, with her escort hovering over her. She had one hand pressed against her chest while the other pushed him away weakly. The man ignored it and crowded close to her, speaking in a low, urgent voice. The woman kept sliding away from him until she was at the edge of the bench.

I pushed him ungently aside. "I think she wants her space from you right now."

"Who are you?" he demanded, his voice shrill. "Are you a physician? Who is this man? Someone fetch a physician at once!" He tried to elbow me aside.

"You!" I pointed to a large sailor sitting at a table. "Take this man and put him over there." My voice snapped like a whip and the sailor jumped to his feet, grabbed the young gentleman by the back of his neck, and scuffed him tidily away.

I turned back to the woman and watched as her perfect mouth opened. She strained and drew in only the barest rasp of a breath. Her eyes were wild and wet with fear. I moved close to her and spoke in my gentlest tones. "You will be fine. All is well," I reassured her. "You need to look in my eyes."

Her eyes fixed on mine, then widened in recognition, in amazement. "I need you to breathe for me." I laid one hand against her straining chest. Her skin was flushed and hot. Her heart was thrilling like a frightened bird. I laid my other hand along her face. I looked deeply into her eyes. They were like dark pools.

I leaned close enough to kiss her. She smelled of sclas flower, of green grass, of road dust. I felt her strain to breathe. I listened. I closed my eyes. I heard the whisper of a name.

I spoke it soft, but close enough to brush against her lips. I spoke it quiet, but near enough so that the sound of it went twining through her hair. I spoke it hard and firm and dark and sweet.

There was a rush of indrawn air. I opened my eyes. The room was still enough that I could hear the velvet rush of her second desperate breath. I relaxed.

She laid her hand over mine, over her heart. "I need you to breathe for me," she repeated. "That's seven words."

"It is," I said.

"My hero," Denna said, and drew a slow and smiling breath.

———

"It were powerful strange," I heard the sailor say on the other side of the room. "There were sommat in his voice. I swear by all the salt in me, I felt like a puppet with my string pulled."

I listened with half an ear. I guessed the deckhand simply knew to jump when a voice with the proper ring of authority told him to.

But there was no sense in telling him that. My performance with Denna, combined with my bright hair and dark cloak, had identified me as Kvothe. So it would be magic, no matter what I had to say about it. I didn't mind. What I had done tonight was worthy of a story or two.

Because they recognized me, folk were watching us, but not coming very close. Denna's gentleman friend had left before we thought to look for him, so the two of us enjoyed a certain privacy in our small corner of the taproom.

"I should have known I'd come across you here," she said. "You're always where I least expect to find you. Have you migrated away from the University at last?"

I shook my head. "I'm playing truant for a couple days."

"Are you heading back soon?"

"Tomorrow, actually. I've got a fetter-cart."

She smiled. "Would you like some company?"

I gave her a frank look. "You must know the answer to that."

Denna blushed a little and looked away. "I suppose I do."

When she looked down her hair cascaded off her shoulders, falling around her face. It smelled warm and rich, like sunshine and cider. "Your hair," I said. "Lovely."

Surprisingly, she blushed even deeper at this and shook her head without looking up at me. "That's what we've come to after all this time?" she said, darting a look up at me. "Flattery?"

It was my turn to be embarrassed, and I stammered. "I . . . I wouldn't . . . I mean, I would . . ." I took a breath before reaching out to lightly touch a narrow, intricate braid, half-hidden in her hair. "Your braid," I clarified. "It almost says *lovely*."

Her mouth made a perfect "o" of surprise, and one hand went self-consciously to her hair. "You can read it?" she said, her voice incredulous, her expression slightly horrified. "Merciful Tehlu, isn't there anything you don't know?"

"I've been learning Yllish," I said. "Or trying to. It's got six strands instead of four, but it's almost like a story knot, isn't it?"

"Almost?" she said. "It's a damn sight more than almost." Her fingers plucked at the piece of blue string at the end of her braid. "Even Yllish folk barely know Yllish these days," she said under her breath, plainly irritated.

"I'm not any good," I said. "I just know some words."

"Even the ones that do speak it don't bother with the knots." She glared sideways at me. "And you're supposed to read them with your fingers, not by looking at them."

"I've mostly had to learn by looking at pictures in books," I said.

Denna finally untied the blue string and began to unfurl the braid, her quick fingers smoothing it back into her hair.

"You didn't have to do that," I said. "I liked it better before."

"That's rather the point, isn't it?" She looked up at me, tilting her chin proudly as she shook out her hair. "There. What do you think now?"

"I think I'm afraid to give you any more compliments," I said, not exactly sure what I'd done wrong.

Her demeanor softened a bit, her irritation fading. "It's just embarrassing. I never expected anyone to be able to read it. How would you feel if someone saw you wearing a sign that said, 'I am dashing and handsome'?"

There was a pause. Before it could grow uncomfortable, I said, "Am I keeping you from anything pressing?"

"Only Squire Strahota." She made a negligent gesture toward her departed escort.

"Pressing, was he?" I gave a half-smile, raising an eyebrow.

"All men press, one way or another," she said with mock severity.

"They're still keeping to their book then?"

Denna's expression grew rueful and she sighed. "I used to hope they'd disregard the book with age. Instead I've found they've merely turned a page." She held up her hand, displaying a pair of rings. "Now instead of roses they give gold, and in the giving they grow sudden bold."

"At least you're being bored by men of means," I said consolingly.

"Who wants a mean man?" she pointed out. "Little matter if his wealth is above or below the board."

I laid a gentling hand on her arm. "You must forgive these men of mercenary thought. These poor, rich men who, seeing that you can't be caught, attempt to buy a thing they know cannot be bought."

Denna applauded delightedly. "A plea of grace for enemies!"

"I merely point out that you yourself are not above the giving of gifts," I said. "As I myself well know."

Her eyes hardened, and she shook her head. "There is a great difference between a gift given freely, and one that's meant to tie you to a man."

"There's truth to that," I admitted. "Gold can make a chain as easily as iron. Still, one can hardly blame a man who hopes to decorate you."

"Hardly," she said with smile that was both wry and weary. "Many of their suggestions are rather indecorous." She looked at me. "What of you? Would you have me decorated or indecorous?"

"I have given some thought to that," I said with a secret smile, knowing I had her ring tucked safely away in my room at Anker's. I made a show of looking her over. "Both have their merits, but gold is not for you. You are too bright for burnishing."

Denna gripped my arm and squeezed it, giving me a fond smile. "Oh my Kvothe, I've missed you. Half the reason I came back to this corner of the world was in the hope of finding you." She stood and held out her arm to me. "Come, take me away from all this."

CHAPTER ONE HUNDRED FORTY-EIGHT

The Stories of Stones

ON THE LONG RIDE back to Imre, Denna and I spoke of a hundred small things. She told me about the cities she had seen: Tinuë, Vartheret, Andenivan. I told her about Ademre and showed her a few pieces of hand-language.

She teased me about my growing fame, and I told her the truth behind the stories. I told her how things had fallen out with the Maer, and she was properly outraged on my behalf.

But there was much we didn't discuss. Neither of us mentioned how we'd parted ways in Severen. I didn't know if she had left in anger after our argument, or if she thought I had abandoned her. Any question seemed dangerous. Such a discussion would be uncomfortable at best. At worst it might reignite our previous argument, and that was something I was desperate to avoid.

Denna carried her harp with her, as well as a large traveling trunk. I guessed her song was finished, and she must be performing it. It bothered me that she would play it in Imre, where countless singers and minstrels would hear and carry it out across the world.

Despite this, I said nothing. I knew that would be a hard conversation, and I needed to pick the time for it carefully.

Neither did I mention her patron, though what the Cthaeh had told me preyed on my mind. I thought on it endlessly. Had dreams about it.

Felurian was another matter we didn't discuss. For all the jokes Denna made about my rescuing bandits and killing virgins, she never mentioned Felurian. She must have heard the song I'd written, as it was much more popular than the other stories she seemed to know so well. But she never mentioned it, and I was not enough of a fool to bring it up myself.

So as we rode there were many things unspoken. The tension built in the air between us as the road jounced away beneath the cart's wheels. There were gaps and breaks in our conversation, silences that stretched too long, silences that were short but terrifyingly deep.

We were trapped in the middle of one of those silences when we finally arrived in Imre. I dropped her off at the Boar's Head, where she planned to take rooms. I helped her carry her trunk upstairs, but the silence was even deeper there. So I skirted hastily around it, bid her a fond farewell, and fled without so much as kissing her hand.

———

That night I thought of ten thousand things I could have said to her. I lay awake, staring at the ceiling, unable to sleep until the deep, late hours of night.

I woke early, feeling anxious and uneasy. I had breakfast with Simmon and Fela, then went to Adept Sympathy where Fenton beat me handily three duels in a row, setting him in the top rank for the first time since I'd returned to the University.

With no other classes, I bathed and spent long minutes looking through my clothes before deciding on a simple shirt and the green vest Fela said set off my eyes. I worked my shaed into a short cape, then decided not to wear it. I didn't want Denna thinking of Felurian when I came to call.

Lastly, I slipped Denna's ring into my vest pocket and set off across the river to Imre.

Once at the Boar's Head I hardly had a chance to touch the door handle before Denna opened it and stepped out onto the street, handing me a basket lunch.

I was more than slightly surprised. "How did you know. . . ?"

She wore a pale blue dress that flattered her and smiled winsomely as she linked arms with me. "Woman's intuition."

"Ah," I said, trying to sound wise. The nearness of her was almost painful. The warmth of her hand on my arm, the smell of her like green leaves and the air before a summer storm. "Do you know where we are bound as well?"

"Only that you will take me there." When she spoke she turned to face me, and I felt her breath against the side of my neck. "I gladly leave my trust in you."

I turned to face her, thinking to say one of the clever things I'd thought of last night. But when I met her eyes all words left me. I was lost in wonder, for how long I cannot even guess. For a long moment I was wholly hers. . . .

Denna laughed, jogging me from a reverie that might have stretched a moment or a minute. We made our way out of town, talking as easily as if there had never been a thing between us but sunlight and spring air.

I led her to a place I'd found earlier that spring, a small dell sheltered by the backs of trees. A stream meandered past a greystone that lay lengthwise on the ground, and the sun shone on a field of bright daisies stretching their faces to the sky.

Denna caught her breath when we crested the ridge and saw the carpet of daisies open out in front of her. "I've waited a long time to show these flowers how pretty you are," I said.

That won me an enthusiastic embrace and a kiss burning on my cheek. Both were over before I knew they'd begun. Bemused and grinning, I led the way through the daisies to the greystone near the stream.

I removed my shoes and socks. Denna kicked off her shoes and tied up her skirts, then she ran to the center of the stream until the water rose past her knees.

"Do you know the secret of stones?" she asked as she reached into the water. The hem of her dress dipped into the stream, but she seemed unconcerned.

"What secret is that?"

She drew up a smooth, dark stone from the stream bed and held it out to me. "Come see."

I finished cuffing up my pants and made my way into the water. She held up the dripping stone. "If you hold it in your hand and listen to it . . ." She did so, closing her eyes. She stood still for a long moment, her face turned upward, like a flower.

I was drawn to kiss her, but I resisted.

Finally she opened her dark eyes. They smiled at me. "If you listen close enough it will tell you a story."

"What story did it tell you?" I asked.

"Once there was a boy who came to the water," Denna said. "This is the story of a girl who came to the water with the boy. They talked and the boy threw the stones as if casting them away from himself. The girl didn't have any stones, so the boy gave her some. Then she gave herself to the boy, and he cast her away as he would a stone, unmindful of any falling she might feel."

I was quiet for a moment, not sure if she was done. "It's a sad stone then?"

She kissed the stone and dropped it, watching as it settled to the sand. "No, not sad. But it was thrown once. It knows the feel of motion. It has trouble staying the way most stones do. It takes the offer that the water makes and moves sometimes." She looked up at me and gave a guileless smile. "When it moves it thinks about the boy."

I didn't know what to make of the story, so I tried to change the subject. "How did you learn to listen to stones?"

"You'd be amazed the things you hear if only you take time to listen." She gestured to the streambed strewn with stones. "Try it. You never know what you might hear."

Not sure what game she was playing at, I looked around for a stone, then cuffed up my shirt sleeve and reached into the water.

"Listen," she prompted earnestly.

Thanks to my studies with Elodin, I had a high tolerance for the ridiculous. I held the stone to my ear and closed my eyes. I wondered if I should pretend to hear a story.

Then I was in the water, wet to the skin and spitting it. I spluttered and struggled to my feet while Denna laughed so hard she doubled over at the waist, barely able to stand.

I moved toward her, but she skipped away with a little shriek that left her laughing even harder. So I held off chasing and made a show of wiping water from my face and arms.

"Give up so easily?" she taunted. "Are you so sudden doused?"

I lowered my hand into the water. "I was hoping to find my stone again," I said, pretending to look around for it.

Denna laughed, shaking her head. "You'll not lure me in that easily."

"I'm serious," I said. "I wanted to hear the end of its story."

"What story was that?" she asked teasingly, not coming any closer.

"It was the story of a girl who trifled with a powerful arcanist," I said. "She mocked him and she scoffed at him. She laughed at him full scornfully. He caught her one day in a brook, and rhyming he did quell her fears. And then the girl forgot to look behind her, and it led to tears."

I grinned at her and pulled my hand out of the water.

She turned in time for the wave to hit her. It was only as high as her waist, but it was enough to unbalance her. She went under in a swirl of dress and hair and bubbles.

The current carried her to me and I helped her to her feet, laughing.

She came to the surface looking three-days drowned. "Not fair!" she spluttered indignantly. "Not fair!"

"I disagree," I said. "You're the fairest water-maid I hope to see today."

She splashed at me. "Flatter all you like, the truth remains for God to see. You cheated. I used honest trickery."

She tried to dunk me then, but I was ready for it. We struggled for a while until we were pleasantly breathless. Only then did I realize how close she was. How lovely. How little our wet clothing seemed to separate us.

Denna seemed to realize it at the same time, and we moved a little apart from each other, as if suddenly shy. The wind stirred, reminding us how wet we were. Denna skipped lightly to the shore and stripped away her dress without a moment's hesitation, tossing it over the greystone to dry. She wore a white shift underneath that clung to her as she made her way back into the water. She gave me a playful push as she passed me by, then crawled atop a smooth black boulder that lay half submerged near the center of the stream.

It was a perfect sunning stone, smooth basalt, dark as her eyes. The whiteness of her skin and the too-revealing shift were a sharp contrast against it, almost too bright to look on. She lay on her back and spread her hair to dry. Its wetness made a pattern against the stone that spelled the name of the wind. She closed her eyes and tipped her face toward the sun. Felurian herself could not have been more lovely, more perfectly at ease.

I moved toward the shore as well and stripped off my sodden shirt and vest. I had to be content with my wet pants, as I had nothing else to wear. "What does that stone tell you?" I asked to fill the silence as I laid my shirt next to her dress on the greystone.

She ran one hand over the smooth surface of the stone and spoke without opening her eyes. "This one is telling me what it is like to live in the water, but not be a fish." She stretched like a cat. "Bring the basket over here, would you?"

I fetched the basket and waded out toward her, moving slowly so as not to splash. She lay perfect and still, as if asleep. But as I watched her mouth curved into a smile. "You're quiet." She said. "But I can smell you standing there."

"Nothing bad I hope."

She shook her head gently, still not opening her eyes. "You smell like dried flowers. Like strange spice smoldering, close to catching flame."

"Like river water too, if I have any guess."

She stretched again and smiled an easy smile, showing the perfect whiteness of her teeth, the perfect pinkness of her lips. She shifted her position on the rock slightly. Almost as if she were making room for me. Almost. I thought of joining her. The stone was large enough for two if they were willing to lie close. . . .

"Yes," Denna said.

"Yes to what?" I asked.

"Your question," she said, tilting her face toward me, her eyes still closed. "You're about to ask me a question." She adjusted her position slightly on the stone. "The answer is yes."

How was I to take that? What should I ask for? A kiss? More? How much was too much to ask? Was this a test? I knew asking too much would only drive her away.

"I was wondering if you would move over a little," I said gently.

"Yes." She shifted again, making more space beside her. Then she opened her eyes, and they went wide at the sight of me standing shirtless above her. She glanced down and relaxed when she saw my pants.

I laughed, but her wide-eyed look of shock pushed me back into caution. I set the basket in the place I had thought to take myself. "What thought was that, my lady?"

She colored a bit, embarrassed. "I didn't think you were the sort to bring a girl her lunch while you were running stark." She gave a little shrug, looked at the basket, at me. "But I like you this way. My own bare-chested slave." She closed her eyes again. "Feed me strawberries."

I was happy to oblige, and so we passed the afternoon.

———

Lunch was long gone and the sun had dried us. For the first time since our fight in Severen, I felt things were right between us. The silences no longer lay around us like holes in the road. I knew it had just been a matter of waiting patiently until the tension passed.

As the afternoon slowly slid by, I knew this was the right time to bring up the subject I had been biting my tongue over for so long. I could see the dull green of old bruises on her upper arms, the remnant of a raised welt on her back. There was a scar on her leg above her knee, new enough that the red of it showed through the white of her shift.

All I needed to do was ask about them. If I phrased things carefully, she'd admit they were from her patron. From there it would be a simple thing to draw her out. To convince her she deserved better. That whatever he was offering her was not worth this abuse.

And for the first time in my life, I was in a position to offer her a way out. With Alveron's line of credit and my work in the Fishery, money would never be a problem for me. For the first time in my life, I was wealthy. I could give her a way to escape. . . .

"What happened to your back?" Denna asked softly, interrupting my train of thought. She was still reclining on her stone, I was leaning against it, my feet in the water.

"What?" I asked, unconsciously turning a foolish half-circle.

"You're scarred all along your back," she said gently. I felt one of her cool hands touch my sun-warm skin, tracing a line. "I could hardly tell they were scars at first. They're pretty." She traced another line down my back. "It looks like some giant-child mistook you for a piece of paper and practiced his letters on you with a silver pen."

She took her hand away, and I turned to face her. "How did you get them?" she asked.

"I caused some trouble at the University," I said somewhat sheepishly.

"They whipped you?" she said, incredulous.

"Twice," I said.

"And you stay there?" she asked as if she still couldn't believe it. "After they did this to you?"

I shrugged it away. "There are worse things than whipping," I said. "There's nowhere else I can learn the things they teach here. When I want a thing it takes more than a little blood to . . ."

It was only then I realized what I was saying. The masters whipped me. Her patron beat her. And we both stayed. How could I convince her my situation was different? How could I convince her to leave?

Denna looked at me curiously, her head tilted to the side. "What happens when you want a thing?"

I shrugged. "I was just saying I'm not easily chased away."

"I've heard that about you," Denna said, giving me a knowing look. "A lot of girls in Imre say you're not easily chaste." She sat upright and began to slide toward the edge of the stone. Her white shift twisted and slid slowly up her legs as she moved.

I was about to comment on her scar, hoping I might still bring the conversation around to her patron when I noticed Denna had stopped moving and was watching me as I stared at her bare legs.

"What do they say, exactly?" I asked, more for something to say than from any curiosity.

She shrugged. "Some think you're trying to decimate Imre's female population." She edged closer to the lip of the stone. Her shift shifted distractingly.

"Decimate would imply one in ten," I said, trying to turn it into a joke. "That's slightly ambitious even for me."

"How reassuring," she said. "Do you bring all of them h—" She made a little gasp as she slipped down the side of the stone. She caught herself just as I was reaching out to help her.

"Bring them what?" I asked.

"Roses, fool," she said sharply. "Or have you turned that page already?"

"Would you like me to carry you?" I asked.

"Yes," she said. But before I could reach for her, she slid the rest of the way into the water, her shift gathering to a scandalous height before she slipped free into the stream. The water rose to her knee, just dampening the hem.

We made our way back to the greystone and silently worked our way into our now-dry clothes. Denna fretted at the wetness at the hem of her shift.

"You know, I could have carried you," I said softly.

Denna pressed the back of her hand to her forehead. "Another seven words, I swoon." She fanned herself with her other hand. "What should a woman do?"

"Love me." I had intended to say it in my best flippant tone. Teasing. Making a joke of it. But I made the mistake of looking into her eyes as I spoke. They distracted me, and when the words left my mouth, they ended up sounding nothing at all the way I had intended.

For a fleet second she held my eyes with intent tenderness. Then a rueful smile quirked up the corner of her mouth. "Oh no," she said. "Not that trap for me. I'll not be one of the many."

I clenched my teeth, stuck somewhere between confusion, embarrassment, and fear. I'd been too bold and made a mess of things, just as I'd always feared. When had the conversation managed to run away from me?

"I beg your pardon?" I said stupidly.

"You should." Denna straightened her clothes, moving with an uncharacteristic stiffness, and ran her hands through her hair, twisting it into a thick plait. Her fingers knitted the strands together and for a second I could read it, clear as day: "Don't speak to me."

I might be thick, but even I can read a sign that obvious. I closed my mouth, biting off the next thing I'd been about to say.

Then Denna saw me eyeing her hair and pulled her hands away self-consciously without tying off the braid. Her hair quickly spun free to fall loose around her shoulders. She brought her hands in front of her and twisted one of her rings nervously.

"Hold a moment," I said. "I'd almost forgotten." I reached into the inner pocket of my vest. "I have a present for you."

Her mouth made a thin line as she looked at my outstretched hand. "You too?" she asked. "I honestly thought you were different."

"I hope I am," I said, and opened my hand. I'd polished it, and the sun caught the edges of the pale blue stone.

"Oh!" Denna's hands went to her mouth, her eyes suddenly brimming. "Is it really?" She reached out with both hands to take it.

"It is," I said.

She turned it over in her hands, then removed one of her other rings and slid it onto her finger. "It is," she said in amazement, a few tears spilling over. "How did you ever...?"

"I got it from Ambrose," I said.

"Oh," she said. She shifted her weight from one foot to the other, and I felt the silence loom up between us again.

"It wasn't much trouble," I said. "I'm just sorry it took so long."

"I can't thank you enough for this." Denna reached out and took my hand between hers.

You would think that would have helped. That a gift and clasped hands would make things right between us. But the silence was back now, stronger than before. Thick enough that you could spread it on your bread and eat it. There are some silences that even words cannot drive away. And while Denna was touching my hand, she wasn't holding it. There is a world of difference.

Denna looked up at the sky. "The weather's turning," she said. "We should probably head back before it rains."

I nodded and we left. Clouds cast their shadows across the field behind us as we went.

Tangled

ANKER'S WAS DESERTED EXCEPT for Sim and Fela sitting at one of the back tables. I made my way toward them and sat with my back to the wall.

"So?" Sim asked as I slumped into my seat. "How did yesterday go?"

I ignored the question, not really wanting to discuss it.

"What was yesterday?" Fela asked curiously.

"He spent the day with Denna," Sim supplied. "The *whole* day."

I shrugged.

Sim lost some of his buoyant manner. "Not so well?" he said carefully.

"Not particularly," I said. I looked behind the bar, caught Laurel's eye, and gestured for her to bring me some of whatever was in the pot.

"Care for a lady's perspective?" Fela asked gently.

"I'd settle for yours."

Simmon burst out laughing, and Fela made a face. "I'll help you in spite of that," she said. "Tell Auntie Fela all about it."

So I told her the bones of it. I tried my best to paint a picture of the situation, but the heart of it seemed to defy explication. It sounded foolish when I tried to put it into words.

"That's all," I said after several minutes of fumbling around the subject. "Or at least that's enough of my talking about it. She confuses me like no other thing in the world." I picked at a splinter in the tabletop with my finger. "I hate not understanding a thing."

Laurel brought me warm bread and a bowl of potato soup. "Anything else?" she asked.

"I'm fine, thanks." I smiled at her, then observed her rear aspect as she made her way back to the bar.

"All right then," Fela said in a businesslike manner. "Let's start with your good points. You're charming, handsome, and perfectly courteous to women."

Sim laughed. "Didn't you see how he looked at Lauren just now? He's the world's first lecher. He looks at more women than I could if I had two heads with necks that spun like an owl's."

"I do," I admitted.

"There's looking and there's *looking*," Fela said to Simmon. "When some men look at you it's a greasy thing. It makes you want to have a bath. With other men it's nice. It helps you know you're beautiful." She ran a hand absently through her hair.

"You hardly need to be reminded," Simmon said.

"Everyone needs to be reminded," she said. "But with Kvothe it's different. He's so serious about it. When he looks at you, you can tell his whole attention is focused on you." She laughed at my uncomfortable expression. "It's one of the things I liked about you when we met."

Simmon's expression darkened, and I tried to look as nonthreatening as possible.

"But since you came back it's almost physical," Fela said. "Now when you look at me, there's something happening behind your eyes. Something all sweet fruit, shadows, and lamplight. Something wild that faerie maidens run from underneath a violet sky. It's a terrible thing, really. I like it." As she said the last, she squirmed slightly in her seat, a wicked glitter in her eye.

It was too much for Simmon. He pushed his chair away from the table and started to get to his feet, making inarticulate gestures. "Fine then . . . I'll just . . . fine."

"Oh sweetling," Fela said, laying a hand on his arm. "Hush. It's not like that."

"Don't hush me," he snapped, but he stayed in his chair.

Fela ran her hand through the hair on the back of Sim's neck. "It's nothing you need to worry over." She laughed as if the thought was ridiculous. "You have me tied to you more tightly than you know. But that doesn't mean I can't enjoy a little flattery from time to time."

Sim glowered.

"Should I cloister myself then?" Fela asked. Irritation crept into her voice, bringing with it the barest lilt of her Modegan accent. "You know how you feel when Mola takes the time to flirt with you?" Simmon gaped and looked as if he were trying to go pale and blush at the same time. Fela laughed at his bewilderment. "Tiny Gods, Sim. Do you think I'm blind? It's a sweet thing, and it makes you feel good. What's the harm in it?"

There was a pause. "Nothing, I suppose," Sim said finally. Looking up, he gave me a shaky grin and brushed his hair back from his eyes. "Just don't ever give me the look she mentioned, okay?" His grin widened, became more genuine. "I don't know if I could handle it."

I grinned back at him without thinking of it. Sim could always make me smile.

"Besides," Fela said to him. "You're perfect just the way you are." She kissed his ear as if to put the seal on his improving mood, then turned back to me. "On the other hand, you couldn't pay me enough to get tangled up with you," she said flatly.

"What do you mean?" I demanded. "What about my look? My dark faerie whateverness?"

"Oh, you're fascinating. But a girl wants more than that. She wants a man devoted to her."

I shook my head. "I refuse to throw myself at her like every other man she's ever met. She hates it. I've seen what happens."

"Have you ever thought she might feel the same way?" Fela asked. "You do have something of a reputation with the ladies."

"Should I cloister myself then?" I said, repeating what she'd said to Sim, though it came out sharper than I'd intended. "Blackened body of God, I've seen her on the arms of ten dozen men! Suddenly it's offensive to her if I take another woman out to see a play?"

Fela gave me a frank look. "You've been doing more than going for carriage rides. Women talk."

"Wonderful. And what do they say?" I asked bitterly, looking down at my soup.

"That you're charming," she said easily. "And polite. You don't have wandering hands, which is actually a source of frustration in some cases, apparently." She smiled a little.

I looked up, curious. "Who?"

Fela hesitated. "Meradin," she said. "But you didn't hear it from me."

"She didn't say twenty words to me over dinner," I said, shaking my head. "And she's disappointed I didn't grope her afterward? I thought she hated me."

"We're a long way from Modeg," Fela said. "People aren't sensible about sex in this part of the world. Some women don't know how to deal with a man that doesn't make bold moves."

"Fine," I said. "What else do they say?"

"Nothing terribly surprising," she said. "While you might not be grabby, it's certainly no challenge to trip you either. You're generous, witty, and . . ." She trailed off, looking uncomfortable.

"Go ahead," I said.

Fela sighed and added, "Distant."

It wasn't the crushing blow I'd expected. "Distant?"

"Sometimes all you're looking for is dinner," Fela said. "Or company. Or conversation. Or for someone to have a friendly grope at you. But mostly you want a man to . . ." She frowned and started over. "When you're with a man . . ." She trailed off again.

I leaned forward. "Say what you mean."

Fela shrugged and looked away. "If we were together, I'd expect you to leave me. Not right away. Not with any malice or meanness. But I know you would. You don't seem like the sort who will settle down with a girl forever. Eventually you'd move on to something more important than me."

I prodded idly at a bit of potato in my soup, not sure of what to think.

"There's got to be more to it than just devotion," Sim said. "Kvothe would turn the world upside down for this girl. You can see that, can't you?"

Fela gave me a long look. "I suppose I can," she said softly.

"If you can see it, then Denna must be able to," Simmon pointed out sensibly.

Fela shook her head. "It's only easy to see because I'm far enough away."

"Love is blind?" Sim laughed. "*That's* the advice you have to offer?" He rolled his eyes. "Please."

"I never said I was in love," I interjected. "I never said that. She confuses me, and I'm fond of her. But it doesn't go further than that. How could it? I don't know her well enough to make any earnest claim of love. How can I love something I don't understand?"

They looked at me in silence for a moment. Then Sim burst out in his boyish laugh as if I'd just said the most ridiculous thing he'd ever heard. He took hold of Fela's hand and kissed it squarely on her multifaceted ring of stone. "You win," he said to her. "Love is blind, and a deaf-mute too. I'll never doubt your wisdom again."

Still feeling out of sorts, I went looking for Master Elodin, eventually finding him sitting under a tree in a small garden next to the Mews.

"Kvothe!" He waved lazily. "Come. Sit." He nudged a bowl toward me with his foot. "Have some grapes."

I took a few. Fresh fruit wasn't a rarity for me these days, but the grapes were lovely nonetheless, just on the verge of being overripe. I chewed pensively, my mind still tangled with thoughts of Denna.

"Master Elodin," I asked slowly. "What would you think of someone who kept changing their own name?"

"What?" He sat up suddenly, his eyes wild and panicked. "What have you done?"

His reaction startled me, and I held up my hands defensively. "Nothing!" I insisted. "It's not me. It's a girl I know."

Elodin's face grew ashen. "Fela?" he said. "Oh no. No. She wouldn't do something like that. She's too smart for that." It sounded as if he were desperately trying to convince himself.

"I'm not talking about Fela," I said. "I'm talking about a young girl I know. Every time I turn around she's picked another name for herself."

"Oh," Elodin said, relaxing. He leaned back against the tree, laughing softly. "*Calling* names," he said with tangible relief. "God's bones, boy, I thought . . ." He broke off, shaking his head.

"You thought what?" I asked.

"Nothing," he said dismissively. "Now. What's this about a girl?"

I shrugged, beginning to regret bringing it up in the first place. "I was just wondering what you'd say about a girl who keeps changing her name. Every time I turn around she's picked a different one. Dianah. Donna. Dyane."

"I'm assuming she's not some fugitive?" Elodin asked, smiling. "Hunted. Doing her best to evade the iron law of Atur. That sort of thing?"

"Not to the best of my knowledge," I said with a faint smile of my own.

"It could indicate she doesn't know who she is," he said. "Or that she does know, and doesn't like it." He looked up and rubbed his nose thoughtfully. "It could indicate restlessness and dissatisfaction. It could mean her nature is changeable and she shifts her name to fit it. Or it could mean she changes her name with the hope it might help her be a different person."

"That's a lot of nothing," I said testily. "It's like saying you know your soup is either hot or cold. That an apple is either sweet or sour." I gave him a frown. "It's just a complicated way of saying you don't know anything."

"You didn't ask me what I *knew* of such a girl," he pointed out. "You asked me what I would say of such a girl."

I shrugged, tiring of the subject. We ate grapes in silence as we watched the students come and go.

"I called the wind again," I said, realizing I hadn't told him yet. "Down in Tarbean."

He perked up at that. "Did you now?" he said, turning to look at me expectantly. "Let's hear it then. All the details. "

Elodin was everything you could want in an audience, attentive and enthusiastic. I related the entire story, not sparing a few dramatic flourishes. By the end of it, I found my mood much improved.

"That's three times this term," Elodin said approvingly. "Sought and found when you had need of it. And not just a breeze but a breath. That's subtle stuff." He looked at me from the corner of his eye, giving me a sly smile. "How long do you think it will be before you can make yourself a ring of air?"

I lifted up my naked left hand, fingers spread. "Who's to say I'm not already wearing it?"

Elodin rocked with laughter, then stopped when my expression didn't change. His brow furrowed a bit as he gave me a speculative look, eyes flickering first to my hand, then back to my face. "Are you joking?" he asked.

"That's a good question," I said, looking him calmly in the eye. "Am I?"

CHAPTER ONE HUNDRED FIFTY

Folly

SPRING TERM ROLLED ON. Contrary to what I'd expected, Denna didn't make any public performances in Imre. Instead, she headed north to Anilin after a handful of days.

But this time she made a special trip to Anker's to tell me she was leaving. I found myself strangely flattered by this and couldn't help but feel it was a sign that things were not entirely sour between us.

The Chancellor fell ill just as the term was coming to a close. Though I didn't know him very well, I liked Herma. Not only did I find him to be a surprisingly easygoing teacher when he had been teaching me Yllish, but he had been kind to me when I was new to the University. Nevertheless, I wasn't particularly worried. Arwyl and the staff of the Medica could do everything just short of bringing people back from the dead.

But days passed and no news came from the Medica. Rumor said he was too weak to leave his bed, plagued with spikes of fever that threatened to burn away his powerful arcanist's mind.

When it became apparent he wouldn't be able to resume his duties as Chancellor anytime soon, the masters gathered to decide who would fill his place. Perhaps permanently, should his condition worsen.

And, to make a painful story short, Hemme was appointed Chancellor. After the shock wore off, it was easy to see why. Kilvin, Arwyl, and Lorren were too busy to take up the extra duties. The same could be said for Mandrag and Dal to a lesser extent. That left Elodin, Brandeur, and Hemme.

Elodin didn't want it, and was generally regarded as too erratic to serve. And Brandeur always faced whatever direction Hemme's own wind was blowing.

So Hemme gained the Chancellor's chair. While I found it irritating, it had little impact on my day-to-day life. The only precaution I took was to step with extra care around even the least of the University's laws, knowing if I were put on the horns now, Hemme's vote would count doubly against me.

As admissions approached, Master Herma remained weak and fevered. So it was with a knot of sour dread in my stomach that I prepared for my first admissions interview with Hemme as Chancellor.

I went through the questioning with the same careful artifice I'd maintained for the last two terms. I hesitated and made a few mistakes, earning a tuition of twenty talents or so. Enough to earn some money, but not enough to embarrass myself too badly.

Hemme, as always, asked double-sided or misleading questions designed to trip me, but that was nothing new. The only real difference seemed to be that Hemme smiled a great deal. It wasn't a pleasant smile either.

The masters had their usual muted conference. Then Hemme read my tuition: fifty talents. Apparently the Chancellor had greater control over these things than I had ever known.

I forced myself to bite my lip to keep from laughing, and arranged my face in a dejected expression as I made my way to the basement of Hollows where the bursar kept his counting room. Riem's eyes brightened at the sight of my tuition slip. He disappeared into his back room and returned in a moment with an envelope of thick paper.

I thanked him and returned to my room at Anker's, maintaining my morose expression all the way. Once I had the door closed, I tore open the heavy envelope and poured its contents into my hand: two gleaming gold marks worth ten talents each.

I laughed then. Laughed until my eyes watered and my sides ached. Then I drew on my best suit of clothes and gathered my friends: Wilem and Simmon, Fela and Mola. I sent a runner boy to Imre with an invitation to Devi and Threpe. Then I hired a four-horse carriage and had the lot of us driven across the river to Imre.

We stopped by the Eolian. Denna wasn't there, but I collected Deoch instead and we made our way to the King's Arms, an establishment of the sort no self-respecting student could ever afford. The doorman looked the motley lot of us over scornfully, as if he would object, but Threpe frowned his best gentleman's frown and ushered all of us safely inside.

Then commenced a night of pleasant decadence the likes of which I have hardly seen equaled since. We ate and drank, and I paid for everything happily. The only water on the table was in the hand bowls. In our cups there was only old Vintish wines, dark scutten, cool metheglin, sweet brand, and every toast we drank was to Hemme's folly.

Locks

K VOTHE DREW A DEEP breath and nodded to himself. "Let's stop there," he said. "Money in my pocket for the first time in my life. Surrounded by friends. That's a good place to end for the night." He idly rubbed his hands together, right hand massaging the left absentmindedly. "If we go much farther, things get dark again."

Chronicler picked up the short stack of finished pages and tapped them on the table, squaring their corners before resting the half-finished page on top. He opened his leather satchel, removed the bright green crown of holly, and slid the pages inside. Then he screwed shut his inkwell and began to dismantle and clean all the pieces of his pen.

Kvothe stood and stretched. Then he gathered up the empty plates and cups, carrying them into the kitchen.

Bast merely sat, his expression blank. He didn't move. He hardly seemed to be breathing. After several minutes Chronicler began to dart glances in his direction.

Kvothe came back into the room and frowned. "Bast," he said.

Bast slowly turned his eyes to look at the man behind the bar.

"Shep's wake is still going on," Kvothe said. "There's not much cleaning up to do tonight. Why don't you head over for the end of it? They'll be glad to have you. . . ."

Bast considered for a moment, then shook his head. "I don't think so, Reshi," he said, his voice flat. "I'm not really in the mood." He pushed himself out of his chair and made his way across the room toward the stairs without looking either of them in the eye. "I'll just turn in."

The hard sounds of his footsteps retreated slowly into the distance, followed by the sound of a closing door.

Chronicler watched him go, then turned to look at the red-haired man behind the bar.

Kvothe was looking at the stairway too, his eyes concerned. "He's just had a rough day," he said, sounding as if he were speaking to himself as much as his guest. "He'll be fine tomorrow."

Wiping off his hands, Kvothe walked around the bar and headed to the front door. "Do you need anything before you turn in?" he asked.

Chronicler shook his head and began fitting his pen back together.

Kvothe locked the front door with a large brass key, then turned to Chronicler. "I'll leave this in the lock for you," he said. "In case you wake up early and feel like having a walk or somesuch. I don't tend to sleep very much these days." He touched the side of his face where a bruise was beginning to mottle his jaw. "But tonight I might make an exception."

Chronicler nodded and shouldered his satchel. Then he delicately picked up his holly crown and headed up the stairs.

Alone in the common room, Kvothe swept the floor methodically, catching all the corners. He finished the dishes, washed the tables and the bar, and rolled down all the lamps but one, leaving the room dimly lit and full of flickering shadow.

For a moment he looked at the bottles behind the bar, then turned and made his own slow climb upstairs.

Bast stepped slowly into his room, closing the door behind himself.

He moved quietly through the dark to stand before the hearth. Nothing but ash and cinder remained from the morning's fire. Bast opened the wood-bin, but there was nothing inside except a thick layer of chaff and chips at the bottom.

The dim light from the window glinted in his dark eyes and showed the outline of his face as he stood motionless, as if trying to decide what to do. After a moment he let the lid of the bin fall closed, wrapped himself in a blanket, and folded himself onto a small couch in front of the empty fireplace.

He sat there for a long while, eyes open in the dark.

There was a faint scuffle outside his window. Then nothing. Then a faint scraping. Bast turned and saw a dark shape outside, moving in the night.

Bast went motionless, then slid smoothly from the couch to stand in front of the fireplace. Eyes still on the window, his hands hunted carefully across the top of the mantel.

There was another scrape at the window, louder this time. Bast's eyes darted away from the window to the mantel, and he caught up something with both hands. Metal gleamed faintly in the dim moonlight as he crouched, his body tense as a coiled spring.

For a long moment there was nothing. No sound. No movement outside the window or in the darkened room.

Tap-tap-tap-tap-tap. It was a faint noise, but perfectly clear in the stillness of the room. There was a pause, then the noise came again, sharp and insistent against the window glass: *tap-tap-tap-tap-tap-tap-tap.*

Bast sighed. Relaxing out of his tense crouch, he walked over to the window, threw the drop bar, and opened it.

"My window doesn't have a lock," Chronicler said petulantly. "Why does yours?"

"Obvious reasons," Bast said.

"Can I come in?"

Bast shrugged and moved back toward the fireplace while Chronicler climbed awkwardly through the window. Bast struck a match and lit a lamp on a nearby table, then carefully set a pair of long knives on the mantel. One was slender and sharp as a blade of grass, the other keen and graceful as a thorn.

Chronicler looked around as light swelled to fill the room. It was large, with rich wood paneling and thick carpets. Two lounging couches faced each other in front of the fireplace, and one corner of the room was dominated by a huge canopy bed with deep green curtains.

There were shelves filled with pictures, trinkets, and oddments. Locks of hair wrapped in ribbon. Whistles carved from wood. Dried flowers. Rings of horn and leather and woven grass. A hand-dipped candle with leaves pressed into the wax.

And, in what was obviously a recent addition, holly boughs decorated parts of the room. One long garland ran along the headboard of the bed, and another was strung along the mantle, weaving in and out through the handles of a pair of bright, leaf-bladed hatchets hanging there.

Bast sat back in front of the cold fireplace and wrapped a rag blanket around his shoulders like a shawl. It was a chaos of ill-matching fabric and faded color except for a bright red heart sewn squarely in the center.

"We need to talk," Chronicler said softly.

Bast shrugged, his eyes fixed dully on the fireplace.

Chronicler took a step closer. "I need to ask you . . ."

"You don't have to whisper," Bast said without looking up. "We're on the other side of the inn. Sometimes I have guests. It used to keep him awake, so I moved to this side of the building. There are six solid walls between my room and his."

Chronicler sat on the edge of the other couch, facing Bast. "I need to ask about some of the things you said tonight. About the Cthaeh."

"We shouldn't talk about the Cthaeh." Bast's voice was flat and leaden. "It's not healthy."

"The Sithe then," Chronicler said. "You said if they knew about this story, they'd kill everyone involved. Is that true?"

Bast nodded, eyes still on the fireplace. "They'd burn this place and salt the earth behind them."

Chronicler looked down, shaking his head. "I don't understand this fear you have of the Cthaeh," he said.

"Well," Bast said, "evidence seems to indicate that you're not terribly smart."

Chronicler frowned and waited patiently.

Bast sighed, finally pulling his eyes away from the fireplace. "Think. The Cthaeh knows everything you're ever going to do. Everything you're going to say . . ."

"That makes it an irritating conversationalist," Chronicler said. "But not—"

Bast's expression went suddenly furious. *"Dyen vehat. Enfeun vehat tyloren tes!"* he spat almost incoherently. He was trembling, clenching and unclenching his hands.

Chronicler went pale at the venom in Bast's voice, but he didn't flinch. "You're not angry at me," he said calmly, looking Bast in the eye. "You're just angry, and I happen to be nearby."

Bast glared at him, but said nothing.

Chronicler leaned forward. "I'm trying to help, you know that, right?"

Bast nodded sullenly.

"That means I need to understand what's going on."

Bast shrugged, his sudden flare of temper had burned itself out, leaving him listless again.

"Kvothe seems to believe you about the Cthaeh," Chronicler said.

"He knows the hidden turnings of the world," Bast said. "And what he doesn't understand he's quick to grasp." Bast's fingers flicked idly at the edges of the blanket. "And he trusts me."

"But doesn't it seem contrived? The Cthaeh gives a boy a flower, one thing leads to another, and suddenly there's a war." Chronicler made a dismissive motion. "Things don't work that way. It's too much coincidence."

"It's not coincidence." Bast gave a short sigh. "A blind man has to stumble through a cluttered room. You don't. You use your eyes and pick the easy way. It's clear to you as anything. The Cthaeh can see the future. All futures. We have to fumble through. It doesn't. It merely looks and picks the most disastrous path. It is the stone that stirs the avalanche. It is the cough that starts the plague."

"But if you know the Cthaeh is trying to steer you," Chronicler said. "You would just do something else. He gives you the flower, and you just sell it."

Bast shook his head. "The Cthaeh would know. You can't second-guess a thing that knows your future. Say you sell the flower to the prince. He uses the flower to heal his betrothed. A year later she catches him diddling the chambermaid, hangs herself in disgrace, and her father launches an attack to avenge her honor." Bast spread his hands helplessly. "You still get civil war."

"But the young man who sold the flower stays safe."

"Probably not," Bast said grimly. "More likely he gets drunk as a lord, catches the pox, then knocks over a lamp and sets half the city on fire."

"You're just making things up to prove your point," Chronicler said. "You're not actually proving anything."

"Why do I need to prove anything to you?" Bast asked. "Why would I care what you think? Be happy in your silly little ignorance. I'm doing you a favor by not telling you the truth."

"What truth is that?" Chronicler said, plainly irritated.

Bast gave a weary sigh, and looked up at Chronicler, his expression utterly empty of all hope. "I would rather fight Haliax himself," he said. "I'd rather face all the Chandrian together than have ten words of conversation with the Cthaeh."

This gave Chronicler a bit of a pause. "They'd kill you," he said. Something in his voice made it a question.

"Yes," Bast said. "Even so."

Chronicler stared at the dark-haired man sitting across from him, wrapped in a rag blanket. "Stories taught you to fear the Cthaeh," he said, disgust plain in his voice. "And that fear is making you stupid."

Bast shrugged, his empty eyes drifting back to the nonexistent fire. "You bore me, manling."

Chronicler stood up, stepped forward, and slapped Bast hard across the face.

Bast's head rocked to the side, and for a moment he seemed too shocked to move. Then he came to his feet in a blur of motion, blanket flying from his shoulders. He grabbed Chronicler roughly by the throat, teeth bared, his eyes a deep, unbroken blue.

Chronicler looked him squarely in the eye. "The Cthaeh set all of this in motion," he said calmly. "It knew you would attack me, and terrible things will come of it."

Bast's furious expression went stiff, his eyes widening. The tension left his shoulders as he let go of Chronicler's throat. He started to sink back down onto the cushions of the couch.

Chronicler drew back his arm and slapped him again. If anything, the sound was even louder than before.

Bast bared his teeth again, then stopped. His eyes darted to Chronicler, then away.

"The Cthaeh knows you fear it," Chronicler said. "It knows I would use that knowledge against you. It's still manipulating you. If you don't attack me, terrible things will come of it."

Bast froze as if paralyzed, trapped halfway between standing and sitting.

"Are you listening to me?" Chronicler said. "Are you finally awake?"

Bast looked up at the scribe with an expression of confused amazement. A bright red mark was blossoming on his cheek. He nodded, sinking slowly back onto the couch.

Chronicler drew back his arm. "What will you do if I hit you again?"

"Beat ten colors of guts out of you," Bast said earnestly.

Chronicler nodded and sat back down on his couch. "I will, for the sake of argument, accept that the Cthaeh knows the future. That means it can control many things." He raised a finger. "But not everything. The fruit you ate today was still sweet in your mouth, wasn't it?"

Bast nodded slowly.

"If the Cthaeh is as malicious as you say, it would harm you in every way possible. But it cannot. It could not keep you from making your Reshi laugh this morning. It could not keep you from enjoying the sun on your face or kissing the rosy cheeks of farmers' daughters, could it?"

A flicker of a grin found Bast's face. "I kissed more than that," he said.

"That," Chronicler said firmly, "is my point. It cannot poison every thing we do."

Bast looked thoughtful, then sighed. "You're right in a way," he said. "But only an idiot sits in a burning house and thinks everything is fine because fruit is still sweet."

Chronicler made a point of looking around the room. "The inn doesn't look like it's on fire to me."

Bast looked at him incredulously. "The whole world is burning down," he said. "Open your eyes."

Chronicler frowned. "Even ignoring everything else," he said, bulling ahead. "Felurian let him go. She knew he'd spoken with the Cthaeh, surely she wouldn't have loosed him on the world unless she had some way to guard against its influence."

Bast's eyes brightened at the thought, then dimmed almost immediately. He shook his head. "You're looking for depth in a shallow stream," he said.

"I don't follow you," Chronicler demanded. "What possible reason could she have for letting him go if he was truly dangerous?"

"Reason?" Bast asked, dark amusement coloring his voice. "No *reason*. She's got nothing to do with reason. She let him go because it pleased her pride. She wanted him to go out into the mortal world and sing her praises. Tell stories about her. Pine for her. That's why she let him leave." He sighed. "I've already told you. My folk are not famous for our good decisions."

"Perhaps," Chronicler said. "Or perhaps she simply recognized the futility of trying to second-guess the Cthaeh." He made a nonchalant gesture. "If whatever you're going to do is wrong, you might as well do whatever you want."

Bast sat quietly for a long moment. Then he nodded, faintly at first, then more firmly. "You're right," he said. "If everything is going to end in tears anyway, I should do what I want."

Bast looked around the room, then came suddenly to his feet. After a moment's searching, he found a thick cloak crumpled on the floor. He gave it a vigorous shake and wrapped it around his shoulders before heading to the window. Then he stopped, came back to the couch, and rummaged in the cushions until he found a bottle of wine.

Chronicler looked puzzled. "What are you doing? Are you going back to Shep's wake?"

Bast paused on his way back to the window, seeming almost surprised to see Chronicler still standing there. "I am going about my business," he said tucking the bottle of wine under his arm. He opened the window and swung one foot outside. "Don't wait up."

———

Kvothe stepped briskly into his room, closing the door behind himself.

He moved about busily. He cleared the cold ashes from the fireplace and set new wood in its place, sparking the fire to life with a fat red sulfur match. He fetched a second blanket and spread it over his narrow bed. Frowning slightly, he picked up the crumpled piece of paper from where it had fallen to the floor and returned it to the top of his desk where it sat next to the two other crumpled sheets.

Then, moving almost reluctantly, he made his way to the foot of his bed. Taking a deep breath, he wiped his hands on his pants and knelt in front of the dark chest that sat there. He rested both hands on the curved lid and closed his eyes, as if listening for something. His shoulders shifted as he tugged against the lid.

Nothing happened. Kvothe opened his eyes. His mouth made a grim line. His hands moved again, pulling harder, straining for a long moment before giving up.

Expressionless, Kvothe stood and walked to the window that overlooked the woods behind the inn. He slid it open and leaned out, reaching down with both hands. Then he drew himself back inside, clutching a slender wooden box.

Brushing away a coating of dust and spiderwebs, he opened the box. Inside lay a key of dark iron and a key of bright copper. Kvothe knelt in front of the chest again and fit the copper key into the iron lock. With slow precision he turned it: left, then right, then left again, listening carefully to the faint clicks of some mechanism inside.

Then he lifted the iron key and fit it into the copper plate. This key he did not turn. He slid it deep into the lock, brought it halfway out, then pushed it back before drawing it free in a smooth, quick motion.

After replacing the keys in their box, he put his hands back on the sides of the lid in the same position as before. "Open," he said under his breath. "Open, damn you. Edro."

He lifted, his back and shoulders tensing with the effort of it.

The lid of the chest didn't budge. Kvothe gave a long sigh and leaned forward until his forehead pressed against the cool dark wood. As the air rushed out of him, his shoulders sagged, leaving him looking small and wounded, terribly tired and older than his years.

His expression, however, showed no surprise, no grief. It was merely resigned. It was the expression of a man who has finally received bad news he'd already known was on the way.

CHAPTER ONE HUNDRED FIFTY-TWO

Elderberry

IT WAS A BAD night to be caught in the open.

The clouds had rolled in late, like a grey sheet pulled across the sky. The wind was chill and gusty, with fits and starts of rain that spattered down heavily before fading into drizzle.

For all this, the two soldiers camped in a thicket near the road seemed to be enjoying themselves. They'd found a woodcutter's stash and built their fire so high and hot that the occasional gust of rain did little more than make it spit and hiss.

The two men were talking loudly, laughing the wild, braying laughter of men too drunk to care about the weather.

Eventually a third man emerged from the dark trees, stepping delicately over the trunk of a nearby fallen tree. He was wet, if not soaked, and his dark hair was plastered flat to his head. When the soldiers saw him, they lifted their bottles and called out an enthusiastic greeting.

"Didn't know if you'd make it," the blonde soldier said. "It's a shit night. But it's only fair you get your third."

"You're wet through," said the bearded one, lifting up a narrow yellow bottle. "Suck on this. It's some fruit thing, but it kicks like a pony."

"Yours is girly piss," the blonde soldier said, holding up his own. "Here. Now this here is a man's drink."

The third man looked back and forth as if unable to decide. Finally he lifted a finger, pointing at one bottle then the other as he began to chant.

Maple. Maypole.
Catch and carry.
Ash and Ember.
Elderberry.

He ended pointing at the yellow bottle, then gripped it by the neck and lifted to his lips. He took a long, slow drink, his throat working silently.

"Hey there," said the bearded soldier. "Save a bit!"

Bast lowered the bottle and licked his lips. He gave a dry, humorless chuckle. "You got the right bottle," he said. "It's elderberry."

"You're nowhere near as chatty as you were this morning," the blonde soldier said, cocking his head to one side. "You look like your dog died. Is everything alright?"

"No," Bast said. "Nothing's alright."

"It ain't our fault if he figured it out," the blonde one said quickly. "We waited a bit after you left, just like you said. But we'd been sitting for hours already. Thought you were never going to leave."

"Hell," the bearded man said, irritated. "Does he know? He throw you out?"

Bast shook his head and tipped the bottle back again.

"Then you ain't got nothing to complain of." The blonde soldier rubbed the side of his head, scowling. "Silly bastard gave me a lump or two."

"He got it back with some to spare." The bearded soldier grinned, rubbing his thumb across his knuckles. "He'll be pissing blood tomorrow."

"So it's all good at the end," the blonde soldier said philosophically, lurching unsteadily as he waved his bottle a little too dramatically. "You got to skin your knuckles. I got a drink of something lovely. And we all made a heavy penny. Everyone's happy. Everyone gets what they wanted most."

"I didn't get what I wanted," Bast said flatly.

"Not yet," the bearded soldier said, reaching into his pocket and pulling out a purse that made a weighty chink as he bounced it in his palm. "Grab a piece of fire and we'll divvy this up."

Bast looked around the circle of firelight, making no move to take a seat. Then he began to chant again as he pointed at things randomly: a nearby stone, a log, a hatchet . . .

Fallow farrow.
Ash and oak.
Bide and borrow.
Chimney smoke.

He ended pointing at the fire. He stepped close, stooped low, and pulled out a branch longer than his arm. The far end was a solid knot of glowing coal.

"Hell, you're drunker than I am," the bearded soldier guffawed. "That's not what I meant when I said grab a piece of fire."

The blonde soldier rolled with laughter.

Bast looked down at the two men. After a moment he began to laugh too. It was a terrible sound, jagged and joyless. It was no human laugh.

"Hoy," the bearded man interrupted sharply, his expression no longer amused. "What's the matter with you?"

It began to rain again, a gust of wind spattering heavy drops against Bast's face. His eyes were dark and intent. There was another gust of wind that made the end of the branch flare a brilliant orange.

The hot coal traced a glowing arc through the air as Bast began to point it back and forth between the two men, chanting:

Barrel. Barley.
Stone and stave.
Wind and water.
Misbehave.

Bast finished with the burning branch pointing at the bearded man. His teeth were red in the firelight. His expression was nothing like a smile.

A Silence of Three Parts

IT WAS NIGHT AGAIN. The Waystone Inn lay in silence, and it was a silence of three parts.

The most obvious part was a hollow, echoing quiet, made by things that were lacking. If there had been a steady rain it would have drummed against the roof, sluiced the eaves, and washed the silence slowly out to sea. If there had been lovers in the beds of the inn, they would have sighed and moaned and shamed the silence into being on its way. If there had been music . . . but no, of course there was no music. In fact there were none of these things, and so the silence remained.

Outside the Waystone, the noise of distant revelry blew faintly through the trees. A strain of fiddle. Voices. Stomping boots and clapping hands. But the sound was slender as a thread, and a shift in the wind broke it, leaving only rustling leaves and something almost like the far-off shrieking of an owl. That faded too, leaving nothing but the second silence, waiting like an endless indrawn breath.

The third silence was not an easy thing to notice. If you listened for an hour, you might begin to feel it in the chill metal of a dozen locks turned tight to keep the night away. It lay in rough clay jugs of cider and the hollow taproom gaps where chairs and tables ought to be. It was in the mottling ache of bruises that bloomed across a body, and it was in the hands of the man who wore the bruises as he rose stiffly from his bed, teeth clenched against the pain.

The man had true-red hair, red as flame. His eyes were dark and distant, and he moved with the subtle certainty of a thief in the night. He made his way downstairs. There, behind the tightly shuttered windows, he lifted his hands like a dancer, shifted his weight, and slowly took one single perfect step.

The Waystone was his, just as the third silence was his. This was appropriate, as it was the greatest silence of the three, wrapping the others inside itself. It was deep and wide as autumn's ending. It was heavy as a great river-smooth stone. It was the patient, cut-flower sound of a man who is waiting to die.